CONTE[

CONTENTS

Drinking beer is good for you – in moderation it reduces the risk of coronary heart disease. That is not the editor of *The Real Ale Pub Guide* talking but two sets of scientists, in Germany and the Czech Republic, whose work was published in the summer of 2001.

The notion that a little red wine has health-giving properties is not a new one. What is new is the discovery that beer is actually even better.

The German scientists concluded that, although drinking alcohol from a variety of sources reduced the factors associated with heart attacks, beer actually does it best. And the Czechs discovered that moderate quantities of beer are a valuable means of increasing the folate and vitamin B_{12} concentrations in the blood, which helps to reduce the risk of cardiovascular disease.

This is exactly the sort of news, and positive press, that the brewing industry needs as it battles with a host of twenty-first century problems. The real ale cause never has it easy – multi-national brewing giants and avaricious pub chains are seeing to that – but more than ever it is a cause which is worth the fight.

The decline in the consumption of cask-conditioned real ale is also levelling out, with regional brewers actually reporting a rise in sales. All the more reason, then, to celebrate with the publication of our 2003 edition.

Welcome to a bigger, better and more extensively researched guide than any that have gone before.

This book is for those for whom the most important thing about a pub they visit is the beer they may find within it. We are not (except in passing) interested in the architecture, the quality of the food or the length of the wine list. Nor are we highlighting the pubs harnessed to the big national and international brewers whose motives are almost exclusively profit-driven. This is not a list of Irish theme pubs nor of those often excellent establishments selling fine wines, organic ciders or continental lagers.

Real ale is the name of our game and we believe there is a gap in the market for an independently produced and critically compiled guide to the pubs right across Britain where you should be guaranteed a high-quality pint of ale – and we mean real ale, that living, breathing, life-giving drink produced by brewers who are real craftsmen and served by licensees whose principal aim is to impress.

In an age when sharp marketing can all too easily obscure a substandard product, where the big brewers' focus is on the next novelty craze that will briefly capture the more fickle imaginations, real ale remains a product that has stood the test of time.

New techniques, the latest equipment, improved levels of hygiene, fresher ingredients and more efficient methods of transport mean real ale can now taste better than ever before. But modern brewing is the result of a seamless tradition, a secret passed down the centuries where quality is still what counts.

Rising property prices, government legislation (or the lack of it), predatory pub chains and a host of other factors make life hard for the independent or micro-brewer, and for the publican who really cares about what emerges from his or her pumps. But this book is a celebration of their work and, we hope, further encouragement for them to continue.

Their mission is our mission – to make your trip to the pub a memorable experience for all the right reasons. Let's all drink to that.

HOW IT ALL BEGAN

We have the Romans to thank for bringing beer to Britain in the first century AD, although the drink has its origins in Mesopotamia perhaps as many as 8000 years before that. The first brewer probably stumbled across the secret by accident, perhaps as a result of airborne wild yeast infecting food, but from there it spread to Greece, Egypt and eventually to Rome.

While the Roman aristocracy still preferred to drink wine, Caesar's invading army appreciated beer as an important source of nutrition and, with water supplies so often contaminated, native Britons soon found it safer, and no doubt more pleasurable, to drink than water.

Beer and brewing continued to thrive in Britain long after the Romans had gone, and more than 40 breweries were listed in the Domesday Book of 1086. Hops, which impart flavour and aroma, and act as a preservative, were initially introduced from Scandinavia in the middle of the tenth century, but they were not widely used until the fifteenth century, when they were grown here, primarily in Kent.

Many of the early brewers were monks, and it was in monasteries that brewing techniques were improved and refined, particularly with the introduction of better varieties of barley. During the Reformation, however, and Henry VIII's break with Rome, the monasteries were shut down and their land and assets seized by the Crown. The noble art thus passed into the hands of farmers and owners of estates, who installed private brewhouses to supply beer for farm workers and staff.

Commercial breweries began to appear during the latter part of the sixteenth century, growing steadily in number until, by the 1870s, some 30,000 were registered in Great Britain. This was a golden age, with beer drinking per head of the population at its all-time peak.

The Beer Act of 1830 had made it easy to obtain a licence to brew and sell beer from home, but increasing taxation on malt and hops made home-brewing less economically viable and so, by the end of the nineteenth century, the market was dominated by commercial brewers.

One hundred years ago, a brewery was to be found serving almost every local community, but as the market became increasingly competitive and preservation techniques and transport improved, the vast majority went out of business, were bought up or simply faded away. Only about 50 of the independent breweries that were in operation at the turn of the last century still brew today.

Of these, Shepherd Neame Ltd at Faversham in Kent is believed to be the oldest. Beer has been produced on the same site without interruption since the brewery's official foundation in 1698. Britain's oldest surviving brewpub is believed to be the Blue Anchor at Helston in Cornwall. It first became a pub around the middle of the sixteenth century, although it seems certain that monks were already brewing beer on the premises long before then.

The title of the oldest pub in Britain is disputed, but it probably belongs to the Trip to Jerusalem in Nottingham, part of which is cut into the rock of the castle and dates from 1189. This was once the malthouse for the castle brewery.

Although brewing technology may have progressed over the centuries, the process and basic ingredients have changed very little. Today, real ales still arrive at the pub with live yeast and fermentable sugars present in the brew, allowing the final stages of fermentation to take place in the cellar. This produces a fresh, pert, rounded flavour and natural effervescence. This is real ale at its very best, and part of the proud tradition which spans the centuries.

While market forces, and the price of real estate, see famous names disappearing every year from the brewing map, new, smaller operations are still springing up to replace them. At least 400 breweries are in business today, a considerable improvement on the situation of just 20 years ago.

WHAT WENT WRONG?

Many pubs originally brewed their own beer, often drawing water from a spring or well beneath. But cask-conditioned beers tended to be unreliable and were too often not properly looked after in the cellar.

To overcome this problem, the larger brewers turned to bottles and keg beers which, though bland and characterless by comparison, were consistent and had a much longer shelf life. They were also easy to transport and look after. Huge investments were made in kegs, equipment and advertising and, by the middle of the 1960s, real ale had all but disappeared from the British pub. This was the age of the ubiquitous Watneys Red Barrel, of Worthington E and Double Diamond; the British brewing industry was on the rocks.

Just four brewpubs remained and, as recently as 1985, there were fewer than 150 independent breweries in operation. Lager, too, although a poor imitation of the excellent continental brews, became increasingly popular with British pub-goers, due largely to advertising campaigns which targeted the trend-conscious younger drinker. The national breweries had imposed their corporate will to increase profits at the expense of quality. Real ale sales declined to the verge of extinction.

Though consistent, keg beer is a poor substitute for the natural product. While it starts life as real ale, the beer is filtered, pasteurised and chilled before being poured into containers. This process destroys and removes the yeast, preventing any further fermentation, and ensures that the beer is clear and bright in the keg.

But the beer is now dead. It produces no natural carbon dioxide and lacks the depth of character that cask-conditioned beers offer. In an effort to overcome this problem, it is now frequently served using a mixture of nitrogen and carbon dioxide, which gives the beer a tighter, creamy head in the glass while reducing the overall fizziness associated with carbon dioxide. But it is still a long way from the real thing.

Keg beer is easy to brew, easy to transport, easy to keep and easy to serve. Very little can go wrong so profits are at a premium and craftsmanship plays no part.

THE REAL ALE REVIVAL

Over the past 30 years, due to the dedication of a number of small brewery owners and the campaigning efforts of CAMRA (the Campaign for Real Ale), Britain's excellent real ales have gradually re-emerged and a great heritage of independent breweries is back on the scene. A change in the law known as the Beer Orders helped, too, permitting pubs previously tied to one brewery for all beer supplies to take a guest beer from elsewhere. This increased considerably the potential market for the smaller independent suppliers.

However, problems remain as the big brewers have found a way of fighting back. The Office of Fair Trading conducted a review of the Beer Orders, which was published in December 2000. It found that the larger brewers no longer owned and ran pubs in the traditional way but had sold them, or divided their business into breweries and pub companies.

So none of the big, national brewers now owns enough pubs for the Beer Orders provisions to apply. Traditional giants such as Bass and Whitbread have sold their brewing businesses to Interbrew, a giant international conglomerate, and are concentrating on their leisure interests instead.

This has caused a huge problem for the licensed trade, because the buying power is concentrated in the hands of large pub companies that buy from the big brewers, who can supply large quantities at knockdown prices. The pub companies then sell that beer to their tenants at the full list price and, because the tenant is tied to the pub company for all the beer sold in the pub, he or she has no choice but to buy what the pub company wants to sell at the price it wants to charge.

The same old problem has re-emerged and many tenants are struggling to meet steep targets set by their landlords, the pub companies. These companies, in turn, are increasingly profitable, enabling them to buy up more freehouses or to pounce when struggling smaller breweries with fewer tied houses go under.

While there are some enlightened exceptions among the all-too-dominant pub companies, fewer and fewer pubs are finding themselves able to buy beer from small breweries. The Government has shown signs that it might step in again, with the Chancellor of the Exchequer announcing in a recent budget that he was 'minded' to introduce a reduced rate of duty for the smaller brewers, allowing them to sell at more competitive prices. Consultations are underway and fingers are crossed, but, while it will certainly help the smaller brewers, it does nothing for those tenants already tied to aggressive and predatory pub companies. Pressure on the Government is growing for an extension of the Beer Orders provisions to be applied to the pub companies.

It is the imagination and inventiveness of the small independent and micro-brewers that has kept the real ale market alive in Britain and, against whatever odds, no doubt they will continue to do so. Before 1991, very few brewers produced seasonal or occasional ales; these days, very few do not. Today, the 400 independent breweries in Britain provide well over 1,000 beers of widely varying styles and character, plus a plethora of one-off special or occasional brews. Wheat, tandoori, garlic, vanilla, melon, coriander, lemon, orange, strawberry and liquorice are just a few of the novel flavours on offer, in addition of course to the whole raft of more traditional beers.

Fortunately, more and more enterprising publicans are now offering these brews and the image of the overweight, ageing and exclusively male real ale drinker is fading as a new generation of emerges. Quality, variety and seasonal sensitivity really do count for something and the market should easily be able to support the current crop of independents. Those that produce good brews of consistent quality and possess sufficient marketing and distribution skills will continue to thrive.

But the national brewers have not gone to sleep. Keg beer, dispensed using mixed gases in an effort to mimic the character of real ale, is still gaining ground on the back of multi-million pound marketing campaigns with which no one can compete. The predatory pub companies, too, are highly professional operations that can afford the soaring cost of land and property and can deliver healthy dividends to shareholders at the same time.

Real ale campaigners have fought long and hard to get British beer back to where it is today. Keeping it there is going to be just as much of a challenge.

THE BREWING PROCESS

The brewing process is a delicate one and most brewers inevitably experience occasional problems. The very nature of real ale makes it impossible to produce a consistently uniform product, barrel after barrel, month after month.

Of course, this is part of the attraction for the drinker. There is nothing like the experience of discovering new tastes and drinking sensations, and it places a premium on the skills and experience of both the brewer and the publican. But this inconsistency is something that the makers of bland, uniform keg beers are also keen to emphasise.

The slightest variations in established practice or, more commonly, yeast infections, equipment failures, changes in water or ingredient sources can upset the brewing process and affect the resulting beer. Often, a combination of these elements causes problems. No matter how much care is taken, it is simply not feasible to expect every new brew to taste and behave just the same as it did the last time.

Even renowned, award-winning beers are sometimes unacceptably inconsistent in quality and flavour. Increased demand during the summer months in particular can lead to beer being sent out 'green', before it is really ready.

Barley started the whole process off when it grew wild in Mesopotamia 8,000 years ago, and it is still a vital ingredient for beer-making today. It is soaked in water, then spread over the floor of the malthouse and gently heated to promote germination. This releases sugars, which are vital for fermentation. The barley is constantly raked to ensure even germination throughout. Once the grains start to produce rootlets, they are roasted to prevent further germination. The higher the temperature, the darker the malt will be, and the beer produced from it will consequently be darker, with a more roasted flavour. Pale malt will impart a sweeter, more delicate flavour to the brew.

At the brewery, the malt is passed through rollers in the malt mill, which crush the grains releasing the soluble starch. It is then put in the mash tun, where it is mixed with hot water or 'liquor'. This is known as 'mashing' and converts the soluble starches into fermentable and non-fermentable sugars. Depending on the type of beer required, a mix of malts may be included.

Water used in the brewing process is usually treated in order to remove any unwanted characteristics, and to improve consistency. The 'mash' is thoroughly stirred, then allowed to stand until it becomes clear, when it is known as 'wort'.

The wort is then run into the copper, where it is boiled and hops are added. At this stage, additional ingredients, such as invert sugar to increase fermentability, may be introduced, although purists might consider this an insult to the brewer's art.

There are many different types of hops and different brews use different hops or different combinations of them. They impart the essential bitterness of flavour and aroma and help to prevent infection in the wort. Of the varieties available, those most commonly used in Britain are still the Golding and the Fuggle, although many others are rapidly finding favour.

The wort remains in the copper for a couple of hours before it is passed through the hop back, where the spent hops are removed. On its way to the fermenting vessel, the wort travels through a heat exchanger, where its temperature is reduced to 20°C. This helps to produce optimum conditions for the yeast, as extremes of temperature will either kill it or result in a sluggish fermentation.

The wort is now 'pitched', as yeast is added to the fermenting vessel. It will remain here for around five days, with the yeast feeding on the fermentable sugars while excreting alcohol and producing carbon dioxide.

A thick creamy head of yeast builds up in the fermenting vessel, and this is skimmed and retained for further use. But, as the yeast in the brew becomes tired and much of the sugar is converted to alcohol, the process slows down. Primary fermentation is now over, and it is at this point that beer produced for the keg will go its separate way from real ale.

At this stage, beer is said to be 'green' and the flavour is harsh. The next stage, then, is its transfer to conditioning tanks, where it will remain for several days and much of the remaining sugar will ferment out to produce a more rounded flavour.

At last, the beer is ready to be put into the cask, or 'racked'. By now, any harsh or undesirable flavours will have disappeared and the brew will be crisp and fresh. Finings, which draw the dying yeast cells to the bottom of the cask, are added allowing the beer to clear, or 'drop bright'.

Some fermentable sugars and living yeast cells remain, so the beer continues to ferment gently in the cask. Sometimes, priming sugar will be added to assist this secondary fermentation. Some additional hops may also be added to impart a hoppier aroma to the brew. Once in the pub cellar, the beer will continue to ferment, producing carbon dioxide, which gives real ale its natural vitality. The finings will clear the beer down and the cask will then be tapped, in preparation for use.

This final stage, which is known as cask-conditioning, typically takes two or three days and brings the beer naturally to perfection. The whole process should have taken well over a week, but the beer should now be served as soon as possible.

Assuming that a beer is in the proper condition when it leaves the brewery, plenty of damage can still be done during distribution. Most beers will 'travel', providing that they are properly handled.

The brew within the cask is a living product that must be treated with respect if it is ultimately to be served at its best. Every time a cask is rolled, the finings, which draw all the solid matter to the bottom of the cask, are activated and these will work effectively for approximately five cask rollings. Better-quality finings are available which will allow more cask rollings, but they are significantly more expensive.

Therefore, a cask from a brewer in Scotland arriving at a pub in Cornwall may well have been moved between wholesalers and rolled a number of times. It may also have been in transit too long, having been left in various stores en route, and so be nearing the end of its life even before it arrives. The result will almost certainly be a lifeless, dull brew lacking in any subtlety of flavour.

Extremes of temperature can also prevent a brew from getting into condition properly and dropping clear and bright. Casks may be left in very hot or cold conditions, in warehouses, garages or on the back of vehicles where there is no temperature control equipment. This, too, may result in a brew being damaged before it arrives at the pub and, unfortunately, the publican will not know about this until it is too late.

Co-operation is the key. Regional and larger independent brewers have, for some time, distributed beers from other breweries and an increasing number of the smaller independents are now offering their product wholesale in an effort to improve turnover and distribution. Delivering beers to a brewery in another part of the country, while collecting that brewery's beer for sale with one's own, is obviously of great benefit to both parties.

So, it is very much in a publican's interest to deal directly with the breweries wherever possible and to avoid brews from wholesalers that may arrive via a devious route. It is important, too, to boycott any source of supply if it proves necessary to return more than the occasional cask. Having said that, there are some excellent real ale wholesalers operating in Britain. The key is to find them and then deal with them only, even if this ultimately limits the range of beers on offer.

A small amount of beer is inevitably lost when spilling and tapping each cask and, no matter how carefully it may be stooped, some beer will always be unservable. For this reason, many licensees prefer to buy larger casks in order to minimise wastage, but this often results in casks remaining on-line in the cellar for too long. Once a beer has worked into condition, it will remain at its best for a relatively short period of time. Every pint pulled draws more air into the cask, increasing the rate of oxidisation. If a beer remains on-line for four or five days, although still drinkable, it will be well past its best.

In order to prevent air being taken into the cask, some cellarmen use a cask breather system, which maintains a blanket of carbon dioxide on top of the beer. The gas is at a much lower pressure than that used for the dispensing of keg beer, so there is relatively little absorbence, although it is often detectable as a pint is served.

This method of dispensing beer has become a very contentious issue and there are few hard and fast rules. Many drinkers object to long 'swan necks' or multi-holed sparklers on the end of a hand pump, although some beers are brewed deliberately to be served in this way. Some beer is at its best served through the conventional, slit-type sparkler and short neck, while other brews lose much of their condition and hoppiness if served through any form of sparkler at all. In such cases, the beer should be served straight from the barrel if its subtleties of flavour are to be enjoyed to the full.

Different beers are at their best served in different ways. To insist that all sparklers are an abomination, or that all beer is at its best straight from the wood, is to misunderstand the nature of cask-conditioned beers. Rest assured, there will undoubtedly be something for everyone – and hopefully enough to go round.

Once, pub shelves heaved under the weight of bottles of light and brown ales, stouts and IPAs. However, these largely disappeared over time, relegated to the corner of the cold cabinet, the bottling lines closed down and dispatched to brewing history. Like keg beer, they were dead, pasteurised and filtered, bland and tasteless.

But in recent years a renaissance has taken place, largely led by the independent breweries, many of whom are now very successfully bottling real ale. Shelves are full again and although there are some pubs and brewery shops offering a good selection of these beers, you are more likely to find them in the supermarket.

Real ale in a bottle, or bottle-conditioned beer, like cask ale, contains live yeast and fermentable sugars. A secondary fermentation takes place in the bottle which develops the beer naturally and maintains its condition. Despite the almost hysterical passion for sell-by dates nowadays, these beers actually mature in the bottle and are likely to be in prime condition for some time. Beers like Fuller's Vintage Ale, produced in 1997 with a sell-by date of the end of 2000, is drinking beautifully now and probably will do so for a long while yet. Obviously, though, you should make your own decision as to whether your particular bottle is drinkable and will not cause you any upset.

Like cask beer, to allow enjoyment of the full complexity of flavour they should be between 55–59 degrees Fahrenheit when consumed. The bottle should be allowed to stand for a sufficient period to allow the sediment to drop to the bottom, then poured carefully, to prevent the sediment rising and clouding the beer. They should never be drunk straight from the bottle. Some, less hoppy, continental beers, can be drunk cloudy, but British bottle-conditioned beers generally should not.

The Hogs Back Brewery at Tongham has an excellent selection of bottle-conditioned beers and the following list represents some of their best-sellers. Tasting notes were produced by David Underwood.

Match the colour numbers to the chart on the back flap to give you an idea of the colour of the ale and therefore its style and taste.

ASH VINE PENGUIN PORTER 4.2% ABV 500 ML
Brewed by Ash Vine Brewery, Unit F, Vallis Trading Estate, Robins Lane, Frome, Somerset BA11 3DT. ☎ (01323) 300041.
Colour: Deep burgundy or dark oak (17).
Head: Brown, dense small bubbles in a small head which subsided into the beer.
Aroma: Rich and fruity with blackcurrant notes.
Taste: Subtle fruit developing, then bitter blackcurrant bursting through in a long, tart fruit aftertaste.
Ease of Decanting: Yeast clings to the base of the bottle and the head stays small, so a nice easy pour.
Opinion: A nice fruity porter which would go down very well with a nice Irish stew.

B&T DRAGON SLAYER 4.5% ABV 500 ML
Brewed by B&T Brewery Ltd, The Brewery, Shefford, Bedfordshire SG17 5DZ.
☎ (01462) 815080.
Colour: Pale golden-yellow (3).
Head: White dense large rocky head.
Aroma: A sweet malty aroma, most unexpected from such a pale beer.
Taste: Initial taste is a delicate yet sweet hop flavour which continues through to the end with a delicate hoppy aftertaste.
Ease of Decanting: Have two glasses ready. Not easy due to the large head, and pouring into one glass from start to finish could be difficult. Best to use the second glass, and watch out for swirls of yeast in the last quarter. Well worth the effort.
Opinion: A pale, delicate, thirst-quenching ale which would be a godsend after a hot curry.

BALLARD'S BEST BITTER 4.2% ABV
Brewed by Ballard's Brewery Ltd, The Old Sawmill, Nyewood, Petersfield, Hampshire GU31 5HA. ☎ (01730) 821301.
Colour: Light orange-brown, copper-coloured ale (10).
Head: White, dense bubbles in a large head which keeps growing even after pouring has finished.
Aroma: Delicate toffee apple and caramel aroma.
Taste: Delicate caramel leading to hops on the side of the tongue, with caramel sweetness blending in to produce a slightly burnt, bitter aftertaste.
Ease of Decanting: Difficult. Due to the head growth I couldn't finish pouring it all into a pint glass, so it may need an hour or two in the fridge just to quieten it down a bit before opening. Worth the effort though.
Opinion: Nice beer with sirloin steak and chips.

BALLARD'S NYEWOOD GOLD 5.0% ABV
Brewed by Ballard's Brewery Ltd, The Old Sawmill, Nyewood, Petersfield, Hampshire GU31 5HA. ☎ (01730) 821301.
Colour: Amber-orange (6).
Head: White dense bubbles in a good head that did not need creating.
Aroma: Sweet and appley.
Taste: Fresh, frothy with apples slightly drying into a subtle cidery finish.
Ease of Decanting: Yeast clung to the base of the bottle. Pour carefully to control the head.
Opinion: An unusually cidery beer, very nice and well worth trying. Would go down well with roast pork and crackling.

BALLARD'S WASSAIL 6.0% ABV 500 ML
Brewed by Ballard's Brewery Ltd, The Old Sawmill, Nyewood, Petersfield, Hampshire GU31 5HA. ☎ (01730) 821301.
Colour: Burgundy-brown (14).
Head: Brown, small head with dense bubbles.
Aroma: Malty with slight fruit notes.
Taste: Definite taste of molasses and malt, balanced with bitter fruits in the aftertaste.
Ease of Decanting: A nice easy-pouring ale with yeast that clings to the bottom of the bottle and a head that doesn't get too excited on pouring.
Opinion: A lovely beer with game pie.

BARUM BREWERY BARUM BARNSTABLASTA 6.6% ABV
Brewed by Barum Brewery, c/o Reform Inn, Reform Road, Pilton, Barnstable, Devon EX31 1PD. ☎ (01271) 329994.
Colour: Oak-burgundy (17).
Head: Small light brown head with small bubbles.
Aroma: Acrid liquorice with blackcurrant.
Taste: Rich blackcurrant and liquorice followed by rich black cherry bitterness that prickles on the tongue, then slides away in a rich black cherry finish.
Ease of Decanting: Yeast was a touch loose at the bottom but the head stayed small, a small amount of care for a huge reward.
Opinion: Packed with flavour, robust enough for liver and bacon with creamy mash potato.

BARUM BREWERY BARUM BREAKFAST 5.0% ABV
Brewed by Barum Brewery, c/o Reform Inn, Reform Road, Pilton, Barnstable, Devon EX31 1PD. ☎ (01271) 329994.
Colour: Ruby-brown (13).
Head: Stayed small, bubbles were white and small.
Aroma: Sweet with slight sulphur tones and a slightly acrid note.
Taste: Smooth initially, sweet like flat Coca Cola maturing to rich fruit cake, then to bitter cherries lightly furring the sides of the tongue in a long aftertaste.
Ease of Decanting: Yeast stayed at the bottom and the head was small, so nice and easy.
Opinion: A very nice beer, would go down well with roast beef and Yorkshire pudding.

BARUM BREWERY BARUM CHALLENGER 5.6% ABV
Brewed by Barum Brewery, c/o Reform Inn, Reform Road, Pilton, Barnstable, Devon EX31 1PD. ☎ (01271) 329994.
Colour: Oak-burgundy (17).
Head: White dense bubbles in a large head.
Aroma: Fragrant butterscotch and burnt toffee.
Taste: Frothy burnt toffee taste with butterscotch maturing to bittersweet demerara in a short aftertaste.
Ease of Decanting: Although yeast stayed at the bottom, the large head presented something of a challenge. Persevere, however, as it is well worth the effort.
Opinion: Would go down very nicely with a nice roast pork dinner on a Sunday afternoon.

BARUM BREWERY BARUM ORIGINAL 4.4% ABV
Brewed by Barum Brewery, c/o Reform Inn, Reform Road, Pilton, Barnstable, Devon EX31 1PD. ☎ (01271) 329994.
Colour: Dark amber-chestnut (11).
Head: Large head with lots of small dense white bubbles.
Aroma: Slight rubber and glue aroma though very subtle.
Taste: Smooth initial taste maturing to slight soft apple flavour that dries to tart bitter crab apple.
Ease of Decanting: Yeast swirls in the last quarter with a big head make this a challenge, well worth the effort though.
Opinion: Would go down very nicely with fish and chips.

BLUE ANCHOR SPINGO 6.6% ABV 275 ML
Brewed by The Blue Anchor Inn, 50 Coinagehall Street, Helston, Cornwall TR13 8EX.
☎ (01326) 562821.
Colour: Deep burgundy ale (19).
Head: Brown, dense bubbles in a large head.
Aroma: Sweet forest fruits aroma.
Taste: Initial sensation is prickling on the tongue, the taste is malty caramel with slight liquorice in a short, refreshing aftertaste.
Ease of Decanting: Well-conditioned ale in a small bottle (275 ml), this makes pouring a bit easier. When poured into a pint glass there is room for the large head with brown dense bubbles.
Opinion: Full-bodied malty ale that would go nice with Irish stew.

BLUE ANCHOR SPINGO MIDDLE 6.6% ABV 500 ML
Brewed by The Blue Anchor Inn, 50 Coinagehall Street, Helston, Cornwall TR13 8EX.
☎ (01326) 562821.
Colour: Orangey-brown ale (10).
Head: Very large white dense head.
Aroma: Burnt sugar and honeycomb, like a spiced fruitcake.
Taste: Smooth with fruit warming on the tongue with a short bitter fruit aftertaste on the middle of the tongue.
Ease of Decanting: Difficult with large head, indicating that this beer is sensitive to temperature. Put in the fridge for an hour to control the head.
Opinion: Malty, easy-drinking ale, nice with a strong Cheddar ploughman's.

BURTON BRIDGE BRAMBLE STOUT 5.0% ABV 500 ML
Brewed by Burton Bridge Brewery, Bridge Street, Burton upon Trent, Staffordshire DE14 1SY.
☎ (01283) 510575.
Colour: Black (20).
Head: Brown, dense, large head.
Aroma: Fruity, blackberry aromas.
Taste: Initial grainy fruit taste which explodes into blackberry sweetness, balanced by fruit bitterness in the aftertaste.
Ease of Decanting: Be careful with this one. Large-headed beer with yeast swirls in the last quarter of the bottle, but well worth the effort.
Opinion: Dark, fruity, interesting ale, good with a nice Stilton ploughman's.

BURTON BRIDGE BURTON PORTER 4.5% ABV 500 ML
Brewed by Burton Bridge Brewery, Bridge Street, Burton upon Trent, Staffordshire DE14 1SY.
☎ (01283) 510575.
Colour: Black with burgundy hints in the light (20).
Head: Brown coloured with small, dense bubbles, stayed small and manageable.
Aroma: Slight vanilla aroma, sweet.
Taste: Fruity initial taste frothing on the tongue leading to vanilla pods and fruit cake, then a short bittersweet fruit aftertaste.
Ease of Decanting: Yeast clings to the base of the bottle and head stays small, so a nice easy pourer.
Opinion: Dark, frothy and easy to drink. Would go down a treat with O'Hagan's sausage and mash.

BUSHY'S ALE OF MAN 4.5% ABV 500 ML
Brewed by The Mount Murray Brewing Co. Ltd, Mount Murray, Castletown Road, Braddan, Isle of Man IM4 1JE. ☎ (01624) 661244.
Colour: Chestnut-coloured ale (11).
Head: Small head with dense, white bubbles.
Aroma: Redcurrant and citrus forest fruit aromas.
Taste: Thin initial taste leading to a sour plum or bitter fruit flavour with a short drying souring aftertaste.
Ease of Decanting: Easy beer to pour, with yeast staying at the bottom and the head staying small.
Opinion: Definitely a sour style of beer reminiscent of a Belgian Iambic. Would complement roast beef with horseradish baguette.

BUTTS GOLDEN BROWN 5.0% ABV 500 ML
Brewed by Butts Brewery Ltd, Northfield Farm, Wantage Road, Great Shefford, Hungerford, Berkshire RG17 7BY. ☎ (01488) 648133.
Colour: Dark amber (11).
Head: White, dense head with small bubbles, pours quite large and clings to side of glass.
Aroma: Slightly sulphury with tar aromas.
Taste: Smooth initial impression leading to fruit with molasses, yet balanced in the aftertaste by bitter fruit and hops.
Ease of Decanting: Not an easy pour, due to the large head, so you will possibly need two glasses and a steady hand. Well worth the effort.
Opinion: Would go down very nicely with a pork pie ploughman's.

CONISTON OLD MAN 5.0% ABV 500 ML
Brewed under contract by Brakspears Brewery.
Colour: Deep brown (15).
Head: Small, white dense head.
Aroma: Floral and fruity.
Taste: Definitely malt in the mouth-feel, but not too sweet and not long in the aftertaste.
Ease of Decanting: Although the head stayed small, there were yeast tendrils in the last quarter of the bottle, so pourable with a little care.
Opinion: This beer is definitely on the sweeter end of the taste spectrum, but without cloying. Nice with roast beef and Yorkshire pudding.

CROPTON BACKWOODS BITTER 5.1% ABV
Brewed by Cropton Brewery at The New Inn, Cropton, Pickering, North Yorkshire YO18 8HH
Colour: Oak-burgundy (17).
Head: Small controllable head with white bubbles.
Aroma: Slightly acrid black cherry aroma.
Taste: Thick caramel, then bitter elderflower maturing to grainy bitter chocolate.
Ease of Decanting: Small head and the yeast clung to the base of the bottle so nice and easy.
Opinion: Rich full-bodied beer, would go down well with a duck pâté ploughman's.

DURHAM BEDES' CHALICE 4.8% ABV
Brewed by The Durham Brewery, Unit 5A, Bowburn North Industrial Estate, Bowburn, County Durham DH6 5PF. ☎ (0191) 377 1991.
Colour: Mid-brown, coppery-coloured (9).
Head: White, dense and small.
Aroma: Aromatically hoppy/flowery aroma.

Taste: Initial hoppiness with the bottle conditioning making its presence known with slight foaming during tasting, making this a refreshing thirst quencher with malt fading in the aftertaste.
Ease of Decanting: Much easier than Cloister. Yeast clings to the base of bottle and the head does not foam up too much.
Opinion: Labelled as suitable for vegetarians, this beer would be excellent with a nice Thai vegetable curry.

DURHAM CLOISTER 4.5% ABV
Brewed by The Durham Brewery, Unit 5A, Bowburn North Industrial Estate, Bowburn, County Durham DH6 5PF. ☎ (0191) 377 1991.
Colour: Golden-orange coloured ale (4).
Head: Pours up with a large white rocky head, with dense bubbles which subside, clinging to the sides of the glass.
Aroma: Subtle fruity malt aroma.
Taste: A complex ale for its strength, Cloister's initial malty aroma actually gives way to an initial hop taste. The malt sweetness then comes through to balance the hops, then slides away leaving a bitter but not astringent hoppy aftertaste.
Ease of Decanting: Be careful with this one. Not easy to pour due to a large creamy head, but well worth the effort. Yeast disturbs whilst pouring so a steady hand and a sharp eye are required.
Opinion: A complex and quaffable ale that would go down very well with fish and chips.

DURHAM SAINT CUTHBERT 6.5% ABV 500 ML
Brewed by The Durham Brewery, Unit 5A, Bowburn North Industrial Estate, Bowburn, County Durham DH6 5PF. ☎ (0191) 377 1991.
Colour: Orangey-amber ale (8).
Head: White dense bubbles in a medium head.
Aroma: Toffee and caramel.
Taste: Sweet malt initial taste with full-bodied sweetness turning into hops and increasing in bitterness through long aftertaste.
Ease of Decanting: Medium head and yeast that clings to the base of the bottle means that this is a nice easy-pouring ale.
Opinion: A lovely full-bodied ale that would go down very nicely with a pork pie.

EDWIN TAYLOR'S EXTRA STOUT 4.5% ABV 500 ML
Brewed by B&T Brewery Ltd, The Brewery, Shefford, Bedfordshire SG17 5DZ.
☎ (01462) 815080.
Colour: Black with ruby tints in the light (20).
Head: Pours with a small head with brown, dense bubbles.
Aroma: A very aromatic ale with earthy blackcurrant notes.
Taste: The theme of this B&T stout is definitely malt. The initial taste is smooth and malty, leading to hints of fruit, yet finishing with a subtle yet refreshing hoppy aftertaste.
Ease of Decanting: Quite easy as the head pours small and tight. Keep an eagle eye out for those yeast tendrils in the last quarter of the bottle – a steady hand wins the day.
Opinion: Very nice example of bottle-conditioned stout from a small brewery. Would be a very nice accompaniment to a roast dinner.

**EDWIN TUCKERS EAST INDIA PALE ALE
6.5% ABV 500 ML**
Brewed by Teignworthy Brewery, The Maltings,
Teign Road, Newton Abbot, Devon TQ12 4AA.
☎ (01626) 332066.
Colour: Rich golden amber (8).
Head: Small head with dense white bubbles.
Aroma: Slightly citrusy with sweet caramel.
Taste: Unexpectedly smooth and sweet initial
taste, smooth caramel continuing into long
warm bitter lingering aftertaste.
Ease of Decanting: Won't take an expert, but not
one to pour for the novice, head was
controllable but yeast swirls in the last quarter.
Opinion: Unexpectedly sweet for an IPA, which
are traditionally very hoppy, nicely balanced.
Would go down well with roast pork

**EDWIN TUCKERS EMPRESS RUSSIAN PORTER
10.5% ABV 275 ML**
Brewed by Teignworthy Brewery, The Maltings,
Teign Road, Newton Abbot, Devon TQ12 4AA.
☎ (01626) 332066.
Colour: Thick dense black (20).
Head: Creamy meniscus that broke to a large
bubbled head if poured from a height which
disappeared into the beer.
Aroma: Rich, acrid and fruity, like dark rum.
Taste: Dense full soft mouth-feel, initial liquorice
with prune developing a hot fermented black
treacle tempered by bitter fruit in the aftertaste.
Ease of Decanting: Easy to pour as the bottle is
275 ml, though it was hard to see the yeast due
to the darkness of the beer
Opinion: Wow! Full-blooded Russian-style porter,
intense and strong, this beer should be drunk
like a port, and would go down well after a good
meal with some good cheese.

**EDWIN TUCKERS VICTORIAN STOCK ALE
12% ABV 275 ML**
Brewed by Teignworthy Brewery, The Maltings,
Teign Road, Newton Abbot, Devon TQ12 4AA.
☎ (01626) 332066.
Colour: Thick dense black (20).
Head: Hardly headed up at all, though English
beers of this strength tend not to.
Aroma: Intense cocoa with bitter chocolate.
Taste: Sweet rich raisins that warm the tastebuds
like liquid Christmas pudding, like a sweet
sherry or dark molasses, intense flavours.
Ease of Decanting: Yeast clung to the base of the
bottle, no head and a small bottle make this easy
to decant.
Opinion: Just when the porter takes you to
heaven, along comes this beer to remind you of
your immortality. A beautiful strong ale to be
savoured like an expensive port.

ENVILLE ALE HONEY BEER 4.5% ABV 500 ML
Brewed by Enville Ales, Enville Brewery, Cox
Green, Enville, Stourbridge, West Midlands DY7
5LG. ☎ (01384) 873728.
Colour: Very pale yellow (1).
Head: Bottle expelled most of the beer on
opening in the form of a very large foamy head.
Once this had subsided, large lumps of yeast
floated throughout the remainder of the beer,
rendering it undrinkable.
Opinion: Excessive secondary conditioning in
the bottle caused the beer to erupt upon
opening.

FREEMINER GRIM REAPER 4.0% ABV 500 ML
Brewed by Freeminer Brewery Ltd, The Laurels,
Sling, Coleford, Gloucestershire GL16 8JJ.
☎ (01594) 810408.
Colour: Amber (7).
Head: White dense bubbles with a small head.
Aroma: Caramel.
Taste: Subtle initial malt taste quickly followed
by strong bitter hops punching through leaving
a long aftertaste of bitter hops breaking on the
side of the tongue.
Ease of Decanting: Yeast clings to the base of the
bottle and the head is not too big, so a nice
easy-pouring ale.
Opinion: Lots of taste for a beer of this strength.
Very nice with a cheese ploughman's.

FREEMINER HURRICANE 4.0% ABV 330 ML
Brewed by Freeminer Brewery Ltd, The Laurels,
Sling, Coleford, Gloucestershire GL16 8JJ.
☎ (01594) 810408.
Colour: Amber (7).
Head: White dense bubbles with a small head.
Aroma: Caramel with subtle hoppy overtones.
Taste: Hops and malt combined, with the hops
finishing long in the aftertaste.
Ease of Decanting: Yeast clings to the base of the
bottle and the head is not too big, so a nice
easy-pouring ale.
Opinion: A nice lunchtime beer which was
perfect with my ham and tomato sandwich.

GALE'S FESTIVAL MILD 4.8% ABV 330 ML
Brewed by George Gale & Co. Ltd, The
Hampshire Brewery, Horndean, Hampshire PO8
0DA. ☎ (0239) 257 1212.
Colour: Black with ruby tints (20).
Head: Brown, dense, small head.
Aroma: Malty and fruity, reminiscent of a
Belgian Bruin.
Taste: Initial fizz prickling on the tongue leads to
bitter fruit taste which tails off in the aftertaste.
Ease of Decanting: Easy to pour due to small
head and yeast that clings to the base of the
bottle.
Opinion: Unusual mild which seems to use bitter
fruit flavours as a substitute for hop bitterness.
Nice with an O'Hagan's sausage.

GALE'S HSB 4.8% ABV 330 ML
Brewed by George Gale & Co. Ltd, The
Hampshire Brewery, Horndean, Hampshire PO8
0DA. ☎ (0239) 257 1212.
Colour: Oak-burgundy (17).
Head: Good natural head with small white
bubbles .
Aroma: Reminded me of Coca Cola.
Taste: Sweet malt, frothy but with lots of body,
maturing to caramel with a hint of burnt
currants.
Ease of Decanting: Yeast stayed at the bottom,
easy to pour due to the 330 ml bottle.
Opinion: A tasty beer that would accompany
liver and onions with mash. Very nice.

GALE'S JUBILEE ALE 12% ABV 275 ML
Brewed by George Gale & Co. Ltd, The
Hampshire Brewery, Horndean, Hampshire PO8
0DA. ☎ (0239) 257 1212.
Colour: Ruby-brown (13).
Head: Did not pour with a head.
Aroma: A faint aroma of warming rich fruity
malt.

Taste: Sweet warming fruit with Jaffa Cake zestiness finishing in a long bittersweet aftertaste.
Ease of Decanting: Another corked bottle, no head and sticky yeast so nice and easy.
Opinion: Wow, this would be best described as a dessert beer. A commemorative ale to be enjoyed with plum pudding and brandy sauce at Christmas.

GALE'S MILESTONES PALE ALE 9.0% ABV 275 ML
Brewed by George Gale & Co. Ltd, The Hampshire Brewery, Horndean, Hampshire PO8 0DA. ☎ (0239) 257 1212.
Colour: Oak-burgundy (17).
Head: Very low creamy head disappeared into the beer.
Aroma: Stewed baked apple, toffee and butterscotch.
Taste: Alcohol warms the mouth, then rich butterscotch matures warming to rich sherry.
Ease of Decanting: A small head and yeast staying in the bottle means that this is an easy beer to pour.
Opinion: Another of those famous Gale's after-dinner beers to be savoured and enjoyed.

GALE'S PRIZE OLD ALE 9.0% ABV 275 ML
Brewed by George Gale & Co. Ltd, The Hampshire Brewery, Horndean, Hampshire PO8 0DA. ☎ (0239) 257 1212.
Colour: Rich-burgundy (19).
Head: Did not pour with a head.
Aroma: Sweet pungent toffee apple.
Taste: Stewed apple and sultana initially, warms the throat and coats the tongue then leaves a sweet fruitcake aftertaste.
Ease of Decanting: After taking the cork out, no problem as the bottle is only 275 ml, no head and yeast that stuck to the base of the bottle.
Opinion: An after-dinner beer to be savoured like a fine port or a brandy, a true classic.

HAMPSHIRE CALIFORNIAN RED 5.0% ABV 500 ML
Brewed by Hampshire Brewery Ltd, Romsey Industrial Estate, Greatbridge Road, Romsey, Hampshire SO51 0HR. ☎ (01794) 830000.
Colour: Oak-burgundy (17).
Head: Large with dense white bubbles.
Aroma: Like a mix of butterscotch and blackcurrant.
Taste: Initially fresh and clean, leading to bitter cherries with slight nuttiness maturing into fruity bitterness in a long aftertaste.
Ease of Decanting: Although the yeast clung to the base of the bottle, the head was lively, so take care when pouring.
Opinion: A lively beer to enjoy with a good Lincolnshire sausage and creamy mash.

HAMPSHIRE GOLD RESERVE 4.8% ABV 500 ML
Brewed by Hampshire Brewery Ltd, Romsey Industrial Estate, Greatbridge Road, Romsey, Hampshire SO51 0HR. ☎ (01794) 830000.
Colour: Straw-coloured ale (2).
Head: Small head with dense white bubbles.
Aroma: Lemon zest with lime high notes.
Taste: Frothy slight banana, warming spices turn to bitter fruit on the tongue, then hops dry the mouth in a long aftertaste.
Ease of Decanting: Yeast clung to the base of the bottle, the head stayed small, so nice and easy.
Opinion: A very nice beer, would go down nicely with a good chicken tikka.

HAMPSHIRE PENDRAGON 4.8% ABV 500 ML
Brewed by Hampshire Brewery Ltd, Romsey Industrial Estate, Greatbridge Road, Romsey, Hampshire SO51 0HR. ☎ (01794) 830000.
Colour: Oak-coloured ale (16).
Head: White, dense bubbles in a large, but controllable, head.
Aroma: Sweet banana and vanilla aromas.
Taste: Initial impression is of fizz and prickle on the tongue, with subtle malt following through and leading to subtle bananas and a long aftertaste of hops drying and maturing on the tongue.
Easy of Decanting: A careful pour will reward the drinker with a smashing glass of beer. The head can be controlled by slow, careful pouring halfway through, keeping a close eye on those yeasty tendrils.
Opinion: A fruity beer with a long, drying, hoppy aftertaste, lovely with roast pork.

HAMPSHIRE PRIDE OF ROMSEY IPA 4.8% ABV 500 ML
Brewed by Hampshire Brewery Ltd, Romsey Industrial Estate, Greatbridge Road, Romsey, Hampshire SO51 0HR. ☎ (01794) 830000.
Colour: Copper-coloured (9).
Head: White, dense bubbles in a small head which is controllable through the height of the pour.
Aroma: Sweet floral, malty aroma.
Taste: Hops on the middle of the tongue that bitter progressively in a long aftertaste.
Ease of Decanting: Nice and easy to pour, with a controllable head and the yeast clinging to the base of the bottle.
Opinion: Nice bitter ale, a good quencher for a hot vindaloo.

HANBY PREMIUM 4.6% ABV 500 ML
Brewed by Hanby Ales Ltd. New Brewery, Aston Park, Soulton Road, Wem, Shropshire, SY4 5SD.
Colour: Rich golden amber (8).
Head: A large white head with small bubbles.
Aroma: Sweet red rhubarb.
Taste: Bitter black cherry zings through the taste buds increasing in fruitiness through to the end.
Ease of Decanting: Yeast swirls in the last quarter and the large head make this beer a difficult beer to pour, well worth the effort though.
Opinion: A beer with bags of taste, would go down nicely with steak and kidney pie.

HANBY RAINBOW CHASER 4.3% ABV 500 ML
Brewed by Hanby Ales Ltd. New Brewery, Aston Park, Soulton Road, Wem, Shropshire, SY4 5SD.
Colour: Amber ale (7).
Head: White, small bubbles and controllable.
Aroma: Molasses and fruit cake.
Taste: Bitter honey like a dry mead, dry honey stays throughout finishing in a bitter flourish.
Ease of Decanting: Yeast clings to the bottom and the head stays small, so nice and easy.
Opinion: A nice thirst-quenching beer to be enjoyed on a hot summer's day with a honey-glazed ham baguette.

HANBY SHROPSHIRE STOUT 4.4% ABV 500 ML
Brewed by Hanby Ales Ltd. New Brewery, Aston Park, Soulton Road, Wem, Shropshire, SY4 5SD.
Colour: Black (20).
Head: Brown dense bubbles in a small controllable head.

Aroma: Unusual aromas, biscuity, chocolatey and with a slight hint of old sock. Strangely pleasant.
Taste: Bitter blackcurrant initially leading to bitter fruit, drying to a bitter cherry and dark chocolate finish that dries on the tongue, a lingering aftertaste of drying dark chocolate.
Ease of Decanting: Head stayed small and yeast stayed at the base of the bottle making this an easy beer to pour.
Opinion: A complex stout, would be beautiful with organic roast lamb.

HARVEY'S IMPERIAL EXTRA DOUBLE STOUT 9.0% ABV 330 ML

Brewed by Harvey & Sons (Lewes) Ltd, The Bridge Wharf Brewery, 6 Cliffe High Street, Lewes, East Sussex, BN7 2AH. ☎ (01273) 480209
Colour: Black (20).
Head: Very brown dense head like drinking chocolate, required pouring from height to create.
Aroma: Mulled wine and vintage port.
Taste: Initially smooth velvety mouth-feel, then powerful liquorice and honey warming to a long bitter liquorice aftertaste.
Ease of Decanting: The 330 ml bottle means that there is more room in the pint glass for this beer, yeast stays at the bottom and head has to be created, so a nice easy beer to pour.
Opinion: This beer has the wow factor, savour it like a fine port as an after-dinner drink.

HOGS BACK A OVER T (AROMAS OVER TONGHAM) 9.0% ABV 275 ML

Brewed by Hogs Back Brewery, Manor Farm, The Street, Tongham, Surrey GU10 1DE.
☎ (01252) 783000.
Colour: Oak-burgundy (17).
Head: Small creamy-coloured head with small bubbles.
Aroma: Sweet and alcoholic, like Christmas pudding.
Taste: Smooth thick caramel and molasses matures into liquorice then dries into thick caramel sweetness.
Ease of Decanting: Yeast stayed at the bottom of the bottle, the head was very small and the bottle was small which meant that it fit easily into my pint glass.
Opinion: A barley-wine style of beer, nice after dinner when appreciated like a fine port or brandy.

HOGS BACK BSA (BURMA STAR ALE) 4.5% ABV 500 ML

Brewed by Hogs Back Brewery, Manor Farm, The Street, Tongham, Surrey GU10 1DE.
☎ (01252) 783000.
Colour: Oak-burgundy beer (17).
Head: Stayed controllable, creamy white dense white bubbles.
Aroma: Subtle Ovaltine aroma, slightly fruity.
Taste: Subtle initial malt, fruit follows through, dries on the tongue, then bitter hops follow in a long aftertaste.
Ease of Decanting: Yeast stayed at the bottom of the bottle and the head can be created to whatever size is required.
Opinion: Nice beer with a cheese ploughman's.

HOGS BACK OTT (OLD TONGHAM TASTY) 6.0% ABV

Brewed by Hogs Back Brewery, Manor Farm, The Street, Tongham, Surrey GU10 1DE.
☎ (01252) 783000.
Colour: Black with burgundy tints (20).
Head: Small head with brown, dense bubbles.
Aroma: Sweet liquorice aroma.
Taste: Frothy, strong liquorice flavour with hops drying on the tongue in a long aftertaste.
Ease of Decanting: Yeast clung to the base of the bottle and the head stayed small and controllable.
Opinion: Would go very nicely with liver and bacon.

HOGS BACK TEA (TRADITIONAL ENGLISH ALE) 4.2% ABV 500 ML

Brewed by Hogs Back Brewery, Manor Farm, The Street, Tongham, Surrey GU10 1DE.
☎ (01252) 783000.
Colour: Orange-brown (10).
Head: Creamy-coloured small head which disappeared into the beer.
Aroma: Citrus zesty pear drops with a touch of blackcurrant.
Taste: Subtle and easy to drink with malt and subtle fruit flavours coming through then drying, then hops hit, then dry in the aftertaste.
Ease of Decanting: Yeast stayed at the bottom of the bottle and head stayed small, so nice and easy.
Opinion: An easy-to-drink bitter that would be a good thirst-quencher for a nice hot Indian curry.

HOGS BACK VINTAGE ALE 6.5% ABV

Brewed by Hogs Back Brewery, Manor Farm, The Street, Tongham, Surrey GU10 1DE.
☎ (01252) 783000.
Colour: Burgundy-coloured beer (17).
Head: Small head with brown, dense bubbles which needed height to create.
Aroma: Powerful liquorice and molasses aroma.
Taste: Full, creamy mouth-feel with sweet chocolate fudge, slowly tempered by a bitter blackberry aftertaste.
Ease of Decanting: A swing-top bottle means that a bottle opener is not needed. Yeast clings to the base of the bottle and the head has to be created by pouring from a height, so a nice easy-pouring ale.
Opinion: Usually sold in a wooden presentation box, this is not a cheap beer. However, it lives up to its billing and is well worth trying. Nice with game pie.

HOGS BACK WOBBLE IN A BOTTLE 7.5% ABV 275 ML

Brewed by Hogs Back Brewery, Manor Farm, The Street, Tongham, Surrey GU10 1DE.
☎ (01252) 783000.
Colour: Ruby-brown (13).
Head: Small head with small dense white bubbles.
Aroma: Citrusy and slightly zesty.
Taste: Sweet caramel to start, then develops into powerful bitter fruits leading to bitter lemon in a long drying aftertaste.
Ease of Decanting: Yeast clings to the bottom of the bottle and head stays small and with the unusual 275 ml bottle, no problems to pour.
Opinion: A nice beer to sip and appreciate with roast pork and all the trimmings.

BOTTLE-CONDITIONED BEERS

HOP BACK CROP CIRCLE 4.2% ABV 500 ML
Brewed by Hop Back Brewery plc, Unit 21–24
Batten Road Industrial Estate, Downton,
Salisbury, Wiltshire SP5 3HU. ☎ (01725) 510986.
Colour: Pale straw-coloured ale (2).
Head: White dense small bubbles, stayed small
and was controllable with care.
Aroma: Aroma of strong bitter lager hops with
hints of elderflower.
Taste: Smooth and frothy with light berries
changing to light fruit, turning slightly bitter in
a short aftertaste.
Ease of Decanting: Yeast behaved impeccably
and the head stayed small, though controlled
with care, worth the effort.
Opinion: A light and refreshing thirst-quenching
bitter which would be a godsend after a hot
spicy curry.

**HOP BACK SUMMER LIGHTNING 5.0% ABV
500 ML**
Brewed by Hop Back Brewery plc, Unit 21–24
Batten Road Industrial Estate, Downton,
Salisbury, Wiltshire SP5 3HU. ☎ (01725) 510986.
Colour: Pale straw-coloured ale (2).
Head: Small white head with small bubbles.
Aroma: Hard to describe, it reminded me of
freshly mown hay.
Taste: Initial frothy sweetness dries to a fruit
salad finish that dries with a slightly bitter
aftertaste.
Ease of Decanting: Yeast swirls in the last
quarter, so a steady hand is needed.
Opinion: A legendary beer, another good beer to
enjoy with a good hot curry.

**HOP BACK TAIPHOON LEMON GRASS BEER
4.2% ABV**
Brewed by Hop Back Brewery plc, Unit 21–24
Batten Road Industrial Estate, Downton,
Salisbury, Wiltshire SP5 3HU. ☎ (01725) 510986.
Colour: Deep golden-coloured ale (4).
Head: White, dense-bubbled head that says small
and manageable, yet clings to the sides of the
glass.
Aroma: Sweet and lemony aroma.
Taste: Initial impression is sweet, light and
refreshing with slight warm spice taste after
frothing subsides, with a long aftertaste of subtle
spice on the tongue.
Ease of Decanting: Yeast clings to the base of the
bottle and the head stays manageable, so a nice
easy pour.
Opinion: Nice beer with a Thai curry.
Surprisingly refreshing and well worth trying
even if the idea of a lemongrass beer does not
appeal.

HOP BACK THUNDERSTORM 5.0% ABV 500 ML
Brewed by Hop Back Brewery plc, Unit 21–24
Batten Road Industrial Estate, Downton,
Salisbury, Wiltshire SP5 3HU. ☎ (01725) 510986.
Colour: Pale amber (5).
Head: White head with small bubbles, stayed
controllable.
Aroma: Like sweet fruit salad.
Taste: Frothy, light and hoppy, but not bitter,
fruit develops and dries in a short aftertaste.
Ease of Decanting: Yeast swirls in the last quarter
so pour gently and reap the rewards.
Opinion: An easy-drinking, thirst-quenching ale,
excellent with a nice hot curry.

ICENI FINE SOFT DAY 4.0% ABV 500 ML
Brewed by Iceni Brewery, 3 Foulden Road,
Ickburgh, Mundford, Norfolk IP26 5BJ.
☎ (01842) 878922.
Colour: Rich golden amber (8).
Head: White small bubble head that stayed
controllable, sunk into beer.
Aroma: Damsons and unripe plums.
Taste: Smooth soft bitter fruits develop their
bitterness then dry in a short bitter aftertaste.
Ease of Decanting: Easy to pour, yeast stayed at
the bottom of the bottle.
Opinion: An easy to drink thirst-quencher,
would cool the mouth after a fiery hot curry.

ICENI IT'S A GRAND DAY 4.5% ABV 500 ML
Brewed by Iceni Brewery, 3 Foulden Road,
Ickburgh, Mundford, Norfolk IP26 5BJ.
☎ (01842) 878922.
Colour: Copper-brown (9).
Head: White large bubbles formed a small head.
Aroma: Slightly peachy aroma.
Taste: Aromatic initial flavours, slightly perfumy
like Parma violet maturing to a flowery taste
which is quite sweet but drying.
Ease of Decanting: Yeast stuck to the base of the
bottle, the head stayed small so a nice easy beer
to decant.
Opinion: A nice thirst-quencher for a hot
madras.

ICENI MEN OF NORFOLK 6.2% ABV 500 ML
Brewed by Iceni Brewery, 3 Foulden Road,
Ickburgh, Mundford, Norfolk IP26 5BJ.
☎ (01842) 878922.
Colour: Black (20).
Head: A brown head with a mixture of small and
large bubbles that was controllable by adjusting
the height of the pour.
Aroma: Molasses and rich warm mince pie.
Taste: Blackcurrant and liquorice with bitter
cherries coming through and drying on the back
of the palate.
Ease of Decanting: A controllable head and yeast
that stayed in the bottle made this an easy beer
to pour.
Opinion: A nice robust ale that would go down
nicely with steak and kidney pudding.

ICENI PORTED PORTER 4.4% ABV 500 ML
Brewed by Iceni Brewery, 3 Foulden Road,
Ickburgh, Mundford, Norfolk IP26 5BJ.
☎ (01842) 878922.
Colour: Black (20).
Head: Stayed small, with small brown bubbles.
Aroma: Liquorice with cough mixture, you can
smell the port.
Taste: Very smooth initial taste with the port
taste coming through, it dries to bitter fruits in
the aftertaste.
Ease of Decanting: Yeast stayed at the bottom
and head stayed small so a nice easy beer to
pour.
Opinion: Unusual beer in that port has been
added to great effect. A nice beer with homemade beef cobbler.

**ICENI RED, WHITE AND BLUEBERRY 4.0% ABV
500 ML**
Brewed by Iceni Brewery, 3 Foulden Road,
Ickburgh, Mundford, Norfolk IP26 5BJ.
☎ (01842) 878922
Colour: Mid-brown (12).

Head: Small head with a mix of large and small white bubbles.
Aroma: Forest berries and fruits.
Taste: Thin initially, bitter and hoppy with delicate underlying fruit, hops zing on the tastebuds then draw the juices in a long aftertaste.
Ease of Decanting: Yeast stayed where it should and the head stayed small, so nice and easy to pour.
Opinion: A nice easy-to-drink beer with a cheese ploughman's.

ICENI THETFORD FOREST MILD 3.6% ABV 500 ML
Brewed by Iceni Brewery, 3 Foulden Road, Ickburgh, Mundford, Norfolk IP26 5BJ.
☎ (01842) 878922.
Colour: Black (20).
Head: Brown fizzing head, sunk into beer and disappeared.
Aroma: Liquorice and faint sherry.
Taste: Lively initial bitterness, light and tasty, soft fruit initially, light burnt liquorice follows and ripens into bitter fruit.
Ease of Decanting: Yeast stayed at the bottom and the head stayed small so nothing to fear.
Opinion: A lovely easy-to-drink mild, nice with gammon and eggs.

KELHAM ISLAND PALE RIDER 5.2% ABV 500 ML
Brewed by Kelham Island Brewery Ltd, 23 Alma Street, Sheffield, South Yorkshire S3 8SA.
☎ (0114) 249 4804.
Colour: Pale yellow ale (1).
Head: White, dense bubbles in a medium-sized head.
Aroma: Beautiful fresh citrusy lemon fruit aroma.
Taste: Sweet initial taste with subtle fruit developing to sweet caramel, then fruity hops dry on the tongue in a short burst of aftertaste.
Ease of Decanting: Nice and easy to pour with the yeast clinging to the base of the bottle, but pour carefully or the head might run away.
Opinion: Beautiful fresh pale ale, nice with game pie.

KELTEK KING 5.1% ABV 500 ML
Brewed by Keltek Brewery, Unit 3a, Restormel Industrial Estate, Liddicost Road, Lostwithiel, Cornwall PL22 0HG. ☎ (01208) 871199.
Colour: Pale amber (5).
Head: Small head with white, dense bubbles.
Aroma: Sweet vanilla and toffee.
Taste: Smooth and fruity sweetness maturing to a fruity hop bitterness with a slightly fruit spice (cloves, nutmeg, etc) aftertaste.
Ease of Decanting: Yeast clings to base of bottle and the head stays small, which makes this beer a pleasure to pour.
Opinion: Clean-tasting ale that would go down nice with fish and chips.

KELTEK KRIPPLE DICK 8.5% ABV 275 ML
Brewed by Keltek Brewery, Unit 3a, Restormel Industrial Estate, Liddicost Road, Lostwithiel, Cornwall PL22 0HG. ☎ (01208) 871199.
Colour: Black with burgundy tints (20).
Head: Small head with dense, brown bubbles.
Aroma: Very alcoholic, like plum pudding steeped in brandy.
Taste: Sweetness suddenly exploding into sweet molasses and brown sugar with a backtaste of warming alcohol.

Ease of Decanting: Yeast clings to the base of bottle and the head stays very controllable, which means pouring from height to achieve head.
Opinion: Strong ale to savour, best drunk after a good meal, as you would a fine port or brandy.

KELTEK REVENGE 7.0% ABV
Brewed by Keltek Brewery, Unit 3a, Restormel Industrial Estate, Liddicost Road, Lostwithiel, Cornwall PL22 0HG. ☎ (01208) 871199.
Colour: Ruby-coloured beer (13).
Head: Have to pour from height to create head, which rapidly disappears into beer.
Aroma: Liquorice with faint cinnamon.
Taste: Molasses creating a velvety mouth-feel leading to masses of bitter fruit which bitters increasingly on the tongue in a long aftertaste.
Ease of Decanting: Yeast clings to the base of the bottle and the head is small and disappearing, so very easy to pour.
Opinion: A lovely beer to enjoy with some nice ripe mature Stilton and biscuits.

MAULDONS BLACK ADDER 5.3% 500 ML
Brewed by Mauldons Brewery, 7 Addison Road, Chiltern Industrial Estate, Sudbury, Suffolk CO10 2YW. ☎ (01787) 311055.
Colour: Black (20).
Head: Small head with brown bubbles that disappeared into the beer.
Aroma: Rich fruity blackcurrant with hints of liquorice.
Taste: Smooth initially, then acrid charcoal and iron, well conditioned, dry acrid creosote flavour dries in a long finish.
Ease of Decanting: Yeast clung to the base of the bottle and the head was small, so easy to pour.
Opinion: A strongly flavoured dark ale, would drink nicely with organic roast lamb with all the trimmings.

ORGANIC BREWHOUSE SERPENTINE 4.5% ABV 500 ML
Brewed by The Organic Brewhouse, Cury Cross Lanes, Helston, Cornwall. ☎ (01326) 241555.
Colour: Oak-burgundy (17).
Head: Small head with dense white bubbles.
Aroma: Glacé to bitter cherry with hot blackcurrant.
Taste: Marzipan and vanilla matures from sweetness to chocolate malt in the aftertaste, has a nice clean texture.
Ease of Decanting: Yeast stayed at the bottom of the bottle, the head stayed small, so nice and easy.
Opinion: Another of those fine beers that would go down nicely with a nice organic liver and bacon meal.

ORGANIC BREWHOUSE WOLF ROCK 5.0% ABV 500 ML
Brewed by The Organic Brewhouse, Cury Cross Lanes, Helston, Cornwall. ☎ (01326) 241555.
Colour: Ruby-brown (13).
Head: White small dense bubbled head.
Aroma: Sweet and fruity with pear drops coming through.
Taste: Smooth fruit initially leading through to pear-drop sweetness, then hop bitterness punching through and drying on the palate in a long bitter aftertaste.

Ease of Decanting: Unusually for bottle-conditioned beers, this comes in a clear bottle making it easy to see the yeast: there were swirls in the last quarter though the head was small, so an easy beer to pour.
Opinion: Organic bottle conditioned beers are rare, bottle-conditioning definitely improves organic beers as this was the best organic beer I have tasted, would accompany cod and chips very nicely.

PITFIELD BREWERY ORGANIC PITFIELDS ECO WARRIOR 4.5% ABV 500 ML
Brewed by Pitfield Brewery, The Beer Shop, 14 Pitfield Street, Hoxton London N1 6EY. ☎ (020) 7739 3701.
Colour: Rich golden amber (8).
Head: White dense bubbles in a small head.
Aroma: Pear drops, lemonade shandy, slightly lemony with a faint aroma of mushy bananas.
Taste: Sweet velvet taste of Caribbean fruit punch, then extreme fruit bitterness, sweet punch comes through near the end, then finishes with fresh fruity bitterness.
Ease of Decanting: Yeast stays at the bottom and the head is small, so nice and easy.
Opinion: An unusual beer that would go down nicely with coronation chicken.

PITFIELD BREWERY PITFIELD SHOREDITCH STOUT 4.0% ABV 500 ML
Brewed by Pitfield Brewery, The Beer Shop, 14 Pitfield Street, Hoxton London N1 6EY. ☎ (020) 7739 3701.
Colour: Black (20).
Head: Small head with brown small bubbles.
Aroma: Molasses and dark chocolate.
Taste: Bitter chocolate powder maturing to subtle bitter fruits in a short aftertaste.
Ease of Decanting: Yeast stayed at the bottom of the bottle and the head stayed small, so nice and easy to pour.
Opinion: A very clean-tasting stout, nice with a Melton Mowbray pork pie.

RCH ALE MARY 5.0% ABV 500 ML
Brewed by RCH Brewery, West Hewish, Weston-super-Mare, Somerset BS24 6RR. ☎ (01934) 834447.
Colour: Orangey, golden beechwood colour (8).
Head: Very large, white, dense head.
Aroma: Fruity and sweet.
Taste: Winter spices initially leading to bitter fruit with slight ginger overtones, then a spiced dry aftertaste.
Ease of Decanting: Difficult due to a large head, though bottoms did not rise into the beer. Worth ensuring that the beer is well cooled before opening to minimise risk of excessive heading.
Opinion: A well-hung pheasant or grouse meal would complement this beer perfectly.

RCH OLD SLUG PORTER 4.5% ABV 500 ML
Brewed by RCH Brewery, West Hewish, Weston-super-Mare, Somerset BS24 6RR. ☎ (01934) 834447.
Colour: Dark, rich burgundy (19).
Head: Medium head, light brown, dense small bubbles stayed throughout, clinging to the sides of the glass.
Aroma: Liquorice with toffee and blackcurrants.

Taste: Bitter fruits quickly lead to very slightly aniseed/liquorice and dark caramel, with sweetness slowly fading, giving a full mouth-feel.
Ease of Decanting: Yeast clings to the base of the bottle and head did not start feeding itself, so a nice easy-pouring ale.
Opinion: Fruity, yet well-balanced with a good finish. Nice beer with game pie or a good goulash.

RINGWOOD FORTYNINER 4.9% ABV 500 ML
Brewed by Ringwood Brewery Ltd, 138 Christchurch Road, Ringwood, Hampshire BH24 3AP. ☎ (01425) 471177.
Colour: Orange-brown (10).
Head: Controllable white head with large and small bubbles.
Aroma: Faint aroma of fruity caramel.
Taste: Smooth initial taste, light fruit comes through and dries on the palate.
Ease of Decanting: Yeast stayed sticky and head was controllable, so an easy beer to decant.
Opinion: Surprisingly easy to drink for its strength, a nice beer with fish and chips.

RINGWOOD XXXX PORTER 4.7% ABV 500 ML
Brewed by Ringwood Brewery Ltd, 138 Christchurch Road, Ringwood, Hampshire BH24 3AP. ☎ (01425) 471177.
Colour: Black with deep burgundy hints in the light (20).
Head: Dense brown head which needs to be poured from height to create the desired head volume.
Aroma: Faint toffee and banana.
Taste: Creamy, light mouth-feel with sweet caramel and chocolate malt maturing into bitter hops developing long into the aftertaste.
Ease of Decanting: Nice easy-pouring ale with yeast that clings to the base of the bottle and a head that responds to what you like. For example, pour close to the glass for no head or pour from three inches for a large, rocky head - it's up to you.
Opinion: Lovely beer with a nice O'Hagan's sausage and mash.

SALOPIAN ENTIRE BUTT ENGLISH PORTER 4.8% ABV 500 ML
Brewed by Salopian Brewing Co. Ltd, 67 Mytton Oak Road, Shrewsbury, Shropshire SY3 8UQ. ☎ (01743) 248414.
Colour: Black with deep burgundy hints (20).
Head: Medium brown, dense-bubbled head, the size of which is controlled by height of pour.
Aroma: Liquorice and black treacle.
Taste: Frothy initial impression maturing into a dark chocolate and burnt caramel taste, finishing with a bittersweet burnt malt frothing on the sides of the tongue.
Ease of Decanting: Yeast clings to the base of the bottle and the head is easy to control.
Opinion: A lovely beer with a nice pork casserole.

SALOPIAN GINGER SNAP 4.7% ABV 500 ML
Brewed by Salopian Brewing Co. Ltd, 67 Mytton Oak Road, Shrewsbury, Shropshire SY3 8UQ. ☎ (01743) 248414.
Colour: Rich, amber-coloured ale (8).
Head: White, dense bubbles in a small, controllable head.
Aroma: Lemony ginger and citrus aromas.

Taste: Initial taste is of gingery sweetness, with the spiciness of the ginger burning through in the mid-taste and lingering on the tongue in a long aftertaste.
Ease of Decanting: Yeast clings to the base of the bottle and head stays manageable, so a nice easy beer to pour.
Opinion: A ginger beer for the connoisseur.

SALOPIAN MINSTERLEY 4.5% ABV 500 ML
Brewed by Salopian Brewing Co. Ltd, 67 Mytton Oak Road, Shrewsbury, Shropshire SY3 8UQ.
☎ (01743) 248414.
Colour: Golden (4).
Head: Small, white with large bubbles, subsiding into beer leaving a brown marble effect on top of the liquid.
Aroma: Fruity/toffee, with a slight aroma of tar.
Taste: Starts out with subtle sweet malt flavours which mature into a tart caramel taste that bitters progressively in a long aftertaste.
Ease of Decanting: Easy to pour as head sinks quickly into the beer.
Opinion: Unusual golden ale in which hops might be expected to be the main flavour. Would go very well with duck and orange pie.

SKEW SUNSHINE ALE 4.6% ABV 500 ML
Brewed by Suthwyk Ales, Offwell Farm, Southwick, Fareham, Hampshire PO17 6DX.
☎ (01392) 325252.
Colour: Straw-coloured or pale yellow-coloured ale (2).
Head: White, dense bubbly large head.
Aroma: Slightly citrus with underlying forest fruit aromas.
Taste: Initial frothy mouth-feel gives way to a sweet malt taste with subtle fruit which matures on the roof of the mouth in a short aftertaste.
Ease of Decanting: Difficult unless kept in the fridge for an hour before pouring. Mine had a very large head and yeast swirls in the last quarter, so be careful. The taste is definitely worth the trouble.
Opinion: Lovely refreshing ale which would go down very well with a nice fresh baguette with ham off the bone and some English mustard.

SPRINGHEAD CROMWELLS HAT 6.2% ABV 500 ML
Brewed by Springhead Brewery, Unit 3, Sutton Workshops, Old Great North Road, Sutton on Trent, Newark, Nottinghamshire NG23 6QS.
☎ (01636) 821000.
Colour: Orange-brown (10).
Head: Very large dense white bubbles.
Aroma: Orange zest and raisins.
Taste: Initial taste of tangy zesty orange peel turning tart and lemony which dries to a warming bitter cherry finish.
Ease of Decanting: A real challenge for the more experienced connoisseur of bottle conditioned beers. Yeast swirls in the last quarter plus a large head required a steady hand to wait until the head had subsided.
Opinion: Unexpected taste, reminiscent of a Belgian cherry beer. Very good with game pie.

SPRINGHEAD THE LEVELLER 5.0% ABV 500 ML
Brewed by Springhead Brewery, Unit 3, Sutton Workshops, Old Great North Road, Sutton on Trent, Newark, Nottinghamshire NG23 6QS.
☎ (01636) 821000.
Colour: Mid-brown (12).

Head: Large head with large, white bubbles.
Aroma: Dryish malt and caramel aromas.
Taste: Initial powerful hops give way to balancing hops in the main taste. A pleasant prickle on the tongue due to excellent conditioning.
Ease of Decanting: Large head and tendrils in the last quarter means that this is a challenging beer to pour, though definitely worth the effort.
Opinion: Excellent accompaniment to a good steak and kidney pie.

TEIGNWORTHY BEACHCOMBER 4.5% ABV 500 ML (BOTTLE CONDITIONED LAGER)
Brewed by Teignworthy Brewery, The Maltings, Teign Road, Newton Abbot, Devon TQ12 4AA.
☎ (01626) 332066.
Colour: Amber (7).
Head: Stayed small, high pour to create the head, white dense bubbles.
Aroma: Fruit salad penny sweets.
Taste: Light bitter fruits maturing to delicate pears with bitter fruit drying the palate in a short aftertaste.
Ease of Decanting: Yeast clung to base of bottle and head controllable by height of pour, so nice and easy to pour.
Opinion: Unusually sweet for a lager but very tasty for it. Would drink nicely with fish and chips.

TEIGNWORTHY MALTSTERS ALE 4.5% ABV 500 ML
Brewed by Teignworthy Brewery, The Maltings, Teign Road, Newton Abbot, Devon TQ12 4AA.
☎ (01626) 332066.
Colour: Burgundy-brown (14).
Head: Small head with dense white bubbles.
Aroma: Pineapple with traces of zesty orange and kiwi fruit.
Taste: Bitter fruit developing to bitter cherry drying to a slightly burnt, long grapefruit aftertaste.
Ease of Decanting: Yeast clinging to the base of the bottle and the small head make this a nice easy beer to pour.
Opinion: Would accompany a nice game pie.

TEIGNWORTHY OLD DOGGIE 4.4% ABV 500 ML
Brewed by Teignworthy Brewery, The Maltings, Teign Road, Newton Abbot, Devon TQ12 4AA.
☎ (01626) 332066.
Colour: Dark amber-chestnut (11).
Head: White dense bubbles with a small head.
Aroma: Like tutti-frutti children's sweets leading to a slightly soapy aroma.
Taste: Lots of body, slightly sweet marmalade leading to a long drying bitter aftertaste.
Ease of Decanting: Yeast clung to the base of the bottle and the head stayed small.
Opinion: Would accompany a good cheese board with soft cheeses like a nice mature warm brie.

TEIGNWORTHY REEL ALE 4.0% ABV 500 ML
Brewed by Teignworthy Brewery, The Maltings, Teign Road, Newton Abbot, Devon TQ12 4AA.
☎ (01626) 332066.
Colour: Orange-brown (10).
Head: Small controllable head that needed height to create.
Aroma: Subtle warming spices with vanilla and caramel notes.
Taste: Sweet Malteser, drying to a long bitter fruit taste, then malty and slightly aromatic finish.

Ease of Decanting: Yeast clung to the base of the bottle and head stayed small, so a nice easy one to pour.

Opinion: A well-crafted session beer, would go down nicely with an authentic spaghetti bolognese.

THREE TUNS CLERIC'S CURE 5.0% ABV 500 ML

Brewed by The Three Tuns Brewing Co. Ltd, The Three Tuns Inn, Salop Street, Bishop's Castle, Shropshire SY9 5BW. ☎ (01588) 638797.

Colour: Pale orange-golden ale (5).

Head: White head with dense bubbles subsiding quickly into the glass.

Aroma: Fresh almonds and marzipan.

Taste: Smooth with sweetness on the middle of the tongue, then bittersweet almonds maturing into hoppy bitterness that spreads from the front to the back of the tongue in a long aftertaste.

Ease of Decanting: Nice and easy, with yeast clinging to the base of the bottle and a small head.

Opinion: Smashing, unusual beer, nice with a gammon sandwich.

TISBURY FANFARE 4.5% ABV 500 ML

Brewed by Tisbury Ltd, Oakley Business Park, Dinton, Salisbury, Wiltshire SP3 5EU. ☎ (01722) 716622.

Colour: Orangey-amber (3).

Head: Large head with white, dense bubbles slowly subsiding to a half-inch white collar.

Aroma: Slightly floral summer fruit.

Taste: Sweet malt initial taste quickly developing to bitter hops, which continues with hops slowly maturing with slight caramel tar in the aftertaste.

Ease of Decanting: Definitely a challenge. The large head feeds upon itself on pouring, creating lots of froth. Have two glasses handy and a very steady hand.

Opinion: Nice bitter ale, well worth the effort of pouring. Refreshing with a hot curry.

TITANIC CAPTAIN SMITH'S 5.2% ABV 500 ML

Brewed by The Titanic Brewery, Harvey Works, Lingard Street, Burslem, Stoke-on-Trent, Staffordshire ST6 1ED. ☎ (01782) 823447.

Colour: Browny-red (13).

Head: White, large bubble head that disperses into the beer.

Aroma: Flowery and slightly acid hops.

Taste: Strong malt which continues though to a drying hoppy finish.

Ease of Decanting: Small head but tendrils to look out for in the last quarter require that all-important eagle eye.

Opinion: Nice beer to accompany beef cobbler.

TITANIC STOUT 4.5% ABV 500 ML

Brewed by The Titanic Brewery, Harvey Works, Lingard Street, Burslem, Stoke-on-Trent, Staffordshire ST6 1ED. ☎ (01782) 823447.

Colour: Black with ruby hints in the light (20).

Head: Brown, dense bubbles in a medium-sized head.

Aroma: Dark chocolate and burnt caramel.

Taste: Initial chocolate malt and molasses maturing into bitter chocolate with full smooth mouth-feel, then hop bitterness maturing on the back of the tongue, balancing the chocolate in a long bitter aftertaste.

Opinion: Strongly flavoured stout with long

bitter aftertaste, a very nice accompaniment to a strong Cheddar ploughman's.

VALE BREWERY BLACK BEAUTY PORTER 4.3% ABV 500 ML

Brewed by Vale Brewery Co Ltd, Thame Road, Haddenham, Buckinghamshire HP17 8BY. ☎ (01844) 290008.

Colour: Black (20).

Head: Small with dense brown bubbles that disappeared into the beer leaving a brown cream meniscus.

Aroma: Rich plum and autumn fruit.

Taste: Surprisingly light initial taste, delicate malt comes through with hops that dry to a blackberry bitter fruit taste, with residual sweetness countering the bitterness.

Ease of Decanting: Small head and yeast clinging to the base of the bottle making this nice and easy to pour.

Opinion: Lovely beer to drink with a beef hotpot.

VALE BREWERY BLACK SWAN DARK MILD 3.3% ABV 500 ML

Brewed by Vale Brewery Co Ltd, Thame Road, Haddenham, Buckinghamshire HP17 8BY. ☎ (01844) 290008.

Colour: Dark brown to black (20).

Head: Brown head was created by pouring from height, stayed small.

Aroma: A subtle fruity with acetate tones.

Taste: Thin bitter taste initially, subtle aftertaste of drying chocolate malt.

Ease of Decanting: Yeast stayed at the bottom and the head needed creating, so no problems with this beer.

Opinion: Would go down nicely with steak and kidney pudding.

VALE BREWERY EDGAR'S GOLDEN ALE 4.3% ABV 500 ML

Brewed by Vale Brewery Co Ltd, Thame Road, Haddenham, Buckinghamshire HP17 8BY. ☎ (01844) 290008.

Colour: Amber (7).

Head: White dense bubbles in a small head.

Aroma: A slightly acrid aroma of fresh cauliflower.

Taste: Initially light, frothy and refreshing, slightly bitter caramelised subtle zesty fruits mature to drying light bitter fruit.

Ease of Decanting: Yeast swirls in the last quarter need to be watched carefully, worth the effort though.

Opinion: A nice beer with a Cheddar ploughman's.

VALE BREWERY GRUMPLING PREMIUM 4.6% ABV 500 ML

Brewed by Vale Brewery Co Ltd, Thame Road, Haddenham, Buckinghamshire HP17 8BY. ☎ (01844) 290008.

Colour: Orange-brown (10)

Head: Small head with dense white bubbles.

Aroma: Subtle aroma of blackcurrant and pears.

Taste: Subtle initial flavour, smooth, slightly fruity blackberry malt, fruity bitterness zings on the sides of the tongue.

Ease of Decanting: A nice easy beer to pour, with the head staying small and the yeast staying at the bottom of the bottle.

Opinion: Goes down well with a cheese ploughman's and sweet pickle.

VALE BREWERY HADDA'S HEAD BANGER 5.0% ABV 500 ML

Brewed by Vale Brewery Co Ltd, Thame Road, Haddenham, Buckinghamshire HP17 8BY. ☎ (01844) 290008.
Colour: Copper-brown (13).
Head: Pour high carefully to create head.
Aroma: Spicy vanilla.
Taste: Fruity initial taste which sweetens on the palate with delicate pear quickly drying to bitter winter fruits.
Ease of Decanting: Although the head was very small, there was yeast swirls in the last quarter making this slightly more difficult to pour than the average, well worth the effort though.
Opinion: Would go nicely with a vegetarian quiche.

VALE BREWERY WYCHERT THE ORIGINAL 3.9% ABV 500 ML

Brewed by Vale Brewery Co Ltd, Thame Road, Haddenham, Buckinghamshire HP17 8BY. ☎ (01844) 290008.
Colour: Dark amber-chestnut (11).
Head: Small with dense white bubbles.
Aroma: Like pear drops or fresh candyfloss.
Taste: Initially light, frothy and easy to drink, slightly sour malt with burnt toffee malt leading to a long bitter dark chocolate aftertaste that lingers.
Ease of Decanting: Yeast clung to the base of the bottle and the head stayed small, so no problems with this beer.
Opinion: Would go down nicely with O'Hagan's sausage, onions and mash.

WESSEX CRAFT BREWERS JOCKSTRAP 4.0% ABV

Brewed by Wessex Craft Brewers, Units 5/7, Stenders Centre, The Stenders, Micheldean, Wiltshire GL17 0ZE. ☎ (01594) 544776.
Colour: Clear, pale straw (2).
Head: White, dense bubbles forming a large foamy head.
Aroma: Fruity and citrusy.
Taste: Initially smooth and creamily malty with malty fruit sweetness maturing into a long drying hoppy aftertaste.
Ease of Decanting: The large head means that all the beer could not be poured. A tricky one, but well worth the effort.
Opinion: Why not follow the name of the beer and try it with haggis, neeps and mash?

WESSEX CRAFT BREWERS OLD GEE SPOT 4.0% ABV

Brewed by Wessex Craft Brewers, Units 5/7, Stenders Centre, The Stenders, Micheldean, Wiltshire GL17 0ZE. ☎ (01594) 544776.
Colour: Amber (7).
Head: Small, dense head which subsides into the beer.
Aroma: Floral yet malty and sweet.
Taste: Initial taste is caramel, maturing into hops that continue into the aftertaste.
Ease of Decanting: Yeast clings to the base of the bottle and takes some shaking to dislodge, so an easy bottle to decant.
Opinion: Definitely aimed at the sweeter or more malty end of the taste spectrum. A good ale with fish and chips.

WESSEX CRAFT BREWERS RUMPY PUMPY 4.0% ABV

Brewed by Wessex Craft Brewers, Units 5/7, Stenders Centre, The Stenders, Micheldean, Wiltshire GL17 0ZE. ☎ (01594) 544776.
Colour: Orangey-amber (6).
Head: White and dense, yet poured up as a small head.
Aroma: Sweet, aromatic and fruity.
Taste: Sweetness maturing into a nutty maltiness with hops coming through near the end. Finishes gently on sweetly malty notes.
Ease of Decanting: Yeast clings to the base of the bottle and head is small and manageable, making this another easy-to-pour ale.
Opinion: Another tasty ale at the sweeter end of the taste spectrum, nice with steak and chips.

WICKWAR INFERNAL BREW 4.8% ABV 500 ML

Brewed by Wickwar Brewing Co., The Old Cider Mill, Station Road, Wickwar, Wootton-under-Edge, Gloucestershire GL12 8NB. ☎ (01454) 294168.
Colour: Crystal amber ale (10).
Head: Very large head with dense white bubbles.
Aroma: Very faint malt and caramel aroma.
Taste: Fruity banana flavour developing into sweet molasses with sweetness continuing long in the aftertaste.
Ease of Decanting: The large head makes handling this beer a challenge. I got yeast swirls in the last quarter of the bottle due to trying to change glasses. Well worth the effort though.
Opinion: Lovely beer with roast pork and crackling.

WICKWAR STATION PORTER 6.1% ABV 500 ML

Brewed by Wickwar Brewing Co. The Old Cider Mill, Station Road, Wickwar, Gloucestershire. GL12 8NB. ☎ (01454) 294168.
Colour: Black (20).
Head: Brown, dense bubbles in a small head.
Aroma: Molasses and black treacle.
Taste: Smooth and sweet with subtle black treacle bittering to stringent hops to balance in the aftertaste.
Ease of Decanting: Nice and easy to pour.
Opinion: A sweet beer, would drink nicely with roast pork and crackling.

WOLF BREWERY CAVELL ALE 3.7% ABV 500ML

Brewed by The Wolf Brewery, 10 Maurice Gaymer Road, Attleborough, Norfolk NR17 2QZ. ☎ (01953) 457775.
Colour: Rich golden amber (8).
Head: White, small dense bubbled head.
Aroma: Zest and citrus with warm spices.
Taste: Light and bubbly leading to bitter hops that sour slightly, then dry in the aftertaste.
Ease of Decanting: The yeast clung to the base of the bottle and the head was small, making this an easy ale to pour.
Opinion: Unusually low in alcohol for a bottle-conditioned beer. Would drink nicely with a doorstep off-the-bone ham and pickle sandwich.

WOLF BREWERY GRANNY WOULDN'T LIKE IT 4.8% ABV 500ML

Brewed by The Wolf Brewery, 10 Maurice Gaymer Road, Attleborough, Norfolk NR17 2QZ. ☎ (01953) 457775.
Colour: Rich burgundy (19).
Head: White, dense head that stayed small.

Aroma: Subtle sweet aroma of cinnamon.
Taste: Bitter fruits dry to rich malt leading to a bitter slightly metallic hop aftertaste.
Ease of Decanting: No problem decanting this beer, yeast stayed where you want it (at the bottom of the bottle) and the head stayed small.
Opinion: A nice thirst-quencher after a hot chilli con carne.

WOLF BREWERY LUPUS LUPUS 5.0% ABV 500ML

Brewed by The Wolf Brewery, 10 Maurice Gaymer Road, Attleborough, Norfolk NR17 2QZ.
☎ (01953) 457775.
Colour: Mid-brown (12).
Head: Controllable head with white dense bubbles.
Aroma: Subtle aroma of caramelised malt.
Taste: Initial bitter fruits, the bitterness changes to hops then finishes on caramelised but bitter fruit.
Ease of Decanting: Yeast clung to the base of the bottle and the head was controllable, so an easy-to-pour bitter.
Opinion: Fantastic beer with a cheese ploughman's.

WOOD BREWERY G££ZER 4.0% ABV 500 ML

Brewed by The Wood Brewery Ltd, Wistanstow, Craven Arms, Shropshire SY7 8DG.
☎ (01588) 627523.
Colour: Maple amber (10).
Head: Poured with a small head which disappeared within one minute.
Aroma: Sweet and malty.
Taste: Initial subtle malty sweetness matures into subtle hops on the back of the tongue, continuing into the aftertaste.
Ease of Decanting: Quite an easy pour, with the head staying small, but look out for those yeast swirls in the last quarter.
Opinion: A nice beer with a pâté ploughman's.

WYE VALLEY BREW 69 5.6% ABV

Brewed by Wye Valley Brewery, 69 Owen Street, Hereford, Herefordshire HR1 2JQ.
☎ (01432) 342546.
Colour: Orange-golden ale (3).
Head: Small head with large white bubbles. The beer has to be poured from height to create head.
Aroma: Fruity and spicy.
Taste: Sweet malt flavour creating a full smooth mouth-feel with bitter hops and an underlying honey sweetness vying for your attention in a short aftertaste.
Ease of Decanting: Yeast clings to the base of the bottle and the head has to be created by pouring from height.
Opinion: Lovely beer with a nice honey-roast pork and mustard sandwich.

WYE VALLEY PLOUGHMAN'S ALE 5.6% ABV 500 ML

Brewed by Wye Valley Brewery, 69 Owen Street, Hereford, Herefordshire HR1 2JQ.
☎ (01432) 342546.
Colour: Deep-brown/dark-red ale (18).
Head: Brown, large bubble head that subsides into the beer.
Aroma: Sweet and malty.
Taste: Sweet, malty, fruity, yet mellow, satisfying ale.
Ease of Decanting: A nice easy-pouring ale with yeast clinging to the base of the bottle and the head staying small.
Opinion: A nice beer with a good rare steak and chips.

The Real Ale Pub Guide is a celebration of the rejuvenated art of brewing in Great Britain. Our concern, deliberately, is not with the often bland and certainly mass-produced market leaders, but simply with the smaller, independent makers of what we consider to be the *real* real ales. For this reason, we do not tell you about the big, multi-national brewers and their products, good or bad. Nor do we tell you about the pubs whose reputation owes more to their impressive location, their excellent cooking or their extensive range of malt whiskies, although we may mention their claim in passing. This is a book about beer and is aimed squarely at those who love drinking it, who want to know more about it and who want to know where to find it at its best.

The entries within England are arranged alphabetically by county, taking into account the boundary changes that came into force in 1996. Unitary authorities (such as Bristol and Leicester) have been incorporated into their most logical county. There are some border towns and villages where the postal town is in one county while the actual place is over the boundary. We have tried to place all the entries in the counties to which they actually belong, but be prepared for some county-hopping along borders. Scotland and Wales are organised first by region and then alphabetically by town.

Each county contains details first of the breweries within it and then the pubs and brewpubs, organised alphabetically by town or village. We have attempted to give as full an address as possible and a telephone number in most cases. Brief directions may also be found within the entry itself but, if you do get lost and there is no one available to ask, a call ahead should keep the inconvenience to a minimum.

Central London is treated slightly differently. London is full of pubs where you can buy a pint of real ale and so the aim which we apply to the rest of the book: to provide details of pubs in which you will find real ales on offer among all the lagers and keg beers, is not especially useful. However, although there is no shortage of 'real ale' pubs, there *is* a vast difference in the quality and range of beers sold in those pubs. There are also huge numbers of chains, such as Wetherspoons, and tied houses, many of which are more or less identical. With this in mind, full entries in London are only given to pubs which we feel truly offer a good, varied selection of interesting beers. Chains and tied houses are listed at the end of each postal area.

Our primary aim is to make this guide as useful to people looking for a place to drink real ale as possible. The criteria, therefore, is that a selection of real ales in proportion to the number of beers sold in total is always available. Tied houses, even those tied to national breweries, are included if they meet this criteria. However, because cask ales are the focus of our project we have usually excluded details of the keg beers available.

Where possible, we have sought to include the licensee's name for we believe that the character and quality of a pub owes much to the person who runs it. Inevitably, these people move on and many enjoy the challenge of taking on a new pub and establishing its place on the map. While every acknowledgement should be made of the nation's finest innkeepers, this is more than just a chance for publicans to see their names in print. We hope that readers will recognise the people who run particularly successful pubs and, as they move, need no other recommendations to visit than that person's name.

Because we believe the beers are the most important thing to be found in a pub, we have sought to give an indication of the names and numbers of ales that you are likely to find when you walk through the door. Of course, there are few hard and fast rules. Availability varies and, on some days, the choice will probably be wider than on others. Nevertheless, a pub that says it has 12 beers on tap should come reasonably close to doing just that. If you discover this is not the case, then we want to know.

There is a short description of the type of pub to be found with each entry, intended to give you an idea of what to expect. If they have told us they specialise in a certain type of food, or have accommodation or other features then we have sought to pass that on. However, as this is not the purpose of our guide we have kept the details to a minimum.

Opening hours are another feature that will inevitably vary, particularly as the Government relaxes the licensing laws. An increasing number of pubs are opening for longer and later than was the case just a few years ago. However, we suggest that, if you are proposing to visit in the middle of the afternoon, a telephone call ahead will ensure that you are not disappointed.

Unfortunately, for a number of reasons it has not been possible to include an entry for every real ale pub in the country. Similarly, there are many pubs about which we have heard favourable reports but which we have been unable to verify first hand. A selection of those pubs appears at the end of each county under the heading 'You Tell Us'. Perhaps if you visit them you can let us know your findings by returning one of the questionnaires at the back of the book. Similarly, if you find a pub does not live up to your expectations or you know of a good pub which is not included, we'd love to hear from you. The pubs already recommended by readers are highlighted with a little 'Reader's Report' logo. Send us your completed questionnaire, or e-mail reception@ foulsham.com with your comments.

The Real Ale Research Team

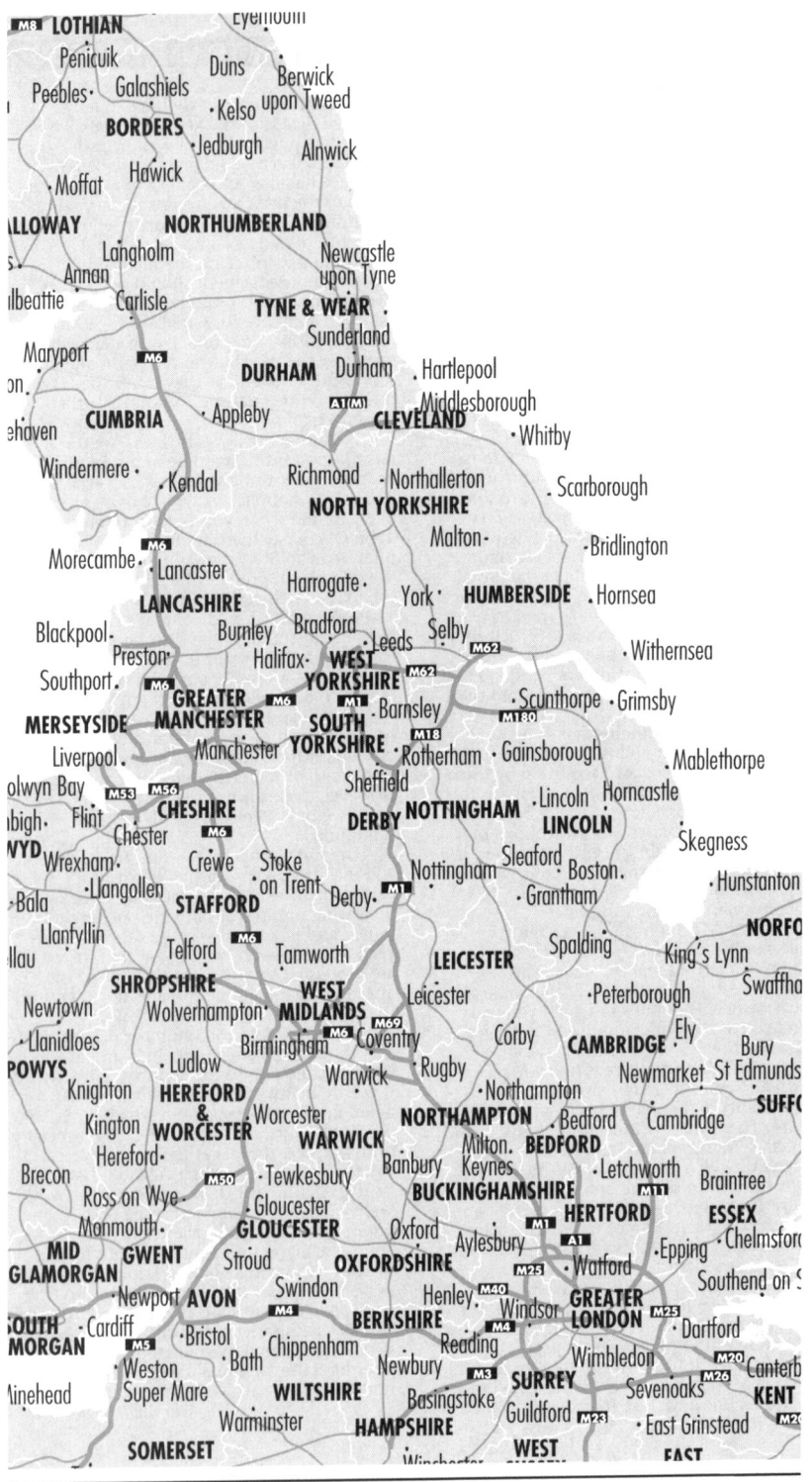

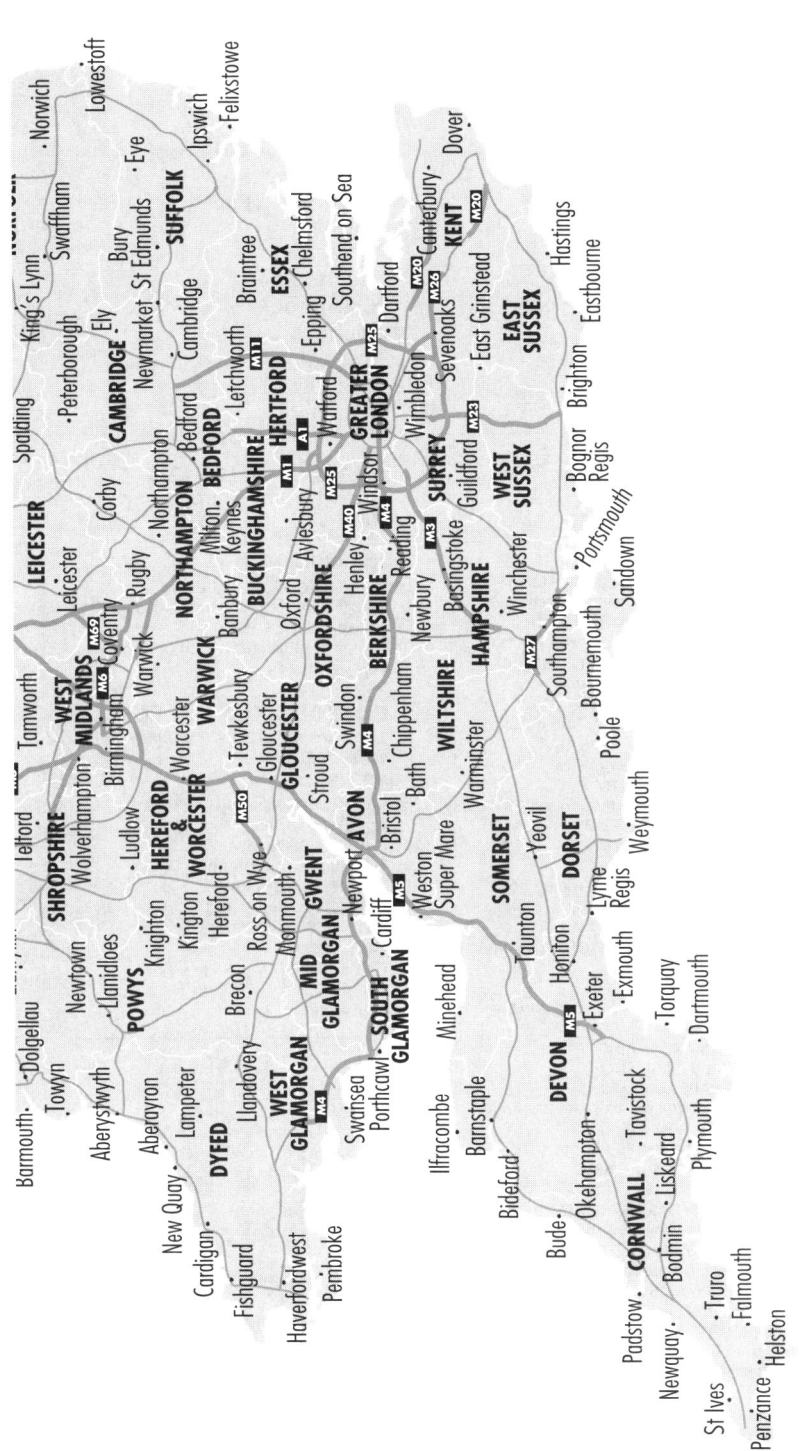

Places Featured:

Bedford	Little Gransden
Biggleswade	Luton
Broom	Millbrook Village
Campton	Potton
Clophill	Ravensden
Dunstable	Ridgmont
Everton	Sharnbrook
Great Barford	Shefford
Harrold	Studham
Henlow	Wingfield
Leighton Buzzard	Yelden

THE BREWERIES

B & T BREWERY LTD

The Brewery, Shefford SG17 5DZ
☎ *(01462) 815080*

 MIDSUMMER ALE 3.5% ABV
Seasonal, easy-drinking brew.

BARLEY MOW 3.8% ABV
Seasonal, quenching hoppy brew.

BEDFORDSHIRE CLANGER 3.8% ABV
Seasonal, crisp and well-hopped.

SHEFFORD BITTER 3.8% ABV
Golden and hoppy with dry hop finish.

SHEFFORD DARK MILD 3.8% ABV
Rich, mellow, dry and hoppy.

SANTA'S SLAYER 4.0% ABV
Seasonal, with sweeter fruit and malt flavour.

TURKEY'S TRAUMA 4.0% ABV
Seasonal, well-balanced beer.

BODYSNATCHER 4.5% ABV
Seasonal, sweetness with balancing hops.

EASTER EGGSTRA 4.5% ABV
Seasonal, with malt throughout.

EDWIN TAYLOR'S EXTRA STOUT 4.5% ABV
Creamy and full-bodied.

GUY FAWKES 4.5% ABV
Seasonal, amber malty beer with good
hoppiness.

ROMEO'S RUIN 4.5% ABV
Seasonal, hoppy and bitter.

SHEFFORD PALE ALE 4.5% ABV
Hoppy with balancing malt and dry finish.

EMERALD ALE 5.0% ABV
Seasonal, green-coloured and rounded.

JULIET'S REVENGE 5.0% ABV
Seasonal, smooth and rounded.

SHEFFORD OLD DARK 5.0% ABV
Deep red, sweet caramel and malt flavour.

SHEFFORD OLD STRONG 5.0% ABV
Hoppy with bitter malty flavour.

BLACK BAT 6.0% ABV
Ruby black, malt and fruit flavour.

2XS 6.0% ABV
Golden, rich aroma and fruit undertones.

SHEFFORD 2000 6.5% ABV
Powerful barley wine.

Plus regular commemorative and celebratory brews.

CHARLES WELLS LTD

*The Eagle Brewery, Havelock Street, Bedford
MK40 4LU*
☎ *(01234) 272766*
www.charleswells.co.uk

 EAGLE 3.6% ABV
Balanced, dry, full-flavoured IPA.

BOMBARDIER 4.3% ABV
Hoppy, well-balanced with dry finish.

Plus seasonal brews.

POTTON BREWING CO.

10 Shannon Place, Potton, Sandy SG19 2PZ
☎ *(01767) 261042*
www.potton-brewery.co.uk

 SHANNON IPA 3.6% ABV
Traditional, hoppy IPA.

PHOENIX 3.8% ABV
Soft, smooth and hoppy.

SHAMBLES 4.3% ABV
Hoppy bitterness with balancing sweetness.

VILLAGE BIKE 4.3% ABV
Hoppy brew.

PRIDE OF POTTON 6.0% ABV
Warming and dry-hopped.

Plus occasional brews.

CHARLES WELLS

BOMBARDIER
PREMIUM
BITTER

THE PUBS

BEDFORD

The Castle
17 Newnham Street, Bedford MK40 3JR
☎ *(01234) 353295* Michael Holmes

 A Charles Wells tenancy. Four guest beers available from a range of 12 per year including Morland Old Speckled Hen, Marston's Pedigree, Young's Special, Brains Bitter and Badger Tanglefoot.

A two-bar public house with country pub atmosphere. Bar food available at lunchtime and evenings. Car park, accommodation. Well-behaved children allowed.

OPEN *12–3pm and 5.30–11pm Mon–Thurs and Sun; all day Fri–Sat.*

De Parys Hotel
45 De Parys Avenue, Bedford MK40 2UA
☎ *(01234) 352121* Joanna Worthy

 A freehouse with Castle Eden, Potton Brewery and Fenland Brewery ales regularly available plus Fuller's London Pride. Beers changed weekly with emphasis on smaller breweries.

Hotel with bar, garden, 100-seater restaurant and 20 rooms. Situated near the park. Food available at lunchtimes and evenings Mon–Sat, and all day Sun. Children allowed.

OPEN *All day, every day.*

The Kent Arms
54 Salisbury Street, Bedford MK41 7RQ
☎ *(01234) 354156* Mr Doran

 Potton's Shambles permanently available plus three pumps rotating the full range of Potton brews.

A community pub on the outskirts of town with two bars and a beer garden. Pool table and darts. No food. Children allowed in the garden only. Located 30 yards from Bedford Park, off Stanley Street.

OPEN *11am–11pm Mon–Sat; 12–10.30pm Sun.*

The Wellington Arms
Wellington Street, Bedford MK40 2JA
☎ *(01234) 308033* Eric Mills (Manager)

 A B&T tied house, with Shefford Bitter, Dragonslayer, Edwin Taylor's Extra Stout, Adnams Bitter, Everards Tiger and a mild always available, plus Two Brewers Bitter (house beer brewed for the pub by B&T), seasonal ales from B&T and six guests from micro-breweries such as Rebellion, Border, North Yorkshire, Castle Rock, Nethergate and Mighty Oak. Hoegaarden and Leffe Belgian beers on draught, plus a guest Belgian beer. A range of 50 Belgian bottled beers and 50 bottle-conditioned ales also served.

This Mecca for real ale drinkers is a traditional local with wooden floors. Regional CAMRA Pub of the Year in 2001. Large collection of real ale memorabilia, including bottles and pump clips. Patio and small car park. Skittles, darts and dominoes. Bar snacks available all day. Children allowed outside only. Situated near the prison.

OPEN *12pm–11pm (10.30pm Sun).*

BIGGLESWADE

The Brown Bear
29 Hitchin Street, Biggleswade SG18 8BE
☎ *(01767) 316161* Mary and Alan

 Eight hand pumps serving a constantly changing range of real ales (2,100 in three years) from micro and other small breweries. Ales from breweries such as Fisherrow, Dwan, Brasserie de la Soif, Vale, Suthwyk, Kichen, Salamander and Mighty Oak have been featured.

A two-bar, open-plan pub with a large non-smoking eating area. Two annual beer festivals are held, plus a mini festival every month. Homemade food available all day. Located on the main street, off the market square.

OPEN *12–3pm and 5–11pm Mon–Thurs; 11am–11pm Fri–Sat; 12–3pm and 7–10.30pm Sun.*

The Wheatsheaf
5 Lawrence Road, Biggleswade SG18 0LS
☎ *(01767) 222220* Mr RE Stimson

Greene King IPA and XX Mild regularly available.

Simple, unspoilt, small and friendly pub known for its well-kept beer. Cask Marque award winner. No food. Beer garden and children's play area.

OPEN *11am–4pm and 7–11pm Mon–Fri; 11am–11pm Sat; 12–10.30pm Sun.*

BROOM

The Cock

23 High Street, Broom
☎ *(01767) 314411* Gerry Lant

 Greene King IPA, Abbot and Ruddles County always available.

A 300-year-old pub in which the beers are served direct from the barrels in the cellar. Food available 12–2.30pm Mon–Sun and 7–9pm Mon–Sat. Children welcome, with family room available. Car park. Campsite available. Situated off the A1 at Biggleswade roundabout.

OPEN *12–3pm and 6–11pm Mon–Fri; 12–4pm and 6–11pm Sat–Sun.*

CAMPTON

The White Hart

Mill Lane, Campton SG17 5NX
☎ *01462 812657* Jerry Cannon

 Hook Norton Best, Marston's Pedigree and Greene King Ruddles County always available, plus two guest ales which could come from any UK independent brewery. Winner of various CAMRA local awards.

A traditionally run village freehouse which has been in the same family for 33 years. A traditional brick and beam interior including inglenook fireplaces, decorated with rural artefacts and antiquities. No pool table. No juke box. No food, except for pre-ordered buffets. Children welcome. Garden with patio, petanque area and children's play area. Large car park. Located off the A507, just outside Shefford.

OPEN *6.30–11pm Mon–Thurs (closed lunchtimes); 12–3pm and 6.30–11pm Fri; 12–11pm Sat; 12–3pm and 6.30–10.30pm Sun.*

CLOPHILL

The Stone Jug

Back Street, Clophill MK45 4BY
☎ *(01525) 860526* Joyce and Vikki Stevens

 B&T's Shefford always available, plus two guests, changed frequently, from breweries across Britain. Occasional house ales.

A traditional back-street country pub, built around 1700 as 3 cottages and converted into a pub in the nineteenth century. One large bar area, front patio and small patio and pond at back. Crib and dominoes. Food available 12–2pm Mon–Sat. Separate room available for children. Phone for directions if required.

OPEN *12–4pm and 6–11pm Mon–Thurs; 12–11pm Fri; 11am–11pm Sat; 12–10.30pm Sun.*

DUNSTABLE

The Victoria

69 West Street, Dunstable LU6 1ST
☎ *(01582) 662682* Dave and Val Hobbs

 Five hand pumps regularly serving a house beer (Victoria Ale) from the Tring Brewery, plus a range of guest beers (approx. 200 per year) from independent breweries such as Fuller's, Vale, Mauldons, Cottage, Wye Valley, York and Fernandes.

A traditional pub just outside the town centre. Bar food is served at lunchtimes only (12–2.30pm), with roasts on Sundays. Well-behaved children allowed. The landlord's policy is to have a session, a premium and a mind-blowing beer always on sale! Regular beer festivals are held in the barn at the rear of the pub. Small patio-style garden where regular barbecues are held in summer.

OPEN *All day, every day.*

EVERTON

Thornton Arms

1 Potton Road, Everton, Sandy SG19 2LD
☎ *(01767) 681149* Michael Hall

 Charles Wells Eagle and IPA and Fuller's London Pride always available, plus two guest ales which change all the time, with local micro-breweries supported as much as possible.

A traditional pub, recently refurbished, with lounge bar and servery bar for restaurant. Food available lunchtimes and evenings including Sunday roasts. Children allowed until 9pm. Beer garden. Located in the centre of the village.

OPEN *12–3pm and 6–11pm Mon–Fri; 11am–11pm Sat; 12–10.30pm Sun.*

GREAT BARFORD

The Golden Cross

2–4 Bedford Road, Great Barford MK44 3JD
☎ *(01234) 870439* Mr Older

 Greene King IPA permanently available, plus four guest beers changed weekly including Hop Back Summer Lightning and brews from Charles Wells, Bateman, Shepherd Neame and Wadworth, among others.

A traditional pub on the main road with an unconventional twist as the rear houses a Chinese restaurant. There is only Chinese food available. Children allowed in restaurant.

OPEN *12.30–2.30pm and 5–11pm Mon–Fri; 11am–11pm Sat; 12–10.30pm Sun.*

HARROLD

The Magpie
54 High Street, Harrold, Bedford MK43 7DA
☎ *(01234) 720071*

A Charles Wells house with Eagle permanently available plus one other Charles Wells ale.

A busy, traditional country pub with beams and open fireplaces. No food. Pool table, garden, car park. Children allowed.

OPEN *12–3pm and 5–11pm Mon–Fri; 12–11pm Sat; 12–10.30pm Sun.*

HENLOW

The Engineers Arms
68 High Street, Henlow SG16 6AA
☎ *(01462) 812284* Kevin Macuin

Everards Tiger, Timothy Taylor Landlord and Fuller's London Pride usually available. Six guest beers are usually served, changing twice weekly, and may include Hop Back Summer Lightning and beers from Cottage, Wolf, Kitchen and many micro-breweries from around the country.

Popular village local with pleasant beer terrace. Sky TV in separate room. Rolls, sandwiches and traditional hot pies available. Children welcome in separate room and garden. Pub in Henlow village, not Henlow Camp.

OPEN *12–11pm (10.30pm Sun).*

LEIGHTON BUZZARD

The Stag
1 Heath Road, Leighton Buzzard LU7 8AB
☎ *(01525) 372710* Bob Patrick

Serves the full range of Fuller's beers, including seasonal specials such as Honey Dew, Summer Ale, Red Fox and Old Winter Ale.

A traditional town pub with food served Mon–Sat lunchtimes (12–2pm) and evenings (6–9.30pm). Children not allowed.

OPEN *12–2.30pm and 6–11pm.*

LITTLE GRANSDEN

The Chequers
Little Gransden, Sandy
☎ *(01767) 677348* Mr R Mitchell

Adnams Bitter is permanently available, and there is one constantly changing guest beer, from breweries such as Milton, Church End, Wye Valley and Nethergate.

Friendly pub with tap room, lounge, games room and large garden. No food. Children welcome until 9pm. Car park.

OPEN *12–2pm and 7–11pm Mon–Fri; 11am–11pm Sat; 12–2pm and 7–10.30pm Sun.*

LUTON

The Bricklayers Arms
High Town Road, Luton LU2 0DD
☎ *(01582) 611017* Alison Taylor

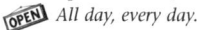Everards Beacon and Tiger, and Bateman Mild usually available with two weekly changing guest beers, perhaps from B&T, Nethergate, Dent, Crouch Vale, Rebellion, Burton Bridge and many others.

Bare boards and barrels set the tone for this traditional pub, first known to be trading in 1834. Lunchtime bar snacks. Car park. No children.

OPEN *12–2.30pm and 5–11pm Mon–Thurs; 12–11pm Fri–Sat; 12–10.30pm Sun.*

The Globe
26 Union Street, Luton LU1 3AN
☎ *(01582) 728681*

Greene King IPA always available, plus two guests from an ever-changing range.

Friendly one-bar pub, situated just outside town centre. Strong local support, with bar games and teams a regular feature. All major sporting events shown. Beer festivals held. Car park plus large patio area. Children allowed until early evening. Food served 11am–3pm Mon–Fri, 10am–3pm Sat.

OPEN *All day, every day.*

Mother Redcap
Latimer Road, Luton LU1 3XD
☎ *(01582) 730913* Bill and Noreen Lauden

A Greene King tied house with IPA, Abbot and Martha Green permanently available, one guest serving ales such as Morland Old Speckled Hen or Ruddles.

A typical drinkers' local in a traditional building. Outside seating at the front. Car park. Pool, darts, juke box and fruit machines. Bar food available at lunchtime. Children allowed lunchtime only.

OPEN *11am–11pm Mon–Sat; 12–10.30pm Sun.*

The Two Brewers
43 Dumfries Street, Luton LU1 5AY
☎ *(01582) 616008* Andy Gill

Two Tring beers (Sidepocket for a Toad and Jack O'Legs) always available, plus four ever-changing guest ales from Crouch Vale, Iceni, Kitchen, Slater's and Hook Norton, amongst others.

A welcoming, old-style, back street pub just two minutes from the town centre. Recently refurbished by Tring Brewery, who are now using the pub as their brewery tap. Food available 12–3pm Mon–Sat. Children allowed.

OPEN *12–11pm (10.30pm Sun).*

The Wheelwright's Arms
34 Guildford Street, Luton LU1 2NR
☎ *(01582) 759321* Alex Dalgarno

A freehouse with Fuller's ESB and London Pride among the beers always available. Two guests might be something else from Fuller's, perhaps seasonal beers such as Summer Ale, Honey Dew, and Red Fox.

Traditional drinkers' pub in a mid-nineteenth-century building, with one large bar, garden and seating. Food available. Pool, snooker, darts. Live music very occasionally. Fifteen letting rooms. Children allowed until early evening. Situated near the bus station.

OPEN *7–8am for breakfast, then 10.30am–11pm (10.30pm Sun).*

MILLBROOK VILLAGE

The Chequers
Millbrook Village MK45 2JB
☎ *(01525) 403835* Thomas

Fuller's London Pride and Hook Norton Old Hooky are regulars, with guests changed weekly.

An Italian family-run pub specialising in pasta, chargrilled meat, fish and award-winning coffee. Food served 12–2pm and 7–9pm. Children allowed in the restaurant. Located off A507 from Ridgmont, opposite the Vauxhall proving ground.

OPEN *11.30am–2.30pm and 6.30–11pm (closed Sun evening and all day Mon).*

POTTON

The Red Lion
1 Station Road, Potton, Sandy SG19 2PZ
☎ *(01767) 262705*

Greene King IPA permanently available during the summer months, and Morland Old Speckled Hen during the winter. Plus seasonal guests.

A one-bar drinkers' pub with pool, skittles, big-screen TV and live music. Beer garden. Parking. No food. No children.

OPEN *5–11pm Mon–Fri (7–11pm in winter); all day Sat–Sun and bank holidays.*

RAVENSDEN

The Blacksmith's Arms
Bedford Road, Ravensden
☎ *(01234) 771496* Pat O'Hara

Fuller's London Pride, Adnams IPA, Greene King Abbot and Marston's Pedigree permanently available, plus occasional guests in summer.

A family-friendly, food-oriented pub and restaurant in traditional style with beams and fireplaces. Garden. Parking.

OPEN *12–3pm and 6–11pm Mon–Sat; 12–10.30pm Sun.*

RIDGMONT

The Rose & Crown
89 High Street, Ridgmont MK43 0TY
☎ *(01525) 280245* Neil McGregor

Adnams Broadside and Mansfield Riding Bitter are regularly available, while other guests may include Morland Old Speckled Hen or a Young's brew.

A traditional, rural pub with food available (12–2pm and 7–9pm). Children allowed.

OPEN *10.30am–2.30pm and 6–11pm Mon–Sat (10.30pm Sun).*

SHARNBROOK

The Swan with Two Necks
High Street, Sharnbrook MK44 1PM
☎ *(01234) 871585* Mr and Mrs Baxter

Charles Wells Eagle IPA and Bombardier plus Morland Old Speckled Hen always on offer, as well as one guest beer.

Village pub with food available (snacks and full menu) 12–2.30pm and 6–9pm Mon–Thurs, 12–2.30pm and 6–10pm Fri–Sat, 12–2.30pm Sun (including roasts). Children welcome. Car park.

OPEN *11.30am–3pm and 5–11pm Mon–Fri; all day Sat–Sun.*

SHEFFORD

The Brewery Tap
14 North Bridge Street, Shefford SG16 5DH
☎ *(01462) 628448* Mr D Mortimer

B&T Shefford Bitter, Dark Mild and Dragonslayer and Everards Tiger always on offer, plus one guest beer, perhaps from Wye Valley or Crouch Vale.

Local beer house. Hot pies and rolls served at lunchtimes. Children allowed. Car park.

OPEN *11.30am–11pm Mon–Sat; 12–10.30pm Sun.*

STUDHAM

The Red Lion at Studham
Church Road, Studham LU6 2QA
☎ *(01582) 872530* Philip Potts

Five real ales available, perhaps including Timothy Taylor Landlord, Greene King Abbot Ale, Fuller's London Pride, Wadworth 6X and Farmers Glory, plus Black Sheep Bitter and Thwaites or Marston brews. The selection changes on a weekly basis.

Traditional country pub with food at lunchtimes and evenings (12–2.30pm and 7–9.30pm). Children allowed at lunchtimes only.

OPEN *11.30am–3pm and 5.30–11pm Mon–Fri; 11am–11pm Sat; 12–10.30pm Sun.*

WINGFIELD

The Plough Inn

Tebworth Road, Wingfield, Leighton Buzzard LU7 9QH
☎ *(01525) 873077* Sue and Jim Carr

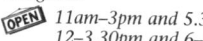 A Fuller's house serving their range of prize-winning ales, Chiswick, London Pride and ESB, together with their seasonal ales, Honey Dew, Summer Ale, Red Fox and Jack Frost. A guest beer is also available.

A thatched olde-English pub. CAMRA South Bedfordshire Pub of the Year 1993 and 1994. Bar and restaurant food available at lunchtimes and evenings (not Sun evenings). Garden with children's play area. From M1 junction 12, follow the A5120 through Toddington to Houghton Regis. Turn off to Wingfield.

OPEN *11am–3pm and 5.30–11pm Mon–Sat; 12–3.30pm and 6–10.30pm Sun.*

YELDEN

The Chequers

High Street, Yelden MK44 1AW
☎ *(01933) 356383* Alistair Bowie

 Thwaites Bitter, Greene King Abbot on gravity, Fuller's London Pride always available plus two rolling guests such as Wadworth 6X, Tamworthy Real Ale, Pott'n'Gold or any Potton Brewery ale.

A traditional village pub, located close to game shooting venues with real beer, real cider and a real fire! Large beer garden. Food available in separate dining area. Children allowed. Pool, darts, skittles (children welcome to play).

OPEN *5–11pm Mon–Tues (closed lunch); 12–2pm and 5–11pm Wed–Fri; 11am–11pm Sat; 12–10.30pm Sun. 11am–11pm Fri in game shooting season.*

YOU TELL US

* *The Old Bell*, Church Road, Totternhoe
* *The Queen's Head*, The Lane, Tebworth

Places Featured:

Aldworth	Pinkneys Green
Ashmansworth	Reading
Aston	Shinfield
Bracknell	Silchester
Brimpton	Sindlesham
Broad Laying	Slough
Burghclere	Sonning
Burghfield Common	Stanford Dingley
Caversham	Sunningdale
Chieveley	Sunninghill
Donnington	Thatcham
Eton	Theale
Frilsham	Tidmarsh
Holyport	Twyford
Hurley	Warfield
Littlewick Green	White Waltham
Lower Inkpen	Windsor Forest
Maidenhead	Winterbourne
Newbury	

THE BREWERIES

BUTTS BREWERY LTD

Unit 6a, Northfield Farm, Wantage Road,
Great Shefford, Hungerford RG17 7BY
☎ *(01488) 648133*

 JESTER 3.5% ABV
Light, easy-drinking.
BITTER 4.0% ABV
Golden and fruity.
BLACKGUARD 4.5% ABV
BARBUS BARBUS 4.6% ABV
Hoppy throughout.
GOLDEN BROWN 5.0% ABV
Hoppy spice flavour.
Plus occasional brews.

THE WEST BERKSHIRE BREWERY

Pot Kiln Lane, Frilsham, Yattendon, Newbury,
RG18 0XX
☎ *(01635) 202638 www.wbbrew.co.uk*

 SKIFF 3.6% ABV
Refreshing session beer.
BRICK KILN BITTER 4.0% ABV
Fruity. Only brewed for the Pot Kiln.
GOOD OLD BOY 4.0% ABV
Hop flavours throughout.
OLD TYLER 4.0% ABV
Brewed for The Bell at Aldworth.
DR HEXTER'S WEDDING ALE 4.1% ABV
Golden and refreshing.
GRAFT BITTER 4.3% ABV
Hoppy, with bitterness in the finish.
GOLDSTAR 5.0% ABV
Brewed with honey.
DR HEXTER'S HEALER 5.0% ABV
Pale and fruity.
Plus occasional brews.

THE PUBS

ALDWORTH

The Bell

Aldworth, Nr Reading RG8 9SE
☎ *(01635) 578272* Mr and Mrs IJ Macaulay

 Arkells 3B and Kingsdown Ale, West
Berkshire Old Tyler and Magnificent
Mild always available, plus a monthly ale
from West Berkshire.

A small, unaltered inn dating from 1340 in
good walking country. Bar food available
at lunchtimes and evenings. Well-behaved
children allowed in the tap room. Country
garden with adjacent cricket ground. Two
miles from Streatley on B4009 to Newbury.

OPEN *Closed all day Mon (except bank
holidays); 11am–3pm and 6–11pm
Tue–Sat; 12–3pm and 7–10.30pm Sun.*

ASHMANSWORTH

The Plough

Ashmansworth, Nr Newbury RG20 9SL
☎ *(01635) 253047* Oliver Davies

 Archers Village, Best and Golden always
available plus one guest which might be
Butts Barbus or Morrells Graduate.

A small, traditional pub serving beer direct
from the cask. Light bar snacks available
12–1.45pm Wed–Sun. No children. Tiny car
park accommodating three cars.

OPEN *6–11pm Tues; 12–2.30pm and 6–11pm
Wed–Sat; 12–2.30pm and 7–10.30pm
Sun (closed Mondays and Tues
lunchtime).*

ASTON

The Flower Pot Hotel

Ferry Lane, Aston, Henley-on-Thames RG9 3DG
☎ *(01491) 574721* AR Read and PM Thatcher

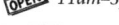Brakspear Mild, Bitter, Special and Old available, plus seasonal brews.

Built around 1890, the Flower Pot has been refurbished to provide modern facilities whilst retaining its Victorian character. Situated in pleasant countryside close to the river and half a mile from Hambledon Lock. Large garden. Bar food served lunchtimes and evenings. Children welcome. Car park.

OPEN *11am–3pm and 6–11pm (10.30pm Sun).*

BRACKNELL

The Green Man

Crowthorne Road, Bracknell RG12 7DL
☎ *(01344) 423667* Alan Cannon

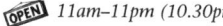Two weekly changing guest beers available. Hundreds of different beers have been served, including Bateman Jolly's Jaunts and Everards Tiger.

A local community pub with two bars. Food available. Pool table, darts. Large garden. No children.

OPEN *11am–11pm (10.30pm Sun).*

BRIMPTON

The Three Horseshoes

Brimpton Lane, Brimpton
☎ *(0118) 971 2183* Mr and Mrs M Holmes

Arkells 3B and Kingsdown always available, plus specials from Arkells such as Summer Ale and Noel.

Small, country pub with and lounge and public bars, off the A4 between Thatcham and Midgham. Recently refurbished, and now includes disabled access and toilets. Food served 12–2pm every day and 7–9.30pm Mon–Sat. Beer garden. Car park. Well-behaved children welcome.

OPEN *11.30am–2.30pm and 6–11pm Mon–Sat; 12–3pm and 7–10.30pm Sun.*

BROAD LAYING

The Rampant Cat

Broad Laying, Wootton Hill, Nr Newbury RG20 9TP
☎ *(01635) 253474* Mr JP Molyneux

Greene King Abbot Ale and IPA and Fuller's London Pride regularly available, plus a guest beer changed every eight weeks, such as Charles Wells Bombardier.

A well-presented pub with good atmosphere and magnificent gardens, set in the beautiful Berkshire countryside. Food served lunchtimes and evenings Tues–Sat, evenings only Mon and lunchtimes only Sun. Car park. Children welcome if eating.

OPEN *12–3pm and 6–11pm Mon–Sat; 12–3pm and 7–10.30pm Sun.*

BURGHCLERE

The Carpenters Arms

Harts Lane, Burghclere, Newbury RG20 9JY
☎ *(01635) 278251* Fiona Thorpe and L Hunt

An Arkells pub with 3B always on offer, with other Arkells beers such as Kingsdown Ale and seasonals Noel and Summer Ale regularly featured.

A tiny country pub with open log fire and beams. Full menu available lunchtimes and evenings (not Sun or Mon evening). Garden, car park. Children allowed. Off the by-pass, over the roundabout, head to Sandringham Memorial Chapel, turn left at the T-Junction, and the pub is on the right.

OPEN *11am–11pm Mon–Sat; 12–10.30pm Sun.*

BURGHFIELD COMMON

The Bantam

Omers Rise, Burghfield Common, Reading RG7 3HJ
☎ *(0118) 983 2763* Trevor James Clark

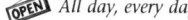An Arkells pub with 3B always on offer, plus seasonal Arkells ales.

A drinkers' pub in a modern building, featuring two bars, pool tables, a juke box and fruit machines. No food. Barbecues occasionally held in summer (weather permitting!). Garden, car park. Children allowed lunchtimes only, in garden. Call for directions.

OPEN *11am–3pm and 6–11pm Mon–Fri; 11am–11pm Sat; 12–3pm and 6–10.30pm Sun.*

CAVERSHAM

Baron Cadogan

22–4 Prospect Street, Caversham, Reading RG4 8JG
☎ *(0118) 947 0626* Philip Ashby

Three hand pumps serving a constantly changing range of guests, with four or five different beers each week. Regulars include Fuller's London Pride, Greene King Abbot, Shepherd Neame Spitfire, Archers Golden, Hogs Back TEA and Morland Old Speckled Hen.

A modern town freehouse with food available all day. No children.

OPEN *All day, every day.*

CHIEVELEY

Olde Red Lion

Green Lane, Chieveley RG20 8XB
☎ *(01635) 248379* Lance and Jackie Headley

Arkells 3B and Kingsdown Ale always available plus other, seasonal Arkells brews.

A traditional pub with bar food available (12–2.30pm and 6.30–10pm). Children welcome. Located just off M4 J13, near the services. Coach parties welcome.

OPEN *11am–3pm and 6–11pm (10.30pm Sun).*

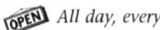
DONNINGTON

The Fox & Hounds
Oxford Road, Donnington, Newbury RG14 3AP
☎ *(01635) 40540* Julia Megarry

An Arkells pub where 3B is always on offer, plus Arkells seasonal ales on a regular basis.

Small country pub with open fire, live music and garden patio. Food served in the 50-seater restaurant. New small private dining room/meeting room. Car park. Children allowed in restaurant. Close to J13 of M4.

OPEN *All day, every day.*

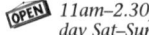
ETON

Waterman's Arms
Brocas Street, Eton SL4 6BW
☎ *(01753) 861001* Mr Collibee

Greene King IPA, Wadworth 6X, Charles Wells Bombardier and a Brakspear brew always available, plus guests from Bateman, Gale's and Felinfoel.

An old English-style pub with food served in a separate restaurant at lunchtimes and evenings. Children allowed.

OPEN *11am–2.30pm and 6–11pm Mon–Fri; all day Sat–Sun.*

FRILSHAM

Pot Kiln
Yattendon, Frilsham RG18 0XX
☎ *(01635) 201366* Philip Gent

West Berkshire Brick Kiln Bitter only available here, plus Morland Original, Arkells 3B and others. Seasonal brews and specials, usually from West Berkshire brewery.

A traditional pub with the West Berkshire micro-brewery in an out-building at the back. Food available (12–1.45pm and 7–9.30pm). Children allowed. From Newbury take B4009 into Hermitage. Turn right at The Fox, follow Yattendon sign. Take second turning on right and continue for a mile. Pub is on the right.

OPEN *12–2.30pm (except Tues) and 6.30–11pm Mon–Sat; 12–3pm and 7–10.30pm Sun.*

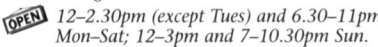

HOLYPORT

The Belgian Arms
Holyport Street, Holyport, Maidenhead SL6 2JR
☎ *(01628) 634468* Alfred G Morgan

Brakspear Bitter and Special are always available.

A typical English country pub situated next to the village pond, with a 250-year-old wisteria plant at the pub's entrance. Cosy in wintertime. Conservatory leading on to attractive beer garden where large willows screen a view of the village pond. Food served 12–2pm and 7–9.30pm on weekdays and 12–2pm Sun. Children allowed in the conservatory but not in the bar area. Car park. From Junction 8/9 on M4 follow signs for Maidenhead, then take A330 Ascot/Bracknell road, turn left at Holyport Green and left again at the village pond.

OPEN *11am–3pm and 5.30–11pm Mon–Sat; 12–3pm and 7–10.30pm Sun.*

HURLEY

The Dew Drop Inn
Batts Green, Honey Lane, Hurley SL6 6RB
☎ *(01628) 824327* CH and BD Morley

Brakspear Mild, Bitter, Special and the seasonal ale regularly available.

Recently refurbished and sensitively extended, cottage-style country pub in an idyllic woodland setting. Fresh, home-cooked food served every lunchtime and evening. Large car park and garden. Well-behaved children welcome. To find the pub, look for a sharp turning halfway along Honey Lane with a smaller lane leading off. Follow this for 300 yards. Pub will be found on the right-hand side.

OPEN *12–3pm and 6–11pm Mon–Sat; 12–3pm and 7–10.30pm Sun.*

LITTLEWICK GREEN

The Cricketers
Coronation Road, Littlewick Green SL6 3RA
☎ *(01628) 822888* Mr Carter

Timothy Taylor Landlord, Fuller's London Pride and Brakspear Pale Ale always available. Other brews rotating regularly may include Shepherd Neame Spitfire, Wadworth 6X, Morland Old Speckled Hen or something from Timothy Taylor.

A traditional village pub situated on the village green close to the old Bath Road (A4). Food available (12–2pm and 7–9pm). Cricket regularly played at weekends. Children allowed.

OPEN *11am–11pm Mon–Sat; 12–10.30pm Sun.*

LOWER INKPEN

Swan Inn
Lower Inkpen, Hungerford RG17 9DX
☎ *(01488) 668326* Mary Harris

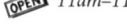Hook Norton Bitter and Mild and Butts Brewery's Traditional and Blackguard regularly available, plus a range of guest beers.

A traditional village hotel with 'freehouse' bar. West Berkshire CAMRA Pub of the Year 2000. Ten bedrooms and a restaurant. AA and English Tourist Board recommended. Bar food also available with organic food a speciality. Organic farm shop and butchery on the premises. Children allowed.

OPEN *11am–11pm (10.30pm Sun).*

MAIDENHEAD

The Hobgoblin
High Street, Maidenhead SL6 1QE
☎ *(01628) 636510* D Dean (Manager)

A Wychwood tied house with at least two seasonal Wychwood ales always available, plus three guests changing weekly, such as Fuller's London Pride, Rebellion ales, Hooray Henley, or Ow'sthat (a cricket celebration ale).

A lively town pub with a young clientele, particularly at weekends. One bar, beer garden. Food available 12–2pm. Children allowed in the garden only.

OPEN *12–11pm Mon–Sat; 3–10.30pm Sun.*

NEWBURY

The Coopers Arms
Bartholomew Street, Newbury RG14 5LL
☎ *(01635) 47469* David Reid

Tied to Arkells, with 2B and 3B always on offer. There are plans to feature guest ales in the future.

Town-centre locals' pub in an old-style building. Pool and darts. Folk/Irish music night on the third Thursday of each month. Car park. No children. Call for directions

OPEN *11am–2.30pm and 5–11pm Tues–Thurs; 11am–11pm Fri–Mon (10.30pm Sun); hours are under review.*

The Hobgoblin
Bartholomew Street, Newbury RG14 5HB
☎ *(01635) 47336* Gay Diss

A Wychwood special always available, plus up to five guest ales such as Wadworth 6X, Brakspear Special or other Wychwood brew. Beers changed every fortnight.

A traditional town pub with one bar, beams and wooden floors. Food available at lunchtime only. Children allowed.

OPEN *12–11pm (10.30pm Sun).*

The Monument
57 Northbrook Street, Newbury RG14 1AN
☎ *(01635) 41964* Simon Owens

Butts Traditional, Butts Barbus Barbus and Morland Old Speckled Hen permanently available, with Gale's HSB an occasional guest.

Now a tenancy, this 350-year-old pub is the oldest in Newbury. Good food available all day and evening, including roasts on Sundays. Children and dogs very welcome. Live music Wed and Thurs, plus a comedian once a month. Covered and heated garden open in summer – the roof is removable. Rotating pool table, free juke box with range of 400 CDs, free internet facility (with a two-drink minimum purchase). Website: www.themonumentonline.co.uk.

OPEN *11am–11pm Mon–Sat; 12–10.30pm Sun.*

The Red House
12 Hampton Road, Newbury RG14 6DB
☎ *(01635) 30584*

Marston's Pedigree is always available, plus one guest, changed monthly, perhaps from Robinson's or Archers.

A local drinkers' pub, with pool and football teams. No food, no garden, no parking, no children.

OPEN *Evenings and weekends only.*

The Woodpecker
Wash Water, Newbury RG20 0LU
☎ *(01635) 43027* Andrew and Janet Cover

An Arkells pub with 2B, 3B and Kingsdown Ale permanently served, plus Noel Ale at Christmas.

Old-fashioned beamed pub with no music, pool or games, just good food and drink! Non-smoking dining area. Outside seating at the front of the pub. Bed and breakfast available during the week. Two car parks. No children.

OPEN *11.15am–2.45pm and 6–11pm Mon–Sat; 12–4pm and 7–10.30pm Sun.*

PINKNEYS GREEN

The Stag & Hounds
Lee Lane, Pinkneys Green, Maidenhead SL6 6NU
☎ *(01628) 630268* Paul Clarke

A freehouse with Brakspear Bitter and Fuller's London Pride always on offer, plus Marston's Pedigree as a regular feature. Three guests available (two changing each week), including beers from local micro-breweries.

A friendly pub in a rural location, with a clientele mainly over the age of 30. Home-made food available. Function room and huge garden. Children allowed.

OPEN *11am–3pm and 6–11pm Mon–Thurs; 11am–11pm Fri–Sat; 12–10.30pm Sun.*

READING

3B's Bar

Old Town Hall, Blagrave Street, Reading RG1 1QH
☎ *(0118) 939 9803* Stefano Buratta

 Four constantly changing real ales from any independent brewery always available. Beers from local breweries such as West Berkshire and Beckett's stocked whenever possible.

A friendly café bar right next to the station. Families welcome. Food available all day.

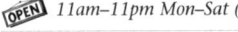 *11am–11pm Mon–Sat (closed Sun).*

Back of Beyond

104–8 Kings Road, Reading RG4 8DT
☎ *(0118) 959 5906* Sean Pickering

 Fuller's London Pride is among the beers always available. Regular guests include Archers Golden and Hogs Back Traditional English Ale plus others from independent breweries such as Cains, Caledonian, Cotleigh, Exmoor, Hardys & Hansons, Smiles, Wychwood and Timothy Taylor.

A traditional JD Wetherspoon's pub with garden, located five minutes from the railway station. Food available all day. No children.

 10am–11pm Mon–Sat; 12–10.30pm Sun.

The Brewery Tap

27 Castle Street, Reading RG1 7SB
☎ *(0118) 957 6280*
Mike Moore (brewer and landlord)

Fuller's London Pride always available, plus one constantly changing guest ale from any micro or independent brewery.

Traditional-style city-centre pub, with games room, four pool tables, darts and a function room. Family-oriented, with food available from 12pm daily. Wide-ranging clientele: business people at lunchtimes and locals in the evenings.

11am–11pm Mon–Sat; 12–10.30pm Sun.

The Hobgoblin

2 Broad Street, Reading RG1 2BH
☎ *(01734) 508119* Duncan Ward

Wychwood beers always available plus up to 700 guests per year exclusively from small independent brewers. No national products are stocked. Also real cider, perry and genuine German lager.

Small, friendly town-centre pub. No juke box, but background R&B etc. Occasional live music, traditional pub games. Bar food at lunchtimes. Supervised children allowed up to 7pm.

All permitted hours.

The Hop Leaf

163–5 Southampton Street, Reading RG1 2QZ
☎ *(0118) 931 4700*

 The full range of Hop Back ales brewed and served on the premises.

This formerly derelict pub on the edge of the town centre was taken over and revitalised as a brewpub by the Hop Back Brewery. A late Victorian building, recently refurbished. Parking can be difficult.

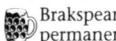 **MILD 3.0% ABV**
GFB 3.5% ABV
EXTRA STOUT 4.0% ABV
HOP LEAF 4.0% ABV
RYE BEER 5.0% ABV
SUMMER LIGHTNING 5.0% ABV
WHEAT BEER 5.0% ABV

 All permitted hours.

The New Inn

Kidmore End, Reading RG4 9AU
☎ *(01189) 723115*

Brakspear Bitter and Special are permanent features.

A country pub with old beams, real fireplace, bronze bric-à-brac and old-fashioned pumps against the walls. Food available in bar and lounge. Large garden and ample car parking. Children allowed only for pre-booked functions.

 12–3pm and 6–11pm Mon–Sat; 12–10.30pm Sun and bank holidays.

Sweeney & Todd

10 Castle Street, Reading RG1 7RD
☎ *(0118) 958 6466* Catherine J Hayward

Wadworth 6X usually available, plus one guest such as Eldridge Pope Royal Oak, Adnams Best and brews from Butts, Itchen Valley, Brakspear, Gale's, Greene King and Young's.

A traditional 'pie and pint' pub. A huge range of pies is served all day in the dedicated restaurant. Children allowed in the restaurant.

11am–11pm Mon–Sat; 12–10.30pm Sun.

Wheelwright's Arms

Davis Way, St Nicholas Hurst, Reading RG10 0TR
☎ *(0118) 934 4100* Kevin Morley

Four Wadworth brews always available, plus four guests perhaps including Adnams Extra, Badger Tanglefoot and others. Guests are changed monthly.

A traditional pub with low beams and a real fire. Food available 12–2pm and 6.30–9pm. Children allowed in restaurant only.

 11.30am–2.30pm and 5.30–11pm Mon–Fri; 11am–11pm Sat; 12–10.30pm Sun.

SHINFIELD

Bell & Bottle

School Green, Shinfield, Reading RG2 9EE
☎ *(0118) 988 3563* Fran Jane

 A freehouse with six cask ales rotated weekly, featuring beers from Beckett's, Cottage, Wychwood, Butts, Smiles, plus Marston's Pedigree, Archers Village and Golden and Wadworth 6X.

A traditional pub, recently extended, with restaurant. Children and dogs welcome.

OPEN *11.30am–11.30pm Mon–Sat; 12–10.30pm Sun.*

SILCHESTER

The Calleva Arms

Silchester Common, Silchester, Reading RG7 2PH
☎ *(01189) 700305* Eileen Maher

 A Gale's pub with HSB, Butser Bitter and GB always on offer, plus one guest, such as Everards Tiger, Timothy Taylor Landlord, Fuller's London Pride, or something from Young's.

A village pub with beams and open fires. Separate dining area and conservatory. Beer garden. Car park. Children allowed.

OPEN *11.30am–2.30pm and 5.30–11pm Mon–Fri; 11.30am–3pm and 6–11pm Sat; 12–3pm and 7–10.30pm Sun.*

SINDLESHAM

The Walter Arms

Bearwood Road, Sindlesham, Wokingham RG41 5BP
☎ *(0118) 978 0260* Brian Howard

 Marston's Pedigree and Young's Special always available.

Upmarket pub with three open fires. Popular with business diners for pre-ordering and rapid service – food is served 12–2.30pm and 6.15–9.30pm (booking essential). Only fresh produce used, with traditional dishes a speciality in the evenings. 'Fish Called Walter' is the adjacent fresh fish and seafood restaurant, open lunchtimes 12–3pm Wed–Fri and 7–10pm Tues–Sat (booking essential). Garden, parking for 80 cars. No children under 14. Situated on the main road. Website: www.thewalterarms.co.uk.

OPEN *12–2.30pm (3pm Sat) and 5–11pm (open from 6pm Sun).*

SLOUGH

Moon & Spoon

86–8 High Street, Slough SL1 1EL
☎ *(01753) 531650*

 Shepherd Neame Spitfire always available, plus two guest beers, changed when the barrel runs out!

A themed JD Wetherspoon's pub with a lively clientele. Food served all day, every day. Children not allowed. At the end of the High Street, opposite the library.

OPEN *10.30am–11pm Mon–Sat; 12–10.30pm Sun.*

The Rose & Crown

213 High Street, Slough SL1 1NB
☎ *(01753) 521114* Mr Jobling

 A freehouse with four pumps serving a range of guest beers, changed every two days. Regular favourites include beers from Mordue and Dwan (Tipperary).

Traditional town pub with two small bars. Patio at front, garden at rear. No food. No children

OPEN *11am–11pm Mon–Sat; 12–10.30pm Sun.*

SONNING

The Bull

High Street, Sonning, Reading RG4 6UP
☎ *(0118) 969 3901*
Christine and Dennis Mason

 A George Gale tied house, permanently serving Gale's HSB, Best and Butser, plus Gale's seasonal specials. Marston's Pedigree often available as a guest.

An old country pub with log fires. Food available lunchtimes and evenings. Children allowed.

OPEN *11am–3pm and 5.30–11pm Mon–Fri; all day Sat–Sun.*

STANFORD DINGLEY

The Boot

Stanford Dingley, Reading RG7 6LT
☎ *(0118) 974 4292* John Haley

Real ales rotated fortnightly usually from Smiles, Archers or West Berkshire breweries.

A traditional, olde-worlde freehouse. Bar food available (12–2.15pm and 7–9.15pm). Children welcome.

OPEN *11am–3pm and 6–11pm Mon–Sat (7–10pm Sun).*

The Bull

Stanford Dingley, Reading RG7 6LS
☎ *(0118) 974 4409* Robert and Kate Archard and Robin and Carol Walker

 West Berkshire Skiff, Good Old Boy, Maggs' Magificent Mild and Resolution, and something from Brakspear regularly available, plus occasional specials.

Traditional family-owned fifteenth-century freehouse in centre of village, with a new dining room and six new bed and breakfast rooms. Menu offers excellent food at pub, not restaurant, prices. Food served 12–2.30pm and 6.30–9.30pm Mon–Sat, 12–2.30pm and 7–9pm Sun. Children welcome, as long as the parents behave! Classic-car owners and motorsport enthusiasts particularly welcome.

12–3pm and 6–11pm Mon–Sat; 12–3pm and 7–10.30pm Sun.

SUNNINGDALE

The Nags Head

28 High Street, Sunningdale SL5 0NG
☎ *(01344) 622725* Dave and Denise West

 Harveys Sussex Mild, Pale Ale and Best Bitter usually available plus a Harveys seasonal brew.

Traditional village pub and the only Harveys pub in Berkshire. Games-orientated public bar and spacious lounge bar. Cask Marque award. 'Pub grub' with daily special served 12–2pm Mon–Sat. Car park. Well-behaved children welcome in lounge bar. Play equipment in large garden. Between A30/A329 in Sunningdale village, nearly opposite the church.

11.30am–11pm Mon–Sat; 12–10.30pm Sun.

SUNNINGHILL

The Dukes Head

Upper Village Road, Sunninghill SL5 7AG
☎ *(01344) 626949* Philip Durrant

 Marston's Pedigree and Greene King Abbot permanently available, plus Greene King seasonal ales as and when available.

A traditional village pub specialising in Thai food (12–2pm and 7–10pm). Owned by Greene King. Well-behaved children allowed. Upper Village Road runs parallel to the High Street. A beer festival is held once a year.

11am–11pm Mon–Sat; 12–10.30pm Sun.

THATCHAM

The White Hart

2 High Street, Thatcham RG19 3JD
☎ *(01635) 863251* Des William

 Wadworth 6X is a permanent feature, plus one guest, changed monthly, including beers such as Fuller's London Pride, Marston's Pedigree, Hyde's A Quick One, Nethergate Suffolk Bitter and many more!

Town-centre pub, catering for business people at lunchtimes and locals in the evenings. Lounge bar with dining area. Food served lunchtimes Mon–Fri and Sun. No darts, pool or TV. Parking at rear and street parking. No children.

11am–11pm Mon–Fri; 11am–3pm and 7–11pm Sat; 12–3pm and 7–10.30pm Sun.

THEALE

The Red Lion Public House

5 Church Street, Theale, Reading RG7 5BU
☎ *(01189) 302394* Mrs FT Mathews

 Marston's Pedigree is always available, plus one regularly changing guest beer, such as Adnams Broadside or Fuller's London Pride.

Village pub with beams, two fires and an old-fashioned cosy atmosphere. Food served 12–2pm Mon–Sat and 12–2.30pm Sun. Small garden, skittle alley (converted for dining during busy periods). Children allowed, and can use skittle alley if not in use. Situated off the High Street.

12–11pm (10.30pm Sun).

TIDMARSH

Greyhound

The Street, Tidmarsh RG8 8ER
☎ *(0118) 984 3557* Martin Ford

 Five real ales including Fuller's London Pride and others rotated monthly from Shepherd Neame, Rebellion, West Berkshire, Coniston, Wadworth and other breweries.

A traditional, twelfth-century village pub serving food at lunchtimes. Children allowed. On the main A340.

11am–3pm and 5.30–11pm Mon–Fri; 11am–11pm Sat; 12–10.30pm Sun.

TWYFORD

The Duke of Wellington

27 High Street, Twyford RG10 9AG
☎ *(0118) 934 0456* Bill Suter

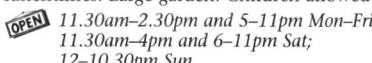A Brakspear tenancy, with Bitter, Special and Mild always on offer, plus seasonal Brakspear beers.

Village local with two public bars and a lounge. Food available Mon–Sat lunchtimes. Large garden. Children allowed.

 11.30am–2.30pm and 5–11pm Mon–Fri; 11.30am–4pm and 6–11pm Sat; 12–10.30pm Sun.

The Golden Cross

38 Waltham Road, Twyford, Reading RG10 9EG
☎ *(0118) 934 0180* Duncan Campbell

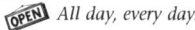Brakspear brews and Fuller's London Pride permanently available, plus guests regularly including Greene King IPA, Marston's Pedigree, and Wadworth 6X.

A locals' pub with restaurant area and beer garden. Food served every lunchtime and Tues–Sat evenings. Children allowed in the garden and restaurant only.

 All day, every day.

WARFIELD

The Cricketers

Cricketers Lane, Warfield RG42 6JT
☎ *(01344) 882910* Dawn and Paul Chance

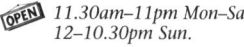Greene King IPA and Abbot always available, plus one guest beer. Previous guests have included Everards Tiger, Wadworth 6X, Brains SA, Batemans XXXB and Wychwood Hobgoblin. Whenever possible, the better-known ales are alternated with more unusual brews, for variety.

A small, rural pub situated in a quiet country lane. Three bars – public, saloon and middle – separate restaurant and garden. Food available 12–3pm and 6–9pm Mon–Fri; 12–9pm Sat–Sun plus Sunday carvery from 12–3pm. Children welcome, play area in garden. Car park. Follow the B3022 from Bracknell towards Windsor and Cricketers Lane is found on the right-hand side of a sharp bend.

 11.30am–11pm Mon–Sat; 12–10.30pm Sun.

WHITE WALTHAM

The Beehive

Waltham Road, White Waltham SL6 3SH
☎ *(01628) 822877* Guy Martin

A Whitbread tied house with four cask ales available, including Fuller's London Pride, a Brakspear brew, plus twice-weekly changing guests, perhaps from the Cottage Brewery, Hampshire Brewery and Rebellion.

A rural pub with two large gardens, one south-facing overlooking cricket pitch, and a separate restaurant. Cask Marque award winner. Food available all day at weekends, lunchtimes and evenings on weekdays. Children welcome. Monthly quiz nights.

 11am–3pm and 5–11pm Mon–Fri; all day Sat–Sun.

WINDSOR FOREST

The Duke of Edinburgh

Woodside Road, Windsor Forest, Nr Windsor SL4 2DP
☎ *(01344) 882736* Nicholas Tilt

Tied to Arkells, with 2B, 3B and Kingsdown Ale always available, plus seasonal Arkells beers.

Traditional 100-year-old pub with restaurant. Public, saloon and back bar – lots of different nooks and crannies! Food available. Garden and car park. Call for directions.

 12–3pm and 5–11pm Mon–Thurs; 11am–11pm Fri–Sat; 12–10.30pm Sun.

WINTERBOURNE

The Winterbourne Arms

Winterbourne, Newbury RG20 8BB
☎ *(01635) 248200* Gordon Fry

Three hand pumps serving a constantly changing range of real ales such as Morland Old Speckled Hen and brews from Badger and West Berkshire breweries. All independent breweries considered.

A one-bar freehouse with restaurant and attractive garden. Food available every lunchtime and Tues–Sat evenings. Children allowed in the restaurant area. Located off the B4494.

 11am–3pm and 6–11pm Tues–Sat; 12–3pm Sun. Closed Sun evening and all day Mon.

YOU TELL US

* *The Crooked Billet*, Honey Hill, Wokingham
* *The Horse & Jockey*, 120 Castle Street, Reading
* *The Vansittart Arms*, 105 Vansittart Road, Windsor

Places Featured:

Ashenden
Asheridge
Aylesbury
Beaconsfield
Bellingdon
Bledlow
Bradwell Common
Chesham
Coleshill
Cublington
Easington
Fawley
Ford
Frieth
Gibraltar
Haddenham
Hedgerley
Ibstone
Little Marlow

Little Missenden
Littleworth Common
Loudwater
Marlow
New Bradwell
Newport Pagnell
North Crawley
Old Amersham
Prestwood
Stoke Poges
Stony Stratford
Tatling End
The Lee
Thornborough
Wendover
Western Turville
Wheeler End
Wing

THE BREWERIES

THE CHILTERN BREWERY

Nash Lee Road, Terrick, Aylesbury HP17 0TQ
☎ *(01296) 613647*
www.chilternbrewery.co.uk

CHILTERN ALE 3.7% ABV
Pale, smooth and a pleasing clean finish.
GOLDEN SOVEREIGN ALE 3.7% ABV
Fine light ale.
BEECHWOOD BITTER 4.3% ABV
Well-rounded, with nut flavours and a long finish.
THREE HUNDREDS OLD ALE 5.0% ABV
Dark, good body and long finish.

REBELLION BEER CO.

Bencombe Farm, Marlow Bottom Road, Marlow SL7 3LT
☎ *(01628) 476594*
www.rebellionbeer.co.uk

IPA 3.7% ABV
Balanced easy quaffer.
SMUGGLER 4.1% ABV
Well-rounded and full-flavoured.
BLONDE BOMBSHELL 4.3% ABV
Summer brew.
MUTINY 4.5% ABV
Smooth and hoppy.
RED OKTOBER 4.7% ABV
Autumn ale.
ZEBEDEE 4.7% ABV
Spring ale.
OLD CODGER 5.0% ABV
Winter ale.
Plus seasonal and monthly brews.

VALE BREWERY CO. LTD

Thame Road, Haddenham HP17 8BY
☎ *(01844) 290008*
www.valebrewery.co.uk

NOTLEY ALE 3.3% ABV
Bitter with a clean taste.
WYCHERT BITTER 3.9% ABV
Smooth and mellow flavours.
EDGAR'S GOLDEN ALE 4.3% ABV
Pale with strong hop flavour.
Plus seasonal and occasional brews.

THE PUBS

ASHENDEN

Gatehangers
Lower End, Ashenden HP18 0HE
☎ *(01296) 651296*

 Wadworth IPA and 6X, Adnams Best and a Badger brew always available plus a guest beer (up to 30 per year) from breweries such as Mole's, Elgood's, Hook Norton, Felinfoel, Everards, Bateman, Smiles or Marston's.

A 300-year-old country pub with traditional atmosphere. Beamed in part with open fires and large L-shaped bar. Bar food at lunchtime and evenings. Car park and garden. Children allowed. Twenty minutes to Oxford. Between the A41 and A418 west of Aylesbury, near the church.

OPEN *12–2.30pm and 7–11pm.*

ASHERIDGE

The Blue Ball
Asheridge, Chesham HP5 2UX
☎ *(01494) 758263* Peter George

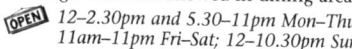 A freehouse, whose June beer festival offers at least 32 real ales. Greene King IPA and Fuller's London Pride are always available plus two guest beers, changed weekly, which may come from Adnams, Brakspear, Cottage, Orkney, Rebellion or Arundel breweries.

A traditional pub built in 1851, two miles north of Chesham, with a mixed clientele. Non-smoking function room, big garden. Food served at lunchtime and evenings. Children allowed in dining area.

OPEN *12–2.30pm and 5.30–11pm Mon–Thur; 11am–11pm Fri–Sat; 12–10.30pm Sun.*

AYLESBURY

The Grapes
36 Market Square, Aylesbury HP20 1TW
☎ *(01296) 483735* Nic Swanson

 Greene King IPA and Ruddles County are the permanent beers here, and one guest is also available.

A locals' haven in the middle of the town centre. Food served 12–3pm daily. Car parking available in adjacent multi-storey.

OPEN *12–11pm (10.30pm Sun).*

BEACONSFIELD

The Greyhound
33 Windsor End, Beaconsfield HP9 2JN
☎ *(01494) 673823* John and Claire Flippance

 Two guest beers are available, changed weekly, mainly from Rebellion and Fuller's. Those previously featured include Rebellion Smuggler and Mutiny, Fuller's ESB and bitters from Ringwood.

A traditional public house with separate dining area. Food served at lunchtime and evenings. Children not admitted.

OPEN *11am–3pm and 5.30–11pm.*

BELLINGDON

The Bull
Bellingdon HP5 2XU
☎ *(01494) 758163* Carl and Kathy Slaughter

 Young's Bitter permanently available, plus one guest, possibly something from Fuller's.

Country pub with one bar and beams, formerly a coaching inn. Food available. Garden, car park, occasional live music. Children allowed.

OPEN *11am–11pm Mon–Sat; 12–10.30pm Sun.*

BLEDLOW

The Lions of Bledlow
Church End, Bledlow HP27 9PE
☎ *(01844) 343345* Mark McKeown

 A freehouse with Wadworth 6X, Marston's Pedigree and Brakspear Bitter always on offer, plus one or two guests, changed twice weekly, such as Vale Edgar's Golden Ale, Rebellion Mutiny or Burton Bridge Bitter. Seasonal ales such as Vale Hadda's Spring Gold and Kelpi (an organic ale made from seaweed) are also featured.

Old, traditional, rambling pub with beams and stone floors. One long bar with two rooms. Food available – there is a separate dining area. Garden, car park. Children allowed in dining area only. Look for the brown tourist sign at the bottom of B4009.

OPEN *12–3pm and 6–11pm (10.30pm Sun); sometimes open longer at weekends.*

BRADWELL COMMON

The Countryman
Bradwell Boulevard, Bradwell Common, Milton Keynes MK13 8EZ
☎ *(01908) 676346* Dave Keating

 A freehouse with eight cask ale pumps. Marston's Pedigree is among the regular brews served.

Aone-bar pub built in 1986 in the middle of the estate. Popular with families. Food available. Children's room. Bradwell Boulevard is the main road through Bradwell Common.

OPEN *11am–11pm Mon–Sat; 12–10.30pm Sun.*

CHESHAM

The Black Horse
The Vale, Chesham HP5 3MS
☎ *(01494) 784656* Mike Goodchild

 Tied to Benskins (Carlsberg-Tetley), with four real ales. Regulars include Morland Old Speckled Hen, Black Stallion (5%, brewed specially by Tring Brewery), Adnams Best Bitter and Young's Special.

Afourteenth-century coaching inn just outside Chesham (with certified ghosts!), mainly operating as a restaurant. Large garden. No children allowed in bar area.

OPEN *12–3pm and 6–11pm Mon–Sat (sometimes all day during summer); 12–10.30pm Sun.*

The Queens Head
120 Church Street, Old Chesham HP5 1JD
☎ *(01494) 783773* Mr Shippey

 A freehouse regularly offering Brakspear Bitter and Special, plus Fuller's London Pride. Other brews served include Brakspear and Fuller's seasonal ales.

Atraditional family pub, offering English and Thai food in the bar, and a Thai restaurant. Children allowed.

OPEN *11am–2.30pm and 5–11pm Mon–Fri; 11am–3pm and 5–11pm Sat; 12–3pm and 7–10.30pm Sun.*

COLESHILL

The Red Lion
Village Road, Coleshill HP7 0LH
☎ *(01494) 727020* John Ullman

 Greene King IPA, Fuller's London Pride and Brakspear Bitter are always on offer, plus one guest, changed weekly, with Vale Wychert Ale and Rebellion Smuggler regular favourites. Seasonal ales such as Rebellion Blonde Bombshell (summer) and Fuller's Winter Ale are featured.

Avillage pub with beams and open fires. Home-cooked food available. Garden front and back, with children's area. Car park. Coleshill is signposted at the Water Tower on A355 Amersham to Beaconsfield road, and the pub is along the village road, opposite the pond and the church.

OPEN *11am–3pm and 5.30–11pm Mon–Fri; 11am–11pm Sat; 12–4.30pm and 7–10.30pm Sun.*

CUBLINGTON

The Unicorn
High Street, Cublington LU7 0LQ
☎ *(01296) 681261*

 A freehouse with Shepherd Neame Spitfire and Master Brew Bitter, and Brakspear Bitter always available, plus two regularly changing guest ales.

Atraditional country pub dating from 1600 with open fires and low beams in the main bar. A very friendly pub with an attractive beer garden and separate smoking and non-smoking areas. Bar food including specials available lunchtimes and evenings Tues–Sat. Car park and garden. Website: www.chilterncountryinns.com. Children allowed.

OPEN *5.30–11pm Mon; 12–3pm and 5.30–11pm Tues–Fri; 12–11pm Sat; 12–10.30pm Sun.*

EASINGTON

The Mole & Chicken
Easington HP18 9EY
☎ *(01844) 208387* Shane Ellis

 A freehouse with Morland Old Speckled Hen, Greene King IPA and something from Hook Norton permanently available, plus one guest. Fuller's London Pride is often featured, and Wychwood The Dog's Bollocks is also a favourite.

Apub and restaurant, with a slate floor, two fireplaces, and an oak bar, plus oak and antique pine furniture. Food available. Beer garden with views over Oxford. Car park and accommodation. Children allowed. Call for directions.

OPEN *12–3pm and 6–11pm Mon–Sat; 12–10.30pm Sun.*

FAWLEY

The Walnut Tree

Fawley RG9 6JE
☎ *(01491) 638360* Adam Dutton

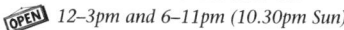A Brakspear pub, with Bitter and Special always served, plus one seasonal guest.

Country pub and restaurant, with garden and patio. Food available. Car park. Accommodation. Children allowed.

 12–3pm and 6–11pm (10.30pm Sun).

FORD

Dinton Hermit

Water Lane, Ford HP17 8XH
☎ *(01296) 747473* Johnny Chick

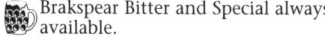Morrells Oxford Blue is a permanent feature. The two guests may include beers from Adnams and Hook Norton.

Sixteenth-century country pub and restaurant, with beams and log fires. Food available. Jazz occasionally in summer. Car park. Children allowed in garden only. Please ring for directions.

 12–2pm and 6–11pm; closed Sun evening and all day Mon.

FRIETH

The Prince Albert

Moors End, Frieth
☎ *(01494) 881683* Steven Anderson

Brakspear Bitter and Special always available.

A seventeenth-century pub, recently refurbished, with original features restored. Food served 12–3pm and 6.30–9.30pm. Large beer garden. Children welcome (no special facilities). From Lane End, turn left before the Frieth signs, towards Fingest.

 12–3.30pm and 5.30–11pm (10.30pm Sun).

GIBRALTAR

The Bottle & Glass

Oxford Road, Gibraltar HP17 8TY
☎ *(01296) 748488* Robert Cambray

Morrells pub with Varsity and Oxford Bitter always available.

Thatched, 'chocolate-box', beamed pub and restaurant. Food available. Beer garden, patio, car park. Children allowed. Located on the main Aylesbury to Thame road.

 11.30am–3pm and 6–11pm (closed Sun evenings).

HADDENHAM

The Rising Sun

9 Thame Road, Haddenham HP17 8EN
☎ *(01844) 291744* Mike and Bev Platt

A freehouse with Charles Wells Eagle IPA and Bombardier plus Vale Wychert Ale always on sale. Guest beers are from a range of micro-breweries, and are changed daily.

A village pub, on the main road from Thame to Aylesbury. Very much a drinker's pub, with bar snacks only. Beer garden. Children allowed until 7.30pm.

 11am–3pm and 5–11pm Mon–Thurs; 11am–11pm Fri–Sat; 12–10.30pm Sun.

HEDGERLEY

The White Horse

Village Lane, Hedgerley, Slough SL2 3UY
☎ *(01753) 643225* Mrs Hobbs and Mr Brooker

Over 1,000 different beers served annually, with seven real ales always available.

CAMRA Slough, Maidenhead and Windsor Pub of the Year 1999–2000. Beer festival held every year at end of May. Bar food available every lunchtime. No machines, no music. Car park, garden. Bird sanctuary nearby.

 11am–2.30pm and 5.30–11pm Mon–Fri; 11am–11pm Sat; 12–10.30pm Sun.

IBSTONE

The Fox

The Common, Ibstone, Nr High Wycombe HP14 3GG
☎ *(01491) 638722* Mrs Banks

Brakspear ales always available plus three guests in summer, two in winter, serving a range of real ales such as Fuller's London Pride or Rebellion. Stocks beers from local breweries whenever possible.

A 300-year-old traditional country inn. Bar and restaurant food available lunchtimes and evenings. Accommodation. Children allowed.

 12–3pm and 6–11pm (10.30pm Sun).

LITTLE MARLOW

The King's Head
Church Road, Little Marlow SL7 3RZ
☎ *(01628) 484407* Tim Pegrum

 Tied to Whitbread with up to six real ales. Fuller's London Pride, Timothy Taylor Landlord and something from Brakspear always on sale. Others, changed every three to four weeks, include Wadworth 6X, Greene King Abbot Ale, Marston's Pedigree and beers from Rebellion, Vale and Eccleshall breweries.

Situated between Marlow and Bourne End, the pub has one large, comfortable bar, a non-smoking dining room, and a function room for 50–80 people. Food is served at lunchtime and evenings Mon–Sat and all day Sun. Children welcome.

OPEN *11am–3pm and 5–11pm Mon–Fri; 11am–11pm Sat; 12–10.30pm Sun.*

LITTLE MISSENDEN

The Crown
Little Missenden HP7 0RD
☎ *(01494) 862571* Mr How

 A freehouse with four beers on pumps and occasionally one from the wood. Marston's Pedigree, Hook Norton Best and Bateman brews are always on offer. Other guests, changed twice weekly, might include Mordue Workie Ticket or something from Greene King, Brakspear, King and Barnes, Adnams, Rebellion or Vale breweries.

A country pub off the A413 coming from Amersham towards Aylesbury, with one bar and two real fires. Mixed clientele, no juke box or machines. Large garden. Food served at lunchtime only. Children allowed, but not in bar area.

OPEN *11am–2.30pm and 6–11pm Mon–Sat; 12–3pm and 7–10.30pm Sun.*

LITTLEWORTH COMMON

The Jolly Woodman
Littleworth Common, Burnham SL1 8PF
☎ *(01753) 644350* Steve and Sandy Moore

 A Whitbread-managed house with no restrictions on the guest beer policy so a good selection is maintained. Brakspear Bitter always available, plus four guests changed twice-weekly, including Rebellion Mutiny and Smuggler, Smiles March Hare, Caledonian Deuchars IPA, Timothy Taylor Landlord, Morland Old Speckled Hen, Wadworth 6X, Marston's Pedigree, Greene King Abbot Ale and seasonal beers.

A traditional seventeenth-century pub in the middle of Burnham Beeches. Lovely walks all around. Beer garden. Food available at lunchtime and evenings. Children allowed until 8pm.

OPEN *11am–11pm Mon–Sat; 12–10.30pm Sun.*

LOUDWATER

Derehams Inn
5 Derehams Lane, Loudwater HP14 3ND
☎ *(01494) 530965*
Graham and Margaret Sturgess

 Eight beers always available including Fuller's London Pride, Young's Bitter, Brakspear Bitter, Timothy Taylor Landlord and two guest beers rotating constantly.

Small and cosy local freehouse. Bar food on weekdays at lunchtime. Car park, garden. Children allowed in the restaurant area. Less than a mile from M40 junction 3.

OPEN *11.30am–3pm and 5.30–11pm.*

MARLOW

The Chequers
51–3 High Street, Marlow SL7 1BA
☎ *(01628) 482053* Neil and Michelle Wass

 A Brakspear-managed house, with Brakspear Bitter and Special permanently on offer, plus Brakspear seasonal ales.

Village pub with two bars and a function room. Small patio on the High Street. Food available. Cask Marque accredited. Children not allowed.

OPEN *11am–11pm Mon–Sat; 12–10.30pm Sun.*

The Prince of Wales
1 Mill Road, Marlow SL7 1PX
☎ *(01628) 482970* RP Robson

 Tied to Whitbread, with Fuller's London Pride and Brakspear Bitter always served. A guest beer changes every three or four weeks. Brakspear Special, Wadworth 6X, Greene King Abbot and ales from Rebellion, Vale and Hook Norton are regular favourites.

A traditional pub just off the high street, with no juke box, pool, darts or alcopops. Food served at lunchtime and evenings. Separate dining area. Accomodation. Children not allowed in the bar area.

OPEN *11am–11pm Mon–Sat; 12–10.30pm Sun.*

The Two Brewers
St Peters Street, Marlow SL7 1NQ
☎ *(01628) 484140* Derek Harris

 Brakspear Bitter, Fuller's London Pride and Wadworth 6X always served, with a guest changed every few months. Beers from Rebellion, such as Blonde Bombshell, are regularly featured.

Traditional pub in a 300-year-old building, with beams and fires. Patio, barn at the back and tables outside, near the river. Food is available, and there is a 50-seater restaurant. Children allowed.

OPEN *11am–3pm and 5–11pm Mon–Thurs; 11am–11pm Fri–Sat; 12–10.30pm Sun.*

NEW BRADWELL

The New Inn

2 Bradwell Road, New Bradwell, Milton Keynes MK13 0EN
☎ *(01908) 312094* Derrick and Rebecca

A Charles Wells managed house. Four real ales always available (Adnams Broadside, Old Speckled Hen, Charles Wells Eagle and Bombardier).

Canalside, family-run traditional pub with beer garden, between Newport Pagnell and Wolverton. Food available in a separate 70-seater restaurant, 12–2.45pm and 6–8.45pm Mon–Sat, plus 12–3.45pm Sun. Restaurant available for dinner-dances on Fri–Sat. Children allowed.

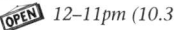 *Winter: 12–3pm and 6–11pm Mon–Thurs; 11am–11pm Fri–Sat; 12–10.30pm Sun. Summer: 12–11pm Mon–Sat; 12–10.30pm Sun.*

NEWPORT PAGNELL

The Bull Inn

33 Tickford Street, Newport Pagnell MK16 9AE
☎ *(01908) 610325* Terry Fairfield

A freehouse serving up to eight cask ales at any one time, with a minimum of two changed each week. Favourites include Young's Special, Fuller's London Pride, Wadworth 6X and Bateman ales. Others might be Shepherd Neame Spitfire, Hampshire Pride of Romsey, Jennings Sneck Lifter, Burton Bridge Top Dog Stout and Ridleys ESX Best, to name but a few.

An old-fashioned coaching inn, just like pubs used to be! No music in lounge. Food at lunchtimes and evenings. Children allowed in restaurant only, if eating. Take M1, junction 14; pub next door to the Aston Martin Lagonda factory

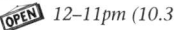 *11.30am–2.30pm and 5–11pm Mon–Fri; 11am–11pm Sat; 12–10.30pm Sun.*

The Green Man

92 Silver Street, Newport Pagnell
☎ *(01908) 611914* James and Justine Cambell

Greene King IPA and Everards Tiger usually available plus one guest beer, such as Marston's Pedigree, Young's Special, Greene King Abbot Ale or Fuller's London Pride.

Busy bar with patio, serving food all day.

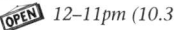 *12–11pm (10.30pm Sun).*

NORTH CRAWLEY

The Cock Inn

16 High Street, North Crawley, Newport Pagnell MK16 9LH
☎ *(01234) 391222* Terry McLaren

Tied to Charles Wells, serving four real ales at any one time. Adnams Broadside and Charles Wells Eagle always available, plus a guest, changed every couple of months, from somewhere like Everards, Wadworth or Young's.

Avery old, oak-beamed pub, built around 1460, next to the church in the village square. A broad cross-section of customers. Two bars and a family room. Food served at lunchtime and evenings, except Sunday evening. Children allowed in family room.

 11am–3pm and 6–11pm Mon–Sat; 12–4pm and 7–10.30pm Sun.

OLD AMERSHAM

The Kings Arms

30 High Street, Old Amersham HP7 0DJ
☎ *(01494) 726333* John Jennison

A freehouse with Rebellion IPA on hand pump always available, plus two weekly changing guests from breweries such as Brakspear, Young's and Vale, served direct from casks behind the bar.

A500-year-old coaching inn, where Oliver Cromwell once stayed. No TV, no music. Food is available in the pub at lunchtimes only, but the restaurant is open Tues–Sat for lunch and dinner, and for Sunday lunch (menus available on website). Car park, beer garden. Small non-smoking area for children. Website: www.kingsarmsamersham.co.uk.

 11am–11pm Mon–Sat; 12–10.30pm Sun.

PRESTWOOD

The King's Head

188 Wycombe Road, Prestwood HP16 0HJ
☎ *(01494) 868101* Simon Wiles

Greene King ales always available, including Abbot and IPA. Special and guest ales are regularly featured.

An old pub tastefully refurbished, offering a full range of meals from 12–10pm daily. Friendly service to tables or at the bar. Large car park. Children tolerated. Garden and barbecue. Take the A4128 from High Wycombe.

 11am–11pm Mon–Sat; 12–10.30pm Sun.

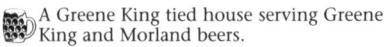

STOKE POGES

Rose & Crown
Hollybush Hill, Stoke Poges SL2 4PW
☎ *(01753) 662148* Mr Holloran

A Greene King tied house serving Greene King and Morland beers.

A traditional village pub with food served at lunchtimes. Well-behaved children allowed.

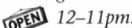 *11am–3pm and 5.30–11pm (10.30pm Sun).*

STONY STRATFORD

Vaults Bar
The Bull Hotel, 64 High Street, Stony Stratford, Milton Keynes MK11 1AQ
☎ *(01908) 567104* Paul Wareing

Fuller's London Pride, Young's Bitter, Eldridge Pope Royal Oak, Wadworth 6X and Adnams Bitter usually available. One guest beer is also available from a very varied list. Timothy Taylor Landlord is the one repeat beer.

Simple, characterful bar in imposing Georgian coaching inn, prominently located in the High Street. Food available 12–10pm. Car park. Children welcome although there are no special facilities.

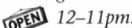 *12–11pm.*

TATLING END

The Tatling Arms
Oxford Road, Tatling End SL9 7AT
☎ *(01753) 883100* Michael McGee

Fuller's London Pride and Charles Wells Bombardier permanently available, plus guests alternating on two pumps. Guests are usually from Brakspear and the local Vale Brewery.

A small 300-year-old listed building with a mixed clientele. Vehicles in the car park range from Rolls Royces to Transits. Food served all day. Children allowed. Located off the old A40 Oxford Road.

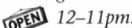 *11am–11pm Mon–Sat; 12–10.30pm Sun.*

THE LEE

The Cock & Rabbit
The Lee, Great Missenden HP16 9LZ
☎ *(01494) 837540*

A freehouse, with four to five real ales always available. Permanent fixtures are Cock and Rabbit Bitter (brewed by Greene King), Fuller's London Pride and Morland Old Speckled Hen. Other guests are changed seasonally.

A classic English pub with an Italian flavour. Restaurant, dining area and garden lounge. Food served lunchtimes and evenings, seven days a week. Children allowed.

 12–2.30pm and 6–11pm Mon–Sat; 12–3pm and 7–10.30pm Sun.

The Old Swan
Swan Lane, Swan Bottom, The Lee, Great Missenden HP16 9NU
☎ *(01494) 837239* Sean Michaelson-Yeats

A freehouse, with something from Adnams and Brakspear always available, plus a guest beer.

A traditional sixteenth-century inn in the Chiltern Hills. Off the beaten track, it lies between Tring, Chesham, Great Missenden and Wendover. Food served at lunchtime and evenings, with fresh fish a speciality. Restaurant area. Large garden. Children allowed.

 12–3pm and 6–11pm Sun–Fri; all day Sat; closed Mon except bank holidays.

THORNBOROUGH

The Lone Tree
Bletchley Road, Thornborough MK18 2DZ
☎ *(01280) 812334* PB Taverner

Five beers available from breweries stretching from Orkney to Cornwall, Norfolk to Wales. Plus one real cider.

Small roadside pub with a large choice of food available at lunchtime and evenings. Car park and garden. Supervised children allowed.

 11.30am–3pm and 6–11pm Mon–Sat; 12–3pm and 6.30–10.30pm Sun.

WENDOVER

The Red Lion Hotel

9 The High Street, Wendover HP22 6DU
☎ *(01296) 622266* Phil Hills

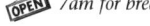Young's Special, Brakspear Pale Ale and Adnams Bitter usually available, plus one monthly changing guest purchased through the Beer Seller.

A sixteenth-century coaching inn situated in beautiful Chilterns countryside, ideal for walkers. One bar, open fires, outside seating. Very busy restaurant serving fresh food all day every day, plus separate bar food available at lunchtimes and evenings. Children allowed. Accommodation.

OPEN *7am for breakfast; 11am–11pm.*

WESTERN TURVILLE

The Chequers Inn

35 Church Lane, Western Turville HP22 5SJ
☎ *(01296) 612079* Sean Witherspoon

Fuller's London Pride, plus Adnams Best and Broadside always available. Two guests, changed fortnightly, may included Wadworth 6X, Vale Notley Ale or something from Bateman. Seasonal ales such as Vale Good King Senseless are also featured.

Sixteenth-century country inn with two bars. Food available – there are two dining areas. Live music outside sometimes during summer. Car park. Children allowed. Ring for directions, as can be difficult to find.

OPEN *12–3pm and 6–11pm (10.30pm Sun); closed Mon lunchtimes.*

WHEELER END

The Chequers

Bullocks Farm Lane, Wheeler End, High Wycombe HP14 3NH
☎ *(01494) 883070*
Stephen Warner and Anna Kaiser

A seventeenth-century Fuller's inn with London Pride, Chiswick and ESB always available, plus one guest pump serving a Fuller's seasonal ale.

A traditional pub with attractive beer gardens and inglenook fireplace. Home-cooked food, freshly prepared on the premises, served every lunchtime and evening. Children welcome in the restaurant. Dog-friendly. Car park at rear.

OPEN *11am–3pm and 5.30–11pm Mon–Fri; 11am–11pm Sat; 12–10.30pm Sun.*

WING

The Cock Inn

26 High Street, Wing, Nr Leighton Buzzard LU7 0NR
☎ *(01296) 688214*
Alberto Marcucci and Stuart Mosley

Four weekly changing guest beers regularly available from a number of different breweries.

Privately-owned, fine English country pub with good home-cooked food available every lunchtime and evening in a separate restaurant and at the bar. Car park. Children welcome, high chairs available.

OPEN *11.30am–3pm and 6–11pm Mon–Sat; 12–3pm and 7–10.30pm Sun.*

YOU TELL US

* *The Greyhound,* West Edge, Marsh Gibbon
* *The King's Arms,* 1 King Street, Chesham
* *The Rose & Crown,* Desborough Road, High Wycombe
* *The Rose & Crown,* Vicarage Lane, Ivinghoe
* *The Stag & Griffin,* Oxford Road, Tatling End

Places Featured:

Abington Pigotts	Longstowe
Ashton	Madingley
Boxworth	March
Brandon Creek	Milton
Cambridge	Needingworth
Castle Camps	Newton
Dogsthorpe	Old Weston
Duxford	Peterborough
Ely	St Ives
Glinton	Six Mile Bottom
Graveley	Stow cum Quy
Hinxton	Thriplow
Holywell	Whittlesey
Huntingdon	Wisbech
Keyston	Woodston
Leighton Bromswold	Yarwell

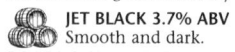

THE BREWERIES

CITY OF CAMBRIDGE BREWERY LTD

19 Cheddars Lane, Cambridge CB5 8LD
☎ *(01223) 353939*
www.real-ale-guide.co.uk/city-of-cambridge

JET BLACK 3.7% ABV
Smooth and dark.
BOAT HOUSE BITTER 3.8% ABV
Refreshing.
HOBSON'S CHOICE 4.1% ABV
Pale and hoppy.
ATOMSPLITTER 4.7% ABV
Full-bodied and hoppy.
PARKER'S PORTER 5.3% ABV
Good fruity hoppiness.
BRAMLING TRADITIONAL 5.5% ABV
Fruity.

ELGOOD AND SONS LTD

North Brink Brewery, Wisbech PE13 1LN
☎ *(01945) 583160*

BLACK DOG MILD 3.6% ABV
Malty, dark mild with good balance.
CAMBRIDGE BITTER 3.8% ABV
Malt fruit flavours with dry finish.
PAGEANT ALE 4.3% ABV
Rounded and balanced with a bittersweet flavour.
OLD BLACK SHUCK 4.5% ABV
November ale.
GOLDEN NEWT 4.6% ABV
Dry and hoppy.
BARLEYMEAD 4.8% ABV
September ale.
GREYHOUND STRONG BITTER 5.2% ABV
Bittersweet flavour.
NORTH BRINK PORTER 5.5% ABV
Winter ale.
REINBEER 5.9% ABV
December ale.
WENCESLAS WINTER WARMER 7.5% ABV
December ale.
Plus seasonal brews.

THE FENLAND BREWERY

Unit 4, Prospect Way, Chatteris PE16 6TZ
☎ *(01354) 696776*

TALL TALE PALE ALE 3.6% ABV
FBB 4.0% ABV
SMOKESTACK LIGHTNING 4.2% ABV
FRACT ALE 4.5% ABV
SPARKLING WIT 4.5% ABV
DOCTOR'S ORDERS 5.0% ABV
RUDOLPH'S ROCKET FUEL 5.5% ABV

MILTON BREWERY CAMBRIDGE LTD

Unit 111, Norman Industrial Estate, Cambridge Road, Milton CB4 6AT
☎ *(01223) 226198*
www.miltonbrewery.co.uk

MINOTAUR 3.3% ABV
Dark mild with rich chocolate malt flavour.

JUPITER 3.5% ABV
A spring/summer session beer.

ARTEMIS 3.7% ABV

NEPTUNE 3.8% ABV
Crisp autumn/winter brew.

PEGASUS 4.1% ABV
Hoppy with balancing fruity, malt finish.

ZEUS 4.2% ABV

BABYLON 4.4% ABV

ELECTRA 4.5% ABV
Malty sweetness and powerful bitter finish.

PHAROS 4.7% ABV

MAUSOLEUM 4.9% ABV

PYRAMID 4.9% ABV

CYCLOPS 5.3% ABV
Rounded malt and fruit flavours.

COLOSSUS 5.6% ABV

MAMMON 7.0% ABV
Dark winter warmer for December.

OAKHAM ALES

80 Westgate, Peterborough PE1 2AN
☎ *(01733) 358300*

JEFFREY HUDSON BITTER 3.8% ABV
WHITE DWARF 4.3% ABV
Slightly cloudy wheat beer.

FIVE LEAVES LEFT 4.5% ABV
Autumn/winter brew.

BISHOP'S FAREWELL 4.6% ABV
Golden and refreshing.

HELTER SKELTER 5.0% ABV
Seasonal.

MOMPESSON'S GOLD 5.0% ABV
Seasonal. Golden, light and full-flavoured.

OLD TOSSPOT 5.2% ABV
Seasonal. Brewed Sept–May.

BLACK HOLE PORTER 5.5% ABV
Black, sweet and rich.

Plus one off brews for special occasions.

ROCKINGHAM ALES

c/o 25 Wansford Road, Elton PE8 6RZ
☎ *(01832) 280722*

FINESHADE 3.8% ABV
Autumn.

FOREST GOLD 3.9% ABV

SAXON CROSS 3.9% ABV

A1 AMBER ALE 4.0% ABV

FRUITS OF THE FOREST 4.1% ABV

SANITY CLAUSE 4.3% ABV
Christmas.

OLD HERBACEOUS 4.5% ABV
Winter brew.

DARK FOREST 5.0% ABV

THE PUBS

ABINGTON PIGOTTS

The Pig & Abbot

High Street, Abington Pigotts, Nr Royston
☎ *(01763) 853515 Miss Sarah Corthorn*

City of Cambridge Boathouse Bitter and IPA plus Adnams Best are always available, plus two guests, possibly Woodforde's Wherry, City of Cambridge Hobson's Choice or Fuller's London Pride, or beers from breweries such as Potton and Jennings.

Cosy, olde-worlde country pub with open fire, beams and a relaxed, friendly atmosphere. Home-cooked food to appeal to all tastes served 12–2.30pm and 6–9.30pm Mon–Fri and 12–9pm Sat–Sun. Restaurant, beer gardens. Children welcome, and high chairs and changing facilities are available. Car park. Turn off the A1198 to Bassingbourn and look for signs.

OPEN *11.30am–3pm and 6–11pm Mon–Fri; 11am–11pm Sat; 12–10.30pm Sun.*

ASHTON

The Chequered Skipper

The Green, Ashton, Nr Arundel, Peterborough
☎ *(01832) 273494 Colin Campbell*

Oakham JHB is a permanent feature, and the four weekly changing guests (200 in the last two years) could include beers such as Black Sheep Bitter, Bateman XXXB, Adnams Broadside or Slaters Premium.

One-bar pub, traditional on the outside but modern inside. Full green, back garden, restaurant. Occasional live music on Bank Holidays. Children allowed.

OPEN *11.30am–3pm and 6–11pm Mon–Fri; 11am–11pm Sat; 12–10.30pm Sun.*

BOXWORTH

The Golden Ball

High Street, Boxworth CB3 8LY
☎ *(01954) 267397 Hilary Paddock*

Beers available include Adnams Broadside and Greene King IPA. Guests include Morland Old Speckled Hen, Ruddles County, Potton Village Bike and many more.

Typical country pub in good walking area. Bar and restaurant food at lunchtime and evenings, with interesting and upmarket fare. Meeting room, car park. Large garden with separate entrance. Children allowed. Ten miles from Cambridge, six miles from St Ives.

OPEN *11.30am–2.30pm and 6.30–11pm.*

BRANDON CREEK

The Ship

Brandon Creek, Downham Market PE38 0PP
☎ *(01353) 676228* Mr A Hook

 A regularly changing range of guest beers which often features something from Adnams, Iceni, Mauldons, Fenland or Kings Head.

Situated by the River Ouse, this is a food-oriented pub offering special weekend carveries on Saturday evening and Sunday lunchtime in winter, Sunday lunchtime in summer. Regular menu available 12–2pm and 6.30–9pm at other times. Car park. Children welcome, but no special facilities.

OPEN *May–Sept: 11am–11pm Mon–Sat; 12–10.30pm Sun. Phone for winter opening times.*

CAMBRIDGE

Ancient Druids

Napier Street, Cambridge CB1 1HR
☎ *(01223) 576324*

 There are plans to expand the range of beers brewed here. They have recently begun producing a dark mild of about 3.3%. Plus a range of guest beers.

There is a history of brewing on the premises. Charles Wells originally set up business here and the present managers took over and restarted production in 1993. This big, bright pub enjoys a laid-back atmosphere, with a wide variety of customers including students and shoppers. Background music. Bar food available all day until 10pm. Children allowed.

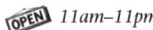 **ELLIES SB 6.0% ABV**

OPEN *11am–11pm.*

The Bird in Hand

73 Newmarket Road, Cambridge CB5 8EG
☎ *(01223) 351919* Trevor Critchlow

 Greene King IPA, XX Dark Mild, Old Speckled Hen and Ruddles County always on offer, plus one guest, changed every two months, such as Brakspear Bitter, Black Sheep Bitter or Jennings Cocker Hoop.

Traditional one-bar town pub with garden. No games or music. A French chef prepares the food on the French menu. Children not allowed. Website: www.bird-in-hand.fsnet.co.uk

OPEN *12–2pm and 5–11pm Mon–Thurs; 12–11pm Fri–Sun (10.30pm Sun).*

Cambridge Blue

85–7 Gwydir Street, Cambridge CB1 2LG
☎ *(01223) 361382* Chris and Debbie Lloyd

 At least six beers always available, focusing on Cambridgeshire breweries. Favourites include City of Cambridge Hobson's Choice and other ales in their range, plus beers from the Milton brewery, such as Pegasus. Stocks a range of East Anglian beers – always open to suggestions.

Terraced side-street pub, totally non-smoking, with large garden and two bars. Healthy bar food at lunchtimes and evenings, seven days a week. Children allowed in conservatory area until 9pm. Off Mill Road on the city side of railway bridge.

OPEN *12–2.30pm (3.30pm Sat) and 6–11pm.*

The Dobblers Inn

184 Sturton Street, Cambridge CB1 2QF
☎ *(012213) 576092* Jackie Lanz

 A Charles Wells-managed house, with Bombardier and Eagle IPA plus Adnams Broadside always on offer. Two guests, changed weekly, may include Morland Old Speckled Hen and Badger Tanglefoot, or seasonal ales such as Viking Summer Solstice.

Lively backstreet boozer – definitely a drinkers' pub – with gaming machine and pool table. 'Pub grub' available. Garden. Children not allowed.

OPEN *12–11pm (10.30pm Sun).*

The Elm Tree

42 Orchard Street, Cambridge CB1 1JT
☎ *(01223) 363005* John Simons

 A Charles Wells tenancy with Bombardier and Eagle IPA always on offer. Two guest beers, such as Adnams Best or Marston's Pedigree, are changed regularly.

A traditional one-bar pub off the city centre, near Grafton Shopping Centre, with large-screen TV and lots of table games (including chess). Rolls only served. No children allowed.

OPEN *12–2.30pm and 4 or 5–11.30pm Mon–Thurs; 11am–11pm Fri–Sat; 12–10.30pm Sun.*

The Free Press

Prospect Row, Cambridge CB1 1DU
☎ *(01223) 368337*
Donna and Martin Thornton

 A Greene King tied house with Abbot, IPA and XX Dark Mild always available, plus guests such as Jennings Cocker Hoop or beers from Black Sheep.

A famous East Anglian real ale house, the first pub in Cambridge to stock real ales when the revival began. A very traditional atmosphere, with table games available and a beer garden. Genuine home-made hot and cold bar food available 12–2pm and 6–9pm Mon–Fri, 12–2.30pm and 6–9pm Sat, and 12–2.30pm Sun. Totally non-smoking. Children welcome. Located near Grafton Shopping Centre.

OPEN *12–2.30pm Mon–Fri; 12–3pm Sat–Sun; 6–11pm Mon–Sat; 7–10.30pm Sun.*

The Kingston Arms

33 Kingston Street, Cambridge CB1 2NU
☎ *(01223) 319414*

 Owned by Suffolk-based Lidstones Brewery, regularly serving real ales on up to ten hand pumps. Guest beers are changed weekly.

A friendly pub, with locals and visitors welcome. No music or machines, just a natural buzz! Traditional English menu served lunchtimes 12–2pm and evenings 6–9pm, with a good wine list, and tables can be pre-booked. Garden open in summer. Children under 14 allowed in the garden until 9pm. Situated just off Mill Road, 15 minutes' walk from city centre.

OPEN *12–2.30pm and 5–11pm (closed Mon lunch); all day Sat–Sun.*

The Locomotive

44 Mill Road, Cambridge CB1 2AS
☎ *(01223) 322190* Mr Foster

 Greene King IPA and Adnams Broadside permanently available, plus a regularly changing guest ale.

Situated near the University, with a student-based clientele. One bar, air-conditioned function room, large-screen TV for sports. Parking at rear. Thai food available in the evenings on a trial basis. Children allowed until 7pm.

OPEN *11am–11pm Mon–Sat; 12–10.30pm Sun.*

Live and Let Live

40 Mawson Road, Cambridge CB1 2EA
☎ *(01223) 460261* Alan Kilker

 At least seven beers available. Extensive and varied guest list (around 250 guest beers per year), including Wood Shropshire Lad, Colleys Dog, Nethergate Golden Gate, Grim Reaper, Tring Jack O'Legs, Anchor Street Porter, Ewesual, Bateman Mild and Nethergate Umbel Ale. The most popular breweries are Nethergate, Tring, Oakham, Adnams, Everards and Banks & Taylor. Mini beer festival every three months.

Situated in central Cambridge, just off Mill Road, popular with students, business people and locals alike. Wooden furniture and walls with real gas lighting. Live music on Sunday nights by a local busker. Extensive home-cooked menu with several vegetarian options available lunchtimes until 2pm and evenings until 9pm (not Sun evenings). Children allowed in eating area. Street parking.

OPEN *11.30am–2.30pm daily; 5.30–11pm Mon–Fri; 6–11pm Sat; 7–11pm Sun.*

The Portland Arms

129 Chesterton Road, Cambridge CB4 3BA
☎ *(01223) 357268* David Thompson

 A Greene King tenancy. Greene King IPA, Abbott, Mild and Ruddles County are permanently served, and there are always two non-Greene King beers available, such as Black Sheep Bitter, Jennings Bitter, Badger Tanglefoot, Morrells Graduate and Everards Tiger.

A pub with three bars, one a traditional saloon, one a music venue (100 capacity), and one an internet bar/café with 5 terminals. Food served in all areas, especially the saloon. Garden and parking. Children allowed. Situated on the outer Ring Road (A10).

OPEN *11am–11pm Mon–Sat; 12–10.30pm Sun.*

St Radegund

129 King Street, Cambridge CB1 1LD
☎ *(01223) 311794* Terry Kavanagh

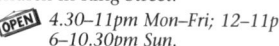 One of the few freehouses in Cambridge, where Bateman XB, Fuller's London Pride and Shepherd Neame Spitfire are always available. Occasional guest beers also served.

The smallest pub in Cambridge. CAMRA-listed from 1991–99 and Pub of the Year 1993–94. No juke box, no games machines. Background jazz music. Filled rolls only. Children not allowed. Opposite the Wesley church in King Street.

OPEN *4.30–11pm Mon–Fri; 12–11pm Sat; 6–10.30pm Sun.*

Tap & Spile
14 Mill Lane, Cambridge CB2 1RX
☎ *(01223) 357026* Peter Snellgrover

 Approx 300 beers per year (nine at any one time) including brews from Adnams, Bateman, Black Sheep, Hadrian, Thwaites, Ushers, Nethergate and many other independent breweries.

Traditional alehouse with oak floors and exposed brickwork in picturesque setting right next to the river (perhaps the biggest beer garden in England?). Punting station nearby. Bar food at lunchtime.

OPEN *11am–11pm Mon–Sat; 12–3pm and 7–10.30pm Sun.*

Wrestlers
337 Newmarket Road, Cambridge CB5 8JE
☎ *(01223) 566553* Tom Goode

 A house tied to Charles Wells, with Eagle IPA and Bombardier always served, plus two guest beers changed fortnightly. Favoured breweries include Lees, Archers, Caledonian and Adnams.

The pub specialises in Thai food. Children allowed.

OPEN *12–3pm and 5–11pm Mon–Sat; closed Sun.*

CASTLE CAMPS

The Cock Inn
High Street, Castle Camps, Cambridge CB1 6SN
☎ *(01799) 584207* Mr Puell

 A freehouse always serving Greene King IPA plus a guest beer, which may be Fuller's London Pride, something from Nethergate or Shepherd Neame Spitfire. Changed weekly.

An olde-worlde drinkers' pub. Snacks available. Children allowed.

OPEN *12–2pm and 7–11pm Sun–Fri; 11am–11pm Sat.*

DOGSTHORPE

The Blue Bell Inn
St Pauls Road, Dogsthorpe, Peterborough PE1 3RZ
☎ *(01733) 554890* Mr PR and Mrs TL Smith

 Elgood's Black Dog Mild, Cambridge Bitter and Greyhound usually available with a weekly changing guest beer such as Bateman XXXB and beers from Hook Norton, Adnams and Burton Bridge.

Good old-fashioned character to this listed, sixteenth-century, Elgood's tied house. Food served 11am–2pm Mon–Fri, but not bank holidays. Car park. Children permitted in small lobby room and garden. Located on the junction of Welland Road/St Pauls Road, near to Dogsthorpe Fire H.Q.

OPEN *11am–2.30pm and 6–11pm Mon–Fri; 11.30am–3pm and 6–11pm Sat; 12–3pm and 7–10.30pm Sun.*

DUXFORD

The Plough Inn
59 St Peters St, Duxford, Cambridge
☎ *(01223) 833170* Julie Nicholls

 Everards Tiger, Original and Beacon, and Adnams Bitter always on offer, plus one guest, perhaps another Adnams beer.

Thatched village pub with beer garden. Food available 12–2pm and 5–9pm Mon–Fri, and 12–6pm Sat–Sun. Live music Saturday. Children welcome (bouncy castle in garden!). Car park.

OPEN *11am–3pm and 5–11pm Mon–Thurs; 11am–11pm Fri–Sat; 12–10.30pm Sun.*

ELY

The Fountain
1 Silver Street, Ely CB7 4JF
☎ *(01353) 663122* John Borland

 A freehouse with Adnams Best and Broadside plus Fuller's London Pride as permanent fixtures. A guest beer, changed frequently, could well be Charles Wells Bombardier.

A Victorian pub, recently renovated and modernised. No food. Children allowed until 9pm.

OPEN *5–11.30pm Mon–Fri; 12–2pm and 6–11.30pm Sat; 12–2pm and 7–11pm Sun.*

GLINTON

The Blue Bell
10 High Street, Glinton, Peterborough PE6 7LS
☎ *(01733) 252285* Mr Mills

 Tied to Greene King brewery and permanently serving IPA and Abbot Ale. Other guests from various breweries available.

A village pub with separate dining area. Food served at lunchtime and evenings. Children allowed.

OPEN *12–2.30pm and 5.30–11pm Mon–Thurs; 12–11pm Fri–Sat; 12–10.30pm Sun.*

GRAVELEY

The Three Horseshoes
23 High Street, Graveley, Huntingdon PE18 9PL
☎ *(01480) 830992* Alfred Barrett

 A freehouse with three pumps serving a variety of guest beers, which change weekly, mainly from independent breweries such as Marston's, Adnams and others.

A very old country inn, with no juke box or pool tables. Non-smoking restaurant. Food at lunchtime and evening. Children allowed.

OPEN *11am–3pm and 6–11pm Mon–Sat; 12–2pm and 7–11pm Sun.*

HINXTON

The Red Lion

32 High Street, Hinxton, Cambridge CB10 1QX
☎ *(01799) 530601* Linda Crawford

 A freehouse with Adnams Best and Woodforde's Wherry Best always on sale. There is also one guest.

A sixteenth-century pub half a mile south of junction 9 off the M11, with one bar and a non-smoking restaurant. Food served at lunchtime and evenings. Children allowed.

 11am–2.30pm and 6–11pm Mon–Sat; 12–2.30pm and 7–10.30pm Sun.

HOLYWELL

The Ferryboat Inn

Holywell PE27 4TG
☎ *(01480) 463227*
David and Niamh Baynham

 Tied to Greene King, with IPA and Abbot always available. Guest beers, mainly available in the summer months, include Ruddles County and Morland Old Speckled Hen.

A remote pub in a rural setting down a country lane and overlooking the River Great Ouse. Ring for directions, if needed! Food-oriented, with meals available all day. Large bar and eating area with function room. Children welcome.

 11.30am–11pm Mon–Sat; 12–10.30pm Sun.

HUNTINGDON

The Old Bridge Hotel

1 High Street, Huntingdon PE29 3TQ
☎ *(01480) 424300* Martin Lee

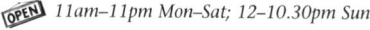 Adnams Best and City of Cambridge Hobson's Choice are always available, along with a guest beer.

A smart townhouse hotel that includes a busy and welcoming bar. Restaurant meals and snacks served every day, with full afternoon teas. Well-behaved children allowed. Occasional live entertainment.

 11am–11pm Mon–Sat; 12–10.30pm Sun.

KEYSTON

The Pheasant

Keyston, Huntingdon PE18 0RE
☎ *(01832) 710241* Clive Dixon

Adnams Southwold always available, plus two guests from a changing selection, with brews from Potton and City of Cambridge appearing regularly.

A thatched inn in a quiet village, with oak beams and large open fires. Quality food served in the pub, and in the small restaurant. Food available lunchtimes and evenings. Car park. Children welcome.

 12–3pm and 6–11pm.

LEIGHTON BROMSWOLD

The Green Man

37 The Avenue, Leighton Bromswold, Nr Huntingdon PE18 0SH
☎ *(01480) 890238* Ms Toni Hanagan

Nethergate Bitter always available plus three guest beers (200 per year) perhaps from Adnams, Nene Valley, Young's, Robinson's, Shepherd Neame, Brakspear, Fuller's, Wychwood, Shepherd Neame or Timothy Taylor.

Seventeenth-century, detached public house with a collection of water jugs and memorabilia. Bar food available at lunchtime and evenings. Car park, garden, children's room. One mile off the A14.

12–3pm and 7–11pm; closed Mon.

LONGSTOWE

The Red House

Old North Road, Longstowe PB3 7UT
☎ *(01954) 718480* Gillian Willis

A freehouse with Potton Shambles a permanent feature. Two guests, changed every few weeks, include favourites such as Ruddles County and beers from Nethergate.

Traditional rural pub with one bar, garden and separate restaurant. No games. Live music occasionally on Sundays. Car parking. Children welcome.

12–2.30pm and 5.30–11pm (10.30pm Sun).

MADINGLEY

The Three Horseshoes

Madingley CB3 8AB
☎ *(01954) 210221* Richard Stokes

Adnams Best is a permanent feature, with two guests also served, City of Cambridge being a regular.

A thatched inn with a bar and large garden. Imaginative food served in the bar, garden and conservatory-restaurant. Meals available 12–2pm and 6.30–9.30pm daily. Car park. Children welcome.

11.30am–2.30pm and 6–11pm Mon–Sat; 12–3pm and 7–10.30pm Sun.

MARCH

The Rose & Crown

41 St Peters Road, March PE15 9NA
☎ *(01354) 652879* Mr D Evans

At least six traditional beers served from a menu that changes on a daily basis. Fuller's London Pride and a mild usually available. Around 300 different ales each year are featured, including some imported ones. The pub also stocks over 100 whiskies.

A 150-year-old suburban pub with a non-smoking lounge. Winner of a CAMRA Gold Award. Bar snacks Thurs–Sat. No juke box, no videos, no television, just a good old-fashioned atmosphere. No children. No dogs.

OPEN *12–2.30pm and 7–11pm Mon–Fri (closed Wed lunchtime); 12–3pm and 7–11pm Sat–Sun (closed 10.30pm Sun).*

MILTON

The Waggon & Horses

39 High Street, Milton CB4 6DF
☎ *(01223) 860313*
Nick and Mandy Winnington

Elgood's Cambridge Bitter, Black Dog Mild, Golden Newt and Greyhound Strong Bitter permanently available, plus one guest ale from a varied range.

Imposing 1930s mock-Tudor building set back from the main road. Large child-friendly garden to rear. Note hat collection and eclectic pictures on walls. Bar billiards and darts. Children allowed in pub under supervision (9pm curfew), as are animals on a lead. Car park.

OPEN *12–2.30pm and 5–11pm Mon–Fri; 12–4pm and 6–11pm Sat; 12–3pm and 7–10.30pm Sun.*

NEEDINGWORTH

The Queen's Head

30 High Street, Needingworth, Nr Huntingdon PE17 2SA
☎ *(01480) 463946* Mr and Mrs Vann

Six beers always available including Smiles Best, Woodforde's Wherry Best and Hop Back Summer Lightning. Approximately 100 guests per year including Nene Valley Old Black Bob, the Reindeer range, Timothy Taylor Landlord, Parish Somerby Premium, Butterknowle Conciliation, Hook Norton Best, Chiltern Beechwood, Sarah Hughes Dark Ruby Mild and brews from Wild's brewery.

Friendly pub. Bar snacks served 12–8pm. Car park and garden. Children allowed in lounge bar. Close to St Ives.

OPEN *12–11pm.*

NEWTON

Queen's Head

Newton, Nr Cambridge CB2 5PG
☎ *(01223) 870436* Mr David Short

Has specialised in Adnams beers for the past 30 years. Best Bitter and Broadside always available, plus seasonal winter ale, Regatta (the seasonal summer ale) and Tally Ho! on Bonfire Night and at Christmas.

A typical early eighteenth-century pub beside the village green. Bar food at lunchtime and evenings. Car park, children's room, various bar games. Three miles from M11 junction 10; less than two miles off the A10 at Harston.

OPEN *11.30am–2.30pm and 6–11pm Mon–Sat; 12–2.30pm and 7–10.30pm Sun.*

OLD WESTON

The Swan

Main Road, Old Weston, Huntingdon PE17 5LL
☎ *(01832) 293400* Jim Taylor

Greene King Abbot, Adnams Best and Broadside are always available in this freehouse, along with two guest beers each week. Hook Norton Old Hooky is regularly featured.

A restaurant/pub, with a fish and chip night each Wednesday. Children allowed.

OPEN *6.30–11.30pm Mon–Fri; 11am–11pm Sat; 12–10.30pm Sun.*

PETERBOROUGH

Bogart's Bar and Grill

17 North Street, Peterborough PE1 2RA
☎ *(01733) 349995*

A house beer brewed by Eldridge Pope plus six guest beers always available from a varied selection (300+ per year) usually ranging in strength from a mild at 3.0% to 5.5% ABV. The pub hosts a regional beer festival at the start of each month, featuring brewers from a specific part of the United Kingdom. Real cider also available.

Bogart's was built at the turn of the century and now has a wide-ranging clientele of all ages. The horseshoe-shaped bar is decorated with film posters and Humphrey Bogart features prominently. There is background music but no juke box or pool table. Bar food available at lunchtime. Car park opposite and beer garden. Children not allowed. Located off the main Lincoln Road.

OPEN *11am–11pm Mon–Sat; closed Sun.*

Charters Bar

Town Bridge, Peterborough PE1 1DG
☎ *(01733) 315700*
Paul Hook (owner)/Damian Miller (manager)

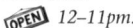Twelve hand pumps serve four permanent and eight guest ales. Oakham JHB and Bishop's Farewell, Fuller's London Pride and Hop Back Summer Lightning are always available, and the guest beers (approx. 500 per year) are from as many independent breweries as possible.

A floating converted Dutch barge moored on the River Nene in the centre of Peterborough. Oriental bar food is served at lunchtimes, and there is an oriental restaurant on the upper deck. Large landscaped beer garden next to the river. Late-night live blues club Fri and Sat nights until 2am.

OPEN *12–11pm.*

The Golden Pheasant

1 Main Road, Etton, Peterborough PE6 7DA
☎ *(01733) 252387* David McLennan

Hop Back Summer Lightning, Oakham Jeffrey Hudson Bitter, Woodforde's Wherry and Adnams Broadside are always available, plus six guests, two of which are changed every fortnight. Regular favourites include Timothy Taylor Landlord, Bateman XXXB, Woodforde's Great Eastern and Nelson's Revenge, Butcombe Best, Abbeydale Absolution and Greene King Abbot. Rare malts and brandies plus exclusive wines also served. Annual beer festival on first weekend of September features over 20 beers.

This pub in an old Georgian rectory is set in an acre and a half of gardens, with a 100-seater marquee permanently available for functions. Food is available 12–2.30pm and 6.30–9.30pm Mon–Sat, plus 12–6pm Sun. The gourmet restaurant, where booking is advisable, features in the *Good Food Guide*, and food is also served in the bar and conservatory. Boules, barbecues, large car park. Children are welcome, and there are family facilities outside. Located close to 'Green Wheel' cycle route.

OPEN *12–3pm and 5–11pm Mon–Thurs (closed Mon lunch); all day Fri–Sun. Open all day, every day in summer (closed Mon lunch).*

Hand & Heart

12 Highbury Street, Peterborough PE1 3BE
☎ *(01733) 564653* Eamon Bracken

Marston's Pedigree is among the beers always on offer, plus two or three guests, changed weekly, from a range including Wolf Granny Wouldn't Like It, Barnsley IPA, Black Dog Stout, Kelham Island Pride of Sheffield and Beckett's Original Bitter.

A local community pub retaining many original 1930s features, with friendly, warm atmosphere. Open fire, wooden floor and large beer garden with lawn and flowers. Crib, darts and dominoes, but no juke box. Sandwiches and rolls are available on request, and hot food may be offered in the future. Children welcome in lounge bar until 6pm. Located 15 minutes' walk from town centre, off Lincoln Road.

OPEN *11am–11pm Mon–Sat; 12–10.30pm Sun.*

ST IVES

The Royal Oak

13 Crown Street, St Ives PE17 4EB
☎ *(01480) 462586* Miss M Pilson

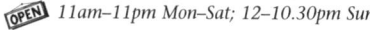Marston's Pedigree always on sale. Six guests, changed weekly, might include something from breweries such as Smiles or Maclays.

An old-style pub with one bar, in a Grade II listed building. Food served from 12–2pm. Children allowed until 7pm.

OPEN *11am–11pm Mon–Sat; 12–10.30pm Sun.*

SIX MILE BOTTOM

Green Man Inn

London Road, Six Mile Bottom CB8 0UF
☎ *(01638) 570373* James Ramselle

At least three beers always available, including Greene King IPA and Adnams Best Bitter, and a guest beer, such as Nethergate Umbel Ale.

A ward-winning, historical, old-fashioned friendly country inn, with open log fire in the bar. Candlelit dining room with famous giant horseracing mural, delightful flower garden, terrace and petanque court. Lunch served 12–2pm Tues–Sun and dinner 6.30–9pm Tues–Sat, prepared by award-winning French chef Jean Christophe Fossard-Schenck. Internet services. Car park. Located on the A1304 near Newmarket. Website: www.SixMileBottom.com.

OPEN *11.30am–2.30pm and 4.30–11pm Tues–Sat; 12–4.30pm Sun (closed Sun evening and all day Mon).*

Prince Albert

Newmarket Road, Stow cum Quy CB5 9AQ
☎ *(01223) 811294* Mr and Mrs Henderson

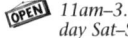 Five beers always available including Greene King IPA. Guests might include Ash Vine Bitter, Stormforce Ten, Worzel Wallop and Shardlow Reverend Eaton's Ale.

Lively roadside pub built in 1830. Bar and restaurant food served at lunchtime and weekend evenings. Private functions catered for. Car park and garden. Children allowed. Just off A14 on the Newmarket road (A1303).

OPEN *11am–3.30pm and 5–11pm Mon–Fri; all day Sat–Sun.*

White Swan

Main Street, Stow cum Quy CB5 9AB
☎ *(01223) 811821* Mr A Cocker

 Among those beers always available are Greene King IPA, Adnams Best, Shepherd Neame Spitfire and Woodforde's Wherry Best plus a guest beer changed fortnightly. Regulars include Everards Tiger, Fuller's London Pride and something from Charles Wells.

A freehouse and restaurant with one small public bar. No smoking. Food served at lunchtime and Tues–Sun evenings. Children allowed but no facilities for them.

OPEN *11am–3pm and 6–11pm Tues–Sat; 12–3pm and 7–10.30pm Sun.*

The Green Man

2 Lower Street, Thriplow SG8 7RJ
☎ *(01763) 208855* Ian Parr

 A freehouse offering an ever-changing selection of up to four real ales. Beers from Milton, Slaters and Oakham have been featured, but brews from almost any brewery could be served.

Open-plan, two-bar pub by the village green with small non-smoking dining area. Formerly Charles Wells. Bar and restaurant food available at lunchtime and evenings (not Sunday). Car park and garden. Children allowed with well-behaved parents! Turn off the A505 near the Imperial War Museum, Duxford.

OPEN *12–3pm and 6–11pm Tues–Sat; 12–3pm Sun (closed Sun evening and all day Mon).*

The Boat Inn

2 Ramsey Road, Whittlesey, Nr Peterborough PE7 1DR
☎ *(01733) 202488*

 Elgood's Cambridge Bitter and Smooth plus Black Dog Mild always available.

A seventeenth-century pub on a site mentioned in the Domesday Book. Large informal bar, plus separate lounge featuring the bow of a boat as the bar. Bed and breakfast accommodation. No food (except breakfasts for those staying). Car park and garden. Ask for directions on reaching Whittlesey.

OPEN *12–11pm (10.30pm Sun).*

The Rose Tavern

53 North Brink, Wisbech PE13 1JX
☎ *(01945) 588335*

 Everards Beacon and Morrells ales always available, plus guest beers.

A 200-year-old listed building forming a comfortable, one-roomed pub on the banks of the river. The closest pub to Elgood's Brewery. Outdoor area, wheelchair access, traditional pub games, accommodation.

OPEN *12–3pm and 5.30–11pm.*

Palmerston Arms

82 Oundle Road, Woodston, Peterborough PE2 9PA
☎ *(01733) 565865* Mrs P Patterson

 A freehouse always offering Hop Back Summer Lightning and Bateman XB, with regular guest beers including Shepherd Neame Spitfire, Church End Vicar's Ruin and RCH Pitchfork.

A traditional pub with lounge and public bar. All beers straight from the barrel from cellar. No food. No children.

OPEN *12–11pm (10.30pm Sun). Closed bank holiday Mondays.*

The Angel

59 Main Street, Yarwell, Peterborough PE8 6PR
☎ *(01780) 782582* Mrs Pamela Turner

 A freehouse with Banks's Best always available. One guest, changed weekly, might be something like Harveys Sussex Best Bitter or Fenland Doctor's Orders.

Traditional two-bar village pub with beams and fires. Pool table, skittles, fruit machine. Bar meals available. Garden. Children allowed in family room.

OPEN *12–2.30pm and 6.30–11pm Mon–Fri (closed Mon evenings); 12–3pm and 6.30–11pm Sat; 12–3pm and 7–10pm Sun.*

Places Featured:

Appleton Thorn	Kingsley
Aston	Langley
Broxton	Macclesfield
Chester	Middlewich
Congleton	Mobberley
Crewe	Nantwich
Frodsham	Penketh
Golborne	Rode Heath
Great Sutton	Sandbach
Halebank	Stalybridge
Handforth	Strines
Hatchmere	Tushingham
Heaton Chapel	Warrington
Heaton Norris	Whitchurch
Higher Hurdsfield	Wrenbury

THE BREWERIES

BEARTOWN BREWERY

Unit 9, Varey Road, Eaton Bank Industrial Estate, Congleton CW12 1UW
☎ *(01260) 299964*
www.beartownbrewery.co.uk

 GOLDIE HOPS 3.5% ABV
Pale and easy drinking.
AMBEARDEXTROUS 3.8% ABV
Copper-coloured and quenching.
BROWN BEAR 3.9% ABV
Full bodied brown ale.
BEAR ASS 4.0% ABV
Aromatic, with smooth, dry malty flavour.
BEARSKINFUL 4.2% ABV
Golden, dry sharp flavour, with a hoppy, rich malt aftertaste.
POLAR ECLIPSE 4.8% ABV
Rich dark oatmeal stout.
BLACK BEAR 5.0% ABV
Smooth, dark ruby mild.
BRUINS RUIN 5.0% ABV
Golden, smooth and full-flavoured.
WHEAT BEER 5.0% ABV
Crisp, refreshing award winner.

COACH HOUSE BREWING CO. LTD

Wharf Street, Howley, Warrington WA1 2DQ
☎ *(01925) 232800*
www.beer.u-net.com

 COACHMAN'S BEST BITTER 3.7% ABV
Smooth, rich malt flavour, with some fruit.
GUNPOWDER STRONG MILD 3.8% ABV
Full flavour, with slight bitter aftertaste.
OSTLERS SUMMER PALE ALE 3.8% ABV
SQUIRES GOLD SPRING ALE 4.2% ABV
INNKEEPER'S SPECIAL RESERVE 4.5% ABV
Crisp and malty with balancing hops.
POSTHORN PREMIUM 5.0% ABV
Rich, smooth and complex.
TAVERNERS AUTUMN ALE 5.0% ABV
BLUNDERBUSS OLD PORTER 5.5% ABV
ANNIVERSARY ALE 6.0% ABV
Strong ale brewed once a year.
Plus seasonal brews.

FREDERIC ROBINSON LTD

Unicorn Brewery, Stockport SK1 1JJ
☎ *(0161) 612 4061*
www.frederic-robinson.com

 HATTERS MILD 3.3% ABV
Fresh, with malt throughout.
OLD STOCKPORT BITTER 3.5% ABV
Golden, with a hoppy flavour.
XB 4.0% ABV
Malt flavour with hoppy bitterness.
BEST BITTER 4.2% ABV
Light in colour with a bitter hop taste and aroma.
FREDERIC'S 5.0% ABV
Smooth and well-balanced.
OLD TOM 8.5% ABV
Superb, mellow winter warmer.

PARADISE BREWING COMPANY

Unit 2, The Old Creamery, Wrenbury Road,
Wrenbury, Nantwich CW5 8EX
☎ *(01270) 780916*

 MARBURY MILD 3.6% ABV
Dark and delicious.
ASTON LIGHT 3.8% ABV
Refreshing, golden, easy-drinking beer.
WRENBURY ALE 4.0% ABV
Slightly dark, crisp after taste.
PARADISE GOLD 4.4% ABV
Lovely gold, well hopped beer.
WYBUNBURY RED 4.5% ABV
Reddish full bodied beer.
DABBER'S GOLD 5.0% ABV
Golden wheat beer.
RUM OLD ALE 6.0% ABV
Dark, mature, strong and well balanced.
Plus bottled beers, seasonal and celebration ales.

THE STORM BREWING CO.

Waterside, Macclesfield SK11 7HJ
☎ *(01625) 432978*

 BEAUFORTS 3.8% ABV
DESERT STORM 4.0% ABV
BITTER EXPERIENCE 4.0% ABV
ALE FORCE 4.2% ABV
WINDGATHER 4.5% ABV
STORM DAMAGE 4.7% ABV

THOMAS HARDY BURTONWOOD LTD

Bold Lane, Burtonwood, Warrington WA5 4PJ
☎ *(01925) 225131*
www.burtonwood.co.uk

 BITTER 3.7% ABV
Rich, smooth malt flavour. Hoppy aroma.
JAMES FORSHAWS BITTER 4.0% ABV
Full bodied and malty.
TOP HAT 4.8% ABV
Rich flavour with dry hop character.
BUCCANEER BITTER 5.2% ABV
Pale golden ale.
Plus monthly specials.

WEETWOOD ALES LTD

The Brewery, Weetwood Grange, Tarporley
CW6 0NQ
☎ *(01829) 752377*

 BEST BITTER 3.8% ABV
Sharp with a hoppy finish.
EASTGATE ALE 4.2% ABV
Golden, with fruity hoppiness.
OLD DOG BITTER 4.5% ABV
Deep colour, smooth and rich.
OASTHOUSE GOLD 5.0% ABV
Pale and hoppy with a dry finish.

THE PUBS

APPLETON THORN

Appleton Thorn Village Hall

Stretton Road, Appleton Thorn, Nr Warrington
WA4 4RT
☎ *(01925) 268370* Mrs Karen Howard

 Seven real ales always available, always different (over 1,500 served in last three years).

A charitable village club operated voluntarily by local residents. Membership not required for entry, though new members always welcome (£4 per year). Car park, garden, playing field, bowling green, pool and darts. Children welcome. From M6 Jct 20 or M56 Jct 10, follow signs for Appleton Thorn. Hall is 100m west of village church. 1995 CAMRA national club of the year.

OPEN *8.30–11pm Thurs–Sat; 8.30–10.30pm Sun. Open lunchtimes (1–4pm) on first and third Sunday of each month.*

ASTON

Bhurtpore Inn

Wrenbury Road, Aston, Nr Nantwich CW5 8DQ
☎ *(01270) 780917* Simon and Nicky George

 Hanby Drawwell always available plus nine guest beers (over 800 per year) which may include a brew from Tomlinson's, Burton Bridge, Weetwood, Adnams, Slaters (Eccleshall), Bateman, Black Sheep and Rudgate. Also real cider and 180 bottled Belgian beers plus three Belgian beers on draught.

The family has been connected with this comfortable, traditional, award-winning pub since 1849. Fresh bar and restaurant food at lunchtime and evenings. Car park, garden. Children allowed in pub at lunchtime and in early evening. Located just west of the A530, midway between Nantwich and Whitchurch.

OPEN *12–2.30pm and 6.30–11pm Mon–Sat; 12–3pm and 7–10.30pm Sun.*

BROXTON

The Egerton Arms

Whitchurch Road, Broxton CH3 9JW
☎ *(01829) 782241* Jim Moneghan

 A Burtonwood house, with Top Hat a permanent feature. One guest beer, changed monthly, could be another Burtonwood ale, or a beer such as Ridleys Rumpus or Everards Tiger.

A rural pub on the main road, with one bar and a restaurant. Garden, car park. Children allowed. Seven letting rooms. Located 10 miles from Chester on the junction of the A41 and A534.

OPEN *11am–11pm Mon–Sat; 12–10.30pm Sun.*

CHESTER

The George & Dragon Hotel

Liverpool Road, Chester CH2 1AA
☎ *(01244) 380714* Tony Chester

A huge range of real ales always available in this freehouse. Castle Eden Ale is a permanent fixture. Regular guests, changed weekly, include Wadworth 6X, Titanic White Star, Timothy Taylor Landlord, Morland Old Speckled Hen, Fuller's London Pride and Greene King Abbot Ale.

A pub with a traditional atmosphere. Separate dining area and background music. Hotel accommodation. Food served at lunchtime and evenings. Children not allowed.

OPEN *11am–11pm Mon–Sat; 12–10.30pm Sun.*

The Mill Hotel

Milton Street, Chester CH1 3NF
☎ *(01244) 350035*

CAMRA Pub of the Year 1996 and Millennium Pub of the Year 2000, offering 15 real ales, including three permanently available, Weetwood Best, Coach House Mill Premium and Cains Traditional Bitter. Guests change daily (approx. 900 served every year) and always include a mild and either a stout or a porter. Requests welcome!

Hotel bar and restaurant on the site of a once-working mill. Bar and restaurant food available at lunchtime and evenings. Canalside patio, restaurant boat lunch and dinner cruises. Accommodation available (expansion to 130 rooms during 2000). Non-smoking area. Sky Sports on TV (with sound turned down). Families most welcome. Ample car parking. Visit our website at: www.millhotel.com.

OPEN *11am–11pm Mon–Sat; 12–10.30pm Sun.*

The Union Vaults

44 Egerton Street, Chester CH1 3ND
☎ *(01244) 322170* Miss Lee

Former Greenalls pub offering Plassey Bitter from Wrexham plus two guests, which are changed weekly.

A little local alehouse, five minutes from Chester train station, this is a drinkers' pub with one bar. No food. Children allowed.

OPEN *11am–11pm Mon–Sat; 12–10.30pm Sun.*

CONGLETON

The Beartown Tap

18 Willow Street, Congleton CW12 1RL
☎ *(01260) 270990* Steve King

The Beartown Brewery tap, with the full range of Beartown beers usually available. Six hand-pulled beers available – Wye Valley Brew 69 and Dwan Tipperary are examples of the guests on offer (one, changed weekly). Cider and Belgian beer on draught, plus over 30 bottled Belgian beers.

Traditional drinkers' town pub, quiet (no juke box), with no swearing allowed! Darts, dominoes and crib. Pre-booked meals and buffet are available. Function room. Extension and garden planned for future. Parking nearby. Children allowed.

OPEN *12–2pm and 4–11pm Mon–Thurs; 12–11pm Fri–Sat; 12–10.30pm Sun.*

CREWE

The Albion Inn

1 Pedley Street, Crewe CW2 7AA
☎ *(01270) 251465* Jacqui Woolhouse

Greene King Abbot always available plus a changing guest, which is sometimes Marston's Pedigree but could be any real ale.

A small, friendly, family-run pub situated close to the railway station and local football ground. Bar, lounge and pool room. Baps available at weekends only. Children only allowed on football days, if accompanied by parents. To find, take first left after the railway station, then right at first traffic lights.

OPEN *5–11pm Mon–Thurs; 12–11pm Fri–Sat; 12–10.30pm Sun.*

FRODSHAM

Netherton Hall

Chester Road, Frodsham WA6 6UL
☎ *(01928) 732342* Mr Rowland

A Jennings brew is a permanent fixture, plus four fine cask ales, perhaps Greene King Abbot and IPA, Timothy Taylor Landlord and something from Adnams.

A typical Cheshire country pub on the main road, with one large bar, half of which is smoking and half non-smoking. Food served at lunchtime and evenings, and all day Friday and Saturday. Well-behaved children allowed.

OPEN *11am–11pm Mon–Sat; 12–10.30pm Sun.*

Helter Skelter

31 Church Street, Frodsham WA6 6PN
☎ *(01928) 733361* Mike Toner and Robin Holt

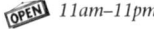 Six real ales always available, including Weetwood Best Bitter (the house bitter) plus five guest beers, changing constantly. There is also one pump serving traditional farmhouse cider.

One-room public bar with restaurant above. Bar and restaurant food at lunchtime and evenings. Restaurant closed Saturday lunchtime and all day Sunday. Parking. Children allowed in restaurant. In the main shopping area, close to British Rail station.

OPEN *11am–11pm.*

GOLBORNE

The Railway Hotel

131 High Street, Golborne, Warrington WA3 3TG
☎ *(01942) 728202* Sarah Porter

 Sarah's Hophouse Brewery is on the premises, and the full range of beers is served, plus Greene King IPA and one ever-changing guest which might be from any brewery.

Community local with darts and pool. Live band every Friday, jam night every Thursday. Sandwiches served through the day. Motorbike-friendly – the pub has a bike club. No special children's facilities, though children allowed until 6pm. From Junction 23 on M6, take the A580 heading to Manchester, and after one mile turn left at the first roundabout; Golborne is half a mile on the right.

   HOPHOUSE BITTER 3.9% ABV
  BLACK MAMBA MILD 4% ABV
AMBER ALE 4.2% ABV
HOP TO IT 4.2% ABV
CHOCOLATE STOUT 4.7% ABV

OPEN *12–11pm Mon–Fri; 11am–11pm Sat; 12–10.30pm Sun.*

GREAT SUTTON

The White Swan Inn

Old Chester Road, Great Sutton, Ellesmere Port CH66 3NZ
☎ *(0151) 339 9284* John and Denise Hardy

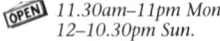 Tied to the Burtonwood Brewery, offering five different brews a week, the Burtonwood range plus guests such as Shepherd Neame Bishop's Finger and Jennings Sneck Lifter.

A community local with Sky TV, off the main road (not signposted). Meals served at lunchtimes 11.30am–2pm Mon–Sat (except Tues) and 12–4pm Sun (Sunday roast available: three choices, £4.50). Children allowed only if dining.

OPEN *11.30am–11pm Mon–Sat; 12–10.30pm Sun.*

HALEBANK

The Cock & Trumpet Inn

Halebank Road, Halebank, Widnes WA8 8NB
☎ *(0151) 4253142* Tom Glover (Manager)

 Two pumps serve Burtonwood Top Hat plus one guest, changed weekly, which may include Jennings Sneck Lifter or Shepherd Neame Bishop's Finger, though the aim is not to repeat beers.

Fairly modern community pub, recently renovated, with two bars (games room and lounge). 'Pub grub' served. Beer garden at back with play area. Barbecues when weather permits. Car park. Children allowed up to 8pm. Located five minutes from Runcorn Bridge, off Ditton Road.

OPEN *11.30am–11pm Mon–Sat; 12–10.30pm Sun.*

HANDFORTH

The Railway

Station Road, Handforth, Wilmslow
☎ *(01625) 523472* Linda Cook

 Robinson's Best Bitter and Hatters Mild usually available with one other Robinson's beer such as Frederics, Old Tom (in winter) and occasionally Hartleys XB.

Friendly, traditional locals' pub. Non-smoking area. Food served 12–2pm Mon–Sat. Car park. Children are welcome at lunchtimes although there are no special facilities. Opposite Handforth railway station.

OPEN *11.45am–3.30pm and 5.30–11pm Mon–Sat; 12–3pm and 7–10.30pm Sun.*

HATCHMERE

Carriers Inn

Delamere Road, Hatchmere, Norley
☎ *(01928) 788258* Karen Ashton

 A Burtonwood house with Bitter and Smooth permanently available, plus one monthly changing guest. York Yorkshire Terrier is a regular feature.

An old-style, one-bar pub with non-smoking restaurant. Food available 12–3pm and 6–8pm daily. Pool table. Large beer garden. Children allowed, with children's play area provided. Located on the B5152.

OPEN *11am–11pm Mon–Sat; 12–10.30pm Sun.*

HEATON CHAPEL

The Hinds Head

Manchester Road, Heaton Chapel, Stockport
SK4 2RB
☎ *(0161) 431 9301* Terence Murphy

 Morland Old Speckled Hen, Timothy Taylor Landlord, Marston's Pedigree and Black Sheep Bitter permanently available, plus one monthly changing guest.

A ward-winning pub with extensive lawned beer garden and lovely hanging baskets, CAMRA listed for its beer and food. Meals are served 12–2pm and 7–9pm Mon–Sat and 12–4.30pm Sun. Children welcome at all times in the beer garden, and inside the pub if dining. Large car park.

OPEN *11.30am–11pm Mon–Sat;*
12–10.30pm Sun.

HEATON NORRIS

The Crown Inn

154 Heaton Lane, Heaton Norris, Stockport
SK4 1AR
☎ *(0161) 429 0549* Graham Mascord

 Ten guest pumps serve a varied and interesting choice of real ales. There are dedicated pumps for Bank Top, Phoenix, Pictish, Whim and Jennings, and many of the independent breweries in the UK are featured. Micro-breweries also favoured. A range of 15 malt whiskies also available, plus real cider.

V ery cosy, old-fashioned multi-roomed boozer, with the focus on real ale for the real ale lover. Hot and cold snacks available during opening hours. Live music. Website: www.thecrown.org.

OPEN *12–3pm and 6–11pm Mon–Thurs;*
12.30–11pm Fri–Sat; 7.30–10.30pm Sun.

HIGHER HURDSFIELD

George & Dragon

61 Rainow Road, Higher Hurdsfield, Macclesfield
SK10 2PD
☎ *(01625) 424300* D Molly Harrison

 A beer from Storm Brewing Co. is among the beers usually available.

T raditional part-seventeenth-century pub with food served 12–2pm Mon–Fri and Sun. Car park. Children welcome, but no special facilities.

OPEN *12–3pm and 7–11pm Mon–Fri; 7–11pm*
Sat; 12–3pm and 7.30–10.30pm Sun.

KINGSLEY

Horseshoe Inn

Hollow Lane, Kingsley WA6 8EF
☎ *(01928) 788466* Ron Varnett

 A Burtonwood pub, with Burtonwood Bitter always on offer. One guest, such as Everards Tiger or something from Ridleys, is changed monthly.

V illage community pub with an L-shaped bar and open fire. Food is available, and there is a dining area. Patio, car park. Children allowed.

OPEN *12–3pm and 5–11pm (10.30pm Sun).*

LANGLEY

Leathers Smithy

Langley, Nr Macclesfield SK11 0NE
☎ *(01260) 252313* Mr McMahon

 Marson's Pedigree always available, plus one guest changed twice weekly, which could be from any independent brewery. Wherever possible, guest beers are not repeated.

A former smithy (originally run by William Leather), built in the sixteenth century in beautiful surroundings on the edge of Macclesfield Forest overlooking the Ridge Gate Reservoir (fishing possible). Food available at lunchtime and evenings. Also 80 different whiskies. Car park, garden, family/function room.

OPEN *12–3pm and 7–11pm Mon–Sat;*
12–10.30pm Sun.

MACCLESFIELD

The Railway View

Byrons Lane, Macclesfield SK11 7JW
☎ *(01625) 423657* David Calvert (Manager)

 A freehouse with beers from Coach House and Cains always available, plus five guests, changed regularly, such as Timothy Taylor Landlord, Charles Wells Bombardier, Sarah Hughes Dark Ruby Mild and Wadworth 6X.

O ne-bar family pub with beams and log fires. Food served. Patio, darts. Children allowed. Ring first for directions.

OPEN *12–3 pm and 6–11pm (not afternoons*
weekdays).

Waters Green Tavern
96 Waters Green, Macclesfield SK11 6LH
☎ *(01625) 422653* Brian McDermott

 Timothy Taylor Landlord and Greene King IPA are always available, plus guests from breweries such as Rooster's, Phoenix, Oakham and Whim, to name but a few.

A traditional pub with a real fire in winter. Local CAMRA Pub of the Year 1999. Home-cooked food served at lunchtime only. Children allowed if dining.

OPEN *11.30am–3pm and 5.30–11pm Mon–Fri; 11am–3pm and 7–11pm Sat; 12–3pm and 7–10.30pm Sun.*

MIDDLEWICH

The Big Lock
Webbs Lane, Middlewich CW10 9DN
☎ *(01606) 833489* Stuart Griffiths

 Greene King Abbot and Black Sheep Bitter permanently available. The two guests, changed every fortnight and not repeated if possible, could be Marston's Pedigree, Charles Wells Pedigree, or anything from Beartown or Adnams.

Traditional pub on the canal bank with outside balcony and benches overlooking the canal. Two public bars, restaurant and function room. Car park. Children allowed. Call for directions.

OPEN *11am–11pm Mon–Sat; 12–10.30pm Sun.*

MOBBERLEY

The Roebuck Inn
Mill Lane, Mobberley WA16 7XH
☎ *(01565) 872757* Dave Robinson

 A freehouse with Timothy Taylor Landlord and Greene King Abbot Ale always available, plus regular guests, changed weekly, that may include Hydes' Anvil Bitter, Shepherd Neame Spitfire or Elgood's Pageant Ale.

A friendly country inn with a contemporary twist, recently refurbished. Fresh food served at lunchtime and evenings. Children allowed.

OPEN *12–3pm and 5.30–11pm Mon–Fri; 12–11pm Sat; 12–10.30pm Sun.*

NANTWICH

The Black Lion
29 Welsh Row, Nantwich CW5 5ED
☎ *(01270) 628711* Jill Llewellyn

A three-pump freehouse with Weetwood Old Dog and Best Bitter plus Titanic Premium always available.

A traditional two-bar pub. Food at lunchtime and evenings. No children.

OPEN *11am–11pm Mon–Sat; 12–10.30 pm Sun.*

Oddfellows Arms
97 Welsh Row, Nantwich CW5 5TL
☎ *(01270) 624758* Mr Drinkwater

 Tied to Burtonwood, with Burtonwood Bitter and Top Hat always on offer. The monthly changing guest could be Jennings Cumberland, Brakspear Special or Ridleys Rumpus, to name but a few.

Locals' pub, with beams and open fires. Food served. Garden. First pub into town from the canal. Children allowed.

OPEN *12–3pm and 6–11pm Mon–Thurs (closed Mon lunch); 12–11pm Fri–Sat; 12–4pm and 7–10.30pm Sun.*

Wilbraham Arms
58 Welsh Row, Nantwich CW5 5EJ
☎ *(01270) 626419*

 Marston's Pedigree and JW Lees Best Bitter always available.

Close to the town centre, near canal, with traditional Georgian frontage, bar and dining area. Bar food available at lunchtime and evenings. Small car park, accommodation. Children allowed in dining room.

OPEN *12–11pm (10.30pm Sun).*

PENKETH

The Ferry Tavern
Station Road, Penketh, Warrington WA5 2UJ
☎ *(01925) 791117* Mr T Maxwell

 Charles Wells Bombardier always available, plus eight to ten guest beers every week (on three pumps). These could be from breweries such as Cottage, Coach House, Daleside, Caledonian, Rebellion or Brakspear, but beers from all over the country, from Orkney to the Isle of Wight, have been featured. A range of 300 whiskies is also on offer, including 50 Irish varieties (one of the best selections outside Ireland).

Built in the eleventh century, the Ferry Tavern has been an alehouse for 300 years and stands in a unique position on an island between the river Mersey and the St Helens canal. CAMRA Pub of the Year for Cheshire 2002. No food – the emphasis is on real ale. Car park. Children welcome. Website: www.ferrytavern.com.

OPEN *12–3pm and 5.30–11pm Mon–Fri; 12–11pm Sat; 12–10.30pm Sun.*

RODE HEATH

The Royal Oak

41 Sandbach Road, Rode Heath ST7 3RW
☎ *(01270) 875670* Christopher Forrester

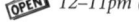Adnams Bitter or Greene King Abbot always available, plus one guest from an independent brewery.

Public house with bar, smoke room, lounge and restaurant. Food served 12–9pm. Children are welcome, and there is a fully equipped play area. Car park. Located on the main Alsager to Sandbach road.

 12–11pm (10.30pm Sun).

SANDBACH

Ring O'Bells

17 Wells Street, Sandbach CW11 1GT
☎ *(01270) 765731* Jane Robson

A Burtonwood house with Bitter and Mild permanently available, plus guests during the winter months.

A traditional one-bar locals' pub with darts, pool and a juke box. No food. Children allowed until 6pm.

 11am–11pm Mon–Sat; 12–10.30pm Sun.

STALYBRIDGE

The Buffet Bar

Stalybridge Railway Station, Stalybridge SK15 1RF
☎ *(0161) 303 0007*

Seven or eight real ales available. Wadworth 6X is a permanent fixture plus a constantly changing range of guest beers from independent breweries.

A unique and authentic buffet bar built in 1855 with a real fire, real ale, and real people! Bar food available at most times. Parking. Children allowed. On platform one at Stalybridge railway station.

11am–11pm Mon–Sat; 12–10.30pm Sun.

Q Inn

3 Market Street, Stalybridge SK15 2AL
☎ *(0161) 303 9157* Ray and Sheena Calland

A Hyde's Brewery tied house serving the full range of Hyde's products, including Dark Mild in the Craft range.

The pub with the shortest name in Britain forms part of the Stalybridge Eight – eight pubs in the town offering 37 different beers. Brick walls and a flagstone floor. Quiz night on Monday, cocktail bar on Friday. Bar snacks available. No children. Next to the railway station.

11am–11pm Mon–Sat; 12–10.30pm Sun.

The White House

1 Water Street, Stalybridge SK15 2AG
☎ *(0161) 303 2288* Ray and Sheena Calland

A Hyde's Brewery tied house serving the full range of Hyde's products, including Dark Mild in the Craft range.

A traditional pub with low ceilings, recently refurbished and very comfortable. Full menu available. No children.

11am–11pm Mon–Sat; 12–10.30pm Sun.

STRINES

The Sportsman's Arms

105 Strines Road, Strines SK12 3AE
☎ *(0161) 427 2888*

Cains Mild and Bitter always available, plus a weekly alternating guest from any independent brewery.

An old, two-roomed pub with a lounge/dining room. Home-cooked food is available at lunchtime and evenings. Car park, garden. On the B6101.

12–3pm and 5.15–11pm Mon–Fri; all day Sat and Sun.

TUSHINGHAM

The Blue Bell Inn

Tushingham, Nr Whitchurch
☎ *(01948) 662172* Patrick and Lydia Gage

Hanby Drawwell Bitter always available plus one or two others (20 per year), perhaps including beers from Plassey, Joule, Four Rivers, Cains and Felinfoel breweries.

Dating from 1667, this claims to be Cheshire's oldest pub, with an American landlord and Russian landlady. Friendly and welcoming. No games machines or loud music. Sunday papers and comfortable settee. Bar and restaurant food available at lunchtime and evenings. Car park and garden. Children and dogs always very welcome. Four miles north of Whitchurch on the A41 Chester road.

12–3pm and 6–11pm Mon–Sat; 7–11pm Sun.

WARRINGTON

The Old Town House

Buttermarket Street, Warrington WA1 2NL
☎ *(01925) 242787* Roy Baxter

A five-pump freehouse, always serving Marston's Pedigree and Morland Old Speckled Hen.

A country town pub with one bar, situated in the main street leading into the town centre. Food served at lunchtime only. Children allowed.

OPEN *11am–11pm Mon–Sat; 12–10.30pm Sun.*

WHITCHURCH

Willeymoor Lock Tavern

Tarporley Road, Nr Whitchurch SY13 4HF
☎ *(01948) 663274* Mrs Elsie Gilkes

Four guest beers served in summer, two in winter. These may include beers from Beartown, Hanby Ales, Kitchen, Cottage, Weetwood, Coach House, Wood, Springhead or Wychwood breweries.

Situated next to a working lock on the Llangollen Canal, this pub was formerly a lock-keeper's cottage. Food served lunchtimes and evenings. Children welcome: there is a large garden with a play area. Car park. Situated two miles north of Whitchurch on A49. Pub found at end of driveway, pub sign on the road.

OPEN *12–2.30pm (2pm winter) and 6–11pm Mon–Sat; 12–2.30pm (2pm winter) and 7–10.30pm Sun.*

WRENBURY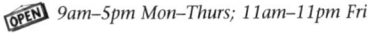

The Old Creamery

Wrenbury Road, Wrenbury, Nantwich CW5 8EX
☎ *(01270) 780916* Nick Platt and John Wood

Home of the Paradise Brewing Company with the full range of Paradise ales always available.

An unusual and fascinating haven for real ale lovers, this is the opposite of a brewpub: a bar inside a brewery. Cold bar snacks available. Parties of 20 or more catered for by prior arrangement.

OPEN *9am–5pm Mon–Thurs; 11am–11pm Fri.*

YOU TELL US

★ *The Swan, 2 Swan Street, Wilmslow*

Places Featured:

Altarnun
Blisland
Bodmin
Boscastle
Charlestown
Crackington Haven
Crantock
Crowlass
Cubert
Edmonton
Falmouth
Golant
Gorran Haven
Gunnislake
Hayle
Helston
Kilkhampton
Launceston
Lerryn
Lostwithiel
Nancenoy
Penzance
Polperro
Port Gaverne
Porthallow
Porthleven
Portreath
Quintrell Downs
St Cleer
St Columb
St Just
Stratton
Trebarwith
Tregrehan
Tresparrett
Trevaunance Cove
Truro
Widemouth Bay
Zelah
Zennor

THE BREWERIES

ALES OF SCILLY BREWERY

Higher Trenoweth, St Mary's, Isles of Scilly TR21 0NS
☎ *(01720) 422419*

SCUPPERED 4.0% ABV
Slightly darker beer with fuller flavour. Name may change.

MAIDEN VOYAGE 4.2% ABV
Light summer quaffing ale, so named because it is the brewer's first venture.

BLACKAWTON BREWERY

Unit 14 Saltash Business Park, Moorlands Trading Estate, Forge Lane, Saltash PL12 6LX
☎ *(01752) 848777*

BITTER 3.8% ABV
Well-hopped. A popular session beer.

DEVON GOLD 4.1% ABV
Summer brew. European style. Light and fresh.

44 SPECIAL 4.5% ABV
Full-bodied with rich nutty flavour.

EXHIBITION 4.7% ABV
Pale, soft and fruity.

HEADSTRONG 5.2% ABV
Rich and powerful with fruit flavour. Deceptively smooth.

Plus occasional brews.

DOGHOUSE BREWERY

Scorrier, Redruth TR16 5BN
☎ *(01209) 822022*

WET NOSE 3.5% ABV
A healthy dog has a wet nose, a healthy beer has a good nose!

DOGHOUSE BITER 4.0% ABV
The hops in this finely balanced beer provide the extra bite to make this a 'biter' not a 'bitter'!

BOW WOW 5.0% ABV
A balance of malty sweetness countered by bitter, aromatic hops.

KELTEK BREWERY

Unit 3a, Restormel Industrial Estate, Liddicoat Road, Lostwithiel PL22 0HG
☎ *(01208) 871199*
www.carnmenellis.demon.co.uk/brewers.htm#keltek

GOLDEN LANCE 3.8% ABV
KELTEK MAGIC 4.2% ABV

KELTEK KING 5.1% ABV
Plus monthly and seasonal brews.

THE ORGANIC BREWHOUSE

Unit 1, Higher Bochym Workshops, Cury Cross Lanes, Helston TR12 7AZ
☎ *(01326) 241555*

LIZARD POINT 4.0% ABV
Refreshing session bitter.

SERPENTINE 4.5% ABV
Malty and hoppy.

BLACK ROCK 4.7% ABV
Stout.

WOLF ROCK 5.0% ABV
Full-bodied premium bitter.

RING O'BELLS BREWERY

Pennygilliam Industrial Estate, Pennygilliam Way, Launceston PL15 7ED
☎ *(01566) 777787*

PORKER'S PRIDE 3.8% ABV
SURF BOAR 4.0% ABV
A golden coloured summer ale. Seasonal.
DREKLY 4.0% ABV
BODMIN BOAR 4.3% ABV
TIPSY TROTTER 5.0% ABV
A winter ale.
SANTA PIG 5.5% ABV
Christmas special.

ST AUSTELL BREWERY CO. LTD

63 Trevarthian Road, St Austell PL25 4BY
☎ *(01726) 74444*
www.staustellbrewery.co.uk

IPA 3.4% ABV
XXXX MILD 3.6% ABV
Dark and distinctive, with malt flavour.
DUCHY BITTER 3.7% ABV
Refreshing and cool.
TINNERS 3.7% ABV
Classic bitter.
TRIBUTE 4.2% ABV
Pale and drinkable.
CELTIC SMOOTH 4.4% ABV
Light, smooth and creamy.
HICKS SPECIAL DRAUGHT 5.0% ABV
Powerful and distinctive.
Plus seasonal brews.

SHARP'S BREWERY

Pityme Industrial Estate, Rock, Wadebridge PL27 6NU
☎ *(01208) 861121*
www.carnmenellis.demon.co.uk/brewers.htm#sharps

CORNISH COASTER 3.6% ABV
DOOM BAR BITTER 4.0% ABV
EDEN ALE 4.2% ABV
OWN 4.4% ABV
WILL'S RESOLVE 4.6% ABV
SPECIAL ALE 5.2% ABV

SKINNER'S BREWING CO.

Riverside View, Newham, Truro TR1 2SU
☎ *(01872) 271885*
www.carnmenellis.demon.co.uk/brewers.htm#skinners

COASTLINER 3.4% ABV
Quenching and well-hopped.
SPRIGGAN ALE 3.8% ABV
Quenching, with flavour of hops.
BETTY STOGS BITTER 4.0% ABV
Light-coloured, with hops throughout.
CORNISH KNOCKER 4.5% ABV
Gold in colour and refreshing.
FIGGY'S BREW 4.5% ABV
Rich and well-rounded.
ICE BLONDE 5.0% ABV
SUMMER BLONDE 5.0% ABV

THE PUBS

ALTARNUN

The Rising Sun

Altarnun, Nr Launceston PL15 7SN
☎ *(01566) 86332* Mr and Mrs Manson

 Up to six beers available, including brews from Sharp's, Hoskins & Oldfield, Cotleigh, Butcombe, Otter, Exe Valley, Cask Force and the Beer Seller. Continually changing.

Sixteenth-century, single-bar pub with open fires and slate/hardwood floor. Bar food available at lunchtime and evenings. Ample parking. Children allowed. One mile off the A30, seven miles west of Launceston.

OPEN 11am–3pm and 5.30–11pm Mon–Fri; 11am–11pm Sat; 12–10.30pm Sun. Open all day, every day, during summer season.

BLISLAND

Blisland Inn

The Green, Blisland, nr Bodmin PL30 4JF
☎ *(01208) 850739* Gary Marshall

 Six pumps with guests changing every couple of days. Cornish ales are regulars.

Country-style freehouse, with lounge, public bar and family room. CAMRA Cornwall Pub of the Year and CAMRA South West Pub of the Year, both in 2000. Separate dining area for bar food served at lunchtime and evenings. Children allowed in family room.

OPEN 11.30am–11pm Mon–Sat; 12–10.30pm Sun.

BODMIN

The Masons Arms

Higherbore Street, Bodmin PL31 2JS
☎ *(01208) 72607* Matt Woods

 A freehouse with Sharp's Cornish Coaster and Timothy Taylor Landlord always on offer. Three guests are rotated a couple at a time, every four days. Crouch Vale Willie Warmer, Sutton XSB and Robinson's Old Tom are regular favourites.

A traditional Cornish drinkers' pub in a seventeenth-century building, with quiet lounge bar and noisy public bar. No food. Pool, darts, beer garden. Car parking. Children allowed, but not in bar area. Located on the main road, so easy to find.

OPEN 11am–11pm Mon–Sat; 12–10.30pm Sun.

BOSCASTLE

The Cobweb Inn

Boscastle PL35 0HE
☎ *(01840) 250278* AI and AP Bright

 St Austell Tinners and Greene King Abbot permanently available, plus a range of guest ales.

Atmospheric, seventeenth-century freehouse, close to the harbour. Food served lunchtimes and evenings. Car park. Children permitted in family room, restaurant and outside seating, but not in bar area. The pub is across the road from the car park at the bottom of the village.

OPEN *11am–11pm Mon–Fri; 11am–midnight Sat; 12–10.30pm Sun.*

CHARLESTOWN

Rashleigh Arms

Charlestown Road, Charlestown, St Austell PL25 3NJ
☎ *(01726) 73635* Glen Price

 A 14-pump freehouse with Wadworth 6X and Sharp's Doom Bar among those always available. Two guests are changed twice a week. Skinner's ales are often featured.

A country pub with family room, TV and juke box, plus entertainment in winter. Food served at lunchtimes and evenings. Children allowed.

OPEN *11am–11pm Mon–Sat; 12–10.30pm Sun.*

CRACKINGTON HAVEN

Coombe Barton Inn

Crackington Haven, Bude EX23 0JG
☎ *(01840) 230345* Mr Cooper
 A freehouse offering eight beers including four guests. Sharp's Doom Bar and Dartmoor Best are always available. Regular guests come from St Austell and Sharp's breweries.

A seaside family-run pub on the sea front, with separate dining area and family room. Six rooms available for bed and breakfast. Food at lunchtime and evenings. Children allowed in family room.

OPEN *Summer: 11am–11pm Mon–Sat; 12–10.30pm Sun; winter: 11am–3pm and 6–11pm.*

CRANTOCK

Old Albion

Langurroc Road, Crantock, Newquay TR8 5RB
☎ *(01637) 830243*
Mr Andrew Brown and Miss S Moses

 Sharp's and St Austell beers always available. Three guests, changed frequently, might include Cotleigh brews, Morland Old Speckled Hen, Exmoor Gold and Fuller's London Pride.

A country pub, which used to be used for smuggling beer, situated next to the church in Crantock. Homemade food served at lunchtime and evenings in bar area. Children allowed in family room.

OPEN *12–11pm.*

CROWLASS

The Star Inn

Crowlass TR20 8DX
☎ *(01736) 740375* Pete Elvin

 Fourteen different brews per week are available at this freehouse. Everards Tiger is regularly served, and Nethergate Umble and beers from Keltek have also been featured. The landlord always tries to keep a local beer on during the summer.

Locals' village pub in a late Victorian purpose-built hotel. No food at present, though there are plans for a restaurant/dining area. Pool, darts, occasional live music. Beer garden, car park. Children allowed.

OPEN *11am–11pm Mon–Sat; 12–10.30pm Sun.*

CUBERT

The Smuggler's Den Inn
Trebellan, Cubert, Newquay TR8 5PY
☎ *(01637) 830209*
Mr SE Hancock and Mr PB Partridge

 During the summer months, Sharp's Cornish Coaster, Skinner's Betty Stogs and St Austell Tribute and HSD are permanently available, plus there are four constantly changing guests which might be from breweries such as Skinner's, Sharp's, Doghouse, Keltek, Greene King, Cottage, St Austell, Fuller's, Brains, Clearwater, Cotleigh, Hook Norton or Badger, to name but a few. Local ales stocked whenever possible. In the winter, there are no permanent ales.

A sixteenth-century thatched country pub with a reputation locally for good ale, wine and food. Real fires, beer garden with children's play area, function room for private hire. Food available lunchtime from 12pm and evenings from 6pm. Children allowed. Car park. Situated on the A3075 Newquay–Redruth road. Turn towards Cubert village and take first left.

OPEN *Summer: 11.30am–11pm (10.30pm Sun). Winter: 11.30am–2.30pm Thurs–Sun (closed lunchtimes Mon–Wed); 6–11pm Mon–Sat; 6–10.30pm Sun.*

EDMONTON

The Quarryman
Edmonton, Wadebridge PL27 7JA
☎ *(01208) 816444* Terrence de-Villiers Kuun

 A four-pump freehouse, with guest beers changed every two or three days. Favourites include Skinner's and Sharp's brews plus Cottage Golden Arrow.

An old Cornish inn with separate restaurant and bar food. Food served at lunchtime and evenings. Well-behaved children allowed.

OPEN *11am–11pm Mon–Sat; 12–10.30pm Sun.*

FALMOUTH

The Quayside Inn
41 Arwenack Street, Falmouth TR11 3JQ
☎ *(01326) 312113*
Paul and Katherine Coombes

 Up to eight beers always available. Sharp's Special, Skinner's Cornish Knocker, Marston's Pedigree, Wadworth 6X, Ringwood Old Thumper and Morland Old Speckled Hen permanently served, plus a range of guests from breweries such as Bateman, Shepherd Neame and Fuller's.

Twice-yearly beer festivals at this quayside pub overlooking the harbour. Two bars – comfy upstairs lounge and downstairs real ale bar. Food available all day, every day in summer, and at lunchtimes and evenings in winter (skillet house with food cooked in skillets). Outside seating on quayside. Parking. Children very welcome – children's menu. On Custom House Quay.

OPEN *Both bars all day in summer. Top bar all day in winter.*

GOLANT

The Fisherman's Arms
Fore Street, Golant, Fowey PL23 1LN
☎ *(01726) 832453* Michael Moran

 Ushers Best and Sharp's Doom Bar Bitter are always on offer.

A village pub on the banks of the River Fowey. Food at lunchtime and evening. Children allowed.

OPEN *12–3pm and 6–11pm Mon–Fri; 11am–11pm Sat; 12–10.30am Sun.*

GORRAN HAVEN

Llawnroc Inn
33 Chute Lane, Gorran Haven, St Austell PL26 6NU
☎ *(01726) 843461*
Alan Freeman and Don Reece

 A Sharp's beer is regularly available.

Relaxing, family-run hotel with beautiful sea views situated in an old fishing village. Food served 12–2.30pm and 6–9.30pm in summer and 12–2pm and 7–9pm in winter. Car park. Children welcome. From St Austell continue past Heligan Gardens and after Gorran Haven, turn right.

OPEN *Summer: 12–11pm Mon–Sat (10.30pm Sun). Winter: 12–3pm and 6.30–11pm Mon–Sat; 12–3pm and 7–10.30pm Sun.*

GUNNISLAKE

Rising Sun Inn

Calstock Road, Gunnislake PL18 9BX
☎ *(01822) 832201* Pauline and David Gray

 A freehouse with Sharp's Cornish Coaster and Skinner's Betty Stogs Bitter always available, plus a range of guest beers.

Seventeenth-century olde-worlde freehouse on the outskirts of Gunnislake. Home-cooked food served lunchtimes and evenings Tues–Sat and lunchtime Sun. Beautiful gardens. Well-behaved children welcome.

OPEN *12–2.30pm and 5–11pm Mon–Sat; 12–3pm and 7–10.30pm Sun.*

HAYLE

Bird in Hand

Trelissick Road, Hayle TR27 4HY
☎ *(01736) 753974* Mr Miller

 A freehouse and brewpub, home of the Wheal Ale Brewery. A range of own brews always available, plus two guest beers, perhaps including Greene King Abbot or Shepherd Neame Spitfire.

An old coach house with one bar. Live music. Food at lunchtime and evenings (summer only). Children allowed.

PARADISE 3.8–4.0% ABV
A light session bitter.
MILLER'S 4.2–4.4% ABV
A medium light bitter.
SPECKLED PARROT 5.5–6.5% ABV
A dark ale.

OPEN *11am–11pm Mon–Sat; 12–10.30pm Sun.*

HELSTON

The Blue Anchor

50 Coinagehall Street, Helston TR13 8EX
☎ *(01326) 562821*

One of only four pubs in Britain which has brewed continuously for centuries and still produces its famous Spingo ales, from a Victorian word for strong beer.

This thatched town pub was originally a monks' rest home in the fifteenth century. Brewing continued on the premises after the Reformation and the Blue Anchor is now believed to be the oldest brewpub in Britain. Bar snacks and meals are available at lunchtime. Garden, children's room, skittle alley, function room. Accommodation available.

MIDDLE 5.0% ABV
BEST 5.3% ABV
SPECIAL 6.6% ABV
CHRISTMAS AND EASTER SPECIAL 7.6% ABV

OPEN *11am–11pm Mon–Sat; 12–10.30pm Sun.*

KILKHAMPTON

The London Inn

Kilkhampton EX23 9QR
☎ *(01288) 321665* John and Angela Leigh

 Sharp's Doom Bar and Eden Ale are always available, plus one guest, such as Fuller's London Pride, Skinner's Betty Stogs Bitter, or another Sharp's brew.

Sixteenth-century pub with unusual hardwood bar front. The pub has a reputation for good-quality food, served in the restaurant or the snug, 12–2pm and 6–9pm. Beer gardens to front and rear – barbecues held regularly. Children and dogs welcome if kept under control. Ample parking space nearby. Located at the centre of the village on the main A39.

OPEN *12–11pm Mon–Fri; 11am–11pm Sat; 12–4pm and 7–10.30pm Sun.*

LAUNCESTON

The Eliot Arms

Tregadillet, Launceston
☎ *(01566) 772051*
Debbie Copper and Jamie Player

 Sharp's Eden and Doom Bar always available, with guests including other Sharp's brews.

Ivy-clad pub with softly lit rooms, open fires, slate floors, high-backed settles and fine Victorian furniture and artefacts. Collection of horse brasses, Masonic regalia and clocks (46, including five grandfather clocks). Food served 12–2pm and 7–9.30pm, with new children's menu recently introduced. Car park. Children and dogs welcome in front rooms.

OPEN *11am–3pm and 6–11pm Mon–Fri; 11am–11pm Sat; 12–10.30pm Sun.*

LERRYN

The Ship

Lerryn, Nr Lostwithiel PL22 0PT
☎ *(01208) 872374* Mr Packer

Four beers available including Sharp's brews and guests such as Exmoor Gold, Morland Old Speckled Hen, Fuller's London Pride and Otter Ale.

A pub since the early 1600s, with a wood burner in the bar and slate floors. Bar and restaurant food available at lunchtime and evenings. Set in a quiet riverside village three miles south of Lostwithiel. Car park, garden, accommodation. Children allowed.

OPEN *11.30am–3pm and 6–11pm Mon–Sat; 12–3pm and 7–10.30pm Sun.*

LOSTWITHIEL

The Royal Oak Inn

Duke Street, Lostwithiel PL22 0AG
☎ *(01208) 872552* Mr and Mrs Hine

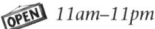 Marston's Pedigree, Sharp's Own and Fuller's London Pride always available. Orkney Skullsplitter, the Blue Anchor Spingos, Woodforde's Headcracker, Exmoor Gold, Ash Vine Bitter, Badger Tanglefoot and Best are among the guest beers (50 per year).

A popular thirteenth-century inn catering for all tastes. Bar and restaurant food at lunchtime and evenings. Car park, garden, children's room. Spacious accommodation. Located just off the A390 going into Lostwithiel.

{OPEN} *11am–11pm.*

NANCENOY

Trengilly Wartha Inn

Nancenoy, Constantine, Nr Falmouth TR11 5RP
☎ *(01326) 340332*
Nigel Logan and Michael MacGuire

 Sharp's Cornish Coaster always available, plus a couple of constantly rotating guests which may include brews from Skinner's, Keltek, St Austell or Exmoor.

A country freehouse and restaurant in six acres of valley gardens and meadows. Bar and restaurant food at lunchtime and evenings. Car park, garden and children's room. Eight bedrooms. Just south of Constantine – follow the signs.

{OPEN} *11am–2.30pm and 6.30–11pm.*

PENZANCE

Globe & Ale House

Queen Street, Penzance TR18 4BJ
☎ *(01736) 364098* Jenny Flewitt

 A freehouse with up to eight real ales always available. Something from local Skinner's and Sharp's usually features, plus a constantly changing range of real ales from any independent or micro-brewery from Cornwall to Orkney!

An alehouse with live music once a week and quiz nights. Food served lunchtimes and evenings, but no separate dining area. No children.

{OPEN} *11am–11pm Mon–Sat; 12–10.30pm Sun.*

Mounts Bay Inn

Promenade, Wherry Town, Penzance TR18 4NP
☎ *(01736) 360863*
Denis Mayor and Shirley O'Neill

 Skinner's Cornish Knocker and Sharp's Doom Bar Bitter always available, plus one guest, changed weekly, which could be from any independent or micro-brewery.

A warm welcome awaits in this characterful olde-worlde pub. Food served lunchtimes and evenings. Local authority car park situated opposite the pub. Quiz nights. No children allowed inside the pub, although welcome on side terrace. Small side terrace with seating.

{OPEN} *11am–11pm Mon–Sat; 12–10.30pm Sun.*

POLPERRO

The Blue Peter Inn

The Quay, Polperro, Nr Looe PL13 2QZ
☎ *(01503) 272743*
Caroline and Steve Steadman

 A selection of Sharp's and St Austell ales permanently available, plus daily guest beers, with the emphasis on minor breweries from all over the country. Local draught scrumpy also served.

Small, atmospheric, traditional pub with beamed ceilings, log fires and a family room. Children and pets welcome. Excellent lunch menu available every day, with local crab and scallops a speciality. Live music Fri and Sat nights plus Sun afternoons. Situation at the end of the fish quay.

{OPEN} *11am–11pm Mon–Sat; 12–10.30pm Sun.*

The Old Mill House

Mill Hill, Polperro PL13 2RP
☎ *(01503) 272362* Anne Peacock

 Sharp's Eden Ale, Special and Cornish Coaster always available.

White-painted, cottage-style pub with a nautical theme. Food available at lunchtimes from 12pm and from 7pm in the evening. Pool table. Log fire in winter. Children not allowed in bar area. Car parking for residents only. Garden.

{OPEN} *Summer: 11am–11pm (10.30pm Sun); Winter: 12–11pm (10.30pm Sun).*

Cornish Real Ale

Coaster
SHARP'S
Traditional
Cask Conditioned Ale
3.6%
ABV
Sharp's Brewery
Rock

PORT GAVERNE

Port Gaverne Inn
Port Gaverne PL29 3SQ
☎ *(01208) 880244* Mrs Hopehill

Sharp's Doom Bar Bitter and Cornish Coaster permanently available, plus one guest, such as Greene King Abbot or Fuller's London Pride.

Sixteenth-century hotel and bar 100 yards from the sea. Restaurant open in evenings, bar food also served during the day. Garden, car park. Accommodation available (17 rooms and 9 cottages/flats). Children allowed in garden and designated areas.

OPEN 11am–2.30pm and 6–11pm Mon–Thurs; 11am–11pm Fri–Sat; 12–10.30pm Sun. All day Easter and throughout summer.

PORTHALLOW

The Five Pilchards
Porthallow, St Keverne, Helston TR12 6PP
☎ *(01326) 280256* Brandon Flynn

A four-pump freehouse with Greene King Abbot Ale and Sharp's Own always available. Two guests, changed fortnightly, might include favourites Skinner's or Sharp's.

An old Cornish seafaring pub, with new conservatory featuring a waterfall. Interesting dispay of ship's accessories, including figure heads, binnacles and telegraphs, plus ship models. Food served lunchtimes and evenings – separate dining area available. Juicing machine which juices whole oranges. Children allowed.

OPEN 12–2.30pm and 6–11pm.

PORTHLEVEN

Atlantic Inn
Peverell Terrace, Porthleven, Helston TR13 9DZ
☎ *(01326) 562439* Leigh and Adrian Santi

A freehouse, with Skinner's ales such as Figgy's Brew and Coastliner regularly featured.

A traditional seaside pub in a village location (signposted), with live entertainment every Saturday. Food served lunchtimes and evenings from an extensive menu, reasonably priced. Children allowed.

OPEN 12–11pm (10.30pm Sun).

PORTREATH

Basset Arms
Tregea Terrace, Portreath TR16 4NS
☎ *(01209) 842277* Craig Moss and Don Reece

Sharp's Doom Bar and Marston's Pedigree regularly available.

Warm and friendly pub situated directly opposite Portreath Bay. Food served 12–2pm and 6.30–9.30pm. Car park. Children's play area.

OPEN Summer: 11.30am–11pm Mon–Sat; 12–10.30pm Sun. Winter: 11.30am– 2.30pm and 6–11pm Mon–Sat; 12–2.30pm and 7–10.30pm Sun.

QUINTRELL DOWNS

The Two Clomes
East Road, Quintrell Downs, Nr Newquay TR8 4PD
☎ *(01637) 871163* Kath/Frank

Approx 100 guest beers per year, three or four at any one time. Beers from Exmoor, Otter, Sharp's Fuller's, Cains and Four Rivers breweries all favoured.

A converted and extended old farm cottage built from Cornish stone with a beer garden and 48-seater restaurant. Open log fires in winter. Bar food available at lunchtime and evenings. Car park. Take the A392 from Newquay to Quintrell Downs, straight on at the roundabout, then second right.

OPEN 12–3pm and 7–11pm (10.30pm Sun).

ST CLEER

The Stag Inn
Fore Street, St Cleer, Liskeard PL14 5DA
☎ *(01579) 342305* Pam Dawson

A seven-pump freehouse, with Sharp's Own, Greene King Abbot and something from Skinner's always available, plus guest ales changed weekly.

A seventeenth-century pub with TV and non-smoking dining area. Food at lunchtimes and evenings. Well-behaved children welcome. En-suite accommodation. Close to the Eden Project.

OPEN 12–11pm (10.30pm Sun).

ST COLUMB

The Queen & Railway Inn
St Columb Road, St Columb TR9 6QR
☎ *(01726) 860343* Mrs Barnes

 Two weekly changing guests are on offer at this freehouse. Regular favourites include beers from Cotleigh, Keltek, Castle and other local breweries. Cotleigh Peregrine, plus Scattor Rock and Orkney brews, have also been featured.

Traditional village pub with open fire, one bar and patio. No food. Pool, darts, juke box. Car park. Children allowed in the early evening only.

OPEN *12–(variable closing time in afternoon) and 7pm–11pm (10.30pm Sun).*

ST JUST

The King's Arms
Market Square, St Just, Penzance TR19 7HF
☎ *(01736) 788545* Jan McCall

 A St Austell Brewery tied house with Tinners and Tribute always on offer, plus HSD when available, and seasonal St Austell ales. Cask Marque awarded.

A fourteenth-century cosy pub with family atmosphere. One bar with lots of nooks and crannies, low ceilings, open fires. Outside seating at the front, parking on the square. Occasional live music weekly in summer, free weekly quiz night. Food available lunchtimes and evenings. Children and dogs welcome.

OPEN *11am–11pm Mon–Sat; 12–10.30pm Sun. Plus early opening for breakfast in summer.*

The Star Inn
1 Fore Street, St Just, Penzance TR19 7LL
☎ *(01736) 788767* Peter and Rosie Angwin

 A St Austell house with HSD, Tinners, Black Prince and Dartmoor permanently available.

Old mining pub with a horseshoe bar and artefacts on the walls. Bar food available at lunchtimes all year round, and in the evenings in summer. Children welcome, children's room provided. Beer garden with outside seating.

OPEN *11am–11pm Mon–Sat; 12–10.30pm Sun.*

STRATTON

King's Arms
Howell's Road, Stratton, Bude EX23 9BX
☎ *(01288) 352396* Steven Peake

 A seventeenth-century freehouse serving Sharp's Own and Doom Bar Bitter and Exmoor Ale. Two guests are changed weekly. Traditional cider served during the summer season.

A traditional pub with TV and sports coverage. Quality, value-for-money bar meals served 12–2pm and 6.30–9pm, including a very popular Sunday lunch. Well-behaved children and nice dogs are welcome. Ten minutes' drive from beautiful beaches and rugged coastal walks. Accommodation.

OPEN *12–2pm and 6.30–11pm Mon–Thurs; 11am–11pm Fri–Sat; 12–10.30pm Sun.*

TREBARWITH

The Mill House Inn
Trebarwith, Tintagel PL34 0HD
☎ *(01840) 770200* Chrissy and Lee

 Eight beers available including Sharp's Own and Doom Bar Bitter. Guest ales served in summer.

A sixteenth-century mill over a trout stream, set in seven acres of woodland half a mile from the sea. Bar and restaurant food available at lunchtime and evenings, featuring excellent cuisine in an informal atmosphere. Car park, garden and terrace. Accommodation. Children welcome. Website: www.themillhouseinn.co.uk.

OPEN *11am–11pm.*

TREGREHAN

The Britannia Inn
Tregrehan Par, Tregrehan PL24 2SL
☎ *(01726) 812889* Richard Rogers

This seven-pump freehouse serves Sharp's Own, Fuller's London Pride, Morland Old Speckled Hen and Greene King Abbot Ale. A guest beer is changed twice weekly. Regulars include Marston's Pedigree and Fuller's ESB.

An eating house with two separate bars; one tends towards the young, the other towards eating. Food served at lunchtime and evenings. Children allowed in the dining area

OPEN *11am–11pm Mon–Sat; 12–10.30pm Sun.*

TRESPARRETT

The Horseshoe Inn
Tresparrett, Camelford PL32 9ST
☎ *(01840) 261240* Mr Kirby

 Sutton's Knickerdroppa Glory and Hospice (brewed especially for The Horseshoe Inn by Sutton Brewery) always available, plus up to four more including others from Sutton's.

A one-bar country pub situated in walking country. Separate dining area, outside seating, food served lunchtime and evening. Six darts teams and two pool teams. Children allowed. Located off the A39.

OPEN *12–3pm and 6.30–11pm (10.30pm Sun).*

TREVAUNANCE COVE

Driftwood Spars Hotel and Driftwood Brewery
Quay Road, Trevaunance Cove, St Agnes TR5 0RT
☎ *(01872) 552428* Jill and Gordon Treleaven

 Six ales always available. Home brew Cuckoo Ale permanently served, plus Sharp's Own and a Hicks or Skinner's ale. Guests are regularly from Skinner's but could also be from any independent brewery.

Built in 1660 as a tin mining chandlery/warehouse, this three-bar pub is situated a stone's throw from the sea, with attractive sea views. Food available all day in summer with Sunday carveries. Children and dogs allowed. Accommodation. Once you are in St Agnes, bear right at the church, go down a steep hill and turn sharp left. Website: www.driftwoodspars.com.

 CUCKOO ALE 4.7% ABV
Plans to produce two new brews shortly.

OPEN *11am–11pm Sun–Thurs; 11am–midnight Fri–Sat.*

TRURO

The Old Ale House
7 Quay Street, Truro TR1 2HD
☎ *(01872) 271122* Mark and Bev Jones

 A house ale brewed by the local Skinner's brewery, Kiddlywink, is permanently available, plus a range of guest ales served straight from the barrel. Regulars include Wadworth 6X, Sharp's Own, Exmoor Stag and Gold, Cotleigh Tawny and Old Buzzard, Fuller's London Pride and Shepherd Neame Spitfire.

An olde-worlde pub in the town centre with old furniture and free peanuts. *The Good Pub Guide* Beer Pub of the Year 2000. Bar food available at lunchtime and evenings with skillets and hands of bread a speciality. Live music twice a week. Children welcome.

OPEN *11am–11pm Mon–Sat; 12–10.30pm Sun.*

WIDEMOUTH BAY

The Bayview Inn
Marine Drive, Widemouth Bay, Bude EX23 0AW
☎ *(01288) 361273*
M Gooder (Licensee)/D Kitchener (Manager)

 A freehouse with Sharp's Own and Sharp's Doom Bar always available, as is Skinner's Kitch's Klassic (exclusive to this pub). One constantly changing guest also served, usually from Skinner's (Betty Stogs, Cornish Knocker, Skilliwidden), but also from Otter, Exmoor, Cotleigh, Cottage or St Austell. Cask-conditioned cider also available.

A traditional old-style seaside pub decorated with the pump clips of beers past! Two bars, garden, children's play area, large car park. Food available at lunchtimes from 12–2.30pm and evenings from 6–9pm. Dining and family room. Accommodation with stunning views of the sea. Children allowed.

OPEN *June–Sept 11am–11pm (10.30pm Sun); Oct–May 12–3pm and 6–11pm (10.30pm Sun).*

ZELAH

Hawkins Arms
High Road, Zelah, Truro TR4 9HU
☎ *(01872) 540339* Stuart Lomas

 A freehouse with seven pumps. Guests change regularly.

A one-bar country-style pub with non-smoking area and beer garden. Food served at lunchtime and evenings. Children allowed. Large car park. Accommodation.

OPEN *11am–3pm and 6–11pm Mon–Sat; 12–3pm and 7–10.30pm Sun.*

ZENNOR

The Tinners Arms
Zennor, St Ives TR27 3BY
☎ *(01736) 796927* David Care

 Sharp's Cornish Coaster is always available, plus two guests, including Sharp's seasonal ales.

Family-run pub in a lovely fourteenth-century building, with stone floor, beams and open fires. Function room is used as a family room in bad weather in summer. Food served. Large garden with tables overlooking coastline. Occasional live music. Children allowed, but not in the main bar. Offers sealed polykeg carry-out service. Follow the Wayside Museum signs.

OPEN *Easter–Sept: 11am–11pm Mon–Sat; 12–10.30pm Sun. Winter: opening times vary.*

Places Featured:

Allonby
Ambleside
Appleby
Barngates
Broughton in Furness
Carlisle
Cartmel
Cockermouth
Coniston
Curthwaite
Dent
Elterwater
Foxfield
Grasmere
Great Corby
Great Langdale

Hayton
Hesket Newmarket
Holmes Green
Ings
Ireby
Kendal
Kirkby Lonsdale
Kirksanton
Lanercost
Nether Wasdale
Silloth
Strawberry Bank
Tirril
Troutbeck
Wasdale Head
Winton

THE BREWERIES

DENT BREWERY

Hollins, Cowgill, Dent LA10 5TQ
☎ *(01539) 625326*
www.dentbrewery.co.uk

 BITTER 3.7% ABV
Mild hop flavour and slightly sweet.
AVIATOR 4.0% ABV
Full, rounded hop flavour.
RAMSBOTTOM STRONG ALE 4.5% ABV
Medium-dark, caramel flavour, hop balance.
KAMIKAZE 5.0% ABV
Very pale, good hop flavour and creamy maltiness.
T'OWD TUP 6.0% ABV
Powerful stout. Roast barley, bite and softness.
Plus monthly brews.

DERWENT BREWERY

*Units 2a–2b, Station Road Indutrial Estate,
Silloth CA5 4AG*
☎ *(01697) 331522*

 CARLISLE STATE BITTER 3.7% ABV
PARSON'S PLEDGE 4.0% ABV
TEACHERS PET 4.3% ABV
WHITWELL & MARK PALE ALE 4.4% ABV
BILL MONK 4.5% ABV
Plus occasional brews.

HESKET NEWMARKET BREWERY

Old Crown Barn, Hesket Newmarket CA7 8JG
☎ *(01697) 478066*
www.bdksol.demon.co.uk/hesket

 GREAT COCKUP PORTER 3.0% ABV
Dark, smooth and malty.
BLENCATHRA BITTER 3.2% ABV
Ruby-coloured and hoppy.
SKIDDAW SPECIAL BITTER 3.7% ABV
Gold-coloured and full-flavoured.
HELVELLYN GOLD 4.0% ABV
Straw coloured and hoppy.
DORIS'S 90TH BIRTHDAY ALE 4.3% ABV
Full-flavoured, with fruit throughout.
KERN KNOTT'S CRACK-ING STOUT 5.0% ABV
CATBELLS PALE ALE 5.1% ABV
Refreshing, easy quaffing brew.
OLD CARROCK STRONG ALE 5.6% ABV
Rich, smooth and strong.

JENNINGS BROS PLC

The Castle Brewery, Cockermouth CA13 9NE
☎ *(01900) 823214*
www.jenningsbrewery.co.uk

BITTER 3.5% ABV
Dark bitter. Nutty and mellow, with malt.
OLD SMOOTHY 3.5% ABV
CUMBERLAND ALE 4.0% ABV
Gold-coloured, rich and smooth.
CRAG RAT 4.3% ABV
Golden coloured bitter.
CROSS BUTTOCK ALE 4.5% ABV
Malty autumn ale.
COCKER HOOP 4.6% ABV
A well-hopped premium bitter.
SNECK LIFTER 5.1% ABV
Robust and slightly sweet.
LA'AL COCKLE WARMER 6.5% ABV
Smooth, Christmas brew.

THE PUBS

ALLONBY

Ship Hotel

Main Street, Allonby CA15 6QF
☎ *(01900) 881017* Steve and Valarie Ward

Yates Bitter and Premium always available, plus Yates seasonal ale (Winter, Summer, Spring or Autumn Fever).

Overlooking Solway Firth, a 300-year-old hotel with considerable history. Home-cooked bar meals served at lunchtime 12–3pm and evenings 6–11pm, Sun 6–10.30pm (no food on Mondays during winter). Car park, accommodation. Dogs welcome.

OPEN *12–3pm and 7–11pm (10.30pm Sun). Closed Monday lunch in winter.*

AMBLESIDE

Queens Hotel

Market Place, Ambleside LA22 9BU
☎ *(015394) 32206* Mr Bessey

A freehouse with Jennings Bitter always available. Two constantly changing guests from a mixture of nationals and independents, with Coniston Bluebird and Old Man Ale, Black Sheep and Yates Bitter regularly offered.

A centrally situated, Victorian-style pub, with two traditional bars. Food available 12–9.30pm daily. Smoking and non-smoking areas, and à la carte restaurant. Children welcome.

OPEN *11am–11pm Mon–Sat; 12–10.30pm Sun.*

APPLEBY

The Royal Oak Inn

Bongate, Appleby CA16 6UB
☎ *(017683) 51463* Tim and Jo Collins

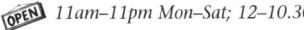Black Sheep Bitter is among those beers permanently available, plus 50 guests per year, including such ales as Thwaites Lancaster Bomber and Charles Wells Summer Solstice. Well-chosen range of wines and malt whiskies for non-beer drinkers!

A long white-washed building, roughly 400 years old with lots of character. Bar snacks are available 12–2.30pm, and food from the à la carte menu is served 12–2.30pm and 6–9pm. Large non-smoking dining room and outside terrace. Children welcome. Nine letting rooms. On the B6542 just outside Appleby town centre.

OPEN *11am–11pm Mon–Sat; 12–10.30pm Sun.*

BARNGATES

The Drunken Duck Inn

Barngates, Ambleside LA22 0NG
☎ *(015394) 36347* Stephanie Barton

The home of the Barngates brewery, with Cracker Ale, Tag Lag, Chester's Strong & Ugly plus Jennings Bitter.

Delightful 400-year-old inn, set in beautiful countryside and oozing olde-worlde charm. Tempting restaurant and modern, stylish accommodation. Amusing story behind the pub name – ask the landlady! Food available 12–2.30pm and 6–9pm. Car park. Children are welcome, but there are no special facilities.

CRACKER ALE 3.9% ABV
Delicate quenching hoppiness with balancing malt.

TAG LAG 4.4% ABV
Pale and fruity with good bitterness.

CHESTER'S STRONG & UGLY 4.9% ABV
Rounded and flavoursome.

OPEN *11.30am–11pm Mon–Sat; 12–10.30pm Sun.*

BROUGHTON IN FURNESS

The Manor Arms

The Square, Broughton in Furness LA20 6HY
☎ *(01229) 716286* David and Scott Varty

Seven well-kept real ales available including 160 guest beers per year from small breweries. New brews, winter warmers – you name it, they have served it!

Eighteenth-century traditional family-run freehouse with a welcoming atmosphere. Regular CAMRA pub of the year award-winner. Bar snacks available all day. Parking and outside seats overlooking a picturesque market square. En-suite accommodation. Children allowed.

OPEN *12–11pm (10.30pm Sun).*

CARLISLE

Fox & Pheasant

Armathwaite, Carlisle CA4 9PY
☎ *(01697) 472400* Mr A Glass

Jennings Bitter and Sneck Lifter always available, plus three guest, often from local Cumbrian breweries.

A seventeenth-century coaching inn with log fires, overlooking the River Eden, in a small village. Outside seating. Food served at lunchtime and evenings in a separate dining area. Children allowed.

OPEN *11am–11pm Mon–Sat; 12–10.30pm Sun.*

Woodrow Wilsons

48 Botchergate, Carlisle CA1 4RG
☎ *(01228) 819942*
Richard Archibald (Manager)

 A Wetherspoon's pub with Greene King Abbot, Derwent Carlisle State Bitter, Thwaites Mild and Shepherd Neame Spitfire always available. Two guests are changed every few days, and may include Hop Back Summer Lightning, Timothy Taylor Landlord or Cotleigh Osprey.

Typical Wetherspoon's town-centre pub in a stone-fronted building. Food available all day. Children not allowed.

OPEN *11am–11pm Mon–Sat; 12–10.30pm Sun.*

CARTMEL

Cavendish Arms

Cavendish Street, Cartmel LA11 6QA
☎ *(01539) 536240* Paul and Sandra Lester

 Marston's Pedigree and Charles Wells Bombardier permanently available, plus two guests in summer which could be any cask-conditioned real ale.

A food-oriented coaching inn, 500 years old, offering bar and restaurant food at lunchtime and evenings. Car park, dining room, non-smoking room, accommodation. Children not allowed in the restaurant during the evenings. For further details visit the website: www.thecavendisharms.co.uk.

OPEN *11am–11pm Mon–Sat; 12–10pm Sun.*

COCKERMOUTH

The Bitter End

15 Kirkgate, Cockermouth CA13 9PJ
☎ *(01900) 828993* Susan Askey

Bitter End Cockersnoot is always available in this freehouse and brewpub, along with four guests, changed weekly, which often include Yates Bitter, Coniston Bluebird, Isle of Skye Red Cuillin or Hesket Newmarket Doris's 90th Birthday Ale. Other home brews when available.

A very traditional pub with background music, non-smoking area at lunchtimes. Food served at lunchtime and evenings. Children allowed.

COCKERSNOOT 3.8% ABV
A golden, clean, refreshing beer.
CUDDY LUGS 4.3% ABV
Strong hop aroma with a dry aftertaste.
SKINNER'S OLD STRONG 5.5%
A rich amber beer, sweet and fruity.

OPEN *11.30am–2.30pm and 6–11pm Mon–Thurs; 11.30am–3pm and 6–11pm Fri–Sat; 11.30am–3pm and 7–10.30pm Sun.*

The Bush

Main Street, Cockermouth CA13 9JS
☎ *(01900) 822064* Maureen Williamson

 A Jennings house with 9 hand pumps. The full Jennings range is always on offer, and the one guest could be any local ale.

A very homely pub with open fires. Food served at lunchtime only. Children allowed.

OPEN *11am–11pm Mon–Sat; 12–10.30pm Sun.*

CONISTON

The Black Bull

Yewdale Road, Coniston LA21 8DU
☎ *(01539) 441335*
Ronald Edward Bradley

A seven-pump freehouse and brewpub, with the Coniston Brewery at the rear of the pub. Always available are Coniston Bluebird and Old Man Ale. Specials include Coniston Opium and Blacksmith's Ale. Guests are rotated on two pumps and changed fortnightly: regulars are Moorhouse's Black Cat, also Saxons Scrumpy Cider. Other guests are all from small independent and micro-breweries.

A sixteenth-century coaching inn in the centre of Coniston, with oak beams and log fire. No juke box or fruit machines. Outside seating area. Separate restaurant. Food served all day. Children allowed.

BLUEBIRD BITTER 3.6% ABV
A session ale. Champion Best Bitter 1998. Also available as bottle-conditioned at 4.2%.
OPIUM 4.0% ABV
A seasonal autumn brew. Dark amber, malty ale.
BLUEBIRD XB 4.2% ABV
A lighter ale brewed with wheat and American hops.
OLD MAN ALE 4.4% ABV
Dark and ruby-coloured.
BLACKSMITH'S ALE 5.0% ABV
A seasonal Christmas brew. Winter warmer.

OPEN *11am–11pm Mon–Sat; 12–10.30pm Sun.*

The Sun Hotel and 16th Century Inn

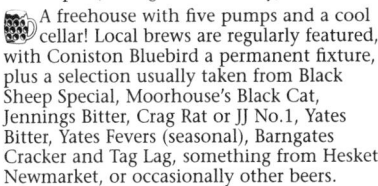

Coniston LA21 8HQ
☎ (01539) 441248
Alan Piper (Manager Keith Brady)

 A freehouse with five pumps and a cool cellar! Local brews are regularly featured, with Coniston Bluebird a permanent fixture, plus a selection usually taken from Black Sheep Special, Moorhouse's Black Cat, Jennings Bitter, Crag Rat or JJ No.1, Yates Bitter, Yates Fevers (seasonal), Barngates Cracker and Tag Lag, something from Hesket Newmarket, or occasionally other beers.

This sixteenth-century pub has a nineteenth-century hotel attached, accommodating 25 people in recently refurbished bedrooms. Situated on rising ground to overlook the village and enjoying excellent mountain views. One bar, a new conservatory and terrace overlooking the beer garden, outside seating at front, side, rear and in garden. Food from à la carte menu and specials board served lunchtimes and evenings in the conservatory restaurant and bar; the wine list has 40 wines. Children and dogs welcome. Situated on the hill leading up to the Old Man of Coniston, 100 yards above Coniston village, turn left at the bridge.

OPEN *11am–11pm (10.30pm Sun).*

CURTHWAITE

The Royal Oak

Curthwaite, Wigton CA7 8BG
☎ (01228) 710219 Mr McQueen

 Derwent Carlisle State Bitter is always on offer, as well as two guest beers.

Seventeenth-century country pub with non-smoking restaurant. Darts. Children allowed.

OPEN *12–2.30pm and 7–11pm (10.30pm Sun); 11am–11pm Sat.*

DENT

The George & Dragon

Main Street, Dent LA10 5QL
☎ (01539) 625256 Mrs Dorothy Goad

 Owned by Dent Brewery, with Dent beers always available.

A country pub, with accommodation. Food served lunchtimes and evenings, separate dining area. Children and dogs allowed. Ten miles from junction 37 of the M6.

OPEN *Summer: 11am–11pm; closed afternoons in winter.*

The Sun Inn

Main Street, Dent LA10 5QL
☎ (01539) 625208 Martin Stafford

 Owned by Dent Brewery. Five Dent brews always available.

A traditional country pub in the cobbled main street. Friendly atmosphere, large beer garden, pool room, non-smoking dining area. Food served lunchtimes throughout the year and evenings (summertime only). Children allowed till 9pm.

OPEN *Winter: 12–2pm and 7–11pm Mon–Fri; 11am–11pm Sat; 12–10.30pm Sun. Summer: 11am–11pm Mon–Sat; 12–10.30pm Sun.*

ELTERWATER

Britannia Inn

Elterwater, Ambleside LA22 9HP
☎ (01539) 437210 Clare Woodhead

A freehouse with Jennings Bitter, Coniston Bluebird and Dent Aviator always on the menu, plus two guests changed frequently.

A country inn with quiz nights on Sundays. Food served lunchtimes and evenings, plus snacks all afternoon. Separate dining area. Large outside seating area. Accommodation. Children and dogs allowed.

OPEN *11am–11pm Mon–Sat; 12–10.30pm Sun.*

FOXFIELD

The Prince of Wales

Foxfield, Broughton in Furness LA20 6BX
☎ (01229) 716238 Stuart Johnson

The home of the Foxfield Brewery. Four to six hand pumps dispense a constantly changing range of beers – over 1,000 different ales sold in the last four years. There is usually a mild and something from Tigertops or Foxfield breweries available. Set up by Stuart and Lynda Johnson of the Tigertops brewery in Wakefield, both breweries brew experimental and varied beer styles. The range in pub and brewery is constantly changing.

A 'no-frills' real ale house, for real ale lovers. Home-made snacks served 12–7pm Fri–Sun. Car park. Bed and breakfast available. Located opposite Foxfield station. Website: www.drink.to/foxfieldbrewery.

OPEN *5–11pm Wed–Thurs; 12–11pm Fri–Sat; 12–10.30pm Sun; closed Mon–Tues.*

GRASMERE

The Traveller's Rest Inn

Grasmere, LA22 9RR
☎ *(01539) 435604* Graham Sweeney

A pub owned by a family of dedicated beer sellers, with four real ales offered at any one time. Always available are Jennings Bitter, Cumberland and Sneck Lifter, and the one guest ale might be Black Sheep Bitter, Coniston Bluebird or another beer from an independent brewery.

A sixteenth-century inn. One bar, beer garden, games room, bed and breakfast (en-suite accommodation). Food served from 12–3pm and 6–9.30pm (winter); 12–9.30pm (summer). Smoking dining area and non-smoking restaurant. Families welcome. Half a mile north of Grasmere village, on A591.

 11am–11pm Mon–Sat; 12–10.30pm Sun.

GREAT CORBY

The Corby Bridge Inn

Great Corby, Carlisle CA4 8LL
☎ *(01228) 560221* Barbara Griffiths

Thwaites Bitter and Mild always available plus a rotating guest, changed at least twice a week, often including Nethergate Old Growler, Charles Wells Bombardier, Fuller's London Pride, Timothy Taylor Landlord, Badger Tanglefoot or a Wychwood brew.

A freehouse built in 1838. Originally a railway hotel. Grade II listed. Approximately four miles from junction 43 of M6. One bar, pool and darts room and non-smoking dining area. Large garden, games area, accommodation. Food served all day Tues–Sun and Bank Holiday Mondays. Well-behaved children welcome.

 12–11pm (10.30pm Sun).

GREAT LANGDALE

Old Dungeon Ghyll Hotel

Great Langdale, Ambleside LA22 9JY
☎ *(01539) 437272* Neil and Jane Walmsley

Seven real ales and scrumpy available in this freehouse. Yates Bitter and Jennings Cumberland Ale always present. Three guests are changed regularly, one barrel at a time. Black Sheep Special is popular.

An interesting National Trust-owned, listed building with real fire. Food served at lunchtime (12–2pm) and evenings (6–9pm). Children allowed.

 11am–11pm Mon–Sat; 12–10.30pm Sun.

HAYTON

Stone Inn

Hayton, Brampton, Nr Carlisle CA8 9HR
☎ *(01228) 670498* Johnnie and Susan Tranter

Four beers from Jennings and Thwaites permanently available plus occasional guest beers, as available.

A traditional village pub. Toasted sandwiches available all day, though the focus is on beer rather than food. There are function facilities, and coach parties can be catered for if booked in advance. The pub has a car park, and is situated seven minutes east of M6 junction 43, just off the A69.

 11am–3pm and 5.30–11pm.

HESKET NEWMARKET

The Old Crown

Hesket Newmarket, Caldbeck, Wigton CA7 8JG
☎ *(01697) 478288* Kim Matthews

A freehouse, but concentrating on the Hesket Newmarket brews, with the brewery situated close by. Old Carrock Strong Ale, Skiddaw Special, Catbells Pale Ale, Doris's 90th Birthday Ale, Pigs Might Fly, Kern Knott's Crack(ing) Stout, Blencathra Bitter and Great Cockup Porter are always on the menu. A guest is changed once a month. Regulars include Coniston Bluebird and Timothy Taylor Landlord.

A small, old-fashioned pub, with two bars. Food served at lunchtime and evenings. Children allowed. On the edge of the Lake District National Park, the only pub in the village.

 5.30–11pm Mon; 12–2.30pm and 5.30–11pm Tues–Sat; 12–2.30pm and 7–10.30pm Sun.

HOLMES GREEN

Black Dog Inn

Broughton Road, Holmes Green, Dalton-in-Furness LA15 8JP
☎ *(01229) 462561* Jack Taylor

A freehouse with Coniston Bluebird and Butterknowle Bitter always available. Five guests might include favourites such as Wye Valley Hereford Pale Ale or York Yorkshire Terrier.

An old country inn half a mile from South Lakes Wildlife Park. Dining area. Food served all day. Children allowed.

 11am–11pm Mon–Sat; 12–10.30pm Sun.

INGS

The Watermill Inn

Ings, Nr Staveley, Kendal LA8 9PY
☎ *(01539) 821309*
AF and B Coulthwaite

 JW Lees Moonraker is among those beers always available, plus up to 15 guest beers (500 per year) which may come from the Hop Back, Cotleigh, Ridleys, Shepherd Neame, Exmoor, Ash Vine, Summerskills, Black Sheep, Coach House, Yates and Wadworth breweries.

Formerly a wood mill, now a traditional, family-run pub full of character with log fires, brasses and beams and a relaxing atmosphere. Two bars. No juke box or games machines. Many times winner of Westmorland Pub of the Year. Bar food at lunchtime and evenings. Car park, garden, seats and tables by the river. Disabled toilets. Children allowed. Accommodation. From the M6, junction 36, follow the A591 towards Windermere. One mile past the second turning for Staveley. Turn left after the garage, before the church.

OPEN *12–11pm (10.30pm Sun).*

IREBY

The Lion

The Square, Ireby, Carlisle CA5 1EA
☎ *(01697) 371460*
Peter Boulton and Karen Spencer

A four-pump freehouse offering Bateman XB, Titanic Premium and Marston's Pedigree, plus one guest, usually from Yates or Hesket Newmarket.

This freehouse was the area's first Irish pub in the late 1980s. Café bar, with traditional oak panels, open fire and wooden floor. Back bar/games room for pool and darts. Food served at lunchtimes, and at lunchtimes and evenings at weekends. Children allowed.

OPEN *5.30–11pm Mon–Fri; 12–3pm and 6–11pm Sat; 12–3pm and 7–10.30pm Sun.*

KENDAL

Burgundy's Wine Bar

19 Lowther Street, Kendal LA9 4DH
☎ *(01539) 733803* Mr Pennington

 A freehouse with Yates Bitter and Kendal Pale Ale permanently featured, plus two guests, changed every three days, usually from local breweries, but sometimes including Timothy Taylor Landlord. Auld Kendal, a beer exclusive to the pub, is also served.

Traditional town pub, built around 1870. Food available. Occasional live music. Children allowed. Situated next to the Town Hall.

OPEN *6.30–11pm Mon; 11am–3.30pm and 6.30–11pm Tues–Sat; 12–3.30pm and 7–10.30pm Sun.*

Ring o' Bells

39 Kirkland, Kendal LA9 5AF
☎ *(01539) 720326* Tony Bibby

 One weekly-changing guest always served from a range of 11, including Bateman XB, Jennings Cumberland, Marston's Pedigree, Brains SA and Adnams Broadside.

An unspoilt seventeenth-century pub in the grounds of the parish church. Bar food available at lunchtime and evenings. Parking. Children allowed. Accommodation. Take M6 junction 36, then follow the A590 and A591 to the A6 in Kendal.

OPEN *12–3pm and 6–11pm Mon–Sat; usual hours Sun.*

KIRKBY LONSDALE

The Snooty Fox

Main Street, Kirkby Lonsdale LA6 2AH
☎ *(01524) 271308* Stuart Rickard

 A freehouse, with Timothy Taylor Landlord regularly available, plus a wide range of guest cask ales.

A seventeenth-century inn, with two bars, stonework and beams. Nine en-suite bedrooms. Food at lunchtime and evenings. Children allowed.

OPEN *11am–11pm Mon–Sat; 12–10.30pm Sun.*

KIRKSANTON

King William IV

Kirksanton, Nr Millom LA18 4NN
☎ *(01229) 772009* Pete and Karen Rodger

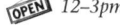 A freehouse with Jennings Cumberland Ale (@ £1.70) always available, with regular guest ales during the summer season.

A 200-year-old country pub with oak beams and real fires. Four letting rooms available for bed and breakfast. Non-smoking dining area. Food at lunchtime and evenings. Children allowed. On the main road from Millom to Whitehaven.

🅾 *12–3pm and 7–11pm.*

LANERCOST

Abbey Bridge Inn

Lanercost, Brampton CA8 2HG
☎ *(016977) 2224* Tim and Sue Hatt

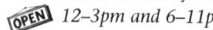 Traditional inn specialising in Cumbrian beers. Yates Bitter and Coniston Bluebird XB always available, plus up to two guests. Brews from Hesket Newmarket and Dent are frequently served.

F ormer temperance inn, recently refurbished, with two bars featuring stone slab floors and open fires. Food is available at lunchtime and evenings, and there is a non-smoking restaurant. Car park, outside seating, children and dogs allowed. Accommodation. Situated close to Hadrian's Wall, Lanercost Priory and riverbank.

🅾 *12–3pm and 6–11pm.*

NETHER WASDALE

The Screes Inn

Nether Wasdale, Seascale CA20 1ET
☎ *(01946) 726262*
Nick Putnam and Rachel Hughes

 A freehouse, with Yates and Black Sheep brews always available. Four guests, changed weekly, come from independents such as Dent.

A n eighteenth-century pub with split-level bar, separate dining area, small function room and five en-suite letting rooms. Magnificent views of the fells. Food served all day. Children allowed. Can be tricky to find. Ring for directions, if necessary.

🅾 *All day, every day (except Christmas Day).*

SILLOTH

The Golf Hotel

Criffel Street, Silloth CA7 4AB
☎ *(01697) 331438* Christine Previtali

 A freehouse with one Derwent brew always available.

A 22-room hotel and restaurant with one bar. Food served. Games machine. Children allowed.

🅾 *11am–11pm Mon–Sat; 12–10.30pm Sun.*

STRAWBERRY BANK

The Mason's Arms

Strawberry Bank, Cartmel Fell LA11 6NW
☎ *(01539) 568486* Mrs Walsh

 Five real ales always available, including Barnsley, Cumberland and Blackpool brews. Other guests are from all over the country, e.g. Young's, Okells and Yates. Good selection of fruit beers and bottle-conditioned beers. Hoegaarden and Budvar also available. The Strawberry Bank Brewery's unique Damson Beer is brewed seasonally, but is always on offer in bottles.

A rural freehouse set in the middle of nowhere! Slate floor and open fires. Terrace with 12 tables overlooking the valley. Self-catering studio apartments available. Homemade food served at lunchtime and evenings, with a good vegetarian and vegan selection. Children allowed.

🛢 **DAMSON BEER 7% ABV**
Brewed when fruit in season, but available all year round in bottles.

🅾 *11.30am–3pm and 6–11pm Mon–Fri; all day Sat–Sun.*

TIRRIL

The Queen's Head

Tirril CA10 2JF
☎ *(01768) 863219* Chris Thomlinson

Offers four house beers, plus one more on a guest pump.

A 300-year-old pub, once owned by William Wordsworth, situated on the B5320, with stone walls and beams. Two bars. The small village of Tirril once boasted two breweries, one being at this inn. It was closed in 1899, and reopened 100 years later in October 1999 by the present landlord, in an outhouse at the rear of the pub. There are plans to move the brewery to nearby Brougham Hall. The pub itself is a Cask Marque winner. Food served at lunchtime and evenings, with a separate dining area available. Cumbrian Beer and Sausage Festival held annually on second weekend of August. Children allowed. Websites: www.queensheadinn.co.uk and www.tirrilbrewery.co.uk.

🛢 **JOHN BEWSHER'S BEST BITTER 3.8% ABV**
BROUGHAM HALL ALE 3.9% ABV
CHARLES GOUGH OLD FAITHFUL 4.0% ABV
THOMAS SLEE'S ACADEMY ALE 4.2% ABV

🅾 *12–3pm and 6–11pm Mon–Fri; 12–11pm Sat; 12–10.30pm Sun.*

TROUTBECK

The Queen's Head Hotel

Troutbeck LA23 1PW
☎ *(01539) 432174* Mark Stewerdson

A freehouse with four guests, which change every few days, and which might include Coniston Bluebird, Old Man Ale, Burton Bridge Amazon or Great Northern.

A food-oriented pub and hotel, with nine rooms and seating area outside. Food served at lunchtime and evenings. Children allowed.

OPEN *11am–11pm (10.30pm Sun).*

WASDALE HEAD

Wasdale Head Inn

Wasdale Head, Nr Gosforth CA20 1EX
☎ *(01946) 726229* Howard Christie

Home of the Great Gable Brewery, with the brewery's own beers always available. Beers from other breweries, such as Jennings, Dent, Derwent, Coniston and Foxfield, are also regularly served.

A traditional pub with a beer garden, set in the Lake District National Park. Food served all day until 8.30pm. Children allowed (if on a lead!). Visit our website at: www.wasdale.com.

GABLE 3.7% ABV
A light, refreshing beer.
WRY'NOSE 4.0% ABV
A zesty, summer rye beer.
WASD'ALE 4.4% ABV
An old-fashioned, robust, flavoursome beer.

OPEN *11am–11pm Mon–Sat; 12–10.30pm Sun.*

WINTON

The Bay Horse Inn

Winton, Kirkby Stephen CA17 4HS
☎ *(01768) 371451* Derek Parvin

A freehouse offering four real ales, two rotated, and all hand-pulled from the cask. Black Sheep Bitter is always on offer. Varied guests, changed twice weekly, may include Coniston Bluebird or perhaps a Harviestoun brew.

A pub dating from the late 1600s, off the A685, two miles north of Kirkby Stephen. Lounge bar, panelled walls, beams, two open fires, flag floors. Public and lounge bars with central servery. Modern 50-seater dining area. Food served at lunchtime and evenings. Children allowed.

OPEN *12–2pm and 7–11pm Mon–Sun (closed Tues lunchtimes). More flexible in summer.*

YOU TELL US

∗ *The Slip Inn,* Barras, Kirkby Stephen

Places Featured:

Brampton
Buxworth
Chesterfield
Cromford
Dale Abbey
Derby
Fenny Bentley
Foolow
Glossop
Hope
Horsley Woodhouse
Ilkeston
Ilkeston Junction
Ingleby
Kirk Ireton
Kniveton
Makeney

Marsh Lane
Matlock
Melbourne
Ockbrook
Old Tupton
Over Haddon
Rowarth
Shardlow
Smalley
Staveley
Swinscoe
Ticknall
Tideswell
Wardlow Mires
Whaley Bridge
Whitehough
Woolley Moor

THE BREWERIES

LEADMILL BREWERY

Park Hall, Parkhall Road, Denby, Ripley DE5 8PX
☎ *(01332) 883577*

 INGOT 3.6% ABV
Single hop session beer.
WILD WEASEL 3.9% ABV
Pale, refreshing and malty.
ARC-LIGHT 4.2% ABV
Dry-hopped, pale and fruity.
ROLLING THUNDER 4.5% ABV
Full-flavoured with some sweetness.
SAIGON 4.5% ABV
Distinctive pale ale.
LINEBACKER 4.6% ABV
Flavoursome, with fruity hop finish.
RED RIVER 4.8% ABV
Full flavoured ruby red ale.
AGENT ORANGE 4.9% ABV
Balanced and hoppy with subtle honey tones.
FIREBIRD 5.0% ABV
Creamy red ale with a hint of blackcurrant.
NIAGARA 5.0% ABV
Malt flavour throughout and dry-hopped.
APOCALYPSE NOW 5.2% ABV
Inviting, well-balanced flavour with some fruit.

TOWNES BREWERY

Speedwell Inn, Lowgates, Staveley, Chesterfield S43 3TT
☎ *(01246) 472252*

 SPEEDWELL BITTER 3.9% ABV
A light, well-hopped and spicy session beer.
BEST LOCKOFORD BITTER 4.0% ABV
A full-bodied, well-balanced bitter beer.
IPA 4.5% ABV
A light, refreshing single-hopped pale ale.
PYNOT PORTER 4.5% ABV
Very dark and wholesome.
STAVELEYAN 4.8% ABV
A robust full-flavoured premium bitter.
Plus monthly brews covering a range of styles.

WHIM ALES

Whim Farm, Hartington, Buxton SK17 0AX
☎ *(01298) 84991*

 ARBOR LIGHT 3.6% ABV
Pale and easy drinking.
MAGIC MUSHROOM MILD 3.8% ABV
Very dark and flavoursome.
HARTINGTON BITTER 4.0% ABV
Pale and refreshing.
HARTINGTON IPA 4.5% ABV
Light and well-balanced.
Plus occasional brews.

THE PUBS

BRAMPTON

The Royal Oak
43 Chatsworth Road, Brampton, Chesterfield S40 2AH
☎ *(01246) 277854* Mr and Mrs M Mount

 A freehouse with Marston's Pedigree and Ruddles (Greene King) always available, plus two guests from local breweries, changed weekly. Other beers featured include Morland Old Speckled Hen, Charles Wells Bombadier and many more (500 per year).

A traditional local pub with timbers and open fire. Friendly staff and regulars of all ages. Live music three times a week, pool and darts. Beer festivals and annual music festival. Traditional pub lunches available. Car park, patio and children's play area.

OPEN *11am–11pm Mon–Sat; 12–10.30pm Sun.*

BUXWORTH

Navigation Inn
Bugsworth Canal Basin, Buxworth, High Peak SK23 7NE
☎ *(01663) 732072* Alan Hall

 A freehouse with Timothy Taylor Landlord and Marston's Pedigree always on the menu, plus regularly changing guest beers, including Abbeydale Moonshine, Greene King Abbot, and many others.

A 200-year-old stone inn on the site of a recently restored canal basin. Full of interesting memorabilia and canalwares. Separate restaurant, play area, pets' corner, games room and stone-floored snug. Website: www.navigationinn.co.uk.

OPEN *11am–11pm Mon–Sat; 12–10.30pm Sun.*

CHESTERFIELD

The Derby Tup
387 Sheffield Road, Whittington Moor, Chesterfield S41 8LS
☎ *(01246) 454316* Mr Hughes

 Black Sheep Bitter, Whim Hartington, Timothy Taylor Landlord, Marston's Pedigree and Greene King Abbot permanently available, plus four hand pumps serving a constantly changing range of guest real ales (500 per year).

Old and original, beamed with three rooms and open fires. Home-cooked food available 11am–2pm daily and 6–8pm Thurs–Sat; Thai, Indian and vegetarian food are specialities. Parking nearby, children allowed.

OPEN *11.30am–3pm and 5–11pm Mon–Sat; 12–4pm and 7–10.30pm Sun.*

The Market
95 New Square, Chesterfield S40 1AH
☎ *(01246) 273641* Keith Toone

 Marston's Pedigree and Greene King Abbot always available. Three guests may include Black Sheep Special, Hop Back Summer Lightning or Ushers Founders Ale.

A one-bar, market pub, with dining area in bar. Food served at lunchtime only. Children allowed in the dining area only and if eating.

OPEN *11am–11pm Mon–Sat; 7.30–10.30pm Sun.*

The Rutland Arms
23 Stephenson Place, Chesterfield S40 1XL
☎ *(01246) 205857* Paul Young

 Tied to Whitbread, serving four ales straight from the barrel and five on pumps. Castle Eden, Marston's Pedigree and Greene King Abbot are always on offer plus guests, changed every ten days, which often include Morland Old Speckled Hen, Bateman XXXB or Black Sheep Best.

Predominantly wooden interior, close to Chesterfield's famous crooked spire church. Non-smoking dining area away from the bar. Food served 11am–9pm Mon–Thurs and 11am–7pm Fri–Sun. No children.

OPEN *11am–11pm Mon–Sat; 12–10.30pm Sun.*

CROMFORD

The Boat Inn
Scarthin, Cromford, Matlock DE4 3QF
☎ *(01629) 823282*
Kevin White and Debbie White

 A freehouse with a Springhead ale and Marston's Pedigree always available plus all sorts of guests, from local microbreweries whenever possible.

A village pub built about 1772, near the market square. Two bars, log fires, beer garden. Regular music nights and pub quizzes, plus an annual beer festival. Bar snacks at lunchtime and evenings plus Sunday lunches. Children allowed. Dogs welcome.

OPEN *11.30am–3pm and 6–11pm Mon–Fri; all day Sat–Sun.*

DALE ABBEY

The Carpenters Arms

Dale Abbey, Ilkeston DE7 4PP
☎ *(0115) 932 5277* John Heraty

Tied to Punch Retail, with Marston's Pedigree and Adnams Bitter always available, plus two other beers from local and national breweries such as Charles Wells and Greene King.

A traditional village pub in picturesque walking country, family run for 70 years. Children's play area and beer garden, family room and large car park. Food served at lunchtimes and evenings. Children not allowed in bar. Three miles from junction 25 off the M1.

OPEN *12–3pm and 6–11pm (7–10.30pm Sun).*

DERBY

The Alexandra Hotel

203 Siddals Road, Derby DE1 2QE
☎ *(01332) 293993* Mark Robins

Bateman XB, Hook Norton Best Bitter and Timothy Taylor Landlord always available plus six guest beers (600 per year) with the emphasis firmly on new and rare micro-breweries. Also traditional cider.

B uilt as a coffee and chop house in 1865. Now trading as a comfortable award-winning pub decorated with a railway and brewery theme. Bar food at lunchtimes and evenings. Car park and garden. Three minutes' walk from Derby Midland Railway Station.

OPEN *11am–11pm Mon–Sat; 12–3pm and 7–10.30pm Sun.*

The Brunswick Inn

1 Railway Terrace, Derby DE1 2RU
☎ *(01332) 290677*

Fourteen pumps serve beer from all around the country, notably Marston's Pedigree and Timothy Taylor Landlord, plus five or six ales from the on-site brewery.

B uilt in 1841–2 as the first purpose-built railwaymen's pub in the world. The birthplace of the Railway Institute, an educational establishment for railway workers. It fell into dereliction in the early 1970s and trading ceased in April 1974. The Derbyshire Historic Buildings Trust started restoration work in 1981. The trust sold it to Trevor Harris, a local businessman, in May 1987. The pub reopened in October 1987 and the installation of the brewing plant followed in 1991. The first beer was produced on June 11 that year. Bar and restaurant food is available at lunchtime and on request in the evening. Parking, garden, children's room, non-smoking room, function room.

RECESSION ALE 3.3% ABV
MILD 3.7% ABV
TRIPLE HOP 4.0% ABV
SECOND BREW 4.2% ABV
RAILWAY PORTER 4.3% ABV
OLD ACCIDENTAL 5.0% ABV

OPEN *11am–11pm Mon–Sat; 12–10.30pm Sun.*

The Crompton Tavern

46 Crompton Street, Derby DE1 1NX
☎ *(01332) 733629* Mr and Mrs Bailey

Marston's Pedigree and Timothy Taylor Landlord always available plus four guest beers (200 per year) perhaps from Fuller's, Coach House, Kelham Island, Banks & Taylor or Burton Bridge breweries. A porter or stout is normally available.

A small pub just outside the city centre. Popular with locals and students. Cobs and sandwiches available daily. Car park and garden. Children allowed in garden.

OPEN *11am–11pm Mon–Sat; 12–10.30pm Sun.*

The Falstaff Brewery

74 Silver Hill Road, Derby DE23 6UJ
☎ *(01332) 342902* Adrian Parkes

Four real ales are permanently on offer. Greene King Abbot Ale is almost always on tap, as is Leatherbritches Hairy Helmet. Two other local beers are also available, one around 5% ABV and one 5.2% or above.

A friendly, 125-year-old former hotel tucked away in the back streets of Derby. One main bar serves three rooms. Real fire in lounge. Outside seating area. Children welcome. Wheelchair access if required. From the city, take the Normanton Road to the painted island, turn right, take the first available right, then the next right.

OPEN *12–11pm (10.30pm Sun).*

The Flowerpot
25 King Street, Derby DE1 3DZ
☎ *(012332) 204955* S Manners

 Marston's Pedigree and Timothy Taylor Landlord always available plus at least seven guest beers (500+ per year) from all over the United Kingdom.

A traditional friendly town pub with parts of the building dating from the late seventeenth century. Age range of regulars is 18 to 95. Ground-level cellar bar has a unique 'beer wall', through which customers can see ale being cared for and dispensed. Homemade bar food served at lunchtime through to evening. Garden area. Function suite with capacity for up to 250 people. Wheelchair access to all areas. Children welcome till 7.30pm. Car park 30 yards away. Situated on the A6 just off the inner ring road, 300 yards north of the Cathedral.

OPEN *11am–11pm Mon–Sat; 12–10.30pm Sun.*

The Friargate
114 Friargate, Derby DE1 1EX
☎ *(01332) 297065* Roger Myring

A freehouse serving Marston's Pedigree straight from the barrel plus up to eight others. Regulars come from Rooster's, Whim and Oakham breweries.

A quiet town pub with one main bar. Acoustic music on Wednesdays. Food served at lunchtime (not Sun). No children.

OPEN *11am–11pm Mon–Sat; 12–3pm and 7–10.30pm Sun.*

The Rowditch Inn
246 Uttoxeter New Road, Derby DE22 3LL
☎ *(01332) 343123* Mr Birkin

A freehouse with at least four real ales always available, including Marston's Pedigree and Hardys & Hansons Kimberley Classic and Kimberley Best Bitter, plus rotating guests.

A traditional beer house with one bar, non-smoking area, snug and beer garden. No food, no children. On the main road.

OPEN *12–2pm Thurs–Sun; 7–11pm daily (10.30pm Sun).*

The Smithfield
Meadow Road, Derby DE1 2BH
☎ *(01332) 370429* Roger and Penny Myring

A freehouse with Whim Hartington IPA and either Whim Arbor Light or Oakham JHB available, plus up to seven guests changing two or three times a week. Beers from Rooster's and Oakham regularly featured.

Traditional, friendly atmosphere. Lounge with open fire and pub games plus a family room. Food served 12–2pm only. Children allowed until 8pm. Ring for directions. Website: www.thesmithfield.co.uk.

OPEN *11am–11pm Mon–Sat; 12–10.30pm Sun.*

FENNY BENTLEY

The Bentley Brook Inn & Fenny's Restaurant
Fenny Bentley, Ashbourne DE6 1LF
☎ *(01335) 350278* Mrs Jeanne Allingham

Home to the Leatherbritches Craft Brewery and Leatherbritches Fine Food shop. Leatherbritches cask- and bottle-conditioned beers, brewed on site, are always available, plus Marston's Pedigree and occasional guest beers.

A traditional, family-run, country inn (AA 2 star) with large garden, children's play area and kitchen herb garden and nursery open to the public. Food served 12–9.30pm. Annual beer festival on bank holiday at end of May.

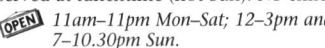 **GOLDINGS 3.6% ABV**
ASHBOURNE 4% ABV
BELTER 4.4% ABV
Light, golden with flowery hoppiness.
BELT N BRACES 4.4%
HAIRY HELMET 4.7% ABV
BESPOKE 5.0% ABV
Ruby-coloured and smooth.
Plus occasional brews.

OPEN *All day, every day.*

The Coach & Horses
Fenny Bentley DE6 1LB
☎ *(01335) 350246* John and Matthew Dawson

A family-run freehouse offering a continually changing range of award-winning cask ales. Marston's Pedigree always available, plus three guests, which may include Abbeydale Moonshine, Coniston Bluebird or Timothy Taylor Landlord.

A traditional seventeenth-century coaching inn with background music and beer garden. Food served every day at lunchtime and evenings. Children welcome.

OPEN *11am–3pm and 5–11pm Mon–Fri; 11am–11pm Sat; 12–10.30pm Sun.*

FOOLOW

The Bull's Head Inn
Foolow, Eyam, Hope Valley
☎ *(01433) 630873* Penelope Walker

Black Sheep Bitter and Shepherd Neame Spitfire are among the beers regularly available.

Claims to be the prettiest pub in the Peak District! Food available 12–2.30pm and 6.30–9pm. Children, dogs and muddy boots welcome. Three delightful en-suite bedrooms. Car park. Take the A623 through Stoney Middleton towards Chapel-en-le-Frith, turn right for Foolow.

OPEN *12–3pm and 6–11pm (10.30pm Sun).*

GLOSSOP

The Old Glove Works
Riverside Mill, George Street, Glossop SK13 8AY
☎ *(01457) 858432*

 Six ever-changing real ales always available, from breweries such as Wye Valley, Shaws, Abbeydale, Kelham Island and Whim Ales.

A grown-up environment, appealing to the over 25s. Food available 12–2pm Mon–Fri. Two outside riverside drinking areas. Live entertainment Thurs and Sun, resident DJ playing music from the 60s–80s Friday and Sat. For further information, visit www.thegloveworksglossop.com.

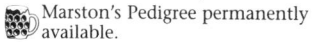 *12–8pm Mon–Wed; 12–11pm Thurs; 12pm–12am Fri–Sat (no admission after 10.45pm); 12–10.30pm Sun.*

HOPE

The Woodroffe Arms Hotel
1 Castleton Road, Hope, Hope Valley S33 6SB
☎ *(01433) 620351* Barry Thomson

 Marston's Pedigree permanently available.

A ttractive one-bar pub with traditional log fires, conservatory restaurant, outside seating and patio with swings for children. Food available every lunchtime and evening with £4.95 specials available Mon–Sat lunchtimes. Children allowed.

OPEN *11.30am–11pm Mon–Sat; 12–10.30pm Sun.*

HORSLEY WOODHOUSE

Old Oak Inn
176 Main Street, Horsley Woodhouse, Ilkeston DE7 6AW
☎ *(01332) 780672* Mr Hyde

 A freehouse with Marston's Pedigree and something from Mansfield always available. Two or three guest beers are offered each week (300 to date). Favourites include Everards Tiger and Morland Old Speckled Hen.

A village pub with background music and beer garden. No food. Children allowed.

OPEN *5.30–11pm Mon–Fri; 11am–11pm Sat; 12–10.30pm Sun.*

ILKESTON

Spring Cottage
1 Fulwood Street, Ilkeston DE7 8AZ
☎ *(0115) 932 3153* Mr Wootton

 Tied to Punch Taverns, with two guests changed daily, that may include Wadworth 6X, Morland Old Speckled Hen, Marston's Pedigree, Greene King Abbot Ale or Shepherd Neame Spitfire.

A traditional town pub with two bars and background music. Children's room. The lounge doubles as a dining area. Food at lunchtime and evenings. Children allowed. Near the main shopping area on one-way system.

OPEN *11am–3pm and 6–11pm Mon–Thur; 11am–4pm and 6–11pm Fri; 11am–5pm and 7–11pm Sat; 12–3pm and 7–10.30pm Sun.*

ILKESTON JUNCTION

The Dewdrop Inn
Station Street, Ilkeston Junction DE7 5TE
☎ *(0115) 9329684* Graham Sargerson (Sarge)

 Timothy Taylor Best plus Whim Hartington Bitter and IPA usually available, with guest beers from Mallard, Nottingham, Oldershaw, Glentworth, Wentworth, Abbeydale, Shardlow, Wye Valley, Burton Bridge, Ossett, Cottage, Brewsters, Broadstone, Kelham Island and Boggart Hole Clough breweries often served. Polish beers Okocim and Zywiec, plus Korenwolf bottled wheat beer also offered.

L arge, unspoilt Victorian pub dating from 1884, complete with ghost (moves things around – bottles, barrels etc!) Real fires in snug and lounge. Dart boards in snug and tap. Real juke box (free) in tap. Families welcome in snug. Food served at all times, with hot black pudding cobs a speciality. Three minutes from M1 (west on A610 from J26, first turning left to A6096 for one mile, then sharp left immediately after railway bridge). Website: www.eggpie.com.

OPEN *11.30am–2.30pm and 7–11pm Mon–Fri; 7–11pm Sat (closed lunchtime); 12–4.30pm and 7–10.30pm Sun.*

INGLEBY

John Thompson Inn
Ingleby, Melbourne DE73 1HW
☎ *(01332) 862469* John Thompson

 Home of the John Thompson Brewery, which re-introduced brewing to Derbyshire in 1977. John Thompson Special plus the seasonal ale is permanently available.

Converted fifteenth-century oak-beamed farmhouse, with a collection of paintings and antiques. Food served from the carvery lunchtimes only. Car park. Children's room and large garden.

 JOHN THOMPSON SPECIAL 4.2% ABV
JOHN THOMPSON PORTER 4.5% ABV
Available in winter.
JOHN THOMPSON SUMMER GOLD 4.5% ABV
Available in summer.

OPEN *10.30am–2.30pm and 7–11pm Mon–Sat; 12–2.30pm and 7–10.30pm Sun.*

KIRK IRETON

The Barley Mow Inn
Kirk Ireton, Ashbourne DE6 3JP
☎ *(01335) 370306* Mary Short

 Marston's Pedigree, Hook Norton Best Bitter and Old Hooky always available plus five guest beers, many from local breweries.

Seventeenth-century village inn with unspoilt interior. Beers served straight from the barrel. Rolls available at lunchtime. Children are permitted inside the pub at lunchtime, but there are no special facilities. Garden area at front. Car park. Accommodation.

OPEN *12–2pm and 7–11pm (10.30pm Sun).*

KNIVETON

The Red Lion
Winksworth Road, Kniveton, Ashbourne DE6 1JH
☎ *(01335) 345504* Angela Tegram

 This freehouse always has something from Burton Bridge and Blanchfield on the menu. A guest beer, changed every few days, is also offered. Black Sheep Special is popular.

A small village pub with separate dining area. Background music only. Food served at lunchtime and evenings. Children allowed.

OPEN *12–2pm and 7–11pm Mon–Fri; 11am–11pm Sat; 12–10.30pm Sun*

MAKENEY

The Holly Bush Inn
Holly Bush Lane, Makeney, Milford
☎ *(01332) 841729* JJK Bilbie

 Marston's Pedigree and Ruddles County (Greene King) always available plus four (200+ per year) guests that may include Morland Old Speckled Hen, Exmoor Gold, Fuller's ESB, Marston's Owd Roger, Greene King Abbot, Timothy Taylor Landlord and brews from Bateman. Also scrumpy cider.

A Grade II listed twelfth-century coaching inn with flagstone floors and open fires. Bar food at lunchtime, barbecues in summer. Car park and children's room. Private parties welcome. Just off the main A6 at Milford, opposite the Makeney Hotel.

OPEN *12–3pm and 6–11pm Mon–Fri; 12–11pm Sat–Sun.*

MARSH LANE

The George Inn
46 Lightwood Road, Marsh Lane, Eckington
☎ *(01246) 433178* Martyn and Christa

 A regularly changing guest beer available perhaps from Everards, Robinson's, Young's, Bateman and others, all 4.2% ABV or above and served in over-sized glasses.

Village freehouse with taproom and lounge, each with real fire and free of any machines or music. Outside seating at front and small garden to rear. No food. Car park. Children welcome during the day. Dogs welcome.

OPEN *1–4pm and 7–11pm Mon–Sat; 12–3pm and 7–10.30pm Sun.*

MATLOCK

The Thorntree Inn
48 Jackson Road, Matlock DE4 3JG
☎ *(01629) 582923* Philip John Sismey

 Timothy Taylor Landlord is always on offer, plus one guest, which might from Black Sheep or any one of a number of different breweries. Twice-yearly real ale festival held.

Traditional country-style community pub with a large covered patio, heated on chilly evenings, offering unrivalled views over the valley. Food available 12–1.45pm Wed–Sat, 7–8.30pm Tues–Sat and 12–5.30pm Sun. Children allowed on the patio, but no special facilities. From Crown Square in Matlock, go up the hill on Bank Road, turn into Smedley Street, then second right into Smith Road, and the pub is at the top on the left.

OPEN *7–11pm Mon–Tues; 12–2.30pm and 7–11pm Wed–Sat; 12–10.30pm Sun.*

MELBOURNE

The Bluebell Inn
53 Church Street, Melbourne DE73 1EJ
☎ *(01332) 865764* Kevin Morgan

 Owned by Shardlow, with Shardlow Reverend Eaton's Ale, Goldenhop and Best Bitter always on offer. One guest, changed weekly, might be something like Brunswick The Usual, Everards Tiger, Shardlow Five Bells or a beer from Springhead.

Traditional family pub frequented by good drinkers! Bar snacks available, plus meals in the small restaurant. Patio, barbecue. Four en-suite letting rooms. Accompanied children allowed. Situated near Melbourne Hall.

OPEN *11am–11pm Mon–Sat; 12–10.30pm Sun.*

The Railway Hotel
222 Station Road, Melbourne DE73 1BQ
☎ *(01332) 862566* Lucy Kelly

 A freehouse with two rotating guest beers, changed weekly. Favourites include Marston's Pedigree.

A small pub within a family-run hotel with seven bedrooms and a restaurant. Food served at lunchtime and evenings. Children allowed.

OPEN *12–3pm and 6–11pm Mon–Thurs; 11am–11pm Fri–Sat; 12–10.30am Sun.*

OCKBROOK

The Royal Oak
Green Lane, Ockbrook DE72 3SE
☎ *(01332) 662378* Mrs Wilson

 Three guest beers are changed up to five times a week, and may include beers from Shardlow, Whim, Brewsters or Burton Bridge.

Village pub built in 1762. The landlady has run the pub for 49 years! Lunch is available every day, and there is a separate dining area. Function room with bar, two beer gardens (one for adults, one for children), darts, car park. Annual beer festival. Children allowed at lunchtimes only.

OPEN *11.30am–2.30pm and 6.30–11pm (10.30pm Sun).*

OLD TUPTON

The Royal Oak Inn
Derby Road, Old Tupton, Chesterfield S42 6LA
☎ *(01246) 862180* John Angus

 Morland Old Speckled Hen always available plus four guests, changed weekly, often including Ruddles County (Greene King), Ushers Founders Ale or Tomintoul Witches Cauldron.

A 100-year-old pub with three rooms. Food at lunchtime and evenings. No children.

OPEN *12–3pm and 5–11pm Mon–Thur; 11am–11pm Fri–Sat; 12–3pm and 7–10.30pm Sun.*

OVER HADDON

Lathkil Hotel
Over Haddon DE45 1JE
☎ *(01629) 812501* Robert Grigor-Taylor

 A freehouse featuring Charles Wells Bombadier plus guests, changed weekly, which may include Timothy Taylor Landlord or Black Sheep Bitter.

A pub with stunning views over the Dales. Occasional TV for sporting events. Food at lunchtime and evenings. Dining area evenings only. Children allowed lunchtimes only.

OPEN *May–Sept: 11.30am–3pm and 6–11pm Mon–Fri; 11.30am–11pm Sat; 12–10.30pm Sun. Winter opening hours vary – check with hotel.*

ROWARTH

Little Mill Inn
Rowarth, High Peak SK22 1EB
☎ *(01663) 743178* Mr Barnes

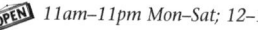 A freehouse always offering Banks's Bitter, Marston's Pedigree, Camerons Strongarm and Hardys & Hansons Kimberley Best. A guest beer, changed weekly, may well be Hartleys SB (Robinson's).

An old-style pub in the middle of nowhere with a waterwheel at the side. Two bars, live music twice a week, quiz and bingo nights. Upstairs restaurant area. Food served all day. Children allowed. Isolated, but fully signposted.

OPEN *11am–11pm Mon–Sat; 12–10.30pm Sun.*

SHARDLOW

The Old Crown

Cavendish Bridge, Nr Shardlow DE72 2HL
☎ *(01332) 792392* P and GR Morton-Harrison

Marston's Pedigree always available plus five guest beers (400 per year) which may include Bateman XXXB, Otter Ale, something from the Shardlow brewery, Eldridge Pope Royal Oak, Shepherd Neame Spitfire or Brewery on Sea Black Rock.

Asmall inn by the River Trent serving bar food at lunchtime. Car park and garden. Children allowed in the bar at lunchtime for food. En-suite accommodation. Turn left on the A6 before the river bridge, before Shardlow from the M1.

 11.30am–3pm and 5–11pm Mon–Sat; 12–3pm and 7–10.30pm Sun.

SMALLEY

The Bell Inn

Main Road, Smalley, Ilkeston DE7 6EF
☎ *(01332) 880635*
Angela Bonsall and Ian Wood

A freehouse with up to seven real ales available at any one time. Adnams Broadside and ales from Mallard, Rooster's and Whim Hartington regularly available.

Atwo-roomed, Victorian-style pub. Food at lunchtime and evenings. Accommodation.

 11.30am–2.30pm and 5–11pm Mon–Fri; all day Sat–Sun.

STAVELEY

Speedwell Inn

Lowgates, Staveley, Chesterfield S43 3TT
☎ *(01246) 472252* Alan Wood

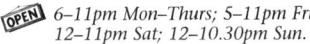A freehouse whose owners run the Townes Brewery on the premises. At least four Townes brews, such as Sunshine and Golden Bud always available, plus occasional guests.

Atraditional pub, refurbished in 1998, with occasional live music. Non-smoking area. No food. No children. Local CAMRA Pub of the Season for Winter 1999 and Pub of the Year 2000.

 6–11pm Mon–Thurs; 5–11pm Fri; 12–11pm Sat; 12–10.30pm Sun.

SWINSCOE

The Dog & Partridge Country Inn

Swinscoe, Ashbourne DE6 2HS
☎ *(01335) 343183* Mr MJ Stelfox

Morland Old Speckled Hen and Ruddles County usually available, plus one or two guest beers such as Charles Wells Bombardier, Hartington Best Bitter, Marston's Pedigree, Burton Bridge Best Bitter or Top Dog.

Seventeenth-century inn, with olde-worlde beamed bar and log fire in winter. Restaurant and garden. Bar and restaurant food available all day, including breakfasts. Car park. Indoor and outdoor children's play areas, highchairs and special children's menu.

 7.30am–11pm.

TICKNALL

The Staff of Life

7 High Street, Ticknall DE73 1JH
☎ *(01332) 862479* Mr Nix

Marston's Pedigree, Everards Tiger, RCH East Street Cream, Timothy Taylor Landlord and Fuller's ESB available plus five guests (200 per year) which may include Exmoor Gold, Hook Norton Old Hooky, Hop Back Summer Lightning, Mauldons Black Adder, Ringwood Old Thumper, Uley Old Spot and Temperance Relief.

Afifteenth-century beamed former bakehouse. Bar and restaurant food at lunchtime and evenings, home-cooked British foods a speciality. Car park, garden and children's room. Now also offers accommodation. At the south end of the village at the intersection between the Ashby-de-la-Zouch and Swadlincote roads.

 11.30am–2.30pm and 6–11pm Mon–Sat; 12–2.30pm and 7–10.20pm Sun.

TIDESWELL

The George Hotel

Commercial Road, Tideswell, Buxton SK17 8NU
☎ *(01298) 871382* Mr Norris

A pub tied to Hardys & Hansons' Kimberley Brewery, so with Kimberley Best and Classic always available. Also four guest beers, changed every six to eight weeks, including Hardys & Hansons seasonal ales.

Acoaching house dating back to 1730, with separate dining area. Food served at lunchtime and evenings. Children allowed.

 11am–3pm and 7–11pm Mon–Sat; 12–3pm and 7–10.30pm Sun.

WARDLOW MIRES

Three Stags' Heads

Wardlow Mires, Tideswell SK17 8RW
☎ *(01298) 872268* Mr and Mrs Fuller

 Broadstone Brewery's Bitter, Abbeydale Black Lurcher (brewed exclusively for The Three Stags' Heads), Absolution and Matins permanently available, plus occasional guests.

A small seventeenth-century Peak District farmhouse pub with stone-flagged bar and its own pottery workshop. Unspoilt, with no frills, no piped muzak, no games machines. Live folk/Irish music at weekends. Bar food at lunchtime and evenings. Car park. Older children allowed (no babes-in-arms or toddlers). On the A623 at the junction with the B6465.

OPEN *7–11pm Fri; 11am–11pm Sat; 12–10.30pm Sun (closed during the week).*

WHALEY BRIDGE

Shepherd's Arms

7 Old Road, Whaley Bridge, High Peak SK23 7HR
☎ *(01663) 732384* Mr and Mrs Smith

 A Marston's tenancy, where Banks's Mild, Marston's Bitter and Pedigree are always available, plus one guest beer, changed monthly.

Old-fashioned, traditional, family-orientated pub, with beautiful large beer garden. Bar snacks available. Children allowed. Families and dogs welcome.

OPEN *4–11pm Mon (12–11pm bank hols); 2–11pm Tues–Fri; 12–11pm Sat; 12–10.30pm Sun.*

WHITEHOUGH

The Oddfellows Arms

Whitehead Lane, Whitehough, Chinley, High Peak SK23 6EJ
☎ *(01663) 750306*
Miss JA Newton and Mr A Holland

 Tied to Marston's, so always offers Marston's Bitter and Pedigree, plus one guest, changed monthly.

A one-bar country pub. Food served 12–7pm Mon–Sat and 12–5pm Sun. Children allowed.

OPEN *11am–11pm Mon–Sat; 12–10.30pm Sun.*

WOOLLEY MOOR

The White Horse Inn

Badger Lane, Woolley Moor, Alfreton DE55 6FG
☎ *(01246) 590319* Keith Hurst (Bar Manager)

 A freehouse with four or five guests which often include Everards Beacon, Bateman Salem Porter, Shepherd Neame Spitfire, Greene King IPA and Black Sheep.

A two-bar pub with non-smoking areas in main lounge, and conservatory for dining. Adventure playground, football goalposts, outside seating on three patios with 25 tables, disabled facilities. Food served 12–2pm and 6–9pm Mon–Sat and 12–8pm Sun. Walkers, children and dogs welcome.

OPEN *11.30am–3pm and 6–11pm Mon–Sat; 12–10.30pm Sun.*

YOU TELL US

★ *The Grouse Inn*, Longshaw

Places Featured:

Barnstaple	Mortehoe
Bideford	Newton Abbot
Blackawton	Newton St Cyres
Branscombe	North Tawton
Brendon	Okehampton
Broadhempston	Ossaborough
Buckfastleigh	Pilton
Chittlehampton	Plymouth
Coleford	Plymstock
Combeinteignhead	Princetown
Combe Martin	Ringmore
Crediton	St Giles in the Wood
Dartmouth	Shaldon
Doddiscombsleigh	Silverton
Exeter	Slapton
Exmouth	Stokenham
Georgeham	Tavistock
Halwell	Teignmouth
Hatherleigh	Topsham
Holbeton	Torquay
Horndon	Torrington
Horsebridge	Tuckenhay
Iddlesleigh	Umberleigh
Instow	West Down
Kingsbridge	Westward Ho!
Lapford	Whimple
Lower Ashton	Winkleigh
Monkley	Yarde Down

THE BREWERIES

BARUM BREWERY

*c/o Reform Inn, Reform Road, Pilton, Barnstaple
EX31 1PD*
☎ *(01271) 329994*
www.barumbrewery.co.uk

 BSE 3.5% ABV
XTC 3.9% ABV
GOLD 4.0% ABV
ORIGINAL 4.4% ABV
LIQUID LUNCH 4.6% ABV
DARK STAR 4.8% ABV
Occasional brew.
BREAKFAST 5.0% ABV
Hoppy bitterness throughout.
BARUMBURG 5.1% ABV
Occasional brew.
TECHNICAL HITCH 5.3% ABV
Occasional brew.
CHALLENGER 5.6% ABV
BARNSTABLASTA 6.6% ABV
Winter only.

THE BRANSCOMBE VALE BREWERY

Great Seaside Farm, Branscombe EX12 3DP
☎ *(01297) 680511*

 BRANOC 3.8% ABV
Golden and malty with a light hop
finish.
DRAYMANS BEST BITTER 4.2% ABV
ANNIVERSARY ALE 4.6% ABV
Light-coloured with clean, crisp hoppy flavour,
Feb only.
OWN LABEL 4.6% ABV
House beer, may be sold under different names.
HELLS BELLES 4.8% ABV
Oct–Mar. Smooth, mellow and hoppy.
SUMMA THAT 5.0% ABV
Golden, light and hoppy throughout, Mar–Oct.
YO HO HO 6.0% ABV
From November onwards. Fruity, and flavour
packed.
Plus occasional brews.

CLEARWATER BREWERY

2 Devon Units, Hatchmoor Industrial Estate, Torrington EX38 7HP
☎ *(01805) 625242*

 CAVALIER 4.0% ABV
BEGGARS TIPPLE 4.2% ABV
1646 4.8% ABV
OLIVER'S NECTAR 5.2% ABV
Plus occasional brews.

EXE VALLEY BREWERY

Silverton, Exeter EX5 4HF
☎ *(01392) 860406; Fax: (01392) 861001*
E-mail: guysheppard@supanet.com

 EXE VALLEY BITTER 3.7% ABV
A full-bodied bitter based on an old West Country recipe.
BARRON'S HOPSIT 4.1% ABV
A well-hopped bitter using Challenger hops.
DOB'S BEST BITTER 4.1% ABV
A finely balanced bitter with that extra touch of hops.
DEVON GLORY 4.7% ABV
A distinctive beer made from the finest Devon malt.
MR SHEPPARD'S CROOK 4.7% ABV
Premium bitter, full flavour of Devon malt and Challenger hops.
EXETER OLD BITTER 4.8% ABV
A smooth, well hopped, strong beer.
Seasonal:
DEVON SUMMER 3.9% ABV
SPRING BEER 4.3% ABV
AUTUMN GLORY 4.5% ABV
DEVON DAWN 4.5% ABV
WINTER WARMER 6.0% ABV
Occasional:
BARRON'S DARK 4.1% ABV
HOPE 4.3% ABV
CURATES CHOICE 4.8% ABV

THE JOLLYBOAT BREWERY

The Coach House, Buttgarden Street, Bideford EX39 2AU
☎ *(01237) 424343*

 BUCCANEERS 3.7% ABV
Nut-brown colour and hoppy.
FREEBOOTER 4.0% ABV
MAINBRACE 4.2% ABV
Light chestnut colour, late hopped for aroma.
PLUNDER 4.8% ABV
Dark red with Caribbean flavours. Fuggles hop.
PRIVATEER 4.8% ABV
Full-flavoured and hoppy. Mixed hop.
CONTRABAND 5.8% ABV
Christmastide feasting ale/porter. Cascade hop.
Plus occasional brews.

O'HANLON'S BREWING CO.

Great Barton Farm, Clyst St. Lawrence EX5 2NY
☎ *(01404) 822 412*
www.ohanlons.co.uk

 FIREFLY 3.7% ABV
WHEATBEER 4.0% ABV
BLAKELEY'S BEST NO.1 4.2% ABV
DRY STOUT 4.2% ABV
MYRICA ALE 4.5% ABV
PORT STOUT 4.5% ABV
RED ALE 4.5% ABV
Plus seasonal brews.

OTTER BREWERY

Mathayes Farm, Luppit, Honiton EX14 4SA
☎ *(01404) 891285*
www.otterbrewery.com

 BITTER 3.6% ABV
Pale brown. Hoppy, fruity aroma.
BRIGHT 4.3% ABV
Light and delicate with long malty finish.
ALE 4.5% ABV
OTTER CLAUS 5.0% ABV
Christmas beer.
HEAD 5.8% ABV
Smooth, strong and malty.

POINTS WEST BREWERY

Plymouth College of Further Education, Kings Road, Devonport, Plymouth PL1 5QG
☎ *(01752) 305700*

 PILGRIM PALE ALE 4.0% ABV
Light and hoppy, made with English hops.
KITCHEN PORTER 4.4% ABV
A Guinness-style porter.
DRAKE'S DRUM 4.8% ABV
Heavier bodied than Pilgrim, but still hoppy.
Seasonal:
ROOSTER 7.5% ABV
Brewed at Christmas, this is a Monastic Ale based on Monasteries in Belgium.

PRINCETOWN BREWERIES LTD

Tavistock Road, Princetown PL20 6QF
☎ *(01822) 890789*

 DARTMOOR IPA/BEST 4.0% ABV
Pale, refreshing and hoppy.
JAIL ALE 4.8% ABV
Plus occasional brews.

SCATTOR ROCK BREWERY
Unit 5, Gidley's Meadow, Christow, Exeter
EX6 7QB
☎ *(01647) 252120*
www.scattorrockbrewery.com

 SCATTY BITTER 3.8% ABV
TEIGN VALLEY TIPPLE 4.0% ABV
SKYLARK 4.2% ABV
DEVONIAN 4.5% ABV
GOLDEN VALLEY 4.6% ABV
VALLEY STOMPER 5.0% ABV
Plus the Tor Collection: two brews each month, named after local Tors.

SUMMERSKILLS BREWERY
Unit 15, Pomphlett Farm Industrial Estate, Broxton Drive, Billacombe, Plymouth PL9 7BG
☎ *(01752) 481283*

 CELLAR VEE/BBB 3.7% ABV
Well-balanced.
BEST BITTER 4.3% ABV
Pale, with malty flavour and honey hints.
TAMAR 4.3% ABV
MENACING DENNIS 4.5% ABV
Occasional. Robust and clean flavour.
WHISTLEBELLY VENGEANCE 4.7% ABV
Dark ruby colour. Hop, dark malt and liquorice flavour.
NINJABEER 5.0% ABV
Winter ale. Rich and golden, with soft malt, hops and toffee flavour.
TURKEY'S DELIGHT 5.1% ABV
Christmas ale.
INDIANA'S BONES 5.6% ABV
Rich, dark winter warmer.

TEIGNWORTHY BREWERY,
The Maltings, Teign Road, Newton Abbot
TQ12 4AA
☎ *(01626) 332066*

REEL ALE 4.0% ABV
Hoppy, dry session beer.
SPRING TIDE 4.3% ABV
Sweet, copper colour brew, with hops throughout.
OLD MOGGIE 4.4% ABV
This is a good golden, hoppy, citrus ale, ideal for hot summer weather.
BEACHCOMBER 4.5% ABV
Light in colour with citrus taste.
MALTSTERS ALE 5.0% ABV
Winter ale, rich and dark but highly drinkable.
CHRISTMAS CRACKER 6.0% ABV
Smooth rich seasonal brew.
Plus occasional brews.

THE PUBS

BARNSTAPLE

The Check Inn
Castle Street, Barnstaple EX31 1DR
☎ *(01271) 375964* Christopher Bates

 Six hand pumps offer a constantly changing range of beers, direct from independent breweries around the UK.

A true freehouse with one bar, a friendly, local atmosphere and the usual pub games. Music (mainly blues/rock) on alternate Fri–Sat evenings. Food served lunchtimes and evenings Mon–Fri, all day Sat–Sun. Car park. Children welcome. Bed and breakfast accommodation available.

OPEN *11am–11pm Mon–Sat; 12–10.30pm Sun.*

The Corner House
108 Boutport Street, Barnstaple EX31 1SY
☎ *(01271) 343528*
Noreen Stevens and Louise Oldfield

 A freehouse with two guests, changed every two days, often include Greene King Abbot, Young's Special or something from Wye Valley.

An old-fashioned drinking pub in the town centre, with pool room and big-screen TV. Live music once a month. Children allowed in the separate lounge room.

OPEN *11am–11pm Mon–Sat; 12–10.30pm Sun.*

BIDEFORD

The Kings Arms
The Quay, Bideford EX39 2HW
☎ *(01237) 475196* Paul Phipps

 Kings Arms Best Bitter, brewed for the pub by Clearwater Brewery, is a permanent feature, plus three guests, changed weekly, which may include Wadworth 6X or Greene King Abbot.

Pleasant market-town pub in a building dating from 1560, with beams and log fires. One big bar, patio. Food served lunchtimes. Children allowed.

OPEN *11am–11pm Mon–Sat; 12–10.30pm Sun.*

BLACKAWTON

The George Inn
Main Street, Blackawton, Totnes TQ9 7BG
☎ *(01803) 712342*
Heather Gates, Vic Hall and Ruth Coe

 Teignworthy Spring Tide and Princetown Jail Ale always on sale in this freehouse. Guest beers change frequently, and often include Harviestoun Belgian White, Wychwood Hobgoblin or Heather Froach Ale.

An old village pub with eating area in the lounge bar. Four en-suite bed and breakfast rooms. Beer garden. Live bands occasionally. Bar snacks served at lunchtime, and a more extensive menu is available in the evening, with local produce used whenever possible. Children welcome.

OPEN *12–2.30pm Tues–Sat (closed Mon lunchtimes); 7–11pm Mon–Sat; 12–3pm and 7–10.30pm Sun.*

BRANSCOMBE

The Fountain Head
Branscombe EX12 3AG
☎ *(01297) 680359* Mrs Luxton

 Branscombe Vale Branoc, Olde Stoker and Summa That often available. Guests (60 per year) include Hook Norton Old Hooky, Crouch Vale Millennium Gold and Freeminer Speculation Ale.

A fourteenth-century pub at the top of the village with flagstone floors, log fires and wood panelling. The lounge bar was formerly the village blacksmith's. Food at lunchtime and evenings. Car park, outside seating, non-smoking area and children's room. Self-catering accommodation.

OPEN *11.30am–2.30pm and 6.30–11pm Mon–Sat; 12–2.30pm and 7–10.30pm Sun.*

BRENDON

The Rockford Inn
Brendon, Nr Lynton EX35 6PT
☎ *(01598) 741214* Barrie Jon Marden

 Regularly changing beers often include Cotleigh Barn Owl and Tawny, Cottage and Clearwater beers or a St Austell ale.

Seventeenth-century riverside inn, in quiet village at the heart of Exmoor. Food served 12–2.30pm and 7–9pm. Small beer garden and accommodation. Car park. Children's room.

OPEN *12–3pm and 6–11pm Mon–Thurs; 12–11pm Fri–Sat; 12–3pm and 6.30–10.30pm Sun*

BROADHEMPSTON

Coppa Dolla Inn
Broadhempston, Totnes TQ9 6BD
☎ *(01803) 812455*
Andrew Greenwood and Philip Saint

 A freehouse with two guest ales, changed every two weeks, always available. These will usually include a local or regional bitter.

A country pub with restaurant area and delightful beer garden. Food at lunchtime and evenings. Children allowed. Easy to find, once you're in Broadhempston.

OPEN *11.30am–3pm and 6.30–11pm (10.30pm Sun).*

BUCKFASTLEIGH

The White Hart
2 Plymouth Road, Buckfastleigh TQ11 0DA
☎ *(01364) 642337* Louise and Chay Mann

 A freehouse with Teignworthy Beachcomber, Green King Abbot and a house ale always on the menu, plus one guest, changed every two days.

An olde-worlde pub, Grade II listed, with flagstone floors and log fires. One bar, background music. Partitioned dining area and family room. Food served at lunchtime and evenings (not Sun evening). Three bed and breakfast rooms (two en suite). Children allowed.

OPEN *6–11pm Mon (closed Mon lunch); 12–2.30pm and 6–11pm Tues–Thurs; 12–11pm Fri–Sat; 12–4pm and 7–10.30pm Sun.*

CHITTLEHAMPTON

The Bell
The Square, Chittlehampton EX37 9QL
☎ *(01769) 540368* Mr and Mrs Jones

 Eight real ales always available, from breweries such as Cotleigh, Clearwater, Barum, Greene King or any independent brewery. Range of 140 different whiskies are also available.

Village community pub in an unusual building on the Square, overlooking the church. Food available. Non-smoking conservatory, dining area, garden, orchard, skittle alley and function room. Children, and dogs on leads, are allowed.

OPEN *11am–3pm and 6–11pm Mon–Fri; 11am–11pm Sat; 12–10.30pm Sun.*

COLEFORD

New Inn

Coleford, Crediton EX17 5BZ
☎ *(01363) 84242* Mr PS Butt

 A freehouse with Otter Ale, Badger Best and Wadworth 6X permanently available, plus one guest.

A thirteenth-century thatched pub, with lots of oak beams. Restaurant and bar meals available. Food served lunchtimes and evenings. Six luxury bedrooms. Well-behaved children allowed.

OPEN *12–2.30pm and 6–11pm Mon–Sat; 7–10.30pm Sun.*

COMBEINTEIGNHEAD

The Wild Goose

Combeinteignhead, Newton Abbot TQ12 4RA
☎ *(01626) 872241* Jerry and Kate

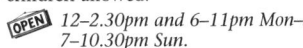 A freehouse offering 40 different real ales a month. Regularly featured are Otter Bright, Princetown Jail Ale, Teignworthy Springtide, Skinner's Betty Stogs and Exe Valley Devon Glory, plus ales from other independent West Country brewers.

A seventeenth century, traditional, family-run country village pub with real open fires. Extensive menu with an emphasis on homemade fare, with fresh fish and vegetarian dishes always available. Separate dining room and beer garden. Down country lanes, is signposted.

OPEN *11.30am–2.30pm and 6.30–11pm Mon–Sat; 12–3pm and 7–10.30pm Sun.*

COMBE MARTIN

The Castle Inn

High Street, Combe Martin EX34 0HS
☎ *(01271) 883706* Chris Franks

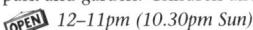 Four real ales are available at this freehouse, from a list of more than 500 guests.

A village pub, with one bar and a big-screen TV. A restaurant opened May 1999. Food served at lunchtime and evenings. Large car park and garden. Children allowed.

OPEN *12–11pm (10.30pm Sun).*

The London Inn

Leigh Road, Combe Martin EX34 0NA
☎ *(01271) 883409* Bob White

Beers from Clearwater are among those permanently available, plus one weekly guest, such as Morland Old Speckled Hen or Barum Breakfast.

An old coaching inn, now a pub, hotel and restaurant. Two bars, garden with river running through, car park for 50 cars. Bar and restaurant meals available. Pool, fruit machines, skittles. Eight en-suite letting rooms and holiday cottage. Children allowed.

OPEN *All day, every day.*

Ye Olde George & Dragon

Castle Street, Combe Martin EX34 0HX
☎ *(01271) 882282* Craig Davey

 A freehouse with beers from Barum and Clearwater always served.

Village pub, club and restaurant in a 400-year-old building, with three bars. Meals served throughout. Pool, darts, patio. Children allowed. Ring for directions, as it is easy to miss.

OPEN *4–11pm Mon–Wed; 4pm–1am Thurs–Sat; 12–10.30pm Sun.*

CREDITON

The Crediton Inn

28A Mill Street, Crediton EX17 1EZ
☎ *(01363) 772882* Diane Heggadon

 A freehouse with Sharp's Doom Bar Bitter always available, plus two guests changed every two days. Examples include Branscombe Vale Branoc and Teignworthy Reel Ale.

A friendly local, with skittle alley and function room. Bar meals and snacks. No children.

OPEN *11am–11pm Mon–Sat; 12–2pm and 7–10.30pm Sun.*

DARTMOUTH

The Cherub Inn

13 Higher Street, Dartmouth TQ6 9RB
☎ *(01803) 832571* Laurie Scott

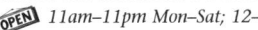 A freehouse with Cherub Best Bitter (Summerskills) and three other real ales that change each month. These are typically from Brakspear, Cains, Everards, Exmoor, Jennings, Shepherd Neame or Young's.

A 600-year-old pub, very small with beams and open fire. Air-conditioned cellar. Bar food at lunchtimes and evenings, plus à la carte restaurant in the evenings. Over-10s only in the restaurant, no under-14s in the bar. See our website at: www.the-cherub.co.uk

OPEN *11am–11pm Mon–Sat; 12–10.30pm Sun.*

DODDISCOMBSLEIGH

The Nobody Inn

Doddiscombsleigh, Nr Exeter EX6 7PS
☎ *(01647) 252394* Nick Borst-Smith

 Nobody's House Ale always available plus two guest beers (at least 70 per year) which may include Blackawton Headstrong, Sarah Hughes Dark Ruby Mild, Otter Bitter and RCH East Street Cream.

A sixteenth-century inn with beams and inglenook fireplaces. Food available in the bar at lunchtimes and in the restaurant in the evenings. Speciality cheeses. Car park and garden. Accommodation unsuitable for children under 14. Three miles southwest of Exeter racecourse.

OPEN *12–2.30pm and 6–11pm.*

EXETER

Double Locks Hotel

Canal Bank, Exeter EX2 6LT
☎ *(01392) 256947* Tony Stearman

 Young's Bitter, Special, Waggle Dance and Winter Warmer, Adnams Broadside, Everards Old Original, Branscombe Vale Branoc, Greene King Abbot and Shepherd Neame Spitfire are always available, as well as up to six guest beers.

Recently acquired by Young's, the pub is located in a 250-year-old building situated by twin locks on the oldest ship canal in the country. Bar food is available all day. Car park, large garden, volleyball, barbecue in summer and children's room. Located on the south-west edge of the city, through the Marsh Barton Trading Estate.

OPEN *11am–11pm Mon–Sat; 12–10.30pm Sun.*

Great Western Hotel

St David's Station Approach, Exeter EX4 4NU
☎ *(01392) 274039* Trevor Crouchen

 Fuller's London Pride, Adnams Broadside and Bitter, plus a beer from Exe Valley always available. Three guests during the week and seven at weekends are also served, and these may include favourites such as Orkney Dark Island and Morland Old Speckled Hen.

A traditional freehouse within a hotel. Exeter and East Devon CAMRA Pub of the Year 2001. Staff pride themselves on looking after their customers. Thirty-five bedrooms with en-suite facilities. Background music. Live music on bank holidays. Food served all day. Children allowed.

OPEN *11am–11pm Mon–Sat; 12–10.30pm Sun.*

The Hole Inn the Wall

Little Castle Street, Exeter EX14 3PX
☎ *(01392) 273341* Mr Kerrigan

 A pub tied to Eldridge Pope, in a back street near the law courts, with five pumps serving real ale. Hardy Country and Royal Oak always on offer.

A two-storey pub with eight pool tables, pub bar at very top. Quiz night on Tuesday. Food at lunchtime only (12–2pm). No children; over-18s only.

OPEN *11am–11pm Mon–Sat; 7–10.30pm Sun and bank holidays.*

The Well House Tavern

Cathedral Yard, Exeter EX1 1HB
☎ *(01392) 495365*
Tracy Cherry and Ian Scanes

 Five guest beers available which may include Morland Old Speckled Hen, Guernsey Sunbeam Bitter and Oakhill Best.

There is live music and a quiz night at this popular pub on alternate Sundays. Bar food is available at lunchtime and evenings. Facing Exeter Cathedral, with a Roman cellar.

OPEN *11am–11pm Mon–Sat; 7–11pm Sun.*

EXMOUTH

The Grove

The Esplanade, Exmouth EX15 2AZ
☎ *(01395) 272101* Mr Doble

 A freehouse with Fuller's London Pride always available. A guest beer is changed monthly. Regulars include Otter Ale and Morland Old Speckled Hen.

A quiet, family-run pub with one bar. Live bands on Fridays. Food at lunchtime and evenings. Children allowed.

OPEN *11am–11pm Mon–Sat; 12–10.30pm Sun.*

GEORGEHAM

The Rock Inn

Rock Hill, Georgeham EX33 1JW
☎ *(01271) 890322* Mr and Mrs Scutts

 Eight real ales usually available. Greene King Abbot and IPA plus St Austell Darmoor Best Bitter are among those permanently served. There are usually four guest beers, two from local breweries such as Cotleigh and Barum, and two from other breweries.

A 400-year-old inn one mile from the sea. CAMRA North Devon Pub of the Year 1994–96. Bar food available at lunchtime and evenings. North Devon Pub Food Silver Award winner in 2000 and 2001. Car park, garden and conservatory. Children's room and children's area.

OPEN *11am–4pm and 6–11pm Mon–Fri; all day Sat–Sun.*

HALWELL

Old Inn

Halwell, nr Totnes TQ9 7JA
☎ *(01803) 712329* Mr Crowther

 A freehouse with RCH East Street Cream always on offer. There is also one guest, changed weekly.

A food and beer pub, with dining area and background music. Food at lunchtime and evenings. Children allowed.

OPEN *11am–3pm and 6–11pm Mon–Sat; 12–3pm and 6–10.30pm Sun.*

HATHERLEIGH

Tally Ho Country Inn

14 Market Street, Hatherleigh EX20 3JN
☎ *(01837) 810306*

 Offers a range of six popular brews which are produced in the micro-brewery on the premises.

Although the present brewery only started brewing in 1990, its history goes back over 200 years. Records show that it was producing ales in 1790, when it was known as The New Inn Brewery. It was destroyed by fire in 1806 but was brewing again in 1824. The brewery finally closed down in the early 1900s, when it could no longer compete with the larger breweries of the time. The new brewery is situated at the back of The Tally Ho Country Inn in what used to be the town bakery and can produce 260 gallons of real ale a week. Bar and restaurant food available at lunchtime and evenings. Car park, garden, accommodation. Children allowed.

MARKET ALE 3.7% ABV
TARKA'S TIPPLE 4.0% ABV
NUTTERS ALE 4.6% ABV
MIDNIGHT MADNESS 5.0% ABV
THURGIA 6.0% ABV

Plus seasonal ales such as Master Jack's Mild (3.5% ABV) and Jollop (6.6% ABV).

OPEN *11am–2.30pm and 6–11pm.*

HOLBETON

Mildmay Colours

Holbeton, Plymouth PL8 1NA
☎ *(01752) 830248* Louise Price

Mildmay Colours Best and SP (Skinner's) always on the menu in this freehouse. Two guests, changed fortnightly, may include Skinner's Cornish Knocker or Bunces Danish Dynamite.

A traditional country pub with upstairs dining and bar area. Occasional rock and jazz bands. Food at lunchtime and evenings. Children allowed.

OPEN *11am–11pm Mon–Sat; 12–10.30pm Sun.*

HORNDON

The Elephant's Nest

Horndon, Nr Mary Tavy PL19 9NQ
☎ *(01822) 810273* Peter Wolfes

Palmers IPA and St Austell HSD always available plus two guest beers (150 per year) including those from Exe Valley, Wye Valley, Cotleigh, Exmoor, Hook Norton, Summerskills and Ash Vine breweries. Also draught cider.

This sixteenth-century Dartmoor inn with a large garden and log fires has a collection of 'Elephant's Nests' written in different languages on the beams in chalk. Bar food at lunchtime and evenings. Car park and children's room. The garden is home to rabbits, ducks and chickens. Travel along the A386 into Mary Tavy. Take the road signposted Horndon for just under two miles.

OPEN *Oct–Apr: 12–3pm and 6–11pm (10.30pm Sun); May–Sept: 12–11pm (10.30pm Sun).*

HORSEBRIDGE

The Royal Inn

Horsebridge TL19 8PJ
☎ *(01822) 870214* Catherine Eaton

A freehouse with Wadworth 6X and a Sharp's brew always available. Two guests also offered.

An old pub with open fires, patio and beer garden. Food at lunchtime and evenings. Children allowed at lunchtime only.

OPEN *12–3pm and 7–11pm (10.30pm Sun).*

IDDESLEIGH

Duke of York

Iddesleigh EX19 8BG
☎ *(01837) 810253* J Stewart

A freehouse, with all real ales served straight from the barrel; no pumps used. Adnams Broadside and Cotleigh Tawny are always available, plus numerous guest beers which change daily. Wye Valley brews are a favourite.

A pub in a rural setting (ring for directions!). No TV, occasional live music. Separate dining area. Food served all day. Children allowed.

OPEN *11am–11pm Mon–Sat; 12–10.30pm Sun.*

INSTOW

The Quay

Marine Parade, Instow EX39 4HY
☎ *(01271) 860624* Steven Lock

 Instow Regatta, from the pub's own Tarka micro-brewery, is always among the beers always on offer, plus one guest.

Traditional seaside pub overlooking estuary of River Torridge, with an emphasis on real ale and food, especially seafood. Impromptu live music. Outside seating, restaurant. Children allowed.

📖 *11am–11pm Mon–Sat; 12–10.30pm Sun.*

KINGSBRIDGE

The Ship & Plough

The Promenade, Kingsbridge TQ7 1JD
☎ *(01548) 852485* Jackie Blewitt

A brewpub, home of Blewitts Brewery with the full range of own brews always available, plus Wadworth 6X. Plans to start a cask-conditioned lager.

A large pub, with beams and open fires, situated in the Sorley Tunnel. The tunnel itself is open to the public (admission charge) and has a children's play area, shop, restaurant and a workshop in which pottery and metalwork are demonstrated. There is also a glass viewing area in which people can watch the brewing process. The pub itself has live music on Thursdays. Food available. Children allowed in family room.

 BLEWITTS BEST 4.0% ABV
Fruity.
BLEWITTS WAGES 4.5% ABV
Made with barley and maize.
BLEWITTS HEAD OFF 5.0% ABV
A fruity, sweet flavour

📖 *11am–11pm Mon–Sat; 12–10.30pm Sun.*

LAPFORD

The Old Malt Scoop Inn

Lapford, Nr Crediton EX17 6PZ
☎ *(01363) 83330* Bryn and Sally Hocking

Adnams Broadside and Marston's Pedigree always available, plus 52 guest beers each year, to include Sharp's Doom Bar and beers from Badger. Also traditional cider.

This sixteenth-century freehouse is open for morning coffee, bar snacks, meals and cream teas. There are inglenook fireplaces, beamed ceilings, panelled walls, skittle alley, beer garden, patio areas and car park. Children are allowed in the sun lounge and one of the bars. Lapford is on the A377 between Crediton and Barnstaple. Follow brown tourist signs near village. The inn is at the centre of the village, opposite the church.

📖 *12–4pm and 6–11pm Mon–Fri; 12–11pm Sat; 12–4pm and 7–11pm Sun.*

LOWER ASHTON

The Manor Inn

Lower Ashton, Teign Valley, Nr Exeter EX6 7QL
☎ *(01647) 252304* GW and CMS Mann

 A freehouse with Teignworthy Reel Ale, RCH Pitchfork and Princetown Jail Ale always on offer, plus one guest, which could be from anywhere!

Informal rural pub in the heart of the scenic Teign Valley. No games machines, no piped music, just good conversation! There is an emphasis on food, served 12–1.30pm and 7–9.30pm Tues–Sun (until 9pm Sun). Children allowed in garden only. Car park. Located on the B3193, about five miles from Chudleigh.

📖 *12–2.30pm and 6.30pm–11pm (10.30pm Sun); closed Mon except bank holidays.*

MONKLEY

The Bell Inn

Monkley EX39 5JS
☎ *(01805) 622338* Sue Smith and Jock Tierney

A freehouse with beers from Barum Brewery permanently available, plus two monthly guests, with ales from Clearwater and West Berkshire regular favourites.

Fifteenth-century thatched village pub with dining area. Food served 12–9pm. Pool and darts, live music, garden. Accommodation available – one single and two double rooms. Car park. Children allowed.

📖 *12–11pm (10.30pm Sun).*

MORTEHOE

The Chichester Arms

Chapel Hill, Mortehoe, Woolacombe EX34 7DU
☎ *(01271) 870411* David and Jane Pugh

 Ushers Best Bitter, Badger Tanglefoot, Barum Original and Gold regularly available, plus a guest beer perhaps from Cains, Robinson's, Cotleigh, Shepherd Neame, Brakspear, Fuller's, Young's, Banks's, Timothy Taylor, Jennings, Exmoor, Thwaites or others.

Mortehoe's original village inn, built as a vicarage in 1620. Converted in 1820, it is basically unchanged since and is still partly gas lit, although it does also have its own electricity generator. Commended for the best pub food in Devon for the past two years. Food served 12–2pm and 6–9pm every day. Children's room and garden. Car park.

📖 *Winter: 12–2.30pm and 6.30–11pm Mon–Fri; 12–11pm Sat; 12–10.30pm Sun. Summer: 11.30am–11pm Mon–Sat; 12–10.30pm Sun.*

NEWTON ABBOT

Dartmouth Inn

63 East Street, Newton Abbot TQ12 2JP
☎ *(01626) 353451*
Malcolm and Brenda Charles

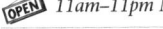Guest beers (300 per year) may include RCH East Street Cream, Sarah Hughes Dark Ruby Mild, Teignworthy Springtide and Sutton Knickerdroppa Glory.

This 450-year-old pub is reputed to be the oldest inn in Newton Abbot. Beautiful beer garden, a previous Bloom of Britain winner. The pub has also won the regional CAMRA Pub of the Year award on several occasions. Five minutes' walk from the station.

OPEN *11am–11pm Mon–Sat; 12–10.30pm Sun.*

The Golden Lion

4 Market Street, Newton Abbot EX39 1PW
☎ *(01626) 367062* Ali Snell

A freehouse always offering Teignworthy Reel Ale. Two guests may include favourites such as Badger Tanglefoot, Fuller's London Pride or something from Scattor Rock.

An olde-worlde one-bar pub, with juke box. Food at lunchtime only. No children. In a back alley, can be hard to find.

OPEN *11am–2.30pm and 5.30–11pm Mon–Fri; 11am–4pm and 6–11pm Sat; 11am–3pm and 7–10.30pm Sun.*

NEWTON ST CYRES

The Beer Engine

Sweetham, Newton St Cyres, Nr Exeter EX5 5AX
☎ *(01392) 851282 Fax (01392) 851876*
Peter and Jill Hawksley

Rail Ale, Piston Bitter and Sleeper Heavy brewed on the premises and always available. Seasonals brewed occasionally.

The brewery was established along with a cellar bar in the basement of a former station hotel in 1983. It has now expanded to produce three brews and supplies a couple of local pubs and wholesalers. Home-made food available at lunchtime and evenings. Car park, garden. Children allowed. Website: www.thebeerengine.co.uk

RETURN TICKET 3.4% ABV
An occasional beer.
RAIL ALE 3.8% ABV
Amber-coloured, malty nose and flavour of fruit.
PISTON BITTER 4.3% ABV
Sweetness throughout, with some bitterness in the finish.
GOLDEN ARROW 4.6% ABV
An occasional beer.
PORTER 4.7% ABV
An occasional beer.
SLEEPER HEAVY 5.4% ABV
Red, with fruit, sweetness and some bitterness.
WHISTLEMAS 6.7% ABV
A Christmas brew.

OPEN *11am–11pm Mon–Sat; 12–10.30pm Sun.*

NORTH TAWTON

Fountain Inn

Exeter Street, North Tawton EX20 2HB
☎ *(01837) 82551* Lesley Whitehouse

A freehouse with Charles Wells Bombardier, St Austell Daylight Robbery and Palmers Copper Ale always available.

A large, lively and friendly pub. Separate dining area. Food at lunchtime and evenings. Well-behaved children allowed.

OPEN *11.30am–2.30pm and 5.30–11pm Mon–Fri; all day Sat–Sun.*

Railway Inn

Whiddon Down Road, North Tawton EX20 2BE
☎ *(01837) 82789* Claire Speak

A freehouse with Teignworthy Reel Ale always available. Regular guests include Teignworthy Beachcomber, Adnams Broadside and ales from Wye Valley.

An old country inn, on the main road but slightly hidden, with one bar and dining area. Bar snacks and evening meals. Children allowed.

OPEN *12–3pm (not Mon) and 6–11pm Mon–Sat; 12–3pm and 7–10.30pm Sun.*

OKEHAMPTON

Plymouth Inn

26 West Street, Okehampton EX20 1HH
☎ *(01837) 53633* Geoff and Jill Hoather

A freehouse, with beers served straight from the barrel. Accent on beers from the West Country, though others are often featured.

A country-style town pub with restaurant, beer garden and function room. Local CAMRA Pub of the Year 2002. Mini beer festivals and occasional folk bands. Food at lunchtime and evenings. Children allowed; function room doubles as children's room.

OPEN *12–3pm and 7–11pm Mon–Fri; 12–11pm Sat and bank holidays; 12–10.30pm Sun.*

OSSABOROUGH

The Old Mill

Ossaborough, Woolacombe EX34 7HJ
☎ *(01271) 870237* D Huxtable

Brains Buckley's Reverend James usually available plus one guest beer from Brains or Barum brewery.

Once a mill, this seventeenth-century country pub has plenty of olde-worlde charm and retains many decorative features. Food is served 12–2pm and 6–9pm. Children welcome, outdoor play area. Car park. Take the first right-hand turning out of Woolacombe.

OPEN *Winter: 12–3pm and 6–11pm (10.30pm Sun); Summer: 11am–11pm (10.30pm Sun).*

PILTON

The Reform Inn

Reform Street, Pilton, Barnstaple EX31 9PD
☎ *(01271) 323164* Esther Hatch

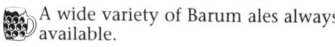 A wide variety of Barum ales always available.

The Reform Inn offers a pool table, darts, shove ha'penny and two computer terminals for games and access to the internet. The Barum Brewery is situated behind the pub, but is separately owned.

 11.30am–11.30pm (10.30pm Sun).

PLYMOUTH

The Clifton

35 Clifton Street, Greenbank, Plymouth PL4 8JB
☎ *(01752) 266563* Mr Rosevear

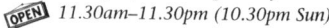 A freehouse with Clifton Classic (house beer brewed by Summerskills) always on offer. Two guests, changed weekly, may include beers from anywhere in the UK, with Orkney Dark Island a particular favourite.

A locals' pub, with one bar and Sky TV for football. No food. No children. Not far from the railway station.

3.30–11pm Mon–Thurs; 11am–11pm Fri–Sat; 12–10.30pm Sun.

The Library

15 Wyndham Street East, Plymouth EX17 6AL
☎ *(01752) 266042* Douglas Russell

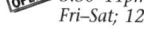 A freehouse with Cornish Rebellion and Sutton XSB always available, plus two guest beers.

A student-style pub, juke box (free on Student Night – Tuesday), one long bar. Big-screen TV/Sky. Live acts or karaoke Wednesdays. Pool room. Food: burgers, hot dogs, chips. No children after 7pm.

11am–11pm Mon and Wed–Sat; 12–5pm and 7–11pm Tues; 12–10.30pm Sun.

The Prince Maurice

3 Church Hill, Eggbuckland, Plymouth PL6 5RJ
☎ *(01752) 771515* Rick and Anne Dodds

 Ten real ales always available, including Badger Tanglefoot, Summerskills Best and Adnams Broadside, plus many and various guest beers.

Small, seventeenth-century freehouse with two bars and log fires. Local CAMRA Pub of the Year 1994, 1995, 2000 and 2001. Weekday lunchtime bar snacks. Car park, patio.

11am–3pm and 7–11pm Mon–Thurs; all day Fri–Sat; 12–4pm and 7–10.30pm Sun.

Porters

20 Looe Street, Plymouth PL4 0EA
☎ *(01752) 662485* Ken Gordon

 Eight real ales are available, changed every two or three days. Morland Old Speckled Hen, Coach House Dick Turpin and St George's Ale plus Greene King Abbot regularly featured.

A town-centre pub with exposed brickwork and lots of bric-à-brac. Background music. Raised area at top of pub for eating. Beer garden. Food served at lunchtimes and evenings. Children allowed.

11am–11pm Mon–Sat; 12–10.30pm Sun.

Thistle Park Brewhouse

32 Commercial Road, Plymouth PL4 0LE
☎ *(01752) 204890*

 A brewpub with home-brewed ales always served. Brewing began in 1993.

Polished wooden floors, maritime relics and oil paintings by a local artist. Bar food and a range of South African cuisine served at lunchtime and evenings. Parking, patio.

DARTMOUTH PRIDE 3.8% ABV
GROMMET 3.8% ABV
PLYMOUTH PRIDE 3.8% ABV
XSB 4.2% ABV
WILD BLONDE 4.4% ABV
SUTTON COMFORT 4.5% ABV
Seasonals:
HOPNOSIS 4.5% ABV
A summer ale.
EDDYSTONE LIGHT 5.0% ABV
KNICKADROPPA GLORY 5.5% ABV
A winter warmer.

11am–1am Mon–Sat; 12–10.30pm Sun.

PLYMSTOCK

The Boringdon Arms

13 Boringdon Terrace, Turnchapel, Nr Plymstock PL9 9TQ
☎ *(01752) 402053*

 Butcombe Bitter, RCH Pitchfork and Summerskills Best among the beers always available plus up to five guests beers (250 per year) from Orkney (north), Butts (south), Skinner's (west), Scott's (east) and all points in between.

An ex-quarrymaster's house with a good atmosphere. No juke box. Live music on Saturday nights. CAMRA's first Plymouth Pub of the Year, and Plymouth CAMRA's Pub of the Year for 1999/2000. Bar food available at lunchtime and evenings. Conservatory and beer garden in the old quarry to the rear of the pub. Accommodation. Bi-monthly beer festivals. Located at the centre of the village, four miles south-east of Plymouth, on south coast footpath. Signposted from the A379. Website: www.bori.co.uk.

11am–11pm Mon–Sat; 12–10.30pm Sun.

PRINCETOWN

The Prince of Wales

Tavistock Road, Princetown PL20 6QF
☎ *(01822) 890219 Mr and Mrs Baker*

 Princetown Jail Ale and Dartmoor IPA are always available, as well as one guest, with beers from St Austell a regular feature.

Family-run bar in a 150-year-old building, full of character. Food available all day, and there is a small restaurant. Children allowed. En-suite bed and breakfast. Car park.

 11am–11pm Mon–Sat; 12–10.30pm Sun.

RINGMORE

The Journey's End

Ringmore, Nr Kingsbridge TQ7 4HL
☎ *(01548) 810205*

 Up to ten brews available including Exmoor Ale and Otter Ale, Badger Tanglefoot, Shepherd Neame Spitfire, Adnams Broadside and Crown Buckley Reverend James Original. Also guests (50 per year) changed weekly including Archers Golden, Greene King Abbot and brews from Fuller's, Cains and Wye Valley.

An eleventh-century thatched inn with flagstone floors and open fires. Bar and restaurant food served at lunchtime and evenings. Conservatory, car park, garden, non-smoking dining room. Accommodation. No children in the bar.

 11.30am–3pm and 6–11pm Mon–Sat; 12–10.30pm Sun.

ST GILES IN THE WOOD

The Cranford Inn

St Giles In The Wood, Torrington EX38 7LA
☎ *(01805) 623309 Richard Ward*

 Fuller's London Pride is permanent here, and Timothy Taylor Landlord, Greene King Abbot and beers from Clearwater are regularly available. There are two guests in summer and one in winter, changed weekly.

Food-oriented country pub in a converted farmhouse, with restaurant, garden and patio. Car parking. Children allowed. On the B3227, the only pub on the road!

 12–2.30pm and 6–11pm (10.30pm Sun).

SHALDON

The Clifford Arms

34 Fore Street, Shaldon, Teignmouth TQ14 0DE
☎ *(01626) 872311 Mr Balster*

 A freehouse with Blackawton Headstrong and Greene King Abbot always on sale. Regular guests include Fuller's London Pride and Shepherd Neame Spitfire.

A one-bar pub with garden, juke box and live music. Food at lunchtime and evenings. Children allowed in certain areas.

 11am–2.30pm and 5–11pm Mon–Fri and Sun; 11am–11pm Sat.

SILVERTON

Silverton Inn

Fore Street, Silverton, Nr Exeter EX5 4HP
☎ *(01392) 860196*

 Exe Valley Dob's Best Bitter always available, plus three guests, changed weekly, from a wide range of breweries. Greene King Abbot is a favourite.

Traditional, cosy wooden pub between Exeter and Tiverton with easy access to sea coasts and shopping towns. Separate upstairs restaurant. Food available at lunchtime and evenings. Recently converted, well-equipped luxury rooms are now available. Nearby parking, beer garden. Children allowed in restaurant. Killerton House, a National Trust property, is nearby.

 11.30am–3pm and 5.30–11pm.

SLAPTON

The Tower Inn

Slapton, Nr Kingsbridge TQ7 2PN
☎ *(01548) 580216 Josh and Nicola Acfield*

 Adnams Best, Dartmoor Best, Exmoor Ale and Badger Tanglefoot always available plus one guest, changed weekly, which may include Gibbs Mew Bishop's Tipple, Blackawton Headstrong, Palmers IPA, Timothy Taylor Landlord and Eldridge Pope Royal Oak. The guest is often a seasonal ale.

A fourteenth-century inn offering accommodation and a superb garden. Bar and restaurant food available at lunchtime and evenings. Car park. Hidden in the centre of the village at the foot of the old ruined tower.

 12–3pm and 6–11pm.

STOKENHAM

The Tradesman's Arms

Stokenham, Kingsbridge TQ7 2SZ
☎ *(01548) 580313*
John and Elizabeth Sharman

 Adnams Southwold and Broadside usually available plus a guest beer from Fuller's or local breweries such as Blewitts.

Welcoming, picturesque country pub, well known locally for its imaginative and interesting food. Good range of malt whiskies. Food served 7–9pm Tues–Sat and lunchtimes Sun. Children welcome Sunday lunchtimes only. Car park. Situated 100 yards off the A379, Kingsbridge to Dartmouth road. Website: www.thetradesmansarms-stokenham.co.uk.

OPEN *6.30–11pm Tues–Sat; 12–2.30pm Sun; closed at other times.*

TAVISTOCK

The Halfway House

Grenofen, Tavistock PL19 9ER
☎ *(01822) 612960* Peter Jones

 A freehouse with Sharp's Doom Bar Ale always available. Two guests are changed weekly and may include beers from Skinner's, Sutton and Sharp's.

A country inn on the A386. Public bar. Background music. Separate dining and lounge bar. Food served every lunchtime and evening. Children allowed. En-suite accommodation available.

OPEN *11.30am–3pm and 5–11pm Mon–Sat; 12–4pm and 6–10.30pm Sun.*

TEIGNMOUTH

The Blue Anchor

Teign Street, Teignmouth TQ14 8EG
☎ *(01626) 772741* Paul Fellows

A freehouse serving Adnams Broadside, Marston's Pedigree and Teignworthy Reel Ale. Three guests, changed two or three times a week, include favourites such as Greene King Abbot, Fuller's ESB or something from Bateman or Branscombe Vale.

A small, very boozy, locals' pub. Old, with log fire. Rolls only. No children.

OPEN *11am–11pm Mon–Sat; 12–10.30pm Sun.*

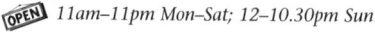

The Golden Lion

85 Bitton Park Road, Teignmouth TQ14 9BY
☎ *(01626) 776442*

 At least two guest beers (approx 50 per year) usually available from regional brewers such as Blackawton, Teignworthy, Exe Valley and Oak Hill.

This is a locals' pub on the main road just out of the town with a public and lounge bar. Darts and pool are played. Bar food is available at lunchtime and evenings. Small car park. Children not allowed.

OPEN *12–4pm and 6–11pm (10.30pm Sun).*

TOPSHAM

Bridge Inn

Bridge Hill, Topsham, Nr Exeter EX3 0QQ
☎ *(01392) 875857* Mrs CA Cheffers-Heard

Nine or ten real ales usually available, which may include Branscombe Vale Branoc, Exe Valley Exeter Old, Otter Ale, Blackawton West Country and Adnams Broadside, plus seasonal brews from local breweries.

This sixteenth-century pub overlooking the River Clyst has been in the same family since 1897 through four generations. Simple bar food at lunchtime. Car park and children's room. Two miles from M5 junction 30. Topsham is signposted from the exit. In Topsham, follow the yellow signpost (A376) to Exmouth. For further information visit the website at www.cheffers.co.uk.

OPEN *12–2pm daily; 6–10.30pm Mon–Thurs; 6–11pm Fri–Sat; 7–10.30pm Sun.*

TORQUAY

Chelston Manor

Old Mill Road, Torquay TQ2 6HW
☎ *(01803) 605142* Peter Uphill

A freehouse with four real ales always available, changed weekly, such as Wadworth 6X, Marston's Pedigree, Sharp's Doom Bar or Fuller's London Pride.

Unique olde-worlde pub in the heart of Torquay. Home-cooked meals served 11.30am–2.30pm and 6–9.30pm daily. Large walled beer garden. Car park. Children welcome. Follow sign for Chelston and Cockington Village.

OPEN *11am–3pm and 5–11pm. Open all day May–Sept.*

Crown & Sceptre

*2 Petitor Road, St Marychurch, Torquay
TQ1 4QA*
☎ *(01803) 328290* Mr R Wheeler

 Eight real ales always available, including two guest ales from around the country.

A traditional pub with two bars, children's room and garden. Live music. Food at lunchtimes only. Children allowed.

OPEN *11am–3pm and 5.30–11pm Mon–Fri;
11am–4pm and 6.30–11pm Sat; 12–3pm
and 7–10.30pm Sun.*

TORRINGTON

The New Market Inn

10 South Street, Torrington EX38 8HE
☎ *(01805) 622289* Mr Pascoe

 Clearwater beers are regularly featured as are ales from Cottage and Barum. The two guest beers are sometimes changed daily!

Family pub and restaurant, with division in the middle. Beams, stone floors, live music and separate nightclub at the back. Garden, accommodation and car park. Children allowed.

OPEN *11am–11pm Mon–Sat; 12–10.30pm Sun.*

TUCKENHAY

Maltsters Arms

Bow Creek, Tuckenhay TQ9 7EQ
☎ *(01803) 732350*
Quentin and Denise Thwaites

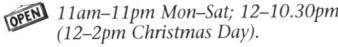 A freehouse with Princetown Dartmoor IPA always available. Two or three guests also served, with regulars including brews from Teignworthy, Scattor Rock, Blackawton, Cottage and Exmoor. Over 100 different guest ales served last year. Young's Special London Ale (bottle conditioned) is also stocked.

A traditional country pub with separate eating area overlooking the river. Bed and breakfast, with themed bedrooms. Barbecues on the river bank. Occasional live music and barbecues. Food served 12–3pm and 6.30–9.30pm every day (except Christmas Day). Children allowed in certain areas. In the middle of nowhere. If you manage to find Tuckenhay, you'll find the pub. Website: www.tuckenhay.com (there is also an e-mail list for news of music events).

OPEN *11am–11pm Mon–Sat; 12–10.30pm
(12–2pm Christmas Day).*

UMBERLEIGH

The Rising Sun

Umberleigh EX37 9DU
☎ *(01769) 560447* Malcolm Andrew Hogg

 Clearwater Cavalier, Cotleigh Tawny Bitter and Jollyboat Freebooter are among the beers regularly available as guests.

Inn in a traditional building, with restaurant, patio and nine bedrooms. Local folk musicians have jamming sessions every Monday (not Bank Holidays). Car park. Children allowed. On the A377 between Barnstaple and Exeter.

OPEN *11.30am–3pm and 6–11pm
(10.30pm Sun).*

WEST DOWN

The Crown Inn

The Square, West Down
☎ *(01271) 862790* Russ Trueman

 Barum Original usually available plus one guest beer. This might be another Barum beer, Wadworth 6X, Greene King Abbot Ale, Marston's Pedigree or local ales of interest.

A small seventeenth-century village pub with open fire, non-smoking area and delightful garden. Food served in separate restaurant 12–2pm and 6–10pm. Children welcome. Car park. Follow the brown tourist signs between Braunton and Ilfracombe and Lynton Cross and Mullacott Cross.

OPEN *12–3pm and 6–11pm Mon–Sat; 12–4pm
and 7–10.30pm Sun.*

WESTWARD HO!

Pig on the Hill

West Pusehill, Westward Ho!, Bideford EX39 5AH
☎ *(01237) 477615*

 Home to the Country Life Brewery, with the four house beers rotated on the pumps. Bottle versions of the home brews also available.

Friendly country inn in rural setting with food available each session. Garden, terrace and children's play area. Games room and giant TV. Petanque club and holiday cottages. The brewery has doubled in size over recent years to keep up with demand, and ales are supplied to outlets all over the country. There are views of the working brewery from the pub through glass screens.

OLD APPLEDORE 3.7% ABV
Dark red colour and quenching.
WALLOP 4.4% ABV
Pale, easy-quaffing, summer brew.
GOLDEN PIG 4.7% ABV
Gold-coloured and well-rounded.
COUNTRY BUMPKIN 6% ABV
Dark, with malty sweetness.

OPEN *Summer: all day, every day. Winter:
12–3pm and 6–11pm Mon–Sat; 12–3pm
and 7–10.30pm Sun.*

WHIMPLE

New Fountain Inn

Church Road, Whimple, Exeter EX5 2TA
☎ *(01404) 822350* Paul Mallett

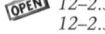 A freehouse with Teignworthy beers and Branscombe Vale Branoc usually on the menu. Guest beers (one from the barrel) come from local independent breweries.

A family-run village inn split into two tiers, the top one used for eating. Food served at lunchtime and evenings. Children and dogs welcome. There are plans to open a heritage centre on the site.

OPEN *12–2.30pm and 6.30–11pm Mon–Sat; 12–2.30pm and 7–10.30pm Sun.*

WINKLEIGH

The Kings Arms

Fore Street, Winkleigh EX19 8HQ
☎ *(01837) 83384* Steve and Ann Kinsey

 Princetown Best Bitter usually available plus two guest beers which may be from local breweries or any independent brand in the country, such as St Austell HSD, Princetown Jail Ale or Fuller's London Pride.

Traditional, thatched country pub in pretty village. Award-winning bar food served 12–2pm and 6.30–9pm (restaurant from 7pm). Bar food only on Sunday nights. No food on Mondays. Children welcome, but no special facilities. Follow signs 'To the village'.

OPEN *11am–3pm and 6–11pm Mon–Fri; 11am–11pm Sat; 12–3pm and 7–10.30pm Sun.*

The Royal Oak

The Square, Winkleigh, Dolton EX19 8QF
☎ *(01805) 804288* John Howarth

 Wadworth 6X is a permanent feature, and beers from Clearwater are regularly served. Other Devon breweries are available as guests.

Large village pub in a fourteenth/sixteenth-century building, with restaurant, two main bars and snug. Food served. Pool table, darts, live music (mainly jazz), skittles, garden. Car parking available. Quite difficult to find, so call for directions.

OPEN *11.30am–3pm and 6.30–11pm (10.30pm Sun); open all day in summer.*

YARDE DOWN

Poltimore Arms

Yarde Down, South Molton EX36 3HA
☎ *(01598) 710381* Richard Austen

 A freehouse with real ales served straight from the barrel. Cotleigh Tawny Ale is always available, and guests, changed weekly, may include Marston's Pedigree, Morland Old Speckled Hen or Greene King Abbot Ale.

Dates back to 1600. Has its own generator for electricity. Food served; a very large menu. Children allowed. In the middle of nowhere; best to ring for directions.

OPEN *12–2.30pm and 6.30–11pm Mon–Sat; 12–2.30pm and 7–10.30pm Sun.*

YOU TELL US

* *Nog Inn*, Sidmouth Junction, Feniton
* *The Welcome Inn*, Haven Banks, Exeter

Places Featured:

Beaminster	Linwood
Benville	Loders
Bournemouth	Lower Burton
Bradpole	Lyme Regis
Branksome	Nettlecombe
Bridport	North Wootton
Burton Bradstock	Plush
Cattistock	Poole
Charmouth	Pulham
Chetnole	Sherborne
Chideock	Shroton
Child Okeford	Spyway
Christchurch	Stourton Caundle
Church Knowle	Studland
Corfe Mullen	Tarrant Monkton
Corscombe	Trent
Cranborne	Verwood
Dorchester	Westbourne
Eype	Weymouth
Hinton St Mary	Winkton
Hurn	Wyke Regis

THE BREWERIES

THE BADGER BREWERY

Blandford St Mary, Blandford Forum DT11 9LS
☎ *(01258) 452141*
www.tanglefoot.co.uk

 BEST BITTER 4.0% ABV
Fruity with refreshing finish.
CHAMPION 4.6% ABV
Delicate hop and citrus flavours.
TANGLEFOOT 5.1% ABV
Pale, full fruit, with bittersweet finish.

GOLDFINCH BREWERY

47 High East Street, Dorchester DT1 1HU
☎ *(01305) 264020*

TOM BROWN'S BITTER 4.0% ABV
Hoppy throughout.
FLASHMAN'S CLOUT 4.5% ABV
Balanced and flavoursome.
MIDNIGHT SUN 4.5% ABV
Replaces Flashman's Clout during the summer.
MIDNIGHT BLINDER 5.0% ABV
Sweet malt with balancing hoppiness.
Plus occasional brews.

JC AND RH PALMER

Palmers Brewery, West Bay Road, Bridport DT6 4JA
☎ *(01308) 422396*
www.palmersbrewery.com

 BRIDPORT BITTER 3.2% ABV
Refreshing, with hops and bitterness throughout.
COPPER ALE 3.7% ABV
Fruity session ale.
DORSET GOLD 3.7% ABV
Golden with delicate fruity hoppiness.
BEST BITTER 4.2% ABV
Well-balanced and good hop character.
200 5.0% ABV
Smooth, full-flavoured and complex.
TALLY HO! 5.5% ABV
Nutty and distinctive.

POOLE BREWERY

68 High Street, Poole BH15 1DA
☎ *(01202) 682345*

BEST BITTER OR DOLPHIN 3.8% ABV
BEDROCK BITTER 4.2% ABV
Occasional.
HOLES BAY HOG 4.5% ABV
BOSUN 4.6% ABV
DOUBLE BARREL 5.5% ABV
Occasional.

THE QUAY BREWERY
Brewers Quay, Hope Square, Weymouth DT4 8TR
☎ *(01305) 777515*

 WEYMOUTH HARBOUR MASTER 3.6% ABV
Rounded and easy-drinking.
SUMMER KNIGHT 3.8% ABV
Award-winning wheat beer. Available MayñOct.
WEYMOUTH SPECIAL PALE ALE 4.0% ABV
Gold and well-balanced.
WEYMOUTH JD 1742 4.2% ABV
Quenching bittersweet flavour.
BOMBSHELL BITTER 4.5% ABV
Sweet and malty.
QUAY STEAM BEER 4.5% ABV
Aromatic and full-flavoured. American hops.
OLD ROTT 5.0% ABV
SILENT KNIGHT 5.9% ABV
Dark wheat beer.
Plus occasional beers.

THOMAS HARDY BREWING LTD
Weymouth Road, Dorchester DT1 1QT
☎ *(01305) 250255*

POPE'S TRADITIONAL 3.8% ABV
HARDY COUNTRY 4.2% ABV
Well-balanced with clean bitterness in
the finish.
ROYAL OAK 5.0% ABV
Warming, excellent balance and smooth finish.
For Morrells:
OXFORD BITTER 3.7% ABV
VARSITY 4.3% ABV
GRADUATE 5.2% ABV

THE PUBS

BEAMINSTER

The Hine Bar
Hogshill Street, Beaminster DT8 3AE
☎ *(01308) 863576* Mr Hart

 Tied to Palmers, with Palmers 200, IPA
and Dorset Gold always on offer.

Early seventeenth-century coaching inn
with a courtyard, now a pub, restaurant
and guest house. Food available, including
weekend carvery. Restaurant at each end (one
non-smoking), with the bar in the middle.
Three en-suite letting rooms. Car park.
Accompanied children allowed.

OPEN *11am–2pm and 6pm–midnight (has
supper licence).*

BENVILLE

The Talbot Arms
Benville, Dorchester DT2 0NN
☎ *(01935) 83381* Richard Moulsdale

 A freehouse serving Branscombe Vale
Drayman's Best Bitter, plus one guest,
which may be another beer from
Branscombe Vale, or one from a wide range
of other breweries.

A country pub/restaurant with beer garden.
The pub features a 'curiosity shop' selling
locally produced goods. Food served at
lunchtime and evenings. Campsite. Children
allowed. Website: www.thetalbotarms.co.uk.

OPEN *9am–11pm*

BOURNEMOUTH

The Goat & Tricycle
27–9 West Hill Road, Bournemouth BH2 5PF
☎ *(01202) 314220* David Maguire

 Wadworth 6X, Henry's Original IPA and
JCB always available, plus four or five
regularly changing guests including Morland
Old Speckled Hen or brews from Bateman
and Hop Back.

A traditional pub with family area and
courtyard. No juke box, background
music only. No children in the bar. Food
served lunchtimes and evenings.

OPEN *12–3pm and 6–11pm Mon–Sat; 12–3pm
and 7–10.30pm Sun.*

Moon in the Square
4–8 Exeter Road, Bournemouth BH2 5AQ
☎ *(01202) 652090* Dave and Terri Lea

 Four guest real ales always available,
with Shepherd Neame Spitfire a regular
feature. Weston's cider also served.

A traditional Wetherspoon's pub, recently
refurbished, with non-smoking bar. Food
served all day. Beer garden. Disabled
facilities. No children.

OPEN *All day, every day.*

BRADPOLE

The King's Head Inn

Bradpole, Bridport DT6 3DS
☎ *01308 422520* Barry Lurkins

 A Palmers house, with Palmers IPA and Bridport Bitter permanently available. Other beers from Palmers, such as 200, Tally Ho! and Dorset Gold, appear as guests.

Traditional 400-year-old village pub with two bars and a dining area. Food available. Entertainment and quiz nights once a month. Garden and patio. Two letting rooms. Car parking. Children allowed. On the main road from Bridport to Yeovil.

OPEN *11am–2.30pm and 6–11pm Mon–Sat; 12–2.30pm and 6–10.30pm Sun.*

BRANKSOME

Branksome Railway Hotel

429 Poole Road, Branksome, Poole BH12 1DQ
☎ *(01202) 769555*
Debbie Ellery and Bill Whiteley

 An Enterprise pub with a guest beer policy. Hampshire Strong's Best always available, plus two weekly changing guests from Cottage, Hop Back, Brains, Fuller's, Jennings and many more.

Victorian pub, built in 1894, recently refurbished. Two bars, games including pool and darts. Live music/disco at weekends, Sunday afternoon entertainment a must! B&B in large, comfortable en-suite accommodation. Located on the A35, opposite Branksome Railway Station.

OPEN *All day, every day.*

BRIDPORT

The Bridport Arms

West Bay, Bridport DT6 4EN
☎ *(01308) 422994* Adrian Collis

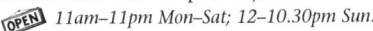 A Palmers Brewery house with Copper Ale, IPA and Palmers 200 always available.

Old thatched pub and hotel by the beach. Non-smoking area, separate dining area with food available lunchtimes and evenings. Children allowed. Outside seating. Accommodation. Campsite adjacent.

OPEN *11am–11pm Mon–Sat; 12–10.30pm Sun.*

The Crown Inn

59 West Bay Road, Bridport DT6 4AX
☎ *(01308) 422037* Noel Cane

 Tied to Palmers, with the full range of the brewery's beers available (Bridport Bitter, Dorset Gold, IPA, 200, Tally Ho!).

Family-run pub in a very old building on the edge of town. One bar, dining area, garden and rear patio. Food available 12–2.30pm and 6–9.30pm. Live music most Saturdays, quiz second Sunday of month. Children allowed. On the main A35, look out for the entrance 50 yards on right-hand side of the B3157.

OPEN *Summer: 11am–11pm Mon–Sat; 12–10.30pm Sun. Call for seasonal opening hours.*

BURTON BRADSTOCK

The Dove Inn

Southover, Burton Bradstock, Bridport DT6 4RD
☎ *(01308) 897897* Neil Walker

 Branscombe Vale Branoc, Otter Ale and Morland Old Speckled Hen are among the brews usually available, plus one regularly changing guest, usually from a local or micro-brewery.

A listed building with thatched roof. Recently refurbished to convert three cottages into one building. One bar, restaurant area, large garden terrace, car park. Food served lunchtimes and evenings. Children allowed. Signposted from Burton Bradstock.

OPEN *All day, every day.*

CATTISTOCK

The Fox & Hounds

Duck Street, Cattistock
☎ *(01300) 320444* Anne Hinton

 Lots of guest beers, two at any one time. These may include Fuller's London Pride, Charles Wells Bombadier and ales from Oakhill and Cottage breweries.

A fifteenth-century village inn with large fires, flagstones and a separate restaurant. Relaxing atmosphere. Bar and restaurant food available at lunchtime and evenings. Parking, garden and play area opposite. Campsite nearby. Accommodation. On the A37, look out for the sign for Cattistock, just past the Clay Pigeon Cafe from Yeovil or the sign on the road from Dorchester.

OPEN *12–2.30pm and 7–11pm.*

CHARMOUTH

The Royal Oak

The Street, Charmouth DT6 6PE
☎ *(01297) 560277* Mr and Mrs Presser

 Tied to Palmers, with Bridport Bitter always on offer, plus two seasonal guest ales, often other Palmers beers such as Tally Ho! and 200.

A village pub built in the 1870s, with beams, open fires in winter and one through bar. Bar snacks available. Children allowed.

OPEN *12–4pm and 7–11pm (10.30pm Sun).*

CHETNOLE

The Chetnole Inn

Chetnole, Sherborne DT9 6NU
☎ *(01935) 872337* David Lowe

 A freehouse with Branscombe Vale Branoc Ale, Butcombe Bitter and Palmers IPA permanently available, plus a range of guest beers.

A two-bar village pub with background music and occasional small live bands. Beer garden and dining area. Food served at lunchtime and evenings. Children welcome. Opposite the church.

OPEN *11am–2.30pm and 6–11pm Mon–Sat; 12–3pm and 7–10.30pm Sun.*

CHIDEOCK

The Anchor Inn

Seatown, Chideock, Bridport DT6 6JU
☎ *(01297) 489215* David and Sadie Miles

 A Palmers house with Copper Ale, IPA and Palmers 200 permanently available, plus Tally Ho! occasionally.

Situated in the centre of a little cove, nestled under the Golden Cap Cliff which is the highest point on the south coast. A World Heritage site, area of outstanding natural beauty, with National Trust land all around. Food available all day in summer, lunchtimes and evenings in winter (except Sun pm). Well-behaved children and dogs allowed. Beer garden with terraces overlooking the sea and the south west coastal path. From A35 travel south to Chideock. For further information visit the website at www.theanchorinn.co.uk.

OPEN *Summer (end May–September): all day, every day. Winter: 11am–2.30pm and 6–11pm (10.30pm Sun).*

CHILD OKEFORD

Saxon Inn

Gold Hill, Child Okeford DT11 8HD
☎ *(01258) 860310* Margaret and Alan

 Three real ales always available, including Ringwood Best, something from Butcombe, and a variety of popular brews from around the country.

A friendly, traditional, old village pub with two cosy log fires. Good, tasty, home-cooked food from a varied menu served every day except Tuesday and Sunday evenings. At the rear of the pub is a country garden with ample seating.

OPEN *11.30am–2.30pm and 7–11pm Mon–Fri; 11.30am–3pm and 7–11pm Sat; 12–3.30pm and 7–10.30pm Sun.*

CHRISTCHURCH

The Ship

48 High Street, Christchurch
☎ *(01202) 484308* Nicole Thomas

 Ringwood Fortyniner is always on offer, plus four guests, including beers such as Ringwood Old Thumper, Hop Back Crop Circle, Archers Golden, Wychwood Hobgoblin and Fuller's London Pride, to name but a few.

Steeped in history, with a welcoming atmosphere and excellent staff, this claims to be the oldest (and busiest!) pub in Christchurch. A wide range of traditional and special food, mostly homemade, is served lunchtimes and until 6pm Mon–Sat and 12–3pm Sun. Children welcome. Car park. Situated on main street opposite Woolworths.

OPEN *11am–11pm Mon–Sat; 12–10.30pm Sun.*

CHURCH KNOWLE

The New Inn

Church Knowle, Wareham BH20 5NQ
☎ *(01929) 480357* Mr M Estop

 Wadworth 6X is a permanent fixture, and the one guest beer might be something like Morland Old Speckled Hen.

Beamed sixteenth-century food-oriented pub that has had the same landlord for 18 years, and has featured in several food guidebooks. Part stone, part thatched, with fires in winter, two bars and non-smoking dining area. Garden, car park. Children allowed in one bar.

OPEN *11am–3pm and 6–11pm (10.30pm Sun); opening hours change in winter, so call first to confirm.*

CORFE MULLEN

Coventry Arms
Mill Street, Corfe Mullen BH21 3RH
☎ *(01258) 857284* John Hugo

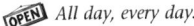 Freehouse serving local beers straight from the barrel, including Ringwood Best and Fortyniner, plus other guests as available.

An old-style, one-bar country pub with food served at lunchtime and evenings in a separate dining area. Children allowed. Located on the main A31.

OPEN *All day, every day.*

CORSCOMBE

The Fox Inn
Corscombe, Nr Beaminster DT2 0NS
☎ *(01935) 891330* Martin and Susie Lee

 Exmoor Ale and Fox, and Fuller's London Pride are the permanent beers here.

Sixteenth-century thatched country pub, with log fire, flagstone floors and beams. No music. A wide variety of food is served in the pub's four dining areas. Garden, car park. Four letting rooms. Well-behaved children allowed. On the Halstock road, on the outskirts of Corscombe.

OPEN *12–3pm and 7–11pm (10.30pm Sun) (afternoon closing times may vary).*

CRANBORNE

The Sheaf of Arrows
The Square, Cranborne BH21 5PR
☎ *(01725) 517456*
Carol Driver and Vicky Donaghue

 Ringwood Best Bitter regularly available plus four constantly changing guest beers. Fuller's London Pride may reappear, but different beers are usually served each time.

Small, friendly village local with lots of passing trade. Open fires in both bars. Garden, pool table, Sky Sports and skittle alley. Home-cooked food served 10–11.30am (breakfast), 12–2pm and 7–9pm daily. No children.

OPEN *10am–2.30pm and 6–11pm Mon–Sat; 12–2.30pm and 7–10.30pm Sun.*

DORCHESTER

Blue Raddle
Church Street, Dorchester DT1 1JN
Arthur and Lesley Ash

 Sharp's Cornish Coaster, Greene King Abbot Ale, Otter Bitter and Raddle Tupping Bitter regularly available, plus two or three guest beers (over 300 in the last five years), perhaps from Hop Back, Tisbury, Oakhill, RCH, Cottage or Sharp's.

Small, market-town pub. Food served 12–2pm Mon–Sat. No children.

OPEN *11.30am–3pm and 7–11pm Mon–Sat; 12–3pm and 7–10.30pm Sun.*

EYPE

The New Inn
Eype DT6 6AP
☎ *(01308) 423254* Jim McClements

 A Palmers tied house, with four pumps serving the range of Palmers brews, changed regularly.

Village pub in a traditional building. Food is available, and there is a separate dining area. Garden, patio. Small car park. Children allowed.

OPEN *12–3pm and 6–11pm Mon–Fri; 12–3pm and 7–10.30pm Sun.*

HINTON ST MARY

The White Horse
Hinton St Mary, Sturminster Newton DT10 1NA
☎ *(01258) 472723* Mr T Spooner-Green

 A freehouse serving a wide range of real ales (8–10 per week) on a rotating basis including Ringwood Best and True Glory plus brews from Tisbury and Cottage Breweries. One light beer (under 3.9% ABV) and one heavy (over 4% ABV) always available. On Fridays one real ale is selected for a special offer at £1 per pint.

A busy nineteenth-century pub. Public bar, lounge bar and beer garden. Restaurant area in the lounge with à la carte menu and specials plus Sunday roasts. Food served at lunchtime and evenings. Children allowed.

OPEN *11.15am–3pm and 6.15–11pm Mon–Sat; 12–3pm and 7–11pm Sun.*

HURN

Avon Causeway Hotel

Hurn, Christchurch BH23 6AS
☎ *(01202) 482714* Keith Perks

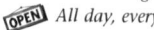Up to seven real ales available, including Red Shoot Forest Gold and Wadworth 6X, plus guests such as Ringwood Best or Old Thumper, to name but two.

A quaint country hotel, ten minutes from Bournemouth. Formerly Hurn railway station, the pub is decorated with lots of railway bric-à-brac. CAMRA and Cask Marque approved. Food served at lunchtime and evenings in a separate large lounge. Murder mystery nights are a feature, and make use of an old Victorian carriage. Beer garden with large children's play area. Inside, children are allowed in dining area only.

OPEN *All day, every day.*

LINWOOD

The Red Shoot Inn

Toms Lane, Linwood, BH24 3QT
☎ *(01425) 475792* Paul and Margo Adams

A Wadworth-managed house which is also the home of the Red Shoot Brewery. The full range of Wadworth ales available plus both Red Shoot ales. Beer festivals held twice a year.

A traditional country brewhouse for lovers of real food and real ale. Prettily situated on the edge of the New Forest. Quiz nights, theme nights and live music. Food available every lunchtime and evening. Children allowed with separate family room and outside children's play area. Well-behaved dogs and muddy boots also welcome. Visit the website at www.redshootinn.co.uk for further details.

OPEN *11am–11pm Mon–Sat; 12–10.30pm Sun.*

LODERS

The Loders Arms

Loders, Nr Bridport DT6 3SA
☎ *(01308) 422431* Helen Flint

Palmers 200, IPA and Bridport Bitter are always available.

Country village pub, a traditional Dorset longhouse, over 200 years old. Food served. Fires, dining area, garden, patio and car park. Two letting rooms, occasional live music in garden. Children allowed.

OPEN *11.30am–3pm and 6–11pm Mon–Sat; 12–10.30pm Sun.*

LOWER BURTON

The Sun Inn

Lower Burton, Nr Dorchester DT2 7RX
☎ *(01305) 250445* Robin Maddex

Three to five constantly changing cask ales available.

A traditional coaching inn with the motto 'Good Beer and Good Cheer'. Garden and disabled facilities. Carvery and bar menu served 12–2.30pm and 6.30–10pm Mon–Sat and 12–9.30pm Sun. Car park. Children's menu and high chairs available. Situated half a mile from Dorchester town centre on the Sherbourne road.

OPEN *11am–11pm Mon–Sat; 12–10.30pm Sun.*

LYME REGIS

The Nag's Head

Silver Street, Lyme Regis DT7 3HS
☎ *(01297) 442312* Mrs Hamon

A freehouse with up to four ales available, perhaps including Ringwood Best.

A traditional one-bar pub with background music and beer garden. Separate dining area. Food served every lunchtime and Mon, Wed, Fri and Sat evenings. Children allowed in the bar or restaurant when eating.

OPEN *11am–3pm and 6–11pm Mon; all day Tues–Sun (10.30pm Sun).*

The Volunteer Inn

31 Broad Street, Lyme Regis DT7 3QE
☎ *(01297) 442214* JP O'Donnell

Fuller's London Pride and house ale Donegal which is brewed by Branscombe Vale are always available. Two constantly changing guest ales served. Regulars include Morland Old Speckled Hen, Adnams Bitter, Young's Bitter, Greene King IPA and Abbot, Otter Bitter and Ale, Hop Back Summer Lightning and Branscombe Vale Branoc.

A small, friendly pub with separate dining area and extensive bar menu; the emphasis is on food, drink and conversation. Food available 12–2.30pm and 6.30–9.30pm Tues–Sat, 12–2.30pm Sun. Children allowed in the dining area only. Located on the main high street, at the top of the hill.

OPEN *11am–11pm Mon–Sat; 12–10.30pm Sun.*

NETTLECOMBE

Marquis of Lorne Inn
Nettlecombe, Nr Bridport DT6 3SY
☎ *(01308) 485236* Julie and David Woodrosse

A Palmers pub with Palmers 200, IPA and Copper permanently served.

Country pub with two bars and a restaurant, in a sixteenth-century farmhouse. The only pub in Dorset that is a member of the Campaign for Real Food, so the focus is on homemade food using local produce. Log fires in winter. Occasional live folk music. Large garden. Car park for 50. Seven double en-suite letting rooms. Children allowed. Half a mile from Powerstock.

 12–2.30pm and 6.30–11pm Mon–Sat; 12–3pm and 7–10.30pm Sun.

NORTH WOOTTON

The Three Elms
North Wootton, Nr Sherborne DT9 5JW
☎ *(01935) 812881* Mr and Mrs Manning

Fuller's London Pride, Shepherd Neame Spitfire Ale, Otter Bitter and Butcombe brews available.

This busy rural roadside pub contains a large collection of 1,500 diecast model cars and lorries in display cabinets around the walls. Bar and restaurant food, including a large vegetarian selection, available at lunchtime and evenings. Children allowed. Accommodation. Situated on the A3030 Sherborne to Sturminster Newton road, two miles from Sherborne.

 11am–2.30pm Mon–Sat, 12–3pm Sun; 6.30–11pm Mon–Thurs, 6–11pm Fri–Sat, 7–10.30pm Sun.

PLUSH

The Brace of Pheasants
Plush DT2 7RQ
☎ *(01300) 348357* Mr Knights

A freehouse with Fuller's London Pride always available, plus one or two weekly rotated guests, including Hop Back Summer Lightning or something from Butcombe, Smiles or Tisbury breweries.

A sixteenth-century thatched village inn. Non-smoking family room, non-smoking restaurant area, large garden. Bar meals and snacks and à la carte restaurant food served lunchtimes and evenings. Children allowed in the garden and family room only. Situated off B3142 Dorchester/Sherborne road.

 12–2.30pm and 7–11pm Mon–Sat; 12–3pm and 7–10.30pm Sun.

POOLE

Bermuda Triangle Freehouse
Parr Street, Lower Parkstone, Poole BH14 0JY
☎ *(01202) 748087* Gisela Crane

Four real ales constantly changing. These may include Timothy Taylor Landlord, Fuller's ESB and London Pride, Adnams Broadside, Hop Back Summer Lightning, Greene King Abbot Ale, Ringwood Old Thumper and Fortyniner. Also Young's, Wychwood, Hampshire, Smiles and Shepherd Neame brews.

An interesting theme pub. German lagers on draught and at least 30 bottled beers from all around the world. Good music, great atmosphere. Bar food at lunchtime. Car park. Near Ashley Cross.

 12–3pm and 5.30–11pm Mon–Fri; all day Sat–Sun.

The Blue Boar
29 Market Close, Poole BH15 1NE
☎ *(01202) 682247* Fax *(01202) 661875*
Jim and Sheila Kellaway and Tim and Clare Welford

A freehouse with five real ales available. Cottage Southern Bitter is a permanent feature, and the two constantly changing guests are from independent breweries.

An unusual three-storey pub in a restored eighteenth-century listed mansion. Cellar bar with live music on Fri and Sun, open-floor music night on Wed, DJ (rock/blues/cajun/jazz/folk/chart) on Sat night. Food served 11.30am–2pm. Pub games (shove ha'penny, darts), children's certificate while meals are served. Comfortable lounge bar on ground floor. Conference facility with bar on first floor.

 11am–3pm and 5–11pm Mon–Sat; 12–4pm and 7–10.30pm Sun.

The Brewhouse
68 High Street, Poole BH15 1DA
☎ *(01202) 685288*

Tied to Milk Street Brewery, with Milk Street Mermaid and Beer always on offer.

A welcoming pub with a varied clientele. Pool table and darts team. Pub has narrow frontage on High Street, so could easily be missed.

 *All day, every day.*

Hogs Head
35–7 High Street, Poole BH15 1AB
☎ *(01202) 670520* David Neil

 A Hogshead-managed pub with six pumps. Marston's Pedigree, Brakspear Bitter, Hook Norton Old Hooky, Ringwood Best and Timothy Taylor Landlord are always available, and Greene King Abbot is often on offer. Seasonal beers are also served.

Town pub in a very old building. Air-conditioned, with excellent staff, games machines, log fires and non-smoking area. Food served 12–9pm (until 7pm Fri–Sat). Car park. Children not allowed. To find the pub, face the High Street and walk towards the Quay from the Dolphin Centre.

OPEN *11am–11pm Mon–Sat; 12–10.30pm Sun.*

Poole Arts Centre
Kingsland Road, Poole BH15 1UG
☎ *(01202) 665334* Keith Dorkar (Bar Manager)

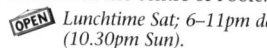 Poole Best Bitter is always on offer, plus one weekly changing guest, such as Ruddles Best, Ringwood Old Thumper or Greene King Abbot.

Freehouse café bar within the Arts Centre, with food available. Children allowed. Situated in the centre of Poole.

OPEN *Lunchtime Sat; 6–11pm daily (10.30pm Sun).*

Sandacres Free House
3 Banks Road, Sandbanks, Poole BH13 7PW
☎ *(01202) 707244* Peter Fay (Manager)

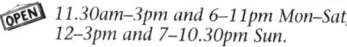 Ringwood Best and Fortyniner and Morland Old Speckled Hen permanently available, plus two guests, usually from smaller local breweries such as Palmers.

A modern-style waterside pub in Poole Harbour with lovely views. One large bar, children's area, outside seating. Disabled facilities with no steps. Food served at lunchtimes and evenings. Children allowed until 9pm. Website: www.thesandacres.co.uk.

OPEN *11.30am–3pm and 6–11pm Mon–Sat; 12–3pm and 7–10.30pm Sun.*

Halsey Arms
Pulham, Dorchester DT2 7DZ
☎ *(01258) 817344* Julyan Letzow

 A freehouse serving beers from Ringwood, Tisbury and Fuller's, plus regular guests such as Mauldons Black Adder and brews from Bath Ales and Cottage Brewery.

A traditional pub with a friendly atmosphere – everyone welcome! Wide-ranging menu available, including carvery on Sunday lunchtimes, children's and over-60s' menus plus a good range of sandwiches. Happy hour. Large car park.

OPEN *12–3pm and 6–11pm Mon–Fri; 11am–11pm Sat; 12–10.30pm Sun.*

The Digby Tap
Cooks Lane, Sherborne DT9 3NS
☎ *(01935) 813148* Peter LeFevre

 Twenty different beers served each week from a range of 100 per year. Brews from the Smiles, Teignworthy, Ringwood, Exmoor, Oakhill, Otter and Cottage breweries, plus many other regional producers.

A traditional, local, one-bar pub with flagstone floors. Bar snacks available at lunchtime (not on Sundays). Children are allowed at lunchtime only. Just 100 yards from the abbey, towards the railway station.

OPEN *11am–2.30pm and 5.30–11pm Mon–Sat; 12–2.30pm and 7–10.30pm Sun.*

The Cricketers
Shroton, Nr Blandford Forum DT11 8QD
☎ *(01258) 860421* George and Carol Cowie

 Ringwood Fortyniner and Fuller's London Pride feature regularly, with many guest ales from various breweries, including Wychwood, Butcombe, Brakspear and Otter.

Very friendly freehouse with pretty, sheltered garden and children's play area, situated between village green and Hambledon Hill. Good for walking. Well-known locally for good food from blackboard menu, available lunchtimes and evenings seven days a week. One luxury en-suite bed and breakfast garden room. Children allowed. Large beer garden. Located just off the A350 between Blandford and Shaftbury.

OPEN *11.30am–2.30pm and 6.30–11pm Mon–Fri; 11.30am–3pm and 6.30–10.30pm Sat; 12–3pm and 6.30–10.20pm Sun.*

SPYWAY

The Spyway Inn
Spyway, Askerswell, Dorchester DT2 9EP
☎ *(01308) 485250*
Mr A Dodds and Mrs LS Nugent

 Greene King IPA and Abbot Ale plus Branscombe Vale Branoc and an Adnams beer usually available with one other Greene King brew.

Old smugglers' lookout, situated in glorious Dorset countryside. Atmospheric bars with oak beams, high-backed settles and vast collection of china cups. Good walks from the pub. Terrace and garden. Food served 12–2pm and 7–9pm Tues–Sat; 12–2pm Sun. Large car park. Separate dining room for families.

OPEN *11am–3pm and 6–11pm Tues–Sat; 12–3pm and 7–10.30pm Sun.*

STOURTON CAUNDLE

Trooper
Stourton Caundle, Sturminster Newton DT10 2JW
☎ *(01963) 362405* Mr Larry Skeats

 A freehouse with something from Palmers always available and an Oakhill brew usually served. Guest beers, changed very frequently, might include Exmoor Ale, Fuller's London Pride, Greene King Abbot, Ringwood Best, Sharp's Doom Bar, Hampshire King Alfred's Bitter or Badger Best.

A very small pub with two bars and a countryside and rural museum. Claims to be the friendliest pub in Dorset! Snacks served at lunchtime. Children allowed at lunchtime only. Situated off the main road, can be difficult to find.

OPEN *12–2.30pm and 7–11pm (closed Monday lunchtimes except on bank holidays).*

STUDLAND

The Banks Arms
Manor Road, Studland BH19 3AU
☎ *(01929) 450225* Mr and Mrs Lightbown

 A freehouse with eight pumps. The one permanent beer is chosen at the annual beer festival, held every August and featuring beers from 30 breweries. The winner remains a permanent fixture for the whole year. The seven guests, changed daily, might be from breweries such as Cottage, Smiles, Wychwood or Badger.

Country village inn overlooking the sea, with two fires, beams and dining area. The only pub in the village! Award-winning food available. Fruit machine, live music, garden. Car park. Eight en-suite letting rooms. Children allowed.

OPEN *11am–11pm Mon–Sat; 12–10.30pm Sun.*

TARRANT MONKTON

The Langton Arms
Tarrant Monkton, Nr Blandford DT11 8RX
☎ *(01258) 830225* Barbara Cassins

 A freehouse serving 30 different guest ales every month through four real ale pumps. A fifth pump permanently serves The Langton's Best, brewed by Ringwood Brewery.

An attractive seventeenth-century thatched inn with a separate restaurant (evenings only). Bar food available lunchtime and evenings. Car park, garden, children's room and play area. Accommodation. Less than two miles off the A354 Blandford to Salisbury road, five miles north of Blandford. Website: www.thelangtonarms.co.uk.

OPEN *All day, every day.*

TRENT

The Rose & Crown
Trent, Nr Sherborne DT9 4SL
☎ *(01935) 850776* Mr and Mrs Crawford

Butcombe Best and Shepherd Neame Spitfire always available plus two guest beers (24 per year) including Wadworth 6X, Charles Wells Bombardier, Otter Ale plus brews from Smiles, Hook Norton and Samuel Smith.

A fifteenth-century part-thatched freehouse opposite Trent church. Bar and restaurant food available at lunchtime and evenings. Car park, garden, children's room and playground. Less than two miles north of the A30 between Sherborne and Yeovil.

OPEN *12–2.30pm and 7–11pm Mon–Sat; 12–3pm and 7–10.30pm Sun.*

VERWOOD

Albion Inn

Station Road, Verwood BH31 7LB

☎ *(01202) 825267* Rex Neville

 An Enterprise Inns pub, with Ringwood Best Bitter always available.

A traditional two-bar layout. Was previously a railway-owned hotel. Food served at lunchtime and evenings (restaurant closed Monday evening). Patio and garden plus children's garden.

OPEN *All day, every day.*

WESTBOURNE

The Porterhouse

113 Poole Road, Westbourne BH4 9BG

☎ *(01202) 768586* Ray Rutter

Ringwood Best, Fortyniner and Old Thumper always available, plus regular guests changed every few days such as Fuller's London Pride, Everards Mild, Hop Back Summer Lightning or Hogs Back Hop Garden Gold.

A traditional one-bar pub on the main road. Food served at lunchtime only. No children under 14.

OPEN *All day, every day.*

WEYMOUTH

King's Arms

15 Trinity Road, Weymouth DT4 8TJ

☎ *(01305) 770055* Martin Taylor

Wadworth 6X and Ringwood Best and Fortyniner always available, plus one regular guest from the Quay Brewery, perhaps Weymouth JD.

An olde-worlde quayside pub owned by Greenalls, with separate dining area. Two bars, pool table. Food served every lunchtime and Wed–Sat evenings. Children allowed.

OPEN *All day, every day.*

The Weatherbury Freehouse

7 Carlton Road North, Weymouth DT4 7PX

☎ *(01305) 786040* Mr and Mrs Cromack

Four beers (200 per year) which may include Townes IPA, Badger Tanglefoot, Wild's Redhead and Fuller's London Pride.

A busy town local in a residential position. Bar and restaurant food available at lunchtime and evenings. Car park, patio and dining area (where children are allowed). Accommodation. Dart board and pool table. Coming in to Weymouth, turn right off the Dorchester road.

OPEN *12–11pm (10.30pm Sun).*

WINKTON

The Lamb Inn

Burley Road, Winkton BH23 7AN

☎ *(01425) 672427* Mr and Mrs J Haywood

Four real ale pumps, one serving Fuller's London Pride, the others with a range of ales such as Ringwood Best Bitter.

Situated on the edge of the New Forest, this pub has a lounge and public bar. Bar and restaurant food available at lunchtime and evenings. Car park and garden. Children are allowed in the restaurant and garden.

OPEN *11am–3pm and 5–11pm Mon–Fri; 11am–11pm Sat; 12–10.30pm Sun.*

WYKE REGIS

The Wyke Smugglers

76 Portland Road, Wyke Regis, Weymouth DT4 9AB

☎ *(01305) 760010* Mick Nellville

Ringwood Old Thumper always available plus two real ales served as guests which change weekly.

A local drinkers' pub, sport orientated. No food. No children.

OPEN *11am–2.30pm and 6–11.30pm.*

YOU TELL US

* *Tom Brown's,* 47 High East Street, Dorchester

Places Featured:

Barnard Castle
Billy Row
Bishop Auckland
Bolam
Consett
Croxdale
Darlington
Durham
Forest in Teesdale
Framwellgate Moor

Great Lumley
Hartlepool
Kirk Merrington
Middlestone Village
Newton Aycliffe
No Place
North Bitchburn
Rookhope
Shadforth
Tantobie

THE BREWERIES

CATHEDRALS BREWERY CO LTD

Court Lane, Durham City DH1 3JS
☎ *(0191) 370 9632*

CATHEDRALS BITTER 3.9% ABV
A light brown, hoppy bitter; session beer.
BISHOP'S STOUT 4.4% ABV
Dry Irish-style stout; black and bitter.
BOBBY'S BEST BITTER 4.5% ABV
Tawny brown in colour with malty caramel notes.
CATHEDRALS LAGER 4.5% ABV
Continental Pilsner-style lager; brewed exclusively with Saaz hops from the Czech Republic.
Seasonal Brewer's Choice:
PRIORY SUMMER ALE 3.2% ABV
EADMER EASTER BEER 3.5% ABV
SUMMER FRUIT ALE 3.7% ABV
GRADUATION ALE 4.0% ABV
DUNELM DARK BEER 4.3% ABV
COURT RUBY ALE 4.5% ABV
CUTHBERTUS WHEAT BEER 4.7% ABV
OLD SHIRE HALL GOLDEN BITTER 4.8% ABV
CASTLE PORTER 5.0% ABV
OLD ELVET WINTER WARMER 5.1% ABV
NEW ELVET IPA 5.5% ABV
ST OSWALD'S CHRISTMAS ALE 6.0% ABV

DARWIN BREWERY,

Unit 5, Castle Close, Crook DL15 8LU
☎ *(01388) 763200*
www.darwinbrewery.com

DARWIN'S BITTER 3.6% ABV
Light, refreshing and fruity. Good hoppiness.
SUNDERLAND BEST 3.9% ABV
Light, smooth and creamy.
DURHAM LIGHT 4.0% ABV
Light colour with good bitter hoppiness.
EVOLUTION ALE 4.0% ABV
Good hoppiness.
HODGE'S ORIGINAL 4.0% ABV
Balanced.
SMUGGLER'S MILD 4.0% ABV
Rich roasted mild ale.
RICHMOND ALE 4.8% ABV
Rounded and smooth.
SAINTS SINNER 5.0% ABV
Dark with powerful roast flavour.
KILLER BEE 6.0% ABV
Powerful honeyed flavour.
EXTINCTION 8.3% ABV
A classic strong ale.

THE DURHAM BREWERY
Unit 5a, Bowburn North Industrial Est.,
Bowburn DH6 5PF
☎ *(0191) 377 1991*
www.durham-brewery.co.uk

The White Range:
 SUNSTROKE 3.6% ABV
Summer ale.
GREEN GODDESS 3.8% ABV
Refreshing and spicy.
MAGUS 3.8% ABV
Pale, well-hopped lager-style beer.
WHITE GOLD 4.0% ABV
Pale, refreshing with citrus fruit flavours.
WHITE SAPPHIRE 4.5% ABV
Quenching and quaffable.
CUTHBERT'S ALE 5.0% ABV
Refreshing, golden and fruity.
The Gold Range:
FROSTBITE 3.6% ABV
Winter ale.
PRIORS GOLD 4.5% ABV
CATHEDRAL GOLD 5.1% ABV
MAGNIFICAT 6.5% ABV
The Dark Range:
BLACK BISHOP 5.5% ABV
Black stout with powerful roast malt flavour.
SANCTUARY 6.0% ABV
Rounded, old ale.
Plus seasonal brews.

TRIMDON CASK ALES
Unit 2c, T G Industrial Estate, Trimdon Grange
TS29 6PA
☎ *(01429) 880967*

BUSTY BITTER 4.3% ABV
TILLEY BITTER 4.3% ABV
HARVEY BITTER 4.9% ABV
PITPROP 6.2% ABV

THE PUBS

BARNARD CASTLE

The Black Horse Hotel
10 Newgate, Barnard Castle DL12 8NG
☎ *(01833) 637234* Mr Landon

Castle Eden pub with Castle Eden Bitter and Nimmo's XXXX always on offer.

Rural pub in a stone building dating from the seventeenth century, formerly a coaching inn. Food available – the pub is famous for its steaks. Function room, pool room, snug area and private dining area for small parties. Occasional live music. Car park at rear. Five letting rooms. Children allowed.

OPEN *7–11pm Mon–Tues; varies on Wed–Thurs; 11am–11pm Fri–Sat; 12–10.30pm Sun.*

BILLY ROW

Dun Cow Inn (Cow Tail)
Old White Lea, Billy Row, Crook
Steve Parkin

One or two Darwin beers regularly available from a changing selection which may include Richmond Ale.

Established in 1740, this pub is only open four nights a week and has a unique atmosphere. 'A bit of a good crack.' The current licensee has been here since 1960. Car park. Well-behaved children welcome.

OPEN *8–11pm Wed, Fri, Sat; 8–10.30pm Sun.*

BISHOP AUCKLAND

Newton Cap
Newton Cap Bank, Bishop Auckland DA14 7PX
☎ *(01388) 605445* Christine Peart

Tied to Castle Eden. One guest ale, changed monthly, is available, and the policy is not to repeat beers if possible.

This has been a pub since the nineteenth century. Pool room, lounge, patio. No food. Car parking space available. Accompanied children allowed, but not in evenings. Situated on the outskirts of town, two miles from the bus station.

OPEN *12–4pm and 7–11pm (10.30pm Sun); closed Tues lunch.*

BOLAM

The Countryman
Bolam, Nr Darlington DL2 2UP
☎ *(01388) 834577* David Clarke

Five guest pumps serve beers from local breweries, such as Mordue Workie Ticket, Northumberland Secret Kingdom, Durham Magus, Rudgate Battleaxe and Black Sheep Bitter, to name but a few. Guests change every couple of days.

A 150-year-old one-bar country pub, with beams and coal fires, that has won awards for its beer and food. Non-smoking dining area, garden, car park for 50 cars. Children allowed. On the A68 between Darlington and West Buckland.

OPEN *12–2pm and 6pm–midnight (10.30pm Sun); closed Mon.*

CONSETT

The Grey Horse
115 Sherburn Terrace, Consett DH8 6NE
☎ *(01207) 502585* Mr and Mrs Conroy

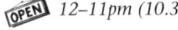Home of the Derwent Rose Brewery, with home beers brewed and always available on the premises, plus up to four other ales.

A brewpub with traditional interior including two log fires in winter. No juke box or loud music. Snacks available, including famous lunchtime doorstep 'sarnies'. No children. Website: www.thegreyhorse.co.uk.

MUTTON CLOG 3.8% ABV
Hoppy, bittersweet beer.
STEEL TOWN 3.8 % ABV
Hop flavours and bitter aftertaste.
RED DUST 4.2% ABV
Ruby coloured, with malt and fruit flavours. Bittersweet in the finish.
SWORDMAKER 4.5% ABV
Fruit and malt flavours, with bitter hop finish.
COAST 2 COAST 5.0% ABV
Balanced, hoppy bitter.
DERWENT DEEP 5.0% ABV
Deep-coloured, with roast barley flavour, and hops in the finish.

OPEN *12–11pm (10.30pm Sun).*

CROXDALE

The Daleside Arms
Front Street, Croxdale, Durham DH6 5HY
☎ *(01388) 814165* Mr Patterson

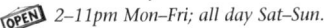A freehouse with Black Sheep Special and Mordue Workie Ticket always available. Four guest beers, which change weekly, include other favourites from Mordue, Black Sheep and Border breweries.

A village pub in a country setting, with en-suite accommodation and two bars (a pub/lounge and restaurant). Food served at lunchtimes only. Children allowed.

OPEN *2–11pm Mon–Fri; all day Sat–Sun.*

Number Twenty 2
Coniscliffe Road, Darlington DL3 7RG
☎ *(01325) 354590* Mr Wilkinson

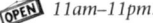Ten ales including Hambleton Nightmare, White Boar and Old Raby always available plus guests (500 per year) such as Dent Ramsbottom, Hadrian Gladiator and Butterknowle's Conciliation.

Traditional town-centre freehouse. Food available at lunchtime and evenings. Parking nearby, children allowed.

OPEN *11am–11pm.*

The Railway Tavern
8 High Northgate, Darlington DL1 1UN
☎ *(01325) 464963* Mr C Greenhow

Tied to Enterprise, this pub offers Wadworth 6X and Bateman XXXB on a fairly regular basis. Guests include beers from Durham, Mordue, Timothy Taylor, Northumberland, Rudgate, Marston Moor and others.

This small local pub was probably the first 'Railway Inn' in the world, as it is situated 150 metres from the first passenger station in the world. The land on which it stands was owned by the Pease family, founders of the Darlington–Stockton Railway. On the main road through Darlington, the pub has two bars, one of which has pool and darts, and features live music on Friday nights. Children allowed if supervised.

OPEN *12–11pm.*

Tap & Spile
99 Bondgate, Darlington DL3 7JY
☎ *(01325) 381679* Marian Holtby

Caledonian Deuchars IPA permanently available, plus up to four guests which regularly include Marston's Pedigree among many others.

Traditional town-centre pub with two bars, a function room and live music Thurs–Sun. Bar food available Mon–Sat lunchtime. Children allowed if eating. Outside café pavement licence. Disabled facilities.

OPEN *11.30am–11pm Mon–Thurs; 11.30am–midnight Fri–Sat; 12–11pm Sun.*

DURHAM

Cathedrals Bar

Court Lane, Durham City DH1 3JS
☎ *(0191) 370 9632*
Richard Lazenby and Simon Lazenby

 A mixture of hand-pulled ales and contemporary copper vessels and fermenting tanks from the on-site Cathedrals Micro-brewery. The micro-brewery produces a range of beers with names incorporating local heritage and flavours reflecting a range of styles, mixing tradition with innovation. House-style cocktails and a large range of hand-selected wines also available.

A traditional pub atmosphere with 'pub grub' available all day, including home-made soup and fresh bread, freshly made pizza, hand-crafted pork pie and pickle or a choice of hot and cold sandwiches with chips or salad. All the food is freshly produced on-site from local, seasonal produce and authentic ingredients by a team of 47 chefs and bakers. Cathedrals also offer a Fine Dine restaurant, Bistro, Coffee House and Pantry. Brewery visits are available with advance booking.

OPEN *11am–11pm Mon–Sat; 12–10.30pm Sun.*

Ye Old Elm Tree

12 Crossgate, Durham DH1 4PS
☎ *(0191) 386 4621* Mr Dave Cruddace

 Regular guests, two rotating every two weeks, may include Fuller's London Pride, Morland Old Speckled Hen or Bateman XXXB.

An alehouse dating from 1601, situated in the centre of Durham city, off Framwellgate Bridge. Two guest rooms, beer garden and patio. The bar is built round an elm tree. Quiz and folk nights held. Light snacks at lunchtime and evenings. Children allowed.

OPEN *12–3pm and 6–11pm Mon–Fri; 11am–11pm Sat; 12–4pm and 7–10.30pm Sun.*

FOREST IN TEESDALE

The High Force Hotel

Forest in Teesdale DL12 0XH
☎ *(01833) 622222* Gary Wilson

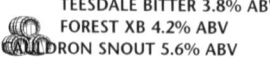 Home of the High Force brewery with three own brews always available.

A country hotel, which is easy to find, serving food at lunchtime and evenings. Children allowed.

TEESDALE BITTER 3.8% ABV
 FOREST XB 4.2% ABV
CAULDRON SNOUT 5.6% ABV

OPEN *11am–11pm Mon–Sat; 12–10.30pm Sun. Opening hours subject to seasonal variation.*

FRAMWELLGATE MOOR

Tap & Spile

27 Front Street, Framwellgate Moor, Durham DH1 5EE
☎ *(0191) 386 5451* Jean McPoland

 Up to nine beers available. Marston's Pedigree and Fuller's London Pride are usually among them.

A traditional pub with a family room, non-smoking room, and games room for darts and billiards. Pet-friendly. Snacks served all day. Children allowed. Two miles north of Durham city centre, on the old A1.

OPEN *11.30am–3pm and 6–11pm Mon–Sat; 12–3pm and 7–10.30pm Sun.*

GREAT LUMLEY

The Old England

Front Street, Great Lumley, Nr Chester le Street DH3 4JB
☎ *(0191) 388 5257* Mr Barkess

 Three or four different ales a week are available in this freehouse, with a good mix of nationals and micro-breweries from all over the country. Regular guests include Hop Back Summer Lightning and brews from Caledonian and Wychwood.

A pub/restaurant set off the road, with a 200-seat lounge, 150-seat bar, separate dining area, darts, dominoes, pool. Food served mostly during evenings, lunchtime at weekends. Children allowed in dining area.

OPEN *11am–11pm Mon–Sat; 12–10.30pm Sun.*

HARTLEPOOL

Tavern

56 Church Street, Hartlepool TS24 7DX
☎ *(01429) 222400* Chris Sewell

 Camerons Strongarm and three guest beers regularly available such as Orkney Dark Island or something from the Jennings range.

Traditional town-centre one-bar pub with upstairs, open-plan dining area. Home-cooked food served 11am–2pm and 5–8pm Mon–Sat, 12–4pm Sun. Children welcome until 8pm and they eat half price. Situated close to the railway station.

OPEN *11am–3pm and 5–11pm Mon–Fri; 11am–11pm Sat; 12–3pm and 7–10.30pm Sun.*

KIRK MERRINGTON

The Half Moon Inn
Crowther Place, Kirk Merrington, Nr Spennymoor DL16 7JL
☎ *(01388) 811598* Mrs Crooks

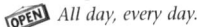 Something from Durham Brewery always available in this freehouse. Favourite guest beers might come from the Kitchen Brewery, or include Elgood's Black Dog and Hart Squirrels Hoards. Anything and everything has been tried.

A traditional pub on the village green, with one room, games area and car park. Bar meals at lunchtime and evening. Children allowed up to 8pm.

OPEN *All day, every day.*

MIDDLESTONE VILLAGE

The Ship Inn
Low Row, Middlestone Village, Bishop Auckland DL14 8AB
☎ *(01388) 810904* Graham Snaith

 A freehouse with up to six real ales available. Ales from local breweries such as Durham, Daleside and Big Lamp are popular.

A well-appointed traditional pub with a small bar and lounge. Built into the hillside in walking country, it offers panoramic views. Restaurant on first-floor balcony doubles as a function room. Food served from 6–9pm Wed–Sat plus Sunday lunchtimes. Children allowed if parents are eating.

OPEN *12–2pm and 5–11pm Mon–Thurs; 12–11pm Fri–Sat; 12–10.30pm Sun.*

NEWTON AYCLIFFE

The Blacksmith's Arms
Preston-le-Skerne, Newton Aycliffe DL5 6JH
☎ *(01325) 314873* Pat Cook

 Three local beers are rotated each week (100 per year). Favourites come from Hambleton, Barnsley and a range of microbrewers.

A country pub in the middle of farmland, in an isolated position two miles from Newton Aycliffe. Two bars, a one-acre beer garden, rabbits and a plant nursery. Ice creams served. Food available at lunchtime and evenings, outdoors in summer. Children allowed.

OPEN *All day, every day in summer. 12–3pm and 6.30–11pm in winter.*

NO PLACE

Beamish Mary Inn
No Place, Nr Stanley DH9 0QH
☎ *(0191) 370 0237* Graham Ford

 Black Sheep Special and Bitter and Jennings Cumberland Ale always available, plus three guests often including No Place, a beer brewed specially by Big Lamp Brewery. Others come from Border and other small local breweries.

Over 100 years old, this pub is a throwback from the Beamish Museum housing many interesting artefacts. Live music four nights a week in the converted stables of the old barn. Food served 12–2pm and 7–9.30pm in a separate restaurant area. B&B. Children allowed.

OPEN *12–3pm and 6–11pm Mon–Thurs; all day Fri–Sun.*

NORTH BITCHBURN

Famous Red Lion
North Bitchburn Terrace, Nr Crook DL15 8AL
☎ *(01388) 763561* Mr Kyte

 A freehouse with Black Sheep Special, Marston's Pedigree and Greene King Abbot always available. There is also an ever-changing guest beer, sourced from local breweries and around the country.

An easy-to-find, typical, olde-worlde inn with open fires, one bar, a small patio and a separate restaurant. Food served at lunchtime and evenings. Children allowed.

OPEN *12–3pm and 7–11pm (10.30pm Sun).*

ROOKHOPE

The Rookhope Inn
Rookhope, Nr Stanhope DL13 2BG
☎ *(01388) 517215* Stephen Thompson

 A freehouse offering a constantly changing choice of beers. A Hexhamshire and a Hadrian (Four Rivers) brew are always available, with Four Rivers Moondance and Hexhamshire Devil's Water particularly popular. Also Butterknowle Conciliation and Fuller's London Pride. No nationals; other guests are sourced as special offers through wholesalers or direct from small breweries.

A seventeenth-century pub with open fires and real beams. Three rooms (games/lounge/restaurant). Prior booking required for restaurant; soup and sandwiches served in bar and lounge. Children allowed in games room and restaurant.

OPEN *7–11pm daily; 12–3pm Sat–Sun (and weekdays by arrangement).*

SHADFORTH

The Plough Inn

South Side, Shadforth, Durham DH6 1LL
☎ *(0191) 372 0375* Jane Barber

 A freehouse with a varied and ever-changing range of beers, which change once or twice a week. Regular guests, which now number in the hundreds, come mainly from independents and micro-breweries. You name it, they've probably served it!

A small, traditional country pub, with one bar and lounge. No food. Children allowed.

OPEN *6.30–11pm Mon–Fri; 11am–11pm Sat; 12–10.30pm Sun.*

TANTOBIE

The Highlander

White-le-Head, Tantobie, Nr Stanley DH9 9SN
☎ *(01207) 232416* Mr CD Wright

Up to 100 beers per year changed weekly including something from Thwaites, Timothy Taylor, Black Sheep and Marston's, plus beers from many other smaller breweries as available.

One bar has games and music (pool, darts, etc). Also a small lounge and dining area. Hot food available on weekday evenings and weekend afternoons. Car park, beer garden and function room. Children welcome. Occasional accommodation. Ring to check. One mile off the A692 between Tantobie and Flint Hill.

OPEN *7.30–11pm Mon–Fri; 12.30–3pm and 7.30–11pm Sat–Sun.*

YOU TELL US

* *Dun Cow,* 43 Front Street, Sedgefield
* *Tap & Spile,* 13 Cockton Hill Road, Bishop Auckland
* *Traders,* Blue Post Yard, Stockton-on-Tees

Places Featured:

Basildon
Billericay
Birdbrook
Black Notely
Brentwood
Brightlingsea
Burnham-on-Crouch
Chelmsford
Colchester
Coxtie Green
Earls Colne
Epping
Feering
Finchingfield
Fyfield
Gestingthorpe
Hatfield Broad Oak
Herongate Tye
High Roding
Horndon on the Hill
Hutton
Leigh-on-Sea
Little Clacton
Little Oakley
Littlebury
Maldon
Manningtree
Mill Green

Moreton
Navestock Heath
Ongar
Orsett
Pebmarsh
Pleshey
Radwinter
Rickling Green
Ridgewell
Rochford
Shalford
South Fambridge
Southend-on-Sea
Southminster
Stanford Rivers
Stisted
Stock
Stow Maries
Tendring
Thornwood Common
Tillingham
Toot Hill
Wendens Ambo
White Roding
Witham
Woodham Ferrers
Woodham Water

THE BREWERIES

CROUCH VALE BREWERY LTD

12 Redhills Road, South Woodham Ferrers, Chelmsford CM3 5UP
☎ *(01245) 322744*
www.crouch-vale.co.uk

ESSEX BOYS BITTER 3.5% ABV
Plenty of malt and hop flavour.
BLACKWATER MILD 3.7% ABV
Smooth, dark and malty.
BEST BITTER 4.0% ABV
Malt and fruit, some hops. Bitter finish.
BREWERS GOLD 4.0% ABV
Hoppy with tropical fruit aromas.
ANCHOR STREET PORTER 4.9% ABV
Rounded, roast barley flavour.
Plus occasional brews.

THE FELSTAR BREWERY

Felsted Vineyard, Crix Green, Felsted CM6 3JT
☎ *(01245) 361504*

ROOSTER'S ALE 3.8% ABV
Traditional, lightly spicy.
CRIX GOLD 4.2% ABV
Light gold coloured and refreshing.
HOPSIN 4.2% ABV
Dry with hint of liquorice and aniseed.
BETTY'S BEST 5.0% ABV
Full bodied.
Seasonals and specials:
ROOSTER'S KNIGHT 3.4% ABV
HOP-HOP-HURRAY 4.0% ABV
HOPPIN' HEN 4.5% ABV
HOPS AND GLORY 4.8% ABV
PECKIN' ORDER 5.0% ABV
HAUNTED HEN 6.0% ABV
ROOSTER'S DOUBLE MALT 7.0% ABV
Plus a range of bottled ales.

MIGHTY OAK BREWING CO.

14B West Station Yard, Spital Road, Mauldon CM9 6TW
☎ *(01621) 843713*

IPA 3.5% ABV
Occasional. Pale golden. Good hoppy bitterness.

OSCAR WILDE 3.7% ABV
Mellow and nutty dark mild. Seasonal.

BURNTWOOD BITTER 4.0% ABV
Copper-coloured, deep hops and rounded malt.

BRASS MONKEY 4.1% ABV
Subtle malt flavour.

ALE DANCER 4.2% ABV
Gentle bitterness with good malt flavour.

SAFFRON GOLD 4.3% ABV
Clean, refreshing bitter after palate.

SIMPLY THE BEST 4.4% ABV
Clean and fragrant with distinctive bitterness.

ESSEX COUNTY ALE 4.6% ABV
Good hoppy bitterness and balancing malt.

MIGHTY OAK BITTER 4.8% ABV
Strong and complex flavours.

SPICE 7.0% ABV
Dark, spicy and complex.

TD RIDLEY AND SONS LTD

Hartford End Brewery, Chelmsford CM3 1JZ
☎ *(01371) 820316*
www.ridleys.co.uk

IPA 3.5% ABV
Flavour of hops, with some malt.

PROSPECT 4.1% ABV
Rich golden ale.

RUMPUS 4.5% ABV
Ruby, with smooth nutty character.

OLD BOB 5.1% ABV
Flavoursome and heartening.

Plus monthly specials and occasional brews.

THE PUBS

BASILDON

The Moon on the Square

11–15 Market Square, Basildon SS14 1DF
☎ *(01268) 520360* Jon and Carol Pyne

 A Wetherspoon's pub. Eight guests, changed weekly, from a list that includes Shepherd Neame Spitfire, Adnams Clipper, Arundel Old Knuckler, Eldridge Pope's Royal Oak, Spinnaker and Hop Back brews amongst other independents.

A busy market pub with one large bar. A mixed clientele of business customers and lunchtime shoppers. Food served all day. No children.

OPEN *11am–11pm Mon–Sat; 12–10.30pm Sun.*

BILLERICAY

The Coach & Horses

36 Chapel Street, Billericay CM12 9LU
☎ *(01277) 622873* Mr J Childs

 Greene King IPA and Abbot and something from Adnams always available, plus weekly changing guest beers. Tries to stock independent breweries' beers whenever possible.

A town pub with one bar. Friendly locals but clientele tend to be business lunchers during the day, regulars in the evening. Food available Mon–Sat. Beer garden. No children. Next to Waitrose.

OPEN *All day Mon–Sat; 12–3.30pm and 7–10.30pm Sun.*

BIRDBROOK

The Plough

The Street, Birdbrook CO9 4BJ
☎ *(01440) 785336* Stuart Walton

 Adnams Best and Greene King IPA always available, plus rotating guest beers.

A sixteenth-century thatched freehouse with a very low beamed ceiling. Two interlinking bars, safe beer garden. Food served every lunchtime and evening except Sunday evenings. Children allowed. Follow signs to Birdbrook from A1017.

OPEN *11.30am–3pm and 6–11pm (10.30pm Sun).*

BLACK NOTELY

The Vine Inn

105 The Street, Black Notely, Nr Braintree CM7 8LJ
☎ *(01376) 324269* Arthur Hodges

 One Adnams brew and Ridleys IPA always available plus three guests changed three or four times a week. Regulars have included Kelham Island Pale Rider and Nethergate Old Growler and Augustinian.

A country freehouse dating from 1640 with an old barn end, stone floor and a minstrel's gallery which is used as a small restaurant and for beer festivals. Food served at lunchtime and evenings. Children allowed. A couple of mile outside Braintree on the Notely Road

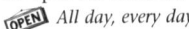 *12–2pm and 6.30–11pm Mon–Fri; all day Sat–Sun.*

BRENTWOOD

The Swan

123 High Street, Brentwood CM14 4RX
☎ *(01277) 211848* Sarah and Gary Eynon

 Young's Special, Fuller's London Pride, Brakspear Bitter, Marston's Pedigree, Wadworth 6X, Greene King IPA and Adnams Best always available, plus four weekly changing guests such as Adnams Broadside, Shepherd Neame Spitfire and seasonal ales from all over the UK.

A thirteenth-century pub with a friendly atmosphere. Mainly a locals' pub with quiet background music. Food served 12–9pm. No children.

 All day, every day.

BRIGHTLINGSEA

The Famous Railway Tavern

58 Station Road, Brightlingsea CO7 0DT
☎ *(01206) 302581* David English

 Crouch Vale Best, a dark mild, a stout and a real cider always available, plus up to five guests from local breweries such as Tolly Cobbold amongst others. Gravity-fed in winter.

A friendly, traditional pub with real fire and floorboards. No fruit machines or juke box in the public bar. Garden, children's room. Table football, shove ha'penny, darts, cribbage, dominoes. Campsite opposite, 11 pubs within walking distance. Buskers' afternoon held once a month between October and April. Annual cider festival held during first week of May.

 CRAB & WINKLE MILD 3.7% ABV
SPAT & OYSTER BITTER 4.3% ABV
BLADDERWRACK STOUT 4.7% ABV

 5–11pm Mon–Thurs; 3–11pm Fri; 12–11pm Sat; 12–3pm and 7–10.30pm Sun.

BURNHAM-ON-CROUCH

The Anchor Hotel

The Quay, Burnham-on-Crouch CM0 8AT
☎ *(01621) 782117* Mr Veal

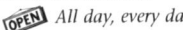 Greene King IPA and Adnams and Crouch Vale brews usually available, plus three guests from breweries such as Titanic or Ridleys. Seasonal ales also stocked.

A locals' pub with a broad clientele in a small seaside town with seating on the sea wall. Two bars, dining area. Food available at lunchtime and evenings. Children allowed.

 All day, every day.

CHELMSFORD

The Queen's Head

30 Lower Anchor Street, Chelmsford CM2 0AS
☎ *(01245) 265181* Mike Collins

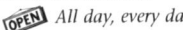 One of two local Crouch Vale-owned houses. Crouch Vale Best and seasonal ales always available, plus guests (400 a year), always including a mild, stout or porter. Guests come from a range of independent breweries such as Elgood's Buffy's, RCH, Titanic and Orkney.

A traditional alehouse a mile from the cricket ground. Built in 1895 but totally refurbished – one bar with real fires, courtyard and beer garden. Pub games, no music. Food available Mon–Sat lunchtimes only, with homemade pies and locally produced beer sausages a speciality. No children.

 12–11pm Mon–Fri; 11am–11pm Sat; 12–10.30pm Sun.

The White Horse

25 Townfield Street, Chelmsford CM1 1QJ
☎ *(01245) 269556* Rob Furber

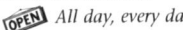 Up to nine cask-conditioned ales served at this pub managed by Wessex Taverns. Morland Old Speckled Hen, Adnams Bitter and Broadside, Young's Bitter, Greene King IPA and Abbot, Wadworth 6X and a regular mild usually available, plus guests.

L arge comfortable one-bar pub with a plethora of traditional pub games. Bar food available at lunchtime. An ideal drop-in after an arduous journey! Turn right from the rear of the railway station.

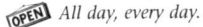 *All day, every day.*

COLCHESTER

Odd One Out

28 Mersea Road, Colchester CO2 7ET
☎ *(01206) 578140* John Parrick

 Tolly Original, Archers Best and a dark ale always available plus up to four guest beers which may include Nethergate Bitter, Tolly Mild, Mauldons Moletrap, Crouch Vale SAS, Swale Kentish Pride. Also up to three traditional ciders.

Friendly pub about 100 yards up the Mersea Road from St Botolph's roundabout. A traditional drinkers' alehouse with garden. Also has a good range of whiskies.

OPEN *4.30–11pm Mon–Thurs; 11am–11pm Fri–Sat; 12–10.30pm Sun.*

The Hospital Arms

123–5 Crouch Street, Colchester CO3 3HA
☎ *(01206) 573572* Mike Blackmore

 An Adnams tied house with all Adnams draught beers permanently available, plus Fuller's London Pride and several constantly changing guest beers, from independent breweries.

Traditional English alehouse with soft background music. Bar food served 12–2pm Mon–Fri only. Outside patio. Children allowed in the garden only. Just outside the town centre, opposite the Essex County Hospital, on Lexden Road. Traditionally known as Ward 9 by the hospital staff regulars (the hospital itself has eight wards!).

OPEN *11am–2.30pm and 5–11pm Mon–Fri; 11am–11pm Sat; 12–3pm and 7–10.30pm Sun.*

COXTIE GREEN

The White Horse

173 Coxtie Green Road, Coxtie Green, Brentwood CM14 5PX
☎ *(01277) 372410* Mr Hastings

 Ridleys Rumpus, Fuller's London Pride and Adnams Bitter always available, plus three rotating guests such as Wolf Brewery's Coyote, Hop Back Summer Lightning, Timothy Taylor Landlord or Crouch Vale, Ash Vine or Mighty Oak brews. Over 100 guest beers served every year. Beer festival held each July with 30–40 real ales.

A semi-rural pub, with public bar and lounge. Darts, large garden. Barbecues in summer, some children's facilities in the garden. Food served at lunchtime Mon–Sat and Sat evenings. Situated off the A128 towards Ongar.

OPEN *All day, every day.*

EARLS COLNE

The Bird in Hand

Coggeshall Road, Earls Colne, Colchester CO6 2JX
☎ *(01787) 222557* Mrs Eldred

 A Ridleys pub with IPA a permanent feature, plus one guest, also from Ridleys, such as Rumpus or Old Bob.

Traditional rural pub with open fire in both bars. Food available. Pool, garden, car park. Children not allowed. On the main road between the villages of Coggeshall and Earls Colne.

OPEN *12–2pm and 6–11pm Mon–Sat; 12–2pm and 7–10.30pm Sun.*

EPPING

The Moletrap

Tawney Common, Epping CM16 7PU
☎ *(01992) 522394* Mr and Mrs Kirtley

 A freehouse with Fuller's London Pride always available plus ever-changing guests from all over the country with the emphasis on independent and micro-breweries.

A 250-year-old listed building which has recently been enlarged. Outside seating. Food served at lunchtime and evenings. Children allowed. Down a rural country lane, but five minutes from Epping.

OPEN *Winter: 12–3pm and 7–11pm. Summer: 11.30am–3pm and 6–11pm.*

FEERING

The Sun Inn

3 Feering Hill, Feering, Nr Kelvedon CO5 9NH
☎ *(01376) 570442* Mr and Mrs Scicluna

 Six ever-changing beers (up to 20 per week). The emphasis is firmly on the more unusual micro-breweries.

A heavily timbered former mansion, richly decorated with carved beams and open fires. Bar and restaurant food is available at lunchtime and evenings. Car park and garden. Two beer festivals every year – Easter and August bank holiday. Small functions (up to 28 persons) catered for. Turn off the Kelveden bypass when coming from the north or south.

OPEN *11am–3pm and 6–11pm Mon–Sat; 12–3pm and 7–10.30pm Sun.*

FINCHINGFIELD

The Red Lion
6 Church Hilll, Finchingfield CM7 4NN
☎ *(01371) 810400* Francis Tyler

 A Ridleys pub with IPA and Old Bob always on offer, plus one monthly changing guest, usually another Ridleys beer such as Rumpus or ESX.

Country village pub, a fifteenth-century coaching inn, with one bar and two gardens. Food is available, and there is a non-smoking restaurant. Live music on bank holidays. Car park. Four letting rooms. Children allowed.

OPEN *11am–11pm Mon–Sat; 12–10.30pm Sun.*

FYFIELD

The Queen's Head
Queen Street, Fyfield, Ongar CM5 0RY
☎ *(01277) 899231*
Daniel Lamprecht and Penelope Miers

 Timothy Taylor Landlord plus Adnams Best and Broadside always available plus three constantly changing guests from a range of independent and micro-breweries.

A friendly freehouse dating from the fifteenth century, with riverside garden and open fires. Food served seven days a week (not Sun evening). No children under 14 years allowed in the bar.

OPEN *11am–3.30pm and 6–11pm Mon–Sat; 12–3.30pm and 7–10.30pm Sun.*

GESTINGTHORPE

The Pheasant
Audley End, Gestingthorpe CO9 3AU
☎ *(01787) 461196* Ian and Kay Crane

 Greene King IPA, Adnams Best and Morland Old Speckled Hen always on offer, supplemented by guest beers in the summer months.

Multi-roomed, 400-year-old freehouse with exposed beams, open fires and a warm friendly atmosphere. There are two bars and a dining area. Comprehensive menu available every lunchtime (except Mon), with roast and bar snacks on Sunday. Garden with extensive views over the Essex coutryside. Car park. Children are welcome and there is a children's menu. Well signposted, just north of Halstead, the only pub in the village.

OPEN *12–3pm and 6–11pm Mon–Fri; 12–4pm and 6–11pm Sat; 12–4pm and 7–10.30pm Sun.*

HATFIELD BROAD OAK

The Cock Inn
High Street, Hatfield Broad Oak CM22 7HF
☎ *(01279) 718273*
Miss Holcroft and Mr Sulway

 Adnams Best and Fuller's London Pride always available, plus four guests changing twice-weekly. Independent brews always included.

A traditional country freehouse with open fires, non-smoking area, private function room, car park, disabled access and outside seating. Food served at lunchtime and evenings. Children allowed.

OPEN *12–2.30pm and 6–11pm Mon–Sat; all day most Sundays.*

HERONGATE TYE

The Old Dog Inn
Billericay Road, Herongate Tye, Brentwood CM13 3SD
☎ *(01277) 810337* Sheila Murphy

 Ridleys IPA and Rumpus plus something from Mauldons, Nethergate, Adnams and Crouch Vale. Also two or three regularly changing guests, such as Fuller's London Pride or Shepherd Neame Spitfire.

A sixteenth-century family-owned and -run Essex weatherboard pub. One bar, garden, background music only. Food served at lunchtime and evenings in a separate dining area. Children allowed. Located off the A128 Brentwood/Tilbury Road.

OPEN *11am–3pm and 6–11pm (10.30pm Sun).*

HIGH RODING

The Black Lion
3 The Street, High Roding, Great Dunmow CM6 1NT
☎ *(01371) 872847* Fiona Day

 Ridleys IPA, ESX Best and Mild are always served at this Ridleys tied house. Other Ridleys ales are regularly available, such as Fisherman's Whopper, Rumpus and Old Bob.

Built in 1397, this olde-worlde country village pub features beams and open fires. Food is served and there is a non-smoking dining area. Occasional festivals and music. Children welcome – the pub has a children's enclosed garden, and one of its two bars is specifically for children to sit in. Lawned area, car park. Two letting rooms. On the main B4187.

OPEN *11am–3pm and 6–11pm Mon–Fri; 11am–11pm Sat; 12–10.30pm Sun.*

HORNDON ON THE HILL

The Bell Inn
High Road, Horndon On The Hill SS17 8LD
☎ *(01375) 642463* John Vereker

 Greene King IPA usually available, with regularly changing guest beers such as Hop Back Summer Lightning, Crouch Vale Millennium Gold and SAS, Young's Special, Shepherd Neame Spitfire, Slaters Top Totty and Mighty Oak Burntwood.

Attractive 600-year-old village inn. Courtyard filled with hanging baskets in summer. Award-winning restaurant and bar food available lunchtimes and evenings (except bank holiday Mondays). Car park. Children welcome in the restaurant and bar eating area. Website: www.bell-inn.co.uk.

OPEN *11am–2.30pm and 5.30–11pm Mon–Fri; 11am–3pm and 6–11pm Sat; 12–4pm and 7–10.30pm Sun.*

HUTTON

Chequers
213 Rayleigh Road, Hutton, Brentwood CM13 1PJ
☎ *(01277) 224980* Peter Waters

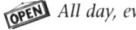 Greene King IPA always available plus a range of guest ales served on one pump. Tends towards the lighter brews.

A seventeenth-century coaching house. Two cosy bars, beer garden, main road location. Bar snacks available at lunchtime. Children allowed. Situated on the main A129 road.

OPEN *All day, every day.*

LEIGH-ON-SEA

The Broker Free House
213–17 Leigh Road, Leigh-on-Sea SS9 1JA
☎ *(01702) 471932* Mrs Short

 Shepherd Neame Spitfire and Tolly Original always available, plus two guests which regularly include Fuller's London Pride, Young's Bitter and beers from Mighty Oak, Woodforde's, Harveys, Mansfield, Bateman and Cottage breweries. Often serves 14 different beers over 10 days.

A family-run, welcoming freehouse, catering for 18–96 year olds! One big bar, beer garden, children's licence and dedicated children's area. Sunday night is live music or quiz night. Food served at lunchtime and evenings (not Sundays). Children allowed. Website: www.brokerfreehouse.co.uk.

OPEN *11am–3pm and 6–11pm (opens 5.30pm Fri).*

The Elms
1060 London Road, Leigh-on-Sea SS9 3ND
☎ *(01702) 474687*
Theo and Leanne Korakianitis

 Shepherd Neame Spitfire available, plus more than 100 guests every year such as Ringwood Old Thumper and Exmoor Beast. Twice-yearly beer festival.

A Wetherspoon's pub. Modern bar with an old-looking exterior. Outside seating. Non-smoking area. Food served 11am–10pm. No children.

OPEN *All day, every day.*

LITTLE CLACTON

The Apple Tree
The Street, Little Clacton CO16 9LF
☎ *(01255) 861026*

 Adnams Southwold Bitter and Greene King Abbot are regularly available, plus seasonal guest beers. All beers are served straight from the barrel.

A refurbished, traditional freehouse with both smoking and non-smoking bars. Food served in a separate non-smoking restaurant at lunchtimes and Friday and Saturday evenings. Car park and garden. Follow the 'old' road into Clacton (i.e. not the bypass).

OPEN *12–11pm (10.30pm Sun). Closed Mon lunchtimes and Sun evenings in winter.*

LITTLE OAKLEY

Ye Olde Cherry Tree Inn
Clacton Road, Little Oakley, Harwich CO12 5JH
☎ *(01255) 880333* Steve and Julie Chandler

 Adnams Best and Broadside and Fuller's London Pride always available, plus two rotating guest, one session and one heavier brew, changing weekly.

A traditional country pub, recently refurbished, with traditional pub games. One bar, beer garden and children's play area. Friendly, family atmosphere, overlooking the sea. Bistro-style restaurant with non-smoking area open Tues–Sat lunchtimes and evenings; bar food served 12–2pm and 7–9pm. Colchester and North East Essex CAMRA Pub of the Year 2000 and 2001. Cask Marque winner. Children allowed. Website: www.cherrytreepub.com.

OPEN *11am–2.30pm and 5–11pm Mon–Fri; all day (subject to trade) Sat–Sun.*

LITTLEBURY
The Queen's Head
High Street, Littlebury, Nr Saffron Walden CB11 4TD
☎ *(01799) 522251* Martin Housden

A Greene King tied house with IPA and Ruddles Best permanently available, plus guest beers.

A sixteenth-century coaching inn with exposed beams, a snug and two open fires. Good food available lunchtimes and evenings, all home-cooked using freshly prepared ingredients to create interesting restaurant-style meals rather than typical pub grub. Non-smoking area, car park, garden. Accommodation. Children allowed. On the B1383, between Newport and junction 9 of the M11.

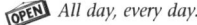*12–4pm and 5.30–11pm Mon–Thurs; 12–11pm Fri–Sat; 12–3pm and 7–10.30pm Sun.*

MALDON
The White Horse
26 High Street, Maldon CM9 5PJ
☎ *(01621) 851708* Mr RJ Wood

A Shepherd Neame tied house. So, Bishop's Finger, Spitfire and Master Brew always available plus one rotating guest.

A typical high-street pub with pub grub served at lunchtime. Children allowed.

All day, every day.

MANNINGTREE
Manningtree Station Buffet
Station Road, Lawford, Manningtree CO11 2LH
☎ *(01206) 391114* Mr Paul Sankey

Adnams Best and IPA permanently available, plus two guest ales.

A station buffet, built in 1846. Food served all day in a 24-seater restaurant. Restaurant menu in evenings, pies and breakfast until 2.30pm. Children allowed.

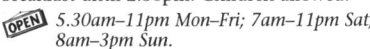*5.30am–11pm Mon–Fri; 7am–11pm Sat; 8am–3pm Sun.*

MILL GREEN
The Viper
Mill Green Road, Mill Green, Nr Ingatestone CM4 0PT
☎ *(01277) 352010* Mr RDM Beard

Five regularly changing real ales always available , including a mild. These may be from Mighty Oak, Nethergate, Wolf, Crouch Vale, Oakham, Ridleys or other breweries around the country. A traditional cider is always available.

A small, traditional, unspoilt country pub with award-winning garden. Bar food available at lunchtime. Car park. Children allowed in garden only. Take the Ivy Barn road off the A12. Turn off at Margaretting. Two miles north-west of Ingatestone.

12–3pm and 6–11pm Mon–Sat; 12–3pm and 7–10.30pm Sun.

MORETON
The Nag's Head
Church Road, Moreton, Nr Ongar CM5 0LF
☎ *(01277) 890239* Richard Keep

Adnams Best and Fuller's London Pride always available plus one rotating guest, perhaps Greene King Abbot, Morland Old Speckled Hen or a Young's brew.

A country freehouse with B&B. Food served at lunchtimes and evenings in a separate dining area. Children allowed.

11.30am–3pm and 6–11pm Mon–Fri; all day Sat–Sun.

NAVESTOCK HEATH
The Plough Inn
Sabines Road, Navestock Heath RM4 1HD
☎ *(01277) 372296*

Marston's Pedigree and Fuller's London Pride among the beers always available in a varied selection of eight real ales (100+ per year) chosen from all across the land.

A one-bar public house with a small dining room and family room. Background music, no juke box, machines or pool table. Bar snacks and meals are available at lunchtime and evenings (except Sunday and Monday). Car park, two gardens, children allowed. The pub is difficult to find, so ring for directions.

11am–11pm Mon–Sat; 12–10.30pm Sun.

ONGAR

The Royal Oak
High Street, Ongar CM5 9DX
☎ *(01277) 363893* Terry Butcher

 Ridleys IPA and Prospect are always on offer.

Traditional local boozer. No food. Darts, folk club every other Tuesday. Children not allowed. Car park.

OPEN *11.30am–3pm and 5.30–11pm Mon–Thurs; 11am–11pm Fri–Sat; 12–10.30pm Sun.*

ORSETT

The Foxhound
High Road, Orsett RM16 3ER
☎ *(01375) 891295* Jackie Firman

 Tied house with one pump offering a regularly changing guest beer, perhaps from Elgood's, Fuller's, O'Hanlon's, Everards, Charles Wells, York, Millennium, Hampshire, Phoenix or Shepherd Neame, among others.

Traditional, two-bar country pub with local pictures and memorabilia covering the walls. Saloon lounge bar with open fire and 'tree'. Bar and restaurant food available every lunchtime and Wed–Sat evenings. Traditional roasts on Sundays. Darts and pub games in public bar. Dogs welcome. Patio. Large car park. Well-behaved children welcome in the restaurant.

OPEN *11am–3.30pm and 6–11pm Mon–Fri; 11am–11pm Sat; 12–3.30pm and 7–10.30pm Sun.*

PEBMARSH

The King's Head
The Street, Pebmarsh, Nr Halstead CO9 2NH
☎ *(01787) 269306*
Anne-Marie and Gary Olmstead

Greene King IPA always available plus three constantly changing guest ales.

An oak-beamed freehouse dating from 1450. Homemade meals available at lunchtime and evenings – fresh fish, Mexican and American dishes are specialities. Barbecues in season. Car park, garden. One mile off the Halstead to Sudbury road.

OPEN *12–3pm and 6–11pm Tues–Sat (closed Mondays); 12–3pm and 7–10.30pm Sun.*

PLESHEY

The White Horse
The Street, Pleshey, Chelmsford CM3 1HA
☎ *(01245) 237281* Mike and Jan Smail

Young's PA, Triple A and Waggle Dance and a selection of Smiles ales always available.

A village pub in very picturesque historic village. One bar and two eating areas, large garden, car park. Food served at lunchtime and evenings during the week and all day at weekends. Children allowed.

OPEN *11am–3pm and 7–11pm Mon–Sat; 12–4pm Sun (closed Sun evening).*

RADWINTER

The Plough Inn
Radwinter, Nr Saffron Walden CB10 2TL
☎ *(01799) 599222*

A freehouse with Adnams Best and Greene King IPA always available, plus two or three rotating guests such as Oakhill Mendip Gold, Jennings Cumberland Ale, Shepherd Neame Spitfire, Timothy Taylor Landlord, Nethergate Golden Gate and Hop Back Summer Lightning.

A seventeenth-century country freehouse with heavy emphasis on food and accommodation. Non-smoking area in the restaurant. Food available at lunchtime and evenings. Children and dogs welcome. At the junction of B1053 and B1054, four miles east of Saffron Walden.

OPEN *12–3pm and 6.30–11pm (10.30pm Sun).*

RICKLING GREEN

The Cricketer's Arms
Rickling Green, Quendon, Saffron Walden CB11 3YG
☎ *(01799) 543210* Tim Proctor

A freehouse with three guest ales always available from a list including Wadworth 6X, Fuller's ESB, one best bitter and one dark mild. The focus is on stronger brews. Also a selection of Belgian beers.

A heavily timbered building dating from 1590, ten en-suite bedrooms, three dining rooms (one non-smoking). Food served daily at lunchtime and evenings. Children not allowed in the main bar area. Facing the cricket green, just off the B1383 at Quendon. Website: www.cricketers.demon.co.uk.

OPEN *All day, every day.*

RIDGEWELL

The White Horse
Mill Road, Ridgewell CO9 4SG
☎ *(01440) 785532* Robin Briggs

A freehouse serving a constantly changing range of real ales, which may include Ridleys IPA, Fuller's London Pride or brews from Shepherd Neame, Belhaven, Cottage or other smaller breweries.

A rural village pub with games room, pool table and darts. Single bar covered in old pennies (4,200 in all). Large restaurant, beer garden and car park. Food served at lunchtime and evenings. Children allowed. Located on the A1017 between Halstead and Haverhill.

 6–11pm Tues; 11am–3pm and 6–11pm Wed–Sat; 12–10.30pm Sun (closed all day Mon except bank holidays).

ROCHFORD

The Golden Lion
35 North Street, Rochford SS4 1AB
☎ *(01702) 545487* Sue Williams

Greene King Abbot Ale and Fuller's London Pride always available, plus three or four guests ales which constantly change. Emphasis on unusual brews from smaller breweries.

A sixteenth-century traditional-style freehouse with one bar with beams and brasses and a small beer garden. South East Essex CAMRA Pub of the Year 2001. Regular live music. Well-behaved children and dogs welcome.

 12–11pm.

SHALFORD

The George Inn
The Street, Shalford CM7 5HH
☎ *(01371) 850207* Mr and Mrs D Buckman

Greene King IPA, Morland Old Speckled Hen and Adnams Broadside always available, plus one changing guest. Regular guests include Badger Best, Morrells Trinity and Shepherd Neame Spitfire.

A country pub, over 500 years old, with restaurant and bar areas. Food available lunchtimes and evenings, including Sunday roasts. Children welcome if eating. Patio and ample parking. Situated on the main road from Braintree to Wethersfield.

 12–3pm and 6.30–11pm (closed Sunday evening).

SOUTH FAMBRIDGE

The Anchor Hotel
Fambridge Road, South Fambridge, Rochford SS4 3LY
☎ *(01702) 203535* Mr Cracknell

Greene King Abbot is one of two beers always available, plus two rotating guests such as Shepherd Neame Bishop's Finger, Smiles Heritage, Ringwood Fortyniner, Morland Old Speckled Hen, Crouch Vale SAS or Young's Special.

A traditional country freehouse with two bars and a restaurant. Four minutes' walk from the sea wall of River Crouch. Good views. Food available at lunchtime and evenings. Children allowed.

 11am–3pm and 6–11pm.

SOUTHEND-ON-SEA

Cork & Cheese
10 Talza Way, Victoria Plaza, Southend-on-Sea SS2 5BG
☎ *(01702) 616914* John Murray

Nethergate Best always available plus three guests (250 per year) including brews from Concertina, Butterknowle, Rooster's, Woodforde's, Titanic, Hop Back, Wild's and Clark's.

An alehouse with a cosmopolitan trade. Separate dining area for bar and restaurant meals. Food available at lunchtime. Multi-storey car park nearby. Patio in summer. Children allowed in the restaurant. Located on the basement floor of the Victoria Circus shopping centre in Southend.

 11am–11pm Mon–Sat; closed Sun.

Last Post
5 Weston Road, Southend-on-Sea SS1 1BZ
☎ *(01702) 431682* Neil Sanderson

Ridleys IPA always available, plus up to five daily-changing guests such as Morland Old Speckled Hen or Hop Back Summer Lightning. Anything and everything from brewers of real ale considered.

A busy two-bar operation with disabled access and toilets. No music, a real drinkers' pub. Two non-smoking areas. Food served all day, every day. No children. Opposite the railway station.

 10am–11pm.

SOUTHMINSTER

The Station Arms
39 Station Road, Southminster CM0 7EW
☎ *(01621) 772225* Martin Park

 Crouch Vale Brewer's Gold and Adnams Bitter always available, plus three guest beers from a range of small independent brewers.

A welcoming, one-bar, Essex weatherboard pub with open fire and traditional pub furniture. CAMRA East Anglia Pub of the Year 1997–98 and Dengie and Mauldon Pub of the Year 2001. Pub games played. Restaurant and courtyard to the rear. Food served in restaurant Thurs–Sat evenings only. Street parking. No children. Three beer festivals held each year, with 30 real ales at each. Just 200 yards from Southminster railway station.

OPEN *12–2.30pm and 6–11pm Mon–Fri; 12–11pm Sat; 12–4pm and 7–10.30pm Sun.*

STANFORD RIVERS

The Woodman
155 London Road, Stanford Rivers, Ongar
☎ *(01277) 362019* Peter Benefield

Shepherd Neame Master Brew, Spitfire and Bishop's Finger regularly available.

Wooden-clad, fourteenth-century inn set in three acres. Food served all day. Car park. Children's play area.

OPEN *11am–11pm Mon–Sat; 12–10.30pm Sun.*

STISTED

The Dolphin
Stisted, Braintree CM7 8EU
☎ *(01376) 321143* George James

Tied to Ridleys, with IPA and ESX Best always on offer, plus other Ridleys beers such as Fisherman's Whopper.

Traditional locals' pub – three cottages knocked into one. Food available. Beer garden, car park. Children not allowed. On the main A120 from Stansted and Colchester

OPEN *12–3pm and 6–11pm Mon–Sat; 12–3pm and 7–10.30pm Sun.*

STOCK

The Hoop
21 High Street, Stock CM4 9BD
☎ *(01277) 841137* Albert and David Kitchen

Up to ten beers available. Brews from Adnams, Crouch Vale, Wadworth and Charles Wells always served. Guests from Bateman, Archers, Ringwood, Hop Back, Jennings, Exmoor, Fuller's, Marston's, Nethergate, Rooster's and Shepherd Neame.

The pub has been adapted from some late fifteenth-century beamed cottages. There is an extensive beer garden to the rear. Bar food available all day. Barbecues at weekends in summer, weather permitting. Parking. Children not allowed. Take the B1007 from the A12 Chelmsford bypass, then take the Galleywood–Billericay turn-off.

OPEN *11am–11pm.*

STOW MARIES

The Prince of Wales
Woodham Road, Stow Maries CM3 6SA
☎ *(01621) 828971* Robert Walster

Fuller's Chiswick always available plus any four guests (too many to count) including a mild and a stout/porter from small independent and the better regional brewers.

A traditional Essex weatherboard pub with real fires and Victorian bakehouse. Bar food available at lunchtime and evenings. Car park, garden and family room. Under two miles from South Woodham Ferrers on the road to Cold Norton.

OPEN *11am–11pm Mon–Sat; 12–10.30pm Sun.*

TENDRING

The Cherry Tree
Crow Lane, Tendring CO16 9AP
☎ *(01255) 830340* Mr Whitnell

Greene King IPA, Abbot and Adnams Best always available, plus a regularly changing guest.

An olde-worlde pub and restaurant. One bar, big garden. Food served at lunchtime and evenings. Well-behaved children allowed.

OPEN *11am–3pm and 6–11pm Mon–Sat; all day Sun.*

THORNWOOD COMMON

The New Carpenter's Arms
High Road, Thornwood Common, Epping CM16 6LS
☎ *(01992) 574208* Des and Christine Rees

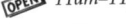Adnams Broadside, McMullen AK, Greene King IPA and Morland Old Speckled Hen always available, plus constantly changing guest beers.

A traditional country pub, recently completely refurbished. Essex Pub of the Year for 1998–1999. New 80-seat fully air-conditioned fish restaurant, Ridgeways, recently built behind pub (open 12 noon to 12 midnight).

OPEN *11am–11pm Mon–Sat; 12–10.30pm Sun.*

TILLINGHAM

Cap and Feathers
8 South Street, Tillingham CM70 7TH
☎ *(01621) 779212* Martin Gale

Crouch Vale Best Bitter and Brewers Gold always available plus at least one guest.

Dates from 1427, an old weatherboard building. Unspoilt, with a relaxed atmosphere. Homemade food available at lunchtime and evenings. Car park, garden, non-smoking family room. Accommodation. Between Southminster and Bradwell.

OPEN *12–3pm and 5.30–11pm Mon–Fri; 12–11pm Sat; 12–10.30pm Sun.*

TOOT HILL

The Green Man and Courtyard Restaurant
Toot Hill, Nr Ongar CM5 9SD
☎ *(01992) 522255* Mr J Roads

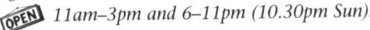Crouch Vale Best always available plus two guests changing twice weekly including, perhaps, an Adnams brew or Fuller's London Pride. No strong bitters over 4.3% ABV.

A country freehouse with two restaurants, one bar, courtyard and beer garden. Food served at lunchtime and evenings. Children aged 11+ allowed.

OPEN *11am–3pm and 6–11pm (10.30pm Sun).*

WENDENS AMBO

The Bell
Royston Road, Wendens Ambo CB11 4JY
☎ *(01799) 540382* David and Sheila Thorp

Adnams Bitter always available plus two guests (150 per year) from micro-breweries.

Built in 1576, beamed with open fires in winter. Bar food available 12–2pm and 6–9pm Mon–Fri, 12–3pm and 6–9pm Sat, 12–3pm Sun (no food Sun and Mon evenings). Car park, large garden, new terrace, crazy golf, pets' corner, wilderness walk. Family-friendly garden.

OPEN *11.30am–2.30pm and 6–11pm Mon–Fri; all day Sat–Sun.*

WHITE RODING

The Black Horse
Chelmsford Road, White Roding CM6 1RF
☎ *(01279) 876322* Michael Miller

A Ridleys house with IPA, Prospect and Old Bob always on offer.

A traditional family-oriented country pub with two bars, a non-smoking dining room and beer garden. Bar food and full à la carte menu available with fish a speciality. Well-behaved children allowed.

OPEN *11.30am–3pm and 5.30–11pm Mon–Fri; 11.30am–3pm and 6–11pm Sat; 12–3pm and 7–10.30pm Sun.*

WITHAM

The Woolpack
7 Church Street, Witham CM8 2JP
☎ *(01376) 511195* Lynda Thomas

Greene King IPA and Tolly Cobbold Original or Best always available, plus one constantly changing guest ale.

A small community locals' drinking pub. Team orientated (darts, pool, cribbage etc). Bar snacks available at lunchtime. No children.

OPEN *All day, every day.*

WOODHAM FERRERS

The Bell Inn
Main Road, Woodham Ferrers, Chelmsford CM3 8RF
☎ *(01245) 320443* DL Giles and S Rowe

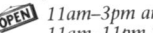Ridleys IPA and Adnams Bitter regularly available, plus five guest beers often from Ridleys, Adnams, Mauldons, Crouch Vale or Cottage.

Friendly village pub with cosy bars and open fire in winter. Freshly cooked food served 12–2.30pm and 7–10pm Mon–Fri, 12–10pm Sat–Sun. Car park. No children.

OPEN *11am–3pm and 6–11pm Mon–Fri; 11am–11pm Sat; 12–10.30pm Sun.*

WOODHAM WATER

The Bell

The Street, Woodham Water, Maldon CM9 6RF
☎ *(01245) 223437* Mr Alan Oldfield

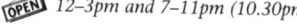 A freehouse with Greene King IPA permanently available, plus two guest pumps serving real ales such as Morland Old Speckled Hen, Fuller's ESB, Hook Norton Old Hooky or Everards Tiger or Triple Gold.

A traditional sixteenth-century village inn with beams, one bar and three adjoining rooms. No music or machines. Beer garden. Food available lunchtimes and evenings in a separate dining room. Children allowed.

OPEN *12–3pm and 7–11pm (10.30pm Sun).*

YOU TELL US

∗ *The Angel,* 36 Bocking End, Bocking
∗ *Boadicea,* St John's Street, Colchester
∗ *The Retreat,* 42 Church Street, Bocking
∗ *The Royal Fusiliers,* Aingers Green Road, Aingers Green

Places Featured:

Apperley
Ashleworth
Avening
Awre
Bedminster
Birdlip
Bishopston
Blaisdon
Bledington
Box
Bristol
Broad Campden
Charlton Kings
Cheltenham
Chipping Campden
Chipping Sodbury
Cirencester
Clearwell
Cockleford
Coleford
Cranham
Didmarton
Duntisbourne Abbots
Dursley
Ebrington
Ford
Frampton Cotterell
France Lynch
Gloucester
Ham
Hanham Mills

Hawkesbury Upton
Kingswood
Lime Street
Littleton upon Severn
Longborough
Longhope
Lower Apperley
Minchinhampton
Newland
Oakridge Lynch
Old Sodbury
Oldbury on Severn
Pill
Pope's Hill
Prestbury
Pucklechurch
Quedgeley
Sapperton
Sheepscombe
Slad
Sling
Snowshill
South Woodchester
Stow-on-the-Wold
Tewkesbury
Todenham
Uley
Waterley Bottom
Westbury on Trym
Whitminster
Winterbourne Down

THE BREWERIES

BATH ALES LTD

Siston Lane, Webbs Heath, Bristol BS30 5LX
☎ *(0117) 907 1797*
www.bathales.com

 **BATH SPA 3.7% ABV**
Pale and quenching.
GEM 4.1% ABV
Well-rounded flavours with balancing hops.
BARNSTORMER 4.5% ABV
Roast malt flavour with some fruitiness.
FESTIVITY 5.0% ABV
Rich, dark and warming.
SPA EXTRA 5.0% ABV
A golden beer with bags of hop character and a bitter finish.
RARE HARE 5.2% ABV
Dry and clean on the palate.
Plus seasonal brews.

DONNINGTON BREWERY

Upper Swell, Stow-on-the-Wold GL54 1EP
☎ *(01451) 830603*

 BB 3.6% ABV
Plenty of flavour for gravity.
SBA 4.6% ABV
Smooth and malty.

FREEMINER BREWERY LTD

Whimsey Road, Stem Mills, Cinderford GL14 3JA
☎ *(01594) 827989*
http://website.lineone.net/freeminer.brewery

 BITTER 4.0% ABV
MORSES LEVEL 4.0% ABV
Hoppy with powerful malty balance.
STRIP AND AT IT 4.0% ABV
IRON BREW 4.2% ABV
SPECULATION ALE 4.8% ABV
CELESTIAL STEAM GALE 5.0% ABV
GOLD STANDARD 5.0% ABV
SHAKEMANTLE GINGER ALE 5.0% ABV
SLAUGHTER PORTER 5.0% ABV
TRAFALGAR IPA 6.0% ABV
DEEP SHAFT 6.2% ABV

GOFF'S BREWERY LTD

9 Isbourne Way, Winchcombe GL54 5NS
☎ *(01242) 603383*

 JOUSTER 4.0% ABV
Fruity, with hop flavours.
TOURNAMENT 4.0% ABV
Amber thirst quenching bitter with delicate
floral aroma.
WHITE KNIGHT 4.7% ABV
Pale, with hoppiness throughout.
Plus seasonal brews.

NORTH COTSWOLD BREWERY

*Unit 3, Ditchford Farm, Moreton-in-Marsh
GL56 9RD*
☎ *(01608) 663947*

 SOLSTICE 3.7% ABV
Straw coloured and lightly hopped.
GENESIS 4.0% ABV
Full bodied with refreshing taste.
FOUR SHIRES 4.2% ABV
Copper coloured, balanced hop flavour.
XMAS SPECIAL 4.4% ABV
Dark with smooth malty taste.

SMILES BREWING CO. LTD

Colston Yard, Colston Street, Bristol BS1 5BD
☎ *(0117) 929 9308*
www.smiles.co.uk

 ORIGINAL 3.8% ABV
BEST BITTER 4.1% ABV
Well-rounded, hop, fruit and malt
flavours.
BRISTOL IPA 4.5% ABV
With a delicate aroma.
HERITAGE 5.2% ABV
Dark and rich with roast malt character.
Plus monthly brews.

STANWAY BREWERY

Stanway, Cheltenham GL54 5PQ
☎ *(01386) 584320*
www.stanwaybrewery.co.uk

 COTTESWOLD GOLD 3.9% ABV
Light refreshing ale only brewed in
summer.
LORDS-A-LEAPING 4.5% ABV
Winter ale.
STANNEY BITTER 4.5% ABV
Quenching, with hoppiness throughout.
Plus seasonal brews.

ULEY BREWERY LTD

*The Old Brewery, The Street, Uley, Dursley
GL11 5TB*
☎ *(01453) 860120*

 HOGSHEAD PALE ALE 3.5% ABV
Light in colour and well-hopped.
ULEY BITTER 4.0% ABV
Balanced and full-flavoured.
OLD RIC 4.5% ABV
OLD SPOT 5.0% ABV
Flagship ale. Powerful malt flavour with fruit and
hops.
PIG'S EAR 5.0% ABV
Smooth IPA.

WICKWAR BREWERY CO.

*The Old Cider Mill, Station Road, Wickwar
GL12 8NB*
☎ *(01454) 294168*
www.wickwarbrewing.co.uk

 COOPERS WPA 3.5% ABV
Quenching, full-flavoured pale ale.
BRAND OAK BITTER (BOB) 4.0% ABV
Characterful and well-balanced.
COTSWOLD WAY 4.2% ABV
Rich amber, smooth, well balanced beer.
OLD ARNOLD 4.6% ABV
OLD MERRYFORD ALE 4.8% ABV
Flavoursome, with hoppy fruit aroma.
MR PERRETT'S TRADITIONAL STOUT 5.9% ABV
A powerful stout with a liquorice and chocolate
taste.
STATION PORTER 6.1%ABV
Intricate, well-rounded blend of flavours.
Plus seasonal and occasional brews.

THE PUBS

APPERLEY

Coal House Inn
Gabb Lane, Apperley GL19 4DN
☎ *(01452) 780211* Mrs McDonald

Wickwar Coopers WPA and Brand Oak Bitter always available plus a changing guest. Traditional underground cellar.

A country freehouse on the east bank of the River Severn. Home-cooked food served lunchtimes and evenings. 'Portuguese Steak on a Stone' a speciality. Large car parks and riverside garden. Children allowed. Moorings for boats (24 hours). Apperley is signposted on B4213 south of Tewkesbury. Follow signs for Coalhouse Wharf from village centre.

OPEN *April–Sept: 11.30am–2.30pm and 6–11pm; Oct–Mar: 11.30am–2.30pm and 7–11pm; 12–3pm and 7–10.30pm Sun (all year).*

ASHLEWORTH

The Boat Inn
The Quay, Ashleworth GL19 4HZ
☎ *(01452) 700272* Mrs Nicholls

Arkells 3B, RCH Pitchfork, Oakhill Yeoman 1767 and Wye Valley brews always available plus at least three constantly changing guest beers served straight from the cask including, for example, Exmoor Gold, Oakhill Somer Ale and Black Magic, Arkells Summer Ale, Smiles Exhibition, brews from Hambleton, Church End, Goff's, Cottage, Sporting Ales and Eccleshall plus various Christmas ales.

A small fifteenth-century cottage pub on the banks of the River Severn which has remained in the same family for 400 years. Bar food available at lunchtime. Car park and garden. Children allowed. Ashleworth is signposted off the A417 north of Gloucester. The Quay is signed from the village.

OPEN *April–Sept: 11am–2.30pm and 6–11pm Mon–Sat; 12–3pm and 7–10.30pm Sun; Oct–Mar: 11am–2.30pm Thurs–Tues, closed Mon and Wed lunchtime; 7–11pm Mon–Sat; 12–3pm and 7–10.30pm Sun.*

AVENING

The Bell
29 High Street, Avening, Tetbury GL8 8NF
☎ *(01453) 836422* Graham Hackney

A freehouse with Wickwar Brand Oak usually available plus two guests.

A traditional Cotswold pub with log fire, dining area and garden. Food served at lunchtime and evenings, every day. Children allowed. Accommodation.

OPEN *12–3pm and 6–11pm (10.30pm Sun).*

AWRE

The Red Hart Inn
Awre, Newnham GL14 1EW
☎ *(01594) 510220* Gerry Bedwell

A freehouse with Fuller's London Pride generally available, plus two guests changing weekly. Examples include something from Wickwar, Archer's or Goff's. The landlord's policy is to support smaller breweries as much as possible.

A beamed hostelry dating from 1483 with one bar area. Non-smoking area. Outside seating in front garden. Bar snacks and à la carte menu available at lunchtime and evenings. Children allowed until 8pm, if well supervised. Accommodation. Set in a tranquil hamlet environment. Turn off A48 between Newnham and Blakeney.

OPEN *6.30–11pm Mon; 12–3pm and 6.30–11pm Tues–Sat; 12–3pm and 7–10.30pm Sun.*

BEDMINSTER

Robert Fitzharding
24 Cannon Street, Bedminster, Bristol BS3 1BN
☎ *(0117) 966 2757* Neil Sykes

A Wetherspoon's pub with Butcombe Bitter always available. Four guest pumps serve a range of 30 guests every quarter. Examples include Coniston Bluebird, Exmoor Beast, Caledonian Deuchars IPA or something from Burton Bridge.

A city suburb pub with non-smoking area. Two beer festivals held each year. Food served all day. Children welcome until 6pm.

OPEN *All day, every day.*

BIRDLIP

The Golden Heart Inn
Nettleton Bottom, Nr Birdlip GL4 8LA
☎ *(01242) 870261*
Mr D Morgan and Miss C Stevens

Timothy Taylor Landlord and Golden Best and something from Young's and Archers always available, plus guest beers.

A sixteenth-century pub with stone floors, beams and bric-à-brac. Bar food available at lunchtime and evenings. The menu features both traditional dishes and exotic fare such as ostrich, crocodile and kangaroo, and there is also an emphasis on English meats from prize-winning stock. Beer festivals held on May and August bank holidays, featuring over 40 real ales plus cider and perry. Live music, barbecues, camping. Also has en-suite accommodation available. Car park, garden, children's room and function room. Situated on the A417 between Cheltenham, Gloucester and Cirencester, two miles from Birdlip.

OPEN *11am–3pm and 5.30–11pm Mon–Thurs; 11am–11pm Fri–Sat; 12–10.30pm Sun.*

GLOUCESTERSHIRE

BISHOPSTON

The Annexe
Seymour Road, Bishopston, Bristol BS7 9EQ
☎ *(0117) 949 3931* Mr Morgan

 Smiles Best, Marston's Pedigree and Morland Old Speckled Hen are permanent plus one guest changing daily.

A town pub with disabled access, children's room, garden, darts etc. Bar food available at lunchtime and restaurant food in the evenings. Children allowed until 8.30pm in the conservatory only.

OPEN *11.30am–2.30pm and 6–11pm Mon–Fri; 11.30am–11pm Sat; 12–10.30pm Sun.*

BLAISDON

The Red Hart Inn
Blaisdon, Nr Longhope GL17 0AH
☎ *(01452) 830477* Guy Wilkins

 Hook Norton Best Bitter regularly available plus three guest beers perhaps from Uley, Wickwar, Berkeley, Freeminer, Goff's, RCH, Timothy Taylor, Wood, Eccleshall, Exmoor, Otter, Hop Back, Adnams, Cotleigh or Greene King.

Traditional English village pub with stone floor, low-beamed ceiling and open fire. Large bar area and separate non-smoking restaurant with food available 12–2pm and 7–9pm Sun–Thurs, 12–2pm and 7–9.30pm Fri–Sat. Barbecue and large garden with children's play area. Car park. Unattended children in the bar are sold as slaves.

OPEN *11.30am–2.30pm and 6–11pm Mon–Sat; 12–3pm and 7–10.30pm Sun.*

BLEDINGTON

The Kings Head Inn
The Green, Bledington OX7 6XQ
☎ *(01608) 658365*
Archie and Nicola Orr-Ewing

 Wadworth 6X and a beer from Hook Norton usually available, plus two guest beers which may include Shepherd Neame Spitfire, Timothy Taylor Landlord, Uley Old Spot or Pigs Ear, Wychwood Hobgoblin or Fiddlers Elbow, Smiles Best, Adnams Broadside amongst many others.

Quintessential, fifteenth-century Cotswold stone inn located on the village green with brook and attendant ducks. Retains olde-worlde charm of pews, settles, flagstone floors, beams, antique furnishings and inglenook fireplace. Tasteful accommodation. Food served 12–2pm and 7–9.45pm. Children welcome, under supervision, in the garden room. Large car park. On the B4450.

OPEN *11am–2.30pm and 6–11pm Mon–Sat; 12–3pm and 7–10.30pm Sun.*

BOX

The Halfway Inn
Minchinhampton, Box, Stroud GL6 9AE
☎ *(01453) 832631* Andrew Johnson

 Wickwar Brand Oak Bitter, Archers Village and Hook Norton Best always available, plus Black Rat Scrumpy cider.

A prettily situated freehouse with recently refurbished bar and 70-seat restaurant. Newly landscaped garden with giant chessboard and Jenga.

OPEN *11am–11pm Mon–Sat; 12–10.30pm Sun.*

BRISTOL

The Bag O'Nails
141 St Georges Road, Hotwells, Bristol BS1 5UW
☎ *(0117) 940 6776* Gordon Beresford

 Up to six different beers served on a guest basis (over 300 offered in two years). Mainly supplied by smaller, independent breweries. The pub's own web page gives details of beers stocked at any one time (www.bagonails.org.uk).

A small, quiet, gas-lit city-centre pub with one bar. Situated just 25 yards from the Dock. Simple lunches only, served 12–2pm. No children.

OPEN *12–2.15pm and 5.30–11pm Mon–Thurs; all day Fri–Sun.*

The Bell Inn
21 Alfred Place, Kingsdown, Bristol BS2 8HD
☎ *(0117) 907 7563* Anna Luke

 A freehouse regularly offering Wickwar Brand Oak Bitter and Uley Old Spot. Also RCH Pitchfork plus occasional guests.

A proper, traditional English pub with a warm and friendly atmosphere. Customers an eclectic mix of all ages. Candlelight in the evenings. No food. No children. Situated off St Michael's Hill, at the back of the BRI hospital.

OPEN *12–2.30pm and 5.30–11pm (10.30pm Sun); closed Tues lunchtime.*

Cadbury House
68 Richmond Road, Montpelier, Bristol BS6 5EW
☎ *(0117) 924 7874* Bernie Perry

 A freehouse serving Wickwar Brand Oak Bitter and Olde Merryford plus two rotating guests. Wickwar Station Porter or other winter ales usually available from October.

A locals' pub in a residential area. Clientele a mix of regulars and students. Large beer garden. Bar meals served 12–6.30pm and traditional Sunday roasts. Children not allowed inside.

OPEN *All day, every day.*

The Cat & Wheel

207 Cheltenham Road, Bristol
☎ *(0117) 942 7862*
Jane Chamberlain and Jim Hill

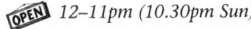A Mole's pub with Mole's Tap Bitter always on offer.

A two-bar pub, famous for its pig-racing nights! One bar has a traditional, relaxed atmosphere, while the other is student-oriented, with pool and juke box. No food. Bands and singers on Fridays 9–11pm – no door charge. Children not allowed.

OPEN *12–11pm (10.30pm Sun).*

Commercial Rooms

43–5 Corn Street, Bristol BS1 1HT
☎ *(0117) 927 9681* John Baldwin

A freehouse serving Butcombe Bitter and Gold plus two guests changing constantly, at least nine different beers in a week.

A town-centre pub with twice-yearly beer festivals in April and October. Food served all day. Children allowed until 6pm.

OPEN *10.00am–11pm.*

Cornubia

142 Temple Street, Bristol BS1 6EN
☎ *(0117) 925 4415* Micheal Blake

A freehouse offering four constantly changing beers from a range of hundreds per year, specialising in micro-breweries from around the country. A dark mild, porter or stout is usually available.

A Georgian listed building situated just behind the old Courage Brewery site, 10 minutes' walk from Temple Meads Station. Traditional town-centre pub atmosphere. Well-behaved children allowed.

OPEN *12–11pm Mon–Fri; 5.30–11pm Sat; closed Sun.*

Hare On The Hill

41 Thomas Street North, Kingsdown
☎ *(0117) 9081982* John Lansdall

Bath Ales SPA, Gem, Barnstormer, SPA Extra (summer) and Festivity (winter) usually available with one or two guest beers, all above 4.8% ABV. Their own Rare Hare is also offered and they specialise in beer swaps.

Popular, Bath Ales award-winning pub. Bar food served lunchtimes and evenings. Sunday roasts 12.30–3.30pm. Well-behaved children welcome, but no special facilities.

OPEN *12–2.30pm and 5–11pm Mon–Thurs; 12–11pm Fri–Sat; 12–10.30pm Sun.*

The Highbury Vaults

164 St Michael's Hill, Cotham, Bristol BS2 8DE
☎ *(0117) 973 3203* Bradd Francis

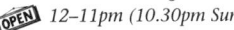A Young's tied house serving Young's Bitter, Special and seasonal ales, plus Smiles Best and Heritage and Brains SA.

Very traditional pub set in the heart of university land with no music, fruit machines, pool tables etc. Lots of atmosphere for young and old, students and locals. Cheap bar food available at lunchtime and evenings (nothing fried). Heated rear garden. Children allowed in garden.

OPEN *12–11pm (10.30pm Sun).*

Smiles Brewery Tap

6–8 Colston Street, Bristol BS1 5BT
☎ *(0117) 921 3668*

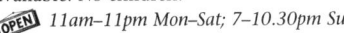Smiles Original, Best, Heritage, IPA and seasonal brews available.

A traditional pub atmosphere awaits in this small horseshoe bar with hops adorning the ceiling. Separate non-smoking room and small bar with wood panelling and chequered tiled floor. Hot food served 12–3pm Mon–Sat; sandwiches always available. No children.

OPEN *11am–11pm Mon–Sat; 7–10.30pm Sun.*

BROAD CAMPDEN

The Bakers Arms

Broad Campden, Chipping Campden GL55 6UR
☎ *(01386) 840515* Sally and Ray Mayo

Charles Wells Bombardier and brews from Stanway and Hook Norton always available, plus two rotating guest ales.

A small, friendly Cotswold country pub with open fire. Bar food available every lunchtime and evening. Car park, garden, patio and children's play area. In a village between Chipping Campden and Blockley.

OPEN *Summer: 11.30am–11pm Mon–Sat; 12–10.30pm Sun. Winter: 11.30am–2.30pm and 4.45–11pm Mon–Fri; 11.30am–11pm Sat; 12–10.30pm Sun.*

CHARLTON KINGS

Merryfellow

2 School Lane, Charlton Kings, Cheltenham GL53 8AU ☎ *(01242) 525883*

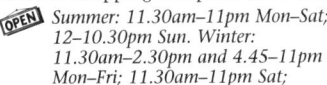Five different beers generally available. Greene King IPA, Gale's HSB, Wadworth 6X and beers from Archers and Black Sheep are regulars.

Classic village pub offering value-for-money food and a selection of ales. No food on Monday night. Car park, garden, skittle alley, function room and pool table. Children welcome.

OPEN *All day, every day.*

CHELTENHAM

Adam & Eve

10 Townsend Street, Cheltenham GL51 9HD
☎ *(01242) 690030* Mrs Gasson

Arkells 2B, 3B and seasonals always on offer.

Simple side-street pub that could be somebody's front room. Skittle alley and darts. Children allowed in patio area.

OPEN *10.30am–2.30pm and 4–11pm Sun–Fri; all day Sat.*

The Kemble Brewery Inn

27 Fairview Street, Cheltenham GL52 2JF
☎ *(01242) 243446* Dennis Melia

An Archers house with Village and Golden usually available plus three guest beers which may include others from Archers or ales from Butcombe, Fuller's, Donnington, Young's or Hook Norton.

This small, friendly local with rear courtyard is one of the few remaining real ale pubs in Cheltenham. Situated behind Fowlers motorcycle shop in the Fairview area. Food served 12–2.30pm Sun–Mon, 6–8.30pm Mon–Fri. Children welcome in courtyard.

OPEN *11.30am–2.30pm and 5.30–11pm Mon–Fri; 11.30am–11pm Sat; 12–4pm and 7–11pm Sun.*

Tailors

4 Cambray Place, Cheltenham GL50 1JS
☎ *(01242) 255453* Mrs Cherri Dandridge

A Wadworth managed house with 6X, IPA and JCB always available.

A comfortable, traditional pub in the town centre, newly refurbished and full of character. Cellar bar is a function room. Two lovely beer gardens. Big-screen TV. Good value pub meals served Mon–Sat lunchtimes only. Children welcome.

OPEN *All day, every day.*

CHIPPING CAMPDEN

The Lygon Arms

High Street, Chipping Camden GL55 6HB
☎ *(01386) 840318* Ivor Porter

Wadworth 6X, Hook Norton Best and Morland Old Speckled Hen permanently available plus two guests, changing frequently, from any independent brewery.

A sixteenth-century, family-run coaching inn. One bar, non-smoking dining area, courtyard and beer garden, car parking at rear. En-suite accommodation. Homemade, traditional English food from local produce. Children allowed.

OPEN *Winter: 10.30am–2.30/3pm and 6–11pm Mon–Fri; 11am–11pm Sat; 12–10.30pm Sun. Summer: 11am–11pm Mon–Sat; 12–10.30pm Sun.*

The Volunteer

Lower High Street, Chipping Campden GL55 6DY
☎ *(01386) 840688* Mrs H Sinclair

North Cotswold Genesis, Stanway Stanney Bitter and Hook Norton Best always available, plus three guests from all around the country.

A country inn with garden. Food served at lunchtime and evenings. Children allowed. Accommodation.

OPEN *11.30am–3pm and 5–11pm Mon–Sat; 12–3pm and 6.30–10.30pm Sun.*

CHIPPING SODBURY

Beaufort Hunt

Broad Street, Chipping Sodbury, Bristol BS37 6AG
☎ *(01454) 312871* Mrs Jarvis

Greene King IPA always available plus two guests including, perhaps, Wickwar Olde Merryford, Fuller's London Pride, Shepherd Neame Bishop's Finger or Everards Tiger.

An olde-style village pub with courtyard. Food available at lunchtime. Children aged 14–18 allowed in lounge bar only if eating. Under 14s not allowed.

OPEN *10.30am–3pm and 5–11pm (10.30pm Sun).*

CIRENCESTER

The Bear Inn

12 Dyer Street, Cirencester GL7 2PF
☎ *(01285) 653472* Paul Rice

A Mole's Brewery tied house. Mole's Best is always available, plus one guest.

A town-centre pub, refurbished in the style of an old coaching inn. Home-cooked food served at lunchtime and evenings. Children allowed.

OPEN *All day, every day.*

Corinium Hotel

12 Gloucester Street, Cirencester GL7 2DG
☎ *(01285) 659711* Tim McGrath

Greene King IPA always available, plus two guest beers that change weekly.

A sixteenth-century wool merchant's house, now a hotel, bar and restaurant with Roman theme. Wide selection of food served lunchtimes and evenings. Children welcome in restaurant and garden.

OPEN *11am–11pm (10.30pm Sun).*

The Drillman's Arms
84 Gloucester Road, Cirencester GL7 2JY
☎ *(01285) 653892* Richard Selby

 A freehouse serving Archers Best and Smiles Original, plus one guest.

A village pub with log fire and function room. Food served at lunchtime and evenings. Children allowed.

 11am–3pm and 5.30–11pm Mon–Fri; all day Sat; 11am–4pm and 7–10.30pm Sun.

CLEARWELL

The Lamb Inn
The Cross, Clearwell, Coleford GL16 8JU
☎ *(01594) 835441* FJ Yates and SY Lewis

 Freeminer Best Bitter always available, with a range of guest beers which may include Goff's Jouster, Bath Ales Gem, Oakhill Best Bitter or beers from Ash Vine, Slater's, Otter, Hampshire, Church End, Wye Valley or Archers.

Nineteenth-century stone-built inn with later additions. No food, machines or music and the beer is served straight from the barrel. Well-behaved children welcome till 8.30pm. Car park. Situated 200 yards from Clearwell Cross on the Newland and Redbrook road.

 6–11pm Mon–Thurs; 12–3pm and 6–11pm Fri–Sat and bank holidays; 12–3pm and 7–10.30pm Sun.

COCKLEFORD

Green Dragon Inn
Cockleford, Cowley, Cheltenham GL53 9NW
☎ *(01242) 870271* Mhari Ashworth

 Goff's Jouster and Hook Norton Best Bitter regularly available, plus one guest, which could be from any one of a range of breweries.

Traditional Cotswold inn with stone-clad floors and roaring log fire in winter. Function room and patio overlooking lake. Accommodation. Food served 12–2.30pm and 6–10pm Mon–Sat, 12–2.30pm and 7–10pm Sun. Car park. Children's menu and high chairs available.

 *11am–11pm Mon–Sat; 12–10.30pm Sun.*

COLEFORD

The Angel Hotel
Market Place, Coleford GL16 8AE
☎ *(01594) 833113* Barry C Stoakes

 Freeminer Speculation usually available plus three guest beers which regularly include other beers from Freeminer, Timothy Taylor and Hook Norton, changing weekly.

Dating from the sixteenth century and situated in the Forest of Dean, this was once used as a town hall but is now a nine-room hotel with real ale bar. Courtyard and beer garden. Separate nightclub attached. Food served lunchtimes and evenings with sandwiches available during the afternoons. Children welcome if dining, until 7pm.

 7am (for breakfast) and 10.30am–11pm daily (1am in nightclub).

CRANHAM

The Black Horse Inn
Cranham, Gloucester GL4 8HP
☎ *(01452) 812217* David Job

 Wickwar Brand Oak Bitter and Hook Norton Best are regular ales plus one guest such as Greene King IPA.

An unspoilt traditional village inn perched on the side of a hill. Cosy lounge, classic country public bar complete with strange stag head, and dining room upstairs. No food on Sunday evening. Car park and garden. Children allowed.

 11.45am–2.30pm and 6.30–11pm (8–10.30pm Sun).

DIDMARTON

The King's Arms
The Street, Didmarton, Nr Badminton GL9 1DT
☎ *(01454) 238245* Nigel and Jane Worrall

 Uley Bitter usually available with two guest ales changing twice weekly.

A coaching inn dating from the seventeenth century, with two bars and a restaurant. The old country pub has recently been refurbished in an Edwardian style. Accommodation – rooms and self-catering cottages. Food available each session. Children welcome. Well-kept, stone-walled garden with boules piste.

 12–3pm and 6–11pm (10.30pm Sun).

DUNTISBOURNE ABBOTS

Five Mile House
Gloucester Road, Duntisbourne Abbots,
Cirencester GL7 7JR
☎ *(01285) 821432* JW Carrier

 A freehouse serving three different distinctive beers of varying strength. Timothy Taylor Landlord is quite often on the list as is Donnington BB and Archers Village.

A traditional country pub with old bar, family room and garden. Food served at lunchtime and evenings in non-smoking restaurant. Children allowed.

OPEN *12–3pm and 6–11pm (7–10.30pm Sun).*

DURSLEY

Old Spot Inn
Hill Road, Dursley GL11 4JQ
☎ *(01453) 542870* Stephen Herbert

 Six ales always available, with Old Ric from the local Uley brewery a permanent feature. Guests are from Wickwar, Abbey, Bath, Wychwood, Fuller's, Young's and Adnams.

Cosy freehouse with log fires, on the Cotswold Way. Lunches served daily. Secluded garden, boule piste. Clean-air policy. Parking.

OPEN *11am–3pm and 5–11pm Mon–Thurs; all day Fri–Sun.*

EBRINGTON

The Ebrington Arms
Ebrington, Nr Chipping Campden GL55 6NH
☎ *(01386) 593223* Graham Springett

 Hook Norton Best and Donnington SBA always available.

An unspoilt traditional Cotswold village pub that has recently been sympathetically refurnished. Gentle music. Traditional games such as darts and cribbage. Bar and restaurant food at lunchtime and evenings (no food Sun and Mon evenings). Car park and garden. Children allowed in the restaurant only. The owner has a pottery in the courtyard where he makes bowls, jugs and cruet sets used in the restaurant. Accommodation.

OPEN *11am–2.30pm and 6–11pm Mon–Sat (closed Monday lunchtime); 12–3pm and 7–10.30pm Sun.*

FORD

The Plough Inn
Ford, Temple Guiting GL54 5RU
☎ *(01386) 584215* Craig Brown

 A Donnington Brewery house always serving BB and SBA.

A thirteenth-century Cotswold stone inn with inglenook fireplace, beams and flagstone floor. Food served at lunchtime and evenings, with a separate dining area. Children allowed. Located on the main road between Stow-on-the-Wold and Tewkesbury, opposite the Jackdaws Castle racing stables.

OPEN *All day, every day.*

FRAMPTON COTTERELL

The Rising Sun
43 Ryecroft Road, Frampton Cotterell, Nr Bristol
BS17 2HN
☎ *(01454) 772330* Kevin Stone

 A popular freehouse with Butcombe Bitter, Wickwar Brand Oak Bitter and Cooper's WPA, Wadworth 6X always available, with up to 80 guest beers per year.

Small, friendly, single-bar local that likes to support the smaller brewers. CAMRA Pub of the Year for Avon in 1995. Bar food available at lunchtimes, including Sunday lunch. Evening food in the restaurant – a large new conservatory.

OPEN *11.30am–3pm and 5.30–11pm Mon–Thurs; 11.30am–11pm Fri–Sat; 12–3pm and 7–10.30pm Sun.*

FRANCE LYNCH

The King's Head
France Lynch, Stroud GL6 8LT
☎ *(01453) 882225* Mike Duff

 A freehouse serving Hook Norton and Archers brews, plus two guests that change frequently.

A small, traditional, country pub with large garden. No juke box. Live music every Monday evening. Food served at lunchtime and evenings. Children's play area.

OPEN *12–2.30pm and 6–11pm Mon–Sat; 12–2.30pm and 7–10.30pm Sun.*

GLOUCESTER

England's Glory

66–8 London Road, Gloucester GL1 3PB
☎ *(01452) 302948* Alban Joseph

A Wadworth-managed house with IPA, 6X and JCB always available. Also two guests, changing every week, which may include Badger Tanglefoot.

A food-oriented pub on the outskirts of town. Disabled access, non-smoking area, beer garden. Food available at lunchtime and evenings. Children allowed in the non-smoking area only.

OPEN *11.30am–2.30pm and 5–11pm Mon–Fri; all day Sat–Sun.*

The Linden Tree

73–5 Bristol Road, Gloucester GL1 5SN
☎ *(01452) 527869* Gordon Kinnear

Wadworth 6X, Henry's IPA, JCB, and Red Shoot Tom's Tipple always available plus up to four guest beers which may include Badger Tanglefoot.

A true country pub in the heart of Gloucester, south of the city centre. Large refurbished Georgian Grade II listed building. Bar food available at lunchtime and evenings (except Sun night). Parking, skittle alley, function room. Children allowed if eating. Accommodation. Cask Marque approved. Follow the Bristol road from the M5.

OPEN *11.30am–2.30pm and 6–11pm Mon–Fri; 11am–11pm Sat; 12–3.30pm and 7–10.30pm Sun.*

The Regal

32 St Aldate Street, King's Square, Gloucester GL1 1RP
☎ *(01452) 332344* Stephen Jordan

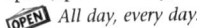A Wetherspoon's pub. Greene King Abbot, Shepherd Neame Spitfire and Goff's Jouster always available plus at least two guests changed on a weekly basis.

A large town pub with non-smoking areas, disabled access and toilets. Beer garden. Food served all day. Children allowed up to 6pm (5pm Saturday). Regular beer festivals.

OPEN *All day, every day.*

HAM

The Salutation Inn

Ham, Berkeley GL13 9QH
☎ *(01453) 810284* Mrs BS Dailly

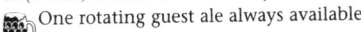One rotating guest ale always available.

Friendly pub set in pleasant countryside. Situated off the A38 towards Berkeley. Food served 12–2pm and 7–9pm. Children are welcome, but there are no special facilities. Car park.

12–3pm and 7–11pm (10.30pm Sun). Closed on Mon and Tues in the winter.

HANHAM MILLS

Old Lock & Weir

Hanham Mills, Bristol BS15 3NU
☎ *(0117) 967 3793* Simon Adams

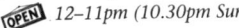A freehouse serving a range of up to six quality real ales, including Marson's Pedigree, Butcombe Bitter, Wadworth 6X and Morland Old Speckled Hen plus two guest ales.

A riverside country pub with dining area and garden. Food available at lunchtimes and evenings. Children allowed in dining area and garden only.

OPEN *All day, every day.*

HAWKESBURY UPTON

The Beaufort Arms

High Street, Hawkesbury Upton GL9 1AU
☎ *(01454) 238217*

Wickwar Brand Oak Bitter, plus two or three guest beers which may include Fuller's London Pride, Greene King Abbot Ale or beers from Bath Ales, Goff's or RCH. More unusual brews are obtained from Ales of the Unexpected.

Traditional Cotswold freehouse with extensive collection of old advertising signs, pub mirrors, bottles and jugs. Dining room and recently added skittle alley. Food served 12–2.30pm and 7–9.30pm every day. Well-behaved children welcome. Disabled facilites. Car park.

OPEN *12–11pm (10.30pm Sun).*

KINGSWOOD

Dinneywicks Inn

The Chippings, Kingswood, Wotton-under-Edge GL12 8RT
☎ *(01453) 843328* Mr and Mrs Thomas

A Wadworth house serving 6X and IPA, with other seasonal guests such as Adnams Broadside.

A recently refurbished village pub with garden and petanque court. Children allowed.

OPEN *11.30am–3pm and 6–11pm (all day Sat in winter); 12–10.30pm Sun.*

LIME STREET

The Greyhound Inn
Lime Street, Eldersfield GL19 4NX
☎ *(01452) 840381* Matthew and Kate Brown

 A freehouse with a Butcombe brew regularly available, plus a weekly changing guest beer from an independent brewery such as Dorothy Goodbody's (Wye Valley), Ledbury, Wickwar, Smiles or Oakhill.

A rural country inn with two bars and real fires, skittle alley/function room. Large garden with play area. Food served every lunchtime and evening except Mondays. Children allowed. Look for Lime Street on the map, not Eldersfield!

OPEN *11.30am–2.30pm Mon–Sat; 12–3pm Sun; 7–11pm Mon; 6–11pm Tues–Sat; 7–10.30pm Sun.*

LITTLETON UPON SEVERN

The White Hart Inn
Littleton upon Severn, Nr Bristol BS12 1NR
☎ *(01454) 412275* Howard and Liz Turner

 A Young's pub always offering Young's Bitter and Special, plus Waggle Dance in the summer and Winter Warmer for the colder months.

Near the Severn Bridges and Thornbury Castle. Bar food at lunchtime and evenings. Children are welcome in the garden room. Leave the M4 at junction 21. Head towards Thornbury, then Elberton village. Signposted from there.

OPEN *12–3pm and 6–11pm Mon–Sat; 12–4pm and 7–10.30pm Sun.*

LONGBOROUGH

The Coach & Horses Inn
Longborough Village, Moreton-in-Marsh GL56 0QJ
☎ *(01451) 830325* Connie Emm

 A Donnington tied house with XXX and Best Bitter served.

Old, original Cotswold locals' inn in lovely village setting with good views from patio. Sandwiches and ploughmans available at lunchtimes, if pre-ordered. Children welcome at lunchtime and early evening. Walkers are very welcome, and can eat their own sandwiches on the premises.

OPEN *11am–3pm and 7–11pm (10.30pm Sun).*

LONGHOPE

The Glasshouse Inn
May Hill, Longhope GL17 0NN
☎ *(01452) 830529* Mr S Pugh

 A freehouse regularly serving Butcombe brews. Guests served straight from the barrel include ales from Adnams and Hook Norton.

An old-fashioned country pub with garden. Food served at lunchtime and evenings, but not on Sundays. Well-behaved children allowed.

OPEN *11.30am–3pm and 6.30–11pm Mon–Sat; 12–3pm and 7–10.30pm Sun.*

LOWER APPERLEY

The Farmer's Arms
Ledbury Road, Lower Apperley GL19 4DR
☎ *(01452) 780307* Judith Karelus

 Wadworth 6X and IPA are permanent ales with a different guest beer each week; Charles Wells Bombadier is a popular one.

An eighteenth-century inn with one bar, oak beams and open fires. Bar and restaurant food available at lunchtime and evenings. Car park and garden. B4213 Ledbury Road, four miles south of Tewkesbury.

OPEN *11.30am–2.30pm and 6–11pm Mon–Sat; 12–3pm and 7–10.30pm Sun.*

MINCHINHAMPTON

The Ragged Cot
Cirencester Road, Hyde, Minchinhampton, Nr Stroud GL6 8PE
☎ *(01453) 884643* Simon Taylor

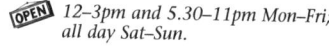 Freehouse generally serving Uley Old Spot and Smiles Best, with a couple of rotating ales such as Wickwar Cotswold Way.

A typical Cotswold coaching inn, first licensed in 1640, with a tasteful light restaurant sympathetically added on. If you arrive by horse the animal can have a drink at the trough while you have a pint. Accommodation and food – pub grub or restaurant menu. Children welcome but no special facilities. Games room that contains pool, TV, darts and electronic games. Garden and patio with strange water feature. Parking.

OPEN *12–3pm and 5.30–11pm Mon–Fri; all day Sat–Sun.*

The Weighbridge Inn

Longfords, Minchinhampton GL6 9AL
☎ *(01453) 832520* Simon and Jane Hudson

 Uley Old Spot and Wadworth 6X usually available with one rotating ale such as Uley Hogshead Bitter.

This part-seventeenth-century building used to serve the local mill and now acts as a community pub. Hundreds of old keys from the mill hang from the ceiling providing a curious decoration. Famous for its 2-in-1 pie – customers choose a second filling to go with cauliflower cheese – a 25-year-old recipe. Food served all day, every day but it is advisable to book. Car park and beer garden. Well-behaved children welcome. Located half way between Minchinhampton and Nailsworth.

OPEN *12–11pm (10.30 Sun).*

NEWLAND

The Ostrich Inn

Newland, Nr Coleford GL16 8NP
☎ *(01594) 833260* Miss Kathryn Horton

 Character country pub boasting eight real ales that are changed continuously. Some of the most frequent and popular include Hook Norton Old Hooky, Exmoor Hound Dog, Timothy Taylor Landlord and Uley Pig's Ear.

This thirteenth-century inn opposite the Cathedral of the Forest has beams, log fire, settles and candles. Well-known for its meals using local produce – bar and restaurant food available at lunchtime and evenings. Garden.

OPEN *12–2.20pm and 6.30–11pm Mon–Fri; 12–3pm and 6–11pm Sat; 12–3pm and 6.30–10.30pm Sun.*

OAKRIDGE LYNCH

Butchers Arms

Oakridge Lynch, Nr Stroud GL6 7NZ
☎ *(01285) 760371* PJ Coupe and BE Coupe

 Archers Best Bitter, Greene King Abbot Ale and Wickwar Brand Oak Bitter regularly available plus an occasional guest beer.

Friendly, 200-year-old village pub with log fires, exposed beams and attractive garden. It has been in the same hands for 16 years. Separate restaurant. Food served in the bar each lunchtime and evening (except Sun evening and all day Monday). Restaurant open 7.30–9.30pm Wed–Sat and Sun lunchtimes. Car park. Children welcome in the restaurant and small dedicated room off bar area. Signposted from the Eastcombe to Bisley road.

OPEN *12–3pm and 6–11pm Mon–Sat; 12–4pm and 7–10.30pm Sun.*

OLD SODBURY

Dog Inn

Old Sodbury, Near Bristol BS37 6LZ
☎ *(01454) 312006* John Harris

 Wadworth 6X, Marston's Pedigree, Wickwar Brand Oak Bitter and Fuller's London Pride are permanent features.

Very popular cosy rural pub with plenty of oak beams. Food available lunchtime and evening each day. Juke box. Accommodation. Children welcome in the large garden which includes a play area. Parking.

OPEN *11am–1pm Mon–Sat; 12–3.30pm and 7–10.30pm Sun.*

OLDBURY ON SEVERN

Anchor Inn

Church Road, Oldbury on Severn BS35 1QE
☎ *(01454) 413331* Alex and Sally De La Porre

 Freehouse offering a Butcombe ale at all times.

A sixteenth-century country pub whose clientele come from far and wide. Two bars and a dining area. Good walks in the area. Boasts one of the largest boules pistes in the country. Children welcome in the dining room. Garden and parking.

OPEN *11.30am–2.30pm and 6.30–11pm Mon–Fri; open all day Sat–Sun.*

PILL

The Star Inn

13 Bank Place, Pill, Nr Bristol BS20 0AQ
☎ *(01275) 374926* Mrs Fey

 Butcombe Bitter always available.

Local village pub with a wide range of customers. Parking. Children allowed in bar. Junction 19 off the M5.

OPEN *All day, every day.*

POPE'S HILL

The Greyhound Inn

The Slad, Pope's Hill, Gloucester GL14 1JX
☎ *(01452) 760344* Mr Pammenter

 A freehouse serving Timothy Taylor brews and Fuller's London Pride. One twice-weekly changing guest from any brewery in the UK. Examples are Exmoor Gold, RCH Pitchfork and brews from Cottage and Hop Back.

A country pub with non-smoking family room and garden. CAMRA Forest of Dean Pub of the Year 1999 and 2001. Food served at lunchtime and evenings. Children allowed in the family room only.

OPEN *11.30am–3.30pm and 5.30–11pm Mon–Sat; 12–3.30pm and 7–10.30pm Sun.*

PRESTBURY

The Royal Oak

43 The Burgage, Prestbury, Cheltenham
GL52 3DL
☎ *(01242) 522344* Simon Daws

 A freehouse offering Wadworth 6X, Timothy Taylor Landlord and an ale from the Archers brewery.

Classic old country pub with hops hanging from the beams. It is claimed to be the most haunted pub in Britain and was formerly owned by cricketer Tom Graveney. Bar and restaurant room – food served every session except Sunday night. Car parking, garden and skittle alley. Children allowed in restaurant and garden.

OPEN *11.30am–3pm and 5.30–11pm Mon–Fri; 11am–11pm Sat; 12–10.30pm Sun.*

PUCKLECHURCH

Rose & Crown

Parkfield Road, Pucklechurch BS16 9PS
☎ *(0117) 9372351* Evan Stewart

 A Wadworth house with 6X, IPA and JCB permanently available.

A popular pub that retains its olde-worlde charm in the quaint front bars, with its stone floors and wooden furniture, but is also heavily orientated towards food with the large dining area at the back. Food every lunchtime and evening except Sunday and Monday nights – best to book in advance. Car park, garden and play area. Children allowed in the dining room. Darts and occasional live music.

OPEN *11.30am–3pm and 6–11pm Mon–Sat; 12–4pm and 7–10.30 Sun.*

QUEDGELEY

Little Thatch Hotel

Bristol Road, Quedgeley, Gloucester GL2 4PQ
☎ *(01452) 720687* Mrs J McDougall

 Berkeley Old Friend and Dicky Pearce usually available plus one or two guest beers often from Goff's, Oakhill or Robinson's plus others from time to time.

Black and white timber-frame hotel built in 1351 with recent addition. Food served 12–2pm and 7–9.30pm Mon–Fri and 7–10pm Sat. Car park. Children welcome.

OPEN *12–2.30pm and 6.30–10.30pm Mon–Fri; 7–10.30pm Sat; 12–3.30pm and 7–10.30pm Sun.*

SAPPERTON

The Daneway

Sapperton, Nr Cirencester GL7 6LN
☎ *(01285) 760297*
Elizabeth and Richard Goodfellow

 Wadworth house offering 6X, Henry's IPA and JCB all year, plus Wadworth seasonal brews.

Built in 1784, this beamed pub is set in some wonderful Gloucestershire countryside. It features a lounge and public bar, plus small non-smoking family room. No music, machines or pool but traditional pub games. Bar food is available at lunchtime and meals in the evening. Car park, garden, children allowed in family room. Less than two miles off the A419 Stroud–Cirencester road.

OPEN *11am–2.30pm and 6.30–11pm.*

SHEEPSCOMBE

The Butcher's Arms

Sheepscombe, Painswick GL6 7RH
☎ *(01452) 812113*
Johnny and Hilary Johnston

 A freehouse with Hook Norton Best always available, plus two constantly changing guests.

A sixteenth-century country pub with panoramic views and sheltered gardens. Bar and restaurant food served lunchtimes and evenings. Car park. Children allowed. Situated off A46 north of Painswick (signposted from main road).

OPEN *11.30am–3pm and 6.30–11pm (10.30pm Sun).*

SLAD

Woolpack Inn

Slad Road, Slad, Stroud GL5 7QA
☎ *(01452) 813429* Dan Chadwick

 Uley Bitter, Old Spot and Pig's Ear regularly available. One or two guest beers are usually served, which may include Wickwar Cooper's WPA or Fuller's London Pride. Draught cider offered in the summer months.

The haunt of the late Laurie Lee (*Cider with Rosie*) and situated in the beautiful Slad Valley. Food served 12–2.30pm and 7–10pm Mon–Sat, 1–4pm (best to book) Sun. Car park. Small garden and terrace. Children welcome.

OPEN *11.30am–3pm and 6–11pm Mon–Fri; 11.30am–11pm Sat; 12–10.30pm Sun.*

The Miners Arms
Sling, Coleford GL16 8LH
☎ *(01594) 836632*

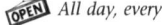Two rotating real ales on offer, including beers from local micro-breweries.

Traditional country inn with one bar, in tourist area. Nice walking and views. Large garden, juke box and live music twice a week. Food served all day. Children's play area. Situated on the main road from Chepstow to Coleford and the Forest of Dean.

OPEN *All day, every day.*

SNOWSHILL

The Snowshill Arms
Snowshill, Broadway WR12 7JU
☎ *(01386) 852653* David J Schad

Donnington SBA and BB usually available.

Rural Donnington-owned, family pub in the heart of the Cotswolds. The open-plan bar has a log fire in winter. Food lunchtimes and evenings. Children welcome, with play area in garden for use under parental supervision. Car park.

OPEN *11am–2.30pm and 6–11pm Mon–Sat; 12–3pm and 7–10.30pm Sun.*

SOUTH WOODCHESTER

The Ram Inn
South Woodchester, Nr Stroud GL5 5EL
☎ *(01453) 873329* Mike McAsey

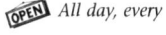Wickwar Brand Oak Bitter, Uley Old Spot and Dwan Ruby Red usually available plus three constantly changing guest beers from around the country. Approximately 400 served each year.

This bustling old Cotswold pub was built around 1601. Beautiful village setting, with wonderful views. Food served 12–2pm and 6–9pm every day. Children welcome. Plenty of outside seating, and real fires in the winter. Car park. Follow brown tourist signs from A46.

OPEN *All day, every day.*

STOW-ON-THE-WOLD

The Golden Ball Inn
Lower Swell, Stow-on-the-Wold GL54 1LF
☎ *(01451) 830247* Steve and Maureen Heath

Tied to the nearby Donnington Brewery, so BB and SBA are always available.

A seventeenth-century, Cotswold stone, village local with log fires in winter. Accommodation available. Typical old pub games played (darts, dominoes, cribbage, Aunt Sally). Bar food served at lunchtime and evenings. Car park and garden. Children and pets welcome. On the B4068, one mile from Stow-on-the-Wold.

OPEN *12–3pm and 6–11pm Mon–Sat; 12–3pm and 7–10.30pm Sun.*

TEWKESBURY

The Berkeley Arms
8 Church Street, Tewkesbury GL20 5PA
☎ *(01684) 293034* Mr Ian Phillips

Wadworth IPA, 6X and JCB always available, plus a seasonal ale and one guest which may include Badger Tanglefoot, Wadworth Old Timer, Morland Old Speckled Hen and Charles Wells Bombardier.

A small, homely fifteenth-century pub. Cask Marque accredited. Bar and restaurant food available. Street parking. The restaurant can be hired for functions. Children allowed in the restaurant.

OPEN *11am–3pm and 5–11pm Mon–Thur; all day Fri–Sun.*

The White Bear
Bredon Road, Tewkesbury GL20 5BU
☎ *(01684) 296614* Gerry and Jane Boazman

A freehouse serving Wye Valley Bitter, plus two guests from breweries such as Wood, Hook Norton, RCH, Wyre Piddle and Banks's.

A games-orientated, male-dominated boozer! No food. Children allowed in the garden only.

OPEN *All day, every day.*

TODENHAM

The Farriers Arms

Todenham, Moreton-in-the-Marsh GL56 9PF
☎ *(01608) 650901* Steve and Sue Croft

 A freehouse with Hook Norton Best always available, plus two monthly changing guests, perhaps Wye Valley Butty Bach, Shepherd Neame Spitfire, or seasonal and celebration ales.

Seventeenth-century brick-built village pub with inglenook fireplace, beams and wood burner. Food is available, and there is a restaurant and private room with two tables. Front patio, car park, and garden. Children allowed in non-bar areas. Signposted from the A429.

OPEN *12–3pm and 6.30–11pm Mon–Sat (closed Monday in the winter); 12–3pm and 7–10.30pm Sun.*

ULEY

Old Crown Inn

The Green, Uley, Dursley GL11 8SN
☎ *(01453) 860502* Mrs Morgan

 A freehouse with Uley Bitter and Pig's Ear regularly available, plus three weekly changing guests from breweries such as Cotleigh, Greene King, Hook Norton, Hampshire or Hop Back.

A village pub with games room, garden and accommodation. Pub food served at lunchtimes and evenings. Children allowed.

OPEN *11.30am–3pm and 7–11pm (10.30pm Sun).*

WATERLEY BOTTOM

The New Inn

Waterley Bottom, North Nibley, Nr Dursley GL11 6EF
☎ *(01453) 543659* Mrs Cartigny

 Greene King Abbot, Cotleigh Tawny, Bath Ales SPA and Gem always available, plus a changing guest (about 100 different beers per year).

A remote freehouse with two bars, set in a beautiful valley. Bar food available at lunchtime and evenings, except Monday. Car park and garden. CAMRA Gloucestershire Pub of the Year 1992–93. Beer festival held on the last weekend in June with 18 different ales. From North Nibley, follow signs for Waterley Bottom.

OPEN *7–11pm Mon; 12–2.30pm and 6–11pm Tues–Fri; all day Sat–Sun.*

WESTBURY ON TRYM

The Post Office Tavern

17 Westbury Hill, Westbury on Trym, Nr Bristol BS9 3AH
☎ *(0117) 940 1233* Rodney Duckett

 Up to ten beers available. Otter Ale, Bath Spa, Smiles Best, Butcombe Bitter and Fuller's London Pride are regulars, plus various other guests.

Early twentieth-century alehouse full of post office memorabilia. Non-smoking lounge. Bar food lunchtime and evenings. Street parking, small patio. No children under 14. On main road in Westbury village.

OPEN *11am–11pm Mon–Sat; 12–3pm and 7–10.30pm Sun.*

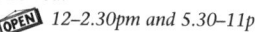

The Victoria Inn

20 Chock Lane, Westbury on Trym, Bristol BS9 3EX
☎ *(0117) 950 0441* Alastair Deas

 A Wadworth tied house with 6X and Henry's IPA always available, plus two weekly changing guests such as Butcombe Bitter and seasonal brews.

A village pub with garden. Food available at lunchtime and evenings. Children allowed.

OPEN *12–2.30pm and 5.30–11pm.*

WHITMINSTER

The Old Forge

Bristol Road, Whitminster GL2 7NY
☎ *(01452) 741306* John and Ginny Owens

A freehouse serving Exmoor Ale, Black Sheep Bitter, Wickwar Cotswold Way plus one rotating guest.

An old, traditional pub with dining area and beer garden. Food served at lunchtime and evenings. Children allowed.

OPEN *5–11pm Mon (closed Mon lunchtimes); 11.30am–3pm and 5–11pm Tues–Fri; all day Sat; 12–4pm and 7–10.30pm Sun.*

WINTERBOURNE DOWN

The Golden Heart

*Down Road, Winterbourne Down, Bristol
BS36 1AU*
☎ *(01454) 773152*
Matthew and Nicky Livingstone

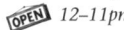 Smiles Original and Wadworth 6X permanently available.

A pub that from the outside looks just like a traditional country local – and it is – but there is also a large dining area attached at the back. Food served lunchtime and evening, and all day Sat and Sun. Car park and huge garden with two play areas. Children allowed in restaurant. Quiz night Wed and 60s, 70s & 80s night on Sun.

[OPEN] *12–11pm (10.30pm Sun).*

YOU TELL US

✶ *Bayshill Inn,* 85 St George's Place, Cheltenham
✶ *The Bristol Brewhouse,* Stokes Croft, Bristol
✶ *The Prince Albert,* Two Mile Hill Road, Kingswood, Bristol
✶ *The Rose & Crown,* High Street, Iron Acton
✶ *The Swan,* Pillowell
✶ *The Twelve Bells,* 12 Lewis Lane, Cirencester

Places Featured:

Aldershot	Horndean
Andover	Lasham
Beauworth	Linwood
Bentworth	Liss
Bishops Waltham	Little London
Chalton	Meonstoke
Charter Alley	Micheldever
Cheriton	Monk Sherborne
Dunbridge	Ovington
Eachingwell	Portsmouth
Easton	Priors Dean
Fareham	Ringwood
Farnborough	Rotherwick
Freefolk Priors	Selborne
Frogham	Shedfield
Froxfield	Southampton
Gosport	Southsea
Hamble	Titchfield
Hartley Wintney	Weyhill
Hawkley	Whitsbury
Hinton Ampner	Winchester

THE BREWERIES

BALLARD'S BREWERY LTD

Unit C, The Old Sawmill, Nyewood, Rogate, Petersfield GU31 5HA
☎ *(01730) 821301*

 MIDHURST MILD 3.5% ABV Winter brew, dark and smooth.
TROTTON BITTER 3.6%
Well-flavoured, well-hopped session bitter.
BEST BITTER 4.2% ABV
Nutty and well-balanced, with hops and bitterness in the finish.
GOLDEN BINE 4.2% ABV
Occasional brew.
ON THE HOP 4.5% ABV
Occasional brew.
WILD 4.7% ABV
Occasional brew.
NYEWOOD GOLD 5.0% ABV
Golden, hoppy brew.
WHEATSHEAF 5.0% ABV
Occasional brew.
WASSAIL 6.0% ABV
Malty and powerful, but not over-sweet.
Plus a powerful Christmas ale.

BECKETT'S BREWERY LTD

8 Enterprise Court, Rankine Road, Basingstoke RG24 8GE
☎ *(01256) 472986*

 OLD TOWN BITTER 3.7% ABV
ORIGINAL BITTER 4.0% ABV
BIER BLONDE 4.3% ABV
Pale with floral hoppiness. May and early July.
LIGHT MILD 4.3% ABV
Amber brown. Smoky and sweeter. May.
OLIVER'S ALE 4.3% ABV
Rounded and malty with delicate hoppiness. Jan.
WHITEWATER 4.3% ABV
Fruity, wheat flavour. Mid July–late Aug.
AMBER 4.5% ABV
Rounded and hoppy. Late Aug–end Sept.
EXTRA MILD 4.5% ABV
Smoky, bitter flavour. Oct–mid Nov.
GOLDEN GRALE 4.5% ABV
LODDON BITTER 4.5% ABV
Amber and aromatic. Mid Mar–end Apr.
COBBETT'S BITTER 4.7% ABV
Hoppy bitterness. Jan–mid Mar.
PORTER 4.7% ABV
Traditional porter-style ale. Mid Nov.
ST NICHOLAS 5.3% ABV
Malty, Christmas brew.

THE CHERITON BREWHOUSE

Cheriton, Alresford SO24 0QQ
☎ *(01962) 771166*

 POTS ALE 3.8% ABV
Golden, with hoppiness throughout.
BEST BITTER 4.2% ABV
Pronounced fruit and malt flavour.
DIGGERS GOLD 4.6% ABV
Powerful hoppiness and bitter finish.
FLOWER POWER 5.2% ABV
TURKEY'S REVENGE 5.9% ABV
A Christmas ale.

GEORGE GALE & CO. LTD

The Hampshire Brewery, Horndean PO8 0DA
☎ *(02392) 571212*
www.gales.co.uk

 BUTSER BREW 3.4% ABV
A sweet brew, with fruit throughout.
GB 4.0% ABV
Malt flavour with some fruitiness. Bitter.
FESTIVAL MILD 4.8% ABV
Sweet and dark, with fruitiness.
HSB 4.8% ABV
Sweet and malty.
Plus seasonal ales.

HAMPSHIRE BREWERY LTD

6–8 Romsey Industrial Estate, Greatbridge Road,
Romsey SO51 0HR
☎ *(01794) 830529*
www.hampshirebrewery.com

 KING ALFRED'S BITTER 3.8% ABV
Amber, light, refreshing and complex.
STRONGS 3.8% ABV
IRONSIDE 4.2% ABV
Amber, with crisp hop flavour and bitter finish.
LIONHEART 4.5% ABV
Refreshing with subtle hop finish.
GOLD RESERVE 4.8% ABV
PENDRAGON 4.8% ABV
Excellent balance. Bursting with malt hops.
PRIDE OF ROMSEY 5.0% ABV
Aromatic with good bitter flavour.
1066 6.0% ABV
Light, powerful pale ale. Clean and subtle.
Plus a range of special brews.

ITCHEN VALLEY BREWERY

Shelf House, New Farm Road, Alresford
SO24 9QE
☎ *(01962) 735111*
www.itchenvalley.com

 GODFATHERS 3.8% ABV
Golden and hoppy with bittersweet
flavour.
EASTER BUNNIES 3.9% ABV
Seasonal brew.
FAGIN'S 4.1% ABV
Balanced and hoppy, with citrus fruitiness.
WYKEHAMS GLORY 4.3% ABV
Smooth maltiness throughout.
JUDGE JEFFREYS 4.5% ABV
Copper coloured, rounded with hoppy
bitterness.
TEA CLIPPER 4.6% ABV
PURE GOLD 4.8% ABV
FATHER CHRISTMAS 5.5% ABV
Seasonal brew.
WATT TYLER 5.5% ABV
Seasonal brew.
Plus occasional brews.

OAKLEAF BREWING COMPANY

Unit 7, Clarence Wharf Industrial Estate,
Mumby Road, Gosport PO12 1AJ
☎ *(02392) 513222*
www.oakleafbrewing.co.uk

 MAYPOLE MILD 3.8% ABV
OAKLEAF BITTER 3.8% ABV
NUPTU'ALE 4.2% ABV
SQUIRREL'S DELIGHT 4.4% ABV
HOLE HEARTED 4.7% ABV
STOCKERS STOUT 5.0% ABV
YODEL WEISS 5.0% ABV
BLAKE'S GOSPORT BITTER 5.2% ABV
IPA 5.5% ABV

PORTCHESTER BREWERY

6 Audret Close, Portchester, Fareham PO16 9ER
☎ *(01329) 512918*
www.portchesterbrewery.co.uk

 BASTION 3.8% ABV
Ordinary bitter.
SLINGSHOT 4.2% ABV
CATAPULT 4.8% ABV
Light coloured, refreshing, strong bitter.
BATTERING RAM 5.0% ABV
Well-hopped, premium English ale.
XP 6.3% ABV
Christmas brew.

RINGWOOD BREWERY LTD

138 Christchurch Road, Ringwood BH24 3AP
☎ *(01425) 471177*
www.ringwoodbrewery.co.uk

BEST BITTER 3.8% ABV
Sweet malt flavour, becoming dry.
Bitterness in the finish.
BOONDOGGLE 3.9% ABV
Available May–Sept.
TRUE GLORY 4.3% ABV
Smooth and malty throughout, with some fruit.
XXXX PORTER 4.7% ABV
Full-bodied, winter brew.
FORTYNINER 4.9% ABV
Hop and malt flavour with malty finish.
OLD THUMPER 5.6% ABV
Golden with various fruit flavours.

TRIPLE FFF BREWING CO.

Old Magpie Works, Unit 3, Station Approach,
Four Marks, Alton GU34 4HN
☎ *(01420) 561422*
www.real-ale-guide.co.uk/triplefff

BILLERICAY DICKIE 3.8% ABV
Hoppy session brew.
PRESSED RAT AND WARTHOG 3.8% ABV
Dark and malty with hoppy bitterness.
MOONDANCE 4.2% ABV
Golden with fruity, hoppy flavour.
DAZED AND CONFUSED 4.6% ABV
Light and hoppy.
STAIRWAY TO HEAVEN 4.6% ABV
Excellent balance.
COMFORTABLY NUMB 5.0% ABV
Dark and fruity.

THE PUBS

ALDERSHOT

The Red Lion

Ash Road, Aldershot GU12 4EZ
☎ *(01252) 403503* Mr Freeth

A freehouse serving a range of up to six
weekly changing beers including
Timothy Taylor Dark Mild, Oakham Perrywig
and many, many more.

A traditional pub with beer garden. No
music or pool. Food available Tues–Fri
lunchtimes. Well-behaved children allowed.

OPEN *All day Mon–Sat; 12–4pm and*
7–10.30pm Sun.

ANDOVER

The George

Vernham Dean, Andover SP11 0JY
☎ *(01264) 737279*
Darren and Juliette Godwin

A Greene King house with IPA and
Morland Old Speckled Hen permanently
available, plus one monthly changing guest.

A traditional country village pub with
exposed beams. Food available lunchtime
and evenings either at the bar or in a
separate dining area. Beer garden and front
patio. Children allowed until 8.30pm.

OPEN *11am–3pm and 6–11pm Mon–Sat;*
12–2.30pm and 7–10.30pm Sun.

BEAUWORTH

The Milbury's

Beauworth, Alresford SO24 0PB
☎ *(01962) 771248* Mr Larden

A freehouse with Milbury's Best (house
beer), Hop Back Summer Lightning and
Best, and Cheriton Best Bitter always
available. Two guests change every couple of
months, and may be something like Timothy
Taylor Landlord.

A seventeenth-century country pub with
dining area and beer garden. Food
available 12–2pm and 6.30–9.30pm Mon–Fri,
12–3pm and 7–9.30pm Sat–Sun. Children
allowed.

OPEN *12–11pm.*

BENTWORTH

The Sun Inn

Bentworth, Nr Alton GU34 5JT
☎ *(01420) 562338* Mary Holmes

Ringwood Best, Cheriton Pots Ale, Hampshire Sun (house beer) and Bunces Pigswill always available, plus at least four guest ales changed weekly. Regulars include Ringwood Old Thumper, Badger Best, Brakspear Bitter, Archers Best, Fuller's London Pride, Gale's HSB and Young's Special.

A pretty seventeenth-century country inn with three connecting rooms. No music or fruit machines. Stone and wooden floors. Food available at lunchtime and evenings. Children allowed.

  12–3pm and 6–11pm Mon–Sat; all day Sun.

BISHOPS WALTHAM

The Hampshire Bowman

Dundridge Lane, Bishops Waltham, Southampton SO32 1GD
☎ *(01489) 892940* Jim Park

A freehouse serving Archers Village and Golden and Ringwood Fortyniner plus guests such as Cheriton Flower Power.

Freehouse in a rural setting with beer garden. Archery next door. Food available at lunchtime and evenings. No children.

  12–2pm and 6–11pm Mon; 11am–2.30pm and 6–11pm Tues–Sat; 12–3pm and 7–10.30pm Sun.

CHALTON

The Red Lion

Chalton, Waterlooville PO8 0BG
☎ *(023) 9259 2246* Mr McGee

A Gale's brewery managed house, serving HSB, Butser Bitter and GB plus one rotating guest changed monthly. This might be Marston's Pedigree, Shepherd Neame Spitfire, Charles Wells Bombardier or Wadworth 6X.

Reputed to be the oldest in Hampshire, this country pub with garden overlooks the Downs. Thatched roof, non-smoking lounge and non-smoking dining area. Food available at lunchtime and evenings (not Sunday evenings). Under 14s allowed only if eating.

  11am–3pm and 6–11pm Mon–Sat; 12–3pm and 7–10.30pm Sun.

CHARTER ALLEY

The White Hart

White Hart Lane, Charter Alley, Tadley RG26 5QA
☎ *(01256) 850048* Howard Bradley

A freehouse with Greene King Abbot Ale always available, plus two guest beers. Brews from Otter and Harveys breweries are popular.

A village pub with dining area, skittle alley and garden. Food available at lunchtime and evenings. Children allowed in certain areas.

  12–2.30pm Mon–Fri; 12–3pm Sat–Sun; 7–11pm Mon–Sat; 7–10.30pm Sun.

CHERITON

The Flower Pots Inn

Cheriton, Alresford SO24 0QQ
☎ *(01962) 771318*
Paul Tickner and Jo Bartlett

The Cheriton Brewhouse is situated very close to this pub, hence the full range of Cheriton brews are always available, plus occasional Cheriton specials. The two businesses are run separately though, and this is not the 'brewpub' that it is often mistaken for.

The pub is an unspoilt traditional inn on the edge of the village. Bar food is available every lunchtime and Mon–Sat evenings. Car park, garden, en-suite accommodation. Children not allowed in the pub. CAMRA regional Pub of the Year 1995.

  12–2.30pm and 6–11pm Mon–Sat; 12–3pm and 7–10.30pm Sun.

DUNBRIDGE

The Mill Arms

Barley Hill, Dunbridge, Nr Romsey SO51 0LF
☎ *(01794) 343401*
Martin and Christine O'Farrell

A freehouse with up to four real ales changed every few days. These often include something from the Hampshire, Ringwood or Badger breweries.

A quiet country pub in the middle of nowhere! Two open fires, conservatory, restaurant, function room, twin skittle alley, bar billiards. Accommodation available in six en-suite rooms, one with four-poster bed. Large garden. Food available at lunchtime and evenings. Children and dogs welcome. Website: www.themillarms.co.uk.

  12–3pm and 6–11pm Mon–Sat; 12–3pm and 7–10.30pm Sun.

EACHINGWELL

The Royal Oak

Eachingwell, Nr Newbury RG20 4UH
☎ *(01635) 298280* Mrs A Noonan and Mr Lay

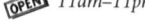Two guest ales, changed weekly, are served straight from the cask. Wadworth 6X and Fuller's London Pride are regulars, but other beers are featured if requested by customers!

Small village pub with two bars, a dining area, fireplaces and beams. Food served. Pool, darts, TV, beer garden, car park. Children allowed. Situated just over 7 miles south of Newbury.

OPEN *11am–11pm Mon–Sat; 12–10.30pm Sun.*

EASTON

The Cricketers Inn

Easton, Winchester SO21 1ET
☎ *(01962) 779353* Geoff Green

A freehouse with a Ringwood brew, Timothy Taylor Landlord and Otter Ale always available. Three weekly changing guests might be beers from Cotleigh or Lloyds.

A traditional village pub with drinking terrace and non-smoking dining area. A drop-home service is provided on Fri and Sat nights. Food available at lunchtime and evenings. B&B. Children allowed.

OPEN *12–3pm and 6–11pm (10.30pm Sun).*

FAREHAM

Osborne View Hotel

67 Hill Head Road, Fareham PO14 3JP
☎ *(01329) 664623* Richard and Denise Bell

A Hall and Woodhouse (Badger) tied pub with up to eight real ales always available. Badger Best, IPA and Tanglefoot always featured, plus a range of ales from Gribble Brewery.

A seafront pub on three levels. Non-smoking area, sea views, parking. Food available at lunchtimes and evenings, and all day on Sundays. Children and dogs welcome.

OPEN *11am–11pm (10.30pm Sun).*

FARNBOROUGH

The Prince of Wales

184 Rectory Road, Farnborough GU14 8AL
☎ *(01252) 545578* Peter Moore

Ten-pump freehouse with Hogs Back TEA, Fuller's London Pride, Badger Tanglefoot, Ringwood Fortyniner and Young's Bitter the permanent beers, plus five guests, changed every month. Session beers below 4.0% ABV appear on a monthly basis. Ales from micro-breweries across the country are featured, plus Brakspear Bitter, Hop Back Summer Lightning and Fuller's Chiswick.

Traditional country drinking pub in an old building on the edge of town. No music, games or darts. Food available Mon–Thurs lunchtimes. Marquee outside during summer, patio area, car park. Children allowed only in marquee. Round the corner from North Farnborough Station (not main Farnborough station).

OPEN *11.30am–2.30pm and 5.30–11pm Mon–Sat; 12–3.30pm and 7–10.30pm Sun.*

FREEFOLK PRIORS

The Watership Down Inn

Freefolk, Nr Whitchurch RG28 7NJ
☎ *(01256) 892254* Mark and Alison Lodge

Real ale on five pumps with Archers Best, Brakspear Bitter and a mild always available plus two constantly changing guests usually from smaller breweries including Ringwood, Otter, Moor, Juwards, Beckett's, Itchen Valley, Oakhill, Triple FFF and Butts.

Built in 1840, renamed after the Richard Adams novel that was set locally, a one-bar pub with an open fire and pretty garden with many outside tables. Bar and restaurant food available at lunchtime and evenings, plus new non-smoking conservatory that seats 30 diners. Car park, children's play area. Children allowed in the restaurant. On the B3400 between Whitchurch and Overton.

OPEN *11.30am–3.30pm and 6–11pm (10.30pm Sun).*

FROGHAM

The Forester's Arms

Abbots Well Road, Frogham, Fordingbridge SP6 2JA
☎ *(01425) 652294* Mr M Harding

A Wadworth tied house with 6X and Henry's IPA always available plus two seasonal or special brews such as Mayhem Odda's Light.

A country inn in the New Forest area. Dartboard, garden children's play area. Food available at lunchtime and evenings in a separate restaurant. Children and dogs welcome.

OPEN *11am–3pm and 6–11pm Mon–Sat; 12–3pm and 7–10.30pm Sun.*

FROXFIELD

The Trooper Inn

Froxfield, Petersfield GU32 1BD
☎ *(01730) 827293* Mr Matini

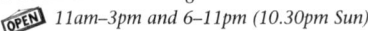A freehouse serving Ringwood Fortyniner and Best plus a couple of weekly changing guests from breweries such as Ballard's.

Acountry pub with dining area, function room and garden. Food available at lunchtime and evenings. Children allowed.

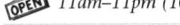 *11am–3pm and 6–11pm (10.30pm Sun).*

GOSPORT

The Clarence Tavern

1 Clarence Road, Gosport PO12 1AJ
☎ *(023) 9252 9726*
Patrick and Teresa Noonan

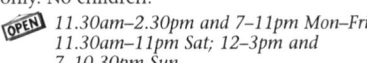Beers from the Oakleaf Brewery range are always available. Beer festivals at Easter and August bank holiday.

AVictorian pub with food available all day in separate dining area. Outside terrace seating. Darts. Golf society. Car park. Function room.

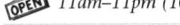 *11am–11pm (10.30pm Sun).*

Queens Hotel

143 Queens Road, Gosport
☎ *(023) 9258 2645* Sue Lampon

Archers Village, Black Sheep Special and Badger Tanglefoot are usually available, plus a porter in winter. Two or three guest beers are also served from a constantly changing selection of breweries.

Popular town pub with good selection of ales. Snacks and rolls served at lunchtimes only. No children.

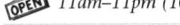 *11.30am–2.30pm and 7–11pm Mon–Fri; 11.30am–11pm Sat; 12–3pm and 7–10.30pm Sun.*

HAMBLE

The King & Queen

High Street, Hamble, Southampton SO31 4HA
☎ *(023) 8045 4247* Kelly Smith

A Whitbread house with Fuller's London Pride, Wadworth 6X, and a Brakspear brew always available, plus a guest from local breweries such as Cottage or Hampshire.

Asailing pub with log fires and bar billiards. Serving food at lunchtime and evenings. Children allowed in the lounge.

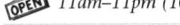 *11am–11pm (10.30pm Sun).*

HARTLEY WINTNEY

The Wagon & Horses

High Street, Hartley Wintney, Nr Hook RG27 8NX
☎ *(01252) 842119* Neil Scott

A freehouse with Gale's HSB always available, plus two guests, often brews from Ringwood but changing all the time.

Atypical village pub with secluded garden. Food available at lunchtime. No children.

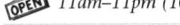 *11am–11pm Mon–Sat; 12–3pm and 7–10.30pm Sun.*

HAWKLEY

The Hawkley Inn

Pococks Lane, Hawkley, Nr Liss GU33 6NE
☎ *(01730) 827205* Al Stringer

Six constantly changing real ales available at any once time, from breweries such as Ballard's, RCH, Itchen Valley, Triple FFF, Ringwood, Beckett's and Weltons, to name but a few. The pub's own cider, Swamp Donkey, is also served.

Small, rural alehouse with fires in winter, large garden, discreet blues music and a handsome landlord! Food served from an interesting menu 12–2pm and 7–9.30pm (not Sun evening). Extremely well-behaved children welcome at lunchtime only. Parking in lane opposite pub. Smokers welcome.

 12–2.30pm and 6–11pm Mon–Fri; 12–3pm and 6–11pm Sat–Sun.

HINTON AMPNER

The Hinton Arms

Hinton Ampner SO24 0NH
☎ *(01962) 771252* Richard Powell

Two beers from Triple FFF are permanently available, Moondance, plus a house bitter brewed especially for the pub, called Hinton Arms Best. One guest, changed every four days, might be something from Wychwood, Smiles or Brakspear, but Otter Ale, RCH East Street Cream, Oakhill Bitter, Butcombe Bitter, Timothy Taylor Landlord have all been featured.

Roadside pub specialising in real ales and food, featuring beams, stone floors and 300 pewter mugs hanging from the ceiling. One very large bar divided into three. Food is available, and there is a non-smoking dining area. Garden, patio and car park. Children allowed.

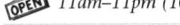 *11am–3pm and 6–11pm (10.30pm Sun).*

HORNDEAN

Ship & Bell Hotel
6 London Road, Horndean, Waterlooville
PO8 0BZ
☎ *(023) 9259 2107* Taff Williams

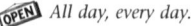A Gale's Brewery house serving Butser, HSB and GB plus seasonal specials and a range of other guests perhaps including Everards Tiger.

A village pub with separate dining area and accommodation. Children allowed if eating.

 All day, every day.

LASHAM

The Royal Oak
Lasham GU34 5SJ
☎ *(01256) 381213* Lawrence Berwick

Ringwood Best is always on offer, plus five guest beers, changed weekly. Hogs Back TEA is a regular favourite, with other beers from Hogs Back and brews from Triple FFF and Hop Back also featured.

Village pub in a building dating from 1780, with beams and real fires. Food available. Occasional live music. Two bars (lounge and public), garden. Children allowed. Located next to Lasham Airfield, which is signposted.

 11am–2.30pm and 6–11pm Mon–Thurs; 11am–11pm Fri–Sat; 12–10.30pm Sun.

LINWOOD

The Red Shoot Inn & Brewery
Toms Lane, Linwood, Ringwood BH24 3QT
☎ *(01425) 475792*
Mr P Adams and Mr AJ Benson

Wadworth 6X, IPA and Farmer's Glory plus Red Shoot's own beers – Forest Gold and Tom's Tipple – usually available. Wadworth seasonal brews also served.

This Wadworth-owned, New Forest pub is home to the Red Shoot Brewery. Food served lunchtimes and evenings. Children welcome. Car park. Signposted from A338 at Ellingham.

 FOREST GOLD 3.8% ABV
TOM'S TIPPLE 4.8% ABV

 Winter: 11am–3pm and 6–11pm Mon–Fri; 11am–11pm Sat; 12–10.30pm Sun; Summer: 11am–11pm Mon–Sat; 12–10.30pm Sun.

LISS

The Bluebell
Farnham Road, Liss GU33 6JE
☎ *(01730) 892107* George Doa

A freehouse with Fuller's London Pride always available plus three guests including, perhaps something from Hogs Back, Triple FFF Moondance, Ballard's Best, Beckett's Original or Gale's GB.

A pub/restaurant, half smoking and half non-smoking. International cuisine served at lunchtime and evenings, with a choice of either à la carte or bar menu. Beer garden. Children allowed.

 11.30am–3pm and 5–11pm (10.30pm Sun).

LITTLE LONDON

The Plough Inn
Silchester Road, Little London, Tadley RG26 5EP
☎ *(01256) 850628* Mr Brown

A freehouse with Ringwood Best and Fortyniner usually available plus a wide selection of guest ales.

A 330-year-old pub with exposed beams and secluded garden for summer, log fires in winter. Hot, filled baguettes served at lunchtime and evening. Children allowed.

 12–2.30pm and 6–11pm Mon–Sat; 12–3pm and 7–10.30pm Sun.

MEONSTOKE

The Bucks Head
Bucks Head Hill, Meonstoke, Southampton
SO32 3NA
☎ *(01489) 877313* Robin Christian

A Greene King house with IPA and Abbot always available, plus two guests. Archers Golden and Everards Tiger are regulars, but many different beers are featured.

A rural country pub on the banks of the river. Tourist Board recommended with separate restaurant and B&B. Food available at lunchtime and evenings. Well-behaved children and dogs allowed. Situated just off the A32 north of Dropsford

 11am–3pm and 6–11pm Mon–Fri; all day Sat–Sun and bank holidays.

MICHELDEVER

Half Moon & Spread Eagle

Winchester Road, Micheldever SO21 3DG
☎ *(01962) 774339*
Belinda Boughtwood and Ray Douglas

 A Greene King tenancy with Greene King ales always available, plus guests.

A popular rural pub with sixteenth-century walls and original beams. Wide selection of mainly home-cooked food served lunchtimes and evenings daily, plus take-away service. Large garden and patio, children's play area overlooking village cricket green. Car park. Less than a mile off the A33, six miles north of Winchester, 12 miles south of Basingstoke.

 12–3pm and 6–11pm Mon–Sat; 12–3pm and 7–10.30pm Sun.

MONK SHERBORNE

The Mole Inn

Ramsdell Road, Monk Sherborne, Nr Tadley RG26 5HS
☎ *(01256) 850033* Chris and Jerry Elliott

 A Greene King house with IPA, Abbot and Morland Original always available, plus one guest during the winter months.

A traditional two-bar pub with separate dining area and beer garden. Country location. Food available lunchtimes and evenings daily. Children allowed until 8.30pm, special children's menu available. Turn left off A340, signposted Monk Sherborne.

 12–2.30pm and 6.30–11pm (10.30pm Sun).

OVINGTON

The Bush Inn

Nr Alresford, Ovington SO24 0RE
☎ *(01962) 732764* Nick Young

 Wadworth 6X and IPA and The Red Shoot brewpub's Tom's Tipple permanently available, plus two guests changing every two weeks. Wadworth Farmer's Glory and Badger Tanglefoot are regular features.

A seventeenth-century up-and-down pub with lots of little rooms and antique memorabilia. Real fires make it cosy in the winter. One main bar in the middle of the pub. Beer garden. Recently refurbished with new toilets. Disabled facilites. Reputation for good food, which is available every lunchtime and Mon–Sat evenings. Well-behaved children allowed. Situated off the A31 towards Winchester.

 11am–3pm and 6–11pm Mon–Sat; 12–3pm and 7–10.30pm Sun.

PORTSMOUTH

The Connaught Arms

119 Guildford Road, Fratton, Portsmouth PO1 5EA
☎ *(023) 9264 6455* Mick and Carol Frewing

 Three guest beers usually available, perhaps Caledonian Deuchars IPA, Fuller's London Pride, Hop Back Summer Lightning, Cheriton Pots Ale, Ringwood Fortyniner or others.

Comfortable pub hidden in the back streets of Fratton, famous for its interesting range of pasties. Bar menu available 11.45am–2.15pm Mon–Sat; pasties available every session. Well-behaved children welcome until 7pm. Situated at the junction of Penhale and Guildford roads.

 11.30am–2.30pm and 6–11pm Mon–Thurs; 11.30am–11pm Fri–Sat; 12–4pm and 7–10.30pm Sun.

The Dolphin

41 High Street, Portsmouth PO1 2LV
☎ *(023) 9282 3595* Giorgio Pitzettu

 Fuller's London Pride, Wadworth 6X, Timothy Taylor Landlord, Gale's HSB, Brakspear Bitter, Greene King Abbot, Morland Old Speckled Hen and Adnams Bitter always available.

A sixteenth-century coaching inn with wood and flagstone floors. Historic area with good walks nearby. The pub boasts Nelson's signature on a piece of glass in the bar! A la carte menu and bar food available at lunchtime and evenings. Small function room. Children allowed. Directly opposite the cathedral in old Portsmouth.

 11am–11pm Mon–Sat; 12–10.30pm Sun.

The Tap

17 London Road, North End, Portsmouth PO2 0BQ
☎ *(023) 9261 4861*

 Up to 11 beers available including Ruddles Best and Ringwood Old Thumper. Guests (100 per year) will include Ringwood Best, Badger Tanglefoot, Gale's HSB and brews from Spinnaker. Micro-breweries particularly favoured.

A one-bar drinking pub in the town centre with no juke box or fruit machines. Formerly the brewery tap for the now defunct Southsea Brewery. Bar meals available at lunchtime. Street parking opposite, small yard, disabled toilet. Children not allowed.

 10.30am–11pm Mon–Sat; 12–10.30pm Sun.

The Wellington

62 High Street, Portsmouth PO1 2LY
☎ *(023) 9281 8965* Mr Western

 Wadworth 6X and Greene King IPA available plus one guest from a brewery such as Fuller's.

A traditional community pub with a reputation for good food served at lunchtime and four evenings per week. Use the harbour entrance. Children allowed.

OPEN *11am–11pm (10.30pm Sun).*

Wetherspoons: The Isambard Kingdom Brunel

2 Guildhall Walk, Portsmouth PO1 2DD
☎ *(023) 9229 5112* Karen and Mark Saunders

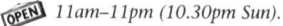 Hop Back Summer Lightning and Shepherd Neame Spitfire always available plus three guest ales. Quality ales at Wetherspoon prices.

A friendly town pub, recently refurbished, in a Grade II listed building. Food served all day with meal deals available. Non-smoking area. Cask Marque approved. No children.

OPEN *10am–11pm Mon–Sat; 12–10.30pm Sun.*

The Winchester Arms

99 Winchester Road, Portsmouth PO2 7PS
☎ *(023) 9266 2443* Dave and Lynn Pickersgill

 Beers from Oakleaf Brewery always served, with Nuptu'Ale, Blake's Gosport Bitter and Hole Hearted (Beer of Hampshire 2002) permanently available.

Small, backstreet, community village pub, where everybody is treated as a friend. Live music from local musicians every Sunday, with occasional karaoke and discos. Light-hearted pub quiz every Monday evening, darts, football and cricket teams. Bar snacks available at most times, Sunday lunches can be booked. Barbecues held in summer. Non-smoking area, children allowed in snug, tap and patio garden.

OPEN *4–11pm Mon; 11am–11pm Tues–Sat; 12–10.30pm Sun.*

The White Horse Inn

Priors Dean, Nr Petersfield GU32 1DA
☎ *(01420) 588387* Mr J Eddleston

 Gale's Festival Mild, HSB and Butser Brew Bitter, Ballard's Best plus Ringwood Fortyniner always available and guest beers (ten per year) including Wadworth 6X, Bateman Summer Breeze, Gale's IPA and Porter, plus a range of one-off brews from Gale's.

An olde-world pub untouched for years, with log fires, rocking chairs, antique furniture and a grandfather clock. Bar food available at lunchtime. Car park and garden. Nearby caravan site. Tricky to find. Between Petersfield and Alton, five miles from Petersfield, seven miles from Alton.

OPEN *11am–2.30pm and 6–11pm Mon–Fri; 11am–3pm and 6–11pm Sat; 12–3pm and 7–10.30pm Sun.*

Inn on the Furlong

12 Meeting House Lane, Ringwood BH24 1EY
☎ *(01425) 475139* Joyce Dean

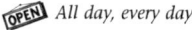 Tied to the Ringwood brewery, so Best, Fortyniner and Old Thumper available, plus a seasonal beer.

An old building with log fire, conservatory and beer garden. Food available at lunchtime. Children allowed.

OPEN *All day, every day.*

The Falcon

The Street, Rotherwick, Hook RG27 9BL
☎ *(01256) 762586*

 An Eldridge Pope tied house with a choice of three real ales, Fuller's London Pride, Brakspear Bitter and a weekly changing guest ale.

A traditional family-run village pub/restaurant with a large garden and car park. Food available 12–2pm and 7–9.30pm Mon–Sat, 12–2.30pm and 7–9pm Sun. Children allowed, but not in bar area. No high chairs.

OPEN *11am–2.30pm and 6–11pm Mon–Fri; 11am–11pm Sat; 12–10.30pm Sun.*

SELBORNE

The Selborne Arms
High Street, Selborne GU34 3JR
☎ *(01420) 511247* Hayley Carter

 A freehouse with Ringwood Fortyniner and Cheriton Pots Ale always on offer, plus guests from a wide range of local breweries.

Traditional village pub in a seventeenth-century building, with original beams, log fires, garden and children's play area. A wide range of imaginative food is served.

🍺 *11am–3pm and 6–11pm Mon–Sat; 12–10.30pm Sun.*

SHEDFIELD

The Wheatsheaf Inn
Botley Road, Shedfield, Southampton SO32 2JG
☎ *(01329) 833024* Mr Rennie

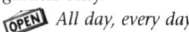 A freehouse serving Cheriton Pots Ale, Mansfield Four Season, Cotleigh Tawny, and Hop Back Summer Lightning plus two different guests every week.

A country pub with garden. Food available at lunchtime. Children allowed in the garden only.

🍺 *All day, every day.*

SOUTHAMPTON

The Alexandra
6 Belle Vue Road, Southampton SO15 2AY
☎ *(023) 8033 5071* Miss Hiles

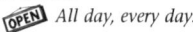 A Whitbread house with Wadworth 6X and Fuller's London Pride always available, plus two guests per week, such as Gale's HSB, Hop Back Summer Lightning or a Ringwood brew.

A town-centre pub with traditional building. One bar with big TV and juke box. Food available at lunchtime. No children.

🍺 *All day, every day.*

Bevois Castle
63 Onslow Road, Bevois Valley, Southampton SO14 0JL
☎ *(023) 8033 0350* Mr D Bulpitt

 Two guest ales served, from any independent brewery – range changes weekly.

Small, traditional pub with real fire and shove ha'penny board. Full menu available 11.30am–3pm and 6.30–9.30pm. Hot pies and pasties available all day. No children's facilities. Car park.

🍺 *11am–11pm (10.30pm Sun).*

The Crown Inn
9 Highcrown Street, Southampton SO17 1QE
☎ *(023) 8031 5033* Jackie Hahyer

 A Whitbread house with Wadworth 6X and Fuller's London Pride always available plus a rotating guest ale, often from Archers.

A city pub and restaurant with food available at lunchtime and evenings. No children under 14 allowed.

🍺 *11am–11pm Mon–Sat; 12–10.30pm Sun.*

The Duke of Wellington
36 Bugle Street, Southampton SO14 2AH
☎ *(023) 8033 9222* Mr Wyle

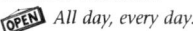 A Wadworth-managed house offering the range of Wadworth ales, plus Ringwood Best. Guests may include Adnams Southwold.

Built in the twelfth century, this is the oldest pub in Southampton. Food available at lunchtime and evenings in a separate dining area. Function room. Children welcome.

🍺 *All day, every day.*

The Eagle
1 Palmerston Road, Southampton SO14 1LL
☎ *(023) 8033 3825* Michelle Wisniak

An Enterprise tenancy with Wadworth 6X and Fuller's London Pride always available, plus four guests from a range of ales such as Gale's HSB, Greene King Abbot and Morland Old Speckled Hen.

A traditional town-centre pub with darts and pool. Food available at lunchtime. No children.

🍺 *All day, every day.*

The South Western Arms
38–40 Adelaide Road, Southampton SO17 2HW
☎ *(023) 8032 4542* Stephen Howey

 Wadworth 6X, Fuller's London Pride, Ringwood Best and Badger Tanglefoot are permanent fixtures, plus a constantly changing range of guest ales, changed at least twice a week.

A split-level pub with the bar on the ground floor and a games area with TV on the first floor. Light lunches and bar snacks available. Families welcome upstairs only. Large beer garden. Selection of country wines. Located opposite St Denys railway station.

🍺 *4–11pm Mon (closed Mon lunchtime); 12–11pm Tues–Sat; 12–10.30pm Sun.*

The Standing Order
30 High Street, Southampton SO14 3HT
☎ *(023) 8022 2121* Ben Foy

A Wetherspoon's pub with Ringwood Fortyniner and Shepherd Neame Spitfire always available, plus about ten different guests per week.

A traditional high-street pub with non-smoking area. Food available all day. No children.

OPEN *10am–11pm Mon–Sat; 12–10.30pm Sun.*

The Stile
163 University Road, Southampton SO17 1TS
☎ *(023) 8058 1124* Matthew Crick

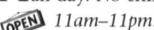Two guest ales always available, such as Brains SA, Ruddles Best or Fuller's London Pride.

A city-based student pub with food served all day. No children.

OPEN *11am–11pm.*

Waterloo Arms
101 Waterloo Road, Southampton SO15 3BS
☎ *(023) 8022 0022* Robert and Linda Roach

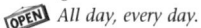A Hop Back pub serving Summer Lightning, Thunderstorm, GFB, Festive Stout and Best, plus guests rotated weekly on one pump, perhaps King and Barnes Festive, Woodforde's Wherry or something from the Hampshire Brewery.

A local, traditional, village pub with garden. Food available at lunchtime and evenings. Children allowed.

OPEN *All day, every day.*

The Wellington Arms
56 Park Road, Freemantle, Southampton SO15 3DE
☎ *(023) 8022 7356* Eduardo Bonniffini

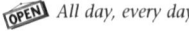A freehouse with Ringwood Old Thumper and Best, Fuller's London Pride and ESB, Timothy Taylor Landlord, Morland Old Speckled Hen and Shepherd Neame Spitfire always available, plus four constantly changing guests. Regular guests include Greene King IPA, Wadworth 6X and Charles Wells Bombardier. Also serves one Belgian and one German brew.

A town pub with garden and à la carte restaurant. Blues/jazz-oriented, with live music twice a month. Bar or restaurant food served 12–3pm and 6–9pm. Children allowed in the garden.

OPEN *All day, every day.*

The Artillery Arms
Hester Road, Southsea PO4 8HB
☎ *(023) 9273 3610* Brian and Eileen Findlay

A freehouse with Gale's, Hampshire and Cheriton brews and Ringwood Old Thumper always available, plus up to four guest ales. Nadder Valley real cider also served.

A traditional pub with garden. Food available at lunchtimes. Children allowed until 8pm (7.30pm Sat–Sun).

OPEN *11am–3pm and 6–11pm Mon–Thurs; all day Fri–Sun.*

The Old Oyster House
291 Lockway Road, Southsea, Portsmouth PO4 8LH
☎ *(023) 9282 7456* Mark and Karen Landon

A constantly changing selection of beers, usually including a mild, is available perhaps from Ash Vine, Hop Back, Packhorse, Teignworthy or Abbey Ales.

Friendly, comfortable and busy pub with separate games bar for pool, darts, table football and big-screen Sky Sport. Large garden and patio. No food. Large public car park opposite. Well-behaved children welcome in the games bar. Located at the end of a mile-long cul de sac.

OPEN *4–11pm Mon–Thurs; 12–11pm Fri–Sat; 12–10.30pm Sun.*

Wine Vaults
43–7 Albert Road, Southsea PO5 2SF
☎ *(023) 9286 4712*
Mike Hughes and Jeremy Stevens

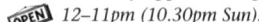Twelve hand pumps serve a range of ales including Fuller's London Pride and beers from Archers, Young's, Greene King, Itchen Valley, Ringwood, Hampshire and Suthwyk breweries.

Friendly, traditional pub with varied clientele and good atmosphere. Food is served 12–9pm daily, and there is a new brasserie menu. Well-behaved over 5s welcome, but there are no special facilities. Located directly opposite Kings Theatre.

OPEN *12–11pm (10.30pm Sun).*

TITCHFIELD

The Wheatsheaf Inn
1 East Street, Titchfield, Fareham PO14 4AD
☎ *(01329) 842965* Adrienne DoNoia

A freehouse serving Fuller's London Pride and Woodforde's Wherry plus two guests changed weekly. Examples may include Hook Norton Best and Exmoor Gold.

A village pub with dining area, open fire, patio and garden. Food available at lunchtime and evenings. Children allowed in the dining area only.

OPEN *12–3pm and 6–11pm Mon–Thurs; all day Fri; 12–3pm and 6–11pm Sat; 12–3pm and 7–10.30pm Sun.*

WEYHILL

Weyhill Fair
Weyhill Road, Weyhill, Nr Andover SP11 0PP
☎ *(01264) 773631* Mr and Mrs Rayner

Fuller's London Pride, Chiswick and ESB always available plus three guest beers (200 per year) including brews from Shepherd Neame, Adnams and Ringwood.

A friendly local freehouse offering bar food at lunchtime and evenings. Cask Marque award winner. Car park, garden and non-smoking family room. On the A342 west of Andover.

OPEN *11am–3pm and 6–11pm Mon–Thurs; 11am–3pm and 5–11pm Fri; 11am–3pm and 6–11pm Sat; 12–3pm and 7–10.30pm Sun.*

WHITSBURY

The Cartwheel
Whitsbury Road, Whitsbury, Nr Fordingbridge SP6 3PZ
☎ *(01725) 518362 Fax (01725) 518886*
Patrick Lewis

Up to six beers always available (120 per year) but brews continually changing. Breweries favoured include Adnams, Shepherd Neame, Bunces, Hop Back, Ringwood and Mole's. Seasonal beers and small breweries preferred.

A relaxed bar with exposed beams and open fire, in good walking country. Bar and restaurant food available at lunchtime and evenings. Car park and garden. Children allowed in the restaurant. Turn west of Salisbury onto the Fordingbridge road at Breamore. Signposted from the A338.

OPEN *11am–2.30pm and 6–11pm; all day Sun in summer.*

WINCHESTER

The Old Gaol House
11 Jewry Street, Winchester SO23 8RZ
☎ *01962 850095* Gareth Hughes

Wadworth 6X, Shepherd Neame Spitfire, Greene King Abbot and Hop Back Summer Lightning are among the beers permanently served, plus four guests from a wide range of independent breweries.

L arge pub offering food 10am–10pm Mon–Sat and 12–9.30pm Sun. Accompanied children welcome 12–5pm if eating, with children's menu, high chairs and baby-changing facilities available.

OPEN *10am–11pm Mon–Sat; 12–10.30pm Sun.*

YOU TELL US

* *The Axford Arms,* Farleigh Road, Axford
* *The Newport Inn,* Newport Lane, Brashfield
* *The Plough,* Ashmansworth
* *The Raven,* Bedford Street, Portsmouth (brewpub)
* *Sir Robert Peel,* Astley Street, Southsea

Places Featured:

Aston Crews	Knightwick
Aymestry	Ledbury
Birtsmorton	Leominster
Bishop's Frome	Letton
Bretforton	Malvern
Broadway	Much Dewchurch
Bromyard	Norton Canon
Dodford	Offenham
Dormington	Ombersley
Evesham	Pensax
Fromes Hill	Pershore
Hampton Bishop	Ross-on-Wye
Hanley-Broadheath	Shatterford
Hanley Castle	Stourport-on-Severn
Hereford	Tenbury Wells
Kempsey	Uphampton
Kidderminster	Wellington
Kington	Worcester

THE BREWERIES

BRANDY CASK BREWING CO.
25 Bridge Street, Pershore WR10 1AJ
☎ *(01386) 555338*

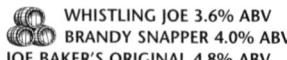
WHISTLING JOE 3.6% ABV
BRANDY SNAPPER 4.0% ABV
JOE BAKER'S ORIGINAL 4.8% ABV

FROME VALLEY BREWERY
Mayfields, Bishop's Frome WR5 5AS
☎ *(01531) 640321*

PREMIUM BITTER 3.8% ABV
FIFTY NOT OUT 4.0 ABV
Plus occasional brews.

HOBSONS BREWERY & CO.
*Newhouse Farm, Tenbury Road, Cleobury
Mortimer, Kidderminster DY14 8RD*
☎ *(01299) 270837*

BEST BITTER 3.8% ABV
Excellent, hoppy session bitter.
TOWN CRIER 4.5% ABV
Smooth, mellow sweetness with balancing hops.
OLD HENRY 5.2% ABV
Darker, smooth and flavoursome.
Plus occasional brews.

MALVERN HILLS BREWERY
*15 West Malvern Road, Great Malvern
WR14 4ND*
☎ *(01684) 560165*
www.malvernhillsbrewery.co.uk

RED EARL 3.7% ABV
BLACK PEAR 4.4% ABV
DOCTOR GULLY'S WINTER ALE 5.2% ABV

MARCHES ALES
*Unit 6, Western Close, Southern Avenue
Industrial Estate, Leominster HR6 0QD*
☎ *(01568) 611084*
www.beerinabox.co.uk

BLACK HORSE BITTER 3.8% ABV
Specially brewed for the Black Horse,
Leominster.
LEMPSTER ORE 3.8% ABV
Hoppy, easy quaffer.
GOLD 4.5% ABV
Pale, award-winner.
PRIORY ALE 4.8% ABV
Smooth, ruby ale.
JENNY PIPES BLONDE BIERE 5.2% ABV
Brewed with Saaz hops.
EARL LEOFRIC'S WINTER ALE 7.2% ABV
Winter warmer, available December.

SP SPORTING ALES LTD
*Cantilever Lodge, Stoke Prior, Leominster
HR6 0LG*
☎ *(01586) 760226*

WINNERS 3.5% ABV
S.I.B.A regional winner 2001.
Amber, refreshing and full-flavoured for
gravity.
DOVES DELIGHT 4.0% ABV
Dark amber, rich and well-balanced.
JOUST BOOTIFUL 4.2% ABV
Pale golden ale.
STING 4.2% ABV
Golden ale with a hint of honey.
JOUST 'PERFIC' 4.5% ABV
Smooth and creamy.
Plus seasonal brews.

SPINNING DOG BREWERY

88 St Owen Street, Hereford HR1 2DQ
☎ *(01432) 342125*

 MUTTLEY'S BARK MILD 3.5% ABV
Superb mild, not to be missed!
CHASE YOUR TAIL 3.6% ABV
An easy quaffer.
MUTTLEY'S MONGREL 3.9% ABV
A blend of three hops, giving a pleasant aroma.
MUTTLEY'S BUTT KICKER 4.2% ABV
MUTTLEY'S PALE ALE 4.2% ABV
TOP DOG 4.2% ABV
A premium, full-bodied ale.
SANTA PAWS 5.2% ABV
A seasonal Christmas ale.
Also brewed: Flannery's Beers.

ST GEORGE'S BREWING CO. LTD

The Old Bakehouse, Bush Lane, Callow End,
Worcester WR2 4TF
☎ *(01905) 831316*

 PRIDE 3.8% ABV
WAR DRUM 4.1% ABV

WOODHAMPTON BREWING CO.

Woodhampton Farm, Aymestrey, Leominster
HR6 9TA
☎ *(01586) 770503*

 RED KITE 3.6% ABV
JACK SNIPE 4.1%ABV
KINGFISHER ALE 4.5% ABV
SILURIAN SPRING 5.0% ABV
WAGTAIL 5.0% ABV

WYE VALLEY BREWERY

Stoke Lacey, Hereford, HR74HG
☎ *(01885) 490505*
www.wyevalleybrewery.co.uk

BITTER 3.5% ABV
HEREFORD PALE ALE 4.0% ABV
DOROTHY GOODBODY'S GOLDEN
  SUMMERTIME ALE 4.2% ABV
WINTER TIPPLE 4.4% ABV
BUTTY BACH 4.5% ABV
DOROTHY GOODBODY'S WHOLESOME STOUT
4.6% ABV
CHRISTMAS ALE 6.0% ABV

WYRE PIDDLE BREWERY

Highgrove Farm, Pinvin, Nr Pershore WR10 2LF
☎ *(01905) 841853*

PIDDLE IN THE HOLE 3.9% ABV
PIDDLE IN THE WIND 4.2% ABV
Plus occasional and seasonal brews.

THE PUBS

ASTON CREWS

The Penny Farthing

Aston Crews, Nr Ross-on-Wye, Herefordshire
HR9 7LW
☎ *(01989) 750366*
Mrs R Blanch, Miss E Mellor and Miss D Mellor

Marston's Pedigree and Bitter and Wadworth 6X always available plus a guest beer (ten per year) which may be Shepherd Neame Spitfire, Morland Old Speckled Hen or from Robinson's or Hook Norton breweries.

A country inn and restaurant. Bar and restaurant food available at lunchtime and evenings. Car park and garden. Children allowed in the restaurant. Turn off the A40 Ross-on-Wye to Gloucester road at Lea, on to the B4222 (signposted to Newent). The Penny Farthing is one mile down this road.

 12–3pm and 7–11pm.

AYMESTRY

The Riverside Inn

Aymestry, Leominster, Herefordshire HL6 9ST
☎ *(01568) 708440* Liz and Richard Gresko

Beers from Wye Valley are featured, including Butty Bach, Dorothy Goodbody's Golden Ale and Hereford Pale Ale. Also one guest, which could be Timothy Taylor Landlord or Black Sheep Best Bitter.

A rural village pub with one bar, dining area and riverside garden. Limited disabled access, but willing. Food available at lunchtime and evenings. Children over seven permitted.

 12–3pm and 6.30–11pm (10.30pm Sun).

BIRTSMORTON

The Farmer's Arms

Birts Street, Birtsmorton, Malvern, Worcestershire
WR13 6AP
☎ *(01684) 833308* Julie Moore

Hook Norton Best and Old Hooky always available plus one guest from breweries such as Ledbury, Cottage or Cannon Royall.

A traditional two-bar country freehouse with beer garden. Food available at lunchtime and evenings in a separate dining area at one end of the bar. Children allowed.

11am–3pm and 6–11pm Mon–Sat;
12–4pm and 7–10.30pm Sun.

BISHOP'S FROME

The Chase Inn

4 Bridge Street, Bishop's Frome, Herefordshire
☎ *(01885) 490234* Tony James

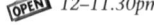 Beers from Wye Valley, Fat God's and Hobsons are permanently available at this freehouse, and the one guest might be Morland Old Speckled Hen or Fat God's Thunder and Lightning.

A country inn offering home-cooked food 12–9pm Mon–Sat and 12–6pm Sun. Five en-suite letting bedrooms. Children welcome. Car park.

OPEN *12–11.30pm (10pm Sun).*

BRETFORTON

The Fleece Inn

The Cross, Bretforton, Worcesterhire WR11 5JE
☎ *(01386) 831173* Graham Brown

 Hook Norton and Uley brews always available, plus guests.

This pub is 650 years old and has been used by the BBC as a film location. Owned by the National Trust, it is also a working museum. Non-smoking family room. East of Evesham, in the middle of the village.

OPEN *11am–3pm and 6–11pm Sun–Fri; all day Sat.*

BROADWAY

The Crown & Trumpet Inn

Church Street, Broadway, Worcestershire WR12 7AE
☎ *(01386) 853202* Andrew Scott

 Morland Old Speckled Hen and Hook Norton Old Hooky permanently available plus a house bitter which is produced especially by the Stanway Brewery. In summer this beer is Cotteswold Gold, and in winter, Lords-a-Leaping.

A seventeenth-century village inn built from Cotswold stone. Seasonal and homemade dishes cooked on the premises are available at lunchtimes and evenings. Beer garden. Accommodation. Well-behaved children allowed. Website: www.cotswoldholidays.co.uk.

OPEN *11am–2.30pm and 5–11pm Sun–Fri; all day Sat.*

BROMYARD

The Rose & Lion Inn

5 New Road, Bromyard, Herefordshire HR7 4AJ
☎ *(01885) 482381* Mrs Herdman

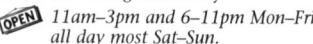 A Wye Valley tied house always serving Bitter, Hereford Pale Ale, Dorothy Goodbody's and Butty Bach beers. One weekly changing guest, sometimes a seasonal Wye Valley ale such as Springtime, or brews such as Coach House Gunpowder Strong Mild.

A two-bar drinking house. Old, traditional building with garden. No food. Children allowed in the garden only.

OPEN *11am–3pm and 6–11pm Mon–Fri; all day most Sat–Sun.*

DODFORD

The Dodford Inn

Whinfield Road, Dodford, Bromsgrove, Worcestershire B61 9BG
☎ *(01527) 832470* Larry Bowen

 Three guests available, from breweries such as Titanic, Evesham and Young's. Some 2000 beers served over five years.

A traditional country pub situated in an historic village. Beamed ceilings, very large garden and campsite plus two patios. Food served at lunchtime and evenings. Children allowed.

OPEN *12–3pm and 6–11pm Mon–Fri; all day Sat; 12–3pm and 6–10.30pm Sun.*

DORMINGTON

The Yew Tree

Priors Frome, Dormington, Herefordshire HR1 4EH
☎ *(01432) 850467* Sue Crofts and Len Gee

Morland Old Speckled Hen permanently stocked. Wye Valley Yew Tree Bitter is served whenever possible, and a varying range of local ales are available on three hand pumps. Spinning Dog, Wye Valley and Dunn Plowman are regular features.

This 200-year-old country pub and restaurant with log fire and wood burner has some beams that are 500 years old! Food available. Three bars, 50-seater restaurant, garden. Car park plus room for coaches. Children allowed.

OPEN *12–2pm and 7–11pm Mon–Wed; 12–2pm and 6–11pm Thurs–Fri; 12–4pm and 6–11pm Sat; 12–4pm and 7–10.30 Sun.*

EVESHAM

The Green Dragon

17 Oat Street, Evesham, Worcestershire WR11 4PJ
☎ *(01386) 443462*

Home of the Evesham Brewery. Two Asum brews produced and sold, 'Asum' being the local pronunciation of 'Evesham'. Other guest ales also offered.

The brewery is housed in the old bottle store. A Grade II listed pub with a cosy lounge. Bar and restaurant food is served at lunchtime and evenings. Car park, garden, large function room. Children allowed.

ASUM ALE 3.8% ABV
A malty session ale.
ASUM GOLD 5.2% ABV
Fruity, malty and sweet strong ale.

11am–11pm Mon–Thur; 11pm–1am Fri–Sat.

The Queens Head & Fat God's Brewery

Iron Cross, Evesham, Worcestershire WR11 5SH
☎ *(01386) 871012* Andy and Kym Miller

Home to the Fat God's Brewery with the whole range of beers usually available.

Rural brewpub on B4088 Evesham to Alcester road opposite Salford Priors. Food served all day. Children welcome. Car park.

FAT GOD'S BITTER 3.6% ABV
Light-coloured and hoppy.
MORRIS DANCER 3.9% ABV
Red-tinged, smooth and full-flavoured.
FAT GOD'S MILD 4.0% ABV
Dark and nutty.
MERRY MILLERS RUSTY DUSTY 4.0% ABV
Reddish golden brown colour. Hoppy. Available Sept–Oct.
PORTER OF THE VALE 4.1% ABV
Black and packed with smooth roast malt flavour.
MERRY MILLERS SUMMER SENSATION 4.3% ABV
Hoppy seasonal brew. Available Jul–Aug.
THUNDER AND LIGHTNING 4.3% ABV
Balanced, malty full-flavoured bitter.
MERRY MILLERS SPRING CELEBRATION 4.5% ABV
Golden and flavour-packed. Available Mar–June.
MERRY MILLERS WINTER WOBBLER 4.9% ABV
Hoppy, easy-drinking seasonal brew. Available Nov–Feb.

All day, every day.

FROMES HILL

Wheatsheaf Inn

Fromes Hill, Ledbury, Herefordshire HR8 1HT
☎ *(01531) 640888* Mr Mirfin

A brewpub serving Fromes Hill Buckswood Dingle and Overture. Also occasional guests.

A country inn with one bar, dining area and garden. Food served at lunchtime and evenings. Children allowed.

BUCKSWOOD DINGLE 3.6% ABV
EIGHTH OVERTURE 4.2% ABV

All day, every day.

HAMPTON BISHOP

Bunch of Carrots

Hampton Bishop, Hereford, Herefordshire HR1 4JR
☎ *(01432) 870237* Paul and Katharine Turner

Hook Norton Best Bitter and three guest beers, often from local breweries, regularly available.

Traditional country inn with open fires and stone-clad floors, beer garden and function room. Situated two miles from Hereford city centre on the B4224, close to the River Wye. Disabled facilities. Carvery and bar food served lunchtimes and evenings. Car park. Children's menu and play area in the garden.

11am–3pm and 6–11pm Mon–Sat; 12–4pm and 7–10.30pm Sun.

HANLEY-BROADHEATH

The Fox Inn

Hanley-Broadheath, Tenbury Wells, Worcestershire
☎ *(01886) 853219* Keith Williams

Batham Best Bitter and a beer from Hobsons usually available.

Set in lovely countryside, part of this pub dates from the sixteenth century. Food available 12–2.30pm (summer only) and 6–9.30pm in separate restaurant. Games room. Car park. Outside children's play area. Situated on the B4204 Tenbury Wells to Worcester road.

12–2.30pm and 6–11pm (10.30pm Sun).

Mutley's Bark Mild
O.G.1035°
Spinning Dog Brewery

HANLEY CASTLE

The Three Kings

Church End, Hanley Castle, Worcestershire
WR8 0BL
☎ *(01684) 592686* Mrs Sheila Roberts

 Thwaites and Butcombe brews available plus three guest beers (more than 150 per year) perhaps from Brandy Cask, Evesham, Mildmay, Fromes Hill, Crouch Vale, Berkeley, Otter, Hop Back, Goff's, Stanway, Wood and Belhaven breweries.

A traditional fifteenth-century freehouse that has been in the same family for over 90 years. Bar food available at lunchtime and evenings. Parking, garden and children's room. CAMRA pub of the Year 1993. Just off the B4211, Upton-upon-Severn to Malvern road. Take the third turn on the left from Upton.

OPEN *11am–3pm and 7–11pm Mon–Sat; 12–3pm and 7–10.30pm Sun.*

HEREFORD

The Barrels

69 Owen Street, Hereford, Herefordshire HR1 2JQ
☎ *(01432) 274968* Cath Roden

 The Wye Valley Brewery is on the premises, so home-brewed ales are served in the pub. Also offers one guest ale, such as O'Hanlon's Red.

A town boozer. One of the last multi-roomed public houses in Hereford. Clientele a mix of old regulars and students. Occasional live music. Outside seating and fishpond. Annual beer festival on August bank holiday weekend, during which over 50 beers and ciders are available. No food. No children.

OPEN *All day, every day.*

Lichfield Vaults

11 Church Street, Hereford, Herefordshire
HR1 2LR
☎ *(01432) 267994* Charles Wenyon

Marston's Pedigree usually available plus up to seven guest ales including, perhaps, Hoskins & Oldfield Ginger Tom, Shepherd Neame Spitfire or a Greene King brew.

A traditional town-centre pub, one bar, patio. Food served at lunchtime only. No children.

OPEN *All day Mon–Sat; 7–10.30pm Sun.*

The Victory

88 St Owen Street, Hereford, Herefordshire
HR1 2QD
☎ *(01432) 274998*
Mr Kenyon and Miss Brooks

Run by the owners of the Spinning Dog Brewery, with seven different real ales always available, five Spinning Dog and two guests from other local independent breweries such as Flannery's. Two annual beer festivals held (May Day and October).

A two-bar boozer with a nautical theme. Live music from Thursday to Sunday. Beer garden. Food served lunchtimes and evenings Mon–Sat, with vegetarian meals available, and traditional roasts on Sundays 12–5pm. Children allowed. Cask Marque accredited. CAMRA Herefordshire Pub of the Year 2001. The publican runs a visitors' book which is an absolute must for 'tickers'! Brewery tours by appointment.

OPEN *All day, every day.*

KEMPSEY

Walter de Cantelupe Inn

Main Road, Kempsey, Worcestershire WR5 3NA
☎ *(01905) 820572* Martin Lloyd Morris

A freehouse with Highgate Special Bitter and Timothy Taylor Landlord among the brews always available, plus one guest from a wide range. Examples include Greene King Abbot, Cannon Royall Arrowhead, Malvern Hills Black Pear, Orkney Raven Ale and Felinfoel Double Dragon.

A Tudor village pub with wooden beams and stone floors. One bar, dining area and garden. Food available Tues–Sun lunchtime and evenings. Children allowed during the day only. Accommodation.

OPEN *12–2.30pm and 6–11pm Mon–Sat; 7–10.30pm Sun.*

KIDDERMINSTER

The Boar's Head

39 Worcester Street, Kidderminster,
Worcestershire DY10 1EA
☎ *(01562) 862450* Andy Hipkiss

Banks's Bitter and Original, Camerons Strongarm and Marston's Pedigree always available plus three guests such as Fuller's London Pride, Cains Formidable and Brewery Bitter or a selection from Bateman.

A two-bar town-centre pub with stone floors and beamed ceilings. Small beer garden and all-weather bricked courtyard covered with a glass pyramid. Live bands on Thurs and Sun nights. Food available Mon–Sat 12–3pm. Children allowed in the courtyard only.

OPEN *12–11pm Mon–Sat; 12–3pm and 7–10.30pm Sun.*

The King & Castle

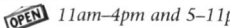

Severn Valley Railway Station,
Comberton Hill, Kidderminster,
Worcestershire
☎ *(01562) 747505* Peter Williamson

Batham Best is among the brews always available plus guest beers (250 per year) from Enville, Hobsons, Hanby, Three Tuns, Timothy Taylor, Holt, Holden's, Berrow, Wood, Burton Bridge and Wye Valley breweries.

The pub is a copy of the Victorian railway refreshment rooms, decorated in the 1930s, GWR-style. Bar food available. Car park and garden. Children allowed until 9pm. Located next to Kidderminster railway station.

[OPEN] *11am–4pm and 5–11pm.*

The Red Man

92 Blackwell Street, Kidderminster,
Worcestershire DY10 2DZ
☎ *(01562) 67555* Richard Burgiff

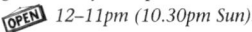

Greene King IPA and Abbot, Adnams Broadside, Fuller's London Pride and Morland Old Speckled Hen are always on offer. Guests, changed at least twice a week, might include Timothy Taylor Landlord, brews from Berrow, or seasonal ales such as Smiles Old Tosser (available for a week around Pancake Day, with pancakes on the menu!).

A country pub in the town, in a 1930s building, with a focus on traditional ale, traditional fayre and traditional values. Claims to be the only pub of this name in the country. Food available 12–7pm every day. A base for local clog dancers on Mondays in winter. Conservatory, 'tardis' garden, darts, three pool tables, pinball. Children allowed in the conservatory and garden only. Car park.

[OPEN] *12–11pm (10.30pm Sun).*

KINGTON

The Queen's Head and Dunn Plowman Brewery

Bridge Street, Kington, Herefordshire HR5 3DW
☎ *(01544) 231106* Michael John Hickey

Home of the Dunn Plowman Brewery with the full range of home brews always available.

A 400-year-old pub in the old market town. Food available all day Tues–Sun. Beer garden. Petanque court. Accommodation. Children allowed.

    BREW HOUSE BITTER 3.8% ABV
    EARLY RISER 4.0% ABV
KINGTON 5.0%
Traditional Bitter.
Also bottled beers sold to other pubs through James Williams distributors.

[OPEN] *11.30am–11pm (10.30pm Sun).*

KNIGHTWICK

Talbot

Knightwick, Worcester, Worcestershire
☎ *(01886) 821235*

Home of the Teme Valley Brewery, with all own beers usually available, plus Hobsons Bitter.

Attractive, 500-year-old country inn standing by the River Teme. Well known locally for its home-produced food. Food available lunchtimes and some evenings. Car park. Children welcome and high chairs are available. Located just off A44 Bromyard to Worcester on B4197 at Knightford Bridge.

    T'OTHER 3.5% ABV
    THIS 3.7% ABV
THAT 4.1% ABV
WOT 6.0% ABV

[OPEN] *11am–11pm Mon–Sat; 12–10.30pm Sun.*

LEDBURY

The Horseshoe Inn

The Homend, Ledbury, Herefordshire HR8 1BP
☎ *(01531) 632770* David Tegg

Timothy Taylor Landlord permanently available, plus one monthly changing guest ale.

A small family inn in Ledbury town with one bar and garden. Food available at lunchtime only. Children allowed.

[OPEN] *All day, every day.*

The Royal Oak Hotel

The Southend, Ledbury, Herefordshire HR8 2EY
☎ *(01531) 632110* Rex Barron

Greene King IPA, Charles Wells Bombardier and Fuller's London Pride always available, plus local guest beers in summer.

Eighteenth-century Georgian coaching hotel situated at the top of the town, recently refurbished, and featuring exposed beams dating from 1420 and 1520, hidden since 1836. Extensive traditional bar menu with many homemade specialities, served in the oak-panelled bar. Off-street parking and quality en-suite accommodation. Well-behaved children and dogs welcome.

[OPEN] *11am–11pm.*

LEOMINSTER

The Black Horse Coach House

South Street, Leominster, Herefordshire HR6 8JF
☎ *(01568) 611946* Peter Hoare

 A freehouse serving Dunn Plowman Black Horse (house ale) and Hobsons Town Crier plus two guests such as Fuller's London Pride, Hobsons Best or other micro-brews. Has served 150 beers over the past 12 months.

A town pub in a traditional building. Two bars, restaurant and garden. Food served every lunchtime and Mon–Sat evenings. Children allowed.

OPEN *11am–2.30pm and 6–11pm Mon–Fri; all day Sat; 12–3pm and 7–10.30pm Sun.*

The Grape Vaults

Broad Street, Leominster, Herefordshire HR6 8BS
☎ *(01568) 611404* PA and JM Saxon

 A freehouse offering Marston's Pedigree and Best and Banks's Mild plus two guests, changing constantly.

A small pub in the town centre. Old-fashioned with log fire, no music. Bar snacks available at lunchtime and evenings. Children allowed if eating.

OPEN *11am–11pm Mon–Sat; 12–10.30pm Sun.*

LETTON

The Swan Inn

Letton, Hereford, Herefordshire HR3 6DH
☎ *(01544) 327304* M Boardman

 Two house bitters brewed for the pub by Wye Valley Brewery: Old Swan Bitter (3.5% ABV) and Butty Bach (4.5% ABV) are always available.

A traditional roadside freehouse with two bars, a pool table, darts and a beer garden with petanque. No background music. Food available until 9.30pm. Children welcome. Car park. Non-smoking accommodation available. Located on the A438 Hereford–Brecon road, 12 miles out of Hereford.

OPEN *11am–3pm and 6–11pm Mon–Tues; 11am–11pm Wed–Sat; 12–3pm and 7–10.30pm Sun.*

MALVERN

Bolly & Bass Bar

Foley Arms Hotel, Worcester Road, Malvern, Worcestershire
☎ *(01684) 573397* Nigel Thomas

 An ever-changing selection of four guest beers usually available, which may include Shepherd Neame Spitfire, Morland Old Speckled Hen, Fuller's London Pride or brews from Malvern Hills, Charles Wells, Hook Norton and many others.

Friendly, cosy, locals' pub, situated in the historic Foley Arms Hotel offering live music on Monday nights. Full bar menu available. Car park. Children very welcome. Situated in middle of Malvern on the A449.

OPEN *12–2.30pm and 5–11pm Mon–Sat; 12–3pm and 7–10.30pm Sun.*

Malvern Hills Hotel

Wynds Point, Malvern, Worcestershire WR13 6DW
☎ *(01684) 540690* Oswald John Dockery

 Hobsons Best Bitter, Malvern Hills Black Pear and Morland Old Speckled Hen usually available. Two guest beers, which may include Fuller's London Pride, Charles Wells Bombardier, Marston's Pedigree or Wye Valley Butty Bach are also regularly served.

High on the western slopes of the Malverns at British Camp with 'one of the goodliest vistas in England', offering walks with breathtaking views. Warm, traditional oak-panelled lounge bar with sun terrace. Bar food and separate restaurant food available every lunchtime and evening. Car park. Children welcome but no special facilities. Situated on the A449 at British Camp hill fort (also known as the Herefordshire Beacon) midway between Malvern and Ledbury.

OPEN *11am–11pm Mon–Sat; 12–10.30pm Sun.*

MUCH DEWCHURCH

The Black Swan Inn

Much Dewchurch, Hereford, Herefordshire HR2 8DJ
☎ *(01981) 540295* A Davies

 Beers from breweries such as Timothy Taylor, Badger and Adnams usually available plus one rotating guest such as Reverend James's Shropshire Lad or a beer from Frome Valley or Hook Norton breweries.

A fourteenth-century freehouse with lounge and public bar. Dining area in lounge. Patio. Food available at lunchtime and evenings. Children allowed.

OPEN *12–3pm and 6–11pm Mon–Fri; 11.30am–3pm and 6–11pm Sat; 12–3pm and 7–10.30pm Sun.*

NORTON CANON

Three Horse Shoes Inn

Norton Canon, Hereford, Herefordshire HR4 7BH
☎ *(01544) 318375* Frank Goodwin

 Home of the Shoes Brewery, with both beers regularly available.

Two bars and games room, with grassed area for summer use. Situated on the A480. No food. Car park. Children welcome.

 NORTON ALE 3.6% ABV
CANON BITTER 4.1% ABV

6–11pm Mon–Tues; 12–3pm and 6–11pm Wed–Fri; 11am–11pm Sat; 12–10.30pm Sun.

OFFENHAM

The Bridge Inn and Ferry

Offenham, Evesham, Worcestershire WR11 5RS
☎ *(01386) 446565* Morris Allan

 Something from Bateman and Caledonian regularly available plus up to six guest beers from breweries around the country.

Independent, historic freehouse on the banks of the River Avon. Large heated patio. Bar and lounge/dining area. Food served 12–2.30pm and 6.30–9pm daily. Car park. Well-behaved children welcome. Follow signs to ferry from main road.

11am–11pm Mon–Sat; 12–10.30pm Sun.

OMBERSLEY

The Crown & Sandys Arms

Main Road, Ombersley, Worcester, Worcestershire WR9 0EW
☎ *(01905) 620252* Richard Everton

 Greene King Abbot Ale, Marston's Pedigree, Adnams Best Bitter and Southwold usually available, plus two guest beers such as Wood Parish Bitter, Hobsons Best Bitter, Wyre Piddle Piddle In The Wind or Cannon Royall Arrowhead.

Seventeenth-century refurbished freehouse with large bar and two busy bistros. Extensive wine list. Food served lunchtimes and evenings Mon–Fri and all day Sat–Sun, with seafood a speciality. Gardens. Car park. Children welcome.

11am–3pm and 5–11pm Mon–Fri; 11am–11pm Sat; 12–10.30pm Sun.

PENSAX

The Bell

Pensax, Abberley, Worcestershire WR6 6AE
☎ *(01299) 896677* John and Trudy Greaves

 At least five beers available at any one time. Regulars include Archers Golden, Timothy Taylor Landlord and brews from Hook Norton. Local beers also featured, such as Woodbury White Goose, Enville Bitter and ales from Hobsons and Wood breweries.

Friendly, rural freehouse with various traditional drinking areas and dining room. Large garden, superb views, three real fires in winter. Beer festival held on Whitsuntide weekend. Seasonal home-cooked bar and restaurant food served at lunchtimes and evenings. Families welcome. Located on the B4202 Great Witley to Cleobury Mortimer road, between Abberley and Clows Top.

5–11pm Mon (closed Mon lunchtimes except bank holidays); 12–2.30pm and 5–11pm Tues–Sat; 12–10.30pm Sun.

PERSHORE

The Brandy Cask

25 Bridge Street, Pershore, Worcestershire WR10 1AJ
☎ *(01386) 552602*

 The ales brewed here now supply 30 outlets. Also Ruddles Best and County available plus guest beers.

Town-centre freehouse. Bar and restaurant food is served at lunchtime and evenings. Large riverside garden. Children allowed.

BRANDY SNAPPER 4% ABV
JOHN BAKER'S ORIGINAL 4.8% ABV

11.30am–2.30pm and 7–11pm.

ROSS-ON-WYE

The Crown Inn

Gloucester Road, The Lea, Ross-on-Wye, Herefordshire HR9 7JZ
☎ *(01989) 750407* Mr F and Mrs S Ellis

 Hook Norton Best and RCH Pitchfork permanently available, plus three guests, often from Wye Valley Brewery. Small, independent breweries favoured.

A splendid fifteenth-century country village pub with a warm welcome always assured. One bar, beer garden. Smoking and non-smoking restaurant. Food available Mon–Sun lunchtimes and Tues–Sat evenings. Children allowed. Situated on the A40 from Ross-on-Wye to Gloucester.

11am–11pm.

The Crown & Sceptre

*Market Place, Ross-on-Wye, Herefordshire
HR9 5NX*
☎ *(01989) 562765* Mr M Roberts

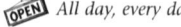 A Whitbread pub serving Archers Best, Fuller's London Pride and Greene King Abbot Ale plus two changing guests such as Morland Old Speckled Hen, Shepherd Neame Spitfire or Gale's HSB.

A town pub with a friendly atmosphere and mixed clientele. One bar with smoking and non-smoking areas, patio and garden. Bar food served all day. Well-behaved children allowed.

OPEN *All day, every day.*

SHATTERFORD

The Red Lion Inn

*Bridgnorth Road, Shatterford, Nr Kidderminster
DY12 1SU*
☎ *(01299) 861221* Richard Tweedie

 Banks's Mild and Bitter plus Batham Bitter usually available. Two guest beers are also served, often from Wood, Wye Valley, Marston's and Cannon Royall breweries.

Truly rural pub, well known locally for its food. Non-smoking areas and restaurant. Food every lunchtime and evening, including traditional Sunday roasts. Two car parks: one in Worcestershire, the other in Shropshire! Children welcome, with special children's menu available.

OPEN *11.30am–2.30pm and 6.30–11pm
Mon–Sat; 12–3pm and 7–10.30pm Sun.*

STOURPORT-ON-SEVERN

The Rising Sun

*50 Lombard Street, Stourport-on-Severn,
Worcestershire DY13 8DU*
☎ *(01299) 822530* Robert Hallard

 Banks's Original, Bitter and Hanson's Mild plus Marston's Pedigree always available, plus one guest such as Goddards Inspiration. Seasonal and celebration ales served whenever available.

A 200-year-old canalside pub. One bar, small dining area and patio. Food available at lunchtime and evenings. Children allowed in the dining room and patio only.

OPEN *All day, every day.*

The Wheatsheaf

*39 High Street, Stourport-on-Severn,
Worcestershire DY13 8BS*
☎ *(01299) 822613* Mr M Webb

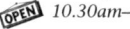 Banks's Mild, Bitter and Hanson's Bitter usually available.

A games-orientated house in the town centre, with relaxing lounge and cosy bar. Food served 10.30am–3pm Mon–Sat and 12–2pm Sun. Children welcome until 9.30pm. Car park.

OPEN *10.30am–11pm.*

TENBURY WELLS

The Ship Inn

*Teme Street, Tenbury Wells, Worcestershire
WR15 8AE*
☎ *(01584) 810269* Michael Hoar

 A freehouse with Hobsons Best always available plus a guest beer such as Fuller's ESB, Morland Old Speckled Hen or Greene King Abbot.

A seventeenth-century, market-town pub that has been under the same ownership for the last 15 years. The pub has daily deliveries of fresh fish and is renowned for its food, which is served at lunchtimes and evenings every day; there are two separate non-smoking restaurants. Recommended in two good-food guides. Pretty beer garden, accommodation. Children allowed.

OPEN *11am–3pm and 7–11pm (10.30pm Sun).*

UPHAMPTON

The Fruiterer's Arms

*Uphampton, Ombersley, Worcestershire
WR9 0JW*
☎ *(01905) 621161*

 Cannon Royall brews produced and served on the premises plus a guest beer.

Brewing began in this converted cider house in July 1993 and the maximum output is now 16 barrels per week. The pub has two bars and a log fire in winter. Bar food is served at lunchtime. Car park. Children allowed.

FRUITERER'S MILD 3.7% ABV
Replaces Millward's Musket Mild.
ARROWHEAD 3.9% ABV
Beer with strong hoppiness in the finish.
BUCKSHOT 4.5% ABV
Rich and malty, leaving a round and hoppy aftertaste.
Plus winter ales, changed annually.

OPEN *12.30–2.30pm and 7–11pm Mon–Fri;
12–3pm and 7–11pm Sat–Sun (10.30pm
Sun).*

WELLINGTON

The Wellington
Wellington, Herefordshire HR4 8AT
☎ *(01432) 830367* Ross Williams

A freehouse with Hobsons Best Bitter among the beers always available, plus two regularly changing guests including Shepherd Neame Spitfire, Robinson's Best, Tomos Watkin OSB, Wood Shropshire Lad and brews from Spinning Dog and Wye Valley.

Traditional country pub in a Victorian building, with a restaurant in the converted stables. No games, no TV. Beer garden, car park. Children allowed.

OPEN *12–2.30pm and 6–11pm (10.30pm Sun).*

WORCESTER

The Dragon Inn
The Tything, Worcester, Worcestershire
☎ *(01905) 25845* RM Appleton

A true ale-lovers' paradise. Up to six guest ales, a stout and a real cider available year-round. They source their own ales and ciders, and regulars include brews from Beowulf, Buffy's, Church End, Anglo-Dutch, Stonehenge, Oakham, Teme Valley and Cannon Royall, to mention just a few.

Late Georgian, Grade II listed alehouse with L-shaped bar and outside patio area for warm summer afternoons. Food served 12–2pm Mon–Sat. Children allowed. Situated a three-minute walk from Foregate Street Station, away from the city centre.

OPEN *12–3pm and 4.30–11pm Mon–Fri; 11am–11pm Sat; 12–3pm and 7–10.30pm Sun.*

The Postal Order
18 Foregate Street, Worcester,
Worcestershire WR1 1DN
☎ *(01905) 22373* Hayley Smithson

Banks's Mild, Greene King Abbot Ale, Shepherd Neame Spitfire and Hop Back Summer Lightning always available. Up to six guest real ales purchased through East West. Weston's Old Rosie cider also served.

An open-plan Wetherspoon's freehouse converted from an old telephone exchange (originally a sorting office). Separate non-smoking area, no music. Food available all day. No children. Situated opposite the cinema.

OPEN *11am–11pm Mon–Sat; 12–10.30pm Sun.*

YOU TELL US

* *Greyhound Inn,* 30 Rock Hill, Eldersfield, Bromsgrove
* *The Halfway House,* Droitwich Road, Bastondford, Fernhill Heath
* *Old Fogey,* 37 High Street, Kington
* *The Plume of Feathers,* Feathers Pitch, Castlemorton
* *The Swan Inn,* Letton
* *Tap & Spile,* 35 St Nicholas Street, Worcester

Places Featured:

Aldbury
Amwell
Arrington
Ashwell
Astwick
Ayot St Lawrence
Baldock
Barkway
Barley
Benington
Bishop's Stortford
Bricket Wood
Chenies Village
Datchworth
Flaunden
Harpenden
Hertford
Hertingfordbury

Hitchin
Ickleford
King's Langley
Much Hadham
Old Knebworth
St Albans
Sawbridgeworth
Stapleford
Stortford
Tonwell
Tring
Tyttenhanger Green
Waltham Cross
Wareside
Whitwell
Widford
Wild Hill

THE BREWERIES

BUNTINGFORD BREWERY CO.

3A Watermill Industrial Estate, Aspenden Road,
Buntingford SG9 9JS
☎ *(07956) 246215*
www.buntingford-brewery.co.uk

 HIGHWAYMAN BEST BITTER 3.7% ABV
Light brown session beer.
HURRICANE FORCE 4.3% ABV
Mid-brown premium bitter.
BUNTINGFORD ORIGINAL BITTER 4.5% ABV
Deep coppery red.
WATERMILL STOUT 4.8% ABV
Traditional English-style stout. Near black in colour.
Seasonals:
SUNSTREAM 4.0% ABV
Summer ale.
DARK TIMES
Winter ale. ABV unconfirmed.

GARDEN BARBER BREWERY

PO Box 23, Hertford SG14 3PZ
☎ *(01992) 504167* Steven Johnson

 REEDY POPS 4.0% ABV
Bitter mild ale, sold locally and for festivals.

GREEN TYE BREWERY

Green Tye, Much Hadham SG10 6JP
☎ *(01279) 841041*
www.gtbrewery.co.uk

 SHOT IN THE DARK 3.6% ABV
Dark ruby colour and hoppy flavour. Available October.
IPA 3.7% ABV
Refreshing, pert hoppiness and dry finish.
MUSTANG MILD 3.7% ABV
Dark mild.
SNOWDROP 3.9% ABV
Quenching, balanced hop flavour, with some sweetness.
FIELD MARSHALL 4.0% ABV
AUTUMN ROSE 4.2% ABV
Red brown best bitter.
GREEN TIGER 4.2% ABV
Light copper-coloured bitter.
MAD MORRIS 4.2% ABV
Golden and quenching with citrus fruit tanginess.
WHEELBARROW 4.3% ABV
Balanced hop, malt and fruit flavours. Easy drinker.
COAL PORTER 4.5% ABV
Flavour-packed porter. Winter brew.
CONKERER 4.7% ABV
Mid brown best bitter.
TUMBLEDOWN DICK 5.3% ABV
Strong and hoppy.

MCMULLEN & SONS LTD

The Hertford Brewery, 26 Old Cross, Hertford SG14 1RD
☎ *(01992) 584911*

ORIGINAL AK 3.7% ABV
Light, well-balanced with good hoppiness.
COUNTRY BEST BITTER 4.3% ABV
Hoppy, fruity aroma and flavour.
GLADSTONE 4.3% ABV
Smooth, with finely rounded bitterness.
STRONGHART 7.0% ABV
Powerful, complex, sweet and dark.
Plus seasonal beers.

THE PUBS

ALDBURY

The Greyhound

19 Stocks Road, Aldbury, Tring HP23 5RT
☎ *(01442) 851228* Rich Coletta

A Badger Brewery pub serving Badger Best, Tanglefoot, IPA and Champion.

A historic inn with an inglenook fireplace, two bars, two dining areas including a non-smoking conservatory, and courtyard garden. Food available every day. Children welcome.

[OPEN] *10am–11pm Mon–Sat; 12–10.30pm Sun.*

AMWELL

Elephant & Castle

Amwell Lane, Amwell, Wheathampstead AL4 8EA
☎ *(01582) 832175*

Amwell Ale brewed specially for the pub is always available plus up to seven other real ales (80 per year) selected from anywhere and everywhere. Strengths generally vary from 3.7% to 5.2% ABV.

This pub is almost 500 years old, with three bars on different levels. There is a 200ft well in the middle of the bar. No music or machines, with the emphasis on good beer and good conversation. Bar meals available at lunchtime and evenings. Car park, two gardens (one for adults only), dining area. Children not allowed in bar. The pub is difficult to find. Ask in Wheathampstead or ring for directions.

[OPEN] *11am–3pm and 5.30–11pm Mon–Fri; all day Sat–Sun.*

ARRINGTON

Hardwicke Arms Hotel

96 Ermine Way, Arrington, Nr Royston SG8 0AH
☎ *(01223) 208802* Mr JR Julius

A freehouse regularly serving Greene King IPA, plus two guest beers, perhaps from Thomas Hardy, Jennings, Bateman, Brakspear, Ridleys, Shepherd Neame, Hop Back, Adnams or Hook Norton.

Thirteenth-century coaching inn, with hotel, restaurant and beer garden. Non-smoking areas. Food served 11.30am–2.15pm and 6.30–9.15pm, including Sunday carvery. Close to Wimpole Hall. Children welcome.

[OPEN] *11.30am–2.15pm and 6.30–11pm Mon–Sat; 12–2.15pm and 7–10.30pm Sun.*

ASHWELL

The Bushel & Strike

Mill Street, Ashwell
☎ *(01462) 742394*
Mrs J Grommann and Mr N Burton

 Charles Wells Eagle and Bombardier usually available plus three guest beers which may include Adnams Broadside or Morland Old Speckled Hen.

A Charles Wells two-bar house with large restaurant, patio, barbecue and small garden. Food served 12–2.30pm Mon–Sun, 7–9pm Mon–Sat. Car park. Special children's menu. From Ashwell village, turn left by the Indian take-away and continue to the car park. The pub is opposite the church tower.

OPEN *11.30am–3pm and 6–11pm Mon–Sat; 12–10.30pm Sun.*

ASTWICK

Tudor Oakes Lodge

Taylors Road, Astwick, Nr Hitchin SG5 4AZ
☎ *(01462) 834133* Mr Welek

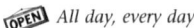 A freehouse serving Mauldons White Adder, Shepherd Neame Spitfire and Wolf Hare of the Dog plus other guests including Oakham Old Tosspot.

A fifteenth-century building with hotel and restaurant, one bar and courtyard. Food available at lunchtime and evenings. Children allowed. Situated off the A1.

OPEN *All day, every day.*

AYOT ST LAWRENCE

The Brocket Arms

Ayot St Lawrence AL6 9RT
☎ *(01438) 820068* Toby Wingfield-Digby

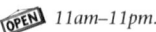 Greene King IPA and Abbot Ale, Young's IPA, Adnams Broadside and Fuller's London Pride always available plus a guest beer, changing weekly, from any independent brewery.

A traditional, oak-beamed pub with a walled garden and accommodation. Bar and restaurant food served at lunchtime and evenings (except Sunday and Monday nights). Parking. For access from the A1 or M1, head for Wheathampstead (B653 and A6129). Then take directions to Shaw's Corner at Ayot St Lawrence. Website: www.brocketarms.com.

OPEN *11am–11pm.*

BALDOCK

The Old White Horse

1 Station Road, Baldock SG7 5BS
☎ *(01462) 893168* Vincent Walker

 A Whitbread tied house with Fuller's London Pride, Timothy Taylor Landlord, Wadworth 6X and a Burton brew usually available, plus other occasional guests.

A town pub with restaurant specialising in Caribbean and English food. Restaurant open from 7pm. Beer garden. Children allowed.

OPEN *11am–3pm Mon–Thurs; all day Fri–Sun.*

BARKWAY

The Tally-Ho

London Road, Barkway SG8 8EX
☎ *(01763) 848389*

 Nine different ales on offer every week, through three barrels at a time. The focus is on a varied spectrum of strengths from all breweries, 650 different beers have been served in 2 years. Genuine real ales only: no nitros.

A traditional pub with traditional values – no fruit machines, no pool tables, no music, no TV. Oak-panelled bar with armchairs, a non-smoking restaurant, two gardens and terraces, petanque pitch, car park. Food available 12–2pm and 7–9pm, all homemade from local produce where possible. Children allowed, with well-behaved parents! Located on the B1368 main road.

OPEN *11.30am–3pm and 5.30–11pm Mon–Sat; 12–6pm Sun (closed Sunday evening).*

BARLEY

The Fox & Hounds

Barley SG8 8HU
☎ *(01763) 848459*

 Morland Old Speckled Hen, Adnams Bitter and IPA always available.

Parts of the heavily beamed pub date back to 1450. Formerly known as The Waggon & Horses, there is an inglenook fireplace and original beams. Bar and restaurant food is available. Non-smoking area in dining room. Bar billiards, games tables, darts etc. Car park, garden, children's room (occasionally used for other functions), disabled toilets, baby-changing facilities. Well-behaved children welcome.

OPEN *12–2.30pm and 6–11pm Mon–Sat; 12–3pm and 7.30–10.30pm Sun.*

BENINGTON

The Lordship Arms
42 Whempstead Road, Benington
☎ *(01438) 869665*

 Young's Special, Fuller's ESB and London Pride always available, plus five guest beers (100 per year). The pub specialises in ales from small independent and micro-breweries. Also draught cider.

A cosy village freehouse with a display of telephone memorabilia. Bar snacks available weekday lunchtimes. Home-cooked roast lunches served on Sundays (booking advisable). Curry night on Wednesdays. Car park and garden. Children not allowed. Take the A602 exit off the A1(M), follow the A602 then turn left. Signposted Aston, Benington.

 12–3pm and 6–11pm Mon–Sat; 12–3pm and 7–10.30pm Sun.

BISHOP'S STORTFORD

The Cock Inn
High Street, Huttfield Broadoak, Bishop's Stortford CM22 7HF
☎ *(01279) 718273* Miss Holcroft

Adnams Best, Greene King IPA and Fuller's London Pride always available plus three guests (up to 150 per year) including Everards Tiger and brews from Robinson's, Oakhill, Marston's and Wadworth.

A sixteenth-century coaching inn, beamed with log fires. Bar and restaurant food available at lunchtime and evenings. Non-smoking room, car park, function room. Children allowed. Easy to find.

12–3pm and 5–11pm Mon–Sat; 12–10.30pm Sun.

The Half Moon
31 North Street, Bishop's Stortford CM23 2LD
☎ *(01279) 834500* Rohan Wong

Adnams Broadside and a mild always available plus up to five others, often including brews from Adnams, Jennings or Bateman.

A town pub with children's room and beer garden. Food available at lunchtimes only. Children allowed in children's room.

All day Mon–Sat; 12–3pm and 7–10.30pm Sun.

DARK RUBY

BRICKET WOOD

Moor Mill
Smug Oak Lane, Bricket Wood, Nr St Albans AL2 3PN
☎ *(01727) 875557* Mr Bambury

A selection of four real ales available from breweries such as Brakspear, Wadworth and Gale's. Seasonal guests also available (50 per year).

An eighteenth-century converted corn mill sitting astride the River Ver. Bar and restaurant food available at lunchtime and evenings. Hotel with 56 bedrooms. Car park, garden and meeting room. Children allowed.

11am–11pm Mon–Sat; 12–10.30pm Sun.

CHENIES VILLAGE

The Red Lion
Chenies Village, Rickmansworth WD3 6ED
☎ *(01923) 282722* Mike Norris

A freehouse with Lion Pride, brewed especially for the pub by Rebellion, plus Wadworth 6X and Vale's Best Bitter (Ben's!), among the beers permanently available. Plus a guest ale from Rebellion.

Owner-run, traditional pub that sells food, not a restaurant that sells beer! Home-cooked meals are served 12–2pm and 6.30–10pm (until 9.30pm Sun). No children. Car park. From Junction 18 on M25, the pub is off the A404 between Little Chalfont and Chorleywood.

11am–2.30pm and 5.30–11pm (6.30–10.30pm Sun).

DATCHWORTH

Tilbury (The Inn off the Green)
1 Watton Road, Datchworth SG3 6TB
☎ *(01438) 812496* Ian Miller

Hides Bitter and Hop Pit Bitter brewed and available on the premises plus two or three rotating guests from independent brewers.

A seventeenth-century, two-bar village pub and micro-brewery. Bar and restaurant food available. Large garden and car park. Well-behaved children allowed. On the Datchworth crossroads, on the road from Woolmer Green to Watton.

 HIDES BITTER 4.0% ABV
 HOP PIT BITTER 4.5% ABV

11am–3pm and 5–11pm Mon–Wed; all day Thurs–Sun.

FLAUNDEN

The Bricklayers Arms
Hog Pits Bottom, Flaunden HP3 0PH
☎ *(01442) 833322* Rob and Liz Mitchell

A freehouse regularly serving at least five real ales, always including brews from London and the Midlands, plus a thoroughly local beer!

This award-winning country pub and restaurant set in beautiful countryside has been welcoming visitors through its oak-beamed doors for over 200 years. Three chefs serve freshly prepared meals, both bar and à la carte, seven days a week. Well-behaved children and dogs welcome. Ample car parking and sheltered garden with heated patios.

OPEN *11.30am–2.30pm (3pm Sat) and 6–11pm Mon–Sat; 12–3pm (4pm in summer) and 7–10.30pm Sun.*

HARPENDEN

The Oak Tree
15 Leyton Green, Harpenden AL5 2TG
☎ *(01582) 763850* Mr Needham

A Charles Wells tied house with Bombardier and Eagle IPA and Adnams Bitter and Broadside permanently available, plus four rotating guests.

A one-bar town freehouse with beer garden. A leaflet is available listing the beers of the month. Home-cooked food available at lunchtime. Children allowed at lunchtimes if eating.

OPEN *All day, every day.*

HERTFORD

The White Horse
33 Castle Street, Hertford SG14 1HH
☎ *(01992) 501950* Nigel Crofts

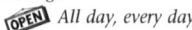Fuller's London Pride, ESB and seasonal brews and Adnams Southwold Bitter usually available, plus up to six guest beers from micro-brewers the length and breadth of the country. Spring and autumn beer festivals held, each featuring up to 60 micro-brewery beers.

Classic fifteenth-century alehouse, renowned for its selection of cask ales, and now offering a traditional bar billiards room upstairs. A varied menu of home-cooked specials is served 12–2pm Mon–Sat, with traditional Sunday lunches also available 12–2pm. Supervised children are welcome in the upstairs non-smoking area. Well-behaved dogs are always welcome.

OPEN *12–2.30pm and 5.30–11pm Mon–Thurs; all day Fri–Sun.*

HERTINGFORDBURY

The Prince of Wales
244 Hertingfordbury Road, Hertingfordbury, Hertford SG14 2LG
☎ *(01992) 581149* Andrew Thomas

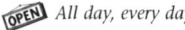A freehouse with Fuller's London Pride, Greene King IPA, McMullen AK and Wadworth 6X always available.

A one-bar country pub with garden. Food available at lunchtime only. Children allowed.

OPEN *All day, every day.*

HITCHIN

The Sunrunner
24 Bancroft, Hitchin SG5 1JW
☎ *(01462) 440717* Jason Hanning

A freehouse with Potton Shannon IPA and Fuller's London Pride permanently available. Up to nine guests, sometimes changed as often as twice a day, are from a huge range, including such beers as Caledonian 80/-, Shepherd Neame Spitfire, Charles Wells Eagle IPA, Potton Dumb Blonde and celebration ales.

Town pub in an old building, with beams and one large bar. Snacks served at luchtimes. Children allowed.

OPEN *12–3pm and 5.30–11pm Mon–Thurs; 11am–11pm Fri–Sat; 12–10.30pm Sun.*

ICKLEFORD

The Cricketers
107 Arlesey Road, Ickleford, Hitchin SG5 3TH
☎ *(01462) 422766* Mathew Walker

A Charles Wells tied house with Bombardier and Eagle IPA and Adnams Bitter and Broadside always available, plus one guest.

A one-bar traditional country pub. Food available at lunchtime. No children.

OPEN *12–3pm and 5–11pm Mon–Fri; all day Sat–Sun.*

The Plume of Feathers
Upper Green, Ickleford, Hitchin SG5 3YD
☎ *(01462) 432729* Teresa Thompson

A Whitbread house with Fuller's London Pride and Wadworth 6X always available plus one rotating guest from a wide range of smaller breweries such as Mauldons or Timothy Taylor. Examples of beers served include Adnams Regatta, Tomintoul Highland Heir and Archers Golden.

A village pub with dining area and garden. Food available at lunchtime and evenings. Well-behaved children allowed.

OPEN *11am–3pm and 6–11pm Mon–Fri; all day most Sat and Sun.*

KING'S LANGLEY

The Unicorn
Gallows Hill, Kings Langley WD4 8LV
☎ *(01923) 262287* Terry Ashcroft

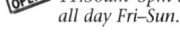An Adnams brew is usually available plus two guests from a range of constantly changing ales. Examples have included Bateman Hill Billy, Nethergate Golden Gate, Beartown Bearskinful and Rebellion Blonde Bombshell.

An upmarket family pub with function room (seats 80 people). Large beer patio. Food served at lunchtime and evenings in a separate dining area. Children allowed if eating.

OPEN *11.30am–3pm and 5–11pm Mon–Thurs; all day Fri–Sun.*

MUCH HADHAM

The Hoops
Perry Green, Much Hadham SG10 6EF
☎ *(01279) 843568*

Greene King IPA and Fuller's London Pride always available, plus a guest ale from Green Tye.

A seventeenth-century, family-run pub in a small hamlet situated close to the Henry Moore Foundation and Sculpture Park and directly opposite Henry Moore's house. Tastefully extended in keeping with the period. Separate non-smoking dining room. Large garden with outside seating, two patios, barbecue and large car park. Food available lunchtimes and evenings Mon–Sat, all day Sun. Children allowed. For further information and directions, visit www.thehoopsinn.co.uk.

OPEN *12–3pm and 6.30–11pm Mon–Sat; 12–10.30pm Sun.*

The Prince of Wales
Green Tye, Much Hadham SG10 6JP
☎ *(01279) 842517* Gary Whelan

A freehouse with the Green Tye Brewery to the rear of the premises. Green Tye beers always available, plus a McMullen ale.

A country pub with beer garden. Food available at lunchtime only. Children allowed.

OPEN *12–2.45pm and 5.30–11pm Mon–Fri; all day Sat–Sun and bank holidays.*

OLD KNEBWORTH

The Lytton Arms
Park Lane, Old Knebworth SG3 6QB
☎ *(01438) 812312* Steven Nye

Fuller's London Pride, Woodforde's Wherry and Young's Special are among those ales always available plus up to six guest beers (200 per year) from Adnams, Nethergate, Cotleigh, Exmoor, B&T, Spinnaker and Elgood's etc. Note also the Belgian beers and malt whiskies.

A traditional freehouse on the edge of Knebworth Park, built in 1837. Beamed with open fires. Bar food available at lunchtime and evenings. Car park, garden and children's room. Located halfway between Knebworth and Codicote.

OPEN *11am–3pm and 5–11pm Mon–Thurs; 11am–11pm Fri–Sat; 12–10.30pm Sun.*

ST ALBANS

The Blacksmith's Arms
56 St Peter's Street, St Albans AL1 3HG
☎ *(01727) 855761* Sue and Noel Keane

Six real ales always available (over 250 a year), with Wadworth 6X and Timothy Taylor Landlord regularly served, plus a wide variety of guests from around the country. The only supplier of City of Cambridge beer in St Albans. Regular Beer of the Month feature, and free tasters on all products. Six Belgian beers also stocked.

A Hogshead pub with one bar. Food served 12–9pm Mon–Thurs, 12–7pm Fri–Sun. Background music. Large garden – children welcome in garden until 5.30pm. Located on the main road.

OPEN *11am–11pm Mon–Sat; 12–10.30pm Sun.*

The Duke of Marlborough
110 Holywell Hill, St Albans AL1 1DH
☎ *(01727) 858982* Eamonn Murphy

Greene King IPA and Young's Special usually available with one guest beer.

Situated on the main road through St Albans, near the park and Abbey railway station. Big-screen TV for sport. Food served 12–3pm daily. Children welcome in beer garden, function and pool rooms. Car park.

OPEN *All day, every day.*

The Farmer's Boy

134 London Road, St Albans AL1 1PQ
☎ *(01727) 766702* Viv Davies

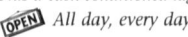 Home of the Verulam Brewery. All own brews available plus Adnams Best and occasionally brews from the Dark Horse Brewery.

A town pub with garden. Food served all day, every day. Children allowed.

SPECIAL 3.8% ABV
A light mild.
IPA 4.0% ABV
A true bitter.
FARMER'S JOY 4.5% ABV
A darker ale.
Plus a cask-conditioned lager 'VB' at 3.8%.

OPEN *All day, every day.*

The Lower Red Lion

34–6 Fishpool Street, St Albans AL3 4RX
☎ *(01727) 855669* Mrs Turner

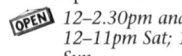 Fuller's London Pride, Oakham JHB and regularly Black Sheep Special plus five guests (500 per year) from all over the country. Two beer festivals held each year (May bank holiday and August bank holiday).

A city two-bar traditional coaching house in the conservation area of St Albans with a wide-ranging clientele. No music or games machines. Bar food is available 12–2.30pm Mon–Sat. Car park and garden.

OPEN *12–2.30pm and 5.20–11pm Mon–Fri; 12–11pm Sat; 12–3pm and 7–10.30pm Sun.*

SAWBRIDGEWORTH

The Gate Public House

81 London Road, Sawbridgeworth CM21 9JJ
☎ *(01279) 722313* Gary and Tom Barnet

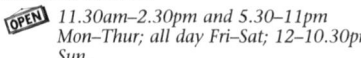 Nine hand pumps serving a constantly changing range of guest ales, always including Timothy Taylor Landlord, with Fuller's London Pride, Charles Wells Bombadier and Greene King Abbot regularly featured. The Sawbridgeworth Brewery is on the premises, so house brews are available.

A traditional pub with two bars, darts and pool. Food available at lunchtime. Children allowed.

OPEN *11.30am–2.30pm and 5.30–11pm Mon–Thur; all day Fri–Sat; 12–10.30pm Sun.*

STAPLEFORD

Papillon at the Woodhall Arms

17 High Road, Stapleford SG14 3NW
☎ *(01992) 535123* Phil Gonzalez

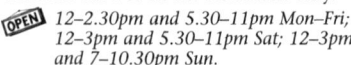 Charles Wells Eagle IPA and Adnams Bitter are always served, and the two guests (15–20 beers a month) might be ales from Young's, Everards, Wychwood or Brains.

Food-oriented French/Continental pub/restaurant, part of the Woodhall Estate. The bar, restaurant and conservatory each seat 50 people, and there is an extra restaurant seating 25, plus a party room for 10. Garden and barked play area – children allowed. Car park for 60 cars. Accommodation available in 12 letting rooms. On the A119 between Hertford and Stevenage.

OPEN *11–3pm and 5–11pm Mon–Sat; 12–4 and 7–10.30pm Sun.*

STORTFORD

The Crown at Elsenham

High Street, Stortford CM22 6DG
☎ *(01279) 812827* Ian and Barbara Goode

Two real ales are always available. Previous regulars have included Adnams Broadside and Crouch Vale Woodham IPA.

A 360-year-old country pub. Food available. Dining area and garden. Children allowed. Car park.

OPEN *12–3pm and 6–11pm Mon–Sat; 12–3pm and 7–10.30pm Sun.*

TONWELL

The Robin Hood

14 Ware Road, Tonwell, Ware SG12 0HN
☎ *(01920) 463352* Mr Harding

Dark Horse brews always available, plus three guests often including Hampshire Brewery's Lion Heart, Nethergate Swift or Shepherd Neame Spitfire.

A 300-year-old, traditional village pub. One bar and non-smoking restaurant. B&B. Food available at lunchtime and evenings. Children allowed in the restaurant only.

OPEN *12–2.30pm and 5.30–11pm Mon–Fri; 12–3pm and 5.30–11pm Sat; 12–3pm and 7–10.30pm Sun.*

TRING

The King's Arms
King Street, Tring HP23 6BE
☎ *(01442) 823318*
Victoria North and John Francis

A freehouse. Wadworth 6X always available plus guests from a wide-ranging list including Adnams Bitter, Brakspear Special or Bee Sting, Hop Back Summer Lightning and local Tring brewery ales.

A town pub with a distinctive covered and heated beer garden. Home-cooked food available at lunchtime and evenings. Non-smoking area. Children allowed at lunchtime only.

OPEN *12–2.30pm and 7–11pm Mon–Sat; 12–4pm and 7–10.30pm Sun.*

TYTTENHANGER GREEN

The Plough
Tyttenhanger Green, Nr St Albans AL4 0RW
☎ *(01727) 857777* Mike Barrowman

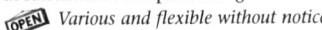Marston's Pedigree, Morland Old Speckled Hen, Wadworth 6X, Fuller's London Pride and ESB, Greene King IPA and Abbot Ale, Tring Ridgeway and Timothy Taylor Landlord always available, plus numerous unusual and interesting guest beers.

These purveyors to the multitude of murky beers and watery spirits specialise in incompetent staff, greasy food and exhorbitant prices in a terrible atmosphere. Ideal for discreet liaisons. Bar food available at lunchtime. Car park and garden.

OPEN *Various and flexible without notice.*

WALTHAM CROSS

The Vault
160 High Street, Waltham Cross EN8 7AB
☎ *(01992) 631600* Mr P Laville

A freehouse with no permanent beers but a regularly changing selection that might include Crouch Vale SAS, Clark's Burglar Bill or a Spinnaker brew. Micro-breweries favoured.

A family- and food-orientated pub with separate dining area. Food available at lunchtime and early evenings. Live bands every Thursday. Beer garden. Children allowed.

OPEN *All day, every day.*

WARESIDE

Chequers Inn
Wareside, Ware SG12 7QY
☎ *(01920) 467010* Mrs Julie Cook

A freehouse with Dark Horse brewery's Chequers Ale and Adnams Best and Broadside usually available plus three regularly changing guests such as Marston's Pedigree, Fuller's London Pride, Shepherd Neame Spitfire or Wadworth 6X.

A tiny old village pub, parts of the building date from the thirteenth century and parts from the seventeenth century. Food available at lunchtime and evenings in a 36-seater restaurant. Bench seating outside, hog roast on bank holidays. Live band on Sundays. Children allowed. Less than three miles outside Ware.

OPEN *12–3pm and 6–11pm Mon–Fri; all day Sat–Sun.*

WHITWELL

Maidens Head
67 High Street, Whitwell, Nr Hitchin SG4 8AH
☎ *(01438) 871392* Mike Jones

A McMullen tied house with AK Original and Country Best available plus one guest, changed monthly, perhaps including Shepherd Neame Spitfire, Everards Tiger or Wadworth 6X.

A two-bar village pub, timbered building with garden seating. Food available Mon–Sat lunchtimes and Tues–Sat evenings. No children.

OPEN *11.30am–3pm and 5–11pm Mon–Fri; 11.30am–4pm and 6–11pm Sat; 12–3pm and 7–10.30pm Sun.*

WIDFORD

The Green Man
High Street, Widford, Ware SG12 8SR
☎ *(01279) 842846* Brian Goodbody

Adnams Bitter and a McMullen ale are the permanent beers at this freehouse, plus two guests, changed every two weeks, perhaps from Green Tye, Moor or Mighty Oak.

Traditional pub with one large bar. Darts, pool, beer garden. Food served at lunchtimes only. Children allowed. Car park. Accommodation available. On main road from Bishop's Stortford to Ware.

OPEN *12–3pm and 5.30–11pm Mon–Fri (open 4.30pm Fri); 11am–11pm Sat; 12–10.30pm Sun.*

WILD HILL

The Woodman

45 Wildhill Lane, Wild Hill, Hatfield AL9 6EA
☎ *(01707) 642618* Graham Craig

 McMullen ales, Greene King Abbot and IPA available plus three guests from independent breweries such as Rooster's, Hampshire, Mighty Oak or York.

A country pub with garden. Sandwiches available at lunchtime (no food on bank holidays). No children.

OPEN *11.30am–2.30pm and 5.30–11pm Mon–Sat; 12–2.30pm and 7–10.30pm Sun.*

YOU TELL US

★ *Eight Bells*, 2 Park Street, Hatfield
★ *The Plume of Feathers*, Pye Corner

4.2% ABV

FALLEN ANGEL

BREWED BY THE DARK HORSE BREWING COMPANY HERTFORD

Places Featured:

Arreton
Bembridge
Brightstone
Chale
Cowes
Godshill
Hulvaston
Newport
Niton
Northwood

Rookley
Ryde
Sandown
Shanklin
Totland Bay
Ventnor
Whippingham
Wroxhall
Yarmouth

THE BREWERIES

GODDARDS BREWERY

Barnsley Farm, Bullen Road, Ryde PO33 1QF
☎ *(01983) 611011*
www.goddards-brewery.co.uk

 ALE OF WIGHT 4.0% ABV
Pale, refreshing and fruity.
SPECIAL BITTER 4.0% ABV
Well-balanced with good hoppiness.
FUGGLE DEE DUM 4.8% ABV
Golden, full-bodied and spicily aromatic.
IRON HORSE 4.8% ABV
Dark, with liquorice/chocolate flavour.
DUCK'S FOLLY 5.2% ABV
Light colour, strong and hoppy.
INSPIRATION ALE 5.2% ABV
Floral and exotic.
WINTER WARMER 5.2% ABV
Dark and smooth.

VENTNOR BREWERY LTD

119 High Street, Ventnor PO38 1LY
☎ *(01983) 856161*
www.ventnorbrewery.co.uk

GOLDEN BITTER 4.0% ABV
Light and fruity. Winner of CAMRA Isle
of Wight Beer of the Year 2002.
ADMIRAL'S ALE 4.0% ABV
SUNFIRE 4.3% ABV
OYSTER STOUT 4.5% ABV
OLD RUBY 4.7% ABV
Traditional, well-hopped ale.
WIGHT SPIRIT 5.0% ABV
ORGANIC HYGEIA ALE 5.2% ABV
Light in colour and flavour.
SANDROCK SMOKED ALE 5.6% ABV
Plus seasonal brews.

YATES BREWERY

*Undercliffe Drive, St Lawrence, Ventnor
PO39 1XG*
☎ *(01983) 854689*
www.yates-brewery.co.uk

 UNDERCLIFFE EXPERIENCE 4.1% ABV
HOLY JO 4.9% ABV
Seasonal:
WIGHT WINTER 5.0% ABV

THE PUBS

ARRETON

The Dairyman's Daughter

Arreton Barns, Arreton
☎ *(01983) 856161* Andrew Gibbs

 Home of the Scarecrow Brewery with the one home-brewed ale always available. Four other ales on offer, often including Ventnor Golden or a Hall and Woodhouse ale.

A family-orientated pub located in a craft village with candlemakers, glass-blowing and wood carving – ideal for a good day out. Bar food and full menu available lunchtimes and evenings. Children welcome, with play area provided. Beer garden. Beershop. Located between Newport and Sandown.

SCARECROW BEST 4.2% ABV
OPEN *11am–11pm Mon–Sat; 12–10.30pm Sun.*

The White Lion

Main Road, Arreton, Newport PO30 3AA
☎ *(01983) 528479* Chris and Katie Cole

 An Enterprise Inns pub with Fuller's London Pride and Badger Best always available.

An old coaching inn in a picturesque country village. One bar, two non-smoking restaurants, family room and patio garden. Food served 12–9pm every day.

OPEN *11am–11pm Mon–Sat; 12–10.30pm Sun.*

BEMBRIDGE

The Crab & Lobster

32 Forelands Field Road, Bembridge PO35 5TR
☎ *(01983) 872244* The Allen family

 A Whitbread pub, with Goddards Fuggle Dee Dum and Greene King IPA always available.

Family pub with bar and non-smoking restaurant, in a traditional building with sea views and patio. Five en-suite letting rooms. Children and dogs allowed. Car park.

OPEN *11am–3pm and 5.30–11pm Mon–Fri; 11am–11pm Sat; 12–10.30pm Sun.*

BRIGHTSTONE

The Countryman

Limerstone Road, Brightstone
☎ *(01983) 740616* Mr R Frost

Badger IPA, Dorset Best and Tanglefoot usually available, plus one guest beer, frequently from Ringwood or Goddards breweries.

Situated in a countryside setting in the south west of the island, with panoramic views of the coast and sea. Well known locally for food. Car park. Families welcome. Functions room. From Brightstone, the pub is about 400 yards along Shorewell Road.

OPEN *11am–3pm and 5.30–11pm.*

CHALE

The Wight House

Church Place, Newport Road, Chale PO38 2H
☎ *(01983) 730431* Roger Burston

Badger Best, Tanglefoot and Champion, Gribble's Fursty Ferret, Harveys Sussex Bitter and Ventnor Golden permanently available. Plus 260 whiskies.

A traditional family pub overlooking the downs to the Needles. Food available all day, every day. Children welcome, there is a covered play area and swings. Front and rear gardens. Plenty of car parking. Accommodation.

OPEN *11am–11pm Mon–Sat; 12–10.30pm Sun.*

COWES

The Anchor Inn

High Street, Cowes PO31 7SA
☎ *(01983) 292823* Andy Taylor

Wadworth 6X and Fuller's London Pride always available plus four guests, usually from local or independent breweries. Goddards Fuggle Dee Dum and Inspiration Ale and Badger Tanglefoot are popular.

A high-street pub built in 1704. Three bars, garden. Stable bar with music Fri–Sat. Food available at lunchtime and evenings. Children allowed in the garden and middle eating area.

OPEN *All day, every day.*

The Duke of York

Mill Hill Road, Cowes PO31 7BT
☎ *(01983) 295171* Barry Caff

Tied to Whitbread, with Morland Old Speckled Hen, Goddards Fuggle Dee Dum and Fuller's London Pride permanently featured.

Old-fashioned town pub and restaurant with a maritime theme. Seafood meals are a speciality. Twelve letting rooms. Children allowed. Car park.

OPEN *11am–11pm (later in summer months) Mon–Sat; 12–10.30pm Sun.*

The Globe Inn

The Parade, Cowes PO31 7QJ
☎ *(01983) 293005* Lee Taylor

Wadworth 6X is among the beers always on offer. Two guests are also served, with beers from Goddards, such as Fuggle Dee Dum and Inspiration Ale, regular favourites.

A town pub with beams, log fires and patio. Bar food is served downstairs and there is an à la carte restaurant upstairs. Live music on Saturdays. Car park. Children allowed until 7pm.

OPEN *11am–11pm Mon–Sat; 12–10.30pm Sun.*

The Ship & Castle

21 Castle Street, East Cowes PO32 6RB
☎ *(01983) 280967* Mrs Malcolm

Morland Old Speckled Hen and Marston's Pedigree always available plus guests such as Badger Brewery ales or local brews from Ventnor Brewery. The preference is for independent beers.

A tiny pub with a friendly, traditional atmosphere. No pool or music. No food but the restaurant across the road delivers food to the pub! Well-behaved children allowed.

OPEN *All day, every day.*

GODSHILL

The Griffin Inn

Godshill PO38 3JD
☎ *(01983) 840039* Andrew Still

Morland Old Speckled Hen and Marston's Pedigree are regular guests, and local beers such as Goddards Special Bitter and Ventnor Golden are also featured.

An open-plan, family pub in a Gothic-style stone building. The superb garden includes a pond, wendy house, play area, basketball hoop, and hedge maze in the shape of a griffin, made up of 2,500 privet trees. Food is served from the Adults' and Children's Menus plus Specials board.

OPEN *10.30am–11pm Mon–Sat; 12–10.30pm Sun.*

HULVASTON

The Sun Inn

Hulvaston, Newport PO30 4EH
☎ *(01983) 741124* Troy Hebden

 Ventnor Golden permanently available, plus guests on two pumps. Regular features include Adnams Bitter, Brakspear Bitter, Ringwood Best and Fortyniner and Greene King Abbot.

A small 600-year-old pub offering views of the Channel. Log burner and fireplace in winter, plus a very large beer garden for use in summer. Food is available 12–2.30pm and 6–9.30pm daily, from an extensive menu and daily specials board. Children are welcome until 10pm. Large car park. The pub is located just off the main Military road, five minutes' drive from Chessel Pottery.

 Winter: 11am–3pm and 6–11pm Mon–Sat; 12–3pm and 6–10.30pm Sun. Summer: all day, every day.

NEWPORT

The Bargeman's Rest

Little London Quay, Newport PO30 5BS
☎ *(01983) 525828*
Dan McCarthy and Debbie Richardson

Badger Best and Tanglefoot, Yates of St Lawrence Undercliffe Experience, Goddards Fuggle Dee Dum, Harveys Sussex Bitter and Ventnor Golden permanently available plus two guests such as Goddards Ale of Wight or Inspiration. Local beers are favoured whenever possible.

A traditional seafaring family pub. The two bars are decorated with artefacts of marine interest, and the pub has an outside terrace and a function room. Food is available all day, every day. Children, dogs and muddy boots are all welcome.

11am–11pm Mon–Sat; 12–10.30pm Sun.

The Blacksmith's Arms

Calbourne Road, Newport PO30 5SS
☎ *(01983) 529263* Edgar Nieghorn

 A freehouse with five real ale pumps serving a range of constantly changing ales. Examples include Fuller's London Pride, Hop Back Summer Lightning, Nethergate Augustinian and Bunces Sign of Spring.

A countryside pub with small restaurant, garden and play area. CAMRA Isle of Wight Pub of the Year 1996–2001. Food available at lunchtime and evenings. Beer festival held every October. Children allowed. Visit the award-winning website: www.blacksmiths-arms.co.uk.

 All day, every day in summer (tourist season); outside tourist season: 11am–3pm and 6–11pm Mon–Fri; 11am–11pm Sat; 12–10.30pm Sun.

NITON

The Buddle

St Catherine's Road, Niton PO38 2N3
☎ *(01983) 730243* John Bourne

Six real ales always on tap, including Adnams Best (the landlord's favourite, so they never run out!), and a local ales from either the Ventnor Brewery or Yates of St Lawrence. Local wine and cider served when available, together with a wide and interesting selection of soft drinks for the non-drinker.

A sixteenth-century, stone-built pub with oak beams, flagstone floors and open fires. Food available at lunchtime and evenings. Car park, dining room and garden. Children allowed. Near St Catherine's Lighthouse.

11am–11pm Mon–Sat; 12–10.30pm Sun.

NORTHWOOD

Traveller's Joy

85 Pallance Road, Northwood, Cowes PO31 8LS
☎ *(01983) 298024* Mr and Mrs D Smith

 Locally brewed Goddards Special Bitter and Ringwood Old Thumper are among the beers on offer, plus a wide range of guest ales from all around the country.

Multiple winner of the local branch of CAMRA's Real Ale Pub of the Year. Food is available at lunchtime and evenings and a traditional roast lunch is served on Sundays. There is a large car park and a garden with a patio, swings and children's play area in addition to two children's rooms. On the main Cowes to Yarmouth road.

11am–2.30pm and 5–11pm Mon–Thurs; 11am–11pm Fri–Sat; 12–10.30pm Sun.

ROOKLEY

The Chequers

Niton Road, Rookley PO38 3NZ
☎ *(01983) 840314* Debbie Lazelle

 Morland Old Speckled Hen and Gale's HSB are permanent features, plus two guests, changed every couple of months.

Traditional pub with beams, log fires and a flagstone floor. Food served all day. Gaming machines, garden, car park. Children allowed – there is a non-smoking family room.

OPEN *11am–11pm Mon–Sat; 12–10.30pm Sun.*

Rookley Country Park

Main Road, Rookley PO38 3LU
☎ *(01983) 721800* Jeff Ledicott

 Fuller's London Pride and Greene King Abbot are always on offer. Two guests, changed fortnightly, might include Goddards Fuggle Dee Dum, Ventnor Golden, Ringwood Fortyniner or Badger Tanglefoot.

A family-oriented pub on holiday park, with stage, restaurant and patio area. Entertainment seven nights a week. Children welcome. From Rookley, take the main road from Newport to Shanklin.

OPEN *All day, every day (except Christmas Day); late licence till 12.30am.*

RYDE

Fowlers & Co

41–3 Union Street, Ryde PO33 2LS
☎ *(01983) 812112* Lydia Hancock

 Tied to Wetherspoon's, with Shepherd Neame Spitfire, Greene King Abbot and Ventnor Golden among the beers always available. Of the twelve pumps, three or four serve guest ales, changing every couple of days, with favourites including Hop Back Summer Lightning, Badger Tanglefoot and Charles Wells Bombardier.

Traditional town pub with non-smoking areas. Food available. No children.

OPEN *10.30am–11pm Mon–Sat; 12–10.30pm Sun; extensions on Bank Holidays.*

The Railway

68 St Johns Road, Ryde
☎ *(01983) 615405* Janet Brown

 Greene King Abbot, Oakleaf Farmhouse, Charles Wells Bombardier, Young's Best and Special and Adnams Broadside permanently available. Up to 5 guest ales which could include any of the following: Brakspear Special, Everards Tiger, Bateman XB and XXXB, Hook Norton Old Hooky, Brains Reverend James or a Jennings ale.

An olde-worlde pub with flagstone floor, stone walls, beamed ceiling and open fire. Food available 6–9pm Mon; 12–3pm and 6–9pm Tues–Sat; 12–3pm Sun. Well-behaved children allowed. No car park. Situated opposite St John's railway station.

OPEN *11am–11pm Mon–Sat; 12–10.30pm Sun.*

The Simeon Arms

Simeon Street, Ryde PO33 1JG
☎ *(01983) 614954* Jamie Clarke

 Wadworth 6X is always on offer, and the weekly changing guest is often a beer from Goddards.

Locals' drinking pub with one bar, function room, darts, shove ha'penny and the best petanque on the island! Food available. Garden with outside seating. Live music Fri/Sat. Children allowed in function room.

OPEN *11am–3pm and 6–11pm Mon–Fri; 11am–11pm Sat; 12–10.30pm Sun.*

The Wishing Well

Pondwell Hill, Ryde PO33 1PX
☎ *(01983) 613222* Mr Adrian Allen

 Goddards Fuggle Dee Dum is permanently available. Two guests might be something like Greene King Abbot and IPA.

Family pub with one main bar, fireplace, patio and wishing well. Games room with pool table and TV. Food served 12–2.30pm and 6–9.30pm. Children allowed, and there are plans for a play area. Car park.

OPEN *11am–11pm Mon–Sat; 12–10.30pm Sun.*

SANDOWN

The Castle Inn

12–14 Fitzroy Street, Sandown PO36 8HY
☎ *(01983) 403169* Penny Wooly

 A freehouse with Wadworth 6X, Gale's HSB and Ventnor Golden always served, plus two guests such as Charles Wells Bombardier or Marston's Pedigree.

Drinkers' town pub with patio. Bar snacks served. No children.

OPEN *12–11pm (10.30pm Sun).*

Old Comical
15 St Johns Road, Sandown PO36 8ES
☎ *(01983) 403848* Rosemary Morris

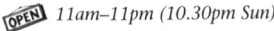Ushers Best and seasonal brews, Badger Bishops Tipple and Greene King Abbot Ale usually available.

Traditional, two-bar town pub with large garden. Barbecues on Sunday evenings in summer. Live music Friday evenings. Bar food served 12–3pm daily. Children welcome. Car park.

OPEN *11am–11pm (10.30pm Sun).*

SHANKLIN

Billy Bunters Freehouse and Restaurant
64 High Street, Shanklin PO37 6JN
☎ *(01983) 867241* Marc Richards

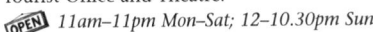A freehouse with a choice of four real ales, including locally brewed Undercliff Experience, from Yates of St Lawrence, and Ventnor Golden Bitter, as well as mainland favourites such as Badger Tanglefoot, Fuller's London Pride and Morland Old Speckled Hen.

Family-friendly, medium-sized town pub with separate restaurant. Live music on Friday, quiz night on Sunday, curry night on Tuesday. Food served all day. Located on the edge of Shanklin Old Village, opposite the Tourist Office and Theatre.

OPEN *11am–11pm Mon–Sat; 12–10.30pm Sun.*

The Crab Inn
High Street, Shanklin PO37 6NS
☎ *(01983) 862363* Derry Derbyshire

Something from Goddards is always available here, and one monthly changing guest beer is also served.

Traditional family dining pub with patio, built in the seventeenth century. No music, games or TV. Children allowed.

OPEN *11am–11pm Mon–Sat; 12–10.30pm Sun.*

The Steamer Inn
Shanklin Esplanade, Shanklin, Isle of Wight PO37 6BS
☎ *(01983) 862641* Duncan Scott (Manager)

Ventnor Golden, Badger Best and Tanglefoot and Goddards Fuggle Dee Dum permanently available, plus two guests which might include Greene King Abbot, Adnams Regatta (in summer) or a Yates of St Lawrence ale.

A nautical theme which includes memorabilia and a seafront terrace. Get 'wrecked' here!! Food, including local seafood, available all day in summer, lunchtimes and evenings in winter. Children welcome, children's menu available.

OPEN *11am–11pm Mon–Sat; 12–10.30pm Sun.*

The Village Inn
Old Village Church Road, Shanklin PO37 6NU
☎ *(01983) 862764* Paul Ockley

Ventnor Golden permanently available, plus a guest ale. There are plans for a house bitter which will be brewed by Ventnor.

A two-bar pub with beams and fireplaces. Children welcome, separate family bar upstairs. Food available 12–2.30pm and 6–10pm daily. Beer garden.

OPEN *11am–11pm Mon–Sat; 12–10.30pm Sun.*

TOTLAND BAY

The Broadway Inn
The Broadway, Totland Bay PO39 0BL
☎ *(01983) 852453* Kim Adriaenffens

House ale Broadway Blip and Yates of St Lawrence Daniel Yara always available plus a range of guests, often including Ventnor Golden, Sunfire, Wight Spirit, Old Trumpet and Valleyho.

A two-bar drinkers' pub with comfy seating and a good atmosphere. The focus is on brilliant and unusual real ale in a brilliant and unusual pub! No food. Children allowed in the back bar. Beer garden.

OPEN *11am–11pm Mon–Sat; 12–10.30pm Sun.*

Highdown Inn
Highdown Lane, Totland Bay PO39 0HY
☎ *01983 752450*
Miss S White and Mr NK Ballantyne

Three real ales are usually available including a selection of Ushers, Greene King or possibly Oakleaf and Goddards.

Ideal ramblers' pub, nestling at the foot of Tennyson Down, only half a mile from Alum Bay and the Needles. Muddy boots and dogs welcome! Known locally as a pub for good food and real ales. Runner-up in the Ushers Food Competition. Food available in a small, newly decorated restaurant, two small bars or garden patio area. Children are catered for with their own menu and play area within a large garden. En-suite accommodation also available. Follow Alum Bay Old Road to Freshwater Bay.

OPEN *Winter: 11am–3pm and 6–11pm; potentially all day in Summer.*

VENTNOR

The Spyglass

The Esplanade, Ventnor PO38 1JS
☎ *(01983) 855338*
Meg Mortimer and Edna Carter

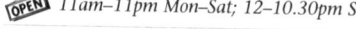 Badger Best and Tanglefoot and Ventnor Golden always available, plus two guests. Goddards Fuggle Dee Dum and beers from Yates of St Lawrence, Hall & Woodhouse, Ventnor Ales and Scarecrow are often available. Two real ale festivals every year, in spring and October.

A seafaring pub situated on the sea wall. Food available all day in summer, lunchtimes and evenings in winter. Large outside terraces. Children, dogs and muddy boots welcome. Live music every evening.

OPEN *11am–11pm Mon–Sat; 12–10.30pm Sun.*

The Volunteer Inn

30 Victoria Street, Ventnor PO38 1ES
☎ *(01983) 852537* Tim Saul

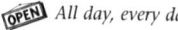 A freehouse with a good range of regularly changing ales. Regulars include Badger Best, Tanglefoot, and the locally produced Ventnor Golden Bitter. Six real ales on hand pump always available.

This award-winning freehouse is the smallest pub on the island, and a haven for adult drinkers. Traditional wooden floors, lively conversation and gourmet pickled eggs, but no chips, children, fruit machines or juke box. Annual October beerfest with over 24 real ales. Muddy boots and (cat-proof) dogs welcome. Website: www.volunteer-inn.com.

OPEN *All day, every day.*

WHIPPINGHAM

Folly Inn

Folly Lane, Whippingham PO32 6NB
☎ *(01983) 297171* Chris and Sue (managers)

 Four pumps serve a range of real ales, changed seasonally, including brews from Goddards, Morland Old Speckled Hen and Wadworth 6X.

Open-plan country pub seating 200, with large patio and garden area. Non-smoking dining area, full menu and specials board (lunches served from 12 noon). Live music Fri and Sat in summer. Based on a river mooring for 230 boats and pontoon with mooring – a water taxi runs from the pontoon to the mooring during summer. Showers available 24 hours. Children allowed. Well signposted.

OPEN *9am (for breakfasts)–11pm (10.30pm Sun).*

WROXALL

Four Seasons

2 Clarence Road, Wroxhall PO38 3BY
☎ *(01983) 854701* Richard Lowe

 Ventnor Golden permanently available, plus two guests which often include Greene King Abbot, Wadworth 6X, other Ventnor ales and occasionally something from Goddards.

A family pub where they pride themselves that nothing is too much trouble. Family area. Food available in the bar or in a separate à la carte restaurant. Garden with outside seating. Located off the main road but visible from it, on the junction with Manor Road.

OPEN *11am–3pm and 6–11pm Mon–Fri; 11am–11pm Sat; 12–10.30pm Sun.*

The Star Inn

Clarence Road, Wroxall, Nr Ventnor PO38 3BY
☎ *(01983) 854701* Mr and Mrs Boocock

Six guest beers available (15 per year), including Eldridge Pope Royal Oak, Mansfield Old Baily and Wadworth 6X.

The Star Inn offers the weary traveller hot and wholesome food and seven real ales. Destroyed by fire in 1980 but since rebuilt. Food available at lunchtime and evenings. Car park and garden. Children allowed. Wroxhall lies in the south of the island, two miles north of Ventnor on the B3327.

OPEN *11am–3pm and 7–11pm.*

YARMOUTH

The Bugle Hotel

The Square, Yarmouth PO41 0NS
☎ *(01983) 760272* John Russell

Morland Old Speckled Hen is a permanent feature, as is a local favourite, Bugle Bitter, brewed on the Island to The Bugle's own recipe. Two guests usually available.

Seventeenth-century coaching inn fronting the town square, with two bars and a beer garden. Food is available, including a specials menu featuring locally caught fresh fish. Nine letting bedrooms. Children always welcome. Non-smoking areas. Car park.

OPEN *All day, every day.*

The Wheatsheaf

Bridge Road, Yarmouth PO41 0PH
☎ *(01983) 760456* Mrs Keen

Goddards Fuggle Dee Dum, Wadworth 6X, Morland Old Speckled Hen and a Brakspear bitter usually available.

A traditional, food-oriented pub with two bar areas, separate eating area, two family areas, conservatory and garden. An extensive menu is available at lunchtime and evenings. Children allowed. Near the ferry.

OPEN *All day, every day.*

YOU TELL US

✶ *The Central Tap,* High Street, Ventnor

Places Featured:

Ashford	Great Chart
Aylesford	Halstead
Badlesmere	Harvel
Barfreston	Hollowshore
Borden	Kennington
Bossingham	Luddesdown
Boughton Aluph	Marden
Boughton Monchelsea	Margate
Boxley	Marsh Green
Burham	Plaxtol
Canterbury	Ramsgate
Charing	Ringlestone
Chatham	Rochester
Chiddingstone	St Mary-in-the-Marsh
Chiddingstone Causeway	Sittingbourne
Dartford	Smarden
Denton	Snargate
Dover	Southborough
East Malling	Southfleet
Elham	Stone Street
Fairseat	Tonbridge
Farningham	Upnor
Faversham	West Malling
Folkestone	West Peckham
Gillingham	Whitstable
Gravesend	Worth

THE BREWERIES

ALES OF KENT BREWERY

The Old Stables, Boxley Grange Farm, Lidsing Road, Boxley, Maidstone ME14 3EL
☎ *(01634) 669296*
www.alesofkentbrewery.co.uk

OLD MA WEASEL 3.6% ABV
WEALDON WONDER 3.7% ABV
DEFIANCE 4.1% ABV
STILTMAN 4.3% ABV
SMUGGLERS GLORY 4.8% ABV
BRAINSTORM 8.0% ABV

THE FLAGSHIP BREWERY

The Historic Dockyard, Chatham ME4 4TZ
☎ *(01634) 832828*
www.real-ale-guide.co.uk/flagship

VICTORY MILD 3.5% ABV
CAPSTAN 3.8% ABV
SPRING PRIDE 4.0% ABV
ENSIGN 4.2% ABV
SPANKER 4.2% ABV
FRIGGIN IN THE RIGGIN 4.7% ABV
CROWS NEST 4.8% ABV
FUTTOCK 5.2% ABV
OLD SEA DOG STOUT 5.5% ABV
Seasonal:
GANG PLANK 5.8% ABV

OLD KENT BREWERY COMPANY

11–13 Western Road, Borough Green, Sevenoaks
TN15 8AL
☎ *(01732) 882111*
www.okbc.co.uk

GOLDEN DUCK 3.6% ABV
FINE EDGE 3.8% ABV
Session ale.
HALF CENTURY 4.0% ABV
OPENER 4.2% ABV
TOP SCORE 4.6% ABV
Dark ale.
FULL PITCH 5.0% ABV
Winter warmer.
LONGHOP 5.0% ABV

P & DJ GOACHER

Unit 8, Tovil Green Business Park, Tovil,
Maidstone ME15 6TA
☎ *(01622) 682112*

REAL MILD ALE 3.4% ABV
Malt taste, slightly bitter.
FINE LIGHT ALE 3.7% ABV
Light with hops and some balancing malt.
BEST DARK ALE 4.1% ABV
Darker bitter brew with malt flavours.
CROWN IMPERIAL STOUT 4.5% ABV
GOLD STAR 5.1% ABV
Pale ale.
OLD 1066 ALE 6.7% ABV
Powerful, dark winter ale.

LARKINS BREWERY LTD

Larkins Farm, Chiddingstone, Edenbridge
TN8 7BB
☎ *(01892) 870328*

TRADITIONAL ALE 3.4% ABV
Malty with balancing hoppiness.
CHIDDINGSTONE BITTER 4.0% ABV
BEST BITTER 4.4% ABV
PORTER 5.2% ABV

RAMSGATE BREWERY

The Ramsgate Royal Harbour Brewhouse & Bakers,
98 Harbour Parade, Ramsgate CT11 8LP
☎ *(01843) 594 758*
www.ramsgatebrewhouse.com

GADDS NO.7 3.8% ABV
GADDS NO.3 5.0% ABV
Plus an extensive range of guest beers.

SHEPHERD NEAME LTD

17 Court Street, Faversham ME13 7AX
☎ *(01795) 532206*
www.shepherd-neame.co.uk

MASTER BREW BITTER 3.7% ABV
Well-hopped and slightly sweet
throughout.
BEST BITTER 4.1% ABV
Rich malt flavour with good hoppiness.
EARLY BIRD 4.3% ABV
Spring ale.
LATE RED 4.5% ABV
Autumn ale.
GOLDINGS 4.7% ABV
Summer ale.
SPITFIRE ALE 4.7% ABV
Well-rounded, commemorative ale.
BISHOP'S FINGER 5.2% ABV
Smooth, well-rounded and complex.

THE SWALE BREWERY CO. LTD

Unit 1, D2 Trading Estate, Castle Road,
Eurolink, Sittingbourne ME10 3RH
☎ *(01795) 426871*
www.swale-brewery.co.uk

KENTISH PRIDE 3.8% ABV
COPPER CAST 4.0% ABV
INDIAN SUMMER PALE ALE 4.2% ABV
KENTISH GRANDE CRU 4.2% ABV
COCKLEWARMER 5.0% ABV

THE PUBS

ASHFORD

Hooden Horse on the Hill
Silver Hill Road, Ashford TN24 0NY
☎ *(01233) 662226*

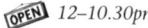Seven beers always available including Hop Back Summer Lightning, Hook Norton Old Hooky and Goacher's Light. Also some 200+ guest beers per year, which may include Greene King Abbot Ale and Hop Back Wheat Beer. Micro-breweries are well represented.

The oldest and busiest pub in Ashford, beamed and candlelit with hops in the ceiling. One bar, friendly staff, background music only. Food available at lunchtime and evenings. Car park and garden. Children allowed. Off the Hythe Road, near the ambulance station.

OPEN *12–10.30pm.*

AYLESFORD

The Little Gem
19 High Street, Aylesford ME20 7AX
☎ *(01622) 717510* Harvey Tox

Fuller's London Pride and ESB always available plus three or four guest beers weekly, which may include Charles Wells Bombardier, Gale's HSB or Morland Old Speckled Hen.

Reputedly the smallest pub in Kent. A former bakery, the building dates back to 1106 in the reign of Henry I. The pub also has a small gallery which seats 12 people. Bar food available at lunchtime Mon–Sat and evenings Mon–Thurs. Next door to the post office.

OPEN *11am–3pm and 6–11pm Mon–Fri; 11am–11pm Sat; 12–10.30pm Sun.*

BADLESMERE

The Red Lion
Ashford Road, Badlesmere, Faversham ME13 0NX
☎ *(01233) 740320* Moira Anderson

A freehouse with Shepherd Neame Master Brew, Fuller's London Pride, Greene King Abbot and a mild always available. Two rotating guest taps serve, perhaps, Timothy Taylor Landlord, Hop Back Summer Lightning or Tomintoul Nessie's Monster Mash.

A sixteenth-century village local. Large garden housing pigs and sheep! Food available at lunchtime and evenings. Children allowed.

OPEN *12–3pm Mon–Thurs; all day Fri–Sun.*

BARFRESTON

Yew Tree Inn
Barfreston, Nr Dover CT15 7JH
☎ *(01304) 831619* Peter and Kathryn Garstin

Five real ales always available, including a cask mild. The beers may be from any small independent brewery or micro-brewery, and local brewers are favoured. A huge range of brewers stocked throughout the year. Two or three Bidden Ciders are also served.

An unspoilt traditional village freehouse with wooden floors and pine-scrubbed tables. Bar food available, and there is also a separate restaurant menu. Food served 12–2.15pm and 7–9.15pm Tues–Sat and 12–2.30pm Sun (no food Mon). Children allowed, but not in bar area. Dogs are welcome, and there is a tethering rail outside for horses. Approximately eight miles south of Canterbury, two miles off the main A2 towards Dover, signposted Barfreston.

OPEN *12–3pm and 6–11pm Mon–Thurs; 12–11pm Fri–Sat; 12–10.30pm Sun.*

BORDEN

The Plough & Harrow
Oad Street, Borden, Sittingbourne ME9 8LB
☎ *(01795) 843351* David Budden

Greene King IPA, Young's Best and Shepherd Neame Master Brew always available, plus a range of guest ales. Examples include Young's Special and Shepherd Neame Early Bird and Spitfire.

A small country pub with two bars and a garden with children's area. Food available at lunchtime daily and evenings Fri–Sat. Children allowed.

OPEN *All day, every day.*

BOSSINGHAM

The Hop Pocket
The Street, Bossingham, Canterbury CT4 6DY
☎ *(01227) 709866* Mr Fuller

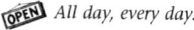A freehouse specialising in local real ales. Guests are from independent breweries across the country and include Timothy Taylor Landlord, Harveys Sussex Best, Hook Norton Old Hooky and brews from Shepherd Neame.

A village pub with a family atmosphere. Victorian building, decorated with hops. Conservatory, garden and meadow with children's area. Extensive menu available at lunchtime and evenings. Children allowed. Parties catered for.

OPEN *12–3pm and 7–11pm (10.30 Sun).*

BOUGHTON ALUPH

The Flying Horse
Boughton Aluph, Ashford TN25 4ET
☎ *(01233) 620914* Tim Chandler

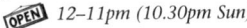 Fuller's London Pride and Greene King IPA are among the beers always available.

Fifteenth-century beamed pub on cricket green. One bar, restaurant, garden. Children allowed in restaurant only. Car park.

OPEN *12–11pm (10.30pm Sun).*

BOUGHTON MONCHELSEA

The Red House
Hermitage Lane, Boughton Monchelsea ME17 4DA
☎ *(01622) 743986* Mr and Mrs Richardson

 Six beers available at any one time (150 per year). Hampshire Strong and Everards Tiger always available, plus guests such as Ringwood Fortyniner, Wolf in Sheep's Clothing, Burton Bridge Porter, Green King Triumph, Cotleigh Barn Owl and Butcombe Bitter. Guests change constantly – check website for current details.

A country freehouse with pool room and two other bars, one with an open log fire. Also a conservatory/children's room, a large garden and camp site. Bar food available at lunchtime and evenings. South off the B2163 at Marlpit, take the Wierton Road, then left down East Hall Hill. OS783488. Website: www.the-redhouse.co.uk.

OPEN *12–3pm and 7–11pm Mon–Fri; 12–11pm Sat; 12–10.30pm Sun. Closed Tues lunch.*

BOXLEY

The King's Arms
Boxley, Maidstone ME14 3DR
☎ *(01622) 755177* Helen and Jon Sutton

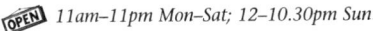 An Enterprise Inns pub with Fuller's London Pride, Adnams Bitter, Greene King IPA and Gale's HSB permanently available, plus one regularly changing guest.

Village pub, with some parts of the building dating from the twelfth century. The large garden is a particular feature. Food served all day Sat and Sun. One open bar divided into two. The pub is dog-friendly, and children are allowed.

OPEN *11am–11pm Mon–Sat; 12–10.30pm Sun.*

BURHAM

The Toastmaster's Inn
65–7 Church Street, Burham, Rochester ME1 3SB
☎ *(01634) 861299* Mr Nik Frangoulis

 A freehouse serving Greene King IPA, Abbot and Triumph, Young's Bitter and Shepherd Neame Spitfire. One guest ale from a range including Marston's Pedigree and King and Barnes Sussex Bitter.

A country pub with back bar, snug and restaurant. Tuesday night is bikers' night. Pub food served all day. Children allowed in the restaurant only. Exit J6 of the M20.

OPEN *All day, every day.*

CANTERBURY

Canterbury Tales
12 The Friars, Canterbury CT1 2AS
☎ *(01227) 768594*
Jacqui Smith and Mark Tunbridge

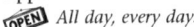 Fuller's London Pride, Shepherd Neame Spitfire, Highgate Dark Mild and Greene King IPA always available, plus one guest beer.

A lively 'country pub in the town', used by locals and actors. Bar food is available all day, and there is a separate restaurant upstairs, 'The Friars', specialising in Mexican and Continental cuisine. Children allowed. Opposite the Marlowe Theatre.

OPEN *All day, every day.*

The Unicorn
61 St Dunstan's Street, Canterbury CT2 8BS
☎ *(01227) 463187* Lorenzo Carnevale-Masse

Shepherd Neame Masterbrew and Fuller's London Pride always available, plus one weekly changing guest either from a local brewery such as Hopdaemon and Swale, or maybe from Young's.

Dating from 1604, this pub has one large bar, bar billiards and a large beer garden. Food available every lunchtime and evening.

OPEN *11am–11pm Mon–Sat; 12–10.30pm Sun.*

CHARING

The Bowl Inn
Egg Hill Road, Charing, Ashford TN27 0HG
☎ *(01233) 712256* Alan Paine

A freehouse with Fuller's London Pride always available plus three guests. The whole Fuller's range is often stocked, also brews such as Badger Tanglefoot, Gale's HSB, Adnams Best or a Harveys ale.

A traditional country freehouse. Unusual revolving pool table. Large beer garden. Bar snacks served until 10pm every day.

OPEN *5–11pm Mon–Thurs; all day Fri–Sun.*

CHATHAM

The Tap & Tin
24 Railway Street, Chatham ME4 4JT
☎ *(01634) 847926* Dave Gould

A range of beers are brewed on the premises by the brewer from the Flagship Brewery. Also one guest ale, often from Greene King.

A lively pub with a largely student clientele. Quiz nights on Tuesday, live music on Thursday and Sunday. No food. Children allowed.

CAULKER'S BITTER 3.7% ABV
A light gold ale, refreshingly dry with hints of fruit and bitter aftertaste.

FLOGGIN 4.1% ABV

CAPTIN'S TACKLE 4.2% ABV
Dry, malty ale with subtle roast tones and a bitter finish.

YARDARM 4.3% ABV
Well-balanced malty ale, slightly nutty with a smooth bitter aftertaste.

OPEN *11am–11pm Mon–Sat; 12–10.30pm Sun.*

CHIDDINGSTONE

The Rock
Chiddingstone, Edenbridge TN8 8BS
☎ *(01892) 870296* Mr Shaw Kew

Larkins Brewery's only pub, with Larkins ales always on offer. These include Traditional Ale, Chiddingstone Bitter, Best Bitter and Porter in the winter.

A 450-year-old rural drinkers' pub with two bars. Food available (not Sun evenings). Garden and car park. Children not allowed. No disabled access. Difficult to find, so phone for directions.

OPEN *11.30am–3pm and 6–11pm Tues–Sat (closed Mon except bank holidays); 12–3pm and 6–10.30pm Sun.*

CHIDDINGSTONE CAUSEWAY

The Little Brown Jug
Chiddingstone Causeway, Nr Tonbridge TN11 8JJ
☎ *(01892) 870318*
Tim Wallis and Tony Gallagher

Greene King IPA and Abbot always available plus guest beers including Morland Old Speckled Hen, Ruddles County, Everards Tiger and Greene King Triumph. Wide selection of New-World wines.

A friendly, family-owned country pub. Bar and restaurant food available at lunchtime and evenings. Car park, garden, conference facilities and accommodation. Children allowed. Website: www.thelittlebrownjug.co.uk.

OPEN *12–11pm (10.30pm Sun).*

DARTFORD

Paper Moon
55 High Street, Dartford DA1 1DS
☎ *(01322) 281127* Joanne Holder

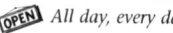A Wetherspoon's pub with Shepherd Neame Spitfire always available plus a selection of four guest ales from any independent brewery or micro-brewery in the United Kingdom.

A traditional one-bar town pub with non-smoking area. Food served all day. Children allowed until 5pm if eating.

OPEN *All day, every day.*

Wat Tyler
80 High Street, Dartford DA1 1DE
☎ *(01322) 272546* Michael Aynge

Brains Bitter permanently available plus one guest ale such as Charles Wells Bombardier, Marston's Pedigree, Brains Reverend James, Flagship Friggin' in the Riggin' or Hardy's Kiss.

A 600-year-old building with beamed ceilings and many historic features. Food available all day with seating in a separate area in the evenings. No children. Traditional Irish music on the first Sunday of the month.

OPEN *10am–11pm Mon–Sat; 12–10.30pm Sun.*

DENTON

The Jackdaw Inn
The Street, Canterbury Road, Denton CT4 6QZ
☎ *(01303) 844663* Caroline Hopkins

Five real ales always on offer, changed two or three times a week. Examples include Swale Kentish Pride and Indian Summer, Flagship Hurricane (brewed for the pub) and Spanker, and beers from Ales of Kent.

Country village pub built in 1645. Used by the Home Guard during the Second World War, and featured in the film *The Battle of Britain*. The 130-seater restaurant is the main focus of the inn, and food is available 12–3pm and 6.30–9.30pm. Garden back and front, parking, occasional beer festivals (call for details). Children allowed.

OPEN *11am–11pm Mon–Sat; 12–10.30pm Sun.*

DOVER

The Mogul
5–6 Chapel Place, Dover CT17 9AS
☎ *(01304) 205072* Mr and Mrs Franklin

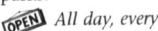Three or four constantly changing real ales always available (over 500 served in two years), with beers from Hop Back, Oakham and Timothy Taylor regularly featured, as well as brews from micro-breweries. Beers served by gravity on stillage behind the bar.

Unspoilt freehouse with wooden floors and log-burning stove. Traditional bar games played, such as quoits and table skittles. Sandwiches available from lunchtime to early evening. No children's licence. From the Snargate–York Street roundabout, take the first left off York Street, first left again, then follow the road around between the car parks.

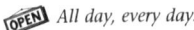 *All day, every day.*

The Louis Armstrong
Maison Dieu Road, Dover CT16 1RA
☎ *(01304) 204759* Jackie Bowles

A freehouse with two guest beers, changed twice a week, featuring beers such as Otter Ale and brews from Wessex and Burton Bridge.

A drinkers' pub with live music three or four times a week. Bar food available. One large bar, garden and car park. Children allowed in the garden only. On the main road into Dover.

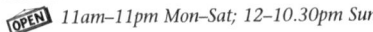 *11am–11pm Mon–Sat; 12–10.30pm Sun.*

EAST MALLING

The Rising Sun
125 Mill Street, East Malling ME19 6BX
☎ *(01732) 843284* Mr Kemp

A freehouse specialising in local ales from breweries such as Goacher's and Shepherd Neame. Up to three guests, usually from micro-breweries such as Bateman or Gale's.

A locals' pub with two bars and a beer garden. Food available at lunchtime Mon–Fri. No children.

 All day, every day.

ELHAM

The Rose & Crown
High Street, Elham, Canterbury CT4 6TD
☎ *(01303) 840226* Denise McNicholas

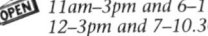A freehouse serving a selection of cask ales, including Hopdaemon Golden Braid, from a range reflecting different styles and strengths.

A sixteenth-century village inn. Full à la carte, bar food and fresh fish menus available lunchtimes and evenings in lounge bar or non-smoking restaurant. En-suite accommodation, patio.

 11am–3pm and 6–11pm Mon–Sat; 12–3pm and 7–10.30pm Sun.

FAIRSEAT

The Vigo Inn
Gravesend Road, Fairseat, Nr Sevenoaks TN15 7JL
☎ *(01732) 822547* Mrs PJ Ashwell

Young's, Harveys and Flagship brews always available, plus guests from the Old Kent Brewery Company and Crouch Vale.

Situated on the North Downs, partly non-smoking. No music or games machines. Bar food is available. Car park. Children allowed in the garden only.

 6–11pm Mon–Fri (closed lunchtimes Mon–Fri); 12–3.30pm and 6–11pm Sat; 12–3.30pm and 7–10.30pm Sun.

FARNINGHAM

The Chequers
High Street, Farningham, Dartford DA4 0DT
☎ *(01322) 865222*
Alan Vowls and Karen Jefferies

A freehouse serving Fuller's ESB and London Pride and Timothy Taylor Landlord plus six guest ales including brews from Hop Back, Bateman, Oakham, Greene King and other small breweries.

A 300-year-old beamed village pub. Close to the river in the Brands Hatch area. Food served 12–2.30pm. Children allowed.

 11am–11pm (10.30pm Sun).

FAVERSHAM

The Elephant Inn
31 The Mall, Faversham ME13 8JN
☎ *(01795) 590157*
Sharon Yates and Aden Brady

 Owned by Flagship Taverns, this freehouse has six hand pumps featuring local ales, always including one mild, constantly changing. Belgian beers and local cider also served.

Traditional, old-fashioned, locals' pub with a friendly atmosphere. Excellent home-made food served every lunchtime and Fri–Sat evenings in the bar or the non-smoking restaurant. Snacks are available all day, and roasts are served on Sundays. Walled garden, families welcome.

OPEN *12–11pm (10.30pm Sun).*

FOLKESTONE

The Lifeboat
42 North Street, Folkestone CT19 6AD
☎ *(01303) 243958* P O'Reilly

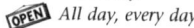 Fuller's London Pride usually available plus three guest beers from a range including Bateman Victory and XXXB and Mansfield Old Bailey.

Largely a locals' pub in a tourist area. One bar and beer garden. Food available at lunchtime and evenings. Children allowed in the garden only.

OPEN *All day, every day.*

GILLINGHAM

Dog & Bone
21 Jeffrey Street, Gillingham ME7 1DE
☎ *(01634) 576829* David Skinner

 Four constantly changing real ales available at any one time, with a large selection of styles and strengths, to suit everyone.

A traditional one-bar pub with large conservatory and restaurant. Food available every lunchtime. Situated just off the high street, 10 minutes from Gillingham Football Ground.

OPEN *11am–11pm Mon–Sat; 12–10.30pm Sun.*

Roseneath
79 Arden Street, Gillingham ME7 1HS
☎ *(01634) 852553*
Mr T Robinson and Mrs H Dobson

 Up to six beers available, perhaps including Greene King Abbot, Bateman XB, Cotleigh Barn Owl, Belchers Best, Charles Wells Bombardier, Adnams Broadside, B&T Dragonslayer, Coach House Gunpowder Strong Mild and many more.

A friendly pub with perhaps the most adventurous selection of beers in north Kent. Doorstep sandwiches. Crazy bar billiards. Just five minutes from the railway station.

OPEN *11am–11.30pm Mon–Sat; 12–10.30pm Sun.*

GRAVESEND

The Jolly Drayman
Wellington Street, Gravesend DA12 1JA
☎ *(01474) 352355* Mr Fordred

 Everards Tiger always available, plus three guests, ranging from 3.5% to 5.5% ABV in strength.

A country-style pub in a town-centre location. Housed in part of the Wellington Brewery building. Patio and garden. Food available at lunchtime (not Sunday), separate restaurant attached. Barbecues on Friday and Saturday evenings, May–Sept. Accommodation. Children allowed in the garden only. Website: www.jollydrayman.com.

OPEN *11.30am–2.30pm and 6–11pm Mon–Thurs; 11.30am–2.30pm and 5.30–11pm Fri; 12–3pm and 7–11pm Sat; 12–3pm and 7–10.30pm Sun.*

Somerset Arms
10 Darnley Road, Gravesend DA11 0RU
☎ *(01474) 533837* Mr and Mrs Cerr

 Six beers always available from a range of hundreds per year. These may include Exmoor Gold, Timothy Taylor Landlord, Kelham Island Pale Rider, Maclays Broadsword, Ash Vine Hop and Glory and brews from Harviestoun, Hoskins & Oldfield, Young's and Fuller's.

A country-style pub. The Best Town Pub in Kent 1993, and winner of Cask Marque award. Bar food available. Children allowed. Opposite Gravesend railway station.

OPEN *11am–midnight.*

GREAT CHART

The Hooded Horse
The Street, Great Chart, Ashford TN23 3AN
☎ *(01233) 625583* Alison Woolford

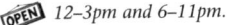Morland Old Speckled Hen and Adnams Bitter permanently available, plus one changing guest.

An old English pub with one bar decorated with hops, and a Mexican restaurant. Beer garden. Food available 12–2pm and 6–10pm. Children allowed.

OPEN *12–3pm and 6–11pm.*

HALSTEAD

The Rose & Crown
Otford Lane, Halstead, Sevenoaks TN14 7EA
☎ *(01959) 533120* Joy Brushneen

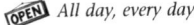Larkins Traditional and a Harveys brew always available plus three guests (over 100 per year) from independent breweries such as Otter, Gale's or Kelham Island.

A rural drinking pub with two bars, pool room and enclosed garden. Food available at lunchtime Mon–Fri. Children allowed in the garden and pool room.

OPEN *All day, every day.*

HARVEL

Amazon & Tiger
Harvel Street, Harvel, Nr Meopham DA13 0DE
☎ *(01474) 814705* Lesley Whitehouse

The three beers served vary on a weekly basis and may include Greene King IPA and Triumph, Morland Old Speckled Hen, Ruddles Best or beers from Brains among many others.

Typical village pub appealing to all age groups, with sporting and games bias. Occasional Friday night entertainment. Food served every lunchtime. Children welcome. Car park.

OPEN *12–3pm and 6–11pm Mon–Fri; 12–11pm Sat; 12–10.30pm Sun.*

HOLLOWSHORE

The Shipwright Arms
Hollowshore, Faversham ME13 7TU
☎ *(01795) 890088* Derek Cole

A freehouse specialising in Kent beers, all gravity-dispensed. Goacher's ales are regular favourites, including Dark Mild, Gold Star and Shipwrecked (brewed especially for the pub). Beers from Hopdaemon and Kent Garden have also been featured.

Seventeenth-century former smugglers' inn by a creek, with one service bar and lots of nooks and crannies! Food available. Occasional beer festivals (phone for details). Garden, car park. Children allowed in designated areas. Difficult to find (they say 'the challenge is to find us!'): go to Oare, then find Davington Primary School and turn opposite, following signpost to The Shipwrights Arms. Call if not sure.

OPEN *11am–3pm and 6–11pm Mon–Fri; 11am–11pm Sat and bank holidays; 12–10.30pm Sun.*

KENNINGTON

The Pilgrim's Rest
Canterbury Road, Kennington TN24 9QR
☎ *(01233) 636863* Mr Killick

Tied to Fuller's, with London Pride and ESB always on offer.

Hotel, restaurant and pub in a nineteenth-century building with a new extension. One bar, five-acre garden, 34 bedrooms, car park. Children allowed. On the main A28 Ashford to Canterbury road.

OPEN *11am–11pm Mon–Sat; 12–10.30pm Sun.*

LUDDESDOWN

The Cock Inn
Henley Street, Luddesdown DA13 0XB
☎ *(01474) 814208* Mr A Turner

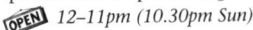Adnams Bitter always available plus six guest beers (two new ones per day). If it is brewed, it has probably been sold here.

A sixteenth-century traditional two-bar public house set in idyllic countryside. Bar food available until 8pm. Seafood specialities. Car park and garden.

OPEN *12–11pm (10.30pm Sun).*

MARDEN

The Stilebridge Inn

Staplehurst Road, Marden, Tonbridge TN12 9BH
☎ *(01622) 831236* Mr and Mrs S Johnson

 A freehouse with a constantly changing, varied range of up to seven real ales. Local and micro-breweries favoured.

A traditional country pub with restaurant, three bars and beer garden. Food available at lunchtime and evenings. Children allowed.

[OPEN] *11.30am–3pm Mon–Sat; 6–11pm Tues–Fri; 6.30–11pm Sat; all day Sun (closed Mon evening).*

MARGATE

The Spread Eagle

25 Victoria Road, Margate CT9 1LW
☎ *(01843) 293396* Renny Dobbs

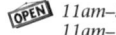 A freehouse serving Greene King IPA, Fuller's London Pride, Adnams Best and Morland Old Speckled Hen, plus guests.

A traditional Victorian pub with bar and dining areas. Food available daytimes and evenings. Children allowed.

[OPEN] *11am–3pm and 5–11pm Mon–Fri; 11am–11pm Sat; 12–10.30pm Sun.*

MARSH GREEN

The Wheatsheaf

Marsh Green, Edenbridge TN8 5QL
☎ *(01732) 864091* Neil Foster

 Harveys brews available plus a good selection of guests (approx 150 per year) including, perhaps, Fuller's London Pride, Timothy Taylor Landlord, Gale's HSB, Young's Ram Rod, or an Adnams brew.

A traditional village pub with four bars, conservatory and beer garden. Food available at lunchtime and evenings. Children allowed.

[OPEN] *11am–3pm and 5.30–11pm Mon–Fri; all day Sat–Sun.*

PLAXTOL

The Golding Hop

Sheet Hill, Plaxtol TN15 0PT
☎ *(01732) 882150* EA Mortimer

 Young's Special and Adnams Best always available plus two guest ales which could come from any independent brewery. Marston's, Smiles and Everards regularly featured. Also Weston's cider.

A whitewashed, cottage-like pub nestling in a valley, with four rooms on three levels. Small selection of 'pub grub' available lunchtimes and Wed–Sun evenings. Large beer garden with petanque and children's play area. Children allowed in the garden only. Car park. Located on the A227 between Borough Green and Tonbridge.

[OPEN] *11am–3pm and 5.30–11pm Mon–Thurs; 11.30–3pm and 5.30–11pm Fri; 11am–11pm Sat; 12–4pm and 7–10.30pm Sun.*

The Papermaker's Arms

The Street, Plaxtol TN15 0QL
☎ *(01732) 810407* Michael Crompton

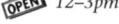 Greene King IPA and Fuller's London Pride always available, plus a monthly changing guest.

A smart pub/restaurant in the picturesque village of Plaxtol, serving bar and restaurant food daily. Beer garden. Families welcome, and there is a play area in the garden. Car park.

[OPEN] *12–3pm and 6–11pm (10.30pm Sun).*

RAMSGATE

The Artillery Arms

36 West Cliff Road, Ramsgate CT11 9JS
☎ *(01843) 853282* Chris and Michele Parry

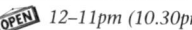 A freehouse serving Charles Wells Bombardier plus four other real ales on a constantly rotating basis. Too many beers to list, from all over the UK. Hoegaarden and real cider also served.

Small pub with a big friendly atmosphere. CAMRA Thanet Pub of the Year 2002. This Grade II listed building features unique leaded stained-glass windows depicting Royal Artillery horse-back scenes, hand-painted by soldiers recovering after the Napoleonic Wars. No modern music on juke box (mainly music from 1950s–1990s). Doorstep sandwiches made fresh to order Mon–Sat.

[OPEN] *12–11pm (10.30pm Sun).*

The Churchill Tavern
19–22 The Paragon, Ramsgate CT11 9JX
☎ (01843) 587862 Sarah Barrett

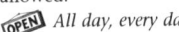 Ringwood Old Thumper, Timothy Taylor Landlord, Morland Old Speckled Hen, Hop Back Summer Lightning and Fuller's London Pride usually available, plus up to seven guests including Cottage Golden Arrow, Exmoor Gold, Wychwood Dog's Bollocks and many more.

A country-style pub in the town. Two bars in a four-storey building, live music at least three times a week, including jazz, folk, blues and Irish music. Annual beer festival. Country Kitchen restaurant (tel: 01843 593805) combines modern brasserie-style with a traditional English pub. Function room (Paragon Room) holds 250. Children allowed.

OPEN *All day, every day.*

RINGLESTONE

Ringlestone Inn
Nr Harrietsham, Maidstone ME17 1NX
☎ (01622) 859900 Michael Millington-Buck

 Five beers always available including Shepherd Neame Best and guests (40 per year) from brewers such as Bateman, Adnams, Young's, Hook Norton, Fuller's, Felinfoel, Harveys and Shepherd Neame, plus seasonal variations.

B uilt as a hospice for monks, a sixteenth-century inn and hotel, beamed with open fires and two bars. Bar and restaurant food. Car parks, garden. Children allowed. Accommodation. From junction 8 of the M20, follow signs to Hollingbourne, drive through Hollingbourne, then at the water tower turn right and straight over at next crossroads.

OPEN *11.30am–3pm and 6–11pm Mon–Fri; all day at weekends and bank holidays.*

ROCHESTER

The Man of Kent
6–8 John Street, Rochester ME1 1YN
☎ (01634) 818771 Mr and Mrs Sandmann

 Five ever-changing beers available at any one time (100 per year) with local breweries such as Goacher's and Flagship favoured. Also Theobald's cask-conditioned cider.

A friendly old-style pub with one L-shaped bar. Games include chess, bar billiards, darts, carpet bowls and shove ha'penny. Bar food is available at lunchtime and evenings. Parking and garden. Off Victoria Street, near the Main Star Hill junction. Near the school.

OPEN *12–11pm (10.30pm Sun).*

The Star Inn
Star Hill, Rochester ME1 1UZ
☎ (01634) 826811 Vana Bartelow

 Fuller's London Pride usually available, plus guests from independents and micro-breweries such as such as Timothy Taylor Landlord or an Adnams ale.

A boozers' pub in the town centre. One bar, old building. No food. No children.

OPEN *All day, every day.*

Who'd Ha Thot It?
9 Baker Street, Rochester ME1 3DN
☎ (01634) 830144

 Six beers always available including Butchers Brew (brewed specially for the pub), Greene King Abbot, Thomas Hardy Royal Oak, Fuller's London Pride. Guests include Goacher's brews and vary in strength from 3.5% to 5.2% ABV. The landlord tries to favour smaller breweries.

A nineteenth-century pub off the main Maidstone Road, refurbished and with an open fire. There is a games bar and lounge bar, no juke box. Bar food available. Street parking, beer garden. Well-behaved children only.

OPEN *12–11pm (10.30pm Sun).*

ST MARY-IN-THE-MARSH

The Star Inn
St Mary-In-The-Marsh, Romney Marsh TN29 0BX
☎ (01797) 362139
Marc and Jenny van Overstreten

 Shepherd Neame Spitfire plus a seasonal brew usually available.

F amily-run freehouse with large beer garden and views of the church and surrounding countryside. Food served 12–2pm and 7–9pm Mon–Sat, 12.30–2pm Sun. No children's facilities. Car park. Accommodation.

OPEN *11am–3pm and 7–11pm Mon–Sat; 12–3pm and 7–10.30pm Sun.*

SITTINGBOURNE

The Barge
17 Crown Quay Lane, Sittingbourne ME10 3JN
☎ (01795) 423291 John Aitken

 Greene King IPA usually available with a guest beer possibly from Young's, Greene King, Tolly Cobbold, Marston's, Brains, Adnams or Charles Wells.

F riendly, two-bar family pub with restaurant area. Very large garden. Live entertainment on Saturday and Sunday. Food available 11.30am–2pm and 7–9pm Mon–Sat. Children welcome. Car park. Located two minutes off the main High Street, on the edge of Eurolink Industrial Estate.

OPEN *11.30am–11pm (10.30pm Sun).*

The Red Lion

58 High Street, Sittingbourne ME10 4PB
☎ *(01795) 472706* Rod Bailey

Fuller's London Pride and one beer from Swale Brewery usually available, plus four others which may include Wadworth 6X, Greene King Abbot Ale or IPA, Gale's HSB, Harveys Best Bitter, Badger Tanglefoot or Charles Wells Bombardier.

A fourteenth-century inn with a wealth of history and a myriad of famous visitors over the centuries. Lovely garden courtyard. Winner of Kent 1999 Town Centre Pub of the Year. Food served daily: snacks and meals at lunchtimes and meals only in the evenings. Children welcome till 6pm, but no special facilities. Small car park at rear.

OPEN *Summer: 11am–3pm and 5–11pm Mon–Thurs; 11am–11pm Fri–Sat; 12–3pm and 7–10.30pm Sun; Winter: 11am–3pm and 6–11pm Mon–Thurs; Fri–Sun as summer.*

SMARDEN

The Bell Inn

Bell Lane, Smarden, Nr Ashford TN27 8PW
☎ *(01233) 770283* Ian Turner

Shepherd Neame Best, Fuller's London Pride, Goacher's IPA, Morland Old Speckled Hen and Marston's Pedigree are always available plus a couple of guest beers, perhaps from breweries such as Bateman and Young's.

A fifteenth-century inn, beamed with stone floors and an inglenook fireplace. Three bars (one non-smoking). Bar food available. Car park, garden, children's room, accommodation.

OPEN *11.30am–2.30pm and 6–11pm Mon–Sat; 12–3pm and 7–10.30pm Sun.*

SNARGATE

The Red Lion

Snargate, Romney Marsh TN29 9UQ
☎ *(01797) 344648* Doris Jemison

Goacher's Light, Hopdaemon Golden Braid and a house beer, 90 Not Out, brewed by Hopdaemon Brewery usually available, plus five guest beers which may include Goacher's Mild, Bateman XB, Black Sheep Best Bitter, Woodforde's Wherry or something from Cottage or Wolf.

U nspoilt, sixteenth-century pub serving real ale drawn straight from the cask. Real fires, traditional pub games and large garden. No food. Car park. Children welcome, but not in main bar.

OPEN *12–3pm and 7–11pm (10.30pm Sun).*

SOUTHBOROUGH

The Bat & Ball

141 London Road, Southborough, Tunbridge Wells TN4 0NA
☎ *(01892) 518085* Sonia Law

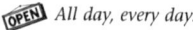A freehouse with five pumps serving a constantly changing range of real ales. These might include Morland Old Speckled Hen, Flagship Nelson's Blood and Destroyer, Fuller's London Pride and brews from Black Sheep, Hook Norton or Larkins.

A n old-fashioned two-bar boozer in a village area. Music. Garden. No food. No children.

OPEN *All day, every day.*

SOUTHFLEET

The Black Lion

Red Street, Southfleet, Gravesend DA13 9QJ
☎ *(01474) 832386*

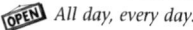A freehouse serving five real ales, plus guests from local micro-breweries.

A traditional two-bar pub with garden. Food available 12–9pm and 12–4.30pm on Sundays, with traditional pies a speciality. Supervised children welcome.

OPEN *All day, every day.*

STONE STREET

The Padwell Arms

Stone Street TN15 0L
☎ *(01732) 761532*

Seven beers always available including Badger Best, Hook Norton Old Hooky and Harveys Best. Also some 300+ guest beers per year mainly from micro-breweries. Definitely no nationals.

A country pub one mile off the A25 between Seal and Borough Green. Features include two real fires and views overlooking apple and pear orchards. Bar food is available at lunchtime. Car park, garden and outside terrace with barbecues in summer. Children allowed under sufferance. Live blues music on the last Saturday of every month.

OPEN *12–3pm and 6–11pm Mon–Sat; 12–3pm and 7–10.30pm Sun.*

TONBRIDGE

The New Drum
54 Lavender Hill, Tonbridge TN9 2AU
☎ *(01732) 365044* Matt Spencer

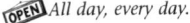 Harveys Best, Fuller's London Pride and Larkins Chiddingstone always available, plus a range of guests including Young's Special, Greene King IPA and Abbot, Tisbury Stonehenge and Charles Wells Bombardier.

A traditional local with one bar and garden. Rolls only available. Children allowed.

OPEN *All day, every day.*

The Royal Oak
Lower Haysden Lane, Tonbridge TN11 9BD
☎ *(01732) 350208* Mr and Mrs Bird

 Adnams Bitter always available plus two or three guest beers (100+ per year), perhaps from Bateman, Wychwood, Ash Vine, Crouch Vale or Harviestoun breweries.

Olde-worlde country pub and restaurant. Bar and restaurant food available at lunchtime. Car park and garden. Children allowed. Follow the signs to Haysden Country Park, south of Tonbridge.

OPEN *11am–11pm Mon–Sat; 12–10.30pm Sun.*

Wonderful Hooden Horse
59 Pembury Road, Tonbridge TN9 2JB
☎ *(01732) 366080* Michelle Crawford

 Greene King IPA always available, plus three guests. Greene King Abbot and Adnams Broadside regularly featured plus customers' choice of guest ales on a weekly basis ('The Ale Spotter's Guide' system).

An old building with great atmosphere. Beer garden. Live music at least once a fortnight. Beer festivals, barbecues and art and craft fairs. Mexican and Mediterranean food available at lunchtime and evenings. Children allowed in the garden and in designated area inside if eating.

OPEN *12–2.30pm and 6–11pm Mon–Thurs; all day Fri–Sun.*

UPNOR

The Tudor Rose
29 High Street, Upnor, Rochester ME2 4XG
☎ *(01634) 715305* Mr Rennie

 A freehouse with six constantly changing real ales always available. Charles Wells Bombardier and Gravesend Shrimpers are regular features.

A 430-year-old pub with one main bar and a small 20-seater restaurant. Large walled garden with children's play area. Food available at lunchtimes and evenings. Children allowed. Near Upnor Castle (follow signs for the castle).

OPEN *11am–11pm Mon–Sat; 12–4pm and 7–10.30pm Sun.*

WEST MALLING

The Lobster Pot
47 Swan Street, West Malling ME19 6JU
☎ *(01732) 843265* Clive Cooper

 A freehouse offering six real ales from breweries such as Goacher's, Adnams and Larkins, as well as lesser-known micro-breweries. Local beers are always a feature.

A traditional 300-year-old pub, runner-up in CAMRA Pub of the Year for Kent in 1999. Two bars, restaurant and function room. Food available at lunchtime and evenings. Children allowed in the restaurant only.

OPEN *12–2.30pm daily; 5–11pm Tues–Fri; 6–11pm Mon and Sat; 7–10.30pm Sun.*

WEST PECKHAM

The Swan on the Green
The Green, West Peckham, Maidstone ME18 5JW
☎ *(01622) 812271* Michelle Harris

 A freehouse and brewpub with a range of real ales brewed on the premises always available. Seasonals and specials also brewed; any celebration is an excuse for a new beer!

A country pub at the heart of a small village community with an emphasis on good food and good beer. Outside seating area. Children allowed. Website: www.swan-on-the-green.co.uk.

Permanent:
WHOOPER 3.5% ABV
TRUMPETER BEST 4.0% ABV
PARLIAMENT 4.8% ABV
SWAN OLD FASHIONED MILD
WHEAT BEER
Seasonal:
GINGER SWAN 3.6% ABV
VALENTINE BEER

OPEN *11am–3pm and 6–11pm Mon–Fri; 11am–4pm and 6–11pm Sat; 12–4pm and 7–10.30pm Sun. (Times can differ seasonally and if there are cricket matches or events on the Green.)*

WHITSTABLE

The Ship Centurion Arminius
111 High Street, Whitstable CT5 1AY
☎ *(01227) 264740*
Janet, Roland and Armin Birks

 One strong bitter always available, such as Cains Formidable, Morland Old Speckled Hen, Nethergate Augustinian, Hop Back Summer Lightning, or Adnams Broadside. Only pub in town to serve cask mild. Adnams Southwold Bitter and Elgood's Black Dog Mild are regular features.

A one-bar town freehouse with disabled access and dining area. Home-cooked bar food served lunchtimes and evenings, Hungarian Goulash Soup and German Bratwurst are specialities. Live music every Thursday night. Children with well-behaved parents allowed in 24-seater sun lounge! Cask Marque award winner on all four casks.

OPEN *11am–11pm Mon–Sat; 12–7pm Sun (closed Sun evening).*

The Wheatsheaf
74 Herne Bay Road, Whitstable
☎ *(01227) 792310* S O'Brien and D Seamans

Greene King IPA and Abbot are always on offer, plus one guest.

Community pub with an emphasis on food, which is served 12–9.30pm Mon–Sat and 12–8pm Sun. Pool, large beer garden. Live music Fridays. Children welcome until 9pm, but no special facilities. Car park.

OPEN *12–11pm (10.30pm Sun).*

WORTH

St Crispin Inn
The Street, Worth, Deal CT14 0DF
☎ *(01304) 612081* Jane O'Brien

 A freehouse serving Shepherd Neame Master Brew plus three guests. Examples include Shepherd Neame Early Bird, Rye and Coriander plus Gale's HSB.

A sixteenth-century oak-beamed pub. One open bar, patio, large beer garden. Bat and chat pitch. Accommodation. Food served at lunchtime and evenings in a separate 28-seater restaurant. Children allowed.

OPEN *Generally all day, every day in summer. 11am–2.30pm and 5–11pm (10.30pm Sun) at other times.*

YOU TELL US

* *The Kings Head,* 38 London Road, Sittingbourne
* *The Red Lion,* 61 High Street, Bluetown, Sheerness
* *The Royal Oak,* 2 High Street, Shoreham

Places Featured:

Accrington
Arkholme
Bispham Green
Blackburn
Blackpool
Bretherton
Burnley
Chorley
Clayton-le-Moors
Clitheroe
Cliviger
Colne
Crawshawbooth
Croston
Dalton
Darwen

Entwhistle
Fleetwood
Great Harwood
Greenhowarth
Haslingden
Heskin
Lea Town
Little Eccleston
Lytham
Ormskirk
Preston
Upholland
Whalley
Wharles
Wheelton
Wrightington

THE BREWERIES

BLACKPOOL BREWERY CO.

6 The Old Dairy, George Street, Blackpool FY1 3RP
☎ *(01253) 304999*

 GOLDEN SMILE 3.7% ABV
Award-winning brew, full-flavoured with hoppy undertones.

BLACKPOOL BITTER 4.0% ABV
A golden blend of strength and flavour that is an original experience.

BPA (BLACKPOOL PALE ALE) 4.2% ABV
Blackpool's very own Pale Ale. Proven to be a great favourite with the North West real ale aficionados.

Seasonal:
BLACK DIAMOND MILD 3.4% ABV
CHRISTMAS LIGHTS 3.9% ABV
SWEET FA 3.9% ABV
LIGHTSOUT 4.4% ABV

BRYSON'S BREWS

1 Summerside, 25 Oxcliffe Road, Heysham LA3 1PU
☎ *(01524) 852150*

 BARROWS BITTER 4.2% ABV
Straw coloured 'bitter' bitter.

ACREMOSS 4.5% ABV
Bitter brewed with amber malt.

Seasonal:
WAMMELLERS 4.0%
A summer ale.
PATRICKS PORTER 4.3%
A winter ale.
Plus other one-offs and specials.

MOORHOUSE'S BREWERY LTD

4 Moorhouse Street, Burnley BB1 5EN
☎ *(01282) 422864*
www.moorhouses.co.uk

 BLACK CAT 3.4% ABV
Refreshing.

PREMIER BITTER 3.7% ABV
Full-flavoured with good hoppiness.

PRIDE OF PENDLE 4.1% ABV
Smooth and well-rounded.

PENDLE WITCHES BREW 5.1% ABV
Complex, sweet malt and fruit flavour.

OLD WHEELTON BREWERY

Dressers Arms, 9 Briers Row, Wheelton, Chorley PR6 8HD
☎ *(01254) 830041*

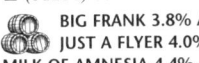 **BIG FRANK 3.8% ABV**
JUST A FLYER 4.0% ABV

MILK OF AMNESIA 4.4% ABV

Seasonal:
wINTER BREW 4.4% ABV
No, this is not a typo! The brewery specify that the 'w' is in lower case and the rest of the beer name in capitals!

PICKS BREWERY
Red Lion Hotel, Willows Lane, Greenhowarth,
Accrington BB5 3SJ
☎ *(01254) 233194*

 MOORGATE MILD 3.5% ABV
PALE ALE 3.7% ABV
BEDLAM BITTER 3.9% ABV
LIONS MANE 4.2% ABV
PORTER 4.5% ABV
LIONS PRIDE 5.4% ABV

PICTISH BREWERY
Unit 9, Canalside Industrial Estate, Woodbine
Street East, Rochdale OL16 5LB
☎ *(01706) 522227*
www.pictish-brewing.co.uk

 BREWER'S GOLD 3.8% ABV
Pale golden session beer with spicy hop
aroma.
CELTIC WARRIOR 4.2% ABV
Mid-brown premium ale.
PICTISH PORTER 4.4% ABV
Complex black beer. Available November–March.
SUMMER SOLSTICE 4.7% ABV
Refreshing blonde ale. Available May–August.
Plus monthly specials.

THE THREE B'S BREWERY
Laneside Works, Stockclough Lane, Fennicowles,
Blackburn BB2 5JR
☎ *(01254) 207686*

 STOKERS SLAK 3.6% ABV
Mild.
BOBBIN'S BITTER 3.8% ABV
TACKLER'S TIPPLE 4.3% ABV
PINCH NOGGIN 4.6% ABV
KNOCKER UP 4.8% ABV
Porter.
SHUTTLE ALE 5.2% ABV
Plus occasional beers.

DANIEL THWAITES BREWERY
PO Box 50, Star Brewery, Blackburn BB1 5BU
☎ *(01254) 686868*
www.thwaites.co.uk

BEST MILD 3.3% ABV
Sweet and full-bodied.
BITTER 3.6% ABV
Amber, distinctive and malty.
CHAIRMAN'S 4.2% ABV
Golden, easy-drinking.
DANIEL'S HAMMER 5.0% ABV
Pale and malty with dry hoppy finish.
Plus occasional beers.

THE PUBS

ACCRINGTON

The George Hotel
185 Blackburn Road, Accrington BB5 0AF
☎ *(01254) 383441*

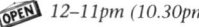 Four beers always available from an ever-changing list that might include Titanic
Stout, Cains FA, Passageway St Arnold and
Goose Eye Bitter.

A friendly freehouse with an open-plan bar
area and separate restaurant in converted
stables. Bar and restaurant food available at
lunchtime and evenings. Street parking,
garden/patio area. Children allowed.
Accommodation. Close to the railway and
bus stations.

OPEN *12–11pm (10.30pm Sun).*

ARKHOLME

The Bay Horse Hotel
Arkholme, Carnforth
☎ *(015242) 21425)* Peter Dawson Jackson

 A guest beer usually available, perhaps
Greene King Abbot Ale, Morland Old
Speckled Hen, Everards Tiger or one of
several other regular beers.

Typical, unspoilt country pub. Food served
Tues–Sun lunchtimes and every evening.
Car park. Children welcome. From junction
35 of the M6, follow the Kirkby Lonsdale
sign for 5 miles.

OPEN *11.30am–3pm and 6–11pm*
(10.30pm Sun).

BISPHAM GREEN

The Eagle & Child
Bispham Green, Nr Ormskirk L40 3SG
☎ *(01257) 462297* John Mansfield

A freehouse with Moorhouse's Black Cat
Mild and Thwaites Bitter always
available. Also five guests from breweries
such as Hanby, Hart or Phoenix. Annual beer
festival on May bank holiday with a selection
of 50 real ales.

An old-fashioned country pub with
flagstone floors, old furniture, bowling
green, croquet lawn and beer garden. Food
served at lunchtime and evenings. Children
allowed.

OPEN *12–3pm and 5.30–11pm Mon–Sat;*
all day Sun.

BLACKBURN

The Cellar Bar
39–41 King Street, Blackburn
☎ *(01254) 698111* Dan Hook

 Two regularly changing beers available often from Moorhouse's, Three B's, Castle Eden, Dent, Jennings or RCH.

Buried underground in the first mayor of Blackburn's family home and the oldest Georgian house in the town, this pub has a cosy, friendly atmosphere, real fire, live music and the biggest beer garden in Blackburn. No food. Car park. Children welcome.

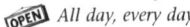 *11am–11pm Mon–Tues; 11am–1am Wed–Fri; 7pm–1am Sat; 7–10.30pm Sun.*

The Postal Order
15 Darwen Street, Blackburn BB2 2BY
☎ *(01254) 676400* Neil and Sharon Longley

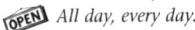 A Wetherspoon's pub serving several guest ales. Thwaites Mild is a regular feature, and other guests might include Exmoor Fox, Gale's GB and Cotleigh Barn Owl.

A large, traditional town pub near the Cathedral. One long bar with two separate areas. Non-smoking dining area. Food served all day. Children welcome.

All day, every day.

BLACKPOOL

The Shovels
Common Edge Road, Blackpool FY4 5DH
☎ *(01253) 762702* Steve and Helen Norris

Six guest beers always available from breweries such as Hart. Micro-breweries favoured whenever possible.

A steak 'n' ale pub in a suburban location. CAMRA Blackpool and Fylde Pub of the Year 2001. One bar, non-smoking area, real fire, front patio, disabled access/toilet. Dining area, conservatory. Food served every day (12–9.30pm). Children allowed, but not near bar area. Situated just off the M55.

All day, every day.

BRETHERTON

The Blue Anchor Inn
21 South Road, Bretherton, Nr Leyland PR26 9AB
☎ *(01772) 600270* Michele Fielden

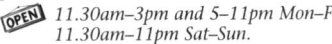 Timothy Taylor Landlord, Marston's Pedigree and Moorehouse's Black Cat are among the beers always available, and the three guests might be something from Hart, Phoenix, Marston's, Moorehouse's, Boggart Hole Clough, Cottage or Blackpool.

Busy traditional village pub with large beer garden and play area. Food served 11.30am–2pm and 5–9.30pm Mon–Fri and all day at weekends. Children welcome. Car park.

11.30am–3pm and 5–11pm Mon–Fri; 11.30am–11pm Sat–Sun.

BURNLEY

The Ministry of Ale
9 Trafalgar Street, Burnley BB11 1TQ
☎ *(01282) 830909* Michael Jacques

 Home of the Moonstone Brewery, with two home ales always available, plus at least two guests which could be a Moonstone special or a beer from any independent brewery, but especially local ones such as Phoenix, Bank Top and Moorehouse's. Over 350 beers featured in the last 18 months, with repeats avoided.

A recently refurbished, modern café-style brewpub situated on the edge of town. No food. No children.

BLACK STAR 3.4% ABV
A mild.
SUNSTONE ANNIVERSARY ALE 3.8% ABV
TIGER'S EYE 3.8% ABV
TRUMPINGTON BITTER 4.2% ABV
CRAGGY'S WOBBLE 4.5% ABV
MOONSTONE DARK 4.5% ABV
RED JASPER 6.0% ABV
A ruby winter ale.

5–11pm Mon–Thurs (closed lunchtimes); 12–11pm Fri–Sat; 12–10.30pm Sun.

The Sparrowhawk Hotel
Church Street, Burnley BB11 2DN
☎ *(01282) 421551* Mr Baker

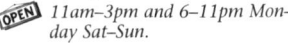 A freehouse specialising in real ales. Moorhouse's Premier and Pendle Witches Brew always available plus Ruffled Feathers (brewed especially for The Sparrowhawk by Moorhouse's) or a Hart Brewery ale.

A country-style inn in the town centre. Two bars, restaurant and accommodation. Food served at lunchtime and evenings. Children allowed.

11am–3pm and 6–11pm Mon–Fri; all day Sat–Sun.

CHORLEY

Malt 'n' Hops
50–2 Friday Street, Chorley PR6 0AH
☎ *(01257) 260967*

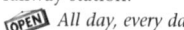 Timothy Taylor Landlord and Coach House Gunpowder Mild always available plus four guest beers (at least one changed every day) perhaps including something from Lloyds Country Beers, Batham, Cains and many other breweries.

A Victorian-style, one-bar pub ideal for trainspotters. Bar food available at lunchtime. Parking. Children allowed. Just 200 yards behind the Manchester to Preston railway station.

OPEN *All day, every day.*

CLAYTON-LE-MOORS

The Albion
243 Whalley Road, Clayton-le-Moors, Accrington BB5 5HD
☎ *(01254) 238585* John Burke

Porter Dark Mild, Bitter, Porter and Sunshine always available plus seasonal ales such as Ginger Beer, Floral Dance, Young Tom and others.

A traditional real ale pub. One bar, darts, beer garden. Mooring spot for barges on the Liverpool to Leeds canal. Sandwiches only. Children allowed in the garden only.

OPEN *5–11pm Mon–Tues; all day Wed–Sun.*

CLITHEROE

The New Inn
Parson Lane, Clitheroe BB7 2JN
☎ *(01200) 423312* Mr and Mrs Lees

A Whitbread house with a guest beer policy serving Fuller's London Pride, Marston's Pedigree and a Moorhouse's brew plus a guest, changed weekly, from smaller breweries if possible. Beers featured have included Greene King Abbot, Gale's HSB and Wadworth 6X.

An old English pub with one bar and an open fire. Four adjoining rooms, plus a non-smoking room. No music or games, but folk club on Friday nights. Children allowed in designated area. No food.

OPEN *All day, every day.*

CLIVIGER

Queens
412 Burnley Road, Cliviger, Nr Burnley
☎ *(01282) 436712* Alec Heap

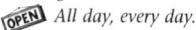 Three guest beers usually available from a wide range of micro-breweries.

Simple alehouse. No pool table, juke box or bandits. No food. Children welcome, but there are no special facilities.

OPEN *1–11pm Mon–Sat; 12–10.30pm Sun.*

COLNE

The Hare & Hounds Inn
Black Lane Ends, Colne BB8 7EP
☎ *(01282) 863070* John Holmes

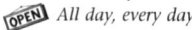 A freehouse serving Timothy Taylor Golden Best and Landlord on a regular basis plus various guests such as Black Sheep Bitter.

A country pub. One bar, real fires, stone and wood floors and beams. Food available all day. Children welcome.

OPEN *All day, every day.*

CRAWSHAWBOOTH

The White Bull
Burnley Road, Crawshawbooth BB4 8AJ
☎ *(01706) 260394* Elaine Bibby

Tied to Beartown, so the six permanent beers are all from the Beartown Brewery (including Bearskinful, Bear Ass, Bruins Ruin, Wheat Beer and Polar Eclipse). One guest is sometimes available, perhaps from Wye Valley or Titanic, and one of the permanent beers is taken off when a guest is to be served.

Quiet traditional village pub, with no alcopops! Old building, with beams, Scottish tartan carpet, Indian restaurant upstairs (no food in the pub) and beer garden. Children allowed. Car park.

OPEN *5–11pm Mon–Fri; 12–11pm Sat; 12–10.30pm Sun.*

CROSTON

The Black Horse
Westhead Road, Croston, Nr Chorley PR5 7RQ
☎ *(01772) 600338* Mr G Conroy

Six traditional cask bitters and one mild always available, from breweries such as Black Sheep, Caledonian, Jennings, Moorhouse's, Greene King and Timothy Taylor, plus smaller micro-breweries. Two beer festivals held each year around April and October.

Completely refurbished in 1997, this traditional village freehouse serves bar and restaurant food at lunchtimes and evenings, at very competitive prices. Car park, beer garden, children's play area, bowling green and French boules pitch are all available, and specially organised parties and meals can be catered for. In the village of Croston, close to Chorley and midway between Preston and Southport.

OPEN *All day, every day.*

DALTON

The Beacon Inn

Beacon Lane, Dalton WN8 7RR
☎ *(01695) 632607* Kevin Balke

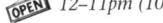Jennings Mild, Bitter and Cumberland regularly available plus a guest beer which may include Fuller's London Pride or something from Castle Eden.

Acquired by Jennings in 1999, this country pub is much used by ramblers as it is situated by Ashurst Beacon Point. Also handy for Beacon Golf Club. Food served 12–2pm Tues–Sat, 12–5pm Sun. Car park. Large beer garden. Children welcome.

OPEN *12–11pm (10.30pm Sun).*

DARWEN

Greenfield Inn

Lower Barn Street, Darwen BB3 2HQ
☎ *(01254) 703945* Carol Wood

Timothy Taylor Landlord, Greene King Abbot and Charles Wells Bombardier always available, plus two guests.

A traditional one-room pub with beer garden. Food served at lunchtime and evenings. Children allowed. Situated on the outskirts of Darwen.

OPEN *12–11pm (10.30pm Sun).*

ENTWHISTLE

The Strawbury Duck

Overshores Road, Entwhistle, Bolton BL7 0LU
☎ *(01204) 852013* Roger and Lisa Boardman

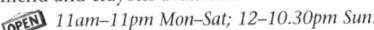Eight real ales available at all times. Moorhouse's Pendle Witches, Timothy Taylor Landlord and Black Sheep Special are permanent fixtures, and a wide variety of guests are also served. Regulars include Morland Old Speckled Hen, Marston's Pedigree and ales from Brains or Caledonian including seasonals.

A 300-year-old pub situated next to Entwhistle Railway Station. One bar, several dining areas, pool room, non-smoking room, beer garden, accommodation. Food served 12–9.30pm Mon–Thurs, all day Fri–Sun. Children welcome, with special menu and crayons available.

OPEN *11am–11pm Mon–Sat; 12–10.30pm Sun.*

FLEETWOOD

Wyre Lounge Bar

Marine Hall, The Esplanade, Fleetwood FY7 6HF
☎ *(01253) 771141*

Eight beers always available including Moorhouse's brews. Also 200+ guest beers per year which may come from Young's, Charles Wells, Banks's and Timothy Taylor.

Part of the Marine Hall Sports Complex in Fleetwood. Food available at lunchtime. CAMRA Pub of the Year. Car park, garden, function room. No children.

OPEN *11am–4.30pm and 7–11pm Mon–Sat; 12–4pm and 7–10.30pm Sun.*

GREAT HARWOOD

The Dog & Otter

Cliffe Lane, Great Harwood, Blackburn BB6 7PG
☎ *(01254) 885760* Catherine Darnley

A Jennings-managed house with Jennings Bitter and Cumberland Ale always available, plus one rotating guest ale, perhaps Fuller's London Pride or a Marston's brew.

A recently refurbished pub/restaurant with one bar and outside tables. Old-style building with extension. Traditional pub food including specials served all day Fri–Sun. Children allowed.

OPEN *All day, every day.*

The Royal Hotel

Station Road, Great Harwood, Blackburn BB6 7BA
☎ *(01254) 883541* Janice and Peter Boothe

A freehouse with seven constantly changing beers (over 350 per year) from a varied selection from around the UK. Regular guests include brews from Phoenix, Hart, Anglo-Dutch, Barngates, Three Bs, Picks and Cropton. An eighth hand pump serves draught Sarsparilla (non-alcoholic).

A Victorian pub/hotel with public bar, separate dining area, separate live music area and beer garden. English Tourist Council 3-diamond accommodation. Food available. No football, no discos, no karaoke! Live music Fri, musicians' jam sessions Mon (mainly blues and folk). Children allowed. Great Harwood is between Blackburn, Accrington and Clitheroe. Website: www.rock-n-royal.co.uk.

OPEN *12–11pm (10.30pm Sun).*

GREENHOWARTH

The Red Lion Hotel

Willows Lane, Greenhowarth, Accrington BB5 3SJ
☎ *(01254) 233194*

 A freehouse situated on the same site as Picks Brewery naturally stocking mostly Picks ales although not a tied house. Five beers always available, usually Moorgate Mild, Bedlam, Porter and Lions Pride and one of either Lions Mane or Pale Ale.

A village pub with games room, lounge and car parking facilities. Food is available 12–2pm daily. Children allowed. Call for directions.

[OPEN] *12–3pm and 7–11pm Mon–Thurs; 12–11pm Fri–Sat; 12–10.30pm Sun.*

HASLINGDEN

The Griffin Inn

84 Hud Rake, Haslingden, Rossendale BB4 5AF
☎ *(01706) 214021* David Porter

Home of the Porter Brewing Company. A brewpub with Dark Mild, Bitter, Porter, Sunshine and Rossendale Ale brewed and served on the premises.

A traditional no-frills alehouse and local community pub on the northern edge of town. No music or TV. No food. No children.

 DARK MILD 3.3% ABV
 BITTER 3.8% ABV
ROSSENDALE ALE 4.2% ABV
PORTER 5.0% ABV
SUNSHINE 5.3% ABV
Plus occasional and seasonal brews.

[OPEN] *All day, every day.*

HESKIN

The Farmer's Arms

85 Wood Lane, Heskin PR7 5NP
☎ *(01257) 451276*
Mr and Mrs Malcolm Rothwell

Castle Eden Ale and Timothy Taylor Landlord are among the beers always available, and the one guest may be something like Wadworth 6X or Morland Old Speckled Hen.

A quaint, white, flowery country village pub in an eighteenth-century building. Food served – there is a non-smoking dining area. Well-behaved children allowed. Garden, five letting rooms, car park.

[OPEN] *12–11pm (10.30pm Sun).*

LEA TOWN

The Saddle Inn

Sidgreaves Lane, Lea Town, Preston PR4 0RS
☎ *(01772) 726616* Carole Buck

A Thwaites tied house, with Thwaites Bitter and Lancaster Bomber permanently featured, plus one seasonal guest beer.

Traditional country pub. Food served all day until 9pm Mon–Sat and until 8pm Sun. Children are welcome, and there is a children's play area. Large car park.

[OPEN] *All day, every day.*

LITTLE ECCLESTON

The Cartford Hotel

Cartford Lane, Little Eccleston, Preston PR3 0YP
☎ *(01995) 670166. Fax (01995) 671785*
Andrew Mellodew

The Hart Brewery operates from the premises producing a range of 16 beers for sale in the hotel and some local freehouses. Fuller's London Pride and Timothy Taylor Landlord are also regularly available plus a range of over 3,000 other beers so far served on a guest basis.

An award-winning, 400-year-old family pub. One large bar, large garden with children's play area. Quiet eating area with food available at lunchtime and evenings. Children allowed. Brewery tours by appointment. Car park. Games room. Accommodation.

GOLD BEACH 3.8% ABV
A true summer session ale, light and hoppy.
SECOND COMING 3.8% ABV
Easter special. Light and sweet.
GOLDEN SQUIRREL 3.9% ABV
A summer ale blending Squirrels Hoard and Gold Beach.
DISHY DEBBIE 4.0% ABV
A year-round session beer. Light and golden with a citrus flavour.
SQUIRRELS HOARD 4.0% ABV
Award-winning session beer. Intense nut taste.
AMBASSADOR 4.2% ABV
A relatively dry beer, red in colour.
NEMESIS 4.5% ABV
Golden premier bitter. Also known as The Goddess.
NO BALLS 4.5% ABV
Christmas ale. Light and refreshing.
CRIMIN ALE PORTER 4.7% ABV
A true porter brewed once a year.
VAL.(ADDICTION) 4.8% ABV
Dark, sweet, easy-drinking beer.
AMADEUS 5.0% ABV
Dark, rich winter warmer.
COBBLESTONE 5.0% ABV
A stout-style beer.
EXCALIBUR 5.0% ABV
A light lager-style beer with citrus taste and sweet finish.
OLD RAM 5.0% ABV
Bronze, full-bodied beer. Brewed more in the winter than summer.
CESTRIAN HART 5.2% ABV
Dark and sweet.
STEAMIN' JACK 5.5% ABV
A version of Nemesis.

OPEN *12–3pm and 6.30–11pm Mon–Sat; all day Sun.*

LYTHAM

The Taps

Henry Street, Lytham FY8 5LE
☎ *(01253) 736226* Ian Rigg

A Whitbread house with an extensive guest beer policy. Hook Norton Old Hooky, Wychwood The Dog's Bollocks, Orkney Dark Island and Moorhouse's Pendle Witches Brew regularly available, plus beers from breweries such as Black Sheep.

A town pub with yard, viewing cellar. Disabled facilities and toilets. Food served at lunchtime only. Children allowed only if dining.

OPEN *All day, every day.*

ORMSKIRK

The Hayfield

County Road, Ormskirk L39 1NN
☎ *(01695) 571157* Godfrey Hedges

Cains Mild is among the beers always on offer, plus eight guests from a variety of breweries, including Jennings, Phoenix, Slaters (Eccleshall), Rooster's, Black Sheep, Weetwood, Moorhouse's and Robinson's, to name but a few!

Busy freehouse with a warm, friendly atmosphere. Food served 12–3pm and 5.30–8.30pm Mon–Sat plus 12–7.30pm Sun. No children's facilities. Car park. On the main A59 road in Ormskirk.

OPEN *12–11pm (10.30pm Sun).*

The Queen's Head

30 Moor Street, Ormskirk L39 2AQ
☎ *(01695) 574380* Gerry Fleming

Up to four guest ales available including Fuller's London Pride, Shepherd Neame Bishop's Finger and Spitfire, Black Sheep Special or Wychwood The Dog's Bollocks.

A traditional one-bar pub with beer garden. Annual themed beer festival. Food served 12–2pm Mon–Sat. Well-behaved children allowed.

OPEN *All day, every day.*

PRESTON

The Hogshead

Moss Cottage, Fylde Road, Preston PR1 2XQ
☎ *(01772) 252870*
Steven Leyshon (assistant manager)

Moorhouse's Pendle Witches and Black Cat Mild are always on offer. Three or four guest ales, changed every few days (20 per month), might include Hook Norton Old Hooky, Timothy Taylor Landlord or something from Brakspear. There is also an Ale of the Month, featuring a beer such as Hoskins & Oldfield Ginger Tom.

Drinkers' pub in a listed building on the outskirts of town. Food available 12–9pm Sun–Thurs and 12–8pm Fri–Sat. Beer garden and patio. Children not allowed. Parking available. Annual beer festivals held (call for more details).

OPEN *11.30am–11pm Mon–Sat;*
12–10.30pm Sun.

The Old Black Bull

35 Friargate, Preston PR1 2AT
☎ *(01772) 823397* Stan Eaton

A beer from Cains is among those permanently served. The eight guest beers are changed every couple of days, and might include Timothy Taylor Landlord and Fuller's London Pride.

Old traditional pub in the town centre. Food served until 4pm. Pool and darts, patio. Live music on Saturday nights. Children allowed during the daytime.

OPEN *10.30am–11pm Mon–Sat;*
12–10.30pm Sun.

The Stanley Arms

Lancaster Road, Preston PR1 1DA
☎ *(01772) 254004* Anthony Quinn

Six ales are always on offer, including three constantly changing guest beers.

A traditional pub in a Grade II listed building. The downstairs bar area has recently undergone a minor refurbishment. Food available 11am–7pm Mon–Sat and 12.30–6pm Sun. Big-screen TV. The newly refurbished restaurant on the second floor is available for hire.

OPEN *All day, every day.*

UPHOLLAND

The White Lion

10 Church Street, Upholland WN8 0ND
☎ *(01695) 622727* Jim and Jean Gardner

Tied to Thwaites, so Thwaites Best Bitter permanently available, plus two guests, changed every couple of months, often including other Thwaites beers such as Swashbuckler, Golden Charmer and Daniel's Hammer.

Village pub built in the sixteenth century, with many of the original features still present. Bar snacks served. Traditional pub games such as darts and dominoes. Non-smoking dining area, patio and car park. Children allowed.

OPEN *5–11pm Mon–Fri; 12–11pm Sat;*
12–10.30pm Sun.

WHALLEY

The Swan Hotel

62 King Street, Whalley BB7 9SN
☎ *(01254) 822195* CD Liz and Sara White

Swan Ale brewed by Moorhouse's permanently available. Black Sheep Bitter usually stocked, plus one changing guest.

A small, friendly, family-run hotel. Food served 12–9pm Mon–Thurs, 12–8pm Fri–Sat, and 12–7pm Sun. Well-behaved children allowed until 9pm. Car park.

OPEN *All day, every day.*

WHARLES

The Eagle & Child Inn

Church Road, Wharles, Nr Kirkham
☎ *(01772) 690312* Brian Tatham

Two guest beers regularly available perhaps from Clark's, Wadworth or Eccleshall.

Relaxed atmosphere and lovely antiques in this Grade II listed thatched country inn (circa 1650) on the Fylde coast. No food. Large car park. Well-behaved children welcome, subject to licensing regulations.

OPEN *7–11pm Mon–Sat; 12–4pm and*
7–10.30pm Sun.

WHEELTON

The Dresser's Arms
9 Briers Brow, Wheelton, Chorley PR6 8HD
☎ *(01254) 830041* Steve and Trudie Turner

A true freehouse with eight hand pumps serving one or two Old Wheelton brews at any one time, plus a selection of ales from Timothy Taylor, Phoenix, Hart, Pictish and any local micro-brewery. The Old Wheelton Brewery is located on the same premises, but operates independently.

A village pub with oak beams, real fires and a cosy atmosphere. Food available with separate Cantonese restaurant upstairs. Beer garden. Car park. Children allowed.

OPEN *11am–11pm Mon–Sat; 12–10.30pm Sun.*

WRIGHTINGTON

Hinds Head
Mossy Lea Road, Wrightington, Nr Wigan WN6 9RN
☎ *(01257) 421168* Mr Ferro

Two guest ales always available such as Morland Old Speckled Hen.

A big traditional pub with restaurant, beer garden and bowling green. Food available. Children allowed.

OPEN *11am–2.30pm Tues–Thurs; 5.30–11pm Mon–Thurs; all day Fri–Sun.*

YOU TELL US

* *Lane Ends Hotel,* Weeton Road, Wesham, Preston
* *The Prince Albert,* 109 Wigan Road, Westhead
* *The Tap & Spile,* Fylde Road, Ashton-on-Ribble, Preston

Places Featured:

Ashby de la Zouch
Aylestone
Barrow on Soar
Barrowden
East Langton
Frisby on the Wreake
Glenfield
Glooston
Hemington
Hose
Kirby Muxloe
Leicester
Loughborough
Market Bosworth
Medbourne

Oadby
Old Dalby
Saddington
Shawell
Shearsby
Somerby
Smisby
Sutton Bassett
Thorpe Satchville
Thurnby
Walcote
Waltham-on-the-Wolds
Wigston Magna
Wymeswold

THE BREWERIES

BELVOIR BREWERY LTD

Woodhill, Nottingham Lane, Old Dalby LE14 3LX
☎ *(01664) 823455*
www.belvoirbrewery.co.uk

 WHIPPLING GOLDEN BITTER 3.6% ABV
Light, refreshing and hoppy.
STAR BITTER 3.9% ABV
Citrus fruit and hoppy flavour.
BEAVER 4.3% ABV
Smooth, balanced with malt flavour and bitter finish.
PEACOCK'S GLORY 4.7% ABV
Golden, fruity and hoppy.
Plus occasional brews.

BREWSTERS BREWING CO. LTD

Penn Lane, Stathern, Melton Mowbray LE14 4JA
☎ *(01949) 861868*
www.brewsters.co.uk

 HOPHEAD 3.6% ABV
MARQUIS 3.8% ABV
MONTY'S MILD 4.0% ABV
BITTER 4.2% ABV
SERENDIPITY VAR. ABV
A range of beers.
CLAUDIA 4.5% ABV
Seasonal brew.
VPA 4.5% ABV
FRAU BRAU 5.0% ABV
Seasonal brew.
BREWSTERS STOCKING 5.5% ABV
Seasonal brew.
DOMEHEAD 5.6% ABV
Seasonal brew.

EVERARDS BREWERY LTD

Castle Acres, Narborough LE9 5BY
☎ *(0116) 2014100*
www.everards.co.uk

 BEACON BITTER 3.8% ABV
Award-winning, fresh, clean taste.
TIGER BEST BITTER 4.2% ABV
Good body, dry hopped and long bitter finish.
OLD ORIGINAL 5.2% ABV
Copper-brown and sweetish.
Plus seasonal beers.

THE FEATHERSTONE BREWERY

Unit 3 King Street Buildings, King Street, Enderby LE9 5NT
☎ *(0116) 275 0952*

HOWS HOWLER 3.6% ABV
BEST BITTER 4.2% ABV
STAGE ALE 4.8% ABV
VULCAN 5.1% ABV
Special.
KINGSTONE BITTER 7.2% ABV

THE GRAINSTORE BREWERY

Davises Brewing Co. Ltd, Station Approach, Oakham LE15 6RE
☎ *(01572) 770065* (Brewery tours)

COOKING 3.6% ABV
Golden and well-balanced.
TRIPLE B 4.2% ABV
Malty sweetness with balancing hop flavours.
STEAMIN' BILLY BITTER 4.3% ABV
TEN FIFTY 5.0 ABV
Easy-drinking sweet maltiness, with bitter finish.
Seasonals:
GOLD 4.5% ABV
SPRINGTIME 4.5% ABV
THREE KINGS 4.5% ABV
TUPPING ALE 4.5% ABV
WINTER NIP 7.3% ABV

HOSKINS & OLDFIELD BREWERY LTD

Moving premises. Brews temporarily being produced by Tower and Leadmill.

 HOB BEST MILD 3.5% ABV
Dark, balanced, traditional mild.

HOSKINS BITTER 4.0% ABV

WHITE DOLPHIN WHEAT BEER 4.0% ABV
Pale, tart wheat beer.

TOM KELLY STOUT 4.2% ABV
Dark and malty with hoppy bitterness.

SUPREME 4.4% ABV
Golden and refreshing.

EXS 5.0% ABV
Golden and well-balanced.

SHARDLOW BREWING CO. LTD

Old Brewery Stables, British Waterways Yard, Cavendish Bridge DE72 2HL
☎ *(01332) 799188*

 CHANCELLOR'S REVENGE 3.6% ABV
Pale session bitter.

CAVENDISH DARK 3.7% ABV
Mild, well-balanced, hoppy bitter.

BEST BITTER 3.9% ABV

GOLDENHOP 4.1% ABV

KILN HOUSE 4.1% ABV
Refreshing with bitter aftertaste.

NARROWBOAT 4.3% ABV

OLD STABLE BREW 4.4% ABV
Hoppy, dark ale blended from three malts.

CAVENDISH GOLD 4.5% ABV

REVEREND EATON'S 4.5% ABV

FESTIVAL 4.6% ABV
Originally a special, now permanent.

MAYFLY 4.8% ABV
Pale premium bitter.

FIVE BELLS 5.0% ABV
Ruby-coloured with bittersweet finish.

PLATINUM BLONDE 5.0% ABV
Powerful and rich.

WHISTLE STOP 5.0 ABV

FROSTBITE 6.0% ABV
Christmas ale.

Plus occasional brews.

WICKED HATHERN BREWERY

46 Derby Road, Hathern, Loughborough LE12 9LD
☎ *(01509) 842364*
www.wicked-hathern.co.uk

 DOBLE'S DOG 3.5% ABV
HAWTHORN GOLD 3.5% ABV
WHB (WICKED HATHERN BITTER) 3.8% ABV
COCKFIGHTER 4.2% ABV
SOAR HEAD 4.8% ABV

THE PUBS

ASHBY DE LA ZOUCH

The Ashby Court Hotel

34 Wood Street, Ashby de la Zouch LE65 1EL
☎ *(01530) 415176* Nigel

 A freehouse with Shardlow Reverend Eaton's Ale and Golden Hop permanently available, plus a weekly changing guest, perhaps Springhead Best Bitter, Everards Tiger or Brunswick The Usual.

Mock-Tudor town pub with spacious restaurant. Occasional live music. Ten en-suite letting rooms. Accompanied children allowed. Car park.

 11am–2.30pm and 5–11pm Mon–Thurs; 11am–11pm Fri–Sat; 12–2.30pm and 7–10.30pm Sun.

AYLESTONE

The Black Horse

65 Narrow Lane, Aylestone
☎ *(0116) 283 2811 Neil Spears*

 Tied to Everards, with Beacon, Tiger and Original always on offer, plus two seasonal guests.

Village community pub in a nineteenth-century building, just about to be refurbished. Lounge bar and snug, garden. Food available. No children

 11am–2.30pm and 6–11pm Mon–Thurs; 11am–11pm Fri–Sat; 12–4pm and 7–10.30pm Sun.

BARROW ON SOAR

The Navigation

Mill Lane, Barrow on Soar LE12 8LQ
☎ *(01509) 412842 Pete Lane*

 Old Laxey Bosun Bitter, Belvoir Star Bitter, Marston's Pedigree and Banks's Bitter are the beers always on offer, and the two guests, changed every three or four days, might feature Greene King Abbot, Shepherd Neame Bishop's Finger or Spitfire, or Morrells Varsity.

Village pub on the river, with garden for 75 people. Food is available, and there is a non-smoking dining area. The pub has two darts teams. Children allowed. Can be difficult to find, so ask locally or phone for directions.

 11am–11pm Mon–Sat; 12–10.30pm Sun.

BARROWDEN

The Exeter Arms

Main Street, Barrowden, Rutland LE15 8EQ
☎ *(01572) 747247* Mr Peter Blencowe

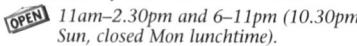A freehouse and home of the Blencowe Brewing Company. A full range of brews is always available (and only sold here). Also various guests such as Fuller's London Pride, Greene King IPA and seasonal ales from various brewers. The aim is only to repeat the guest beers a maximum of three times a year.

A very traditional country pub, situated off the beaten track. One bar, huge garden. Brewery tours by appointment only. Food available Tues–Sun lunchtimes and Tues–Sat evenings. Accommodation consists of two twin rooms and one double. Children allowed. Ring for directions. Website: www.exeterarms.com.

BARROWDEN BOYS 3.6% ABV
A year-round session bitter.
BEACH BOYS 3.8% ABV
Brewed mainly in summer.
LOVER BOYS 3.8% ABV
Valentine's Day special.
YOUNG BOYS 4.1% ABV
BIG BOYS 4.5% ABV
DANNY BOY 4.5% ABV
An autumn-winter stout.
STRONG BOYS 5% ABV
Brewed mainly in autumn and winter.

11am–2.30pm and 6–11pm (10.30pm Sun, closed Mon lunchtime).

EAST LANGTON

The Bell Inn

Main Street, East Langton, Market Harborough
☎ *(01858) 545278*

A freehouse and home of the Langton Brewery. Both home brews always available plus a range of real ales. Greene King Abbot and IPA, Timothy Taylor Landlord, Marston's Pedigree and Jennings ales are regular features but unusual brews are stocked whenever possible. Also a good range of wines.

A traditional county pub in the heart of the Leicestershire countryside. Friendly village pub atmosphere. Freshly prepared food available every lunchtime and evening, from light bites to full meals. Traditional roasts on Sundays. Accommodation. Located 5 miles north of Market Harborough on the B6047. Visit the website at www.thebellinn.co.uk for further details.

CAUDLE BITTER 3.9% ABV
BOWLER STRONG ALE 4.8% ABV

11am–2.30pm and 7–11pm (10.30pm Sun).

FRISBY ON THE WREAKE

The Bell Inn

2 Main Street, Frisby on the Wreake LE7 2NJ
☎ *(01664) 434237* Mr Wells

A freehouse with Charles Wells Bombardier, Greene King Abbot and IPA among the beers permanently available, plus two guests.

A 250-year-old village pub. One bar serves two rooms. Outside seating and conservatory restaurant. Food served at lunchtime and evenings. Children allowed if eating.

12–2.30pm and 6–11pm (10.30pm Sun).

GLENFIELD

The Dominion

Tournament Road, Glenfield
☎ *(0116) 231 3789* Peter Flaherty

An Everards pub with Beacon and Tiger constantly available, plus one guest, perhaps Everards Original, or a seasonal beer.

Estate community pub offering pool, snooker, darts and games machines. Food served. Garden and patio, car park. Children allowed.

11am–3pm and 5–11pm Mon–Thurs; 11am–11pm Fri–Sat; 12–10.30pm Sun.

GLOOSTON

The Old Barn Inn

Andrews Lane, Glooston, Nr Market Harborough LE16 7ST
☎ *(01858) 545215* Phillip Buswell

Four beers (30 per year) always available from brewers such as Adnams, Hook Norton, Fuller's, Wadworth, Oakhill, Nene Valley, Ridley, Bateman, Thwaites, Leatherbritches, Mauldons, Cotleigh, Greene King and Tolly Cobbold.

A sixteenth-century village pub in rural location with a log fire, no juke box or games machines. Bar and restaurant food available in evenings and Sunday lunchtime. Car park. Catering for parties, receptions and meetings. Well-behaved children and dogs welcome. Accommodation. On an old Roman road between Hallaton and Tur Langton.

12–2.30pm Tues–Sun; 7–11pm Mon–Sat; 7–10.30pm Sun.

HEMINGTON

The Jolly Sailor
Main Street, Hemington, Derby DE74 2RB
☎ *(01332) 810448* Margaret and Peter Frame

 The permanent beers include Greene King Abbot, Marston's Pedigree and Everards Beacon, while the two guests could be something like Abbeydale Absolution, Leadmill Sidewinder, Whim Hartington IPA, Timothy Taylor Landlord, Oakham Jeffery Hudson Bitter, Bateman XXXB or something from Burton Bridge.

Aseventeenth-century village pub, full of character and with a hospitable atmosphere. Food is served 12–2pm Tues–Sat and 6–8.30pm Fri–Sat. Evening meals are available in the non-smoking restaurant annexe. The two patios are heated. No children's facilities. Car park. Next to Castle Donington (Junction 24 on M1).

 11am–2.30pm and 4–11pm Mon–Fri; 11am–11pm Sat; 12–10.30pm Sun.

HOSE

The Rose & Crown
43 Bolton Lane, Hose LE14 4JE
☎ *(01949) 860424* Brian Morley

 Greene King Abbot and IPA are permanently available, plus three other real ales, changing constantly.

Not easy to find at the back of the village, this modernised open-plan bar has an olde-worlde lounge with open fire, attractive bar with darts and pool plus background music. Beamed restaurant open Thurs–Sun is available for functions. Large car park and gardens.

 12–2.30pm and 7–11pm (5–11pm Fri); closed Mon, Tues, Wed lunchtimes.

KIRBY MUXLOE

The Royal Oak
Main Street, Kirby Muxloe, Leicester LE9 2AN
☎ *(0116) 239 3166* Mr Jackson

 An Everards house with Tiger, Beacon and Old Original always available. Also two guest pumps serving beers such as Greene King Abbot Ale, Nethergate Old Growler or an Adnams brew.

Afood-oriented village pub. Modern building with traditional decor. Function facilities. Disabled access. Garden. Food available at lunchtime and evenings. Children allowed.

11am–3pm and 5.30–11pm (10.30pm Sun).

LEICESTER

The Ale Wagon
27 Rutland Street, Leicester LE1 1RE
☎ *(0116) 262 3330* Stephen Hoskins

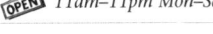 A Hoskins Brewery house with four Hoskins ales always available, plus two or three guests from other micro-breweries.

A1930s red brick corner pub, originally built as a hotel. Food available lunchtimes and evenings. Located on the corner of Rutland Street and Charles Street.

11am–11pm Mon–Sat; 12–10.30pm Sun.

The Barley Mow
93 Granby Street, Leicester LE1 6SB
☎ *(0116) 254 4663* Lee Boyd (manager)

Everards Tiger and Beacon are always on offer. Lazy Daze, also from Everards, is often featured as one of the two weekly changing guests, and beers such as Jennings Cocker Hoop and Clark's Ram's Revenge have also been served.

Regulars' pub in the city, with one main bar and another upstairs, used when necessary. Food available. Karaoke on Wednesdays. No children allowed. One minute from the station on the way to the city centre.

11am–11pm Mon–Fri; 12–11pm Sat; closed Sun.

The Globe
43 Silver Street, Leicester
☎ *(0116) 262 9819* Hugh Kerr

Tied to Everards, so Beacon, Tiger and Original are pemanent fixtures. Monthly guests include seasonal beers such as Everards Lazy Daze.

Built in 1723, this town drinkers' pub has three bars and a restaurant. Children not allowed.

11am–11pm Mon–Sat; 12–10.30pm Sun.

The Hat & Beaver
60 Highcross Street, Leicester LE1 4NN
☎ *(0116) 2622157* Mr A Cartwright

Hardys & Hansons tied house serving Mild, Best Bitter and Kimberley Classic.

Traditional town-centre pub. Rolls served at lunchtime. Children welcome in beer garden only.

12–11pm (10.30pm Sun).

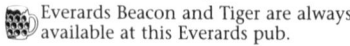

Molly O'Gradys

14 Hotel Street, Leicester LE1 5AW
☎ *(0116) 251 8992* Margaret and Kevin Flynn

 Everards Beacon and Tiger are always available at this Everards pub.

Traditional city-centre drinkers' pub in an old building, with fireplaces and wooden interior, known for its live music. Food served at lunchtimes, six days a week. Children not allowed. Situated just off the market place.

OPEN *11am–11pm Mon–Thurs; 11am–1am Fri–Sat; 12–10.30pm Sun.*

The North Bridge Tavern

Frog Island, Leicester LE3 5AG
☎ *(0116) 251 2508* Rod Woodward

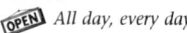 A freehouse with Marston's Pedigree always available plus one guest, often from a small local brewery such as Tom Hoskins.

A food-oriented town pub. One bar, function room. Non-smoking dining area. Traditional building with disabled access. Food available all day. Children allowed.

OPEN *All day, every day.*

The Swan and Rushes

19 Infirmary Square, Leicester LE1 5WR
☎ *(0116) 233 9167* Grant Cook

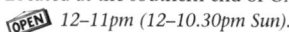 Hardys & Hansons Kimberley Best Bitter and Oakham JHB permanently available, plus up to five guests which often include Oakham Bishop's Farewell, Burton Bridge Golden Delicious, Newby Wyke White Squall, Hardys & Hansons Kimberley Mild. There is usually a mild on at least one pump. No nationals. Seasonal beers come from all over the UK. Also a range of imported beers including ales from the Czech Republic and Belgium, and 150 top-quality bottled beers

A triangular pub, built in the 1920s, with a comfortable interior and a small garden with outside seating. Food available every lunchtime and Mon–Sat evenings. Weekly quiz nights, occasional live entertainment. Located at the southern end of Oxford Street.

OPEN *12–11pm (12–10.30pm Sun).*

The Vaults

1 Wellington Street, Leicester LE1 6HH
☎ *(0116) 255 5506* Mr Spencer

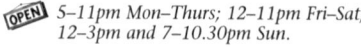 A freehouse offering 15 to 18 real ales, which change weekly, from micro- and smaller breweries. More than 2,300 beers served in the past five years.

A traditional pub with cellar bar. One bar area. Music on Sundays with an admission charge. No food. No children.

OPEN *5–11pm Mon–Thurs; 12–11pm Fri–Sat; 12–3pm and 7–10.30pm Sun.*

LOUGHBOROUGH

The Albion Inn

Canal Bank, Loughborough LE11 1QA
☎ *(01509) 213952* Mr Hartley

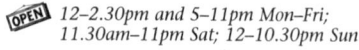 Robinson's Best, Brains Dark and something from the Wicked Hathern Brewery always available plus guests such as Shepherd Neame Spitfire and Early Bird, Black Sheep Special or brews from Greene King.

A traditional two-bar pub with garden, situated on the canal bank. Disabled access. Food available at lunchtimes and early evenings. Well-behaved children allowed. Car park.

OPEN *11am–3pm and 6–11pm (10.30pm Sun).*

The Swan in the Rushes

21 The Rushes, Loughborough
☎ *(01509) 217014*
Ian Bogie and Angela O'Neill

 Archers Golden and Castle Rock Swan's Gold always available plus seven guest beers (including a mild) at any one time, to include absolutely anything!

A cosmopolitan town-centre alehouse, smart yet down to earth, with a friendly atmosphere. Home-cooked bar food is available at lunchtimes and weekday evenings. Two bars and one non-smoking room. Car park and recently refurbished accommodation. Children allowed in designated areas. On the A6, behind Sainsbury's.

OPEN *11am–11pm Mon–Sat; 12–10.30pm Sun.*

Tap & Mallet

36 Nottingham Road, Loughborough LE11 1EU
☎ *(01509) 210028* Steve Booth

Marston's Pedigree permanently available, plus five guest beers. Regular guests include beers from Abbeydale, Archers, Brewster's, Church End, Cottage, Hook Norton, Mallard, Rooster's, Shardlow, Stonehenge, Oakham and Oldershaw. Many other breweries used but on a less frequent basis. Traditional scrumpy also served.

The pub features a good selection of well-kept beers, plus a large garden, which includes a children's play area and pets' corner with rabbits and birds.

OPEN *12–2.30pm and 5–11pm Mon–Fri; 11.30am–1pm Sat; 12–10.30pm Sun.*

The Three Nuns

30 Churchgate, Loughborough LE11 1UD
☎ *(01509) 611989* Steve Wesson

 An Everards pub serving Tiger, Beacon and Original, plus two guests, changed every six weeks, often including Everards Lazy Daze and Perfick.

The second oldest pub in town, with wood-panelled interior. Food available. Live rock bands on Saturdays. Garden seating area, car park. Children allowed until 8pm.

OPEN *11am–11pm Mon–Sat; 12–10.30pm Sun.*

MARKET BOSWORTH

Ye Olde Red Lion

1 Park Street, Market Bosworth CV13 0LL
☎ *(01455) 291713* Eddie Davies

 Tied to Banks's, with Bitter and Original plus Marston's Pedigree among the beers always on offer. The two guests are changed every few days, and include something from Frankton Bagby once a month, with beers from Church End, Lloyds and Cottage making regular appearances. Seasonal and celebration ales are also featured.

Small market-town pub, over 400 years old, very close to the countryside. Beams and fires in winter. Food is served every day at lunchtime, plus Tues–Sat evening, and there is a non-smoking dining area. Live jazz once a month, quiz night on first Sunday of month, Irish music four times a year (call for details). Patio, car park, four letting rooms. Children allowed.

OPEN *11am–2.30pm and 5.30–11pm Mon–Fri; 11am–11pm Sat; 11am–3pm and 7–10.30pm Sun.*

MEDBOURNE

The Nevill Arms

Medbourne, Market Harborough LE16 8EE
☎ *(01858) 565288* Mr and Mrs N Hall

 A freehouse with Adnams Bitter, Greene King Abbot and Fuller's London Pride always available plus two guests changing every month. Guests are often seasonal.

A traditional, two-bar country pub. Outside seating on benches near a brook. Bed and breakfast accommodation available in 6-bedroom cottage next door. Bar food served at lunchtime and evenings. Function room available for hire (suitable for weddings and parties for up to 70 people). Well-behaved children allowed.

OPEN *12–2.30pm and 6–11pm Mon–Sat; 12–3pm and 7–10.30pm Sun.*

OADBY

The Cow & Plough

Stoughton Farm Park, Gartree Road, Oadby LE2 2FB
☎ *(0116) 272 0852* Barry and Elisabeth Lount

 A freehouse with an ever-changing range of beers, many from micro-breweries. Home of Steamin' Billy beers (brewed by Grainstore), with Grand Prix Mild and Steamin' Billy Bitter always available. Steamin' Billy seasonals include BSB, Country Bitter, Lazy Summer and Skydiver.

A converted barn on a working farm, with ornate Victorian bar and large non-smoking conservatory. Twice CAMRA East Midlands Pub of the Year. Large car park.

OPEN *5–10pm Mon–Wed; 12–3pm and 5–10pm Thurs–Fri; 12–10pm Sat; 12–4pm and 7–10pm Sun.*

OLD DALBY

The Crown Inn

Debdale Hill, Old Dalby, Nr Melton Mowbray LE14 3LF
☎ *(01664) 823134* Ms Lynn Busby

 A range of ales is available, some served straight from the cask behind the bar, including Marston's Pedigree, Charles Wells Bombadier and something from Banks's. Regular guests are featured, often from the local Belvoir brewery.

Built in 1590, a pub with six small rooms, oak beams, open fires, antique furniture and prints. Large patio and terrace with orchard at bottom of the garden. Beer served from cellar near back door. Bar and restaurant food served at lunchtime and evenings. Car park, petanque pitch. Take the A46 Nottingham to Leicester road. Turn off at Willougby Hotel, left for Upper Broughton, right for Old Dalby.

OPEN *12–3pm and 6–11pm.*

SADDINGTON

The Queens Head

Main Street, Saddington
☎ *(0116) 2402536*
Christine and Steve Bebbington

 Everards Beacon and Tiger plus Adnams Southwold Bitter usually available. Also one guest beer, supplied through Everards.

A nicely situated, award-winning country inn and restaurant. Leicestershire Tourist Board Pub Meal of the Year winner for the last three years. Food served 12–2pm and 6.30–9pm, but not on Sunday evenings. Large car park. Situated near to Fleckney.

OPEN *11am–3pm and 5.30–11pm (10.30pm Sun).*

SHAWELL

White Swan Inn
Main Street, Shawell, Nr Lutterworth LE17 6AG
☎ *(01788) 860357* Mike and Susan Walker

Greene King Abbot and IPA always available, plus a regularly changing guest ale.

Built in the main street of a small hamlet in around 1700, it retains many original features. Local skittles in the bar. Non-smoking restaurant and separate dining area for smokers. Seating to the front of the pub. Food served all opening times. Accommodation available, with plans for log-cabin accommodation in 2003. Car park. Children welcome. Located 5 minutes from M1, M6, A14 and A5.

OPEN *7–11pm Tues–Fri; 12–3pm Sun (closed all day Mon, Tues–Sat lunchtimes and Sun evenings).*

SHEARSBY

Chandler's Arms
Village Green, Shearsby, Nr Lutterworth LE17 6PL
☎ *(0116) 247 8384* Mr Ward

Fuller's London Pride and Marston's Pedigree and Bitter always available plus four guests. Beers featured include Greene King Abbot, Wadworth 6X, Exmoor Gold or brews from Timothy Taylor or Jennings.

A seventeenth-century red-brick pub overlooking the village green, with a three-tier prize-winning garden. Two lounges. AA recommended. International cuisine served at lunchtime and evenings. Children allowed.

OPEN *12–2.30pm and 6.30–11pm (10.30pm Sun).*

SMISBY

The Anwell Inn (also known as Mother Hubbard)
Anwell Lane, Smisby, Ashby de la Zouch LE65 2TA
☎ *(01530) 413604* Chris and Kathleen

Three real ales always available. Favourites include Ruddles brews and Marston's Pedigree.

An olde-worlde pub situated in the heart of a farming community, known locally as The Mother Hubbard in honour of the previous landlady. Exposed beams and a bar built from old church fittings. Separate restaurant/function room. Food available 12–2.30pm Wed–Sat; 6–9.30pm Mon–Sat; 12–6pm Sun. Children allowed until 9.30pm, if eating. Beer garden with barbecue area.

OPEN *12–2.30pm Wed–Sat (closed Mon–Tues lunch); 5.30–11pm Mon–Sat; 12–6pm Sun.*

SOMERBY

The Old Brewery Inn
High Street, Somerby, Leicester LE14 2PZ
☎ *(01664) 454777* Barrie Parish

Home of the Parish Brewery and John O'Gaunt Brewery. Robin a Tiptoe, Cropped Oak and Coat o'Red always available plus a good range of Parish bitters such as Somerby Premium, Poachers Ale and Special. Other celebration ales, as appropriate, for instance Life Sentence, which was brewed for the landlady's wedding!

Three bars, restaurant, function room and beer garden. Disabled access. Brewery visits permitted if quiet or pre-arranged. Food served at lunchtime and evenings Tues–Sun. Children allowed.

John o'Gaunt:
ROBIN A TIPTOE 3.9% ABV
CROPPED OAK 4.4% ABV
COAT O'RED
Parish:
MILD 3.5% ABV
SPECIAL BITTER 3.8% ABV
FARM GOLD 4% ABV
SOMERBY PREMIUM 4% ABV
PORTER 4.8% ABV
POACHERS ALE 6% ABV
BAZ'S BONCE BLOWER 11% ABV
BAZ'S SUPER BREW 23% ABV

OPEN *11.30am–3pm and 6–11pm Mon–Fri; all day Sat–Sun.*

The Stilton Cheese Inn
High Street, Somerby LE14 2PZ
☎ *(01664) 454394* Jeff Evans

Marston's Pedigree and Grainstore Ten Fifty permanently available, plus one or two constantly changing guests. Over 1,000 beers served in five years. Guest cider also offered, plus over 20 malt whiskies and a good wine list.

A sixteenth-century stone building with beams, two rooms and upstairs restaurant. Decorated with hops and hunting prints. Food available 12–2pm and 6–9pm daily. Children allowed in the restaurant and small bar. Small patio with seating for 20.

OPEN *12–3pm and 6–11pm.*

SUTTON BASSETT

The Queen's Head

Sutton Bassett, Market Harborough LE16 8HP
☎ *(01858) 463530* Mario Cancelliere

A freehouse with up to eight real ales including Timothy Taylor Landlord and Adnams Bitter plus a selection of guests including Fuller's London Pride and Morland Old Speckled Hen.

A friendly country pub with traditional decor, real fires, front and back bars. Disabled facilities on ground floor. Patio and petanque court. Food served at lunchtime and evenings (pub food in the bar and Italian food in restaurant upstairs). Large parties and functions catered for. Children allowed. Prettily situated with views of the Welland valley.

OPEN *11.45am–3pm and 6.30–11pm Mon–Sat; 12–3pm and 7–10.30pm Sun.*

THORPE SATCHVILLE

The Fox Inn

Main Street, Thorpe Satchville LE14 2DQ
☎ *(01664) 840257* Celia Frewe

A freehouse offering John O'Gaunt Robin a Tiptoe and Coat O' Red.

Country pub built in 1935. Food is available, and the pub has a restaurant area. Skittle alley, petanque, garden and patio. Children allowed. Car park

OPEN *12–3pm and 6–11pm (10.30pm Sun); closed Mon lunch.*

THURNBY

The Swallow

Station Road, Thurnby LE7 9PU
☎ *(0116) 241 9087* Ross Allibone

Everards Tiger, Beacon and Old Original are always served at this Everards tied house. The two guests might include Morland Old Speckled Hen, something from Adnams, or seasonals such as Everards Lazy Daze.

Community pub built in the sixties, with two bars, conservatory, garden and play area. Food is served, and there is a non-smoking restaurant area. Live music Sat and Sun evenings. Disabled facilities, car park. Children allowed until 8pm.

OPEN *11.30am–11pm Mon–Fri; 11am–11pm Sat; 12–10.30pm Sun.*

WALCOTE

The Black Horse

Lutterworth Road, Walcote LE17 4JU
☎ *(01455) 552684* Mrs Tinker

HOB Bitter (Hoskins & Oldfield), Timothy Taylor Landlord, Greene King Abbot and Oakham Jeffrey Hudson Bitter always available plus two guest beers (75 per year) always from independent breweries.

A one-bar village pub. Bar and restaurant food available at lunchtime and evenings. Authentic Thai cooking. Car park, garden and children's room. One mile east of M1 junction 20.

OPEN *7–11pm Mon–Thurs; 12–2pm and 5.30–11pm Fri; 6.30–11pm Sat; 12–3.30pm and 6.30–10.30pm Sun.*

WALTHAM-ON-THE-WOLDS

The Marquis of Granby

High Street, Waltham-on-the-Wolds LE14 4HA
☎ *(01664) 464212* Melanie Dawson

An Everards pub with Tiger and Original plus something from Adnams permanently available, together with one guest, changed every couple of weeks, often a beer from Everards such as Perfick.

A 400-year-old village pub with beams and fires. Food served. Occasional live music. Garden and patio. Children allowed.

OPEN *12–2.30pm and 5.30–11.30pm; 11am–11pm Sat; 12–10.30pm Sun.*

WIGSTON MAGNA

The Horse & Trumpet

Bull Head Street, Wigston Magna LE18 1PB
☎ *(0116) 288 6290* Andy Moone

 Tied to Everards, and always featuring Original, Tiger and Beacon, plus one guest, changed seasonally.

Characterful community local in a very old building, with one open-plan bar. Food served at lunchtimes. Live music on Thurs evenings. Patio, car park. Children allowed.

 11am–2.30pm and 5–11pm Mon–Fri; 11am–2.30pm and 6–11pm Sat; 12–3pm and 7–10.30pm Sun.

WYMESWOLD

The Hammer & Pincers

5 East Road, Wymeswold LE12 6ST
☎ *(01509) 880735* Mrs T Williomson

 A freehouse with Ruddles County and Marston's Pedigree always on offer, plus one weekly changing guest from the Grainstore brewery, such as Ten Fifty or Gold.

Traditional country village pub dating from the sixteenth century, with beams and fires. Food available. Garden, patio and car park. Children allowed.

 12–2.30pm and 6–11pm Mon–Fri; 12–3pm and 6–11pm Sat; 12–3pm and 7–10.30pm Sun.

The Three Crowns

45 Far Street, Wymeswold LE12 6TZ
☎ *(01509) 880153* Robert Herrick

 Marston's Pedigree and Adnams Bitter are permanent features. The two guests, changed regularly, are often beers from Castle Rock (such as Hemlock) or from Belvoir (such as Whippling), but other regular breweries include Cottage, Wye Valley, Oldershaw and Eccleshall.

Country pub, over 300 years old, with a traditional atmosphere (no TV). Food available at lunchtimes. One bar with segregated room, garden and car park. Annual beer festivals in autumn (call for details). No children allowed. In the middle of the village, opposite the church.

 12–2.30pm and 5.30–11pm Mon–Sat (open 6pm Sat); 12–3pm and 7–10.30pm Sun.

YOU TELL US

* *The Crown & Anchor*, Oadby
* *The Old Crown*, Cavendish Bridge
* *The Three Cranes Hotel*, 82 Humberstone Gate, Leicester

Places Featured:

Allington
Aslackby
Aubourn
Barnack
Boston
Caythorpe
Dyke
Frognall
Gainsborough
Grainthorpe
Grantham
Harmston
Laughterton

Lincoln
Little Bytham
Louth
North Kelsey
Rothwell
Scamblesby
Scawby Brook
Seacroft
Spalding
Stamford
Whaplode St Catherine
Woolsthorpe-by-Belvoir

THE BREWERIES

GEORGE BATEMAN & SON LTD

Salem Bridge Brewery, Mill Lane, Wainfleet, Skegness PE24 4JE
☎ *(01754) 880317*
www.bateman.co.uk

 DARK MILD 3.0% ABV
Dark and fruity, some roast malt, hoppy finish.
XB 3.7% ABV
Distinctive, refreshing dry bitterness.
YELLABELLY 4.2% ABV
Organic beer.
SALEM PORTER 4.7% ABV
Dry, nutty, rich malt and superb hop flavours.
XXXB 4.8% ABV
Multi-faceted malt and fruit character.
Plus a seasonal and special selection.

DARKTRIBE BREWERY

25 Doncaster Road, Gunness, Scunthorpe DN15 8TG
☎ *(01724) 782324*

DIXIE'S MILD 3.6% ABV
Dark, tasty award-winner.
HONEY MILD 3.6% ABV
Dark with a hint of honey.
FULL AHEAD 3.8% ABV
Dry-hopped bitter.
ALBACORE 4.0% ABV
Beautifully pale and hoppy.
GUNNESS STOUT 4.1% ABV
Traditional dark stout. Occasional brew.
FUTTOCKS 4.2% ABV
Easy-quaffing and hoppy.
DIXIE'S BOLLARDS 4.5% ABV
Ginger beer.
DR GRIFFIN'S MERMAID 4.5% ABV
Dark bitter.
OLD GAFFER 4.5% ABV
Traditional bitter.
AEGIR ALE 4.7% ABV
Flavour-packed.
GALLEON 4.7% ABV
Popular award-winner.
TWIN SCREW 5.1% ABV
Powerful, occasional brew.
SIXTEEN BELLS 6.5% ABV
Easy-drinking for gravity. Occasional brew.

HAPPY HOOKER BEERS

30 St Edmunds Road, Sleaford NG34 7LS
☎ *(01529) 307499*
www.happyhookerbeers.com

UP & UNDER 3.9% ABV
LOOSEHEAD 4.2% ABV
TIGHTHEAD 4.8% ABV
STAY ON YOUR FEET 5.8% ABV

HIGHWOOD BREWERY LTD

Melton Highwood, Barnetby DN38 6AA
☎ *(01652) 680020*

 TOM WOOD BEST BITTER 3.5% ABV
Well-hopped and refreshing.
TOM WOOD SHEPHERD'S DELIGHT 4.0% ABV
Easy-quaffing and full-flavoured.
TOM WOOD BARN DANCE 4.2% ABV
Seasonal brew.
TOM WOOD LINCOLNSHIRE LEGEND 4.2% ABV
Good, hoppy bitterness throughout.
TOM WOOD HARVEST 4.3% ABV
Soft and full-flavoured.
TOM WOOD SUMMER DAYS 4.4% ABV
Seasonal brew.
TOM WOOD OLD TIMBER 4.5% ABV
Smooth and full-flavoured.
TOM WOOD BOMBER COUNTY 4.8% ABV
Red, with good hoppy flavour.

NEWBY WYKE BREWERY

*Willoughby Arms Cottages, Station Road,
Little Bytham NG33 4RA*
☎ *(01780) 410276*

 SIDEWINDER 3.8% ABV
BRUTUS 4.0% ABV
SKIPPER EDDIES ALE 4.0% ABV
BEAR ISLAND 4.6% ABV
WHITE SQUALL 4.8% ABV
WHITE SEA 5.2% ABV

Seasonals and specials:
SUMMER SESSION BITTER 3.8% ABV
BARDIA 4.0% ABV
LORD ANCASTER 4.0% ABV
Summer brew for Willoughby Arms, Little
Bytham.
SLINGSHOT 4.2% ABV
SLIPWAY 4.2% ABV
RED SQUALL 4.4% ABV
STAMFORD GOLD 4.4% ABV
Occasional brew for the Green Man, Stamford.
BLACK SQUALL PORTER 4.6% ABV
LORD WILLOUGHBY 4.8% ABV
Winter brew for Willoughby Arms, Little
Bytham.
DISTANT GROUNDS 5.2% ABV
KINGSTON AMBER 5.2% ABV
THE DEEP 5.4% ABV
HOMEWARD BOUND 6.0% ABV

OLDERSHAW BREWERY

12 Harrowby Hall Estate, Grantham NG31 9HB
☎ *(01476) 572135*
www.oldershawbrewery.co.uk

 HARROWBY BITTER 3.6% ABV
Occasional brew.
HIGH DYKE 3.9% ABV
Gold-coloured with good hoppiness.
SUNNYDAZE 4.0% ABV
Bright, quenching, summer wheat beer.
NEWTON'S DROP 4.1% ABV
Golden and hoppy.
VETERAN ALE 4.1% ABV
Traditional, gently bitter brew.
CASKADE 4.2% ABV
Light, clean-tasting.
ERMINE ALE 4.2% ABV
Pale and refreshing hoppiness.
AHTANUM GOLD 4.3% ABV
Golden and hoppy. New Zealand hops.
GRANTHAM STOUT 4.3% ABV
Dark and moreish occasional brew.
REGAL BLONDE 4.4% ABV
Cask-conditioned lager.
TOPERS TIPPLE 4.5% ABV
Autumn/winter brew.
OLD BOY 4.8% ABV
Golden chestnut colour with good balance.
YULETIDE 5.2% ABV
Powerful flavours. Christmas brew.
Plus seasonal brews.

POACHER BREWERY

457 High Street, Lincoln LN5 8NJ
www.poachersbeer.co.uk

SUMMA SHY TALK BITTER 3.7% ABV
POACHERS PRIDE 4.0% ABV
POACHERS DEN 4.2% ABV
POACHERS TRAIL 4.2% ABV
POACHERS DICK 4.5% ABV

WILLY'S BREWERY

17 High Cliff Road, Cleethorpes DN35 8RQ
☎ *(01472) 602145*

WILLY'S ORIGINAL 3.7% ABV
WILLY'S LAST RESORT 4.3% ABV
WILLY'S WEISS BOUY 5.0% ABV
Pronounced 'vice boy'!
WILLY'S OLD GROYNE 6.2% ABV
Plus seasonals and celebration ales.

THE PUBS

ALLINGTON

The Welby Arms

The Green, Allington, Grantham NG32 2EA
☎ *(01400) 281361* Matt Rose and Anna Cragg

Timothy Taylor Landlord and Fuller's London Pride always available, plus two guests perhaps including Wadworth 6X, Phoenix Wobbly Bob or Greene King Abbot.

A traditional village pub with log fires and terrace. Disabled access. Baguettes or soup available at lunchtime in the bar, plus restaurant food at both lunchtime and evenings. En-suite accommodation. Well-behaved children allowed.

OPEN *12–2.30pm and 6–11pm (10.30pm Sun).*

ASLACKBY

Robin Hood & Little John

Aslackby, Sleaford NG34 0HL
☎ *(01778) 440681* Mike Wickens

A freehouse with Greene King Abbot always available, plus one guest pump serving a real ale such as, perhaps, Adnams Broadside or a Wood or Oldershaw ale.

A traditional country pub, one bar, function room, restaurant. Food available at lunchtime and evenings. Children's garden with sheep next door, children allowed in designated area only.

OPEN *11am–3pm and 5.30–11pm (10.30pm Sun).*

AUBOURN

The Royal Oak

Royal Oak Lane, Aubourn LN5 9DT
☎ *(01522) 788291*

Bateman XB and XXXB and Samuel Smith OBB always available plus three guest beers from breweries stretching from the Orkneys to Cornwall.

A traditional village pub with character. Bar food available at lunchtime and evenings. Car park and garden. Children welcome at lunchtime and evenings in the function room until 8.30pm. South of Lincoln, off the A46.

OPEN *12–2.30pm and 7–11pm (10.30pm Sun).*

BARNACK

The Millstone Inn

Millstone Lane, Barnack, Nr Stamford PE9 3ET
☎ *(01780) 740296* Aubrey Sinclair-Ball

Everards Old Original and Tiger plus Adnams Southwold usually available. A regularly changing guest beer is supplied through Everards.

The inn was built in 1672 of Barnack rag stone which was quarried nearby. The interior is olde-worlde with beamed ceilings. Walled courtyard. Food served 11.30am–2pm Mon–Sun and 6.30–9pm Mon–Sat. Children welcome. Car park.

OPEN *11.30am–2.30pm and 5.30–11pm Mon–Sat; 12–4pm and 7–10.30pm Sun.*

BOSTON

The Carpenter's Arms

Witham Street, Boston PE21 6PU
☎ *(01205) 362840* Tessa Barrand

A Bateman house with XB always available plus two changing guests which are often other Bateman brews but also sometimes Marston's Pedigree, Morland Old Speckled Hen or Fuller's London Pride. A wider selection of real ales is available in the summer than during the winter.

A traditional one-bar town pub. Games room, real fires, outside seating. No food. Well-behaved children allowed.

OPEN *11am–11pm Mon–Sat; 12–10.30pm Sun.*

The Eagle

144 West Street, Boston PE21 8RE
☎ *(01205) 361116* Mr Andy Watson

Timothy Taylor Landlord, Adnams Broadside and Banks's Bitter always available, plus up to three guests such as Exmoor Gold, Hop Back Summer Lightning or Castle Rock brews. May operate up to eight real ales during beer festivals.

A traditional local on the outskirts of Boston town centre. Two bars, real fires, beer garden. Food served 12–2pm Mon–Sat, including homemade specials and doorstep sandwiches. Curry nights available for groups, subject to room availability. Function room is venue for monthly meetings of folk club. Regular beer festivals held throughout the year.

OPEN *11am–11pm Mon–Sat; 12–10.30pm Sun.*

CAYTHORPE

The Red Lion Inn

62 High Street, Caythorpe, Grantham NG32 3DN
☎ *(01400) 272632* Ann Roberts

 A freehouse serving Adnams Best plus up to three guests from every possible brewery. Glentworth and Slaters (Eccleshall) brews are particular favourites.

A seventeenth-century traditional country inn with two gardens and two bars. No music or games machines. Disabled access. Food available at lunchtime and evenings in a separate restaurant. Children allowed in the restaurant and one of the bars only.

OPEN *11am–2.30pm and 6–11pm (10.30pm Sun).*

DYKE

The Wishing Well Inn

Main Street, Dyke, Bourne PE10 0AF
☎ *(01778) 422970* Mr BF Creaser

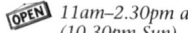 Everards Beacon and Tiger and Greene King Abbot usually available plus two constantly changing beers from micro-breweries around the country.

A attractive country inn with accommodation and a large restaurant. Food served 12–2pm and 6.30–9.30pm daily. Children welcome. Large car park. One mile north of Bourne, off A15. Look for signs.

OPEN *11am–2.30pm and 6–11pm (10.30pm Sun).*

FROGNALL

The Goat

155 Spalding Road, Frognall, Deeping St James, Nr Peterborough PE6 8SA
☎ *(01778) 347629* Peter Wilkins

 Five guest beers available from a variety of micro-breweries and brewpubs. Over the past six years, more than 1,750 different guests have been served, from more than 400 breweries.

A country pub dating from 1647. Full bar menu served every lunchtime and evening, including seasonal specials as available. Functions catered for. Car park, large beer garden with play equipment, family dining area. Situated on the B1525 between Market Deeping and Spalding.

OPEN *11.30am–2.30pm (3pm Sat) and 6–11pm Mon–Sat; 12–3pm and 6–10.30pm Sun.*

GAINSBOROUGH

The Eight Jolly Brewers

Ship Court, Caskgate Street, Gainsborough DN21 2DL
☎ *(01427) 677128* Alex Craig

 Timothy Taylor Landlord and Caledonian Deuchars IPA always available plus a varied range of guest ales. No national beers served, micro-breweries favoured. Examples include Highwood Bitter and Glentworth Light Year.

A 300-year-old town-centre freehouse with two bars in a traditional building. Small outdoor area and patio. Sandwiches available at lunchtime only. No children. Located near the Guildhall.

OPEN *11am–11pm Mon–Sat; 12–10.30pm Sun.*

GRAINTHORPE

The Black Horse Inn

Mill Lane, Grainthorpe, Louth LN11 78U
☎ *(01472) 388229* Mrs Donaghue

 A freehouse serving Bateman ales plus a guest such as Timothy Taylor Landlord. Micro-brewery on premises, so own ales served in pub.

A cosy country village pub with a real ale theme. Open fires, beer garden with children's area. Food served every evening and at lunchtime at weekends and during the summer. Children allowed, if eating.

MOLLY'S MILD 3.6% ABV
DANNIE BOY BITTER 4.0% ABV

OPEN *7–11pm and lunchtime at weekends and during the summer.*

GRANTHAM

The Blue Bull

64 Westgate, Grantham NG31 6LA
☎ *(01476) 570929* Mr P Mitchell

 Three cask ales always available, always including something from Newby Wyke, plus two other guest beers, perhaps from Greene King, Black Sheep or Shepherd Neame.

C AMRA Lincolnshire Pub of the Year 1995. Dates from the 1850s. Bar food available at lunchtimes. Car park. Children allowed. Three minutes from the main line BR railway station.

OPEN *11am–11pm Mon–Sat; 12-10.30pm Sun.*

HARMSTON

The Thorold Arms
High Street, Harmston, Lincoln LN5 9SN
☎ *(01522) 720358* Darren Hedges

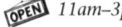Four guest ales always on offer, one of which will be a Lincolnshire brew, while the other three could be any independent ales.

A rural pub with traditional decor and log fire. Disabled access and toilets. Food available at lunchtime and evenings in a separate dining area. Small functions catered for. No children.

OPEN *11am–3pm and 6–11pm (10.30pm Sun).*

LAUGHTERTON

The Friendship Inn
Main Road, Laugherton, Lincoln LN21 2JZ
☎ *(01427) 718681* Diane Humphries

A freehouse with Marston's Pedigree and Mansfield Friendship Bitter always available plus guests, which may well be something from Brewsters, Slaters (Eccleshall) or another micro-brewery.

A traditional, friendly one-bar village pub. Log fires, garden, disabled access. Food available at lunchtime and evenings (except Sun evening) in a designated dining area. Children allowed.

OPEN *11.30am–2.30pm and 6–11pm Mon–Sat; 12–3pm and 7–10.30pm Sun.*

LINCOLN

The Golden Eagle
21 High Street, Lincoln LN5 8BD
☎ *(01522) 521058* James and Liz Middleton

A freehouse with Everards Beacon and Bateman XB always available plus one real cider. Four guest ales, rotating continually.

A locals' pub with two bars, one with no music or games machines, half a mile from the city centre. Snacks menu served 11am–7pm Mon–Fri. Car park and garden. Children not allowed in the pub.

OPEN *11am–11pm Mon–Sat; 12–10.30pm Sun.*

The Portland Arms
50 Portland Street, Lincoln
☎ *(01522) 513912*
Lisa Nicholson and David Spiers

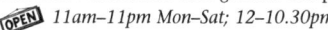Fuller's London Pride permanently available, plus four guests which could be from any independent brewery.

Relaxed, games-orientated pub with music and TV. Beer garden. Bar food available 11am–6pm Mon–Sat and 11am–2pm Sun. Children welcome in beer garden. Car park.

OPEN *11am–11pm Mon–Sat; 12–10.30pm Sun.*

Sippers Freehouse
26 Melville Street, Lincoln LN5 7HW
☎ *(01522) 527612* Philip Tulley

Morland Old Speckled Hen, Marston's Pedigree and two regularly changing guest beers (mostly from micro-breweries) usually available.

Traditional city-centre pub. Food served lunchtime and evenings Mon–Fri, lunchtime only Sat. No food Sun. No children.

OPEN *11am–2pm and 5–11pm Mon–Thurs; 11am–2pm and 4–11pm Fri; 11am–2pm and 7–11pm Sat; 7–10.30pm Sun.*

The Tap & Spile
21 Hungate, Lincoln LN1 1ES
☎ *(01522) 534015* Mr and Mrs Cay

Eight beers always available but the range changes daily. Approx 150 brews per year including Charles Wells Fargo, Thwaites Craftsman and Greene King IPA.

Formerly the White Horse, a city-centre pub with stone and wood floors, bare brick and plaster walls. Bar food available at lunchtime. Pay and display car park opposite. Children not allowed. At the top of the high street turn left, then 200 yards on the left near the police station.

OPEN *11am–11pm Mon–Sat; 12–3pm and 7–10.30pm Sun.*

The Victoria
6 Union Road, Lincoln LN1 3BJ
☎ *(01522) 536048* Mr Renshaw

Up to ten beers always available including a mild, Castle Rock Union Gold, Timothy Taylor Landlord, Bateman XB and Oldershaw Regal Blonde. Plus four guests (up to 1,000 per year) including Orkney Raven Ale, Brains Bitter, Exmoor Gold, Hop Back Summer Lightning and Adnams brews.

A traditional, two-bar Victorian terraced pub with a small patio, in the city by the west gate of the castle. Bar food available at lunchtime. Regular beer festivals and brewery feature nights.

OPEN *11am–11pm Mon–Sat; 12–10.30pm Sun.*

LITTLE BYTHAM

The Willoughby Arms
Station Road, Little Bytham, Grantham
NG33 4RA
☎ *(01780) 410276* Neil and Claire Salisbury

A freehouse with Sidewinder and Lord Ancaster, brewed by the award-winning Newby Wyke Brewery at the rear of the pub, always on offer. Four other guest beers also available, all from micro-breweries from around the country.

Beamed country pub, around 150 years old, with open fire and garden with superb views over open countryside. Bar meals are available every lunchtime and evening, and there is a non-smoking dining room. Live music several times a month, especially during the twice-yearly beer and music festivals held over bank holiday weekends at the end of May and August. Six mini beer festivals are also held during the year. En-suite accommodation available. Website: www.willoughbyarms.co.uk.

OPEN *12–2pm and 5–11pm Mon–Fri; 12–11pm Sat; 12–10.30pm Sun.*

LOUTH

The Woodman Inn
134 Eastgate, Louth LN11 9AA
☎ *(01507) 602100* Dave Kilgour

Greene King Abbot always available plus two guests. Among those featured are Wadworth 6X, Charles Wells Bombardier and brews from Cotleigh and Abbeydale. Other specials from micro-breweries stocked when possible.

Situated on the edge of town, this pub has a film theme. Two bars, one a live rock and blues music venue. Food available at lunchtime only. Children allowed.

OPEN *11am–4pm and 7–11pm Mon–Fri; all day Sat; 12–3.30pm and 7–10.30pm Sun.*

NORTH KELSEY

The Butchers Arms
Middle Street, North Kelsey, Market Rasen
LN7 6EH
☎ *(01652) 678002* Steve Cooper

A freehouse predominantly serving Tom Wood Highwood beers, plus one constantly changing guest.

A small, old-style village pub. One bar. No music or games. Outside seating. Sandwiches, salads and ploughmans available at weekends. Children allowed.

OPEN *4–11pm Mon–Fri; 12–11pm Sat–Sun.*

ROTHWELL

The Blacksmith's Arms
Hillrise, Rothwell LN7 6AZ
☎ *(01472) 371300* Mike Hubbard

A constantly changing range of real ales is served, including Bateman XXXB and 12-Bore and the award-winning Tom Wood Lincolnshire Legend from the Highwood Brewery.

A 400-year-old haunted pub, formerly a blacksmiths, with oak beams, real fires and candles. Bar and restaurant food available at lunchtime and evenings. Car park, garden and function room/entertainment room. Restaurant open 12–3pm and 7–11pm Tues–Sat and 12–8pm Sun. Two miles off the A46 between Caistor and Swallow.

OPEN *11am–11pm Mon–Sat; 12–10.30pm Sun.*

SCAMBLESBY

The Green Man
Old Main Road, Scamblesby, Louth LN11 9XG
☎ *(01507) 343282* Tim and Anne Eyre

An ever-changing selection of real ales always available. Regular features include Tom Wood, Rebellion and Cottege brews.

A country pub with lounge and public bar. Sky TV. Pub meals served 12–9pm every day. Children allowed.

OPEN *12–11pm (10.30pm Sun).*

SCAWBY BROOK

The Horse & Cart
185 Scawby Road, Scawby Brook, Brigg DN20 9JX
☎ *(0152) 652150* Paul Brown

Daleside Best Bitter permanently available, plus at least two guests, changing constantly, from breweries such as Wychwood, Castle Rock, Jennings and Cottage. Themed beer festivals held every Easter and August. At one time this was the home of the Faint Hope Brewery, but brewing is suspended at present.

Built in late 1960s with a large bar and lounge with small dining area. Food available lunchtimes and evenings, including Sunday roasts. Children allowed. Beer garden with swings for children. Large car park. Paddock area which can be used for camping.

OPEN *12–2pm and 5–11pm Mon–Fri; 11am–11pm Sat; 12–10.30pm Sun.*

SEACROFT

The Vine Hotel
Vine Road, Seacroft, Skegness PE25 3DB
☎ *(01754) 610611* Kathy Brown

 Tied to Bateman, and featuring XB, XXXB and Mild. One monthly guest is also served.

Country hotel with AA 3-star restaurant. The oldest building in Skegness, it dates from 1660, and has two bars, beams and coal fires. Food available. Garden, car park, 21 letting rooms. Very occasional live music and beer festivals. Children allowed.

11am–11pm Mon–Sat; 12–10.30pm Sun.

SPALDING

The Lincolnshire Poacher
11 Double Street, Spalding PE11 2AA
☎ *(01775) 766490* Gary Bettles

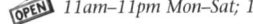 Four real ales available at any one time, including three constantly changing guests.

A large, airy pub with two bars. Food available at lunchtimes and early evenings (5.30–7.30pm). Children allowed. Large patio with tables and seating.

11am–11pm Mon–Sat; 12–10.30pm Sun.

STAMFORD

The Green Man
29 Scotgate, Stamford PR9 2YQ
☎ *(01780) 753598* Tony Shilling

Six real ales always available, usually including Stamford Gold, a house ale brewed by Newby Wyke, Rooster's Man of Green and Oakham's Two Tanners plus guests from breweries far and wide. Two beer festivals held every year: one at Easter for four days and one in September for three days.

Olde-worlde pub with oak beams, low ceilings and wooden floors. Food available at lunchtimes. Children allowed until 7pm. Beer garden. Located on the old A1 through Stamford.

11am–11pm Mon–Sat; 12–10.30pm Sun.

The Periwig
Red Lion Square, Stamford PE9 2AG
☎ *01780 762169* William Fry

A freehouse offering Oakham JHB, Hop Back Summer Lightning, Adnams Southwold and Fuller's London Pride, plus two guests (six per week), usually including something from Oakham, though Abbeydale Moonshine and RCH Pitchfork are also regulars.

A town pub in a seventeenth-century building with modernised interior. Food available 12–2.30pm Mon–Sat. Live band once a month. Beer festivals twice a year (call for details). Children allowed.

11am–11pm Mon–Sat; 12–10.30pm Sun.

WHAPLODE ST CATHERINE

Blue Bell Inn & Brewery
Cranesgate South, Whaplode St Catherine, Holbeach PE12 6SN
☎ *(01406) 540300* Mr Pilkington

 All three of the beers brewed on the premises are usually available.

A pub and restaurant with one main bar and a separate smoking room. Pool and darts. Beer garden with occasional barbecues in summer. Separate restaurant open evenings only. Children allowed. Situated in the middle of nowhere, so do ring for directions.

OLDE SESSION ALE 3.7% ABV
OLDE HONESTY 4.1% ABV
Award-winning, East Anglian ale
OLDE FASHIONED 4.5% ABV

7–11pm Mon–Fri; 12–4pm and 7–11pm Sat–Sun.

WOOLSTHORPE-BY-BELVOIR

The Chequers
Main Street, Woolsthorpe-by-Belvoir, Grantham NG32 1LV
☎ *(01476) 870701* Mr Potter

A freehouse with Marston's Bitter and Pedigree always served, plus two guest ales available seasonally, such as Timothy Taylor Landlord or Greene King Abbot plus beers from local breweries such as Brewsters.

A country pub with olde-worlde decor. Five-acre garden and private cricket field. Accommodation. Restaurant food available at lunchtime and evenings. Children allowed.

12–3pm and 7–11pm (10.30pm Sun).

YOU TELL US

∗ *Ebrington Arms*, Main Street, Kirkby on Bain, Woodhall Spa

THE BREWERIES

BATTERSEA BREWERY COMPANY
43 Glycena Road, Battersea SW11 5TP
☎ *(020) 7978 7978*

 BATTERSEA BITTER 4.0% ABV
Copper-coloured with hints of malt.
POWER STATION PORTER 4.9% ABV
Dark, dry, traditional London beer.

FULLER, SMITH & TURNER PLC
Griffin Brewery, Chiswick Lane South, W4 2QB
☎ *(020) 8996 2000*

 CHISWICK BITTER 3.5% ABV
Quenching, with flowery hop character.
SUMMER ALE 3.9% ABV
Seasonal. Lager-style beer.
LONDON PRIDE 4.1% ABV
Smooth and rounded, with excellent balance.
ORGANIC HONEY DEW 4.3% ABV
Seasonal. Golden smooth and honeyed
sweetness.
RED FOX 4.3% ABV
Seasonal. Tawny, mellow and well-rounded.
JACK FROST 4.5% ABV
Winter ale with blueberries among the
ingredients.
ESB 5.5% ABV
Powerful, rounded and well-balanced.

HAGGARDS BREWERY
*c/o The Imperial, 577 King's Road, Chelsea
SW6 2EH*
☎ *(020) 7731 3780*

 IMPERIAL BEST BITTER 4.3% ABV
Light, balanced, easy-drinking, with
bittersweet finish.

PITFIELD BREWERY
The Beer Shop, 14 Pitfield Street, Hoxton N1 6EY
☎ *(020) 7739 3701*

ORIGINAL BITTER 3.7% ABV
EAST KENT GOLDINGS 4.2% ABV
ECO WARRIOR 4.5% ABV
HOXTON HEAVY 4.8% ABV
BLACK EAGLE 5.0% ABV
1850 LONDON PORTER 5.0% ABV
*Plus seasonal and occasional brews.
Certified organic brewery.*

SWEET WILLIAM BREWERY
King William IV, 816 High Road, Leyton E10 6AE
☎ *(020) 8556 2460*

 EAST LONDON MILD 3.6% ABV
JUST WILLIAM 3.8% ABV
WILLIAM THE CONQUEROR 4.4% ABV
Plus seasonal and occasional brews such as:
E10 RED 4.1% ABV
RISING SUN 4.1% ABV
WONDERFULLY WHEATY 4.3% ABV
CREAM STOUT 4.5% ABV
SPICED WINTER ALE 5.0% ABV
GINGER BEER 5.5% ABV

YOUNG & CO.
*The Ram Brewery, High Street, Wandsworth
SW18 4JD*
☎ *(020) 8875 7000*

BITTER 3.7% ABV
Pale and bitter throughout.
TRIPLE 'A' 4.0% ABV
Light, easy-quaffer.
DIRTY DICK'S 4.1% ABV
Seasonal beer.
SPECIAL 4.6% ABV
Excellent malt and hop balance.
WAGGLE DANCE 5.0% ABV
Golden, smooth, honeyed flavour.
WINTER WARMER 5.0% ABV
Rich, smooth and sweet seasonal brew.

LONDON CENTRAL

EC1

The Artillery Arms

102 Bunhill Row EC1V 8ND
☎ *(020) 7253 4683* Helen Thomas

 A Fuller's pub with Chiswick, London Pride and ESB available plus seasonal brews and a guest ale from a wide range of independent breweries.

A Victorian building tucked away behind Old Street. Named after the Honourable Artillery Company, based over the road. Food available 12–3pm Mon–Fri. Upstairs function room.

⊖ Nearest Tube: Old Street.

OPEN *11am–11pm Mon–Fri; 12–11pm Sat; 12–10.30pm Sun.*

The Eagle

139 Farringdon Road EC1
☎ *(020) 7837 1353* Michael Belben

 Four hand pumps, with Charles Wells IPA and Bombardier always available.

A gastro pub with a reputation for good food, which is available 12.30–2.30pm Mon–Fri (3.30pm Sat and Sun) and 6.30–10.30pm Mon–Sat. On a busy main road close to *The Guardian* newspaper offices. Outside seating.

⊖ Nearest Tube: Farringdon.

OPEN *12–11pm Mon–Sat; 12–5pm Sun. Closed bank holidays.*

Hogshead

171–76 Aldersgate Street EC1
☎ *(020) 7600 5852*

 Brakspear Bitter, Fuller's London Pride, Marston's Pedigree and Wadworth 6X always available plus guest beers every month.

Recently opened addition to the chain on the ground floor of a former office block. Outside drinking on narrow balcony. Food available 12–9pm Mon–Thurs, 12–7pm Fri.

⊖ Nearest Tube: Barbican.

OPEN *12–11pm Mon–Fri; closed Sat–Sun.*

Jerusalem Tavern

55 Britton Street, Clerkenwell EC1M 5NA
☎ *(020) 7490 4281* Bruce Patterson

 A St Peter's Brewery tied house serving the range of St Peter's brews such as Best Bitter, Strong Bitter, Wheat Beer, Golden Ale, Fruit Beer (elderberry), Summer Ale and Winter Ale. Available on draught and in bottles.

A small, restored coffee house with plenty of atmosphere, no music or machines. Some outside seating. Food available at lunchtime from 12–2.30pm and toasted sandwiches in the evenings. Children allowed.

⊖ Nearest Tube: Farringdon.

OPEN *9am (for coffee)–11pm Mon–Fri; closed Sat–Sun.*

The Leopard

33 Seward Street, Clerkenwell EC1V 3PA
☎ *(020) 7253 3587* Malcolm Jones

 A freehouse with Gibbs Mew (Ushers) Salisbury always available, plus three guests such as Greene King Abbot or brews from O'Hanlon's, Nethergate, Eccleshall and Cottage plus other micros and independents. Guests are changed daily.

A one-bar pub, a mixture of modern and traditional, with wooden floors, conservatory, dining area, disabled facilities and small outside seating area. Food available from 12.30–9pm. Children allowed in conservatory.

⊖ Nearest Tube: Old Street.

OPEN *11am–11pm Mon–Fri; closed Sat–Sun.*

O'Hanlon's

8 Tysoe Street, Islington EC1
☎ *(020) 7278 7630* Paul Stevens

 Former home of the O'Hanlon's Brewery, which has moved to a site in Devon. Despite the change of ownership, still serving the O'Hanlon's range plus Fuller's Chiswick, London Pride and a guest beer.

Traditional street-corner local near Sadlers Wells. Some seats outside in summer. Food served 12–3pm and 6–9pm. Children welcome until early evening.

⊖ Nearest Tube: Angel.

OPEN *8.30am–12am Mon–Fri; 12pm–12am Sat; 12–6pm Sun.*

Ye Olde Mitre

13 Ely Place, Off Hatton Garden EC1
☎ *(020) 7405 4751* Don O'Sullivan

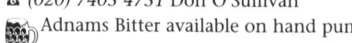 Adnams Bitter available on hand pump.

Unspoilt, historic tavern built in 1547 within the grounds of what was the Bishop of Ely's London palace. Two bars. Standing area outside. Bar snacks served 11am–9.15pm.

⊖ Nearest Tube: Chancery Lane.

OPEN *11am–11pm Mon–Fri; closed Sat–Sun and bank holidays.*

OTHER REAL ALE PUBS IN EC1

The Bishops Finger (SHEPHERD NEAME)
9–10 West Smithfield EC1 ☎ *(020) 7248 2341*

Butcher's Hook & Cleaver (FULLER'S)
61–3 West Smithfield EC1A 9DY
☎ *(020) 7600 0615*

City Pride (FULLER'S)
28 Farringdon Lane, Clerkenwell EC1R 3AU
☎ *(020) 7608 0615*

Hogshead
Cowcross Street EC1 ☎ *(020) 7251 3813*

Melton Mowbray (FULLER'S)
18 Holborn EC1 2LE ☎ *(020) 7405 7077*

Sekforde Arms (YOUNG'S)
34 Sekforde Street EC1 0HA ☎ *(020) 7253 3251*

Sir John Oldcastle (WETHERSPOON)
29–35 Farringdon Road, Farringdon EC1M 3JF
☎ *(020) 7242 1013*

The Masque Hunt (WETHERSPOON)
168–72 Old Street EC1V 9PB
☎ *(020) 7251 4195*

One of Two (FULLER'S)
67–9 Cowcross Street, Smithfield EC1M 6BP
☎ *(020) 7250 3414*

Sutton Arms
15 Great Sutton Street EC1V 0BX
☎ *(020) 7253 2462*

EC2

Crowders Well
185 Fore Street, Barbican EC2Y 5EJ
☎ *(020) 7628 8574* Tom Nicholson

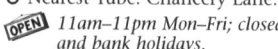 A freehouse with a varied range of guest ales always available.

An old, traditional city-centre pub. Food available from 12–3pm and 6–9pm Mon–Fri and 12–4pm Sun. Function room available for hire free of charge with buffet supplied. Coach parties welcome. No children.

⊖ Nearest Tube: Moorgate.

OPEN *All day Mon–Fri; closed Sat–Sun.*

OTHER REAL ALE PUBS IN EC2

Bill Bentley's (YOUNG'S)
202 Bishopsgate EC2M 4NR
☎ *(020) 7283 1763*

City House (YOUNG'S)
86 Bishopsgate EC2N 4AU
☎ *(020) 7256 8325*

Dirty Dicks (YOUNG'S)
202 Bishopsgate EC2M 4NR
☎ *(020) 7283 5888*

Finch's (YOUNG'S)
12a Finsbury Square EC2A 1AS
☎ *(020) 7588 3311*

Fleetwood (FULLER'S)
36 Wilson Street EC2M 2TE
☎ *(020) 7247 2241*

49 Gresham Street (FULLER'S)
49 Gresham Street EC2
☎ *(020) 7606 0399*

The Greene Man (WETHERSPOON)
1 Poultry, Bank Station EC2R 8EJ
☎ *(020) 7248 3529*

Hamilton Hall (WETHERSPOON)
Unit 32, Liverpool Street Station EC2M 7PY
☎ *(020) 7247 3579*

Hogshead
26 Throgmorton Street EC2N 2AN
☎ *(020) 7588 7289*

The Old Monk
128–48 Bishopsgate EC2 4QX
☎ *(020) 7377 9555*

One of Two (FULLER'S)
45 Old Broad Street EC2N 12HU
☎ *(020) 7588 4845*

One of Two (FULLER'S)
130 Wood Street EC2V 6DL
☎ *(020) 7600 9642*

Red Herring (FULLER'S)
49 Gresham Street EC2V 7ET
☎ *(020) 7606 0399*

EC3

The Hoop & Grapes
47 Aldgate High Street EC3
☎ *(020) 7265 5171* Hugh Ede

 Fuller's London Pride always available, plus three guests which could well include Timothy Taylor Landlord, Brakspear Special and Best, Badger Best, Adnams Bitter and Extra, Charles Wells Bombardier, Eagle or IPA, Shepherd Neame Spitfire, Hook Norton Old Hooky or Wychwood Hobgoblin or Special. An average of 50 different beers served every year.

A 400-year-old pub just inside the Square Mile. Bar food served every lunchtime 12–3pm, with table service available. No children.

⊖ Nearest Tube: Aldgate.

OPEN *11am–10pm Mon–Wed; 11am–11pm Thurs–Fri; closed Sat–Sun.*

OTHER REAL ALE PUBS IN EC3

Bill Bentley's (Young's)
5 Minories EC3N 1BJ ☎ *(020) 7481 1779*

Bill Bentley's By The Monument (Young's)
1 St George's Lane EC3R 8DR
☎ *(020) 7929 2244*

Chamberlain Hotel (Fuller's)
132 Minories EC3N 1NT
☎ *(020) 7680 1500*

Counting House (Fuller's)
50 Cornhill EC3V 3PD
☎ *(020) 7283 7123*

The Crosse Keys (Wetherspoon)
9 Gracechurch Street EC3V 0DR
☎ *(020) 7623 4824*

The Eastern Monk (Old Monk)
133 Houndsditch EC3A 7BX
☎ *(020) 7929 0902*

Elephant (Young's)
119 Fenchurch Street EC3M 5BA
☎ *(020) 7623 8970*

Fine Line (Fuller's)
124–27 The Minories EC3 1NT
☎ *(020) 7481 8195*

Fine Line (Fuller's)
1 Bow Churchyard EC4M 9PQ
☎ *(020) 7248 3262*

Hogshead
America Square EC3
☎ *(020) 7702 2381*

Hogshead
29 St Mary Axe EC3A 8AA
☎ *(020) 7929 0245*

Hung Drawn and Quartered
(Fuller's)
26–7 Great Tower Street EC3R 5AQ
☎ *(020) 7626 6123*

Lamb Tavern (Young's)
10–12 Leadenhall Market EC3V 1LR
☎ *(020) 7626 2454*

The Liberty Bounds (Wetherspoon)
15 Trinity Square EC3N 4AA
☎ *(020) 7481 0513*

Mint (Fuller's)
Royal Mint Court, 12 East Smithfield EC3
☎ *(020) 7702 0371*

The Old Monk
80 Leadenhall Street EC3 3DH
☎ *(020) 7621 0850*

Swan (Fuller's)
Ship Tavern Passage, 77–80 Gracechurch Street EC3V 0AS
☎ *(020) 7283 7712*

Three Lords (Young's)
27 Minories EC3N 1DD
☎ *(020) 7481 4249*

Walrus & Carpenter (Young's)
45 Monument Street EC3R 8BU
☎ *(020) 7626 3362*

Willy's Wine Bar (Young's)
107 Fenchurch Street EC3 5JB
☎ *(020) 7480 7289*

Wine Lodge (Young's)
Sackville House, 145 Fenchurch Street EC3M 6BL
☎ *(020) 7626 0918*

EC4

The Old Bank of England
194 Fleet Street EC4 2LT
☎ *(020) 7430 2255* Victoria Meadows

 A Fuller's flagship alehouse with London Pride, Chiswick and ESB always available plus the usual seasonal brews.

A n impressive conversion of a Victorian building that was once part of the Bank of England annexed to the law courts. Styled in brass and wood. Two separate rooms for dining (smoking and non-smoking) in which food is available 12–9pm Mon–Thurs and 12–4pm Fri. Full bar menu, including popular pies. No children.

⊖ Nearest Tube: Temple.

OPEN *11am–11pm Mon–Fri; closed Sat–Sun, although available for private party hire.*

Black Friar

174 Queen Victoria Street EC4
☎ *(020) 7236 5650* Mr Becker

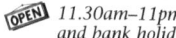 Adnams Bitter, Fuller's London Pride and Marston's Pedigree available.

Popular and original pub on a triangular site on the edge of The City. Bar food available 12–2.30pm Mon–Fri. Children allowed. Outside standing area.

⊖ Nearest Tube: Blackfriars.

OPEN *11.30am–11pm Mon–Fri; closed Sat–Sun and bank holidays.*

The Hogshead

100 Ludgate Hill EC4
☎ *(020) 7329 8517* Mike Wren

 Marston's Pedigree, Morland Old Speckled Hen, Fuller's London Pride and a beer from Adnams and Brakspear usually available plus up to four guests. These might be from Bateman or almost any independent brewery.

A modern-style pub which retains an authentic feel. Previously known as The Old King Lud. Food available all day Mon–Thurs. No children.

⊖ Nearest Tube: Blackfriars.

OPEN *11.30am–11pm Mon–Fri; closed Sat–Sun.*

Hoop & Grapes

80 Farringdon Street EC4A 4BL
☎ *(020) 7353 8808* D Peregrine

 Acquired by Hall & Woodhouse two years ago, so serving Sussex Bitter, Best and Tanglefoot.

Formerly known as Samuels, saved from demolition and refurbished by the new owners. Outside seating. Restaurant and function room upstairs. Food available all day.

⊖ Nearest Tube: Farringdon.

OPEN *11am–11pm Mon–Fri; available for private hire on Sat.*

St Bride's Tavern

1 Bridewell Place EC4
☎ *(020) 7353 1614* Carol Partridge

 Greene King IPA and Abbot always available and one guest pump which regularly features Everards Tiger.

A traditional City pub. Food available lunchtimes only. Children allowed.

⊖ Nearest Tube: Blackfriars.

OPEN *11am–11pm Mon–Fri; closed Sat–Sun.*

Williamson's Tavern

1 Groveland Court EC4
☎ *(020) 7248 6280* Russ McGilvrey

Adnams beers usually available plus up to six guest ales from breweries such as Brakspear. Fewer guests available in winter.

An old, three-bar pub situated off Bow Lane. Food available 11.30am–3pm and 5–9pm. Well-behaved children allowed.

⊖ Nearest Tube: Mansion House.

OPEN *11.30am–11pm Mon–Fri; closed Sat–Sun.*

OTHER REAL ALE PUBS IN EC4

Banker (FULLER'S)
Cousin Lane EC4R 3TE
☎ *(020) 7283 5206*

City Retreat (YOUNG'S)
74 Shoe Lane EC4 3BQ
☎ *(020) 7353 7904*

Fine Line (FULLER'S)
1 Bow Churchyard EC4M 9PQ
☎ *(020) 7248 3262*

Hogshead
5 Fetter Lane EC4A 1BR
☎ *(020) 7353 1387*

The Old Monk
1 Fleet Street, Holborn Viaduct EC4M 7RA
☎ *(020) 7236 4262*

Shaws Booksellers (FULLER'S)
31–4 St Andrew's Hill EC4V 5DE
☎ *(020) 7489 7999*

WC1

Calthorpe Arms

252 Gray's Inn Road WC1X 8JR
☎ *(020) 7278 4732* Adrian and Tessa Larner

Popular Young's pub serving Bitter, Special and seasonal brews.

One-bar street-corner local. Upstairs dining room. Food served at lunchtime.

⊖ Nearest Tube: Russell Square.

OPEN *11am–11pm Mon–Sat; 12–10.30pm Sun.*

Cittie of Yorke

22 High Holborn WC1
☎ *(020) 7242 7670* Stuart Browning

Sam Smith's London flagship, serving Old Brewery Bitter at a competitive price.

Recently restored and impressively huge with a history dating back to 1430. Enormous back bar with side booths and adjoining wood-panelled room. Bar food available 12–9pm Mon–Sat. Well-behaved children allowed.

⊖ Nearest Tube: Chancery Lane.

OPEN *11.30am–11pm Mon–Sat; closed Sun and bank holidays.*

The College Arms
18 Store Street WC1E 7DH
☎ *(020) 7436 4697* Paul Davies

A freehouse serving Greene King IPA, Adnams Broadside or Regatta, Shepherd Neame Spitfire plus one guest rotating monthly, such as Fuller's London Pride.

Formerly The University Tavern, now a one-bar pub with large open-plan basement seating area situated next door to England & Wales College of Law, so very student-oriented. Bare and basic traditional pub, with wooden floors, large-screen TVs and outside seating. Food available 12–4pm and 5–9pm Mon–Fri. No children or dogs. Situated off Tottenham Court Road.

⊖ Nearest Tube: Goodge Street.

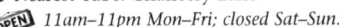*11am–11pm Mon–Fri; closed Sat–Sun except for major sporting events.*

The King's Arms
11a Northington Street, Bloomsbury WC1N 2JF
☎ *(020) 7405 9107* Clive Gilbert

Greene King IPA, Marston's Pedigree and Wadworth 6X usually available, plus occasional guests but no very strong ales.

A one-bar, office workers' pub in the midst of a legal and media professional area. Food available at lunchtime only. No children.

⊖ Nearest Tube: Chancery Lane.

11am–11pm Mon–Fri; closed Sat–Sun.

The Lamb
92–4 Lamb's Conduit Street WC1N 3LZ
☎ *(020) 7405 0713* Michael and Joanne Hehir

Young's brews always available including seasonal ales.

A popular Young's pub in a Grade II listed building. Upstairs dining room. Food available at lunchtime every day (except Sat) and Mon–Fri evenings. Children in eating area only.

⊖ Nearest Tube: Russell Square.

11am–11pm Mon–Sat; 12–4 and 7–10.30pm Sun.

The Museum Tavern
49 Great Russell Street WC1
☎ *(020) 7242 8987* Tony Williamson

Up to six beers usually available, including Fuller's London Pride.

Traditional, Victorian pub situated opposite the British Museum. The front and back bars are listed buildings. Food available all day. Outside seating area. No children.

⊖ Nearest Tube: Holborn/Tottenham Court Road.

11am–11pm Mon–Sat; 12–10.30pm Sun and bank holidays.

The Oarsman
2 New Oxford Street WC1A 1EE
☎ *(020) 7404 5009* Leigh Sullivan-Plews

Two real ales always available. Charles Wells Bombardier is a regular but other, more unusual, ales from independent breweries are also served as available.

A small one-bar pub with outside seating. Homemade food available all day. Children allowed.

⊖ Nearest Tube: Tottenham Court Road.

12–11pm Mon–Fri; closed Sat–Sun, except for private hire.

Overdraught's
6 Dane Street WC1R 4BL
☎ *(020) 7405 6087*

Three real ales usually available, perhaps including Thwaites Best and Forge Smithy, Rebellion Smugglers and something from Greene King.

Tiny, unpretentious street-corner pub beneath residential premises off High Holborn. Separate bar/function room available downstairs.

⊖ Nearest Tube: Holborn.

11.30am–11pm Mon–Fri; closed Sat–Sun.

Pakenham Arms
1 Pakenham Street WC1X 0LA
☎ *(020) 7837 6933* Pat Mulligan

Up to seven real ales that might include beers from Fuller's, Young's, Slaters, Adnams, Ringwood plus other smaller breweries such as North Yorkshire and Fisherrow.

Large, popular local near Mount Pleasant sorting office with extended opening hours as a result. Breakfast, lunch and dinner available. Some brews sold at reduced prices.

⊖ Nearest Tube: King's Cross.

9.30–1.30am Mon–Sun.

Rugby Tavern
19 Great James Street WC1N 3ES
☎ *(020) 7405 1384*

Formerly Fuller's, now Shepherd Neame. Serving Master Brew, Best, Spitfire, Bishop's Finger and seasonal brews such as Early Bird.

Recently refurbished, popular locals' pub. Outside seating. Food available at lunchtime and evenings.

⊖ Nearest Tube: Holborn.

11am–11pm Mon–Fri; 12–3pm and 6–11pm Sat (summer only); closed Sun.

Swan
7 Cosmo Place WC1
☎ *(020) 7837 6223*

Up to six real ales always available including Greene King IPA and Abbot, plus guests.

One-bar pub down pedestrian alley between Southampton Row and Queen's Square. Outside seating. Food available all day.

⊖ Nearest Tube: Russell Square.

OPEN *11am–11pm Mon–Sat; 12–10.30pm Sun.*

OTHER REAL ALE PUBS IN WC1

The Old Monk
39–41 Gray's Inn Road WC1X 8PP
☎ *(020) 7242 9094*

Penderel's Oak (WETHERSPOON)
283–8 High Holborn, Holborn WC1V 7PF
☎ *(020) 7242 5669*

Three Cups (YOUNG'S)
21–2 Sandland Street WC1R 4PZ
☎ *(020) 7831 4302*

WC2

The Crown
43 Monmouth Street WC2H 9DD
☎ *(020) 7836 5861* Mr Brocklebank

An Adnams ale is usually available plus up to four guest ales. Morland Old Speckled Hen and Marston's Pedigree are regular features.

A traditional, two-bar pub near Seven Dials. Generally quiet, with background music and a mixed clientele. Food available all day. No children.

⊖ Nearest Tube: Leicester Square.

OPEN *11am–11pm Mon–Sat; closed Sun.*

Edgar Wallace
40 Essex Street WC2
☎ *(020) 7353 3120*

Adnams Bitter, Wadworth 6X and Charles Wells Bombardier among those brews always available, plus a couple of guests.

Listed building down small side street between the river and the Strand.

⊖ Nearest Tube: Temple.

OPEN *11am–11pm Mon–Fri; closed Sat–Sun.*

Knights Templar
95 Chancery Lane WC2A 1DT
☎ *(020) 7831 2660*
Gerard Swards and Steven Morris

Fuller's London Pride, Bateman XXXB, Shepherd Neame Spitfire, Hop Back Summer Lightning and Greene King Abbot available.

Another huge Wetherspoon's conversion right in the legal heart of the city. Food available all day.

⊖ Nearest Tube: Chancery Lane.

OPEN *11am–11pm Mon Sat; 12–10.30pm Sun.*

Lamb & Flag
33 Rose Street WC2
☎ *(020) 7497 9504* Terry Archer

Marston's Pedigree, Young's Bitter and Special and one or two guests available.

Popular, Elizabethan pub in the heart of Covent Garden, once known as the Cooper's Arms. Bar food available at lunchtime (12–2pm). Children in eating area only.

⊖ Nearest Tube: Leicester Square.

OPEN *11am–11pm Mon–Sat; 12–10.30pm Sun.*

Moon Under Water
105–7 Charing Cross Road WC2H 0BP
☎ *(020) 7287 6039* Nic Harper

One of Central London's finer Wetherspoon's establishments serving Fuller's London Pride, Shepherd Neame Spitfire, Greene King Abbot and several other brews. Regular beer festivals.

An impressive conversion of the former Marquee Club. Modern and huge, spread over three floors. Food served all day. No children. Cask Marque approved.

⊖ Nearest Tube: Tottenham Court Road.

OPEN *11am–11pm Mon–Sat; 12–10.30pm Sun.*

The Round House
1 Garrick Street, Covent Garden WC2E 9AR
☎ *(020) 7836 9838* Ollie McClorey

Greene King Abbot and IPA and Marston's Pedigree usually available, plus a minimum of two guests per week from independent and micro-breweries far and wide.

A small, one-bar real ale house with no juke box or machines. Food available all day. Children allowed at weekends only.

⊖ Nearest Tube: Leicester Square.

OPEN *11am–11pm Mon–Sat; 12–10.30pm Sun.*

The Round Table
26 St Martin's Court WC2N 4AL
☎ *(020) 7836 6436* Suzanne Simpson

Charles Wells Bombardier and Fuller's London Pride always on offer.

A lively pub with a friendly atmosphere just off Charing Cross Road. Full menu available all day. Children allowed until 7pm. Separate function room available.

⊖ Nearest Tube: Leicester Square.

OPEN *11am–11pm Mon–Sat; 12–10.30pm Sun.*

The Seven Stars
53 Carey Street WC2A 2JB
☎ *(020) 7242 8521* Roxy Beaujolais

Adnams Best, Broadside and Regatta always available plus seasonal Adnams brews and a guest beer such as Harveys Best.

O riginally known as The League of Seven Stars in honour of the Dutch sailors who settled in the area, this unspoilt, 400-year-old two-bar freehouse behind the Law Courts has been tactfully restored and enhanced. A new kitchen means food is now served in the smaller bar until 7.30pm Mon–Fri and 10.30pm Sat.

⊖ Nearest Tube: Holborn/Temple.

OPEN *11am–11pm Mon–Sat; closed Sun and some holidays.*

Ship & Shovell
1–3 Craven Pasage WC2N 5PH
☎ *(020) 7839 1311* A O'Neill

Owned by Hall and Woodhouse, so Badger IPA, Dorset Best and Tanglefoot always available plus seasonal brews.

E nlarged pub on either side of pedestrian passage near Trafalgar Square.

⊖ Nearest Tube: Embankment.

OPEN *11am–11pm Mon–Fri; 12–9pm Sat; closed Sun.*

OTHER REAL ALE PUBS IN WC2

Columbia Bar (YOUNG'S)
69 Aldwych WC2B 4RW
☎ *(020) 7831 8043*

Fine Line (FULLER'S)
77 Kingsway WC2B 6SR
☎ *(020) 7405 5004*

Hogshead
5 Lisle Street, Leicester Square WC2H 7BF
☎ *(020) 7437 3335*

Hogshead
23 Wellington Street WC2E 7DA
☎ *(020) 7836 6930*

Marquess of Anglesey (YOUNG'S)
39 Bow Street WC2E 7AU
☎ *(020) 7240 3216*

The Moon under Water (WETHERSPOON)
28 Leicester Square WC2H 7LE
☎ *(020) 7839 2837*

Shakespeare's Head (WETHERSPOON)
Africa House, 64–8 Kingsway, Holborn WC2B 6BG
☎ *(020) 7404 8846*

LONDON EAST

E1

Pride of Spitalfields
3 Heneage Street, Spitalfields E1 5LJ
☎ *(020) 7247 8933* Ann Butler

Fuller's Chiswick, London Pride and ESB are available, plus seasonals and a weekly changing guest, such as Crouch Vale IPA or Woodham IPA.

F riendly, small and comfortable, one-bar, side-street pub, attracting good mixed clientele. Homemade food served at lunchtime. Children welcome. Turn left out of Algate East tube station (Whitechapel Art Gallery end), left again then take the third side street on the left.

⊖ Nearest Tube: Aldgate East.

OPEN *11am–11pm Mon–Sat; 12–10.30pm Sun.*

OTHER REAL ALE PUBS IN E1

The Half Moon (Wetherspoon)
213–23 Mile End Road, Stepney Green E1 4AA
☎ *(020) 7790 6810*

Mint (Fuller's)
12 East Smithfield E1 9AP ☎ *(020) 7702 0370*

The Old Monk
32 Leman Street E1 8EW ☎ *(020) 7680 4006*

The Old Monk
94–8 Middlesex Street E1 7DA
☎ *(020) 7247 1727*

The Old Monk
Thomas More Square, Nesham Street E1W 1YY
☎ *(020) 7702 9222*

Shooting Star (Fuller's)
125–9 Middlesex Street E1 7JF
☎ *(020) 7629 6818*

The White Swan (Shepherd Neame)
21 Alie Street E1 ☎ *(020) 7702 0448*

E2

The Approach Tavern
47 Approach Road, Bethnal Green E2 9LY
☎ *(020) 8980 2321 Caroline Apperley*

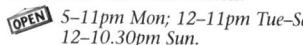 A freehouse with Morland Old Speckled Hen, Fuller's London Pride, Wadworth 6X, Adnams Bitter and Marston's Pedigree usually available. Guests stocked occasionally.

A friendly pub with good atmosphere, decorated with photographs. Gallery, beer garden. Food available at lunchtime and evenings Tues–Sun. Children and dogs on lead welcome.

⊖ Nearest Tube: Shoreditch.

OPEN *5–11pm Mon; 12–11pm Tue–Sat; 12–10.30pm Sun.*

OTHER REAL ALE PUBS IN E2

The Camden's Head (Wetherspoon)
456 Bethnal Green Road, Bethnal Green E2 0EA
☎ *(020) 7613 4263*

E3

The Coburn Arms
8 Coburn Road, Bow E3 2DA
☎ *(020) 8980 3793 Peter and Norma Footman*

 A Young's pub with Bitter and Special always available.

A busy one-bar locals' pub. Food available 12–2pm and 6.30–9pm Mon–Fri and 1–9pm Sat–Sun. Outside seating. No children.

⊖ Nearest Tube: Bow Road/Mile End.

OPEN *11am–11pm Mon–Sat; 12–10.30pm Sun.*

The Crown
223 Grove Road E3
☎ *(020) 8981 9998*
Esther Boulton and Sangeeta Singh

 One of the few direct outlets for the Pitfield Brewery, who provide a special house ale (Singhboulton), Pitfield Eco Warrior and Black Eagle plus St Peter's Organic Best. Also organic lager and cider.

Organic food and organic drink only at this popular gastro-freehouse opened in 2000 in a Victorian building overlooking Victoria Park. Restaurant food and bar snacks available at lunchtime and evenings. Outside seating. Children welcome. See also the Duke of Cambridge (N1) and The Pelican (W11).

⊖ Nearest Tube: Bow Road/Mile End.

OPEN *5–11pm Mon; 10.30am–11pm Tues–Sat; 10.30am–10.30pm Sun.*

E4

Kings Ford
250–2 Chingford Mount Road, Chingford E4 8JL
☎ *(020) 8523 9365*

 Popular Wetherspoon pub so with the chain staples such as Greene King Abbot, Wadworth 6X, Shepherd Neame Spitfire etc plus three or four guests at any one time.

A busy pub not far from Walthamstow Greyhound Stadium beyond the North Circular Road. Food served all day.

OPEN *11am–11pm Mon–Sat; 12–10.30pm Sun.*

E5

The Anchor & Hope
15 High Hill Ferry, Clapton E5 9HG
☎ *(020) 8806 1730 Leslie Heath*

 A Fuller's pub, serving ESB and London Pride.

A small, popular, single-bar establishment beside the River Lea near Walthamstow Marshes. No food. Children allowed outside only.

OPEN *11am–3pm and 5.30–11pm Mon–Sat; 12–10.30pm Sun.*

OTHER REAL ALE PUBS IN E5

Princess of Wales (Young's)
146 Lea Bridge Road, Clapton E5 9QB
☎ *(020) 8533 3463*

E6

Millers Well

419–23 Barking Road, East Ham E6 2JX
☎ *(020) 8471 8404*

A Wetherspoon pub with six regular brews including Greene King Abbot, Wadworth 6X and Shepherd Neame Spitfire plus a couple of guests.

A former wine bar, converted and extended. Food available all day every day.

⊖ Nearest Tube: Plaistow.

OPEN *11am–11pm Mon–Sat; 12–10.30pm Sun.*

E7

The Old Spotted Dog

212 Upton Lane, Forest Gate E7 9NP
☎ *(020) 8472 1794* Ray Saunders

Marston's Pedigree and Morland Old Speckled Hen always available, plus two guests, changing weekly.

A Tudor pub with two large bars, restaurant, family room and children's play area. Bar snacks available at lunchtime, restaurant food available every evening (7–10pm). Children allowed.

⊖ Nearest Tube: Upton Park.

OPEN *11am–11pm Mon–Sat; 12–10.30pm Sun.*

OTHER REAL ALE PUBS IN E7

The Hudson Bay (WETHERSPOON)
1–5 Upton Lane, Forest Gate E7 9PA
☎ *(020) 8471 7702*

E10

The Drum

557–9 Lea Bridge Road, Leyton E10 7EQ
☎ *(020) 8539 6577*

A Wetherspoon pub with all the usual suspects always available plus a couple of more interesting guests.

A busy local recently reopened and refurbished after a fire. Food available at lunchtime and evenings.

⊖ Nearest Tube: Walthamstow Central.

OPEN *11am–11pm Mon–Sat; 12–10.30pm Sun.*

King William IV

816 High Road, Leyton E10 6AE
☎ *(020) 8556 2460* Michael Debono

A popular brewpub with up to ten cask ales available at any one time. Home brews always available include Just William, William the Conqueror and East London Mild, plus seasonal brews. Fuller's London Pride and ESB also always available together with an ever-changing menu of interesting guests sourced from all over the country.

A traditional and genuine East London freehouse with two large bars and a micro-brewery in a converted stable at the back. Food available 12–3pm and 5.30–8.30pm Mon–Sat, 12.30–5pm Sun. Children welcome until 7pm. Quiz on Sunday evenings.

⊖ Nearest Tube: Leyton/Walthamstow Central.

OPEN *11am–11pm Mon–Sat; 12–10.30pm Sun.*

E11

The Birkbeck Tavern

45 Langthorne Road, Leytonstone E11 4HL
☎ *(020) 8539 2584* Roy Leach

A freehouse with a house brew (Rita's Special 4%) named after a previous landlady always available. Plus Fuller's London Pride, Marston's Pedigree and two guests changed at least twice a week.

A friendly, backstreet community pub in a late Victorian building. Two bars, function room and garden. Sandwiches only available at lunchtime. Children allowed in the garden.

⊖ Nearest Tube: Leyton.

OPEN *11am–11pm Mon–Sat; 12–10.30pm Sun.*

The Sir Alfred Hitchcock

147 Whipps Cross Road, Leytonstone E11 1NP
☎ *(020) 8532 9662*
Jason Flack and Michelle Laverty

A freehouse with five beers usually available, perhaps including Black Sheep Bitter, Brakspear Bitter, Wadworth 6X and Fuller's London Pride.

L arge, rambling pub opposite Hollow Ponds with several inter-connecting rooms and a rear terrace. Refurbished restaurant specialising in steaks, burgers and seafood and serving at lunchtimes and evenings. Plus Sunday carvery. Quiz nights. Children welcome.

⊖ Nearest Tube: Leytonstone.

OPEN *11am–11pm Mon–Sat; 12–10.30pm Sun*

OTHER REAL ALE PUBS IN E11

The George (WETHERSPOON)
High Street, Wanstead E11 2RL
☎ *(020) 8989 2921*

The Walnut Tree (WETHERSPOON)
857–61 High Street, Leytonstone E11 1HH
☎ *(020) 8539 2526*

E14

The Grapes
76 Narrow Street, Limehouse E14
☎ *(020) 7987 4396* Barbara Haigh

Adnams Bitter and Marston's Pedigree always available.

Popular, long, narrow riverside pub with a considerable history and splendid views. Bar and restaurant food (especially seafood) available at lunchtime and evenings (not Sun evening).

⊖ Nearest Tube: Limehouse/Westferry DLR.

OPEN *12–3pm Mon–Sun; 5.30–11pm Mon–Sat; 7–10.30pm Sun.*

The Oporto Tavern
43 West India Dock Road E14 8EZ
☎ *(020) 8987 1530* Steve Baldwin

Three guest beers. Wadworth 6X, Greene King IPA and a Brains brew among those regularly available. Other guests changed monthly.

A traditional male-dominated boozer set in a Victorian building retaining some original features. One bar, TV, darts, pool and racing club. Hot food, including specials, and baguettes available 12–3pm. Children allowed in the paved area at front with bench seating.

⊖ Nearest Tube: Westferry DLR.

OPEN *11am–11pm Mon–Sat; 12–10.30pm Sun.*

OTHER REAL ALE PUBS IN E14

Cat & Canary (FULLER'S)
Building FC2, 1–24 Fisherman's Walk, Canary Wharf E14 4DJ
☎ *(020) 7512 9187*

Fine Line (FULLER'S)
10 Cabot Square, Canary Wharf E14 4QB
☎ *(020) 7513 0255*

Queens Head (YOUNG'S)
8 Flamborough Street E14 7LS
☎ *(020) 7791 2504*

E15

The Golden Grove
146–148 The Grove, Stratford E15 1NS
☎ *(020) 8519 0750* Sue Guyatt

Greene King Abbot Ale and Shepherd Neame Spitfire always available plus three guests such as Hop Back Summer Lightning.

A large, popular Wetherspoon pub with one bar, non-smoking dining area, no music, disabled access and beer garden. Food available all day. No children.

⊖ Nearest Tube: Stratford.

OPEN *11am–11pm Mon–Sat; 12–10.30pm Sun.*

King Edward VII
47 Broadway, Stratford E15 4BQ
☎ *(020) 8221 9841* Paul Taylor

Fuller's London Pride and two guest beers usually available, which may include Shepherd Neame Bishop's Finger, Morland Old Speckled Hen, Badger Tanglefoot, Adnams Bitter, Wychwood Dog's Bollocks, Hop Back Summer Lightning or Timothy Taylor Landlord.

Original, three-bar London tavern with lots of wood, beams and mirrors. Air-conditioned. Prize quiz nights Sunday and Wednesday. Food served 12–7pm every day. No children.

⊖ Nearest Tube: Stratford.

OPEN *12–11pm (10.30pm Sun).*

E17

The Village
31 Orford Road, Walthamstow E17 9NL
☎ *(020) 8521 9982* Gary Leader

Five real ales always available, with Fuller's London Pride, Caledonian Deuchars IPA and Bateman XB usually on offer, plus two guests which could come from any independent brewery, although Hook Norton, Everards and Adnams brews are regular favourites.

A refurbished residential pub with one bar and one snug. Large garden. Food available every lunchtime and some evenings. No children.

⊖ Nearest Tube: Walthamstow Central.

OPEN *11am–11pm (10.30pm Sun).*

E18

Hogshead
184 George Lane, South Woodford E18 1AY
☎ *(020) 8989 8542*

LONDON NORTH

N1

Compton Arms
4 Compton Avenue, Islington N1
☎ *(020) 7359 6883* Paul Fairweather

 A Greene King pub, so with Abbot and IPA plus seasonal brews always available.

Asmall, unspoilt local tucked away near Highbury Corner. Food available at lunchtime and evenings (not Tues). Small, part-covered garden. Children by day only.

⊖ Nearest Tube: Highbury and Islington.

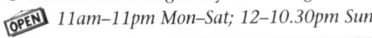 *11am–11pm Mon–Sat; 12–10.30pm Sun.*

Duke of Cambridge
30 St Peter's Street N1 8JT
☎ *(020) 7359 9450*
Esther Boulton and Sangeeta Singh

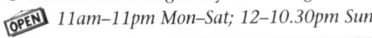 One of the few direct outlets for the Pitfield Brewery, who provide a special house ale (Singhboulton), Pitfield Eco Warrior and Black Eagle plus St Peter's Best. Also organic lager and cider.

Organic food and organic drink only at this popular, refurbished street-corner gastro-freehouse. Restaurant food and bar snacks available at lunchtime and evenings. Outside seating. Children welcome. A sister pub (The Crown E3) followed its lead in Bow during 2000 and a third (The Pelican W11) opened in Ladbroke Grove in 2001.

⊖ Nearest Tube: Angel.

 5–11pm Mon; 12–11pm Tues–Sat;
12–10.30pm Sun.

The Wenlock Arms
26 Wenlock Road, Hoxton N1 7TA
☎ *(020) 7608 3406* Steven Barnes

 A genuine freehouse with up to eight real ales always available. At least one Adnams brew always on offer plus a mild and something from the nearby Pitfield Brewery. The rest of the menu is an ever-changing selection from brewers up and down the country.

Apopular street-corner, one-bar pub with a big real ale reputation. Sandwiches and pasties only available. No children after 9pm. Live music on Sat evening and Sun lunchtime. Quiz on Thurs.

⊖ Nearest Tube: Old Street/Angel.

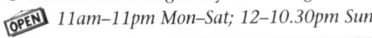 *12–11pm (10.30pm Sun).*

OTHER REAL ALE PUBS IN N1

The Angel (WETHERSPOON)
3–5 High Street, Islington N1 9LQ
☎ *(020) 7837 2218*

The Crown (FULLER'S)
116 Cloudesley Road, Islington N1 0EB
☎ *(020) 7837 7107*

Earl of Radnor (FULLER'S)
106 Mildmay Grove N1
☎ *(020) 7241 0318*

George & Vulture (FULLER'S)
63 Pitfield Street, Hoxton N1 6BU
☎ *(020) 7253 3988*

Hogshead
77 Upper Street, Islington N1 0NU
☎ *(020) 7359 8052*

Hope and Anchor (GREENE KING)
207 Upper Street N1
☎ *(020) 7354 1312*

Marquess Tavern (YOUNG'S)
32 Canonbury Street, Islington N1 2TB
☎ *(020) 7354 2975*

The White Swan (WETHERSPOON)
255–6 Upper Street, Islington N1 1RY
☎ *(020) 7288 9050*

N2

Madden's Ale House
130 High Road, East Finchley N2 7ED
☎ *(020) 8444 7444*

 Greene King Abbot, Wadworth 6X, Fuller's London Pride and Adnams Broadside always available plus up to eight guests (300 per year) including Ridleys Witchfinder Porter, Gibbs Mew Bishop's Tipple, Ringwood Old Thumper and Fortyniner etc. Also country wines.

Aconverted shop on the High Road. Bar food available at lunchtime. Children allowed.

⊖ Nearest Tube: East Finchley.

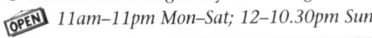 *11am–11pm Mon–Fri; 12–10.30pm Sun.*

N4

The White Lion of Mortimer
(WETHERSPOON)
125–7 Stroud Green Road, Stroud Green
N4 3PX
☎ *(020) 7561 8880*

The Old Suffolk Punch
(WETHERSPOON)
10–12 Grand Parade, Green Lanes, Haringey
N4 1JX
☎ *(020) 8800 5912*

N6

The Flask
77 Highgate West Hill N6 6BU
☎ *(020) 8340 7260* Rupert Reeves

Adnams Bitter, Harveys Sussex, Timothy Taylor Landlord, Hopback Summer Lightning and Fuller's London Pride typically available. Other guests and seasonal beers may come from Smiles, Highgate (in the East Midlands), Bateman or similar breweries.

Popular, former coaching inn in the heart of Highgate village. Built in 1663, still with many original features. There is a large paved outside seating area. Food available 12–3pm and 6–10pm (9.30pm Sun). Children and dogs welcome.

⊖ Nearest Tube: Highgate.

OPEN *11am–11pm Mon–Sat; 12–10.30pm Sun.*

OTHER REAL ALE PUBS IN N6

The Gatehouse (WETHERSPOON)
1 North Road, Highgate N6 4BD
☎ *(020) 8340 8054*

N7

The Coronet (WETHERSPOON)
338–46 Holloway Road, Holloway N7 6NJ
☎ *(020) 7609 5014*

N8

The Hogshead
33–5 Crouch End Hill, Crouch End N8 8DH
☎ *(020) 8342 8465* Nichola Cripps

Wadworth 6X, Marston's Pedigree, Fuller's London Pride among the brews always available, plus up to six guests, which might well include Young's Bitter and beers from O'Hanlon's and Shepherd Neame.

A one-bar pub in the heart of Crouch End (so some distance from a Tube). Disabled access, background music, fruit machines, internet games. Food available 12–9pm Mon–Thurs, 12–8pm Fri–Sun. No children.

⊖ Nearest Tube: Finsbury Park.

OPEN *11am–11pm Mon–Sat; 12–10.30pm Sun*

OTHER REAL ALE PUBS IN N8

The Toll Gate (WETHERSPOON)
26–30 Turnpike Lane N8 0PS
☎ *(020) 8889 9085*

N9

The Lamb Inn
52–54 Church Street, Lower Edmonton N9 9PA
☎ *(020) 8887 0128* Dave and Brenda Andrews

A freehouse with Greene King IPA and Fuller's London Pride among the brews always available, plus up to five guests including, perhaps, Greene King Abbot Ale and Fuller's ESB.

A modern, community pub with one large bar, non-smoking dining area and disabled access. Food available all day. Children allowed.

OPEN *All day, every day.*

N12

Elephant Inn (FULLER'S)
283 Ballards Lane, Finchley N12 8NR
☎ *(020) 8445 0356*

The Tally Ho (WETHERSPOON)
749 High Road, North Finchley N12 0BP
☎ *(020) 8445 4390*

N13

The Whole Hog (WETHERSPOON)
430–4 Green Lanes, Palmers Green N13 5XG
☎ *(020) 8882 3597*

N14

The New Crown (WETHERSPOON)
80–4 Chase Side, Southgate N14 5PH
☎ *(020) 8882 8758*

N16

The Rochester Castle
145 Stoke Newington High Street, Stoke Newington N16 0YN
☎ *(020) 7249 6016*

Greene King Abbot and Shepherd Neame Spitfire always available plus six guests each week, rotated on three hand pumps. Regulars include Hop Back Summer Lightning and Fuller's London Pride.

A huge Wetherspoon pub with one big bar, patio, disabled access and facilities. No music. Board games – chess, backgammon etc. Non-smoking dining area. Food available all day. Children allowed.

OPEN *All day, every day.*

OTHER REAL ALE PUBS IN N16

The Daniel Defoe (CHARLES WELLS)
102 Stoke Newington Church Street N16
☎ *(020) 7254 2906*

N17

The New Moon
413 Lordship Lane, Tottenham N17 6AG
☎ *(020) 8801 3496* Tom Connelly

A freehouse with Wyre Piddle Piddle in the Wind always available, plus three guests stocked to customer order. Customers tick a list of suggested ales each month and the ones with the most ticks win! Badger Tanglefoot is popular.

A large town pub with three bars, dining area, patio, disabled access and facilities. Food available at lunchtimes and evenings. Children allowed.

OPEN *All day, every day.*

N18

The Gilpin's Bell (WETHERSPOON)
50–4 Fore Street, Upper Edmonton N18 2SS
☎ *(020) 8884 2744*

N21

The Orange Tree
18 Highfield Road, Winchmore Hill N21 3HD
☎ *(0208) 360 4853* John Maher

Greene King IPA and Abbot, Ruddles Best and County usually available with a guest frequently from B&T Brewery, Fuller's or Adnams.

Comfortable, traditional one-bar house with pub games and beer garden. Regional CAMRA award winner. Food served 12–2.30pm daily plus all day on Sat. Children welcome in the beer garden. No car park but plenty of parking nearby. Located off Green Lanes, enter through Carpenter Gardens.

OPEN *12–11pm (10.30pm Sun).*

N22

Wetherspoon's
*5 Spouters Corner, High Road,
Wood Green N22 6EJ*
☎ *(020) 8881 3891*

The Phoenix Bar
Alexandra Palace N22 ☎
(020) 8365 2121

LONDON NORTH WEST

NW1

Head of Steam
1 Eversholt Street, Euston NW1 1DN
☎ *(020) 7388 2221* John Craig-Tyler

Nine real ales always available. Shepherd Neame Master Brew, Hop Back Summer Lightning and brews from O'Hanlon's, Cottage, B&T and Brakspear, including one mild, usually featured. Three other brews also served, perhaps from Arundel, Phoenix, Black Sheep, Eccleshall or Barnsley breweries. Monthly beer festivals feature up to 24 beers.

Congenial upstairs freehouse with polished wood floors, featuring regular exhibitions of railway paintings. Food served 12–2.30pm and 5–8pm Mon–Fri, 12–3pm Sat. Children's certificate until 9pm. Situated in front of the bus station outside the mainline railway station.

⊖ Nearest Tube: Euston.
OPEN *11am–11pm Mon–Sat; 12–10.30pm Sun.*

Spread Eagle
141 Albert Street, Camden NW1 7NB
☎ *(020) 7267 1410* Gill Pipes

A Young's house serving Bitter and Special at all times plus the full seasonal range as appropriate.

Traditional, Victorian pub off Parkway in the heart of Camden, not far from Regents Park and London Zoo. Food served until 7.30pm Mon–Sat and 5pm Sun. Outside seating. No facilities for children.

⊖ Nearest Tube: Camden Town.
OPEN *11am–11pm Mon–Sat; 12–10.30pm Sun.*

OTHER REAL ALE PUBS IN NW1

The Albert
11 Princess Road, Primrose Hill NW1
☎ *(020) 7722 1886*

The Engineer
65 Gloucester Avenue, Primrose Hill NW1
☎ *(020) 7722 0950*

The Euston Flyer (FULLER'S)
83–7 Euston Road NW1 2RA
☎ *(020) 7383 0856*

Hogshead
128 Albert Street, Camden NW1 7NE
☎ *(020) 784 1675*

The Lansdowne
90 Gloucester Avenue, Primrose Hill NW1
☎ *(020) 7483 0409*

The Man in the Moon (WETHERSPOON)
40–2 Chalk Farm Road, Camden NW1 8BG
☎ *(020) 7482 2054*

The Metropolitan Bar (Wetherspoon)
7 Station Approach, Marylebone Road NW1 5LA
☎ *(020) 7486 3489*

Queens (Young's)
49 Regents Park Road, Primrose Hill NW1 8XD
☎ *(020) 7586 9498*

Square Tavern (Young's)
26 Tolmers Square NW1 2PE
☎ *(020) 7388 6010*

NW2

The Beaten Docket
55–6 Cricklewood Broadway, Cricklewood NW2 3DT
☎ *(020) 8450 2972* John Hand

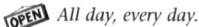Shepherd Neame Spitfire and Greene King Abbot always available, plus at least two constantly changing guests from the Wetherspoon range.

A two-bar Wetherspoon pub on the A5 (Edgware Road) as it passes through Cricklewood with dining area and patio. Music, but no games. Food available all day. No children.

⊖ Nearest Tube: Kilburn Park.
(OPEN) *All day, every day.*

NW3

The Duke of Hamilton
23 New End, Hampstead NW3
☎ *(020) 7794 0258* Mary Wooderson

Freehouse serving Fuller's brews plus guests.

Close to the New End Theatre, a 200-year-old pub that has won several awards recently thanks to the quality of its beer. Snacks only. Outside seating. Children allowed.

⊖ Nearest Tube: Hampstead
(OPEN) *12–11pm (10.30pm Sun).*

OTHER REAL ALE PUBS IN NW3

Flask (Young's)
Flask Walk, Hampstead NW3 1HE
☎ *(020) 7435 4580*

The Hollybush
22 Holly Mount, Hampstead NW3
☎ *(020) 7435 2892*

The Spaniards
Spaniards Road, Hampstead NW3
☎ *(020) 8731 6571*

The Three Horseshoes (Wetherspoon)
28 Heath Street, Hampstead NW3 6TE
☎ *(020) 7431 7206*

NW4

Greyhound (Young's)
Church End NW4 4JT
☎ *(020) 8457 9730*

NW6

Queens Arms (Young's)
1 High Road, Kilburn NW6 4SE
☎ *(020) 7624 5735*

NW8

The Clifton Hotel
96 Clifton Hill, St John's Wood NW8 0JT
☎ *(020) 7372 3427* John Hale

Adnams Best and Fuller's London Pride always available, plus two weekly changing guests such as Timothy Taylor Landlord

A converted house in St John's Wood with a garden at the front and a patio at the back. A mainly business clientele (average age 25–35ish). Food available 12–3.30pm and 6.30–10pm Mon–Sat and 12–6pm Sun (for traditional roasts). Children allowed if eating, but not at the bar. Situated off Abbey Road, close to Lord's cricket ground.

⊖ Nearest Tube: St John's Wood.
(OPEN) *11am–11pm (10.30pm Sun).*

Crocker's Folly
24 Aberdeen Place, Maida Vale NW8 8JR
☎ *(020) 7286 6608* Juanita Kirk

A freehouse serving up to seven real ales, perhaps including Brakspear Bitter, Adnams Bitter, Greene King Abbot and Morland Old Speckled Hen.

Built in 1898, originally the Crown Hotel, not far from Lord's cricket ground and close to the Regents Canal, with three large bars and outside seating. Food available 12–3pm and 6–9pm Mon–Fri; 12–2pm and 6–8pm Sat and 12–9pm Sun. While attempts to convert it into flats have fallen through, this pub was sold in summer 2002 and its future remains uncertain

⊖ Nearest Tube: St John's Wood/Warwick Avenue.
(OPEN) *11am–11pm Mon–Sat; 12–10.30pm Sun.*

NW9

JJ Moons (Wetherspoon)
553 Kingsbury Road, Kingsbury NW9 9EL
☎ *(020) 8204 9675*

The Moon Under Water
(Wetherspoon)
10 Varley Parade, Colindale NW9 6RR
☎ *(020) 8200 7611*

NW10

The Coliseum (WETHERSPOON)
25–6 Manor Park Road, Harlesden NW10 4JE
☎ *(020) 8961 6570*

Grand Junction Arms (YOUNG'S)
Canal Bridge, Acton Lane, Willesden NW10 7AD
☎ *(020) 8965 5670*

Green Man (FULLER'S)
109 High Street, Harlesden NW10
☎ *(020) 8965 7307*

The Outside Inn (WETHERSPOON)
312–14 Neasden Lane, Neasden NW10 0AD
☎ *(020) 8452 3140*

William IV
786 Harrow Road, Kensal Green NW10
☎ *(020) 8969 5944*

LONDON SOUTH EAST

SE1

Bunch of Grapes
2 St Thomas Street, Borough SE1 9RS
☎ *(020) 7403 2070 Ron and Maggie Wileman*

 Young's Bitter, Special and Triple A always available.

A busy Young's house close to Guy's Hospital. Beer garden. Bar snacks served at lunchtime (12–2.30pm) and evenings (7–10pm).

⊖ Nearest Tube: London Bridge.

11am–11pm Mon–Fri; 12–5pm Sat; closed Sun.

The Fire Station
150 Waterloo Road SE1
☎ *(020) 7620 2226 Philippe Ha Yeung*

Adnams Best, Brakspear Bitter, Young's Bitter, and a special house brew usually available, plus occasional and seasonal guests.

Popular conversion of a huge fire station beside Waterloo station. Bar and restaurant food served at lunchtime and evenings and all day at weekends. Children welcome.

⊖ Nearest Tube: Waterloo.

11am–11pm Mon–Sat; 12–10.30pm Sun.

The George Inn
77 Borough High Street, Borough SE1 1NH
☎ *(020) 7407 2056 George Cunningham*

 Fuller's London Pride, Morland Old Speckled Hen and Greene King Abbot plus a house brew (brewed by Adnams) among the beers always available, plus at least one guest (often seasonal).

A famous galleried seventeenth-century pub, owned by the National Trust. Large courtyard, one bar, servery, courtyard and function room. Food available 12–3pm Mon–Fri (12–4pm Sat–Sun) and 6–9.30pm Mon–Sat in restaurant. Children allowed.

⊖ Nearest Tube: London Bridge.

11am–11pm Mon–Sat; 12–10.30pm Sun.

The Globe Tavern
8 Bedale Street SE1 9AL
☎ *(020) 7407 0043*

 An Adnams and Young's brew always available, plus a guest such as Greene King Abbot, Morland Old Speckled Hen or Marston's Pedigree.

A traditional pub close to Borough Market made famous by its appearance in the film *Bridget Jones's Diary*. Background music, bar billiards, game machines. Disabled access. Bar snacks available 12–3pm. No children.

⊖ Nearest Tube: London Bridge.

11am–11pm Mon–Fri; closed Sat–Sun but available for private hire.

The Market Porter
9 Stoney Street SE1 9AA
☎ *(020) 7407 2495 Tony Hedigan*

Harveys Sussex Best always available, plus up to eight often-changing guests from a huge range of independent breweries small and large.

A traditional pub recently refurbished within Borough Market. Food available at lunchtime. Function room available seven days per week for private functions, meetings, etc. NB early-morning opening.

⊖ Nearest Tube: London Bridge.

6.30–8.30am and 11am–11pm Mon–Sat; 12–10.30pm Sun.

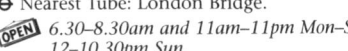

Royal Oak
44 Tabard Street SE1
☎ *(020) 7357 7173* John Porteous

Well-kept Harveys XX Mild, Pale, Best Bitter and Armada always available, plus seasonal brews.

The capital's only Harveys tied house, tucked away off Borough High Street. An unspoilt oasis and well worth uncovering. Two bars plus upstairs function room. Food available at lunchtime and evenings. No children.

⊖ Nearest Tube: Borough.

OPEN *11am–11pm Mon–Fri; closed Sat–Sun.*

OTHER REAL ALE PUBS IN SE1

Barrow Boy & Banker (FULLER'S)
6–8 Borough High Street SE1 9QQ
☎ *(020) 7403 5415*

Founders Arms (YOUNG'S)
52 Hopton Street, Blackfriars SE1 9JH
☎ *(020) 7928 1899*

Hogshead
52 Stamford Street SE1
☎ *(020) 7261 9642*

Leather Exchange (FULLER'S)
15 Leathermarket Street SE1 3HN
☎ *(020) 7407 0295*

Lord Clyde
27 Cleman Street SE1
☎ *(020) 7407 3397*

Mad Hatter (FULLER'S)
3–7 Stamford Street SE1 9NT
☎ *(020) 7401 9222*

Mulberry Bush (YOUNG'S)
89 Upper Ground SE1 9PP
☎ *(020) 7928 7940*

The Pommeler's Rest (WETHERSPOON)
196–8 Tower Bridge Road SE1 2UN
☎ *(020) 7378 1399*

Prince William Henry (YOUNG'S)
217 Blackfriars Road SE1 8NL
☎ *(020) 7928 2474*

Ship (FULLER'S)
68 Borough Road SE1 1DX
☎ *(020) 7403 7059*

Wetherspoon's
Metro Central Heights, Newington Causeway, Elephant and Castle SE1 6PB
☎ *(020) 7940 0890*

Wheatsheaf (YOUNG'S)
6 Stoney Street, Borough Market SE1 9AA
☎ *(020) 7407 7242*

SE3

The British Oak
109 Old Dover Road, Blackheath SE3
☎ *(020) 8858 1082*

SE4

The Brockley Barge (WETHERSPOON)
184 Brockley Road, Brockley SE4 2RR
☎ *(020) 8694 7690*

SE5

Fox on the Hill
149 Denmark Hill, Camberwell SE5 8EH
☎ *(020) 7738 4756* Peter Martin

Shepherd Neame Spitfire and Hop Back Summer Lightning among the brews always available plus a wide range of guests.

A large, modern Wetherspoon's pub with one bar, non-smoking dining area, garden and disabled facilities. Food available all day. Children allowed in the non-smoking area only.

OPEN *All day, every day.*

Hermit's Cave
28 Camberwell Church Street, Camberwell SE5 8QU
☎ *(020) 7703 3188*

Twelve beers available including Morland Old Speckled Hen, Marston's Pedigree, Gale's HSB, Fuller's London Pride and Adnams Best. Micro-brewers provide the guest beers.

Built in 1902, this beamed pub serves bar food at lunchtime and evenings. Street parking. Children not allowed.

OPEN *11am–11pm Mon–Sat; 12–10.30pm Sun.*

SE6

Catford Ram (YOUNG'S)
9 Winslade Way, Catford SE6 4JU
☎ *(020) 8690 6206*

The London & Rye (WETHERSPOON)
109 Rushey Green, Catford SE6 4AF
☎ *(020) 8697 5028*

Rutland Arms
55 Perry Hill, Catford SE6
☎ *(020) 8291 9426*

The Tiger's Head (WETHERSPOON)
350 Bromley Road, Catford SE6 2RZ
☎ *(020) 8698 8645*

SE8

The Dog & Bell
116 Prince Street, Deptford SE8 3JD
☎ *(020) 8692 5664*

Five beers always available. Brews might include Fuller's London Pride and ESB, Shepherd Neame Spitfire, Nethergate Bitter and something from Larkins, Archers or a host of other independents.

Freehouse built in 1850 and recently extended. Bar food available on weekdays 12–2pm and 6–9pm. Street parking, garden. Children aged 14 and over allowed. Pub quiz (Sun). Tucked away, not far from the railway station.

OPEN *11am–11pm Mon–Sat; 12–10.30pm Sun.*

SE9

The Banker's Draft (WETHERSPOON)
80 High Street, Eltham SE9 1FT
☎ *(020) 8294 1FT*

SE10

Ashburnham Arms (SHEPHERD NEAME)
25 Ashburnham Grove, Greenwich SE10
☎ *(020) 8692 2007*

Richard I (YOUNG'S)
52–4 Royal Hill, Greenwich SE10 8RT
☎ *(020) 8692 2996*

SE12

Crown (YOUNG'S)
117 Burnt Ash Hill, Lee SE12 0AJ
☎ *(020) 8857 6607*

The Edmund Halley (WETHERSPOON)
25–7 Lee Gate Centre, Lee Green SE12 8RG
☎ *(020) 8318 7475*

SE13

The Watch House
198–204 Lewisham High Street, Lewisham SE13 6JP
☎ *(020) 8318 3136 Mark Stevenson*

Shepherd Neame Spitfire and Hop Back Summer Lightning among the brews always available plus up to five guests from breweries such as Bateman, Ash Vine, JW Lees, Nethergate and Cotleigh.

A town-centre Wetherspoon pub with a mature clientele. No music. Patio, non-smoking area, disabled facilities. Food available all day. Children allowed until 7pm.

OPEN *All day, every day.*

OTHER REAL ALE PUBS IN SE13

Hogshead
354 Lewisham High Street, Lewisham SE13
☎ *(020) 8690 2054*

SE15

The Kentish Drovers (WETHERSPOON)
77–9 Peckham High Street, Peckham SE15 5RS
☎ *(020) 7277 4283*

SE16

Blacksmiths Arms (FULLER'S)
257 Rotherhithe Street SE16 1EJ
☎ *(020) 7237 1349*

Moby Dick (FULLER'S)
6 Russell Place, Greenland Dock SE16 1PL
☎ *(020) 7231 5482*

Ship (YOUNG'S)
39–47 St Marychurch Street, Rotherhithe SE16 4JE
☎ *(020) 7237 4103*

The Surrey Docks (WETHERSPOON)
185 Lower Road, Rotherhithe SE16 2LW
☎ *(020) 7394 2832*

SE18

Prince Albert (aka Rose's)
49 Hare Street, Woolwich SE18 6NE
☎ *(020) 8854 1538 Dave Evans*

Three brews at any one time, from a huge and varied range. Always changing, with 20–25 different beers a week.

Popular, one-bar, wood-panelled pub. Bar snacks available all day.

OPEN *11am–11pm Mon–Sat; 12–3pm Sun.*

OTHER REAL ALE PUBS IN SE18

The Great Harry (WETHERSPOON)
7–9 Wellington Street, Woolwich SE18 6NY
☎ *(020) 8317 4813*

SE19

The Postal Order (WETHERSPOON)
33 Westow Street, Crystal Palace SE19 3RW
☎ *(020) 8771 3003*

Railway Bell (YOUNG'S)
14 Cawnpore Street SE19 1PF
☎ *(020) 8670 2844*

SE20

Moon & Stars
164–6 High Street, Penge SE20 7QS
☎ *(020) 8776 5680* Iain Thomson

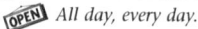Shepherd Neame Spitfire, Greene King IPA and Abbot and Hop Back Summer Lightning among the beers always available, plus up to three guests.

A large Wetherspoon pub. Disabled facilities. Non-smoking dining area, beer garden. Food available all day. No children.

OPEN *All day, every day.*

SE21

Crown & Greyhound (aka The Dog)
73 Dulwich Village SE21
☎ *(020) 8299 4976* Ann Taylor

Young's Bitter, Fuller's London Pride and an Adnams brew usually available.

Formerly two pubs, this huge alehouse sits in the heart of Dulwich. With garden and conservatory. Food available at lunchtime and evenings. Children welcome in parts.

OPEN *11am–11pm Mon–Sat; 12–10.30pm Sun.*

SE22

The Clock House (Young's)
196a Peckham Rye SE22 9QA
☎ *(020) 8693 2901*

SE23

The Capitol (Wetherspoon)
11–21 London Road, Forest Hill SE23 3TW
☎ *(020) 8291 8920*

SE25

The Alliance
91 High Street, South Norwood SE25 6EA
☎ *(020) 8653 3604* Mr Goodridge

Greene King Abbot, Fuller's London Pride and Shepherd Neame Spitfire alternating on one hand pump plus one guest which might be Timothy Taylor Landlord, Hook Norton Old Hooky, Hop Back Summer Lightning, Cotleigh Barn Owl or another brew from an independent.

A traditional, popular pub built in 1860 with leaded windows and wooden beams. Bar snacks available on weekday lunchtimes. No children's room.

OPEN *11am–11pm Mon–Sat; 12–10.30pm Sun.*

Clifton Arms
21 Clifton Road, South Norwood SE25
☎ *(020) 8771 2443*

Adnams Bitter, Greene King IPA, Fuller's London Pride and a couple of guest beers usually available.

Popular pub, close to Selhurst Park, so particularly busy on football days/ evenings. Food available lunchtime and evenings (Mon–Sat).

OPEN *12–11pm Mon–Fri; 11am–11pm Sat; 12–10.30pm Sun.*

Portmanor
Portland Road, South Norwood, SE25 4UF
☎ *(020) 8655 1308* Joan Brendan Kelly

Fuller's London Pride, Greene King Abbot Ale and up to five guest beers regularly available, perhaps from Hogs Back, Flagship or other small independents.

Popular freehouse with a good atmosphere and upstairs restaurant. Food served 11am–3pm and 5–9.30pm Mon–Fri, 12–9pm Sat (7pm Sun). No children. Quiz night (Thurs). Disco at weekends.

OPEN *11am–11pm Mon–Sat; 12–10.30pm Sun.*

OTHER REAL ALE PUBS IN SE25

Goat House (Fuller's)
2 Penge Road, South Norwood SE25 4EX
☎ *(020) 8778 5752*

The William Stanley (Wetherspoon)
7–8 High Street, South Norwood SE25 6EP
☎ *(020) 8653 0678*

SE26

The Windmill
125–31 Kirkdale, Sydenham SE26 4QJ
☎ *(020) 8291 8670* Steve Jarvis

A Wetherspoon pub with Fuller's London Pride and Shepherd Neame Spitfire usually available plus at least three guests.

A recently refurbished and reopened former furniture shop. Spacious premises with non-smoking area and garden. Food available all day.

OPEN *11am–11pm Mon–Sat; 12–10.30pm Sun.*

OTHER REAL ALE PUBS IN SE26

Bricklayers' Arms (Young's)
189 Dartmouth Road, Sydenham SE26 4QY
☎ *(020) 8699 1260*

Dulwich Wood House (Young's)
39 Sydenham Hill SE26 6RS
☎ *(020) 8693 5666*

SE27

Hope (YOUNG'S)
49 High Street, West Norwood SE27 9JS
☎ *(020) 8670 2035*

LONDON SOUTH WEST

SW1

The Captain's Cabin
4–7 Norris Street SW1Y 4RJ
☎ *(020) 7930 4764* Mervyn and Julie Wood

Greene King IPA and Abbot usually available plus two constantly changing guests.

Two bars with a central staircase and open balcony. Food served all day. Cash-back facilities available! Top bar available for private hire. No children.

⊖ Nearest Tube: Piccadilly Circus.

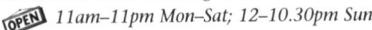 *11am–11pm Mon–Sat; 12–10.30pm Sun.*

Jugged Hare
172 Vauxhall Bridge Road, Victoria SW1V 1DX
☎ *(020) 7828 1543* Ben Bagguley

A Fuller's pub serving Chiswick, London Pride, ESB and the seasonal range.

Another bank conversion serving food at lunchtimes and evenings (not Fri).

⊖ Nearest Tube: Victoria.

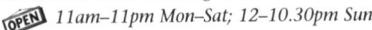 *11am–11pm Mon–Sat; 12–10.30pm Sun.*

Lord Moon of the Mall
16–18 Whitehall, SW1A 2DY
☎ *(020) 7839 7701* James Langan

A Wetherspoon pub with Fuller's London Pride and Shepherd Neame Spitfire always available, plus four guests such as Ridleys Rumpus, Hop Back Summer Lightning, Everards Tiger, Exmoor Gold, Smiles Golden and Bateman XXXB.

An impressive former bank with high ceilings, arches and oak fittings. Non-smoking area, disabled facilities. Food available all day. No children.

⊖ Nearest Tube: Charing Cross.

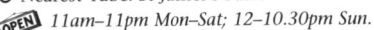 *11am–11pm Mon–Sat; 12–10.30pm Sun.*

Sanctuary House Hotel
33 Tothill Street SW1 9LA
☎ *(020) 7799 4044* Liz McLelland

Another Fuller's pub, so with Chiswick, London Pride, ESB and the appropriate seasonal brew available.

Bar attached to small hotel in the heart of Westminster serving food until 9pm every day. Children welcome.

⊖ Nearest Tube: St James's Park.

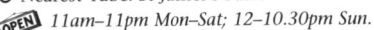 *11am–11pm Mon–Sat; 12–10.30pm Sun.*

Star Tavern
6 Belgrave Mews West SW1 8HH
☎ *(020) 7235 3019* TJ and Christine Connell

A Fuller's tied pub with Chiswick, London Pride and ESB always available.

Tucked away down a small, cobbled mews street off Belgrave Square. Bars on two floors (upstairs available for functions). Food available at lunchtime (12–2.30pm) and evenings (6–9pm).

⊖ Nearest Tube: Hyde Park Corner/ Knightsbridge.

OPEN *All day Mon–Fri; 11.30am–3pm and 6.30–11pm Sat; 12–3pm and 7–10.30pm Sun.*

Westminster Arms
9 Storey's Gate SW1
☎ *(020) 7222 8520* Gerry and Marie Dolan

A freehouse with a range of real ales always available that might include Brakspear Bitter, Greene King Abbot, Wadworth 6X and a special house brew.

A large, busy, politician's pub handy for Westminster, serving restaurant food on weekday lunchtimes (not Wednesdays) and bar snacks at other times. Children in the restaurant only.

⊖ Nearest Tube: St James's Park/ Westminster.

OPEN *All day Mon–Fri; 11am–8pm Sat; 12–6pm Sun.*

OTHER REAL ALE PUBS IN SW1

Buckingham Arms (YOUNG'S)
62 Petty France, Westminster SW1H 9EU
☎ *(020) 7222 3386*

Cask & Glass (SHEPHERD NEAME)
39–41 Palace Street, Victoria SW1
☎ *(020) 7834 7630*

Fox & Hounds (YOUNG'S)
29 Passmore Street SW1W 8HR
☎ *(020) 7730 6367*

Grouse & Claret (HALL & WOODHOUSE)
14–15 Little Chester Street SW1X 7AP
☎ *(020) 7235 3438*

The Monk Exchange (OLD MONK)
61–71 Victoria Street SW1 0HW
☎ *(020) 7233 2248*

Morpeth Arms (YOUNG'S)
58 Millbank SW1 4RW
☎ *(020) 7834 6442*

The Old Monk
Unit 22 Great Minister, 51 Horseferry Road SW1
☎ *(020) 7802 0047*

Paviours Arms (FULLER'S)
Page Street, Westminster SW1P 4LR
☎ *(020) 7834 2150*

Rising Sun (YOUNG'S)
46 Ebury Bridge Road, Pimlico SW1W 8PZ
☎ *(020) 7730 4088*

Royal Oak (YOUNG'S)
2 Regency Street SW1 4EZ
☎ *(020) 7834 7046*

Wetherspoon's
Unit 5 Victoria Island, Victoria Station SW1V 1JT ☎ *(020) 7931 0445*

The Willow Walk (WETHERSPOON)
25 Wilton Road, Victoria SW1V 1LW
☎ *(020) 78282953*

SW2

The Crown & Sceptre
2a Streatham Hill, Brixton SW2 4AH
☎ *(020) 8671 0843 Sean Pulford*

Shepherd Neame Spitfire among the brews always available plus two guests such as Hop Back Summer Lightning and ales from Adnams or Cotleigh.

A Wetherspoon conversion with a big bar, non-smoking dining area, front and rear patios. Food available all day. Children allowed in the garden only.

⊖ Nearest Tube: Balham.

OPEN *All day, every day.*

OTHER REAL ALE PUBS IN SW2

Hope & Anchor (YOUNG'S)
123 Acre Lane, Brixton SW2 5UA
☎ *(020) 7274 1787*

SW3

The Crown
153 Dovehouse Street, Chelsea SW3 6LB
☎ *(020) 7352 9505*
Alan Carroll and Karen Moore

Adnams Best Bitter, Fuller's London Pride plus a guest beer usually available.

Traditional central London pub, recently refurbished. Food served 12–3pm Mon–Fri plus some evenings. Well-behaved over 14s welcome. Situated 100 yards off Fulham Road, between the Brompton and Royal Marsden hospitals.

⊖ Nearest Tube: South Kensington.

OPEN *11am–11pm Mon–Sat; 12–10.30pm Sun.*

Cooper's Arms
87 Flood Street, Chelsea SW3 5TB
☎ *(020) 7376 3120 Simon and Caroline Lee*

A Young's pub serving Bitter, Special and Triple A.

Street-corner tied house just off the King's Road. Upstairs function room. Food served 12.30–3pm and 6–10pm (not Sun evenings).

⊖ Nearest Tube: Sloane Square.

OPEN *11am–11pm Mon–Sat; 12–10.30pm Sun.*

OTHER REAL ALE PUBS IN SW3

The Blenheim (HALL & WOODHOUSE)
27 Cale Street, Chelsea SW3 3 QP
☎ *(020) 7349 0056*

Moore Arms
61–3 Cadogan Street, Chelsea SW3
☎ *(020) 7376 3120*

Phene Arms
9 Phene Street, Chelsea SW3
☎ *(020)7352 3294*

SW4

Bread & Roses
68 Clapham Manor Street, Clapham SW4 6DZ
☎ *(020) 8498 1779 Peter Dawson*

A freehouse owned by the Workers Beer Company with Adnams Best and Workers Ale (a house ale brewed by Smiles) always available, plus two guests, perhaps Adnams Regatta, Old Ale or Broadside, Oakhill Mendip Gold or O'Hanlon's Red Ale.

A bright, modern pub. Bar and function room, front and rear garden, disabled access and toilets. Food available at lunchtime and evenings. Children allowed during the day in the non-smoking area only.

⊖ Nearest Tube: Clapham Common.

OPEN *11am–11pm Mon–Sat; 12–10.30pm Sun.*

Windmill
South Side, Clapham Common SW4 9DE
☎ *(020) 8673 4578 Peter and Jenny Hale*

A Young's house with Bitter, Special and seasonal brews available.

A substantial and popular Victorian pub, built on the site of the home of the founder of Young's brewery. Recently refurbished with good accommodation very close to the common. Bar and restaurant food available 12–10pm Mon–Fri (9pm Sat–Sun). Children welcome in the family room, which doubles as a function room available for private hire. Outside seating.

⊖ Nearest Tube: Clapham Common/ Clapham South.

OPEN *11am–11pm Mon–Sat; 12–10.30pm Sun.*

OTHER REAL ALE PUBS IN SW4

Fine Line (FULLER'S)
182–4 Clapham High Street SW4 7UG
☎ *(020) 7622 4436*

SW5

Blackbird (FULLER'S)
209 Earls Court Road SW5 9AR
☎ *(020) 7835 1855*

SW6

The White Horse
1 Parsons Green, Fulham SW6 4UL
☎ *(020) 7736 2115 Fax (020) 7610 6091*
Mark Dorber

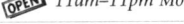Harveys Sussex Best, Adnams Broadside and Highgate Mild always available plus guests including Rooster's Yankee and all sorts of seasonal brews, plus a wide range of bottled beers from around the world.

A large, comfortable Victorian pub overlooking Parsons Green. Recently refurbished, the 'Sloany Pony' now features the non-smoking 'Coach House' restaurant. Brunch is also served on Saturdays, 11am–4pm, and on Sundays. Regular beer festivals, including an Old Ale Festival (last Saturday of November), a Wheat Beer Festival (May) and the 'Beauty of the Hops' competition (June). Function room for private dinner parties, tastings and presentations. Parking, terrace/garden. Children allowed.

⊖ Nearest Tube: Parsons Green.
OPEN *11am–11pm Mon–Sat; 12–10.30pm Sun.*

The Imperial
577 King's Road SW6 2EH
☎ *(020) 7736 8549 Andrew and Tim Haggard*

Haggards Imperial Best and Charles Wells Bombardier always available. The pub lease belongs to the owners of Haggards Brewery and this is the principal outlet for their beer, which is brewed in Battersea.

A bright, airy, modern town pub with covered rear garden. Lively atmosphere. Food served every lunchtime and weekday evenings. Traditional roasts on Sundays. No children. Situated on the junction with Cambria Street.

⊖ Nearest Tube: Fulham Broadway.
OPEN *11am–11pm Mon–Sat; 12–10.30pm Sun.*

OTHER REAL ALE PUBS IN SW6

Duke of Cumberland (YOUNG'S)
235 New King's Road, Fulham SW6 4XG
☎ *(020) 7736 2777*

SW7

The Anglesea Arms
15 Selwood Terrace, Chelsea SW7 3GG
☎ *(020) 7373 7960 Andrew Ford*

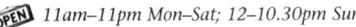Six real ales always available, including Adnams Best and Broadside, Brakspear Special and Bitter, and Fuller's London Pride. Guests beers are rotated on the remaining pump.

A lively, easy-to-find, 200-year-old pub with a traditional atmosphere – no background music or juke box. Bar and restaurant food available at lunchtime and evenings Mon–Fri, 12–9pm Sat–Sun in a wood-panelled dining room. Terraced garden area at front. Cask Marque winner. Children over 14 allowed. Just off the Fulham Road.

⊖ Nearest Tube: South Kensington.
OPEN *11am–11pm Mon–Sat; 12–10.30pm Sun.*

SW8

The Priory Arms
83 Lansdowne Way, Stockwell SW8 2PB
☎ *(020) 7622 1884 Gary Morris*

Adnams Bitter and Broadside, and Harveys Best Bitter always available, plus three guests, mainly from smaller regional breweries and especially micro-breweries.

Popular, genuine freehouse. Regular CAMRA regional pub of the year. Bar food available at lunchtimes, with traditional roasts on Sundays. Quiz night (Sun). Outside seating.

⊖ Nearest Tube: Stockwell.
OPEN *11am–11pm Mon–Sat; 12–10.30pm Sun.*

OTHER REAL ALE PUBS IN SW8

Mawbey Arms (SHEPHERD NEAME)
7 Mawbey Street, Lambeth SW8
☎ *(020) 7622 1936*

Plough Inn (YOUNG'S)
518 Wandsworth Road, Lambeth SW8 3JX
☎ *(020) 7622 2777*

Surprise (YOUNG'S)
16 Southville, South Lambeth SW8 2PP
☎ *(020) 7622 4623*

SW9

The Beehive
407–9 Brixton Road, Brixton SW9 7DG
☎ *(020) 7738 3643* Peter Martin

Shepherd Neame Spitfire always available, plus three guests such as Hop Back Summer Lightning, Greene King Abbot or Strawberry Blonde.

A one-bar Wetherspoon pub with a non-smoking dining area, disabled access. Food available all day. No children.

⊖ Nearest Tube: Brixton.

OPEN *All day, every day.*

OTHER REAL ALE PUBS IN SW9

Hogshead
409 Clapham Road SW9
☎ *(020) 7274 2472*

Trinity Arms (YOUNG'S)
45 Trinity Gardens, Stockwell SW9 8DR
☎ *(020) 7274 4544*

SW10

Chelsea Ram
32 Burnaby Street, Chelsea SW10 0PL
☎ *(020) 7351 4008* James Symington

A Young's tied house selling Bitter, Special and seasonal brews.

Popular, colourful, cheerful pub off the King's Road. Children welcome. Outside seating. Good food served 12.30–3pm and 7–10pm.

⊖ Nearest Tube: Fulham Broadway.

OPEN *11am–11pm Mon–Sat; 12–10.30pm Sun.*

OTHER REAL ALE PUBS IN SW10

Finch's (YOUNG'S)
190 Fulham Road SW10 9PN
☎ *(020) 7351 5043*

Fine Line (FULLER'S)
236 Fulham Road SW10 9NB
☎ *(020) 7376 5827*

The World's End (HALL & WOODHOUSE)
459 King's Road, Chelsea SW10 0LR
☎ *(020) 7376 8946*

SW11

The Asparagus (WETHERSPOON)
1–13 Falcon Road, Battersea SW11 2PT
☎ *(020) 7801 0046*

Beehive (FULLER'S)
197 St John's Hill, Wandsworth SW11 1TH
☎ *(020) 7207 1267*

The Castle (YOUNG'S)
115 High Street, Battersea SW11 3JR
☎ *(020) 7228 8181*

Duke of Cambridge (YOUNG'S)
228 Battersea Bridge Road SW11 3AA
☎ *(020) 7223 5662*

Fine Line (FULLER'S)
31–7 Northcote Road, Battersea SW11 1NJ
☎ *(020) 7924 7387*

The Latchmere
503 Battersea Park Road, Battersea SW11
☎ *(020) 7223 3549*

Plough (YOUNG'S)
89 St John's Hill, Clapham Junction SW11 1SY
☎ *(020) 7228 9136*

Woodman (HALL & WOODHOUSE)
60 Battersea High Street SW11 3HX
☎ *(020) 7228 2968*

SW12

Moon Under Water
194 Balham High Road, Balham SW12 9BP
☎ *(020) 8673 0535* James Glover

Hop Back Summer Lightning and Shepherd Neame Spitfire permanently available, plus two guest beers.

A friendly, Wetherspoon local. No music. Large and relatively peaceful non-smoking area. Food served all day, every day. No children.

⊖ Nearest Tube: Balham.

OPEN *11am–11pm Mon–Sat; 12–10.30pm Sun.*

OTHER REAL ALE PUBS IN SW12

Duke of Devonshire (YOUNG'S)
39 Balham High Road SW12 9AN
☎ *(020) 7673 1363*

Grove (YOUNG'S)
39 Oldridge Road, Balham SW12 8PN
☎ *(020) 8673 6531*

Jackdaw & Rook (FULLER'S)
96–100 Balham High Road SW12 9AA
☎ *(020) 8772 9021*

Nightingale (YOUNG'S)
97 Nightingale Lane, Balham SW12 8NX
☎ *(020) 8673 1637*

SW13

Bulls Head
373 Lonsdale Road, Barnes SW13 9PY
☎ *(020) 8876 5241* Dan and Liz Fleming

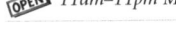A Young's pub serving Bitter, Special, Triple A and seasonal brews such as Winter Warmer as appropriate.

Beside the Thames on the south side of Barnes Bridge with a reputation for live jazz music every evening and on Sundays. Bar and restaurant food available from 12–9pm (12–3pm Sun). Children welcome in eating area. Popular on Boat Race day. Outside seating.

🍺 *11am–11pm Mon–Sat; 12–10.30pm Sun.*

Coach & Horses
27 High Street, Barnes SW13 9LW
☎ *(020) 8876 2695* Nichola Green

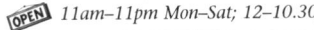A Young's house serving Bitter, Special, Triple A and seasonal brews.

Popular former coaching inn with large garden. Food available at lunchtime. Function room available for hire. Children welcome in the garden.

🍺 *11am–11pm Mon–Sat; 12–10.30pm Sun.*

Rose of Denmark
28 Cross Street, Barnes SW13
☎ *(020) 8392 1761*
Hugh Davidson and Susan Gamble

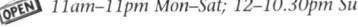Genuine freehouse serving Brakspear Bitter, Woodforde's Wherry and Timothy Taylor Landlord.

Tucked-away, street-corner local once owned by Watney's. Outside seating. Food served all day every day.

🍺 *11am–11pm Mon–Sat; 12–10.30pm Sun.*

OTHER REAL ALE PUBS IN SW13

Red Lion (Fuller's)
2 Castlenau, Barnes SW13 9RU
☎ *(020) 8748 2984*

White Hart (Young's)
The Terrace, Riverside, Barnes SW13 9NR
☎ *(020) 8876 5177*

SW14

Charlie Butler (Young's)
40 High Street, Mortlake SW14 8SN
☎ *(020) 8878 2310*

Hare and Hounds (Young's)
216 Upper Richmond Road, Sheen SW14 8AH
☎ *(020) 8876 4304*

Jolly Gardeners (Young's)
36 Lower Richmond Road, Mortlake SW14 7EX
☎ *(020) 8876 1721*

Railway Tavern (Hall & Woodhouse)
11 Sheen Lane, Mortlake SW14 8HY
☎ *(020) 8878 7361*

SW15

The Railway
202 Upper Richmond Road, Putney SW15 6TD
☎ *(020) 8871 4497* Julie Allen

A Wetherspoon house serving the usual suspects such as Green King Abbot and Shepherd Neame Spitfire plus guests.

Another in the chain, but with a railway theme. Serving standard Wetherspoon food all day. Non-smoking area, upstairs bar. Children welcome.

⊖ Nearest Tube: East Putney.

🍺 *11am–11pm Mon–Sat; 12–10.30pm Sun.*

OTHER REAL ALE PUBS IN SW15

Angel (Young's)
11 High Street, Roehampton SW15 4HL
☎ *(020) 8788 1997*

Castle (Young's)
220 Putney Bridge Road, Putney SW15 2NA
☎ *(020) 8788 0972*

Duke's Head (Young's)
8 Lower Richmond Road, Putney SW15 1JN
☎ *(020) 8788 2552*

Green Man (Young's)
Putney Heath, Putney SW15 3NG
☎ *(020) 8788 8096*

Half Moon (Young's)
93 Lower Richmond Road, Putney SW15 1EU
☎ *(020) 8780 9383*

Maltese Cat (Young's)
Aubyn Square, Roehampton SW15 5NT
☎ *(020) 8876 7534*

P Shannon and Sons (Fuller's)
46–8 High Street, Putney SW15
☎ *(020) 8780 5437*

Spotted Horse (Young's)
122 Putney High Street SW15 1RG
☎ *(020) 8788 0246*

Whistle and Flute (Fuller's)
46–8 High Street, Putney SW15 1SQ
☎ *(020) 8780 5437*

SW16

Bedford Park (Young's)
233 Streatham High Road, Streatham SW16 6EN
☎ *(020) 8769 2836*

The Holland Tringham
(Wetherspoon)
107–109 Streatham High Road,
Streatham SW16 1HJ ☎ *(020) 8769 3062*

Hogshead
Streatham High Road, Streatham SW16 1DA
☎ *(020) 8696 7582*

The Moon Under Water
(Wetherspoon)
1327 London Road, Norbury SW16 4AU
☎ *(020) 8765 1235*

Pied Bull (Young's)
498 Streatham High Road SW16 3BQ
☎ *(020) 8764 4033*

SW17

Castle (Young's)
38 High Street, Tooting SW17 0RG
☎ *(020) 8672 7018*

Gorringe Park (Young's)
29 London Road, Tooting SW17 9JR
☎ *(020) 8648 4478*

JJ Moons (Wetherspoon)
56a High Street, Tooting SW17 0RN
☎ *(020) 8672 4726*

Leather Bottle (Young's)
538 Garratt Lane, Tooting SW17 0NY
☎ *(020) 8946 2309*

Prince of Wales (Young's)
646 Garratt Lane, Tooting SW17 0PB
☎ *(020) 8946 2628*

SW18

The Rose & Crown
134 Putney Bridge Road, Wandsworth SW18 1NP
☎ *(020) 8871 4497* Barry O'Hare

Wetherspoon pub with regulars such as Shepherd Neame Spitfire, Greene King Abbot, Timothy Taylor Landlord and various guests usually available.

Recently refurbished member of the Wetherspoon stable, so with food served all day. Outside drinking area, no-smoking area, children welcome.

⊖ Nearest Tube: East Putney/Putney Bridge.

OPEN *All day, every day.*

The Spotted Dog
72 Garratt Lane, Wandsworth SW18 4DJ
☎ *(020) 8875 9531* Colin Daniels

Fuller's London Pride and ESB and Greene King IPA and Abbot always available, plus two guests such as Jennings Cocker Hoop, Fuller's Summer Ale and Greene King Centenary. Beers changed weekly.

A traditional one-bar town pub with food available 12–4pm. Disabled facilities. Patio. Children allowed if dining.

OPEN *All day, every day.*

OTHER REAL ALE PUBS IN SW18

Alma (Young's)
499 Old York Road, Wandsworth SW18 1TF
☎ *(020) 8870 2537*

Brewer's Inn (Young's)
147 East Hill, Wandsworth SW18 2QB
☎ *(020) 8874 4128*

Brewery Tap (Young's)
68 High Street, Wandsworth SW18 2LB
☎ *(020) 8875 7005*

The Cat's Back
86 Point Pleasant, Wandsworth SW18
☎ *(020) 8877 0818*

County Arms (Young's)
345 Trinity Road, Wandsworth SW18 3SH
☎ *(020) 8874 8532*

Crane (Young's)
14 Armoury Way, Wandsworth SW18 3EZ
☎ *(020) 8874 2450*

Fox & Hounds (Young's)
29 Passmore Street SW18 8HR
☎ *(020) 7730 6367*

Gardeners Arms (Young's)
268 Merton Road, Southfields SW18 5JL
☎ *(020) 8874 7624*

Grapes (Young's)
39 Fairfield Street, Wandsworth SW18 1DX
☎ *(020) 8874 8681*

The Grid Inn (Wetherspoon)
22 Replingham Road, Southfields SW18 5LS
☎ *(020) 8874 8460*

Halfway House (Young's)
521 Garratt Lane, Earlsfield SW18 4SR
☎ *(020) 8946 2788*

Kings Arms (Young's)
96 High Street, Wandsworth SW18 4LB
☎ *(020) 8874 1428*

Old Sergeant (Young's)
104 Garratt Lane, Wandsworth SW18 4DJ
☎ *(020) 8874 4099*

Pig & Whistle (YOUNG'S)
481 Merton Road SW18 5LB
☎ *(020) 8874 1061*

Queen Adelaide (YOUNG'S)
35 Putney Bridge Road, Wandsworth SW18 1NP
☎ *(020) 8874 1695*

Ship (YOUNG'S)
41 Jew's Row, Wandsworth SW18 1TB
☎ *(020) 8870 9667*

Spread Eagle (YOUNG'S)
71 High Street, Wandsworth SW18 4LB
☎ *(020) 8877 9809*

Wheatsheaf (YOUNG'S)
30 Putney Bridge Road, Wandsworth SW18 1HS
☎ *(020) 8874 5753*

SW19

The Brewery Tap
68–9 High Street, Wimbledon Village SW19 5EE
☎ *(020) 8947 9331* John and Heather Grover

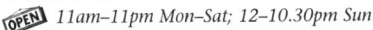 Freehouse serving five rotating cask ales from independent breweries, including Fuller's London Pride, Adnams Best and a mild.

Small and cosy freehouse in the heart of Wimbledon village. Food available every lunchtime and Mon and Wed evenings. Children allowed.

⊖ Nearest Tube: Wimbledon

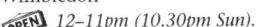 *11am–11pm Mon–Sat; 12–10.30pm Sun.*

The Sultan
78 Norman Road, South Wimbledon SW19 1BT
☎ *(020) 8544 9323* Angela Shaw

 The only pub in London owned by the Salisbury-based Hop Back Brewery, so serving GFB, Thunderstorm, Summer Lightning, Crop Circle and others.

All beers sold at reduced price (£1.50) on Wednesdays. Garden. Quiz night (Tues). No food.

⊖ Nearest Tube: Colliers Wood/South Wimbledon

12–11pm (10.30pm Sun).

OTHER REAL ALE PUBS IN SW19

Alexandra (YOUNG'S)
33 Wimbledon Hill Road, Wimbledon SW19 7NE
☎ *(020) 8947 7691*

Crooked Billet (YOUNG'S)
15 Crooked Billet, Wimbledon Common SW19 4RQ
☎ *(020) 8946 4942*

Dog & Fox (YOUNG'S)
24 Wimbledon High Street SW19 5EA
☎ *(020) 8946 6565*

Hand in Hand (YOUNG'S)
6 Crooked Billet, Wimbledon Common SW19 4RQ
☎ *(020) 8946 5720*

Kings Head (YOUNG'S)
18 High Street, Merton SW19 1DN
☎ *(020) 8540 7992*

Princess of Wales (YOUNG'S)
98 Morden Road, Merton SW19 3BP
☎ *(020) 8542 0573*

Rose and Crown (YOUNG'S)
55 High Street, Wimbledon SW19 5BA
☎ *(020) 8947 4713*

Wibbas Down Inn (WETHERSPOON)
6–12 Gladstone Road, Wimbledon SW19 1QT
☎ *(020) 8540 6788*

LONDON WEST

W1

Ain't Nothin' But ... Blues Bar
20 Kingly Street W1R 5LB
☎ *(020) 7287 0514* K Hillier

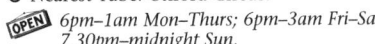 Adnams Best and Broadside usually available, plus a guest beer that changes every few days, such as Fuller's London Pride, Young's Waggle Dance, Charles Wells Bombardier, Morland Old Speckled Hen, Everards Tiger or something from Badger Brewery.

London's only blues bar venue. Good old-fashioned drinkers' bar with mixed clientele. Open late with live music every night. Food served during opening hours. No children. Situated between Regent Street and Carnaby Street behind Hamley's Toy Shop.

⊖ Nearest Tube: Oxford Circus.

6pm–1am Mon–Thurs; 6pm–3am Fri–Sat; 7.30pm–midnight Sun.

The Argyll Arms
18 Argyll Street W1 1AA
☎ *(020) 7734 6117* Mike Tayara

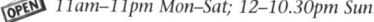 Seven beers always available including Wadworth 6X and an ever-changing selection that might feature Everards Daredevil, Hop Back Summer Lightning, Felinfoel Double Dragon, Timothy Taylor Landlord, Charles Wells Bombardier and brews from Jennings, Ringwood or Tomintoul.

A 300-year-old pub just off Oxford Circus owned by the Duke of Argyll. Air-conditioned. Bar and restaurant food available at lunchtime and evenings. Function room, non-smoking area. Children allowed in play area.

↔ Nearest Tube: Oxford Circus.
[OPEN] *11am–11pm Mon–Sat; 12–10.30pm Sun.*

The Carpenters Arms
12 Seymour Place W1 5WF
☎ *(020) 7723 1050* Steed Sherriff

Fuller's London Pride and Young's Special usually available plus a guest beer such as Hop Back Summer Lightning, Everards Tiger, Wadworth 6X or something from Harveys, Hardys & Hansons or Oakhill.

A charming traditional tavern with a warm welcome. Small and intimate one-bar house which is a great favourite with locals, business people and tourists alike. Food served all day, every day. Cask Marque winner.

↔ Nearest Tube: Edgware Road/Marble Arch.
[OPEN] *11am–11pm Mon–Sat; 12–10.30pm Sun.*

The Clachan
34 Kingly Street W1R 5LB
☎ *(020) 7734 2659*

A Nicholson's house serving up to four ales that may well include Fuller's London Pride, Greene King IPA Timothy Taylor Landlord and guests.

Behind Liberty's, just off Carnaby Street, a one-bar central London alehouse with upstairs function room. Food served at lunchtime and evenings.

↔ Nearest Tube: Oxford Circus.
[OPEN] *11am–11pm Mon–Sat; closed Sun.*

The Guinea
30 Bruton Place, Berkeley Square W1J 6NL
☎ *(020) 7409 1728* Carl and Pauline Smith

A Young's pub serving the brewery's Bitter, Special and seasonal brews.

Tucked away in a Mayfair mews street with a fine restaurant next door. Bar food served on weekday lunchtimes.

↔ Nearest Tube: Bond Street.
[OPEN] *11am–11pm Mon–Fri; 6.30–11pm Sat; closed Sun.*

Shaston Arms
4–6 Ganton Street W1S 7QN
☎ *(020) 7287 2631* Sally Graham

Owned by Hall & Woodhouse, so serving Badger Best and Tanglefoot, plus King & Barnes Sussex.

Opened in December 2000 in a former wine bar off Carnaby Street. The curious layout sees the bar in one room with much of the seating next door. Food available until 5pm.

↔ Nearest Tube: Oxford Circus.
[OPEN] *11am–11pm Mon–Sat; closed Sun.*

OTHER REAL ALE PUBS IN W1

Dog & Duck
18 Bateman Street, Soho W1
☎ *(020) 7494 0697*

Fuller's Ale Lodge (FULLER'S)
11 Avery Row, Mayfair W1X 9HA
☎ *(020) 7629 1643*

Golden Eagle
59 Marylebone Lane W1
☎ *(020) 7935 3228*

Hogshead
72 Grafton Way W1
☎ *(020) 7387 7923*

Jack Horner (FULLER'S)
236 Tottenham Court Road W1P 9AE
☎ *(020) 7636 2868*

The Moon and Sixpence
(WETHERSPOON)
183–5 Wardour Street W1V 3FB
☎ *(020) 7734 0037*

The Old Monk
24–6 Maddox Street W1R 9PG
☎ *(020) 7499 3775*

One Tun (YOUNG'S)
58–60 Goodge Street W1T 4ND
☎ *(020) 7209 4105*

Pillars of Hercules
7 Greek Street, Soho W1
☎ *(020) 7437 1179*

Ship (FULLER'S)
116 Wardour Street W1F 0TT
☎ *(020) 7437 8446*

Spice of Life (McMULLEN'S)
37–9 Romilly Street, Soho W1
☎ *(020) 7437 7013*

Sun & 13 Cantons (FULLER'S)
21 Great Pultney Street W1R 3DB
☎ *(020) 7734 0934*

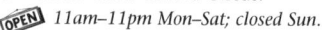
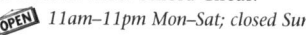

Wargrave Arms (Young's)
42 Brendon Street W1H 5HS
☎ *(020) 7723 0559*

Windmill (Young's)
6–8 Mill Street W1R 9TE
☎ *(020) 7491 8050*

W2

Archery Tavern
4 Bathurst Street W2 2SD
☎ *(020) 7402 4916* Tony O'Neil

A Hall & Woodhouse tied pub with Badger Best, Tanglefoot and Sussex Ale always available, plus two guests such as Gribble Black Adder II or Golden Champion Ale.

A three-room, one-bar traditional pub on the north side of Hyde Park near the riding stables. Fruit machines, quiz machine, darts. Food available 12–10pm. Well-behaved children allowed. Outside seating.

⊖ Nearest Tube: Lancaster Gate

OPEN *11am–11pm Mon–Sat; 12–10.30pm Sun.*

Fountain's Abbey
109 Praed Street W2 1RL
☎ *(020) 7723 2364* David Harrison

Greene King Abbot Ale, Charles Wells Bombardier and Morland Old Speckled Hen always available, plus one rotating guest ale. Approximately six different guests served every month.

A large, Victorian-style alehouse with outside seating and food available all day. Children allowed until 6pm. Upstairs function room for hire.

⊖ Nearest Tube: Paddington.

OPEN *11am–11pm Mon–Sat; 12–10.30pm Sun.*

OTHER REAL ALE PUBS IN W2

Mad Bishop & Bear (Fuller's)
1st Floor, The Lawn, Paddington Station W2 1HB
☎ *(020) 7402 2441*

Monkey Puzzle (Hall & Woodhouse)
30 Southwick Street W2 1JQ
☎ *(020) 7723 0143*

Prince Edward (Hall & Woodhouse)
73 Princes Street, Bayswater W2 4NY
☎ *(020) 7727 2221*

The Tyburn (Wetherspoon)
20 Edgware Road W2 2EN
☎ *(020) 7723 4731*

Victoria (Fuller's)
10A Strathearn Place W2 2NH
☎ *(020) 7724 1191*

W3

Castle (Fuller's)
Victoria Road, North Acton W3 6UL
☎ *(020) 8992 2027*

Kings Arms (Fuller's)
Acton Vale, Acton W3 7JT
☎ *(020) 8743 2689*

Kings Head (Fuller's)
214 High Street, Acton W3 9NX
☎ *(020) 8992 0282*

The Red Lion & Pineapple
(Wetherspoon)
281 High Street, Acton W3 9PJ
☎ *(020) 8896 2248*

W4

The Bell & Crown
11–13 Thames Road, Strand on the Green, Chiswick W4 3PL
☎ *(020) 8994 4164* Frank McBrearty

A Fuller's tied house with London Pride, Chiswick and ESB permanently on offer. Fuller's seasonal ales served as available.

Backing on to the Thames, with excellent views, this substantial pub has a 40-seater non-smoking dining area/conservatory and outside seating. Food available 12–10pm daily. Children allowed, under supervision.

⊖ Nearest Tube: Gunnersbury.

OPEN *11am–11pm Mon–Sat; 12–10.30pm Sun.*

OTHER REAL ALE PUBS IN W4

Crown & Anchor (Young's)
374 Chiswick High Road, Chiswick W4 5TA
☎ *(020) 8995 2607*

Duke of York (Fuller's)
107 Devonshire Road, Chiswick W4 2HU
☎ *(020) 8994 4624*

George IV (Fuller's)
185 Chiswick High Road, Chiswick W4 1DR
☎ *(020) 8994 4624*

George & Devonshire (Fuller's)
8 Burlington Lane, Chiswick W4 2QE
☎ *(020) 8994 1859*

Hogshead
34 Chiswick High Road, Chiswick W4
☎ *(020) 8742 0021*

Mawson Arms and Fox & Hounds (Fuller's)
Mawson Lane, Chiswick W4 2QD
☎ *(020) 8994 2936*

Old Pack Horse (Fuller's)
434 Chiswick High Road, Chiswick W4 5TF
☎ *(020) 8994 2872*

W5

The Red Lion

13 St Mary's Road, Ealing W5 5RA
☎ *(020) 8567 2541* Jonathan and Victoria Lee

Fuller's Chiswick, London Pride and ESB plus a seasonal brew usually available.

Small, traditional, Grade II listed, one-bar Fuller's pub. No music or machines. Large patio garden. Food served 12–2.30pm and 6–9pm. Children allowed in garden only. Situated opposite Ealing Studios.

⊖ Nearest Tube: Ealing Broadway.

[OPEN] *11am–11pm Mon–Sat; 12–10.30pm Sun.*

TJ Duffy

282 Northfield Avenue, Ealing W5 4UB
☎ *(020) 8932 1711*

Fuller's London Pride always available plus guests from Adnams, Charles Wells, Timothy Taylor etc.

Guest beers are sold at a reduced price on Tuesdays at this west London freehouse. Food served at lunchtimes and evenings. Quiz nights, live music.

⊖ Nearest Tube: Northfields.

[OPEN] *11am–11pm Mon–Sat; 12–10.30pm Sun.*

OTHER REAL ALE PUBS IN W5

Castle (FULLER'S)
36 St Mary's Road, Ealing W5 5RG
☎ *(020) 8567 3285*

Fox & Goose Hotel (FULLER'S)
Hanger Lane, Ealing W5 1DP
☎ *(020) 8998 5864*

Hogshead
46–7 The Mall, Ealing W5 3TJ
☎ *(020) 8579 3006*

Plough Inn (FULLER'S)
297 Northfield Avenue, Ealing W5 4XB
☎ *(020) 8567 1416*

Rose & Crown (FULLER'S)
Church Place, St Mary's Road, Ealing W5 4HN
☎ *(020) 8567 2811*

Townhouse (FULLER'S)
The Broadway, Ealing W5 2PH
☎ *(020) 8810 0304*

Wheatsheaf (FULLER'S)
41 Haven Lane, Ealing W5 2HZ
☎ *(020) 8997 5240*

W6

The Cross Keys

57 Black Lion Lane, Hammersmith W6 9BG
☎ *(020) 8748 3541* Paul Lees and Kerry Poole

Fuller's Chiswick, London Pride and ESB usually available.

A traditional pub with back garden open in summer. Food served 12–2.30pm Mon–Fri and Sun. Children welcome before 9pm.

⊖ Nearest Tube: Stamford Brook.

[OPEN] *11am–11pm (10.30pm Sun).*

Dove

Upper Mall, Hammersmith W6 9TA
☎ *(020) 8748 5405* Andrew Ward

A Fuller's house, so with Chiswick, London Pride and ESB always available plus the seasonal brews.

Backing on to the Thames near Hammersmith Bridge. Owned by Fuller's since 1796. Features allegedly the smallest bar in Britain, but with plenty of space (inside and out) elsewhere. Bar and restaurant food available until 9pm. No machines or music. No children.

⊖ Nearest Tube: Hammersmith.

[OPEN] *11am–11pm Mon–Sat; 12–10.30pm Sun.*

OTHER REAL ALE PUBS IN W6

Andover Arms (FULLER'S)
57 Aldensley Road, Hammersmith W6 0DL
☎ *(020) 8741 9794*

Blue Anchor
13 Lower Mall, Hammersmith Bridge W6
☎ *(020) 8748 5774*

Brook Green (YOUNG'S)
170 Shepherds Bush Road, W6 7PB
☎ *(020) 7603 2516*

Hammersmith Ram (YOUNG'S)
81 King Street, Hammersmith W6 9HW
☎ *(020) 8748 4511*

Latymers (FULLER'S)
157 Hammersmith Road, Hammersmith W6 8BS
☎ *(020) 8748 3446*

Salutation (FULLER'S)
154 King Street, Hammersmith W6 0QU
☎ *(020) 8748 3668*

Thatched House (YOUNG'S)
115 Dalling Road, Hammersmith W6 0ET
☎ *(020) 8748 6174*

The William Morris (WETHERSPOON)
2–4 King Street, Hammersmith W6 0QA
☎ *(020) 8741 7175*

W7

The Dolphin

13 Lower Boston Road, Hanwell W7 3TX
☎ *(020) 8810 1617* John Connoly

Marston's Pedigree, Brakspear Bitter, Morland Old Speckled Hen, Fuller's London Pride, Wadworth 6X or Gale's HSB usually available. A guest beer such as Badger Tanglefoot often on offer, too.

Olde-worlde character pub with wooden floors, lovely beer garden and restaurant. Food served 12–2.30pm and 6–9pm Tues–Sun. Kitchen closed Sun evening and Monday. Children welcome, with separate children's menu available. Small car park. Located off one-way system to Uxbridge Road or follow Boston Road to end.

OPEN *12–11pm (10.30pm Sun).*

The Fox

Greene Lane, Olde Hanwell W7
☎ *(020) 8567 3912*

Fuller's London Pride, Timothy Taylor Landlord and Kelham Island Pale Rider plus ever-changing guests.

Freehouse built in 1853 close to the Grand Union Canal serving food at lunchtime and evenings. Garden. Quiz night. Occasional live music and beer festivals.

OPEN *11am–11pm Mon–Sat; 12–10.30pm Sun.*

OTHER REAL ALE PUBS IN W7

Viaduct (FULLER'S)

221 Uxbridge Road, Hanwell W7 3TD
☎ *(020) 8567 1362*

White Hart (FULLER'S)

324 Greenford Avenue, Hanwell W7 3DA
☎ *(020) 8578 1708*

W8

Churchill Arms

119 Kensington Church Street W8 7LN
☎ *(020) 7727 4242* Gerry O'Brien

Another Fuller's house, so with Chiswick, London Pride, ESB and seasonal brews available.

A popular, atmospheric, 1930s, award-winning locals' pub with plenty of Churchill family memorabilia (they celebrate his birthday in style). Thai food available. Conservatory.

⊖ Nearest Tube: Notting Hill Gate

OPEN *11am–11pm Mon–Sat; 12–10.30pm Sun.*

OTHER REAL ALE PUBS IN W8

Britannia (YOUNG'S)

1 Allen Street, Kensington W8 6UX
☎ *(020) 7937 6905*

W9

The Truscott Arms

55 Shirland Road, Maida Vale W9 2JD
☎ *(020) 7286 0310* Barbara Slack

Fuller's London Pride, Greene King IPA and Abbot usually available, plus other Fuller's beers.

Local community pub with one large centre bar. Secluded rear beer garden. Food served 12–3pm and 6–9pm Mon–Sat, plus 12–3pm Sun for traditional roasts and summer barbecues (weather permitting). Children are welcome until 7pm.

⊖ Nearest Tube: Warwick Avenue.

OPEN *11am–11pm Mon–Sat; 12–10.30pm Sun.*

Warrington Hotel

93 Warrington Crescent, Maida Vale W9 1EH
☎ *(020) 7286 2929* J Brandon

Brakspear Special, Young's Special, Fuller's London Pride and ESB usually available, plus one or two guest beers perhaps from Rebellion or Kitchen.

A splendid example of a Victorian public house with art nouveau stained glass, marble bar and fireplace. A family-owned freehouse which has been a popular meeting place for many years. Thai food served in the bar 12–2.30pm and in the upstairs restaurant 6–11pm. No children. Outside seating.

⊖ Nearest Tube: Warwick Avenue.

OPEN *11am–11pm Mon–Sat; 12–10.30pm Sun.*

W11

The Pelican

All Saints Road, Ladbroke Grove W11
☎ *(020) 7792 3073*
Esther Boulton and Sangeeta Singh

Pitfield Singhboulton, Eco Warrior and St Peter's Organic Best always available plus seasonal beers from the Pitfield Brewery.

The third in this chain of organic gastro-pubs (see Duke of Cambridge N1 and The Crown E3), opened in 2001. Large ground-floor bar plus upstairs restaurant. Food served 12.30–3.30pm and 6.30–10.30pm.

⊖ Nearest Tube: Ladbroke Grove.

OPEN *5–11pm Mon; 12–11pm Tues–Sat; 12–10.30pm Sun.*

OTHER REAL ALE PUBS IN W11

Duke of Wellington (YOUNG'S)

179 Portobello Road W11 2ED
☎ *(020) 7727 6727*

W12

Crown and Sceptre (Fuller's)
57 Melina Road, Shepherds Bush W12 9HY
☎ (020) 8743 6414

Vesbar (Fuller's)
15–19 Goldhawk Road, Shepherds Bush W12 8QQ
☎ (020) 8762 0215

W13

Drayton Court Hotel (Fuller's)
2 The Avenue, Ealing W13 8PH
☎ (020) 8997 1019

Kent Hotel (Fuller's)
Scotch Common, Ealing W13 8DL
☎ (020) 8997 5911

W14

Britannia Tap (Young's)
150 Warwick Road, West Kensington W14 8PS
☎ (020) 7602 1649

Seven Stars (Fuller's)
253 North End Road, Kensington W14 9NS
☎ (020) 7385 3571

Warwick Arms (Fuller's)
160 Warwick Road, Kensington W14 9OS
☎ (020) 7603 356

Places Featured:

Barking	Isleworth
Barnet	Kingston-upon-Thames
Bexleyheath	Laleham
Brentford	North Cheam
Bromley	Petts Wood
Carshalton	Pinner
Croydon	Purley
Egham	Richmond
Farnborough	Romford
Feltham	Staines
Hampton	Stanmore
Harrow	Surbiton
Heathrow	Twickenham
Hounslow	Uxbridge
Ilford	Woodford Green

THE PUBS

BARKING

The Britannia

1 Church Road, Barking, Essex IG11 8PR
☎ *(020) 8594 1305* Mrs Pells

 A Young's pub with Special and Bitter always available, plus a winter warmer from October and various specials in summer.

An old-fashioned community alehouse with public bar, saloon/lounge bar and snug. Patio. Food available at lunchtime and evenings. No children. Can be extremely difficult to find – ring if need be.

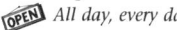 *11am–3pm and 5–11.30pm Mon–Fri; all day Sat–Sun.*

BARNET

Moon Under Water

148 High Street, Barnet, Hertfordshire EN5 5XP
☎ *(020) 8441 9476* Gareth Fleming

 A Wetherspoon's pub with Greene King IPA and Abbot plus Shepherd Neame Spitfire always available. Also three guests such as Hop Back Summer Lightning which are changed on a weekly basis.

An olde-worlde town pub with one large bar, a non-smoking dining area and big beer garden. Food available from 11am–10pm. No children.

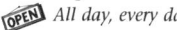 *All day, every day.*

BEXLEYHEATH

Robin Hood & Little John

78 Lion Road, Bexleyheath, Kent DA6 8PF
☎ *(020) 8303 1128* Mr Johnson

 A freehouse with Shepherd Neame Spitfire and Golding, Burtonwood Bitter, plus Flagship Destroyer and Futtock, Timothy Taylor Landlord and others regularly available. The least popular brew is dropped each month to try something different. Up to eight pumps in operation.

A one-bar, village-type pub with wood panel walls and old Singer sewing machine tables. Beer garden. Food available at lunchtime only, Mon–Sat. No children.

 11am–3.30pm and 6–11pm (7–11pm Sat–Sun).

Wrong Un

234–6 The Broadway, Bexleyheath
☎ *(0208) 298 0439* Timothy Shepherd

 Hop Back Summer Lightning and Greene King Abbot Ale regularly available plus four or five guest beers such as Shepherd Neame Spitfire, Bateman XXXB, Brains SA, Hook Norton Old Hooky, Hop Back Thunderstorm or something from Ash Vine or Marston's.

Light, spacious pub with relaxed atmosphere and large non-smoking area. Extensive menu available 10am–10pm Mon–Sat, 12–10.30pm Sun. Disabled facilities. Car park. No children.

 10am–11pm Mon–Sat; 12–10.30pm Sun.

BRENTFORD

The Magpie & Crown
128 High Street, Brentford, Middlesex TW8 8EW
☎ *(020) 8560 5658* Charlie and Steve Bolton

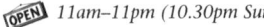A freehouse with four pumps serving a range of ales such as Brakspear Bitter, Greene King IPA, something from Cottage and many, many more.

A mock-Tudor pub. One bar. No food. No children.

OPEN *11am–11pm (10.30pm Sun).*

BROMLEY

The Red Lion
10 North Road, Bromley, Kent BR1 3LG
☎ *(020) 8460 2691*
Chris and Siobhan Humphrey

Greene King Abbot and IPA plus something from Harveys always available. The two guest pumps offer a wide selection of ales from various breweries, changed at least twice weekly.

Friendly local offering food Mon–Sat.

OPEN *11am–11pm (10.30pm Sun)*

CARSHALTON

The Racehorse
17 West Street, Carshalton, Surrey SM5 2PT
☎ *(020) 8647 6818* Julian Norton

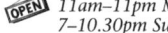A freehouse with Gale's Butser and HSB and Greene King IPA always on offer, plus two guests ales, usually from Fuller's, Morland, Marston's or Brakspear.

A locals' pub with two bars, dining area, disabled access and patio. Food available at lunchtime and evenings (not Sunday pm).

OPEN *11am–11pm Mon–Sat; 12–4pm and 7–10.30pm Sun.*

CROYDON

Claret Free House
5 Bingham Corner, Lower Addiscombe Road, Croydon CR0 7AA
☎ *(020) 8656 7452* Mike Callaghan

Palmers IPA, Shepherd Neame Spitfire plus a Cottage brew usually available. Three regularly changing guests are also served (200 per year).

Small, friendly and comfortable community pub. No food. No children. Adjacent to new Tramlink station.

OPEN *11.30am–11pm Mon–Sat; 12–10.30pm Sun.*

EGHAM

The Crown
38 High Street, Egham, Middlesex TW20 9DP
☎ *(01784) 432608* Lin Bowman

The permanent beers are Adnams Broadside in winter and Adnams Regatta in summer, and the two or three guests, changed weekly, are from a wide range of breweries.

Very busy town pub with one bar, dining area and garden. Plenty of food available! Twice-yearly beer festivals held, with around 10 beers at each. Occasional live music.

OPEN *11.30am–11pm Mon–Sat; 12–10.30pm Sun.*

FARNBOROUGH

The Woodman
50 High Street, Farnborough BR6 7BA
☎ *(01689) 852663* Sharon Pritchard

Shepherd Neame Master Brew, Spitfire and a seasonal brew usually available.

A village pub in a quiet location, with a large garden, grapevine canopy and many hanging baskets, window boxes and tubs. Food served 12–2pm and 7–9pm Mon–Sat and lunchtime roasts every Sunday. Children welcome. Car park. Located just off the A21, three miles from Bromley, sign posted 'Farnborough Village'.

OPEN *12–3.30pm and 5–11pm Mon–Wed; all day Thurs–Sun.*

FELTHAM

Moon on the Square
30 The Centre, Feltham, Middlesex TW13 4AU
☎ *(020) 8893 1293* Phil Cripps

Fuller's London Pride and Marston's Pedigree always available, plus four guests changing all the time, from breweries such as Brakspear, Cotleigh, Hook Norton and Exmoor.

One big bar plus non-smoking dining area in which food is available all day. No children.

OPEN *All day, every day.*

HAMPTON

The White Hart

70 High Street, Hampton, Middlesex TW12 2SW
☎ *(020) 8979 5352* Mrs Macintosh

Greene King Abbot is among those beers always available plus six guest beers (hundreds per year) including ales from Ringwood, Pilgrim, Nethergate, Hop Back, Archers, Hogs Back, Brakspear, Gale's, Shepherd Neame, Charles Wells, Titanic, Woodforde's and Harviestoun breweries.

Mock-Tudor pub in an historical area with a log fire in winter and large patio area. No darts or pool. Homemade bar food served at lunchtime and a Thai restaurant in the evenings. Car park, garden and function room with bar. Close to Hampton BR station. Easy access from the M3 and A316. On main bus routes from Richmond, Heathrow and Wimbledon.

OPEN *11am–3pm and 5–11pm Mon–Fri; 11.30am–11pm Sat–Sun.*

HARROW

The Castle

30 West Street, Harrow, Middlesex HA1 3EF
☎ *(020) 8422 3155* Helena Ackroyd

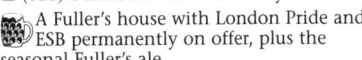A Fuller's house with London Pride and ESB permanently on offer, plus the seasonal Fuller's ale.

A quiet pub with no music or pool. Central bar and beer garden. Food served 12–9pm Mon–Sat and lunchtime roasts on Sundays. Children and dogs welcome. Follow signs to Harrow School and Harrow on the Hill, West Street is located next to Harrow School Outfitters shop.

OPEN *11am–11pm Mon–Sat; 12–10.30pm Sun.*

The Moon on the Hill

373–5 Station Road, Harrow, Middlesex HA1 2AW
☎ *(020) 8863 3670* Scott Hellery

A JD Wetherspoon's pub with up to four guest ales. Hop Back Summer Lightning, Shepherd Neame Spitfire and Greene King Abbot are among the regulars, but brews from any independent brewery are stocked when possible.

A friendly town-centre pub, with a traditional atmosphere – no music. Food available every day until 10pm. Children allowed if eating. Non-smoking area.

OPEN *11am–11pm Mon–Sat; 12–10.30pm Sun.*

HEATHROW

The Tap & Spile

Upper Concourse, Terminal One, Heathrow Airport, Middlesex UB5 4PX
☎ *(020) 8897 8418* John Heaphy

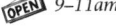Marston's Pedigree always available plus up to nine guest beers (50 per year) including Rooster's Bitter, Charles Wells Eagle, Brains SA, Nethergate IPA and Adnams Best.

Cosy and relaxing refuge with a 1930s feel overlooking the anarchy of the check-in area. Bar food available at lunchtime and evenings. Car park and children's room. On the catering balcony at departure level in terminal one.

OPEN *9–11am for breakfast, then 11am–11pm.*

HOUNSLOW

Moon Under Water

84–6 Staines Road, Hounslow, Middlesex TW3 3LF
☎ *(020) 8572 7506* Peter Johnson

Hop Back Summer Lightning and Greene King Abbot permanently available, plus three to five guests which are constantly changing.

A Wetherspoon's pub with non-smoking area, patio, disabled facilities. Food available all day from 11am–10pm. Children allowed until 5pm – separate children's area.

OPEN *All day, every day.*

ILFORD

The Rose & Crown

16 Ilford Hill, Ilford, Essex IG1 2DA
☎ *(020) 8478 7104*

Marston's Pedigree and Adnams Best always available along with a monthly selection which might include Shepherd Neame Spitfire or a special brew. Three guest pumps.

A town pub just off the high street with beams and log fires. One bar with dining area and a small terrace. Food available 12–3pm Mon–Fri. Children allowed if eating.

OPEN *11am–11pm Mon–Sat; 12-10.30pm Sun.*

ISLEWORTH

The Red Lion

94 Linkfield Road, Isleworth, Middlesex TW7 6QJ
☎ *(020) 8560 1457* Nikki Redding

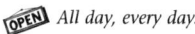A freehouse with up to seven beers available at any one time. Brakspear Bitter and Special are permanent offerings. Beer of the Month promotions have featured Marston's Pedigree and Timothy Taylor Landlord, and other regular guests include beers from Cottage, Wye Valley, Burton Bridge, Brains, Hampshire, Rebellion, O'Hanlons, Eccleshall, Hogs Back and Mole's breweries.

A large, friendly, locals' pub in a back street near the station, situated in an early-Victorian residential area close to Twickenham Rugby Ground and Richmond. Regular live music, own theare company and a relaxed atmosphere. Two bars and a large landscaped garden with regular BBQs in the summer. Food served 12–3pm Mon–Fri. Corporate hospitality facilities available. Children allowed in the garden.

OPEN *All day, every day.*

KINGSTON-UPON-THAMES

The Canbury Arms

49 Canbury Park Road, Kingston-upon-Thames, Surrey KT2 6LQ
☎ *(020) 8288 1882* Paul Adams

Six real ales usually available which may include Wadworth 6X, Morland Old Speckled Hen, Marston's Pedigree or Greene King Abbot Ale. Over 650 beers from more than 100 independent/micro-breweries served so far. Regularly changing real cider and annual Easter cider festival.

B ack-street pub with mock-Tudor interior. Large-screen TV for sport. Extensive reference library. Live music on Friday and Saturday evenings, quiz nights on Sunday. Beer garden with patio. Dog the size of a Shetland pony! No food. Car park with secure motorcycle parking. No children.

OPEN *All permitted hours.*

The Fighting Cocks

56 London Road, Kingston-upon-Thames, Surrey KT2 6QA
☎ *(020) 8546 5174* Natalie Salt

Wadworth 6X among the brews always available plus two guests such as Marston's Pedigree.

A town pub with wooden floors and panelled walls. Two bars and courtyard. No food. Children allowed.

OPEN *11am–11pm.*

The Kelly Arms

Alfred Road, off Villiers Road, Kingston-upon-Thames, Surrey KT1 2UB
☎ *(020) 8296 9815* Vanessa McConnon

Four real ales usually available, featuring beers from Wolf, Hogs Back and Cottage breweries. Stowford Press cider from H. Weston also served.

A back-street locals' pub with a friendly atmosphere. One big bar. Pool table, Tornado football table, darts, pinball, Sky TV. Garden with BBQ. Food available all day, every day. Children allowed if eating or in garden. Functions catered for.

OPEN *11am–11pm Mon–Sat; 12–10.30pm Sun.*

The Willoughby Arms

Willoughby Road, Kingston-upon-Thames, Surrey, KT2 6LN
☎ *(020) 8546 4236* Rick Robinson

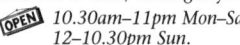Timothy Taylor Landlord, Fuller's London Pride, Caledonian Deuchars IPA and Marston's Pedigree permanently available, plus one guest ale which is sold at £1.50 per pint. The pub is the HQ of the Kingston branch of the Society of Preservation of Beers from the Wood. Two annual beer festivals held on St George's Day and Hallowe'en.

A recently refurbished Victorian corner local. Rolls available at lunchtime, barbecues on Sundays (weather permitting). Children allowed in the large garden which has a pond and waterfall. Large-screen TV, bric-à-brac. Quiz night Sundays. Can be difficult to find, so ring if you get lost.

OPEN *10.30am–11pm Mon–Sat; 12–10.30pm Sun.*

LALEHAM

The Feathers

The Broadway, Laleham, Staines, Middlesex TW18 1RZ
☎ *(01784) 453561*
Keith John Graham and Louise Jackson

Fuller's London Pride is a permanent fixture, and the three guest ales might include beers from Hogs Back, Smiles, Adnams, Shepherd Neame, Badger or Hop Back, to name but a few.

W arm, friendly, traditional village pub with a secluded beer garden. An excellent range of freshly cooked meals is served 12–3pm and 6–9pm Mon–Thurs, 12–8.30pm Fri, 12–9.30pm Sat and 12–8pm Sun, and the pub has a separate dining area with two log fires. Children and families welcome. Car park.

OPEN *11am–11pm Mon–Sat; 12–10.30pm Sun.*

NORTH CHEAM

Wetherspoons
552–6 London Road, North Cheam, Surrey SM3 9AA
☎ *(020) 8644 1808* Dean Kelly

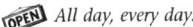A Wetherspoon's pub with Fuller's London Pride always available plus two guests such as Shepherd Neame Spitfire. Guests changed every three days.

One large bar and non-smoking dining area. Food available all day. Disabled facilities. No children.

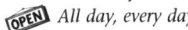 *All day, every day.*

PETTS WOOD

Sovereign of the Seas
109 Queensway, Petts Wood, Orpington, Kent BR5 1DG
☎ *(01689) 891606* Robert Barfoot

A Wetherspoon's pub with Shepherd Neame Spitfire among the brews always available. Two guests might include Hop Back Summer Lightning, or Timothy Taylor Landlord. Guests changed weekly.

A community pub with one big bar, a non-smoking dining area and disabled facilities. Outside patios in summer. Food available all day. No children.

 *All day, every day.*

PINNER

The Village Inn
402–8 Rayners Lane, Pinner, Middlesex HA5 5DY
☎ *(020) 8868 8551* Mark Daniels (Manager)

Shepherd Neame Spitfire permanently available, plus three constantly changing guest ales.

A JD Wetherspoon's house with food available all day, every day. Children allowed, baby-changing facilities provided. Disabled access and facilities. Non-smoking area. Small garden with outside seating. Car park. To find, turn left at the station.

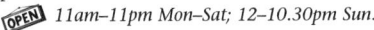 *11am–11pm Mon–Sat; 12–10.30pm Sun.*

PURLEY

Foxley Hatch
8–9 Russell Hill Road, Purley CR8 2LE
☎ *(020) 8763 9307* Andy Rimmer

A Wetherspoon's pub with Shepherd Neame Spitfire and Greene King Abbot permanently available, plus two guest beers from around the country. Three or four festivals are also held each year offering up to 20 beers at a time.

Friendly, locals' pub free of music and television. Non-smoking area and easy access for the disabled. Food served all day, every day. No children.

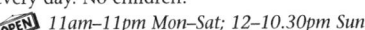 *11am–11pm Mon–Sat; 12–10.30pm Sun.*

RICHMOND

The Triple Crown
15 Kew Foot Road, Richmond, Surrey TW9 2SS
☎ *(020) 8940 3805*

Fuller's London Pride and Timothy Taylor Landlord regularly available. Four guest beers are also served, from a list running into several hundreds.

Traditional, one-bar house. Food served 12–2.30pm. Children welcome.

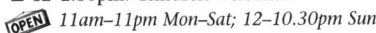 *11am–11pm Mon–Sat; 12–10.30pm Sun.*

ROMFORD

The Moon & Stars
103 South Street, Romford, Essex RM1 1NX
☎ *(01708) 730117* Sarah Saye

A Wetherspoon's pub with Greene King Abbot and Shepherd Neame Spitfire among the beers always available. Four guest ales change on a weekly basis.

Large bar, non-smoking dining area, outside seating, disabled facilities. Food available all day. Children allowed outside only.

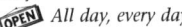 *All day, every day.*

STAINES

The Angel Hotel
Angel Mews, High Street, Staines, Middlesex TW18 4EE
☎ *(01784) 452509* John Othick

A freehouse with two beers from Hogs Back and two from Ushers always available, varying according to the season.

A town pub and restaurant with patio and 12 bedrooms. Food available all day.

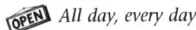 *All day, every day.*

The Bells
124 Church Street, Staines, Middlesex TW18 4ZB
☎ *(01784) 454240* Mr and Mrs Winstanley

Tied to Young's, with Young's Special and Triple A always served, plus one guest from Smiles.

Village pub with village atmosphere, with two bars, function room and beer garden. Food available. Children allowed in designated areas.

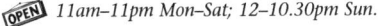 *11am–11pm Mon–Sat; 12–10.30pm Sun.*

The George

2–8 High Street, Staines, Middlesex TW18 4EE
☎ *(01784) 462181* Jim Conlin

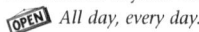 Fuller's London Pride and Greene King Abbot among the beers always available plus four guests such as Marston's Pedigree, Shepherd Neame Spitfire and Morland Old Speckled Hen. Always a good selection of brews from all over the UK. Guests changed monthly.

A large, two-level Wetherspoon's pub. No music, non-smoking dining areas upstairs and down, disabled access and toilets. Food available all day. No children.

 All day, every day.

The Hobgoblin

14–16 Church Street, Staines, Middlesex TW18 4EP

☎ *(01784) 452012* Del Woolsgrove

Wychwood Special, Shires XXX and Hobgoblin always available. Three guests could include Marston's Pedigree, Charles Wells Bombardier and beers from Hampshire and Rebellion breweries.

A town-centre, regulars' pub, frequented by the 23–35 age group in evenings, with an older clientele at lunchtimes. An old building with wooden floors and beams, one bar and courtyard. Food available 12–2.30pm. Children allowed in courtyard if open.

 12–11pm Mon–Sat (10.30pm Sun).

STANMORE

The Malthouse

7 Stanmore Hill, Stanmore, Middlesex HA7 3DP
☎ *(020) 8420 7265* Charles Begley

A freehouse serving a range of four constantly changing real ales. Favourites include Wadworth 6X and beers from breweries such as Rebellion, Slaters, Ringwood, Cottage and Greene King.

A modern pub decorated in an old style. Late licence. Garden, disabled access. Food available lunchtimes only. Children allowed.

 11am–11pm Mon–Tues; 11am–midnight Wed–Thurs; 11am–1am Fri–Sat; 11am–10.30pm Sun.

SURBITON

Coronation Hall

St Mark's Hill, Surbiton, Surrey KT6 4TB
☎ *(020) 8390 6164* Emma Wales

A Wetherspoon's pub with Shepherd Neame Spitfire and Fuller's London Pride always available. Three guest pumps changed twice a week, which might include Hop Back Summer Lightning.

Large bar area, non-smoking dining area and disabled facilities. Food available all day. No children.

 All day, every day.

The Lamb Inn

73 Brighton Road, Surbiton KT6 5NF
☎ *(020) 8390 9229* Ian Stewart

Greene King IPA and Young's Special permanently available plus one guest changed every two or three days. A good choice of regional ales is offered, from the Isle of Wight to the Isle of Man.

A true old-fashioned community locals' pub. Darts, bar games and a friendly welcoming atmosphere. Large beer garden with grassed area for children. Bar food available every lunchtime. Children allowed in the garden only. From J10 of M25, take left turn towards Kingston; eventually you come to Brighton Road.

 11am–11pm Mon–Sat; 12–10.30pm Sun.

TWICKENHAM

The Eel Pie

9–11 Church Street, Twickenham TW1 3NJ
☎ *(020) 8891 1717* Tom and Kate McAuley

Badger Best, Tanglefoot and IPA and King and Barnes Sussex always available, plus two guests which may include Gribble Brewery's Fursty Ferret or Pig's Ear, or possible from time to time, Timothy Taylor Landlord, Oakham JHB or Slaters Top Totty.

A cosy, traditional pub with laid-back atmosphere situated just off the main street in Twickenham. A newcomer is welcome either to keep themselves to themselves, or to be the life and soul of the party! Food available 12–4pm daily. Children allowed, children's menu available.

 11am–11pm Mon–Sat; 12–10.30pm Sun.

Up 'N' Under

33–5 York Street, Twickenham, Middlesex TW1 3JZ
☎ *(020) 8891 3940* William Upton (manager)

Five cask ales stocked, and changed on a monthly basis. Charles Wells Bombardier is a particular favourite.

A stylish bar and upstairs restaurant serving traditional food, which is available all day. Children welcome.

 12–11pm (10.30pm Sun).

UXBRIDGE

The Load of Hay
Villier Street, Uxbridge, Middlesex UB8 2PU
☎ *(01895) 234676* Heather Winsbottom

A freehouse with Buckley's Best always available plus three guests from breweries such as Wye Valley, Everards, Rebellion and Cottage – a different one appears each week. Local breweries, micros and small independents favoured.

Situated on the outskirts of town, near the university. University clientele during the daytime, and locals in the evenings. Two bars. Beer garden. Food available every lunchtime and Mon–Sat evenings. Children allowed in the smaller bar area and the garden. In a secluded location – ring for directions if necessary.

OPEN *11am–3pm and 5.30–11pm Mon–Fri; 11am–3pm and 7–close Sat–Sun.*

The Swan and Bottle
Oxford Road, Uxbridge, Middlesex UB8 1LZ
☎ *(01895) 234047* Claire Chapman

Morland Old Speckled Hen permanently available plus one guest which changes fortnightly.

A Chef & Brewer pub/restaurant. Family-friendly with children welcome, plus disabled toilet, parking and access. Food available daily. Beer garden.

OPEN *11am–11pm Mon–Sat; 12–10.30pm Sun.*

The Three Tuns
24 High Street, Uxbridge, Middlesex UB8 1JN
☎ *(01895) 233960* Brian Gallagher

Marston's Pedigree, Fuller's London Pride and Adnams Bitter are always on offer.

Traditional town-centre pub with beams, fires, conservatory, beer garden and patio for 80 people. Food available (not Sundays), and there is a separate dining area. Children allowed if eating. Opposite the Tube Station.

OPEN *11am–11pm Mon–Sat; 12–10.30pm Sun.*

WOODFORD GREEN

The Cricketers
299–301 High Road, Woodford Green, Essex IG8 9EG
☎ *(020) 8504 2734* Mr and Mrs Woolridge

Owned by McMullen, so AK Original, Gladstone and Country Best Bitter always served, with specials and seasonals when available.

A semi-rural pub with lounge and public bars and beer garden. Food available 12–2pm Mon–Sat, with OAP specials Mon–Thurs. Children allowed till 6.30pm in the lounge bar only. Situated near the statue of Winston Churchill.

OPEN *11am–11pm Mon–Sat; 12–10.30pm Sun.*

YOU TELL US

* *The Albany,* Station Yard, Twickenham
* *The Beaconsfield Arms,* 63 West End Road, Southall
* *The Brewery at the Hog & Stump,* 88 London Road, Kingston-upon-Thames
* *The Cricketer's Arms,* 21 Southbridge Place, Croydon
* *The Cricketers,* 93 Chislehurst Road, Orpington
* *The Five Bells,* Church Road, Chelsfield, Orpington
* *The George,* 17 George Street, Croydon
* *The Greyhound,* 82 Kew Green, Kew
* *The Royal Standard,* 39 Nuxley Road, Upper Belvedere

Places Featured:

Altrincham	Hawkshaw
Ashton-under-Lyne	Heywood
Atherton	Hindley
Bolton	Hyde
Bury	Manchester
Castleton	Nangreaves
Cheetham	Oldham
Chorlton	Rochdale
Delph	Salford
Denton	Stalybridge (see Cheshire)
Edgeley	Uppermill
Failsworth	Wigan

THE BREWERIES

BANK TOP BREWERY

Unit 1, Back Lane, Vernon Street, Bolton BL1 2LD
☎ *(01204) 528865*

 BRYDGE BITTER 3.8% ABV
DARK MILD 4.0% ABV
FLAT CAP 4.0% ABV
GOLD DIGGER 4.0% ABV
GOLDEN BROWN 4.2% ABV
HAKA 4.2% ABV
SAMUEL CROMPTON'S ALE 4.2% ABV
VOLUNTEER BITTER 4.2% ABV
CLIFFHANGER 4.5% ABV
SANTA'S CLAWS 5.0% ABV
Christmas brew.
SATANIC MILLS 5.0% ABV
SMOKESTACK LIGHTNIN' 5.0% ABV
Plus seasonal brews.

BOGGART HOLE CLOUGH BREWING COMPANY

13 Brookside Works, Clough Road, Moston, Manchester M9 4FP
☎ *(0161) 277 9666*
www.boggart-brewery.co.uk

BOGGART PUNNET 3.6% ABV
BOGGART BITTER 3.8% ABV
BOG STANDARD 4.0% ABV
LOG END 4.0% ABV
ANGEL HILL 4.2% ABV
BOGGART'S BREW 4.3% ABV
DARK SIDE 4.4% ABV
SUN DIAL 4.7% ABV
STEAMING BOGGART 9.0% ABV

CHESHIRE CAT ALES

Old Market Tavern, Old Market Place, Altringham W14 4DN
☎ *(0161) 927 7062*

POESJE'S BOLLEKES 4.1% ABV

J W LEES & CO.

Greengate Brewery, Middleton Junction, Manchester M24 2AX
☎ *(0161) 643 2487*
www.jwlees.co.uk

 GB MILD 3.5% ABV
Smooth and sweet, with a malt flavour and a dry finish.
BITTER 4.0% ABV
Refreshing maltiness, with a bitter finish.
MOONRAKER 7.5% ABV
Rounded sweetness, with balancing bitterness.
Plus a changing brew every two months between 4.0% ABV and 5.0% ABV.

JOSEPH HOLT PLC

Derby Brewery, Empire Street, Cheetham, Manchester M3 1JD
☎ *(0161) 834 3285*

 MILD 3.2% ABV
Malty with good hoppiness.
BITTER 4.0% ABV
Powerful, hoppy and bitter throughout.

HYDES: THE MANCHESTER BREWER

46 Moss Lane West, Manchester M15 5PH
☎ *(0161) 266 1317*
www.hydesbrewery.co.uk

 BLACK 3.5% ABV
HYDE'S MILD 3.5% ABV
HYDE'S LIGHT 3.5% ABV
HYDE'S TRADITIONAL BITTER 3.8% ABV
JEKYLL'S GOLD 4.0% ABV
SMOOTH 4.0% ABV

MAYFLOWER BREWERY

Mayflower House, 15 Longendale Road,
Standish, Wigan WN6 0UE
☎ *(01257) 400605*
www.mayflowerbrewery.co.uk

BLACK DIAMOND 3.4% ABV
MAYFLOWER BEST BITTER 3.8% ABV
SACK RACE 4.1% ABV
WIGAN BIER 4.2% ABV
HIC BIBI 5.0% ABV
Plus seasonal brews.

PHOENIX BREWERY

Oak Brewing Co., Green Lane, Heywood, Greater
Manchester OL10 2EP
☎ *(01706) 627009*

BANTAM BITTER 3.5% ABV
OAK BEST BITTER 3.9% ABV
HOPWOOD BITTER 4.3% ABV
OLD OAK ALE 4.5% ABV
THIRSTY MOON 4.6% ABV
BONNEVILLE 4.8% ABV
DOUBLE DAGGER 5.0% ABV
WOBBLY BOB 6.0% ABV
Plus seasonal brews.

SHAW'S BREWERY

The Old Stables, Park Road, Dukinfield SK16 5LX
☎ *(0161) 330 547*

BEST BITTER 4.0% ABV
GOLD MEDAL 4.4% ABV
JUBILEE ALE 5.0% ABV

THE PUBS

ALTRINCHAM

The Old Market Tavern

Old Market Place, Altrincham W14 4DN
☎ *(0161) 927 7062* Wayne Reece

No permanent real ales, but 11 constantly changing beers (30 each week), such as Hop Back Summer Lightning, Young's Special, Brakspear Special, Robinson's Old Tom, Oakham Helter Skelter, and RCH PG Steam, to name but a few.

A traditional pub, with no games, no music, but lots of real ale! Food available. Children not allowed. Garden.

OPEN *11am–11pm Mon–Sat; 12–10.30pn Sun.*

ASHTON-UNDER-LYNE

The Station

2 Warrington Street, Ashton-under-lyne OL6 6XB
☎ *(0161) 330 6776* Susan Watson

Marston's Pedigree and Station Bitter (a special brew) among the beers always available, plus up to six guests, perhaps including Timothy Taylor Landlord and Hydes' Anvil Bitter.

A traditional Victorian freehouse filled with railway memorabilia. Beer garden, happy hours on weekdays from 3–8pm, 4–8pm (Sat) and 12–5pm (Sun). Entertainment on Friday and Saturday nights. Food served at lunchtime and evenings. Children allowed.

OPEN *12–11pm (10.30pm Sun).*

The Witchwood

152 Old Street, Ashton-under-Lyne OL6 7SF
☎ *(0161) 344 0321* Pauline Town

Marston's Pedigree and Moorhouse's Pendle Witches Brew are among the beers always available, plus four guests from a range of 15 independent brewers.

A real ale bar and live music venue six days a week. Two bars, beer garden. Food available. No children.

OPEN *12–11pm (10.30pm Sun).*

ATHERTON

The Pendle Witch

2–4 Warburton Place, Atherton, Manchester
M46 0EQ
☎ *(01942) 884537* Joan Houghton

Tied to Moorhouse's with Premier and Pendle Witches Brew always available plus a couple of others, perhaps Moorhouse's seasonal ales or specials such as Bursting Bitter, Black Witch, Black Panther, Thunder Struck, Black Cat or Easter Ale.

A 100-year-old cottage pub. Light snacks only available. Beer garden. Children allowed inside in the afternoons, or in the garden. Situated off Market Street.

OPEN *All day, every day.*

BOLTON

The Hen & Chickens

Deansgate, Bolton BL1 1EX
☎ *(01204) 389836* Anthony Coyne

Three guests are served, and change so quickly that they are too numerous to mention!

A traditional pub situated near the post office. Homemade food served at lunchtime only. Children allowed at lunchtime only.

OPEN *11.30am–11pm Mon–Sat;*
7–10.30pm Sun.

Howcroft Inn

36 Pool Street, Bolton BL1 2JU
☎ *(01204) 526814* Clive Nightingale

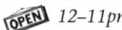 Timothy Taylor Landlord and beers from Bank Top are always available, plus guests, often from micro-breweries.

A traditional pub with a broad clientele. Appears on the CAMRA/English Heritage Pub Interiors list. Beer garden and bowling green. Food served every lunchtime, including Sundays. Home to the largest pub beer festival in the country, held in the second week of October, and featuring over 200 beers. Children allowed.

OPEN *12–11pm.*

BURY

Dusty Miller

87 Crostons Road, Bury BL8 1AL
☎ *(0161) 764 1124* Sue Johnson

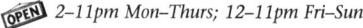 A Moorhouse's pub with Premier, Pendle Witches Brew and Black Cat Mild always available. A selection of guest ales is also served.

A traditional local pub. No food. No car park. No children. Located between Walshaw and Bury.

OPEN *2–11pm Mon–Thurs; 12–11pm Fri–Sun.*

CASTLETON

Midland Beer Company

826 Manchester Road, Castleton, Rochdale OL11 3AW
☎ *(01706) 750873* Mr Welsby

A freehouse serving Thwaites Bitter plus two guests such as Timothy Taylor Best and Landlord, Mallard IPA or a Cottage Brewery ale.

A traditional pub in an old bank building with beer garden. Food available. Children allowed. Opposite Castleton railway station.

OPEN *All day, every day.*

CHEETHAM

The Queen's Arms

Honey Street, Cheetham M8 8RG
☎ *(0161) 834 4239*

Eight beers always available, usually including Timothy Taylor Landlord and Phoenix Bantam. Others change constantly. Also a wide range of Belgian beers.

A traditional town pub built in the 1800s and subsequently extended. Bar food available at lunchtime and until 8pm. Street parking, children's play area and garden.

OPEN *12–11pm (10.30pm Sun)*

CHORLTON

The Marble Beer House

57 Manchester Road, Chorlton M21 9PW
☎ *(0161) 881 9206* David Yuill

 Marble Arch Brewery pub, with the totally organic Marble Beers always on offer. Two guests, changed every couple of days, include favourites such as Harviestoun Schiehallion and beers from Phoenix. Seasonal Marble Beers include Organic Ginger in summer and Organic Chocolate (Heavy) in winter.

Café bar with wooden floors and tasteful furniture, reminiscent of an Amsterdam Brown Café. Conservatory, front seating. No cooked food, but out-of-the-ordinary healthy snacks are available. Children allowed till 5pm. Situated in the heart of Chorlton.

OPEN *12–11pm (10.30pm Sun).*

DELPH

Royal Oak Inn

Broad Lane Heights, Delph, Saddleworth OL3 5TX
☎ *(01457) 874460* Michael and Sheila Fancy

A freehouse with Moorhouse's Black Cat Mild and Bitter always available plus four guest ales often including Fuller's London Pride or brews from Black Sheep or Jennings.

Built in 1767 this is an unspoilt pub with low beams, open fires and dining area. Situated in a remote setting off the Delph–Denshaw road, with good views over Saddleworth Moor. Food available Fri–Sun only. Children allowed.

OPEN *7–11pm Mon–Fri (closed lunchtime); 12–3pm and 7–11pm Sat–Sun.*

DENTON

Lowes Arms

301 Hyde Road, Denton M34 3FF
☎ *(0161) 336 3064* Peter and Gillian Wood

A brewpub, home of The LAB Brewery with four own brews: Haughton Weave, Frog Bog, Broomstairs Bitter and Old Stands plus Pictish Celtic Warrior always available. Home-brewed seasonals and specials.

A large pub with traditional decor and a friendly atmosphere. Separate lounge, dining area and vault bar. A fully qualified in-house chef provides full menus at lunchtime and evening. Children allowed if eating.

 FROG BOG 3.9% ABV
OLD STANDS 4.2% ABV
BROOMSTAIRS BITTER 4.3% ABV
HAUGHTON WEAVE 4.5% ABV
Seasonals:
GOLDEN BALLS 4.1% ABV
Began brewing for World Cup 2002.
WILD WOOD 4.1% ABV
BROKEN BROOM 4.2% ABV
JUBILEE BITTER 4.5% ABV
HAZY HAUGHTON WHEAT BEER 5.2% ABV

OPEN *12–3pm and 5–11pm Mon–Fri; 12–11pm Sat; 12–10.30pm Sun.*

EDGELEY

Olde Vic

1 Chatham Street, Edgeley, Stockport SK3 9ED
☎ *(0161) 480 2410*
Steve Brannan and Johanne Quinn

Five pumps serve a wide range of constantly changing beers, often changed daily (350 served so far by the current licensees. Chilled Weston's cider also on offer.

A small cosy pub with coal fire in the winter and a large, secure beer garden (complete with marquee-style covering for inclement weather!). No food. Situated two minutes' walk from Stockport railway station.

OPEN *5–11pm Mon–Fri; 7–11pm Sat; 7–10.30pm Sun (closed every lunchtime).*

FAILSWORTH

The Millgate

Ashton Road West, Failsworth M35 0ES
☎ *(0161) 681 8284* David McConvile

A freehouse with Joseph Holt Bitter and Willy Booth's Best (a house beer supplied by Bridgewater Ales) plus two guests such as Liverpool Blondie.

A family-oriented pub with log fires, restaurant, beer garden and children's play area. Food available. Children allowed.

OPEN *11am–11pm (10.30pm Sun).*

HAWKSHAW

The Red Lion Hotel

81 Ramsbottom Road, Hawkshaw, Bury BL8 4JS
☎ *(01204) 856600* Carl Owen

A freehouse with one Jennings brew and one Bank Top ale permanently served, plus occasional guests.

A traditional pub and restaurant. Bar and restaurant food available. Children allowed.

OPEN *12–3pm and 6–11pm Mon–Sat; all day Sun.*

HEYWOOD

The Wishing Well

89 York Street, Heywood OL10 4NS
☎ *(01706) 620923* Mr TM Huck

A freehouse with Moorhouse's Pendle Witches Brew and Premier, Phoenix Hopwood, Jennings Cumberland and Timothy Taylor Landlord usually available, plus two rotating guests from a vast range of independent and micro-breweries.

A traditional pub with dining area. Food available at lunchtime and evenings. Children allowed.

OPEN *All day, every day.*

HINDLEY

The Edington Arms

186 Ladies Lane, Hindley
☎ *(01942) 259229*

A Joseph Holt tied house, with Holt Mild and Bitter always available.

An old coaching house with two large, comfortable rooms. No food. Parking and garden. Children allowed. A CAMRA pub of the year. Function room upstairs. Next to Hindley railway station.

OPEN *All day, every day.*

HYDE

The Sportsman

58 Mottram Road, Hyde SK14 2NN
☎ *(0161) 368 5000* Geoff Oliver

A freehouse with Plassey Bitter and Hartington Bitter always available, plus two guests from an ever-changing list including Timothy Taylor Landlord, Whim Magic Mushroom Mild or a Robinson's brew.

A traditional alehouse with open fires. Bar food available at lunchtime. Well-supervised children allowed. Near the railway station at Newton St Hyde Central.

OPEN *All day, every day.*

MANCHESTER

The Beer House

6 Angel Street, Manchester M4 4BR
☎ *(0161) 839 7019* Philip Chapman

Twelve real ales usually on offer, including Phoenix Lancashire Lightning and Timothy Taylor Landlord as permanent features, plus ten guests, changed every three days. Thwaites Bitter is a regular favourite, and Mighty Oak Oscar Wilde Mild, Pictish Ginger Ale and beers from Goose Eye have all been served.

Traditional pub with one bar and function room. Food available. Juke box and gaming machine, yard area with seating. Beer festivals held approximately every 8 weeks throughout the year (phone for further details). No children.

OPEN *11.30am–11pm Mon–Sat; 12–10.30 Sun.*

Bar Fringe

8 Swan Street, Manchester M4 5JN
☎ *(0161) 835 3815* Ms Carmen Contreras MBII

A freehouse with four cask ales available. Beers from Bank Top and Boggart Hole Clough are permanently featured, and the two guest, changed regularly, could be brews from Spinning Dog, Salamander, Cottage or Derwent breweries. Traditional cider, plus draught Belgian and fruit beers are also stocked, and there are regular promotional offers. Wide selection of foreign bottled beers, and guest crisps!

A pub on the outskirts of the town centre, in a building over 100 years old, with traditional long, narrow, Belgian brown bar. Food available 12–6pm every day. One bar, pinball table, garden. Three beer festivals held every year, with plans to increase this in future. Well-behaved children allowed.

OPEN *12–11pm (10.30pm Sun).*

The Lass o'Gowrie

36 Charles Street, Manchester M1 7DB
☎ *(0161) 273 6932* Chris Nagy

A brewpub with both of the home-brewed ales always available. The seven guest ales constantly change. Approximately 1000 are served every year, and regulars include Morland Old Speckled Hen and Black Sheep Best.

A Victorian tiled pub with an open view to the brewery, and gas lighting. Bar food available at lunchtime. Close to BBC North. Parking nearby. Children allowed.

LASS ALE 4.1% ABV
AWLD MUKKA 5.0% ABV

OPEN *11am–11pm Mon–Sat; 12–10.30pm Sun.*

Marble Arch Inn

73 Rochdale Road, Manchester M4 4HY
☎ *(0161) 832 5914* Mr P Chapman

Claiming to be the only organic brewpub in England, this is the home of the Marble Brewery, with five totally organic ales produced and served on tap. All beers are approved by the Soil Association and the Vegan Society. Brewery tours are available. The micro-brewery was installed in December 1998 and turned vegan organic in 2000.

A Victorian pub dating from 1880, with a mosaic floor, brick ceiling with ornate frieze made of marble. Bar food available 11.30am–3pm (not Sun).

N/4 3.8% ABV
CLOUDY MARBLE 4.0% ABV
THE NEW MANCHESTER BITTER 4.2% ABV
GINGER MARBLE 4.5% ABV
UNCUT AMBER 4.7% ABV
Seasonal ale.
OLD LAG 5% ABV
CHOCOLATE HEAVY 5.5% ABV
Seasonal ale.

OPEN *11.30am–11pm Mon–Fri; 12–11pm Sat; 12–10.30pm Sun.*

Sand Bar

120 Grosvenor Street, All Saints, Manchester M1 7HL
☎ *(0161) 273 3141* Rob Loyeau

A freehouse with Phoenix Bantam and Charles Wells Bombardier always available, plus three guests from breweries such as Abbeydale, Goose Eye, Kelham Island, Eccleshall, Burton Bridge and Phoenix. Also selling the biggest range of bottled beers in Manchester (70 in total, mainly German and Belgian).

A city café bar in an old Georgian building. One main bar and benches outside. Food available 12–3pm Mon–Fri. Children allowed. Located off the A34 by the University.

OPEN *11am–11pm Mon–Fri; 12.30–11pm Sat; 5–10.30pm Sun.*

NANGREAVES

The Lord Raglan
Walmersley Old Road, Nangreaves, Bury BL9 6SP
☎ *(0161) 764 6680* Brendan Leyden

The home of the Leyden Brewing Company with the full range of ales brewed on the premises and permanently available. Will occasionally swap one of the home brews with another local micro-brewery. Two annual beer festivals held end June/early July and September.

A Victorian two-bar pub and restaurant. Food available lunchtimes and evenings Mon–Sat and all day Sun. Beer garden. Car park. Children allowed. Brewery visits by arrangement. Take the M66 to J1 Burnley, left and left at first lights. The pub is 1½ miles on the left.

NANNY FLYER 3.8% ABV
A very drinkable session bitter with an initial dryness, a hint of citrus followed by a strong malty finish.
BLACK BEARD 3.9% ABV
A very drinkable dark creamy beer brewed using oats and roasted malt.
LIGHT BRIGADE 4.2% ABV
Gold in colour with a complex fruit and hop taste.
RAGLAN SLEEVE 4.6% ABV
A dark amber beer with a good balance of chocolate malt bitterness and hops.
HEAVY BRIGADE 4.7% ABV
A traditional strong bitter, pale in colour with malt and a touch of bitterness coming through in the finish.
Plus seasonals.

 12–2.30pm and 7–11pm Mon–Fri; 12–3pm and 7–11pm Sat; 12–10.30pm Sun.

OLDHAM

Hark to Topper
Bow Street, Oldham OL1 1SJ
☎ *(0161) 624 7950* Harry Hurn

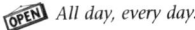A Samuel Smith pub with two hand pumps, always serving the brewery's ale.

A small, refurbished country-style pub located near the town centre. Open fires. Food available at lunchtime and evenings. Children allowed.

 All day, every day.

ROCHDALE

The Albion Freehouse & Bistro
600 Whitworth Road, Rochdale OL12 0SW
☎ *(01706) 648540* KR Robinson

Timothy Taylor Best Bitter and Landlord are the permanent beers here, together with Hyde's Dark Mild and JW Lees Bitter. Guest ales from a variety of brewers are also featured.

Traditional three-roomed freehouse with open fires and a welcoming atmosphere. One TV room, no machines. Pub food is available. The 32-seater non-smoking bistro serves high-quality meals of English and African cuisine (e.g. ostrich, springbok, warthog). Catering for small weddings, functions, business meeting, etc. Situated on A671 in the foothills of the Pennines a mile and a half from Rochdale town centre, with nearby moorland making for good walks.

 12–2.30pm and 5–11pm Mon–Fri; 12–11pm Sat; 12–10.30pm Sun.

Cask & Feather
1 Oldham Road, Rochdale OL16 1UA
☎ *(01706) 711476* Jackie Grimes

Home of the Thomas McGuinness Brewery, so beers from the range of own brews always available on five hand pumps.

A small brewery founded in 1991 by Thomas McGuinness, who died in early 1993. Expansion plans are in hand. An old-style castle-fronted pub dating from 1814 and close to the town centre. Bar and restaurant food available at lunchtime and evenings. Parking. Children allowed. Located on the main road near the station.

FEATHER PLUCKER MILD 3.4% ABV
Dark in colour, rich maltiness throughout.
BEST BITTER 3.8% ABV
Well-hopped and quenching, with some fruitiness.
SPECIAL RESERVE BITTER 4.0% ABV
Malt flavour, with sweetness and some fruitiness.
JUNCTION BITTER 4.2% ABV
Strong malt flavours.
AUTUMN GLORY 4.6% ABV
Seasonal brew.
CHRISTMAS CHEER 4.6% ABV
Seasonal brew.
SUMMER TIPPLE 4.6% ABV
Seasonal brew.
WINTER'S REVENGE 4.6% ABV
Seasonal brew.
TOMMY TODD PORTER 5.0% ABV
A warming winter brew.

 All day, every day.

Cemetery Inn

470 Bury Road, Rochdale OL11 5EU
☎ *(01706) 645635* Miss Joanne Stewart

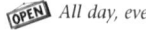 A freehouse always offering Timothy Taylor Best and Landlord plus Marston's Pedigree. Something from Jennings is often available, and the three guests, changed weekly, are usually from local breweries.

A Victorian pub with log fires, dating from 1865. Food currently available at weekends and for functions only. Children allowed.

OPEN *All day, every day.*

SALFORD

The Crescent

20 The Crescent, Salford M5 4PF
☎ *(0161) 736 5600* Mrs J Davies

 Crescent Bitter (house beer) always available plus up to ten others (150 per year) primarily from local breweries, including Oak, Moorhouse's, Titanic and Marston's. Other guests from all around the country. Occasional beer festivals.

A sprawling pub with a comfortable atmosphere, frequented by students and locals alike. Car park. Traditional pub games. Opposite Salford University. The nearest station is Salford Crescent, on the main A6.

OPEN *12–11pm Mon–Fri; 7.30–11pm Sat; 12–3pm and 7.30–10.30pm Sun.*

The Old Pint Pot

2 Adelphi Street, Salford M3 6EN
☎ *(0161) 939 1514*
Thomas and Peter Morrison

 A freehouse with small micro-brewery producing Bridgewater. Two guest ales, such as Liverpool Blondie or Greene King Abbot, also served.

A riverside pub in a converted convent, with a largely student clientele. Food available. Children allowed. Beer garden. Situated next to Salford University, below road level.

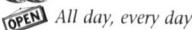 **BRIDGEWATER % ABV VARIES**

OPEN *All day, every day.*

UPPERMILL

The Church Inn and Belfry Function Suite

Church Lane, Off Church Road, Uppermill, Saddleworth
☎ *(01457) 820902 or 872415*
Julian Paul Taylor

 Home of the Saddleworth Brewery with all brews usually available, plus occasional guest beers. Brewery visits by arrangement.

Country freehouse set in a beautiful, historic location with panoramic views and lovely patio area. Peacocks, horses, ducks, geese, cats, dogs and hens too. Caters for all age groups. Log fires in winter. Non-smoking room. Food served lunchtimes and evenings Mon–Fri and all day Sat–Sun. Children welcome. Car park. Situated in Uppermill village, turn into New Street and continue to Church Road. Pub will be found near the church.

SADDLEWORTH MORE 3.8% ABV
Amber-coloured, full-bodied session beer.
AYRTONS ALE 4.1% ABV
Fruity, strawberry blonde, not too bitter.
BERT CORNER 4.1% ABV
Very pale, smooth bitter – a real winner with the ladies.
BOOMTOWN BITTER 4.1% ABV
Smooth golden bitter. A celebration ale brewed to commemorate 150 years of Oldham Borough Council.
HARVEST MOON 4.1% ABV
A light, golden, refreshing beer. Slightly sweet taste with a bitter aftertaste.
HOPSMACKER 4.1% ABV
A clean, pure, refreshing bitter, brewed using five different hops.
PETE'S DRAGON 4.6% ABV
A smooth bitter with light amber colour.
SADDLEWORTH MORE GOLD 4.6%
Amber, full-bodied bitter, much stronger version of Saddleworth More.
SHAFTBENDER 5.4% ABV
A black porter/stout bitter, extremely smooth. Nicknamed The Truth Drug – don't expect to drink too much of this and keep secrets!
CHRISTMAS CAROL 7.4% ABV
Seasonal. Liquid Christmas pudding.
Plus seasonal brews.

OPEN *12–11pm (10.30pm Sun).*

WIGAN

The Beer Engine
69 Poolstock, Wigan WN3 5DF
☎ *(01942) 321820* John Moran

Moorhouse's Pendle Witches Brew and Beer Engine Bitter always available plus up to five guest beers (186 per year) with the emphasis on supporting the smaller brewer.

Food available 12–2pm Mon–Fri and 12–6pm Sat–Sun. Function room with a capacity of 250 for hire. Three full-size snooker tables and a pool table. Crown green bowling. Annual beer, pie and music festival in October. Twice winner of CAMRA Pub of the Year. Children allowed. Well known in Wigan, five minutes' walk from the railway station and town centre.

OPEN *11am–11pm Mon–Sat; 12–10.30pm Sun.*

Moon Under Water
Market Place, Wigan WN1 1PE
☎ *(01942) 323437* Paul Hammond

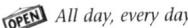A Wetherspoon's pub with Cains Mild among the beers always available, plus two guests often from East-West Ales, perhaps Brakspear Bee Sting. Two annual beer festivals.

A very busy town-centre pub with no music. Food available. No children.

OPEN *All day, every day.*

The Orwell
Wigan Pier, Wallgate, Wigan WN3 4EU
☎ *(01942) 323034* Robin Harston

A freehouse. Three or four guest beers always available from micro-breweries whenever possible. Brews from Moorehouse's, Pictish, Phoenix, Mayflower, Slaters, Bank Top and Wye Valley are regular features.

A tourists' pub on the edge of town on the pier. Styled as a traditional Victorian cotton warehouse. Local CAMRA Pub of the Year 2001. Three bars, non-smoking dining area, baby changing facilities, disabled toilets, passenger lift to all floors. Benches outside. Food available lunchtimes only. Children allowed.

OPEN *Summer: all day, every day. Winter: 11.30am–2.30pm and 5–11pm Mon–Thurs; 11am–11pm Fri–Sun.*

The Tudor House Hotel
New Market Street, Wigan
☎ *(01942) 700296* Mr Miller

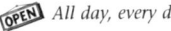A freehouse with Moorhouse's Pendle Witches Brew among the beers always available plus up to four guests including Everards Tiger, Hop Back Summer Lightning, Wychwood Hobgoblin, O'Hanlon's Summer Gold and Phoenix Wobbly Bob.

A predominantly student pub with open fires, a beer garden and accommodation. Food available at lunchtime and evenings. Children allowed during the day.

OPEN *All day, every day.*

YOU TELL US

* *The Crown*, Heaton Lane, Standish
* *The Malt & Hops*, Bradshawgate, Bolton
* *Mash & Air*, 40 Chorlton Street, Manchester (brewpub)
* *The Swan Inn*, The Square, Dobcross
* *Tandle Hill Tavern*, Thornham Lane, Middleton, Manchester

Places Featured:

Bebington
Birkenhead
Formby
Irby
Liverpool

Rainhill
St Helens
Southport
Wavertree

THE BREWERIES

CAMBRINUS CRAFT BREWERY (ASPINALLS)

Home Farm, Knowsley Park, Knowsley L34 4AQ

RENAISSANCE 3.3% ABV
Mild.

RESTAURANCE 3.6% ABV
A coloured bitter.

HERALD 3.7% ABV

YARDSTICK 4.0% ABV
Mild.

DELIVERANCE BITTER 4.2% ABV

ENDURANCE 4.3% ABV
An IPA.

Plus seasonals and specials.

ROBERT CAIN & CO. LTD

The Robert Cain Brewery, Stanhope Street, Liverpool L8 5XJ
☎ *(0151) 709 8734*
www.cainsbeer.com

DARK MILD 3.2% ABV
Very dark and distinctive.

DR DUNCAN'S IPA 3.5% ABV

TRADITIONAL BITTER 4.0% ABV
Occasional brew.

CAINS FA 5.0% ABV

Plus seasonal brews.

THE PUBS

BEBINGTON

Traveller's Rest Hotel

169 Mount Road, Bebington, Wirral L63 8PJ
☎ *(0151) 608 2988* Alan Irving

Greene King Abbot and Cains Traditional always available, plus two guests from breweries such as Timothy Taylor, Enville, Wye Valley, Hart, Cumberland and Morland.

A rural village pub bordering fields with a view of Wales. Open fires, non-smoking lounge. Food available. No children.

OPEN *All day, every day.*

BIRKENHEAD

The Crown & Cushion

60 Market Street, Birkenhead L41 5BT
☎ *(0151) 647 8870* Sue and Debs

Cains Bitter permanently available, plus new guest ales every week, perhaps Highgate Dark Mild or Morland Old Speckled Hen.

A traditional town-centre pub. Sandwiches available. All-day happy hours. Children allowed until 7pm. Accommodation.

OPEN *All day, every day.*

The Crown Hotel

128 Conway Street, Birkenhead L41 6JE
☎ *(0151) 647 0589* Kevin Oates

Ten cask ales usually available, with regulars being Cains Traditional Bitter and Mild.

A typical old alehouse. Bar food available. Parking, darts/meeting room, beer garden. Children allowed. Head for Birkenhead town centre, not far from the Birkenhead tunnel (Europa Park).

OPEN *11.30am–11pm Mon–Sat; 12–3pm and 7–10.30pm Sun.*

The Dispensary
20 Chester Street, Birkenhead CH41 5DQ
☎ *(0151) 649 8259* Dean Hornby

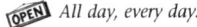A Cains tied house, with Traditional and Dark Mild always available, plus a selection of seasonal and special ales with at least one new one each month.

A modern, refurbished building with raised glass ceiling. Formerly a chemist, hence the new name. Used to be known as The Chester Arms. Food available at lunchtime only. Children allowed only if eating.

OPEN *All day, every day.*

The Old Colonial
167 Bridge Street, Birkenhead CH41 1AY
☎ *(0151) 650 1110* Jayne Loftus

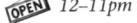Cains Traditional Bitter, Mild and Doctor Duncans IPA, plus seasonal brews usually available.

A friendly, traditional pub. Cask Marque award winner. Food served 12–3pm and 5–7pm Mon–Fri; 12–3pm Sat–Sun. Car park. Children welcome until 7pm, but no special facilities.

OPEN *12–11pm (10.30pm Sun).*

FORMBY

Freshfield Hotel
Massams Lane, Formby L37 7BD
☎ *(01704) 874871* Les Nuttall

Moorhouse's Black Cat Mild, Fuller's London Pride, Marston's Pedigree, Wadworth 6X and Castle Eden Ale usually available, plus five guest beers, often Jennings Cumberland or Bitter, Moorhouse's Pendle Witches Brew, Yates Premium, Timothy Taylor Landlord, Robinson's Best or something from Dent.

A traditional pub with polished wooden floor and log fire. Beer garden and separate music/conference room at rear. Food served 12–2pm Mon–Fri. Car park. No children.

OPEN *12–11pm (10.30pm Sun).*

IRBY

Shippons Inn
Thingwall Road, Irby, Wirral CH61 3UA
☎ *(0151) 648 0449* Stephen Thompson

Thwaites Best, Thoroughbred and Lancaster Bomber always available, plus regularly changing guests.

A rustic pub with beams and stone floor. Food available 12–2.30pm. No children.

OPEN *All day, every day.*

LIVERPOOL

The Baltic Fleet
33A Wapping, Liverpool L1 8DQ
☎ *(0151) 709 3116* Simon Holt

A brew pub, home of Wapping Beers, with a range of home-brewed ales always available.

Town pub in a 350-year-old building next to the Albert Dock and featuring beams and fireplaces. Food available. Small patio for use by pub customers, function room (25–30 people), restaurant area (can be hired for private parties). Children allowed in restaurant only until 8pm.

WAPPING BITTER 3.6% ABV
SUMMER ALE 4.2% ABV
EXTRA BITTER 4.5% ABV
Plus seasonals and specials.

OPEN *11.30am–11pm Mon–Fri; 11am–11pm Sat; 12–10.30pm Sun.*

The Brewery
21–3 Berry Street, Liverpool L1 9DF
☎ *(0151) 709 5055*

Home of the Liverpool Brewing Company. At least six beers available from the six-barrel plant. Plus occasional seasonal brews.

The Brewery, previously called The Black Horse & Rainbow, was renamed when it was sold in 1996. It is still a student-based brewpub, serving real ales brewed on the premises. Bar food available.

BERRY STREET MILD 3.4% ABV
YOUNG STALLION 3.6% ABV
RED 3.8% ABV
BLONDIE 4.1% ABV
FIRST GOLD 4.2% ABV
BITTER 4.3% ABV
ROCKET 4.3% ABV
CELEBRATION 4.8% ABV

OPEN *12pm–2am.*

The Brewery Tap
Stanhope Street, Liverpool L8 5XJ
☎ *(0151) 709 2129* John Wright

Tied to the Robert Cain brewery, so Cains Bitter, Dark Mild and Formidable Ale (FA) always available, plus seasonal and special brews such as Sundowner and Dr Duncans. Also four guests, perhaps Timothy Taylor Landlord, Bateman XB and XXXB, Derwent Bitter or Exmoor Gold and Stag.

Built in 1869, winner of CAMRA's New Heritage Award 1994. Food available. Children allowed if eating.

OPEN *All day, every day.*

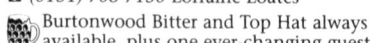

The Cambridge
Mulberry Street, Liverpool L7 7EE
☎ *(0151) 708 7150* Lorraine Loates

Burtonwood Bitter and Top Hat always available, plus one ever-changing guest.

One of the few traditional pubs in the area, this has a friendly atmosphere and is popular with students and lecturers. Food available 11.30am–2pm Mon–Fri. No children. Outside drinking area.

OPEN *11.30am–11pm (10.30pm Sun).*

The Cambridge Pub
28 Picton Road, Liverpool L15 4LH
☎ *(0151) 280 5126* Joan Adali

A freehouse with Chester's Mild among the brews always available, plus two twice-monthly changing guests.

A modern pub with music. No food. No children.

OPEN *All day, every day.*

Coopers Bar
Lime Street, Liverpool L1 1JD
☎ *(0151) 709 0076* Karen Lee

A good range of real ales available.

A modern pub refurbished in summer 1999. Serving food. No children.

OPEN *7am (for breakfast)–11pm.*

Dr Duncan
St John's Building, St John's Lane, Liverpool L1
☎ *(0151) 709 5100* Fiona Watkins

A Cains pub with Traditional, Dr Duncans IPA, Formidable Ale and Dark Mild permanently served, plus four guests, changed daily. Cains seasonal ales are usually available, and beers such as Eccleshall Top Totty, Mauldons Midsummer Gold and Oakham White Dwarf are featured. Rooster's Maax is brewed for especially for the pub.

City-centre pub in a traditional listed building from the turn of the last century, a National Heritage Award winner. Food served throughout the pub, and there is a non-smoking dining area. Function rooms, patio. Beer festivals held every two or three months, usually with a theme (e.g. wheat, Belgian, German). Children allowed up to 7pm in non-smoking area.

OPEN *11.30am–11pm Mon–Sat; 12–10.30 Sun.*

Everyman Bistro
5–9 Hope Street, Liverpool L1 9BH
☎ *(0151) 708 9545* Joe Power (Bar Manager); Alan Crowe (General Manager)

A freehouse with a Cains beer always available, plus a constantly changing range of guests, usually including Timothy Taylor Landlord, Marston's Pedigree, Black Sheep Bitter or a beer from Castle Eden.

A lively pub with a bohemian atmosphere, situated between the cathedrals. Popular with an eclectic mix of people. Food always available – menu, with meat and vegetarian options, changes twice daily (choices can be limited outside main lunchtime and evening periods). More of a pub than a bistro after 8pm. Children allowed until 9pm. Website: www.everyman.co.uk.

OPEN *Bistro: 12–midnight Mon–Wed; 12–1am Thurs; 12–2am Fri–Sat (closed Sun). Foyer Café Bar: 10am–2pm Mon–Fri.*

The Ship & Mitre
133 Dale Street, Liverpool L2 2JH
☎ *(0151) 236 0859* David Stevenson

Hydes' Anvil Bitter and Dark Mild always available, plus something from Rooster's and Passageway. Up to eight guests also served (650 different ales per year), plus beers from Belgium, Germany and the Czech Republic on draught.

A town-centre pub, popular with students and council staff. Four-times winner of CAMRA Merseyside Pub of the Year. Good value food served lunchtimes Mon–Fri. The pub has a starred entry in the book *Good Pub Food*. Pay and display car park opposite. Children not allowed. Near the Mersey tunnel entrance, five minutes' walk from Lime Street station and Moorfields station.

OPEN *11.30am–11pm Mon–Fri; 12.30–11pm Sat; 2.30–10.30pm Sun.*

The Swan Inn
86 Wood Street, Liverpool L1 4DQ
☎ *(0151) 709 5281* Clive Briggs

A freehouse with Marston's Pedigree, Phoenix Wobbly Bob and a Cains brew always available, plus three constantly changing guests from breweries such as Hanby Ales, Durham, Cottage, Wye Valley (Dorothy Goodbody's) or Belhaven.

A traditional backstreet pub with wooden floors. Food served in separate dining area. No children. Located off Berry Street at the back of Bold Street

OPEN *All day, every day.*

The Vernon Arms
69 Dale Street, Liverpool L2
☎ *(0151) 236 4525* Alex Bauched

Tied to Liverpool Brewing Company. Coach House Gunpowder is always on offer, and the six guest beers, sometimes changed every day, could be anything from Eccleshall, Cottage or Archers.

Old Victorian one-bar town pub in the business district. Food available. No children.

⟨OPEN⟩ *11.30am–11pm Mon–Fri; 12–11pm Sat; closed Sun.*

Ye Cracke
13 Rice Street, Liverpool L1 9BB
☎ *(0151) 709 4171* Paul Moss

Oak Best, Phoenix Wobbly Bob, a Cains brew and Timothy Taylor Landlord always available, plus two guests from independent and micro-breweries whenever possible. Examples include Cottage, Weetwood, Wye Valley and Hanby.

A traditional local with beer garden. Food available until 6pm. Children allowed in the pub until 6pm. Located in a back street off Hope Street.

⟨OPEN⟩ *All day, every day.*

The Manor Farm
Mill Lane, Rainhill, Prescot L35 6NE
☎ *(0151) 430 0335* Brian Maguire

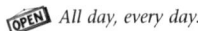A Burtonwood tied house always serving Burtonwood brews. Two other guests from a range including Wyre Piddle Piddle in the Hole.

A traditional seventeenth-century pub with restaurant and beer garden. No juke boxes. Food available. Children allowed.

⟨OPEN⟩ *All day, every day.*

Beechams Bar & Brewery
Water Street, St Helens
☎ *(01744) 623420* Robert Barrett

Home to the Beecham Brewery with all beers usually available plus Thwaites Bitter, Daniels Hammer and Chairmans Bitter. A new brewer will be brewing his own recipe beers every four/six weeks. Six-week brewery courses available.

Situated under Beecham's clock, this is a traditional real ale house. Sandwiches available at lunchtimes. Nearby public car park. No children.

BELL TOWER 4.7% ABV
CRYSTAL WHEAT 5.0% ABV

⟨OPEN⟩ *12–11pm Mon–Sat; closed Sun.*

Barons Bar in The Scarisbrick Hotel
Lord Street, Southport PR8 1NZ
☎ *(01704) 543000* George Sourbutts

A freehouse serving a wide variety of cask-conditioned ales, ranging from Timothy Taylor Landlord to the hotel's very own brew, 'Flag & Turret', a session beer of 3.8% ABV. There are also at least four ever-changing guest ales, with the main emphasis on the smaller breweries from around the UK.

Newly refurbished, while retaining a baronial look and feel! The hotel's adjoining facilities can be enjoyed. Annual beer festival starts on 1 May and lasts for one week. Children allowed in the family room until 6pm.

⟨OPEN⟩ *All day, every day.*

The Berkeley Arms
19 Queens Road, Southport PR9 9HN
☎ *(01704) 500811* Philip Ball

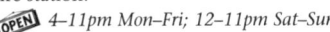Banks's Bitter, Holt Bitter, Marston's Pedigree, Adnams Bitter, Fuller's London Pride, Moorhouse's Black Cat Mild and Pendle Witches Brew always available, plus one guest beer changed at least once a week.

A family-run freehouse just outside the town centre, anxious to promote the real ale cause, with an extended bar. Music. Pizzas served from 5–11pm. Children allowed. Car park and accommodation. Look behind the fire station.

⟨OPEN⟩ *4–11pm Mon–Fri; 12–11pm Sat–Sun.*

Wetherspoons
93 Lord Street, Southport PR8 1RH
☎ *(01704) 530217* Donna Pagett

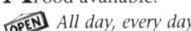A Wetherspoon's pub. Regular guest beers served on two pumps include Cotleigh Osprey, Hop Back Summer Lightning and beers from Burton Bridge, Spinnaker (Brewery on Sea), Hook Norton, Everards, Ash Vine and Banks and Taylor.

An old-fashioned, quiet, drinkers' pub. Food available.

⟨OPEN⟩ *All day, every day.*

WAVERTREE

The Willow Bank

329 Smithdown Road, Wavertree, Liverpool
☎ *(0151) 733 5782* Tracy Hughes

Up to eight hand pumps serving up to 15 real ales every week. Regular breweries featured include Cains, Wychwood, Hop Back, Robinson's and JW Lees, but the range comes from far and wide. Well-known locally for real ales.

A friendly pub, popular with locals, students and real-ale lovers. Beer festivals held every three months. Food available 12–8pm Mon–Fri and 12–4pm Sat–Sun. Beer garden. Quiz nights. Car park. Children allowed in the garden only.

OPEN *12–11pm (10.30pm Sun).*

YOU TELL US

* *Bonaparte's,* 21 Clarence Street, Liverpool
* *Crosby,* 75 Liverpool Road, Crosby
* *The Turks Head,* 40–51 Morley Street, St Helens
* *United Powers,* 66–8 Tithebarn Street, Liverpool
* *The White Star,* 2–4 Rainford Gardens, Liverpool

Places Featured:

Attleborough
Barford
Blickling
Briston
Burnham Thorpe
Burston
Cantley
Coltishall
Colton
Downham Market
East Runton
Erpingham
Fakenham
Foulden
Gorleston
Great Cressingham
Great Yarmouth
Gressenhall
Happisburgh
Heacham
Hilborough
Hingham
Hockwold
Ingham
Kenninghall
King's Lynn
Larling
Little Dunham

Lynford
Mundford
Northwold
Norwich
Pulham St Mary
Reedham
Reepham
Ringstead
Sheringham
Stiffkey
Stowbridge
Swanton Morley
Thornham
Tibenham
Toft Monks
Upton
Walsingham
Warham
West Rudham
West Somerton
Whinburgh
Windham
Winterton-on-Sea
Wiveton
Woodbastwick
Wreningham
Wymondham

THE BREWERIES

BUFFY'S BREWERY

Mardle Hall, Rectory Road, Tivetshall St Mary NR15 2DD
☎ *(01297) 680511*
www.buffys.co.uk

NORFOLK TERRIER 3.6% ABV
Light and quenching with good hop character.
BITTER 3.9% ABV
Easy-drinking, well-hopped brew.
MILD 4.2% ABV
Smooth, dark mild.
POLLY'S FOLLY 4.3% ABV
Traditional bitter.
IPA 4.6% ABV
Superb, genuine IPA.
HOLLYBERRY 4.8% ABV
POLLY'S EXTRA FOLLY 4.9% ABV
Stronger version of Polly's Folly.
ALE 5.5% ABV
Well-rounded and hoppy.
STRONG ALE 6.5% ABV

CHALK HILL BREWERY

Rosary Road, Thorpe Hamlet, Norwich NR1 4DA
☎ *(01603) 477077*

TAP BITTER 3.6% ABV
CHB 4.2% ABV
DREADNOUGHT 4.9% ABV
FLINTKNAPPER'S MILD 5.0% ABV
OLD TACKLE 5.6% ABV

HUMPTY DUMPTY BREWERY

Church Road, Reedham NR13 3TZ
☎ *(01493) 701818*
www.humptydumptybrewery.com

 NORD ATLANTIC 3.7% ABV
Red-coloured, easy quaffer.
FERRYMAN 3.8% ABV
LITTLE SHARPIE 3.8% ABV
Pale and quenching.
LEMON AND GINGER 4.0% ABV
SWINGBRIDGE ALE 4.0% ABV
TENDER BEHIND 4.0% ABV
Spicy wheat beer.
OPS ON TRAIN 4.1% ABV
Dry-hopped, gold-coloured beer.
UN PETIT DEUX PETITS 4.1% ABV
BRIEF ENCOUNTER 4.3% ABV
CLAUD HAMILTON 4.3% ABV
Oyster stout.
IRON DUKE 4.6% ABV
BUTT JUMPER 4.8% ABV
Sweet malt flavour.
RAILWAY SLEEPER 5.0% ABV
Good hoppy bitterness throughout.

THE ICENI BREWERY

3 Foulden Road, Ickburgh, Mundford IP26 5BJ
☎ *(01842) 878922*
www.stevedunks.demon.co.uk/iceni

 BOADICEA 3.8% ABV
Full-flavoured and hoppy with some fruit.
CELTIC QUEEN 4.0% ABV
Flavoursome easy drinker.
FINE SOFT DAY 4.0% ABV
Maple syrup and hops give bittersweet flavour.
FEN TIGER 4.2% ABV
Malty with coriander.
FOUR GRAINS 4.2% ABV
Rounded, fruity flavour.
CÚ CHULAINN 4.3% ABV
Slightly sweet ale.
DEIRDRE OF THE SORROWS 4.4% ABV
Amber and complex.
ROISIN DUBH 4.4% ABV
Dark with sweet flavour.
KIWI 4.5% ABV
Smooth and easy-drinking, with kiwi fruit.
ICENI GOLD 5.0% ABV
Golden and refreshing.
WINTER LIGHTNING 5.0% ABV
Light and crisp.
Plus seasonal brews.

OLD CHIMNEYS BREWERY

The Street, Market Weston, Diss IP22 2NZ
☎ *(01359) 221411*

MILITARY MILD 3.4% ABV
SWALLOWTAIL IPA 3.6% ABV
Plus seasonal and occasional brews.

REEPHAM BREWERY

Unit 1, Collers Way, Reepham NR10 4SW
☎ *(01603) 871091*

 GRANARY BITTER 3.8% ABV
RAPIER PALE ALE 4.2% ABV
NORFOLK WHEATEN 4.5% ABV
VELVET STOUT 4.5% ABV
Plus seasonal brews.

SPECTRUM BREWERY

The Cock Inn, Watton Road, Barford NR9 4AS
☎ *(0794) 925 4383*

LIGHT FANTASTIC 3.2% ABV
Pale golden session bitter.
BEZANTS 4.0% ABV
Golden, hoppy bitter.
REAPER 4.4% ABV
Dark wheat beer.
WIZZARD 4.9% ABV
Full-flavoured strong bitter.

TINDALL ALE BREWERY

Former Stables, Toad Lane, Seething NR35 2EQ
☎ *(01508) 483844*

FUGGLED UP 3.7% ABV
A late hopping of fuggles hops.
TINDALL BEST BITTER 3.7% ABV
A good all-round session bitter, the most popular Tindall ale with a smooth hop taste.
TINDALL MILD 3.7% ABV
A good dark mild.
RESURRECTION 3.8% ABV
A lighter ale using cascade hops for a fruitier finish.
ALLTIME 4.0% ABV
A slightly stronger session bitter, as the name suggests a good drink all the time.
DITCHINGHAM DAM 4.2% ABV
A good dark ale with a hint of ginger. Brewed in support of the local chickens residing at Ditchingham Dam.
TINDALL ALE EXTRA 4.5% ABV
A slightly darker ale with extra colour, taste and strength.
NORFOLK 'N' GOOD 4.6% ABV
Again using cascade hops a real good pint.
HONEYDEW 5.0% ABV
A lighter ale with a mellow honey taste.
Seasonal:
SUMMER LOVING 3.6% ABV
A light refreshing summer ale.
AUTUMN BREW 4.0% ABV
A full-bodied beer with a pleasant ruby colour.
LOVERS ALE 4.0% ABV
CHRISTMAS CHEER 4.0% ABV

WINTER'S BREWERY

8 Keelan Close, Norwich NR6 6QZ
☎ *(01603) 787820*

 MILD 3.6% ABV
Mild in strength but strong in flavour.
BITTER 3.8% ABV
Session bitter made with East Anglian barley and Kent hops.
REVENGE 4.7% ABV
Gold-coloured and well-hopped, sweetish.
STORM FORCE 5.3% ABV
Light amber, malty and sweetish.
TEMPEST 6.2% ABV
Strong ale.

WOLF BREWERY

*10 Maurice Gaymer Road, Attleborough
NR17 2QZ*
☎ *(01953) 457775*
www.wolf-brewery.ltd.uk

 GOLDEN JACKAL 3.6% ABV
99 3.7% ABV
WOLF IN SHEEPS CLOTHING 3.8% ABV
Smooth and malty.
WOLF 3.9% ABV
COYOTE 4.3% ABV
Golden with floral hoppiness.
BIG RED 4.5% ABV
LUPINE 4.5% ABV
WERWOLF 4.5% ABV
GRANNY WOULDN'T LIKE IT 4.8% ABV
Complex, malty flavour.
WOILD MOILD 4.8% ABV
Dark, smooth and fruity.
PRAIRIE 5.0% ABV
RED & GINGER 5.0% ABV
TIMBER WOLF 5.8% ABV
Plus occasional brews.

WOODFORDE'S NORFOLK ALES

*Broadland Brewery, Slad Lane, Woodbastwick,
Norwich NR13 6SW*
☎ *(01603) 720353*
www.woodfordes.co.uk

 MARDLER'S 3.5% ABV
Light, mid-coloured mild.
KETT'S REBELLION 3.6% ABV
Balanced, easy drinker.
WHERRY 3.8% ABV
Superb, well-hopped session ale.
GREAT EASTERN ALE 4.3% ABV
Golden with malt flavour.
NELSON'S REVENGE 4.5% ABV
Flavoursome throughout.
NORFOLK NOG 4.6% ABV
Smooth chocolate malt flavour.
ADMIRAL'S RESERVE 5.0 % ABV
Traditional Strong Ale.
HEADCRACKER 7.0% ABV
Fruity and easy to drink for gravity.
NORFOLK NIP 8.5% ABV
Rare barley wine.
Plus seasonal brews.

THE PUBS

ATTLEBOROUGH

The Griffin Hotel

Attleborough NR17 2AH
☎ *(01953) 452149* Richard Ashbourne

 Wolf Best and Coyote plus Greene King Abbot always available. Also two hand pumps serving guest ales from a range of small breweries.

A sixteenth-century freehouse in the centre of town. Beams, log fires, dining area, accommodation. Food available at lunchtime and evenings. Children allowed.

OPEN *10.30am–3.30pm and 5.30–11pm
Mon–Thurs; 11am–11pm Fri–Sat;
10.30am–3.30pm and 5.30–10.30pm
Sun.*

BARFORD

The Cock Inn

Watton Road, Barford NR9 4AS
☎ *(01603) 757646* Peter Turner

 Home of the Blue Moon Brewery, with the home-brewed Hingham, Darkside and Easy Life and either Moondance or Milk of Amnesia always available, plus seasonals and specials, and brews from Spectrum Brewery (which shares the Blue Moon plant).

Two hundred years old with rustic character and lots of nooks and crannies. Two bars, separate dining areas and a beer garden with bowling green and petanque pitch. Food available lunchtimes and evenings. Children allowed at lunchtime only. Situated four miles west of Norwich on the B1108.

 EASY LIFE 3.8% ABV
Light aromatic session bitter.
DARKSIDE 4.0% ABV
Mild shamelessly fashioned after Marston's Merry Monk.
SEA OF TRANQUILITY 4.2% ABV
Premium best bitter.
MOONDANCE 4.7% ABV
Lighter-coloured bitter, much more hoppy character. A bit seasonal but very popular.
HINGHAM HIGH 5.0% ABV
Malty ale.
MILK OF AMNESIA 5.2% ABV
Old-fashioned mild with a hint of cinnamon.
Seasonal:
LIQUOR MORTIS 7.5% ABV
Deep red-coloured barley wine.
TOTAL ECLIPSE 8.5% ABV
Very heavy, like drinking a slice of Christmas cake, fruity and dark.

OPEN *12–2.30pm and 6–11pm Mon–Sat;
12–3pm and 7–10.30pm Sun.*

BLICKLING

The Buckinghamshire Arms
Blickling, Nr Aylsham NR11 6NF
☎ *(01263) 732133*

A Humble Inns pub, with Woodforde's Wherry and Blickling (house beer from Woodforde's) plus Adnams brews usually available.

An olde-English, food-oriented freehouse with small bar, log fires and beer garden. Food available at lunchtime and evenings in separate restaurant. Accomodation, with four-poster beds. Well-behaved children allowed in the garden, or if eating.

OPEN *11.30am–3pm and 6–11pm.*

BRISTON

The John H Stracey
Westend, Briston NR24 2JA
☎ *(01263) 860891 RE Fox*

A freehouse with Ruddles County a permanent feature, plus one guest, perhaps Morland Old Speckled Hen, Greene King Triumph, Morland Tanner's Jack or something from Reepham.

Country pub, built in 1565, with 46-seat restaurant, fires, beams and oak furniture. Garden and car park. One twin and two double letting rooms available. Children allowed. On the B1354 in Briston.

OPEN *11am–2.30pm and 6.30–11pm; 12–2.30pm and 7–10.30pm Sun.*

BURNHAM THORPE

The Lord Nelson
Walsingham Road, Burnham Thorpe, King's Lynn PE31 8HN
☎ *(01328) 738241 Miss L Stafford*

A Greene King house with Abbot, IPA and XX Mild always available, plus Woodforde's Wherry.

A 355-year-old village pub in the birthplace of Nelson. Log fires, beer garden. Food available at lunchtime and evenings. Children allowed.

OPEN *11am–3pm and 6–11pm Mon–Sat; 12–3pm and 7–10.30pm Sun.*

BURSTON

The Crown
Crangreen/Millwood Road, Burston IP22 5TW
☎ *(01379) 741257 Mrs Whitehead*

Adnams Bitter is always on offer. Guests, often changed two or three times a week, might be something from Hampshire, Old Chimneys or Robinson's.

Rural village pub and restaurant in a late sixteenth-century building, with two bars, fires and beams. Food served. Non-smoking lounge, garden and patio. Children allowed only if eating. There are plans for holiday accommodation with special disabled facilities. Car park. On the corner of Crangreen and Millwood Road with large green in front (large gypsy cart on green with pub name on!).

OPEN *12–2.30pm and 7–11pm Mon–Sat (all day in summer); 12–10.30pm Sun.*

CANTLEY

The Cock Tavern
Manor Road, Cantley NR13 3JQ
☎ *(01493) 700895 Mr and Mrs Johnson*

Adnams Best Bitter always available plus four guest beers (100+ per year) including Greene King Abbot, Old Speckled Hen, beers from Iceni Brewery, and many more.

A traditional country pub not far from Norwich with many separate areas, a beamed ceiling and two open fires. Bar food is available at lunchtime and evenings. Car park, garden and children's room. Caravan Club campsite adjacent. Turn right off the A47 (Norwich to Yarmouth road) near Acle, then signposted Cantley. Approx four miles from the turn.

OPEN *11am–3.30pm and 6–11pm Mon–Fri; 7–11pm Sat; 12–4pm and 7–10.30pm Sun.*

COLTISHALL

The Red Lion
77 Church Street, Coltishall NR12 7DW
☎ *(01603) 737402 Mrs Melanie Lamb*

Adnams Southwold Bitter and Greene King Abbot Ale usually available plus a guest, often from Woodforde's, who also brew Weaselpis, the house beer.

Olde-worlde, 350-year-old pub full of nooks and crannies, with oak beams and log fires. Food served lunchtimes and evenings Mon–Fri and all day Sat–Sun and bank holidays. Car park. Large beer garden with children's play area, plus indoor soft-play area.

OPEN *11am–3pm and 5–11pm Mon–Fri; 11am–11pm Sat and bank holidays; 12–10.30pm Sun.*

COLTON

The Ugly Bug Inn
High House Farm Lane, Colton, Norwich
☎ *(01603) 880794* Natalie Mallam

Wolf Ugly Bug Ale, Greene King Abbot Ale and four guest beers usually available, perhaps from Fuller's, Woodforde's, Elgood's, Shepherd Neame, Buffy's, Iceni or Bateman.

Farm building conversion with informal atmosphere. Restaurant, grounds and lakes of three acres. Food served 12–2pm and 7–9.30pm daily. Patio dining in summer. Beer festival with 25–30 beers held every August. Accommodation. Ample parking. Children welcome, provided they are supervised if near the deep lakes.

OPEN *12–3pm and 5.30–11pm Mon–Thurs;*
11am–11pm Fri–Sat; 12–10.30pm Sun.

DOWNHAM MARKET

The Crown Hotel
Bridge Street, Downham Market PE38 9DH
☎ *(01366) 382322* Mrs N Hayes

A freehouse with Bateman XB and Charles Wells Bombardier always available, plus a guest which might be Wyre Piddle Piddle in the Wind, Shepherd Neame Spitfire or Charles Wells Summer Solstice.

An olde-worlde pub with open fires. Food available at lunchtime and evenings in two restaurants. No children.

OPEN *11am–2.30pm and 5–11pm Mon–Thurs; all day Fri–Sat; 12–10.30pm Sun.*

EAST RUNTON

The White Horse
High Street, East Runton, Nr Cromer NR27 9NX
☎ *(01263) 519530* Mr Tarrison

Adnams Bitter, Greene King Abbot, and something from Woodforde's always available, plus one or two guests, changed weekly, including beers such as Wolf Mild, Timothy Taylor Landlord, Marston's Pedigree and Reepham brews.

Village family pub, built in 1910. Food served. Two bars, function room, garden/patio, car park. Live music. Children allowed.

OPEN *12–3pm and 7–11pm (10.30pm Sun) during low season; 12–11pm (10.30pm Sun) in summer.*

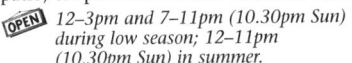

ERPINGHAM

The Spread Eagle
Erpingham, Norwich NR11 7QA
☎ *(01263) 761591* Billie Carder

Six real ales are always on offer. Woodforde's Wherry and Nelson's Revenge, plus Adnams Best and Broadside are permanent features, and the two guests could include Greene King Abbot or Exmoor Hound Dog. The pub also has an exclusive wine list and offers house wines from around the world.

A traditional pub with open fires, non-smoking dining area, pool room and new garden bar. Live music every Saturday night. Food available at lunchtime and evenings, with roasts on Sundays (booking advisable). Well-behaved children and dogs welcome.

OPEN *11am–3pm and 6.30–11pm Mon–Sat; 12–3pm and 7–10.30pm Sun (garden bar will remain open on summer afternoons).*

FAKENHAM

The Bull
Bridge Street, Fakenham NR21 9AG
☎ *(01325) 862560* Graham Blanchfield

Home of Blanchfields Brewery. At least three beers brewed and served on the premises. Other seasonal ales as available.

A nineteenth-century pub with two small bar rooms and a dining area. Food available at lunchtime only. Children allowed. Brewery viewing by arrangement.

BLACK BULL MILD 3.6% ABV
A traditional dark mild.
BULL BEST BITTER 3.9% ABV
Full of hop flavours.
THE WHITE BULL 4.4% ABV
A seasonal wheat beer available in summer only.
RAGING BULL 4.9% ABV
Powerful malt-flavoured bitter. Also available in bottles.

OPEN *11am–3pm and 7–11pm Mon–Wed; 11am–11pm Thurs–Sat; 12–10.30pm Sun.*

FOULDEN

The White Hart Inn
White Hart Street, Foulden, Thetford IP26 5AW
☎ *(01366) 328638* Sylvia Chisholm

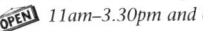A freehouse serving Greene King IPA, Mild, XS and Abbot plus two guests such as Shepherd Neame Spitfire or other customer requests.

A traditional pub with dining area, fires and beer garden. Live music on Friday or Saturday. Biker-friendly. Food available at lunchtime and evenings. Children allowed.

OPEN *11am–3.30pm and 6–11pm.*

GORLESTON

The Cliff Hotel
Gorleston NR31 6DH
☎ *(01493) 662179* Vaughan Cutter

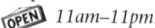 Fuller's London Pride, Greene King IPA, Woodforde's Wherry and Marston's Pedigree usually available.

Hotel with two bars and two restaurants overlooking Gorleston beach and harbour. Food served 12–2.30pm and 7–9.30pm every day. Children welcome in gardens or hotel only, not in the bars. Two car parks.

OPEN *11am–11pm.*

The Short Blue
47 High Street, Gorleston, Great Yarmouth NR31 6RR
☎ *(01493) 602192* Kevin Duffield

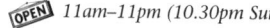 Greene King IPA and Adnams Best Bitter always available, plus one regularly changing guest ale. Whenever possible, guest ales are from a local brewery such as Woodforde's.

Dating from 1693, this traditional olde-worlde pub houses carved wood, stained glass and wooden barrels. No juke box or pool table. Food available 12–2pm Mon–Sun and 6–10.30pm Fri. Riverside garden with covered patio, children allowed in the garden only. Roadside parking in Riverside Road.

OPEN *11am–11pm (10.30pm Sun).*

GREAT CRESSINGHAM

The Olde Windmill Inn
Water End, Great Cressingham, Watton IP25 6NN
☎ *(01760) 756232* Caroline and Michael Halls

 Greene King IPA and Adnams Best Bitter and Broadside are always available, plus two guests, changed regularly, normally one local beer and one from elsewhere in the UK.

Olde-worlde country pub dating from 1650, with five acres of park land and paddocks, three bars, five family rooms, games room and conservatory. Food is served 12–2pm and 6–10.30pm Mon–Sat, and 12–2pm and 6.30–10pm Sun. There is an extensive bar menu. Children are welcome in the family rooms, the beer garden and the play area, and the pub has high chairs and a children's menu. Conferences, meetings and private parties are a speciality. Car parks front and back (80 cars). Just off the A1065 Swaffham–Brandon road, or the B1108 Watton–Brandon road.

OPEN *11.30am–3pm and 6–11pm Mon–Sat; 11.45am–3.30pm and 6.30pm–10.30pm Sun.*

GREAT YARMOUTH

The Mariner's Tavern
69 Howard Street South, Great Yarmouth NR30 1LN
☎ *(01493) 332299* Mr Adams

 Fuller's London Pride, Highgate Dark, Greene King Abbot and beers from Adnams always available. One guest changed each weekend. Previous guest beers have included Thwaites Bloomin Ale and Greene King Triumph.

A small traditional pub with log fires. Full bar menu available lunchtimes. Children allowed. Ring for directions.

OPEN *11am–11pm Mon–Sat; 12–10.30pm Sun.*

The Red Herring
24–5 Havelock Road, Great Yarmouth NR30 3HQ
☎ *(01493) 853384* Sylvia and Barry Haslett

 A freehouse with Adnams Best and seven alternating guest ales always available. Guest beers could be from local or national independent breweries.

An old-fashioned, country-style pub in a town location. Darts, pool and regular quiz nights. No food. No children. Ring for directions.

OPEN *12–2.30pm and 6–11pm Mon–Fri; 12–3pm and 6–11pm Sat; 12–3pm and 7–10.30pm Sun.*

GRESSENHALL

The Swan
The Green, Gressenhall, Dereham NR20 4DU
☎ *(01632) 860340* Mr Mansfield

 Greene King IPA always available, plus two guests such as Marston's Pedigree or Young's Bitter.

A family-oriented country pub with dining area, log fires and beer garden. Food available at lunchtime and evenings. Children allowed.

OPEN *12–2.30pm and 6–11pm Mon–Sat; 12–3pm and 7–10.30pm Sun.*

HAPPISBURGH

Hill House
Happisburgh NR12 0PW
☎ *(01692) 650004* Clive and Sue Stockton

Buffy's Hill House Elementary Ale, Shepherd Neame Spitfire and two guest beers regularly available, perhaps from Church End, Black Sheep, Wolf, Adnams, Concertina or Ossett.

Coastal coaching inn known for its Sherlock Holmes connection. Restaurant and large garden. Food served 12–2.30pm and 7–9.30pm daily. 'Kids' Bar' open during school holidays. Car park.

OPEN *Winter: 12–3pm and 7–11pm (10.30pm Sun). Summer: 12–11pm (10.30pm Sun).*

HEACHAM

Fox & Hounds

22 Station Road, Heacham PE31 7EX
☎ *(01485) 570345* Mark Bristow

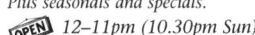Home of the Fox Brewery with own brews Heacham Gold, Grace & Favour and Red Knob permanently available. Occasional guests and seasonal and special home brews.

A large 1920s traditional pub with beer garden. Food available 12–2pm and 6–9pm daily. Children allowed. Brewery on site, tours available. Function room.

HEACHAM GOLD 3.9% ABV
RED KNOB 3.9% ABV
GRACE & FAVOUR 4.4% ABV
Brewed for Peterborough Beer Festival.
OOPS A DAISY 4.4%
HEACHAM GOLD EXTRA 4.6%
Plus seasonals and specials.

OPEN *12–11pm (10.30pm Sun).*

HILBOROUGH

The Swan

Hilborough, Thetford IP26 5BW
☎ *(01760) 756380* Mr Wallis

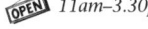Greene King Abbot and IPA, Bateman Mild and an Adnams beer always available, plus a guest which changes once a fortnight and may well be a Greene King seasonal or special brew.

An olde-worlde pub with log fires, beer garden and accommodation. Smallholding with animals. Food available at lunchtime and evenings. Children allowed.

OPEN *11am–3.30pm and 6–11pm.*

HINGHAM

The White Hart Hotel

3 Market Place, Hingham, Norwich NR9 4AF
☎ *(01953) 850214 Fax (01953) 851950*
Les and Carol Foster

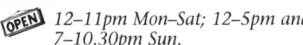Greene King IPA and Abbot always available plus two guests.

The only pub in Hingham, this is a family-oriented pub and restaurant with beer garden and accommodation. Food available at lunchtime and evenings. Children allowed.

OPEN *12–11pm Mon–Sat; 12–5pm and 7–10.30pm Sun.*

HOCKWOLD

The Red Lion

Main Street, Hockwold IP26 4NB
☎ *(01842) 828875* Mrs Miles

Greene King IPA always available plus two guests which change fortnightly. A beer festival is held each August bank holiday.

A village pub and restaurant. Children allowed.

OPEN *12–2.30pm and 6–11pm Sun–Fri; 12–11pm Sat.*

INGHAM

The Swan Inn

Mill Road, Ingham NR12 9AB
☎ *(01692) 581099* Sandra and Malcolm Potts

A Woodforde's pub with Wherry, Nelson's Revenge, Great Eastern and Mardler's Mild the permanent beers. One of these is sometimes taken off in order to feature a seasonal or celebration ale.

Fourteenth-century thatched village pub with fireplaces and beams. Food is available, and there is a non-smoking restaurant. Patio, car park, five letting rooms. Children allowed only if eating.

OPEN *Summer: 11am–11pm Mon–Sat; 12–10.30pm Sun. Please call for seasonal opening hours.*

KENNINGHALL

The Red Lion

East Church Street, Kenninghall, Diss NR16 2EP
☎ *(01953) 887849* Mandy and Bruce Berry

A freehouse offering Greene King IPA and Abbot, Woodforde's Wherry and Mardler's, plus one guest, such as a beer from Wolf.

A one-bar village pub with beams, open fires, bare stone floors and floorboards. A listed building with a snug, one of only two snugs in the area. Bar snacks and restaurant food available at lunchtimes and evenings every day. Rear patio garden. Beer garden. Children allowed, but not in the bar area. Bed and breakfast accommodation available.

OPEN *12–3pm and 6.30–11pm Mon–Thurs; 12–11pm Fri–Sat; 12–10.30pm Sun.*

KING'S LYNN

Stuart House Hotel

35 Goodwins Road, King's Lynn PE30 5QX
☎ *(01553) 772169* David Armes

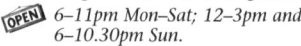Adnams Best Bitter and Broadside plus Woodforde's Wherry and Greene King IPA usually available. One guest beer is also served, such as Timothy Taylor Landlord, Fuller's London Pride, Woodforde's Nelson's Revenge, Oakham JHB or Mompesson's Gold.

A family-run hotel, quietly situated within its own grounds in the centre of King's Lynn. Cosy bar with a real fire in winter and doors that open on to the garden in summer. Regular entertainment. Bar menu and à la carte restaurant. Food served 7–9.30pm daily. Car park. Well-behaved children welcome until 8.30pm. Pets' corner in garden.

OPEN *6–11pm Mon–Sat; 12–3pm and 6–10.30pm Sun.*

LARLING

The Angel Inn

Larling, Norwich NR16 2QU
☎ *(01953) 717963* Andrew Stammers

Adnams Southwold Bitter and four guest beers usually available, perhaps from Iceni, Woodforde's, Wolf, Mauldons, Orkney or Cottage.

A 400-year-old village pub with quarry-tiled, beamed public bar, real fire and local atmosphere. Live music Thursday evening. Two dining rooms. En-suite accommodation. Food served lunchtimes and evenings. Car park. Children welcome in the lounge and picnic area. Small, fenced play area outside.

OPEN *10am–11pm Mon–Sat; 12–10.30pm Sun.*

LITTLE DUNHAM

The Black Swan

The Street, Little Dunham, King's Lynn PE32 2DG
☎ *(01760) 722200* Paul and Christine

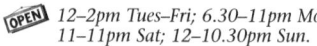A freehouse with two constantly changing real ales always available.

A country pub with log fires, restaurant and beer garden. Food available lunchtimes and evenings. Children allowed. Located off the A47.

OPEN *12–2pm Tues–Fri; 6.30–11pm Mon–Fri; 11–11pm Sat; 12–10.30pm Sun.*

LYNFORD

Lynford Hall

Lynford, Thetford IP26 5HW
☎ *(01842) 878351* Peter Scopes

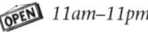Woodforde's Wherry, St Peter's Ale and an Iceni brew always available.

Pub located within Lynford Hall, a stately home and tourist attraction open to the public. Separate restaurant and beer garden. Food available. Children allowed.

OPEN *11am–11pm.*

MUNDFORD

The Crown Hotel

Crown Street, Mundford, Nr Thetford IP26 5HQ
☎ *(01362) 637647* Barry Walker

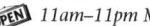Seven beers always available including Samuel Smith OBB, Woodforde's Norfolk Wherry and Marston's Pedigree plus more than 100 guests per year including all Iceni brews, Morland Old Speckled Hen and brews from Nethergate and Wolf.

A sixteenth-century beamed pub with open fires in winter. Bar and restaurant food available at lunchtime and evenings. Pool and darts, car park, garden, function room, accommodation. Children allowed.

OPEN *11am–11pm Mon–Sat; 12–10.30pm Sun.*

NORTHWOLD

The Crown Inn

High Street, Northwold, Thetford IP26 5LA
☎ *(01366) 727317* Michael and James Archer

A freehouse with five traditional ales (Ruddles County, Morland Tanner's Jack, Adnams Best, Old Speckled Hen and Greene King IPA) permanently available, plus one guest ale which changes every week.

A village pub, recently refurbished, with log fires and beer garden. Food available 12–2.30pm and 6.30–9.30pm daily. Children allowed.

OPEN *12–3pm and 6.30–11pm Mon–Fri; 12–11pm Sat; 12–10.30pm Sun.*

NORWICH

Alexandra Tavern

Stafford Street, Norwich NR2 3BB
☎ *(01603) 627772* JL Little

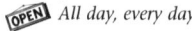A freehouse with Chalk Hill Best, Flintknapper's Mild and Tap always available. Guests on two hand pumps tend to be brews such as Exmoor Gold.

A traditional local with log fires in winter. Bar snacks always available, and bar meals are served 2–7pm. Children allowed until 7pm.

OPEN *All day, every day.*

Billy Bluelight

27 Hall Road, Norwich NR1 3MQ
☎ *(01603) 623768* Simon Morgan

 A Woodforde's house with a good range of Woodforde's ales always available. Mild, Bluelight, Wherry, Great Eastern, Nelson's Revenge, Admiral's Reserve, Norfolk Nog and Headcracker usually on offer, plus seasonals and specials.

Themed 1930s/1940s-style pub. No fruit machine, juke box or pool table. Beer garden with petanque, piste and full-size skittle alley in the function room. Food served lunchtimes and evenings every day. Children welcome until 9pm each day. Located on the junction of Queens and Hall roads.

OPEN *12–11pm (10.30pm Sun).*

Coach & Horses

82 Thorpe Road, Norwich NR1 1BA
☎ *(01603) 477077* Bob Cameron

 At least seven constantly changing ales on at any one time. The pub is situated on the same site as Chalk Hill Brewery (tours available by arrangement), so the full range of Chalk Hill ales always on offer.

Busy old-style pub with an open fire and wooden floors. Wide range of food available 12–9pm daily. Children allowed.

OPEN *11am–11pm Mon–Sat; 12–10.30pm Sun.*

The Eaton

75 Mount Pleasant, Norwich NR2 2DQ
☎ *(01603) 453048*
Mr I Tilbury and Mr M Dormer

Adnams Best, Charles Wells Bombardier, Greene King Abbot, Chalk Hill Best and Wolf Brewery's Old Eatonian permanently available, plus a guest. Fuller's London Pride, Bateman's XXXB, Young's Special, Adnams Broadside and Morland Old Speckled Hen are among the ales on rotation.

A traditional corner pub, under major renovation in 2002. Bar snacks available food. Children welcome (under close supervision) until 7pm.

OPEN *12–11pm Mon–Fri; 11.30am–11pm Sat; 12–10.30pm Sun.*

The Fat Cat

49 West End Street, Norwich NR2 4NA
☎ *(01603) 624364*

 Up to 25 beers available at any one time. Regulars include Adnams Best, Woodforde's Nelson's Revenge, Kelham Island Pale Rider, Greene King Abbot and a guest list that now runs into thousands. Belgian beers (four on draught, plus bottles) also stocked.

A traditional Victorian pub decorated with breweriana and pub signs. Bar food available at lunchtime. Street parking. Children not allowed.

OPEN *12–11pm Mon–Thurs; 11am–11pm Fri–Sat; 12–10.30pm Sun.*

The Jubilee

26 St Leonards Road, Norwich NR11 4BL
☎ *(01603) 618734*
Tim Wood and Teresa Santos

 Wadworth 6X, Fuller's London Pride, Greene King Abbot, Jubilee Ale and Triumph always available, plus three other guests such as Hop Back Summer Lightning.

A traditional freehouse with beer garden and adults' games room. Food available at lunchtime only. Children allowed until 5pm.

OPEN *All day, every day.*

The Kings Arms

22 Hall Road, Norwich NR1 3HQ
☎ *(01603) 766361* John Craft

 A freehouse permanently offering Adnams Southwold Best, Wolf Coyote Bitter and Greene King Abbot, plus ten guests. The emphasis is on East Anglian breweries, with beers such as Mauldons Cuckoo and Eatonswill Old, Tindall Best Bitter and Iceni Fine Soft Day being featured. One hand pump is dedicated to fruit beer or spiced ale, changed every three or four days, for example St Peter's Elderberry Beer. Another pump serves a mild, such as Tindall, and is changed every two days.

One-bar drinkers' pub in the city, a pub since 1831. Local CAMRA Pub of the Year 1998–1999. Only rolls are available – customers are encouraged to bring their own food, and cutlery is provided. Garden. No children.

OPEN *11am–11pm Mon–Sat; 12–10.30pm Sun.*

The Mustard Pot

101 Thorpe Road, Norwich NR1 1TR
☎ *(01603) 432393* Jason Bates

An Adnams house with Best, Broadside and Extra always available, plus Regatta when in season. A range of guest ales such as Charles Wells Summer Solstice or Fuller's London Pride is also served.

A drinkers' pub with beer garden and food available at lunchtime and evenings. No children.

OPEN *All day, every day.*

The Old White Lion

73 Oak Street, Norwich NR3 3AR
☎ *(01603) 620630* Nick Ray (Manager)

Greene King IPA, Woodforde's Wherry, Fuller's London Pride and Adnams Southwold always available, plus around eight guest beers every week.

A 450-year-old pub with old beams, slate floors, and lots of wood and brass. Colourfully decorated with flowers on the outside. Candles every evening. Food available 12–10.30pm – phone orders taken. On the inner ring road going anti-clockwise, first left before river on the east side.

OPEN *11am–11pm Mon–Sat; 12–10.30pm Sun.*

The Ribs of Beef

24 Wensum Street, Norwich NR3 1HY
☎ *(01603) 619517* Joolia and Gary Gilvey

A freehouse serving 11 cask ales such as Marston's Pedigree, Woodforde's Wherry and Rib Cracker, Iceni It's a Grand Day and Adnams brews, plus guests changing weekly. These might be something like Brakspear Bee Sting, Hogs Back TEA or Timothy Taylor Landlord.

A popular local situated near the river with private jetty. Food available 12–2.30pm Mon–Fri and 12–5pm Sat–Sun. Children's room. Website: www.ribsofbeef.co.uk.

OPEN *All day, every day.*

Rosary Tavern

95 Rosary Road, Norwich NR1 4BX
☎ *(01603) 666287* Ian and Nina Bushell

At least seven real ales always available. Adnams Best and Black Sheep Best are on permanently plus five constantly changing guests. Also sells real Norfolk cider.

A traditional pub with a friendly atmosphere. Bar food available at lunchtimes only, including roasts on Sun. Car park, beer garden and function room. Easy to find, near the yacht and railway station, and the football ground.

OPEN *11.30am–11pm Mon–Sat; 12–10.30pm Sun.*

St Andrew's Tavern

4 St Andrews Street, Norwich NR2 4AF
☎ *(01603) 614858* Jenny Watt and Alan Allred

An Adnams house serving nine cask ales, including the full range of Adnams brews. A cask mild is always available, and guests may come from Jennings, Bateman, Fuller's, Elgood's, Badger, Robinson's or Charles Wells.

A friendly, traditional city-centre pub. Good value food available at lunchtimes, including home-cooked specials. Terrace garden and cellar bar. Children not allowed. At the junction of Duke Street and St John Maddermarket opposite St Andrews car park.

OPEN *All day, every day.*

Seamus O'Rourke's

92 Pottergate, Norwich NR2 1DZ
☎ *(01603) 626627* Phil Adams

A freehouse with Adnams Best and O'Rourke's Revenge (house beer) always available, plus up to eight guests including Charles Wells Bombardier, Wolf Coyote, Iceni Fine Soft Day, Scott's Blues and Boater or a Burton Bridge beer.

Irish sports themed pub with open fires and food available at lunchtime. No children.

OPEN *All day, every day (except Christmas Day 12–3.30pm).*

The Steam Packet

39 Crown Road, Norwich NR1 3DT
☎ *(01603) 441545* Clive Ravetta

An Adnams house with Best permanently available, plus guests served on three pumps. Other Adnams ales such as Broadside and Millennium, and seasonal ales like Regatta are featured, plus a few beers from other breweries, such as Fuller's London Pride.

A 200-year-old traditional local. The pub has a 'bring your own food' policy – cutlery and condiments are provided. Blues music played. Children welcome. Separate room available for booking.

OPEN *Summer: 12–11pm (10.30pm Sun). Winter: closed Sun lunchtime.*

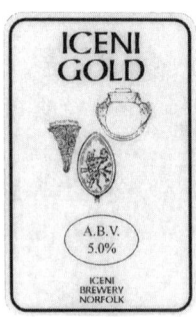

ICENI GOLD

A.B.V. 5.0%

ICENI BREWERY NORFOLK

The Trafford Arms

61 Grove Road, Norwich NR1 3RL
☎ *(01603) 628466* Chris and Glynis Higgins

 Adnams Bitter, Woodforde's Mardler's and Barley Boy house bitter brewed by Woodforde's, usually available. A mild is always served and guest beers may include Sarah Hughes Ruby Mild, Burton Bridge Porter, Bateman Dark Mild, Elgood's Black Dog Mild, Timothy Taylor Landlord or brews from Mauldons, Rooster's or Reepham.

A welcoming community pub, just out of the city centre. Cosmopolitan collection of customers from all walks of life. No loud music, just a cacophony of chatting voices. Food served lunchtimes only (or evenings by arrangement). Limited parking. No children. Situated very close to Sainsbury's on Queens Road. Website: www.traffordarms.co.uk.

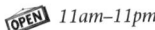 *11am–11pm Mon–Sat; 12–10.30pm Sun.*

The York Tavern

1 Leicester Street, Norwich NR22 2AS
☎ *(01603) 620918* Mr Verret

 Adnams ales usually available, plus guests such as Wadworth 6X, Marston's Pedigree or Morland Old Speckled Hen.

An old-fashioned London-style pub with open fires, restaurant and beer garden. Food available at lunchtime and evenings. Children allowed in the restaurant only.

 11am–11pm.

PULHAM ST MARY

The King's Head

The Street, Pulham St Mary IP21 4RD
☎ *(01379) 676318* Graham Scott

Brews from Buffy's and Adnams always available plus two guests including Marston's Pedigree, Wadworth 6X, Shepherd Neame Spitfire, Woodforde's Wherry and brews from Brains, Robinson's and Fuller's.

Built in the 1600s, this pub has an old oak timber frame with exposed beams. Bar and restaurant food available at lunchtime and evenings. Non-smoking dining area, games room, bowling green, paddock, car park, garden, children's area, accommodation. Off the A140 to Harlesdon, on the B1134.

June–Aug: all day, every day. Sept–May: 11.30am–3pm and 5.30–11pm Mon–Fri; all day Sat–Sun.

REEDHAM

The Railway Tavern

17 The Havaker, Reedham NR13 3HG
☎ *(01493) 700340*
James Lunn and Christina Felix

 Adnams ales always available plus many guest beers including those from the local Humpty Dumpty brewery. Eighteen beer festivals held so far.

A listed Victorian railway hotel freehouse. CAMRA award. No fruit machines. Bar and restaurant food is available at lunchtime and evenings. Car park, garden and children's room. Accommodation available in the Garden Room. Take the A47 south of Acle, then six miles on the B1140. By rail from Norwich, Gt Yarmouth or Lowestoft.

 12–3pm and 6.30–11pm Mon–Thurs; all day Fri–Sat; normal Sun hours.

REEPHAM

The Crown

Ollands Road, Reepham, Norwich NR10 4EJ
☎ *(01603) 870964* Mr Good

Marston's Pedigree and Greene King Abbot among the beers always available.

A village pub with dining area and beer garden. Food available at lunchtime and evenings. Children allowed.

 12–3pm and 7–11pm Mon–Sat; 12–5pm and 7–10.30pm Sun.

The Kings Arms

Market Place, Reepham, Norwich NR10 4JJ
☎ *(01603) 870345* Steve Capel

A freehouse with Woodforde's Wherry, Adnams Best and Greene King Abbot permanently available.

A village community pub with restaurant area, courtyard and garden. Jazz on Sundays in summer. Children welcome. Car park.

 11.30am–3pm and 5.30–11pm (10.30pm Sun); all day Sat–Sun in summer.

The Old Brewery House Hotel

Market Place, Reepham, Norwich NR10 4JJ
☎ *(01603) 870881* Sarah Gardener

A freehouse with Greene King Abbot, Adnams beers and a house bitter always available, plus one changing guest which will be something like Morland Old Speckled Hen, Adnams Regatta or another local brew.

An olde-worlde pub with beams, log fires, restaurant, beer garden and accommodation. Food available at lunchtime and evenings. Children allowed.

 11am–11pm.

RINGSTEAD

The Gin Trap Inn

Ringstead, Nr Hunstanton PO36 5JU
☎ *(01485) 525264* Brian and Margaret Harmes

A freehouse with a house beer brewed by Woodforde's called Gin Trap always available, plus Norfolk Nog, Greene King Abbot and an Adnams ale. One other guest served.

A350-year-old traditional English pub. Dining area, beer garden, self-catering accommodation. Food available at lunchtime and evenings. Children allowed. Ring for directions.

OPEN *11.30am–2.30pm and 6.30–11pm Mon–Sat; 12–2.30pm and 6.45–10.30pm Sun.*

SHERINGHAM

The Windham Arms

15 Wyndham Street, Sheringham NR26 8BA
☎ *(01263) 822609* Roger Thake

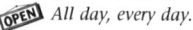Woodforde's Wherry, Chalk Hill Flintknapper's Mild and the pub's own in-house brew, Leopard's Head, always available, plus a wide selection of guest ales served on three hand pumps (never the same beer twice). An annual beer festival is held on the first weekend in July with 20 different guest beers on offer.

Alarge pub with restaurant, log fires, beer garden. Food available at lunchtime and evenings. Children allowed.

OPEN *All day, every day.*

STIFFKEY

The Red Lion

44 Wells Road, Stiffkey, Wells-next-the-Sea NR23 1AJ
☎ *(01328) 830552* Matthew Rees

A freehouse with Woodforde's Wherry, Adnams Best and Greene King Abbot always available, plus two guests, perhaps seasonal Woodforde's ales such as Great Eastern in Summer or Norfolk Nog in Winter, or Elgood's Black Dog Mild, Wolf Best, or something from Nethergate, Green Jack or other local breweries.

An old, rustic pub with tiled floor, log fires and beer garden. Food available at lunchtime and evenings. Children and dogs welcome. Located on the main A149.

OPEN *11am–3pm and 6–11pm.*

STOWBRIDGE

The Heron

Station Road, Stowbridge, King's Lynn PE34 3PH
☎ *(01366) 384147* The Luckey Family

A freehouse with Greene King IPA and Abbot plus Adnams Best always available. Also three guests including, perhaps, Woodforde's Wherry, Charles Wells Bombardier or Morland Old Speckled Hen.

A150-year-old traditional pub with log fires and beer garden. Bar food and separate restaurant food served 12–2pm and 7–9.30pm. Families welcome. Situated between two rivers, ring for directions if necessary. Riverside moorings available.

OPEN *12–3pm and 5–11pm Mon–Fri; 12–3pm and 6–11pm Sat; 12–3pm and 7–10.30pm Sun.*

SWANTON MORLEY

The Angel Inn

Greengate, Swanton Morley, Norwich NR20 4LX
☎ *(01362) 637407* David Ashford

A freehouse with Samuel Smith Old Brewery Bitter always available, plus two guests such as Greene King Abbot.

Acountry village pub dating from 1609 with log fires, beer garden and bowling green. No food. Children allowed.

OPEN *12–11pm Mon–Sat; 12–3pm and 7–10.30pm Sun.*

Darby's Freehouse

1 Elsing Road, Swanton Morley, Dereham NR20 4JU
☎ *(01362) 637647*
John Carrick and Louise Battle

A freehouse serving eight real ales. Adnams Best and Broadside, Woodforde's Wherry, Badger Tanglefoot and Greene King IPA are permanent features, and three guests are also served.

Agenuine, family-owned and -run freehouse converted from two derelict farm cottages. Traditional English and Thai cuisine available at lunchtime and evenings. Attached to a nearby farmhouse that offers accommodation and camping. Car park, garden and children's room and playground. Take the B1147 from Dereham to Bawdeswell, turn right on to Elsing Road at Swanton Morley.

OPEN *11.30am–3pm and 6–11pm Mon–Fri; 11am–11pm Sat; 12–10.30pm Sun.*

THORNHAM

The Lifeboat Inn
Ship Lane, Thornham, Hunstanton PE36 6LT
☎ *(01485) 512236* Mr and Mrs Coker

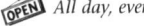Adnams, Greene King and Woodforde's ales always available plus a couple of guest beers, mainly from small independents including Tolly Cobbold.

A sixteenth-century smugglers' alehouse with wood beams, hanging paraffin lamps and open fires overlooking salt marshes. Bar and restaurant food available at lunchtime and evenings. Car park, garden and accommodation. Children allowed. Turn first left when entering the village from Hunstanton.

OPEN *All day, every day.*

TIBENHAM

The Greyhound
The Street, Tibenham NR16 1PZ
☎ *(01379) 677676* David and Colleen Hughes

Greene King IPA and something from Adnams always on offer, plus one guest, which might be Timothy Taylor Landlord, Brakspear Special, Tindall Honeydew, Shepherd Neame Spitfire, Early Bird or Late Red, Black Sheep Special, Young's Special or Waggle Dance or Fuller's London Pride.

Traditional village freehouse in extensive grounds. The lounge bar has low beams and a wood fire, the public bar features darts, and there is a pool room. Two beer gardens, children's playground, large car park. There are plans to serve traditional pub food daily until 9pm, from the end of 2002. Camping and caravanning facilities.

OPEN *6.30–11pm Mon, Wed, Thurs (closed all day Tues); 12–11pm Fri–Sat; 12–10.30pm Sun.*

TOFT MONKS

Toft Lion
Toft Monks, Nr Beccles NR34 0EP
☎ *(01502) 677702* Jan and Giles Mortimer

Adnams Bitter and Broadside regularly available. Two weekly changing guest beers, often from local breweries, are also served.

The Toft Lion has been a pub since 1650 and offers home-cooked food, log fires, beer garden and en-suite accommodation. Dogs and well-behaved children welcome.

OPEN *11.30am–2.30pm and 5–11pm (10.30pm Sun).*

UPTON

The White Horse
17 Chapel Road, Upton, Norwich
☎ *(01493) 750696* Raymond Norman

Adnams Best, Greene King IPA and St Peter's Best always available, plus two or three guest ales. Emphasis on local breweries; guests come from breweries such as Woodforde's, Wolf, Elgood's, Adnams, Morland, Buffy's and Mauldons.

Dating from the nineteenth-century, full of character with two inglenook fireplaces, a snug and a main bar with two further rooms. Food available 12–3pm and 6.30–9.30pm daily. Children and dogs welcome. Conservatory. Beer garden with aviary. Regular live music and summer events. Taxi service available for parties.

OPEN *11am–11pm Mon–Sat; 12–10.30pm Sun.*

WALSINGHAM

The Bull Inn
Common Place, Shire Hall Plain, Walsingham NR22 6BP
☎ *(01328) 820333* Philip Horan

Tolly Original and Marston's Pedigree among the beers always available.

A 600-year-old olde-worlde pub with open fires, restaurant, beer garden and accommodation. Food available at lunchtime and evenings. Children allowed.

OPEN *11am–3pm and 6–11pm Mon–Sat; 12–3pm and 7–10.30pm Sun.*

WARHAM

The Three Horseshoes
Bridge Street, Warham, Wells-next-the-Sea NR23 1NL
☎ *(01328) 710547* Mr Salmon

Woodforde's Wherry and Greene King IPA always available plus a guest (changed each week) such as Greene King Abbot, Morland Old Speckled Hen, Woodforde's Nelson's Revenge and Wadworth 6X.

Traditional cottage pub in the centre of the village with gas lighting and open fires. Bar food available at lunchtime and evenings. Car park, garden, function room, non-smoking room, accommodation. Children allowed.

OPEN *11.30am–2.30pm and 6–11pm Mon–Sat; 12–3pm and 6–10.30pm Sun.*

WEST RUDHAM

The Duke's Head

West Rudham, King's Lynn PE31 8RW
☎ *(01485) 528540* Mr Feltham

A range of Woodforde's ales (usually including Great Eastern, Wherry and Kett's Rebellion) always available. Occasional guests.

A fifteenth-century coaching inn. Food oriented with separate dining area and food available at lunchtime and evenings. Children allowed.

OPEN *11am–3pm and 7–11pm Mon–Sat (closed Tues); 12–2.30pm and 7–10.30pm Sun.*

WEST SOMERTON

The Lion

West Somerton, Great Yarmouth
☎ *(01493) 393289*
Mr GI Milroy and SM Milroy

Greene King IPA and Abbot usually available plus two guest beers, often Hampshire Lionheart and a Mauldons ale.

Traditional country pub with children's room. Food served 11.30am–3pm and 6–9.30pm. Car park.

OPEN *11.30am–3.30pm and 6–11pm Mon–Sat; 12–3.30pm and 6–10.30pm Sun.*

WHINBURGH

The Mustard Pot

Dereham Road, Whinburgh, Dereham NR19 1AA
☎ *(01362) 692179* Ricky and Amanda Fox

A freehouse with Adnams Bitter permanently available, plus guest ales served on four pumps, from local independent breweries.

An old village pub with open fireplace and beer garden. Good pub food available 12–2pm and 6.30–8.45pm Mon–Sat, with Sunday lunches served until 2pm (no food Sun evening). Children welcome.

OPEN *11am–11pm Mon–Sat; 12–10.30pm Sun.*

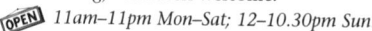

WINDHAM

The Feathers

Windham, Norfolk NR18 0PN
☎ *(01953) 605675*
Eddie Aldus and Lorna Palmer

A freehouse offering Adnams Best, Greene King Abbot, Marston's Pedigree, Fuller's London Pride and Feather Ticklers (brewed for the pub by Mauldons), plus two guests, changed every couple of days, such as Adnams Broadside or something from Buffy's or Mauldons.

Regulars' town pub, with one bar and function room. Food available. Gaming machines, darts, garden. Children allowed.

OPEN *11am–2.30pm and 7–11pm Mon–Sat (open 6pm Fri); 12–2.30pm and 7–10.30pm Sun.*

WINTERTON-ON-SEA

The Fisherman's Return

The Lane, Winterton-on-Sea, Great Yarmouth NR29 4BN
☎ *(01493) 393305* Kate and John Findlay

A freehouse with Woodforde's Wherry, Great Eastern and Norfolk Nog always available, plus two guests changing at least twice a week. These will include something like Mauldons Cuckoo, Buffy's Mild, Cottage Our Ken or Woodforde's Nelson's Revenge.

A 300-year-old brick and flint pub with open fires and beer garden. Food available at lunchtime and evenings. No children.

OPEN *11am–2.30pm and 6.30–11pm Mon–Fri; all day Sat–Sun.*

WIVETON

The Wiveton Bell

The Green, Wiveton, Blakeney NR25 7TL
☎ *(01263) 740101* John and Lucy Olsen

A freehouse with Adnams Bitter permanently available, plus guests during the summer from local independent breweries such as Wolf.

A traditional, beamed village pub with a non-smoking conservatory restaurant. Beer garden. Adjoining cottage to let. Food available at lunchtimes and evenings. Well-behaved children and dogs welcome.

OPEN *Summer: 11.30am–3pm and 6–11pm. Winter opening hours vary.*

WOODBASTWICK

The Fur & Feather Inn
Woodbastwick, Norwich NR13 6HQ
☎ *(01603) 720003* Tim and Penny Ridley

 The Woodforde's brewery tap, situated next door to the brewery and specialising in the range of Woodforde's ales: Fur and Feather Bitter, Admiral's Reserve, Wherry Best, Mardler's Mild, Great Eastern, Nelson's Revenge, Norfolk Nog and Headcracker.

A thatched country pub/restaurant with beer garden. Food available at lunchtimes and evenings Mon–Sat and all day Sun. Children allowed. Dogs welcome in the garden.

 11.30am–3pm and 6–11pm Mon–Sat; 12–10.30pm Sun.

WRENINGHAM

Bird in Hand
Church Road, Wreningham NR16 1BH
☎ *(01508) 489438* Mrs Carol Turner

A freehouse with Woodforde's Wherry, Fuller's London Pride and an Adnams brew always available, plus one guest, perhaps Greene King Abbot.

A traditional pub with wood burners, restaurant and beer garden. Food available at lunchtime and evenings. Children allowed if eating. Ring for directions.

11.30am–3pm and 6–11pm Mon–Sat; 12–3pm and 6–10.30pm Sun.

WYMONDHAM

The Feathers Inn
Town Green, Wymondham NR18 0PN
☎ *(01953) 605675* Eddie Aldours

 Adnams Best, Marston's Pedigree and Greene King Abbot among the brews always available, plus two guests such as Fuller's London Pride, Adnams Regatta, Elgood's Greyhound, Brakspear Bee Sting or Adnams Broadside.

A town freehouse with open fires and beer garden. Food available at lunchtime and evenings. Children allowed.

11am–2.30pm and 7–11pm Mon–Sat; 12–2.30pm and 7–10.30pm Sun.

YOU TELL US

★ *Dock Tavern*, Dock Tavern Lane, Gorleston, Great Yarmouth
★ *The White Horse*, Brandon

Places Featured:

Ashton
Barnwell
Brackley
Bugbrooke
Corby
Desborough
Eastcote
Finedon
Fotheringhay
Gayton
Geddington
Great Brington
Great Houghton
Grendon
Higham Ferrers
Holcot
Kettering

Litchborough
Little Brington
Little Harrowden
Marston St Lawrence
Mears Ashby
Milton Keynes
Northampton
Orlingbury
Ravensthorpe
Southwick
Stoke Bruerne
Sudborough
Sulgrave
Towcester
Wellingborough
Woodford
Woodnewton

THE BREWERIES

FROG ISLAND BREWERY

The Maltings, Westbridge, St James Road,
Northampton NN5 5HS
☎ *(01604) 587772*
www.frogislandbrewery.co.uk

BEST BITTER 3.8% ABV
Golden, quenching and well-hopped.
Malty finish.
SHOEMAKER 4.2% ABV
Malty with delicate hoppiness and bitter finish.
NATTERJACK 4.8% ABV
Sweet and malty, pale and dangerously
drinkable.
FIRE-BELLIED TOAD 5.0% ABV
Pale gold, single hop award winner.
Plus monthly special brews, usually around
5.0% ABV.

THE PUBS

ASHTON

The Chequered Skipper

Ashton, Oundle PE8 5LD
☎ *(01832) 273494* Ian Campbell

Oakham JHB is always on offer, plus
three weekly changing guests, such as
Adnams Broadside, Young's Special, Gale's
HSB or something from Rockingham.

Thatched village pub and restaurant with
modern minimalist interior, with
stunning village green front drinking area
and rear beer garden. Food available. Events
include beer festivals with live music, the
World Conker Champsionships and Morris
dancing – phone for details. Children
allowed.

OPEN *11.30am–3pm and 6–11pm Mon–Fri;*
11am–11pm Sat; 12–10.30pm Sun.

BARNWELL

The Montagu Arms

Barnwell, Oundle, Peterborough PE8 5PH
☎ *(01832) 273726* Ian Simmons

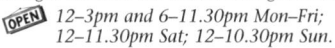 Adnams Southwold and Broadside served with two or three guest beers such as Ash Vine Hop & Glory, Hop Back Summer Lightning or Shepherd Neame Spitfire.

A traditional country inn built in 1601 and retaining many original features. Heavily beamed bar area and more modern non-smoking restaurant. Food served 12–2.30pm and 7–10pm daily. Free children's facilities include log swings and activity centre. Car park. Accommodation. To be found just past bridge. Website: www.themontaguarms.co.uk.

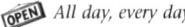 *12–3pm and 6–11.30pm Mon–Fri; 12–11.30pm Sat; 12–10.30pm Sun.*

BRACKLEY

The Greyhound Inn

Milton Malsor, Brackley, Borthampton NN7 3AP
☎ *(01604) 858449* Mr and Mrs Rush

 At least six beers always available, with Morland Old Speckled Hen among them.

A fifteenth-century inn, cosy atmosphere with real fires. Large beer garden. Food available. Children allowed. Situated on the main road into the village.

 All day, every day.

BUGBROOKE

The Wharf Inn

Cornhill Lane, Bugbrooke NN7 3QB
☎ *(01604) 832585* Dave Pownall

 A freehouse with Frog Island Best Bitter always on offer, plus two guests, perhaps Morland Old Speckled Hen or another Frog Island beer.

Canalside pub/restaurant with modern exterior and traditional interior, featuring a giant pile of 10p pieces! There is a balcony for eating, a garden lawned to the canal and a boules area, venue for the Frog Island Boules Competition. Live easy-listening entertainment on Fridays from 9pm. Well-behave children allowed, if eating. 'Busy Bee' canal boat trips run at weekends, or midweek day/evening by private charter (tel 07721 372 569). Situated on the outskirts of the village, heading out towards the A5.

 12–3pm and 6–11pm Mon–Thur; 11am–11pm Fri–Sat; 12–10.30pm Sun.

CORBY

Knight's Lodge

Towerhill Road, Corby NN18 0TH
☎ *(01536) 742602* Fred Hope

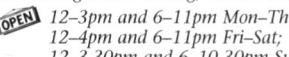 An Everards house with Tiger, Beacon and Old Original always available. Two other guests including, perhaps, Morland Old Speckled Hen, Wadworth Farmers Glory or Perfick, Nethergate Old Growler, Everards Equinox, Charles Wells Fargo or Wood Shropshire Lad.

A traditional seventeenth-century inn linked to Rockingham Castle by a network of tunnels. Food available in dining area Fri–Sun. Children allowed in the dining area if eating, and in the garden.

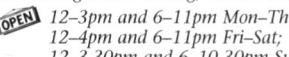 *12–3pm and 6–11pm Mon–Thurs; 12–4pm and 6–11pm Fri–Sat; 12–3.30pm and 6–10.30pm Sun.*

DESBOROUGH

The George

79 High Street, Desborough NN14 2NB
☎ *(01536) 760271* Mr Fairy

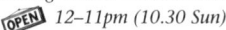 Tied to Everards, with Beacon and Tiger permanently available. The weekly guest beer might be something from Everards, Morland Old Speckled Hen, or a winter seasonal ale.

Drinkers' pub in the town centre, with two bars. No food. Pool, darts, skittles and pigeon club. Patio, car park, eight en-suite letting rooms. Children allowed.

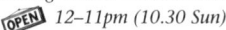 *12–11pm (10.30 Sun).*

EASTCOTE

The Eastcote Arms

6 Gayton Road, Eastcote, Towcester NN12 8NG
☎ *(01327) 830731* John and Wendy Hadley

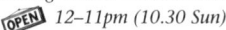 Fuller's London Pride, Adnams Southwold and Greene King IPA always available, plus one guest, constantly changing. An annual beer festival takes place over the Whitsun bank holiday.

A 330-year-old freehouse with dining area and beer garden. Food served at lunchtime and Thurs–Sat evenings. Children allowed in the dining area only. Ring for directions.

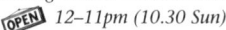 *6–11pm Mon; 12–2.30pm and 6–11pm Tues–Sat; 12–3pm and 7–10.30pm Sun.*

FINEDON

The Bell Inn
Bell Hill, Finedon, Nr Wellingborough NN9 5ND
☎ *(01933) 680332* Denise Willmott

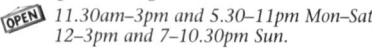 A freehouse with Fuller's London Pride always available, plus three guests perhaps from Woodforde's, Cottage, York or Frog Island.

An ancient pub, apparently dating from 1042. Food served at lunchtime and evenings in dining area. Children allowed.

OPEN *11.30am–3pm and 5.30–11pm Mon–Sat; 12–3pm and 7–10.30pm Sun.*

FOTHERINGHAY

The Falcon Inn
Fotheringhay, Oundle, Peterborough PE8 5HZ
☎ *(01832) 226254* Ray Smikle

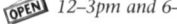 Adnams Best Bitter and Old, and Greene King IPA always available, plus one weekly changing guest.

A pub and restaurant in a historic village. Emphasis on good food, served in the pub and restaurant at lunchtimes and evenings. Darts and dominoes, function room, car park. Children allowed.

OPEN *12–3pm and 6–11pm.*

GAYTON

Eykyn Arms
20 High Street, Gayton, Northampton NN7 3HD
☎ *(01604) 858361* Robert Pattle

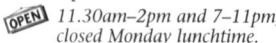 Charles Wells Eagle, Shepherd Neame Spitfire and a Hook Norton brew usually available. One guest beer is served which may be Fuller's London Pride or another beer from Shepherd Neame.

Traditional freehouse with accommodation. Snacks served by prior arrangement. Car park. Children welcome, but no special facilities.

OPEN *11.30am–2pm and 7–11pm; closed Monday lunchtime.*

GEDDINGTON

The Star Inn
2 Bridge Street, Geddington, Kettering NN14 1AD
☎ *(01536) 742386*
Jim Grimmett and Natalie Britchford

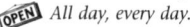 A freehouse with six real ales available, generally including Marston's Pedigree, Wadworth 6X and Fuller's London Pride, plus local brews from Grainstore and Frog Island breweries.

A traditional pub steeped in history set in the heart of Geddington, in front of the Queen Eleanor cross and near the memorial to US fighter pilots. Good range of food, from freshly filled baguettes to pheasant and game dishes, served in separate smoking and non-smoking dining areas. Located off the A43 between Kettering and Corby.

OPEN *All day, every day.*

GREAT BRINGTON

The Fox & Hounds
Althorp Coaching Inn, Great Brington, Northampton NN7 4JA
☎ *(01604) 770651* Peter Krempels

 A freehouse with 11 real ales always available. Greene King IPA and Abbot are permanent features, and there is usually something from Adnams. Other guests are from all over the country.

A sixteenth-century coaching inn with log fires, exposed beams and stone/wood floors. Dining area and beer garden. Food served at lunchtime and dinner, 'Rosette Standard' cooking. Children and dogs allowed. Walkers and horses welcome. Take the A428 from Northampton past Althorp House, then first left turn before railway bridge.

OPEN *Summer: 11am–11pm Mon–Sat; 12–10.30pm Sun (phone for winter hours).*

GREAT HOUGHTON

The Old Cherry Tree
Cherry Tree Lane, Great Houghton, Northampton NN4 7AT
☎ *(01604) 761399* Mr Carr

A Charles Wells house with Bombardier and Eagle always available, plus one other guest such as Adnams Broadside

A pub and restaurant. Children allowed in the restaurant only. Located off the A428 from Northampton to Bedford. Three miles out of Northampton. Turn right into the village, then first left.

OPEN *12–3pm and 6–11.30pm (10.30pm Sun).*

GRENDON

The Half Moon
42 Main Road, Grendon
☎ *(01933) 663263* Frederick Maffre

Charles Wells Eagle, IPA and one guest beer usually available.

A 300-year-old thatched pub with low ceilings and original beams. Beer garden. Food served lunchtimes and evenings Mon–Sat and Sun lunchtimes only. Car park. Children's menu.

12–2.30pm and 6–11pm Mon–Fri; 12–2.30pm and 6.30–11pm Sat; 12–2.30pm and 7–10.30pm Sun.

HIGHAM FERRERS

The Green Dragon
College Street, Higham Ferrers, Rushden NN10 8DZ
☎ *(01933) 312088* Joy Ormond

A freehouse with Fuller's London Pride and Greene King Abbot always available. Guests are numerous and varied and come mostly from small local breweries.

A seventeenth-century coaching inn with open fires, restaurant, beer garden, accommodation. Food served lunchtimes and evenings. Children allowed.

12–2.30pm and 5–11pm Mon–Thurs; all day Fri–Sun.

The Griffin Inn
High Street, Higham Ferrers, Rushden NN10 8BW
☎ *(01933) 312612* Ray Gilbert

Charles Wells Eagle, Greene King Abbot, Fuller's London Pride and Wadworth 6X always available, plus a range of guests constantly changing but often including Marston's Pedigree and Morland Old Speckled Hen.

A luxurious seventeenth-century freehouse with leather Chesterfield, inglenook fireplace and conservatory. Patio. Food served at lunchtime and evenings in a 50-seater restaurant. Children allowed in the restaurant only.

11am–3pm and 5.30–11pm.

HOLCOT

The White Swan Inn
Main Street, Holcot, Northampton NN6 9SP
☎ *(01604) 781263* David Hodgson

A freehouse with Greene King IPA and a Hook Norton brew always available.

A thatched country pub with two bars, games room and garden. B&B. Food available at lunchtime and evenings. Families welcome.

12–2.30pm and 5.30–11pm Mon–Fri; all day Sat–Sun.

KETTERING

Park House/The Milestone Restaurant
Kettering Venture Park, Kettering NN15 6XE
☎ *(01536) 523377* Rachael Early

Banks's Bitter and Original always available.

A traditional pub and restaurant. Children allowed.

11.30am–11pm Mon–Sat; 12–10.30pm Sun.

LITCHBOROUGH

The Old Red Lion
Banbury Road, Litchborough, Towcester NN12 8HF
☎ *(01327) 830250* Mr and Mrs O'Shey

Banks's Bitter and a Marston's ale always available.

A small, 300-year-old pub with log fires and beer garden. Food available Tues–Sat, lunchtime and evenings. Children allowed.

11.30am–2.30pm and 6.30–11pm Mon–Sat; 12–3pm and 7–10.30pm Sun.

LITTLE BRINGTON

The Saracen's Head
Little Brington, Northampton NN7 4HS
☎ *(01604) 770640* Mo and Anne Farsad

A freehouse offering beers from Shepherd Neame, Hook Norton, Greene King and Ridleys.

The only pub in Little Brington. Open fires and beer garden. Food available in two restaurants. Children allowed throughout. En-suite accommodation available. Function room, beer & skittles nights.

12–2.30pm and 6–11pm Mon–Fri; 12–11pm Sat–Sun.

LITTLE HARROWDEN

The Lamb Inn
Orlingbury Road, Little Harrowden, Wellingborough NN9 5BH
☎ *(01933) 673300* Sheila Field

A Charles Wells house with Eagle and Bombardier always available, plus three constantly changing guests.

A traditional seventeenth-century Northampton inn. Skittles table. Beer garden. Food, which is homemade from fresh produce, is available in separate dining area during all opening hours (until 10pm). Children allowed until 9pm.

12–2.30pm and 6–11pm Mon–Fri; 12–11pm Sat; 12–10.30pm Sun.

MARSTON ST LAWRENCE

Marston Inn

Marston St Lawrence, Banbury OX17 2DB
☎ *(01295) 711906*
Ms Claire Ellis and Mr Paul Parker

 Hook Norton tied house with a different guest beer served each month, with Gale's HSB, Shepherd Neame Spitfire, Badger Tanglefoot, Fuller's ESB or Caledonian 80/- among the popular ones.

Fifteenth-century, 'roses-round-the-door' village pub. Converted from three cottages, the pub features oak beams, real fire, two dining rooms (one non-smoking), cosy bar, lounge and gardens. Traditional pub games. Food served 12–2pm Tues–Sun and 7–9.30pm Tues–Sat. Car park. Children welcome in garden or if pre-booked for Sunday lunch.

OPEN *7–11pm Mon; 12–3pm and 7–11pm Tues–Sat; 12–4pm and 7–10.30pm Sun.*

MEARS ASHBY

The Griffin's Head

Wilby Road, Mears Ashby, Northampton NN6 0DX
☎ *(01604) 812945* Philip Tompkins

 Marston's Pedigree, Charles Wells Eagle and Everards Beacon always available, plus two guests including, perhaps, Everards Tiger or an Adnams brew. Also seasonal ales.

A cosy freehouse with log fires, restaurant and beer garden. Food served at lunchtime and evenings. Children allowed if eating. Can be difficult to find (ring for directions).

OPEN *11.30am–3pm and 5.30–11pm Mon–Fri; 12–3pm and 6–11pm Sat; 11.30am–10.30pm Sun.*

MILTON KEYNES

The Navigation Inn

Thrupp Wharf, Castlethorpe Road, Cosgrove, Milton Keynes
☎ *(01908) 543156* Mr H Willis

 Greene King IPA and Abbot Ale plus two weekly changing guest beers usually available.

Family-run pub set on the Grand Union Canal with unspoilt views over open countryside. Restaurant, sun terrace and family garden. Bar food available lunchtimes and evenings Mon–Sat and all day Sun. Restaurant open evenings only Mon–Sat and all day Sun. Children welcome when dining and in the family garden.

OPEN *12–3pm and 6–11pm Mon–Fri; 12–11pm Sat–Sun.*

NORTHAMPTON

The Malt Shovel Tavern

121 Bridge Street, Northampton NN1 1QF
☎ *(01604) 234212*

 A freehouse with four regular ales, including Frog Island Natterjack, Fuller's London Pride and Banks's Bitter plus up to eight constantly changing guests such as Oakham JHB, Skinner's Cornish Knocker and Timothy Taylor Dark Mild.

A traditional pub with beer garden. Food served at lunchtime and early evenings. Children allowed in the garden only. Located opposite the Carlsberg Brewery.

OPEN *11.30am–3pm and 5–11pm Mon–Sat; 12–3pm and 7–10.30pm Sun.*

Moon On The Square

6 The Parade, Market Place, Northampton NN1 2EE
☎ *(01604) 634062*
Nigel Abbott and Olivia Jenkinson

 Marston's Pedigree, Greene King Abbot Ale and Shepherd Neame Spitfire usually available, plus two guest beers from a wide selection supplied by the excellent East-West Ales.

Large city-centre pub with disabled access and no music or games tables. Food served all day, every day. No children.

OPEN *10.30am–11pm Mon–Sat; 12–10.30pm Sun.*

The Old Black Lion

Black Lion Hill, Northampton NN1 1SW
☎ *(01604) 639472* Mr Wilkinson

 Frog Island Natterjack is among the beers always served, with other Frog Island beers featured as guests.

Very old building on the outside of the town centre, near the station. Refurbished interior, with one bar, function room and patio. Food available. Children allowed.

OPEN *11am–11pm Mon–Sat; 12–10.30pm Sun.*

ORLINGBURY

The Queen's Arms

11 Isham Road, Orlingbury NN14 1JD
☎ *(01933) 678258*

 Up to six guest ales available, changing weekly.

A country freehouse and restaurant with beer garden. Food served at lunchtime and evenings. Children allowed. Local CAMRA Pub of the Year 1994 (and runner-up 1999).

OPEN *12–2.30pm and 6–11pm Mon–Fri; all day Sat–Sun.*

RAVENSTHORPE

The Chequers

Chequer's Lane, Ravensthorpe NN6 8ER
☎ *(01604) 770379* Gordon Walker

A freehouse with five hand pumps, serving Fuller's London Pride, Greene King Abbot, something from Thwaites and Jennings, plus one guest.

A cosy village pub serving traditional English fare. Restaurant and bar food served lunchtimes and evenings. Beer garden and children's play area – children welcome.

OPEN *12–3pm and 6–11pm Mon–Fri; all day Sat; 12–3pm and 7–10.30pm Sun.*

SOUTHWICK

The Shuckburgh Arms

Main Street, Southwick, Nr Oundle, Peterborough PE8 5BL
☎ *(01832) 274007* Nicola Stokes

Fuller's London Pride and Marston's Pedigree usually available, plus one constantly changing guest, such as Shepherd Neame Spitfire, Jennings Best, Timothy Taylor Landlord or beers from Bateman and Cains among others.

Small, thatched, family-run freehouse with log fire and beams. Darts and dominoes regularly played. Food served 12–1.30pm Wed–Sun, 6–9pm Wed–Sat, 6–8.30pm Sun in summer only. Large car park. Small family room and children's play equipment in garden. Situated three miles east of Oundle.

OPEN *12–2pm Wed–Sat; 6–11pm Mon–Sat; 12–3pm and 7–10.30pm Sun (6–10.30pm in summer). Closed Mon–Tues lunchtimes.*

STOKE BRUERNE

The Boat Inn

Stoke Bruerne, Nr Towcester NN12 7SB
☎ *(01604) 862428*
Andrew and Nicholas Woodward

A freehouse with Banks's Bitter, Marston's Bitter and Pedigree, Frog Island Best Bitter, Mansfield Dark Mild and Adnams Southwold the permanent beers. A guest beer is sometimes served, often from the Wolverhampton & Dudley Head Brewers' Choice scheme.

Canalside pub, run by the same family since 1877. The original part of building has a thatched roof, stone floors and open fires. Food is available – there is an 80-seater restaurant, plus an extension with lounge bar, bistro and cocktail bar. A 40-seater passenger narrowboat is available for hire for party trips all year. Live music at least once a month and cabarets at Christmas in restaurant. The local Rose & Castle Morris team meet here on Wednesday nights. Children allowed. Approximately six minutes from M1 Juntion 15. Website: www.boatinn.co.uk.

OPEN *Summer: 9am–11pm (10.30pm Sun); winter: 9am–3pm and 6–11pm Mon–Thurs; 9am–11pm Fri–Sat; 9am–10.30pm Sun.*

SUDBOROUGH

The Vane Arms

Main Street, Sudborough NN14 3BX
☎ *(01832) 733223* Graeme Walker

Nine different beers changed regularly (150 per year) including Hoskins & Oldfield Ginger Tom, Hop Back Summer Lightning, Woodforde's Headcracker, Adnams Broadside, RCH East Street Cream, Oakham Old Tosspot and Bishop's Farewell.

A centuries-old listed thatched village inn. Bar and restaurant food available at lunchtime and evenings. Mexican specials. Car park, games room. Children allowed. Accommodation. Just off the A6116 between Thrapston and Corby.

OPEN *12–3pm and 5.30–11pm.*

SULGRAVE

The Star Inn

Manor Road, Sulgrave OX17 2SA
☎ *(01295) 760389*
Mr and Mrs R Jameson King

 Hook Norton Best Bitter and Old Hooky usually available plus a guest beer from a micro- or independent brewery.

Idyllic country inn on the South Northants/Oxon borders. Food served 12–2pm and 6.30–9pm Mon–Sat, 12–4pm Sun. Car park. Children welcome in non-smoking restaurant and garden. Follow brown signs for Sulgrave Manor.

OPEN *11am–2.30pm and 6–11pm Mon–Sat; 12–5pm Sun.*

TOWCESTER

The Plough Inn

Market Square, Towcester NN12 6BT
☎ *(01327) 350738*
Geraldine, Matthew and Bob Goode

 A Charles Wells tied house with Eagle permanently available, plus Adnams Broadside.

Cosy, 400-year-old, award-winning pub which has been in the same hands for over 30 years. Food served 11.30am–10pm and the pub is Egon Ronay recommended. Car park. Children's eating area.

OPEN *11am–11pm Mon–Sat; 12–10.30pm Sun.*

WELLINGBOROUGH

Red Well

16 Silver Street, Wellingborough NN14 1PA
☎ *(01933) 440845*
Steve Frost and Tina Garner

A freehouse with five guest ales always available. Regulars include Hop Back Summer Lightning, Nethergate Old Growler, Morland Old Speckled Hen, Cotleigh Osprey, Ash Vine Frying Tonight and Adnams Regatta. Beer festivals held three times a year.

A new-age pub, no music, no games. Separate non-smoking area, disabled access, garden. Food available all day, every day. Children allowed in the garden only.

OPEN *All day, every day.*

WOODFORD

The Dukes Arms

High Street, Woodford, Nr Kettering NN14 4HE
☎ *(01832) 732224* Mr and Mrs Keith Wilson

 Fuller's London Pride, Morland Old Speckled Hen, Banks's Best Bitter and Shepherd Neame Spitfire usually available.

Delightful setting for the oldest pub in the village which prides itself on good real ale and down-to-earth food. Garden and restaurant. Food served lunchtimes and evenings. Children welcome, but no special facilities. Car park.

OPEN *12–2.30pm and 7–11pm (10.30pm Sun).*

WOODNEWTON

The White Swan Inn

Main Street, Woodnewton PE8 5EB
☎ *(01780) 470381* David and Susan Hydon

Bateman House Bitter, Otter Bright and something from Adnams usually available, plus one guest.

Friendly pub, situated in the next village to the historic village of Fotheringhay. Boules played in summer. Bar and restaurant food served 12–1.45pm and 7–9pm daily (not Sunday evenings). Car park. Children welcome in garden if supervised (no special facilities).

OPEN *12–2pm and 7–11pm Tues–Thurs; 12–2pm and 6–11pm Fri; 12–2pm and 6.30–11pm Sat; 12–3pm Sun (closed Sun evening and all day Mon).*

YOU TELL US

* *The Exeter Arms*, Main Street, Wakerley
* *The Old Plough Inn*, 82 High Street, Braunston, Daventry

Places Featured:	Great Whittington
Acomb	Haltwhistle
Allendale	Hedley on the Hill
Alnmouth	Hexham
Alnwick	High Horton
Ashington	Longframlington
Bedlington	Low Newton
Berwick-upon-Tweed	Morpeth
Blyth	Shotley Bridge
Cramlington	Tweedmouth
Featherstone	Wylam

THE BREWERIES

HEXAMSHIRE BREWERY

Leafields, Ordley, Hexham NE46 1SX
☎ *(01434) 606577*

DEVIL'S ELBOW 3.6% ABV
SHIRE BITTER 3.8% ABV
DEVIL'S WATER 4.1% ABV
WHAPWEASEL 4.8% ABV
Plus seasonal:
OLD HUMBUG 5.5% ABV

THE NORTHUMBERLAND BREWERY

Earth Balance, West Sleekburn Farm, Bomarsund, Bedlington NE22 7AD
☎ *(01670) 822122*

CASTLES 3.8% ABV
Hoppy session bitter.
COUNTY 4.0% ABV
Well-balanced, easy-drinking brew.
BALANCE 4.2% ABV
As the name suggests … well-balanced!
SECRET KINGDOM ALE 4.3% ABV
Smooth and rich.
BEST 4.5% ABV
Rounded and full-flavoured.
BOMAR 5.0% ABV
Pale and refreshing.

WYLAM BREWERY

South Houghton, Heddon-on-the-Wall NE15 0EZ
☎ *(01661) 853377*
www.wylambrew.co.uk

HEDONIST 3.8% ABV
A pale, session ale.
TURBINIA 4.0% ABV
A highly hopped bitter with rich colour and flavour.
ROCKET 4.4% ABV
Best bitter.
YOUR HOUSE SPECIAL 4.6% ABV
Complex, full-flavoured and aromatic.
THE HAUGH 5.1% ABV
Dark porter.

THE PUBS

ACOMB

The Miner's Arms

Main Street, Acomb, Hexham NE46 4PW
☎ *(01434) 603909* Joan Crozier

A freehouse serving Yates Bitter, Federation Northumbria Smooth and Ushers Founders Ale, plus a range of guest ales. Regular features include Durham White Velvet and Magus, Mordue Five Bridge Bitter and Black Sheep Bitter.

An unspoilt old-style stone pub, dating from 1750, and recently refurbished. Two bar areas, outside garden and barbecue. Home-cooked food served at lunchtimes (weekends) and evenings. Function facilities. Children allowed until 9pm.

5–11pm Mon–Fri (closed lunchtimes); 11am–11pm Sat; 12–10.30pm Sun; also open 12–3pm Mon–Fri seasonally and on bank holidays, according to demand.

ALLENDALE

The King's Head Hotel

Market Place, Allendale, Hexham NE47 9BD
☎ *(01434) 683681* Margaret Taylor

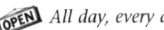A freehouse with Jennings Cumberland Ale and Greene King Abbot always available, plus three guests such as Timothy Taylor Landlord, Mordue Workie Ticket, Morland Old Speckled Hen, Marston's Pedigree, Northumberland Cat 'n' Sawdust or one of many Durham Brewery ales.

A cosy quiet pub with two bars, fires and a function room. No music or games. Food served at lunchtime and evenings. Children allowed.

All day, every day.

ALNMOUTH

The Famous Schooner Haunted Hotel & Restaurant

Northumberland Street, Alnmouth NE66 2RS
☎ *(01665) 830216* John Orde (Director)

 Schooner Parson's Smyth Ale 3.6% (brewed for the Schooner Hotel) permanently available plus five guests often featuring Marston's Pedigree, Ruddles County, Charles Wells Bombardier, Border Noggins Nog or Mythic Brews, or other ales from Jennings, Border, Orkney or Northumberland breweries.

A seventeenth-century haunted hotel with Chase Bar and Long Bar, conservatory and terraced beer garden. Two real ale beer festivals held every year at the Whitsun Bank Holiday and the weekend before the August Bank Holiday. Two restaurants with full menus, one specialising in seafood and local game, plus bar food at lunchtimes and all day at weekends and school holidays. Children welcome. Ghostly bouncy castle! Website: www.schooner.sagehost.co.uk.

OPEN *All day, every day.*

ALNWICK

The John Bull Inn

12 Howick Street, Alnwick NE66 1UY
☎ *(01665) 602055* S Belcher and D Odlin

 A freehouse offering three ever-changing guest beers from micro-breweries nationwide, as well as local breweries such as Hadrian/Border, Wylam, Mordue and Northumberland. Almost 600 different ales served in three years. Over 60 single-malt whiskies and over 40 Belgian beers also stocked.

Old-fashioned backstreet boozer, purpose-built as a pub in 1831, with walled beer garden. No food. Cards, dominoes, Jenga, chess and lots of board games, but no music, TV or games machines. Beer festivals in June (phone for further details). Difficult to find – ring for directions, or ask at Tourist Information. Visit the website at: www.John-Bull-Inn.co.uk.

OPEN *12–3pm and 7–11pm Mon–Fri (closed Wed lunchtime); 11am–3pm and 7–11pm Sat; 12–3pm and 7–10.30pm Sun.*

The Market Tavern

Fenkle Street, Alnwick NE66 1HW
☎ *(01665) 602759* Ken Hodgson

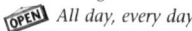 Young's Waggle Dance is among the beers always available, plus a rotating guest including, perhaps, Morland Old Speckled Hen or Charles Wells Bombardier. Other seasonal guests such as Wye Valley Winter Tipple when appropriate.

A traditional town-centre pub with one bar, restaurant, disabled access and accommodation. Food available at lunchtime and evenings. Children allowed.

OPEN *All day, every day.*

ASHINGTON

The Black Diamond

29 Southview, Ashington NE63 0SS
☎ *(01670) 851500* Paul Gray

 Black Diamond Bitter is the house beer at this freehouse, and is always available. A guest beer is sometimes served.

Town-centre pub with lounge/diner and public bar. Pool, darts, gaming machines. Four letting rooms. Children allowed. Car park.

OPEN *11am–11pm Mon–Sat; 12–10.30pm Sun.*

Bubbles Wine Bar

58a Station Road, Ashington NE63 9UJ
☎ *(01670) 850800* David Langdown

 A freehouse with three pumps serving a range of real ales. Too many to list; all breweries stocked as and when available.

A town-centre pub for all ages. One bar, back-yard area, entertainment and discos. Food served at lunchtimes and evenings. There is a nightclub on the premises, open Fri and Sat nights. Children allowed.

OPEN *11am–3pm and 6–11pm Mon–Thurs (extension to midnight on Thurs); all day Fri–Sat; 7–12.30am Sun.*

BEDLINGTON

The Northumberland Arms

112 Front Street East, Bedlington
☎ *(01670) 822754* Mrs Mary Morris

 Three regularly changing guest beers served, such as Timothy Taylor Landlord, Fuller's ESB or London Pride, Charles Wells Bombardier, Shepherd Neame Spitfire or Bishop's Finger, Black Sheep Bitter or Special and Bateman XXXB.

Friendly pub with interesting beer range. Food served 11.30am–2.30pm Thurs–Sat.

OPEN *7–11pm Mon–Tues; 11am–11pm Wed–Sat; 12–10.30pm Sun.*

BERWICK-UPON-TWEED

Barrels Ale House
Bridge Street, Berwick-upon-Tweed TD15 1ES
☎ *(01289) 308013* Mark Dixon

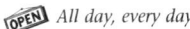A freehouse with Fuller's London Pride, Timothy Taylor Landlord and Exmoor Gold the permanent beers, plus five different guests per week, rotated on two handpumps.

A traditional two-bar pub, one up, one down. Dining area, real fires. Renowned music and comedy venue in basement. Food served at lunchtime and evenings. Children allowed in certain areas.

OPEN *All day, every day.*

BLYTH

The Joiners Arms
Coomassie Road, Blyth
☎ *(01670) 352852* Mrs Ann Holland

Northumberland Secret Kingdom plus a guest beer usually available.

Small, friendly, one-bar pub with entertainment on Thursday, Saturday and Sunday evenings. Seating area at side of pub. Sandwiches and toasties available. Car park. Children welcome.

OPEN *12–11pm (10.30pm Sun).*

CRAMLINGTON

The Plough
Middle Farm, Cramlington NE23 9DN
☎ *(01670) 737633* Roy Apps

Three guest beers are available every week.

A two-bar village freehouse with dining area and two beer gardens. Food served every lunchtime, including traditional Sunday roasts. Well-behave children welcome 12–3pm only. Two function rooms. Big-screen TV in bar.

OPEN *11am–3pm and 6–11pm Mon–Wed; all day Thurs–Sun.*

FEATHERSTONE

The Wallace Arms
Featherstone, Nr Haltwhistle
☎ *(01434) 321872* Allan Blackburn

Big Lamp Bitter and Prince Bishop Ale are the permanent beers here, and one guest is also served.

Traditional country pub with large garden, adjacent to the South Tyne Trail, with bar, snug and pool room. Food served 12–2pm and 6–7.30pm (Sunday lunches by order only). Children and dogs welcome. Car park.

OPEN *12–3pm and 6–11pm Mon–Fri (closed all day Tues); 11am–11pm Sat; 12–10.30pm Sun.*

GREAT WHITTINGTON

The Queens Head Inn
Great Whittington, Newcastle upon Tyne NE19 2HP
☎ *(01434) 672267* Ian J Scott

Queens Head Bitter (brewed by Nick Stafford), Hambleton Best Bitter and Black Sheep Bitter usually available plus one guest. Hambleton Stud, Black Sheep Special, Northumberland Secret Kingdom and Durham Magus feature frequently.

A fifteenth-century coaching inn which incorporates a restaurant. Comfortable bar with open fires. Food served Tues–Sat. Car park. Well-behaved children welcome. Situated four miles north of Corbridge, off the Military Road (B6318) towards Newcastle.

OPEN *12–2.30pm and 6–11pm Tues–Sat; 12–3pm and 7–10.30pm Sun.*

HALTWHISTLE

The Black Bull
Market Square, Haltwhistle NE49 0BL
☎ *(01434) 320463* Mr Sandford

Jennings Cumberland Ale always available plus a good range of guests on five additional pumps, plus extra barrels at weekends. Beers are sometimes brewed on the premises and these are served as available.

A small, quiet freehouse with one main bar and a small side room. No music or machines. No food. Children allowed at lunchtime only in the smaller area.

OPEN *7–11pm Mon–Wed; 12–3pm and 7–11pm Thurs–Fri; 12–4pm and 7–11pm Sat; 12–3pm and 7–10.30pm Sun.*

HEDLEY ON THE HILL

The Feathers Inn Freehouse
Hedley on the Hill, Stocksfield NE43 7SW
☎ *(01661) 843607* Marina Atkinson

Mordue Workie Ticket among the beers always available, plus a range of guests from local breweries such as Big Lamp and Northumberland whenever possible. Otherwise Fuller's London Pride and Chiswick or beers from Yates or Wylam breweries.

A traditional, attractive pub with log fires, beams and stone walls. No music or games. Outside tables. Food served Tues–Sun evenings and lunchtime at weekends. Children allowed.

OPEN *6–11pm Mon–Fri; 12–3pm and 6–11pm Sat; 12–3pm and 7–10.30pm Sun.*

HEXHAM

The Dipton Mill Inn
Dipton Mill Road, Hexham NE46 1YA
☎ *(01434) 606577* Mr Brooker

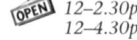A freehouse not far from the Hexhamshire brewery, so Hexhamshire beers such as Devil's Elbow, Shire Bitter, Devil's Water and Whapweasel usually available.

An old-fashioned country pub with real fires. No music or games. One bar, garden, disabled access. Food served at lunchtime and evenings. Children allowed.

OPEN *12–2.30pm and 6–11pm Mon–Sat; 12–4.30pm and 7–10.30pm Sun.*

The Tap & Spile
Battle Hill, Hexham NE46 1BA
☎ *(01434) 602039* Sandra Kelf

Black Sheep Best Bitter is always on offer, plus five guests, changed daily, such as Timothy Taylor Landlord, Jennings Cumberland Ale, Morland Old Speckled Hen, Ruddles County, Fuller's London Pride, Hook Norton Best, Marston's Pedigree, Exmoor Gold and beers from Mordue, to name but a few!

A pub since 1862, this is a traditional town-centre bar in a listed building. Pub food and snacks served 12–2pm Mon–Sat. Northumbrian music once a month. Children allowed in one room. Situated on the main road.

OPEN *11am–11pm Mon–Sat; 12–3pm and 7–10.30pm Sun.*

HIGH HORTON

The Three Horseshoes
Hathery Lane, High Horton, Blythe NE24 4HF
☎ *(01670) 822410* Malcolm Farmer

Greene King Abbot is among the permanent beers at this freehouse. The four guests (usually 10–15 different ones each week) might include Morland Old Speckled Hen, Adnams Broadside, Bateman XXXB, Charles Wells Bombardier or Northumberland Secret Kingdom.

A pub on the outskirts of town, with beamed ceiling, conservatory, restaurant area and beer garden. Food available. Gaming machines. Children allowed. Car park. The pub is a large white building overlooking the A189.

OPEN *11am–11pm Mon–Sat; 12–10.30pm Sun.*

LONGFRAMLINGTON

The Anglers Arms
Weldon Bridge, Longframlington, Morpeth NE65 8AX
☎ *(01665) 570655* John Young

A freehouse offering one guest, changed daily, with an emphasis on seasonal and celebration ales from local breweries. Charles Wells Bombardier is also a favourite.

Seventeenth-century country inn with beams and fireplaces. Food is available, and there is a non-smoking restaurant. Garden, car park, five letting rooms. Children allowed.

OPEN *11am–3pm and 6–11pm Mon–Sat; 12–3pm and 7–10.30pm Sun.*

LOW NEWTON

The Ship Inn
Newton Square, Low Newton, Alnwick NE66 3EL
☎ *(01665) 576262* Christine Forsythe

Up to four guest beers in summer, less in winter. Beers changed as often as every day, including brews such as Border Farne Island and Rampart, Black Sheep Bitter and Old Barn Sheepdog.

A drinkers' pub in a building dating from 1790, situated 20 yards from the sea in a tiny fishing village. Lunchtime bar snacks available (crab, soup, ham and local cheeses). Outside seating on the green. The National Trust holds music festivals on the green in summer. Live music on occasions. Flat to let (sleeps 4). Beer festivals planned – call for details. Children and dogs welcome.

OPEN *Summer: 11am–11pm Mon–Sat; 12–10.30pm Sun; winter: closed Mon; 12–3pm and 8–11pm Tues–Fri; 11am–5pm and 8–11pm Sat; 12–5pm and 8–10.30pm Sun.*

MORPETH

Tap & Spile
Manchester Street, Morpeth NE61 1BH
☎ *(01670) 513894* Mrs Boyle

Beers from breweries such as Cumberland, Adnams, Black Sheep, Jennings, Bateman and Fuller's. Also celebration and seasonal ales when available.

An old-fashioned pub with small lounge and bar area. Open fires. No food except on special occasions. Children allowed in the lounge only.

OPEN *12–2.30pm and 4.30–11pm Mon–Thurs; all day Fri–Sun.*

SHOTLEY BRIDGE

The Manor House Inn
*Carterway Heads, Shotley Bridge, Nr Consett
DH8 9LX*
☎ *(01207) 255268* Mr and Mrs C Brown

Four beers at any one time with an emphasis on a rolling guest ale programme. Beers from all the local brewers (Mordue, Durham, Northumberland, North Yorkshire, Castle Eden) plus a wide range from all over the country, including Hampshire, Morland and many others.

A converted farmhouse, with open log fires in winter. Stunning views over the Derwent Valley. Bar and restaurant food available at lunchtime and evenings. Large car park, garden, accommodation. Children welcome.

OPEN *11am–3pm and 6–11pm Mon–Sat;
12–3pm and 7–10.30pm Sun; all day Sat
and Sun in school summer holidays.*

TWEEDMOUTH

The Angel Inn
11 Brewery Bank, Tweedmouth
☎ *(01289) 303030* Kirsty Turton

Hadrian and Border Brewery's Cowie – a good session ale at 3.6% ABV – permanently available and sold exclusively at £1.25 per pint. Also three guest ales which could be from any independent or micro-brewery. Black Sheep Masham, Fuller's London Pride, Timothy Taylor Best and Landlord, Hadrian and Border Rampart and Mordue Workie Ticket are all regular features; beers from Iceni brewery are also often available and very popular.

K nown locally as the Berwick Rangers supporters' pub, pride is taken over the range and quality of the real ales on offer, as well as the laid-back, friendly atmosphere. Separate lounge and bar. No food. Children welcome, with beer garden for families. Car park. Situated in the main street.

OPEN *5–11pm Mon–Thurs; 12–11pm Fri–Sun.*

WYLAM

The Boat House
Station Road, Wylam
☎ *(01661) 853431* GN and M Weatherburn

A constantly changing selection of nine real ales is on offer. Timothy Taylor Landlord, Wylam Rocket and Border Farne Island Pale Ale usually available, plus five or six guest beers, often from Border, Northumberland, Castle Eden, Wylam, Marston's or many other independent breweries.

W arm, friendly pub on the south bank of the Tyne. Northumberland CAMRA Pub of the Year 2001. Unspoilt bar with real fire. Home-prepared food served lunchtimes and evenings Mon–Thurs, 12–6pm Fri–Sat and 12–5pm Sun. Car park. Children welcome in the beer garden and lounge until 9pm. Continue through Wylam village, the pub is situated just over the bridge.

OPEN *11am–11pm Mon–Sat; 12–10.30pm Sun.*

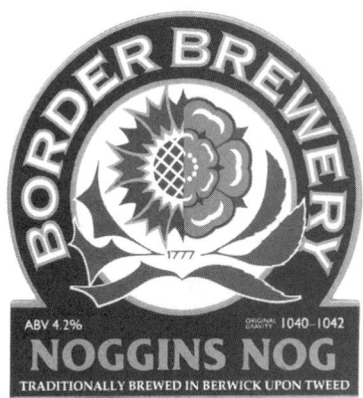

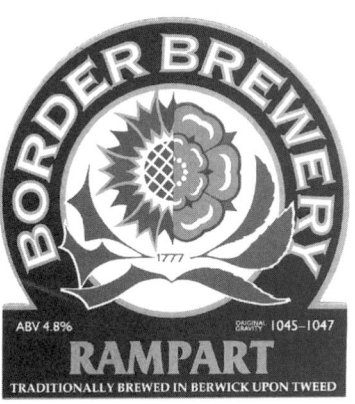

Places Featured:

Barnby in the Willows	Mapperley
Basford	Newark
Beeston	Nottingham
Carlton on Trent	Ollerton
Caythorpe	Radcliffe on Trent
Colston Bassett	Radford
Dunham on Trent	Retford
Hoveringham	Upper Broughton
Kimberley	Upton
Mansfield	Worksop

THE BREWERIES

ALCAZAR BREWING CO.

At The Fox & Crown, 33 Church Street, Old Basford, Nottingham NG6 0GA
☎ *(0115) 942 2002*
www.alcazarbrewingco.com

 ALCAZAR ALE 3.7% ABV
NEW DAWN MILLENNIUM ALE 4.5% ABV
BRUSH BITTER 4.9% ABV
VIXEN'S VICE 5.2% ABV
MAPLE MAGIC 5.5% ABV
Winter brew.
WINDJAMMER IPA 6.0% ABV
Plus the Sherwood Forest selection and other occasional & seasonal brews.

BROADSTONE BREWING CO.

Waterside Brewery, Retford DN22 7ZJ
☎ *(01777) 719797*
www.broadstonebrewery.com

 BROADSTONE BEST BITTER 3.8% ABV
STONEBRIDGE MILD 4.0% ABV
CHARTER ALE 4.6% ABV
BROADSTONE GOLD 5.0% ABV
WAR HORSE 5.8 % ABV
Winter brew.

CASTLE ROCK BREWERY

Queens Bridge Road, The Meadows, Nottingham NG2 1NB
☎ *(0115) 985 1615*

 NOTTINGHAM PALE ALE 3.6% ABV
DAZE (COLLECTION) 3.8% ABV
Summer, winter and Christmas.
HEMLOCK 4.0% ABV
SNOW WHITE 4.2% ABV
BENDIGO 4.5% ABV
Autumn ale.
SALSA 4.5% ABV
Spring ale.
ELSIE MO 4.7% ABV
TRENTSMAN 4.8% ABV
Seasonal.
BLACK JACK STOUT 4.9% ABV
Winter brew.
STAIRWAY 5.2% ABV

CAYTHORPE BREWERY

3 Gonalston Lane, Hoveringham NG14 7JH
☎ *(0115) 966 4376*

 DOVER BECK BITTER 4.0% ABV
OLD NOTTINGHAM EXTRA PALE ALE 4.2% ABV
BIRTHDAY BREW 4.5% ABV
Plus seasonal and occasional brews.

HARDYS & HANSONS PLC

Kimberley Brewery, Nottingham NG16 2NS
☎ *(0115) 938 3611*

 KIMBERLEY BEST MILD 3.1% ABV
Dark red and nutty with good roast malt flavour.
KIMBERLEY BEST BITTER 3.9% ABV
Golden and well-balanced with pleasing bitter flavour.
KIMBERLEY CLASSIC 4.8% ABV
Overflowing with malt, fruit and hop flavours.
Plus seasonal brews.

HOLLAND BREWERY

5 Brown Flats, Brewery Street, Kimberley NG16 2JU
☎ *(0115) 938 2685*

 GOLDEN BLONDE 4.0% ABV
LIP SMACKER 4.0% ABV
CLOGHOPPER 4.2% ABV
DOUBLE DUTCH 4.5% ABV
HOLLY HOP 4.7% ABV
DUTCH COURAGE 5.0% ABV

MALLARD BREWERY

15 Hartington Avenue, Carlton NG4 3NR
☎ *(0115) 952 1289*
www.mallard-brewery.co.uk

 DUCK AND DIVE 3.7% ABV
WADDLERS MILD 3.7% ABV
BEST BITTER 4.0% ABV
DUCKLING 4.2% ABV
SPITTIN' FEATHERS 4.4% ABV
DRAKE 4.5% ABV
DUCK DOWN STOUT 4.6% ABV
Black, fruity occasional brew.
OWD DUCK 4.8% ABV
FRIAR DUCK 5.0% ABV
D.A. 5.8% ABV
Complex winter ale.
QUISMAS QUACKER 6.0% ABV
Dark, smoky, coffee-flavoured Christmas ale.

MAYPOLE BREWERY

North Laithes Farm, Wellow Road, Eakring
NG22 0AN
☎ *(01623) 871690*

 MAYFAIR 3.8% ABV
Available Mar–Oct.
LION'S PRIDE 3.9% ABV
CELEBRATION 4.0% ABV
CENTENARY ALE 4.2% ABV
FLANAGAN'S STOUT 4.4% ABV
Available Mar–Apr.
MAYDAY 4.5% ABV
Available May.
MAE WEST 4.6% ABV
OLD HOMEWRECKER 4.7% ABV
Available Nov–Dec.
POLE AXED 4.8% ABV
Available Oct–Mar.
DONNER & BLITZED 5.1% ABV
Available Dec–Jan.
Plus occasional brews.

NATHAN'S FINE ALES

Dovecote Brewery, The Old Ale House, Top Street,
Elston
☎ *(01636) 525197*

STANDARD BEST BITTER 3.6% ABV
AUTUMN ALE 4.2% ABV
Seasonal
Plus other seasonals and celebration ales.

SPRINGHEAD BREWERY

Unit 3, Sutton Workshops, Old Great North
Road, Sutton on Trent, Newark NG23 6QS
☎ *(01636) 821000*
www.springhead.co.uk

 HERSBRUCKER WEIZENBIER 3.6% ABV
Wheat beer. Available Mar–Sept.
PURITAN'S PORTER 4.0% ABV
Dark and easy-drinking.
SPRINGHEAD BITTER 4.0% ABV
Refreshing and well-hopped session beer.
ROUNDHEAD'S GOLD 4.2% ABV
Quenching and moreish.
GOODRICH CASTLE 4.4% ABV
Pale with rosemary flavour.
THE LEVELLER 4.8% ABV
Rich and rounded.
ROARING MEG 5.5% ABV
Pale and sweet with balancing hoppy, dry
aftertaste.
CROMWELL'S HAT 6.0% ABV
Oct–Mar. Herby flavours.

THE PUBS

BARNBY IN THE WILLOWS

The Willow Tree

Front Street, Barnby in the Willows, Newark
NG24 2SA
☎ *(01636) 626613* H Roberts

 Timothy Taylor Landlord and two guest
beers available, from a wide range of
breweries.

Eighteenth-century village inn with quaint
interior and low beams. Cosy log fires and
candlelit tables in winter. There is a beautiful
floral courtyard, ideal for early-evening
drinks in summer. Food served every evening
from 7pm and at weekend lunchtimes.
Traditional Sunday lunches available.
Spacious en-suite letting rooms. Live jazz
evenings on last Friday of every month.

OPEN *7–11pm Mon–Fri; 12–3pm and 7–11pm*
Sat; 12–3pm and 7–10.30pm Sun.

BASFORD

The Lion Inn
Mosley Street, Basford, Nottingham NG7 7FG
☎ *(0115) 970 3506* Jim Louth

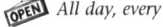 Ten real ales are on offer at this Bateman-owned pub, usually including three Bateman ales, plus guests such as Charles Wells Bombardier, Kelham Island Pale Rider, Castle Rock Elsie Mo, Everards Tiger or Bateman XXXB. Other seasonal celebration beers on bank holidays, at Christmas and Easter etc.

A traditional pub with wooden floorboards, open fires, beer garden and play area. A broad clientele. Live bands on Fri and Sat nights, plus jazz at Sun lunchtimes. Quiz on Mon, open-mike on Thurs. An extensive menu served at lunchtime only. Regular beer festivals. Children allowed.

OPEN *All day, every day.*

BEESTON

The Victoria Hotel
85 Dovecote Lane, Beeston, Nr Nottingham NG9 1JG
☎ *(0115) 925 4049*

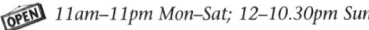 A constantly changing range of twelve cask beers are served, including a mild and a stout or porter. Also 120 whiskies and extensive wine list.

Refurbished and redecorated Victorian railway pub with high ceilings. *Times* Pub of the Year runner-up 2002, Nottinghamshire Food Pub of the Year 2002. Bar and restaurant food is available at lunchtime and evenings, and the restaurant menu includes a wide vegetarian range. Car park, garden, conference room. Accompanied children allowed in the restaurant and garden until 8pm only. Off Queens Road, behind Beeston railway station.

OPEN *11am–11pm Mon–Sat; 12–10.30pm Sun.*

CARLTON ON TRENT

The Great Northern Inn
Ossington Road, Carlton on Trent, Newark NG23 6NT
☎ *(01636) 821348* Ken and Fran Munro

 A freehouse with four pumps serving a range of real ales. No permanent beers but guests might include Timothy Taylor Landlord, Marston's Pedigree or a Bateman ale. Local micro-breweries supported whenever possible, including Springhead, Maypole and Brewsters.

A family-oriented pub with two bars, family room, restaurant, outside playground and large car park. CAMRA Pub of the Season for Spring 2000. Food served at lunchtime and evenings, including a children's menu. Traditional roasts available on Sundays. Located 100 yards from the A1, with easy return access to the A1.

OPEN *12–2.30pm and 5–11pm Mon–Thurs; all day Fri–Sun and bank holidays.*

CAYTHORPE

The Black Horse
29 Main Street, Caythorpe, Nottingham NG14 7ED
☎ *(0115) 966 3520* Miss Sharron Andrews

 A freehouse and brewpub with up to four hand-pulled beers on offer. Home-brewed Dover Beck Bitter always available, plus guest beers from micro-breweries such as Brewsters, Mallard, Oldershaw and Maypole, as well as brews from Adnams, Timothy Taylor and Black Sheep.

A traditional village pub with coal fires, two beamed bar areas, garden and car park. Freshly prepared food served at lunchtime and evenings (booking necessary for evenings). No hot food on Sunday lunchtimes, but fresh sandwiches are available. Good location for walkers and cyclists. No children, no music.

DOVER BECK BITTER 4% ABV

OPEN *12–2.30pm and 5.30–11pm Mon–Fri (closed Mon lunch except bank holidays); 12–2.30pm and 6–11pm Sat; 12–4pm and 7–10.30pm Sun (8–10.30pm in winter).*

COLSTON BASSETT

The Martins Arms Inn

School Lane, Colston Bassett NG12 3FD
☎ *(01949) 81361* Miss L Bryan

Seven beers always available (200 per year), with regulars including Marston's Best and Pedigree, Castle Rock Hemlock, Timothy Taylor Landlord and brews from Black Sheep and Bateman.

This village freehouse was built in 1700 as a farmhouse set in 100 acres owned by the local squire. Now set in one acre with original stables surrounded by National Trust parkland. Antique furniture, prints, old beams, Jacobean fireplace and bar. Bar and restaurant food available at lunchtime and every evening except Sunday. Les Routiers Gold Plate Award 2001. Five of the stables have been converted into an antiques and interiors shop (open 11am–7.30pm). Car park, large garden with croquet, children's room. Accommodation. On the A46 Newark to Leicester road.

OPEN *12–3pm and 6–11pm.*

DUNHAM ON TRENT

The Bridge Inn

Main Street, Dunham on Trent, Newark NG22 0TY
☎ *(01777) 228385* David Ollerenshaw

A freehouse with three pumps serving a range of ales, with local breweries featured when possible.

A traditional village pub with two bars, non-smoking restaurant and beer garden. Disabled access. Food available at lunchtime and evenings. No children.

OPEN *12–3pm and 5–11pm Mon–Fri; all day Sat–Sun.*

HOVERINGHAM

The Marquess of Granby

Main Street, Hoveringham NG14 7JH
☎ *(0115) 966 3080* David Cross

A freehouse serving two guests, changed three times a week, with beers from Caythorpe regularly featured. Oldershaw Old Boy and Badger Tanglefoot might also be on offer, or perhaps a celebration ale.

Old cottage-type country village pub with beams, log fires and garden. Food available. Pool and darts. Beer festivals planned for future – please call for details. Children allowed. Car park.

OPEN *11am–3pm and 5.30–11pm (10.30pm Sun).*

KIMBERLEY

The Nelson & Railway

Station Road, Kimberley NG16 2NR
☎ *(0115) 938 2177* Harry Burton

Three real ales always available including Hardys & Hansons Kimberley Best and Classic. Also an interesting guest from a range of six per year.

Opposite the Hardys & Hansons brewery. A Victorian, family-run village pub with dining area, including non-smoking section. Cask Marque accredited. Bar food available at lunchtime and evenings. Car park, garden, skittle alley and games. Accommodation. Children allowed in dining area for meals. One mile north of M1 junction 26. Website: www.nelsonandrailway.fsnet.co.uk.

OPEN *11.30am–11pm Mon–Sat; 12–10.30pm Sun.*

MANSFIELD

The Plough

180 Nottingham Road, Mansfield NG18 4AF
☎ *(01623) 623031* Lee Everett

Four real ales are always available, changed every few days. Examples include Wadworth 6X, Marston's Pedigree, Black Sheep Bitter and Best, Timothy Taylor Landlord and Morland Old Speckled Hen.

Welcoming, spacious pub situated on the outskirts of Mansfield. Quiz night on Sundays. Big-screen sports. Food served 12–7.30pm Mon–Sat and 12–5pm Sun. Car park. Restaurant facilities for babies/children.

OPEN *11am–11pm Mon–Sat; 12–10.30pm Sun.*

MAPPERLEY

The Duke of Cambridge

548 Woodborough Road, Mapperley NG3 5FH
☎ *(0115) 956 6150* David Hill

Caythorpe Dover Beck, Marston's Pedigree and Charles Wells Bombardier are always on offer, plus one guest.

Traditional one-room community pub, recently refurbished, with feature fireplace. Food available. Non-smoking area, function room. Children not allowed. Car park.

OPEN *12–3pm and 6–11pm Mon–Fri; 11am–11pm Sat; 12–10.30pm Sun.*

NEWARK

The Old Malt Shovel

25 North Gate, Newark NG24 1HD
☎ *(01636) 702036* Tim Purslow

 Timothy Taylor Landlord, Adnams Broadside, Everards Tiger and Caledonian Deuchars IPA usually available plus one or two guest beers. These may be from Brewsters, Cains, Black Sheep, York, Rudgate, Glentworth, Hop Back, Cottage, Morrells, Shepherd Neame, Oakham, Exmoor, Badger or many, many other independent breweries from around the UK.

Popular, 400-year-old pub situated 200 yards from the River Trent with lovely walks nearby. Home-cooked food available 12–2.30pm and 5.30–9.30pm Mon–Sat and 12–4pm Sun, both as bar meals and in a continental-style restaurant (non-smoking). Beer garden. Monthly meetings of the RAT (Real Ale Tasting) Society held in pub. Children welcome in the restaurant. Located midway between North Gate and Castle stations.

OPEN *11.30am–3pm and 5.30–11pm Mon–Tues; 11.30am–11pm Wed–Sat; 12–10.30pm Sun.*

NOTTINGHAM

The Bunkers Hill Inn

36–8 Hockley, Nottingham NG1 1FP
☎ *(0115) 910 0114* Jon Holland

 Marston's Pedigree, Ruddles County, Greene King Abbot and IPA and Morland Old Speckled Hen are the permanent beers here. Two guest pumps, with ales changed weekly, might offer Everards Lazy Daze, Caledonian Golden Promise, Fuller's ESP, local Nottingham ales or celebration ales.

Drinkers' pub on the outskirts of town, previously a Barclays Bank. Food is served from a limited menu 11am–2pm daily. TV, live music, function room. Beer festivals held in conjunction with Nottingham Beer Festival. Quiet children allowed. Situated next to Ice Stadium.

OPEN *11am–11pm Mon–Sat; 12–10.30pm Sun.*

Fellows

54 Canal Street, Nottingham NG1 7EH
☎ *(0115) 950 6795* Les Howard

 Home of the Fellows, Morton and Clayton Brewhouse Company, with Fellows Bitter and Posthaste always available, plus Timothy Taylor Landlord, Fuller's London Pride or a Castle Eden brew. Other guests served on four pumps could included brews from Cains or from local breweries such as Mallard.

A traditional pub leased from Whitbread with a brewery on the premises. One bar, garden area and restaurant. Food served 12–9.30pm Mon–Sat and 12–6pm Sun. Children allowed in the restaurant and garden only.

 FELLOWS BITTER 3.9% ABV
POSTHASTE

OPEN *All day, every day.*

The Forest Tavern

Mansfield Road, Nottingham NG1 3FT
☎ *(0115) 947 5650* Marianne Atkinson

Castle Rock Hemlock, Woodforde's Wherry, Greene King Abbot and Bateman Yella Belly (organic) always available. Range of continental bottled beers and draught products also served.

A traditional building on the outside, inside a continental café. Piped music. Night club at the back of premises. Food served until 10.30pm. No children.

OPEN *4–11pm Mon–Thurs; 12–11pm Fri–Sat; 12–10.30pm Sun.*

The Golden Fleece

105 Mansfield Road, Nottingham NG1 3FN
☎ *(0115) 947 2843* Steven Greatorex

 Marston's Pedigree, Cains Mild, Adnams Bitter and Greene King IPA permanently available, plus one guest cask ale from an independent brewery.

A nineteenth-century pub with an L-shaped bar and wooden floor. Roof garden available in summer. There is a 40-foot cellar with a glass trap-door visible from the pub. Live music Fri–Sat, folk music Sun, open-mike Mon–Tues. Food served 11am–8pm daily. Children allowed if eating.

OPEN *All day, every day.*

The Limelight Bar

Nottingham Playhouse, Wellington Circus,
Nottingham NG1 5AF
☎ (0115) 941 8467 Andrew Milton-Ayres

Bateman XB, Marston's Pedigree, Fuller's
London Pride and Adnams Bitter among
those beers always available, plus an ever-
changing range of guest beers.

Freshly cooked bar and restaurant food is
available from 12–8pm Mon–Sat and
12–2.30pm Sunday. Bookings available on
request. Large outdoor seating area. Function
room for hire. Children welcome in the
restaurant and outside. Adjacent to
Nottingham Playhouse and Nottingham
Albert Hall.

OPEN *11am–11pm Mon–Sat; 12–10.30pm Sun.*

Lincolnshire Poacher

161–3 Mansfield Road, Nottingham NG1 3FR
☎ (0115) 941 1584 Paul Montgomery

Bateman XB, XXXB and Victory plus
Marston's Pedigree at all times. Also up
to five guest beers, mostly from small
independent brewers such as Kelham Island,
Springhead, Shardlow, Highwood etc.

A traditional alehouse. No juke box, no
games machines, lots of conversation. Bar
food available at lunchtimes and evenings.
Parking and garden. Children allowed at the
management's discretion. Just north of the
city centre on the left-hand side. On the
A612 Newark to Southwell road.

OPEN *11am–3pm and 5–11pm Mon–Thurs;*
11am–11pm Fri–Sat; 12–10.30pm Sun.

O'Rourkes Bar

10 Raleigh Street, Nottingham
☎ (0115) 970 1092 Mrs Rhodes

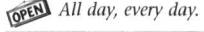Adnams Bitter and Greene King Abbot
Ale usually available.

Friendly, cosy pub with hand-painted
murals. Big-screen entertainment, karaoke,
pool and quiz nights. Food served 12–2.30pm
and 4–7pm Mon–Fri, 12–4pm Sat–Sun.
Children permitted only if eating. Car park.

OPEN *All day, every day.*

The Vat & Fiddle

Queensbridge Road, Nottingham NG2 1NB
☎ (0115) 985 0611 Jerry Divine

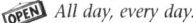The full range of Castle Rock ales brewed
and served on the premises. Plus guest
ales such as Archers Golden, Whim
Hartington IPA or Everards Tiger also
available. Micro-breweries favoured.

An old-fashioned alehouse, no machines,
TV or music. Small beer garden. Situated
on the edge of Nottingham, near the railway
station. Food served 12–3pm daily, plus
Mon–Sat 6–8pm. Children allowed if eating.

OPEN *All day, every day.*

Ye Olde Trip to Jerusalem

Brewhouse Yard, Castle Road, Nottingham
NG1 6AD
☎ (0115) 947 3171
Claire Underdown (Manager)

A Hardys & Hansons tied house with
Kimberley Mild, Classic and Best always
available, plus Marston's Pedigree. Other
seasonal Kimberley ales available as guests.

A three-bar pub built inside raw sandstone
caves in the Castle Rock. Two courtyards.
No music or juke box. Food served
11am–6pm Mon–Sat and 12–6pm Sun.
Children welcome during food service times,
in top bar, snug room or outside only.
Website: www.triptojerusalem.com.

OPEN *All day, every day.*

OLLERTON

The Olde Red Lion

Eakring Road, Nr Ollerton, Wellow NG22 0EG
☎ (01623) 861000 Vaughan Mitchell

A freehouse with Maypole Lion's Pride
and Shepherd Neame Spitfire always
available plus three guests, regularly
including Charles Wells Bombardier.

A 400-year-old country village pub. No
music or games. Food available at
lunchtime and evenings in a separate dining
area. Beer garden. Children allowed.

OPEN *11am–3.30pm and 6–11pm Mon–Fri;*
11.30am–4pm and 6–11pm Sat; all day
Sun. (Hours may vary during the winter.)

RADCLIFFE ON TRENT

The Royal Oak

Main Road, Radcliffe on Trent NG12 2FD
☎ (0115) 933 3798 Gaynor Taylor

Up to 10 brews available including
Marston's Pedigree, Timothy Taylor
Landlord, Morland Old Speckled Hen and
Castle Eden Ale. Also various guest beers
throughout the year, including Exmoor Gold
and Black Sheep Bitter.

An old, traditional-style pub in the village
centre. Cosy lounge and extended public
bar, which includes pool table and large-
screen TV. No food available at present.
Large, private car park.

OPEN *11am–11pm Mon–Sat; 12–10.30pm Sun.*

RADFORD

The Plough Inn

17 St Peter's Street, Radford NG7 3EN
☎ *(0115) 942 2649* PW Darby

Home of the Nottingham Brewery, with Rock Bitter, Mild, Legend, Bullion and EPA brewed on the premises and always available. Up to five rotating guests, either own brews or guests from micro-breweries.

Dating from 1792 but rebuilt, this is a traditional pub with two bars, a dining area and real fires. Food available lunchtimes and evenings including Sunday roasts. Well-behaved children allowed. Beer garden. Car park. Located off Ilkeston Road going out of Nottingham.

ROCK BITTER 3.8% ABV
An original Nottingham Brewery recipe, first brewed in the 1800s to refresh the factory workers of the city.

ROCK MILD 3.8% ABV
The complement to the bitter, a smooth dark biscuity flavour.

LEGEND 4.0% ABV
Traditional amber session ale, malty and hoppy.

EXTRA PALE ALE (EPA) 4.2% ABV
Light-coloured, well-balanced smooth ale.

DREADNOUGHT 4.5% ABV
Rich ruby-coloured premium bitter.

BULLION 4.7% ABV
Single malt, lighter than its ABV suggests.

OATMEAL STOUT 4.8% ABV
Classic oatmeal stout.

NOTTINGHAM SUPREME 5.2% ABV
Premium beer, easy-drinking strong ale.

 12–3pm and 5–11pm Mon–Wed; 12–11pm Thurs–Sat; 12–10.30pm Sun.

RETFORD

Market Hotel

West Carr Road, Ordsall, Nr Retford DN22 7SN
☎ *(01777) 703278* Graham Brunt

Exmoor Gold, Greene King Abbot Ale, Marston's Pedigree and Bitter, Timothy Taylor Landlord, Thwaites Bitter and Marston's Head Brewer's Choice usually available, plus three guest ales from local brewers.

Family-run traditionally decorated pub. Bar food available at lunchtime and evenings. Car park, conservatory restaurant, large banqueting suite. Children allowed. Located two minutes through the subway from the railway station.

 11am–3pm and 6–11pm Mon–Fri; all day Sat; 12–4pm and 7–10.30pm Sun.

UPPER BROUGHTON

The Golden Fleece

Main Road, Upper Broughton LE14 3BG
☎ *(01664) 822262* Andrew Carnachan

Belvoir Beaver and Marston's Pedigree usually available.

A traditional family pub with beer garden and children's play area, situated on the edge of the Vale of Belvoir. Live jazz on the last Sunday of every month. Food served all day, every day. Car park.

 11am–11pm Mon–Sat; 12–10.30pm Sun.

UPTON

Cross Keys

Main Street, Upton, Nr Newark NG23 5SY
☎ *(01636) 813269* Mr and Mrs Sharp

A selection of between two and five cask ales available at all times.

A seventeenth-century listed freehouse and restaurant. Open fires, beams, brasses etc. The former dovecote has been converted into a restaurant, the tap room has carved pews from Newark parish church. Home-cooked bar food, with an emphasis on Mediterranean-style dishes, fresh fish and tapas, is available at lunchtime and evenings. A la carte restaurant with separate menu open Friday and Saturday evenings and Sunday lunch. Car park, garden, children's area.

 11.30am–2.30pm and 5.30–11pm Mon–Sat; 12–2.30pm and 7–10.30pm Sun.

WORKSOP

Mallard

Worksop Railway Station, Station Approach, Worksop S81 7AG
☎ *(01909) 530757* Sarah Cadman

No permanent beers here, just two regularly changing guests from micro- and small breweries.

A Grade II listed building, part of Worksop Station. Occasional beer festivals are held in the cellar bar. Car park. Sandwiches and snacks available. No children.

 5–11pm Mon–Thurs; 2–11pm Fri; 12–11pm Sat; 12–4pm Sun (closed Sun evening).

Manor Lodge Hotel

*Manor Lodge, off Mansfield Road, Worksop
S80 3DL*
☎ *(01909) 474177* Miss D Edington

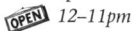Daleside Old Legover and Greengrass,
and Black Sheep Bitter always available,
plus two guest beers.

A freehouse in a Grade I listed building, a
sixteenth-century Elizabethan manor.
Features pub, restaurants and function
rooms. Food available 12–9pm daily, with
Sunday carvery. Accommodation. Murder-
mystery nights, medieval banquets, weddings
and christenings catered for. Follow the
Manor Lodge tourist sign on the A60 into
Worksop.

OPEN *12–11pm.*

YOU TELL US

* *The Red Lodge,* Fosse Way, Screveton
* *Tom Hoskins,* Queen's Bridge Road,
  Nottingham

Places Featured:

Bampton
Bloxham
Bodicote
Brightwell-cum-Sotwell
Burford
Chadlington
Chalgrove
Charlbury
Childrey
Chipping Norton
Clifton
Cowley
Crowell
East Hendred
Eynsham
Faringdon
Fewcott
Fifield

Great Tew
Henley-on-Thames
Highmoor
Murcott
North Leigh
Oxford
Ramsden
Ratley
Shutford
South Moreton
Sparsholt
Stoke Lyne
Thame
Wantage
West Hanney
Witney
Woodcote

THE BREWERIES

HENRY'S BUTCHER'S YARD BREWERY

c/o JR Kench, 25 High Street, Chipping Norton OX7 5AD
☎ *(01608) 645334*

 CHIPPY BEST 3.8% ABV
Malty and bitter, very pale, made using Maris Otter malt.

THE HOOK NORTON BREWERY CO. LTD

The Brewery, Hook Norton, Banbury OX15 5NY
☎ *(01608) 737210*
www.hooknortonbrewery.co.uk

 MILD 3.0% ABV
Easy-drinking mild.
BEST BITTER 3.4% ABV
Good well-hopped session bitter.
OLD HOOKY 4.6% ABV
Complex. Rounded and highly drinkable.
DOUBLE STOUT 4.8% ABV
Full-bodied and smooth.
HAYMAKER 5.0% ABV
Smooth and full-bodied.
TWELVE DAYS 5.5% ABV
Nutty, malt flavour. Dec–Jan.
Plus seasonal beers.

OLD LUXTERS WINERY AND BREWERY

Vineyard, Winery and Brewhouse, Hambledon, Henley-on-Thames RG9 6JW
☎ *(01491) 638330*
www.luxters.co.uk

 BARN ALE BITTER 4.0% ABV
Refreshing, well-hopped session bitter.
BARN ALE SPECIAL 4.5% ABV
Golden and smooth.
Plus occasional brews.

OXFORD BREWERY

PO Box 256, Kidlington OX5 2FR
☎ *(01865) 841836*
www.oxfordbrewery.com

 **CAVALIER BITTER 3.9% ABV**
OXFORD DRAUGHT ALE 4.4% ABV

W H BRAKSPEAR & SONS PLC

The Brewery, New Street, Henley-on-Thames
RG9 2BU
☎ *(01491) 570200*
www.real-ale-guide.co.uk/brakspear

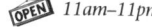 **MILD 3.0% ABV**
Sweet and full-flavoured.
BITTER 3.4% ABV
Session bitter with hops throughout.
GENERATION 4.0% ABV
FIRST LIGHT 4.3% ABV
May–June.
STEAMING ON 4.4% ABV
Sept–Oct.
COPPER ALE 4.8% ABV
DOUBLE STOUT 4.8% ABV
Jan–Feb.
HAYMAKER 5.0% ABV
Jul–Aug.
TWELVE DAYS 5.5% ABV
Nov–Dec.

THE WYCHWOOD BREWERY CO. LTD

Eagle Maltings, The Crofts, Witney OX8 7AZ
☎ *(01993) 702574*
www.wychwood.co.uk

SHIRES XXX 3.7% ABV
Fruit and malt flavour throughout.
FIDDLER'S ELBOW 4.1% ABV
HOBGOBLIN 4.5% ABV
Rich roast malt flavour with some fruit and
hops.

Plus seasonal and occasional brews.

THE PUBS

BAMPTON

The Romany Inn

Bridge Street, Bampton OX18 2HA
☎ *(01993) 850237* Trevor Johnson

Archers Village always available, plus
monthly promotions of guest beers.

A seventeenth-century Grade II listed pub
with Saxon arches in the cellar. Bar and
restaurant food is available at lunchtime and
evenings. Car park, garden, picnic tables and
children's play area. Accommodation.
Bampton is situated on the A4095 Witney to
Faringdon road. The pub is in the centre of
the village.

 11am–11pm.

BLOXHAM

The Red Lion Inn

High Street, Bloxham, Banbury OX15 4LX
☎ *(01295) 720352* Mr and Mrs Cooper

A freehouse with Wadworth 6X and
Adnams Best always available, plus two
guests such as Morland Old Speckled Hen or
something from breweries such as
Hampshire, Wychwood or Fuller's. Session
bitters are generally popular.

A two-bar village pub with large garden and
car park. Food served at lunchtime and
evenings. Children very welcome if eating:
children's menu and play area. Occasional
'children's days', with bouncy castles, etc.

11.30am–2.30pm and 7–11pm Mon–Fri;
12–3pm and 7–11pm Sat–Sun
(10.30 Sun).

BODICOTE

The Plough Inn

Goose Street, Bodicote, Banbury OX15 4BZ
☎ *(01295) 262327* JW Blencowe

Home of the Bodicote Brewery, which
was established in 1982, with Bodicote
Bitter and No. 9 always available, plus
seasonal specials.

A small village pub with separate lounge/
diner and saloon. Early Tudor building,
'Cruck' cottage design. Food served at
lunchtime and evenings. Children allowed if
eating.

 BODICOTE BITTER 3.9% ABV
3 GOSLINGS 4.1% ABV
A summer ale, light in colour.
BODICOTE NO.9 4.3% ABV
PORTER 4.5% ABV
A black porter.
XXX 6.0% ABV
A winter ale.

 11am–3pm and 6–11pm.

BRIGHTWELL-CUM-SOTWELL

The Red Lion

Brightwell-cum-Sotwell
☎ *(01491) 837373* William Prince

Something from Brakspear, West Berkshire and Hook Norton plus a guest beer often from West Berkshire usually available.

Fifteenth-century thatched freehouse with tables at the front and in the courtyard. Garden and restaurant area. Food served lunchtimes and evenings Tues–Sat, lunchtimes only Sun. Children welcome in the beer garden or restaurant area at lunchtimes only. Car park.

OPEN *6–11pm Mon; 11am–3pm and 6–11pm Tues–Sat; 12–3pm and 7–10.30pm Sun.*

BURFORD

The Lamb Inn

Sheep Street, Burford OX18 4LR
☎ *(01993) 823155* Richard De Wolf

Wadworth 6X, Hook Norton Best Bitter and Badger Dorset Bitter regularly available.

A traditional Cotswold inn with log fires and gleaming copper and brass. Tranquil walled garden with a profusion of cottage-garden flowers. Bar food available Mon–Sat lunchtimes; restaurant open 7–9pm Mon–Sat, 12.30–3pm and 7–9pm Sun. Smaller portions available for children. Residents' car park. Descending Burford High Street, take the first turning on the left.

OPEN *11am–2.30pm and 6–11pm Mon–Sat; 12–2.30pm and 7–10.30pm Sun.*

CHADLINGTON

The Tite Inn

Mill End, Chadlington OX7 3NY
☎ *(01608) 676475* Michael Willis

Tite Inn Bitter, brewed by Brakspear, always available, plus three guest beers (50 per year) which may include Fuller's London Pride, Charles Wells Bombardier, Young's Special or Brakspear Special. Draught cider, usually Biddenden's, also served.

A sixteenth-century Cotswold stone pub with superb country views. Bar and restaurant food is available at lunchtime and evenings. Car park, garden and garden room. Children allowed. Chadlington is just over two miles south of Chipping Norton off the A361. Website: www.titeinn.com.

OPEN *12–3pm and 6.30–11pm Tues–Sun; closed Mon (except bank holidays).*

CHALGROVE

The Red Lion

High Street, Chalgrove, Oxford OX44 7SS
☎ *(01865) 890625* Jonathan Hewitt

A freehouse with Fuller's London Pride and an Adnams brew always available. Plus guests such as Timothy Taylor Landlord or Fuller's seasonal ales.

A rambling village pub with a stream and log fires. A separate dining area serves homemade food every lunchtime and evening except Sundays. Beer garden. Children allowed.

OPEN *12–3pm and 6–11pm Mon–Sat; 12–3pm and 7–10.30pm Sun.*

CHARLBURY

The Rose & Crown

Market Street, Charlbury, Chipping Norton OX7 3PL
☎ *(01608) 810103* Mr T Page

Archers Best and Fuller's London Pride always available plus three guest beers (100 per year) from breweries such as Lichfield, Coach House, Smiles, Butcombe, Marston's, Timothy Taylor, Robinson's, Badger and Hook Norton. Range of Belgian bottled beers also available.

A popular one-room Victorian pub with a courtyard. No food. Parking, garden and children's room. Located in the town centre. Website: www.topbeerpub.co.uk.

OPEN *12–11pm Mon–Fri; 11am–11pm Sat; 12–10.30pm Sun.*

CHILDREY

Hatchet

Childrey, Nr Wantage
☎ *(01235) 751213* Ian James Shaw

Morland Original Bitter usually available, plus four guest beers often from Adnams, Brains, Brakspear, Charles Wells, Fuller's, Gale's, Greene King, Hook Norton, Mansfield, Marston's, Ridleys, Shepherd Neame, Wadworth, Young's, Jennings, Vale, West Berkshire or Butts.

Welcoming one-bar village pub. Food served 12–2pm daily. Car park. Garden play area for children.

OPEN *12–2.30pm and 7–11pm Mon–Fri; 12–3pm and 7–11pm Sat; 12–4pm and 7–11pm Sun.*

CHIPPING NORTON

The Bell Inn
West Street, Chipping Norton OX7 5ER
☎ *(01608) 642521* Brian Galbraith

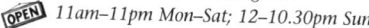 A range of real ales usually available, with the emphasis on quality rather than quantity.

Community local in an old stone building, with beams and a wooden floor. Two bars (sports bar and lounge), pool, darts. Food available from a limited menu. Children allowed in the garden only. Car park. On the road from Churchill to Bledington.

OPEN *11am–11pm Mon–Sat; 12–10.30pm Sun.*

Stones
Market Place, Chipping Norton OX7 5NH
☎ *(01608) 644466* Brian and Jan Galbraith

 A freehouse with Greene King IPA constantly available, plus two guests, changed every fortnight. There is always a beer at 4% ABV such as North Cotswold Genesis, Goff's Jouster or Hook Norton Generation, plus one at 4.3–5% ABV, from breweries such as Eccleshall (a Slaters brew), Wye Valley, St George's and North Cotswold.

Town pub in a listed stone building, with modern interior and traditional values! Annual beer festival (phone for details). Food is available and there is a non-smoking dining area. A good selection of coffees is available. The pub's terrace overlooks the marketplace. Car parking available. Children allowed.

OPEN *10am–11pm (10.30pm Sun).*

CLIFTON

The Duke of Cumberland's Head
Clifton OX15 0PE
☎ *(01869) 338534*

Four beers always available including Hook Norton Best, Adnams Bitter and Wadworth 6X. Guests may include Hampshire King Alfred.

Built in the late 1600s, this thatched Oxfordshire village pub serves bar and restaurant food. Car park, attractive gardens, accommodation. Children allowed.

OPEN *12–3pm and 6.30–11pm.*

COWLEY

The Original Swan
Oxford Road, Cowley OX4 2LF
☎ *(01865) 778888*
Andre and Debbie Lemasurier

Tied to Arkells, with Arkells 3B and 2B always on offer, plus two guests, often seasonals from Arkells, or celebration ales.

Community pub in a building dating from 1902, with two bars, function room and patio. Food available. Occasional live music. Accompanied children allowed. Car park.

OPEN *12–3pm and 6–11pm Mon–Fri; 11am–11pm Sat; 12–10.30pm Sun.*

CROWELL

The Shepherd's Crook
The Green, Crowell, Nr Chinnor OX9 4RR
☎ *(01844) 351431* Mr Scowen

Hook Norton Best, Bateman XB, Batham Best, Timothy Taylor Landlord and Donnington Best usually available.

A quiet, one-bar country pub, no music or games. Beer garden. Food served 12–2.30pm and 7–9.30pm. Fish is a speciality. Bookings taken. Children allowed.

OPEN *11.30am–3pm and 5–11pm Mon–Fri; all day Sat–Sun.*

EAST HENDRED

Eyston Arms
High Street, East Hendred, Wantage OX12 8JY
☎ *(01235) 833320* Bernadine Winfield

Wadworth 6X and Fuller's London Pride permanently available, plus guest ales form West Berkshire, Cottage and Wye Valley breweries.

Traditional, beamed village pub with log fire in winter and non-smoking tea room. Darts, dominoes, pool and Aunt Sally. Car park. Bar snacks such as toasties, jacket potatoes and pies available all day. Children welcome until 7pm.

OPEN *11am–11pm Mon–Sat; 12–10.30pm Sun.*

EYNSHAM

The Talbot Inn

Oxford Road, Eynsham OX21 4BT
☎ *(01865) 881348* Charles and Arthur Biggers

 An Arkells pub with 3B and Kingsdown permanently offered, plus one seasonal Arkells ale.

Family-run country pub, recently refurbished, in an eighteenth-century Cotswold stone building, with one bar and a partitioned restaurant. Bar food and an à la carte menu available every lunchtime and evening, with the emphasis on fresh local produce and fresh fish. Lawn area with seating at front. Three letting rooms. Children allowed.

OPEN *11am–3pm and 5.30–11pm (10.30pm Sun).*

FARINGDON

The Bell

Market Place, Faringdon SN7 7HP
☎ *(01367) 240534*
Andrew and Angela MacLachlan MBII

 Wadworth 6X and IPA always available, plus a seasonal Wadworth ale such as Old Timer, Summersault and Malt and Hops, with JCB served inbetween!

A sixteenth-century coaching inn, located in the centre of town, with cobbled courtyard recently fully refurbished. AIR-Charter compliant, with smoking in designated areas, ventilation and filtration. Well-known for its floral displays in summer at the back of the hotel. A la carte restaurant and bar food is available at lunchtime and evenings. Eight en-suite bedrooms, car park, children welcome. Website: www.bell-hotel-faringdon.co.uk.

OPEN *10.30am–11pm Mon–Sat; 12–3pm and 7–10.30pm Sun.*

FEWCOTT

The White Lion

Fewcott, Bicester OX6 9NZ
☎ *(01869) 346639* Paul and Carol King

 Four regularly changing beers which may include brews from Hook Norton, Wadworth, Bateman, Ash Vine, Archers, Rectory, Moor or Holt.

Cotswold stone, country village pub with large beer garden. No food. Car park. Children welcome.

OPEN *7–11.30pm Mon–Fri; 12–11.30pm Sat; 12–4pm and 7–10.30pm Sun.*

FIFIELD

Merrymouth Inn

Stow Road, Fifield OX7 6HR
☎ *(01993) 831652* Mr Andrew Flaherty

 A freehouse with Hook Norton Best and one regularly changing guest ale always available.

An old-style, one-bar pub and restaurant with garden. Large non-smoking areas. Accommodation. Food available 12–2pm and 6.30–9pm. Children allowed.

OPEN *11.30am–2.30pm and 6–11pm Mon–Sat; 12–2.30pm and 7–10.30pm Sun.*

GREAT TEW

The Falkland Arms

Great Tew OX7 4DB
☎ *(01608) 683653*
Paul Barlow-Heal and Sarah-Jane Courage

 Seven beers available from hand pumps at any one time from a range of about 350 per year. Wadworth Henry's IPA, 6X and JCB all favoured. Smaller brewers and some regionals preferred. Also a selection of country wines and draught cider.

A sixteenth-century Oxfordshire village inn with a vast inglenook fireplace, smooth flagstone floor, high-backed settles, oak beams and panelling and sparkling brasses. Bar food 12–2pm daily. Evening food served in a small dining room 7–8pm Mon–Sat, booking essential. Beer garden to the rear of the pub with picturesque view over the Great Tew Estate. Live folk music every Sunday evening. En-suite accommodation. Filled clay pipes and snuff for sale, in keeping with the picture of a traditional English country inn. Off the B4022, seven miles east of Chipping Norton.

OPEN *11.30am–2.30pm and 6–11pm Mon–Sat; 12–3pm and 7–10.30pm Sun. Open all day Sat–Sun in summer.*

HENLEY-ON-THAMES

Bird in Hand

61 Greys Road, Henley-on-Thames RG9 1SB
☎ *(01491) 575775* Graham Steward

 A freehouse with Brakspear Mild and Bitter and Fuller's London Pride always available, plus guests on two hand pumps. Examples include Timothy Taylor Landlord, Coniston Bluebird and Mordue Workie Ticket.

An old-fashioned one-bar pub. No music, fruit machines or pool table, not even a till! Large garden. Food served at lunchtime only.

OPEN *11.30am–2.30pm and 5–11pm Mon–Fri; all day Sat–Sun.*

The Horse & Groom

New Street, Henley-on-Thames RG9 2BT
☎ (01491) 575719 Martin Constable

 A Greene King house with IPA and Morland Old Speckled Hen always available. Up to three weekly changing guests from any independent brewery in the UK.

A three-bar pub with a large garden, serving bar food every lunchtime. Children allowed in the garden only.

(OPEN) *11am–11pm Mon–Sat; 12–10.30pm Sun.*

HIGHMOOR

The Dog & Duck

Nettlebed, Highmoor, Henley-on-Thames RG9 5DL
☎ (01491) 641261 Mr Taylor

 A Brakspear tenancy with Brakspear Bitter and Special permanently available.

One-bar country pub with all-over dining area and garden. Food available. Children allowed.

(OPEN) *12–2pm and 7–11pm (10.30pm Sun); closed Mon.*

MURCOTT

The Nut Tree Inn

Murcott, Kidlington OX5 2RE
☎ (01865) 331253 Gordon Evans

 Wadworth Henry's IPA and 6X served, plus a guest beer, perhaps from Wychwood, Hook Norton, Black Sheep or Charles Wells.

Quaint, white, thatched pub with duck pond, set in a peaceful hamlet. Noted for good steaks and fresh fish. Food served 12–2pm and 6.30–9.30pm Mon–Sat. No food Sun. Car park. Children welcome in the conservatory or outside.

(OPEN) *11am–3pm and 6.30–11pm Mon–Sat; 12–3pm and 7–10.30pm Sun.*

NORTH LEIGH

The Woodman Inn

New Yatt Road, North Leigh, Nr Witney OX8 6TT
☎ (01993) 881790 Colin Dickenson

 Wadworth 6X, Hook Norton Best and Wychwood Shires always available plus two guest beers (150 per year) from breweries such as Adnams, Shepherd Neame, Timothy Taylor, Cotleigh and Charles Wells. The Oxfordshire beer festival takes place here twice a year.

A local village pub on the edge of town, overlooking the Windrush valley. Bar food served at lunchtime and evenings. Car park and garden. Children allowed. Accommodation. Located off the A4095 Witney to Woodstock road.

(OPEN) *12–2.30pm and 6–11pm Mon–Fri; 12–3pm and 6–11pm Sat; 12–10.30pm Sun.*

OXFORD

The Eagle Tavern

28 Magdalen Road, Oxford OX4 1RB
☎ (01865) 204842 Mr and Mrs Tom Quinn

 Arkells 2B and 3B are the permanent beers at this Arkells house.

A refurbished pub in an old building on the outskirts or town, with one bar and garden. Bar snacks available. Live music occasionally. Children allowed if kept under control.

(OPEN) *11.30am–3pm and 7–11pm (10.30pm Sun).*

Folly Bridge Inn

38 Abingdon Road, Oxford OX1 4PD
☎ (01865) 790106
Kelvin and Marianne Stevens

 A Wadworth house with 6X, IPA, JCB and seasonal guest beers always available, plus Badger Tanglefoot.

A traditional English pub on the edge of Oxford. Disabled access, patio. Food served at lunchtime and evenings in an environment as smoke-free as possible (there are big smoke extractors). Children allowed.

(OPEN) *All day, every day.*

Turf Tavern

4 Bath Place, Oxford OX1 3SU
☎ (01865) 243235 Darren Kent

Eleven pumps serve a range of real ales, with favourites including Morland Old Speckled Hen, Gale's HSB, Wadworth 6X and Greene King Abbot, but also more unusual beers from independent breweries around the country (hundreds of different brews every year).

One of the oldest pubs in Oxford, this is a country-style pub in the city centre. Two bars plus outside alehouse. Three patios. Food available 12–7.30pm. Children allowed.

(OPEN) *11am–11pm Mon–Sat; 12–10.30pm Sun.*

Wharf House

14 Butterwyke Place, St Ebbes, Oxford
☎ *(01865) 246752* Tony Flatman

Hook Norton Best Bitter and RCH Pitchfork usually available plus two regularly changing guest beers, perhaps from Rebellion, Vale, York, Holt, Moor, Beowulf or Fat God's. Large range of foreign beers also stocked.

Small, basic but friendly pub on the edge of the city centre, close to the Thames. Sandwiches available at lunchtime. Small car park. Children welcome in the outside seating area, may be allowed inside during bad weather at lunchtime and early evening. Situated at the junction of Thames and Speedwell streets.

 11am–3pm and 5.30–11pm Mon–Fri (open 6pm in winter); 11am–11pm Sat; 12–4pm and 7–10.30pm Sun.

RAMSDEN

The Royal Oak

High Street, Ramsden OX7 3AW
☎ *(01993) 868213* John Oldham

Hook Norton Best and Archers Golden always available plus a guest (40 per year) such as Brakspear Special, Banks's Bitter, Caledonian 80/- and Titanic Premium.

A sixteenth-century pub, a former coaching inn, situated in a small village. Bar and restaurant food available. Car park and garden. Ramsden is halfway between Witney and Charlbury off the B4022.

 11.30am–2.30pm and 6.30–11pm Mon–Sat; 12–3pm and 7–10.30pm Sun.

RATLEY

The Rose & Crown

Featherbow Lane, Ratley, Nr Banbury OX15 6DS
☎ *(01295) 678148* Nigel Folker

A freehouse always offering Charles Wells Eagle IPA and Bombardier and Morland Old Speckled Hen, plus one guest beer.

Small, traditional pub, reputedly dating from 1098. Food served 12–2.30pm and 7–9.30pm (Sundays until 8.30pm). Children are welcome, but no special facilities. The pub is on the MacMillan Way, so walkers are also welcome. Bed and breakfast available (two rooms). Car park. Ratley is a small, picturesque village off the A422 Stratford Road, and the pub is at the far end of the village.

 12–3pm and 6.30–11pm (10.30pm Sun).

The George & Dragon

Church Lane, Shutford, Banbury OX15 6PG
☎ *(01295) 780320* Allison Law

Hook Norton Best and Fuller's London Pride usually available, plus a guest such as Adnam's Best, Timothy Taylor Landlord, Greene King IPA and Black Sheep Bitter.

A traditional country pub with log-burning stove in winter, beer garden in summer. Food available in an informal restaurant 12–2pm and 6–9.15pm Tues–Sat and 12–3pm Sun. Children allowed before 9pm although there are no special facilities. To find Shutford, take the Shipston on Stour road from Banbury.

 12–3pm and 6–11pm Tues–Sat; 12–10.30pm Sun (closed Mondays).

SOUTH MORETON

The Crown Inn

High Street, South Moreton, Nr Didcot OX11 9AG
☎ *(01235) 812262* Mr and Mrs Cook

Wadworth IPA and 6X, Badger Tanglefoot and Adnams Best always available.

An attractive village pub. Bar and restaurant food available. Car park and garden. Children allowed. The village is signposted from both Didcot and Wallingford.

 11am–3pm and 5.30–11pm.

SPARSHOLT

The Star Inn

Watery Lane, Sparsholt, Nr Wantage OX12 9PL
☎ *(01235) 751539* Alan Fowles

Morland Original always on offer, plus two weekly changing guests, which regularly include Shepherd Neame Spitfire, Fuller's London Pride and Brakspear Special. Other guests served have included Branscombe Vale Summa That and beers from Cottage.

A 400-year-old country inn with beams and fireplaces. Food is available, and there is a 30-seater dining room. Eight en-suite letting rooms, converted barn, live music occasionally. Children and dogs allowed.

 12–3pm and 6–11pm Mon–Fri; 11am–11pm Sat; 12–10.30pm Sun.

STOKE LYNE

The Peyton Arms
Stoke Lyne, Bicester OX27 8SD
☎ *(01869) 345285* Charlie Edwards

 Hook Norton Mild, Best Bitter, Generation, Old Hooky and a seasonal beer usually available.

Friendly, unspoilt pub situated in a small village. All beers are gravity dispensed, Best Bitter from the wood. Large garden. Bar snacks and specialist sausages available lunchtimes only. Car park. Children and dogs welcome.

OPEN *6–11pm Mon; 12–2.30pm and 6.30–11pm Tues–Thurs; 12–2.30pm and 6–11pm Fri; 12–11pm Sat; 12–10.30pm Sun.*

THAME

The Abingdon Arms
21 Cornmarket, Thame OX9 2BL
☎ *(01844) 216116* W Bonner

 Wadworth 6X, Hook Norton Bitter and Fuller's London Pride usually available, plus two guest beers which may include Vale Wychert Ale or Notley Ale, Hampshire Lionheart or Fuller's ESB.

A sixteenth-century coaching inn which was extensively rebuilt after a fire in 1991. Separate Sky TV, non-smoking section and log fires. Food served lunchtimes and evenings Mon–Fri and all day Sat–Sun. Children welcome, with nappy-changing facilities and high chairs provided, plus play equipment and sand pit. Car park.

OPEN *11am–11pm (10.30pm Sun).*

The Swan Hotel
9 Upper High Street, Thame OX9 3ER
☎ *(01844) 261211* Sue Turnbull

 One Brakspear and one Hook Norton brew usually available plus two guest beers perhaps from Eccleshall, Castle Rock, Hampshire, Rebellion, Timothy Taylor, Shepherd Neame, Clark's, Wye Valley, Flagship, Wychwood, Kitchen and many more.

A sixteenth-century coaching inn situated in the heart of Thame and retaining many original features. Medieval restaurant, oak-beamed bar, log fire, comfortable Chesterfields and seven en-suite bedrooms. Food served lunchtimes and evenings Sun–Fri and all day Sat. Large, free public car park close by. Children permitted before 8pm away from main bar area, but there are no special facilities.

OPEN *11am–11pm Mon–Sat (10.30pm Sun).*

WANTAGE

The Royal Oak Inn
Newbury Street, Wantage OX12 8DF
☎ *(01235) 763129* Paul Hexter

 West Berkshire Brewery's Dr Hexter's Healer, Dr Hexter's Wedding Ale, Maggs' Magnificent Mild and Wadworth 6X permanently available, plus up to six guests. Over 100 malt whiskies also served, including Dr Hexter's Medicinal Malt.

Fair deals and no frills at this freehouse. Navy paraphernalia decorates the bar. CAMRA Pub of the Year 2000 for Berkshire, Buckinghamshire and Oxfordshire. Accommodation.

OPEN *5.30–11pm Mon–Fri; 12–2.30pm and 7–11pm Sat; 12–2pm and 7–10.30pm Sun.*

WEST HANNEY

The Lamb Inn
West Hanney OX12 0LA
☎ *(01235) 868917* Peter Hall

 A freehouse with Young's Special, Oakham Jeffrey Hudson Bitter and Shepherd Neame Spitfire always available, plus two guests changed four times a week from smaller and micro-breweries generally. The landlord tries to stock special beers and not repeat them.

A traditional freehouse. One bar, split into two, children's play area, garden. No juke box, but live music once a week. Annual beer festival on August bank holiday. Food served at lunchtime and evenings. Children allowed in the back room and garden.

OPEN *11.30am–2.30pm and 6–11pm.*

House of Windsor

31 West End, Witney OX8 6NQ
☎ *(01993) 704277*
Prue, Stuart and David Thomas

 Timothy Taylor Landlord, Hook Norton Best and Fuller's London Pride permanently available, plus one constantly changing guest ale which could be from any independent brewery. Regular examples include beers from Wadworth, Shepherd Neame, Archers, Gale's, Jennings and Hop Back.

No machines, no pool or darts in this friendly pub. Coal fire in winter. Bar and restaurant food is available Wed–Sat evenings and Sat–Sun lunchtimes. Large beer garden. Children allowed. Off the A40 and straight across two mini-roundabouts.

OPEN *6–11pm Mon–Fri; 12–3pm and 6–11pm Sat; 12–4.30pm and 6–10.30pm Sun.*

The Highwayman

Exlade Street, Woodcote, Nr Reading RG8 0UE
☎ *(01491) 682020*

 Ever-changing selection of guest beers (60–70 per year) served, which could include Fuller's London Pride, Wadworth 6X, Gibbs Mew Bishop's Tipple, Adnams Broadside, Timothy Taylor Landlord, Hook Norton Old Hooky, Shepherd Neame Spitfire or something from Rebellion.

Rambling seventeenth-century country inn with two-roomed bar, beams and open fire. Bar and restaurant food available at lunchtime and evenings. Car park, garden, accommodation. Children allowed in restaurant. Signposted from the A4074 Reading to Wallingford Road.

OPEN *11am–11pm Mon–Sat; 12–10.30pm Sun.*

YOU TELL US

* *The Old Anchor Inn,* St Helen Wharf, Abingdon
* *The Red Lion,* Peppard Common, Rotherfield Peppard

Places Featured:

Aston on Clun
Atcham
Bishops Castle
Bouldon
Bridgnorth
Cardington
Church Aston
Cleobury Mortimer
Clun
Coalbrookdale
Craven Arms
Ellerdine Heath
Ironbridge
Little Stretton
Lowtown

Much Wenlock
Munslow
Oakengates
Oldwoods
Oswestry
Pontesbury
Port Hill
Ratlinghope
Shifnal
Shrewsbury
Upper Farmcote
Wellington
Welsh Frankton
Wistanstow
Worfield

THE BREWERIES

HANBY ALES LTD

New Brewery, Aston Park, Soulton Road, Wem SY4 5SD
☎ *(01939) 232432*

 BLACK MAGIC MILD 3.3% ABV
Dry, dark and malty award winner.
DRAWWELL BITTER 3.9% ABV
Light, golden medium-strength beer.
ALL SEASONS ALE 4.2% ABV
Quenching, balanced with good hoppiness.
RAINBOW CHASER 4.3% ABV
Rounded, lagerish style.
SHROPSHIRE STOUT 4.4% ABV
Four malts produce powerful flavours.
WEM SPECIAL 4.4% ABV
Straw-coloured and well-rounded.
CASCADE BITTER 4.5% ABV
Very pale, with clean, refreshing hoppiness.
GOLDEN HONEY 4.5% ABV
Brewed with Australian honey.
SCORPIO PORTER 4.5% ABV
Complex coffee and chocolate flavours.
PREMIUM 4.6% ABV
Amber-coloured, rounded and malty.
OLD WEMIAN ALE 4.9% ABV
TAVERNERS ALE 5.3% ABV
Smooth, fruity full-bodied old ale.
CHERRY BOMB BITTER 6.0% ABV
Rich, maraschino cherry taste.
JOY BRINGER BITTER 6.0% ABV
Powerful ginger beer. Too easy to drink.
NUTCRACKER BITTER 6.0% ABV
Full-bodied, balanced and distinctive.
Plus seasonal ales and occasional brews.

THE SALOPIAN BREWING CO LTD

67 Mytton Oak Road, Shrewsbury SY3 8UQ
☎ *(01743) 248414*

 SHROPSHIRE GOLD 3.8% ABV
Pale, with refreshing fruit and hop flavours.
CHOIR PORTER 4.5% ABV
Mellow porter.
GINGERSNAP 4.5% ABV
Dark, wheat beer with ginger.
MINSTERLEY ALE 4.5% ABV
Smooth and malty with crisp hoppiness.
JIGSAW 4.8% ABV
Black wheat beer.
PUZZLE 4.8% ABV
Cloudy, white wheat beer.
GOLDEN THREAD 5.0% ABV
Golden, refreshing and moreish.
IRONBRIDGE STOUT 5.0% ABV
Dark with powerful flavours.
Plus occasional brews.

THE WOOD BREWERY LTD

Wistantow, Craven Arms SY7 8DG
☎ *(01588) 672523*

WOOD'S WALLOP 3.4% ABV
Dark, easy-drinking session bitter.
SAM POWELL ORIGINAL 3.7% ABV
Rounded with hop and grain flavours.
PARISH BITTER 4.0% ABV
Light-coloured, refreshing and hoppy.
SPECIAL BITTER 4.2% ABV
Well-rounded and fruity with good hoppiness.
SHROPSHIRE LAD 4.5% ABV
Complex and full of flavours.
SAM POWELL OLD SAM 4.6% ABV
Copper-coloured, rounded and hoppy.
WONDERFUL 4.8% ABV
Powerful flavours. Excellent winter warmer.
Plus seasonal and occasional beers.

THE WORFIELD BREWING COMPANY LTD

1A The Bullring, Station Lane, Hollybush Road,
Bridgenorth WV16 4AR
☎ *(01746) 769606*

 HOPSTONE BITTER 4.0% ABV
NAILER'S OBJ 4.2% ABV
SHROPSHIRE PRIDE 4.5% ABV
BURCOTE PREMIUM PALE 4.9% ABV
REYNOLD'S REDNECK 5.5% ABV
An occasional brew.

THE PUBS

ASTON ON CLUN

The Kangaroo Inn

Clun Road, Aston on Clun SY7 8EW
☎ *(01588) 660263* Michelle Harding

 A freehouse with Charles Wells
Bombardier and Roo Brew (a house beer
produced by the Six Bells Brewery) always
available, plus up to three guests from local
or micro-breweries whenever possible.
Examples of previous guests include brews
from Burton Bridge, Holden's and
Moorhouse's.

A prettily situated olde-worlde pub with
scenic views. Friendly atmosphere, cosy
fire, beer garden and barbecue. Daily
newspapers and 'quiet room' available. Food
available in separate dining area at lunchtime
and evenings. Monthly quizzes, gourmet
nights, live music. Children allowed. Situated
on the B4368 towards Clun.

7–11pm Mon–Tues; 12–3pm and 7–11pm
Wed–Thurs; all day Fri–Sun.

ATCHAM

Mytton & Mermaid Hotel

Atcham, Shrewsbury
☎ *(01743) 761220* Danny and Ann Ditella

Up to two guest ales, usually offering
local real ales such as Wood Shropshire
Lad, Six Bells Bishops Castle, or Salopian or
Hanby ales.

A casual country house hotel bar with oak
floorboards and a large open fireplace.
Comfy sofas add to the relaxed feel. Lunches
12–2.30pm, afternoon teas and evening
meals from 6.30–10pm. Children welcome.
Car park.

11am–11pm (10.30pm Sun).

BISHOPS CASTLE

The Six Bells

Church Street, Bishops Castle SY9 5AA
☎ *(01588) 638930*
Neville Richards and Colin Richards

 A freehouse and brewpub, home of
The Six Bells Brewery. Three home brews
are permanent fixtures plus seasonal ales
such as Spring Forward and Old Recumbent
when available. An annual beer festival takes
place on the second weekend in July.

A Grade II listed building dating mainly
from the eighteenth century, tastefully
renovated and restored with original
fireplaces, stone and timberwork. Food
available Thurs–Sun lunchtimes and
Thurs–Sat evenings. No music or games.
Children allowed. Patio. Brewery tours
available.

 BIG NEV'S 3.8% ABV
Pale and moderately hopped, a local
favourite.
MARATHON ALE 4.0% ABV
Malty and ruby-coloured.
CLOUD NINE 4.2% ABV
Hoppy with citrus flavours. Award-winner.
Seasonals:
SPRING FORWARD 4.6% ABV
BREW 101 4.8% ABV
CASTLE RUIN 4.8% ABV
FESTIVAL PALE 5.2% ABV
OLD RECUMBENT 5.2% ABV
7 BELLS 5.5% ABV

5–11pm Mon (closed lunchtime);
12–2.30pm and 5–11pm Tues–Fri; all
day Sat–Sun.

The Three Tuns Inn

Salop Street, Bishops Castle SY9 5BW
☎ *(01588) 638797* Jan Cross

 A freehouse and brewpub with the range
of three own brews always available plus
seasonals and celebration ales three or four
times a year. There is an annual beer festival
in July.

An old-fashioned, town-centre brewpub;
both the pub and the beer recipe date
from 1642. Three bars, dining area,
garden/yard. Brewery tours and brewery
museum. Food available at lunchtime and
evenings. Children allowed. Website:
www.thethreetunsinn.co.uk

 SEXTON 3.7% ABV
XXX 4.3% ABV
A best bitter.
OFFA'S ALE 4.9% ABV
A strong bitter.
SCROOGE 6.5% ABV
A Christmas winter warmer.

12–3pm and 5–11pm Mon–Thurs;
all day Fri–Sun.

BOULDON

The Tally Ho Inn

Bouldon, Nr Craven Arms SY7 9DP
☎ *(01584) 841362* JG Woodward

A selection of real ales always available on one or two hand pumps, featuring a wide variety of independent breweries.

A traditional one-bar village pub with garden. Bar snacks available on weekday evenings and at weekends 12–3pm and from 7pm. Children allowed.

OPEN *6–11pm Mon; closed Tues–Wed; 6–11pm Thurs–Fri; 12–3pm and 7–11pm Sat; 12–3pm and 7–10.30pm Sun.*

BRIDGNORTH

The Bear Inn

Northgate, Bridgnorth WV16 4ET
☎ *(01746) 763250* R Brewer and A Jennings

Timothy Taylor Landlord, Morland Old Speckled Hen, Greene King Abbot and Fuller's London Pride permanently available, plus three daily changing guests from any independent brewery, with Hop Back and Shepherd Neame regular favourites.

A two-bar town pub with large beer garden. Food available at lunchtime only. Accommodation.

OPEN *1–3pm and 5pm–12am Mon–Sat; 12–3pm and 7–10.30pm Sun.*

The Railwayman's Arms

Severn Valley Railway, The Railway Station, Bridgnorth WV16 5DT
☎ *(01746) 764361* Mary Boot

Batham Bitter and Hobsons Best Bitter are always on offer, together with Batham or Hobsons Mild. Three guests, constantly changing, are also served, from breweries such as Hobsons, Holden's, Olde Swan, Burton Bridge, Wye Valley, Cannon Royall, RCH, Stonehenge, Berrow, Cottage, Eccleshall and many, many more from all over the country.

The bar is on Platform One of the Severn Valley Railway's northern terminus and is housed in part of the original station building which dates back to the days of the Great Western Railway. The older part of the bar is the original licensed refreshment room. Filled rolls served during opening hours. Accompanied children welcome until 9pm. Car park.

OPEN *April–Sept: 11.30am–4pm and 6–11pm Mon–Fri; 11am–11pm Sat; 12–10.30pm Sun. Oct–Mar: 12–3pm and 6–11pm Mon–Fri; 11am–11pm Sat; 12–10.30pm Sun.*

The Swan Inn

Knowle Sands, Bridgenorth WV16 5JL
☎ *(01746) 763424* Mr Cleaves

A freehouse offering three guest beers (two changed per fortnight), with Wood Shropshire Lad a regular favourite. Smiles Maiden Leg Over, Shepherd Neame Spitfire and ales from Brakspear might also be served.

Refurbished pub on the outskirts of Bridgnorth, with one bar and log-burning stoves. Food available. Function room, conservatory, six letting rooms, garden, wishing well. Children allowed. Car park.

OPEN *12–3pm and 5–11pm Mon–Fri; 11am–11pm Sat; 12–10.30pm Sun.*

CARDINGTON

The Royal Oak

Cardington, Church Stretton SY6 7JZ
☎ *(01694) 771266* David and Christine Baugh

Wood Shropshire Lad, Hobsons Best and Marston's Pedigree always available.

The oldest pub in Shropshire, this is an unspoilt country freehouse, situated in a picturesque hiking/cycling area. One bar, dining room and patio. Food available Tues–Sun lunchtime and Tues–Sat evenings. Children allowed.

OPEN *Closed Mon, except bank holidays; 12–3pm and 7–11pm Tues–Sun.*

CHURCH ASTON

The Last Inn

Wellington Road, Church Aston, Newport TF10 9EJ
☎ *(01952) 820469* Sheila J Austin

Everards Tiger and Original, Hobsons Best Bitter, Bank's Bitter and Original, and one Salopian ale always available plus two guests which could be Hobsons Town Crier, Marston's Pedigree, Everards Lazy Daze or an ale from Timothy Taylor, Slaters, Cottage, Worfield or Wood.

A busy nineteenth-century country pub with a large conservatory and patio/terrace overlooking the Wrekin and Shropshire countryside. Recently refurbished. Food available 12–2.30pm and 6–9.30pm Mon–Thurs; 12–2.30pm and 6–10pm Fri–Sat; 12–9.30pm Sun. Large car park. Under 10s welcome in the conservatory and garden up to 8pm.

OPEN *12–11pm (10.30pm Sun).*

CLEOBURY MORTIMER

The King's Arms Hotel

High Street, Cleobury Mortimer DY14 8BS
☎ *(01299) 270252* Miss Jackie Tinglett

 Hobsons Town Crier and Best are the permanent beers, with three guests also served, and changed every couple of months. Brews from Hook Norton are regular features, but Greene King Abbot or something from Adnams might also be on offer.

A village pub in a seventeenth-century coaching inn, with beams and fires. Food available. Garden, parking at front, five letting rooms. Live music once a month. Children allowed.

OPEN *11am–11pm Mon–Sat; 12–10.30pm Sun.*

CLUN

The White Horse Inn

The Square, Clun SY7 8JA
☎ *(01588) 640305* Jack Limond

 Salopian Shropshire Gold and Wye Valley Butty Bach permanently available, plus two constantly changing guest beer and a real cider (Weston's First Quality). Cask Marque award winner.

Set in the beautiful Clun Valley, close to the castle, serving homemade meals in the cosy bar or garden. Food served 12–2pm and 6.30–8.30pm daily. Children welcome, but no special facilities.

OPEN *Winter: 12–2.30pm and 5.30–11pm Mon–Fri; 12–11pm Sat; 12–10.30pm Sun. Summer: 12–11pm (10.30pm Sun).*

COALBROOKDALE

The Coalbrookdale Inn

12 Wellington Road, Coalbrookdale, Telford TF8 7DX
☎ *(01952) 433953* Mike Fielding

Fuller's London Pride and Adnams Broadside always available plus five guest ales from micro-breweries, both local and across the country.

A traditional village pub with no fruit machines, pool table or juke box. One bar, plus a non-smoking area, air filtration systems and a small patio area. Food served 12–2pm and 6–8pm Mon–Sat. Children allowed in designated areas.

OPEN *12–3pm and 6–11pm Mon–Sat; 12–3pm and 7–10.30pm Sun.*

CRAVEN ARMS

The Stokesay Castle Inn

School Road, Craven Arms SY7 9PE
☎ *01588 672304* Mark Lewis (manager)

A freehouse with a house beer called Discovery, brewed by SP Sporting Ales. A range of twelve guests are regularly rotated, with six at a time being available. Morland Old Speckled Hen, Marston's Pedigree, Bateman XXXB, Charles Wells Bombardier, Banks's Bitter and Adnams Bitter are examples of the beers offered.

Hotel inn dating from 1894 on the outskirts of Craven Arms village, with oak-panelled restaurant and oak-beamed bar with fireplace. Twelve en-suite rooms. Pool, darts, dominoes. Karaoke once a month. Garden, car park for 36 cars. Children allowed, plus pets by arrangement. From Ludlow, take the first turning right as you enter Craven Arms village. From Shrewsbury, take the last turning on the left in the village. Next to the Secret Hills Discovery Centre (signposted).

OPEN *10am (for coffees and pastries)– 12 midnight (restaurant licence).*

The Sun Inn and Corvedale Brewery

Corfton, Craven Arms SY7 9DF
☎ *(01584) 861503* Norman and Teresa Pearce

 Home brews Norman's Pride and Secret Hop are permanently available, plus special own brews. These are all available in bottles as well as on draught. Two guests are also served, from micro-breweries such as Cottage and Hanby.

A friendly country freehouse with two bars, a quiet lounge and a non-smoking dining area. Food available every lunchtime and evening. Exceptionally good disabled facilities, which have been commended by the Heart of England Tourist Board 'Tourism for All' and British Gas's 'Open to All' award, and have made the pub a National Winner of The Ease of Access Award. Children's certificate. Situated on the B4368.

TERESA'S PRIDE 4.0% ABV
NORMAN'S PRIDE 4.3% ABV
SECRET HOP 4.5% ABV
DARK AND DELICIOUS 4.6% ABV
A black bitter.

OPEN *11am–2.30pm and 6–11pm (10.30pm Sun).*

ELLERDINE HEATH

The Royal Oak (The Tiddly)
Ellerdine Heath, Telford TF6 6RL
☎ *(01939) 250300* Barry Colin Malone

Hobsons Bitter, Salopian Shropshire Gold, Shepherd Neame Master Brew and Wye Valley Hereford Pale Ale usually available, plus a guest from any small independent brewery. Young's Special, Exmoor Gold and Fuller's London Pride make regular appearances.

Lovely country pub in a quiet backwater, yet only a short distance from Telford. Food served during the week 12–2pm and 6–9pm (except Tues), 12–3pm and 5–9pm Sat, 12–2pm and 7–9pm Sun. Children's certificate and play area. Car park. Located halfway between the A53 and A442.

OPEN *12–11pm Mon–Fri; 11am–11pm Sat; 12–10.30pm Sun.*

IRONBRIDGE

The Golden Ball Inn
1 Newbridge Road, Ironbridge, Telford TF8 7BA
☎ *(01952) 432179* Matt Roland

Timothy Taylor Landlord is among the beers always available, and the three guests might be from Phoenix, Ossett or Wood.

Dating from 1728, this pub in a village setting has two bars, a restaurant, a courtyard and garden. Well-behaved children allowed (no play area). Three letting rooms. Car parking. Tucked away, but signposted off Padley Road.

OPEN *12–3pm and 5–11pm Mon–Fri; 11am–11pm Sat; 12–10.30pm Sun.*

Ironbridge Brasserie & Wine Bar
29 High Street, Ironbridge, Telford TF8 7AD
☎ *(01952) 432716* Mr Hull

A freehouse with ales from the local Hobsons brewery always available plus two constantly changing guests. Brains SA is a regular feature, among many others.

A village pub/wine bar/restaurant. One bar, dining area and patio. Food available Fri–Sun lunchtime and Tues–Sun evenings. Children allowed.

OPEN *6.30–11pm Mon–Thurs (closed lunchtimes); 12–2pm and 6.30–11pm Fri–Sun.*

LITTLE STRETTON

The Ragleth Inn
Ludlow Road, Little Stretton, Church Stretton SY6 6RB
☎ *(01694) 722711* D Chillcott

A freehouse with Hobsons Best always available plus two alternating guests that might include Morland Old Speckled Hen, Shepherd Neame Spitfire, Hobsons Town Crier or Brains Reverend James. Large range of malt whiskies also available.

A traditional two-bar country pub with dining area and garden. Limited disabled access. Food available at lunchtime and evenings. Children allowed. Website: www.theragleth inn.co.uk.

OPEN *12–2.30pm and 6–11pm; all day Sat–Sun.*

LOWTOWN

Black Horse
4 Bridge Street, Lowtown, Bridgnorth
☎ *(01746) 762415*

Two pumps always serve Banks's beers, and seven guest ales, changed daily, might include something from Hobsons, Wood, Holden's, Wychwood or Brakspear.

A 250-year-old village pub in a listed building on the banks of the River Severn. Food is available and there is a non-smoking area. Two bars plus lounge and courtyard, and seating by the river. Live music once a month. Beer festival once a year in summer (call for details). Seven letting rooms. Children allowed. Car park,

OPEN *6–11pm Mon–Fri; 12–11pm Sat; 12–10.30pm Sun.*

MUCH WENLOCK

The George & Dragon
2 High Street, Much Wenlock TF13 6AA
☎ *(01952) 727312* Milton Monk

A real ale pub with a fine selection of cask ales rotating frequently. Morland Old Speckled Hen, Greene King Abbot and IPA, Hobsons Town Crier, Banks's Original Mild, Adnams Broadside, Charles Wells Bombardier and JW Lees Summer Scorcher are regular features.

Small country town pub, first mentioned in records in 1496, but possibly used by monks since the eleventh century. Food is available 12–2pm and 6–9pm daily, and there is a restaurant area (no restaurant service on Wed and Sun evenings). The pub participates in Shropshire Beer Week Festival. Children allowed. Public car park.

OPEN *Jun–Sept: 12–11pm (10.30pm Sun). Oct–May: 12–3pm and 6–11pm Mon–Thurs; 12–11pm Fri–Sun (10.30pm Sun).*

MUNSLOW

The Crown
Munslow, Craven Arms SY7 9ET
☎ *(01584) 841205* Richard and Jane Arnold

 A selection of Holden's and Hobsons ales of different strengths always available, plus seasonal guests from those breweries.

Winner of the best restaurant in Shropshire 2002, with food prepared by a Masterchef of Great Britain served 12–2pm and 7–9pm. Car park. Children welcome. Situated on the B4368 between Aston Munslow and Beambridge.

OPEN *12–2.30pm and 7–11pm (10.30pm Sun).*

OAKENGATES

Crown Inn
Market Street, Oakengates, Telford TF2 6EA
☎ *(01952) 610888. Fax (01952) 617659*
John Ellis

 A freehouse with Hobsons Best Bitter and Burton Bridge ales always available plus up to ten guest beers changing two or three times a week, plus hand-pulled cider. So far, some 2,000 ales have been served in seven years. Hundreds of breweries featured. Wood, Worfield, Hanby Ales, Hook Norton, Wye Valley, Slaters and Lichfield are just a few of the regulars. Only Shropshire beers are sold during the Shropshire Beer Week at the end of July. What are claimed to be the world's biggest pub-based, hand-pulled beer festivals held twice a year on the first weekends (Thurs–Mon) in May and October, featuring 29 hand pulls specialising in up to 60 new beers.

A homely, traditional town-centre pub with three drinking areas and a small yard with picnic tables. No food available, though there are a number of eateries within two minutes' walk of the pub. Quality live music on Thurs evenings (except August). Children allowed in designated areas. Located near the bus and railway stations. Visit our website at: www.crownoakengates.com.

OPEN *12.30–3pm and 7–11pm Mon–Wed; 12–11pm Thurs–Sat; 12.30–10.30pm Sun.*

The Duke of York
Market Street, Oakengates, Telford TF2 6DU
☎ *(01952) 612741* Miss PA Taggart

 Banks's Bitter and Original are always available, plus occasional seasonal guest beers.

Drinkers' town pub in a building dating from the sixteenth century, with two bars (public and lounge) and patio. No food. Live music Thursday, Friday and Saturday. Children allowed until 6.30pm. Car park.

OPEN *11am–11pm Mon–Sat; 12–10.30pm Sun.*

OLDWOODS

The Romping Cat
Oldwoods, Shrewsbury SY4 3AS
☎ *(01939) 290273* Mr Simcox

 A freehouse with Fuller's London Pride among the brews always available, plus four guests from breweries such as Adnams, Bateman or Greene King and local breweries such as Salopian.

A traditional rural pub with one bar, no machines or music. Beer garden. No food. No children.

OPEN *11am–3pm Mon, Tues, Thurs (closed Wed and Fri lunchtimes); 7–11pm Mon–Fri; 12.30–3.30pm and 7–11pm Sat; 12–2.30pm and 7–10.30pm Sun.*

OSWESTRY

The Old Mill Inn
Candy, Oswestry SY10 9AZ
☎ *(01691) 657058* Mr and Mrs Atkinson

 Morland Old Speckled Hen always available plus two guests, perhaps an Adnams or Wood brew.

A traditional one-bar country pub with restaurant, garden and children's area. Disabled access. B&B. Food available at lunchtime and evenings. Children allowed.

OPEN *12–3pm Wed–Sun (closed all day Mon and Tues); 7–11pm Wed–Thurs; 6–11pm Fri–Sat; 7–10.30pm Sun.*

PONTESBURY

The Horseshoes Inn
Minsterley Road, Pontesbury, Shrewsbury SY5 0QJ
☎ *(01743) 790278* Mrs Scott

 A freehouse with up to four guest ales. Regulars include Fuller's London Pride, but all breweries are featured.

A rural pub with one bar. Food available at lunchtime and evenings. Children allowed if eating. Accommodation.

OPEN *12–3pm and 7–11pm (10.30pm Sun).*

PORT HILL

The Boathouse Inn
New Street, Port Hill, Shrewsbury SY3 8JQ
☎ *(01743) 362965*

 Six guest ales are usually served, regularly rotated (fifteen different ones a week in summer). Examples include regular favourite Marston's Pedigree, plus Greene King Abbot, Salopian Golden Thread and Morland Old Speckled Hen.

A pub on the outskirts of Shrewsbury town dating from before the seventeenth century, with beams and fireplaces. Food available. Two bars, garden, car park. Children allowed in certain areas.

 11am–11pm Mon–Sat; 12–10.30pm Sun.

RATLINGHOPE

The Horseshoe Inn
(also known as The Bridge)
Bridges, Nr Ratlinghope SY5 0ST
☎ *(01588) 650260* Colin and Hilary Waring

 Shepherd Neame Spitfire, Adnams Bitter and Timothy Taylor Landlord permanently available.

A 400-year-old countryside pub in an isolated beauty spot. Food available 12–3pm and 6–9pm Mon–Fri; all day Sat–Sun. Children allowed. Beer garden with tables and seating. Phone for directions.

11am–11pm Mon–Sat; 12–10.30pm Sun.

SHIFNAL

The White Hart
High Street, Shifnal TF11 8BH
☎ *(01952) 461161* Andy Koczy

A freehouse with Enville Ale, Chainmaker Mild and Simpkiss Bitter permanently available, plus two guests from micro-breweries whenever possible. Examples include Exmoor Gold and Moorhouse's Pendle Witches Brew.

A coaching inn in a traditional timbered building, two bars, beer garden. Food available at lunchtime only. Children allowed.

12–3pm and 6–11pm Mon–Thurs; all day Fri–Sun.

SHREWSBURY

The Dolphin Inn
48 St Michael's Street, Shrewsbury SY1 2EZ
☎ *(01743) 350419* Nigel Morton

 Home of the Dolphin Brewery, with Dolphin Best Bitter and Dolphin Brew always available, as well as one or two guest beers from other breweries. Cask cider also served.

A brew pub dedicated to real ales. No lager or beers from national breweries. Traditional decor, wide-ranging, friendly clientele. Coffee available. No food. No children.

DOLPHIN BEST 4.0% ABV
DOLPHIN BREW 5.0% ABV

5–11pm only.

The Peacock Inn
42 Wenlock Road, Shrewsbury SY2 6JS
☎ *(01743) 355215* C Roberts

 Marston's ales are a speciality here, with Pedigree and Owd Roger always available, plus seasonal brews and other guests such as Banks's Mild on one hand pump.

A pub/restaurant with one bar, beer garden, disabled access. Food available at lunchtime and evenings in separate dining area. Children allowed.

11.30am–3pm and 6–11pm (10.30pm Sun).

The Three Fishes
Fish Street, Shrewsbury SY1 1UR
☎ *(01743) 344793* Mr AP Wardrop

 Timothy Taylor Landlord, Fuller's London Pride, and Adnams Best Bitter usually available, plus at least one guest beer such as Salopian Golden Thread or Minsterly Ale, Six Bells Big Nev's or Cloud Nine, or beers from Holden's, Hobsons, Hanby, Greene King or Enville.

Old, town-centre, non-smoking pub, serving a variety of real ales and traditional, homemade meals. Food lunchtimes and evenings Mon–Sat; no food Sun. No under 14s.

11.30am–3pm and 5–11pm Mon–Thurs; 11.30am–11pm Fri–Sat; 12–3pm and 7–10.30pm Sun.

UPPER FARMCOTE

The Lion O'Morfe
Upper Farmcote WV15 5PS
☎ *(01746) 710678* Dave Chantler

 A freehouse offering six guest beers, usually changed every three days, with Wood Shropshire Lad a regular favourite, but beers from Cottage, Shepherd Neame, Burton Bridge and SP Sporting Ales also featured.

A country pub built in the nineteenth century. Food available. Two bars, garden and car park. Live music weekly. Pool. Children allowed.

OPEN *12–2.30pm (closed Mon lunch) and 7–11pm Mon–Fri; hours vary on Sat/Sun.*

WELLINGTON

The Cock Hotel
148 Holyhead Road, Wellington, Telford TF1 2DL
☎ *(01952) 244954* Peter Arden

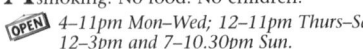 A freehouse with four guests, which might include Hobsons Town Crier, Enville White and occasionally Heaven's Gate, a house brew produced for the hotel by the Salopian Brewery.

A traditional pub with two bars, one non-smoking. No food. No children.

OPEN *4–11pm Mon–Wed; 12–11pm Thurs–Sat; 12–3pm and 7–10.30pm Sun.*

WELSH FRANKTON

The Narrowboat Inn
Welsh Frankton, Oswestry
☎ *(01691) 661051*
Gary Hughes (asst. bar manager)

 Tied to Carlsberg Tetley, but with Bateman XB permanently available, plus two weekly changing guests, such as beers from Greene King and Charles Wells. The pub's regulars dictate which guests are served.

Country pub and restaurant in the shape of a narrowboat, with low ceiling. Bar at one end, plus non-smoking restaurant. The gardens overlook the canal. Children allowed. Car park. On the main road to Ellesmere.

OPEN *11am–3pm and 6–11pm Mon–Sat; 12–3pm and 6–10.30pm Sun.*

WISTANSTOW

The Plough Inn
Wistanstow, Craven Arms SY7 8DG
☎ *(01588) 673251* Denis and Debbie Harding

 The brewery tap to Shropshire's Wood Brewery, serving up to five of their beers.

A traditional two-bar country pub with restaurant and patio. Food is prepared on the premises using only local produce to ensure freshness and quality, and is available at lunchtimes and evenings.

OPEN *11.30am–2.30pm and 6.30–11pm (10.30pm Sun).*

WORFIELD

The Dog Inn and Davenports Arms
Main Street, Worfield WV15 5LF
☎ *(01746) 716320* Vic Pocock

 Charles Wells Bombardier and Highgate Bitter and Mild are among the permanent beers. One guest, changed twice a month, might be something from Hobsons, Smiles, Young's or Holden's.

Seventeenth-century village pub with beams and log burner. Food is available and there is a non-smoking restaurant. Patio, car park. Occasional live music. Children allowed. Follow signs to Worfield from Bridgenorth Road – the pub is in the village.

OPEN *12–2.30pm and 7–11pm Mon–Sat; 12–3pm and 7–10.30pm Sun.*

YOU TELL US

* *All Nations Inn,* Coalport Road, Madeley, Telford (brewpub)
* *The Castle Vaults Inn,* Castle Gates, Shrewsbury
* *The Fox & Hounds,* High Street, Stottesdon
* *The Horseshoe Inn,* Bridges
* *The Old Vaults,* High Street, Ironbridge
* *The Railway Inn,* Yorton

Places Featured:

Allerford Crossing	Lower Odcombe
Ashcott	Luxborough
Axbridge	Martock
Babcary	Nailsea
Barrington	Nether Stowey
Bath	Nettlebridge
Blagdon	North Curry
Bleadon	Norton St Philip
Bridgwater	Norton Sub Hamdon
Burnham on Sea	Pitminster
Chard	Pitney
Chelynch	Rode
Chew Magna	Rowberrow
Churchill	Shurton
Compton Martin	Sparkford
Congresbury	Stanton Wick
Crewkerne	Taunton
Culmhead	Trudoxhill
Exford	Wanstrow
Farleigh Hungerford	Wellington
Faulkland	Wellow
Frome	Wells
Glastonbury	West Cranmore
Hardington Moor	Weston-super-Mare
Hinton Blewitt	Williton
Horsington	Wincanton
Huish Episcopi	Winsford
Kelston	Wiveliscombe
Langford Budville	Wookey
Langley Marsh	Wookey Hole
Langport	Yeovil
Leigh Common	

THE BREWERIES

ABBEY ALES LTD

The Abbey Brewery, 2 Lansdown Road, Bath BA1 5EE
☎ *(01225) 444437*
www.abbeyales.co.uk

 **BELLRINGER 4.2% ABV**
Golden, hoppy award winner.
BATH STAR 4.5% ABV
Amber, strong hoppy taste.
CHORISTER 4.5% ABV
Mid-brown fruity beer.
TWELFTH NIGHT 5.0% ABV
Christmas brew.

BERROW BREWERY

Coast Road, Berrow, Burnham-on-Sea TA8 2QU
☎ *(01278) 751345*

 BBBB/4BS 3.9% ABV
CARNIVALE 4.0% ABV
Available late Oct–mid Nov.
MILLENNIUM MASH/MM 4.7% ABV
BERROW PORTER 4.8% ABV
Mellow and fruity.
CHRISTMAS ALE 5.0% ABV
Available Dec–Jan.
TOPSY TURVY 5.9% ABV
Golden, fruity and refreshing.

BUTCOMBE BREWERY LTD
Butcombe, Bristol BS40 7XQ
☎ *(01275) 472240*

 BITTER 4.0% ABV
A dry, clean-tasting bitter with strong hop flavour.
GOLD 4.7% ABV
Golden and moreish.

COTLEIGH BREWERY
Ford Road, Wiveliscombe, Taunton TA4 2RE
☎ *(01984) 624086*
www.cotleighbrewery.co.uk

 TAWNY 3.8% ABV
Flavoursome and well-hopped.
GOLDEN EAGLE 4.2% ABV
A clean golden best bitter.
BARN OWL 4.5% ABV
Smooth, refreshing and hoppy.
OLD BUZZARD 4.8% ABV
Dark, complex winter brew.
Plus occasional and seasonal brews.

COTTAGE BREWING CO.
The Old Cheese Dairy, Lovington, Castle Cary BA7 7PS
☎ *(01963) 240551*
www.cottagebrewing.com

 SOUTHERN BITTER 3.8% ABV
BROAD GAUGE BITTER 3.9% ABV
MALLARD 4.0% ABV
WHEELTAPPERS ALE 4.0% ABV
BRUNEL'S BITTER 4.1% ABV
CHAMPFLOWER 4.2% ABV
FULL STEAM AHEAD 4.2% ABV
MALLARD IPA 4.3% ABV
SOMERSET AND DORSET ALE 4.4% ABV
GOLDEN ARROW 4.5% ABV
OUR KEN 4.5% ABV
WINDSOR CASTLE 4.6 % ABV
MIDNIGHT EXPRESS 4.7% ABV
WESTERN GLORY 4.7% ABV
JOHNSONS SINGLE 4.8% ABV
STEPHENSON'S GOLD 4.8% ABV
GOLDRUSH 5.0% ABV
HOP AND DROP 5.0% ABV
NORMAN'S CONQUEST MM 5.0% ABV
STANIER BLACK 5 5.0% ABV
NORMAN'S CONQUEST 7.0% ABV
Plus monthly special brews.

EXMOOR ALES LTD
The Brewery, Golden Hill, Wiveliscombe, Taunton TA4 2NY
☎ *(01984) 623798*

 ALE 3.8% ABV
Smooth and full-flavoured, with malt throughout.
HOUND DOG 4.0% ABV
Mar–May.
FOX 4.2% ABV
Easy-drinking and flavour-packed.
WILD CAT 4.4% ABV
Sept–Nov.
GOLD 4.5% ABV
Initially sweet, with a hoppy finish.
HART 4.8% ABV
Malty, with balancing hoppiness.
EXMAS 5.0% ABV
Christmas brew.
STAG 5.2% ABV
Well-balanced with lingering finish.
BEAST 6.6% ABV
Dark, with powerful roast malt flavour.
Plus occasional brews.

MOOR BEER COMPANY
Whitley Farm, Whitley Lane, Ashcott, Bridgwater TA7 9QW
☎ *(01458) 210050*

 WITHY CUTTER 3.8% ABV
AVALON SPRINGTIME 4.0% ABV
MERLINS MAGIC 4.3% ABV
PEAT PORTER 4.5% ABV
PINDER'S PRIDE 4.7% ABV
SOMERLAND GOLD 5.0% ABV
OLD FREDDY WALKER 7.3% ABV
Plus occasional brews.

OAKHILL BREWERY
The Old Maltings, Oakhill, Bath BA3 5BX
☎ *(01749) 840134*
www.oakhillbrewery.co.uk

 BITTER 3.5% ABV
Light and hoppy.
BEST BITTER 4.0% ABV
Malty and refreshing.
BLACK MAGIC STOUT 4.0% ABV
Rich malty flavour with some hoppiness.
CHARIOTEER 4.2% ABV
Distinctive and balanced with fruity aftertaste.
MENDIP GOLD 4.5% ABV
Golden, smooth and rounded.
MENDIP 2K 4.8% ABV
Full-bodied ruby ale. Smooth, fruity hop flavour.
MERRY MALTINGS 4.8% ABV
Hoppy, fruity aroma.
YEOMAN 5.0% ABV
Balanced fruit and hop flavours.

RCH BREWERY

West Hewish, Nr Weston-super-Mare BS24 6RR
☎ *(01934) 834447*

HEWISH IPA 3.6% ABV
Delicate flavours throughout.
PG STEAM 3.9% ABV
Bursting with flavours. Full-bodied for gravity.
PITCHFORK 4.3% ABV
Golden, refreshing and dangerously drinkable.
OLD SLUG PORTER 4.5% ABV
Very dark, traditional porter.
PUXTON CROSS 4.5% ABV
Single-hop award winner. Occasional brew.
25A 4.7% ABV
Pale and hoppy with good malt character.
EAST STREET CREAM 5.0% ABV
Refreshing, clean flavour, fruity and deceptive.
FIREY LIZ 5.0% ABV
Golden, hoppy, occasional brew.
DOUBLEHEADER 5.3% ABV
Golden hoppy beer.
FIREBOX 6.0% ABV
Powerful bitter with a multitude of flavours.
SANTA FE' 7.3% ABV
Dark, bittersweet Christmas special.

THE PUBS

ALLERFORD CROSSING

The Victory Inn

Allerford Crossing, Norton Fitzwarren,
Nr Taunton TA4 1AL
☎ *(01823) 461282* Janet Amos

RCH Pitchfork, Cotleigh Tawny, Exmoor Ale are always available plus two guests usually something like Timothy Taylor Landlord, Morland Old Speckled Hen, Smile's Best or Greene King Abbot Ale.

Recently refurbished to enhance the olde-worlde charm and character. Food is available at lunchtime and evenings. Car park, gardens, patio, family room, skittle alley, children's play area. Rooms are available for hire.

OPEN *12–3pm and 6–11pm.*

ASHCOTT

Ring o'Bells

High Street, Ashcott, Bridgwater TA7 9PZ
☎ *(01458) 210232* John Foreman

A freehouse with three hand pumps serving a range of constantly changing real ales. The local Moor Beer Company in Ashcott is regularly supported, plus smaller independents and micros, too many to mention.

A medium-sized village pub with three bars, non-smoking dining area and beer garden. Food available at lunchtime and evenings. Children allowed.

OPEN *12–2.30pm and 7–11pm (10.30pm Sun).*

AXBRIDGE

The Lamb Hotel

The Square, Axbridge BS26 2AP
☎ *(01934) 732253* Sandy Currie

Butcombe Bitter and Gold, and Wadworth 6X are on offer here.

Family pub, approximately 400 years old, set in quiet town centre. Opposite beautiful mediaeval building, formerly a hunting lodge, now the museum. One curiosity is the bar that has bottles of wine set in concrete underneath it. Accommodation. Food available except on Sunday night. Children welcome. Parking in market square. Small garden. Skittle alley.

OPEN *11am–3pm and 6–11pm Mon–Wed;*
all day Thurs–Sun.

BABCARY

Red Lion
Main Street, Babcary TA11 7ED
☎ *(01458) 223230* Simon Donnelly

Freehouse with the beers changing all the time, more than 200 in a year, favouring West Country micros such as Hop Back and Otter.

A relaxed old-fashioned country pub with large flagstones and thatched roof in remote rural Somerset. Pub skittles and shove ha'penny. Food, with fish speciality, every session except Sunday night and Monday night. Car park and garden. Children welcome. Halfway between Shepton Mallet and Yeovil.

OPEN *12–2.30pm and 6–11pm.*

BARRINGTON

The Royal Oak
Barrington, Nr Ilminster TA19 0JB
☎ *(01460) 53455* Ray Brown

At least three, sometimes four, real ales available (300 per year).

A sixteenth-century Grade II listed building. Food served lunchtimes and evenings. Car park, garden, skittle alley and function room for larger parties. Follow the National Trust signs for Barrington Court.

OPEN *12–3pm and 5.30–11pm Tues–Fri; 12–11pm Sat; 12–3pm and 6–10.30pm Sun.*

BATH

The Bell
103 Walcot Street, Bath, BA1 5BW
☎ *(01225) 460426* Don Pilliner

Abbey Bellringer, Bath Ales Gem and something from Smiles are always available plus three or four guests.

Eclectic and lively city-centre pub with music a central focus. One bar and a table football room. Live music three times a week. Beer garden. Vegetarian rolls. Children welcome.

OPEN *11.30am–11pm Mon–Sat; 12–10.30pm Sun.*

Hatchett's
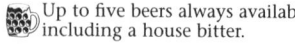
6–7 Queen Street, Bath BA1 1HE
☎ *(01225) 425045* Mr and Mrs Cruxton

Up to five beers always available including a house bitter.

A nineteenth-century pub in Bath city centre with bars upstairs and down. The house bitter is available at £1.75. All beers at reasonable prices. Bar food available at lunchtime. Down a side street in the city centre.

OPEN *11am–11pm Mon–Sat; 12–10.30pm Sun.*

The Hobgoblin
47 St James' Parade, Bath BA8 1UZ
☎ *(01225) 460785* Fidelma Tracey (manager)

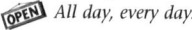A freehouse specialising in Wychwood ales, so Hobgoblin and Wychwood Special always available plus three guests.

A lively town pub with a student clientele. Two bars, tables outside. Food available Mon–Wed 12–2.30pm, Thurs–Fri 12–5pm and Sat 12–4pm. Children allowed.

OPEN *All day, every day.*

The Old Farmhouse
1 Lansdown Road, Bath BA1 5EE
☎ *(01225) 316162* John Bradshaw

Wadworth 6X and IPA, Badger Tanglefoot and beers from Butcombe and Abbey Ales always available, plus one occasional guest.

A town pub with two bars, live jazz four nights a week. Patio. Food available. Well-behaved children allowed.

OPEN *All day, every day.*

The Old Green Tree
12 Green Street, Bath BA1 2JZ
☎ *(01225) 448259*
Nick Luke and Tim Bethune

Only stocks draught beer from micro-breweries within a 60-mile radius. Six beers always available including RCH Pitchfork and Wickwar Brand Oak Bitter. Others rotated regularly including brews from Uley, Church End, Abbey and Stonehenge.

Small oak-lined city-centre pub. A traditional pub, no recorded music or machines. Bar food at lunchtime. On a small street in city centre between Milsom Street and the post office.

OPEN *11am–11pm Mon–Sat; 12–10.30pm Sun.*

The Pig & Fiddle
2 Saracen Street, Bath BA1 5BR
☎ *(01225) 460868*
Sean Bentley and Jo Humphrey

A freehouse with Abbey Bellringer and something from Bath Ales always available plus three guests, often from Butcombe or Badger. Real cider offered.

Very busy town-centre pub but with relaxed atmosphere. Large beer garden. Bar food available 12–7pm Sun–Thurs and 12–6pm Fri–Sat. Children allowed in garden. Opposite the Hilton Hotel.

OPEN *11am–11pm Mon–Sat; 12–10.30pm Sun.*

The Salamander
John Street, Bath BA1 2JL
☎ *(01225) 428889* Robert Wenny

 A Bath Ales house, with Bath Gem, SPA and Barnstormer usually available, plus an occasional guest beer, perhaps something from one of the smaller breweries.

Grade II listed Georgian pub, refurbished but with some original features retained. Food is available, and there is a non-smoking dining area. Children allowed in dining area.

OPEN *11am–11pm (closed Sun evening).*

Star Inn
23 Vineyards, Bath BA1 5NE
☎ *(01225) 425072*
Terry Langley and Julie Schofield

 Abbey Bellringer, Bateman XXXB and Charles Wells Bombadier always available plus five rotating guests.

A timeless local with a friendly atmosphere within the wonderful old interior. One bar with four small rooms including 'death row' where the old people sit. Traditional games such as shove ha'penny.

OPEN *12–3pm and 5.30–11pm Mon–Thur; all day Fri–Sun.*

BLAGDON

New Inn
Church Street, Blagdon BS40 7SB
☎ *(01761) 462475* Anne and Pat McCann

 Wadworth IPA, 6X and JCB plus Butcombe Bitter always available.

Welcoming country pub with fantastic views of Blagdon Lake from the car park. Log fire in the winter. Two out of three bar areas are non-smoking. Children welcome. Garden and large parking area.

OPEN *11am–2.30pm and 7–11pm Tue–Sat; 12–3pm and 7–10.30pm Sun; closed all day Monday.*

Queen Adelaide
High Street, Blagdon BS40 7RA
☎ *(01761) 462573* Terry Beardshaw

 Butcombe ales always available.

Small quaint village pub in a Grade II listed building. Food is served during each session in the one bar. Small beer garden and car park. No children.

OPEN *12–2.30pm and 7–11pm (10.30 Sun).*

BLEADON

The Queen's Arms
Celtic Way, Bleadon, Nr Weston-super-Mare BS24 ONF
☎ *(01934) 812080* Anita and Chris Smith

 Palmers IPA and Copper, Butcombe Bitter, Badger Tanglefoot and Ringwood Old Thumper always available, plus different guest beers each week.

A friendly sixteenth-century freehouse with flagstone floors and settles, specialising in good food and real ales served straight from the barrel. A good stop for refreshment on the Mendip Walk. Food served daily lunchtime and evening, except Sunday evening when the pub holds a very popular quiz night. Skittle alley also available. Website: www.queensarms.co.uk.

OPEN *11.30am–2.30pm and 5.30–11pm Mon–Fri; 11.30am–11pm Sat; 12–10.30pm Sun.*

BRIDGWATER

Annie's Bar
North Street, Bridgwater TA6 3PW
☎ *(01278) 433053* Mr Truman

 A freehouse with Butcombe Bitter constantly available, plus two weekly changing guests, such as beers from Teignworthy, Stonehenge and Cottage.

Country pub on the outskirts of town in an old, traditional building with beams and fireplaces. Back bar and front bar. Food available (back bar for dining). Garden. Children allowed until 9.30pm.

OPEN *5–11.30pm Mon–Fri; 11am–11pm Sat; 12–3pm and 6–10.30pm Sun.*

The Fountain Inn
1 West Quay, Bridgwater TA6 3HL
☎ *(01278) 424115* Elizabeth O'Toole

 Seven real ales always available, including Wadworth 6X and IPA and Butcombe Bitter, plus two guests such as Red Shoot Brewery's Forest Gold, Tom's Tipple or seasonal Wadworth ales like Summer Sault.

A traditional one-bar town-centre pub. Background music. Full bar menu available lunchtime and evenings. Several beer festivals held every year, one main festival and then two or three smaller ones throughout the year with up to 18 beers on at a time. No children.

OPEN *6–11pm Mon–Thurs; 11am–11pm Fri; 11am–5pm and 6–11pm Sat; 12–3pm and 7–10.30pm Sun.*

The Horse & Jockey

1 Durleigh Road, Bridgwater TA6 7HU
☎ *(01278) 424283* Ron Chedgey

 Beers from Exmoor and Teignworthy are always on offer. Four guests, often changed daily, might include Timothy Taylor Landlord or something from Oakhill or Shepherd Neame.

Out-of-town, traditional pub in a coaching house dating from 1770. Currently being extended to make the dining area bigger (it will be a steak house – work expected to be finished by end of 2002). Two function rooms. Children may be allowed following refurbishment (call to confirm).

OPEN *2pm–11pm (will change to all-day opening when building work completed – phone for details).*

BURNHAM ON SEA

The Crown

74 Oxford Street, Burnham on Sea TA8 1EW
☎ *(01278) 782792* Kevin Tippetts

 A freehouse with Fuller's London Pride and Greene King IPA as permanent beers plus one guest, with Berrow 4Bs a regular. RCH East Street Cream, Hop Back Summer Lightning and Bateman XXXB might also be on offer, plus beers from a wide range of micro-breweries.

Locals' pub just off the town centre, frequented by local sports teams, and hosting six skittles teams and two darts teams. Skittle alley, dartboards, separate pool room. No food. Lounge and public bar, patio area with seating. Children allowed. Car park.

OPEN *4–11pm Mon–Fri; 12–11pm Sat; 12–10.30pm Sun.*

The Royal Clarence Hotel

31 The Esplanade, Burnham on Sea TA8 1BQ
☎ *(01278) 783138* Andrew Neilson

RCH Pitchfork and Butcombe Bitter always available plus one other guest, changed throughout the year.

An old coaching hotel. Hosts two beer festivals per year and many cabaret attractions. Bar food available all day. Conference facilities. Sports bar with giant TV. Parking, accommodation. Children allowed. Take M5 junction 22, then make for the sea front. The hotel is by the pier.

OPEN *11am–11pm Mon–Sat; 12–10.30pm Sun. Sports bar has a late licence (1am).*

CHARD

The Bell & Crown Inn

Combe Street, Chard TA20 1JP
☎ *(01460) 62470* Marilyn Randall

 Otter Bitter is a permanent fixture, plus four guests, usually from West Country breweries, or seasonal and celebration ales.

A quiet, old-fashioned pub with gas lights. No music. Beer garden. Food available Tues–Sun lunchtime. Children allowed.

OPEN *12–3pm and 7–11pm (10.30pm Sun).*

CHELYNCH

Poacher's Pocket

Chelynch, Shepton Mallet BA4 4PY
☎ *(01749) 880220* Stephanie and Ken Turner

 Freehouse serving Oakhill Bitter, Butcombe Bitter and Wadworth 6X with a guest beer at the weekend.

A traditional village pub with various different rooms off the one bar; has been licensed since the seventeenth century. Food every session. Children and dogs allowed if well-behaved. Skittle alley and shove ha'penny. Folk club once a month. Beer festival end of September. Car park and garden.

OPEN *12–3pm and 6–11pm.*

CHEW MAGNA

The Bear & Swan

13 South Parade, Chew Magna BS40 8SL
☎ *(01275) 331100* Mr Nigel Pushman

Butcombe Bitter is always available plus one guest, often Greene King IPA or Charles Wells Bombardier.

Pub and restaurant at the centre of the village. Food served 12–2pm and 7–9.45pm (not Sun evenings). No children's facilities. Car park.

OPEN *11am–11pm Mon–Sat; 12–6pm Sun.*

CHURCHILL

The Crown Inn

The Batch, Skinners Lane, Churchill, Nr Bristol
☎ *(01934) 852995* Tim Rogers

 RCH PG Steam and Palmers Best always available straight from the barrel, plus up to five guest beers (100+ per year) to include Exe Valley Devon Glory, Tomintoul Wild Cat, Otter Bright and Hop Back Summer Lightning.

An old pub with small rooms and flagstone floors. Large fires in winter. Food made and prepared to order with fresh local produce when practical. Parking, garden, children's room. Children not allowed in bar area. South of Bristol, just off the A38, not far from M5.

OPEN *All day, every day.*

COMPTON MARTIN

Ring O' Bells

Compton Martin BS40 6JE
☎ *(01761) 221284*

 Freehouse serving Butcombe Bitter and Gold, Wadworth 6X and a rotating guest such as Fuller's London Pride

A quiet yet busy typical English pub with low ceilings and wooden beams, popular for food. It has previously won a local CAMRA award. Two bars and a restaurant room with food served at every session. Large car park and garden. Children welcome in family room. Darts and shove ha'penny.

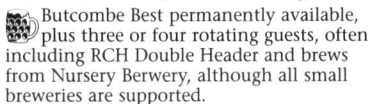 *11.30am–2.30pm and 6.30–11pm Mon–Fri; 11.30am–3pm and 6.30–11pm Sat; 12–3pm and 6.30–10.30pm Sun.*

CONGRESBURY

The Plough Inn

High Street, Congresbury BS49 5JA
☎ *(01934) 832475* Jackie Armstrong

 Butcombe Best permanently available, plus three or four rotating guests, often including RCH Double Header and brews from Nursery Berwery, although all small breweries are supported.

A 200-year-old alehouse, an old-fashioned ale lover's pub. No food. Children and dogs allowed.

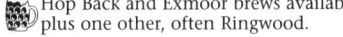 *11am–3.30pm and 4.30–11pm Mon–Thurs; all day Fri–Sun.*

CREWKERNE

The Crown Inn

34 South Street, Crewkerne TA18 8DB
☎ *(01460) 72464* Trevor and Angela Roberts

 Hop Back and Exmoor brews available, plus one other, often Ringwood.

T raditional sixteenth-century coaching inn with two bars, offering comfortable, good value bed and breakfast. Bar snacks available until 9.30pm. Children welcome.

 *6.30–11pm Mon–Sat; 12–3pm and 7–10.30pm Sun.*

CULMHEAD

Holman Clavel Inn

Culmhead, Taunton TA3 7EA
☎ *(01823) 421432* Cara Lawrence

 A freehouse with Butcombe Bitter always available plus three weekly changing guests such as Butcombe Gold, Otter Ale, Church End Vicar's Ruin and What the Fox's Hat, Concertina Bengal Tiger or a Juwards brew.

A fourteenth-century rural pub with garden. Food available at lunchtime and evenings. Children allowed.

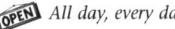 *12–3pm and 5–11pm; 12–3pm and 6–11pm Sat; 12–3pm and 7–10.30pm Sun.*

EXFORD

Exmoor White Horse Inn

Exford, Exmoor TA24 7PY
☎ *01643 831229* Peter Hendrie

Exmoor Ale, Exmoor Gold, Marston's Pedigree and Morland Old Speckled Hen are always available and there is one guest changing every week.

A sixteenth-century family-run inn with plenty of character, attracting both locals and tourists. Accommodation. Food, lunchtime and evening, has an emphasis on local produce. Car park and terrace overlooking the river. Children welcome up to 9pm. Large selection of malt whiskies.

All day, every day.

FARLEIGH HUNGERFORD

Hungerford Arms

Farleigh Hungerford, Nr Bath BA3 6RX
☎ *(01225) 752411* Craig Stewart

Freehouse offering Wadworth 6X, Otter Bright and Bitter, plus one rotating guest.

A n old roadside pub overlooking Farleigh Hungerford Castle. One partitioned bar and a restaurant. Food every session. Children welcome. Car park and patio.

11am–3pm and 5.30–11pm Mon–Thur; all day Fri–Sun.

FAULKLAND

Tucker's Grave

Faulkland, Nr Radstock BA3 5FX
☎ *(01373) 834230* Ivan and Glenda Swift

Butcombe Bitter served straight from the cask.

A really traditional rural pub – basic but with plenty of friendly rustic charm. Ploughman's lunch available. Skittle alley and shove ha'penny. Car park and garden.

11am–3pm and 6–11pm (10.30pm Sun).

FROME

The Griffin

25 Milk Street, Frome BA11 3DB
☎ *(01373) 467766* Nick Branwell

 Home of the Milk Street Brewery with the full range of home brews always available.

A traditional country pub for real ale lovers. Food available only on Sunday. No children.

OPEN *5–11pm (10.30pm Sun).*

The Horse & Groom

East Woodlands, Frome BA11 5LY
☎ *(01373) 462802* Kathy Barrett

 Greene King IPA, Wadworth 6X, Branscombe Vale Branoc and a Butcombe brew always available, plus one guest, changing weekly, which might be Bateman XB or a Brakspear brew.

A two-bar country freehouse with log fires, flag floors, restaurant, conservatory and beer garden. Restaurant and bar food available at lunchtime and evenings. Children allowed in the restaurant, lounge and garden only.

OPEN *11.30am–2.30pm and 6.30–11pm (10.30pm Sun).*

GLASTONBURY

Who'd A Thought It

17 Northload Street, Glastonbury BA6 9JJ
☎ *(01458) 834460* Andrew and Eileen Davis

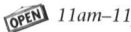 Tied to the Palmers brewery, regularly serving IPA and 200, and occasionally others such as Tally Ho!

A real curiosity of a pub, full of bric-à-brac, old features and loads of character – there's an old red telephone kiosk in the corner, a bike attached to the ceiling and award-winning loos. Strong emphasis on homemade food (every day). Car park and patio. Children allowed in dining area. Accommodation.

OPEN *11am–11pm.*

HARDINGTON MOOR

The Royal Oak Inn

Moor Lane, Hardington Moor, Yeovil BA22 9NW
☎ *(01935) 862354* 'Hag' Harris

 Ales from Butcombe and Branscombe always available plus two guests such as Slaters (Eccleshall) brews. Annual themed beer festival held in May each year.

A rural farmhouse freehouse. Two bars, dining area, beer garden, motorcycle-friendly. Food available Tues–Sun lunchtime and evenings. Children allowed.

OPEN *12–2.30pm and 7–11pm (10.30pm Sun). Closed Monday lunchtime.*

HINTON BLEWITT

Ring O'Bells

Hinton Blewitt, Nr Bristol BS39 5AN
☎ *(01761) 452239* Jon Jenssen

 Abbey Bellringer and Wadworth 6X usually available with two guest beers, perhaps from Young's, Fuller's, Butts, Wickwar, Badger or Oakhill.

T raditional country pub with lovely views. Food served 12–2pm and 7–10pm. Car park. Children welcome. Garden.

OPEN *12–3.30pm and 5–11pm (10.30pm Sun).*

HORSINGTON

Half Moon Inn

Horsington, Templecombe BA8 0EF
☎ *(01963) 370140*
Andrew and Philippa Tarling

 Freehouse with Wadworth 6X permanently available, plus four or five guests rotating all the time but favouring the stronger ones such as Hop Back Summer Lightning, Badger Tanglefoot and Adnams Broadside.

A typical community country pub that tries to present a traditional front yet has some modern extras such as a cash machine – a pretty exterior, pleasant interior and a friendly atmosphere. Accommodation. Darts, table football and skittle alley. Food except Sunday night. Car park and garden.

OPEN *12–2.30pm and 6–11pm Mon Fri; 12–3pm and 6–11pm Sat; 12–3pm and 7–10.30pm Sun.*

HUISH EPISCOPI

The Rose & Crown (Eli's)

Huish Episcopi, Langport TA10 9QT
☎ *(01458) 250494* Steve Pittard

A freehouse with a Teignworthy ale always available plus three guests of varying strengths usually from local breweries.

A traditional country pub with central servery and lots of smaller adjoining rooms, which has been in the same family for over 130 years. Beer garden. Food available at lunchtime and evenings until 8pm. Children allowed.

OPEN *11.30am–2.30pm and 5.30–11pm Mon–Thurs; all day Fri–Sun.*

KELSTON

The Old Crown
Bath Road, Kelston, Nr Bath
☎ *(01225) 423032* C Cole

 Butcombe Bitter and Gold, Bath Ales Gem and Wadworth 6X always available plus Wadworth Old Timer in winter only.

Traditional old-English pub and restaurant with open fire, original flagstones, candle-light and good atmosphere. Food every lunchtime and every evening except Sun and Mon. Car park and garden. No children under 14 inside. On A43 Bitton to Bath road, three miles outside Bath.

 11.30am–2.30pm and 5–11pm Mon–Fri; all day Sat and Sun.

LANGFORD BUDVILLE

Martlet Inn
Langford Budville, Wellington TA21 0QZ
☎ *(01823) 400262* Richard Owen

 A freehouse with Cotleigh Tawny and Barn Owl and Exmoor Ale always available, plus one guest.

A traditional country pub with dining area and beer garden. Food available at lunchtime and evenings. No juke box or games machines. Children allowed in designated areas.

 12–2.30pm Tues–Sat (closed Mon lunchtimes); 7–11pm Mon–Sat; 12–3pm and 7–10.30pm Sun.

LANGLEY MARSH

The Three Horseshoes
Langley Marsh, Wiveliscombe, Nr Taunton TA4 2UL
☎ *(01984) 623763* John Hopkins

 Palmers IPA, Otter Best and Fuller's London Pride always available plus guest beers which may inclue Harveys Sussex Best and Timothy Taylor Landlord.

An old, unspoilt, no-nonsense traditional pub. No juke box or games machines. Bar and restaurant food is available at lunchtime and evenings. Holiday cottages in grounds. Car park, garden and children's room. Children allowed in the restaurant. Follow the B3227 to Wiveliscombe, then follow signs to Langley Marsh.

 12–2.30pm and 7–11pm (10.30pm Sun); closed Mondays in winter.

LANGPORT

The Black Swan
North Street, Langport
☎ *(01458) 250355*
David Brown and Teresa Sleet

 Fuller's London Pride and Palmers Copper regularly available, plus a guest beer changing every week such as Palmers Dorset Gold.

Characterful inn with restaurant, skittle alley and beer garden. Food served 12–2pm and 7–9.30pm every day except Tuesday. Car park. Children welcome.

 11am–2.30pm and 6–11pm Mon–Thur; all day Fri–Sun.

LEIGH COMMON

Hunters Lodge Inn
Leigh Common, Wincanton BA9 8LD
☎ *(01747) 840439* Mr Bent

 A freehouse but with Oakhill Brewery ales usually available.

A country pub with bars, dining area and beer garden. Food available at lunchtime and evenings. Children allowed.

 11am–3pm and 6–11pm (10.30pm Sun).

LOWER ODCOMBE

Mason's Arms
41 Lower Odcombe, Yeovil BA22 8TX
☎ *(01935) 862591* Mr and Mrs Charteris

 Home of Odcombe Ales with the two Odcombe Higher and Lower brews produced on the premises and exclusively available in the bar. Occasional honey beer called Buzz. Other independent ales also available from breweries such as Otter and Butcombe.

A traditional pub with skittle alley. Food offered Wednesday to Saturday, lunchtime and evening, plus Sunday lunches and special curry nights on Thursdays. Beer garden. Children allowed in the garden. Camping.

 7–11pm Mon–Tues (closed lunchtime); 1–3pm and 7–11pm Wed–Fri; 12–3pm and 7–11pm Sat; 12–3pm and 7–10.30pm Sun.

LUXBOROUGH

Royal Oak of Luxborough

Exmoor National Park, Luxborough, Nr Dunster
TA23 0SH
☎ *(01984) 640319* James Waller

A freehouse with Cotleigh Tawny, Exmoor Gold, Palmers 200 and Acorn Ale always available plus occasional guest.

An unspoilt rural pub with loads of beams, flagstones etc. Farmhouse tables. Bar food offered at lunchtime, restaurant menu available at both sessions. Car park and beer garden. Children allowed in the restaurant. En-suite accommodation. Off the A396, four miles south of Dunster.

 12–2.30pm and 6–11pm Mon–Sat;
12–2.30pm and 7–10.30pm Sun.

MARTOCK

The Nag's Head

East Street, Martock TA12 6NF
☎ *(01935) 823432* Christopher Bell

A freehouse with Otter Bitter among the brews always available, plus two weekly changing guests such as Timothy Taylor Landlord, RCH East Street Cream, Badger Tanglefoot or other seasonal and celebration ales.

A local village pub with two bars (lounge and public), non-smoking dining area, beer garden, children's play area, accommodation, disabled access at rear. Well-known locally for its good homemade food, available lunchtimes and evenings. Families welcome. Happy hour for food and drink between 6 and 7pm. Can be difficult to find, but worth it! Phone for directions.

 12–3pm Tues–Sun (closed Mon
lunchtime); 6–11pm daily.

NAILSEA

The Blue Flame Inn

West End, Nailsea BS48 4DE
☎ *(01275) 856910* Mick Davidson

Fuller's London Pride always available plus two or three guest beers at any time, including beers from Oakhill, Butcombe, Wickwar and Smiles.

Charming, 200-year-old real country pub between Nailsea and Clevedon, popular with locals, joggers, riders and walkers. Three rooms and a bar, all with real character. Furnished with mismatched tables and chairs, as far as you can get from high-street theme pubs. Large garden with swings, covered drinking area and a barbecue. Children allowed everywhere except the public bar. Car park. No food.

 12–3pm and 6–11pm.

NETHER STOWEY

The Rose & Crown

St Mary Street, Nether Stowey TA5 1LJ
☎ *(01278) 732265* Malcolm and Gill Bennett

A freehouse with three hand pumps always serving cask ales from breweries such as Cottage, Moor, Oakhill, Cotleigh, Slaters, Scattor Rock, Stonehenge and Otter.

A traditional fifteenth-century coaching inn. One bar, lounge and beer garden. Food at lunchtime and evenings. Separate restaurant is open Wed–Sat. B&B. Children and well-behaved dogs allowed.

 12–11pm Mon–Sat; 12–5pm and
7–10.30pm Sun.

NETTLEBRIDGE

Nettlebridge Inn

Nettlebridge, Nr Oakhill
☎ *(01749) 841360* Mr, Mrs and Miss Piner

Oakhill Best Bitter and Wadworth 6X regularly available.

Olde-worlde, two-bar pub with non-smoking area and lots of hanging baskets in summer. Food served lunchtime and evening, and all day Sunday. Car park. Children welcome.

 12–3pm and 6–11pm Mon–Sat; all day
Sun and bank holidays.

NORTH CURRY

The Bird in Hand

1 Queen Square, North Curry, Taunton TA3 6LT
☎ *(01823) 490248* James Mogg

A freehouse with Butcombe Gold and Otter Bitter always available, plus a constantly changing guest.

A traditional one-bar country pub with log fires and patio. Food is available during all opening hours Tues–Sun, in both the bar and the pretty à la carte restaurant. Children allowed.

 12–3pm and 7–11pm Tues–Fri; 12–4pm
and 7–11pm Sat–Sun (10.30pm Sun).

NORTON ST PHILIP

Fleur de Lys

High Street, Norton St Philip, Nr Bath BA2 7LQ
☎ *(01373) 834333* Simon Shannon

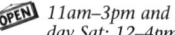A Wadworth house with 6X and IPA, plus Butcombe Bitter.

An old building and an old-style pub that prides itself on its food. Two bars and a restaurant above. Darts and skittles. Children welcome in one bar. Food served lunchtime and evening seven days a week. Parking.

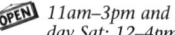 *11am–3pm and 5–11pm Mon–Fri; all*
day Sat; 12–4pm and 7–10.30pm Sun.

NORTON SUB HAMDON

Lord Nelson
Rectory Lane, Norton Sub Hamdon TA14 6SP
☎ *(01935) 881473* Mark Bloomer

 Teignworthy Reel Ale always available with two rotating guest beers.

A freehouse with the atmosphere of a traditional local village pub. A real fire as well as real beer. Children, dogs and muddy boots welcome. Food available lunchtime and evening every day. Live music once a month. Car park.

OPEN *12–3pm and 6.30–11pm Mon–Fri; 12–11pm Sat; 12–10.30pm Sun.*

PITMINSTER

The Queen's Arms
Pitminster, Nr Taunton TA3 7AZ
☎ *(01823) 421529*
Bob Cartman and Sharon Isidoro

 Cotleigh Tawny, Otter Bitter, Butcombe Bitter and Gold always available plus occasional guest beers.

A traditional stone-built pub with an attached fourteenth-century building. No games machines. Home-cooked food served at lunchtime and evenings. Car park and garden. Children allowed in the lounge, which has books and toys. Follow the signs for Corfe from Taunton and turn right in Corfe.

OPEN *11am–11pm Mon–Sat; 12–10.30pm Sun.*

PITNEY

Halfway House
Pitney, Nr Langport TA10 9AB
☎ *(01458) 252513* J Litchfield

 Up to ten beers available, including brews from Teignworthy, Cotleigh, Butcombe, Otter and Hop Back breweries, plus others.

A real ale pub with flagstone floors and log fires. No music or games machines. Bar food is available at lunchtime and evenings. Car park and garden. Well-behaved children allowed. CAMRA Somerset Pub of the Year 1997. On the main road between Somerton and Langport (B3151).

OPEN *11.30am–3pm and 5.30–11pm.*

RODE

The Bell Inn
13 Frome Road, Rode BA3 6PW
☎ *(01373) 830356* Richard Vestey

 A freehouse with Butcombe Bitter regularly available plus two guests.

A food-oriented country pub specialising in seafood. Two bars, dining area and beer garden. Food available at lunchtime and evenings. Children allowed.

OPEN *12–3pm and 7–11pm (10.30pm Sun).*

ROWBERROW

Swan Inn
Rowberrow, Winscombe BS25 1QL
☎ *(01934) 852371* Bob Flaxman

 Butcombe Bitter and Gold always on offer, plus a rotating guest.

Gimmick-free country pub that lets the customers create the atmosphere. Two spacious bars. Parking and garden areas. Food available lunchtime and evening seven days a week. No children under 14. Just off the A38.

OPEN *12–3pm and 6–11pm Mon–Sat; 12–3pm and 7–10.30pm Sun.*

SHURTON

The Shurton Inn
Shurton, Bridgwater TA5 1QE
☎ *(01278) 732695* Aly Critchley

 A freehouse with Exmoor Ale and Butcombe Bitter always available, plus a guest ale changing weekly. Beer festival held in June.

An unspoilt traditional pub with a large bar, with three seating areas on two levels, a restaurant area and a large beer garden. Home-cooked food available lunchtimes and evenings. Accommodation. Live music once a fortnight. Car park in front and to rear of pub. Children's licence.

OPEN *12–2.30pm and 6–11pm Mon–Sat; 12–3pm and 7–10.30pm Sun.*

SPARKFORD

Sparkford Inn
High Street, Sparkford BA22 7JH
☎ *(01963) 440218* Paul Clayton

 Four real ales available at any one time but changing frequently, brews from Butcombe and Otter are regulars.

A fifteenth-century coaching inn that is quite large yet retains a cosy olde-worlde atmosphere with window seats and interesting furnishing. Food every session. Children welcome. Accommodation. Car park and small garden.

OPEN *11am–11pm.*

STANTON WICK

Carpenters Arms
Stanton Wick, Nr Pensford BS39 4BX
☎ *(01761) 490202* Simon and Sharon Pledge

 Freehouse offering Butcombe Bitter and Wadworth 6X.

Quaint traditional pub with restaurant, situated just off the A368. Cosy window seat by large fire. Accommodation and disabled facilities. Food available in bar and restaurant lunchtimes and evening every day. Car park. Children's menu.

OPEN *11am–11pm Mon–Sat; 12–10.30pm Sun.*

TAUNTON

The Eagle Tavern

South Street, Taunton TA1 3AF
☎ *(01823) 275713* Barry and Nicola Turner

 Timothy Taylor Landlord permanently available and guests from breweries such as Smiles, Cotleigh and Brakspear.

A country-style pub in the town, with wooden floors and open fire. Beer garden. Food available whenever open. Children not allowed.

OPEN *5–11pm Mon–Thur; all day Fri–Sun.*

Perkin Warbeck

22 East Street, Taunton TA1 3LP
☎ *(01823) 335830* Ian and Leanne Borsing

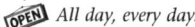 A Wetherspoon's pub with Shepherd Neame Spitfire, Exmoor Gold and Butcombe Bitter always available, plus up to four regularly changing guest ales.

A two-bar town-centre pub. Non-smoking areas, patio. Food available all day, every day. Children allowed for dining.

OPEN *All day, every day.*

TRUDOXHILL

The White Hart

Trudoxhill, Nr Frome BA11 2DT
☎ *(01373) 836324* Adrian Boone

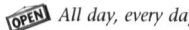 Butcombe Bitter, Wadworth 6X and RCH Hewish IPA regularly available plus a couple of guests.

A sixteenth-century country pub. One bar, restaurant, garden and children's play area. Food available 11.30am–9pm daily. Children allowed.

OPEN *All day, every day.*

WANSTROW

Pub at Wanstrow

Station Road, Wanstrow, Shepton Mallet BA4 4SZ
☎ *(01749) 850455* Paul and Daria Stevens

 Greene King IPA and Hop Back Entire Stout regularly available plus usually four other ales being served, such as Smiles Original and Hop Back Summer Lightning, supporting local breweries as much as possible.

A very friendly little village local with a strong emphasis on the beer. Food every session except Monday and Sunday night. Children allowed. Car park and small garden. Bar billiards, darts and skittle alley.

OPEN *12–2.30pm and 6–11pm Mon–Sat (closed Mon lunchtimes); 12–2.30pm and 7–10.30pm Sun.*

WELLINGTON

The Cottage Inn

Champford Lane, Wellington TA21 8BH
☎ *(01823) 664650* A and L Sullivan

 Greene King IPA, Otter Bitter and Fuller's London Pride permanently available, plus one other changing real ale.

Traditional town-centre pub. Pagoda-style garden with seating for 30. Food served 12–2pm daily. Children welcome, but no special facilities. Car park. Directions: in Wellington town centre, go past cinema on the left and take the second turning on the left.

OPEN *11am–3pm and 6–11pm Mon–Sat; 12–4pm and 7–10.30pm Sun.*

WELLOW

The Fox & Badger

Railway Lane, Wellow, Bath BA2 8QG
☎ *(01225) 832293* Eric and Susanne Hobbs

 Wadworth 6X, Butcombe Bitter and Badger Best usually available. Traditional ciders also served.

Sixteenth-century pub set in picturesque countryside, with conservatory, courtyard and skittle alley. Food served each lunchtime and evening – specialising in traditional ploughman's lunches with a variety of Cheddars. Ample village parking. Children and dogs welcome. Website: www.foxandbadger.co.uk for more details.

OPEN *11.30am–3pm and 6–11pm Mon–Thurs; 11.30am–11pm Fri–Sun.*

WELLS

Fountain Inn

1 St Thomas's Street, Wells BA5 2UU
☎ *(01749) 672317* Adrian and Sarah Lawrence

 Greene King IPA and Butcombe Bitter are served.

Popular inn with a good reputation for its food, which is served every session. Non-smoking area. Car park. Children welcome.

OPEN *12–3pm and 6–11pm (7–10.30pm Sun).*

WEST CRANMORE

Strode Arms

West Cranmore, Shepton Mallet BA4 4QJ
☎ *(01749) 880450*
Mr R McBain and Mrs H MacCullum

Wadworth 6X, JCB and Henry's IPA on offer plus one rotating guest.

A traditional and unpretentious country pub overlooking the village duck pond. One main bar and a restaurant. Food every session. Children allowed in restaurant and over 14 in the bar. Car park and garden.

OPEN *11am–2.30pm and 5–11pm Mon–Sat; 12–3pm and 7–10.30 Sun.*

WESTON-SUPER-MARE

Off The Rails

Pub on the Station, Railway Station, Weston-super-Mare BS23 1XY
☎ *(01934) 415109* Mr Hicks

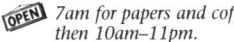RCH Bitter is constantly available, with two guests, changed weekly, perhaps including Slaters Shining Knight, Oakhill Mendip Gold, Sharp's Cornish Coaster, Tisbury Old Wardour or something from Berrow.

Traditional pub in a building dating from 1880, with one bar and buffet in the railway station. Food available in the buffet area. Children allowed in the buffet area.

OPEN *7am for papers and coffee, then 10am–11pm.*

The Regency

22–4 Lower Church Road, Weston-super-Mare BS23 2AG
☎ *(01934) 633406* Mark Short

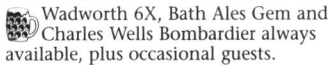Wadworth 6X, Bath Ales Gem and Charles Wells Bombardier always available, plus occasional guests.

A traditional, comfortable pub with pool room and beer yard. Food available at lunchtimes. Children allowed in the pool room. Situated oppostive Weston College.

OPEN *10am–11pm Mon–Sat; 12–10.30pm Sun.*

The Woolpack Inn

Shepherds Way, St Georges, Weston-super-Mare BS22 7XE
☎ *(01934) 521670* PW Sampson

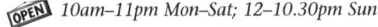Four beers always available, 30 per year to include Charles Wells Bombardier and Oakhill Best.

Village freehouse in 200-year-old building. Bar and restaurant food at lunchtime and evenings. Car park, garden, conservatory and function room. No children. Off M5, junction 21.

OPEN *12–2.30pm and 6–11pm Mon–Sat; 12–3pm and 7–10.30pm Sun.*

WILLITON

The Egremont Hotel

1 Fore Street, Williton, Taunton TA4 4PX
☎ *(01984) 632500* A Yon

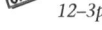A freehouse serving Fuller's London Pride and Exmoor Ale, plus guest beers.

A town-centre hotel with two bars, one mainly serving ciders. Restaurant, beer garden, accommodation. Food available at lunchtime and evenings. Children allowed.

OPEN *All day, every day.*

The Forester's Arms Hotel

Long Street, Williton, Taunton TA20 3PX
☎ *(01984) 632508* Mr I Petrie

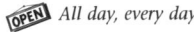A freehouse with Cotleigh Tawny always available, plus three or four others.

A two-bar village pub with dining area, beer garden, accommodation. Pool room and two dart boards. Food served at lunchtime and evenings. Children allowed during the daytime.

OPEN *All day, every day.*

WINCANTON

The Bear Inn

12 Market Place, Wincanton BA9 9LP
☎ *(01963) 32581* Ian Wainwright

A freehouse with Greene King Abbot always available plus three guests. Regulars include Ringwood Best and Fortyniner, Butcombe and many more.

An old coaching inn with food available at lunchtime and evenings in a separate dining area. Accommodation. Children allowed.

OPEN *All day, every day.*

WINSFORD

Royal Oak Inn

Winsford, Exmoor National Park, Nr Minehead TA24 7JE
☎ *(01643) 851455* Charles Steven

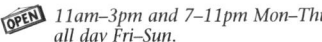Freehouse offering Exmoor Ale and Cotleigh Barn Owl, plus Cotleigh Tawny in the summer.

A cosy twelfth-century thatched inn situated in a beautiful village. Two bars and a quiet atmosphere. Accommodation. Food served lunchtime and evening. Car park and small garden. Children allowed in the back bar.

OPEN *11am–3pm and 7–11pm Mon–Thur; all day Fri–Sun.*

WIVELISCOMBE

The Bear Inn

10 North Street, Wiveliscombe TA4 2JY
☎ *(01984) 623537* Mr A and Mrs H Harvey

Cotleigh Tawny and Golden Eagle, plus Otter Bitter regularly available, plus one guest beer.

Welcoming locals' pub with large, well-laid-out garden and patio. Food served 12–2.30pm and 6–9pm daily. Car park. Family room and large, safe beer garden with children's play equipment. Pool table. Disabled toilets.

OPEN *11am–11pm Mon–Sat; 12–10.30pm Sun.*

WOOKEY

Burcott Inn

*Wookey Road, Wookey, Nr Wells, Somerset
BA5 1NJ*
☎ *(01749 673874)* Ian Stead

Three cask-conditioned ales offered in the summer, two in the winter. Sharp's Doom Bar often available, also something from Cotleigh, Branscombe or Teignworthy but more than 60 different beers tried in a year.

Old stone traditional pub with real beer, real fires and real homemade food. Two bars in one large room. Food available except Sun and Mon evening. Children welcome in games room, garden and restaurant. Parking and large garden. Traditional games such as darts, cribbage and shove ha'penny.

OPEN *11.30am–2.30pm and 6–11pm Mon–Fri; 12–3pm and 6–11pm Sat; 12–3pm and 7–10.30pm Sun.*

WOOKEY HOLE

Wookey Hole Inn

Wookey Hole, Nr Wells BA5 1BP
☎ *(01749) 676677* Mark Hay

Four constantly rotating ales are on offer here.

From the outside this looks like an ordinary pub, from the inside it has a very different and modern feel. Open-plan, it is a pub that is almost a restaurant. High quality, but not cheap, food. Accommodation with rooms in a Japanese style. Well-behaved children welcome. Board games. Live music Fri and Sun nights. Large garden with sculptures and a fountain. Car park.

OPEN *11.30am–3pm and 6–11pm (10.30pm Sun); the restaurant stays open a further hour.*

YEOVIL

The Armoury

1 The Park, Yeovil BA20 1DY
☎ *(01935) 471047* Mark Deegan

Wadworth 6X, IPA and JCB and a Butcombe brew always available plus two guest ales such as Adnams Broadside.

A traditional real ale house with one environmentally controlled bar. Patio and skittle alley. Food available at lunchtime and evenings. Children allowed in one bar.

OPEN *11am–3pm and 5–11pm Mon–Wed; all day Thurs–Sun.*

YOU TELL US

* *The Cooper's Arms Hotel*, Market Street, Highbridge
* *The Crown*, Keynsham
* *The King's Head Inn*, Main Street, Higham
* *The Queens Arms Inn*, Corton Denham
* *The Ring of Bells*, Pit Hill Lane, Moorlinch, Bridgewater

Places Featured:

Abbots Bromley
Alsagers Bank
Bignall End
Burston
Burton upon Trent
Cheslyn Hay
Dosthill
Eccleshall
Etruria
Fazeley
Great Chatwell
Harriseahead

Ipstones
Kidsgrove
Kinver
Leek
Lichfield
Marston
Penkridge
Shraley Brook
Stafford
Stoke-on-Trent
Stone
Whiston

THE BREWERIES

THE ECCLESHALL BREWERY

*The St George Hotel, Castle Street, Eccleshall
ST21 6DF*
☎ *(01785) 850300*

SLATERS BITTER 3.6% ABV
Balanced easy-quaffer.
TOP NOTCH 3.8% ABV
Summer brew.
SLATERS ORIGINAL 4.0% ABV
Complex and smooth.
TOP TOTTY 4.0% ABV
Well-balanced with good hoppiness.
SLATERS PREMIUM 4.4% ABV
Full-bodied and deceptively smooth.
SLATERS SUPREME 4.7% ABV
Creamy, full-bodied and hoppy.

MARSTON, THOMPSON & EVERSHED PLC

*The Brewery, Shobnall Road, Burton upon Trent
DE14 2BW*
☎ *(01283) 531131*

BITTER 3.8% ABV
Well-balanced, easy-drinking brew.
PEDIGREE 4.5% ABV
Smooth and rounded.
OWD RODGER 7.6% ABV
Dark and powerful, with some sweetness.
Plus seasonal brews.

OLD COTTAGE BEER CO.

*Unit 3, Brian Eccleshall Yard, Eccleshall Business
Park, Hawkins Lane, Burton upon Trent
DE14 1PT*
☎ *(01283) 540969*

SHADOW ALE 4.5% ABV
PRIDE PARK 4.7% ABV
COTTAGE PRIDE 4.8% ABV
QUINTAN ALE 5.8% ABV
Trade dictates that beers change frequently.

THE TITANIC BREWERY

*Unit G, Harvey Works, Lingard Street, Burslem,
Stoke-on-Trent ST6 1ED*
☎ *(01782) 823447*
www.titanicbrewery.co.uk

BEST BITTER 3.5% ABV
Quenching and hoppy.
MILD 3.5% ABV
Full of roast malt.
LIFEBOAT 4.0% ABV
Fruit and bittersweet flavour, with a dry finish.
ICEBERG 4.1% ABV
Summer brew.
PREMIUM BITTER 4.1% ABV
Golden, with hoppiness throughout.
STOUT 4.5% ABV
Rich flavour and hoppiness.
WHITE STAR 4.8% ABV
Pale, quenching and deceptively drinkable.
CAPTAIN SMITH'S STRONG ALE 5.2% ABV
Smooth, rounded roast flavour with good
hoppiness.
WRECKAGE 7.2% ABV
Classic winter brew.

THE PUBS

ABBOTS BROMLEY

The Crown Inn

Market Place, Abbots Bromley, Nr Rugeley WS15 3BS
☎ *(01283) 840227* Frank Robertson

Two guest beers are served, at least one of which is changed every week. Regulars include Morland Old Speckled Hen, Greene King Abbot Ale and Fuller's London Pride, but Adnams Broadside and Regatta, Wadworth 6X, brews from Wychwood and seasonal ales are also featured.

Traditional village pub, part of which was a nineteenth-century coaching inn, refurbished internally. Food available, including children's menu. Lounge and bar, separate dining area, function room, six letting rooms, garden. Car park. Situated in the centre of the village, so once you've found the village, you've found the pub!

OPEN *12–3pm and 6–11pm Mon–Fri; 11am–11pm Sat; 12–3pm and 7–10.30pm Sun.*

ALSAGERS BANK

The Gresley Arms

High Street, Alsagers Bank ST7 8BQ
☎ *(01782) 720297* Linda Smith

A freehouse offering six regular guests, changed daily, mainly from micro-breweries. Traditional cider/scrumpy also available.

A 220-year-old country village pub that claims to have the best views in Staffordshire – it is high up, and nine counties can be seen, plus the Welsh mountains. One central bar, lounge and games room, dining room, garden and play area. Children allowed. Car park for 30 cars. Three miles from Newcastle under Lyme (look for signs for Alsagers Bank, not Alsagers).

OPEN *12–3pm and 6–11pm Mon–Sat; 12–10.30pm Sun.*

BIGNALL END

The Plough

Ravens Lane, Bignall End, Stoke-on-Trent
☎ *(01782) 720469* Paul Holt

Banks's Bitter permanently available, plus an ever-changing range of guest ales served on four hand pumps.

A traditional roadside pub. Food available lunchtimes and evenings. Children allowed if eating. Car park. Beer garden.

OPEN *12–3.30pm and 7–11pm Mon–Thurs; 12–11pm Fri–Sat; 12–10.30pm Sun.*

BURSTON

The Greyhound Inn

Burston, Stafford ST18 0DR
☎ *(01889) 508263* Alan Jordan

Three hand pumps always available, with guest ales from around the country.

Traditional seventeenth-century country freehouse with restaurant, in attractive village. Food served lunchtimes and evenings Mon–Sat and all day Sun. Large car park. Children welcome.

OPEN *11.30am–3pm and 6–11pm Mon–Sat; 12–10.30pm Sun.*

BURTON UPON TRENT

The Alfred

Derby Street, Burton upon Trent DE14 2LD
☎ *(01283) 562178*
Martin Page AMBII and Lesley Greenslade

A Burton Bridge Brewery tenancy with Bridge Bitter, Golden Delicious, Festival Ale, Burton Porter, Mild and XL Bitter permanently available. Plus one constantly changing guest which often includes a Titanic or RCH brew. Leatherbritches and Iceni also supported. Two beer festivals every year: one at Easter and one in November.

A two-bar town pub with dining area and beer garden. Food served every lunchtime and Mon–Sat evenings. Full-sized boules pitch. Children allowed.

OPEN *12–11pm (10.30pm Sun).*

Bass Museum

Hornington Street, Burton on Trent DE14 1YQ
☎ *(0845) 600 0598* Darren Robinson

Although clearly owned by international brewing giant Bass, this museum bar houses its own micro-brewery, The Museum Brewing Company, which uses traditional brewing methods and old equipment to produce cask ales. A range of home brews and guest ales from local breweries are sold alongside the Bass beers. Always a variety of strengths on offer, from 3.5%–10.5% ABV.

The Burton Bar is situated inside the Museum of Brewing History, also available for exhibition and private hire. Food served 11am–2.30pm daily. Children allowed with activity/play area provided. Entrance free to CAMRA members. Happy hour 5–7pm Mon–Fri. Brewery tours.

VICTORIA 3.5% ABV
OSSILERS OF DERBY 4.0% ABV
JOULES OF STONE 4.1% ABV
WORTHING WHITE SHIELD 5.6% ABV
Brewed and bottled.
Plus monthly specials.

OPEN *Museum: From 10am, last admission 4pm daily. Burton Bar: 11am–7pm Mon–Fri; 11am–5pm Sat; 12–5pm Sun.*

Burton Bridge Inn

Bridge Street, Burton upon Trent DE14 1SY
☎ *(01283) 536596* Kevin McDonald

Home of the Burton Bridge Brewery with Bridge Bitter, Porter and Festival Ale always available. Seasonal ales always a feature, for example Summer Ale or Gold Medal Ale. Other guests rotated on two pumps including beers from Timothy Taylor and York breweries.

A town brewpub with two rooms (one non-smoking) and a central bar. One room features oak panelling, a quarry-tiled floor and a feature fireplace. Dining area, patio. Food served lunchtimes. Children allowed.

GOLDEN DELICIOUS 3.8% ABV
A light golden bitter.
XL BITTER 4.0% ABV
BRIDGE BITTER 4.2% ABV
Normal brown bitter.
PORTER 4.5% ABV
A dark beer.
SPRING ALE 4.7% ABV
Seasonal.
STAFFORDSHIRE KNOT BROWN ALE 4.8% ABV
Brewed each autumn.
BATTLE BREW 5.0% ABV
Brewed each July.
HEARTY ALE 5.0% ABV
A Christmas brew.
TOP DOG STOUT 5.0% ABV
A winter ale.
FESTIVAL ALE 5.5% ABV
Slightly sweet with a bitter finish.
Plus one new beer each month, always called Gold Medal Ale and at 4.5% ABV, but brewed to varying recipes.

OPEN *11.30am–2.30pm and 5–11pm.*

The Devonshire Arms

86 Station Street, Burton-upon-Trent DE14 1BT
☎ *(01283) 562392* Deborah Reiblein-Stubb

A Burton Bridge Brewery house with Stairway to Heaven, Bridge Bitter and Golden Delicious plus either Top Dog (stout) or Porter always available. Also one weekly changing guest ale which could be from any independent brewery.

A friendly real ale pub dating from the nineteenth century, on the outskirts of Burton. Public and lounge bars decorated with photographs from 1860. Food available Mon–Fri lunchtimes and Sundays for traditional roasts. Children allowed. Non-smoking area, outside patio. No loud music.

OPEN *11am–2.30pm and 5.30–11pm Mon–Thurs; 11am–11pm Fri–Sat; 12–3pm and 7–10.30pm Sun.*

The Roebuck

Station Street, Burton upon Trent DE14 1BT
☎ *(01283) 568660* Tim and Lisa Salt

Marston's Pedigree, Greene King Abbot, Adnams Broadside, Morland Old Speckled Hen and Ruddles County always available, plus occasional guests.

Fringe-of-town pub with one open-plan room, small patio, accommodation. Bar food, including Staffordshire oatcakes, served 12–2pm Tues–Fri. Weekly quiz. No children.

OPEN *11am–11pm Mon–Sat; 12–3pm and 7–10.30pm Sun.*

Thomas Sykes Inn

Anglesey Road, Burton upon Trent DE14 3PF
☎ *(01283) 510246* Norman Goddard

A freehouse with Marston's Pedigree usually available, plus seven or eight different guests beers per week.

A town pub born in a stable(!), with a cobblestone floor and brewery memorabilia. Bar and snug. No food. Children allowed.

OPEN *11.30am–2.30pm and 5–11pm Mon–Thurs; all day Fri; 11.30am–2.30pm and 7–11pm Sat; 12–2.30pm and 7–10.30pm Sun.*

CHESLYN HAY

The Woodman Inn

Woodman Lane, Cheslyn Hay WS6 7ES
☎ *(01922) 413686* Mr Arton

Three guest beers, changed weekly, often include Charles Wells Bombardier, but Gale's HSB, Everards Original and Tiger, Bateman XXXB and Marston's Pedigree might also feature.

Traditional village pub dating from the 1870s, with beamed ceiling in the lounge. Having been recently extended, it now has a conservatory, two bars, a non-smoking dining area and garden. Occasional live music. Car park. Children allowed. Can be difficult to find, as it is in a cul-de-sac location, so call for directions.

OPEN *12–3pm and 7–11pm (midnight for diners) Mon–Thurs; 11am–11pm Fri–Sat; 12.30–3pm and 7–11pm Sun.*

DOSTHILL

The Fox

105 High Street, Dosthill B77 1LQ
☎ 01827 280847 Mr Gwyn

 Greene King Abbot is one of the beers permanently on offer, with the two guests often including something from Church End, or perhaps Fuller's London Pride, Everards Lazy Daze or a Burton Bridge brew.

Village pub on the outskirts of Tamworth in a traditional Victorian building, more than 140 years old. Food available. Lounge and bar, non-smoking dining area, conservatory/ restaurant, garden. Children allowed in lounge if eating, but not in the bar. Car park. On the main road out of Tamworth.

 12–3pm and 6–11pm Mon–Sat; 12–3pm and 7–10.30pm Sun.

ECCLESHALL

The George Hotel

Castle Street, Eccleshall ST21 6DF
☎ (01785) 850300 Gerard and Moyra Slater

 The Eccleshall Brewery is located on the premises, so the Slaters Ales range of up to six beers are brewed and available here plus a variety of guests.

Opened in March 1995 by Gerard and Moyra Slater. The beer is brewed by their son, Andrew. The brewery is a 20-barrel plant. The George is a sixteenth-century coaching inn with olde-worlde beams, log fires, real ales, malt whisky. Bar and restaurant food available. Car park. Accommodation. Children and dogs welcome.

 All day, every day.

ETRURIA

The Plough Inn

147 Etruria Road, Stoke-on-Trent
☎ (01782) 269445 Rob Ward

A Robinson's tied house serving Dark Mild, Best Bitter, Old Stockport Bitter and Frederics Premium Ale, plus seasonal ales.

Country-style pub with a collection of valve radios, old TVs, gramophones, telephones, bottled beers and local pictures, plus a preserved classic bus. Beer garden. Well-known locally for good food, which is available 12–2pm Mon–Sat and 7–9pm Mon–Sun. Car park. Children welcome if dining.

12–2.30pm and 7–11pm Mon–Sat; 7–10.30pm Sun.

FAZELEY

The Plough & Harrow

Atherstone Street, Fazeley B78 3RF
☎ (01827) 289596 Paul Kilby

 Two brews always available plus two guests such as Morland Old Speckled Hen, Wadworth 6X, Thwaites Daniel's Hammer or Fuller's London Pride.

A one-bar village pub. Beer garden. En-suite accommodation. Restaurant with food served at lunchtime and evenings. Children allowed.

 11.30am–3pm and 5.30–11pm Mon–Thurs; all day Fri–Sun.

GREAT CHATWELL

The Red Lion Inn

Great Chatwell, Nr Newport TF10 9BJ
☎ (01952) 691366 Mrs Paula Smith

 Everards Beacon Bitter and Tiger regularly available, plus three guest beers, perhaps from Charles Wells, Robinson's, Wood, Hook Norton, Mansfield, Shepherd Neame, Eccleshall, Lichfield and many others.

Traditional, ivy-clad pub, attracting a mixed clientele. Food served evenings only Mon–Fri, all day at weekends and bank holidays. Car park. Children's play area with animals and birds.

 6–11pm Mon–Fri; 12–11pm Sat and bank holidays; 12–10.30pm Sun.

HARRISEAHEAD

The Royal Oak

42 High Street, Harriseahead, Stoke-on-Trent ST7 4JT
☎ (01782) 513362 Barry Reece

 A freehouse with Fuller's London Pride and Charles Wells Bombardier often available plus a couple of others from independent and micro-breweries whenever possible. Beers from the Isle of Man are especially favoured.

A traditional village pub with one bar and a lounge. Car park. No food. No children.

 7–11pm Mon–Fri; 12–3pm and 7–11pm Sat–Sun.

IPSTONES
The Linden Tree
47 Froghall Road, Ipstones, Stoke-on-Trent ST10 2NA
☎ *(01538) 266370* Graham Roberts

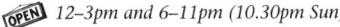 A freehouse with Timothy Taylor Landlord permanently available, plus two guest ales.

A country pub with separate 50-seater non-smoking restaurant. Beer garden. Food served at lunchtime and evenings. Children allowed. Website: www.thelindentree.co.uk.

OPEN *12–3pm and 6–11pm (10.30pm Sun).*

KIDSGROVE
The Blue Bell
25 Hardingswood, Kidsgrove, Stoke-on-Trent ST7 1EG
☎ *(01782) 774052* David Washbrook

 A genuine freehouse serving Thwaites Bitter, plus five frequently changing guests (1150 in four years) from small and micro-breweries, including beers from Whim, Titanic, Oakham, Burton Bridge, Eccleshall, and many more.

Smallish, four-room, out-of-town pub just north of the Potteries, on an island at the junction of the Rivers Trent and Mersey and the Macclesfield Canal. CAMRA Potteries Pub of the Year for the last four years, and CAMRA Staffordhsire Pub of the Year for the last three. Outside drinking area to the front and garden to the rear. Basic snacks at weekends. Dog-friendly, no children. Car Park. Five minutes' walk from Kidsgrove Station along the towpath.

OPEN *7.30–11pm Tues–Fri; 1–4pm and 7–11pm Sat; 12–4pm and 7–10.30pm Sun; closed Mon except bank holidays.*

KINVER
The Plough & Harrow
High Street, Kinver DY7 6HD
☎ *(01384) 872659* Mrs Shirley

 Four pumps serve bitter and three serve mild, with Batham Bitter and Mild always on offer.

Traditional village pub, over 100 years old, with L-shaped lounge and small patio area. Food is available from a limited menu. Live music Thursday evenings. Car park. Well-behaved children allowed. Four miles from Stourbridge.

OPEN *6–11pm Mon–Thurs; 5–11pm Fri; 11am–11pm Sat; 12–10.30pm Sun.*

LEEK
The Bull's Head
35 St Edward Street, Leek ST13 5DS
☎ *(01538) 370269* Vicki and Chris

 A freehouse with Beartown Bearskinful currently available as a permanent feature, plus one or two guests, always including another Beartown brew. The newly formed Leek Brewing Company is expected to begin production of two or three beers during 2002, and the pub will then feature these brews. Weston's cider also served.

Long, thin pub, with a lively atmosphere at weekends and quieter in the week. Pool table and darts at one end, pin-ball machine at the other. Ample street parking. Children and dogs welcome.

OPEN *5–11pm Mon, Tues, Thurs; 12–11pm Wed and Fri; all day Sat–Sun.*

Den Engel
23 St Edward Street, Leek ST13 5DR
☎ *(01538) 373751* Geoff and Hilary Turner

Four constantly changing guest beers are on offer, and small independents and micros are favoured.

Imposing street-corner building, housing impressive continental-style bar. Excellent beer selection, including over 120 Belgian bottled beers and 6 Belgian beers on tap. Bar food available Wed–Thurs and Sun evenings, lunchtime and evening Fri and lunchtimes only Sat. A separate restaurant is open Thurs–Sat evenings. Ample street parking.

OPEN *5–11pm Mon–Thurs; 12–11pm Fri–Sat; 12–3pm and 7–10.30pm Sun.*

The Swan Hotel
2 St Edward Street, Leek ST13 5DS
☎ *(01538) 382081* David and Julie Ellerton

Three or four rotating guests on offer. Wadworth 6X, Wychwood Hobgoblin and Robinson's Frederics are regular features, plus seasonal specials.

A four-bar town-style pub in moorlands, with an additional bar called JD's attached, which is a young person's modern themed sports bar. Food served at lunchtime and evenings. Children allowed. Function room. Bridal suite. Past winner of CAMRA's Pub of the Year and Pub of the Month.

OPEN *11am–3pm and 7–11.30pm.*

The Wilkes Head
16 St Edward Street, Leek ST13 5DA
☎ *(01538) 383616*

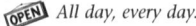The Whim Ales flagship pub, with Hartington Bitter and IPA, Magic Mushroom Mild, and Whim Arbor Light always available, plus an ever-changing range of guest ales from around the country. Seasonal ales such as Whim Black Christmas and Old Isaak stocked when available.

An award-winning town pub, famous for its ales. Small and cosy with large beer garden. Children and dogs welcome.

OPEN *All day, every day.*

LICHFIELD

The Hogshead
12–14 Tamworth Street, Lichfield WS13 6JJ
☎ *(01543) 258925* Mia Higgins

Hook Norton Old Hooky, Timothy Taylor Landlord and Marston's Pedigree are among the permanent beers here. Two guests, changed monthly, sometimes include a brew from Lichfield Brewery.

A one-bar drinkers' pub, with food available. Beer festivals held two or three times a year (call for details). Children not allowed. Situated in the town centre.

OPEN *11am–11pm Mon–Sat; 12–10.30pm Sun.*

The Queen's Head
Queen Street, Lichfield WS13 6QD
☎ *(01543) 410932* Roy Harvey

Adnams Best, Timothy Taylor Landlord and Marston's Pedigree always available, plus two guests, rotating weekly, including beers from all over the British Isles.

A traditional, small, backstreet pub. No music, small TV, one games machine. Bar food available at lunchtime (12–2.30pm), but the pub is really famous for its selection of cheeses, of which up to 20 different ones are available all day.

OPEN *All day Mon–Sat; 12–3pm and 7–10.30pm Sun.*

MARSTON

The Fox Inn
Marston, Nr Church Eaton ST20 0AS
☎ *(01785) 84072*

Eight beers available including Coach House (Joule) Old Priory, Mansfield Old Baily and Charles Wells Eagle. Plus Lloyds and Wood brews and guests from Wychwood, Timothy Taylor etc.

An unadulterated alehouse in the middle of nowhere. Bar and restaurant food available at lunchtime and evenings. Car parking and children's room. Field for tents and caravans. Accommodation.

OPEN *12–3pm and 6–11pm.*

PENKRIDGE

The Star Inn
Market Place, Penkridge, Stafford ST19 5DJ
☎ *(01785) 712513* George G Hedges

Banks's Original and Bitter usually available plus one guest ale from Mansfield or Marston's.

An olde-worlde traditional pub set in a scenic village. Food available 12–4pm. Children welcome. Car park.

OPEN *11am–11pm Mon–Sat; 12–10.30pm Sun.*

SHRALEY BROOK

The Rising Sun
Knowle Bank Road, Shraley Brook, Stoke-on-Trent ST7 8DS
☎ *(01782) 720600* Jill Holland

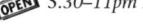Home of the Shraley Brook Brewing Company with the range of three home brews avaiable plus guest beers such as Cottage Golden Arrow, RCH Pitchfork and Archers' Golden.

A traditional country pub with three serving rooms, real fires, function room, restaurant, beer garden and a one-acre paddock with Shetland ponies. Plans for brewery tours. Homemade food served at lunchtime and evenings, including real chips! Children allowed.

OPEN *5.30–11pm Mon–Thurs; all day Fri–Sun.*

STAFFORD

The Stafford Arms
43 Railway Street, Stafford
☎ *(01785) 253313* Marie Mullaney

Titanic Best and White Star always available, plus seven guests, a traditional cider and various imported bottled beer.

A traditional pub with bar food available at lunchtimes. CAMRA Pub of the Year 1994. West Midlands Charity Pub of the Year 2001, with regular charity events held. Car park, bar billiards. Just by the railway station.

OPEN *12–11pm Mon–Sat; 12–4pm and 7–10.30pm Sun.*

Tap & Spile
Peel Terrace, Stafford ST16 3HE
☎ *(01785) 223563* Mr S Tideswell

A selection of eight constantly changing cask ales always available (around 1000 per year).

A village pub. CAMRA Stafford and Stone Pub of the Year 2002. Non-smoking dining area, beer garden. No food. No children.

OPEN *All day, every day.*

STOKE-ON-TRENT

Hogshead

2–6 Percy Street, Hanley, Stoke-on-Trent ST1 1NF
☎ *(01782) 209585* Brett Ritzkowski

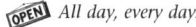 A Whitbread house with an extensive range of cask ales always available. Morland Old Speckled Hen and Wadworth 6X on permanently, plus a range of six guests such as Titanic Best or Premium. Each month one beer is featured as Beer of the Month on special offer (buy three get one free).

A town pub in a city-centre location. One bar, disabled access and lift. Non-smoking area. Food available all day. Children allowed before 6pm.

OPEN *All day, every day.*

The Tontine Alehouse

20 Tontine Street, Hanley, Stoke-on-Trent ST1 1AQ
☎ *(01782) 263890* Becky Smith

 Marston's Pedigree always available, plus four weekly changing guest ales from independent breweries all over the country.

A one-bar, city-centre pub with beer garden. Food served at lunchtime only. Children allowed, if eating.

OPEN *All day Mon–Sat; closed Sun.*

STONE

The Pheasant Inn

Old Road, Stone ST15 8HS
☎ *(01785) 814603* Mrs Glover

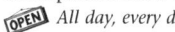 A range of traditional cask ales from independent breweries always available.

A Victorian two-bar pub on the outskirts of town, with a dining room and a child-safe beer garden with lockable access though the pub. Darts and traditional pub games. Food available at lunchtime, bookings only for evenings. Children allowed, if accompanied and if eating.

OPEN *All day, every day.*

The Star Inn

Stafford Road, Stone ST15 8QW
☎ *(01785) 813096* Michael Wheeler

Banks's Bitter and Original and Marston's Pedigree always available plus two guests such as Camerons Strongarm.

An edge-of-town pub situated by the canal with access to the towpath. Two bars, garden and patio. Food available all day. Children allowed.

OPEN *All day, every day.*

WHISTON

The Swan Inn

Whiston, Nr Penkridge ST19 5QH
☎ *(01785) 716200* Jim Davis

Holdens Bitter and Banks's Original permanently available plus two or three guests mostly from smaller breweries such as Titanic, Church End, Wood, Hanby, Jennings and Slaters. Some 300 different beers served over two years.

Set in six acres in a rural location, this pub has open fireplaces, a non-smoking dining room and a beer garden with children's play area. Food available in the evenings, plus Sunday lunch. Children allowed. Car park. Situated two miles off the main road, find Whiston and you find the pub!

OPEN *6–11pm Mon–Sat (closed lunch); 12–10.30pm Sun.*

YOU TELL US

* *The Cooper's Tavern,* Cross Street, Burton-upon-Trent
* *The Crossways,* Nelson Place, Newcastle-under-Lyme
* *The White Swan,* Coventry Road, Kingsbury, Tamworth

Places Featured:

Aldeburgh
Barham
Bildeston
Boxford
Brandon
Brome
Bungay
Bury St Edmunds
Carlton Colville
Earl Soham
East Bergholt
Edwardstone
Felixstowe
Framsden
Freckenham

Gislingham
Great Wenham
Hasketon
Ipswich
Kersey
Lavenham
Laxfield
Lowestoft
Market Weston
Oulton
Pin Mill
Southwold
Stowmarket
Swilland
Wingfield

THE BREWERIES

ADNAMS & CO. PLC

Sole Bay Brewery, East Green, Southwold IP18 6JW
☎ *(01502) 727200*
www.adnams.co.uk

 BITTER 3.7% ABV
Clean and well-hopped, with fruity flavours.
REGATTA 4.3% ABV
Seasonal Apr–Aug.
FISHERMAN 4.5% ABV
Seasonal Sep–end Feb.
BROADSIDE 4.7% ABV
Powerful malty brew with balancing hoppiness.
TALLY HO % ABV VARIABLE
Seasonal Dec. Gravity decided on brew day.
Plus seasonal brews.

BARTRAMS BREWERY

8 Thurston Granary, Station Hill, Thurston,
Bury St Edmunds IP31 3QU
☎ *(01359) 233303*

 MARLD 3.4% ABV
Flavoursome dark mild.
PREMIER 3.7% ABV
Light and hoppy.
LITTLE GREEN MAN 3.8% ABV
Lighter version of Green Man.
RED QUEEN 3.9% ABV
IPA-style brew.
GREEN MAN 4.0% ABV
Organic beer with a hint of coriander.
PIERROT 4.0% ABV
Very light with Tettnang and Saaz hops.
BEES KNEES 4.2% ABV
With honey and coriander.
JESTER 4.4% ABV
Full-bodied, easy quaffer.
CAPTAIN BILL BARTRAMS BEST BITTER 4.8% ABV
Full-bodied and strong.
THURSTON QUENCHER 5.0% ABV
A blend of five hops.
CAPTAINS STOUT
Traditional-style stout also available with cherry or damson.

COX & HOLBROOK

Manor Farm, Buxhall IP14 3DY
☎ *(01449) 736323*

SHELLEY DARK 3.6% ABV
CROWN DARK MILD 3.8% ABV
OLD MILL BITTER 3.8% ABV
GOODCOCK'S WINNER 5.0% ABV
IRONOAK SINGLE STOUT 5.0% ABV
STORM WATCH 5.0% ABV
STOWMARKET PORTER 5.0% ABV
UNCLE STAN 5.0% ABV
EAST ANGLIAN PALE ALE 6.0% ABV
PRENTICE 7.0% ABV

GREEN JACK BREWING CO. LTD

Oulton Broad Brewery, Unit 2, Harbour Road
Industrial Estate, Oulton Road, Lowestoft
NR32 3LZ
☎ *(01502) 587905*

 MILD 3.0% ABV
Occasional.
BITTER 3.5% ABV
CANARY 3.8% ABV
HONEY BUNNY 4.0% ABV
Spring brew.
OLD THUNDERBOX 4.0% ABV
Winter brew.
SUMMER DREAM 4.0% ABV
Summer brew.
GRASSHOPPER 4.2% ABV
ORANGE WHEAT BEER 4.2% ABV
GOLD FISH 4.8% ABV
GONE FISHING 5.0% ABV
NORFOLK WOLF PORTER 5.2% ABV
Occasional.
LURCHER STRONG ALE 5.4% ABV
Occasional.
RIPPER 8.5% ABV
Plus seasonal and occasional brews.

GREENE KING PLC

Westgate Brewery, Bury St Edmunds IP33 1QT
☎ *(01284) 763222*
www.greeneking.co.uk

 IPA 3.6% ABV
Hoppy session bitter.
RUDDLES BEST BITTER 3.7% ABV
TRIUMPH 4.3% ABV
RUDDLES COUNTY 4.9% ABV
ABBOT ALE 5.0% ABV
Rounded and flavoursome.
RUDDLES ORGANIC 5.1% ABV
MORLAND OLD SPECKLED HEN 5.2% ABV
RUDDLES WHEAT 5.3% ABV

KINGS HEAD BREWERY

132 High Street, Bildeston IP7 7ED
☎ *(01449) 741434*
www.bildestonkingshead.co.uk

 NSB 2.8% ABV
Low alcohol beer.
BEST BITTER 3.8% ABV
LYNX 3.9% ABV
BLONDIE 4.0% ABV
FIRST GOLD 4.3% ABV
Very bitter.
HERSBRUCKER BIER 4.3% ABV
APACHE 4.5% ABV
BILLY 4.8% ABV
CROWDIE 5.0% ABV
JJ'S LEMON BITTER 5.0% ABV
DARK VADER 5.4% ABV
Complex, roast character.

LIDSTONES BREWERY

Coltsfoot Green, Wickhambrook, Newmarket
CB8 8UW
☎ *(01440) 820232*

ROWLEY MILD 3.2% ABV
SESSION BITTER 3.7% ABV
LUCKY PUNTER 4.3% ABV
OAT STOUT 4.4% ABV
RAWALPINDI IPA 5.0% ABV
Plus seasonals and celebration ales.

MAULDONS

7 Addison Road, Chilton Industrial Estate,
Sudbury CO10 2YW
☎ *(01787) 311055*
www.mauldons.co.uk

MAULDONS BITTER 3.6% ABV
MOLETRAP 3.8% ABV
Rounded easy-quaffer.
DICKENS 4.0% ABV
Pale with hoppy fruit flavour and dry finish.
MIDSUMMER GOLD 4.0% ABV
PICKWICK BITTER 4.2% ABV
Formerly known as Squires.
PLOUGHMANS 4.3% ABV
SUFFOLK PRIDE 4.8% ABV
Powerful hoppiness throughout.
BLACK ADDER 5.3% ABV
Stout.
WHITE ADDER 5.3% ABV
Easy-drinking and well-hopped.

NETHERGATE BREWERY CO. LTD
11–13 High Street, Clare CO10 8NY
☎ *(01787) 277244*

 IPA 3.5% ABV
Clean hop flavour.
PRIORY MILD 3.5% ABV
UMBEL ALE 3.8% ABV
Distinctive hoppy and coriander flavours.
SUFFOLK COUNTY BEST BITTER 4.0% ABV
Malty and bitter.
AUGUSTINIAN ALE 4.5% ABV
OLD GROWLER 5.0% ABV
Soft, chocolate malt flavours.
UMBEL MAGNA 5.0% ABV
Porter with coriander.
Plus monthly, seasonal brews.

ST PETER'S BREWERY CO. LTD
St Peter's Hall, St Peter South Elmham, Bungay NR35 1NQ
☎ *(01986) 782322*
www.stpetersbrewery.co.uk

 BEST BITTER 3.7% ABV
Light, easy-quaffer.
EXTRA 4.4% ABV
Hoppy, porter-style beer.
FRUIT BEER (ELDERBERRY) 4.7% ABV
Wheat beer with added elderberry.
FRUIT BEER (GRAPEFRUIT) 4.7% ABV
Refreshing citrus fruit flavour.
GOLDEN ALE 4.7% ABV
Golden, lager-style beer.
MILD 4.7% ABV
Smooth and delicate traditional mild.
SPICED ALE 4.7% ABV
Spicy lemon and ginger flavour.
WHEAT BEER 4.7% ABV
Refreshing and clear with an individual taste.
HONEY PORTER 5.1% ABV
Original-style porter with honey.
OLD STYLE PORTER 5.1% ABV
Original porter. Blend of old ale and younger bitter.
STRONG ALE 5.1% ABV
Smooth, soft and well-rounded.
SUMMER ALE 6.5% ABV
Superb balance and easy to drink.

TOLLEMACHE & COBBOLD BREWERY
Cliff Road, Ipswich IP3 0AZ
☎ *(01473) 231723*
www.tollycobbold.co.uk

 MILD 3.2% ABV
Dark with smooth, rich chocolate flavour.
BITTER 3.5% ABV
Hoppy aroma and clean, sharp taste.
ORIGINAL BEST BITTER 3.8% ABV
Full-bodied, with malt and fruit flavours.
COBBOLD'S IPA 4.2% ABV
Golden, hoppy easy-quaffer.
Plus seasonal and occasional brews.

THE PUBS

ALDEBURGH

The Mill Inn
Market Cross Place, Aldeburgh IP15 5BJ
☎ *(01728) 452563 Ted and Sheila Flemming*

Tied to Adnams, with Adnams Bitter and Broadside always on offer, plus seasonal Adnams guests, usually Regatta in summer and Fisherman in winter.

Seaside pub in a seventeenth-century building next to the the beach. Food available. Three small bars, restaurant, letting rooms (three doubles, one single). Children allowed.

 Summer: 11am–11pm Mon–Sat; 12–10.30pm Sun. Winter: 11am–3pm and 6–11pm Mon–Thurs; 11am–11pm Fri–Sat; 12–10.30pm Sun.

BARHAM

The Sorrel Horse
Old Norwich Road, Barham IP6 0PG
☎ *(01473) 830327 Matt Smith*

Tolly Cobbold Best Bitter and IPA are among the beers always on offer. One guest, changed every six months, might be something from Adnams.

Country pub in a building dating from the fifteenth century, with one large bar, beams and open fireplaces. Food is available, and there is a dining area. Garden, eight letting rooms. Very occasional live music. Children allowed. Large car park. Situated opposite the Health Farm.

11am–3pm and 5–11.30pm Mon–Fri; 11am–11.30pm Sat; 12–10.30pm Sun.

BILDESTON

The Kings Head Hotel
132 High Street, Bildeston, Ipswich IP7 7ED
☎ *(01449) 741434/741719*
James Kevin Harrison

The Kings Head Brewery is located on the same premises, although run as a separate concern. However, Kings Head Best Bitter, First Gold, Billy and Old Chimneys Mild regularly available, plus a guest beer often from Old Chimney, Iceni, Buffy's, Wolf, Mighty Oak, Mauldons or Nethergate.

Fifteenth-century timber-framed building with original wattle and daub, situated in a small village. Food served 12–3pm and 7–9.30pm daily. Car park. Children welcome. Accommodation and holiday flat available.

 11am–3pm and 5–11pm Mon–Fri; 11am–11pm Sat; 12–10.30pm Sun.

BOXFORD

White Hart Inn
Broad Street, Boxford CO10 5DX
☎ *(01787) 211071* Marilyn and Barry Hayton

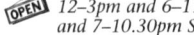Greene King IPA and Adnams Broadside regularly available, plus two guest beers perhaps from Adnams, Fuller's, Mauldons, Lidstones, Cottage, Wye Valley, Bartrams, Bateman, Charles Wells or Hobgoblin.

Sixteenth-century village pub with garden and separate non-smoking dining-room, home to the local cricket and classic motorcycle clubs. Free quiz night every Sunday. Food served 12–2.30pm and 6–9.30pm Mon–Sat, 12–2.30pm and 7–8.30pm Sun. Children welcome and smaller food portions provided. Website: www.white-hart.co.uk.

 12–3pm and 6–11pm Mon–Sat; 12–3pm and 7–10.30pm Sun.

BRANDON

The White Horse
White Horse Street, Brandon IP27 0LB
☎ *(01842) 815767* David Marsh

Tolly Cobbold Original, Greene King IPA and Iceni Fine Soft Day usually available plus a variable number of guests, perhaps from Iceni, Mauldons, Wolf, Nethergate, Old Chimneys, Greene King or Tolly Cobbold.

Friendly, family-run freehouse with sporting bias, supporting several darts teams and a successful football team. No food. Car park. Well-behaved children welcome until 8pm. From London Road (by industrial estate), turn into Crown Street. Take the second of two close left turns into White Horse Street.

11am–11pm Mon–Sat; 12–10.30pm Sun.

BROME

Cornwallis
Brome, Eye IP23 8AJ
☎ *(01379) 870326*
Jeffrey Ward and Richard Leslie

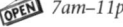St Peter's Best Bitter and a beer from Adnams usually available. A guest such as Fuller's London Pride, Woodforde's Wherry and other St Peter's Brewery beers served.

A former Dower House built in 1561, heavily timbered with a well in the bar. Set in 20 acres of gardens with fine yew topiary, water gardens and ducks. Food served 12–10pm every day, breakfast 7–10am. Children welcome.

7am–11pm (10.30pm Sun).

BUNGAY

The Chequers Inn
23 Bridge Street, Bungay NR35 1HD
☎ *(01986) 893579* Michael and Kim Plunkett

A freehouse with Adnams Best, Fuller's London Pride, Timothy Taylor Landlord and Woodforde's Wherry always available plus five other real ales, changing frequently.

A seventeenth-century, two-bar traditional town alehouse with log fire, large beer garden and patio. Food available Mon–Sun 12–2.30pm (ish!). Large play area for children. Outside bar facilities available.

All day, every day.

The Green Dragon
29 Broad Street, Bungay NR35 1EE
☎ *(01986) 892681* William and Rob Pickard

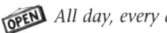Adnams Best is always available and the four beers from the Green Dragon range are brewed and served on the premises.

The pub was bought in 1991 from Brent Walker by William and Rob Pickard. The three-barrel brewery was built and the pub refurbished. Due to increased demand, a second brewery was then built and the capacity expanded to eight barrels. The Green Dragon is a popular pub with a friendly atmosphere. Bar food is available at lunchtime and evenings. Car park, garden, children's room.

 MILD 3.4% ABV
CHAUCER ALE 3.7% ABV
BRIDGE STREET BITTER 4.5% ABV
DRAGON 5.5% ABV

11am–3pm and 5–11pm Mon–Thurs; 11am–11pm Fri–Sat; 12–3pm and 7–10.30pm Sun.

BURY ST EDMUNDS

The Old Cannon Brewery

86 Cannon Street, Bury St Edmunds IP33 1JP
☎ *(01284) 768769* Carole and Richard Locker

 The full range of Cannon Brewery beers are brewed on the premises and are permanently available in the pub. Also featuring Adnams Best Bitter, two guest beers usually from local Suffolk or Norfolk independents and two German Weiss beers.

Half restaurant, half bar, with unique stainless steel brewery sited in the bar. Brewing is done on Mondays, so pub is closed at lunchtime that day. Food available every other lunchtime and every evening. No children. B&B accommodation. Situtated parallel to Northgate Street, off the A14.

OLD CANNON BEST BITTER 3.8% ABV
POWDER MONKEY 4.6% ABV
GUNNER'S DAUGHTER 5.5% ABV

12–3pm Tues–Sun; 5–11pm Mon–Sat; 7–10.30pm Sun.

The Queen's Head

39 Churchgate Street, Bury St Edmunds IP33 1RG
☎ *(01284) 761554* Alistair Torkington

 A freehouse with Adnams Broadside and Nethergate IPA always available, plus the house special bitter and guests rotating on two other hand pumps, including, perhaps, Elgood's Black Dog Mild. Regular long happy hours, with 40p off most ales.

A town-centre pub with a young clientele, particularly in the evenings. One big bar, restaurant, beer garden, conservatory and games room. Food available 12–9pm. Children allowed in the conservatory, garden, games room and restaurant only.

All day, every day.

The Rose & Crown

48 Whiting Street, Bury St Edmunds IP33 1NP
☎ *(01284) 755934* AP and AE Fayers

 Greene King XX Dark Mild, IPA and Abbot are permanently served, plus occasional guests.

An original street-corner local in the same street as the Greene King Brewery. The pub has been with the same family for almost 30 years. Food served 12–2pm Mon–Sat.

11.30am–11pm Mon–Fri; 11.30am–3pm and 7–11pm Sat; 12–2.30pm and 7–10.30pm Sun.

CARLTON COLVILLE

The Bell Inn

82 The Street, Carlton Colville, Lowestoft NR33 8JR
☎ *(01502) 582873*

 Oulton Bitter and Nautilus always available, plus seasonal specials from Oulton Ales and guest breweries, all served straight from the barrel.

A village pub and restaurant with original flagstone floor and open fires. One long bar, disabled access, beer garden. Food available at lunchtime and evenings. Children allowed.

11am–3pm and 4–11pm Mon–Thurs; all day Fri–Sun.

EARL SOHAM

The Victoria

Earl Soham, Woodbridge IP13 7RL
☎ *(01728) 685758* Paul Hooper

Home to the Earl Soham Brewery, the full range is usually available.

A very traditional pub with tiled floors, wooden decor and several interesting pictures of Queen Victoria. No frills, just good beer, food and conversation. Food served lunchtimes and evenings. Car park. Children welcome. Beer garden.

GANNET MILD 3.0% ABV
Dark and flavoursome.
VICTORIA BITTER 3.6% ABV
Tasty with good hop character.
EDWARD ALE 4.0% ABV
Summer only.
SIR ROGER'S PORTER 4.0% ABV
Winter only.
ALBERT ALE 4.6% ABV
Full-bodied and malty.
JOLABRUG 5.0% ABV
Christmas ale.
Plus occasional and seasonal brews.

11.30am–3pm and 5.30–11pm Mon–Sat; 12–3pm and 7–10.30pm Sun.

EAST BERGHOLT

The Red Lion

The Street, East Bergholt CO7 6TB
☎ *(01206) 298332* Rick and Dawn Brogan

Tied to Tolly Cobbold, with IPA and Best Bitter the permanent beers. One seasonal Tolly Cobbold guest is also served.

Village country pub, 300–400 years old, with three fireplaces. Two bars – one has restaurant/family room attached. Live music in garden occasionally on bank holidays. Car park, letting rooms and one family en-suite room. Children allowed in family eating area. Centrally located in the village.

11am–3pm and 6–11pm Mon–Fri; 11am–11pm Sat; 12–10.30pm Sun.

EDWARDSTONE

The White Horse Inn
Mill Green, Edwardstone, Sudbury CO10 5PX
☎ *(01787) 211211* Mrs Baker

A freehouse with Greene King IPA plus a frequently changing mild always available (perhaps Elgood's Black Dog). Also two guests from local breweries such as Tolly Cobbold or further afield such as Cottage.

A two-bar village pub with log fires in winter. Beer garden. Caravan and camping club on site for five caravans. There are two self-catering cottages, each sleeping up to six people, in the pub grounds, available for holiday lets. Food available at lunchtime and evenings. Children allowed.

OPEN *12–2pm Tues–Sun (closed Mon lunchtime) and 6.30–11pm Mon–Sat (10.30pm Sun).*

FELIXSTOWE

The Half Moon
303 High Street, Walton, Felixstowe
☎ *(01394) 216009* Patrick Wroe

An Adnams tied house, so Adnams beers always available, plus two guests, such as Fuller's London Pride or Everards Tiger.

Old-fashioned, friendly alehouse. No food, no fruit machine, no music. Darts, cribbage, backgammon. Garden, children's play area, car park.

OPEN *12–2.30pm and 5–11pm Mon–Fri; 12–11pm Sat; 12–3pm and 7–10.30pm Sun.*

FRAMSDEN

The Dobermann
The Street, Framsden IP14 6HG
☎ *(01473) 890461* Sue Frankland

Adnams Best and Broadside always available and guests such as Mauldons Moletrap and Woodforde's Dobermann Ale.

A 400-year-old, traditional thatched and beamed Suffolk village pub. Extensive menu of bar food available. Non-smoking area. Car park, garden, accommodation. No children. Easy to find off B1077.

OPEN *12–3pm and 7–11pm (10.30pm Sun); closed Mon except bank holidays.*

FRECKENHAM

The Golden Boar
The Street, Freckenham, Bury St Edmunds IP28 8HZ
☎ *(01638) 723000* Alan Strachan

A freehouse with four pumps serving a range of real ales. Adnams Best, Woodforde's Wherry and Nethergate brews are regulars, plus specials and seasonals such as Charles Wells Summer Solstice.

The only pub in Freckenham, this is a restored old-style country village pub with old brickwork and fireplaces, separate dining area and garden. Food available at lunchtime and evenings. Children allowed. En-suite accommodation available.

OPEN *All day Mon–Sat; 12–4pm and 7–10.30pm Sun.*

GISLINGHAM

Six Bells
High Street, Gislingham, Eye IP23 8JD
☎ *(01379) 783349* Mr Buttle

A freehouse with Adnams Best Bitter always available plus two guests changing monthly and not repeating, if possible. Shepherd Neame Spitfire and Brakspear ales are examples of previous guests.

A traditional one-bar village pub with non-smoking dining area and disabled facilities. No fruit machines, no pool table. Food available Tues–Sun lunchtimes and evenings. Children allowed. Function room. Situated near Thornham Walks.

OPEN *12–3pm and 6.30–11pm (10.30pm Sun).*

GREAT WENHAM

The Queen's Head
Great Wenham
☎ *(01473) 310590* M Harris

A freehouse with Adnams Southwold and Greene King IPA and Abbot always on offer, plus one guest, perhaps from Mauldons, Crouch Vale, Woodforde's, Bateman or Fuller's.

Early-Victorian red-brick cottage-style pub in a pleasant rural location, kept by the same licensee for thirteen years and catering for a mixed clientele (mainly aged over 25). English and Indian food is served 12–2pm and 7–9pm (not Sun evenings or Mondays), and booking is advisable. A recent extension has created a non-smoking dining area. Children allowed at lunchtimes only, and not in the bar (advisable to phone in advance). Car park.

OPEN *12–2.30pm and 6.30–11pm Mon–Sat; 12–2.30pm and 7–10.30pm Sun.*

HASKETON

The Turk's Head Inn
Low Road, Hasketon, Woodbridge IP13 6JG
☎ *(01394) 382584* Kirsty Lambert

 Ales from Tolly Cobbold, Greene King and Adnams always on offer, plus guest beers.

A country village pub with huge log fires and low beams, decorated with brewery memorabilia and antiques. Food available at lunchtimes and evenings, ranging from light snacks to a full menu. Children's menu. No food on Mondays. Beer garden and patio. Camping and caravaning in three acres of meadow. Children welcome.

OPEN *6–11pm Mon (closed Mon lunchtime); 12–3pm and 6–11pm Tues–Sat; 12–4pm and 7–10.30pm Sun.*

IPSWICH

The Cricketers
51 Crown Street, Ipswich IP1 3JA
☎ *(01473) 225910* Nicola Harney

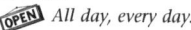 A Wetherspoon's pub. Shepherd Neame Spitfire is among the brews always available plus three guests such as Hop Back Summer Lightning and a range of bottled beers.

A town-centre pub. Large non-smoking area and two beer gardens. Food available all day. Children allowed up to 6pm if eating.

OPEN *All day, every day.*

The Fat Cat
288 Spring Road, Ipswich IP4 5NL
☎ *(01473) 726524* John Keatley

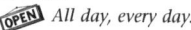 A freehouse with up to 18 real ales served straight from the barrel and rotating all the time. Woodforde's Wherry and Adnams brews are regular features.

A spit and sawdust pub with wooden floor, no music or machines. One bar, beer garden. CAMRA Suffolk Pub of the Year 1998 and 2002. Rolls available at lunchtime. Well-behaved children allowed. On the outskirts of town.

OPEN *All day, every day.*

The Steamboat
78 New Cut West, Ipswich IP2 8HW
☎ *(01473) 601902* Alfred Codona

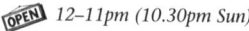 A Tolly Cobbold tenancy serving IPA, Mild, Original and Best Bitter, plus one seasonal beer from Tolly Cobbold.

Old, food-oriented pub/restaurant on the outskirts of town near the river. Live music/karaoke every weekend. Horseshoe-style bar, massive beer garden. Private pub hire, catering and disco available. Website: www.steamboat.fsnet.co.uk.

OPEN *12–11pm (10.30pm Sun).*

KERSEY

The Bell
Kersey
☎ *(01473) 823229* Paul Denton

 Three or four beers always available plus brews from a guest list including Shepherd Neame Spitfire, Fuller's London Pride, Adnams Bitter and Greene King Abbot.

Built in 1380, a timber-framed Tudor-style property with log fires and cobbles. Bar and restaurant food available at lunchtime and evenings. Car park, garden, private dining room. Children allowed. Signposted from Hadleigh.

OPEN *11am–3pm and 6.30–11pm Mon–Sat; 12–3pm and 7–10.30pm Sun.*

LAVENHAM

The Angel Hotel
Market Place, Lavenham CO10 9QZ
☎ *(01787) 247388*
Roy and Anne Whitworth and John Barry

 Adnams Bitter, Nethergate Suffolk County, Greene King IPA and Abbot usually available, plus one guest beer such as Mauldons White Adder or Woodforde's Wherry.

Family-run inn in the centre of Lavenham, first licensed in 1420 and specialising in beers from East Anglia. Food served 12–2.15pm and 6.45–9.15pm Mon–Sun. Bookings advisable for weekends. Children welcome, high chairs supplied. Car park. Eight en-suite bedrooms.

OPEN *11am–11pm Mon–Sat; 12–10.30pm Sun.*

LAXFIELD

The King's Head Inn
Gorams Mill Lane, Laxfield, Woodbridge IP13 8DW
☎ *(01986) 798395*
George and Maureen Coleman

 A freehouse with all beers served straight from the barrel in the tap room. Adnams Best and Broadside always available plus a selection of guest ales. Low House Bitter, brewed by Earl Soham Brewery, is a speciality.

Known locally as The Low House, this is a well-preserved 600-year-old country village pub. East Anglian and Suffolk CAMRA Pub of the Year 2000. Food served 12–2pm and 7–9pm daily. Beer garden. Music on Tuesdays. Carriage rides from nearby Tannington Hall. Separate dining room and card room. Children allowed.

OPEN *11am–3pm and 6–11pm Mon, Wed–Sat; all day Tuesday; 12–3pm and 7–10.30pm Sun.*

LOWESTOFT

The Crown Hotel
High Street, Lowestoft NR32 1HR
☎ *(01502) 500987* Mandy Henderson

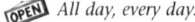 A Scott's Brewery house with Blues and Bloater and Hopleaf always available, plus seasonal specials such as Golden Best.

A town pub with wooden floors and winter fires. Food available at lunchtime only. Patio. Children allowed if eating.

OPEN *All day, every day.*

Elizabeth Denes Hotel
6 Corton Road, Lowestoft NR32 4PL
☎ *(01502) 564616*
Colin Cassels Brown and Elizabeth O'Doherty

 An Adnams brew plus one guest (depending on the time of year), perhaps from Tolly Cobbold.

Friendly, small hotel with cosy beamed bar, carvery, steakhouse restaurant and 12 en-suite rooms. Food served 12–2.30pm and 6–9.30pm Mon–Sat, plus 12–8pm Sun, carvery. Car park. Children welcome, but no special facilities. Located off the A12 between Lowestoft and Great Yarmouth. On corner at the turn-off to Corton.

OPEN *11am–11pm Mon–Sat; 12–10.30pm Sun.*

The Oak Tavern
73 Crown Street West, Lowestoft NR32 1SQ
☎ *(01502) 537246* Jim and Debbie Baldwin

 Woodforde's Oak Tavern Ale and Greene King Abbot Ale usually available plus two guest beers, perhaps from Woodforde's, Buffy's, Wolf, Elgood's, Adnams or Bateman breweries.

Friendly community pub, specialising in real ale and Belgian beers, with a separate pool and darts area, plus Sky Sports wide-screen TV. Five minutes from Lowestoft college. Car park. No food. No children.

OPEN *10.30am–11pm.*

The Triangle Tavern
29 St Peter's Street, Lowestoft NR32 1QA
☎ *(01502) 582711* Bob Vipers

 Green Jack Bitter, Grasshopper, Gone Fishing and Orange Wheat Beer always available plus other Green Jack brews and a selection of constantly changing guests – up to ten available at any one time. Real cider also served.

Owned by the Green Jack Brewing Company and based in the High Street next to the recently developed Triangle Market Place, a two-bar pub with real fire, fully refurbished in December 1998. Customers are welcome to bring their own food. Live music weekly. Beer festivals held at Easter, Hallowe'en and Christmas. Parking.

OPEN *11am–11pm Mon–Sat; 12–10.30pm Sun.*

Welcome Free House
182 London Road North, Lowestoft NR32 1HB
☎ *(01502) 585500* Gavin Crawford

 Adnams Southwold Bitter and Greene King Abbot Ale usually available, plus guest beers such as Marston's Pedigree, Everards Tiger, Charles Wells Eagle or Bombardier, Morland Old Speckled Hen, Brakspear Bitter or Elgood's Greyhound.

A traditional real ale town pub. No food. No children.

OPEN *10.30am–4pm and 7.30–11pm (10.30pm Sun).*

MARKET WESTON

The Mill Inn
Bury Road, Market Weston, Nr Diss IP22 2PD
☎ *(01359) 221018* Miss Leacy

 Adnams Bitter, Greene King IPA and something from Old Chimneys (usually a bitter and mild, but changes occasionally) are the permanent beers at this freehouse.

Village pub in a nineteenth-century former mill house. Food available until 9.30pm. One large bar, garden, patio and restaurant with wood burner. Car park. Children allowed. On the B1111.

OPEN *12–3pm and 7–11pm Tues–Sat (closed Mon); 12–3pm and 7–10.30pm Sun.*

OULTON

The Blue Boad
28 Oulton Street, Oulton, Lowestoft
☎ *(01502) 572160* SJ Battrick

A house beer, Sinbad's Treasure, is a permanent fixture, and the four ever-changing guests (rarely the same one twice) have included beers from Buffy's, Humpty Dumpty, Woodforde's, Green Jack and Elgood's.

A pub with two bars (public and lounge), games room, function room, large beer garden, patio and barbecue area. Food is served 12–2.30pm and 7–9pm. Children welcome in games room and garden area. Car park.

OPEN *12–3pm and 7–11pm Mon–Thurs; 12–11pm Fri–Sat; 12–3pm and 7–10.30pm Sun.*

PIN MILL

The Butt & Oyster

Pin Mill, Chelmondiston, Ipswich IP9 1JW
☎ *(01473) 780764* Dick Mainwaring

 Tolly Cobbold Mild, Bitter, Original, IPA and Shooter always available plus other specials. One guest ale served straight from the cask, generally from a local brewery.

A sixteenth-century inn with one bar, smoking room and riverside seating area. Food available at lunchtime and evenings. Children allowed.

OPEN *All day, every day in summer; 11am–3pm and 7–11pm Mon–Fri and all day Sat–Sun in winter.*

SOUTHWOLD

The Lord Nelson

East Street, Southwold IP18 6EJ
☎ *(01502) 722079* Mr Illstone

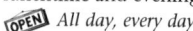 An Adnams house with Best and Broadside always available, plus seasonal ales such as Regatta in summer or celebration ales such as Millennium.

A traditional town pub by the seaside. Beer garden, disabled access. Food available at lunchtime and evenings. Children allowed.

OPEN *All day, every day.*

STOWMARKET

The Stag Tavern

44-46 Bury Street, Stowmarket IP14 1HF
☎ *(01449) 613980* Pat Murphy

Home of the Bury Street Brewery with three real ales on at any time, including at least two own brews. Guests come from independents such as Nethergate, and barrels are sometimes swapped with other breweries giving a wide range.

A traditional drinker's pub with two bars. Bar snacks available at lunchtime. Well-behaved children allowed.

MR MURPHY'S MILD 3.6% ABV
Dark and chocolatey.

BLONDE BOMBSHELL 3.7% ABV
Very pale, straw-coloured, hoppy and citrus.

TAWNY OWL 3.7% ABV
Darkish-coloured bitter.

STAG IPA 3.8% ABV
Best bitter.

PAT MURPHY'S PORTER 4.0% ABV
Very dark, roast chocolatey flavour and fruity.

TAWNY EXTRA 4.2% ABV
Similar to Tawny Owl but with more dry-hopped character to balance its extra strength.

Plus seasonals and specials

OPEN *11am–11pm Mon–Sat; 12–10.30pm Sun.*

SWILLAND

The Moon & Mushroom

High Road, Swilland, Ipswich IP6 9LR
☎ *(01473) 785320* Clive John Goodall

 Green Jack Bitter and Grasshopper, Nethergate Umbel Ale, Woodforde's Wherry and Norfolk Nog, Wolf Bitter, and Buffy's Hopleaf usually available.

A welcoming atmosphere awaits in this unspoilt pub which supports local microbreweries. Food served 12–2pm and 6.30–8.15pm Tues–Sat. Children welcome in the garden only.

OPEN *6–11pm Mon; 11am–2.30pm and 6–11pm Tues–Sat; 12–2.30pm and 7–11pm Sun.*

WINGFIELD

The De La Pole Arms

Church Road, Wingfield, Diss IP21 5RA
☎ *(01379) 384545*

 Tied to St Peter's, with no less than 16 St Peter's beers (on draught or by bottle) always available, including Best Bitter.

A well-restored two-bar dining pub with beams and log fires. Garden, car park. Children allowed. Phone for directions (though once you are in Wingfield, you can't miss the pub!).

OPEN *11am–3pm and 6–midnight Tues–Sat (closed Mon); 12–3pm Sun. (Hours under review, so call first to confirm.)*

YOU TELL US

* *Fleetwood's,* 25 Abbeygate Street, Bury St Edmunds
* *The Hare & Hounds,* Heath Road, East Bergholt
* *The Lion,* The Street, Theburton
* *The White Horse,* Hopton Road, Thelnetham

Places Featured:

Ash	Milford
Bletchingley	Newdigate
Churt	Puttenham
Claygate	Redhill
Coldharbour	Shackleford
Dorking	Shamley Green
Englefield Green	West Byfleet
Epsom	West Clandon
Farnham	Woking
Godalming	Woodstreet Village
Guildford	Wrecclesham
Knaphill	

THE BREWERIES

HOGS BACK BREWERY

Manor Farm, The Street, Tongham GU10 1DE
☎ *(01252) 783000*
www.hogsback.co.uk

 HAIR OF THE HOG 3.5% ABV
TRADITIONAL ENGLISH ALE 4.2% ABV
Smooth, well-balanced flavours.
BLACKWATER PORTER 4.4% ABV
Distinctive, occasional brew.
HOP GARDEN GOLD 4.6% ABV
Refreshing with good fruity hoppiness.
RIP SNORTER 5.0% ABV
Balanced and well-rounded.
Plus commemorative and seasonal brews.

PILGRIM ALES

The Old Brewery, West Street, Reigate RH2 9BL
☎ *(01737) 222651*
www.pilgrim.co.uk

 SURREY BITTER 3.7% ABV
Hoppy, with a good mixture of flavours.
PORTER 4.0% ABV
Dark with roast malt flavour.
PROGRESS 4.0% ABV
Red and malty.
CRUSADER 4.9% ABV
Gold, with hops and malt flavour.
SPRING BOCK 5.2% ABV
Wheat beer.
Plus seasonal brews.

THE PUBS

ASH

The Dover Arms

31 Guildford Road, Ash GU12 6BQ
☎ *(01252) 326025* Errol George Faulkner

 Marston's Pedigree, Wadworth 6X and, once a month, three beers from Sharp's Brewery. A guest from Hogs Back, Triple FFF or Hampshire breweries also regularly served.

Rural village pub with football game, pool and darts. Food served 12–2pm and 7–9pm daily. Car park. Garden. Children welcome.

 11.30am–2.30pm and 6–11pm (10.30pm Sun).

BLETCHINGLEY

William IV

Little Common Lane, Bletchingley, Redhill RH1 4QF
☎ *(01883) 743278* Sue Saunders

Young's Special, Fuller's London Pride and Adnams Best always available plus three monthly changing guests such as a Harveys brew, Shepherd Neame Spitfire, Morland Old Speckled Hen or Adnams Broadside.

An unspoilt Victorian country pub on the edge of the village. Two small bars, dining room and beer garden. Food available at lunchtime and evenings. Children allowed in dining room and garden only.

11.30am–3pm and 6–11pm Mon–Sat; 12–10.30pm Sun.

CHURT

The Crossways Inn
Churt, Nr Farnham GU10 2JE
☎ *(01428) 714323* Paul Ewens

 A freehouse with Cheriton Best,
Ringwood Fortyniner and Shepherd
Neame Bishop's Finger always available, plus
at least four guests such as Shepherd Neame
Spitfire or Hampshire Lionheart. At least ten
different beers are served every week, with
more from micro-breweries than not. Also
real cider from the barrel.

A country village local, winner of Summer
Pub of the Year 1999. Two bars, beer
garden. Food available at lunchtime only.
Well-behaved children allowed. On the main
road.

OPEN *11am–3.30pm and 5–11pm Mon–Thurs;
all day Fri–Sat; 12–4pm and 7–10.30pm
Sun.*

CLAYGATE

The Griffin
58 Common Road, Claygate, Esher KT10 0HW
☎ *(01372) 463799* Tom Harrington

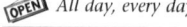 A freehouse with Fuller's London Pride
and Badger Dorset Best always available
plus two constantly changing guests such as
Bateman XB or a Pilgrim ale. Micro-breweries
and smaller independents favoured.

A traditional two-bar village pub with log
fires, beer garden and disabled access.
Food available every lunchtime plus Friday
and Saturday evenings. Children allowed.

OPEN *All day, every day.*

The Swan
Hare Lane, Claygate KT10 9BS
☎ *(01372) 462582* Timothy Kitch

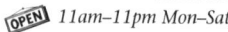 A freehouse with Fuller's London Pride a
permanent feature, plus three guest
beers, perhaps Greene King IPA or something
from Brakspear or Adnams.

Country pub in a building dating from
1804, with beams, Victorian ceiling, 20-
foot bar, large garden and a field for use
during festivals. Food is available, and there
is a Thai restaurant. Annual beer festival in
August, usually at the bank holiday (80 beers
over 4 days). Superior en-suite
accommodation. Children allowed.

OPEN *11am–11pm Mon–Sat; 12–10.30pm Sun.*

COLDHARBOUR

The Plough Inn
*Coldharbour Lane, Coldharbour, Nr Dorking
RH5 6HD*
☎ *(01306) 711793* Mr and Mrs Abrehart

Nine beers always available from
Ringwood, Hogs Back, Timothy Taylor,
Adnams and Shepherd Neame. Two beers
brewed on the premises under the name of
the Leith Hill Brewery. Seasonal brews,
guests, topical and special beers. Also a farm
cider on hand pump.

A traditional family-run seventeenth-
century pub in a beautiful rural setting.
Allegedly the highest freehouse in south-east
England. Bar and restaurant food served at
lunchtime and evenings. Car parking.
Children allowed. Accommodation. Just over
three miles south-west of Dorking.

🍺 **CROOKED FURROW 4.2% ABV**
Hoppy, light bitter.
TALLYWHACKER 5.6% ABV
Very dark ale. Strong, roasted barley flavour.

OPEN *11.30am–3pm and 6.30–11pm Mon–Fri;
11am–11pm Sat–Sun.*

DORKING

The King's Arms
45 West Street, Dorking RH4 1BU
☎ *(01306) 883361* Mr Yeatman

Fuller's London Pride, Wadworth 6X,
Marston's Pedigree and Eldridge Pope
Royal Oak (Thomas Hardy) always available.
Two guests changing every week from micro-
breweries and independents – the smaller
and more unusual, the better!

A country-style pub in a town location, this
is the oldest building in Dorking. More
than 500 years old with oak beams,
inglenook fireplace, restaurant and courtyard
garden. Food available lunchtimes and
evenings. Children allowed.

OPEN *11am–11pm (10.30pm Sun).*

The Water Mill
Reigate Road, Dorking RH4 1NN
☎ *(01306) 887831* Peter Baker

 A freehouse with Shepherd Neame
Bishop's Finger, Fuller's London Pride
and Hogs Back TEA the permanent beers.
Two guests, changed weekly, might include
Pilgrim Surrey Bitter, Ringwood Fortyniner,
Badger Best and Tanglefoot or beers from
Exmoor (Ale, Fox, Stag and Hart).

Traditional pub on the outskirts of town,
built in the 1930s. Food available,
including carvery. Two function rooms,
restaurant, three bars and garden. Live music
(folk/jazz) weekly, monthly live rock band,
plus live DJ at all functions. Children
allowed. Car park.

OPEN *11am–3pm and 6–11pm (10.30pm Sun);
has 2am licence but not in operation at
all times.*

ENGLEFIELD GREEN

The Beehive

34 Middle Hill, Englefield Green, Nr Egham TW20 0JQ
☎ *(01784) 431621* Roy McGranaghan

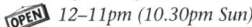 Fuller's London Pride, Hop Back Summer Lightning and Gale's HSB and Best always available plus four guest beers, changing weekly, from breweries such as Adnams, Bateman, Everards, Hoskins & Oldfield, Kemptown, Nethergate, Oldbury, Orkney, Thwaites and Young's. Beer festivals at May and August bank holidays.

A country pub now surrounded by expensive houses. Real homemade food available at lunchtime and evenings. Open log fire in winter. Car park and garden. Just off the A30 between Ferrari's and Royal Holloway College. Children welcome

OPEN *12–11pm (10.30pm Sun).*

EPSOM

The Rising Sun

14 Heathcote Road, Epsom KT18 5DX
☎ *(01372) 740809* Ruth Roberts

 Two or three Pilgrim beers always on draught, plus a guest beer from a small brewery. O'Hara's Stout (from Ireland) and several imported beers are also offered on draught, as well as French cider and 35 imported bottled beers.

Originally two cottages, the pub was extended back into the main building at the end of the nineteenth century, and was tastefully redecorated in 1999. Food is available every evening except Sunday, with 'prix fixe' meals on Friday and Saturday evenings using fresh and seasonal produce. Quarterly beer festivals (see www.pilgrim.co.uk for details). Dogs welcome, plus other animals, including children, if well-behaved. Parking nearby.

OPEN *12–3pm and 5–11pm Mon–Fri (all day during summer months); all day Sat–Sun.*

FARNHAM

The Ball & Wicket

104 Upper Hale Road, Farnham GU9 0PB
☎ *(01252) 735278* Debbie Neale

 Fuller's London Pride, Young's Ordinary and Hogsback TEA are the permanent beers here, and an occasional guest is offered.

A friendly, 200-year-old village pub with an open fire and a warm atmosphere. Live entertainment, quiz nights, darts. No food. Children allowed. Car park.

OPEN *4–11pm Mon–Fri; 12–11pm Sat; 12–3pm and 7–10.30pm Sun.*

The Duke of Cambridge

East Street, Farnham GU9 7TH
☎ *(01252) 716584 Fax (01252) 716549*
Karen and David Newland

 A freehouse with seven pumps serving a constantly changing range of real ales from large breweries to micro-breweries. Hundreds of different beers have been served in recent years. The aim is variety of choice and the perfect pint every time! Up to 20 single malt whiskies also available.

A family-owned pub dating from the 1830s. Food served every lunchtime and Mon–Thurs and Sat evenings in a separate dining area. Regular music, including jazz on Tuesdays. Hotel-standard B&B. Website: www.dukeofcambridge.co.uk.

OPEN *12–3pm and 5.15–11pm Mon–Thurs; 12–11pm Fri–Sat; 12–10pm Sun.*

Exchange

Station Hill, Farnham GU9 8AD
☎ *(01252) 726673*
Mr T Devaney and Ms A Fanning

 Greene King IPA and Triumph usually available, with one guest such as Ruddles Best, Wadworth 6X or Bateman XXXB.

Traditional, recently refurbished bar. Garden and patio. Extensive menu, specialising in steaks, available 12–2.30pm and 6.30–9pm daily. Car park. Children welcome, but no special facilities. Located next to Farnham Station.

OPEN *10.30am–3pm and 5.30–11pm Mon–Thurs; all day Fri–Sun.*

The Shepherd & Flock

Moor Park Lane, Farnham GU9 9JB
☎ *(01252) 716675* Steven Hill

 A freehouse with Hampshire 1066, Hogs Back TEA, Fuller's London Pride and Gale's HSB always available plus three guests, such as Hop Back Summer Lightning, Badger Tanglefoot or Beckett's brews.

Situated on the outskirts of town, on Europe's biggest inhabited roundabout! A well-known local meeting place, close to the North Downs. Old building with one bar and 50-seater dining room. Food available lunchtimes and evenings. Beer garden. Children allowed in the dining room only.

OPEN *11am–3pm and 5.30–11pm Mon–Thurs; all day Fri–Sun.*

GODALMING

The Anchor Inn
110 Ockford Road, Godalming GU7 1RG
☎ *(01483) 417085* John and Vanessa Nelson

 Fuller's London Pride, Hop Back Summer Lightning and Gale's HSB are among the beers always available.

A real-ale pub under new ownership, with bar billiards and a good mixed clientele. Simple bar food, with a new fuller menu, available at lunchtimes and until 9pm. Parking and large rear garden. On the edge of town on the main road.

OPEN *12–3pm and 5.30–11pm.*

The Old Wharf
5 Wharf Street, Godalming GU7 1NN
☎ *(01483) 419543* John Louden

 A wide selection of cask ales available on six hand pumps. Examples have included Fuller's London Pride and Hogs Back TEA.

A traditional town pub. Food available 12–9pm Sun–Thurs; 12–7pm Fri–Sat. Traditional roasts served on Sundays. No children.

OPEN *All day, every day.*

GUILDFORD

The George Abbot
7–11 High Street, Guildford GU2 4AB
☎ *(01483) 456890* John Dunn

 The permanent beers here include Fuller's London Pride, Wadworth 6X, Gale's HSB and Marston's Pedigree. The four guests are changed every two to five days, and may include beers such as Hogs Back TEA, Young's Best, plus many others.

D rinkers' town pub in a traditional building, with beams, fireplaces and a friendly atmosphere. Food available. Food available. Fruit and quiz machines. No children.

OPEN *11am–11pm Mon–Sat; 12–10.30pm Sun.*

KNAPHILL

The Hooden Takes a Knap
134 High Street, Knaphill GU21 2QH
☎ *(01483) 473374*
Paul Crisp and Elizabeth Williamson

 An ever-changing selection of beers from around the country is available, such as brews from Fuller's, Adnams, Greene King, Hop Back, Young's, Brains and Shepherd Neame.

A bistro-style country pub, previously known as The Garibaldi. One small bar, beer garden and BBQ. Food available lunchtimes and evenings in a separate dining area. Mexican food is a speciality, but traditional English, Italian and Indian dishes are also served. Live blues on alternate Thursdays, quiz night on last Sunday of the month, plus regular theme nights. Children allowed. On the crossroads of Knaphill High Street.

OPEN *12–2.30pm and 5.30–11pm Mon–Thurs; all day Fri–Sun.*

MILFORD

The Red Lion
Old Portsmouth Road, Milford, Godalming GU8 5HJ
☎ *(01483) 424342* Lou-Ann Marshall

 A Gale's house with Butser Bitter, GB and HSB always available plus guests such as Badger Tanglefoot, Everards Tiger, Hampshire Glory and Marston's Pedigree changing fortnightly. Tries not to repeat the beers.

A village pub with skittle alley. Two bars, non-smoking and smoking dining areas, beer garden and children's play area, good disabled access. Food available every lunchtime and Mon–Sat evenings. Children allowed.

OPEN *11am–2.30pm and 5.30–11pm Mon–Fri; all day Sat–Sun.*

NEWDIGATE

Surrey Oaks

Parkgate Road, Newdigate, Dorking RH5 5DZ
☎ *(01306) 631200* Ken Proctor

Adnams Southwold Bitter and Fuller's London Pride usually available, plus two guest pumps. Five or six guest beers served each week and favourites include Timothy Taylor Landlord, Hop Back Summer Lightning, Woodforde's Wherry and something from Hogs Back, Harveys, Pilgrim or Weltons.

Timber-beamed country pub, original parts of which date back to 1570. Two small bars, one with a magnificent inglenook fireplace and stone-flagged floors. Games room and restaurant. Food served lunchtimes and evenings Tues–Sat; lunchtimes only Sun–Mon. Large car park. Children's play area in garden. Situated one mile from Newgate village on the Charlwood road.

OPEN *11.30am–2.30pm and 5.30–11pm Mon–Fri; 11.30am–3pm and 6–11pm Sat; 12–3pm and 7–10.30pm Sun.*

PUTTENHAM

The Good Intent

62 The Street, Puttenham, Guildford GU3 1AR
☎ *(01483) 810387* Bill Carpenter

A pub serving only cask-conditioned real ales. Four guests might include beers such as Branscombe Vale Branoc, Ringwood Fortyniner, Young's Waggle Dance or something from Brakspear.

A traditional country pub dating from the sixteenth century and situated on the North Downs Way. A wide variety of food is available lunchtimes and evenings (except Sun and Mon evenings), including fish and chips to eat in or take away every Wednesday night, and superb roast Sunday lunch. Enclosed beer garden. Families welcome.

OPEN *11am–3pm and 6–11pm Mon–Fri; all day Sat–Sun.*

REDHILL

The Hatch

44 Hatchlands Road, Redhill RH1 6AT
☎ *(01737) 764593* Naomi Newman

A Shepherd Neame house with Bishop's Finger, Spitfire and Master Brew always available, plus up to three seasonal or celebration ales such as Goldings or 1698.

A town pub with horseshoe-shaped bar, log-effect fires and oak beams. Beer garden, front patio, pool room. Food available 12–2pm daily. Families very welcome. Situated on the A25.

OPEN *12–3pm Mon–Sun; 5.30–11pm Mon–Sat; 7–10.30pm Sun.*

SHACKLEFORD

The Cyder House

Pepperharrow Lane, Shackleford, Godalming GU8 6AN
☎ *(01483) 810360* Phillip Nisbett

Badger Best, Tanglefoot and Golden Champion always available, plus at least two guest beers.

A light and airy Victorian country pub situated in a pretty village. Extensive blackboard menu offers a range of fine meals and snacks made with fresh seasonal produce. Large patio garden, plenty of parking space. Children and dogs welcome.

OPEN *11am–3pm and 5.30–11pm Mon–Fri; all day Sat–Sun.*

SHAMLEY GREEN

The Bricklayer's Arms

The Green, Shamley Green GU5 0UA
☎ *(01483) 898377* Kim Campbell

Gale's HSB is among the beers constantly available. One guest ale, changed according to level of consumption, might be Fuller's London Pride or something from Adnams, Arundel or Brakspear.

Situated on the green, this is the only pub in the village. Food is available, and there is a small restaurant. Patio and garden. Bands and discos in winter, quiz every Monday in winter, plus music quiz every other Thursday. Car park. Children allowed in restaurant.

OPEN *11am–11pm Mon–Sat; 12–10.30pm Sun.*

WEST BYFLEET

The Plough Inn

104 High Road, West Byfleet KT14 7QT
☎ *(01932) 353257* Carol Wells

A freehouse with nine pumps serving ever-changing brews, all from independents.

A traditional two-bar village pub with beams and two log fires. Beer garden, non-smoking conservatory, car park. Food available Mon–Fri 12–2pm plus Sunday roasts in winter and Wed evenings. Monthly trivia quiz in winter. Children allowed in conservatory until 7pm.

OPEN *11am–3pm and 5–11pm (10.30pm Sun).*

WEST CLANDON

The Onslow Arms

The Street, West Clandon, Guildford GU4 7TE
☎ *(01483) 222447* Alan Peck

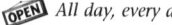 A freehouse with Fuller's London Pride and brews from Young's, Brakspear and Hogs Back always available plus one rotating guest such as Ringwood Old Thumper, Morland Old Speckled Hen or Greene King Abbot. Also celebration ales as available.

A well-known sixteenth-century coaching inn with four bars and excellent food available at lunchtime and evenings in a restaurant and a carvery bistro. Large car park, disabled access. Garden and patio with arbours. Cocktail lounge. Function rooms. Helipad. Children allowed.

OPEN *All day, every day.*

WOKING

Wetherspoons

51 Chertsey Road, Woking GU21 5AJ
☎ *(01483) 722818* Gary Hollis

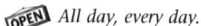 Hogs Back TEA and Shepherd Neame Spitfire permanently available, plus at least three guest ales.

A one-bar town pub with no music or TV. Front drinking terrace, disabled access and toilets. Food available all day (11am–10pm) with a non-smoking seating area available. No children.

OPEN *All day, every day.*

WOODSTREET VILLAGE

The Royal Oak

89 Oak Hill, Woodstreet Village, Guildford GU3 3DA
☎ *(01483) 235137* Tony Oliver

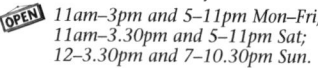 A freehouse with Hogs Back TEA always available plus four constantly changing guests, always including a mild. Hop Back Summer Lightning and Cottage Wheeltappers are just two examples from a huge range (1,600 in seven years).

A good old-fashioned country pub. One bar, beer garden. Food available Mon–Sat lunchtime. Over 14s only allowed.

OPEN *11am–3pm and 5–11pm Mon–Fri; 11am–3.30pm and 5–11pm Sat; 12–3.30pm and 7–10.30pm Sun.*

WRECCLESHAM

The Bat & Ball

Bat & Ball Lane, Wrecclesham, Farnham GU10 4RA
☎ *(01252) 792108*
Andy Bujok and Sally Stockbridge

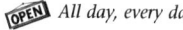 A freehouse with Young's Special, Fuller's London Pride and a Brakspear ale always available, plus four guests including brews such as Archers Golden, Harveys Best, Hop Back Summer Lightning and many, many more.

A traditional country pub with open fires, two bars, restaurant, children's room and play area, beer garden, disabled access. Food available at lunchtime and evenings. Children allowed. Bat & Ball Lane is off Upper Bourne Lane via Sandrock Hill Road.

OPEN *12–11pm (10.30pm Sun).*

The Sandrock

Sandrock Hill Road, Wrecclesham, Farnham GU10 4NS
☎ *(01252) 715865* Mr A Baylis

Eight beers available. Batham, Enville and Brakspear brews always on offer plus guests (100 per year) from Holden's, Hampshire, Ballard's, Hogs Back and Cheriton etc.

A small, no-frills pub. Bar food available at lunchtime (except Sunday). Car park and garden. Ten-day beer festival held first two weeks of March. Children allowed. Along the bypass, left at roundabout onto the A325, left into School Hill, over the crossroads into Sandrock Hill Road. Visit our website at: www.sandrockpub.co.uk.

OPEN *All day, every day.*

YOU TELL US

* *Aitch's Bar-Café*, Angel Court, High Street, Godalming
* *H G Wells' Planets*, Crown Square, Woking
* *The Hedgehog & Hogshead*, 2 High Street, Sutton
* *The Moon on the Hill*, 5–9 Hill Road, Sutton

Places Featured:

Amberley	Horsted Keynes
Arundel	Hove
Ashurst	Icklesham
Balcombe	Isfield
Battle	Lewes
Beckley	Litlington
Berwick Village	Maplehurst
Bexhill-on-Sea	Midhurst
Bognor Regis	Nutbourne
Brighton	Nuthurst
Burpham	Old Heathfield
Caneheath	Oving
Compton	Pett
Crawley	Portslade
Eastbourne	Robertsbridge
East Grinstead	Rudgwick
East Hoathly	Rustington
Exceat Bridge	Rye
Fernhurst	St Leonards on Sea
Firle	Seaford
Fishbourne	Sedlescombe
Fletching	Shoreham
Frant	Stoughton
Graffham	Tarring
Hailsham	Thakeham
Halfway Bridge	Ticehurst
Hastings	Uckfield
Haywards Heath	West Ashling
Heathfield	West Chiltington
Herstmonceux	Worthing
Horsham	Yapton

THE BREWERIES

ARUNDEL BREWERY

*Ford Airfield Estate, Arundel, West Sussex
BN18 0BE*
☎ *(01903) 733111*

1999 3.5% ABV
CASTLE 3.8% ABV
Well-balanced and malty with some fruitiness.
HAIRY MARY 3.8% ABV
Summer seasonal brew.
ARUNDEL GOLD 4.2% ABV
Gold-coloured with good hoppiness.
FOOT SLOGGER 4.4% ABV
Golden seasonal brew.
CLASSIC 4.5% ABV
Malty with some sweetness.
SUMMER DAZE 4.7% ABV
Seasonal brew.
BLACK BEASTY 4.9% ABV
Seasonal brew.

BULLS EYE 5.0% ABV
Golden seasonal brew.
STRONGHOLD 5.0% ABV
Rounded and full-flavoured.
OLD KNUCKLER 5.5% ABV
All the flavours are here. Winter brew.
Plus seasonal brews.

BALLARDS BREWERY LTD

The Old Sawmill, Nyewood, Petersfield GU31 5HA
☎ *(01730) 821362/301*
www.ballardsbrewery.org.uk

MIDHURST MILD 3.5% ABV
TROTTON 3.6% ABV
BEST BITTER 4.2% ABV
NYEWOOD GOLD 5.0% ABV
WASSAIL 6.0% ABV
Plus seasonal brews.

THE CUCKMERE HAVEN BREWERY
Exceat Bridge, Cuckmere Haven, Seaford, West Sussex BN25 4AB
☎ *(01323) 892247*

 BEST BITTER 4.1% ABV
SAXON KING STOUT 4.2% ABV
GENTLEMEN'S GOLD 4.5% ABV
GUV'NER 4.7% ABV

DARK STAR BREWING CO.
55–56 Surrey Street, Brighton BN1 3PB
☎ *(01273) 701758*
www.real-ale-guide.co.uk/dark-star

ALE TRAIL ROAST MILD 3.5% ABV
PALE ALE 3.7% ABV
PENGUIN STOUT 4.2% ABV
GOLDEN GATE BITTER 4.3% ABV
DARK STAR 5.0% ABV

HARVEY & SONS (LEWES) LTD
The Bridge Wharf Brewery, 6 Cliffe High Street, Lewes, East Sussex BN7 2AH
☎ *(01273) 480209*
www.harveys.org.uk

 XX MILD 3.0% ABV
Dark in colour, soft and sweet.
SUSSEX PALE ALE 3.5% ABV
Balanced and well-hopped.
SUSSEX BEST BITTER 4.0% ABV
Hoppiness throughout.
ARMADA ALE 4.5% ABV
Golden and hoppy, with dryness in the aftertaste.
Plus seasonal brews.

HEPWORTH & CO BREWERS (THE BEER STATION)
The Railway Yard, Horsham RH12 2NW
☎ *(01403) 269696. Fax (01403) 269890*
www.thebeerstation.co.uk

 PULLMAN 4.2% ABV
Named after the renowned railway carriage, Pullman has a crisp bitterness and clean flavour.
IRON HORSE 4.8% ABV
Named after Richard Trevithick's first steam-powered engine on rails. A premium bitter with a dense flavour and subtle sweetness.

WJ KING & CO.
3–5 Jubilee Estate, Foundry Lane, Horsham RH13 5EU
☎ *(01403) 272102*
www.kingfamilybrewers.co.uk

HORSHAM BEST BITTER 3.8% ABV
RED RIVER ALE 4.8% ABV

RECTORY ALES
The Rectory, Plumpton Green
☎ *(01273) 890570*
www.rectory-ales.co.uk

 RECTOR'S PLEASURE 3.8% ABV
RECTOR'S LIGHT RELIEF 4.0% ABV
RECTOR'S REVENGE 5.4% ABV
Plus seasonal brews.

ROTHER VALLEY BREWING CO.
Station Road, Northiam TN31 6QT
☎ *(01797) 253535*

HOUSE BITTER 3.6% ABV
WEALDEN BITTER 3.7% ABV
LEVEL BEST 4.0% ABV
SPIRIT LEVEL 4.6% ABV
BLUES 5.0% ABV
Winter brew.
Plus seasonal and occasional brews.

SUSSEX BREWERY (PREVIOUSLY KNOWN AS FORGE BREWERY)
The Two Sawyers, Pett, Nr Hastings, East Sussex TN35 4HB
☎ *(01424) 813927*

FORGE BITTER 3.2% ABV
BROTHER'S BEST 3.9% ABV
OLD BLACK PETT 4.6% ABV
Stout.
PETTS PROGRESS 4.6% ABV
SUMMER ECLIPSE 4.6% ABV

WELTONS NORTH DOWN BREWERY
Chipman House, Railway Goods Yard, Nightingale Road, Horsham RH12 2NW
☎ *(01403) 242901*
www.weltons.co.uk

DORKING'S PRIDE 2.8% ABV
NORTH DOWNS 3.8% ABV
OLD COCKY 4.3% ABV
TOWER POWER 5.0% ABV

WHITE BREWING CO.
The 1066 Country Brewery, Pebsham Farm Ind. Est., Pebsham Lane, Bexhill
☎ *(01424) 731066*

1066 COUNTRY ALE 4.0% ABV
M2 4.5% ABV
Available upon request.
WHITE CHRISTMAS 4.5% ABV
Seasonal brew.

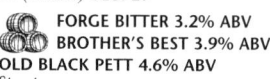

THE PUBS

AMBERLEY

The Sportsman's Inn
Crossgates, Amberley, Arundel, West Sussex
BN18 9NR
☎ *(01798) 831787* Chris and Jenny Shanahan

 A freehouse with Young's Bitter, Fuller's London Pride, Harveys Best and a house ale called Miserable Old Bugger (brewed especially by Weltons of Horsham). Occasional guests, particularly porters in winter.

An edge-of-village pub with panoramic views over Amberley Wildbrooks. Three bars, patio area, hexagonal pool table, dining area in conservatory. Home to the Miserable Old Buggers Club. Food served at lunchtime and evenings. En-suite bed and breakfast available. Well-behaved children and dogs welcome. Visit the website at: www.thesportsmanamberley.com.

OPEN *11am–2.30pm and 6–11pm Mon–Fri; 12–3pm and 7–10.30pm Sun.*

ARUNDEL

Arundel Swan Hotel
27–9 High Street, Arundel, West Sussex
☎ *(01903) 882314* David Vincent

 Part of the family-owned George Gale & Co Ltd, featuring the award-winning Gale's HSB, plus Gale's GB and Butser. A guest beer is always available, perhaps Hop Back Summer Lightning or Shepherd Neame Spitfire.

Restored to its original Victorian splendour, a very popular meeting place for locals and tourists alike. Situated in the heart of Arundel, close to the castle and river. Food served 12–2.30pm and 6.30–9.30pm daily. Car park behind the hotel.

OPEN *11am–11pm Mon–Sat; 12–10.30pm Sun.*

The King's Arms
36 Tarrant Street, Arundel, West Sussex
BN18 9DN
☎ *(01903) 882312* Charlie Malcolmson

 A freehouse always serving Fuller's London Pride and Young's Special plus two guests such as Hop Back Summer Lightning, Rye and Coriander or Crop Circle, or brews from Harveys or Cottage. Small producers always well-represented.

A small, country-style pub dating from 1625, situated out of the town centre. Two bars, patio, table seating at the front. Sandwiches available Mon–Thurs lunchtimes, bar menu Fri–Sun lunchtimes. Children allowed.

OPEN *11am–3pm and 5.30–11pm Mon–Fri; 11am–11pm Sat; 12–10.30pm Sun.*

ASHURST

The Fountain Inn
Ashurst, Nr Steyning, West Sussex BN44 3AP
☎ *(01403) 710219*
Mark and Christopher White

 Harveys Best and Fuller's London Pride plus a constantly changing range of guests, which may include Harveys Gold or Gale's HSB.

An unspoilt sixteenth-century inn with low beams, a flagstone floor and large inglenook fireplace. Picturesque cottage garden and large duck pond. No machines or music. Bar and restaurant food served at lunchtime and evenings (light snacks only Sunday pm and Monday pm). Large car park and garden. Children under 14 not allowed inside the pub. Located on the B2135 north of Steyning.

OPEN *11.30am–2.30pm and 6–11pm Mon–Sat; 12–3pm and 7–10.30pm Sun.*

BALCOMBE

The Cowdray Arms
London Road, Balcombe, Haywards Heath, West Sussex RH17 6QD
☎ *(01444) 811280* Gerry McElhatton

 Harveys Best Bitter, Greene King Abbot, IPA and Mild always available plus two guests such as Greene King Triumph or Arundel, Bateman, Elgood's or Harveys brews.

A one-bar Victorian pub with high ceilings. Non-smoking dining area, traditional pub games. Garden and car park. Food served at lunchtime and evenings. Children allowed.

OPEN *11am–3pm and 5.30–11pm Mon–Sat; 12–3pm and 7–10.30pm Sun.*

BATTLE

The Squirrel Inn
North Trade Road, Battle, East Sussex TN33 9LJ
☎ *(01424) 772717* Mr and Mrs Coundley

 Harveys ales always available plus several guests (200 per year) including Rother Valley Level Best and brews from Gale's and Mansfield etc. New and seasonal beers ordered as and when available.

An eighteenth-century old drover's pub in beautiful countryside surrounded by fields. Family-run freehouse. Unspoilt public bar with log fires. Restaurant (suitable for functions and weddings). Two large beer gardens, ample parking, purpose-built children's room. Families welcome. Located just outside Battle on the A271.

OPEN *11.30am–3pm and 6–11pm Mon–Thurs; 11.30am–11pm Fri–Sat; 12–10.30pm Sun.*

BECKLEY

The Rose & Crown

Northiam Road, Beckley, Nr Rye, East Sussex
TN31 6SE
☎ *(01797) 252161* Alice Holland

 Harveys Best, Hook Norton Best, Badger IPA, Timothy Taylor Landlord and Fuller's ESB always available plus two constantly changing guests from independent breweries.

An old coaching inn on a site which has been occupied by a pub since the twelfth century. Dining area, large garden, petanque. Food available at lunchtime and evenings. Well-behaved children allowed.

OPEN *11.30am–3pm and 5–11pm Mon–Thurs; all day Fri–Sun.*

BERWICK VILLAGE

The Cricketers Arms

Berwick Village, Nr Polegate, East Sussex
BN26 6SP
☎ *(01323) 870469* Peter Brown

 A Harveys tied house with Best Bitter and a seasonal brew usually available.

Three-roomed, cottage-style country pub with stone floors, two open fires and picturesque gardens. Situated near the South Downs Way and very popular with walkers and cyclists. Food served each lunchtime and evening. Car park. Children welcome in designated room. Located west of Drusillas roundabout; signposted to Berwick church.

OPEN *11am–3pm and 6–11pm Mon–Fri; 11am–11pm Sat; 12–10.30pm Sun.*

BEXHILL-ON-SEA

The Rose & Crown

Turkey Road, Bexhill-on-Sea, East Sussex
TN39 5HH
☎ *(01424) 214625*
Stephen and Sarah Newman

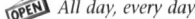 Greene King Abbot and IPA always available, with Harveys Sussex Best a regularly featured guest. Another guest, changed monthly, could be something like Ruddles County or Morland Old Speckled Hen.

One bar, dining area, big-screen sports, darts, bar billiards and Bexhill in Bloom-winning beer garden. 'Hungry Horse' menu includes big plate specials and bar snacks. Food is served 12–10pm Mon–Sat and 12–9.30pm Sun. Disabled toilets. Under 14s allowed until 9pm in designated area only.

OPEN *All day, every day.*

BOGNOR REGIS

Old Barn

42 Felpham Road, Bognor Regis, West Sussex
PO22 7DF
☎ *(01243) 821564* Brian Griffith

 Ringwood Best Bitter, Shepherd Neame Master Brew and Hop Back Summer Lightning regularly available, plus one or two guest beers perhaps from Hop Back, Gale's, Ringwood, Greene King and others.

Thatched, converted barn on the edge of the village behind Butlin's. Pool, darts and Sky TV. Popular with all ages, locals and Butlin's staff, etc. Food available 11am–7pm. Small car park. Well-behaved children welcome.

OPEN *11am–11pm Mon–Sat; 12–10.30pm Sun.*

BRIGHTON

The Cobbler's Thumb

10 New England Road, Brighton, East Sussex
BN1 4GG
☎ *(01273) 605636*
Jude Bergmann and Pascal Fullerton

 A freehouse serving Harveys Best Bitter, plus weekly changing guest ales.

A traditional locals' pub, revamped with an Australian theme! Australian speciality drinks are served at the bar, and there is an 'outback' beer garden (heated). Pool table (free Sun, Mon and 3–6pm Tues–Sat), darts, big-screen TV (movies, Sky), pub games and a variety of entertainment (live music, quiz, DJs, pool league). Food available 12–3pm Mon–Sat, plus barbecues on Sunday in summer and Sunday roasts in winter. Dogs welcome.

OPEN *11am–11pm Mon–Sat; 12–10.30pm Sun.*

The Evening Star

55–6 Surrey Street, Brighton, East Sussex BN1 3PB
☎ *(01273) 328931* Peter Skinner, Matt Wickham and Janine Mayhew

 The home of the Dark Star Brewing Company, though the brewery is no longer on the same site as the pub. Seven real ales always available, including beers from Dark Star and a rotating guest list. Two real ciders also served.

A specialist real-ale house, recently renovated, with wooden floors. Bar food is available 12–3pm Mon, 12–3pm and 6–9pm (curry night) Wed, 12–7pm Thurs, 12–6pm Fri, 12–4pm Sat, 1–5pm Sun. Children not allowed. Just 150 yards from railway station. Visit the websites at: www.EveningStarBrighton.co.uk and www.DarkStarBrewing.co.uk.

OPEN *12–11pm Mon–Fri; 11.30am–11pm Sat; 12–10.30pm Sun.*

Hand In Hand

33 Upper St James's Street, Brighton, East Sussex BN2 1JN
☎ *(01273) 699595* Brenda and Bev Robbins

 Home of the Kemptown Brewery with all Kemptown brews usually available, plus Badger Best and Tanglefoot.

Cosy, street-corner pub, probably the smallest tower brewery in England. Food served 12–3pm. No children.

BRIGHTON BITTER 3.6% ABV
KEMPTOWN BITTER 4.0% ABV
YE OLDE TROUT 4.5% ABV
STAGGERING IN THE DARK 5.2% ABV
OLD GRUMPY 6.2% ABV
December brew.
Plus seasonal and occasional brews.

 12–11pm (10.30pm Sun).

The Lion & Lobster

24 Sillwood Street, Brighton, East Sussex BN1 2PS
☎ *(01273) 327299* Gary Whelan

 Five guest beers (200 per year) which might include Morland Old Speckled Hen, Harveys Best, Gale's HSB or something from Cottage or Dark Star.

An Irish family-run pub with a great atmosphere. All ages welcome. Bar and restaurant food available at lunchtime and evenings. Live music weekly, including jazz and Irish music on Thurs and Sun. Bed and breakfast accommodation. Located 200 yards from the seafront, in between the Bedford Hotel and Norfolk Hotel.

 11am–11pm Mon–Wed; 11am–midnight Thurs–Sat; 12–10.30pm Sun.

The Miller's Arms

1 Windmill Street, Brighton, East Sussex BN2 2GN
☎ *(01273) 380580*
Kim Yallop and Ian Harradine

 Five real ales permanently available: Harveys Best, Fuller's London Pride, Young's Special, Adnams Best and Shepherd Neame Spitfire.

Situated upon a hill with panoramic views of Brighton below. A one-bar pub, with no games except darts. Well-maintained beer garden. Members of the CAMRA Ale Trail. Food available at lunchtime. Barbecues held in summer. Children and dogs very welcome.

 All day, every day.

Prince Albert

48 Trafalgar Street, Brighton, East Sussex BN1 4ED
☎ *(01273) 730499* Chris Steward

 Young's Special and a Harveys brew usually available with two guest beers such as Fuller's London Pride, Morland Old Speckled Hen, Timothy Taylor Landlord or a Bateman or Forge beer.

Large, Grade II listed former Victorian hotel, which was completely refurbished as a pub in 1999. Food served 12–3pm and 5–9pm daily. Children welcome until 5pm. Situated next to Brighton Station, under the Trafalgar Street Bridge.

 11am–11pm Mon–Sat; 12–10.30pm Sun.

The Sussex Yeoman

7 Guildford Road, Brighton, East Sussex BN1 3LU
☎ *(01273) 327985* Rosie Dunton

 Greene King IPA and Abbot plus a Harveys ale are always available. Also occasional seasonal guests.

A trendy pub decorated in orange and blue with a young clientele (25–40) and a relaxed atmosphere. Games nights feature board games, or a pop quiz on Wednesday evenings. Bar snacks and fuller menu available until 9.30pm. No children.

 12pm–close.

Tap & Spile

67 Upper Gloucester Road, Brighton, East Sussex BN1 3LQ
☎ *(01273) 329540*

 Up to four brews. Shepherd Neame Spitfire, Badger Tanglefoot or beers from Bateman and other smaller breweries are among the regular guests. Seasonals and specials as available.

A quaint 1930s-style alehouse, with church pews, wooden floor and a pool room with quarry tiles. A locals' pub, nice and friendly. No food. No children.

 12–3pm and 5–11pm Mon–Thurs; all day Fri–Sun.

BURPHAM

The George & Dragon

Burpham, Nr Arundel, West Sussex BN18 9RR
☎ *(01903) 883131* James Rose

 Arundel Best and Harveys Best always available plus five guest beers (100 per year) from breweries such as Woodforde's, Hop Back, Cotleigh, Harviestoun, Ash Vine etc.

Located in a small village two miles from Arundel off the main track, with some of the best views of the Arun valley. Excellent walking all around. Bar and restaurant food available (restaurant evenings and Sunday lunch only). Car park. Children over 12 allowed.

OPEN *11am–2.30pm and 6–11pm Mon–Sat; 12–3pm and 7–10.30pm Sun.*

CANEHEATH

The Old Oak Inn

Caneheath, Arlington, Nr Polegate, East Sussex
☎ *(01323) 482072*

 Harveys Best Bitter and Badger Best usually available plus a guest beer, perhaps from Rother Valley, Fuller's, Young's or Charles Wells breweries.

Situated between the South Downs and Michelham Priory, with oak-beamed bar and restaurant, beer garden and barbecue. Food served 12–2pm Mon–Sun and Tues–Sat evenings. Car park. Children welcome, but no special facilities.

OPEN *11am–3pm and 6–11pm Mon–Sat; 12–3pm and 7–11pm Sun.*

COMPTON

The Coach & Horses

Compton, Nr Chichester, West Sussex PO18 9HA
☎ *(01705) 631228* David Butler

 Fuller's ESB always available plus five guest beers (100s per year) from breweries including Cheriton, Adnams, Cottage, Hop Back, Timothy Taylor and Hook Norton.

Situated on the Sussex Downs, a coaching inn built in 1500 with exposed beams and a Victorian extension. Bar and restaurant food is available at lunchtime and evenings. Car parking, garden and skittle alley. Children allowed. Good walking. Take the signed road to Uppark House (B2146).

OPEN *11am–2.30pm and 6–11pm Mon–Sat; 12–3pm and 7–10.30pm Sun.*

CRAWLEY

The Swan Inn

Horsham Road, Crawley, West Sussex RH11 7AY
☎ *(01293) 527447* Louise and David Baker

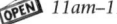 Fuller's London Pride always on offer, plus four guests (200 per year) such as Adnams Broadside, Orkney Skullsplitter, Shepherd Neame Spitfire and King Red River to name but a few. Guests change very frequently.

Traditional local with two bars, wooden floors and friendly staff and locals of all ages. Live music every Friday and every other Saturday, with jazz on first Sunday of the month and resident DJ on Thursday. Pool table, juke box, darts, cribbage and beer garden. Bar food served lunchtimes and evenings Tues–Fri, plus Sunday roasts and monthly curry nights. Well-behaved children and dogs welcome.

OPEN *11am–11pm Mon–Sat; 12–10.30pm Sun.*

EASTBOURNE

The Lamb Inn

36 High Street, Old Town, Eastbourne, East Sussex BN21 1HH
☎ *(01323) 720545* Mrs Hume

 Tied to Harveys Brewery, so Harveys Bitter always available.

An old-style, three-bar pub with seating at the side. Food available at lunchtime and evenings. Children allowed.

OPEN *10.30am–3pm and 5.30–close Mon–Thurs; all day Fri–Sat; 12–4pm and 7–10.30pm Sun.*

The Windsor Tavern

165 Langney Road, Eastbourne, East Sussex BN22 8AH
☎ *(01323) 726206* Shirley Verhulpen

Wadworth 6X and Greene King Abbot always available. Also Hoegaarden Belgian lager.

A quiet country-style pub in the middle of town. Large garden, no juke box or pool table. Food available at lunchtime and evenings. Children allowed in the garden or up to 8pm inside.

OPEN *All day Mon–Sat; 12–3pm and 7–10.30pm Sun.*

EAST GRINSTEAD

The Ship Inn

Ship Street, East Grinstead, West Sussex RH19 4RG
☎ *(01342) 312089* Mr R Connor

 A Young's-owned pub, always serving Young's Bitter, Special, Triple A and Winter Warmer (seasonal).

An olde-worlde locals' pub decorated with Guinness memorabilia. Large bar, restaurant and function room. Huge beer garden. Darts, pool, football and golf teams. Three letting bedrooms. Homemade food available Mon–Sat 12–2pm. Situated off the High Street.

OPEN *10am–11pm Mon–Sat; 12–10.30pm Sun.*

EAST HOATHLY

The King's Head

1 High Street, East Hoathly, Lewes, East Sussex BN8 6DR
☎ *(01825) 840238* Robert and Tracie Wallace

 A freehouse with Harveys Best and Fuller's London Pride always available plus three guests such as Hop Back Summer Lightning or Morland Old Speckled Hen.

Seventeenth-century pub, formerly a coaching inn, in a conservation village. Character bar, restaurant, function room, enclosed garden. Home-cooked food available at lunchtime and evenings. Period cottage available for letting as holiday accommodation. Children and dogs welcome. Visit the website at: www.ferncottageholidays.co.uk.

OPEN *11am–4pm and 6–11pm Mon–Sat; 11am–4pm and 7–10.30pm Sun.*

EXCEAT BRIDGE

The Golden Galleon

Exceat Bridge, Cuckmere Haven, Seaford, East Sussex BN25 4AB
☎ *(01323) 892247* Stefano Diella

 Home of the Cuckmere Haven Brewery, with Cuckmere Haven Best etc always available plus a range of guests (300 per year) including beers from Harveys, Shepherd Neame, Adnams, Timothy Taylor, Sussex, Fuller's and Oakhill.

They have been brewing here since 1994 and in late 2000 recycled a redundant plant in order to increase production. The new brewery can be viewed from the pub conservatory. The pub is a prominent black and white timbered building in the Cuckmere valley with beams and open fires in winter. Bar and restaurant food available all day. Car park, garden, conservatory, non-smoking room, function room. Children allowed, but not near the bar. Off the A259 on the River Cuckmere. Two miles from Seaford railway station. Website: www.goldengalleon.co.uk.

OPEN *11am–11pm Mon–Sat; 12–10.30pm Sun in summer; 12–4pm Sun in winter.*

FERNHURST

The King's Arms

Midhurst Road, Fernhurst, West Sussex GU27 3HA
☎ *(01428) 652005* Annabel and Michael Hurst

 King's Arms Ale (brewed especially by Ventnor Brewery), Ringwood Best and Hogs Back TEA always available plus two guests (500 in six years) perhaps including Hop Back Summer Lightning, Timothy Taylor Landlord, Ringwood Fortyniner and RCH Pitchfork.

A seventeenth-century freehouse with oak beams and fireplaces. An L-shaped bar with servery to dining area, plus hay barn for live bands, weddings etc. Surrounded by farmland, customers may come by horse or helicopter. Food available at lunchtime and evenings. Children allowed until 7pm, over 14s thereafter.

OPEN *11.30am–3pm and 5.30–11pm Mon–Sat; 12–3pm only Sun.*

FIRLE

The Ram Inn

Firle, Nr Lewes, East Sussex BN8 6NS
☎ *(01273) 858222*
Michael and Keith Wooller and Nikki Bullen

 Harveys Best Bitter permanently available, plus two regularly changing guest beers perhaps from Otter or Ringwood breweries.

Simple and unspoilt seventeenth-century coaching inn, situated in attractive village. Log fires during the winter months and large enclosed garden. Regular live folk music. Full bar menu served 12–9pm daily; cream teas available 3–5.30pm daily. Car park. Families very welome – special facilities include three children's menus, family room with toys (for use in winter), microwave for heating baby food, nappy changing facilities, high chairs and outdoor play equipment.

OPEN *11.30am–11pm Mon–Sat; 12–10.30pm Sun.*

FISHBOURNE

The Bull's Head

99 Fishbourne Road, Fishbourne, Nr Chichester, West Sussex PO19 3JP
☎ *(01243) 839895* Roger and Julie Pocock

 Gale's HSB, GB and Butser, plus Fuller's London Pride always available, plus five ever-changing guest ales.

A converted seventeenth-century farmhouse with a country atmosphere, just one mile from the city centre. Bar and restaurant food available at lunchtime and evenings except Sunday. Car park, garden and children's room. On the A259.

OPEN *11am–3pm and 5.30–11pm Mon–Fri; 11am–11pm Sat; 12–10.30pm Sun.*

FLETCHING

The Griffin Inn

Fletching, Nr Uckfield, East Sussex TN22 3SS
☎ *(01825) 722890*
Nigel and James Pullan and John Gatti

 Harveys Best and Badger Tanglefoot usually available, plus two guest beers such as Rother Valley Level Best or a Black Sheep brew.

Sixteenth-century, Grade II listed coaching inn situated in an unspoilt village. Two acres of gardens with lovely views towards Sheffield Park. Restaurant and bar food served every lunchtime and evening. Car park. Children welcome. Eight en-suite rooms.

OPEN *12–3pm and 6–11pm (10.30pm Sun).*

FRANT

Abergavenny Arms

Frant Road, Frant, East Sussex TN3 9DB
☎ *(01892) 750233* John and Debbie Playford

 Several beers available including Rother Valley Level Best, Fuller's London Pride, Timothy Taylor Landlord and Harveys brews, plus three rotating guests (250 per year). Regulars include beers from Arundel, Somerset and Exmoor.

Built in the 1430s, a large, two-bar country inn with non-smoking restaurant. The lounge bar was used as a courtroom in the eighteenth century, with cells in the cellar. Bar and restaurant food available at lunchtime and evenings. Three letting rooms (one family suite of two rooms, and one double en suite). Car park, garden. Children allowed. Easy to find.

OPEN *12.30–3pm and 5–11pm Mon–Fri; 12–11pm Sat; 12–10.30pm Sun.*

GRAFFHAM

The Foresters Arms

Graffham, Petworth, West Sussex GU28 0QA
☎ *(01798) 867202* Lloyd Pocock

 Cheriton Pots Ale plus four guest beers available which often include Hop Back Summer Lightning, beers from Harveys and an ever-changing selection from local breweries and micros.

Heavily beamed country freehouse dating from circa 1609. Situated at the foot of the South Downs with big log fires in winter and large garden for the summer. Food served every lunchtime and evening. Car park. Children are permitted in certain areas of the bar and restaurant, but there are no special facilities.

OPEN *11am–2.30pm and 5.30–11pm Mon–Sat; 12–3pm and 7–10.30pm Sun.*

HAILSHAM

The Bricklayers Arms

1 Ersham Road, Hailsham, East Sussex BN27 3LA
☎ *(01323) 841587* Ray Gosling

Fuller's ESB, Shepherd Neame Bishop's Finger and Greene King Abbot always available straight from the barrel, plus occasional seasonal guests.

Two bars, pool and billiards. Hot snacks available until 8pm. Beer garden. Children allowed in the garden only.

OPEN *11am–3pm and 5–11pm (10.30pm Sun).*

HALFWAY BRIDGE

Halfway Bridge Inn
*Halfway Bridge, Nr Petworth, West Sussex
GU28 9BP*
☎ *(01798) 861281* Simon and James Hawkins

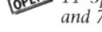 Cheriton Pots Ale and Gale's HSB always available plus two guests (100 per year) changed each week often from Spinnaker, Hampshire or Arundel breweries. Also local cider.

Built in 1710 on the A272 halfway between Midhurst and Petworth, an authentic staging post on the Dover to Winchester road. Four rooms around a central serving area, inglenook fireplace. Bar and restaurant food at lunchtime and evenings. Car park, garden, non-smoking area, traditional games. Children over 10 allowed.

OPEN *11–3pm and 6–11pm Mon–Sat; 12–3pm and 7–11pm Sun.*

HASTINGS

The Carlisle
Pelham Street, Hastings, East Sussex TN34 1PE
☎ *(01424) 420193* Mike Ford

A freehouse serving brews from various local breweries, including Arundel and White, plus seasonal guests.

A bikers' pub but with a mixed clientele. Rock music, bar games. Large function room. Outside seating on concrete mushrooms. Food available at lunchtime and evenings. Children allowed until 7pm.

OPEN *All day, every day.*

First In Last Out
*14–15 High Street, Hastings, East Sussex
TN34 3EY*
☎ *(01424) 425079* Mr Bigg

Three beers brewed on the premises, with two always available. Two guest ales such as Hop Back Rye and Coriander, but always changing. Smaller breweries favoured and normally their stronger brews. Occasional beer festivals.

Definitely a real ale house, known locally as FILO, recently refurbished, with lots of character and charisma. No pool or machines. Food available 12–3pm Mon–Sat in a separate restaurant. Quizzes or live music on Sunday evenings. Covered outside area with protection from inclement weather! Children allowed during the daytime only. Website: www.thefilo.co.uk.

 CROFTERS BEST BITTER 4.0% ABV
FILO GOLD 4.3% ABV
A light summer ale with 'punch'.
CARDINAL SUSSEX PORTER 4.6% ABV

OPEN *All day, every day.*

HAYWARDS HEATH

The Star
*1 The Broadway, Haywards Heath, West Sussex
RH16 3AQ*
☎ *(01444) 413267* Jason Flexen

 Up to 12 beers. Brakspear Bitter, Wadworth 6X, Harveys Sussex and Marston's Pedigree are regularly available, plus guests including Timothy Taylor Landlord, Sussex Pett Progress and Hop Back Summer Lightning. Monthly '4 for 3' offers on selected ales. Micro beer festival in April (25 ales) and two-week festival in October (50 ales and ciders).

A large, refurbished real ale house in the town centre. Food served all day, every day. Car park and outside seating. Part of the Hogshead pub group.

OPEN *11am–11pm Mon–Sat; normal hours Sun.*

HEATHFIELD

The Prince of Wales
*Hailsham Road, Heathfield, East Sussex
TN21 8DR*
☎ *(01435) 862919* Vivienne and Ted Archer

Regularly changing beers may include Harveys Best, Greene King Abbot Ale and brews from Rother Valley, Sussex, Wadworth or Charles Wells, as per customer request.

A freehouse partly dating back to the early nineteenth century, when it was used as a drovers' stop-over alehouse. Now enlarged to include two bars, restaurant and conservatory. Food served every day, lunchtime and evenings. Well-behaved children welcome. Car park.

OPEN *11am–3pm and 5–11pm Mon–Tues; 11am–11pm Wed–Sun.*

HERSTMONCEUX

The Brewer's Arms
*Gardner Street, Herstmonceux, East Sussex
BN27 4LB*
☎ *(01323) 832226* Barry Dimmack

 A freehouse with Harveys Best always available, plus up to four real ales, constantly rotating. Harveys seasonals regularly feature, as do beers from small independent brewers.

An Elizabethan pub dating from 1580. Food available until 7pm every day. Two well-equipped bars. Large-screen TV, pool and darts in the back bar. Children welcome in the back bar until 8pm.

OPEN *12–2.30pm and 6–11pm Mon–Sat; 12–3pm and 7–10.30pm Sun.*

HORSHAM

The Foresters Arms

43 St Leonards Road, Horsham, West Sussex
RH13 6EH
☎ *(01403) 254458* Jo Mainstone

 Three real ales including brews from Shepherd Neame always available.

A small pub with a large garden for outdoor games which is also child- and dog-friendly. Barbecues, quiz nights, happy hours etc. Food only on special occasions (such as BBQs). Children allowed in garden only.

OPEN *12–3.30pm and 6–11pm Mon–Fri; all day at weekends.*

The Malt Shovel

Springfield Road, Horsham, West Sussex
RH12 2PG
☎ *(01403) 254543* Steve Williams

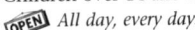 Adnams Bitter, Brakspear Bitter and Black Sheep Bitter always available, plus up to six guests, often including Timothy Taylor Landlord. A beer festival is held in February or March.

A traditional pub with floorboards, real fires, one bar, patio and car park. Food served until 7pm (9.30pm on Mondays). Children over 14 allowed.

OPEN *All day, every day.*

HORSTED KEYNES

The Green Man

The Green, Horsted Keynes, West Sussex
RH17 7AS
☎ *(01825) 790656*
Ramsay and Margaret Atkinson

 The permanent beers are Greene King IPA, Ruddles County, and Morland Old Speckled Hen, and the one guest is often Harveys Best Bitter.

Rural pub with a traditional feel, where a quiet drink and good food can be enjoyed either inside, or out on the green. No gaming machines or pool tables. The background music is usually classical at lunchtimes. Food served 12–2.30pm and 6.30–9.30pm Mon–Sat, and 12–2.30pm and 7–9pm Sun. There is a small, family dining area (no children under 5 allowed); children under 14 are not allowed in the bar area. Car park.

OPEN *11.30am–3.30pm and 5.30–11pm Mon–Fri; 11.30am–3.30pm and 6–11pm Sat; 12–3.30pm and 6–10.30pm Sun.*

HOVE

Farm Tavern

13 Farm Road, Hove, East Sussex
☎ *(01273) 325902* Tanya and D'Arcy Gander

 Greene King IPA, Abbot Ale and Triumph usually available. One or two guest beers served such as Fuller's HSB.

Quaint, old-fashioned pub situated near the town centre. Food served 12–3pm daily. Cinema Club. No children. Website: www.thefarmpub.co.uk.

OPEN *11am–11pm Mon–Sat; 12–10.30pm Sun.*

ICKLESHAM

The Queen's Head

Parsonage Lane, Icklesham, Winchelsea, East Sussex TN36 4BL
☎ *(01424) 814552* Ian Mitchell

 A freehouse with Greene King IPA and either Old Forge or Brother's Best from the Sussex Brewery always available, plus two fortnightly changing guests such as Greene King Abbot, Ringwood Old Thumper and Hop Back Summer Lightning.

A Jacobean pub dating from 1632. Farm implements on ceiling, boules pitch, function room, beer garden overlooking Rye. Food available at lunchtime and evenings. Under 12s allowed until 8.30pm. Situated off the A259.

OPEN *11am–11pm Mon–Sat; 12–5pm and 7–10.30pm Sun.*

ISFIELD

The Laughing Fish

Station Road, Isfield, Nr Uckfield, East Sussex TN22 5XB
☎ *(01825) 750349* Linda and Andy Brooks

 Greene King IPA, Morland Original and Greene King Abbot always available, plus at least one changing guest beer.

Rural village pub with real fires, offering real home-cooked food 12–2.30pm and 6.30–9.30pm every day, with rolls and sandwiches available all the time. Ingredients are sourced as far as possible from local producers. Families welcome. Car park, garden and play area. Situated just off the A26 between Uckfield and Lewes, next door to the Lavender Line Preserved Railway at Isfield Station.

OPEN *12–3pm and 4.30–11pm Mon–Fri; 11.30am–11pm Sat; 12–10.30pm Sun.*

LEWES

The Black Horse Inn
55 Western Road, Lewes, East Sussex BN7 1RS
☎ *(01273) 473653* Vic Newman

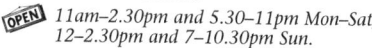Greene King IPA, Triumph and Abbot and a Harveys ale always available, plus two guests from a range of independent brewers.

Built in 1800 as a hotel, this is a quiet, two-bar pub situated on the main road through Lewes. Bar billiards, darts, cribbage, beer garden. Bar snacks available at lunchtime. No children.

[OPEN] *11am–2.30pm and 5.30–11pm Mon–Sat; 12–2.30pm and 7–10.30pm Sun.*

The Brewer's Arms
91 High Street, Lewes, East Sussex BN7 1XN
☎ *(01273) 475524* Kevin Griffin

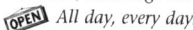A freehouse with Harveys Best always available plus up to four real ales constantly rotating. Harveys seasonals regularly featured, as well as brews such as Fuller's London Pride, Rother Valley Spirit Level or something from Arundel, Spinnaker, Northdown, Bateman, Cuckmere, Rector Ales, Larkins, Hampshire and Cottage. Also real ciders.

There has been a pub on this site since 1540. Well-equipped, with two bars, children's room, extractor fans (for smokers), pool and large-screen TV. Bar food available until 7pm, snacks until 11pm. Children welcome, and dogs if on a lead.

[OPEN] *All day, every day.*

The Elephant & Castle
White Hill, Lewes, East Sussex BN2 2DJ
☎ *(01273) 473797* Dave Whiting

A freehouse with Harveys Best, Morland Old Speckled Hen and Charles Wells Bombardier always available.

An old Sussex pub with one bar and a function room. Meeting place for the Bonfire Society. A themed menu is available at lunchtimes only. Children allowed.

[OPEN] *All day, every day.*

The Gardener's Arms
46 Cliffe High Street, Lewes, East Sussex BN7 2AN
☎ *(01273) 474808* Andy Fitzgerald

A constantly changing range of real ales from independent breweries across the UK is served on up to nine hand pumps.

A small traditional pub. Sandwiches available at lunchtime. Dogs welcome. Country walks nearby.

[OPEN] *11am–11pm Mon–Sat; 12–10.30pm Sun.*

LITLINGTON

The Plough & Harrow
Litlington, Nr Alfriston, East Sussex BN26 5RE
☎ *(01323) 870632* Barry and Ros Richards

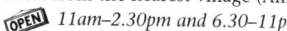Badger Best and Tanglefoot always available plus four guests from a large list including Wadworth 6X, Charles Wells Bombardier and Eagle IPA, Fuller's London Pride and brews from Harveys and Federation.

A fifteenth-century freehouse with oak beams, two bars and a busy restaurant. Bar and restaurant food available. Car park and garden. Children allowed in the restaurant. Three miles south of the A27, two miles from the nearest village (Alfriston).

[OPEN] *11am–2.30pm and 6.30–11pm.*

MAPLEHURST

The White Horse Inn
Park Lane, Maplehurst, Horsham, West Sussex RH13 6LL
☎ *(01403) 891208* Simon Johnson

A freehouse with Weltons Dorking Pride and Harveys Best always available, plus four guests, changed weekly, such as Hogs Back TEA, King and Barnes Best, Butcombe Gold, Harveys Armada or something from Spinnaker. Smaller independents and micro-breweries favoured.

A traditional three-bar pub with no juke box, machines or piped music. Non-smoking area, conservatory, garden with good views. Food served at lunchtime and evenings. Children allowed. Situated less than two miles north of the A272 and south of the A281.

[OPEN] *12–2.30pm and 6–11pm Mon–Sat; 12–3pm and 7–10.30pm Sun.*

MIDHURST

The Crown Inn
Edinburgh Square, Midhurst, West Sussex GU29 9NL
☎ *(01730) 813462* L Williams and R Cox

Fuller's London Pride and Badger Tanglefoot always available with up to five constantly changing real ales from independent brewers from across the UK. Gravity and hand-pump served.

A sixteenth-century freehouse with wooden floors and open fires. Three bar areas including pool and games room and 50-inch plasma TV in main bar. Courtyard. Behind and below the church in the old part of town.

[OPEN] *11am–11pm Mon–Sat; 12–10.30pm Sun.*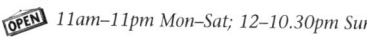

NUTBOURNE

The Rising Sun

The Street, Nutbourne, Pulborough, West Sussex RH20 2HE
☎ *(01798) 812191* Regan Howard

 A freehouse serving Fuller's London Pride, Greene King Abbot and King and Barnes Sussex Ale plus a minimum of two guests such as Harveys Sussex and Hogs Back TEA, or something from an independent such as Cottage.

A 400-year-old pub with Victorian frontage in walking country. Two bars, wooden floors, dining area, mixed clientele with very friendly landlord! Food served at lunchtime and evenings. Children allowed.

 *11am–3pm and 6–11pm (10.30pm Sun).*

NUTHURST

The Black Horse Inn

Nuthurst Street, Nuthurst, West Sussex RH13 6LH
☎ *(01403) 891272* Clive Henwood

 Harveys Sussex, one King brew and one Welton brew always available, plus guests on up to three pumps, which always include a regional ale.

A seventeenth-century pub with front terrace and stream-side rear beer garden. Lots of original features including a spitroast inglenook fireplace, exposed wattle and daub walls, two bars one with a Horsham stone floor, a snug and a restaurant. Food, including daily specials, available every lunchtime and evening, including Sunday roasts. Children welcome with children's menu provided. Dogs also welcome. Located three miles south of Horsham.

 12–3pm and 6–11pm Mon–Fri; 11am–11pm Sat; 12–10.30pm Sun.

OLD HEATHFIELD

The Star

Church Street, Old Heathfield, East Sussex TN21 9AH
☎ *(01435) 863570* Mr and Mrs Chappell

Harveys brews and Fuller's London Pride always available plus a guest (50 per year) such as Harviestoun Ptarmigan, Hop Back Summer Lightning, Black Sheep Best; also Daleside Old Legover, Gravesend Shrimpers, NYBC Flying Herbert, Daleside Monkey Wrench and Burton Bridge Hearty Ale etc.

A freehouse built in 1348, licensed in 1388. Original beams and open fires. Famous gardens and views. Bar and restaurant food served at lunchtime and evenings. Car park and garden. Children allowed. At a dead end of a road to the rear of Old Heathfield church.

 11.30am–3pm and 5.30–11pm.

OVING

The Gribble Inn & Brewery

Oving, Nr Chichester, West Sussex PO20 6BP
☎ *(01243) 786893* Brian and Cyn Elderfield

Gribble Ales all available. Wobbler only from September to March.

The Gribble Inn's brewery is now in its thirteenth year and still going strong. Rob Cooper, the head brewer, is constantly developing new beers, using only the best quality hops and malts with no additives or extra sugars, the latest in his range of fine ales and beers being known as Fursty Ferret, a nut-brown beer. This picturesque sixteenth-century inn is a traditional country pub, serving good, wholesome home-cooked food at both lunchtime and evenings, seven days a week. Car park, large garden, non-smoking area, children's room, skittle alley.

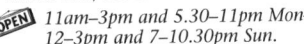

KING AND BARNES MILD 3.5% ABV
Acclaimed beer, in demand throughout Sussex.
FURSTY FERRET 4% ABV
Golden beer with light nutty and slightly hoppy flavour. Easy on the palate.
GRIBBLE ALE 4.1% ABV
A medium-strength hoppy bitter.
REG'S TIPPLE 5.0% ABV
Smooth nutty flavour with a pleasant after-bite.
PLUCKING PHEASANT 5.2% ABV
A light, dry hopped beer, deceptive in colour and easy to drink.
PORTERHOUSE 5.2% ABV
Old-fashioned porter with a full malt flavour and a subtle hint of liquorice.
PIG'S EAR 5.8% ABV
Full-bodied ale with a rich ruby-brown colour.
WOBBLER 7.2% ABV
A winter beer, not for the faint-hearted!

 11am–3pm and 5.30–11pm Mon–Sat; 12–3pm and 7–10.30pm Sun.

PETT

The Two Sawyers

Pett Road, Pett, Nr Hastings, East Sussex TN35 4HB
☎ *(01424) 812255*
Clive Soper, and John and Karen Perkins

A freehouse with the Sussex Brewery located on the premises, but run separately – this is not a brewpub. Sussex Pett Progress and Brother's Best always available, plus seasonals as available. Weekly changing guests selected from numerous nationwide micro-breweries.

An olde-worlde pub with two bars, comfortable restaurant, large beer garden, boules piste and B&B. Live music on Friday nights, quiz night on Wednesday. Food available at lunchtime and evenings. Children allowed in the restaurant, garden or snug. Website: www.twosawyers.com.

 11am–11pm.

PORTSLADE

The Stanley Arms

*47 Wolseley Road, Portslade, East Sussex
BN41 1SS*
☎ *(01273) 701590* Pat and Roy Bond

Three regularly changing beers served.

Traditional, street-corner pub with attractive garden. Barbecues in summer and live blues/rock music most weekends. Sandwiches available. Children welcome in the lounge and garden until 8pm. Situated 400 yards north of Fishersgate station.

OPEN *1pm–11pm Mon–Thurs; 12–11pm
Fri–Sat; 12–10.30pm Sun.*

ROBERTSBRIDGE

The Seven Stars Inn

High Street, Robertsbridge, East Sussex TN32 5AJ
☎ *(01580) 880333* John Mason and Jo Bowell

Harveys Best Bitter and Mild always available, plus Harveys seasonal brews.

Claims to be Britain's oldest haunted pub, dating from the fourteenth century. Homemade food available, including freshly prepared pizzas. Car park, beer garden.

OPEN *All day, every day.*

RUDGWICK

Thurlow Arms

*Baynards, Rudgwick, Nr Horsham, West Sussex
RH12 3AD*
☎ *(01403) 822459* Mr Gibbs

Fuller's London Pride, Hogs Back TEA, Ringwood Best Bitter, Badger Tanglefoot and Dorset Best regularly available.

Large Victorian pub situated on the South Downs Way, with railway memorabilia relating to the closure of Baynards station in 1965. Games room with darts and pool, restaurant, dining rooms and large garden. Food served 12–2pm and 6.15–9.30pm Mon–Fri, 12–2.15pm and 6.15–9.30pm Sat, and 12–2.30pm and 7–9pm Sun. Large car park. Children's play castle and menu.

OPEN *11am–3pm and 6–11pm Mon–Sat;
12–10.30pm Sun.*

RUSTINGTON

The Fletcher Arms

Station Road, Rustington, West Sussex BN16 3AF
☎ *(01903) 784858*
Mr R and Mrs C Dumbleton

Fuller's London Pride, Greene King Abbot Ale, Marston's Pedigree, Ringwood Best and Adnams Broadside permanently available, plus a daily changing guest beer perhaps from Wolf, Ballard's, Wild, Timothy Taylor, Hogs Back, Fuller's, Ringwood, Gale's, or many others from around the country.

Large, friendly, 1920s pub, winner of many awards including Cask Marque. Live entertainment, public and saloon bar and olde-worlde barn. Food available 11.30am–2.30pm and 6–9pm Mon–Sat, 12–2.30pm Sun. Large car park. Large garden with pets' corner, swings and bouncy castle. Accommodation.

OPEN *All day, every day.*

RYE

The Inkerman Arms

*Harbour Road, Rye Harbour, Rye, East Sussex
TN31 7TQ*
☎ *(01797) 222464* Peter and Dawn

A freehouse serving a selection of real ales from one of two local brewers (Sussex or Rother Valley). Guest ales always available.

A traditional pub with one bar, lounge and dining area. Boules pitch, garden. Food served 12–2.20pm and 7–9.20pm daily. Well-behaved children and dogs welcome. Car park.

OPEN *12–3pm Mon (closed Mon evenings except
bank holidays); 12–3pm and 7–11pm
Tues–Sat; closed Sun.*

The Ypres Castle Inn

Gungarden, Rye, East Sussex TN31 7HH
☎ *(01797) 223248*
Tom Cosgrove and Michael Gage

A freehouse with Harveys Bitter always available plus up to four regular guests such as Charles Wells Bombardier, Adnams Broadside, Young's Bitter and Sussex Pett Progress.

A traditional weatherboarded pub dating from the seventeenth century. No juke box or gaming machines. Non-smoking area, safe garden with lovely river views. Live music Fridays. Food using local produce available at lunchtimes and evenings (except Sunday evening) – reservations recommended. Children allowed in separate area and garden at lunchtime, and until 9pm in an evening, but only if eating.

OPEN *12–3pm and 7–11pm (10.30pm Sun); all
day at peak times in summer.*

ST LEONARDS ON SEA

The Dripping Spring

34 Tower Road, St Leonards on Sea, East Sussex RN37 6JE
☎ *(01424) 434055* Mr and Mrs Gillitt

 Goacher's Light and Fuller's London Pride served, plus ales from local breweries. Other guests from as far afield as possible, preferably 4% ABV and over – more than 1600 guest ales to date.

Asmall two-bar public house with attractive courtyard to the rear. Sussex CAMRA Pub of the Year 1999, 2000 and 2001, National CAMRA Pub of the Year runner-up 2001. Bar food available at lunchtime. Car parking. Situated in a side street off the A21.

OPEN *11am–3pm and 5–11pm Mon–Thurs; all day Fri–Sun.*

SEAFORD

The Wellington

Steyne Road, Seaford, East Sussex BN25 1HT
☎ *(01323) 890032* Mr Shaw

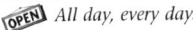 Fuller's London Pride, Greene King IPA, Abbot and Harveys Best Bitter always available. Also one guest from an independent or micro-brewery, changing daily.

Acommunity pub with two bars and a function room. Parking nearby. Food available at lunchtime only. Children allowed.

OPEN *All day, every day.*

The White Lion

74 Claremont Road, Seaford, East Sussex
☎ *(01323) 892473* Carole PE Tidy

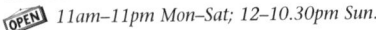 Harveys Sussex Best Bitter, Old, Porter and Fuller's London Pride regularly available, plus one or two guest beers perhaps from Greene King, Shepherd Neame or Harveys.

Friendly, small, family-run hotel by the seafront. Food served every lunchtime and evening. Car park. Large conservatory and separate non-smoking area. Children welcome. En-suite accommodation.

OPEN *11am–11pm Mon–Sat; 12–10.30pm Sun.*

SEDLESCOMBE

The Queen's Head

The Green, Sedlescombe, Battle, East Sussex TN33 0QA
☎ *(01424) 870228* Tony Fisher

 Young's Bitter always available plus one guest from an independent brewery. Rother Valley and Sussex brews are popular choices.

Acountry pub with beams and brasses, on the village green. Beer garden, car park. Food served 12–2.30pm, including fish and chips, jacket potatoes and sandwiches. There is also a free seafood Sunday lunch. Children allowed.

OPEN *10am–11pm Mon–Sat; 12–10.30pm.*

SHOREHAM

The Lazy Toad

88 High Street, Shoreham-by-Sea, West Sussex BN43 5DB
☎ *(01273) 441622* Mr Cederberg

 Greene King Abbot, Badger Tanglefoot, Shepherd Neame Spitfire and Gale's Festival Mild among the beers always available plus up to three guests.

Asmall, friendly freehouse with one big bar. Food served only at lunchtime. Children over 14 allowed.

OPEN *All day, every day.*

The Red Lion

Old Shoreham Road, Shoreham-by-Sea, West Sussex BN43 5TE
☎ *(01243) 453171* James and Natalie Parker

Harveys Best Bitter and four or five guest beers regularly available, perhaps from Hop Back, Adnams, Arundel, Fuller's or many more. Annual Easter beer festival features 50–60 beers, live music and barbecue.

Widely considered to be Shoreham's premier country pub, with low beams, inglenook and secluded beer garden. Good atmosphere, full of tales and history. Separate non-smoking eating area. Food served lunchtimes and evenings Mon–Sat, lunchtimes only Sun. Children welcome. The car park is situated some distance from the pub: pass the pub on your left, turn left at mini roundabout then first left again. Follow the road to church and the car park is opposite.

OPEN *11.30am–3pm and 5.30–11pm Mon–Fri; 11.30am–11pm Sat; 12–10.30pm Sun. Jul–Sept: open all day Mon–Fri.*

STOUGHTON

The Hare & Hounds

Stoughton, West Sussex
☎ *(01705) 631433*

 Adnams Broadside, Ringwood Best and Gale's HSB always available plus four guest beers (from an endless list) such as Hop Back Summer Lightning, Timothy Taylor Landlord, Fuller's ESB, Brakspear etc.

More than 300 years old, a flint-built pub nestling on the Sussex Downs. Bar food available at lunchtime and evenings. Car park and garden. Children allowed. Signposted at Walberton off the B2146.

OPEN *11am–3pm and 6–11pm Mon–Sat; 12–4pm and 7–10.30pm Sun.*

TARRING

The Vine Inn

High Street, Tarring, Worthing, West Sussex BN14 7NN
☎ *(01903) 202891* Nick Black and Lisa Carey

 Badger Dorset Best, Champion Ale and Tanglefoot, King and Barnes Sussex, Ringwood True Glory, Hop Back Summer Lightning and Gribble Inn Fursty Ferret always available, plus two guests from the Gribble Inn at Ovington. Beer festivals held regularly throughout the year, the main one being in September.

An old-fashioned pub in a listed building dating from 1645. Cask Marque accredited. Live entertainment on Mondays plus a quiz every Thursday. Enormous garden and courtyard, car park. Food available 12–2.30pm and 6–9pm Mon–Sat and 12–2.30pm Sun. Children and dogs welcome.

OPEN *12–3pm and 6–11pm Mon–Thurs; 11am–11pm Fri–Sat; 12–10.30pm Sun.*

THAKEHAM

The White Lion Inn

The Street, Thakeham Village, West Sussex RH20 3EP
☎ *(01798) 813141* Judi Gehlcken

 A freehouse with Greene King Abbot and IPA plus Fuller's London Pride always available, together with one regularly changing guest.

Traditional pub in a Grade II listed building in the centre of a picturesque village. Food is available, and is freshly prepared in an open-plan kitchen.

OPEN *11am–3pm and 5.30–11pm Mon–Sat; 12–10.30pm Sun.*

TICEHURST

The Bull Inn

Dunster Mill Lane, Three Legged Cross, Nr Ticehurst, East Sussex TN5 7HH
☎ *(01580) 200586* Mrs Josie Wilson-Moir

 Up to seven brews always available including Rother Valley Level Best, Sussex and Harveys ales plus hundreds of guests per year including brews from Adnams, Iceni etc.

Whealden Hall House was built between 1385 and 1425 in good walking country and has been a pub for 100 years. There are two bars with an adjoining restaurant. Food available at lunchtime and evenings. Car park, garden, children's play area. Bed and breakfast now available. Coming into Ticehurst from the north on the B2099, turn left beside corner house called Tollgate just before village.

OPEN *11am–11pm Mon–Sat; 12–10.30pm Sun.*

UCKFIELD

Alma

Framfield Road, Uckfield, East Sussex
☎ *(01825) 762232* Mrs Joy Hughes

 A Harveys house with Mild, IPA, Best Bitter and seasonal brews usually available.

Traditional, family-run (third generation) pub, with Cask Marque award. Food served 12–2pm Mon–Sat and 6–9pm Mon–Fri. Car park. Separate family and non-smoking rooms.

OPEN *11am–2.30pm and 6–11pm Mon–Sat; 12–2pm and 7–10.30pm Sun.*

The Peacock Inn

Shortbridge, Piltdown, Uckfield, East Sussex TN22 3XA
☎ *(01825) 762463* Matthew Arnold

 Harveys Best Bitter, Fuller's London Pride, Morland Old Speckled Hen and King Horsham Best Bitter are permanent features, and the guest beer might also be from the King Brewery.

A sixteenth-century inn, heavily beamed, with bar, restaurant, inglenook, front and rear garden and patio. Snacks and meals are served 12–2.30pm and 6–10pm, with snacks and afternoon teas available 3–5.30pm. Children are welcome, and the pub has a climbing frame in the rear garden, high chairs and children's menu. Car park. On the A272 Haywards Heath to Lewes road, turn right at Piltdown Garage.

OPEN *11am–11pm.*

WEST ASHLING

The Richmond Arms

Mill Road, West Ashling, West Sussex PO18 8EA
☎ *(01243) 575730* John and Linda Cutler FBII

 Greene King Abbot and IPA always available, plus guest ales.

A comfortable and cosy Victorian pub. Open fires, skittle alley, pool, darts etc. Patio at the front. Traditional home-cooked bar and à la carte meals available at lunchtime and evenings. Well-behaved children allowed in skittle alley. Small functions catered for. Situated one mile from Funtington and three miles from Chichester.

OPEN *11am–2.30pm and 6–11pm Mon–Sat; 12–3pm and 7–10.30pm Sun.*

WEST CHILTINGTON

The Five Bells

Smock Alley, West Chiltington, West Sussex RH20 2QX
☎ *(01798) 812143* Mr Edwards

 Five beers always available from an ever-changing range. Favoured brewers include Ballards, Adnams, Bateman, Black Sheep, Brakspear, Bunces, Cheriton, Exmoor, Fuller's, Gale's, Greene King, Guernsey, Harveys, Hogs Back, Hook Norton, Jennings, King & Barnes, Mansfield, Palmers, St Austell, Shepherd Neame, Smiles, Samuel Smith, Timothy Taylor and Young's.

A n attractive Edwardian-style version of a Sussex farmhouse. Bar and restaurant food available at lunchtime and evenings. Car park, conservatory and beer garden. Well-behaved children allowed. Ask for directions.

OPEN *12–3pm and 6–11pm.*

WORTHING

The Richard Cobden

2 Cobden Road, Worthing, West Sussex BN11 4BD
☎ *(01903) 236856* John Davies

 Greene King IPA and Abbot plus two other real ales always available.

A traditional Victorian alehouse built in 1868. The focus is on the old values of the trade – no fruit machines, no juke box, just old-fashioned sociability and enjoyment of life! Genuine home-cooked food served at lunchtimes (not Sunday).

OPEN *11am–3pm and 5.30–11pm Mon–Thurs; all day Fri–Sat; 12–3pm and 7–10.30pm Sun.*

YAPTON

The Lamb Inn

Bilsham Road, Yapton, Arundel, West Sussex BN18 0JN
☎ *(01243) 551232* John Etherington

 Harveys Sussex Ale and Greene King Abbot always available, plus one guest changing regularly.

A n edge-of-village pub on the road side. Brick floors, large open fire, non-smoking dining area, car park, garden with children's play area, and petanque/boules. Food served every lunchtime and evening. Children allowed. Located on a minor road between the A259 and Yapton village.

OPEN *11am–3pm and 5.30–11pm Mon–Thurs; 11am–3pm and 5–11pm Fri; 12–3.30pm and 6–11pm Sat; 12–4.30pm and 6.30–10.30pm Sun. Open all day at weekends during the summer.*

The Maypole Inn

Maypole Lane, Yapton, Arundel, West Sussex BN18 0DP
☎ *(01243) 551417* Keith McManus

 A freehouse with Ringwood Best always available plus up to six guests. Hop Back Summer Lightning, Cheriton Pots Ale or something from Skinner's may be featured. Smaller breweries well-represented.

A country pub with public and lounge bars, log fires, skittle alley, small garden. Bar snacks available at lunchtime and Sunday roasts. Children allowed in the public bar only until 8.30pm.

OPEN *11am–3pm and 5.30–11pm Mon–Fri; all day Sat; 12–3pm and 6–10.30pm Sun.*

YOU TELL US

* *The Cock Robin*, Station Hill, Wadhurst
* *The Earl of March*, Lavant Road, Lavant
* *Hatter's*, 2–10 Queensway, Bognor Regis
* *The Horse & Groom*, Singleton
* *The Linden Tree*, 47 High Street, Lindfield, Haywards Heath
* *The Ostrich Hotel*, Station Road, Robertsbridge
* *Vinols Cross*, 8 Top Road, Sharpthorne

Places Featured:

Byker
Felling
Gosforth
Hebburn
Jesmond
Low Fell
Newburn
Newcastle upon Tyne
North Hylton

North Shields
Old Ryton Village
South Shields
Sunderland
Sunniside
Wardley
Washington
Westmoor
Whitley Bay

THE BREWERIES

BIG LAMP BREWERS

Big Lamp Brewery, Grange Road, Newburn,
Newcastle upon Tyne NE15 8NL
☎ *(0191) 267 1687*
www.petersen-stainless.co.uk/keelman/blb.html

SUNNY DAZE 3.6% ABV
BITTER 3.9% ABV
KEELMANS 4.3% ABV
SUMMERHILL STOUT 4.4% ABV
PRINCE BISHOP ALE 4.8% ABV
PREMIUM 5.2% ABV
WINTER WARMER 5.5% ABV
KEELMAN BROWN 5.7% ABV

DARWIN BREWERY

63 Tatham St Back, Sunderland SR1 2QE
☎ *(0191) 514 4746*
www.darwinbrewery.com

DARWINS BITTER 3.6% ABV
SUNDERLAND BEST 3.9% ABV
DURHAM LIGHT ALE 4.0% ABV
EVOLUTION ALE 4.0% ABV
RICHMOND ALE 4.8% ABV
Plus a range of specialist beers.

HADRIAN & BORDER BREWERY

Unit 10 Hawick Crescent Ind Estate, Newcastle
upon Tyne NE6 1AS
☎ *(0191) 276 5302*

VALLUM BITTER 3.6% ABV
Rich, golden bitter.
GLADIATOR 3.8% ABV
A rich, dark ruby-coloured session bitter.
FARNE ISLAND 4.0% ABV
Amber-coloured, blended malt and hops.
FLOTSAM 4.0% ABV
Dark golden-coloured.
LEGION ALE 4.2% ABV
SECRET KINGDOM 4.3% ABV
Dark, rich and full-bodied bitter.
REIVER'S IPA 4.4% ABV
Award-winning dark golden bitter with a clean
citrus palate and aroma.
NORTHUMBRIAN GOLD 4.5% ABV
Dark golden ale, malty and not bitter.
CENTURION BITTER 4.5% ABV
Award-winning, pale-coloured, hoppy bitter,
fruity and quenching.
JETSAM 4.8% ABV
RAMPART 4.8% ABV
Gold-coloured, characterful bitter.

MORDUE BREWERY

Unit 21a, West Chirton North Industrial Estate,
Shiremoor NE29 8SF
☎ *(0191) 296 1879*
www.morduebrewery.com

FIVE BRIDGE BITTER 3.8% ABV
GEORDIE PRIDE 4.2% ABV
WORKIE TICKET 4.5% ABV
RADGIE GADGIE 4.8% ABV
Seasonal:
SUMMER TYNE 3.6% ABV
AUTUMN TYNE 4.0% ABV
SPRING TYNE 4.0% ABV
WALLSEND BROWN ALE 4.6% ABV
WINTER TYNE 4.7% ABV

THE PUBS

BYKER

The Cumberland Arms
Byker Buildings, Byker, Newcastle upon Tyne NE6 1LD
☎ *(0191) 265 6151*

 A wide range of constantly changing real ales always available.

An unchanged pub established in 1832 overlooking the Ouseburn Valley. Well known for its live music (traditional and rock). Sandwiches always available. Parking. Children allowed in the function room. Over Byker Bridge, then first right, second right, above farm.

OPEN *12–11pm (10.30pm Sun).*

The Free Trade Inn
St Lawrence Road, Byker, Newcastle upon Tyne NE6 1AP
☎ *(0191) 265 5764* Richard Turner

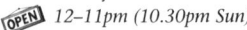 Mordue Workie Ticket and a Mordue seasonal ale always available, plus four rotating guest beers, from local breweries such as Hadrian, Border, Wylam or Cropton.

A traditional town pub with a lovely view of the River Tyne. Two beer gardens, one bar. Sandwiches available. Children allowed during the daytime and early evening only.

OPEN *11am–11pm (10.30pm Sun).*

The Ouseburn Tavern
33 Shields Road, Byker, Newcastle upon Tyne NE6 1DJ
☎ *(0191) 276 5120* Peter Bland

Twelve beers always available from a constantly changing range (450 per year) with Bateman Valiant, Charles Wells Eagle and Black Sheep Bitter among them.

Beamed theme pub with open fires and friendly atmosphere. Bar food available at lunchtime and evenings. Car park. Children allowed. Easy to find.

OPEN *12–11pm (10.30pm Sun).*

FELLING

The Old Fox
13 Carlisle Street, Felling, Gateshead NE10 0HQ
☎ *(0191) 420 0357* Val White

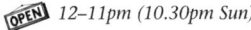 A freehouse with a Banks's ale and Fuller's London Pride always available plus three guests from breweries such as Durham. Beers also stocked at customers' request – previous examples have included Marston's Pedigree, Black Sheep Bitter and Fuller's London Pride.

A real ale pub in town location, with two coal fires, one bar and garden. Bar meals available until 7pm. Children allowed if eating, up to 7pm. Various entertainment on most evenings. Bed and breakfast available.

OPEN *12–11pm (10.30pm Sun).*

The Wheatsheaf
26 Carlisle Street, Felling, Gateshead NE10 0HQ
☎ *(0191) 420 0659* Jim Storey

A range of Big Lamp beers such as Bitter, Price Bishop, Premium Ale, Sandgates or Keelman Bitter always available.

An old-fashioned community pub with one bar. Sandwiches and pies available. Children allowed until 7pm.

OPEN *12–11pm (10.30pm Sun).*

GOSFORTH

Gosforth Hotel
High Street, Gosforth
☎ *(0191) 285 6617* Yvonne Goulden

Charles Wells Bombardier, Fuller's London Pride and Marston's Pedigree always available, plus two guests, such as Black Sheep Bitter, Timothy Taylor Landlord and Shepherd Neame Spitfire.

A busy two-bar pub, recently refurbished, with a friendly atmosphere. Bar food available 12–2.30pm Mon–Sat. Function room available for hire. Car parking opposite pub. No children.

OPEN *12–11pm (10.30pm Sun).*

HEBBURN

Dougie's Tavern
Blackett Street, Hebburn NE31 1ST
☎ *(0191) 428 4800* Paul Hedley (proprietor), Allan Holstead (manager)

 Freehouse offering four cask ales, including two ever-changing guests from breweries and micro-breweries all over the country.

A family-run pub, traditional by day and lively at night. Lunches served. Quiz on Tues, karaoke on Wed, live bands on Thurs, DJ on Fri, Sat and Sun. Children's play equipment in landscaped gardens. Large, floodlit car park.

OPEN *11am–12.30am Mon–Sat; 12–12.30am Sun.*

JESMOND

Legendary Yorkshire Heroes

Archibold Terrace, Jesmond
☎ *(0191) 281 3010* Colin Colquhoun

Nine beers always available from a rotating list including Black Sheep Bitter and brews from Jennings, Big Lamp and Thwaites.

A lively refurbished modern pub within an office complex. Bar food available on weekday lunchtimes. Four pool tables, big-screen sports, live bands Thursday to Saturday. Children allowed at lunchtimes only.

OPEN *11am–11pm Mon–Sat; 12–10.30pm Sun.*

LOW FELL

The Ale Taster

706 Durham Road, Low Fell, Gateshead NE9 6JA
☎ *(0191) 487 0770* Lawrence Gill

Mordue Workie Ticket and Radgie Gadgie always available plus up to six guests such as Timothy Taylor Landlord, Badger Tanglefoot or an Ash Vine brew. Two beer festivals held every year in May and September, serving 30 extra beers.

An old coaching inn with beams and wooden floors, in the town centre. One bar, snug area, large courtyard with children's play area. Food available until 6pm. Children allowed.

OPEN *11am–11pm Mon–Sat; 12–10.30pm Sun.*

NEWBURN

Keelman

Grange Road, Newburn, Newcastle upon Tyne
☎ *(0191) 267 1689* Lee Goulding

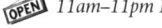Big Lamp Bitter, Prince Bishop Ale, Premium, Summerhill Stout plus other Big Lamp brews regularly available.

Superb conversion of nineteenth-century water board building into a traditional family pub. Situated next to the leisure centre in Newburn Country Park, on the River Tyne. Food served daily 12–3pm and 5–9pm in winter, 12–9pm in summer. Car park. Children's play area.

OPEN *11am–11pm Mon–Sat; 12–10.30pm Sun.*

NEWCASTLE UPON TYNE

The Bodega

125 Westgate Road, Newcastle upon Tyne NE1 4AG
☎ *(0191) 221 1552* Ben Rea

Mordue Workie Ticket, Geordie Pride and Durham Magus among the brews permanently available, plus two guests from breweries such as Hadrian and Border, Shepherd Neame, Black Sheep and Ridleys. Beers changed every three days.

A traditional real ale pub on the outskirts of the town centre. One bar, food available 11am–2.30pm Mon–Sat and 12–2.30pm Sun. No children.

OPEN *11am–11pm Mon–Sat; 12–10.30pm Sun.*

The Bridge Hotel

Castlegart, Newcastle upon Tyne NE1 1RQ
☎ *(0191) 232 6400* Christine Cromarty

A freehouse with Black Sheep Bitter and Mordue Workie Ticket always featured, plus three constantly changing guest beers, perhaps Hadrian and Border Gladiator, Castle Eden Nimmo's 4X, Hexhamshire Whapweasel, or something from Caledonian, Everards, Ridleys or Adnams.

A 100-year-old town-centre real ale pub with a function room, terrace and garden overlooking the Tyne Bridge and the quayside. Food available at lunchtimes (12–2pm and 12–3pm Sun). Live music in function room, folk club Monday night, jazz on Tuesdays. No children. Situated opposite the castle and above the quayside.

OPEN *11.30am–11pm Mon–Sat; 12–10.30pm Sun.*

The Head of Steam

2 Neville Street, Newcastle upon Tyne NE1 5EN
☎ *(0191) 232 4379* David Campell

A freehouse with Black Sheep Bitter always available plus up to three guests from a wide range of breweries including, among others, Castle Eden and Hambleton.

A two-bar, city-centre pub with food available all opening hours. No children.

OPEN *3–11pm Mon–Thurs; 12–11pm Fri–Sat; 12–10.30pm Sun.*

The Hotspur
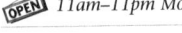
Haymarket, Newcastle upon Tyne
☎ *(0191) 232 4352* Jim Freeman (manager)

Four guests available, changing once or twice a week. Mordue Workie Ticket and Greene King Ruddles County are among the most popular ales. A wide range is purchased through the Beer Seller.

A very busy pub, part of the T&J Bernard chain, attracting mainly students and young professionals. Food available all day. Wide selection of wines and whiskies. Beer alley with big-screen TV for sport. No children. Located opposite Haymarket Bus Station.

OPEN *11am–11pm Mon–Sat; 12–10.30pm Sun.*

The Tap & Spile
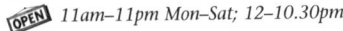
1 Nun Street, Newcastle upon Tyne
☎ *(0191) 232 0026*

Twelve beers always available from a constantly changing range (200 per year) with names such as Durham Canny Lad and Magus, Mordue Workie Ticket and Bateman Yella Belly.

More than 100 years old, with a ground-floor and basement bar. Bar food available at lunchtime. Children allowed for meals. Live bands in the cellar. Two minutes from the railway station and Greys Monument.

OPEN *11am–11pm Mon–Sat; 12–10.30pm Sun.*

The Tut & Shive
52 Clayton Street West, Newcastle upon Tyne NE1 4EX
☎ *(0191) 261 6998*

A Castle Eden ale and Black Sheep Bitter always available.

A friendly, relaxed city-centre pub with a mixed clientele, from students to o.a.p.s! Weekly promotional discounts on draught and bottles. No food. Live music up to five nights a week, plus pool knockouts every Sunday. No children. Two minutes from the Central Station.

OPEN *11am–11pm (12–11pm in summer) Mon–Sat; 12–10.30pm Sun.*

NORTH HYLTON

The Three Horseshoes
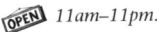
Washington Road, North Hylton, Sunderland SR5 3HZ
☎ *(0191) 536 4183* Frank Nicol

Four guest ales such as Morland Old Speckled Hen and Charles Wells Bombardier. Annual beer festival held at the end of July.

A traditional country pub with two bars (public and lounge), separate dining area, open fire, pool, darts etc. Food available lunchtimes and evenings. Children allowed. Follow signs for Air Museum, by Nissan entrance.

OPEN *11am–11pm.*

NORTH SHIELDS

Chain Locker
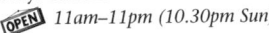
New Quay, North Shields NE29 6LQ
☎ *(0191) 258 0147* Peter McAlister

A freehouse with Mordue Workie Ticket and Radgie Gadgie always available plus four daily changing guests including, perhaps, Mordue Five Bridges and Timothy Taylor Landlord.

A riverside pub by a ferry landing on a fresh fish quay. One bar, styled in a nautical theme, plus separate dining area and beer garden. Food available at lunchtime only. Children allowed.

OPEN *11am–11pm (10.30pm Sun).*

The Garricks Head
Saville Street, North Shields NE30 1NT
☎ *(0191) 296 2064* Ken Ladell

A freehouse with four pumps all serving a range of weekly changing real ales. Morland Old Speckled Hen, Charles Wells Bombardier, Young's Special and Hartleys XB are examples.

A traditional two-bar town pub with function room and restaurant. Food available at lunchtime and evenings. Children allowed in the restaurant only.

OPEN *11am–11pm Mon–Sat; 12–10.30pm Sun.*

Magnesia Bank

1 Camden Street, North Shields
☎ *(0191) 257 4831* Richard Slade

Durham Magus, Mordue Workie Ticket and Black Sheep Bitter and Special always available plus up to four guests which might include Shepherd Neame Spitfire, Fuller's London Pride or Chiswick, Young's Waggle Dance, Bateman XB or Harviestoun Bitter and Twisted.

A true freehouse with a long tradition of supporting local micro-breweries. Winner of the *Morning Advertiser*'s Freehouse of Britain 2001. Good range of food, specialising in fresh fish and local lamb and beef, available lunchtimes and evenings Mon–Wed and all day Thurs–Sun. Live music three nights a week. Children allowed until 9pm. Situated close to North Shields fish quay, opposite the Bean Centre shoppers' car park.

OPEN *11am–11pm Mon–Wed; 11am–midnight Thurs–Sat; 12–10.30pm Sun.*

The Porthole

11 New Quay, North Shields NE29 6LQ
☎ *(0191) 257 6645* Mike Morgan

Five beers always available from a large list (156+ per year) including Fuller's London Pride and Adnams Broadside.

An old-fashioned friendly pub with a maritime theme, on the banks of the Tyne. Bar food served at lunchtime and evenings. Car park. Children allowed. Near the North Shields ferry landing.

OPEN *11am–11pm Mon–Sat; 12–10.30pm Sun.*

Shiremoor House Farm

Middle Engine Lane, North Shields NE29 8DZ
☎ *(0191) 257 6302* Bill Kerridge

A freehouse with Mordue Workie Ticket always available plus up to five guests such as Moorhouse's Pendle Witches Brew, Jennings Cumberland, Timothy Taylor Landlord, Swale India Summer Pale Ale or Durham Brewery's Celtic. Beers changed two or three times a week.

A converted farmhouse with two bars, stone floors and separate restaurant. CAMRA award winner for best pub conversion. Food available 12–10pm daily. Children allowed.

OPEN *11am–11pm (10.30pm Sun).*

The Tap & Spile

184 Tynemouth Road, North Shields NE30 1EG
☎ *(0191) 257 2523*

Castle Eden Bitter and Nimmo's XXXX always available plus six guests from a large and varied list. Beers from Harviestoun and Durham breweries usually available.

A real ale bar with a friendly atmosphere. Bar food served at lunchtime. Parking. Opposite the magistrates court in North Shields.

OPEN *12–11pm Mon–Fri; 11.30am–11pm Sat; 12–10.30pm Sun.*

OLD RYTON VILLAGE

Ye Olde Cross

Barmour Lane, Old Ryton Village, Gateshead NE40 3QP
☎ *(0191) 413 4689*
Diane Armstrong and Dennis Armstrong

The beers always on offer include Timothy Taylor Landlord, Charles Wells Bombardier and Black Sheep Bitter, and the guest is often Mordue Workie Ticket.

An olde-worlde pub overlooking the village green, with one open-plan room downstairs, restaurant upstairs, and secret garden. No pool, darts or juke box. Bar meals and snacks served downstairs in the pub at all times; the Italian-style restaurant upstairs is open evenings and Sunday lunchtimes. Children welcome. Communal car park.

OPEN *Summer: 12–11pm. Winter: 4–11pm Mon–Fri; 12–11pm Sat–Sun.*

SOUTH SHIELDS

The Dolly Peel

137 Commercial Road, South Shields NE33 1SQ
☎ *(0191) 427 1441*

A freehouse with Timothy Taylor Landlord, Black Sheep Bitter and something from Mordue always available, plus two guest pumps serving local ales in particular, but also real ales from breweries throughout the UK.

A traditional suburban pub with two bars and outside seating. Named after an eighteenth-century smuggler – details on request! No juke box, no pool table, no darts, no bandits, just good conversation and good beer in pleasant surroundings. Previous local CAMRA Pub of the Year. Sandwiches only. No bottled beers. No children.

OPEN *11am–11pm Mon–Sat; 12–3pm and 6.30–10.30pm Sun.*

Holborn Rose & Crown

Hill Street, South Shields NE33 1RN
☎ *(0191) 455 2379* Bob Overton

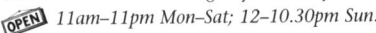 Two guest beers usually served, often from Marston's, Bateman, Fuller's, Black Sheep or Mordue breweries.

One-roomed traditional freehouse with beer garden, opposite the old middle docks. Toasted sandwiches available. Children welcome during daytime only.

OPEN *11am–11pm Mon–Sat; 12–10.30pm Sun.*

Riverside

3 Mill Dam, South Shields NE33 1EE
☎ *(0191) 422 0411* Paul Hedley (proprietor), John Mackay (manager)

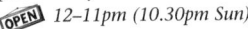 Timothy Taylor Landlord and Black Sheep Special regularly available plus two guest beers often from local micro-breweries and from elsewhere around the UK. Real cider also served.

Well-decorated, one-roomed pub with background music. Can be very busy at weekends. About half a mile from the town centre, tends to attract people 25 years and older. Sandwiches served at lunchtimes. Car park nearby.

OPEN *12–11pm (10.30pm Sun).*

SUNDERLAND

Fitzgeralds

10–12 Green Terrace, Sunderland SR1 3PZ
☎ *(0191) 567 0852* Matt Alldis

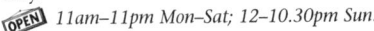 This freehouse held a beer festival a few years ago. It was so successful that it is now run constantly! No permanent ales, just a range of up to ten constantly changing guests, often including brews from Black Sheep, Darwin, Jennings, Hexhamshire and Mordue.

Traditional city-centre bar in an old building with fireplaces. Food is available, and there is a dining area. Quiz machine, beer garden. Children allowed at lunchtimes only.

OPEN *11am–11pm Mon–Sat; 12–10.30pm Sun.*

The Tap & Barrel

Nelson Street, Sunderland SR2 8EF
☎ *(0191) 514 2810* Michael Riley

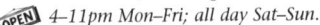 Everards Tiger and Timothy Taylor Landlord among the brews always available, plus four or five guests from a large selection including Banbury Old Vic and Thwaites Bloomin' Ale. Beers changed weekly.

An old-fashioned pub with two bars and a separate dining area. Food available 4–8pm Mon–Fri and 12–4pm Sat–Sun. Children allowed, if eating.

OPEN *4–11pm Mon–Fri; all day Sat–Sun.*

The Tap & Spile

Salem Street, Hendon, Sunderland
☎ *(0191) 232 0026* Janice Faulder

 Nine beers always available from a list of 400+ including North Yorkshire Best, Bateman XB, Charles Wells Bombardier and Marston's Pedigree.

Traditional three-bar alehouse with bare boards and exposed brickwork. Bar food available at lunchtime. Function room. Children allowed in eating area.

OPEN *11am–11pm Mon–Sat; 12–3pm and 7–10.30pm Sun.*

SUNNISIDE

The Potter's Wheel

Sun Street, Sunniside, Newcastle upon Tyne NE16 5EE
☎ *(0191) 488 6255* Liz Donnelly (manager) and David Rawlinson

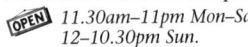 The permanent beers are Timothy Taylor Landlord and Black Sheep Bitter, and the four guests might include Mordue Workie Ticket, Five Bridges or Geordie Pride, Jennings Cumberland Ale or Bitter, Durham Celtic or Magus, or Fuller's London Pride.

Friendly, traditional community pub with bar, lounge, dining area and beer terrace. A 'Britain in Bloom' winner for four consecutive years. Food served 12–2pm and 5.30–9pm Mon–Sat and 12–3pm Sun. Children's certificate. Car park.

OPEN *11.30am–11pm Mon–Sat; 12–10.30pm Sun.*

WARDLEY

The Green

White Mare Pool, Wardley, Gateshead NE10 8YB
☎ *(0191) 495 0171* Deborah Mackay

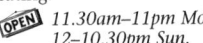 A freehouse with six guest ales always available. Timothy Taylor Landlord, Jennings Cumberland, Big Lamp Bitter, Black Sheep Special and Oakham American Blonde are some of the regular features.

A traditional village pub with one bar and one lounge. Patio and restaurant. Disabled facilities. Food available all day, every day. Children allowed in the lounge if eating.

OPEN *11.30am–11pm Mon–Sat; 12–10.30pm Sun.*

WASHINGTON

The Sandpiper
Easby Road, Washington NE38 7NN
☎ *(0191) 416 0038* Lynda Margaret Bewick

 Up to six guests such as Marston's Pedigree, Black Sheep Bitter, Fuller's London Pride, something from Daleside or Phoenix Wobbly Bob.

A locals' village community pub with two bars, games area and patio. Charity events held. Food available at lunchtime only. Children allowed until 7pm, if supervised.

 11am–11pm (10.30pm Sun).

WESTMOOR

George Stephenson Inn
Great Lime Road, Westmoor, Newcastle upon Tyne NE12 0NJ
☎ *(0191) 268 1073* Richard Costello

Four real ales are always available, including two constantly changing guests, one of them usually from a local micro-brewery.

A community beer drinker's pub with lounge, bar and garden. Adult clientele, no games, live music every Wednesday, Thursday and Saturday. No food. No children.

12–11pm (10.30pm Sun).

WHITLEY BAY

The Briar Dene
71 The Links, Whitley Bay NE26 1UE
☎ *(0191) 252 0926* Mrs Gibson

 Mordue Workie Ticket and Summertime, Black Sheep Riggwelter and a Yates ale always available, plus five or six guests such as Mordue Radgie Gadgie among others. Six beer festivals held each year with 50–60 brews at each.

A seaside pub with one bar, family room, lounge and children's play area. Food available 11am–2.30pm and 5–10pm. Children allowed in the family room and play room only.

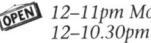 *11am–11pm Mon–Sat; 12–10.30pm Sun.*

The Fat Ox
278 Whitley Road, Whitley Bay NE26 2TG
☎ *(0191) 251 3852* Mr Carling

Eight monthly changing guest beers on offer, including favourites such as Marston's Pedigree, Black Sheep Bitter and Morland Old Speckled Hen, plus beers from a wide range of breweries around the UK.

A traditional one-bar town-centre pub. Live bands on Saturday nights, big-screen TV. No food. No children. Disabled facilities.

12–11pm Mon–Fri; 11am–11pm Sat; 12–10.30pm Sun.

YOU TELL US

* *The Archer,* Archbold Terrace, Jesmond
* *Benton Ale House,* Front Street, Benton, Newcastle upon Tyne
* *The Melvich Hotel,* Melvich, Sunderland
* *Shipwrights Arms Hotel,* Rotherfield Road, North Hylton, Sunderland
* *The Station Hotel,* Hills Street, Gateshead

Places Featured:

Alcester	Henley-in-Arden
Armscote	Ilmington
Ashby St Ledgers	Kenilworth
Bedworth	Leamington Spa
Berkswell	Long Lawford
Bishops Tachbrook	Nuneaton
Chapel End	Rugby
Church Lawford	Shipston-on-Stour
Eathorpe	Stratford-upon-Avon
Edgehill	Studley
Great Wolford	Warwick
Hampton Lucy	Whichford
Hartshill	

THE BREWERIES

CHURCH END BREWERY

Ridge Lane, Nuneaton CV10 0RD
☎ *(01827) 713080*
All beers available on a seasonal or occasional basis. No fully permanent ales.

POACHER'S POCKET 3.5% ABV
ALTAR ALE 3.6% ABV
PHEASANT PLUCKER 3.7% ABV
AVON ALE 3.8% ABV
CUTHBERTS 3.8% ABV
GOATS' MILK 3.8% ABV
GRAVEDIGGERS' ALE 3.8% ABV
ANCHOR BITTER 4.0% ABV
SHAKES BEER 4.0% ABV
THINGEE 4.0% ABV
HOP GUN 4.1% ABV
'V' REG 4.1% ABV
ANCHOR GOLD 4.5% ABV
DROP GOAL 4.5% ABV
OLD HERBACIOUS 4.5% ABV
PEWS PORTER 4.5% ABV
RED OCTOBER 4.5% ABV
SHREDDIES 4.5% ABV
WHATEVER HAPPENED TO U-REG? 4.5% ABV
BALOO-THE-BEER 4.6% ABV
STOUT COFFIN 4.6% ABV
SUNSHINE 4.6% ABV
CUTTING ALE 4.8% ABV
SUPER P 4.8% ABV
FALLEN ANGEL 5.0% ABV
INDIA PALE ALE 5.0% ABV
OLD GRAVEL TREADER 5.0% ABV
CHARTER ALE 5.5% ABV
OLD PAL 5.5% ABV
ARTHUR'S WIT 6.0% ABV
OLD FATHER BROWN 6.0% ABV
REST IN PEACE 7.0% ABV

FRANKTON BAGBY BREWERY

The Old Stables, Green Lane, Church Lawford, Rugby CV23 9EF
☎ *(02476) 540770; Fax: (07977) 570779*

BARNSTORMER 3.7% ABV
Flowery, golden bitter.
OLD CHESTNUT 4.0% ABV
CHICKEN TACKLE 4.1% ABV
A bright hoppy beer with a hint of ginger.
SQUIRES BREW 4.2% ABV
RUGBY SPECIAL 4.5% ABV
CHRISTMAS PUD 7.0% ABV
Sumptuous, strong and complex dark beer.

WARWICKSHIRE BEER CO. LTD

Cubbington Brewery, Queen Street, Cubbington, Leamington Spa CV32 7NA
☎ *(01926) 450747*
www.warwickshirebeerco.co.uk

BEST BITTER 3.9% ABV
LADY GODIVA 4.2% ABV
FALSTAFF 4.4% ABV
ST PATRICK'S ALE 4.4% ABV
CASTLE 4.6% ABV
GOLDEN BEAR 4.9% ABV
KING MAKER 5.5% ABV
Plus seasonal and occasional brews.

THE PUBS

ALCESTER

Lord Nelson
69 Priory Road, Alcester B49 5EA
☎ *(01789) 762632* Dennis and Brenda Stubbs

 Fuller's London Pride usually available, plus two other real ales, varying weekly.

Parts of this pub date back 600 years. There is a mature beer garden, a bar with darts and bar billiards and a restaurant area. Food is available 7–9am, 12–2pm and 7–9pm Mon–Sat, with just lunchtime roasts on Sundays. Car park. Children welcome. Accommodation.

OPEN *12–3pm and 6–11pm Mon–Sat; 12–3pm and 7–10.30pm Sun.*

The Three Tuns
34 High Street, Alcester B49 5AB
☎ *(01789) 762626* P Burdett

 Hobsons Best and Goff's Jouster permanently available, plus six guest ales from independent breweries, with Greene King and Salopian brews making regular appearances.

A sixteenth-century public house with open-plan bar, converted back from a wine bar. Beer festivals are held every three months.

OPEN *12–11pm (10.30pm Sun).*

ARMSCOTE

The Fox & Goose
Armscote, Stratford-upon-Avon CV37 8DD
☎ *(01608) 682293* Miss Sue Gray

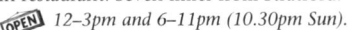 A freehouse always serving a house beer, Fox & Goose Bitter, brewed by Brakspear. North Cotswold Genesis is a regular guest (two are offered, changed weekly), but beers from Hook Norton and seasonal ales are also featured.

Village pub, restaurant and hotel in a 150-year-old stone building adjoining a thatched cottage. Food available. Garden and decking. Four double en-suite letting rooms. Jazz occasionally in garden. Children allowed in restaurant. Seven miles from Stratford.

OPEN *12–3pm and 6–11pm (10.30pm Sun).*

ASHBY ST LEDGERS

The Olde Coach House Inn
Ashby St Ledgers, Nr Rugby CV23 8UN
☎ *(01788) 890349*
Pete and Christine Ballinger

 St Ledger Ale (house brew) and Everards Old Original always available plus five guest ales (200 per year) including Hop Back Summer Lightning, Hook Norton Haymaker, Frog Island Natterjack, Adnams Broadside and beers from Frankton Bagby and Timothy Taylor.

An olde-English converted farmhouse in the middle of an historic village. Lots of family tables and small intimate nooks and crannies. Large secure garden for children and plenty of parking space. Bar and restaurant food available at lunchtime and evenings. Car park. Accommodation. Three miles from M1 junction 18, close to M6 and M40 and adjacent to A5. Daventry three miles to the south, Rugby four miles to the north.

OPEN *12–2.30pm and 6–11pm Mon–Fri; 12–11pm Sat; 12–2.30pm and 7–10.30pm Sun.*

BEDWORTH

The White Swan
All Saints Square, Bedworth
☎ *(02476) 312164* Paul Holden

 Charles Wells Eagle, IPA and Bombardier usually served, plus one guest beer such as Morland Old Speckled Hen, Badger Tanglefoot or Adnams Broadside.

Central pub, catering for mixed clientele of all ages. Food served 12–2pm daily. Car parks close by. Children welcome at lunchtime.

OPEN *11am–11pm (10.30pm Sun).*

BERKSWELL

The Bear
Spencer's Lane, Berkswell CV7 7BB
☎ *(01676) 533202* Nick Lancaster

Two guests, changed fortnightly, might include Marston's Pedigree or Warwickshire Lady Godiva.

Chef & Brewer pub in village location, in an old building. Food is available, and there is a dining area. Garden, car park. Children allowed.

OPEN *11am–11pm Mon–Sat; 12–10.30pm Sun.*

BISHOPS TACHBROOK

The Leopard
Oakley Wood Road, Bishops Tachbrook,
Nr Leamington Spa CV33 9RN
☎ *(01926) 426466* Ian Richardson

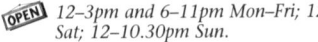 Hook Norton Best, Timothy Taylor Landlord and Greene King Abbot are usually available, plus one changing guest.

Country pub and restaurant in an old A-frame building dating back to 1066. Garden. Food available. Children allowed. Car park.

OPEN *12–3pm and 6–11pm Mon–Fri; 12–11pm Sat; 12–10.30pm Sun.*

CHAPEL END

The Salutation Inn
Chancery Lane, Chapel End, Nuneaton CV10 0PB
☎ *(01203) 392382* Becky Gardner

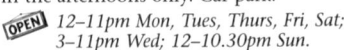 Tied to Banks's, with Banks's Bitter always available.

Very old out-of-town pub, formerly a coaching inn. No food. Children allowed in the afternoons only. Car park.

OPEN *12–11pm Mon, Tues, Thurs, Fri, Sat; 3–11pm Wed; 12–10.30pm Sun.*

CHURCH LAWFORD

Old Smithy
Green Lane, Church Lawford, Nr Rugby
CU23 9EF
☎ *(02476) 542333* John O'Neill

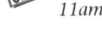 Frankton Bagby Anvil Ale, plus Greene King IPA and Abbot Ale usually available. A guest beer frequently comes from the Frankton Bagby Brewery which adjoins the pub.

Traditional freehouse situated on the village green. Food served lunchtimes and evenings. Car park. Beer garden and children's play area.

OPEN *11am–3pm and 5.30–11pm Mon–Fri; 11am–11pm Sat; 12–10.30pm Sun.*

EATHORPE

Eathorpe Park Hotel
The Fosse, Eathorpe, Leamington Spa CV33 9DQ
☎ *(01926) 632632* Mrs Grinnell

A Church End ale always available plus two guests from breweries such as Hook Norton and Fat God's.

A hotel and restaurant with one bar and accommodation. Disabled access. Bar and restaurant food available at lunchtime and evenings. Children allowed.

OPEN *All day, every day.*

EDGEHILL

The Castle Inn
Edgehill, Nr Banbury OX15 6DJ
☎ *(01295) 670255* NJ and GA Blann

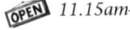 Hook Norton Best, Generation, Old Hooky and the seasonal brew usually available, plus a guest beer which may be from Shepherd Neame, King & Barnes, Wadworth or Wye Valley.

The inn is situated on the summit of Edgehill near the civil war battle site. Built as a folly in the eighteenth century to commemorate the centenary of the battle, it is a copy of Guy's Tower at Warwick Castle. Food served every session. Car park. Original en-suite bedrooms.

OPEN *11.15am–2.30pm and 6.15–11pm.*

GREAT WOLFORD

The Fox & Hounds
Great Wolford CV36 5NQ
☎ *(01608) 674220* Wendy Veale

 Hook Norton Best is always available plus at least three guest beers each week, including Frankton Bagby Old Chestnut, Wyre Piddle Piddle in the Hole, Charles Wells Bombardier and brews from Cottage, Wye Valley, Adnams, Thwaites and Wychwood.

An unspoilt sixteenth-century village inn with stone-flagged floors, log fires, hops, faded hunting pictures – and an infamous pub sign! Seasonal, local produce used for blackboard specials and bar food menu (please enquire for times). Car park, terrace, and charming en-suite bed and breakfast accommodation.

OPEN *12–2.30pm and 6–11pm (10.30pm Sun); closed Mondays.*

HAMPTON LUCY

The Boars Head
Hampton Lucy CV35 8BE
☎ *(01789) 840533* Sally Gilliam

Hook Norton Best Bitter and Shepherd Neame Spitfire usually available, plus one or two guest beers often from Warwickshire, Church End, Frankton Bagby, Timothy Taylor, Fuller's or many others.

Traditional English pub with log fire and great atmosphere. Home-cooked food and nice garden with ample seating. Food served 12–2.15pm and 7–10pm. Car park. Well-behaved children welcome, but no special facilities.

OPEN *11.30am–3pm and 6–11pm Mon–Sat; 12–3pm and 7–10.30pm Sun.*

HARTSHILL

The Anchor Inn
Mancetter Road, Hartshill, Nuneaton CV1 0RT
☎ *(02476) 398839* Mr Anderson

 Tied to Everards, with Tiger and Original constantly available. Morland Old Speckled Hen is a regular guest (two served, changed every four weeks), but other Everards beers such as Lazy Daze, Equinox and Beacon are also featured.

Rural canalside pub with two restaurants and two bars, in a 150-year-old building. Karaoke on Mondays, other entertainment on Thursdays in winter. Garden with access to towpath. Children allowed.

[OPEN] *11am–11pm Mon–Sat; 12–10.30pm Sun.*

HENLEY-IN-ARDEN

The White Swan Hotel
100 High Street, Henley-in-Arden B95 5BY
☎ *(01564) 792623* Nigel May

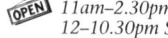 One guest, changed weekly, might be something like Everards Beacon, Bateman XB, Morland Old Speckled Hen, Wadworth 6X or a seasonal or celebration ale.

Situated in the centre of the smallest market town in England, this black and white coaching inn dates from 1352. Food available. One bar, restaurant, garden, ten letting rooms. Jazz on Wednesdays. Children allowed. Car park.

[OPEN] *11am–11pm Mon–Sat; 12–10.30pm Sun.*

ILMINGTON

The Howard Arms
Lower Green, Ilmington CV36 4LJ
☎ *(01608) 682226* Mr and Mrs Greenstock

 Everards Tiger and North Cotswold Genesis are the permanent ales at this freehouse, which also offers one guest, changed fortnightly, perhaps Timothy Taylor Landlord, Shepherd Neame Sptifire, Ruddles County or something from Adnams.

Village pub in a sixteenth-century building with inglenook fireplaces. Food available. Non-smoking area, garden, three letting rooms. Children allowed until the early evening only. Visit the website at: www.howardarms.com.

[OPEN] *11am–2.30pm and 6–11pm Mon–Sat; 12–10.30pm Sun.*

KENILWORTH

The Wyandotte Inn
Park Road, Kenilworth
☎ *(01926) 863219* Mrs Jaeger

 Banks's Bitter plus Marston's Bitter and Pedigree regularly available.

Street-corner local with split-level single room and log fire in winter. Beer garden. Pool table, monthly quiz and regular musical events. No food. Car park. No children.

[OPEN] *5–11pm Mon–Thurs; 3–11pm Fri; 12–11pm Sat; 12–10.30pm Sun; also lunchtimes in summer holidays.*

LEAMINGTON SPA

Benjamin Satchwell
112–14 The Parade, Leamington Spa CV32 4AQ
☎ *(01926) 883733* Andy Tompkins

 Hop Back Summer Lightning, Greene King Abbot and Shepherd Neame Spitfire are among the permanent beers at this twelve-pump pub. The six guests, changed every two days, might include Wyre Piddle Piddle in the Wind, Castle Eden Nimmo's 4X or something from Mordue.

Traditional open-plan Wetherspoon's town pub, holding beer festivals throughout the year (call for details). Food available. No children.

[OPEN] *11am–11pm Mon–Sat; 12–10.30pm Sun.*

LONG LAWFORD

The Sheaf & Sickle
Coventry Road, Long Lawford, Rugby CV23 9DT
☎ *(01788) 544622* Steve Townes

 Two guests available from breweries such as Eldridge Pope, Church End, Ash Vine and Judges. Aims not to repeat the beers.

An old village coaching inn with saloon, lounge and restaurant. Beer garden. Food available at lunchtime and evenings. Children allowed.

[OPEN] *12–2.30pm and 6–11pm Mon–Fri; all day Sat–Sun.*

NUNEATON

The Brewery Tap
Ridge Lane, Nuneaton CV10 0RD
☎ *(01827) 713080* Stewart Elliot

 Located on the site of the Church End Brewery, serving Gravediggers' Ale plus a range of the Church End ales at the point of production.

A brewery tap room run as a pub. Brewing can be viewed through a window in the bar. Non-smoking. No children. No food served at present although there are plans to do so in the future. Large, meadow-style garden. Brewery tours available (phone for details).

[OPEN] *11am–11pm Fri–Sat; 12–10.30pm Sun (closed Mon–Thurs).*

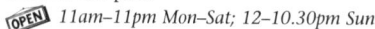

RUGBY

The Alexandra Arms
72 James Street, Rugby CV21 2SL
☎ *(01788) 578660* Julian Hardy

 Marston's Pedigree and Greene King Abbot Ale permanently available, plus two guest beers from a wide selection. Beowolf, Burton Bridge, Church End and Wye Valley feature regularly.

A ward-winning pub with bar billiards, table skittles and pool. Garden. Food available 12–2.30pm and 5–8.30pm. No children. Situated near the main post office.

OPEN *11.30am–3pm and 5–11pm Mon–Thurs; 11.30am–11pm Fri–Sat; 12–10.30pm Sun.*

The Three Horseshoes Hotel
Sheep Street, Rugby CV21 3BX
☎ *(01788) 544585* Christopher Bingham

 Greene King IPA, Abbot Ale and Ruddles County usually available, plus one or two guest beers, often from Frankton Bagby, Church End or Adnams breweries.

C entral, seventeenth-century inn with open fires and beamed restaurant. Food available 12–2pm and 7–10pm daily. Car park. Children welcome. Accommodation.

OPEN *11am–2.30pm and 7–11pm Mon–Sat; 12–2.30pm and 7–10.30pm Sun.*

The Victoria Inn
1 Lower Hillmorton Road, Rugby CV21 3ST
☎ *(01788) 544374* Mrs White

 A freehouse with Cottage Champflower among the brews always available plus two guests such as Hartley XB (Robinson's), Greene King IPA, Hook Norton and Shepherd Neame brews.

A locals' pub just outside the town centre. Two bars, original mirrors in both rooms. Disabled access. Food available at lunchtime only. No children.

OPEN *12–3pm and 6–11pm Mon–Thurs; 12–3pm and 5–11pm Fri; all day Sat; 12–3pm and 7–10.30pm Sun.*

SHIPSTON-ON-STOUR

The Coach & Horses
16 New Street, Shipston-on-Stour CV36 4EM
☎ *(01608) 661335* Bob Payne

 Hook Norton Best always available plus three guests from a long list including Hook Norton Haymaker, Wye Valley Brew 69, Dorothy Goodbody's Summertime Ale, Ash Vine Toxic Waste, Bateman XXXB and XB.

A 250-year-old village pub in the Cotswolds serving bar and restaurant food at lunchtime and evenings. Car park, garden, accommodation. On the A3400 Birmingham to Oxford road, on the Oxford side of town.

OPEN *11am–11pm (10.30pm Sun).*

The Horseshoe Inn
6 Church Street, Shipston-on-Stour CV36 4AP
☎ *(01608) 661225* Lorraine Stinton

 Greene King Ruddles Best is one of the beers always on offer. Two guests, changed frequently, might include Wadworth 6X or something from North Cotswold, such as Genesis or Four Shires.

S mall town pub with restaurant, in a sixteenth-century Grade II listed building with beams and fires. Fruit machines, live music Wednesdays, beer garden, bed and breakfast. Parking. Children allowed. On the main A34.

OPEN *11am–3pm and 6–11pm Mon–Thurs; 11am–11pm Fri–Sat; 12–10.30pm Sun.*

STRATFORD-UPON-AVON

The Queen's Head
53 Ely Street, Stratford-upon-Avon CV37 6LN
☎ *(01789) 204914* Martin Jones

 A freehouse with Adnams Bitter among the beers always on offer. Guests are either Highgate Saddlers Celebrated Best Bitter or Greene King IPA in summer, and one extra during winter, for example Wychwood Hobgoblin or Jennings Sneck Lifter.

A good old-fashioned pub in a traditional sixteenth-century building in the centre of Stratford. Food available at lunchtimes only. One bar, beer garden, live music once a month, five B&B rooms. Children allowed until 7pm only.

OPEN *11.30am–11pm Mon–Fri; 11am–11pm Sat; 12–10.30pm Sun.*

STUDLEY

The Little Lark
108 Alcester Road, Studley B80 7NP
☎ *(01527) 853105* Mark Roskell

 Ushers Best Bitter, Founders and a seasonal brew normally available, plus traditional cider.

A n interesting selection of printing paraphernalia is a feature in this real ale house. Food available lunchtimes and evenings every day. No children.

OPEN *12–3pm and 6–11pm Mon–Fri and Sun; 12–11pm Sat.*

WARWICK

The Old Fourpenny Shop Hotel

27–9 Crompton Street, Warwick CV34 6HJ
☎ *(01926) 491360* Jan Richard Siddle

 Six guest beers usually served from an extensive selection including Timothy Taylor Landlord, RCH Pitchfork, Greene King Abbot and IPA, and beers from Church End, Abbey, Frankton Bagby, Warwickshire, Eccleshall, Litchfield, Burton Bridge, Bateman and many other independent breweries.

Popular real ale house with restaurant. Food served 12–2pm and 7–10pm daily. Car park. Children over 10 years old welcome. Accommodation available, with 11 newly refurbished bedrooms.

[OPEN] *12–2.30pm and 5.30–11pm Mon–Thurs; 12–3pm and 5–11pm Fri; 12–3pm and 6–11pm Sat–Sun (10.30pm Sun).*

WHICHFORD

The Norman Knight

Whichford, Shipston-on-Stour CV36 5PE
☎ *(01608) 684621* Mike Garner

 Four-pump freehouse with Hook Norton Best Bitter always on offer, plus three guests, changed every couple of days, perhaps North Cotswold Genesis, Eccleshall Slaters Original or Cottage Golden Arrow.

Village pub in a nineteenth-century building, part stone, part brick. Food available. Garden, darts, occasional live music. Self-catering holiday accommodation, caravans and camping. Children allowed. Car park.

[OPEN] *12–2pm and 7–11pm Mon–Fri; 12–2.30pm and 7–11pm Sat–Sun (closed 10.30pm Sun).*

YOU TELL US

* *The Griffin Inn,* Church Road, Shustoke
* *The Navigation,* Old Warwick Road, Lapworth
* *Raglan Arms,* 50 Dunchurch Road, Rugby

Places Featured:

Allesley	Hockley
Alvechurch	Lower Gornal
Amblecote	Netherton
Barston	Oldbury
Bentley	Pelsall
Bilston	Sedgley
Birmingham	Shelfield
Bloxwich	Shustoke
Bordesley Green	Smethwick
Brierley Hill	Solihull
Chapelfields	Stourbridge
Coseley	Tipton
Coventry	Walsall
Cradley Heath	Wednesbury
Dudley	West Bromwich
Enville	Willenhall
Halesowen	Wollaston
Highgate	Wolverhampton

THE BREWERIES

DANIEL BATHAM & SON LTD

The Delph Brewery, Delph Road, Brierley Hill DY5 2TN
☎ *(01384) 77229*
www.bathams.co.uk

 MILD ALE 3.5% ABV
BEST BITTER 4.5% ABV
No better brew when on form.
XXX 6.5% ABV
Christmas ale.

THE BEOWULF BREWING CO.

Waterloo Buildings, 14 Waterloo Road, Yardley, Birmingham B25 8JR
☎ *(0121) 706 4116*
www.beowolf.co.uk

NOBLE BITTER 4.0% ABV
Dry, with powerful bitterness.
WIGLAF 4.3% ABV
Golden and malty with strong hoppy flavours.
SWORDSMAN 4.5% ABV
Pale, refreshing and fruity.
HEROES BITTER 4.7% ABV
Golden and hoppy with some sweetness.
MERCIAN SHINE 5.0% ABV
Pale and hoppy with dry finish.
Plus seasonal brews.

ENVILLE ALES

Enville Brewery, Cox Green, Hollies Green, Stourbridge DY7 5LG
☎ *(01384) 873728*
www.envilleales.com

CHAINMAKER MILD 3.6% ABV
Dark, with some sweetness and smooth malty finish.
BEST BITTER 3.8% ABV
Bitter, well-balanced with good hoppiness.
SIMPKISS BITTER 3.8% ABV
Gold-coloured, quenching and well-hopped.
NAILMAKER MILD 4.0% ABV
Dark and sweeter with dry finish.
CZECHMATE SAAZ 4.2% ABV
Dry and fruity in the Czechoslovakian style.
WHITE 4.2% ABV
A clear, refreshing wheat beer.
ALE 4.5% ABV
Pale yellow, honeyed sweetness and hoppy finish.
GINGER BEER 4.6% ABV
Excellent summer brew, delicate ginger flavour.
OLD PORTER 4.8% ABV
Dark, complex roast malt and fruit, and dry finish.
PHOENIX IPA 4.8% ABV
Superb IPA using new Phoenix hop variety.
GOTHIC ALE 5.2% ABV
Black and rich, with honey flavours.
Plus occasional brews up to 8% ABV.

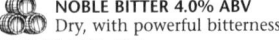

GOLDTHORN BREWERY & CO.

Imex Unit 60, Sunbeam Street, Wolverhampton WV2 4NU
☎ *(01902) 75692*
www.goldthornbrewery.co.uk

 GILT SUM OMMER 3.8% ABV
NO NAME 3.8% ABV
SILVER BULLET 4.0% ABV
WULFRUN GOLD 4.3% ABV
JUNIPER BLONDE 4.5% ABV
TWO TUN BITTER 4.5% ABV
NUMBER 3 4.5% ABV
HUMPSHIRE ALE 5.0% ABV
PREMIUM 5.0% ABV
DEADLY NIGHTSHADE 6.0% ABV

HIGHGATE & WALSALL BREWING CO LTD

Sandymount Road, Walsall WS1 3AP
☎ *(01922) 644453*
www.highgatebrewery.co.uk

HIGHGATE MILD 3.4% ABV
World No.1 dark beer champion.
FOX'S NOB 3.8% ABV
HIGHGATE SPECIAL BITTER 3.8% ABV
SADDLERS PREMIUM BITTER 4.3% ABV
Plus huge range of seasonal brews.

HOLDEN'S BREWERY

Hopden Brewery, George Street, Woodsetton, Dudley DY1 4LN
☎ *(01902) 880051*
www.holdensbrewery.co.uk

STOUT 3.5% ABV
Dark with bitter, malty flavour.
MILD 3.7% ABV
Malty and well-balanced.
BITTER 3.9% ABV
Gold-coloured, quenching session beer.
XB 4.1% ABV
Refreshing and hoppy with some sweetness.
SPECIAL 5.1% ABV
Golden, balanced and far too easy to drink.
OLD XL ALE 6.9% ABV
Christmas only.

THE WOLVERHAMPTON & DUDLEY BREWERIES PLC

PO Box 26, Park Brewery, Bath Road, Wolverhampton WV1 4NY
☎ *(01902) 711811*
www.fullpint.co.uk

BANKS'S ORIGINAL 3.5% ABV
MANSFIELD CASK DARK MILD 3.5% ABV
BANKS'S BITTER 3.8% ABV
Hoppy, with a good combination of flavours.
MANSFIELD CASK ALE 3.9% ABV
SMOOTH CREAMY ALE 3.9% ABV
PEDIGREE 4.5% ABV
Plus monthly specials.

THE PUBS

ALLESLEY

Rainbow Inn and Brewery

73 Birmingham Road, Allesley Village, Coventry CV5 9GT
☎ *(024) 7640 2888*

 Piddlebrook brewed and served on the premises plus one guest beer.

Brewing started in October 1994 providing ale only for the pub and a few beer festivals. Production at the two-barrel plant takes place twice a week. An unpretentious pub in a village location. Grade II listed building dating from around 1650. Bar and restaurant food served at lunchtime and evenings. Parking, garden. Children allowed. Just off the main A45 at Allesley.

PIDDLEBROOK 3.8% ABV

OPEN *11am–11pm.*

ALVECHURCH

The Coach & Horses Inn

Weatheroak Hill, Alvechurch B48 7EA
☎ *(01564) 823386* Philip Meads

 Home of the Weatheroak Brewery with all home brews always available plus Black Sheep Special, Morland Old Speckled Hen and Wood Special. Regular guests from Frankton Bagby and Slaters.

A country pub set in four acres with separate 100-seater restaurant. Food available 12–2pm and 6–9.30pm Mon–Sat and 12–2.30pm Sun. Area Real Ale Pub of the Year winner 2000 and 2001. Well-behaved children allowed. Large beer garden with outside seating and children's play area. From J3 of the M42, follow signs for Weatheroak.

LIGHT OAK 3.6% ABV
WEATHEROAK ALE 4.1% ABV
REDWOOD 4.8% ABV
TOBY'S TTT 5.2% ABV

OPEN *11.30am–2.30pm and 5.30–11pm Mon–Thurs; 11am–11pm Fri–Sat; 12–10.30pm Sun.*

AMBLECOTE

The Maverick

Brettell Lane, Amblecote, Stourbridge DY8 4BA
☎ *(01384) 824099* Mark Boxley

 A freehouse with Banks's Bitter and Mild always available plus one guest pump serving ales from around the country, changed weekly.

A town pub with an American Western theme. One bar, beer garden. Bar snacks available all day. Live music on Fridays. Children allowed.

OPEN *All day, every day (except Tues–Thurs: 3–11pm).*

The Robin Hood Inn

*196 Collis Street, Amblecote, Stourbridge
DY8 4EQ*
☎ *(01384) 821120*

Bathams Bitter, Enville Ale, Everards Beacon, Tiger and Old Original always available plus three guests (120 per year) such as Timothy Taylor Landlord, Badger Tanglefoot, Shepherd Neame Bishop's Finger, Fuller's ESB, Exmoor Gold and Hook Norton Old Hooky.

A family-run, cosy Black Country freehouse. Good beer garden. Non-smoking dining room. Bar and restaurant food available. Parking. Children allowed in the pub when eating. Accommodation.

OPEN *12–3pm and 6–11pm Mon–Sat;
12–10.30pm Sun.*

The Swan

10 Brettell Lane, Amblecote, Stourbridge
☎ *(01384) 76932 Mr G Cook*

Two weekly changing guest beers served, often from Eccleshall, Batham, Cains, Smiles, Hook Norton, Young's, Lees, Elgood's, Brakspear, Ruddles, Daleside or Tisbury.

A traditional town pub with comfortable lounge, bar, darts and juke box. Beer garden. No food. No children.

OPEN *12–2.30pm and 7–11pm Mon–Fri;
12–11pm Sat; 12–3pm and 7–10.30pm
Sun.*

BARSTON

The Bull's Head

Barston Lane, Barston, Solihull B92 0JV
☎ *(01675) 442830 Mr M Bradley*

Something from Adnams plus a guest beer regularly available from a large countrywide selection.

Traditional village pub with garden, dating back to the 1490s. Solihull CAMRA Pub of the Year 2000 and 2002. No machines or music. Food served 12–2pm and 7–8.30pm Mon–Sat. Car park. Children welcome.

OPEN *11am–2.30pm and 5.30–11pm Mon–Fri;
11am–11pm Sat; 12–10.30pm Sun.*

BENTLEY

Highgate Hall

Churchill Road, Bentley WS2 0HR
☎ *(01922) 621950 Marie McFadden*

A Highgate Brewery house with Mild and Bitter always available, plus one guest.

A locals' pub in the middle of a housing estate, under new ownership. Fairly modern in style with a large car park. No food. No children.

OPEN *12–11pm (10.30pm Sun).*

The Lane Arms

Wolverhampton Road West, Bentley WS2 0BX
☎ *(01922) 623490*

Tied to Highgate, with Dark Mild and Special Bitter always on offer. (Pub has recently changed hands, so details are subject to change.)

Town pub built in the 1940s, with three bars, patio and garden. Food is available, and there is a non-smoking dining area. Karaoke on Thursdays, disco on Fridays and Sundays, live music on Saturdays. Children allowed up to 8pm. Car park.

OPEN *12–3pm and 5–11pm Mon–Thurs;
11am–11pm Fri–Sat; 12–10.30pm Sun.*

BILSTON

The Olde White Rose

20 Lichfield Street, Bilston WV14 0AG
☎ *(01902) 498339 John Denston*

Twelve real ale pumps serve the crème de la crème from Shepherd Neame, Hop Back and all the other popular independent and micro-breweries; the list is endless!

Situated in the heart of the Black Country, this is a lounge-style pub, recently extended to include upstairs restaurant and downstairs bier keller. Food available every day until 9pm. Children allowed, with designated play outside. Beer garden. Easy accessible on the Snowhill–Wolverhampton Metro (tram) although be careful not to confuse it with The White Rose in the same town.

OPEN *12–11pm Mon–Sat; 12–4pm and
7–10.30pm Sun.*

Trumpet

58 High Street, Bilston WV14 0EP
☎ *(01902) 493723 Ann Smith*

Holden's Special, Black Country Bitter, Mild and Golden Glow always on offer, plus one guest every week from any one of a range of breweries. Jennings, Hanby Ales, Mauldons, Salopian, Burton Bridge, Cotleigh and many others have been featured.

A jazz pub with jazz music played every evening 8.30–11pm and Sunday lunchtimes, 1–3pm. Only pre-ordered food available at lunchtimes. Beer garden. Children allowed in the garden only. Car park. For more information, see www.trumpetjazz.org.

OPEN *11am–3pm and 7.30–11pm
(10.30pm Sun).*

BIRMINGHAM

The Anchor

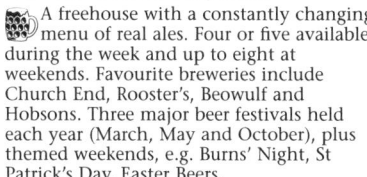

308 Bradford Street, Birmingham B5 6ET
☎ *(0121) 622 4516* Gerry Keane

A freehouse with a constantly changing menu of real ales. Four or five available during the week and up to eight at weekends. Favourite breweries include Church End, Rooster's, Beowulf and Hobsons. Three major beer festivals held each year (March, May and October), plus themed weekends, e.g. Burns' Night, St Patrick's Day, Easter Beers.

Situated outside the city centre, a well-preserved three-bar pub in a Grade II listed building. Birmingham CAMRA Pub of the Year 1996 and 1998. Food available at lunchtime and evenings. Children allowed in the beer garden May–October (weather permitting!).

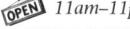 *11am–11pm (10.30pm Sun).*

Figure of Eight

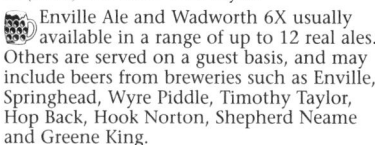

236–9 Broad Street, Birmingham B1 2HG
☎ *(0121) 633 0917* Tom Taylor

Enville Ale and Wadworth 6X usually available in a range of up to 12 real ales. Others are served on a guest basis, and may include beers from breweries such as Enville, Springhead, Wyre Piddle, Timothy Taylor, Hop Back, Hook Norton, Shepherd Neame and Greene King.

Busy JD Wetherspoon's freehouse, popular with all ages, serving the largest number of real ales in the area. Food available 10am–10pm Mon–Sat and 12–9.30pm Sun. No children.

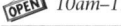 *10am–11pm Mon–Sat; 12–10.30pm Sun.*

The Old Fox

54 Hurst Street, Birmingham B5 4TD
☎ *(0121) 622 5080* Pat Murray

Marston's Pedigree and Morland Old Speckled Hen always available plus two guests, changed twice-weekly, such as Wychwood The Dog's Bollocks, Trash and Tackle or Burton Bridge brews.

An eighteenth-century town freehouse with stained-glass windows, situated in a modern area near the Hippodrome. Food available 12–7.30pm. Outside seating. No children.

 11.30am–11pm Mon–Thurs; 11am–2am Fri–Sat; 11.30am–11pm Sun.

The Old Joint Stock

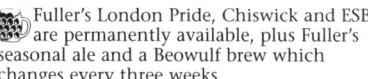

Temple Row West, Birmingham B2 5NY
☎ *(0121) 200 1892* Alison Turner

Fuller's London Pride, Chiswick and ESB are permanently available, plus Fuller's seasonal ale and a Beowulf brew which changes every three weeks.

A Fuller's Ale and Pie House. Large pub in traditional style, balcony area, club room and function room for hire. Food served 12–8.30pm Mon–Sat. Patio area. No children.

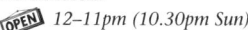 *11am–11pm Mon–Sat; closed Sun.*

The Pavilion

229 Alcester Road South, Kings Heath, B14 6DT
☎ *(0121) 441 3286* Peter Galley

Banks's Original and Bitter plus Marston's Pedigree regularly available.

Friendly community local. Food served every lunchtime and evening. Car park. No children.

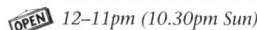 *12–11pm (10.30pm Sun).*

BLOXWICH

The Royal Exchange

24 Stafford Road, Bloxwich, Walsall WS3 3NL
☎ *(01922) 494256* Mr Beattie

Highgate Mild and Bitter are the permanent beers here, and four weekly changing guests might be something from Batham, Bateman or Lichfield.

Community local in Grade II listed building, formerly a coaching inn. Four bars, garden area. Live music Wednesdays and Saturdays. Beer festivals August Bank Holiday and Easter (call to confirm). No food. Well-behaved children allowed. Car park.

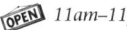 *12–11pm (10.30pm Sun).*

BORDESLEY GREEN

The Tipsy Gent

157 Cherrywood Road, Bordesley Green, Birmingham B9 4XE
☎ *(0121) 772 1858* Paul and Jackie Rackam

A freehouse with Fuller's London Pride among its permanent features, plus one guest, such as Exmoor Gold, changed weekly. Smaller and independent brewers favoured.

A traditional one-bar town pub with stone floors and open fires. Food available Mon–Fri lunchtimes only. Beer garden. No children.

11am–11pm (10.30pm Sun).

BRIERLEY HILL

The Bull & Bladder

10 Delph Road, Brierley Hill DY5 2TN
☎ *(01384) 78293* Mr Wood

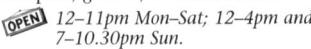Bathams Mild, Best and XXX always available.

Also known as The Vine, this is the brewery tap for Bathams, which is situated behind. A multi-roomed pub with open fires. Bar food available at lunchtime. Car park, garden, children's room.

OPEN *12–11pm Mon–Sat; 12–4pm and 7–10.30pm Sun.*

CHAPELFIELDS

The Nursery Tavern

38–9 Lord Street, Chapelfields, Coventry CV5 8DA
☎ *(024) 7667 4530* Harry Minton

Four guest ales usually featured from breweries such as Church End, Fat God's, Wolf, RCH and Hampshire.

A small, 150-year-old, village-style pub in a town location. Beams, wooden floors. Bar snacks available Mon–Fri; breakfasts Sat–Sun and Sunday lunches. Children allowed in the back room and garden.

OPEN *11am–11pm Mon–Sat; 12–10.30pm Sun.*

COSELEY

Spread Eagle

Birmingham New Road, Coseley, Wolverhampton WV14 9PR
☎ *(01902) 663564* David Mark Ralph

Banks's Original always available, plus a changing range of guest ales.

Separate public bar and lounge, the lounge is comfortably furnished with live entertainment Mon, Wed, Fri evenings. The public bar has pub games and Sky TV. Bar snacks and restaurant food available 12–3pm and 6–9pm Mon–Sat, 12–3pm Sun. Children welcome and children's menu available. Beer garden with children's play area. Large car park. Functions catered for. Located on the main A4123 Wolverhampton to Birmingham road, approximately 3 miles from Wolverhampton city centre.

OPEN *12–11pm Mon–Sat (10.30pm Sun).*

COVENTRY

The Old Windmill

22 Spon Street, Coventry CV1 3BA
☎ *(024) 7625 2183* Lynn Ingram

Marston's Pedigree, Morland Old Speckled Hen and a Banks's ale always available, plus two guests such as Badger Tanglefoot or beers from breweries such as Church End, Orkney and other micros.

A Grade II listed Tudor building situated in the town centre. The oldest pub in Coventry with beams, stone floor, old range in one bar and inglenook fireplaces. Food available at lunchtime in non-smoking restaurant. Children allowed in the restaurant only.

OPEN *11am–11pm Mon–Sat; 12–3pm and 7–10.30pm Sun.*

CRADLEY HEATH

The Waterfall

132 Waterfall Lane, Cradley Heath B64 6RG
☎ *(0121) 561 3499*
Barbara Woodin and Ray Bowater

Ten beers always available including brews from Bathams. Also Enville Ale, Holden's Special, Hook Norton Old Hooky, Marston's Pedigree and Cains Formidable Ale. Plus guests such as Oak Double Dagger, Titanic White Star, RCH Fiery Liz and Gibbs Mew Bishop's Tipple plus something from Burton Bridge and Wood.

A traditional Black Country pub. Cask Marque accredited. Bar food available at lunchtime and evenings. Car park, garden with waterfall, children's room. Also function room for party and quiz nights, etc. Up the hill from the old Hill Station.

OPEN *12–3pm and 5–11pm Mon–Thurs; all day Fri–Sun.*

DUDLEY

Little Barrel

68 High Street, Dudley DY1 1PY
☎ *(01384) 235535*
Brendan Vernon and Chris Sandy

Wadworth 6X always available plus three guests such as Morland Old Speckled Hen, Holden's XB, Shepherd Neame Bishop's Finger, Wychwood Hobgoblin or King & Barnes brews. Seasonal and celebration beers as available.

A small, traditional town pub with wooden floors. One bar, dining area. Food available at lunchtime only. No children.

OPEN *11am–11pm (10.30pm Sun).*

ENVILLE

The Cat Inn

Bridgenorth Road, Enville DY7 5HA
☎ *(01384) 872209* Lisa Johnson

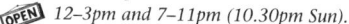A freehouse with Everards Beacon and Enville Ale always on offer. Four weekly changing guests might include Hop Back Summer Lightning or something from Greene King, Sarah Hughes or Ringwood, and where possible the beers are not repeated.

Four-bar sixteenth-century village pub with beams and fireplaces. Food is available and there is a non-smoking dining area. Pool room, darts, garden, car park. Children allowed until 9pm.

OPEN *12–3pm and 7–11pm (10.30pm Sun).*

HALESOWEN

Edward VII

88 Stourbridge Road, Halesowen B63 3UP
☎ *(0121) 550 4493* Patrick Villa

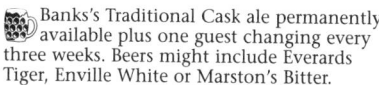Banks's Traditional Cask ale permanently available plus one guest changing every three weeks. Beers might include Everards Tiger, Enville White or Marston's Bitter.

Beautiful, well-thought-out, comfortable pub/restaurant with two bars and outside seating. Food served every lunchtime and Tues–Sat evenings. Children allowed. Located on the A458, next to Halesowen Town Football Club.

OPEN *12–3pm and 5–11pm Mon–Thurs; 11am–11pm Fri–Sat; 12–10.30pm Sun.*

The Waggon & Horses

21 Stourbridge Road, Halesowen B63 3TU
☎ *(0121) 550 4989* Bob Dummons

Bathams Bitter, Enville Ale and something from Oakham always available plus up to ten guests (800 per year) from far and wide.

A West Midlands Victorian boozer. Bar food available at lunchtime.

OPEN *12–11pm (10.30pm Sun).*

HIGHGATE

The Lamp Tavern

157 Barford Street, Highgate, Birmingham B5 6AH
☎ *(0121) 622 2599* Eddie Fitzpatrick

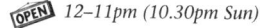A freehouse with Stanway Stanney Bitter, Everards Tiger, Marston's Pedigree and Church End Grave Digger always available, plus one guest pump serving beers such as Shepherd Neame Bishop's Finger or Church End What the Fox's Hat.

A small, friendly village pub situated near the town. Bar snacks available at lunchtime. No children.

OPEN *All day Mon–Sat; 12–3pm and 8–10.30pm Sun.*

HOCKLEY

Black Eagle

16 Factory Road, Hockley, Birmingham B18 5JU
☎ *(0121) 523 4008* Tony Lewis

Marston's Pedigree, Timothy Taylor Landlord and something from Beowulf regularly available plus two guest beers, perhaps from Wye Valley, Church End or Burton Bridge.

Popular award-winning pub with two small front lounges, a large back lounge, snug and restaurant. Original Victorian back bar. Beer garden. Well known locally for good food. Bar meals 12.15–2.30pm and 5.30–9.30pm, restaurant 7–10.30pm. Children welcome to eat.

OPEN *11.30am–2.30pm and 5.30–11pm Mon–Fri; 11.30am–11pm Sat; 12–10.30pm Sun.*

The Church Inn

22 Great Hampton Street, Hockley, Birmingham B18 6AQ
☎ *(0121) 515 1851* Mr Wilkes

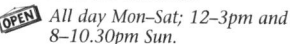Morland Old Speckled Hen and a Bathams ale always available, plus one guest.

A Victorian town pub with one servery and two adjoining rooms. Food available at lunchtime and evenings. Children allowed.

OPEN *11.45am–11pm Mon–Fri; 11.45am–3pm and 6–11pm Sat; closed Sun.*

LOWER GORNAL

The Fountain Inn

8 Temple Street, Lower Gornal
☎ *(01384) 24277* Alan Davis

Enville Ale, Holden's Special, Everards Tiger and Old Original always available, plus five rotating guests. Two real ciders also served.

A comfortable freehouse with a warm and pleasant atmosphere. Bar food served at lunchtime and evenings. Parking, garden and function room. Children allowed.

OPEN *12–3pm and 6–11pm Mon–Fri; 12–11pm Sat; 12–4pm and 7–10.30pm Sun.*

NETHERTON

The Old Swan

89 Halesowen Road, Netherton, Dudley DY2 9PY
☎ *(01384) 253075* Mr Newey

A brewpub, home of the Old Swan Brewery with only home brews available: Old Swan, Dark Swan and Old Swan Entire plus one seasonal or celebration ale.

One of the original four home-brew pubs dating from the 1970s, this is a Victorian tower brewery with a pub which is unchanged since 1863, including original mirrored back bar and enamel plate ceiling. Separate bar, lounges and smoking room plus function room. A quiet, real ale drinkers' pub with no juke boxes, games machines or music. Food available 12–3pm and 6–9.30pm Mon–Sat, and 12–3pm Sun. Courtyard seating. Strictly over 14s only. Brewery tours by arrangement.

OLD SWAN ORIGINAL 3.4% ABV Brewed since 1835.
DARK SWAN (MILD) 3.9% ABV
OLD SWAN ENTIRE 4.4% ABV
Plus one seasonal or celebration ale.

OPEN *11am–11pm Mon–Sat; 12–10.30pm Sun.*

OLDBURY

The Waggon & Horses

Church Street, Oldbury B69 3AD
☎ *(0121) 552 5467* Andrew Gale

Enville Ale, Marston's Pedigree, plus something from Holden's always available. Also a traditional mild. Many guests (200 per year) including Bateman Yellow Belly, Timothy Taylor Landlord, Berrow Topsy Turvy, Greene King Abbot Ale, Brains Reverend James Original and many more.

A Victorian, Grade II listed building with tiled walls, copper ceiling and original brewery windows. Bar food available at lunchtime and evenings. Car parking. Children allowed when eating. Function room with capacity for 40 people. At the corner of Market Street and Church Street in Oldbury town centre, next to the library.

OPEN *12–3pm and 5–11pm Mon–Thur; 12–11pm Fri–Sat; 12–3pm Sun (closed Sun evening).*

PELSALL

The Sloan Inn

Wolverhampton Road, Pelsall, Walsall WS3 4AD
☎ *(01922) 694696* Miss Catherine Yeats

Highgate Dark Mild and Saddlers Celebrated Best Bitter are always on offer.

The oldest pub in Pelsall, with a homely atmosphere. Food is available 12–2.30pm and 6–9pm Tues–Sat and 12–2.30pm Sun. Children allowed. Car park.

OPEN *11am–11pm Mon–Sat; 12–10.30pm Sun.*

SEDGLEY

The Beacon Hotel

129 Bilston Street, Sedgley, Dudley DY3 1JE
☎ *(01902) 883380*

Sarah Hughes Pale Amber, Suprise and Dark Ruby always available, plus Snowflake from Nov to Feb. Various guest beers (150 per year) served on a daily basis.

The Sarah Hughes Brewery, which operates on the premises, reopened in 1987 after a 30-year closure, and now supplies around 500 pubs with guests beers. Visitors welcome for brewery tours, but booking is essential. Children's room, plus beer garden with play area.

PALE AMBER 4.0% ABV
SURPRISE 5.0% ABV
DARK RUBY MILD 6.0% ABV
SNOWFLAKE 8.0% ABV

OPEN *12–2.30pm and 5.30–10.45pm Mon–Thur; 12–2.30pm and 5.30–11pm Fri; 11.30am–3pm and 6–11pm Sat; 12–3pm and 7–10.30pm Sun.*

SHELFIELD

The Four Crosses Inn

1 Green Lane, Shelfield, Walsall WS4 1RN
☎ *(01922) 682518* Mr Holt

A freehouse with Marston's Pedigree and Banks's Bitter and Mild always available, plus two weekly changing guests from smaller and micro-breweries such as Burton Bridge and Ash Vine.

A traditional two-bar pub on the outskirts of town. Games in the bar, beer garden. No food. No children.

OPEN *All day Mon–Sat; 12–3pm and 7–10.30pm Sun.*

SHUSTOKE

The Griffin Inn

Church Road, Shustoke B46 2LP
☎ *(01675) 481567*

At least two Church End brews plus Marston's Pedigree always available. Also 200 guest beers per year.

A large country freehouse with oak beams and open fires set in large grounds. The Church End brewery is next to the pub. Bar food is available at lunchtime (except Sunday). Car park, garden. Children allowed in the conservatory and grounds. Take the B4114 from Coleshill.

GRAVEDIGGERS 3.8% ABV
WHAT THE FOX'S HAT 4.2% ABV
WHEAT A BIX 4.2% ABV
M-REG GTI 4.4% ABV
PEWS PORTER 4.5% ABV
OLD PAL 5.5% ABV

OPEN *12–3pm and 7–11pm Mon–Sat; 12–2.30pm and 7–10.30pm Sun.*

SMETHWICK

The Bear Tavern
500 Bearwood Road, Smethwick B66 4BX
☎ *(0121) 429 1184* Brendan Gilbride

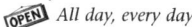Marston's Pedigree and Morland Old Speckled Hen always available plus five weekly changing guests. Regulars include Hardys and Hansons Kimberley Best and Greene King Abbot.

Alocals' pub built after the Second World War, although there has been a pub on the site for 300 years. A mix of the traditional and modern. Four bars, fireplace, beer garden, disabled access. Food available all day. Children allowed.

OPEN *All day, every day.*

SOLIHULL

The Harvester
Tanhouse Farm Road, Solihull B92 9EY
☎ *(0121) 742 0770* Mrs Harwood

A freehouse with Charles Wells Bombardier always available plus two guests such as Morland Old Speckled Hen. Beers served are always between 3.7% and 5% ABV.

Amodern community pub with two bars, pool room, dining area in lounge, garden. Food available at lunchtime and evenings. Children allowed.

OPEN *12–2.30pm and 6–11pm Mon–Thurs; 12–3pm and 6–11pm Fri–Sat; 12–3pm and 7–10.30pm Sun.*

STOURBRIDGE

Hogshead
21–6 Foster Street, Stourbridge DY8 1EL
☎ *(01384) 371040* David Collins

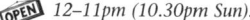Fourteen beers including ten guest ales regularly available. Examples include Enville White, Fuller's London Pride, Timothy Taylor Landlord, Marston's Pedigree, Wadworth 6X or something from Black Sheep, Brakspear or many others.

Hogshead original design, town-centre pub with ten beers on long front bar and four gravity-dispensed beers on back bar. Background music during the day, livelier in the evenings. Air-conditioned. Food available all day. Children welcome in designated areas until 8pm. Situated in pedestrian precinct.

OPEN *12–11pm (10.30pm Sun).*

TIPTON

The Port 'n' Ale
178 Horseley Heath, Great Bridge, Tipton DY4 7DS
☎ *(0121) 557 7249* Kevin Taylor

A freehouse with Greene King Abbot, RCH Pitchfork, Moorhouse's Pendle Witches and Badger Tanglefoot always available, plus two guest pumps regularly serving RCH beers or something like Burton Bridge Summer Ale or Cotleigh Barn Ale.

AVictorian pub situated out of town. Bar, lounge and beer garden. Basic food served, including fish and chips and sandwiches. Children allowed in the garden only. Just down the road from Dudley Port railway station.

OPEN *12–3pm and 5–11pm Mon–Fri; 12–11pm Sat; 12–4.30pm and 7–10.30pm Sun.*

The Rising Sun
116 Horseley Road, Tipton DY4 7NH
☎ *(0121) 530 9780* Penny McDonald

Burton Bridge Bitter, Banks's Bitter and Original, plus three regularly changing guest beers usually available, perhaps from Burton Bridge, Church End, Hobsons, Holden's, Beowulf, Wye Valley, Cottage, Eccleshall or many others.

Friendly, locals' pub with large beer garden. National CAMRA Pub of the Year 1999, Dudley and South Staffs CAMRA Pub of the Year 1998, 1999, 2000 and 2001. Food served 12–2pm Mon–Sat. No children.

OPEN *12–2.30pm and 5–11pm Mon–Fri; 12–3pm and 5–11pm Sat; 12–3pm and 7–10.30pm Sun.*

WALSALL

The Rising Sun
90 Ablewell Street, Walsall WS1 2EU
☎ *(01922) 626575* Reg Turner

A Highgate pub with Mild and Saddlers Celebrated Best Bitter the permanent beers. One guest beer, changed as consumption demands, could be Highgate Fox's Nob or Old Ale, or any one of the Wyre Piddle brews.

Traditional pub in an old building with cobbles outside, on the edge of the town centre. Excellent atmosphere. Food available. Rock-music-oriented at weekends – popular with bikers. Two bars, dining area, massive garden, frequent live music, disco Tues, Fri and Sat – call for details.

OPEN *12–11pm Mon–Wed; 12–1am Thurs–Sat; 12–10.30pm Sun.*

Tap & Spile

5 John Street, Walsall WS2 8AF
☎ *(01922) 627660* John Davies

Charles Wells Eagle IPA usually available plus seven guest beers which change regularly, totalling around 40 per month. These may include beers from Bateman, Wychwood, Arundel, Hoskins, Fuller's, Harviestoun, Hydes', Hop Back, Highwood, Hook Norton, Orkney or any other independent brewery.

Small, traditional backstreet pub with great atmosphere. Friendly staff and chatty customers. Food available 12–2pm Mon, 12–2pm and 6.30–9pm Tues–Sat. Children welcome.

OPEN *12–3pm and 5.30–11pm Mon–Thurs; 12–11pm Fri–Sat; 12–3pm and 7–10.30pm Sun.*

The Wharf

10 Wolverhampton Street, Walsall WS2 8LS
☎ *(01922) 613100* Steve Bratt (manager), Kevin Cryan (licensee)

Tied to Highgate, with Saddlers Celebration Best Bitter and Special Bitter constantly available. The two guests, changed weekly or fortnightly, often include other Highgate brews.

Town pub in a new building with modern interior and a patio. Food is available, and there is a non-smoking dining area. Children allowed until 6.30pm. Car park.

OPEN *11am–11pm Mon–Wed; 11am–1am Thurs–Sat; 12–10.30pm Sun.*

WEDNESBURY

The Forge

Franchise Street, Wednesbury WS10 9RG
☎ *(0121) 526 2777* Paul Pugh

Owned by Highgate, with Highgate Mild Ale a permanent fixture. One seasonal guest is also served.

Two-bar community pub, purpose-built in 1935 by Highgate Brewery. No food. Live music Fri, Sat and Sun. Children allowed. Car park. Situated behind IKEA.

OPEN *12–2pm and 5–11pm Mon–Thurs; 11am–11pm Fri–Sun.*

WEST BROMWICH

The Old Crown

56 Sandwell Road, West Bromwich B70 8TG
☎ *(0121) 525 4600* Mr Patel

A freehouse with three hand pumps serving an ever-changing selection of ales such as Fuller's London Pride, Young's Special, Cottage Somerset or something from Church End, Enville, Burton Bridge, Wye Valley or Hydes' Anvil, to name but a few.

An open-plan town pub. Food available at lunchtime and evenings in a non-smoking area – home-cooked curries, balti and tikka masala are specialities. Children allowed in the non-smoking area only, until 9pm.

OPEN *11am–4pm and 5–11pm Sun–Fri; all day Sat.*

The Vine

152 Roebuck Street, West Bromwich B70 6RD
☎ *(0121) 553 2866* Mr Patel

A freehouse with one real ale always available. Breweries featured include Wood, Lichfield and Wye Valley, among others.

A traditional two-bar pub with beams and gardens. Children's play area. Food available at lunchtime and evenings – barbecues and curries are specialities. Children allowed. Situated out of town. Website: www.sukis.co.uk.

OPEN *11.30am–2.30pm and 5–11pm Mon–Thurs; all day Fri–Sun.*

WILLENHALL

The Brewer's Droop

44 Wolverhampton Street, Willenhall WV13 2PS
☎ *(01902) 607827*

An Avebury Taverns tenancy with Enville Ale and Charles Wells Eagle IPA always available, plus a range of guests changing twice-weekly, such as Holden's Special and Badger Tanglefoot.

A traditional town-centre pub decorated with bric-à-brac, particularly relating to motorbikes. Two bars, pool table. Food available at lunchtime and evenings. Children allowed until 9pm.

OPEN *12–3.30pm and 6–11pm Mon–Thurs; all day Fri–Sat; 12–4pm and 7–10.30pm Sun.*

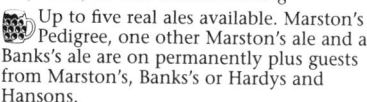

The Falcon Inn

Gomer Street West, Willenhall WV13 2NR
☎ *(01902) 633378* Mick Taylor

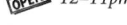 A freehouse with RCH PG Steam, Pardoe's Dark Swan (from Old Swan) and Greene King Abbot and Pitchfork always available, plus five guest beers, usually including a stout or a porter. All beers are hand-pulled and served in oversized glasses. Range of malt whiskies also on offer.

A 1930s traditional backstreet pub near the town centre. Walsall CAMRA commended in 2000. Two rooms – bar and lounge – with no price difference! Both rooms are air-filtered. Non-smoking area in lounge. Bar snacks (pies and pasties) available. Beer garden. Plenty of on-street parking.

OPEN *12–11pm (10.30pm Sun).*

WOLLASTON

The Princess

115 Bridgnorth Road, Wollaston, Stourbridge DY8 3NX
☎ *(01384) 443687* Ralph and Kay Vines

 Wadworth 6X, Charles Wells Bombardier, Greene King Abbot Ale and Banks's Original are permanent fixtures, plus a monthly changing guest beer.

Single bar with wooden floor, quarry tiles and an interesting selection of mirrors and artefacts. Food served lunchtimes only. Car park. Children welcome, but no special facilities.

OPEN *11am–11pm Mon–Sat; 12–10.30pm Sun.*

WOLVERHAMPTON

Chindit

113 Merridale Road, Wolverhampton
☎ *(01902) 425582* John Ralph Smith

 Four guest beers available, changing daily, and totalling around 350 different beers each year. Favourite breweries include Hop Back, Harviestoun, Daleside and Wychwood. The Chindit holds an annual beer festival with over 30 different beers over the May Bank Holiday.

Cosy, two-roomed pub named after a Second World War regiment – the only pub in the world so named. Cask Marque accredited. Live music on Friday evenings and barbecues in summer, weather permitting. Children welcome until 7pm. Play area. Located one mile from city centre, on the west side of Wolverhampton.

OPEN *12–11pm (10.30pm Sun).*

The Exchange Vaults

Cheapside, Wolverhampton WV1 1TS
☎ *(01902) 714219* Steven Durling

 Up to five real ales available. Marston's Pedigree, one other Marston's ale and a Banks's ale are on permanently plus guests from Marston's, Banks's or Hardys and Hansons.

The old Corn Exchange, this is the only pub in the Civic Centre area. One bar, outside seating, food available every day from 11am–5pm. Children allowed if eating. Situated between St Peter's Church and the Civic Centre.

OPEN *11am–11.30pm (10.30pm Sun).*

Great Western

Sun Street, Wolverhampton
☎ *(01902) 351090* Kevin Michael Gould

 Batham Bitter, Holden's Mild, Black Country Bitter and Special Bitter regularly available.

Friendly pub with non-smoking dining room. Food served 11.45am–2.15pm Mon–Sat. Car park. Situated two minutes' walk from railway station. Children welcome in conservatory if dining.

OPEN *11am–11pm Mon–Sat; 12–3pm and 7–10.30pm Sun.*

Moon Under Water

53–5 Lichfield Street, Wolverhampton WV1 1EQ
☎ *(01902) 422447* Edel Crehan

 Shepherd Neame Spitfire, Hop Back Summer Lightning and Greene King Abbot Ale permanently available, plus at least two guests. Regular guests include Springhead Roaring Meg and Bitter, Brains SA and Batemans' XXXB.

A JD Wetherspoon's pub in the city centre, frequented by locals and shoppers, with a young crowd in the evenings at weekends. Food available all day. Children allowed until 6pm if eating.

OPEN *10am–11pm Mon–Sat; 12–10.30pm Sun.*

Newhampton

Riches Street, Wolverhampton WV6 0DW
☎ *(01902) 745773* Betty Carnegie

 Marston's Pedigree, Charles Wells Bombardier and a daily changing guest beer regularly available, such as Timothy Taylor Landlord or something from Enville.

Traditional community pub, an 'oasis' with with bowling green, garden and children's play area. Homemade food served 12–2pm and 6–9pm daily. Children very welcome.

OPEN *11–11pm Mon–Sat; 12–10.30pm Sun.*

Tap & Spile

35 Princess Street, Wolverhampton
WV1 1HD
☎ *(01902) 713319* Michael Stokes

Banks's Bitter and Mild are the permanent beers, plus up to six guest ales which could be from any brewery around the UK.

A locals' town pub with wooden floors, open fire, one main bar and snug rooms. Food available 12–4pm. Beer garden. Children allowed until 7pm.

OPEN *10am–11pm Mon–Sat; 12–10.30pm Sun.*

YOU TELL US

* *Biggin Hall Hotel,* Binley Road, Copsewood, Coventry
* *The Black Horse,* 52 Delph Road, Brierley Hill
* *The Brown Lion,* 33 Wednesbury Road, Pleck, Walsall
* *The Clarendon Hotel,* 38 Chapel Ash, Wolverhampton
* *The Dry Dock,* 21 Windmill End, Netherton
* *The Old Blue Ball,* 19 Hall End Road, Wednesbury
* *The Park Inn,* George Street, Woodsetton, Dudley
* *The Queen's Tavern,* 23 Essex Street, Birmingham
* *The Red Hen,* 78 St Anne's Road, Cradley Heath
* *The Starving Rascal,* Brettell Lane, Amblecote, Stourbridge
* *The Swan Inn,* Wolverhampton Road, Pelsall, Walsall
* *Tap & Spile,* 33 High Street, Brierley Hill
* *Unicorn,* 145 Bridgnorth Road, Wollaston, Stourbridge
* *The Vine Inn,* Bell Street, Wednesbury

Places Featured:

Abbey Meads	Kington St Michael
Axford	Lacock
Berwick St John	Langley Burrell
Bowden Hill	Limpley Stoke
Box Hill	Little Cheverell
Bradford-on-Avon	Lower Chicksgrove
Bratton	Malmesbury
Brokerswood	Marlborough
Broughton Gifford	Marston Meysey
Charlton	Melksham
Chippenham	North Wroughton
Coate	Pewsey
Compton Bassett	Purton
Corsham	Quemerford
Corsley	Rowde
Corton	Salisbury
Cricklade	Shaw
Derry Hill	Shrewton
Devizes	South Marston
East Knoyle	Stratton St Margaret
Easton Royal	Swindon
Ebbesbourn Wake	Upton Lovell
Enford	Wanborough
Ford	Warminster
Hamptworth	Winterbourne Monkton
Highworth	Wootton Bassett
Hilmarton	Wroughton
Holt	

THE BREWERIES

ARCHERS ALES LTD

Penzance Drive, Churchyard, Swindon SN5 7JL
☎ *(01793) 879929*

 VILLAGE BITTER 3.6% ABV
Malty, with hop and fruit notes.
BEST BITTER 4.0% ABV
Bitter with some sweetness.
BLACK JACK PORTER 4.6% ABV
Dark, roasted malt, winter brew.
GOLDEN BITTER 4.7% ABV
Superb balance, a classic beer.
Plus seasonal brews.

ARKELLS BREWERY LTD

Kingsdown Brewery, Swindon SN2 6RU
☎ *(01793) 823026*
www.swindonweb.com/arkells

 2B 3.2% ABV
Light and quenching with good bitter hoppiness.
3B 4.0% ABV
Amber, balanced and hoppy.
KINGSDOWN ALE 5.0% ABV
Smooth, rounded and flavour-packed.
Plus seasonal brews.

HERITAGE ALES AND ASH VINE BREWERY

Oakley Business Park, Dinton, Salisbury SP3 5EU
☎ *(01722) 716622*
www.heritageales.com

Heritage Ales:

ONE X BITTER 3.5% ABV
High on flavour, but moderate on alcohol. This dark amber ale balances a rounded malty flavour with a bitter palate and a full hoppy aroma.

STONEHENGE 3.8% ABV
A classic session bitter that is full of flavour with an amazing amount of body. A fruity, hoppy after taste with a nice amber colour.

BLACK BESS STOUT 4.0% ABV
A classic dark full of wonderful chocolate flavour. Smooth creamy and pretty well perfect!

CHALLENGER BEST BITTER 4.1% ABV
A perfectly balanced best bitter with a deep mahogany colour. Satisfying fruit and malt flavour lead to a clean finish.

AVEBURY ALE 4.3% ABV
Named after the famous stone circle. A beautifully coloured well-balanced bitter with plenty of crystal malt. The strong hop flavour provides a distinct and desirable finish.

ALE FRESCO 4.5% ABV
April to August. A deceptively light-bodied, straw-coloured ale made with Hersbrucker hops. A fresh hoppy nose and palate with a clean refreshing finish.

C.S.B 4.5% ABV
Aug–Nov. A glorious golden colour with a floral nose and clean fresh finish. Captures the essence of autumn.

HOB HOB 4.5% ABV
February to April. Light gold in colour, the pale and cara malt provide an excellent base for the spicy, nutty cascade hop from America. A most unique bitter-sweet character.

HOP AND GLORY 5.0% ABV
A wonderful strong pale ale. This is a beer to respect, as the perfect combination of malt and hops make this too moreish!

OLD WARDOUR 5.0% ABV
Strong, dark rich and mysterious. Wonderfully smooth with a long lingering finish.

DECADENCE STRONG BITTER 6.0% ABV
Strong, smooth and totally addictive, this is a beer to respect. Plenty of strength is balanced by a silky male character and clean fruit flavours.

HOBDEN'S WESSEX BREWERY

Farm Cottage, Norton Ferris, Warminster BA12 7HT
☎ *(01985) 844532*

BA (BLACKMORE ALE) 3.5% ABV
High in flavour, but moderate in alcohol, this rich amber ale balances a rounded malty flavour, with a hint of chocolate, against a slightly bitter palate and hoppy aroma.

NAUGHTY FERRET 3.5% ABV
Flavoursome ordinary bitter.

BEST BITTER 3.9% ABV
Full bodied, tawny, full flavoured. Moderately bitter, with full fruity and malty flavours; a classic best bitter.

CROCKERTON CLASSIC 4.1% ABV
Full flavoured best bitter.

GOLDEN DELIRIOUS 4.5% ABV
Golden premium ale.

P.Z (PALE ZEALS ALE) 4.5% ABV
Pale golden ale, light bodied yet flavoursome, with delicate hoppy flavour and aroma and clean finish.

LOFT DOG IN THE DARK 4.5%
Porter.

OLD DEVERILL 5.0% ABV
Blackmore Ale's big brother. Rich red colour and a rounded bitter/fruit/malt and hops flavour. Fruitcake in a glass.

WESSEX GIANT 6.0% ABV
Strong in all departments! Hops, malt and fruit collide in a memorable confusion.

THE HOP BACK BREWERY PLC

Unit 21–4, Batten Road Industrial Estate, Downton, Salisbury SP5 3HU
☎ *(01725) 510986*
www.hopback.co.uk

GFB 3.5% ABV
Smooth and full-flavoured for gravity.

BEST BITTER 4.0% ABV
Well-balanced, easy-drinking.

CROP CIRCLE 4.2% ABV
Pale with wonderful thirst quenching properties.

ENTIRE STOUT 4.5% ABV
Powerful roast malt flavour.

SUMMER LIGHTNING 5.0% ABV
Superb, pale and quenching with good hoppiness.

THUNDERSTORM 5.0% ABV
Mellow wheat beer.

Plus seasonal and occasional brews.

MOLE'S BREWERY

5 Merlin Way, Bowerhill, Melksham SN12 6TJ
☎ *(01225) 708842*
www.our.co.uk/is.molesbrewery

 TAP 3.5% ABV
Malty with clean, balancing bitterness.
BEST BITTER 4.0% ABV
Golden with quenching, hoppy finish.
BARLEYMOLE 4.2% ABV
Pale, hoppy brew with malty finish. Occasional.
MOLEGRIP 4.3% ABV
Rounded, balanced Autumn ale.
LANDLORD'S CHOICE 4.5% ABV
Darker, with hops, fruit and malt.
MILLENNIUM 4.5% ABV
Fruit, caramel and malty overtones.
HOLY MOLEY 4.7% ABV
Good malt flavour with hop balance. Occasional.
BREW 97 5.0% ABV
Malty with fruity sweetness and good hoppiness.
MOEL MOEL 6.0% ABV
Winter warmer.

STONEHENGE ALES (BUNCES BREWERY)

The Old Mill, Mill Road, Netheravon, Salisbury SP4 9QB
☎ *(01980) 670631*
www.stonehengeales.sagenet.co.uk

 BENCHMARK 3.5% ABV
Malt flavours with good balancing hoppy bitterness.
PIGSWILL 4.0% ABV
Mellow and hoppy.
BODYLINE 4.3% ABV
Darkish beer.
HEEL STONE 4.3% ABV
Quenching fruity flavour.
DANISH DYNAMITE 5.0% ABV
Golden and far too easy to drink!
Plus seasonal brews.

WADWORTH & CO. LTD

Northgate Brewery, Devizes SN10 1JW
☎ *(01380) 723361*
www.wadworth.co.uk

 HENRY'S ORIGINAL IPA 3.6% ABV
Well-balanced and smooth, with malt throughout.
SUMMERSAULT 4.0% ABV
Quenching, lager-style beer.
6X 4.3% ABV
Rich, with malt flavours.
MALT HOPS 4.5% ABV
Sweet and nutty.
JCB 4.7% ABV
Unique palate with chewy bite.
OLD TIMER 5.8% ABV
Ripe fruit and hop aromas.

THE PUBS

ABBEY MEADS

The Jovial Monk

Highdown Way, St Andrews Ridge, Abbey Meads, Swindon SN25 4YD
☎ *(01793) 728636* Sheila and Oliver Cleary

 An Arkells tied house with 2B and 3B permanently available plus Summer Ale, Noel or Kingsdown on a guest basis.

A community character-built pub with beams and hard and soft furnishing. Big-screen Sky TV. Food available in separate restaurant area. Children allowed. Patio. Car park. Accommodation. Disabled access. Situated directly behind the Motorola building.

OPEN *11am–11pm.*

AXFORD

The Red Lion

Axford, Nr Marlborough SN8 2HA
☎ *(01672) 520271* Sarah Grey

 Hook Norton Best and Wadworth 6X permanently available plus guest ales such as Gale's HSB or Hop Back Crop Circle.

A sixteenth-century restaurant and pub with two bars, two beer gardens and a patio. Children allowed.

OPEN *11.30am–3pm and 6.30–11pm Mon–Sat; 12–3pm and 7–10.30pm Sun.*

BERWICK ST JOHN

The Talbot Inn

The Cross, Berwick St John, Nr Shaftsbury SP7 0HA
☎ *(01747) 828222* Chris and June Eason

 Hop Back Summer Lightning and Wadworth 6X regularly available.

Typical country inn in Chalke Valley below Cranbourne Chase. Food served lunchtimes and evenings Tues–Sat. Car park. Children welcome at lunchtime.

OPEN *12–2.30pm and 6.30–11pm Mon–Sat; 12–4pm (closed Sun evening).*

BOWDEN HILL

The Bell Inn

The Wharf, Bowden Hill, Lacock, Chippenham SN15 2PJ
☎ *(01249) 730308*
Alan and Heather Shepherd

 A freehouse with four hand pumps serving Wadworth 6X plus a selection of real ales of varying strengths from local breweries, including smaller and micro-breweries. Farmhouse cider also available.

A traditional rural pub built in converted canal cottages on the edge of a National Trust village. One bar, dining area, beer garden, children's play area. Two boules pistes. Food available every session and all day on Saturday and Sunday. Children allowed.

OPEN *Summer: 11.30am–2.30pm and 6–11pm Tues–Fri. Winter: 11.30am–2.30pm and 7–11pm Tues–Fri; all day Sat–Sun all year round; closed all day Monday except Bank Holidays.*

The Rising Sun

32 Bowden Hill, Lacock, Nr Chippenham SN15 2PP
☎ *(01249) 730363* Howard and Sue Sturdy

 Five beers always available including Mole's Tap, Best, Landlord's Choice, Molecatcher and Black Rat. Guests ales also served.

A Cotswold stone pub with flagstone floors and open fires. Bar food available at lunchtime and evenings (not Mon or Sun evenings), roasts served on Sun until 3.30pm. Car park, garden. Live music Wed evenings plus alternate Sun from 3pm. Children and dogs allowed. Turn into village, then go up Bowden Hill.

OPEN *12–3pm and 6–11pm Mon–Sat; 12–10.30pm Sun.*

BOX HILL

The Quarrymans Arms

Box Hill, Corsham SN13 8HN
☎ *(01225) 743569* John Arundel

 Wadworth 6X, Mole's Best Bitter and Butcombe Bitter regularly available. Two or three guest beers are also served, often from Bath Ales, Abbey Ales or Cottage.

A 300-year-old miners' pub, tucked away in the Wiltshire countryside, high above the Colerne Valley. Popular with pot-holers, cavers, walkers and cyclists. Food served 12–3pm and 7–10pm daily. Car park. Children welcome. Very difficult to find, so ring for directions. Visit the website: www.quarrymans-arms.co.uk.

OPEN *11am–3pm and 6–11pm Mon–Thurs; 11am–11pm Fri–Sat; 12–10.30pm Sun.*

BRADFORD-ON-AVON

The Beehive

Trowbridge Road, Bradford-on-Avon BA15 1UA
☎ *(01225) 863620* Mrs C Crocker

 A freehouse with Butcombe ales always available plus five guests such as Fuller's London Pride, Burton Bridge Draught Excluder, Dobbins' Drop, Blackpool Bitter and Stairway to Heaven (aka Celestial Gateway).

A pub situated next to the bed and breakfast of John Benjamin, on the side of the canal. One bar, no music, open fires. Beer garden features a boules pitch and an antique pump dating from 1880. Also open for coffee. Food available every lunchtime and Tue–Sat evening. Children allowed.

OPEN *12–2.30pm and 7–11pm (10.30pm Sun).*

Bunch of Grapes

14 Silver Street, Bradford on Avon BA15 1JY
☎ *(01225) 863877* John Williams

Smiles Best, Young's Bitter and Special, plus a rotating ale from either Young's or Smiles.

Town-centre pub that is supposedly haunted. Food available lunchtime and evening, every day. Children allowed.

OPEN *12–11pm (10.30pm Sun).*

BRATTON

The Duke at Bratton

Bratton, Nr Westbury BA13 4RW
☎ *(01380) 830242* Ian Overend

Mole's Best permanently available plus a rotating guest.

Community village pub close to the Westbury White Horse, which has won awards for its roast lunch and its loos. Bar food and restaurant menu – restaurant closed Sun night and all day Mon. Cottage-style accommodation. Well-behaved children welcome. Garden and car park.

OPEN *11.30am–3pm and 7–11pm.*

BROKERSWOOD

Kicking Donkey

Brokerswood, Westbury BA13 4EG
☎ *(01373) 823250* Paul Taylor

Freehouse always serving Mole's Tap, Wadworth 6X and Hoofmark (specially brewed for the pub by Stonehenge), plus a couple of guests, often a beer from Hop Back.

A rustic country pub with stone floors and a terracotta paint effect that highlights the unevenness of the walls. One long bar for two separate areas. Food every session with an à la carte menu in the evening. Children welcome. Garden with bouncy castle and swings. Car park.

OPEN *11.30am–3pm and 6–11pm Mon–Thur; all day Fri–Sun.*

BROUGHTON GIFFORD

Bell on the Common

Broughton Gifford, Nr Melksham SN12 8LX
☎ *(01225) 782309*
Anthony and Dorothy Stanley

 A Wadworth pub offering 6X, Henry's IPA and one other from the Wadworth range.

A popular country pub in attractive surroundings and with a prize-winning beer garden. Two bars and a restaurant – food served twice daily, seven days a week. Darts, cribbage, pool and a boules piste. Parking on the edge of the common. Well-behaved children welcome. Winner of the 2001 Real Coal Fire Pub of the Year.

 11am–11pm Mon–Sat; 12–10.30 Sun.

CHARLTON

The Horse & Groom

The Street, Charlton, Malmesbury SN16 9DL
☎ *(01666) 823904* Nicola King

 Archers Village and Wadworth 6X always available, plus three guests such as Uley Old Spot, Smiles Best, Abbey Bell Ringer or Ridleys Spectacular.

A traditional country village pub with beams, fires and wooden floors. Two bars, beer garden, accommodation. Food served at lunchtime and evenings in a separate dining area. Well-behaved children allowed.

 *12–3pm and 7–11pm Mon–Fri; all day Sat–Sun.*

CHIPPENHAM

Four Seasons

6 Market Place, Chippenham SN15 3HD
☎ *(01249) 444668* Bob Gillett

Fuller's ESB and London Pride plus a guest beer.

Pleasant, homely no-frills pub in the centre of town. Food available lunchtime and evening seven days a week. Children allowed if eating with adults. Karaoke Thurs and Sun, music Fri and Sat.

11am–11pm Mon–Thurs; 11am–1am Fri–Sat; 12–10.30pm Sun.

The Peterborough Arms

Dauntsey Lock, Chippenham SN15 4HD
☎ *(01249) 890409* John Howard

 Wadworth pub serving 6X, JCB and Henry's IPA, plus Wadworth seasonals.

A two-bar, traditional country pub with oak beams, fires and non-smoking dining area. Large beer garden. Boules piste and putting green. Extensive menu of home-made food changes weekly and includes vegetarian options plus traditional Sunday roasts. Children and dogs welcome. Ample parking.

 12–2.30pm and 6–11pm Mon–Fri; all day Sat–Sun and spring/autumn bank holidays.

Pheasant Inn

Bath Road, Chippenham SN14 0AE
☎ *(01249) 444083* Danny and Tammy Clark

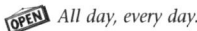 Wadworth 6X, IPA and JCB with occasional guests such as Everard Tiger.

Large edge-of-town pub popular for food and activities, described by the landlord as 'the place for all occasions'. Skittle alley. Pool. Large-screen TV. Car park. Children welcome.

11am–11pm Mon–Sat; 12–10.30pm Sun.

COATE

The Sun Inn

Marlborough Road, Coate, Swindon SN3 6AA
☎ *(01793) 523292* Neil and Karen Shergold

 An Arkells tied house with 2B and 3B permanently available plus Summer Ale, Noel or Kingsdown on a guest basis.

A refurbished country pub with family areas (including children's play area), non-smoking areas and large beer garden. Food available. Live music Sat and Sun.

All day, every day.

COMPTON BASSETT

The White Horse

Compton Bassett, Calne SN11 8RG
☎ *(01249) 813118* John Phillips

A freehouse offering Wadworth 6X and Badger Tanglefoot on a permanent basis and four other constantly changing guests.

Popular and friendly country pub with a good reputation for food. Meals every session. Children allowed in the restaurant. Large car park. Skittle alley, pool and darts. North West Wilts CAMRA Pub of the Year 2002.

11am–3pm and 5–11pm Mon–Sat; 12–3pm and 7–10.30pm Sun.

CORSHAM

The Two Pigs

38 Pickwick, Corsham SN13 0HY
☎ *(01249) 712515* Dickie and Ann Doyle

Stonehenge Pigswill always available plus three guests (200 per year) including Church End brews, Hop Back Summer Lightning, Greene King Abbot and Wood Shropshire Lad. Guest ales rotating constantly, two in ABV range 4.1–4.6% and one at 5%+ ABV.

A traditional wood-panelled pub with stone floors. No food. Parking nearby. Covered courtyard. No children. Live blues music on Monday. On the A4 between Chippenham and Bath.

OPEN *7–11pm Mon–Sat; 12–2.30pm and 7–10.30pm Sun.*

CORSLEY

The Cross Keys

Lyes Green, Corsley, Nr Warminster BA12 7PB
☎ *(01373) 832406* Frank Green

Wadworth house offering IPA, 6X and seasonal ale plus a rotating guest.

Homely and comfortable village pub. Food available except Sun and Mon evenings. Children allowed. Non-smoking room for families. Car park and beer garden. Skittle alley and bar games. Live music on the third Sun of each month.

OPEN *12–2.30pm and 6.30–11pm (10.30pm Sun).*

The White Hart

Lane End, Corsley, Nr Warminster BA12 7PH
☎ *(01373) 832805* Mr S and Mrs E Middleton

Oakhill Best Bitter, Mendip Gold, Yeoman and 2K regularly available.

Welcoming, traditional pub with good mix of clientele and comprehensive menu. Food served lunchtimes and evenings. Car park. Children's room, menu and high chairs.

OPEN *11.30am–depends on custom; 6–11pm Mon–Sat; 12–3pm and 7–10.30pm Sun.*

CORTON

The Dove Inn

Corton, Nr Warminster BA12 0SZ
☎ *(01985) 850109* W Harrison-Allan

Hop Back GFB and Butcombe Bitter always available plus one guest.

Tastefully refurbished, traditional pub tucked away in a beautiful and tranquil village close to the River Wylye. Restaurant and garden. Food served 12–2.30pm and 7–9.30pm every day. Car park. Children welcome. En-suite accommodation. For further information, visit the website at www.thedove.co.uk.

OPEN *12–3pm and 6.30–11pm Mon–Sat; 12–4pm and 7–10.30pm Sun.*

CRICKLADE

The White Hart Hotel

High Street, Cricklade SN6 6AA
☎ *(01793) 750206*
William Finch and Norma Brooks

An Arkells tied house with 2B, 3B and Smooth permanently available, plus Arkells seasonal guests.

An old coaching inn built in 1628, now a small town pub/restaurant. Food available. Live music on Saturday nights. Beer garden. Children allowed but no dogs. Car park. Accommodation.

OPEN *11am–11pm Mon–Sat; 12–10.30pm Sun.*

DERRY HILL

Lansdowne Arms

Church Road, Derry Hill, Nr Calne SN11 9NS
☎ *(01249) 812422* John Chester

Wadworth 6X, JCB and Henry's IPA plus seasonals and guests.

An imposing nineteenth-century coaching inn with scenic views across the Avon valley and close to Bowood House. Food every session except Sunday evening. Car park and garden. Children allowed.

OPEN *11.30am–2.30pm (3pm Sat) and 6–11pm Mon–Sat; 12–3pm and 7–10.30pm Sun.*

DEVIZES

The British Lion

9 Estcourt Street, Devizes SN10 1LQ
☎ *(01380) 720665* Michael Dearing

Three or four real ales available but constantly changing. The pub likes to support the West Country micro-breweries as much as it can. Beer range regularly includes stout, porter and mild, and two real ciders are permanently served.

A popular single-bar character freehouse. Car park and large, sunny garden at the rear. On the main Swindon (A361) road, opposite The Green.

OPEN *11am–11pm Mon–Sat; all day Sun.*

EAST KNOYLE

The Fox & Hounds

The Green, East Knoyle, Salisbury SP3 6BN
☎ *(01747) 830573* Gordon Beck

A Young's tied house with the full range of Young's beers always available, plus one guest which may be from Smiles Brewery or other independents.

A country village pub with beams, slate floors, conservatory and garden. Food available at lunchtime and evenings. Children allowed in the conservatory and garden.

OPEN *11am–2.30pm and 6–11pm (10.30pm Sun).*

EASTON ROYAL

Bruce Arms
Easton Royal, Nr Pewsey SN9 5LR
☎ *(01672) 810216* WJ and JA Butler

 Wadworth 6X and Fuller's London Pride usually available. Other guests such as Ringwood Best Bitter may also be served.

Popular, traditional pub with many original features, situated on the B3087. Only cheese and onion rolls/sandwiches served lunchtimes and evenings. Car park. Children welcome in lounge, skittle alley or pool room. Website: www.brucearms.co.uk.

[OPEN] *11am–2.30pm and 6–11pm Mon–Sat; 12–2.30pm and 7–10.30pm Sun.*

EBBESBOURN WAKE

The Horseshoe Inn
Ebbesbourne Wake SP5 5JF
☎ *(01722) 780474* Tony Bath

 Wadworth 6X, Ringwood Best and Adnams Broadside always available straight from the barrel, plus a guest (12 per year) perhaps from Bateman, Poole, Felinfoel, or Fuller's.

A remote, old-fashioned unspoilt pub hung with old tools of a bygone age. Bar and restaurant food available lunchtime and evenings (except Monday and Sunday night). Car park, garden, accommodation. Children are allowed if eating. From Salisbury (A354), turn right to Bishopston, Broadchalke then on to Ebbesbourne Wake.

[OPEN] *12–3pm and 6.30–11pm. Closed Monday lunchtime.*

ENFORD

The Swan
Longstreet, Enford, Nr Pewsey SN9 6DD
☎ *(01980) 670338* Mike Burton

A good choice of real ales available, changing regularly but usually including brews from Stonehenge and possibly from Fuller's, Ringwood or Shepherd Neame.

Old thatched and beamed pub with open fires. Bar food available at lunchtime and evenings. Carvery Sunday lunchtime. Car park, garden, restaurant. Easy to find.

[OPEN] *12–3pm and 7–11pm Mon–Sat; 12–4pm and 7–10.30pm Sun.*

FORD

The White Hart
Ford, Nr Chippenham SN14 8RP
☎ *(01249) 782213* Colin Rolfe

 Wadworth 6X and Bybrook Ale are permanent with two guest beers.

Old coaching inn off the A420 on the edge of a river. One main bar, restaurant and buttery. Bar food available at lunchtime. Restaurant open at lunchtime and evenings. Car parks, river terrace, accommodation. Children allowed in the buttery.

[OPEN] *11am–3pm and 5–11pm Mon–Sat; usual hours Sun.*

HAMPTWORTH

The Cuckoo Inn
Hamptworth Road, Hamptworth, Nr Salisbury SP5 2DU
☎ *(01794) 390302* Janet Bacon

 Wadworth 6X, Badger Tanglefoot, Cheriton Pots Ale, Hop Back Summer Lightning and GFB always available plus three guest beers from a long list including brews from Bunces, Adnams, Ringwood, Hampshire, Shepherd Neame and Cottage breweries.

A 300-year-old thatched pub in the New Forest. Bar food available at lunchtimes and evenings (except Sunday and Monday evenings). Car park, garden, play area, petanque area. Just off the A36 near Hamptworth golf course.

[OPEN] *11.30am–2.30pm and 6–11pm Mon–Fri (except Mon 7–10.30pm); all day Sat, Sun and Bank Holidays.*

HIGHWORTH

The Plough Inn
Lechlade Road, Highworth, Swindon SN6 7HF
☎ *(01793) 762224* Julie Snook

 An Arkells tied house with 2B and 3B permanently available.

A locals' country pub. Separate lounge, bar and pool room. Bar snacks available. Live music some Saturdays. Children allowed. Beer garden. Accommodation. Parking available.

[OPEN] *4–11pm Mon–Fri (closed lunchtimes); 11am–11pm Sat; 12–10.30pm Sun.*

HILMARTON

The Duke Hotel

Hilmarton, Nr Calne SN11 8SD
☎ *(01249) 760634* Alan & Nyki Martin

 An Arkells house with 3B permanently available, plus an Arkell seasonal ale.

An old-style pub with a separate à la carte restaurant. Bar food also available 12–3pm and 6–10pm Tues–Sat. Children allowed. Large beer garden with children's play area. Quiz nights twice a month. Located on the main road between RAF Lynham and Calne.

OPEN *12–3pm and 6–11pm Mon–Sat; 12–8pm Sun.*

HOLT

Tollgate Inn

Ham Green, Holt, Nr Bradford on Avon BA14 6PX
☎ *(01225) 782326*
Mr A Venables and Miss A Ward-Baptiste

 A freehouse that changes its selection twice weekly, using breweries such as West Berkshire, Exmoor, Abbey Ales, Bath Ales and the Quay Brewery.

A country pub that prides itself on its food – local produce freshly cooked, and no chips. Armchairs in the bar give a different but comfortable feel. Accommodation. Car park and garden. No children.

OPEN *11.30am–3pm and 6–11pm (10.30 Sun).*

KINGTON ST MICHAEL

The Jolly Huntsman

Kington St Michael, Chippenham
☎ *(01249) 750305* MI and CVS Lawrence

 Wadworth 6X, Morland Original, Hall & Woodhouse IPA, Greene King Abbot Ale and Ruddles Best regularly served, plus one or two guest beers from a wide selection of independent breweries around the country.

Welcoming village pub with en-suite accommodation. Food served lunchtimes and evenings. Car park. Children welcome.

OPEN *11.30am–2.30pm and 6.30–11pm Mon–Sat; 12–3pm and 7–10.30pm Sun.*

LACOCK

George Inn

4 West Street, Lacock, Nr Chippenham SN15 2LH
☎ *(01249) 730263* John Glass

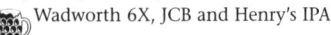 Wadworth 6X, JCB and Henry's IPA.

A very old inn that has been licensed continuously since 1361, with lots of character including a turn spit in the fireplace. Food every session. Car park and garden. Children allowed.

OPEN *10am–3pm and 5–11pm Mon–Fri; all day Sat and Sun.*

LANGLEY BURRELL

Brewery Arms

41 The Common, Langley Burrell, Chippenham SN15 4LQ
☎ *(01249) 652707* Mr P Jones

 Wadworth 6X and Fuller's London Pride are permanents and there are occasional guests.

Known locally as the Langley Tap, this is a traditional village pub providing real ales and good food at reasonable prices. Meals every session. Children allowed in eating area. Function room. Car park and garden. Live music and quizzes.

OPEN *11.30am–3pm and 6.30–11pm Mon–Sat; 12–3pm and 7–10.30pm Sun.*

LIMPLEY STOKE

Hop Pole

Woods Hill, Limpley Stoke, Nr Bath BA2 7FS
☎ *(01225) 723134* Mich and Bob Williams

 A freehouse always serving Butcombe Bitter with one rotating guest ale.

A typical old English village pub characterised by the dried hops hanging from the beams and the wood panelling. Food served lunchtime and evening. Car parking. Children welcome. Large garden overlooking the valley.

OPEN *11am–2.30pm and 6–11pm Mon–Sat; 12–3pm and 7–10.30 Sun.*

LITTLE CHEVERELL

The Owl

Low Road, Little Cheverell, Devizes SN10 4JS
☎ *(01380) 812263*
Paul Green and Jamie Carter

A freehouse with Wadworth 6X always available plus three constantly changing guests from independent breweries such as Hop Back, Oak Hill, Ash Vine, Ringwood or Uley.

A country pub with beams and a woodburning stove. One bar, separate dining area. Large streamside beer garden. Food available at lunchtime and evenings. Children allowed.

OPEN *11am–3pm and 6.30–11pm Mon–Sat; 12–4pm and 7–10.30pm Sun. Open all day in the summer.*

LOWER CHICKSGROVE

The Compasses Inn

Lower Chicksgrove, Tisbury, Salisbury SP3 6NB
☎ *(01722) 714318* Alan and Susie Stoneham

A freehouse with Wadworth 6X always available, plus guests.

A beamed pub with open fires and wooden floors situated in a country hamlet. Small dining area, beer garden, accommodation. Food available Tues–Sun lunchtime and Tues–Sat evenings. Well-behaved children allowed.

OPEN *12–3pm and 6–11pm (10.30pm Sun); closed Mon except bank holidays, but then closed Tues.*

MALMESBURY

The Smoking Dog

62 High Street, Malmesbury SN16 9AT
☎ *(01666) 825823* Ian and Sara Shackleton

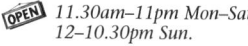Wadworth 6X, Brains SA, Bitter and Reverend James Original, and Archers Best always available, plus at least two guests. These might be Gibbs Mew Bishop's Finger, Fuller's London Pride or a Young's ale, or seasonal and more obscure ales from smaller breweries.

A traditional small-town pub with log fires, beams and wooden floor. Occasional live music. Food available in an à la carte restaurant, plus bar snacks lunchtime and evening. Beer garden. Children allowed.

OPEN *11.30am–11pm Mon–Sat; 12–10.30pm Sun.*

MARLBOROUGH

The Bear Hotel

1 High Street, Marlborough SN8 1AA
☎ *(01672) 515047* Andrew and Victoria Hall

Arkells 3B permanently available plus Arkells seasonal guests.

A 200-year-old brick-built town-centre pub designed in the style of a galleon. Food available every day – famous locally for fish and chips. Beer garden. Occasional live music. Children allowed. Function room for medieval banquets. Situated opposite the Town Hall.

OPEN *11am–11pm Mon–Sat; 12–10.30pm Sun.*

MARSTON MEYSEY

The Old Spotted Cow

Marston Meysey SN6 6LQ
☎ *(01285) 810264* James and Denise Kelso

Fuller's London Pride, Wickwar Brand Oak Bitter and Timothy Taylor Landlord usually available, plus a regularly changing mystery guest beer. Sometimes it's guess what it is and you win four pints!

Friendly, attractive, nineteenth-century country inn with large, yet intimate, open stone bar and two feature fireplaces. Situated on the edge of award-winning village. Food served lunchtimes and evenings, every day. Separate restaurant. Car park. Large, safe children's play area with activities. Accommodation. Touring caravan parking facilities.

OPEN *11.30am–11pm Mon–Sat; 12–10.30pm Sun.*

MELKSHAM

The Red Lion

1–3 The City, Melksham SN12 8DA
☎ *(01225) 702960* Margaret Bright

A Bath Ales beer and Wadworth 6X are regularly available, plus guest beers which might be from Wood, Mighty Oak, Wychwood, Exmoor, Brakspear, Fuller's, Smiles, Greene King, Hydes, Anvil, Young's, Bateman, Wickwar or Marston's.

Grade II listed building dating from 1220, claims to be the only real ale pub in town. Food served 12–2pm Mon–Fri. Car park. No children. Located opposite the Avon Rubber Tyre Factory.

OPEN *11am–2.30pm and 5–11pm Mon–Thurs and Sat; 11am–11pm Fri; 12–3pm and 7–10.30pm Sun.*

NORTH WROUGHTON

The Check Inn

Woodland View, North Wroughton, Nr Swindon SN4 9AA

☎ *(01793) 845584* Doug Watkins

 Eight hand pumps serve a constantly changing range of beers from around the UK and Eire.

Single bar pub with separate lounge (eating) area and extension. Family- and dog-friendly. Traditional pub games and barbecue. Food served lunchtimes and evenings Mon–Fri and all day at weekends. Accommodation. Car park. Children welcome. Directions: from the A361 Swindon–Devizes, take immediate first right after the dual carriageway over the M4.

OPEN *11.30am–3.30pm and 6.30–11pm Mon–Thurs; 11.30am–11pm Fri–Sat; 12–10.30pm Sun.*

PEWSEY

The Cooper's Arms

37–9 Ball Road, Pewsey SN9 5BL

☎ *(01672) 562495* Michael Orpen-Palmer

 A freehouse with Wadworth 6X always available, plus three guests, changed weekly, from local breweries.

A thatched country pub in a picturesque area. Food, but not Sunday night or Tuesday. Beer garden. Live music every Friday. Children allowed.

OPEN *12–2.30pm and 6–11pm Mon, Wed, Thurs; closed Tues; 12–2.30pm and 6–11.30pm Fri; 12–11pm Sat; 12–10.30pm Sun.*

PURTON

The Angel

High Street, Purton SN5 9AB

☎ *(01793) 770248*

Chris Benton and Linda Lee

An Arkells tied house with 2B and 3B permanently available plus Arkells seasonal guests such as Summer Ale and Noel.

A village pub dating from 1704 with beams and open fireplaces. Food available. Children allowed. Beer garden. Car park.

OPEN *11am–3pm and 6–11pm Mon–Fri; 11am–11pm Sat; 12–10.30pm Sun.*

QUEMERFORD

The Talbot Inn

Quemerford, Calne SN11 0AR

☎ *(01249) 812198* Sharon Godwin

Wadworth 6X, Greene King IPA and Morland Old Speckled Hen are regularly available.

A village pub with a reputation for good food and real ales. One bar, wooden floors, beams, large beer garden and car park. Conservatory doubles as dining area. Food available at lunchtime and evenings. Children allowed in the conservatory and garden only.

OPEN *12–11pm Mon–Sat (10.30pm Sun).*

ROWDE

The George & Dragon

High Street, Rowde, Devizes SN10 2PN

☎ *(01380) 723053* Tim Withers

A freehouse with three hand pumps serving just one beer at a time. Real ales from local West Country breweries are featured whenever possible, or other smaller and micro-breweries. Breweries regularly used include Abbey Ales, Bath Ales, Stonehenge and Hop Back.

A seventeenth-century village pub with beams, wooden floor and open fires. One bar, dining area and beer garden. Food available Tues–Sat lunchtime and evenings. Children allowed.

OPEN *12–3pm and 7–11pm (10.30pm Sun).*

SALISBURY

The Deacon Arms

118 Fisherton Street, Salisbury SP2 7QT

☎ *(01722) 504723* Frank Keay

A freehouse with Hop Back GFB and Summer Lightning always available as are Cheriton Best and Village Elder.

A community pub with two bars, wooden floors, open fires in winter and air conditioning in summer. Accomodation. No food. Children allowed.

OPEN *5–11pm Mon–Fri; 12–11pm Sat; 12–10.30pm Sun.*

Devizes Inn

53–5 Devizes Road, Salisbury SP2 7LQ

☎ *(017220) 327842* Brian Corrigan

 Ringwood Best permanently available, plus one other real ale, often Hop Back Summer Lightning, but constantly varying.

Locals' town pub near the railway station. En-suite accommodation. No food. Car park. Children welcome.

OPEN *4.30–11pm Mon–Thurs; 2–11pm Fri; 12–11pm Sat; 12–10.30pm Sun.*

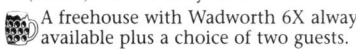
Tom Brown's

225 Wilton Road, Salisbury SP2 7JY
☎ *(01722) 335918*

 A Goldfinch Brewery tied house with a range of Goldfinch beers rotated on three pumps and always available: Tom Brown's Best, Flashman's Clout, Midnight Blinder and Midnight Sun.

A basic one-bar town pub for real ale drinkers. No food. No children.

OPEN *6–11pm Mon–Fri; 12–3pm and 6–11pm Sat; 12–3pm and 6–10.30pm Sun.*

The Village Freehouse

33 Wilton Road, Salisbury SP2 7EF
☎ *(01722) 329707* Joe Morris

 Timothy Taylor Landlord and Abbey Bellringer are always available. Also three guests, constantly changing, including a mild and a stout or porter.

A small street-corner pub with a friendly atmosphere. Salisbury and South Wiltshire CAMRA Pub of the Year 2001. Bar snacks available at lunchtime and evenings. No children allowed. Two minutes from Salisbury railway station.

OPEN *4–11pm Mon; 12–11pm Tues–Sat; 12–5pm and 7–10.30pm Sun.*

The Wig & Quill

1 New Street, Salisbury SP1 2PH
☎ *(01722) 335665* Ken Stanforth

 A Wadworth tenancy with 6X, JCB and IPA from the wood, and a seasonal ale plus a guest ale from The Red Shoot brewery, Mayhem brewery and others.

A city-centre pub with an atmosphere that resembles a village local. A mix of the traditional and modern with one bar and three adjoining areas, open fires and beer garden. Food served at lunchtime 12–2.30pm. Children welcome.

OPEN *11am–11pm Mon–Sat; 12–3pm and 7–10.30pm Sun.*

SHAW

The Golden Fleece

Folly Lane, Shaw, Nr Melksham SN12 8HB
☎ *(01761) 702050* Mr Netherwood

 A freehouse offering Marston's Pedigree, Wickwar Brand Oak Bitter, Butcombe Bitter and Gold.

Classic country pub with beams and low ceiling. Quiet but popular. Boasts its own cricket field and team. Food available every session. Garden. Darts. Car park.

OPEN *11.30am–2.30pm and 6–11pm Mon–Fri; 11.30am–3pm and 6.30–11pm Sat; 12–3pm and 7–10.30pm Sun.*

SHREWTON

The George Inn

London Road, Shrewton, Salisbury SP3 4DH
☎ *(01980) 620341* Tony Clift

 A freehouse with Wadworth 6X always available plus a choice of two guests.

A remote country pub with traditional beams, open fires, one main bar, large covered patio area, beer garden, skittle alley and a 26-seater restuarant. Food available at lunchtime and evenings. Children allowed. Beer festival held every August Bank Holiday.

OPEN *11.30am–3pm and 6–11pm Mon–Fri; all day Sat–Sun in summer, regular hours in winter.*

SOUTH MARSTON

The Carriers Arms

Highworth Road, South Marston, Nr Swindon
☎ *(01793) 822051* Nick and Bridie Smith

 Ushers Best and seasonal brews usually available, plus one guest.

Traditional, village-centre, two-bar pub with separate dining area and patio. Car park. Children welcome when eating, but no special facilities.

OPEN *12–2.30pm and 6.30–11pm Mon–Sat; 12–3pm and 7–10.30pm Sun.*

STRATTON ST MARGARET

The Rat Trap

Highworth Road, Stratton SN3 4QS
☎ *(01793) 823282*
Mark and Claire Richardson

 An Arkells tied house with 2B and 3B permanently available plus occasional Arkells seasonal guests.

A traditional village two-bar pub with garden. Food available. Pool and darts. Live disco once a month. Children allowed. Car park.

OPEN *11am–3pm and 5–11pm (10.30pm Sun).*

The Wheatsheaf

Ermin Street, Stratton St Margaret, Swindon SN3 4NH
☎ *(01793) 823149* Alun Rossiter

 Arkells 2B and 3B are always on offer, and the one guest is often an Arkells beer.

Small, cosy, clean pub with patio and garden. Food served 12–2pm Mon–Fri. Children allowed until 7pm (no special facilities). Car park.

OPEN *11.30am–2.30pm and 5–11pm Mon–Thur; 11am–11pm Fri–Sat; 12–10.30pm Sun.*

SWINDON

The Famous Ale House

146 Redclife Street, Swindon SN2 2BY
☎ *(01793) 522503* Nigel Smith

 Wadworth 6X always available plus a choice of four to six guest ales such as Morland Old Speckled Hen or Caledonian Golden Promise. New beers on once a week.

An olde-worlde locals' community pub. One bar, restaurant and garden. Food served lunchtime and evening, except Sunday evening. Children allowed in the garden only.

[OPEN] *12–11pm (10.30pm Sun).*

The Glue Pot Inn

5 Emlyn Square, Swindon SN1 5BP
☎ *(01793) 523935*
Eamonn Kemp and Dawn Iles

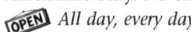 Young's Bitter and Special, plus Mole's Best regularly available, with five rotating guests.

A town pub in the centre of Swindon, located by the old railway museum. One small bar, patio. Bar snacks available at lunchtime only. No children.

[OPEN] *All day, every day.*

The Savoy

38 Regent Street, Swindon SN1 1JL
☎ *(01793) 533970* Kelly Young

 A Wetherspoon's pub. Greene King Abbot, Wadworth 6X, Archers Best and Shepherd Neame Spitfire always available, plus at least one guest beer (usually three or four), with Archers Golden and Village sometimes featured. Beer festivals held every March and October, with 50 real ales at each.

A one-bar town-centre pub. No music. Games machines. Food available all day. Non-smoking dining area. Children allowed until 6pm.

[OPEN] *10.30am–11pm Mon–Sat; 12–10.30pm Sun.*

The Wheatsheaf

32 Newport Street, Old Town, Swindon SN1 3DP
☎ *(01793) 523188*
Andrew Day and Gemma Knights

 A Wadworth house with IPA, 6X, JCB and seasonal brews served. A wide range of guest beers used, two at any one time.

Traditional town pub with wooden floors and outside seating. Back bar very popular with students. Food available 12–2pm and 6–8.30pm, Sunday lunchtime only. Children welcome. Accommodation.

[OPEN] *12–3pm and 5.30–11pm (10.30pm Sun).*

The White Hart

Oxford Road, Swindon SN3 4JD
☎ *(01793) 822272* Steve Cummins

 An Arkells house with 2B and 3B permanently available plus Summer Ale, Noel or other Arkells seasonals on a guest basis.

Situated on the outskirts of Swindon Town, off the A419, this is a three-bar pub with separate non-smoking restaurant plus function room and skittle alley. Big-screen TV. Live music on Fridays and occasionally on Sundays. Children allowed in the restaurant only, plus play area outside.

[OPEN] *11am–3pm and 5–11pm Mon–Fri; all day Sat–Sun.*

UPTON LOVELL

Prince Leopold

Upton Lovell, Nr Warminster BA12 0JP
☎ *(01985) 850460*
Graham and Pamela Waldron-Bradley

 Ringwood Best Bitter and a twice-monthly changing guest beer usually available.

Single-bar freehouse, with garden, pleasantly situated by the River Wylye. En-suite accommodation. Food served 12–3pm and 7–9.30pm daily, with a good reputation locally. Car park. Children welcome. Website: www.princeleopoldinn.co.uk.

[OPEN] *12–3pm and 7–11pm; closed Sunday evening and all day Monday except Bank Holiday lunchtimes.*

WANBOROUGH

The Black Horse Inn

Wanborough, Swindon SN4 0DQ
☎ *(01793) 790305* Roy Samsum

 An Arkells house with 2B and 3B and seasonal guests.

Small and beautiful, with views across the Vale of the White Horse, large garden and car park. Food available every lunchtime and evening. Children allowed. Marquee available for functions. Located on the Bishopston Road out of Wanborough.

[OPEN] *12–3pm and 6–11pm (10.30pm Sun).*

The Brewers Arms

High Street, Wanborough SN4 0AE
☎ *(01793) 790707* Jackie Kitchen

An Arkell house with 2B and 3B plus an Arkell seasonal ale always available.

A family pub with conservatory, dining area, large garden featuring a children's play area and a selection of animals (chickens, rabbits, a horse). Food available lunchtimes and evenings including Sunday roasts. Children welcome.

[OPEN] *11.30am–2.30pm and 6–11pm Mon–Sat; 12–3pm and 7–10.30pm Sun.*

WARMINSTER

The George Inn

Longbridge Deverill, Warminster
BA12 7DG
☎ *(01985) 840396* Nichola Broady

Wadworth 6X permanently available plus two guests changed regularly. Ruddles County, Charles Wells Bombardier, Morland Old Speckled Hen and brews from breweries such as Brakspear or Butcombe are featured, plus customer recommendations.

A prettily situated pub with the River Wylye running through the large beer garden. Two bars, terrace, function room and accommodation. Children's play area. Bar food is served lunchtimes and evenings. Children allowed. Located on the main A350.

OPEN *11am–11pm (10.30pm Sun).*

WINTERBOURNE MONKTON

The New Inn

Winterbourne Monkton, Swindon SN4 9NW
☎ *(01672) 539240*
Mick Folliard and Lynda Atkin

Greene King IPA and Wadworth 6X permanently on offer, plus two regularly changing guest beers, one strong (over 5.0% ABV) and one lighter ale (3.8%–4.3% ABV).

A traditional country inn with old pub memorabilia. Overlooks Marlborough Downs and is close to Avebury stone circle. Charming restaurant, en-suite accommodation. Food served 12–2.30pm and 7–9pm daily. Car park. Children's play equipment in garden.

OPEN *12–2.30pm and 6–11pm Mon–Fri; 12–3pm and 6–11pm Sat; 12–3pm and 7–10.30pm Sun.*

WOOTTON BASSETT

Sally Pusseys Inn

Swindon Road, Wootton Bassett, Swindon
SN4 8ET
☎ *(01793) 852430*
Michael Rundall and Nora Thomas

An Arkells tied house with five real ale pumps, and with 2B and 3B permanently available.

A pub/restaurant dating from the nineteenth-century, with modern additions. Situated in out-of-town location, not walking distance from anywhere. Close to M4. Food available. Well-behaved children allowed.

OPEN *All day, every day.*

WROUGHTON

The Carter's Rest

High Street, Wroughton SN4 9JU
☎ *(01793) 812288* Pete Smith

Eight constantly changing real ales always available.

A country village pub with two bars and a patio area. Food available at lunchtime only. Children allowed.

OPEN *11.30am–2.30pm and 5–11pm Mon–Fri; all day Sat–Sun.*

YOU TELL US

* *Angel,* 3 Church Street, Westbury
* *Black Horse,* Main Road, Cherhill, Nr Calne
* *Black Horse,* Wroughton
* *Cross Keys,* 65 Bradenstoke, Bradenstoke
* *Dumb Post,* Dumb Post Hill, Bremhill, Calne
* *George's Railway,* 5 Union Road, Chippenham
* *Goddard Arms,* Wood Street, Clyffe Pypard
* *The Mermaid Inn,* Main Road, Christian Malford
* *Prince of Wales,* 94 High Street, Dilton Marsh, Westbury
* *Shepherd's Rest,* Foxhill, Swindon
* *Wyndham Arms,* 27 Estcourt Road, Salisbury

Places Featured:

Allerton Bywater
Atwick
Barkisland
Barnsley
Batley
Batyeford
Beck Hole
Bradford
Brearton
Bridlington
Brompton
Burley
Cawood
Chapel Haddlesey
Chapel-le-Dale
Chapeltown
Cleckheaton
Cray
Cropton
Denby Dale
Dewsbury
Dishforth
Doncaster
Driffield
Ecclesfield
Elland
Elslack
Flaxton
Greetland
Guisborough
Gunnerside
Halifax
Harrogate
Haworth
Hebden Bridge
Helperby
Holmfirth
Horbury
Huddersfield
Hull
Idle
Ilkley
Ingleton
Keighley
Kirkbymoorside
Knaresborough
Knottingley

Langdale End
Leeds
Linthwaite
Liversedge
Longwood
Lund
Malton
Marsden
Melmerby
Mexborough
Middlesbrough
North Duffield
North Howden
Northallerton
Old Mixenden
Ossett
Outwood
Pontefract
Pool-in-Wharfedale
Pudsey
Quarmby
Ripon
Ripponden
Rotherham
Scarborough
Selby
Sheffield
Shipley
Skipton
Sowerby Bridge
Staveley
Stokesley
Sutton upon Derwent
Thorne
Thornton-in-Lonsdale
Threshfield
Tockwith
Todmorden
Upperthong
Wakefield
Walsden
Weaverthorpe
Wentworth
Whitby
Wombwell
Wortley
York

THE BREWERIES

ABBEYDALE BREWERY
Unit 8, Aizlewood Road, Sheffield, South Yorkshire S8 0XX
☎ *(0114) 281 2712*
www.abbeydalebrewery.co.uk

 MATINS 3.6% ABV
Pale and flavoursome for gravity.
BEST BITTER 4.0% ABV
Smooth and malty with good hoppiness.
BLACK BISHOP 4.2% ABV
MOONSHINE 4.3% ABV
Fruity easy quaffer.
WHITE KNIGHT 4.5% ABV
ABSOLUTION 5.3% ABV
Golden, smooth and refreshing.
BLACK MASS 6.6% ABV
Stout, with good hoppiness.
LAST RITES 11.0% ABV
Smooth toffee sweetness.
Seasonals:
TURNING POINT 4.5% ABV
ARCHANGEL 4.7% ABV
Pale and quenching.
DARK ANGEL 4.7% ABV
Dark and rounded.
FIRE ANGEL 4.7% ABV
STORMBRINGER 4.7% ABV
WHITE CHRISTMAS 5.0% ABV
Plus The Beer Works range of occasional brews.

ANGLO-DUTCH BREWERY
Unit 12 Savile Bridge Mills, Mill Street East, Dewsbury WF13 6QQ
☎ *(01924) 457772*
www.yorkshire-ale.org.uk/anglo-dutch

 KLETSWATER 3.9% ABV
GHOST ON THE RIM 4.5% ABV

BARNSLEY BREWERY CO. LTD
Wath Road, Elsecar, Barnsley, South Yorkshire S74 8HJ
☎ *(01226) 741010*

 BITTER 3.8% ABV
Brewed to the original Barnsley Bitter recipe.
OAKWELL 4.0% ABV
Golden, hoppy and smooth.
IPA 4.2% ABV
Malty, pale and full-bodied.
MAYFLOWER 4.5% ABV
Golden and hoppy. Brewed with American hops.
BLACK HEART 4.6% ABV
Stout.
GLORY 4.8% ABV
Ruby-coloured, with rich, smooth flavour.
Plus seasonal and occasional brews.

THE BLACK SHEEP BREWERY
Wellgarth, Masham, Ripon, North Yorkshire HG4 4EN
☎ *(01765) 689227*
www.blacksheep.co.uk

 BEST BITTER 3.8% ABV
Golden, well-hopped and refreshing.
SPECIAL 4.4% ABV
Good body, hoppy and bitter.
YORKSHIRE SQUARE ALE 5.0% ABV
Richly flavoured golden ale.
RIGGWELTER 5.9% ABV
Mouthfilling flavours.

BRISCOE'S BREWERY
16 Ash Grove, Otley, West Yorkshire LS21 3EL
☎ *(01943) 466515*

 ROMBALD'S REVIVER 3.8% ABV
PUDDLED AND BARMY ALE 5.8% ABV

BROWN COW BREWERY
Brown Cow Road, Barlow, Selby, North Yorkshire YO8 8EH
☎ *(01757) 618974*
www.browncowbrewery.f9.co.uk

 JUST 4U 3.9% ABV
Brewed for the Jug Inn, Chapel Haddlesey.
HOW NOW 4.5% ABV
WOLFHOUND 4.5% ABV
Plus occasional brews.

CONCERTINA BREWERY
9a Dolcliffe Road, Mexborough S64 9AZ
☎ *(01709) 580841*

 BEST BITTER 3.9% ABV
CLUB BITTER 3.9% ABV
OLD DARK ATTIC 3.9% ABV
ONE-EYED JACK 4.0% ABV
BENGAL TIGER 4.6% ABV
DICTATORS 4.7% ABV
ARIEL SQUARE FOUR 5.2% ABV

CROWN BREWERY
Hillsborough Hotel, 57–8 Langsett Road, Sheffield S6 2UB
☎ *(0114) 223 2100*
www.crownbrewery.com

 FIFTH TEST 3.8% ABV
SECOND TEST 4.0% ABV
THIRD TEST 4.0% ABV
LOXLEY GOLD 4.5% ABV
STANNINGTON STOUT 5.0% ABV
MAPPINS IPA 5.2% ABV
FIRST CHRISTMAS 5.5% ABV

DALESIDE BREWERY

Camwal Road, Starbeck, Harrogate, North Yorkshire HG1 4PT
☎ *(01423) 880022*
www.dalesidebrewery.ltd.btinternet.co.uk

 BITTER 3.7% ABV
BLONDE 3.9% ABV
OLD LEGOVER 4.1% ABV
OLD LUBRICATION 4.1% ABV
GREEN GRASS OLD ROGUE ALE 4.5% ABV
MONKEY WRENCH 5.3% ABV
MOROCCO ALE 5.5% ABV
RIPON JEWEL ALE 5.8% ABV

FERNANDES BREWERY

The Old Malthouse, Savison Yard, Kirkgate, Wakefield, West Yorkshire WF1 1VA
☎ *(01924) 291709*

 MALT SHOVEL MILD 3.8% ABV
CHANCERY BITTER 3.9% ABV
ALE TO THE TSAR 4.1% ABV
ODDFELLOWS ALE 4.3% ABV
WAKEFIELD PRIDE 4.5% ABV
DOUBLE SIX 6.0% ABV
EMPRESS OF INDIA 6.0% ABV

FRANKLIN'S BREWERY

Bilton Lane, Bilton, Harrogate, North Yorkshire HG1 4DH
☎ *(01423) 322345*

FRANKLIN'S BITTER 3.8% ABV
FRANKLIN'S BLOTTO 4.7% ABV
FRANKLIN'S DT'S 4.7% ABV
MY BETTER HALF 4.8% ABV

GARTON BREWERY

Station House, Station Road, Garton-on-the-Wold, Driffield YO25 3EX
☎ *(01377) 252340*

WOLDSMAN BITTER 4.5% ABV
Very light, straw-coloured bitter.
STUNNED MULLET 5.0% ABV
Very deep red bitter.
LIQUID LOBOTOMY 8.0% ABV
Heavy-duty stout.
Plus seasonals and specials.

GLENTWORTH BREWERY

Glentworth House, Crossfield Lane, Skellow, Doncaster, South Yorkshire DN6 8PL
☎ *(01302) 725555*
www.greatbritishbeer.co.uk/brewerydetails

LIGHTYEAR 3.9% ABV
NORTHERN STAR 3.9% ABV
BRASSED OFF 4.1% ABV
DONNY ROVER 4.1% ABV
AMBER GAMBLER 4.3% ABV
HAPPY HOOKER 4.3% ABV
DIZZY BLONDE 4.5% ABV
OLD FLAME 4.5% ABV
POT 'O GOLD 4.5% ABV
FULL MONTY 5.0% ABV
HENPECKED 5.0% ABV

GOLCAR BREWERY

Swallow Lane, Golcar, Huddersfield HD7 4NB
☎ *(01484) 64424*

 GOLCAR MILD 3.2% ABV
GOLCAR BITTER 3.8% ABV
WINKLE WARMER 4.2% ABV
Winter ale.
Plus specials

GOOSE EYE BREWERY

Ingrow Bridge, South Street, Keighley, West Yorkshire BD21 5AX
☎ *(01535) 605807*
www.goose-eye-brewery.co.uk

 BARMPOT 3.8% ABV
BRONTE BITTER 4.0% ABV
Malty and well-balanced.
NO EYE DEER 4.0% ABV
WHARFEDALE BITTER 4.5% ABV
POMMIE'S REVENGE 5.2% ABV
Straw-coloured, soft and smooth.
Plus occasional brews.

H B CLARK & CO. (SUCCESSORS) LTD

Westgate Brewery, Wakefield, West Yorkshire WF2 9SW
☎ *(01924) 372306*

TRADITIONAL BITTER 3.8% ABV
Amber-coloured, with some fruitiness.
CITY GENT 4.2% ABV
Pale golden, fruity and quenching.
FESTIVAL ALE 4.2% ABV
Pale with refreshing fruit flavours.
BLACK CAP BITTER 4.4% ABV
Powerful maltiness with hoppy aroma.
BURGLAR BILL 4.4% ABV
Full-bodied and well-hopped throughout.
GOLDEN HORNET 5.0% ABV
Golden and hoppy.
Plus seasonal brews.

HALIFAX STEAM BREWERY

172 Healy Wood Road, Brighouse HD6 3RW
☎ *(01484) 715074*

 TOP 'O' THE MORNING 4.1% ABV
COCK 'O' THE NORTH 4.7% ABV

HAMBLETON ALES

The Brewery, Holme on Swale, Thirsk, North Yorkshire YO7 4JE
☎ *(01845) 567460*
www.hambletonales.co.uk

 BITTER 3.6% ABV
WHITE BOAR 3.7% ABV
For Village Brewer.
BULL 4.0% ABV
For Village Brewer.
GOLDFIELD 4.2% ABV
STALLION 4.2% ABV
STUD 4.3% ABV
OLD RABY 4.8% ABV
For Village Brewer.
NIGHTMARE 5.0% ABV
Plus 4% monthly/seasonal brews.

KELHAM ISLAND BREWERY

23 Alma Street, Sheffield, South Yorkshire S3 8SA
☎ *(0114) 249 4804*
www.kelhambrewery.co.uk

 BITTER 3.8% ABV
SHEFFIELDS BEST 4.0% ABV
EASY RIDER 4.3% ABV
WHEAT BIER 5.0% ABV
Annual brew.
PALE RIDER 5.2% ABV
BETE NOIRE 5.5% ABV
January.
GRANDE PALE 6.6% ABV
August.

MARSTON MOOR BREWERY

Crown House, Kirk Hammerton, York, North Yorkshire YO26 8DD
☎ *(01423) 330341*

 CROMWELL BITTER 3.6% ABV
Light and refreshing with distinctive hop flavour.
HOLLYDAZE 4.0% ABV
December brew.
PILSENER 4.0% ABV
Refreshing, brewed with Czechoslovakian hops.
PRINCE RUPERT MILD 4.0% ABV
Delicate yet flavoursome light mild.
ROMANCER 4.0% ABV
February special brew.
SUMMER DAZE 4.0% ABV
August brew.
BREWERS PRIDE 4.2% ABV
Smooth, balanced hop flavour.
GEM(INI) 4.5% ABV
June special brew.
HARVEST MOON 4.5% ABV
September brew.
MAD HATTER 4.5% ABV
April special brew.

MERRIE MAKER 4.5% ABV
Award-winning, Yorkshire-style brew.
SCORPIO 4.5% ABV
November brew.
BREWER'S DROOP 5.0% ABV
Easy-drinking, sweeter brew.
TROOPER 5.0% ABV
Dry-hopped version of Brewer's Droop.

NORTH YORKSHIRE BREWING CO.

Pinchinthorpe Hall, Pinchinthorpe, Guisborough TS14 8HG
☎ *(01287) 630200*

 BEST BITTER 3.6% ABV
Pale, refreshing and hoppy.
GOLDEN GINSENG 3.6% ABV
Gold-coloured and hoppy. May.
MILLENNIUM MILD 3.6% ABV
Dark, with caramel hints and hoppy aftertaste.
PRIOR'S ALE 3.6% ABV
Quenching and very hoppy.
ARCHBISHOP LEE'S RUBY ALE 4.0% ABV
Rounded, Northern ale.
BORO BEST 4.0% ABV
Northern, full-bodied style.
CRYSTAL TIPS 4.0% ABV
Rounded, malty September special.
LOVE MUSCLE 4.0% ABV
February, golden special brew.
HONEY BUNNY 4.2% ABV
Mar–Apr brew.
XMAS HERBERT 4.4% ABV
A festive version of Flying Herbert.
CEREAL KILLER 4.5% ABV
June–July wheat beer.
FOOL'S GOLD 4.6% ABV
Pale and hoppy.
GOLDEN ALE 4.6% ABV
Powerful hoppiness.
FLYING HERBERT 4.7% ABV
Smooth and well-balanced.
LORD LEE 4.7% ABV
Smooth, full-flavoured malt.
WHITE LADY 4.7% ABV
Pale, hoppy October brew.
DIZZY DICK 4.8% ABV
Dark and smooth August brew.
NORTHERN STAR 4.8% ABV
Golden and well-balanced.
ROCKET FUEL 5.0% ABV
Golden brew for November.

OAKWELL BREWERY

Pontefract Road, Barnsley
☎ *(01226) 296161*

 BARNSLEY BITTER 3.8% ABV
OLD TOM 3.8% ABV

OLD MILL BREWERY
Mill Street, Snaith, Goole DN14 9HU
☎ *(01405) 861813*

 TRADITIONAL MILD 3.4% ABV
TRADITIONAL BITTER 3.9% ABV
OLD CURIOSITY 4.5% ABV
BULLION STRONG BITTER 4.7% ABV
Seasonal:
January: **BLACK JACK 5.0% ABV**
February: **CUPIDS STUNT 4.5% ABV and BLACK JACK 5.0% ABV**
March: **SPRINGS ETERNAL 4.0% ABV and FINNIGANS STOUT 5.0% ABV**
April: **SPRINGS ETERNAL 4.0% and ST GEORGE 4.2%**
May: **NELLIE DENE 4.2% and WILLOWS WOOD 4.2%**
June: **NELLIE DENE 4.2%**
July: **SUNSHINE 4.0%**
August: **WILLOWS WOOD 4.2%**
September: **AUTUMN BREEZE 4.2%**
October: **HALLOWEEN SURPRISE 3.9%**
November: **GUY FAWKES REVENGE 4.2%**
December: **WINTER WARMER 4.5% and NICKS NOGGIN 4.5%**
Occasional:
BREWERS CHOICE 4.2% ABV
BULLION STRONG BITTER 4.7% ABV
OLD MILL CELEBRATION

OSSETT BREWING COMPANY
Low Mill Road, Ossett WF5 8ND
☎ *(01924) 261333*
www.ossett-brewery.co.uk

 PALE GOLD 3.8% ABV
SILVER FOX 4.1% ABV
IPA 4.3% ABV
SILVER KING 4.3% ABV
BOBBY DAZZLER 4.5% ABV
SILVER LINK 4.6% ABV
FINE FETTLE 4.8% ABV
EXCELSIOR 5.2% ABV
Plus seasonal and specials.

ROOSTER'S BREWERY
Unit 20, Claro Court Business Centre, Claro Road, Harrogate, North Yorkshire HG1 4BA
☎ *(01423) 561861 www.roosters.co.uk*

 SPECIAL 3.9% ABV
Pale, with citrus-fruit freshness.
HOOLIGAN 4.3% ABV
Pale, with some hoppy bitterness.
SCORCHER 4.3% ABV
Pale, with citrus flavours and good hoppiness.
YANKEE 4.3% ABV
Pale, soft and fruity.
CREAM 4.7% ABV
Smooth and soft, with fruit flavours.
ROOSTER'S 4.7% ABV
Golden brown, sweet and fruity.
NECTOR 5.0% ABV
Pale, soft, bitter beer. Christmas.
Plus occasional and seasonal brews. Additional brews produced under the Outlaw Brewing Co. label.

RUDGATE BREWERY
2 Centre Park, Marston Business Park, Rudgate, Tockwith, York, North Yorkshire YO26 8QF
☎ *(01423) 3588832*
www.rudgate-beers.co.uk

 VIKING 3.8% ABV
BATTLEAXE 4.2% ABV
RUBY MILD 4.4% ABV
Plus monthly brews.

SALAMANDER BREWING CO.
Harry Street, Dudley Hill, Bradford BD4 9PH
☎ *(01274) 652323*

BEE'S SPRING BITTER 3.7% ABV
A pale-amber coloured dry-hopped session ale.
OWD AMOS 3.8% ABV
Chestnut coloured, easy drinking malty session ale.
SUMMER ALE 3.8%
A light coloured session bitter.
MUDPUPPY 4.2% ABV
Dark amber, malty and refreshing.
STOUT 4.5% ABV
Brewed with roast and flaked barley.
GENT 4.7% ABV
Russet-coloured premium bitter.
GOLD LAZARUS 4.8% ABV
Pale coloured with a distinctive aroma of Bramling Cross hops.
HELLBENDER 4.8% ABV
Amber-coloured strong ale, fruity nose and clean hop bitterness.
HAMMER & TONG 5.0% ABV
Very pale and bitter.

SAMUEL SMITH OLD BREWERY
High Street, Tadcaster, North Yorkshire LS24 9SB
☎ *(01937) 832225*

 OLD BREWERY BITTER 4.0% ABV
Rounded and flavoursome.

SUNSET CIDER AND WINE COMPANY
Leggers Inn, Saville Town Wharf, Mill Street East, Dewsbury WF12 9BD
☎ *(01942) 502846*

 CANAL NO. 5 3.8% ABV
MARRIOTT'S MILD 4.0% ABV
PROSPECT ROAD 4.0% ABV
GOLDEN EYE 700 4.2% ABV
PHAROAH'S CURSE 4.6% ABV
Plus seasonals and specials such as:
CANAL NO. 7 5.0% ABV
JACK TYE 5.0% ABV
CANAL NO. 9 6.0% ABV

TIMOTHY TAYLOR & CO. LTD
Knowle Spring Brewery, Keighley, West Yorkshire BD21 1AW
☎ *(01535) 603139*
www.timothy-taylor.co.uk

 DARK MILD 3.5% ABV
Mellow and malty with balancing hoppiness.
GOLDEN BEST 3.5% ABV
Balanced, crisp and hoppy.
PORTER 3.8% ABV
Sweeter winter brew.
BEST BITTER 4.0% ABV
Refreshing, hoppy and bitter.
LANDLORD 4.3% ABV
Distinctive combination of malt, hops and fruit.
RAM TAM 4.3% ABV
Landlord with added caramel.

TIGERTOPS BREWERY
22 Oakes Street, Wakefield, West Yorkshire WF2 9LN
☎ *(01942) 378538*

Constantly changing beer range, specialises in continental beer styles.

UPPER AGBRIGG BREWERY
Unit 12, Honley Business Centre, New Mill Road, Honley, Holmefirth HD9 6QB
☎ *(01484) 660008*

 HOLME VALLEY BITTER 3.8% ABV
BLACK BEAUTY PORTER 4.5% ABV
OATMEAL STOUT 5.0% ABV
Plus seasonals, festival specials and a range of German-style bottled beers.

WAWNE BREWERY
Tickton Arms, Main Street, Tickton, Beverley, East Yorkshire HU17 9SH
☎ *(01482) 679876*
Brewery may move shortly.

MONKS MILD 3.2% ABV
INFRINGEMENT BITTER 3.8% ABV
HODGSONS BEST BITTER 3.9% ABV
MELSA 4.3% ABV
Plus occasional brews.

YORK BREWERY
Toft Green, Micklegate, York YO1 1JT
☎ *(01904) 621162*
www.yorkbrew.demon.co.uk

STONEWALL 3.7% ABV
Malty with hoppy finish.
BITTER 4.0% ABV
Well balanced with full bitter flavour.
YORKSHIRE TERRIER 4.2% ABV
Gold-coloured with good bitter finish.
YORK IPA 5.0% ABV
Balanced tawny ale with pleasant finish.
CENTURION'S GHOST ALE 5.4% ABV
Millennium brew.
Seasonals:
GUZZLER 3.6% ABV
Jan–Feb.
SWING LOW 4.8% ABV
Feb–Mar.
FINAL WHISTLE 3.9% ABV
Apr–Jun.
BUSY LIZZIE 4.1% ABV
May–Jun.
GOLDEN REIGN 4.1% ABV
Jul–Aug.
WONKEY DONKEY 4.5% ABV
Sept–Feb.
BLACK BESS STOUT 4.2% ABV
Oct–Nov.
STOCKING FILLER 4.8% ABV
Dec.

THE PUBS

ALLERTON BYWATER

The Boat Inn & Boat Brewery

Boat Lane, Allerton Bywater, Castleford,
West Yorkshire WF10 2BX
☎ *(01977) 552216* Kieron Lockwood

All Boat Brewery ales brewed on the premises and permanently available. One other monthly special guest.

A small pub with moorings directly outside. Food available every day in a large restaurant with non-smoking areas. Children allowed. For further information, visit the web site at www.boatpub.co.uk.

 MAN IN THE BOAT MILD 3.5% ABV
AIRTONIC 3.6% ABV
Session bitter.
RATTLER 4.3 % ABV
Light beer.

OPEN *12–3pm and 6–11pm Mon–Fri;*
all day Sat–Sun.

ATWICK

The Black Horse Inn

The Green, Atwick, East Yorkshire YO25 8DQ
☎ *(01964) 532691* Brian Thompson

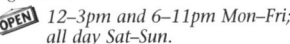Three or four different beers are available each week, with favourites including Morland Old Speckled Hen and Charles Wells Bombardier.

Unspoilt village pub, with home-cooked food served 12–2pm (12–3pm Sun) and 6–9pm. Curry nights on Wednesday. Children welcome. Car park. On B1242, one mile north of Hornsea.

OPEN *11.30am–11pm Mon–Sat;*
12–10.30pm Sun.

BARKISLAND

The Fleece Inn

Ripponden Bank, Barkisland, Halifax,
West Yorkshire
☎ *(01422) 822598* Stewart Taylor

Black Sheep Best and Charles Wells Bombardier permanently available plus up to six guest ales. Timothy Taylor Landlord, Black Sheep Special and Riggwelter and Fuller's London Pride are regular features, but different ales are stocked whenever possible.

A country pub with a warm welcome. Beamed ceilings and open fires. Beer garden with impressive views across the Calder valley and Ryburn valley. Food available 12–2.30pm and 6–9pm Mon–Sat, 12–7pm Sun. Live music twice weekly. Children allowed, with play areas outside and inside. Car park.

OPEN *12–11pm (10.30pm Sun).*

BARNSLEY

The Cherry Tree

High Hoyland, Barnsley, South Yorkshire S75 4BE
☎ *(01226) 382541* Ken Burnett

Eastwood & Sanders Nettlethrasher and Black Sheep Special permanently available plus other guests, usually from Barge & Barrel.

Country pub with beautiful views. Food available. Children allowed. Outside seating. Car park.

OPEN *12–2.30pm and 5–11pm Mon–Fri;*
11am–11pm Sat; 12–10.30pm Sunday.

Miller's Inn

Dearne Hall Road, Barnsley, South Yorkshire
S75 1LX
☎ *(01226) 382888* Mr and Mrs Alan Dyson

A freehouse with Timothy Taylor Landlord and Oakwell Barnsley always available, plus one guest from breweries such as Shepherd Neame or Fuller's.

A riverside two-bar village pub with separate dining area and garden. Food available Wed–Sun lunchtime and Sun–Mon, Wed–Thurs evenings. Children allowed.

OPEN *11.30am–2.30pm and 5.15–11pm*
Sun–Thurs (closed Tues lunchtime);
all day Fri–Sat.

The Orchard Brewery Bar

15 Market Hill, Barnsley, South Yorkshire S72 PX
☎ *(01226) 288906* Gabriel Savage

The full range of home brews are always available.

A Yorkshire brewpub, with separate fish restaurant upstairs. Food available all day Mon–Sat. Children allowed.

MORETONS 3.9% ABV
ORCHARD BEST BITTER 3.9% ABV
TYKE 4.6% ABV

OPEN *11am–11pm (10.30pm Sun).*

BATLEY

The Oaklands

Bradford Road, Batley, West Yorkshire WF17 5PS
☎ *(01924) 444181*

Up to six beers available. Always something from local breweries plus at least three guests from Timothy Taylor or Tomlinson's.

A busy circuit pub. Car park, garden.

OPEN *7–11pm Thurs–Sat; 7–10.30pm Sun.*

Airedale Heifer

*53 Stocksbank Road, Batyeford, Mirfield,
West Yorkshire WF14 9QB*
☎ *(01924) 493547* Melvin Charles

 Eastwood & Sanders Bargee
permanently available plus occasional
seasonal guests.

An old village pub, recently renovated.
Food available 12–3pm Tues–Sun. Beer
garden. Children allowed. Car park. Live
music once a month and odd events
throughout the year – call for details or see
the website: www.airedale-heiffer.i12.com.

OPEN *3–11pm Mon; 12–11pm Tues–Sat;
12–10.30pm Sun.*

Birch Hall Inn

Beck Hole, Goathland, North Yorkshire YO22 5LE
☎ *(01947) 896245*

 A wide choice of beers always available,
including Black Sheep Bitter and local
brews from Cropton, Black Dog and Daleside
Brewery. Many more guests through the year
from further afield.

Tiny, traditional unspoilt pub with two
bars dating from 1600s. CAMRA Pub of
the Year. No juke box or games machines. Bar
food available at lunchtime and evenings.
Garden. Children allowed. Between Pickering
and Whitby.

OPEN *11am–11pm in summer; usual hours in
winter.*

The Beehive Inn

*583 Halifax Road, Bradford, West Yorkshire
BD6 2DU*
☎ *(01274) 678550* Kevin Guthrie

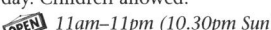 At least two guest ales always available,
one from a local brewery such as
Salamander, Ossett, Eastwood & Sanders, and
Daleside. The other guest will be from the
Cask Marque seasonal range.

A one-bar locals' pub on the outskirts of
the city centre. Bar snacks available all
day. Children allowed.

OPEN *11am–11pm (10.30pm Sun).*

The Castle Hotel

*20 Grattan Road, Bradford, West Yorkshire
BD1 2LU*
☎ *(01274) 393166* James Duncan

 Mansfield Riding and Riding Mild always
available plus seven guest beers (200 per
year) from brewers such as Goose Eye,
Ridleys, Brains, Moorhouse's, Marston's,
Eldridge Pope, Jennings, Wadworth,
Shepherd Neame and many more.

A pub built like a castle in 1898. Bar food is
served at lunchtime from Monday to
Thursday and until 7.30pm on Friday and
Saturday. Parking at weekends and evenings.
Children not allowed. Located in the city
centre.

OPEN *11.30am–11pm Mon–Sat; closed Sun.*

The Corn Dolly

*110 Bolton Road, Bradford, West Yorkshire
BD1 4DE*
☎ *(01274) 720219* Neil Dunkin

 Eight beers always available.
Moorhouse's Bitter, Black Sheep Bitter,
Everards Tiger and something from Timothy
Taylor always available, plus four ever-
changing guest beers from all over the
country, including breweries such as
Durham, Ossett, Coach House and Exmoor.

A freehouse with a friendly atmosphere.
Bradford CAMRA Pub of the Year
1993,1994, 2000 and 2001. Food is available
at lunchtimes Mon–Fri; buffets catered for.
Beer garden and car park. Situated just off
the city centre (Forster Square).

OPEN *11.30am–11pm.*

The Fighting Cock

*21–3 Preston Street, Bradford, West Yorkshire
BD7 1JE*
☎ *(01274) 726907* Kevin Quill

 At least ten beers on sale. Brews from
Timothy Taylor and Black Sheep always
available plus many guests (200 per year)
from Greene King, Fuller's, Archers, Jennings
and Ringwood etc.

A friendly back-to-basics original alehouse.
Bar food available at lunchtime. Go left
on Thornton Road from the former cinema
in the city centre, then left again at the
lights.

OPEN *11am–11pm Mon–Sat; 11am–3pm and
7–10.30pm Sun.*

Haigy's Bar

31 Lumb Lane, Bradford, West Yorkshire BD8 7QU
☎ *(01274) 731644* David and Yvonne Haig

 A freehouse serving Greene King Abbot and beers from Ossett and Black Sheep, plus guests.

An edge-of-town pub with traditional decor, painted in Bradford City colours, but with a modern feel. Games, pool, disco at weekends. Disabled access, beer garden. Food available at lunchtime and evenings. Children allowed in the afternoons only.

OPEN *5pm–1am Mon–Thurs; 12pm–1am Fri–Sat; 12–7pm Sun (10.30pm Sun if Bradford Bulls or Bradford City are playing at home!).*

The Idle Cock

Bolton Road, Bradford, West Yorkshire BD2 4HT
☎ *(01274) 639491* Jim Wright

 Samuel Smith OBB, Black Sheep Special and Timothy Taylor Landlord always available plus several guests (130 per year) including Tomintoul Stag, Hop Back Summer Lightning, Fuller's London Pride, Daleside Old Legover, Joseph Holts etc.

A York stone pub with two separate bars, part wood, part flagstone floors, wooden bench seating. A proper no-frills alehouse. Bar food is available. Parking and garden. Follow the 'Idle' signs along Bolton Road for approximately two miles from the city centre.

OPEN *11.30am–11pm Mon–Sat; 12–3pm and 7–10.30pm Sun.*

The New Beehive Inn

171 Westgate, Bradford, West Yorkshire BD1 3AA
☎ *(01274) 721784* William Wagstaff

 Kelham Island Bitter, Timothy Taylor Landlord, a Salamander ale and Ryeburn Dark Mild permanently available, plus numerous guests from independent breweries across the UK. Listed on CAMRA's National Inventory.

A classic Edwardian inn, barely altered over the years, with unique gas lighting. Six separate drinking rooms. Bar food available all day. Children allowed. Accommodation. Situated on the outskirts of the city centre.

OPEN *11am–11pm (10.30pm Sun).*

The Shearbridge

111 Great Horton Road, Bradford, West Yorkshire BD7 1PS
☎ *(01274) 732136* David Cheshire

 Up to four guests on offer, such as Harviestoun Schiehallion or a Black Sheep ale.

A students' pub with beams, wooden floors and beer garden. There are plans to serve food in the near future. Children welcome.

OPEN *12–11pm (10.30pm Sun).*

Sir Titus Salt

Windsor Baths, Morley Street, Bradford, West Yorkshire BD6 1AQ
☎ *(01274) 732853* Adam Johnson (Manager)

 A JD Wetherspoon's pub with Timothy Taylor Landlord and Shepherd Neame Spitfire permanently available, plus a selection of regularly changing guests from breweries such as Hook Norton, Highgate, Rooster's, Banks & Taylor and Springhead. Beer festivals held.

A large open pub which used to be a swimming pool! Food available all day every day. Children allowed. Small outside area with seating.

OPEN *11am–11pm (10.30pm Sun).*

BREARTON

The Malt Shovel

Brearton, Harrogate, North Yorkshire HG3 3BX
☎ *(01423) 862929* Les Mitchell

 Five beers always available – up to 100 guests per year. Favourites include Daleside Nightjar, Durham Magus, Rudgate Ruby Mild, Black Sheep Bitter and Daleside brews.

A sixteenth-century beamed village inn, with open fires in winter. Bar food available at lunchtime and evenings (except Sunday evenings). Car park, garden. Children allowed. Off the B6165.

OPEN *12–2.30pm and 6.45–11pm Tues–Sat; 12–2.30pm and 7–10.30pm Sun.*

BRIDLINGTON

The Old Ship Inn

90 St John's Street, Bridlington, East Yorkshire YO16 7JS
☎ *(01262) 670466*

 Up to seven beers always available.

A two-bar country pub with dining area and beer garden. Food available. Children allowed.

OPEN *11am–11pm (10.30pm Sun).*

BROMPTON

The Crown Inn

Station Road, Brompton, Northallerton, North Yorkshire DL6 2RE
☎ *(0160) 977 2547* Mrs Addington

 Two guest ales such as Marston's Pedigree in addition to the two regular brews.

A traditional country inn with one bar, coal fires and a small garden. No food. Children allowed.

OPEN *12–3pm and 7–11pm Mon–Thurs; all day Fri–Sun.*

BURLEY

The Fox & Newt

*9 Burley Street, Burley, Leeds, West Yorkshire
LS3 1LD*
☎ *(01132) 432612* Roy Cadman

A wide range of guest ales always available. Regulars include Young's Special, Greene King Abbot, Timothy Taylor Landlord, Wadworth 6X, Marston's Pedigree, Fuller's London Pride and Caledonian 80/-. The beers are changed weekly.

An old-style pub with a wooden floor. Food available at lunchtime only in a separate dining area. Children allowed for lunches only.

OPEN *All day, every day.*

CAWOOD

The Ferry Inn

*2 King Street, Cawood, Selby, North Yorkshire
YO8 3TL*
☎ *(01757) 268515* Lynn Moore, Phillip Daggitt and Dee Ellershaw

A freehouse serving Mansfield Bitter, Black Sheep Special and Timothy Taylor Landlord plus one constantly changing guest ale.

A sixteenth-century village inn with stone floor, beams, log fires and beer garden. Bar food available at lunchtime and evenings. Separate dining area planned. Children allowed. Near the river.

OPEN *5–11pm Mon–Tues; 12–3pm and 5–11pm Wed–Thurs; 12–11pm Fri–Sun.*

CHAPEL HADDLESEY

The Jug Inn

Chapel Haddlesey, Selby, North Yorkshire
☎ *(01757) 270307* Sydney Bolton

A Brown Cow brew is usually available, plus three guest beers, often from Glentworth, Rudgate, Barnsley, Cropton, Eccleshall, Goose Eye, Kelham Island or Tigertops.

Welcoming village pub with beamed ceilings and open coal fires. Food served 12–2.30pm and 6–9.30pm daily in small dining room. Beer garden. Car park. Children's play area in beer garden.

OPEN *12–2.30pm and 6–11pm Mon–Fri; 12–11pm Sat; 12–10.30pm Sun.*

CHAPEL-LE-DALE

The Hill Inn

*Chapel-le-Dale, Ingleton, North Yorkshire
LA6 3AR*
☎ *(015242) 41246* Mrs Sabena Martin

A pub permanently serving Black Sheep Best, Special and Riggwelter plus Dent Bitter and Aviator.

Ancient inn with lots of character, nestling between Ingleborough and Whernside, and close to the White Scar Caves and the Ribblehead Viaduct. Home-cooked food available 12.30–2.30pm and 7–9pm (currently not on Mondays, or Tuesday lunchtimes, but phone to check), with puddings a speciality! Booking advisable. Well-behaved children allowed. Car park.

OPEN *6–11pm Tues; 12–3pm and 6–11pm Wed–Fri; 12–11pm Sat; 12–10.30pm Sun (opening times may change, so phone to check).*

CHAPELTOWN

The Commercial

107 Station Road, Chapeltown, Sheffield, South Yorkshire S35 2XF
☎ *(0114) 246 9066* Paul Manzies

Wentworth Brewery ale permanently available plus between six and ten guest ales every week from a range of independent breweries including Durham, Barnsley, Slaters of Eccleshall and Daleside. Beer festivals twice a year.

A town pub dating from 1889. Food available. No children. Beer garden. Car park.

OPEN *12–3pm and 5.30–11pm Mon–Fri; 11am–11pm Sat; 12–10.30pm Sun.*

CLECKHEATON

Wheatsheaf Inn & Restaurant

95 Gommersall Lane, Little Gommersall, Cleckheaton, West Yorkshire BD19 4JQ
☎ *(01274) 873661* Bill Leather

Black Sheep Best, Greene King Abbot and Marston's Pedigree always available.

A 300-year-old village pub with beams and fireplaces. Food available in non-smoking restaurant. Children allowed. Beer garden. Car park. Village can be difficult to find so call for directions.

OPEN *7–11pm Mon; 12–11pm Tues–Sat; 12–10.30pm Sun.*

CRAY

The White Lion

Cray, Skipton, North Yorkshire BD23 5JB
☎ *(01756) 760262* Kevin and Debbie Roe

Four hand pumps all serving a constantly changing range of real ales. Moorhouse's Pendle Witch and Premier, Goose Eye No Eye Deer, Barm Pot and Wharfedale, Timothy Taylor Landlord and Golden Best, Cottage Champflower and Norman Conquest, Ossett Silver King, Rooster's Yankee and Special, Daleside Blonde and Monkey Wrench and Black Sheep Best, Special and Yorkshire Square are among the beers on regular rotation, although many others are also featured. Emphasis on local ales where possible.

Formerly a Drovers' Hostelry dating from the seventeenth century, this is a peaceful pub in the Yorkshire Dales. Situated in a popular walking area of outstanding natural beauty. Food available 12–2.15pm and 5.45–8.45pm daily, tea and coffee available all day. Outside seating in a beer garden, and also beside the cascading Cray Gill. Superior accommodation with seasonal special offers. Children welcome, baby listening service available to residents. Directions available from Grassington National Park centre.

OPEN *10am–11pm (10.30pm Sun).*

CROPTON

The New Inn

Cropton, Nr Pickering, North Yorkshire YO18 8HH
☎ *(01751) 417310* Sandra Lee

Home of the Cropton Brewery, so a selection of Cropton beers always available.

Cropton Brewery was established in 1984 in the basement of the New Inn in this tiny moorland village. It owes its existence to the deep-seated local fear that, one day, the harsh moors winter weather would prevent the beer waggon from getting through. The brewery's reputation has since spread and, as demand exceeded capacity, a new purpose-built brewery was constructed in an adjacent quarry. Bar and restaurant food is served at lunchtime and evenings. Car park, garden, children's room, accommodation.

- KING BILLY BITTER 3.6% ABV
- TWO PINTS BEST BITTER 4.0% ABV
- HONEY GOLD 4.2% ABV
- SCORESBY STOUT 4.2% ABV
- UNCLE SAM'S BITTER 4.4% ABV
- BACKWARDS BITTER 4.7% ABV
- MONKMAN'S SLAUGHTER BITTER 6.0% ABV

OPEN *11am–3pm and 6.30–11pm; all day Sat.*

DENBY DALE

The White Hart

380 Wakefield Road, Denby Dale, Huddersfield, West Yorkshire HD8 8RT
☎ *(01484) 862357* Mrs Donna M Brayshaw

Between two and four guest beers usually available, often from the Eastwood & Sanders Brewery.

Friendly, village-centre pub with an open fire in winter. Beer garden and Tuesday night quiz with free buffet. Homemade food served 12–2pm daily. Car park. Children welcome when eating.

OPEN *12–11pm (10.30pm Sun).*

DEWSBURY

West Riding Licensed Refreshment Rooms

Dewsbury Railway Station, Wellington Road, Dewsbury, West Yorkshire WF13 1HF
☎ *(01924) 459193*
Challcia Banks and Mike Field

A freehouse with Black Sheep Bitter and Timothy Taylor Landlord always available, plus up to six guests from breweries such as Ossett, Durham, Salamander and the pub's own micro-brewery, Anglo-Dutch. Close links with local breweries.

Situated in the railway station and doubling as a waiting room, this is a real ale pub with one central bar, wooden floors and beer garden. Live music on Thursdays. Music festival venue. Food available every lunchtime, plus Tuesday nights (Pie Nights) and Wednesday nights (Curry Nights). Children allowed in designated areas. On Trans-Pennine route – four trains an hour in each direction.

OPEN *11am–11pm (10.30pm Sun).*

DISHFORTH

The Crown Inn

Main Street, Dishforth, North Yorkshire YO7 3JU
☎ *(01845) 577398* Alison Craddock

Charles Wells Bombardier plus Timothy Taylor Landlord and Golden Best are always on offer, plus four or five guest beers, perhaps Badger Tanglefoot, Morland Old Speckled Hen, or brews from Durham, Salamander and Goose Eye.

Small country pub with pool room, easily accessible from A1 and A19. Food available 12–3pm and 6–9.30pm Tues–Sun. Children very welcome. Car park.

OPEN *12–3pm and 6–midnight (supper licence) Tues–Sun; closed all day Monday.*

DONCASTER

The Hallcross
33–4 Hallgate, Doncaster, South Yorkshire DN1 3NL
☎ (01302) 328213

 Home of the Stocks Brewery, so Stocks brews produced and served on the premises.

The brewery was established in 1981 behind the pub. It is owned and run by Cooplands, a Doncaster bakers, on the site of the first shop, which was opened in 1931 to sell home-made sweets. The pub is of traditional Victorian style with a beer garden. Bar food is served at lunchtime and evenings. Parking, children allowed.

 BEST BIT 3.9% ABV
Light hoppy ale brewed for the northern taste.

SELECT 4.7% ABV
Premium ale of smooth and slightly malty character.

ST LEDGER PORTER 5.1% ABV
Award-winning, almost black, full-flavoured ale with deep fruit and roast malt flavours. A hoppy finish.

GOLDEN WHEAT 4.7% ABV

OLD HORIZONTAL 5.4% ABV
Strong ale with a distinctive nutty flavour, good body and excellent head retention, flavoured with a delicate blend of Fuggles and Goldings hops.

OPEN *11am–11pm.*

The Salutation
14 South Parade, Doncaster, South Yorkshire DN1 2DR
☎ (01302) 340705 Debbie Chetwood

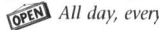 A renowned real ale pub with Marston's Pedigree always available, plus at least five guests (perhaps more that 500 per year), changed very frequently.

A 300-year-old coaching inn with strong connections with Doncaster Racecourse. A one-roomed bar with lots of cosy corners and a real fire in winter. Food available every day – Sunday lunch a speciality. Sunny beer garden and large function room.

OPEN *All day, every day.*

DRIFFIELD

Bell In Driffield
46 Market Place, Driffield, East Yorkshire YO25 6AN
☎ (01377) 256661 Mr GAF Riggs

 Two beers available weekdays and three or four at weekends from a range of around 30 local beers, often including something from York, Hambleton or Highwood.

Characterful, eighteenth-century inn retaining many original features. Food served 12–1.30pm and 7–9.30pm daily. Car park.

OPEN *11am–2.30pm and 6–11pm Mon–Sat; 12–3pm and 7–10.30pm Sun.*

ECCLESFIELD

The Black Bull
18 Church Street, Ecclesfield, Sheffield, South Yorkshire S35 9WE
☎ (0114) 246 7763 Peter and Amanda Down

 One Eastwood & Sanders ale always available with plans to introduce another regular real ale.

Large traditional village pub, mentioned in the Domesday Book, with tap room, function room, snug and bar. Large car park and enclosed seating, cobbled floor. Live music and karaoke every Saturday, Country & Western on Wednesdays. Bar snacks available. Children allowed. Located opposite Ecclesfield Church 'Minster on the Moor' which was once known as Sheffield Cathedral.

OPEN *11am–11pm Mon–Sat; 12–10.30pm Sun.*

ELLAND

Barge & Barrel
10–20 Park Road, Elland, West Yorkshire HA5 9HB
☎ (01422) 373623 Mark Dalton

Eastwood & Sanders Bargee, Nettlethrasher and Best, Black Dump, Coronation Class and Black Sheep Special permanently available plus three constantly changing guests which could be ales such as Greene King Abbot, Phoenix Wobbly Bob, Fuller's London Pride, brews from Goose Eye or any Eastwood & Sanders seasonal ale.

A canalside pub, just outside the small town. Food available in non-smoking dining area. Children allowed if eating. Waterside garden. Live music occasionally. Car park.

OPEN *12–11pm (10.30pm Sun).*

ELSLACK

The Tempest Arms

Elslack, Nr Skipton, North Yorkshire
☎ *(01282) 842450*
Veronica Clarkson (manager)

 Owned by Individual Inns, with Timothy Taylor Landlord and Best Bitter plus Black Sheep Bitter always on offer. Good range of wines served by the glass and bottle.

A pub situated in glorious countryside. Food served lunchtimes and evenings Mon–Sat and all day on Sunday. Function room for up to 100 guests, plus ten en-suite bedrooms. Just outside Elslack, an ancient hamlet close to the Yorkshire Dales.

 11am–11pm Mon–Sat; 12–10.30pm Sun.

FLAXTON

The Blacksmiths Arms

Flaxton, York, North Yorkshire YO60 7RJ
☎ *(01904) 468210* Mrs Alison Jordan

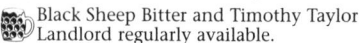 Black Sheep Bitter and Timothy Taylor Landlord regularly available.

A 250-year-old country freehouse with separate non-smoking dining area serving home-cooked food Mon–Sat evening, lunchtime and evening Sun. Car park. Children welcome.

 7–11pm Tues–Sat (closed Mon); 12–3pm and 7–10.30pm Sun.

GREETLAND

The Druids Arms

2–4 Spring Lane, Greetland, Halifax,
West Yorkshire HX4 8JL
☎ *(01422) 372465* Keith Mallinson

Timothy Taylor Golden Best, Best Bitter and Landlord permanently available plus three constantly changing guest ales. Regular features include: Rooster's Cream, Durham White Sapphire or ales from Halifax Steam or Eastwood & Sanders. Micro-breweries supported.

A homely country pub with comfy sofas, real fires in winter, seating area outside in summer and a friendly atmosphere. No food. Children allowed until 8.30pm. Live music once a month. Car park. May be difficult to find; ring for directions.

 5–11pm Mon–Fri; 12–11pm Sat; 12–10.30pm Sun.

GUISBOROUGH

The Tap & Spile

11 Westgate, Guisborough, North Yorkshire
TS14 6BG
☎ *(01287) 632983* Angela Booth

Big Lamp Bitter always available plus six guests (200 per year) which may include Hambleton ales and those from Cotleigh, Big Lamp and Durham.

P lenty of olde-worlde charm, a beamed ceiling, non-smoking room, snug and beer garden. Bar food available at lunchtime. Parking. Children allowed. Situated on the main street in Guisborough.

 11.30am–11pm Mon–Sat; 12–3pm and 7–10.30pm Sun.

GUNNERSIDE

The Kings Head

Gunnerside, North Yorkshire DL11 6LD
☎ *(01748) 886261* Fred and Christine Bristow

The brewery tap for the Swaled Ale Brewery at Gunnerside.

T raditional Dales walkers' pub. Hot and cold snacks served at lunchtimes, with home-cooked meals available 6.30–8pm (booking advisable). Children allowed in designated area.

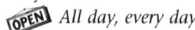 *11.30am–11pm Mon–Sat; 12–10.30pm Sun (reduced hours in winter – ring for details).*

HALIFAX

Tap & Spile

1 Clare Road, Halifax, West Yorkshire HX1 2HX
☎ *(01422) 353661* Chris Dalton

Black Sheep Bitter, Big Lamp Bitter and Fuller's London Pride always available, plus up to four guests, not repeated if possible, from breweries such as Broughton Ales, Fuller's, Hop Back and Hambleton.

A traditional town pub in a listed building, with one bar and a dining area. Plans for a beer garden. Food available at lunchtime only. No children.

 *All day, every day.*

The Three Pigeons

1 Sunfold, South Parade, Halifax, West Yorkshire HX1 2LX

☎ *(01422) 347001* Geoff Amos

 Award-winning, family-run freehouse with seven cask ales on offer. Regulars are Timothy Taylor Landlord and Best Bitter, plus Black Sheep Bitter. Guest ales are drawn from breweries throughout the UK, with mild beers featured on a weekly basis.

A unique, unspoilt 1930s Art Deco pub just a few minutes' walk from the railway station. Real fires, one bar and three parlour rooms. Patio at front. Food available on weekday lunchtimes only, with a curry night on Monday evenings. Children allowed in designated area. Visit the website at: www.threepigeons.demon.co.uk.

OPEN *12–11pm (10.30pm Sun).*

HARROGATE

The Old Bell Tavern

6 Royal Parade, Harrogate, North Yorkshire HG1 2SZ

☎ *(01423) 507930*
Jamie Allan and Gina Andrew

 Timothy Taylor Landlord, Black Sheep Bitter and Caledonian Deuchars IPA always available, plus five regularly changing guests, from local breweries whenever possible. Also Erdinger WeissBier (a Belgian ale) and two guest Belgian beers, plus a range of Belgian bottled beers.

A traditional period town-centre bar with large non-smoking room. Air conditioned. Food available every day in an upstairs dining room/brasserie. Children allowed in the brasserie only. Situated close to the Pump Room Museum and Valley Gardens.

OPEN *12–11pm (10.30pm Sun).*

The Tap & Spile

Tower Street, Harrogate, North Yorkshire HG1 1HS
☎ *(01423) 526785* Roger Palmer

No permanent beers, but a constantly changing range of guest ales. Rooster's and Daleside are regular breweries featured, but two new beers are served every week.

A two-bar pub situated just off the town centre. Stone walls, half-carpet in public bar and lounge, one non-smoking, fireplace. Patio at front. Food available at lunchtime only. Children allowed in non-smoking room only.

OPEN *All day, every day.*

HAWORTH

The Fleece

Main Street, Haworth, Nr Keighley, West Yorkshire BD22 8DA
☎ *(01535) 642172* Mr and Mrs Fletcher

 The complete range of Timothy Taylor beers (six in all) are always on offer. A Taylor's tied house, but special in that they always stock the complete range and most pubs only stock one or two.

T raditional old coaching inn with three small rooms downstairs and a meeting room upstairs. Pool room, outside seating. No food. Well-behaved children allowed.

OPEN *12–11pm (10.30pm Sun).*

HEBDEN BRIDGE

The Fox & Goose

9 Heptonstall Road, Hebden Bridge, West Yorkshire HX7 6AZ
☎ *(01422) 842649* Robin Starbuck

 Daleside Blonde Bitter always available plus three guest beers (300 per year) including Exmoor Gold, Old Mill Bitter, Fuller's London Pride and Orkney Dark Island. Many foreign beers and 30 different malt whiskies also stocked.

A small, friendly three-roomed pub with a wide variety of customers. Garden. No food. Children and dogs allowed, if kept under control. Off the A646.

OPEN *11.30am–3pm and 7–11pm.*

Stubbing Wharfe

King Street, Hebden Bridge, West Yorkshire HX7 6LU
☎ *(01422) 844107*
Dean Batty and Shelley Cockayne

 Up to four permanent real ales: Timothy Taylor Landlord, Greene King IPA, Black Sheep Bitter plus four guests such as Phoenix Wobbly Bob, Abbeydale Absolution, Archers Golden and Jennings Sneck Lifter.

S ituated on the edge of Hebden Bridge toward Todmorden, this is an eighteenth-century canal- and riverside pub, offering homemade food everyday and a function room to seat 50 people. Bridge Rats Motorcycle Club meet every Tuesday, Wednesday folk night and quiz night on Thursday, jazz, blues and storytelling are other regular events.

OPEN *11am–11pm Mon–Sat; 12–10.30pm Sun.*

The Golden Lion Inn

Main Street, Helperby, York, North Yorkshire
YO61 2NT
☎ *(01423) 360870* Pippa and Richard Heather

 A freehouse with four guest beers always available, including premium and strong beers for adventurous drinkers!

A traditional village country inn with stone floor and two log fires. Bar food always available. Home-cooked meals and 'nibbles' menu available weekends and weekday evenings (except Mon–Tues). A warm welcome for all, including families.

OPEN *12–11pm (10.30pm Sun).*

HOLMFIRTH

The Farmer's Arms

2–4 Liphill Bank Road, Holmfirth,
West Yorkshire, HD7 7DE
☎ *(01484) 683713* Mr Greensides

 Eastwood & Sanders Bargee, Black Sheep Special, Fuller's London Pride and something from Timothy Taylor permanently available, plus two constantly changing guests, such as Adnams Bitter or Broadside, Greene King Abbot and Eastwood's Best.

A traditional country village pub. No food. Children allowed until 8.30pm. Car park. From Compo's Café take the second turning on the right.

OPEN *5–11pm Mon–Fri; 11am–11pm Sat; 12–10.30pm Sun.*

HORBURY

Boon's

6 Queen Street, Horbury, Wakefield,
West Yorkshire WF4 6LP
☎ *(01924) 280442* John Bladen

 Timothy Taylor Landlord and Clark's Bitter regularly available, with up to four guest beers often from Adnams, Orkney, Shepherd Neame, Wychwood, Elgood's, Everards, Weltons, Ushers, Thwaites, Rebellion, Nethergate, Jennings, Hoskins, Greene King, Fuller's, Daleside, Bateman or Burton Bridge.

Traditional, single-bar olde-worlde pub with patio and beer garden. Established as a pub c.1710, it retains an open fire, beams and flagged floor. Walls hung with sporting pictures. Children welcome in beer garden and patio only.

OPEN *11am–3pm and 5–11pm Mon–Thur; 11am–11pm Fri–Sat; 12–10.30pm Sun.*

The King's Arms

27 New Street, Horbury, Wakefield,
West Yorkshire WF4 6NB
☎ *(01924) 264329* Mike Davidson

 A Marston's house with Pedigree, Bitter and others available, plus one guest pump regularly featuring a Banks's ale.

A one-bar village pub with wooden floors in bar area. Pool and games area. Conservatory, dining area, garden. Food currently available 5–7 pm. Children allowed.

OPEN *3–11pm Mon–Thurs; 12–11pm Fri–Sat; 12–4pm and 7–10.30pm Sun.*

HUDDERSFIELD

The Old Court Brewhouse

Queen Street, Huddersfield, West Yorkshire
HD1 2SL
☎ *(01484) 454035*

 Four Old Court Brewery beers produced and served on the premises.

A brewpub with the brewery part raised up from the lower floor and visible from the public bar. This listed building was formerly the county court. Bar and restaurant food available at lunchtime and evenings (Mon–Sat). Metered parking, garden.

COPPERS 3.4% ABV
M'LUD 3.5% ABV
1825 4.5% ABV
MAXIMUM SENTENCE 5.5% ABV

OPEN *Ring for details.*

Rat & Ratchet

40 Chapel Hill, Huddersfield, West Yorkshire
HD1 3EB
☎ *(01484) 516734*

 Fourteen ales at all times. Three home brews plus Adnams Best, Bateman Mild, Mansfield Old Baily, Marston's Pedigree, Timothy Taylor Landlord and several more.

The brewery opened at the Rat and Ratchet in December 1994. A popular pub with beer festivals and special events held regularly.

THE GREAT GNAWTHERN 4.0% ABV
THE GREAT ESCAPE 4.2% ABV
CRATCHET'S CHRISTMAS CRACKER 4.3% ABV

OPEN *12–11pm.*

HULL

Minerva Hotel

Nelson Street, Hull, East Yorkshire HU1 1XE
☎ *(01482) 326909* Eamon (Scotty) Scott

One or two guest beers regularly available, often from Orkney, Aviemore, Tomintoul, Harviestoun, Broughton, Rooster's, Young's, Abbeydale, Concertina, Woodforde's, West Yorkshire or Oakham.

Traditional, nineteenth-century pub built on the banks of the River Humber and packed with maritime memorabilia. Three main bars, plus nooks and possibly the smallest snug in Britain which seats three. Large portions of home-cooked food served lunchtimes and evenings Mon–Thurs, lunchtimes only Fri–Sun. Children welcome if taking a meal. Situated at the top of Queens Street.

11am–11pm Mon–Sat; 12–10.30pm Sun.

Springbank Tavern

29 Spring Bank, Hull, East Yorkshire HU3 1AS
☎ *(01482) 581879* Belinda Beaumont

Banks's Original always available plus two guest beers which could be something like Bateman XXXB or Brakspear Special.

A one-room alehouse with traditional games (darts, dominoes and pool). Students and locals provide mixed clientele. Background music, but no juke box. Bar food available 12–2pm daily (12–6pm Sunday). Beer garden. Street parking, disabled facilities. Children allowed in the bar for meals. Just off the city centre.

11am–11pm Mon–Sat; 12–10.30pm Sun.

Ye Olde Black Boy

150 High Street, Hull, East Yorkshire HU1 1PS
☎ *(01482) 326516* Lee Kirman

Six weekly changing guest beers served (300 per year), from breweries such as Rooster's, Timothy Taylor, Hop Back, Greene King, Titanic and Harviestoun.

The original building dates back to 1331. Traditional wood-panelled walls and floors. Upstairs bar open for food at lunchtimes and on Friday and Saturday evenings. Bar food available at lunchtime and evenings. Function room, pool and darts. Parking. Children allowed in the upstairs bar when having food. Situated on the Old High Street, next to the River Hull.

12–11pm (10.30pm Sun).

IDLE

Symposium

7 Albion Road, Idle, Bradford, West Yorkshire BD10 9PY
☎ *(01274) 616587* Karen Harker

Timothy Taylor Landlord always available plus five guests from northern breweries. Also a guest Belgian ale, often Erdinger WeissBier, and a range of over 30 bottled Belgian and German beers.

A traditional ale and wine bar with a non-smoking snug. Separate restaurant with food available every day. Children allowed at the landlord's discretion. Situated in the centre of Idle village, close to the Green.

12–2.30pm and 5.30–11pm Mon–Thurs; 12–11pm Fri–Sat; 12–10.30pm Sun.

ILKLEY

Bar T'At

7 Cunliffe Road, Ilkley, West Yorkshire LS29 9DZ
☎ *(01943) 608888* Simon Wright

Timothy Taylor Landlord always available plus three guests from northern breweries. Erdinger WeissBier (a Belgian beer) also always on offer and a range of over 30 bottled Belgian and German beers.

A traditional ale and wine bar on two floors. Non-smoking area in the 'cellar'. Food available every day. Children allowed in the 'cellar' only. Adjacent to the central main car park.

12–11pm (10.30pm Sun).

INGLETON

The Wheatsheaf Inn

22 High Street, Ingleton, North Yorkshire LA6 3AD
☎ *(01524) 241275* Mr Thompson

A freehouse with Black Sheep Bitter, Special and Riggwelter plus Moorhouse's Pendle Witches Brew among the beers always available.

An olde-worlde one-bar country pub with dining area and beer garden. Disabled access. Accommodation. Food available at lunchtime and evenings. Children allowed.

12–11pm (10.30pm Sun).

The Old White Bear

6 Keighley Road, Crosshills, Keighley,
West Yorkshire BD20 7RN
☎ *(01535) 632115* The Naylor Family

 One brew produced and served on the premises, plus guests beers such as Timothy Taylor Landlord.

The pub was built in 1735 and retains its original beams. Brewing began in the old stables here in 1993. The current owners took over in 2001, and the pub's new brewer (since May 2002) intends to extend the range of beers produced. Bar and restaurant food available at lunchtime and evenings. Car park, small garden. Children allowed if kept under control.

 BEST BITTER 3.9% ABV

 11.30am–3pm and 5–11pm Mon–Thurs (not Mon lunch); 11.30am–11pm Fri–Sat; 12–4pm and 7–10.30pm Sun.

The Worth Valley Inn

1 Wesley Place, Halifax Road, Keighley,
West Yorkshire BD21 5BB
☎ *(01535) 603539* Kevin Sutcliffe

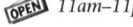 Castle Eden ale permanently available, plus a range of changing guest real ales.

Situated very near to the Keighley and Worth Valley railway, this is a small local with passing trade from the railway. Food available lunchtimes and evenings. Children allowed.

 11am–11pm Mon–Sat; 12–10.30pm Sun.

The George & Dragon Hotel

17 Market Place, Kirkbymoorside,
North Yorkshire YO62 6AA
☎ *(01751) 433334* Mrs E Walker

 A Black Sheep ale and a selection of guest beers usually available.

Cosy, beamed bar with blazing log fire in winter, plus a collection of cricket, rugby and golf memorabilia for the sports enthusiast. Food served 12–2.15pm and 6.30–9.15pm Mon–Sat and 7–9.15pm Sun. Car park. Children welcome – there is an enclosed garden, but no other special facilities.

 10am–11pm Mon–Sat; 12–10.30pm Sun.

Blind Jacks

19 Market Place, Knaresborough, North Yorkshire
HG5 8AL
☎ *(01423) 869148*
Paul and Debbie Holden-Ridgway

 Eight real ales always available. Timothy Taylor Landlord, Village Brewer's White Boar, Daleside Green Grass Old Rogue Ale and Black Sheep Bitter are always on offer, and the four guests, which always include a mild, regularly feature beers from Rooster's, Daleside, Durham and Boat breweries.

A seventeenth-century listed building, beamed with wooden floors and lots of mirrors. Non-smoking room available. No food. No children. Parking nearby. Dogs allowed.

 5.30–11pm Mon; 4–11pm Tues–Thur; 12–11pm Fri–Sat; 12–10.30pm Sun.

The Steam Packet Inn

Racca Green, Knottingley, West Yorkshire
WF11 8AT
☎ *(01977) 677266*
Colin (Jack) and Margaret Horner

 A John Smith's house stocking a good range of changing guest ales on two hand pumps. Charles Wells Bombardier and Phoenix ales are regular features, but all independent breweries are possible.

A small-town pub, recently refurbished, with lounge bar, public bar, function room and beer garden. Food available 12–4pm Mon–Fri. Children allowed but not at the bar.

 All day, every day.

Moorcock Inn

Langdale End, Scarborough, North Yorkshire
☎ *(01723) 882268* Susan Mathewson

 A Daleside beer and Malton Golden Chance are regularly available, plus a guest beer.

Unspoilt, two-bar country pub with hatch servery. No music or machines. Food served every lunchtime and evening during the summer; Thur–Sun evenings and Sat–Sun lunch in the winter. Well-behaved children welcome until 9pm. Situated at the Scarborough end of Forrest Drive.

 Summer: 11.30am–2.30pm and 6.30–11pm Mon–Sat; 12–3pm and 7–10.30pm; Winter: 6.30–11pm Wed–Sat; 7–10.30pm Sun (N.B. RING FIRST TO BE SURE).

LEEDS

The City of Mabgate
45 Mabgate, Leeds, West Yorkshire LS9 7DR
☎ *(01132) 457789 Mr K Broughton*

Black Sheep Bitter and Timothy Taylor Landlord among the brews always available plus up to four guests such as Fuller's London Pride or other beers from smaller breweries such as Rooster's and Durham. Beers change frequently, usually every day; the record is Eldridge Pope Royal Oak, which changed after two hours!

A town-centre pub, winner of CAMRA's Pub of the Year 1998. Two bars, non-smoking area and garden. Food available 12–2pm Mon–Fri. Children allowed until 7pm.

12–11pm Mon–Sat; 12–4pm and 7.30–10.30pm Sun.

The Duck & Drake
43 Kirkgate, Leeds, West Yorkshire LS2 7DR
☎ *(0113) 246 5806 Mr and Mrs Morley*

Timothy Taylor Landlord always available plus six guests (300 per year) from breweries including Jennings, Clark's, Exmoor, Rooster's and Pioneer. Also real cider.

A traditional alehouse with wooden floors, coal fires, bare boards and live bands. Bar food served at lunchtime. Get to Leeds market and ask for directions.

All day, every day.

The Eagle Tavern
North Street, Sheepscar, Leeds, West Yorkshire LS2 1AF
☎ *(0113) 245 7146 Mr Vaughan*

A Samuel Smith tied house. Old Brewery Bitter always available, plus other seasonal ales.

An 1826 Georgian building close to the city centre. CAMRA Yorkshire Pub of the Year 1995. Bar food available at lunchtime and evenings. Occasional live music. Parking. Ten minutes' walk out of the city centre. B&B accommodation.

11.30am–2.30pm and 5.30–11pm Mon–Fri; 11.30am–2.30pm and 6–11pm Sat; 12–3pm and 7–10.30pm Sun.

The Old Vic
17 Whitecote Hill, Leeds, West Yorkshire LS13 3LB
☎ *(0113) 256 1207 Craig Seddon*

A freehouse with Timothy Taylor Landlord and Black Sheep Bitter among the brews always available, plus four guests from breweries such as Coach House and Hambleton.

Three rooms plus a function room decorated with old Bramley photographs. Patio. Disabled access and toilets. Situated on the outskirts of town. No food. Well-behaved children allowed.

4–11pm Mon–Thurs; 2–11pm Fri; 11am–11pm Sat; 12–3pm and 7–10.30pm Sun.

LINTHWAITE

Sair Inn
Lane Top, Linthwaite, Huddersfield, West Yorkshire HD7 5SG
☎ *(01484) 842370*

Ten Linfit beers are brewed and served on the premises.

Home of the award-winning Linfit Brewery, which began production in 1982 for the Sair Inn and free trade. The pub is a traditional nineteenth-century inn with four rooms, stone floors and open fires. Parking in road. Children allowed in any of the three rooms away from the bar.

DARK MILD 3.0% ABV
BITTER 3.7% ABV
CASCADE 4.2% ABV
GOLD MEDAL 4.2% ABV
SPECIAL 4.3% ABV
AUTUMN GOLD 4.7% ABV
ENGLISH GUINEAS STOUT 5.3% ABV
OLD ELI 5.3% ABV
LEADBOILER 6.6% ABV
ENOCH'S HAMMER 8.0% ABV

7–11pm Mon–Thurs; 5–11pm Fri; 12–11pm Sat and public holidays; 12–10.30pm Sun.

LIVERSEDGE

The Black Bull

37 Halifax Road, Liversedge, West Yorkshire
WF15 6JR
☎ *(01924) 403779* Mr Toulson

 A freehouse with Timothy Taylor Landlord and Black Sheep Special always available, plus four guests such as Samuel Smith Old Brewery Bitter, Glentworth Light Year or a Clark's brew. Also seasonals, specials and celebration ales as available.

Two bars, beamed ceilings. Disabled access at rear. No food. Children allowed in the afternoons only. Situated out of town.

12–4pm and 7–11pm Mon–Thurs; all day Fri; 11am–4pm and 7–11pm Sat; 12–4pm and 7–10.30pm Sun.

The Cross Keys

283 Halifax Road, Liversedge, West Yorkshire
WF15 6NE
☎ *(01274) 873294* Paul George Stephenson

 Marston's Bitter and Pedigree regularly available.

Open-plan, community-style pub, with Sky TV and regular quiz nights. Food served Sat–Sun lunchtimes and Wed–Sat evenings. Car park.

5–11pm Mon–Fri; 11am–11pm Sat; 12–10.30pm Sun.

LONGWOOD

Dusty Miller

2 Giled Road, Longwood, Huddersfield,
West Yorkshire HD4
☎ *(01484) 651763* John Drummond

 Black Sheep Special, Eastwood & Sanders Best and Timothy Taylor Landlord and Best always available plus a guest from Phoenix, Golden Hill or Brakspear.

A seventeenth-century village pub for real ale lovers – a drinkers' pub. No food. Children allowed. Patio.

5–11pm Mon–Fri; 11am–11pm Sat; 12–10.30pm Sun.

LUND

The Wellington Inn

19 The Green, Lund, Driffield, East Yorkshire
YO25 9TE
☎ *(01377) 217294* Russell Jeffrey

 A freehouse with Timothy Taylor Landlord and Dark Mild and Black Sheep Best always available, plus one other constantly changing guest ale, usually from local Yorkshire micro-breweries.

A two-bar country village pub with three log fires, flag floors and patio. Bar food available at lunchtime and a separate restaurant is open in the evenings. Children allowed

7–11pm only Mon; 12–3pm and 7–11pm Tues–Sat (10.30pm Sun).

MALTON

The Kings Head

5 Market Place, Malton, North Yorkshire
YO17 7LP
☎ *(01653) 692289* Caroline Norris

 Four guest beers regularly available, which may include Ruddles County, Marston's Pedigree or Morland Old Speckled Hen.

Traditional-style pub with lounge bar and tap room. A la carte menu and sandwiches available 12–2.30pm and 7–9pm Tues–Sat, and 12–2.30pm Sun. Car park opposite pub. No children.

11am–3pm and 7–11pm Mon–Sat; 12–3pm and 7–10.30pm Sun.

Suddaby's Crown Hotel

Wheelgate, Malton, North Yorkshire YO17 7HP
☎ *(01653) 697580* RN Suddaby

Malton Double Chance, Pickwick's Porter and Auld Bob available, plus guests.

The Malton Brewery Company was formed in 1984 in the converted stables behind Suddaby's Crown Hotel. The first pint was pulled in February 1985. The pub is a traditional inn, full of character and located in the town centre. It is popular with locals and visitors alike. No background music or juke box, but pub games and TV showing the latest starting prices for the day's horse racing meetings. Bar food served lunchtimes Fri–Sat. Sandwiches available Mon–Thurs lunchtimes. Parking, children's room. Accommodation.

DOUBLE CHANCE BITTER 3.8% ABV
Fruity with good hoppy bitterness.
GOLDEN CHANCE 4.2% ABV
Dark, flavoursome and fruity.
PICKWICK'S PORTER 4.2% ABV
Dark, smooth and malty.
RYEDALE LIGHT 4.5% ABV
Refreshing straw-coloured bitter.
Plus seasonal and occasional brews.

11am–11pm Mon–Sat; 12–4pm and 7–10.30pm Sun.

MARSDEN

Riverhead Inn
2 Peel Street, Marsden, Huddersfield,
West Yorkshire HD7 6BR
☎ *(01484) 841270* Philip Holdsworth

 Home of the Riverhead Brewery with seven pumps selling only Riverhead ales which are brewed on the premises.

A real pub for drinking and chatting with no juke box or bandit machines. View into the brewery from the pub to watch the brewing. No food.

SPARTH MILD 3.6% ABV
BUTTERLY BITTER 3.8% ABV
DEERHILL PORTER 4.0% ABV
CUPWITH LIGHT BITTER 4.2% ABV
BLACKMOSS STOUT 4.3% ABV
MARCH HAIGH BITTER 4.6% ABV
REDBROOK PREMIUM 5.5% ABV

Occasional celebration and seasonal ales including Ruffled Feathers which is brewed for the local Cuckoo Festival.

OPEN *5–11pm Mon–Thurs (closed lunchtimes); 4–11pm Fri (closed lunchtime); 11am–11pm Sat; 12–10.30pm Sun.*

MELMERBY

The George & Dragon Inn
Main Street, Melmerby, Nr Ripon,
North Yorkshire
☎ *(01765) 640970* Mike Halladay

 Black Sheep Bitter and Hambleton Best Bitter always available, plus one guest which might be a Village Brewer or Daleside ale.

Specialising in good ale, wine and food, this pub has two comfortable bars and a small dining room. Food available 6–9pm Tues–Fri; 12–2pm and 6–9pm Sat–Sun (no food Mon). Children welcome. Car park.

OPEN *5–11pm Mon–Fri; 12–11pm Sat; 12–10.30pm Sun.*

MEXBOROUGH

The Falcon
12 Main Street, Mexborough, South Yorkshire
S64 9DW
☎ *(01709) 513084* Mr Seedring

Old Mill Bitter always available plus several seasonal, celebration or guest ales.

A traditional brewery tap room situated out of the town centre. No food. No children.

OPEN *All day Mon–Sat; 12–3pm and 7–10.30pm Sun.*

MIDDLESBROUGH

Doctor Brown's
135 Corporation Road, Middlesbrough,
North Yorkshire TS1 2RR
☎ *(01642) 213213* Tony Linklater

 At least three regularly changing guest ales are always available, plus a selection of seasonal ales.

It is claimed that this town-centre pub, built in 1868, feels nothing like a town-centre pub! Live music every Fri and Sat. Food available at lunchtimes on weekdays and match days. Outdoor café-style seating area (weather permitting!). Disabled facilities. The pub is within easy reach of Middlesbrough centre and Riverside Stadium.

OPEN *All day, every day.*

The Isaac Wilson
61 Wilson Street, Middlesbrough, North
Yorkshire TS1 1SB
☎ *(01642) 247708* Norma Hardisty

 Up to six guests, with Timothy Taylor Landlord a regular feature.

A town pub with food available 11am–10pm daily. No music or TV. Non-smoking area, disabled access. Children allowed 11am–5pm, if eating.

OPEN *All day, every day.*

NORTH DUFFIELD

The King's Arms
Main Street, North Duffield, Selby,
North Yorkshire YO8 5RG
☎ *(01757) 288492* Martin Lamb

 A freehouse with Black Sheep Bitter always available plus up to three guests such as Timothy Taylor Landlord or ales from Greene King, Adnams or local independent brewers.

A village pub with one bar, beamed ceilings and inglenook fireplace. Bar food available, plus restaurant menu in non-smoking restaurant during evenings only. Children allowed. Beer garden.

OPEN *4–11pm Mon–Fri; all day Sat–Sun.*

NORTH HOWDEN

Barnes Wallis Inn

Station Road, North Howden, Nr Goole,
East Yorkshire DN14 7LF
☎ *(01430) 430639* Philip Teare

 Hambleton Best Bitter and Black Sheep Best Bitter regularly served, with a constantly changing range of three guest beers which are rarely repeated unless requested. Previous beers have been from Black Dog, Whitby, Kitchen, York, Brown Cow, Selby, Malton, Cropton, Marston Moor, Eccleshall, Rooster's and many more.

Traditional, small, real ale house with a permanent exhibition of Barnes Wallis (and other) prints. Large main garden and small sheltered one. Barbecue. Food available Sat evening and Sun lunch (bookings only). Large car park. Children welcome, but no special facilities. Situated adjacent to railway station.

OPEN *7–11pm Mon; 5–11pm Tues–Fri;*
12–11pm Sat; 12–10.30pm Sun.

NORTHALLERTON

Tithe Bar & Brasserie

2 Friarage Street, Northallerton, North Yorkshire
DL6 1DP
☎ *(01609) 778482* Mr Grimston

Timothy Taylor Landlord, Black Sheep Bitter and a Hambleton ale always available, plus three guests. Regular breweries featured include Moorhouse, Hadrian and Border, Salamander, North Yorkshire, Boat, Rudgate, Ossett, Wentworth, Pheonix and Goose Eye. Also a range of Belgian beers.

Built in the old tithe barn of Northallerton, this is a traditional real ale house. Extensive menu with food served from 12–3pm and 6–9.30pm daily in an upstairs brasserie restaurant. Children allowed before 7pm, if accompanied. Located just off the High Street, close to Friarage Hospital.

OPEN *12–11pm Mon–Sat; 12–10.30pm Sun.*

OLD MIXENDEN

The Hebble Brook

2 Mill Lane, Old Mixenden, Halifax,
West Yorkshire HX2 8UH
☎ *(01422) 242059* Teresa Ratcliffe

 Black Sheep Special always available plus Old Mill Nellie Dean most of the time. Also up to five guests such as Thwaites Bloomin' Ale and Daniel's Hammer or Banbury Old Vic.

A country community pub with lounge and games room. Stone floors in the games room, open fires, wooden ceilings in lounge, garden. Food currently available at lunchtime. No children.

OPEN *12–3pm and 5.30–11pm Mon–Thurs;*
all day Fri–Sun.

OSSETT

The Brewer's Pride

Low Mill Road, Healey Road, Ossett,
West Yorkshire WF5 8ND
☎ *(01924) 273865* Sally Walker

 A brewpub, home of the Ossett Brewing Company. Excelsior and Special Bitter always available as well as Timothy Taylor Landlord. Also up to four guests from breweries such as Durham, Morland, Coach House and Cottage.

A traditional real ale house in an old stone building in the old Healy Mills area. No music, etc. Open fires, beer garden. The Ossett Brewing Co. is on site with brewery tours available. Food available 12–2pm Mon–Sat, and Wednesday evenings. Children allowed up to 8pm.

OPEN *12–3pm and 5.30–11pm Mon–Thurs;*
all day Fri–Sun and bank holidays

The Red Lion

73 Dewsbury Road, Ossett, West Yorkshire
WF5 9NQ
☎ *(01924) 273487* Peter Trafford

A brewpub, home of Red Lion Ales, with White Lion and at least one other home ale always available. Plus one guest which may be from breweries such as Phoenix, RCH and Rooster's.

A traditional old English pub with low ceiling, beams, brasses, dining area, and outside seating between the brewery and the pub. Food available every lunchtime and Tues–Sat evening. Sunday roasts available 12–8pm. Children allowed. Located off J40 of the M1, towards Dewsbury.

WHITE LION 4.3% ABV
GOLDEN LION 4.5% ABV
YAKIMA PALE ALE 4.5% ABV
MAJESTIC 5.2% ABV
Plus specials.

OPEN *12–11pm (10.30pm Sun).*

OUTWOOD

The Kirklands Hotel

605 Leeds Road, Outwood, Wakefield,
West Yorkshire WF1 2LU
☎ *(01924) 826666* Christopher D Cook

Old Mill Traditional Bitter and Bullion are permanently served, plus another Old Mill brew of 4.0–4.2% ABV, changed monthly, such as Summer Sunshine.

An olde-worlde hotel with bar featuring brick fireplaces and a library. Food served 12–2pm Mon, 12–2pm and 6–9pm Tues–Sat, 12–5pm Sun. Children welcome, but no special facilities. Car park. Situated on main Wakefield to Leeds road, next door to the church in Outwood.

OPEN *11am–11pm.*

PONTEFRACT

The Counting House

Swales Yard, Pontefract, West Yorkshire WF8 1DG
☎ *(01977) 600388* Helen Clayworth

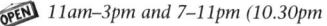 No permanent beers, just a changing range of up to eight ales from breweries such as Black Sheep, Jennings and Old Mill.

A town pub on two levels in a medieval building. Food available at lunchtime only. Children allowed.

 11am–3pm and 7–11pm (10.30pm Sun).

POOL-IN-WHARFEDALE

The Hunter's Inn

Harrogate Road, Pool-in-Wharfedale, Nr Otley, North Yorkshire LS21 2PS
☎ *(0113) 284 1090* Geoff Nunn

Seven guest beers always available (300+ per year), including brews from Abbeydale, Black Sheep, Cropton, Daleside, Durham, Enville, Everards, Fuller's, Goose Eye, Hook Norton, Sarah Hughes, Jennings, Kelham Island, Moorhouse's, Oakham, Greene King, Rooster's, Outlaw, Ossett, Rudgate, Slaters (Eccleshall), Hambleton, Black Dog, Marston Moor and many others from all over the country.

P ub with real ale, real fire and real characters, from bikers to business people. Warm, friendly welcome. Bar food available 12–2.30pm every day except Tuesdays. Car park, garden patio with tables and chairs, pool table, juke box, stone fireplace. Children are allowed but not encouraged too much (no play area). One mile from Pool-in-Wharfedale, on the Harrogate road. Seven miles from Harrogate.

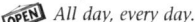 *All day, every day.*

PUDSEY

The Commercial Hotel

48 Chapetown, Pudsey, West Yorkshire LS28 8BS
☎ *(0113) 2577153* Michelle Farr

A freehouse serving a range of real ales.

A lively town pub with Friday evening disco, Saturday evening '60s and '70s music and live entertainment once a month. Free dripping and black pudding on the bar on Sundays. Patio. No children.

 *All day, every day.*

QUARMBY

Field Head

Quarmby Road, Quarmby, West Yorkshire HD3 4FB
☎ *(01484) 654581* Russ Beverly

 Up to three guest ales from breweries such as Adnams, Bateman, Fuller's and Greene King.

A community village pub built 1920. Live country music on Tuesdays. No food. Children allowed. Beer garden. Car park.

 4–11pm Mon–Thurs; 3–11pm Fri; 12–11pm Sat; 12–10.30pm Sun.

RIPON

One Eyed Rat

51 Allhallowgate, Ripon, North Yorkshire HG4 1LQ
☎ *(01765) 607704* Les Moon

Timothy Taylor Landlord and Black Sheep Bitter always available, plus four guests, constantly changing, which may be from Rooster's, Durham, Hambledon, Fuller's or any other independent brewery. No beers from national breweries served. A real freehouse.

U nspoilt, terraced pub, very popular. Superb beer garden. No food, no music, no TV, but fine ales and good conversation. Children allowed in beer garden only. Website: www.oneeyedrat.co.uk.

 6–11pm Mon–Wed; 12–3.30pm and 6–11pm Thur–Fri (open 5.30pm Fri); 12–11pm Sat; 12–3.30pm and 7–10.30pm Sun.

RIPPONDEN

The Old Bridge Inn

Priest Lane, Ripponden, Sowerby Bridge, West Yorkshire HX6 4DF
☎ *(01422) 822595* Tim and Lindsay Walker

Moorhouse's Premier, Black Sheep Best Bitter, Timothy Taylor Golden Best, Best Bitter and Landlord regularly available, plus a guest beer which might be from Kitchen, Old Mill, Burton Bridge, Joseph Holt, Fuller's, St Austell or Gale's.

H istoric pub in lovely riverside setting. Open fires in winter and flowers in summer. Award-winning window boxes and hanging baskets all year round. Homemade food prepared on the premises: full bar menu on weekday evenings and Sat–Sun lunchtimes; help-yourself carved buffet served during the week. Car park. Children welcome until 8.30pm.

12–3pm and 5.30–11pm Mon–Fri; 12–11pm Sat; 12–10.30pm Sun.

ROTHERHAM

Limes

38 Broom Lane, Rotherham, South Yorkshire
☎ *(01709) 363431* E Daykin

 Camerons Strongarm, plus Banks's Bitter and Original regularly available.

This is a popular hotel situated on the outskirts of the town centre with a small hotel atmosphere. Food served all day, every day. Car park. Children welcome, but no special facilities.

OPEN *11am–11pm Mon–Sat; 12–10.30pm Sun.*

The Waverley

Brinsworth Road, Catcliffe, Rotherham, South Yorkshire S60 5RW
☎ *(01709) 360906* Ron Woodthorpe

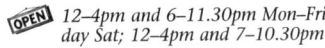 A freehouse with four hand pumps serving a range of guest brews. Regular breweries supported include Glentworth, Slaters (Eccleshall), Drummonds, Banks's and Timothy Taylor.

A large suburban pub with separate lounge and children's room, garden and play area. Disabled access and toilets. Food available at lunchtime and evenings. Children allowed in children's room only.

OPEN *12–4pm and 6–11.30pm Mon–Fri; all day Sat; 12–4pm and 7–10.30pm Sun.*

SCARBOROUGH

Cellar's

35–7 Valley Road, Scarborough, North Yorkshire YO11 2LX
☎ *(01723) 367158* Brian Witty

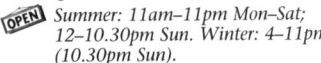 Black Sheep Bitter permanently available, plus one constantly changing guest. Ales from Rudgate, Slaters or Durham are regularly featured.

A basement real ale bar with holiday flats and a restaurant above. Beer garden and patio, past winner of Scarborough in Bloom Award. Bar food available at lunchtime and evenings in summer only. Children allowed.

OPEN *Summer: 11am–11pm Mon–Sat; 12–10.30pm Sun. Winter: 4–11pm (10.30pm Sun).*

The Cricketers

119 North Marine Road, Scarborough, North Yorkshire YO1 7HU
☎ *(01723) 365864* Stuart Neilson

 York Yorkshire Terrier and Timothy Taylor Landlord always available, plus two rotating guest ales. All brews from all breweries are stocked when available. Also Weston's Old Rosie Cloudy Scrumpy available on hand pump.

A friendly real ale pub for anyone. Two bars, sea views, beer garden. Food, specialising in steaks and Stuart's Steak and Ale Pie, available until 9pm daily. Children allowed. Disabled access and facilities. Situated opposite the Cricket Ground.

OPEN *11am–11pm Mon–Sat; 12–10.30pm Sun.*

The Highlander

15–16 The Esplanade, Scarborough, North Yorkshire YO11 2AF
☎ *(01723) 373426* Mrs Dawson

 Young's IPA among the brews always available, plus up to five guests such as Barnsley Bitter, Black Dog Whitby Abbey Ale, Wyre Piddle Piddle in the Wind, Wychwood Dog's Bollocks and Fisherman's Whopper. Also a good selection of whiskies.

On the South Cliff Esplanade, a traditional pub with real fires. Food available at lunchtime only in a separate dining area. Children allowed until 6pm. Patio. Accommodation.

OPEN *11am–11pm (10.30pm Sun).*

The Hole in the Wall

26–30 Vernon Road, Scarborough, North Yorkshire YO11 2PS
☎ *(01723) 373746* Cheryll Roberts

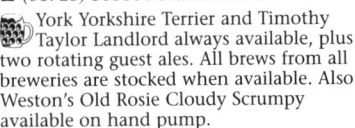 Four to six guest beers on offer each month, from breweries such as Caledonian, Jennings, Ridleys, Brains, Gale's, Everards, Hyde's, Charles Wells, St Austell, Brakspear, Old Mill, Smiles, Aviemore, Bateman and Timothy Taylor, to name but a few!

A traditional wooden-floored real ale pub in a town location, recently refurbished. No music, no games. Home-cooked pub grub available all day Mon–Sat, and Sun 12–3pm. Children welcome until 8pm if eating. Dogs welcome.

OPEN *11am–11pm Mon–Sat; 12–10.30pm Sun.*

Indigo Alley

4 North Marine Road, Scarborough,
North Yorkshire YO12 7PD
☎ *(01723) 381900* Graham Forrest

 A freehouse with six regularly changing guest beers perhaps from Rooster's, Timothy Taylor, Kelham Island, Swale or Hambleton, but could be from anywhere in the UK (over 1,000 different ones in three years). Belgian beers such as Leffe (Brun and Blond) and Hoegaarden also stocked.

Wooden-floored, town-centre bar specialising in ever-changing guest beers and live music on Tues, Wed, Thurs and Sun evenings. No food. No children.

OPEN *3–11pm Mon–Fri; 1–11pm Sat;*
1–10.30pm Sun.
Extra hours Fri–Sun Jun–Sept.

The Scalby Mills Hotel

Scalby Mills Road, Scarborough, North Yorkshire
YO12 6RP
☎ *(01723) 500449* Lorna Baxter

 A selection of Daleside and Black Sheep ales permanently available, plus a choice of four guests, changing all the time.

A seaside freehouse built in an old mill with the Cleveland Way behind it. Two bars, original stonework and beams. Outside seating. Food available at lunchtime only. Children allowed until 6pm. Dogs allowed in the smaller of the two bars. Situated near the Sealife Centre.

OPEN *All day, every day.*

The Tap & Spile

94 Falsgrave Road, Scarborough, North Yorkshire
YO12 5AZ
☎ *(01723) 363837* IM Kilpatrick and V Office

Big Lamp Bitter always available plus guest ales including Bateman, Jennings and Old Mill brews and Tap & Spile Premium. Also two guest ciders.

A lovely old coaching inn with low beams, old Yorkshire stone floor and non-smoking room. Bar food available 11.30am–3pm Mon–Fri, 11.30am–4.30pm Sat, 12.30–3pm Sun. Car park, garden, children's room. Turn left out of the railway station, going towards the roundabout.

OPEN *11am–11pm.*

SELBY

The Albion Vaults

1 The Crescent, New Street, Selby, North
Yorkshire YO8 4PT
☎ *(01757) 213817* Patrick Mellors

An Old Mill Brewery tied house serving only Old Mill ales. Old Traditional and Bullion always available, plus either Old Curiosity, Springs Eternal or Nellie Dean.

An old dark-wood pub with brick fireplaces, taproom and lounge. Beer garden, disabled access. Food available at lunchtime and evenings. Organises brewery tours of The Old Mill Brewery, which is four miles away, during October–April. Children allowed up to 7pm.

OPEN *12–11pm (10.30pm Sun).*

The Royal Oak

70 Ousegate, Selby, North Yorkshire YO8 4NJ
☎ *(01757) 291163* Simon Compton

 Three guest pumps with ales such as Timothy Taylor Landlord, Eccleshall Top Totty or Swale Indian Summer Pale Ale.

A real ale pub comprising a balance of the traditional and the modern: live music in a Grade II listed building with wooden floors and original beams. Beer garden. No food. Children allowed on Sunday afternoons only.

OPEN *12–11pm (10.30pm Sun).*

SHEFFIELD

The Broadfield

Abbeydale Road, Sheffield, South Yorkshire S7 1FR
☎ *(0114) 255 0200*
Hannah Creasy and Martin Bedford

Guests such as Morland Old Speckled Hen, Wadworth 6X and brews from Kelham Island and Black Sheep are served. Only popular beers, such as Kelham Island Pale Rider, are repeated, and requests are encouraged!

A two-bar pub with snooker and pool room and beer garden. Just out of the town centre. Food available 12–7pm daily, plus Sunday breakfast at 11am. Children allowed if eating.

OPEN *11am–11pm Mon–Sat; 11am*
(for breakfast)–10.30pm Sun.

Cask & Cutler

1 Henry Street, Infirmary Road, Sheffield,
South Yorkshire S3 7EQ
☎ *(0114) 249 2295* Neil Clarke

 Seven regularly changing guest beers (4000 beers served to date), including a pale, hoppy bitter, a mild and a stout or porter. Main breweries used are Durham, Glentworth, Ossett, Tigertops, Townes and Oldershaw. No nationals. Also serve Weston's Old Rosie cider and Gwatkins Perry. There is a micro-brewery at the rear of the pub which is currently brewing on a small scale, mainly for festivals. There are plans to run the brewery at a full capacity in the future.

A largely unspoilt street-corner local with two rooms, one non-smoking. Sheffield CAMRA Pub of the Year 2001 (also 1995 and 1999). On-street parking. Real fire in cold weather. Beer garden. Situated 100 yards from Shalesmoor supertram stop. Adjacent to the junction of the A61 and B6079, one mile north of the city centre.

OPEN *5.30–11pm Mon; 12–2pm and 5.30–11pm Tues–Thur; 12–11pm Fri–Sat; 12–3pm and 7–10.30pm Sun.*

East House

19 Spital Hill, Sheffield, South Yorkshire S4 7LG
☎ *(0114) 272 6916* Rita Fielding

 A freehouse with Timothy Taylor Landlord and Abbeydale Moonshine among the beers always available, plus one guest such as Morland Old Speckled Hen or Timothy Taylor Dark Mild or Golden Best.

A student pub, situated conveniently close to the local curry houses! No food. Children allowed until 8pm.

OPEN *Closed during day; 6–11pm Mon–Sat; 7–10.30pm Sun.*

The Fat Cat

23 Alma Street, Sheffield, South Yorkshire S3 8SA
☎ *(0114) 249 4801*

 Three beers from its own Kelham Island brewery and something from Timothy Taylor always available, plus six alternating guest beers.

This olde-worlde pub is a Kelham Island Brewery tap, situated a short walk from the city centre, with separate smoking and non-smoking rooms. Voted one of the top five urban pubs in Britain in *The Times*, 1999. No music, no fruit machines. Award-winning home-cooked food is served at lunchtimes, and always includes vegetarian and vegan dishes. Beer garden, open fires. Children- and animal-friendly. Privately owned and fiercely independent! Website:www.thefatcat.co.uk.

OPEN *12–3pm and 5.30–11pm Mon–Sat; 12–3pm and 7–10.30pm Sun.*

The Frog & Parrot

Division Street, Sheffield, South Yorkshire S1 4GF
☎ *(0114) 272 1280* Mr Perkins

 A brewpub with Roger and Out always available, plus four guest beers, changed weekly.

A one-bar town pub, a young person's venue, particularly at weekends. Bar food available at lunchtime from 12–2pm and 12" pizzas served in the evenings until 11pm. No children.

ROGER AND OUT 12.6% ABV
Served in third-of-a-pint measures.

OPEN *11am–11pm (10.30pm Sun).*

The Gardener's Rest

105 Neepsend Lane, Sheffield, South Yorkshire S3 8AT
☎ *(0114) 272 4978* Pat Wilson

 Timothy Taylor Landlord, Golden Best, Porter and Best Bitter, Wentworth Needle's Eye and WPA (Wentworth Pale Ale) permanently available, plus four guests from breweries all over the UK plus some from France and Belgium. There is always a wheat and a fruit beer on.

A traditional backstreet pub with modern conservatory and beer garden on the river bank. No juke box but traditional pub games like bar billiards. Disabled access and facilities, non-smoking room. No food. Situated close to the city centre and on bus and tram routes, but ring for directions if necessary.

OPEN *12–11pm (10.30pm Sun).*

The Hillsborough Hotel

54–8 Langsett Road, Sheffield, South Yorkshire S6 2UB
☎ *(0114) 232 2100* Del Tilling

 A brewpub with home-brewed ales Loxley Gold, Stannington Stout and Hillsborough Pale Ale always available. Guest beers served on five other pumps. Regulars include Oakham JHB and beers from independents such as Durham, Wentworth and other local micro-breweries. Festival specials and seasonals stocked where possible.

A hotel with a dedicated real ale bar where the landlord is a real ale buff. Quiet, traditional atmosphere with no juke box. Baguettes and bar snacks available all opening hours. Well-behaved children allowed. Sun terrace and conservatory. Located on the super tram route.

HILLSBOROUGH PALE ALE 3.9% ABV
LOXLEY GOLD 4.5% ABV
STANNINGTON STOUT 5.0% ABV

OPEN *4.30–11pm Thurs–Sun only.*

The New Barrack Tavern
*601 Penistone Road, Sheffield, South Yorkshire
S6 2GA*
☎ *(0114) 234 9148* James Birkett

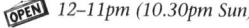Abbeydale Moonshine, Wentworth WPA, Barnsley Bitter and five guest beers usually available. Breweries featured include Abbeydale, Wentworth, Rooster's, Wye Valley, Kitchen, Kelham Island, Concertina, Swale, Ossett, Rudgate, Okells, Timothy Taylor, Brakspear, Holt, Hydes' Anvil, Woodforde's, Beartown, Cains, Oakham, Skinner's, Hop Back, Daleside and many others.

Large, award-winning pub offering a wide selection of draught and bottled beers and excellent food. Regular live music. Non-smoking room and attractive beer garden. Food served 12–2.30pm and 6–8pm Mon–Fri, 12–2.30pm Sat–Sun. Children welcome in the back room and beer garden only.

12–11pm (10.30pm Sun).

The Old Grindstone
3 Crookes, Sheffield, South Yorkshire S10 1UA
☎ *(0114) 266 0322* Margaret Shaw

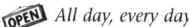Up to six guest ales on offer, from a varied range from around the country. The repeating of beers is generally avoided.

A one-bar local community pub. Food available at lunchtime and evenings. No children.

All day, every day.

Sheaf View
25 Gleadless Road, Sheffield, South Yorkshire S2 3AA
☎ *(0114) 249 6455* Richard Corker (Mgr)

Barnsley Bitter, Abbeydale Moonshine and Wentworth WPA permanently available plus up to four guest ales which may be Pictish Celtic Warrior or a brew from Springhead, Phoenix, Glentworth, Berrow, Rudgate or Townes.

A community pub. Children allowed in the garden only. Car park. Can be difficult to find so call for directions.

5–11pm Mon; 12–11pm Tues–Sat; 12–10.30pm Sun.

Fanny's Ale & Cider House
63 Saltaire Road, Shipley, Nr Bradford, West Yorkshire
☎ *(01274) 591419* S Marcus Lund

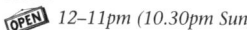Timothy Taylor Golden Best and Landlord regularly available, plus eight guest beers such as Fuller's London Pride, Timothy Taylor Ram Tam, Black Sheep Bitter, Glentworth Whispers, Daleside Monkey Wrench, Rooster's Yankee or Cream and many others.

Olde-worlde alehouse with wooden floorboards and open fire, full of brewery memorabilia. Gas lighting still used in the lounge bar. Extra seating area upstairs. Coffee served 12–6pm. Free car park nearby. Children welcome at lunchtimes only.

5–11pm Mon; 11.30am–11pm Tues–Sat; 12–10.30pm Sun.

The Narrow Boat
38 Victoria Street, Skipton BD23 1JE
☎ *(01756) 797922* Graham and Louise Caunt

Timothy Taylor Landlord, Black Sheep Bitter and Caledonian Deuchars IPA always available, plus five regularly changing guests, from local breweries whenever possible. Also Erdinger WeissBier (a Belgian ale), a guest Belgian beer and a range of Belgian bottled beers.

A traditional ale and wine bar with non-smoking bar – smoking permitted in the Gallery upstairs. Food available every day. Children allowed. Situated close to the canal basin.

12–11pm (10.30pm Sun).

The Moorcock Inn
Norland, Sowerby Bridge, West Yorkshire HX6 3RP
☎ *(01422) 832103* Mr Kitson

A freehouse with Samuel Smith Old Brewery Bitter always available plus two guest ales including, perhaps, Coach House Innkeeper's Special Reserve or Phoenix Old Oak Bitter.

A one-bar country pub with wooden beams, restaurant and outside area. Food available at lunchtime and evenings. Children allowed. Disabled access.

12–3pm and 5.30–11pm (10.30pm Sun).

The Moorings

*Canal Basin, Sowerby Bridge, West Yorkshire
HX6 2AG*
☎ *(01422) 833940* Emma O'Connell

 Black Sheep Special and Ruddles County always available plus two guests, perhaps Marston's Pedigree or something from Greene King.

A small pub with good quality beers, food and service. Beams, stone walls, wooden floors. Seating on canal side. Food available at lunchtime and evenings. Children allowed if dining.

OPEN *12–11pm (10.30pm Sun).*

The Navigation Inn

*Chapel Lane, Sowerby Bridge, West Yorkshire
HX6 3LF*
☎ *(01422) 831636* Trish Rushforth

 Eastwood & Sanders Best Bitter and Black Sheep Bitter are among the beers usually available, plus guests, often other Eastwood & Sanders brews such as Nettlethrasher and Bargee.

A charming canalside pub with historic fireplace dating from before 1722. Beer garden. Homemade food available 12–2.30pm and 5.30–8.30pm Mon–Sat and 1–6pm Sun.

OPEN *12–3pm and 5.30–11pm Mon–Thurs; 11am–11pm Fri–Sat; 12–10.30pm Sun.*

STAVELEY

The Royal Oak

*Main Street, Staveley, Nr Knaresborough,
North Yorkshire HG5 9LD*
☎ *(01423) 340267*

 Four beers always available plus two guests (25 per year) from small independent breweries.

A typical country pub, cosy, friendly, with open fires and two bars. Bar and restaurant food available at lunchtime and evenings, and 12–8pm (no food on Monday in winter). Car park, garden, children's play area.

OPEN *12–3pm and 6–11pm Mon–Sat; 12–5pm and 7–10.30pm Sun.*

STOKESLEY

The White Swan

*1 West End, Stokesley, Middlesbrough, North
Yorkshire TS9 5BL*
☎ *(01642) 710263*
Jonathan and Elizabeth Skipp

 A brewpub with the full range of Captain Cook Brewery beers brewed on site and always available in the pub. Also guests such as Castle Eden Ale.

A market town pub with one bar, open fire, background music and traditional pub games. Brewery on premises, tours available. Winner of the National Ploughman's Award 1997. Ploughman's, homemade pâtés and bar snacks available 12–2.30pm (not Sun).

🛢 **SUNSET 4.0% ABV**
🛢 **BLACK PORTER 4.2% ABV**
SLIPWAY 4.2% ABV
RED GOLD 4.4% ABV

OPEN *11.30am–3pm and 5.30–11pm Mon–Thurs; all day Fri; 11–3pm and 7–11pm Sat; 11–3pm and 7–10.30pm Sun.*

SUTTON UPON DERWENT

St Vincent Arms

Main Street, Sutton upon Derwent, East Yorkshire
☎ *(01904) 608349* Philip Hopwood

 Fuller's Chiswick, London Pride and ESB and Timothy Taylor Landlord always available plus guests including Adnams Extra, Old Mill Bitter, Charles Wells Bombardier and seasonal and special ales.

A bout 200 years old, with white-washed walls. Two bars, four rooms, open fires. Bar and restaurant food available at lunchtime and evenings. Car park, beer garden, non-smoking room. Children allowed. On main road through village.

OPEN *11.30am–3pm and 6–11pm Mon–Sat; 12–3pm and 7–10.30pm Sun.*

THORNE

Canal Tavern

*South Parade, Thorne, Doncaster, South
Yorkshire DN8 5DZ*
☎ *(01405) 813688* Mr Murrigton

 A freehouse with one guest ale changing weekly and not repeated if at all possible. Examples have included Thwaites Bloomin' Ale, Greene King Triumph and Marston's Pedigree.

A two-bar canalside country pub with dining area. Coal fires in winter, waterside beer garden. Food available at lunchtime and evenings. Children allowed, if eating.

OPEN *11am–3pm and 5.30–11pm Mon–Fri; all day Sat–Sun.*

THORNTON-IN-LONSDALE

The Marton Arms Hotel

*Thornton-in-Lonsdale, Carnforth
LA6 3PB*
☎ *(01524) 241281* Colin Elsdon

A freehouse with sixteen real ales always on offer! Timothy Taylor Golden Best, Black Sheep Bitter and Oakhill Bitter are permanent fixtures, and the guest beers, often changed daily, might include Moorhouse's Black Cat Mild or Pendle Witches, plus seasonal brews such as Wood Summer That and Ushers Summer Madness.

Seventeenth-century coaching inn, now a country house hotel with restaurant. Bar billiards, patio and garden. Children allowed. Car parking. Twelve letting rooms.

 11am–11pm Mon–Sat; 12–10.30pm Sun.

THRESHFIELD

Old Hall Inn

*Threshfield, Grassington, Skipton,
North Yorkshire*
☎ *(01756) 752441* Ronald C Matthews

Timothy Taylor Best Bitter and Landlord regularly available.

Traditional country pub with dining room, patio and beer garden. Food served 12–2pm and 6–9.30pm daily. Car park. Children welcome.

 12–3pm and 6–11.30pm Mon–Sat; 12–3pm and 7–10.30pm Sun.

TOCKWITH

The Spotted Ox

*Westfield Road, Tockwith, York, North Yorkshire
YO26 7PY*
☎ *(01423) 358387* James Ray

A freehouse with a selection of three cask ales always available, constantly changing.

A country pub with three bars decorated with the pump clips of past beers sold. Food available at lunchtime and evenings. Beer garden. Children allowed.

 *All day in summer; in winter 11am–3pm and 5.30–11pm Mon–Thurs; all day Fri–Sun.*

TODMORDEN

Masons

*1 Bacup Road, Todmorden, West Yorkshire
OL14 7AN*
☎ *(01706) 812180* Ian Murray

Barnsley Bitter permanently available plus two guests from breweries such as Phoenix, Hart or Moorhouse's.

A traditional drinkers' pub dating from 1830. Beamed ceiling, fireplace. No food. Children allowed. Can be difficult to find, call for directions.

 3–11pm Mon–Fri; 12–11pm Sat; 12–10.30pm Sun.

UPPERTHONG

The Royal Oak

*19 Towngate, Upperthong, Holmfirth,
West Yorkshire HD9 3UX*
☎ *(01484) 680568* David Sutton

Black Sheep Special, Eastwood & Sanders Bargee, Greene King Abbot, and Timothy Taylor Landlord are usually available.

A 200-year-old village pub with beamed ceiling and fireplaces. Food available in bistro Tues–Sat evening. Children allowed. garden. Car park. Call for directions.

 5–11pm Mon–Fri; 12–11pm Sat; 12–10.30pm Sun.

WAKEFIELD

The White Hart

*77 Westgate End, Wakefield, West Yorkshire
WF2 9RL*
☎ *(01924) 375887* David Hobson

Six real ales always available from a wide range of independent breweries. Beers changed weekly.

A traditional alehouse with flagstone floors and real log fires in winter. All-year-round beer garden, which is covered and heated in winter. Quiz night on Tuesdays. Free supper served on Tuesdays, Wednesdays and Sundays. Well-behaved children allowed.

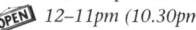 *12–11pm (10.30pm Sun).*

WALSDEN

The Cross Keys Inn

*649 Rochdale Road, Walsden, Todmorden,
West Yorkshire*
☎ *(01706) 815185* Ken Muir

Timothy Taylor Landlord, Black Sheep Bitter, Charles Wells Bombardier and three weekly changing guest beers usually available.

Lively pub, set on the side of the Rochdale Canal. Food served 12–2pm and 5–8pm Mon–Sat, 12–8pm Sun. Children welcome.

 12–11pm (10.30pm Sun).

WEAVERTHORPE
Star Country Inn
*Weaverthorpe, Malton, North Yorkshire
YO17 8EY*
☎ *(01944) 738273*
Susan and David Richardson

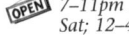Two regularly changing guest beers usually available (only one in winter), from a wide range of breweries around the country, such as Durham, Eccleshall, Hall and Woodhouse (Badger), Adnams, Bateman, Hop Back, Daleside, Rebellion, Black Sheep and Orkney, to name but a few!

Traditional country inn, well known locally for good food. Food served 7–9pm Wed–Mon and 12–2pm Sat–Sun. Car park. Children welcome, but no special facilities. Accommodation. For further information, visit the website at www.thestarinn.net.

OPEN *7–11pm Mon–Fri; 12–4pm and 7–11pm Sat; 12–4pm and 7–10.30pm Sun.*

WENTWORTH
The George & Dragon
85 Main Street, Wentworth, Rotherham, South Yorkshire S62 7TN
☎ *(01226) 742440* Gary and John Sweeting

A freehouse always serving Timothy Taylor Landlord, plus a good selection of guests, not repeated if possible, from breweries such as Ossett, Glentworth and Oakham.

A country village pub with two bars, two real fires and stone floors. Breakfast served 10am–12; lunch served 12–2.30pm and evening meals served 5.30–9pm in a separate dining area. Large beer garden with children's playground. Children allowed if eating.

OPEN *10am–11pm (10.30pm Sun).*

WHITBY
The Duke of York
Church Street, Whitby, North Yorkshire YO22 4DE
☎ *(01947) 600324* Laurie Bradley

Black Dog Special often available plus two guests such as Timothy Taylor Landlord and Adnams Regatta.

A seafaring pub, a mix of the traditional and the modern, with oak beams and modern decor. Food available 12–9pm. Children allowed.

OPEN *All day, every day.*

Tap & Spile
New Quay Road, Whitby, North Yorkshire YO21 1DH
☎ *(01947) 603937* Mr Fleming

Black Sheep Bitter always available, plus up to five guests. Almost 700 beers served since December 1994. Celebration and seasonal ales served where possible. Lindisfarne fruit wine and Old Rosie traditional cider also on offer.

A three-roomed town pub with two bars, wooden floors and beams and one non-smoking room. Food available every day from 12. Children allowed in designated area. Entertainment most nights (music on Mon, Tues, Wed and Fri at 9pm; quiz on Thurs at 9.30pm; open folk session on Sun at 8.30pm). Located by the railway station.

OPEN *All day, every day.
Closed 4.30–7pm Sun in winter.*

WOMBWELL
Royal Oak Hotel
13 Burch Street, Wombwell, South Yorkshire
☎ *(01254) 883541* Helen Jones

Five real ales available from a long list including Brewery on Sea Spinnaker Bitter and Bateman brews.

A 1920s-style town-centre pub. Bar food available at lunchtime and evenings. Car park, accommodation. Children allowed at restricted times.

OPEN *11am–11pm Mon–Sat; 12–10.30pm Sun.*

WORTLEY
Wortley Arms Hotel
Halifax Road, Wortley, South Yorkshire S35 7DB
☎ *(0114) 288 2245* Brian Morrisey

Timothy Taylor Landlord and Dark Mild, Wortley Bitter and Oakwell Barnsley Bitter always available, plus a range of guests. Also offers the widest selection of malt whiskies in the area.

A classic sixteenth-century coaching inn with inglenook fireplace. No background music, no gaming machines. Food served 12–8.30pm daily. Car park, children's room, non-smoking room. En-suite accommodation. Popular with walkers and cyclists on Trans-Pennine and Timberland trails.

OPEN *12–11pm (10.30pm Sun).*

YORK

The Blue Bell
*53 Fossgate, York, North Yorkshire
YO1 9TF*
☎ *(01904) 654904* Jim Hardie

Camerons Strongarm Ruby Red, Timothy
Taylor Landlord, Greene King Abbot,
Caledonian Deuchars IPA and Adnams Bitter
always available, plus rotating guests

The smallest pub in York with an original,
untouched, Edwardian interior which
dates from 1903, but has been cleaned since!
No juke box. Substantial sandwiches
available 11am–6pm. No children.

11am–11pm Mon–Sat; 12–10.30pm Sun.

The Maltings
Tanners Moat, York, North Yorkshire YO1 16HU
☎ *(01904) 655387* Maxine Collinge

Black Sheep Bitter always available plus
six guests changing daily (700 per year).
Too many to mention but with an emphasis
on small, independent brewers. Beer festivals
twice a year. Also Belgian bottled and
draught beers, fruit wines and four
traditional ciders.

Small city-centre freehouse. CAMRA
Yorkshire Pub of the Year 1994–95 and
Cask Ale Pub of Great Britain 1998. Pub grub
served at lunchtime. Situated on Lendal
Bridge. Further information available on
website: www.maltings.co.uk.

11am–11pm Mon–Sat; 12–10.30pm Sun.

Spread Eagle
98 Walmgate, York, North Yorkshire
☎ *(01904) 635868* Ian Taylor

Six beers always available, including
Marston's Pedigree, Mansfield Riding
Bitter, Banks's Bitter and Original Mild,
something from Camerons, plus guests.

Recently refurbished Victorian-style pub.
Full menu available daytimes. Live bands
Sunday lunchtimes and weekend evenings.
Garden. Children allowed at restricted times.

*11.30am–11pm Mon–Sat;
12–10.30pm Sun.*

The Tap & Spile
29 Monkgate, York, North Yorkshire
☎ *(01904) 656158* Andy Mackay

Eight cask ales always available, usually
including a beer from Black Sheep, Big
Lamp or Rooster's. Traditional ciders and a
range of fruit wines also served.

A traditional alehouse, with bar food and
full menu available at lunchtimes only,
plus traditional roasts on Sundays. Car park,
beer garden. Cask Marque accredited.
Evening Press Town Pub of the Year 1999 and
local CAMRA Pub of the Season, Spring 2000.

*11.30am–11.30pm Mon–Sat;
12–10.30pm Sun.*

YOU TELL US

* *The Ackthorne*, St Martin's Lane, Micklegate, York
* *The Brewer's Arms*, 10 Pontefract Road, Snaith
* *The Elm Tree*, 5 Elm Tree Square, Embsay
* *The Keighley & Worth Railway Buffet Car*, The Station, Keighley
* *Keystones*, 4 Monkgate, York
* *The Lord Rosebery*, 85–7 Westborough, Scarborough
* *The Lundhill Tavern*, Beechhouse Road, Hemingfield
* *Milestone*, 12 Peaks Mount, Waterthorpe, Sheffield
* *The Mission*, Posterngate, Hull
* *The Queen's Head*, Wednesday Market, Beverley
* *The Ram's Head*, Wakefield Road, Sowerby Bridge (brewpub)
* *Scholars Bar*, The Bedford Hotel, Somerset Terrace, Scarborough
* *The Station Hotel*, Knott Lane, Easingwold
* *The Tap & Spile*, Flemingate, Beverley
* *The Tap & Spile*, Spring Bank, Hull
* *The Vine Tree*, Newton Bar, Wakefield
* *The Waggon & Horses*, 48 Gillygate, York
* *The Zetland Hotel*, 9 High Street, Marske

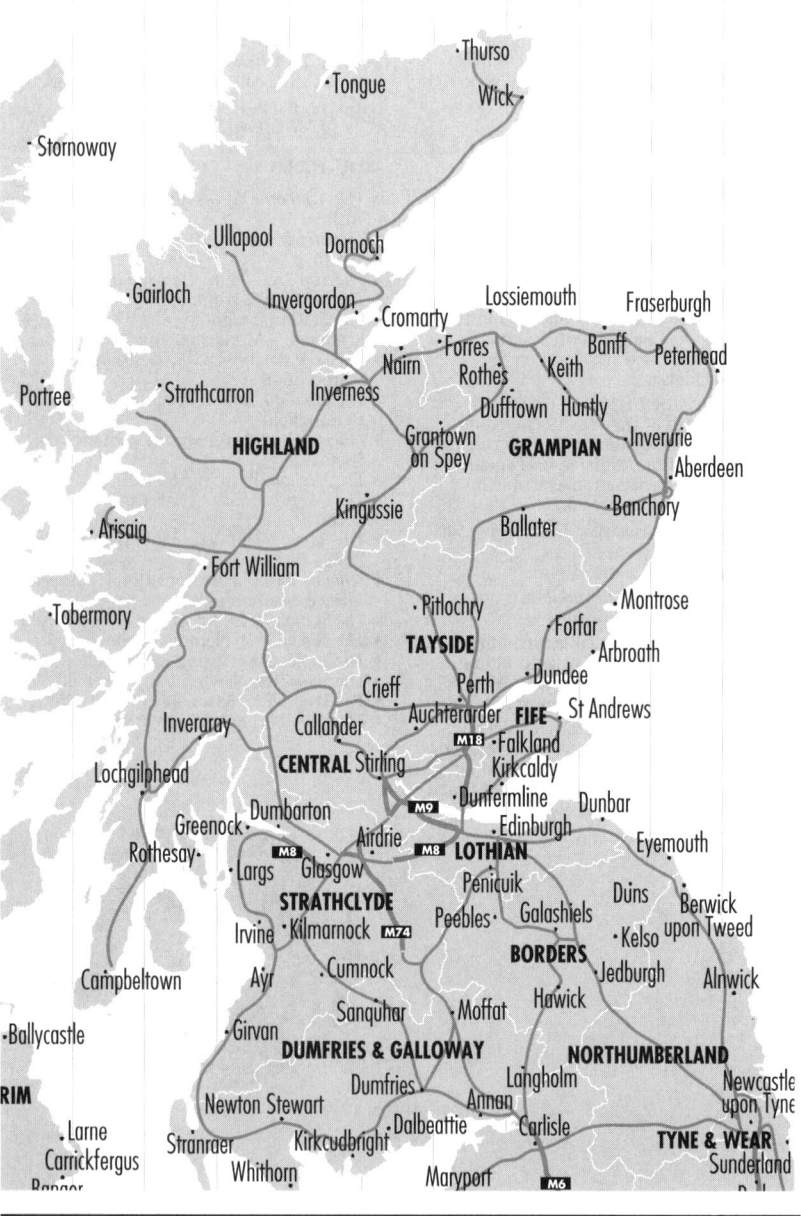

THE BREWERIES

ARRAN BREWERY
Cladach, Brodick, Isle of Arran KA27 8DE
☎ *(01770) 302353*
www.arranbrewery.co.uk

 ARRAN ALE 3.8% ABV
DARK 4.3% ABV
BLONDE 5.0% ABV

ATLAS BREWERY LTD
Lab Rd, Kinlochleven, Argyll PH50 4SG
☎ *(01855) 831111*
www.atlasbrewery.com

 LATITUDE PALE ALE 3.6% ABV
TEMPEST WHEAT BEER 4.9% ABV

BELHAVEN BREWERY CO.
Spott Road, Dunbar EH42 1RS
☎ *(01368) 862734*
www.belhaven.co.uk

 BEST 3.2% ABV
BEST EXTRA COLD 3.2% ABV
80/- 4.2% ABV
Malty and nutty.
ST ANDREW'S ALE 6.0% ABV
Well-balanced and distinctive with dry after-palate.

BRIDGE OF ALLAN BREWERY
Queen's Lane, Bridge of Allan, Central FK9 4NY
☎ *(01786) 834555*
www.bridgeofallan.co.uk

 STIRLING BITTER 3.7% ABV
STIRLING BRIG 4.1% ABV
BANNOCKBURN 4.2% ABV
BRAMBLE ALE 4.2% ABV
GLENCOE WILD OAT STOUT 4.5% ABV
ALEOWEEN PUMPKIN ALE 4.2% ABV
Seasonal.
LOMOND GOLD 5.0% ABV
Seasonal.

BROUGHTON ALES LTD
The Brewery, Broughton, Biggar ML12 6HQ
☎ *(01899) 830345 (Brewery tours)*
www.broughton-ales.co.uk

GREENMANTLE ALE 3.9% ABV
Maltiness, with bittersweet flavour, and hoppy finish.
MERLIN'S ALE 4.2% ABV
Gold-coloured, with dry hop flavour combined with malt.
SCOTTISH OATMEAL STOUT 4.2% ABV
Powerful, malty flavour and hoppy bitterness.
THE GHILLIE 4.5% ABV
Hoppy fruit flavours throughout.
BLACK DOUGLAS 5.2% ABV
Dark and malty.
OLD JOCK 6.7% ABV
Dark copper-coloured, with fruit and roast flavours.

CAIRNGORM BREWING COMPANY LTD
Unit 12 Dalfaber Estate, Aviemore, Inverness-shire PH22 1PY
☎ *(01479) 812222*
www.cairngormbrewery.com

 RUTHVEN BREW 3.8% ABV
Copper-coloured ale with hoppy aroma.
STAG 4.1% ABV
Good hop character.
NESSIE'S MONSTER MASH 4.4% ABV
Malty full-flavoured beer.
CAIRNGORM GOLD 4.5% ABV
Delicious golden beer.
RED MURDOCH 4.8% ABV
WILD CAT 5.1% ABV
Complex malt, fruit and hop flavour.

CALEDONIAN BREWING CO.
42 Slateford Road, Edinburgh EH11 1PH
☎ *(0131) 3371286 (Brewery tours)*
www.caledonian-brewery.co.uk

 DEUCHARS IPA 3.8% ABV
Pale, well-hopped and quenching. Ever-popular.
80/- ALE 4.1% ABV
Golden, full-flavoured award winner.
GOLDEN PROMISE 5.0% ABV
Light-coloured, hoppy organic beer.
Plus monthly special brews.

CRAIGMILL BREWERY
Craigmill, Strathaven ML10 6PB
☎ *(01357) 529029*
www.heatherale.co.uk

 FRAOCH 4.1% ABV
Brewed from malted barley and heather.
KELPIE 4.4% ABV
Rich chocolate.
GROZET 4.5% ABV
Gooseberry and wheat ale.
EBULUM 5.8% ABV
Elderberry black ale.
ALBA 6.0% ABV
Pine and spruce.

FISHERROW BREWERY
Unit 12, Duddingston Yards, Duddingston Park South, Edinburgh EH15 3NX
☎ *(0131) 621 5501*
www.fisherrow.co.uk

 INDIA PALE ALE 3.8% ABV
Golden, refreshing and full-bodied for gravity.
BURGH BITTER 4.2% ABV
Golden and refreshing with some sweetness.
HOPPING MAD 4.2% ABV
Aromatic spring ale.
NUT BROWN ALE 4.8% ABV
Full-flavoured, traditional brown ale.
EXPORT PALE ALE 5.2% ABV
Pale, refreshing easy-quaffer.
Plus monthly brews.

FORTH BREWING COMPANY

Eglington, Kelliebank, Alloa, Clackmannanshire
FK10 1NU
☎ *(01259) 725511*

DARK ALLOA LAGER 4.0% ABV
Full-bodied, well-hopped, clean and refreshing.
PUFFER ALE 4.1% ABV
Strong well-balanced hop character, slightly peppery on the tongue.
SAAZ 4.2% ABV
Organic lager.

FYNE ALES

Achadunan, Cairndow, Argyll PA26 8BJ
☎ *(01499) 600120 (brewery)*
☎ *(01499) 600238 (office)*

PIPER'S GOLD 3.8% ABV
Light, golden ale for easy drinking.
MAVERICK 4.2% ABV
Dark robust ale with distinctive character.
HIGHLANDER 4.8% ABV
Traditional strong ale with full malt flavour.

HARVIESTOUN BREWERY LTD

Devon Road, Dollar FK14 7LX
☎ *(01259) 742141*

WEE STOATER 3.6% ABV
BROOKER'S BITTER & TWISTED 3.8% ABV
Blond with clean citrus fruit flavours.
TURNPIKE 4.1% ABV
PTARMIGAN 4.5% ABV
Pale, with Bavarian hops.
SCHIEHALLION 4.8% ABV
Superb, real cask lager.
Plus seasonal and occasional brews.

THE INVERALMOND BREWERY

1 Inveralmond Way, Inveralmond, Perth
PH1 3UQ
☎ *(01738) 449448*
www.inveralmond-brewery.co.uk

INDEPENDENCE 3.8% ABV
Full-flavoured malt and hops with some spiciness.
OSSIAN'S ALE 4.1% ABV
Golden and hoppy.
THRAPPLEDOUSER 4.3% ABV
Deep golden, refreshing with good hoppiness.
LIA FAIL 4.7% ABV
Smooth, dark and full-flavoured.

THE ISLE OF SKYE BREWING CO. (LEANN AN EILEIN) LTD

The Pier, Uig IV51 9XY
☎ *(01470) 542477 (Brewery tours)*
www.skyebrewery.co.uk

YOUNG PRETENDER 4.0% ABV
Gold-coloured and lightly hopped with dry after taste.
RED CUILLIN 4.2% ABV
Slightly malty, with some fruit and hoppy finish.
HEBRIDEAN GOLD 4.3% ABV
Smooth with good hoppy bitterness.
BLACK CUILLIN 4.5% ABV
Stout-like, with hints of chocolate and honey.
BLAVEN 5.0% ABV
Golden, fruity and well-balanced.
Plus seasonal brews.

KELBURN BREWING CO LTD

10 Muriel Lane, Barrhead, Glasgow G7 1QB
☎ *(0141) 881 2138*
www.kelburnbrewery.com

GOLDI HOPS 3.8% ABV
Golden and hoppy!
RED SMIDDY 4.1% ABV
Smooth dry ale.

MOULIN BREWERY

11–13 Kirkmichael Road, Moulin, By Pitlochry,
Perthshire PH16 5EW
☎ *(01796) 472196*
www.moulin.u-net.com

MOULIN LIGHT ALE 3.7% ABV
BRAVEHEART 4.0% ABV
ALE OF ATHOL 4.5% ABV
OLD REMEDIAL 5.2% ABV
Scottish Tourist Board 2* visitor attraction, tours and shop.

McCOWAN'S BREWHOUSE

Unit 1, Fountain Park, Dundee Street, Edinburgh
EH11 1AG
☎ *(0131) 228 8198*

IPA 3.7% ABV
Sweet ale, fruity aroma and resinous aftertaste.
GOLDEN POWER SHOWER 3.8% ABV
Golden pale ale with added spice.
DARKSIDE 4.0% ABV
Sweet Scottish-style stout.
DOMNHUL 4.5% ABV
Dark bitter.
MCCOWAN'S 80/- 4.5% ABV
Bitter-sweet with roast burnt caramel aroma.
FINLAYS 5.0% ABV
Cask-conditioned premium lager.
Seasonal:
AULD SUMMER SHINER 4.0% ABV
Light refreshing English-style bitter with fruity citrus aroma and taste.
Plus other seasonals and specials.

THE ORKNEY BREWERY

Quoyloo, Stromness KW16 3LT
☎ *(01856) 841802 (Brewery tours)*
www.orkneybrewery.co.uk

 RAVEN ALE 3.8% ABV
Superb malt, hop, citrus fruit flavours and nuttiness.

DRAGONHEAD STOUT 4.0% ABV
Black, powerful roast maltiness, with nutty flavours.

NORTHERN LIGHT 4.0% ABV
Golden, refreshing and mellow.

RED MACGREGOR 4.0% ABV
Mellow and malty with nut and hoppy finish.

DARK ISLAND 4.6% ABV
Smooth, flavour-packed and easy to drink.

SKULLSPLITTER 8.5% ABV
Beautifully smooth and hoppy with dry finish.
Plus several special brews.

SULWATH BREWERS LTD

The Brewery, 209 King Street, Castle Douglas DG7 1DT
☎ *(01556) 504525*
www.sulwathbrewers.co.uk

 CUIL HILL 3.6% ABV
Pale amber, and bursting with fresh malt and hops.

JOHN PAUL JONES 4.0% ABV
Malty occasional brew.

THE BLACK GALLOWAY 4.4% ABV
Nourishing porter.

CRIFFEL 4.6% ABV
Rounded malt and hop flavours with delicate bitterness.

KNOCKENDOCH 5.0% ABV
Deep roast malt flavour and hoppy aftertaste.

GALLOWAY GOLD 5.0% ABV
Thirst quenching lager with citrus aftertaste.
Plus occasional brews.

TRAQUAIR HOUSE BREWERY

Traquair Estate, Innerleithen EH44 6PW
☎ *(01896) 830323 (Brewery tours)*
www.traquair.co.uk

 ROYAL STUART 4.5% ABV
Summer brew.

BEAR ALE 5.0% ABV
Full-bodied and fruity with good dryness in the hoppy finish.

VALHALLA BREWERY

New House, Baltasound, Unst, Shetland ZE2 9DX
☎ *(01957) 711658*
www.valhallabrewery.co.uk

SUMMER DIM 4.0% ABV
AULD ROCK 4.5% ABV
Smooth, malty and full-bodied robust hoppiness.

WHITE WIFE 4.8% ABV

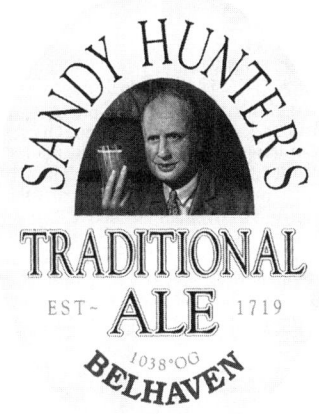

THE PUBS

ALLANTON

The Allanton Inn
Allanton, Duns, Berwickshire TD11 3JZ
☎ *(01890) 818260* Jack Philp

A freehouse with three pumps offering a range that changes weekly, featuring guest ales from small and large Scottish and English breweries.

A listed country inn with pool, darts and a cosy restaurant. En-suite bedrooms. Food served at lunchtimes and evenings. Children welcome.

12–2.30pm and 6–11pm Mon–Wed; 12–2.30pm and 6–12pm Thurs; 12–2.30pm and 5pm–1am Fri; 12pm–1am Sat–Sun.

AUCHENCROW

The Craw Inn
Auchencrow, Berwickshire
☎ *(018907) 61253* Trevor Wilson

Caledonian Deuchars IPA plus a regularly changing guest, perhaps from Orkney, Caledonian or other Scottish and small English regional breweries.

Family-run, eighteenth-century, listed country inn in small, attractive Borders village. Bar and restaurant food served 12.30–2.30pm and 7–9.30pm daily. Car park. Children welcome. En-suite accommodation.

12–2.30pm and 6–11pm Mon–Thurs; 12–12 Fri–Sat; 12.30–11pm Sun.

BONCHESTER BRIDGE

Horse & Hound Hotel
Bonchester Bridge, Hawick TD9 8JN
☎ *(01450) 860645* Mr and Mrs Hope

Maclay, Charles Wells and Border brews always available plus a guest beer (20 per year) perhaps from Longstone, Bateman, Jennings, Caledonian, Belhaven or Holt breweries.

A former coaching inn dating from 1704 with comfortable accommodation and non-smoking areas. Bar and restaurant food is available at lunchtime and evenings. Car park. Children's certificate. Hawick is seven miles from Carter Bar on the England–Scotland border.

11.30am–3pm and 6–11pm.

DENHOLM

Auld Cross Keys Inn
Main Street, Denholm, Roxburghshire TD9 8NU
☎ *(01450) 870305* Peter Ferguson

A freehouse with two cask pumps promoting mainly Scottish ales on a rotation basis, supplied by Broughton and Caley.

Public bar, lounge bar, dining and function room. Meals served lunchtimes and evenings, plus Sunday carvery. Children allowed. Two en-suite rooms available.

5–11pm Mon; 11am–2.30pm and 5–11pm Tues–Wed; 11am–2.30pm and 5pm–midnight Thurs; 11am–2pm and 5pm–1am Fri; all day Sat and Sun.

EYEMOUTH

The Ship Hotel
Harbour Road, Eyemouth, Berwickshire TD14 5HT
☎ *(01890) 750224* Mr RD Anderson

Leased from Carlsberg Tetley, this pub has Caledonian 80/- and Border Farne Island Pale Ale always available. A guest, changed frequently in summer, is also offered. Caledonian Deuchars IPA is a popular choice.

A local fishermen's pub and family-run hotel near the harbour with lounge bar and separate dining area. Food at lunchtime and evenings. Children allowed.

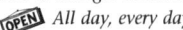*All day, every day.*

GALASHIELS

Ladhope Inn

33 High Buckholmside, Galashiels, Borders TD1 2HR
☎ *(01896) 752446* Mrs Johnston

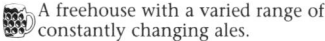 A freehouse with a varied range of constantly changing ales.

On the main road; first pub on the A7. Toasted sandwiches only. Children allowed.

OPEN *All day, every day.*

GREENLAW

Cross Keys Inn

3 The Square, Greenlaw, Duns TD10 6UD
☎ *(01361) 10247* Mary O'Brian

 Two real ales always available, regulars including Timothy Taylor Landlord and Caledonian Deuchars IPA.

A very old-fashioned freehouse with one bar and a restaurant area. Food at lunchtime and evenings. Children allowed.

OPEN *Closed daily between 2.30 and 5pm.*

INNERLEITHEN

Traquair Arms Hotel

Traquair Road, Innerleithen, Borders EH44 6PD
☎ *(01896) 830229* Gig and Dianne Johnston

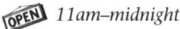 A freehouse with real ales on three pumps offering the local Traquair House Bear Ale on draught. Broughton Greenmantle Ale and 80/- also often available plus occasional others.

A country-style pub with one bar and separate dining area. Food served all day. Children allowed.

OPEN *All day, every day.*

NEWCASTLETON

The Grapes Hotel

16 Douglas Square, Newcastleton, Roxburghshire TD9 0QD
☎ *(01387) 375245* Jim McDonald

Up to eight pumps operating, with Caledonian Deuchars IPA among the beers always available. Guests are changed monthly.

A small hotel with restaurant. Food at lunchtimes and evenings. Children allowed until 8.30pm (residents later).

OPEN *All day, every day.*

PAXTON

Cross Inn

Paxton, Berwickshire
☎ *(01289) 386267* Mr M Caulfield

Orkney Dark Island and Caledonian 80/- permanently available plus a guest which is usually a Scottish ale from either Broughton, Orkney or Caledonian.

A seventeenth-century village pub with a warm and friendly bar and separate dining room. Food available all opening hours. Children welcome. Car park.

OPEN *12–2.30pm and 6.30–9pm Tues–Sun (closed Mon).*

PEEBLES

Green Tree Hotel

41 Eastgate, Peebles EH45 8AD
☎ *(01721) 720582* Mervyn Edge

Caledonian 80/- is permanently available, plus one or two guest beers such as Timothy Taylor Landlord or something from Broughton Ales.

Lively, traditional hotel bar. Food served 12–2.30pm and 5–8.30pm. Car park. Children welcome.

OPEN *11am–midnight.*

ST MARY'S LOCH

Tibbie Shiels Inn

St Mary's Loch, Selkirk, Borders TD7 5LH
☎ *(01750) 42231* Mrs Brown

A freehouse offering Broughton Greenmantle Ale and Belhaven 80/-.

A remote coaching inn with a non-smoking dining area. Food at lunchtime and evenings. Children allowed.

OPEN *All day, every day (closed Mon–Wed from November–Easter).*

Places Featured:

Alva
Bridge of Allan
Dollar
Dunblane
Falkirk

Pool of Muckhart
Sauchie
Stirling
Tillicoultry

THE PUBS

ALVA

Cross Keys Inn
120 Stirling Street, Alva, Clackmannanshire FK12 5EH
☎ *(01259) 760409* Mrs Michie

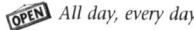 Tied to Belhaven with up to three guests, available. Brains Buckley's Best or Maclay 80/- and Wallace IPA are examples.

An old-fashioned pub with two bars. Food at lunchtime and evenings. Children allowed.

OPEN *All day, every day.*

BRIDGE OF ALLAN

The Queen's Hotel
24 Henderson Street, Bridge of Allan, Stirling, Stirlingshire FK9 4HD
☎ *(01786) 833268* Mr Ross

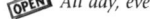 A freehouse with beers Stirling Brig, Bitter, IPA and Dark Mild from the local Bridge of Allan Brewery permanently available, plus seasonal specials. Also Burton brews.

A two-bar pub with restaurant and occasional live entertainment. Food at lunchtime and evenings. Children allowed.

OPEN *All day, every day.*

DOLLAR

Castle Campbell Hotel
11 Bridge Street, Dollar, Clackmannanshire FK14 7DE
☎ *(01259) 742519* Tara Watters

A freehouse with real ale on two pumps. Usually Fuller's London Pride and one of the local Harviestoun ales.

A traditional, very busy pub with a separate dining area and lounge bar. Food at lunchtime and evenings. Children allowed.

OPEN *All day, every day.*

The King's Seat
19 Bridge Street, Dollar, Clackmannanshire FK14 7DE
☎ *(01259) 742515* Mr and Mrs Nelson

Four beers always available from a constantly changing range including Harviestoun Brooker's Bitter and Twisted, Morland Old Speckled Hen, Marston's Pedigree and many more..

A village inn serving families (with a children's certificate). Bar and restaurant food available at lunchtime and evenings. Parking. Dollar is on the main A91 road between Stirling and St Andrews.

OPEN *11am–2.30pm and 5pm–midnight Mon–Sat; 12.30–2.30pm and 6.30–11pm Sun.*

The Lorne Tavern
17 Argyll Street, Dollar, Clackmannanshire FK14 7AR
☎ *(01259) 743423* Jim Nelson

A freehouse with Harviestoun and Abbeydale brews always available. Two pumps, changed every four days, offer guests which include regulars from Backdykes and Inveralmond breweries. Others featured include the Maclay range.

A traditional local with separate restaurant. Children allowed in the dining room.

OPEN *All day, every day.*

DUNBLANE

The Tappit Hen
Kirk Street, Dunblane, Perthshire FK15 0AL
☎ *(01786) 825226* Danny Mitchel

Two ales from Belhaven always available, plus five guests, changed weekly.

A community bar with a warm, welcoming atmosphere, situated opposite the cathedral. No food. No children.

OPEN *All day, every day.*

FALKIRK

Eglesbrech Brewing Company

Upstairs At Behind The Wall, 14 Melville Street, Falkirk FK1 1HZ
☎ *(01324) 633338* C Morris

 The Eglesbrech range of beers is normally available, plus a Caledonian brew and a range of guest beers often from Harviestoun, Caledonian, Broughton, Maclay, Belhaven and Orkney.

Town-centre complex with restaurant, café bar and conservatory. Food served all day. Car park opposite. Children welcome.

OPEN *11am–midnight Sun–Thurs; 11am–1am Fri–Sat.*

POOL OF MUCKHART

The Muckhart Inn

Pool of Muckhart, Muckhart, Clackmannanshire FK14 7JN
☎ *(01259) 781324* Derek Graham

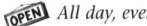 A freehouse and micro-brewery serving Devon Original, Pride and Thick Black plus others.

A one-bar pub with beamed ceilings and log fires. Food at lunchtime and evenings. Children allowed.

OPEN *All day, every day.*

SAUCHIE

Mansfield Arms

7 Main Street, Sauchie, Nr Alloa, Clackmannanshire FK10 3JR
☎ *(01259) 722020* John Gibson

The home of Devon Ales micro-brewery, with three beers brewed and served on the premises.

CAMRA Scottish Pub of the Year in 1993, started brewing in May 1994. The four-barrel brewhouse was built from spare parts and discarded equipment and now produces cask ales in the English tradition. Food is available in the bar until 9pm. Car park, garden. Children allowed. Just north of Alloa.

🛢 **DEVON ORIGINAL 3.8% ABV**
🛢 **DEVON THICK BLACK 4.1% ABV**
DEVON PRIDE 4.6% ABV

OPEN *11am–midnight.*

STIRLING

The Birds & Bees

Easter Cornton Road, Causewayhead, Stirling FK9 5PB
☎ *(01786) 463384* Lesley Anderson

 A freehouse with three real ales on the menu. Caledonian 80/- always available, plus two guests per week.

A traditional farmhouse-style pub with log fires, beer garden and French boules. Voted one of the best places to eat in local Tourism Awards 2000 – food available lunchtimes and evenings. Children welcome.

OPEN *11am–3pm and 5pm–midnight Mon–Thurs; all day Fri–Sun.*

TILLICOULTRY

The Woolpack

1 Glassford Square, Tillicoultry, Clackmannanshire FK13 6AH
☎ *(01259) 750332* Mr D McGhee

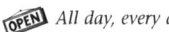 A freehouse with Harviestoun Ptarmigan 85/- and Orkney Dark Island always available. A guest beer, changed every two days, is also offered.

Built around 1700, a one-bar pub with restaurant and children's room. Food served all day. No children in the bar. Off the beaten track, no signposts. Head towards the Glen.

OPEN *All day, every day.*

Places Featured:

Bladnoch	Haugh of Urr
Canonbie	Kirkcudbright
Castle Douglas	Langholm
Dalbeattie	Lockerbie
Dumfries	Newton Stewart
Gatehouse of Fleet	Portpatrick
Glenluce	Thornhill

THE PUBS

BLADNOCH

The Bladnoch Inn
Bladnoch, Wigtown, Nr Newton Stewart, Wigtownshire DG8 9AB
☎ *(01988 402200)* Peter McLaughlin

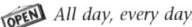Freehouse with up to nine beers available including Sulwath Criffel and Morland Old Speckled Hen. Others from breweries such as Belhaven are rotated twice weekly.

A country inn and restaurant overlooking the river next to the old distillery. Food at lunchtime and evenings. Children allowed.

(OPEN) *All day, every day.*

CANONBIE

The Riverside
Canonbie DG14 0UX
☎ *(013873) 71512* Mr Ed Baxter

Caledonian 80/- and Yates Bitter always available, plus an organic lager.

A civilised English-style country inn on the River Esk. Bar and restaurant food available at lunchtime and evenings (featured in a good food guide). Car park and garden. Accommodation. Children allowed. Situated 14 miles north from the M6 junction 44.

(OPEN) *12–2.30pm and 6.30–11pm Mon–Sat; 12–2.30pm and 7–10.30pm Sun.*

CASTLE DOUGLAS

The Royal Hotel
17 King Street, Castle Douglas, Kirkcudbrightshire DG7 1AA
☎ *(01556) 502040* Mrs Bennett

A freehouse with Orkney Dark Island and Caledonian Deuchars IPA always available.

A small, family-run hotel with two bars and a separate restaurant. Children allowed.

(OPEN) *All day, every day.*

DALBEATTIE

The Pheasant Hotel
1 Maxwell Street, Dalbeattie DG5 4AH
☎ *(01556) 610345* Bill Windsor

A freehouse, the only real ale outlet in Dalbeattie. A local brew such as Caledonian Deuchars IPA or Sulwath Cuil Hill always available.

A high-street community pub with TV and second-floor dining area. Food at lunchtime and evenings. Children allowed.

(OPEN) *All day, every day.*

DUMFRIES

Douglas Arms
Friars Vennel, Dumfries DG1 2RQ
☎ *(01387) 256002* Mrs A Whitefield

Broughton Greenmantle Ale, Merlin's Ale, The Ghillie, Black Douglas and Old Jock always available plus one guest beer (150 per year) to include Whim Magic Mushroom Mild and Hartington Bitter.

An old-style pub with a real coal fire. No food available. Situated in the town centre.

(OPEN) *11am–11pm Sun–Thurs; 11am–midnight Fri–Sat.*

The New Bazaar
38 Whitesands, Dumfries DG1 2RS
☎ *(01387) 268776*
George and Graham Schneider

A freehouse with Belhaven St Andrews and Sulwath Knockendoch always available plus two guest beers daily (over 300 a year) from a list of breweries including Bateman, Adnams, Titanic, Moorhouse's, Tomintoul and Greene King, as well as many new brews.

A traditional Victorian public house consisting of public bar, lounge, family room and beer garden. The public bar has an old-fashioned gantry stocked with more than 200 malt and other whiskies. Lounge has real coal fire. No food available. Car park. Wheelchair access. The pub overlooks the River Nith.

(OPEN) *All day, every day.*

The Ship Inn

St Michael Street, Dumfries DG1 2P7
☎ *(01387) 255189* Mr T Dudgeon

Timothy Taylor Landlord, Morland Old Speckled Hen, Charles Wells Bombardier, Marston's Pedigree and two regularly changing guest beers usually available, perhaps from Orkney, Everards, Brakspear, Harviestoun, Broughton, Fuller's, Badger, Greene King, Holt, Hook Norton, Hop Back, Jennings or Adnams.

Seven ales on hand pump and four directly from the barrel in this friendly alehouse. No TV or music, just good conversation. No food. No children.

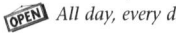 *11am–2.30pm and 5–11pm Mon–Sat; 12.30–2.30pm and 6.30–11pm Sun.*

Tam O'Shanter

117 Queensberry Street, Dumfries DG1 1BH
☎ *(01387) 254055* Doreen Johnston

Caledonian Deuchars IPA always available plus four guests, changed frequently, from a broad selection.

A traditional pub with upstairs restaurant. Food all day. Children allowed.

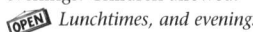 *All day, every day.*

GATEHOUSE OF FLEET

Masonic Arms

Ann Street, Gatehouse of Fleet, Nr Castle Douglas Kirkcudbrightshire DG7 2HU
☎ *(01557) 814335* Paul Irvin

A freehouse with up to seven ales available.

A traditional, English-style country inn with one bar, restaurant and conservatory. Food at lunchtime and evenings. Children allowed.

 Lunchtimes, and evenings from 5pm.

GLENLUCE

Kelvin House Hotel

53 Main Street, Glenluce, Newton Stewart, Wigtownshire DG8 0PP
☎ *(01581) 300303* Christine Holmes

A freehouse offering three real ales, one changed once or twice a week. Orkney Red MacGregor and Burtonwood Top Hat always on the menu, with one guest from a good selection that may include Timothy Taylor Landlord and Orkney Dark Island.

A hotel off the A75, with residents' lounge, dining lounge, public bar and restaurant. Food at lunchtime and evenings, all day at weekends. Children allowed.

11am–3pm and 5–11.30pm Mon–Fri; all day Sat–Sun.

HAUGH OF URR

Laurie Arms Hotel

Haugh of Urr, Castle Douglas, Kirkcudbrightshire DG7 3YA
☎ *(01556) 660246* William Rundle

A freehouse offering four real ales including Timothy Taylor Landlord and Orkney Red MacGregor, with guests from many different breweries changed weekly.

An old country pub with log fires and separate dining area. CAMRA Pub of the Year for Scotland 1999. Food at lunchtime and evenings. Children allowed.

11.45am–2.30pm and 5.30pm–midnight.

KIRKCUDBRIGHT

Selkirk Arms Hotel

High Street, Kirkcudbright, Kirkcudbrightshire DG6 4JG
☎ *(01557) 330209* Mr and Mrs J Morris

A freehouse with Sulwath Criffel always available. A guest, changed weekly, might be Fuller's London Pride or other independent ale.

A Georgian hotel with public and lounge bars and a bistro. Food at lunchtime and evenings. Children allowed.

All day, every day.

LANGHOLM

The Crown Hotel

High Street, Langholm DG13 0JH
☎ *(01387) 380247*
Mr A Barrie and Ms B Bailey

Orkney brews always available in this freehouse plus a guest beer changed weekly.

An eighteenth-century coaching house with five bars and a dining area. Food served. Children allowed.

All day, every day.

LOCKERBIE

Somerton House Hotel

35 Carlisle Road, Lockerbie DG11 2DR
☎ *(01576) 202583* Alex Arthur

A freehouse always offering Caledonian Deuchars IPA and Broughton Greenmantle. A guest is changed each week. Favourites include beers from Fuller's, Jennings and Caledonian breweries.

A hotel built in the 1880s with a separate dining area. Food served at lunchtime and evenings. Children allowed.

All day, every day.

NEWTON STEWART

The Creebridge House Hotel

Newton Stewart, Wigtownshire DG8 6NP
☎ *(01671) 402121* Miss Joanne Allison

 A freehouse with Sulwath Criffel and Cuil Hill ales always available. Two guests served each week, with favourites such as Bridge of Allan Sheriff Muir and Timothy Taylor Landlord.

A country-style hotel built in 1760, with one large bar, brasserie and restaurant. Award-winning food available for lunch and dinner. Children's certificate.

OPEN *12–2.30pm Mon–Sun; 6–11pm Mon–Thurs; 6pm–midnight Fri–Sat; 6.30–11pm Sun.*

PORTPATRICK

Harbour House Hotel

53 Main Street, Portpatrick, Stranraer, Wigtownshire DG9 8JW
☎ *(01776) 810456* Ian Cerexhe

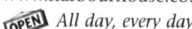 A freehouse with Houston Killellan on offer all year round, plus Houston Peter's Well in summer.

Central hotel on the seafront with lounge bar overlooking the harbour. Outside seating and music most weekends. Separate dining area. Food at lunchtime and evenings. Children allowed. Visit the website: www.harbourhouse.co.uk.

OPEN *All day, every day.*

THORNHILL

Buccleuch & Queensberry Hotel

112 Drumlanrig Street, Thornhill, Dumfriesshire DG3 5LU
☎ *(01848) 330215* David and Naomi Spencer

A freehouse with Caledonian 80/- permanently available, plus one guest, changing weekly, perhaps from Marston's, Timothy Taylor, Orkney, Harviestoun or Jennings, to name but a few.

This 150-year-old hotel stands prominently at the centre of a picturesque conservation village. Traditional old-style lounge bar, log fires and friendly staff. A haven for fishermen, walkers and golfers. Freshly prepared food served every lunchtime and evening. Car park. Children welcome.

OPEN *11am–midnight Mon–Wed; 11am–1am Thurs–Sat; 12.30pm–midnight Sun.*

Places Featured:

Aberdour	Kettlebridge
Anstruther	Kirkcaldy
Ceres	Leslie
Earlsferry	Leven

THE PUBS

ABERDOUR

Cedar Inn
20 Shore Road, Aberdour KY3 0TR
☎ *(01383) 860310* Janet Cadden

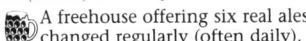 A freehouse offering six real ales, changed regularly (often daily).

A friendly locals' pub with two bars and lounges. Food at lunchtime and evenings. Children allowed.

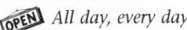 *All day, every day.*

ANSTRUTHER

Dreel Tavern
16 High Street, Anstruther KY10 3DL
☎ *(01333) 310727* Barry Scarsbrook

 A freehouse with Orkney Dark Island a permanent fixture. Two guest beers, changed at least once a week, are also offered and these may include ales from Harviestoun, Broughton, Inveralmond, Houston, Timothy Taylor and Fuller's.

A sixteenth-century coaching inn offering smoking and non-smoking dining areas, plus a garden bar for summer days. Food available 12–2pm and 5.30–9pm (children's menu until 7pm).

 All day, every day.

CERES

Ceres Inn
The Cross, Ceres, Cupar KY15 5NE
☎ *(01334) 828305* Ms LA and Miss JAL Rout

Two guest beers regularly available, perhaps Harviestoun Bitter and Twisted, Caledonian Deuchars IPA, Belhaven IPA or 80/- or something from Houston Brewery.

Traditional olde-worlde bar with good atmosphere, situated in the centre of Ceres. Bar food served 12–2pm Wed–Mon, high teas 4.30–7pm Sat–Sun. Car park. Children's menu.

11.30am–3pm and 5–late.

EARLSFERRY

Golf Tavern (19th Hole)
Links Road, Earlsferry KY9 1AW
☎ *(01333) 330 610* Douglas Duncanson

 Caledonian Deuchars IPA, Broughton Greenmantle and an occasional guest beer served.

Small village pub with wood panelling and gas lamps in the bar. Homemade soup and snacks available. Children welcome in the lounge bar until 8pm.

11am–1am in season; 11am–2.30pm and 5pm–1am out of season.

KETTLEBRIDGE

Kettlebridge Inn
9 Cupar Road, Kettlebridge
☎ *(01337) 830232* James Alkman

 Five beers always available from a list that runs into hundreds.

A traditional village coaching inn in Fife golfing country on the A914 road to St Andrews. Open fires, lounge bar and restaurant. Local CAMRA Pub of the Year 1994 and 1999. Bar and restaurant food available at lunchtime and evenings. Street parking, garden. Children allowed in restaurant only.

12–2.30pm Mon–Sat; 5–7pm Mon; 5–11pm Tues–Thurs; 5pm–midnight Fri–Sat; 12.30–2.30pm and 5–11pm Sun.

KIRKCALDY

Betty Nicol's
297 High Street, Kirkcaldy KY1 1JL
☎ *(01592) 642083* Sandy Haxton

 A freehouse with Caledonian Deuchars IPA and 80/- always available, plus a guest. Morland Old Speckled Hen, Timothy Taylor Landlord and Fuller's London Pride are regularly featured but many others also stocked as available.

Olde-worlde pub with separate lounge for private functions. Food available 12–2pm.

All day, every day.

Harbour Bar

469 High Street, Kirkcaldy KY1 2SN
☎ *(01592) 264270*

Home of the Fyfe Brewing Company offering the full range of Fyfe beers. Also guests from Belhaven Brewery and elsewhere.

The brewery is located in an old sailworks behind and above the pub. Auld Alliance, the first brew, was launched in May 1995 and there are now five more beers available, with further plans for expansion. The plant size is for two and a half barrels, with a ten-barrel per week restriction. The Harbour Bar is a traditional alehouse. Scottish CAMRA Pub of the Year 2000 and runner-up in national awards. Fife CAMRA Pub of the Year for six consecutive years up to 2001. Snacks are available at lunchtime and evenings. Parking. Children not allowed.

ROPE OF SAND 3.7% ABV
Golden IPA-style brew.
AULD ALLIANCE 4.0% ABV
Ruby-coloured and heavily hopped.
LION SLAYER 4.2% ABV
Golden bitter.
FIRST LYTE 4.3% ABV
Lyte-coloured, using First Gold hops.
FYFE FYRE 4.8% ABV
Straw-coloured and fruity.
CAULD TURKEY 6.0% ABV
Dark and dangerous.

OPEN *11am–2.30pm and 5pm–midnight Mon–Thurs; 11am–midnight Fri–Sat; 12.30pm–midnight Sun.*

Burns Tavern

187 High Street, Leslie, Glenrothes KY6 3DB
☎ *(01592) 741345* Margaret Wilkie

A freehouse, but with an agreement with Carlsberg-Tetley for a limited period, offering a very varied selection of real ales, with Caledonian 80/- and Timothy Taylor Landlord always available. Customers' requests are welcome at all times.

A very friendly traditional Scottish pub offering en-suite accommodation. Snacks available all day, and functions are catered for. Extensive beer garden to rear.

OPEN *All day, every day.*

Hawkshill Hotel

Hawkslaw Street, Leven KY8 4LS
☎ *(01333) 427033* Mrs Rossiter

A freehouse with Timothy Taylor Landlord always available, plus a guest beer changed weekly. Favourites include Orkney Dark Island, Exmoor Gold and Kelham Island Pale Rider.

A family inn with function room, separate dining area and beer garden. Food available lunchtimes and evenings. Children allowed.

OPEN *11am–2.30pm and 6pm–midnight Mon–Thurs; 11am–midnight Fri–Sat; 12–12 Sun.*

Places Featured:

Aberdeen
Elgin
Findhorn
Methlick

Portsoy
Ruthven
Stonehaven
Tomintoul

THE PUBS

ABERDEEN

Archibald Simpson
5 Castle Street, Aberdeen AB9 8AX
☎ *(01224) 621365* Jason Dullea

Caledonian 80/- and Deuchars IPA regularly served plus one or two guest beers. Tomintoul Wild Cat often available.

It's not difficult to imagine this Grade I listed building as it used to be: a Clydesdale Bank. Now a JD Wetherspoon freehouse situated on the corner of Union and King Streets. Food served all day, every day. Children welcome until 6pm if eating a meal.

OPEN *11am–midnight Mon–Thurs;
11am–1am Fri–Sat.*

The Blue Lamp
121–3 Gallowgate, Aberdeen AB25 1BU
☎ *(01224) 647472* Mr Brown

A freehouse with Caledonian 80/- and Deuchars IPA always available, plus up to five guest beers. Regulars include Isle of Skye Young Pretender and many others from small Scottish breweries.

A pub combining the traditional and the contemporary, with live entertainment at weekends. Two bars, one with an early 1960s feel, the other spacious. Small function room available to hire. Sandwiches only. No children.

OPEN *All day Mon–Sat; 12.30–3.30pm and
6.30–11pm Sun.*

Carriages Bar & Restaurant
101 Crown Street, Aberdeen AB11 6HH
☎ *(01224) 595440/571593* Jim Byers

Caledonian Deuchars IPA and a Castle Eden brew are among the five beers permanently available, plus five guests, changing weekly, such as Marston's Pedigree, Wadworth 6X, Fuller's London Pride, Shepherd Neame Spitfire, Greene King Abbot Ale, Orkney Dark Island or something from Aviemore, Isle of Skye, Tomintoul, Houston or any other independent brewery.

Carriages is a freehouse and part of the Brentwood Hotel. Personally run by the director/licensee, who is a fount of local knowledge, it has a relaxed, informal atmosphere. A hot buffet lunch is served 12–2pm Mon–Fri; dinner in the restaurant 6–9.45pm Mon–Sun. Car park. Children welcome in lounge area and restaurant, when eating. Special children's menu available. Website: www.brentwood-hotel.co.uk.

OPEN *12–2.30pm and 5pm–midnight Mon–Sat;
6–11pm Sun.*

Old Blackfriars
Castle Street, Aberdeen, Grampian AB11 5BB
☎ *(01224) 581922* Fiona Smith

A Belhaven Brewery house with nine real ale pumps. Belhaven 80/- and St Andrews plus Caledonian 80/-, Deuchars IPA and Inveralmond Ossian permanently available. Up to two guests which may be from breweries such as Orkney, Smiles or Hop Back. Thousands of guest ales have been featured over the years and repeats are avoided.

An 80-year-old city-centre pub in a sixteenth-century building. Original ceiling, old cellar, very traditional atmosphere. Food available in non-smoking dining area at lunchtime. Children allowed for meals only.

OPEN *11am–midnight Mon–Sat;
12.30–11pm Sun.*

The Prince of Wales
7 St Nicholas Lane, Aberdeen AB10 1HF
☎ *(01224) 640597* Steven Christie

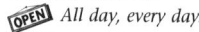A freehouse with Inveralmond Prince of Wales and Caledonian 80/- always on the menu. Four guest beers, changed weekly, may include Isle of Skye Red Cuillin and Young Pretender, Timothy Taylor Landlord or Orkney Dark Island, but ales from other independents also available as and when.

A classic city-centre Victorian bar. No music. Food available at lunchtime. Children allowed.

OPEN *All day, every day.*

Tap & Spile
Aberdeen Airport, Dyce, Aberdeen
☎ *(01224) 722331* J and R Tennent

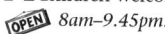Two guest beers regularly served, such as Caledonian IPA, 80/- or Marston's Pedigree.

Airport bar. Food served 8am–5pm. Children welcome.

OPEN *8am–9.45pm.*

ELGIN

Sunninghill Hotel
Hay Street, Elgin, Morayshire IV30 1NH
☎ *(01343) 547799* Winnie Rose

A freehouse offering five real ales. Guests changed weekly, from Scottish breweries such as Isle of Skye, Orkney and Tomintoul.

A hotel lounge bar. Food at lunchtime and evenings. Children allowed.

OPEN *11am–2.30pm and 5–11pm Mon–Fri; 11am–11pm Sat; 12.30–11pm Sun.*

FINDHORN

Crown & Anchor Inn
Findhorn, Nr Forres, Morayshire IV36 3YF
☎ *(01309) 690243* Mrs Heather Burrell

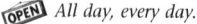A freehouse serving at least four real ales and up to seven in summer. Regulars include Timothy Taylor Landlord, Fuller's ESB and Bateman brews.

Built in 1739, a pub offering bed and breakfast accommodation, live entertainment and a lounge area. Food at lunchtime and evenings. Children allowed.

OPEN *All day, every day.*

Kimberley Inn
Findhorn, Nr Forres, Morayshire IV36 3YG
☎ *(01309) 690492* Mrs Lorraine Hessel

A freehouse with real ales changing regularly, including Caledonian Deuchars IPA, Black Sheep Bitter, Orkney The Red MacGregor and guest ales from Orkney, Black Isle or Aviemore.

A village seafood pub with two separate non-smoking areas. Views across the bay, with outside seating and heating. Fresh seafood daily, including 'catch of the day', salmon, langoustines, mussels, and much more! Food served all day, every day in summer, and at lunchtime and evenings during winter. Children welcome until 8pm.

OPEN *All day, every day.*

METHLICK

The Gight House Hotel
Sunnybrae, Methlick, Ellon, Aberdeenshire AB41 7BP
☎ *(01651) 806389* Les Ross

Three real ale pumps serve a regularly changing range of beers, with Timothy Taylor Landlord, Black Sheep Bitter and Marston's Pedigree featured often, plus Scottish brews such as Isle of Skye Red Cuillin.

A freehouse with lounge, restaurant, two conservatories, children's play area and large garden with putting green. Food served at lunchtime and evenings Mon–Sat and all day Sun. Situated about 20 miles from Aberdeen. Find Methlick and you will not be far away!

OPEN *12–2.30pm and 5pm–midnight Mon–Fri; all day Sat–Sun.*

PORTSOY

The Shore Inn
The Old Harbour, Church Street, Portsoy, Banffshire AB45 2QR
☎ *(01261) 842831* Mr Hill

A freehouse with Isle of Skye Red Cuillin among the brews always available. A guest, changed weekly, is also offered.

A traditional, 300-year-old pub, overlooking a seventeenth-century harbour. Separate restaurant. Food all day. Children allowed.

OPEN *All day, every day.*

RUTHVEN

Borve Brew House

Ruthven, Huntley, Aberdeenshire AB54 4SR
☎ *(01466) 760343*

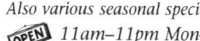 The full range of Borve Brews are produced and available on the premises.

The Borve Brew House is a former school house converted into a small brewery. It relocated to Ruthven, a hamlet in the foothills of the Grampian mountains, in 1988, having originated at Borve, on the Isle of Lewis, in 1983. The beer is available bottled or on draught. No food. Car park. Children not allowed.

BORVE ALE 4.0% ABV
A session ale.
TALL SHIPS IPA 5.0% ABV
BORVE EXTRA STRONG 10% ABV
A connoisseur's beer.
Also various seasonal specials.

 11am–11pm Mon–Sat; 11am–2.30pm and 6.30–11pm Sun.

STONEHAVEN

The Marine Hotel

9–10 Shorehead, Stonehaven AB3 2JY
☎ *(01569) 762155* Mr Phil Duncan

Timothy Taylor ales always available plus five guests (200 per year) perhaps from Orkney, Harviestoun and Tomintoul breweries, plus a wide range of English ales.

The pub overlooks the harbour and has a large bar with a juke box. Bar and restaurant food served at lunchtime and evenings. Local seafood and game. Parking. Follow the signs to the harbour.

9am–1am Mon–Sat; 9am–midnight Sun.

TOMINTOUL

The Glen Avon Hotel

1 The Square, Tomintoul, Ballindalloch, Banffshire AB37 9ET
☎ *(01807) 580218* Robert Claase

A freehouse always offering Tomintoul Wild Cat, Stag and Nessie's Monster Mash. Guest beers changed weekly on two pumps in summer.

A country pub with log fires and separate dining area. Food at lunchtime and evenings. Children allowed.

All day, every day.

Places Featured:

Aviemore	Lochranza
Avoch	Melvich
Carrbridge	Nairn
Clachaig	Rosemarkie
Fort William	Sligachan
Inverness	Stromness
Kingussie	Ullapool

THE PUBS

AVIEMORE

Old Bridge Inn

Dalfaber Road, Aviemore, Inverness-shire PH22 1PX
☎ *(01479) 811137* Mr Reid

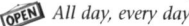Aviemore Ruthven Brew and a house bitter always available in this freehouse, plus a varied selection of guests.

Set in a rural location next to the River Spey. Separate dining area. Food at lunchtime and evenings. Children allowed.

OPEN *All day, every day.*

AVOCH

The Station Hotel

Bridge Street, Avoch, Moray, Ross-shire IV9 8GG
☎ *(01381) 620246* David Graham

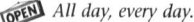A freehouse with two guests, changed twice weekly, from a good range of beers.

A country village pub with two bars and a conservatory. Food at lunchtime and evenings. Children allowed.

OPEN *All day, every day.*

CARRBRIDGE

Cairn Hotel

Carrbridge, Inverness-shire PH23 3AS
☎ *(01479) 841212* AE Kirk

Black Isle Red Kite, Caledonian 80/- and Deuchars IPA, Isle of Skye Red Cuillin, Aviemore Ruthven and Cairngorm regularly available, plus something perhaps from Houston or Tomintoul.

Family-owned, traditional freehouse in ideal touring area. Situated in the centre of the village, well visited by locals and tourists alike. Food served 12–2.15pm and 6–8.30pm. Car park. Children's certificate. En-suite accommodation.

OPEN *11am–midnight Mon–Fri; 11am–1am Sat; 12.30–11pm Sun.*

CLACHAIG

Clachaig Inn

Clachaig, Glencoe, Argyll PH49 4HX
☎ *(01855) 811252* Guy and Ed Daynes

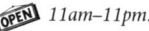Isle of Skye Red Cuillin and Black Cuillin and Heather Ale always available plus daily changing guests from Houston, Isle of Skye, Aviemore and Atlas.

A pub and hotel, popular with hillwalkers. Food available 12–9pm daily. Children allowed in the lounge bar. Beer garden. Accommodation. For further information visit the web site at www.clachaig.com.

OPEN *11am–11pm.*

FORT WILLIAM

Grog and Gruel

66 High Street, Fort William PH33 6AE
☎ *(01397) 705078* Neil Dennison

Up to eight ales on offer in regular rotation, including beers from the new Atlas Brewery in Kinlochleven, Heather and Houston. Seasonal and celebration ales, and occasional festivals.

A traditional town pub in an old building. Bar and restaurant food available. Beer garden. Children allowed daytimes only. Website: www.grogandgruel.co.uk.

OPEN *12–12 Mon–Wed; 12–1am Thurs–Sat; 12–11pm Sun.*

ORKNEY
DARK ISLAND

THE ORKNEY BREWERY
QUOYLOO
SANDWICK
ORKNEY

INVERSNESS

No 27

27 Castle Street, Inverness, Highlands IV2 3DU
☎ *(01463) 241999* Alison Mackenzie

A freehouse serving two constantly changing real ales which in winter could be Scottish or English ales but in summer are always traditional Scottish ales. Regular breweries featured include Black Isle (in summer), Isle of Skye, Arran, and ales such as Timothy Taylor Landlord, Morland Old Speckled Hen, and Fuller's London Pride.

A traditional town pub in an old building with wood panelling, stone floor and fireplace. Bar and restaurant food available. Occasional live music for special events. Children allowed.

OPEN *11am–11pm Mon–Wed; 11am–1am Thurs–Fri; 11am–12.30am Sat; 12.30–11.00pm Sun.*

Blackfriars

93–5 Academy Street, Inverness
☎ *(01463) 233881* Alexander MacDiarmid

Three or four guest beers regularly available, often from Morland and Black Isle.

Old Scottish alehouse, situated close to Inverness bus and railway stations. Food available. Children's certificate.

OPEN *11am–midnight Mon–Wed; 11am–1am Thur–Fri; 11am–11.45pm Sat; 12.30–11pm Sun.*

Clachnaharry Inn

17–19 High Street, Clachnaharry Road, Inverness PH38 4NG
☎ *(01463) 239806* David Irwin

A freehouse offering four real ales, three from the cask. Regular favourites include Tomintoul Wild Cat and Nessie's Monster Mash, Adnams Broadside and Morland Old Speckled Hen.

A traditional old coaching inn next to the railway and canal. Lounge and public bar. The beer garden used to be a train platform. Food served all day. Children allowed in lounge only.

OPEN *All day, every day.*

The Heathmount Hotel

Kingsmills Road, Inverness IV2 3JU
☎ *(01463) 235877* Fiona Newton

A freehouse with Maclay 80/- and Isle of Skye Red Cuillin always on offer. Plus a couple of guests that might include Shepherd Neame Spitfire.

Newly renovated pub, modern with an old touch. Smoking and non-smoking areas in the restaurant. Food at lunchtime and evenings. Children allowed. One minute from the town centre.

OPEN *All day, every day.*

KINGUSSIE

The Royal Hotel

High Street, Kingussie, Inverness-shire PH21 1HX
☎ *(01540) 661898* Fiona McIsaac (manager)

Part of the NKB group (Newtonmore and Kingussie Brewery Limited), and the major outlet for group's micro-brewery. Three regular home brews from NKB always available, including Piper's Brew and Highland Mist, plus a minimum of three guest ales.

This 52-room hotel has a main bar that holds about 200 people and offers live entertainment at weekends and mid-week in season. Food available until 9.30pm. Beer festival with over 50 real ales on offer held throughout November (special rates available). Well-behaved children and dogs welcome.

NKB3 HIGHLAND MIST 3.6% ABV
NKB1 4.0% ABV
NKB2 PIPER'S BREW 4.2% ABV

OPEN *All day, every day.*

LOCHRANZA

Catacol Bay Hotel

Catacol, Lochranza, Brodick, Isle of Arran KA27 8HN
☎ *(01770) 830231* Dave Ashcroft

A freehouse with Arran Brewery ales always available plus up to three guest beers.

Easy-going, family-orientated hotel, with lounge bar, dining room and pool and games room. Food all day till 10pm, plus buffet every Sunday 12–4pm. Acoustic music sessions every Friday. The pub has a children's certificate and outdoor play area. Website: www.catacol.co.uk.

OPEN *All day, every day.*

MELVICH

Melvich Hotel & Far North Brewery

Melvich, Thurso, Caithness & Sutherland KW14 7YJ
☎ *(01641) 531 206* Peter Martin

Beers from the Far North range are always on offer.

A country hotel with two bars and a restaurant, overlooking the Pentland Firth to Orkney. Food served 6–8.15pm daily. Car park. Children welcome.

REAL MACKAY 3.8% ABV
SPLIT STONE PALE ALE 4.2% ABV
PFR 4.8% ABV
EDGE OF DARKNESS 7.0% ABV

OPEN *All day, every day.*

NAIRN

The Invernairne Hotel

Thurlow Road, Nairn, Moray IV12 4EZ
☎ *(01667) 452039* Mrs Wilkie

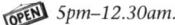Isle of Skye Red Cuillin always available plus one or two guests, changed fortnightly, which may include Belhaven brews or Fuller's London Pride.

A freehouse with a lounge bar and dining area. Regular live music. Food served evenings only. Children allowed.

OPEN *5pm–12.30am.*

ROSEMARKIE

The Plough Inn

High Street, Rosemarkie, Highlands
☎ *(01381) 620164* Rob Brutherstone

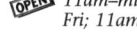A Black Isle Brewery house with Red Kite, Hibernator, Porter and Golden Eye permanently available, plus seasonal guests.

A country village pub dating from 1691. Beer garden. Bar and restaurant food available. Car park. Children allowed.

OPEN *11am–midnight Mon–Thurs; 11am–1am Fri; 11am–11.45pm Sat–Sun.*

SLIGACHAN

The Sligachan Hotel

Sligachan, Isle of Skye IV47 8SW
☎ *(01478) 650204* Iain Campbell

A freehouse with eight real ale pumps in the public bar and one in the lounge bar. Beers from the Isle of Skye Brewery always available, plus frequently changing guest ales such as Caledonian 80/- and Deuchars IPA.

A 100-year-old building with a main public bar, lounge bar, pool tables. Live music. The only pub on the island that is licensed to open at 11am on Sundays! Food at lunchtime and evenings. Children allowed until 8pm – the pub has the largest outdoor play area on the island.

OPEN *All day, every day.*

STROMNESS

The Stromness Hotel

The Pier Head, Stromness, Isle of Orkney KW16 3AA
☎ *(01856) 850298* Leona Macleod

A freehouse with Orkney The Red MacGregor and Dark Island always available.

The largest three-star hotel in Orkney, with 42 bedrooms. A separate restaurant serves food at lunchtime and evenings. Children allowed. For further information visit the website at www.stromnesshotel.com.

OPEN *All day, every day.*

ULLAPOOL

The Ferryboat Inn

Shore Street, Ullapool, Ross-shire IV26 2UJ
☎ *(01854) 612366* Richard Smith

A freehouse offering six real ales. Regulars come from the Orkney brewery, others from further afield such as Wadworth 6X.

An old-fashioned one-bar pub with coal fire and separate restaurant area. Food served at lunchtime and evenings. Children allowed.

OPEN *All day, every day.*

Places Featured:
Belhaven
East Linton
Edinburgh
Haddington
Linlithgow

Mid-Calder
North Berwick
St Andrews
South Queensferry

THE PUBS

BELHAVEN

The Mason's Arms
8 High Street, Belhaven, Dunbar, East Lothian EH42 1NP
☎ *(01368) 863700* Peter Sullivan

Belhaven 80/- or St Andrew's Ale usually available, or occasionally Sandy Hunter's Traditional Ale.

Traditional country inn, situated between West Barns and Dunbar. Bar, separate lounge and restaurant. Bar snacks served 12–2pm Mon–Tues, full bar menu 12–2pm and 6.30–9pm Wed–Sun. Children welcome until 9pm, with grass play area set within the beer garden.

[OPEN] *12–3pm and 5–11pm Mon–Thurs; 12–1am Fri–Sat; 12–11pm Sun.*

EAST LINTON

The Drover's Inn
5 Bridge Street, East Linton, East Lothian EH40 3AG
☎ *(01620) 860298* Alison and John Burns

A freehouse with Adnams Broadside and Caledonian Deuchars IPA always on the menu. Two guests, changed most weeks, include regular choices such as Greene King Abbot, Fuller's London Pride or Orkney Red MacGregor.

An old-fashioned pub-restaurant with one bar. Smoking and non-smoking dining areas and bistro. Live entertainment and folk bands monthly. Food at lunchtime and evenings. Courtesy coach for parties of six or more operates within 25-mile radius. Children allowed.

[OPEN] *Summer: 11.30am–11pm Mon–Wed; 11.30am–1am Thurs–Sat; 12.30pm–midnight Sun. Winter: times as above, except closed 2.30pm–5pm Mon–Sat.*

EDINBURGH

The Bow Bar
80 West Bow, Edinburgh EH1 2HH
☎ *(0131) 226 7667* Helen McLoughlin

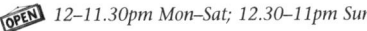Belhaven 80/-, Caledonian Deuchars IPA and Timothy Taylor Landlord always available, plus five constantly changing guests, including a couple from Scotland and the rest from other independent breweries – from Orkney to Cornwall.

Take a step back in time to a genuine freehouse offering an unparalleled selection of real ales and malt whiskies. Bar food at lunchtime. Children not allowed.

[OPEN] *12–11.30pm Mon–Sat; 12.30–11pm Sun.*

Carter's Bar
185 Morrison Street, Edinburgh EH3 8DZ
☎ *(0131) 623 7023* Shane Mallon

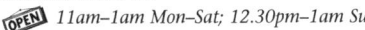Calendonian 80/- and Deuchars IPA permanently available, plus a wide selection of guest ales from all over the UK.

Local bar in the heart of the capital city, with friendly atmosphere downstairs and pleasant, relaxing surroundings in the gallery upstairs. Live music. Food available, including free buffet on Friday evenings. Happy hours 11am–6.30pm Mon–Sat. No children under 14.

[OPEN] *11am–1am Mon–Sat; 12.30pm–1am Sun.*

The Cask & Barrel
115 Broughton Street, Edinburgh EH1 3RZ
☎ *(0131) 556 3132* Patrick Mitchell

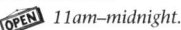Caledonian 80/- and Deuchars IPA are among the brews permanently available plus five guest beers from breweries such as Hop Back, Harviestoun, Mauldons, Hambleton, Cotleigh, Coach House, Shepherd Neame and Larkins.

A large horseshoe bar with a wide range of customers. Food available at lunchtime. From the east end of Queen Street, turn left off York Place.

[OPEN] *11am–midnight.*

Cloisters Bar

26 Brougham Street, Edinburgh EH3 9JH
☎ *(0131) 221 9997* Benjamin Budge

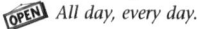 A freehouse with Caledonian Deuchars IPA always available. Guests changed once or twice a week. Dent Aviator, Timothy Taylor Landlord and Caledonian 80/- are regularly featured. Others include B&T, Smiles Golden Brew, Spinnaker Buzz and Ringwood Fortyniner.

A central, old-fashioned, church-like pub, with one bar. No TV or music. Food lunchtimes only. Children allowed.

OPEN *All day, every day.*

The Cumberland Bar

1–3 Cumberland Street, Edinburgh EH3 6RT
☎ *(0131) 558 3134*
RD Simpson (owner), A Douglas (manager)

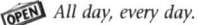 Caledonian Deuchars IPA and 80/-, Timothy Taylor Landlord and Orkney Dark Island always on the menu. The four guests, changed weekly, may include Hop Back Summer Lightning, Fuller's ESB or Greene King Abbot Ale.

A traditional one-bar alehouse. Food served every lunchtime, with toasties, panninis and soup available in the evenings. Children allowed in part of the bar if under control.

OPEN *All day, every day.*

The Guildford Arms

1 West Register Street, Edinburgh EH2 2AA
☎ *(0131) 556 4312* Paul Cronin

 Caledonian 80/-, Deuchars IPA, Orkney Dark Island, Harviestoun Waverley 70/- and Schiehallion permanently available plus seven guest beers (260+ per year) including Traquair Bear Ale and Festival Ale, plus a massive selection from all over England.

A beautiful Jacobean pub. Restaurant food available at lunchtime. At the east end of Princes Street, behind Burger King.

OPEN *11am–11pm Mon–Wed; 11am–midnight Thurs–Sat; 12.30–11pm Sun.*

Halfway House

24 Fleshmarket Close, High Street, Edinburgh EH1 1BX
☎ *(0131) 225 7101* John Ward

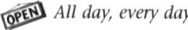 Three real ales on offer, with Caledonian, Fisherrow, Inveralmond and Houston regulars among many visitors. Possibly the best prices for real ale in the Old Town. Also a fine range of malts.

One of the smallest and friendliest pubs in the Old Town, very close to Waverley station and the Royal Mile. Good value homemade food including Stovies with Oat Cakes (£1.90) and Fresh Crab Bisque (£2.40). Food available all day, subject to not being sold out!

OPEN *All day, every day.*

Homes Bar

102 Constitution Street, Leith, Edinburgh EH6 6AW
☎ *(0131) 553 7710* Patrick Fitzgerald

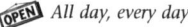 A freehouse with five real ales served on custom-made hand pumps. Guest beers a speciality.

A traditional one-room friendly bar, with interesting decor featuring antiques and memorabilia. Snacks served 12–3pm daily.

OPEN *All day, every day.*

Leslie's Bar

45 Ratcliffe Terrace, Edinburgh EH9 1SU
☎ *(0131) 667 5957* Gavin Blake

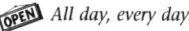 A freehouse with real ale on six pumps. Belhaven 80/-, Caledonian 80/- and Deuchars IPA, plus Timothy Taylor Landlord always available. One guest beer also offered, which is often a Maclay brew.

Unchanged in 100 years, with an old-fashioned gantry and open fire. One bar. Pies only. No children.

OPEN *All day, every day.*

Old Chain Pier

32 Trinity Crescent, Edinburgh EH5 3ED
☎ *(0131) 552 1233* Mr Nicol

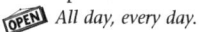 Caledonian Deuchars IPA, Black Sheep Best Bitter and Timothy Taylor Landlord are more or less permanent fixtures here, plus one guest, changed every two days. Regulars include brews from Harviestoun and Moorhouse's.

A local with very mixed clientele, young and old. Non-smoking area. Food served 12–9.30pm. Children allowed.

OPEN *All day, every day.*

Royal Ettrick Hotel

13 Ettrick Road, Edinburgh EH10 5BJ
☎ *(0131) 228 6413* Mrs EM Stuart

 Caledonian 80/- and Maclay Kanes Amber Ale always available, plus four guest beers from a large range that may include Timothy Taylor Landlord, Castle Eden Conciliation Ale, Titanic Best, Hook Norton Old Hooky, or Broughton, Greene King and Adnams ales.

Part of a mansion and conservatory built in 1875 in the leafy suburbs. Bar and restaurant food available at lunchtime and evenings. Morning and afternoon teas also served. Car park, garden, banqueting and conference facilities. Weddings catered for. Children allowed. Accommodation.

OPEN *11am–midnight Mon–Sat; 12.30pm–midnight Sun.*

Southsider
3–7 West Richmond Street, Edinburgh EH8 9EF
☎ *(0131) 667 2003* Liz Walls

One Maclay brew always available plus three guests. The emphasis is on smaller breweries, and a large selection of lager-style beers is also served.

Alounge and public bar, popular with locals and students. Extensive menu available 12–2.30pm and 6–9pm daily. Fully refurbished. No children or animals (except guide dogs). Car park in the city centre.

OPEN *11am–midnight Mon–Wed; 11am–1am Thurs–Sat; 12.30pm–midnight Sun.*

The Starbank Inn
64 Laverock Road, Edinburgh EH5 3BZ
☎ *(0131) 552 4141* Scott Brown

A freehouse with Belhaven 80/-, IPA, St Andrew's Ale, Sandy Hunter's Traditional Ale and Timothy Taylor Landlord always available. Five guests, changed weekly, may include Tomintoul brews or those from Aviemore and other small and micro-brewers.

Traditional, old-fashioned pub with one bar, overlooking the River Forth. Separate non-smoking dining area. Food at lunchtime and evenings. Children allowed.

OPEN *All day, every day.*

The Steading
118–20 Biggar Road, Edinburgh EH10 7DU
☎ *(0131) 445 1128* William Store

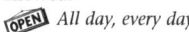A freehouse with Caledonian Deuchars IPA, Timothy Taylor Landlord and Orkney and Belhaven brews always available. Plus a guest, changed weekly. Brains Reverend James Original Ale is a favourite.

Acountry inn with two bars, one smoking, one non-smoking, plus a separate dining area. Food served all day. Children allowed.

OPEN *All day, every day.*

HADDINGTON

Waterside Bistro and Restaurant
1–5 Waterside, Nungate, Haddington, East Lothian EH41 4BE
☎ *(01620) 825674* James Findlay

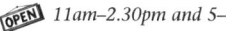Regular guests in this freehouse include Belhaven brews, Caledonian Deuchars IPA, Marston's Pedigree and Timothy Taylor Landlord.

An old, restored cottage overlooking the River Tyne and the abbey. Separate dining area. Food at lunchtime and evenings. Children allowed.

OPEN *11am–2.30pm and 5–11pm.*

LINLITHGOW

The Four Marys
65 High Street, Linlithgow EH49 7ED
☎ *(01506) 842171* Eve and Ian Forrest

Belhaven 80/- and St Andrew's, Caledonian Deuchars and an Orkney ale always available plus nine guest beers (400 per year) that may include Morland Old Speckled Hen, and something from Harviestoun or Timothy Taylor.

Atraditional pub with antique furniture and stone walls. Local CAMRA Pub of the Year 2000, and *Sunday Mail* Pub of the Year 2002. The bar has masses of mementoes of Mary Queen of Scots, who was born at Linlithgow Palace. Food available lunchtimes and evenings Mon–Fri and all day Sat–Sun. Parking. Children allowed. Two real ale festivals held every year, with 20 real ales at each. Opposite the entrance to Linlithgow Palace.

OPEN *12–11pm Mon–Wed; 12pm–12.45am Thurs–Sat; 12.30–11pm Sun.*

MID-CALDER

Torpichen Arms
36 Bank Street, Mid-Calder, Livingston, West Lothian EH53 0AR
☎ *(01506) 880020* Helen Hill

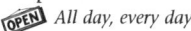Caledonian 80/- and Deuchars IPA always available, plus guests, changed weekly. Harviestoun, Nethergate, Robinson's, Tomintoul and Cains breweries are regularly featured.

Old village pub with weekend entertainment. Bed and breakfast. Lunches only. Children allowed until 8.30pm.

OPEN *All day, every day.*

NORTH BERWICK

Nether Abbey Hotel
20 Dirleton Avenue, North Berwick, East Lothian EH39 4BQ
☎ *(01620) 892802* Stirling Stewart

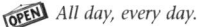A freehouse with Belhaven beers always on the menu. Guests may include Caledonian Deuchars IPA, Marston's Pedigree, Orkney Dark Island, Kelham Island Pale Rider and Timothy Taylor Landlord.

Ahotel with a warm, friendly atmosphere, situated in a leafy Victorian avenue, and run by the Stewart family for the past 40 years. One main bar, brasserie and beer garden, plus first-class accommodation. Lunches, suppers, bar snacks and children's menu always available. Annual beer festival every February features over 50 ales, plus live music and all-day food. Free parking. Families welcome – the hotel has a children's outdoor play area. For more details visit our website at: www.netherabbey.co.uk.

OPEN *All day, every day.*

ST ANDREWS

Drouthy Neebors

209 South Street, St Andrews, Fife KY16 9EF
☎ *(01334) 479952* Mr Shug

 A Belhaven tied house with St Andrew's and 80/- permanently available plus four guest ales. Regular features include Orkney Dark Island and Raven Ale, plus Ridleys Rumpus.

A real mixed-bag clientele here: students, locals, tourists. Food available. Children allowed. Car parking.

OPEN *11am–midnight Mon–Thurs; 11am–1am Fri–Sat; 12.30–midnight Sun.*

SOUTH QUEENSFERRY

The Ferry Tap

36 High Street, South Queensferry, Nr Edinburgh EH30 9HN
☎ *(0131) 331 2000* Brian Inglis

A freehouse always offering Caledonian 80/- and Deuchars IPA plus Orkney Dark Island. Guests are changed weekly, one in winter, two in summer.

O ld-fashioned real ale house with one bar and lounge. Food served at lunchtimes; snacks only in evenings. No children.

OPEN *All day, every day.*

STRATHCLYDE

Places Featured:

Arrochar	Hamilton
Ayr	Houston
Biggar	Inverary
Castlecary	Inverkip
Cove	Johnstone
Darvel	Kilmarnock
Dumbarton	Largs
Dundonald	Lochwinnoch
Furnace	Paisley
Glasgow	Troon
Gourock	

THE PUBS

ARROCHAR

The Village Inn

Arrochar, Lochlong, Argyll and Bute G83 7AX
☎ *(01301) 702279* Josie Andrade

A pub owned by Maclay Brewery, with Maclay Wallace IPA always on the menu. Two guests are changed weekly and may include Orkney Dark Island.

O lde-worlde village pub with two bars and separate dining area. Food served all day. Children allowed.

OPEN *All day, every day.*

AYR

Burrowfields Café Bar

13 Beresford Terrace, Ayr KA7 2EU
☎ *(01292) 269152* Daniel Kelly

Real ale on three pumps in this freehouse. Regular guests, changed weekly, include brews from Caledonian, Clearwater, Greene King and Cains.

L ive music once a week, TV and lounge bar. Food at lunchtime and evenings. Children allowed at lunchtime.

OPEN *All day, every day.*

Geordie's Byre

103 Main Street, Ayr KA8 88U
☎ *(01292) 264325*

 Caledonian 80/- and Deuchars IPA always available plus three guest beers (450 per year) from Orkney (Skullsplitter) to Cornwall and Devon (Summerskill Whistle Belly Vengeance).

A friendly freehouse managed by the owners. Decorated with memorabilia and Victoriana. No food. Children not allowed. Located 50 yards from the police headquarters on King Street.

OPEN *11am–11pm (midnight Thurs–Sat); 12.30–11pm Sun.*

BIGGAR

The Crown Inn

109–11 High Street, Biggar, Lanarkshire ML12 6DL
☎ *(01899) 220116* Mr and Mrs A Barrie

 A freehouse offering real ale on four pumps, two in each bar. Regular guests include Adnams Broadside, Morland Old Speckled Hen, Shepherd Neame Spitfire and Wadworth 6X.

A seventeenth-century pub with two bars, recently refurbished. Food served all day. Beer garden. Children allowed.

OPEN *All day, every day in summer; lunchtimes and evenings in winter.*

CASTLECARY

Castlecary House Hotel

Main Street, Castlecary, Cumbernauld, Lanarkshire G68 0HB
☎ *(01324) 840233* Mr McMillan

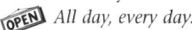 Freehouse with a good rotation of ales, such as Harviestoun Brooker's Bitter and Twisted, Orkney Dark Island and Houston Peter's Well.

Friendly, family-run hotel with 55 cottage-style bedrooms surrounding the main building, three lounges and a restaurant. Traditional pub food served lunchtimes and evenings, with Camerons Restaurant serving lunch plus à la carte meals in the evening. Children allowed. Just off the A80 between Glasgow and Stirling. Visit the website: www.castlecaryhotel.com.

OPEN *All day, every day.*

COVE

Knockderry House Hotel

204 Shore Road, Cove, Nr Helensburgh, Argyll G84 0NX
☎ *(01436) 842283* Murdo MacLeod

 A freehouse with real ale on three pumps. Regular guests, changed weekly, include brews from Orkney, Maclay Wallace IPA and Broadsword, Isle of Skye Red Cuillin and Black Cuillin.

A 10-bedroom, recently refurbished hotel on the shores of Loch Long, built in 1851. Food served in bar and restaurant. Children allowed.

OPEN *All day, every day.*

DARVEL

Loudoun Hill Inn

Darvel, Ayrshire KA17 0LY
☎ *(01560) 320275* Graham and Janet Wellby

Something from Belhaven Brewery is always on offer. The guest beer is changed weekly, and Heather Fraoch Ale and Grozet are usually available in bottles.

An old, one-bar coaching inn with real fire, restaurant and function room. Food served 12–2pm and 5–8pm during opening hours. Well-behaved children welcome. Accommodation available (three en-suite bedrooms). The pub is on the main A71, one mile east of Darvel, and offers access to the Irvine Valley Paths network. Website: www.loudoun-hill-inn.co.uk.

OPEN *12–2.30pm and 5–11pm Mon–Thurs (but closed Tues night, except for residents, and Wed lunch); 12–2.30pm and 5pm–midnight Fri; 12–12 Sat; 12.30–2.30pm and 4.30–11pm Sun.*

DUMBARTON

Cutty Sark

105 High Street, Dumbarton G82 1LF
☎ *(01389) 762509* Mr Fennell

Tied to Punch Taverns, with Belhaven St Andrew's Ale always available. A weekly guest beer might well be Orkney Dark Island.

A town-centre pub with lounge bar and a mixed clientele. Food at lunchtime only. Children allowed.

OPEN *All day, every day.*

DUNDONALD

Castle View

29 Main Street, Dundonald, Kilmarnock,
Ayrshire KA2 9HH
☎ *(01563) 851112* Iain Fisher

Part of the Wilson Boyle development. Caledonian 80/- or Deuchars IPA are regularly featured. Alternatives from Orkney and Harviestoun.

Restaurant-dominated, with two bars. Food at lunchtime and evenings. Children allowed. Just off the B739.

OPEN *All day, every day.*

FURNACE

Furnace Inn

Furnace, Inverary, Argyll PA32 8XN
☎ *(01499) 500200* Gordon Pirie

A freehouse with four or five beers always available. Guests, changed weekly, often include brews from Orkney and Clearwater.

A country-style pub, with one bar, oak beams and fires. Food served all day. Children allowed.

OPEN *All day, every day.*

GLASGOW

Athena Greek Taverna

780 Pollokshaws Road, Strathbungo, Glasgow,
Lanarkshire G42 2AE
☎ *(0141) 424 0858* Nicholas Geordiades

Six beers always available from a list of 200 guests that may include Otter Bright and beers from Rooster's, Yates, Belhaven, Caledonian and Shardlow breweries.

A café-style bar and adjacent Greek Cypriot restaurant serving Greek and European food. Children allowed. Situated beside Queen's Park railway station, not far from Shawlands Cross.

OPEN *11am–2.30pm and 5–11pm Mon–Sat;*
closed Sun.

The Counting House

2 St Vincent Place, Glasgow, Lanarkshire G1 2DH
☎ *(0141) 248 9568* Stuart Coxshall

This freehouse hosts a real ale festival in the spring, when there may be 50 brews on sale. The rest of the time, Caledonian 80/- and Deuchars IPA are among the beers always available. Guests change weekly, and Hop Back Summer Lightning is a regular.

A converted Bank of Scotland building with original fixtures and fittings, including the safe. Ninety tables. Food available all day. No children.

OPEN *All day, every day.*

Maclachlan's Bar

57 West Regent Street, Glasgow G2AE
☎ *(0141) 332 0595*

A range of own brews and Heather Ale always available plus two guests, usually from Scottish breweries.

A very Scottish bar with slate floor and stone bar. Around 100 malt whiskies also available. Food (specialising in venison, pheasant and salmon) available every day. No children.

MACLACHLAN'S IPA 3.8% ABV
KOLSH 4.1% ABV
Lager-style beer.
STRAWBERRY BLONDE 4.1% ABV
Fruit beer.
KIRKCULLEN 6.5% ABV
Winter ale. Porridge beer made with porridge oats.

OPEN *11am–11.45pm Mon–Sat;*
12.30–11.45pm Sun.

Station Bar

55 Port Dundas Road, Glasgow, Lanarkshire
☎ *(0141) 332 3117*
Michael McHugh and George Davie

A freehouse with Caledonian Deuchars IPA always available plus a guest, which might be Caledonian Edinburgh Strong Ale or Fuller's ESB.

A traditional city-centre local with one bar. Snacks, rolls and other tasty food available.

OPEN *All day, every day.*

Tap

1055 Sauchiehall Street, Glasgow G3 7UD
☎ *(0141) 339 0643* Gary Hamilton

Caledonian Deuchars IPA and 80/- usually served, with guest beers such as Heather Ale and Marston's Pedigree.

Traditional bar in a residential area catering mainly for student clientele. Specialising in jazz, with live music at weekends. A light-hearted and welcoming pub favoured by musicians and arty types. Food served 12–9pm. No children. Situated directly opposite Kelvingrove Art Gallery in West End.

OPEN *12–11pm Sun–Thurs; 12–12 Fri–Sat.*

Tennents Bar
191 Byres Road, Hillhead, Glasgow G12
☎ *(0141) 341 1024* Alison O'Conner

Up to 12 beers available from a guest list (100 per year) that may include Fuller's London Pride, Morland Old Speckled Hen and Marston's Pedigree.

A large public bar with a friendly atmosphere and no music. Bar and restaurant food is available at lunchtime and evenings. Adjacent to Glasgow University and Hillhead subway.

OPEN *11am–11pm Mon–Thurs; 11am–midnight Fri–Sat; 12.30–11.30pm Sun.*

The Three Judges
141 Dumbarton Road, Partick Cross, Glasgow G11 6PR
☎ *(0141) 337 3055* Helen McCarroll

Caledonian Deuchars IPA always available plus eight guest beers from independent and micro-breweries, old and new.

A lively West End pub. Bar food is served at lunchtime and evenings. Parking available. Near Kelvin Hall underground.

OPEN *11am–11pm Sun–Thurs; 11am–midnight Fri–Sat.*

GOUROCK

Spinnaker Hotel
121 Albert Road, Gourock, Renfrewshire
☎ *(01475) 633107* Stewart McCartney

Belhaven 80/- regularly available, plus three guest beers often from Caledonian, Orkney, Houston or Castle Eden.

Small hotel, situated a quarter of a mile west of the town centre, with panoramic views over the River Clyde and Cowal Peninsula. Food available all day every day. Children welcome.

OPEN *11am–midnight Mon–Thurs; 11am–1am Fri–Sat; 12.30pm–midnight Sun.*

HAMILTON

The George Bar
18 Campbell Street, Hamilton, Lanarkshire ML3 6AS
☎ *(01698) 424225* Lynn Adams

A pub tied to Belhaven, with three rotating guest beers always available. Regulars include the Belhaven Cask range and Heather Fraoch Ale.

A traditional-style, town-centre pub with small back room. Cask Marque award winner. Food at lunchtime. Children allowed. Can be tricky to find because of the one-way system!

OPEN *All day, every day.*

HOUSTON

The Fox & Hounds
South Street, Houston, Johnstone, Renfrewshire PA6 7EN
☎ *(01505) 612991* Jonathan Wengel

A freehouse and brewpub. Home of the Houston Brewing Company, so home brews are always on the menu, plus guests, changed weekly, such as Isle of Skye Red Cuillin or Coniston Bluebird.

A traditional coaching inn with three bars and a separate restaurant area. Food at lunchtime and evenings. Children allowed.

**KILLELLAN 3.7% ABV**
Golden, mellow ale.
BAROCHAN 4.0% ABV
Ruby-coloured and smooth.
ST PETER'S WELL 4.2% ABV
Fruity wheat beer made with continental hops.
FORMAKIN 4.3% ABV
Clean, tawny-coloured and nutty.

OPEN *All day, every day.*

INVERARY

The George Hotel
Main Street East, Inverary, Argyll PA32 8TT
☎ *(01499) 302111* Donald Clark

Real ale on up to three pumps in this freehouse. Guests are changed weekly, regulars include Broughton Greenmantle Ale and Belhaven St Andrew's Ale. Others might well come from the Houston Brewing Company.

An old-fashioned country house with two bars and a function room. Beer garden. Food served all day. Children allowed.

OPEN *All day, every day.*

INVERKIP

Inverkip Hotel
Main Street, Inverkip, Greenock, Renfrewshire PA16 0AS
☎ *(01475) 521478* Mr Hardy and Mr Cushley

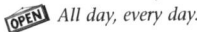A freehouse with real ale on two pumps. Belhaven and Caledonian Breweries tend to supply much of the range.

A family-run inn with dining area and separate restaurant. TV in the public bar. Food at lunchtime and evenings. Children allowed.

OPEN *All day, every day.*

JOHNSTONE

Coanes

26 High Street, Johnstone, Renfrewshire PA5 8AH
☎ *(01505) 322925* Michael Coane

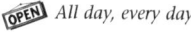 A freehouse always offering Caledonian 80/- and Deuchars IPA and Orkney Dark Island. Guests, changed weekly, may include favourites such as Orkney The Red MacGregor, Greene King Abbot Ale, Adnams Broadside or Marston's Pedigree or other occasional features.

An olde-worlde pub with a bar and lounge. Food available at lunchtime and evenings from Wed to Sat. Children allowed up to 8pm if eating.

OPEN *All day, every day.*

KILMARNOCK

The Hunting Lodge

14–16 Glencairn Square, Kilmarnock, Ayrshire KA1 4AH
☎ *(01563) 322920* Mr Little

A freehouse with real ale on up to seven pumps. Caledonian Deuchars IPA and Shepherd Neame Spitfire always available. Guests, changed weekly might include Timothy Taylor Landlord, Morland Old Speckled Hen, Greene King Abbot Ale and Fuller's London Pride.

Olde-worlde Georgian pub with three bars and a separate eating area. Food at lunchtime and evenings. Children allowed.

OPEN *11am–3pm and 5pm–midnight Mon–Wed; all day Thurs–Sun.*

LARGS

The Clachan Bar

14 Bath Street, Largs, Ayrshire KA30 8BL
☎ *(01475) 672224* Linda Maxwell

Tied to the Belhaven brewery. One real ale always available, such as Belhaven St Andrew's Ale.

A traditional pub with pool room. Bar snacks served 11am–3pm daily, with toasties available all day. Children welcome if eating.

OPEN *All day, every day.*

LOCHWINNOCH

The Brown Bull

33 Main Street, Lochwinnoch, Renfrewshire PA12 4AH
☎ *(01505) 843250*

A freehouse with Orkney Dark Island always on offer plus three guest pumps with ales changing weekly.

Olde-worlde one-bar pub and restaurant. Coal fire in winter. Restaurant open Fri–Sat evenings (booking advised), and bar meals are served 12.30–2.30pm and 5.30–7.30pm daily. Children allowed until 8pm.

OPEN *All day, every day.*

PAISLEY

Gabriels

33 Gauze Street, Paisley, Renfrewshire PA1 1EX
☎ *(0141) 887 8204* Michael O'Hare

A freehouse with Caledonian Deuchars IPA and ales from the Houston Brewing Company always available. Guests change weekly and may include Fuller's London Pride, Cotleigh and Harviestoun ales.

An oval bar with traditional decor on the walls. Separate dining area and restaurant. Food all day. Children allowed.

OPEN *All day, every day.*

TROON

Dan McKay's Bar

69 Portland Street, Troon KA10 6QU
☎ *(01292) 311079* Dan McKay

A freehouse with Belhaven 80/-, Caledonian 80/- and Deuchars IPA always on offer. Plus a guest beer, changed once or twice a week, which might be Timothy Taylor Landlord, Wadworth 6X, Young's Special or Fuller's London Pride.

Traditional establishment, leaning towards a café bar, with TV, live music and jazz. Food at lunchtime and evenings. Children allowed during the day.

OPEN *All day, every day.*

Places Featured:

Abernethy	Dundee
Blair Atholl	Inverkeilor
Blairgowrie	Kinross
Broughty Ferry	Moulin
Carnoustie	Perth
Clova	Strathtummel
Comrie	

THE PUBS

ABERNETHY

Cree's Inn
Main Street, Abernethy, Perthshire PH2 9LA
☎ *(01738) 850714* Brian Johnston

 A freehouse offering beers on four pumps. The range changes every week, but favourites include Belhaven 80/-, Marston's Pedigree, Greene King Abbot Ale and Caledonian Deuchars IPA and 80/-.

A one-bar country pub with separate restaurant attached, open all day. Children allowed. Accommodation.

OPEN *11am–2.30pm and 5–11pm Mon–Fri; all day Sat–Sun.*

BLAIR ATHOLL

The Bothy Bar
Atholl Arms Hotel, Old North Road, Blair Atholl, Perthshire
☎ *(01796) 481205*

 The sister hotel to the Moulin Hotel, with the full range of Moulin Brewery ales usually available.

This 'bothy' (the word means a place of refuge and comfort) was recently rebuilt using beams and wood from the old hotel stables. Food served all day. Gardens and children's play area. Disabled access and facilities.

OPEN *All day, every day.*

BLAIRGOWRIE

Rosemount Golf Hotel
Golf Course Road, Blairgowrie, Perthshire PH10 6LJ
☎ *(01250) 872604* Mr E Walker

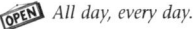 A freehouse with beers from Inveralmond Brewery always available, plus a guest, changed more frequently in summer. Caledonian Deuchars IPA is one favourite.

A family-run hotel, with one bar and a dining area with overspill for non-smokers. Food at lunchtime and evenings. Children allowed.

OPEN *All day, every day.*

The Stormont Arms
101 Perth Street, Blairgowrie, Perthshire PH10 6DT
☎ *(01250) 87312* Lewis Forbes Paterson

 Three beers usually available often from Caledonian, Inveralmond, Houston, Belhaven, Tomintoul or Orkney.

Traditional pub with lots of mirrors, favoured by sporting types. No food. Car park. No facilities for children.

OPEN *11am–2.30pm and 5–11pm Mon–Thurs; 11am–11pm Fri–Sun.*

BROUGHTY FERRY

Fisherman's Tavern
10–16 Fore Street, Broughty Ferry, Dundee DD5 2AD
☎ *(01382) 775941* Mr J McInally

 Belhaven 60/-, 70/-, 80/- and St Andrew's Ale always available. Also four guest beers (700 per year) which include Timothy Taylor Landlord, Fuller's London Pride, Arran Ale, Caledonian Deuchars IPA, Harviestoun Brooker's Bitter and Twisted, and Morland Old Speckled Hen, plus beers from every corner of the UK.

A 300-year-old listed building, formerly a fisherman's cottage. Winner of Scottish Licence Trade News's Best Poured Pint in Scotland award in 2001. Restaurant food available at lunchtime and evenings. Also 11 en-suite rooms in hotel with walled garden. Children welcome. Situated by the lifeboat station at Broughty Ferry.

OPEN *11am–midnight Mon–Wed; 11am–1am Thurs–Sat; 12.30pm–midnight Sun.*

CARNOUSTIE

The Stag's Head Inn
61 Dundee Street, Carnoustie, Angus DD7 7PN
☎ *(01241) 852265* Mr Duffy

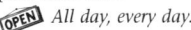 A freehouse with real ale on four pumps. Guest ales, which change constantly, may include Timothy Taylor Landlord, Caledonian 80/- or Orkney Dark Island.

A locals' pub with two bars. Food served at lunchtime and evenings in the summertime. Children only allowed in the pool table area.

OPEN *All day, every day.*

CLOVA
Glen Clova Hotel
Glen Clova, By Kirriemuir, Angus DD8 4QS
☎ *(01575) 550350*
Denise Binnie and Stuart Whisker

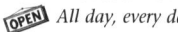 A freehouse with Caledonian Deuchars IPA and 80/- plus Orkney Red MacGregor always available.

A country hotel that has recently undergone a major refurbishment. Food served 12–9pm. Accommodation available in ten en-suite bedrooms and a 40-bed bunk house. Website: www.clova.com.

OPEN *All day, every day.*

COMRIE
Royal Hotel
Melville Square, Comrie, Perthshire
☎ *(01764) 679200* Edward Gibbons

Caledonian 80/-, Deuchars IPA and guest beer such as Caledonian Golden Promise, Timothy Taylor Landlord or something from Aviemore, Harviestoun or Inveralmond may be available.

L arge open fireplace, church pews and stone walls with ornate, hardwood gantry and bar counter. Pool table and Sky TV. Food served lunchtimes and evenings Mon–Fri, and all day Sat–Sun and bank holidays. Car park. Children welcome in the lounge bar or in large walled beer garden.

OPEN *11am–11pm Mon–Thurs; 11am–midnight Fri–Sat; 12–11pm Sun.*

DUNDEE
Drouthy Neebors
142 Perth Road, Dundee, Angus DD1 4JW
☎ *(01382) 202187* Kirstin Wilson

 A pub tied to the Belhaven Brewery, so their range is generally served, but Caledonian 80/- and others may be available as well.

O ld, traditional Scottish pub. Food served at lunchtime and evenings. Children allowed from 12–3pm.

OPEN *All day, every day.*

Mickey Coyle's
21–3 Old Hawkhill, Dundee
☎ *(01382) 225871* Ann Taylor

Caledonian Deuchars IPA and 80/- are always available, plus occasional guests.

T raditional pub. Food available lunchtimes and evenings Mon–Sat. Car park. Well-behaved children welcome.

OPEN *11am–3pm and 5–11.30pm Mon–Thurs; 11am–11.30pm Fri–Sat; 7–11pm Sun.*

The Phoenix Bar
103 Nethergate, Dundee, Angus DD1 4DH
☎ *(01382) 200014* Alan Bannerman

A freehouse always offering Orkney Dark Island, Caledonian Deuchars IPA and Timothy Taylor Landlord.

A traditional, one-bar pub with TV and music. Food served lunchtimes and evenings. No children.

OPEN *All day, every day.*

Speedwell Bar
165–7 Perth Road, Dundee, Tayside DD2 1AS
☎ *(01382) 667783* Jonathan Stewart

A freehouse with real ale on three pumps. Erdinger Wheat Beer, the world's biggest selling wheat beer (live and cask-conditioned) is permanently available, plus two other ales often including Timothy Taylor Landlord, Fuller's London Pride, Belhaven brews and Caledonian Deuchars IPA.

A n Edwardian pub, unchanged since 1902. One bar, two rooms (one non-smoking). Bar snacks only. No children.

OPEN *All day, every day.*

INVERKEILOR
The Chance Inn
Main Street, Inverkeilor, Arbroath, Angus DD11 5RN
☎ *(01241) 830308* Mrs Lee

A freehouse offering three real ales, changed weekly.

T wo bars, two recommended restaurants plus accommodation. Food served lunchtimes and evenings. Children allowed. Scottish Tourist Board 3 Star rated, and Tayside CAMRA award winner.

OPEN *12–3pm and 5pm–midnight Tues–Fri; all day Sat–Sun.*

KINROSS
The Muirs Inn
49 Muirs, Kinross
☎ *(01577) 862270* Paul Chinnock

A selection of Scottish real ales always available, including Belhaven 80/- plus up to six guest beers (100 per year) perhaps from the Harviestoun or Border breweries. Also Scottish whiskies.

A traditional Scottish country inn. Bar and restaurant food available at lunchtime and evenings. Car park and courtyard. Children allowed. Accommodation. M90 junction 6, then follow signs for the A922. At the T-junction, the inn is diagonally opposite to the right.

OPEN *All day, every day.*

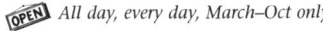

MOULIN

Original Moulin Inn

Moulin Hotel, 11–3 Kirkmichael Road, Moulin,
By Pitlochry, Perthshire
☎ *(01796) 472196* Heather Reeves

 A Moulin Brewery tied house – the brewery is located on the same premises. The full range of Moulin ales normally available.

Seventeenth-century coaching inn situated in the village square, with open fires, beams and stone walls. Originally, it was the traditional meeting house for the Parish. Extended in 1880 and again in 1970. Food served all day, every day. Car park. Children welcome away from the bar area.

OPEN *12–11pm Sun–Thurs;*
12–11.45pm Fri–Sat.

PERTH

Greyfriars

15 South Street, Perth, Perthshire PH2 8PG
☎ *(01738) 633036* Pauline Marshall

 A freehouse with Friar's Tipple, the exclusive house ale brewed locally by Inveralmond Brewery, always available. Guests include regular favourites Caledonian Deuchars IPA, Timothy Taylor Landlord and Morland Old Speckled Hen.

An old-fashioned pub with stone walls and non-smoking dining room upstairs. The clientele tends to be 25 and upwards. Home-made food at lunchtime only. Accompanied children welcome at lunchtimes.

OPEN *All day, every day.*

Lovat Hotel

90–2 Glasgow Road, Perth, Tayside PH2 0LT
☎ *(01738) 636555* Mr Graeme Gillon

 A freehouse with real ale on four pumps, one rotated each week. The nearby Inveralmond brewery suppplies Lia Fail, Ossian and others.

Two bars, accommodation, food at lunchtime and evenings. Children allowed. On the outskirts of Perth, a mile from Broxton roundabout.

OPEN *11am–2.30pm and 5pm–midnight.*

STRATHTUMMEL

Loch Tummel Inn

Strathtummel, Nr Pitlochry, Perthshire PH16 5RP
☎ *(01882) 634272* Michael Marsden

A freehouse with Moulin Braveheart always available.

An old coaching in with six bedrooms, loch views and log fires (one in bathroom!). Home-cooked food is served, with smoked salmon a speciality.

OPEN *All day, every day, March–Oct only.*

YOU TELL US

* ✴ *Allan Ramsay Hotel*, Main Street, Carlops
* ✴ *The Cross Keys Inn*, The Green, Ancrum
* ✴ *The Cellar Bar*, 79 Stirling Street, Airdrie
* ✴ *The Crow's Nest*, Tomintoul
* ✴ *Goblin'ha Hotel*, Main Street, Gifford
* ✴ *Hoolit's Nest*, Paxton
* ✴ *Weston Tavern*, 27 Main Street, Kilmaurs
* ✴ *Wynd Tower*, 57–63 High Street, Fraserburgh

Whitehaven

CUMBRIA

Windermere ·

· Kendal

stle

Peel

· Ramsey

· Douglas

Morecambe ·

M6

· Lancaster

LANCASHIRE

Blackpool ·

Burnle

Preston·

H

Southport ·

M6

**GREATER
MANCHESTER**

MERSEYSIDE

Liverpool ·

· Mancheste

Holyhead

Llandudno ·

· Colwyn Bay

M53

M56

CHESHIRE

Denbigh ·

Flint

Chester

M6

Caernarvon

CLWYD

Wrexham ·

Crewe

S

Portmadoc ·

GWYNEDD · Bala

· Llangollen

STAFFORD

Llanfyllin

Barmouth ·

· Dolgellau

Telford

M6

· Towyn

SHROPSHIRE

Newtown

Wolverhampton ·

Aberystwyth

· Llanidloes

· Ludlow

Birn

POWYS

Knighton

HEREFORD

Aberayron

&

New Quay ·

Lampeter

Kington

WORCESTER

W

Cardigan ·

DYFED

Hereford ·

Fishguard

Brecon

M50

Llandovery

Ross on Wye ·

Gl

Haverfordwest

**WEST
GLAMORGAN**

Monmouth ·

GLO

Pembroke

M4

**MID
GLAMORGAN**

GWENT

Stroud

Swansea

· Newport

AVON

Porthcawl ·

SOUTH

· Cardiff

· Bristol

GLAMORGAN

M5

· Bath

Ilfracombe

Minehead

Weston
Super Mare

W

THE BREWERIES

BRAGDY CEREDIGION BREWERY
2 Brynderwen, Llangrannog SA44 6AD
☎ *(01223) 965 4099*

 GWRACH DU (BLACK WITCH) 4.0% ABV
Porter.
BARCUD COCH (RED KITE) 4.3% ABV
Red in colour, with fruit flavours.
CWRW 2000 (ALE 2000) 5.0% ABV
Red, with fruit and chocolate flavours.
CWRW GWYL (FESTIVAL ALE) 5.0% ABV
Gold-coloured and smooth.
Y DDRAIG AUR (THE GOLD DRAGON) 5.0% ABV
Gold in colour and full-flavoured.
YR HEN DARW DU (THE OLD BLACK BULL) 6.2% ABV
Powerful stout.

BULLMASTIFF BREWERY
14 Bessemer Close, Leckwith, Cardiff CF1 8DL
☎ *(02920) 665292*
www.bullmastiffbrewery.com

 GOLD BREW 3.8% ABV
BEST BITTER 4.0% ABV
EBONY DARK 4.0% ABV
JACK THE LAD 4.1% ABV
CARDIFF DARK 4.2% ABV
GENTLEMAN JACK 4.3% ABV
JACK THE NIPPER 4.3% ABV
SPRING FEVER 4.5% ABV
Seasonal.
SUMMER MOULT 4.5% ABV
Seasonal.
THOROUGHBRED 4.5% ABV
SOUTHPAW 4.7% ABV
Seasonal.
BRINDLE 5.0% ABV
SON OF A BITCH 6.0% ABV
MAD DOG 8.2% ABV
Christmas brew.
MOGADOG 10.0% ABV

COTTAGE SPRING BREWERY
Gorse Cottage, Graig Road, Upper Cwmbran, Trofaen, Gwent NP44 5AS
☎ *(01237) 477615*

 DRAYMAN'S BITTER 3.5% ABV
DRAYMAN'S GOLD 3.8% ABV
CROW VALLEY BITTER 4.2% ABV
FULL MALTY 5.2% ABV
Malty cross between a bitter and mild.

FELINFOEL BREWERY CO. LTD
Farmers Row, Felinfoel, Llanelli SA14 8LB
☎ *(01554) 773357*
www.felinfoel-brewery.com

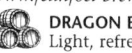 **DRAGON BITTER 3.4% ABV**
Light, refreshing and hoppy.
CAMBRIAN BEST 3.8% ABV
Easy-drinking, hoppy brew.
DOUBLE DRAGON 4.2% ABV
Rich, malty and smooth with balancing hoppiness.

PEMBROKE BREWERY CO.
Eaton House, 108 Main Street, Pembroke SA71 4HN
☎ *(01646) 682517 (Brewery tours)*

 DARKLIN MILD 3.5% ABV
TWO CANNONS EXTRA 3.6% ABV
SAND WHISTLE 3.8% ABV
Summer ale.
DIAMOND LAGER 4.1% ABV
GOLDEN HILL ALE 4.5% ABV
OLD NOBBY STOUT 4.5% ABV
OFF THE RAILS 5.1% ABV
SIGNAL FAILURE 6.0% ABV
Winter ale.
Plus occasional brews.

PLASSEY BREWERY
The Plassey, Eyton, Wrexham LL13 0SP
☎ *(01978) 780922 (Brewery tours)*
www.plasseybrewery.co.uk

PLASSEY BITTER 4.0% ABV
BLACK DRAGON STOUT 4.5% ABV
FUSILIER 4.5% ABV
CWRW TUDNO 5.0% ABV
DRAGON'S BREATH 6.0% ABV

SA BRAIN AND CO. LTD
The Old Brewery, Crawshaw Street, Cardiff CF10 5TR
☎ *(029) 2040 2060 (Brewery tours)*
www.sabrain.com

BUCKLEY'S IPA 3.4% ABV
BRAINS DARK 3.5% ABV
Chocolate and nut flavours, dry finish.
BRAINS BITTER 3.7% ABV
Refreshing. Well-balanced with some sweetness.
BUCKLEY'S BEST BITTER 3.7% ABV
Smooth and nutty with balancing hoppiness.
BRAINS SA 4.2% ABV
Powerful malt flavour with bittersweet finish.
BUCKLEY'S REVEREND JAMES 4.5% ABV
Full-flavoured and complex.

TOMOS WATKIN AND SONS LTD

Phoenix Brewery, Unit 3 Century Park, Valley Way, Swansea Enterprise Park
Swansea SA6 8RP
☎ *(01792) 775333 (Brewery tours)*
www.tomoswatkin.com

WATKINS WHOOSH 3.7% ABV
Dark amber beer with light bitterness.
WATKINS BB 4.0% ABV
Malty, with moderate bitter flavour and floral hoppiness.
MERLINS STOUT 4.2% ABV
Dark, with powerful liquorice flavour.
WATKINS OSB 4.5% ABV
Award-winning, malty with delicate hoppiness.
Plus seasonal ales.

WARCOP COUNTRY ALES

Newhouse Farm, St Brides, Wentlooge NP10 8SE
☎ *(01633) 680058*

PIT SHAFT 3.4% ABV
Dark mild.
PITSIDE 3.7% ABV
Delicate and malty.
ARC 3.8% ABV
Light, hoppy session beer.
PIT PROP 3.8% ABV
Dark mild.
BLACK AND AMBER 4.0% ABV
Pale ruby bitter.
CASNEWYDD 4.0% ABV
Light, quaffer.
DRILLERS 4.0% ABV
Lightly hopped yellow ale.
HILSTON PREMIER 4.0% ABV
Dry and refreshing.
STEELER'S 4.2% ABV
Red and malty.
RAIDERS 4.3% ABV
Lightly hopped strong yellow ale.
ROLLERS 4.3% ABV
Light ruby coloured bitter.
ZEN 4.4% ABV
FURNACE 4.5% ABV
Ruby, malty beer with dry finish.
RIGGERS 4.5% ABV
Golden version of Furnace.
DEEP PIT 5.0% ABV
Ruby full bodied beer.
DOCKER'S 5.0% ABV
Golden, fruity and full-bodied.

Places Featured:

Aberedw
Aberystwyth
Cwmann
Goginan
Howey
Llanbadarn Fynydd
Llanidloes
Llanwrtyd Wells

Machynlleth
Montgomery
Pengenffordd
Pisgah
Rhayader
Rhydowen
Tregaron

THE PUBS

ABEREDW

The Seven Stars Inn

Aberedw, Builth Wells, Powys LD2 3UW
☎ *(01982) 560494 Deena Jones*

A freehouse with four pumps and two guests from a range that has included Shepherd Neame Early Bird, Everards Tiger, Wood Shropshire Lad, Wye Valley brews and many others from micro- and small breweries.

A traditional, two-bar olde-worlde pub with log fires, oak beams, no fruit machines or juke box. Winner of CAMRA South and Mid-Wales Pub of the Year 1997. Bar and restaurant food available at lunchtime and evenings. Children welcome. Accomodation.

OPEN *12–3pm and 6.30–11pm (10.30pm Sun).*

ABERYSTWYTH

The Coopers Arms

Northgate Street, Aberystwyth, Ceredigion SY23 2JT
☎ *(01970) 624050 Mrs Somers*

A Felinfoel Brewery tied house with two pumps serving Felinfoel ales and occasional guests.

Live music, no juke box or fruit machines. Well-mixed clientele of locals and students. No food. Children allowed.

OPEN *11am–11pm Mon–Sat; 12–10.30pm Sun.*

The Ship & Castle

High Street, Aberystwyth, Dyfed SY23 1JG
☎ *(01970) 612334 Pete and Dee Fraser*

A freehouse and micro-brewery serving own beers plus two guests such as Fuller's London Pride. The guests change weekly.

An old one-bar pub with food available at lunchtime and evenings. Children allowed.

SHIP ORIGINAL 3.6% ABV
OATMEAL STOUT 4.4% ABV
Winter ale
HARVEST MOON 4.5% ABV
RHEIDOL RESERVE 4.8% ABV
MUTLEY'S REVENGE 4.9% ABV
Plus a range of seasonal ales.

OPEN *11am–11pm Mon–Sat; 12–10.30pm Sun.*

CWMANN

The Ram Inn

Cwmann, Lampeter, Carmarthenshire SA48 8ES
☎ *(01570) 422556 Wynne and Mary Davies*

A freehouse offering Archers Golden Bitter plus one or two guest beers changed frequently, from national and smaller breweries.

An old drover's pub one mile outside Lampeter on the Llandovery Road, dating from around 1560, with a dining room, bar and garden. CAMRA Best Pub in Wales 1997 and 4th Best Pub in Britain 1997. Food available at lunchtime and evenings. Children allowed.

OPEN *All day, every day.*

GOGINAN

The Druid Inn

Goginan, Aberystwyth, Ceredigion SY23 3NT
☎ *01970 880650* William John Howell

 A freehouse with three real ales always available. Banks's Bitter and Brains brews are regulars, while other guests changed monthly might include Cottage Champflower Ale.

The building dates back to 1730, when it was used by the local mining community. Bar, pool room, function room. No juke box or games machines. Food available all day in a separate dining room. Children allowed. On the A44 heading into Aberystwyth.

OPEN *11am–11pm Mon–Sat; 12–10.30pm Sun.*

HOWEY

The Drovers Arms

Howey, Llandrindod Wells, Powys LD1 5PT
☎ *(01597) 822508* Mr Day

 A freehouse serving its own Drovers Ale, plus guests, usually Welsh.

A stylish Victorian red-brick inn. Back bar for drinking has real fire, no juke box, no fruit machines and no pool table. Non-smoking dining room serves fresh, traditional, award-winning food lunchtimes and evenings. British Cheese Board Award and Heart Beat Wales Award. No children under 14 please. Accommodation available. Website: www.drovers-arms.co.uk.

OPEN *12–2.30pm and 7–11pm (10.30pm Sun); closed Tues lunchtime.*

LLANBADARN FYNYDD

The New Inn

Llanbadarn Fynydd, Llandrindod Wells, Powys LD1 6YA
☎ *(01597) 840378* Robert Barton

 A freehouse with two real ale pumps changed at least monthly. Wood Shropshire Lad and brews from Eccleshall (Slaters) and Wye Valley are among those usually stocked.

A traditional ale and food house with log fires. Food available lunchtimes and evenings in a separate restaurant. Children allowed. Located on main A483 between Newton and Llandrindod Wells.

OPEN *10.30am–3pm and 5.30–11pm in summer; 12–2.30pm and 7–11pm in winter.*

LLANIDLOES

The Red Lion

8 Longbridge Street, Llanidloes, Powys SY18 6EE
☎ *(01686) 412270* Mandy James

 A freehouse serving Banks's brews, plus one guest beer.

A modernised, ten-bedroom hotel with a friendly atmosphere. Open fires, patio garden. Restaurant food and bar meals available lunchtimes and evenings. Children allowed in the restaurant only.

OPEN *11.30am–3pm and 7–11pm (10.30pm Sun).*

LLANWRTYD WELLS

Stonecroft Inn

Dolecoed Road, Llanwrtyd Wells, Powys LD5 4RA
☎ *(01591) 610332/610327*

 Four regularly changing beers, perhaps from Brains, Dunn Plowman, Wye Valley or Flannerys.

Welcoming country pub situated in the smallest town in Britain and popular with cyclists and visitors. Large riverside beer garden. Bar food served Fri–Sun lunchtime and every evening. Hot basket snacks available at other times. Car park. Children welcome. For further information, visit the website at www.stonecroft.co.uk.

OPEN *5–11pm Mon–Thurs; 12–11pm Fri–Sat; 12–10.30pm Sun.*

MACHYNLLETH

The Wynnstay Hotel

Maengwyn Street, Machynlleth, Powys SY20 8AE
☎ *(01654) 702941* Charles Dark

 A freehouse with an ever-changing variety of real ales, some big brands such as Morland Old Speckled Hen, Greene King IPA and Timothy Taylor Landlord, alongside some Welsh brands such as Brains and a representative selection from micro-breweries. Organic ales and seasonal brews included. Also traditional cider on draught.

A comfortable bar in an old coaching inn with very large real open fire. Restaurant (evenings) and quality bar meals (lunchtimes and evenings). Children welcome. Accommodation. Parking.

OPEN *Main pub: lunchtimes and evenings; Stable bar: 11am–11pm.*

MONTGOMERY

The Dragon Hotel
1 Market Square, Montgomery, Powys SY15 6PA
☎ *(01686) 668359* Mrs Michaels

A freehouse serving guest beers on one pump. Brains brews and Fuller's London Pride are regular favourites.

A hotel bar with food available at lunchtime and evenings. Children allowed.

OPEN *11am–11pm Mon–Sat; 12–10.30pm Sun.*

PENGENFFORDD

The Castle Inn
Pengenffordd, Talgarth, Powys LD3 0EP
☎ *(01874) 711353* Paul Mountjoy

A freehouse with three pumps serving alternating guest ales. Brains Rev James Original, Shepherd Neame Spitfire and Bateman XXXB are often, plus others from breweries such as SP Sporting Ales, Cottage and others.

A rural country inn with separate dining area. B&B, plus barn-style dormitory accommodation in the middle of the hills: a good walking area at 1,000 feet. Food available at lunchtimes and evenings. Children allowed.

OPEN *11am–3pm and 7–11pm (10.30pm Sun).*

PISGAH

The Halfway Inn
Devil's Bridge Road, Pisgah, Aberystwyth, Dyfed SY23 4NE
☎ *(01970) 880631* David Roberts

Badger Dorset Best and Felifoel Double Dragon always available, plus one constantly changing guest during the summer months.

A traditional olde-worlde hostelry 700 feet up with magnificent views of the Cambrian mountains and Rheidol Valley. Bar and restaurant food available at lunchtime and evenings. Pool table. Car park and garden. Children allowed. Accommodation. Free overnight camping for customers. Located halfway along the A4120 Aberystwyth to Devil's Bridge road. Note, this is not the Pisgah near Cardigan.

OPEN *12–2pm and 6.30–11pm (10.30pm Sun). Times may vary in winter.*

RHAYADER

The Cornhill Inn
West Street, Rhayader, Powys LD6 5AB
☎ *(01597) 811015* Richard Parker

Greene King Abbot Ale and Brains Reverend James Original regularly available, plus a frequently changing guest beer.

A seventeenth-century freehouse with olde-worlde charm. Low beams and open fires. Bar food available at lunchtimes and evenings. Parking. Children allowed. Accommodation. On the road to Elan Valley.

OPEN *11am–3pm and 7–11pm (10.30pm Sun).*

RHYDOWEN

The Alltyrodyn Arms
Rhydowen, Llandysul, Ceredigion SA44 4QB
☎ *(01545) 590319* Derrick and Jean Deakin

A freehouse serving three or four real ales. Archers Golden and Everards Tiger are regularly available plus hundreds of others constantly changing.

A sixteenth-century pub with a restaurant serving food all day, a pool room, beer garden with fish pond and waterfall. B&B and self-catering accommodation available. Children allowed in the bar until 9pm.

OPEN *11am–11pm Mon–Sat; 12–4pm Sun.*

TREGARON

The Talbot Hotel
Main Square, Tregaron, Ceredigion SY25 6JL
☎ *(01974) 298208* Graham Williams

A freehouse with three hand pumps serving a wide range of real ales.

An old, traditional pub offering a friendly welcome. Beer garden. Open fires, separate restaurant, accommodation, beer garden. Restaurant and bar food available at lunchtime and evenings. Ample parking. Children allowed.

OPEN *11am–11pm Mon–Sat; 12–10.30pm Sun.*

Places Featured:

Abergele	Gresford
Bangor	Gwernaffield
Betws-y-Coed	Gwernymynydd
Betws-yn-Rhos	Halkyn
Blaenau Ffestiniog	Llandudno
Bodedern	Llangollen
Bodfari	Llay
Broughton	Lloc
Brynford	Marchweil
Cadole	Meliden
Caernarfon	Mochdre
Caerwys	Morfa Nefyn
Cilcain	Northop
Clawdd-Newdydd	Old Colwyn
Colwyn Bay	Penysarn
Connah's Quay	Rhewl
Cymau	Rhyd Ddu
Denbigh	Rossett
Dulas	Ruthin
Ffrith	St Asaph
Gorsedd	Waunfawr

THE PUBS

ABERGELE

The Bull Hotel
Chapel Street, Abergele, Conwy LL22 7AW
☎ *(01745) 832115* Alan Yates

 Lees GB Mild and JW Bitter regularly available.

Family-run pub situated just outside Conwy town on the Llanwrst road. Restaurant and music-free main bar. Food served Wed–Mon 11am–2pm and 6.30–8.30pm. Car park. Children welcome. Accommodation.

 11am–3pm and 6–11pm Wed–Mon; 11am–3pm and 7–11pm Tues.

BANGOR

The Castle (Hogshead)
Glanrafon, off High Street, Bangor, Gwynedd LL57 1LH
☎ *(01248) 355866* Mark Fisher

 A Whitbread tied house with up to ten hand pumps plus four beers served straight from the barrel. Regular guests include Timothy Taylor Landlord, Fuller's London Pride, Caledonian 80/- and Marston's Pedigree.

A roomy pub with a large open single floor, dark wood floors, background music. Non-smoking area, wheelchair access. Food available 12–7pm. Children allowed. Opposite the Cathedral, close to the railway station.

OPEN *11am–11pm Mon–Sat; 12–10.30pm Sun.*

The Tap & Spile
Garth Road, Bangor, Gwynedd LL57 2SW
☎ *(01248) 370835* Dean Ibbetson

Greene King IPA and Abbot, Morland Old Speckled Hen, Marston's Pedigree and Wadworth 6X permanently available, plus two constantly changing guests which might be something like Otter Ale or Marquis Bitter.

A suburban pub with B&B. Food served lunchtimes and evenings. Located by the pier.

OPEN *All day, every day.*

BETWS-Y-COED

Pont-Y-Pair Hotel

Holy Head Road, Betws-y-Coed LL24 0BN
☎ *(01690) 710407* E Adam and Ann Watkins

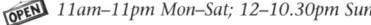 Marston's Pedigree and Greene King Abbot Ale usually available.

Small hotel situated in the heart of Snowdonia with lots of rural pursuits close by. Home-cooked food available 11am–2pm and 6–9pm daily. Children welcome.

OPEN *11am–11pm Mon–Sat; 12–10.30pm Sun.*

BETWS-YN-RHOS

The Wheatsheaf

Betws-yn-Rhos, Abergele, Conwy LL22 8AW
☎ *(01492) 680218* Raymond Perry

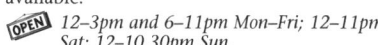 Greene King IPA and Wadworth 6X regularly available.

Inn with olde-worlde atmosphere and lots of brass, first licensed in 1640. Food every lunchtime and evening. Car park. Beer garden with Wendy house and high chairs available.

OPEN *12–3pm and 6–11pm Mon–Fri; 12–11pm Sat; 12–10.30pm Sun.*

BLAENAU FFESTINIOG

Rhiw Goch Inn

Bron Aber, Transfynydd, Blaenau Ffestiniog LL41 4UY.
☎ *(01766) 540374* Mr Norman Bond

 Ales changed either weekly or bi-weekly – include Jennings Cumberland Bitter, Greene King IPA and a range of others.

Pub is set on a Norwegian log cabin tourist site, which enables proprietor to keep his selection of real ales going.

OPEN *12–11pm all year round apart from quiet month of November when opening hours may be reduced.*

BODEDERN

The Crown Hotel

Church Street, Bodedern, Nr Holyhead, Anglesey
☎ *(01407) 740 734* Robert Aled Michael

 Burtonwood Best Bitter regularly available.

Traditional two-bar pub with pool room. Real fires in winter. Food served 12–2pm and 6–8pm daily. Car park. Children welcome, but no special facilities.

OPEN *12–2pm and 5–11pm Mon–Sat; 12–10.30pm Sun.*

BODFARI

Dinorben Arms Inn

Bodfari, Denbigh LL16 4DA
☎ *(01745) 710309* Mr David Rowlands

 Ales include Brains SA, Morland Old Speckled Hen and something from Banks's. Rotated every few weeks.

Pretty hillside setting for pub with views of surrounding countryside. Restaurant and carvery meals available, with meals also served outdoors on timber-framed balconies adorned with hanging baskets. Historic glass-topped well inside the pub. Ample car parking space. The pub is up a winding hilly lane.

OPEN *12–3pm and 6–11pm.*

BROUGHTON

The Spinning Wheel Tavern

The Old Warren, Broughton CH4 0EG.
☎ *(01244) 531068* Mr Mike Vernon

 Guest beers regularly rotated, including Jennings Cumberland Bitter, Greene King IPA and Fuller's London Pride.

Family-run pub in a secluded spot well off the main road, with a popular restaurant.

OPEN *11.30am–3pm and 6–11pm.*

BRYNFORD

The Llyn y Mawn Inn

Brynford Hill, Brynford, Flintshire CH8 8AD
☎ *(01352) 714367*
Mandy McManus and John McLoughlin

A freehouse serving up to six brews every week. Welsh ales are favoured, plus others from small breweries.

CAMRA Welsh Pub of the Year 1995 and 1997. Typical Welsh long house with restaurant and gardens. Real fires, background music. Food available weekday lunchtimes 12–3pm and evenings 6–9.30pm, 12–9.30pm weekends. Booking is advisable for food. Well-behaved children allowed. Adjacent to the A55 expressway, and can be seen from there.

OPEN *12–3pm and 5.30–11pm Mon–Fri; 12–11pm Sat; 12–10.30pm Sun.*

CADOLE

Colomendy Arms
Gwernaffield Road, Cadole, Mold CH7 5LL
☎ *(01352) 810217* Elsie Butler

 Five different guests on pumps. Shepherd Neame Master Brew offered all the time, with other guest examples including Ridleys Prospect, Orkney The Red McGregor, Bateman Jewel in the Crown (a special brew for the Golden Jubilee) and Shepherd Neame Early Bird.

Small, cosy, but extremely friendly pub, with bar, small lounge and beer garden, located in tiny village just off main Mold to Ruthin road. Selection of other real ale pubs nearby. Beer festival was held to celebrate the Golden Jubilee 2002 and other events planned for future.

OPEN *7–11pm Mon–Wed; 6–11pm Thurs; 4–11pm Fri (closed weekday lunchtimes); 12–11pm Sat; 12–10.30pm Sun.*

CAERNAFON

The Alexandra Hotel
North Road, Caernarfon, Gwynedd LL55 1BA
☎ *(01286) 672871* Ken Moulton

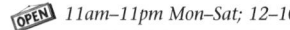 A Whitbread tied house serving a range of guests. Regulars include Wadworth 6X, Morland Old Speckled Hen and Marston's Pedigree. The guest list changes fortnightly.

A local pub with B&B accommodation. Tables outside. No food. Children allowed in the afternoons only.

OPEN *11am–11pm Mon–Sat; 12–10.30pm Sun.*

The Prince of Wales Hotel
Bangor Street, Caernarfon, Gwynedd LL55 1AR
☎ *(01286) 673367* Vivien and John Minshall

Marston's Bitter is always on offer, as are Welsh Highland Bitter and Haf, both from the Snowdonia Brewery. The one guest beer could be from any independent brewery.

A traditional pub within a hotel in a townscape setting, half a mile from Caernarfon Castle and half a mile from the yacht marina. An ideal base for Snowdonia and the Irish ferries. Breakfast is served 7–9.30am, lunch 11.30am–2pm and dinner 6–8.30pm, and the emphasis is on home cooking. Children and dogs are welcome, and the pub has designated family rooms. Car park. Visit the website at: www.smoothhound.co.uk/princewa.

OPEN *11am–11pm Mon–Sat; 12–10.30pm Sun.*

Y Goron Fach
Hole in the Wall Street, Caernarfon, Gwynedd LL55 1RF
☎ *(01286) 673338* Mr Williams

 A freehouse permanently serving Flannery's Celtic Ale, plus Fuller's London Pride, Brains St David's Ale and Adnams bitters as regular guests on two pumps.

A town pub with two bars and a garden. Food served at lunchtimes and evenings in the summer, lunchtime only in winter. Children allowed.

OPEN *All day, every day.*

CAERWYS

The Travellers' Inn
Pen y Cefn, Caerwys, Mold CH7 5BL
☎ *(01352) 720251* Kevin Jones

A freehouse and brewpub with Marston's Pedigree regularly available plus various other guests rotated on the two remaining pumps.

A family pub and restaurant with food available all day. Children allowed. Located on the A55

🛢 **ROY MORGAN'S ORIGINAL 3.8–3.9% ABV**
🛢 **OLD ELIAS 5.2% ABV**

OPEN *11am–11pm Mon–Sat; 12–10.30pm Sun.*

CILCAIN

The White Horse
The Square, Cilcain, Mold, Flintshire CH7 5NN
☎ *(01352) 740142* Mr Jeory

 A freehouse with two hand pumps serving a wide range of beers on rotation. Exmoor Gold, Greene King Abbot, Marston's Pedigree and Fuller's London Pride are regularly featured. Others might include beers from Wood or Cottage breweries. The range changes every other day.

A small, cosy village pub, unspoilt for 150 years, spread over four rooms with real fires and beams. No juke box or pool table. Food available at lunchtime and evenings. No children.

OPEN *12–3pm and 6.30–11pm Mon–Fri; 11am–11pm Sat; 12–10.30pm Sun.*

CLAWDD-NEWYDD

Glan Llyn Inn
Clawdd-Newydd, Ruthin LL15 2NA
☎ *(01824) 750754* Mrs Pauline Bowdler

Morland Old Speckled Hen permanently on the pumps with other guests regularly rotated, including Hook Norton Old Hooky and Greene King Abbot.

Old-style, typical village pub. Food available 7.30–11pm Mon–Thurs; 7–11pm Fri; 6–9pm Sat.

OPEN *2–11pm Mon–Sat; 4–11pm Sun.*

COLWYN BAY

Rhos Fynach
Rhos Promenade, Colwyn Bay, LL28 4NG
☎ *(01492) 548185* Mr Robert Skellie

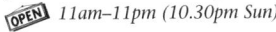 Marston's Pedigree and Banks's Bitter always on offer. Guest ales rotated approximately every two weeks.

Historic pub central to Colwyn Bay, family friendly with spacious beer garden and restaurant. Also caters for weddings and parties. Food served 12–9pm.

OPEN *11am–11pm (10.30pm Sun).*

The White Lion Inn
Llanelian-yn-Rhos, Colwyn Bay, Conwy LL29 8YA
☎ *(01492) 515807* Simon Cole

 A freehouse with three real ales usually available from a wide range that changes fortnightly.

A traditional stone-built Welsh country inn with slate floor, log fires and beams. B&B accommodation and non-smoking dining area. Food available at lunchtime and evenings. Children allowed. For further information visit the website at www.whitelioninn.co.uk.

OPEN *11am–3pm and 6–11pm Mon–Sat; 12–3pm and 7–10.30pm Sun.*

CONNAH'S QUAY

Sir Gawain and the Green Knight
Golftyn Lane, Connah's Quay, Deeside, Flintshire CH5 4BH
☎ *(01244) 812623* David E Leyland

 A Samuel Smith house with Old Brewery Bitter always available.

An old farmhouse fitting the traditional image of a small country pub. Split-level lounge inside, no pool table, no juke box. Outside there are hanging baskets and large garden areas. Food available 12–2pm Mon–Fri. Children welcome in the garden. Car park. Located just off the main road in Connah's Quay.

OPEN *12–3pm and 5.30–11pm Mon–Fri; 12–11pm Sat; 12–10.30pm Sun.*

CYMAU

Ye Olde Talbot Inn
Cymau Lane, Cymau, Nr Wrexham
☎ *(01978) 761410* LJ Mee

 Hydes' Anvil Bitter permanently available, plus a changing seasonal beer every two months.

A traditional drinkers' pub. No food. Car park. Children welcome.

OPEN *7–11pm Mon–Thurs; 12–4pm and 7–11pm Fri–Sat; 12–4pm and 7–10.30pm Sun.*

DENBIGH

Cymro Inn
Llanynys Road, Llanrhaeadre, Denbigh LL16 4NU
☎ *(01745) 890529* Mrs Elizabeth Griffiths

 Regularly rotating mainly Welsh beers, including Brains Bitter and Rev James Original.

Family pub with a conservatory and restaurant, beer garden and children's play area. Also bed and breakfast facility available and pitches for camping.

OPEN *4–11pm Mon–Fri; all day Sat–Sun and school holidays.*

The Eagle Inn
Back Row, Denbigh, Denbighshire LL16 3TE
☎ *(01745) 813203* Mr Evans

 A freehouse serving up to eight real ales. Morland Old Speckled Hen is popular but all real ales are considered.

A large pub with a snooker room, pool, darts etc. The pub runs quiz nights and a cricket team. Food available at lunchtime. Children allowed if eating.

OPEN *11am–11pm Mon–Sat; 12–10.30pm Sun.*

DULAS

Pilot Boat Inn
Dulas, Amlwch, Anglesey
☎ *(01248) 410205* Mark Williams

 A Robinson's tied house serving Best Bitter.

Traditional country pub in an area of outstanding natural beauty. Popular with locals and tourists alike. Food served 12–9.30pm daily. Car park. Children's menu and play area. Situated on the A5025.

OPEN *11.30am–11pm Mon–Sat; 12–10.30pm Sun.*

FFRITH

The Poacher's Cottage
High Street, Ffrith, Wrexham LL11 5LG
☎ *(01978) 756465* Mr David Griffiths

Morland Old Speckled Hen and Fuller's London Pride constantly available.

Old-style pub in countryside setting with open fires. Spacious car park. Restaurant open at same time as pub.

OPEN *7–11pm Mon–Fri; all day Sat–Sun.*

GORSEDD

The Druid Inn

Gorsedd, Holywell, Flintshire CH8 8QZ
☎ *(01352) 710944* Ken Doherty

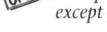 A freehouse usually serving Marston's Pedigree plus four or five others from an extensive range that favours the smaller and micro-breweries rather than nationals.

A listed twelfth-century long house, with oak beams and log fires. The separate restaurant serves food every evening and Sunday lunchtime. Children allowed. Located off the A5026, two miles west of Holywell.

OPEN *7–11pm Mon–Sat (closed lunchtimes except Sun); 12–3pm and 7–10.30 Sun.*

GRESFORD

Pant yr Ochain

Old Wrexham Road, Gresford, Wrexham LL12 8TY
☎ *(01978) 853525*
Lindsey du Prole and Graham Arathoon

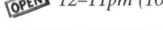 Locally brewed Plassey beers permanently available here, along with changing guests, including ales such as Wadworth 6X.

L arge pub set in its own grounds with big garden. Several dining areas and food served day and evening. Attracts clientele from all around the locality and further afield.

OPEN *12–11pm (10.30pm Sun).*

GWERNAFFIELD

Miner's Arms

Church Lane, Gwernaffield CH7 5DT
☎ *(01352) 740803* Mr Jim Foster

Mansfield Ales regularly available, along with Camerons bitter. Previous guests have included Banks's ales.

Q uiet rural pub in former mining village, catering for mainly local clientele. There is a lounge and bar with darts and pool table.

OPEN *All day, every day.*

GWERNYMYNYDD

Owain Glyndwr

Glyndwr Road, Gwernymynydd, Near Mold, Flintshire CH7 5LP
☎ *(01352) 752967* Richie and Maureen Smith

Ales include Shepherd Neame Bishop's Finger and Marston's Pedigree.

R ural pub with bed and breakfast accommodation and restaurant offering home-cooked food with good choice of vegetarian meals and Sunday roasts. Log fires and homely atmosphere. There is a pool table. Pub situated in remote location some distance away from village centre.

OPEN *5–11pm Mon–Sat; 7–10.30pm Sun.*

The Rainbow Inn

Ruthin Road, Gwernymynydd, near Mold, Flintshire CH7 5LG
☎ *(01352) 752575* John and Victoria Rowley

Ales include Cains Bitter.

V illage pub, popular with walkers and for Sunday lunches. Food served daily, lunchtime and evening. Spacious beer garden. Darts tournaments regularly held here.

OPEN *12–3pm and 7–11pm.*

HALKYN

Brittania Inn

Pentre Road, Halkyn, Flintshire CH8 8BS
☎ *(01352) 780272* K Pollitt

A JW Lees house with Traditional Bitter and GB Mild always available, plus a seasonal Lees ale.

A traditional country pub overlooking the Dee and Mersey estuaries – you can see as far as Blackpool Tower! Two bars, a family area, games room and a separate conservatory restaurant/function room. Homemade food specialising in local produce available 12–2.30pm and 6.30–9pm Mon–Sun. Children welcome, high-chairs available. Small beer garden. Disabled access and facilities. Car park.

OPEN *11.30am–11pm Mon–Sat; 12–10.30pm Sun.*

LLANDUDNO

The Queen Victoria

Church Walks, Llandudno, Conwy LL30 2HL
☎ *(01492) 860949* Mr J Vaughan-Williams

A freehouse serving Banks's brews and up to five others.

A Victorian pub, comfortable, family-orientated. Food is a speciality, served in a separate restaurant and available at lunchtime and evenings. Children allowed. Situated near the pier.

OPEN *11am–11pm Mon–Sat; 12–10.30pm Sun.*

LLANGOLLEN

The Sun Inn

49 Regent Street, Llangollen, Denbighshire LL20 8HN
☎ *(01978) 860233*
Alan Adams and Paul Lamb

A freehouse offering six real ales that could well include Weetwood Old Dog and Wye Valley brews. Four Belgian beers and two real ciders also available.

A friendly, old, beer-drinkers' pub with a good atmosphere. Food available at lunchtime and early evening. Take the A5 towards Llangollen.

OPEN *11am–11pm Mon–Sat; 12–10.30pm Sun.*

LLAY

Crown Inn

Llay, Wrexham LL12 ONT
☎ *(01978) 852380* Mr Ian Sandall

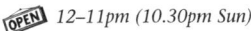 Guests changed weekly, include beers from Marston's, Banks's, Mansfield, Hanson's and Camerons.

Family-friendly pub with large children's play area and beer garden. Very popular with local families in summer.

OPEN *12–11pm (10.30pm Sun).*

LLOC

The Rock Inn

Lloc, Nr Holywell, Flintshire CH8 8RD
☎ *(01352) 710049* T Swift

Burtonwood Bitter and at least one guest bitter always available.

Small, friendly, family-run two-bar pub with dining room. Large car park with picnic benches. Food available lunchtimes and evenings except Tues. Children welcome.

OPEN *12–11pm (10.30pm Sun).*

MARCHWIEL

The Kiln Inn

Cross Lanes, Marchwiel LL13 0TG
☎ *(01978) 780429* Mr Markus Imfeld

Wide range of real ales regularly available, rotated twice a month, include local Plassey beers, Hanby Jubilee Regina, Coach House Honeypot, Shepherd Neame Master Brew and brews from Brains.

A 300-year-old-pub, with cosy atmosphere, log fires, real beams, brasses and a ghost! Restaurant open every day except Monday evening.

OPEN *7–11pm Mon–Fri; 12–close Sat–Sun.*

MELIDEN

Melyd Arms

23 Ffordd Talargoch, Meliden LL19 8LA
☎ *(01745) 852005* Mrs Patricia Giles

 Marston's Bitter and Pedigree permanently available here.

Popular village-centre pub, with split-level eating area, log fires, pleasant atmosphere, friendly landlady.

OPEN *11.30am–11pm Mon–Sat; 12–10.30pm Sun.*

MOCHDRE

The Mountain View

7 Old Conwy Road, Mochdre, Colwyn Bay, Conwy LL28 5AT
☎ *(01492) 544724* Shirley and Nick Pretty

A Burtonwood Brewery tied house serving Burton Best and Top Hat permanently plus regular rotating guests including, perhaps, Everards Tiger, Bateman XXXB, Gales HSB and Caledonian brews. Also a 'Brewery Choice' of a seasonal brew like Black Parrot.

A village pub with restaurant and large garden. Food available at lunchtimes and evenings. Children allowed.

OPEN *All day, every day.*

MORFA NEFYN

Cliffs Inn

Beach Road, Morfa Nefyn, Gwynedd LL53 6BY
☎ *(01758) 720356* Glynne Roberts

A freehouse with two pumps usually serving one English and one Welsh ale, the Welsh brew usually from Brains.

A food-orientated pub with good beer. Outside patio. Food available at lunchtime and evenings in a separate dining area. Children allowed.

OPEN *12–3pm and 6–11pm (10.30pm Sun).*

NORTHOP

Stables Bar at Soughton Hall

Soughton Hall Country House Hotel and Restaurant, Northop, Flintshire CH7 6AB
☎ *(01352) 840577* Mr Rodenhurst (owner); Alexander John (bar manager)

A freehouse serving real ales from Flannery's and Hanby Breweries. There are three dedicated Flannery pumps and three others serving brews rotated weekly. Small and micro-breweries preferred.

An unusual location, set in the old stable block of the hotel complex. The hayloft has been converted into a restaurant. Beer garden and wine shop. Food available at lunchtime and evenings. Children allowed. Located off the A55 Flint/Northop junction

OPEN *11am–11pm Mon–Sat; 12–10.30pm Sun.*

OLD COLWYN

The Red Lion

385 Abergele Road, Old Colwyn, Colwyn Bay, Conwy LL29 9PL
☎ *(01492) 515042* Wayne Hankie

 A freehouse serving seven cask ales, four of which are constantly rotated. Brains SA, Charles Wells Bombardier, Greene King Abbot Ale and Morland Old Speckled Hen usually available plus many, many more.

A village pub on the main road with a double lounge bar, open fires and no music in lounge. The public bar has a pool table, TV and juke box. No food. Children not allowed. A regional pub of the year.

OPEN *5–11pm Mon–Fri; 11am–11pm Sat; 12–10.30pm Sun.*

PENYSARN

Y Bedol

Penysarn, Anglesey, Gwynedd LL69 9YR
☎ *(01407) 832590* Steven and Sheila Hughes

 A selection of three Robinson's ales always available.

Warm, friendly pub with beer garden, pool room, karaoke and quiz nights and occasional local Welsh entertainment. Bar food available evenings. Children allowed. Credit cards accepted.

OPEN *12–11pm Mon–Sat; 12–10.30pm Sun.*

RHEWL

The Drovers Arms

Rhewl, Ruthin, Denbighshire LL15 2UD
☎ *(01824) 703163* Charles Gale-Hasleham

 A freehouse serving three real ales. Tries to specialise in Welsh beers from small and micro-breweries. Coach House Honeypot and brews from Vale and Flannery's Breweries are often featured.

A 300-year-old pub and an old meeting place for drovers. An English Civil War skirmish took place on the bridge outside the pub. Large garden with tables, barbecues in nice weather. Food available at lunchtime and evenings. Well-behaved children allowed. The landlord used to own the Vale and Clwyd (now Flannery's) Breweries.

OPEN *7–11pm Mon (closed lunchtime); 12–3pm and 7–11pm Tues–Sat; 12–10.30pm Sun.*

RHYD DDU

The Cwellyn Arms

Rhyd Ddu, Gwynedd LL54 6TL
☎ *(01766) 890321* Graham Bamber

 A freehouse serving nine real ales, perhaps Dorothy Goodbody's Warming Wintertime Ale (Wye Valley), Cottage Great Western Ale, Young's Special, Fuller's London Pride, Thwaites Bitter, Wadworth 6X and Old Timer, Gale's HSB, Charles Wells Bombardier, Adnams Broadside, Coach House Gunpowder Strong Mild or McGuinness Feather Plucker Mild.

A country inn with B&B accommodation and cottages to let. Restaurant, beer garden, children's adventure playground. Bunkhouses and camping on nearby 25-acre area leading to Cwellyn Lake. Food available all day every day. At the foot of Mount Snowdon, on the Caernarfon/Beddgelert road.

OPEN *11am–11pm Mon–Sat; 12–10.30pm Sun.*

ROSSETT

The Golden Grove

Llyndir Lane, Burton Green, Rosett
☎ *(01244) 570445* Mr Dennis Ames

 Five cask bitters regularly on the pumps, including Camerons Strong Arm, Banks's Original and Bitter and Marston's Pedigree. In past have offered Mansfield Rich and Mansfield Original, plus Marston's Best. Rotating guests also include Banks's World Cup and Morrells Original.

Family-friendly, warm and cosy, but spacious thirteenth-century coaching inn and restaurant, with beamed ceilings, open fires and olde-worlde charm. Large garden area. Unusual location on border between Chester and North Wales. Also offers selection of fine wines.

OPEN *11.30am–11pm Tues–Sun (closed Mon).*

RUTHIN

Red Lion

Cyffylliog, Ruthin, Denbighshire LL15 2DN
☎ *(01824) 710664* Mrs CF Kimberley Jones

 JW Lees Bitter regularly available and also seasonal beers from the same brewery.

Friendly, family-run country pub with lots of character. Caters for everyone, including family meals and bed and breakfast. Food served 7–10pm Mon–Fri and 12–10pm Sat–Sun. Car park. Children welcome.

OPEN *7–11pm Mon–Fri; 12–11pm Sat–Sun.*

Three Pigeons

Graigfechan, Ruthin LL15 2EU
☎ *(01824) 703178* Heather Roberts

 Wide selection of ales changed regularly and including Enville ales and Plassey beers, from the local Wrexham brewery, such as Fusilier.

Seventeenth-century inn, well supported by locals. Restaurant open every day except Sunday and Monday evenings. Live music by local bands, plus a drop-in session on a Sunday night. Charity music festivals held in a field with a stage at the back of the pub have raised up to £9,000 for good causes. Camping sites available. Pub offers jugs of beer from the cellar.

 Summer: 12–11pm. Winter: 12–3pm and 5.30–11pm.

ST ASAPH

The Kentigern Arms

High Street, St Asaph LL17 0RG
☎ *(01745) 584157* Mrs Redgrave

 A freehouse offering up to seven real ales. Popular brews come from Marston's, Cottage and other smaller breweries. The varied and unusual range changes every two weeks.

A seventeenth-century coaching inn with beams and open fires. A separate small room can be used for children or as a dining room. Four bedrooms available. Food available at lunchtimes only. Children allowed.

12–3pm and 7–11pm (10.30pm Sun).

WAUNFAWR

The Snowdonia Parc Hotel

Beddgelert Road, Waunfawr, Gwynedd LL55 4AQ
☎ *(01286) 650409* Karen Humphreys

A brewpub in which the landlady's son Gareth provides the beer, usually to around 5% ABV. Marston's Bitter and Pedigree are among a range of real ales always available, plus occasional local beers. Up to four beers in total in summer.

A village pub in beautiful surroundings. Campsite, family room. Food available at lunchtime and evenings. Play area with play equipment and safety surface. On the A4085 Roman road from Caernarfon to Beddgelert. Nearby terminus for the Welsh Highland Railway from Caernarfon.

Summer: 11am–11pm Mon–Sat and 12–10.30pm Sun. Winter: 12–2pm and 6–11pm.

Places Featured:

Abercrave	Llanvihangel Crucorney
Bassaleg	Machen
Beaufort	Mamhilad
Bettws Newydd	Monknash
Bishopston	Mumbles
Blackmill	Newport
Blaenavon	Ogmore
Bridgend	Pant
Cardiff	Penallt
Chepstow	Pontardawe
Clytha	Raglan
Cowbridge	Risca
Cwmbran	St Brides Major
East Aberthaw	Sebastopol
Gilwern	Shirenewton
Glan-y-Llyn	Swansea
Gower	Talybont-on-Usk
Gwaelod-y-Garth	Tintern
Heol y Plas	Tondu
Kenfig	Tredunnock
Llanbedr	Trellech
Llandogo	Upper Cwmtwrch
Llandovery	Upper Llanover
Llangorse	Upper Torfora
Llangynwyd	Usk
Llantilio Crossenny	Wick
Llantwit Major	Ystalyfera

THE PUBS

ABERCRAVE

The Copper Beech Inn

133 Heol Tawe, Abercrave, Swansea SA9 1XS
☎ *(01639) 730269 Mr and Mrs Messer*

 A family-run freehouse with five guest ales changing weekly. Wye Valley brews are popular and usually featured.

A locals' pub, with function room and beer garden. Families welcome. Bar and restaurant food available all day. Accomodation.

[OPEN] *12–11.30pm (10.30pm Sun).*

BASSALEG

The Tredegar Arms

4 Caerphilly Road, Bassaleg, Newport NP1 9LE
☎ *(01633) 893247 David Hennah*

A Whitbread tied house with up to nine hand pumps and six beers from the barrel. Up to 13 brews available, changing weekly. Regulars include Shepherd Neame Spitfire, Timothy Taylor Landlord and beers from Wychwood and Caledonian. Two beer festivals are held each year, in May and August.

A busy wayside inn, near junction 28 of the M4. Large beer garden, ample car parking. Food available lunchtime and evenings. Children allowed.

[OPEN] *11am–11pm Mon–Sat; 12–10.30pm Sun.*

BEAUFORT

Rhyd y Blew Inn

Rassau Road, Beaufort, Ebbw Vale, Blaenau Gwent NP23 5PW
☎ *(01495) 308935* Ron and Corrina Squire

 Gale's HSB and Brains SA are permanently on offer, plus one guest, supplied in consultation with customers, who have not been disappointed so far!

Semi-rural, sporting community pub with an open-plan bar area and a beer garden. Live entertainment every Friday, plus disco every Wednesday. Food available 12–2pm Mon–Sun and 6.30–8.15pm Fri–Sat (bookings necessary for evenings meals and Sunday lunches). Functions catered for. Annual beer festival held in September. Children welcome if under adult supervision. Located just off the A465 (Heads of the Valley), convenient for local tourist beauty spots and outdoor activities.

OPEN 12–3.30pm and 6.30–11pm Mon–Fri; 12–11pm Sat; 12–3.30pm and 7–10.30pm Sun (sometimes open all day Sun).

BETTWS NEWYDD

The Black Bear

Bettws Newydd, Usk, Monmouthshire NP15 1JN
☎ *(01873) 880701*
Gillian and Stephen Molyneux

 A freehouse with four real ales available at any one time, all straight from the barrel. The range changes every couple of weeks.

An old one-bar country pub with fine restaurant and beer garden. Families welcome. Food available at lunchtime and evenings except Sunday evening. Accommodation. Children allowed. Three miles outside Usk.

OPEN 12–2pm and 6–11pm Mon–Sat (closed Mon lunch); 12–10.30pm Sun; all day on bank holidays.

BISHOPSTON

The Joiners' Arms

50 Bishopston Road, Bishopston, Swansea SA3 3EJ
☎ *(01792) 232658* Ian, Kathleen and Phil

 Home of the Swansea Brewing Company. Up to seven pumps serving all the home brews, plus Marston's Pedigree and a range of guests.

A traditional village pub with mixed clientele, no juke box. CAMRA winner for 2002. Food available at lunchtime and in the evenings. Children allowed.

BISHOPSWOOD BITTER 4.3% ABV
THREE CLIFFS GOLD 4.7% ABV
THE ORIGINAL WOOD 5.2% ABV

OPEN 11.30am–11pm Mon–Sat; 12–10.30pm Sun.

BLACKMILL

The Ogmore Junction Hotel

Blackmill, Bridgend CF35 6DR
☎ *(01656) 840371* John Nicholas

 Up to six pumps serving a range of beers that changes regularly.

A country pub with beams and log fires, beer garden and car park. Backs on to the River Ogmore. Food is available in the separate restaurant at lunchtime and evenings. Children allowed in a designated area. Situated not far from the M4 on the main road to the Rhondda Valley. A fortnightly sheep sale is held behind the pub from the end of July to the end of December.

OPEN 11am–11pm Mon–Sat; 12–10.30pm Sun.

BLAENAVON

Cambrian Inn

Llanover Road, Blaenavon, Torfaen NP4 9HR
☎ *(01495) 790327* J and P Morgans

 Blaenavon Pride and Glory and Brains brews always available, plus a guest (50 per year) such as Morland Old Speckled Hen.

A typical Welsh mining village pub. Darts, pool, cards, etc. No food. Street parking opposite the pub. Children not allowed.

OPEN 6–11pm Mon–Thurs; 12–11pm Sat; 12–3pm and 7–10.30pm Sun.

BRIDGEND

The Pen y Bont Inn

Derwen Road, Bridgend CF31 1LH
☎ *(01656) 652266* Ruth and Jim Simpson

 Marston's Pedigree always available, plus something from Brains, changing frequently.

A small, friendly, comfortable pub. Food available 12–6pm Mon–Sat, with fresh rolls served all day Sunday. A new menu has recently been introduced, and bookings for meals outside the usual food times are welcome. No children allowed. Located near the railway station – formerly the Railway Hotel. Function room available for meetings and functions (50 people).

OPEN 11am–midnight Mon–Sat; 12–10.30pm Sun.

CARDIFF

Cayo Arms

36 Cathedral Road, Cardiff CF11 9LL
☎ *(02920) 391910* Gregson Davies

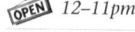Recently taken over by Celtic Inns, there are nine pumps on the one bar serving all Tomos Watkins ales including BB, OSB, Whoosh and Merlin Stout, plus the one special Celtic Best.

Lively pub with a front garden and pergola at the back of the converted Victorian townhouse. Expect rugby fixtures to be shown on the screens inside and to hear Welsh spoken at the bar. Children are welcome and food is served all day until 8pm. Gets very busy at weekends.

 12–11pm (10.30pm Sun).

Chapter Bar

Chapter Arts Centre, Market Road, Canton, Cardiff CF5 1QE
☎ *(02920) 311050* Dave Morgan (manager)

Three pumps serving British guest ales and one with Brains Rev James Original as well as three regular German weissbeers and pilsners. In addition, the bar is stocked with 250 bottled European beers including Belgian Leffe and Duvel and German ales and pilsners and an impressive array of single malt whiskies.

Situated in a popular arts centre and cinema, this is an impressive bar where children are welcome. Nearby café in the centre. Popular beer festivals in May and October.

 6–11pm Mon–Wed; 5–11pm Thurs; 5pm–12.30am Fri; 6–11pm Sat; 7–11pm Sun.

Owain Glyndwr

St John's Street, Cardiff CF10 1XR
☎ *(02920) 22 1980* Glyn White

Five pumps serving regularly changing cask ales including Hook Norton Haymaker, Fuller's London Pride and many others. There is usually Weston's Old Rosie cask cider available too.

A small, former Hogshead chain pub is linked to popular night haunt RSVP next door, but has a charm of its own – not least the single friendly bar. Children are usually allowed in the daytime, but this pub gets quite busy in the evening – especially at weekends – and in the summer tables and chairs are put out in the bustling church square. Excellent food is served all day every day.

 12–11pm (10.30pm Sun).

CHEPSTOW

The Coach & Horses

Welsh Street, Chepstow, Monmouthshire NP6 5LN
☎ *(01291) 622626* Nic Meyrick

A Brains tied pub, with the brewery's ales on three pumps and three guests. Regular visitors include Morland Old Speckled Hen. Additional range of beers available in the summer.

A family pub with B&B accommodation and food available at lunchtime and evenings in a separate dining area.

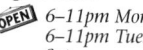 *11am–11pm Mon–Sat; 12–10.30pm Sun.*

CLYTHA

Clytha Arms

Clytha, Monmouthshire NP7 9BW
☎ *(01873) 840206* Mr and Mrs Canning

Hook Norton Best is among those beers permanently available, plus three guests (360 per year) from breweries such as Freeminer, Felinfoel, RCH, Wye Valley, Jennings, Fuller's, Harviestoun, Exmoor and Adnams. A mild is always available.

A large old dower house with restaurant and traditional bar. Bar and restaurant food available at lunchtime and evenings. Car park, garden, accommodation. Children allowed. Located on the old Abergavenny to Raglan road.

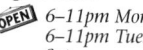 *6–11pm Mon; 11.30am–3pm and 6–11pm Tues–Fri and Sun; 11am–11pm Sat.*

COWBRIDGE

Bear Hotel

63 High Street, Cowbridge, Vale of Glamorgan CF71 7AF
☎ *(01446) 774814* Georgina Woodall

Up four different cask ales such as Wye Valley Butty Bach, Elgood's Greyhound and Cottage Mallard.

Part smart county hotel, part friendly local pub, the Bear Hotel's two bars are always busy with locals and residents. The building dates back to the twelfth century, has open fires and two beer gardens. Children are welcome and bar food is served from 12–9.30pm. Situated right on the main shopping street in Cowbridge where you'll find interesting individual shops and be hard pushed to find a single chain store.

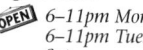 *12–11pm (10.30pm Sun).*

The Bush Inn
St Hilary, Cowbridge, Vale of Glamorgan CF71 7OP
☎ *(01446) 772745* Mark Hitchcock

 Morland Old Speckled Hen, locally produced scrumpy cider straight from the barrel and a regular guest cask ale available at the bar.

This is a traditional sixteenth-century inn set in a beautiful village with two friendly locals' bars, a smaller side bar with a warming inglenook fireplace and a restaurant in the back. Food is served 12–2.30pm and 6.45–9.30pm Mon–Sat and 12–3pm and 6.30–8.30pm Sun. Children are welcome all day and there is a beer garden at the back of the pub.

OPEN *11am–11pm (10.30pm Sun).*

CWMBRAN

The Bush
Craig Road, Cwmbran, Torfaen NP44 5AN
☎ *(01633) 483764* Robert Lewis

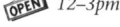 A beer from Cottage Spring is always available here, as are beers from Cwmbran Brewery.

Country pub in an eighteenth-century building, with one bar and garden. No food. Disco held every other Saturday. Car park. Children welcome. Call or ask for directions.

OPEN *12–3pm and 7–11pm (10.30pm Sun).*

EAST ABERTHAW

The Blue Anchor Inn
East Aberthaw, Vale of Glamorgan CF62 3DD
☎ *(01446) 750329* Jeremy Colman

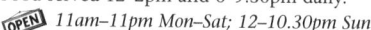 A freehouse offering six pumps, with Wadworth 6X, Brains Buckley's Bitter and Marston's Pedigree the beers regularly available, plus one changing guest ale.

Dating back to the thirteenth century with various cubby-holes and rooms arranged around a central bar. Open fires and a homely atmosphere in winter. Function room/restaurant upstairs. Small beer garden. Food served 12–2pm and 6–9.30pm daily.

OPEN *11am–11pm Mon–Sat; 12–10.30pm Sun.*

GILWERN

Bridgend Inn
Main Road, Gilwern, Bridgend
☎ *(01873) 830939* Mrs PD James

 Up to four real ales always available including Felinfoel brews. Guests include Fuller's London Pride and ESB, also Wadworth 6X and Greene King IPA.

Canalside, olde-worlde pub. Bar and restaurant food available at lunchtime and evenings. Car park, patio and garden. Children allowed for meals.

OPEN *12–2pm and 7–11pm Mon–Thurs; 12–11pm Fri–Sat; 12–10.30pm Sun.*

GLAN-Y-LLYN

Fagin's Ale & Chop House
Cardiff Road, Glan-y-Llyn, Cardiff
☎ *(02920) 811800* Jeff Butler

Five beers always available from a range that may include Shepherd Neame Bishop's Finger, Greene King Abbot, Morland Old Speckled Hen and many more.

A converted terraced house. Former CAMRA Pub of the Year. Bar and restaurant food available at lunchtime and evenings. Function room. Children allowed.

OPEN *12–11pm (10.30pm Sun).*

GOWER

Greyhound Inn
Old Walls, Gower, Swansea SA3 1HA
☎ *(01792) 391027* Paul Stevens (also of the King's Head Hotel, Llangennith)

A freehouse with a total of eight real ale pumps always serving at least four real ales including Marston's Pedigree.

Eighteenth-century pub, popular with walkers, locals and holidaymakers. Two bars and a function room. Food available all day including locally caught fresh fish and homemade curries. Beer garden. Children welcome. Live folk music on Sunday nights.

OPEN *11am–11pm Mon–Sat; 12–10.30pm Sun.*

King's Head Hotel
Llangennith, Gower, Swansea SA3 1HU
☎ *(01792) 386212* Mr and Mrs Stevens

A freehouse with seven pumps serving at least two real ales, often more. Stalwarts include Wadworth 6X and beers from the nearby Felinfoel brewery.

Situated in the centre of a picturesque Gower village, the pub is a Mecca for daytrippers, campers and surfers from nearby Rhossili beach. Food served until 9.30pm daily. Children are welcome until 9pm and the beer garden is a popular suntrap. Very busy on summer evenings.

OPEN *11am–11pm Mon–Sat; 12–10.30pm Sun.*

GWAELOD-Y-GARTH

Gwaelod-y-Garth Inn

Main Road, Gwaelod-y-Garth, Cardiff CF15 9HH
☎ *(02920) 810408* Robert Dodd

 Four cask ale pumps serving Shepherd Neame Spitfire and Tomos Watkin OSB as well as regular guest ales.

Friendly seventeenth-century freehouse, perched in the shadow of Garth Hill, this is a popular haunt for walkers and tourists who rub shoulders with locals. Food available 12–2.30pm and 6–10pm daily in upstairs restaurant. Beer garden overlooking the valley. Children welcome.

OPEN *12–11pm (10.30pm Sun).*

HEOL Y PLAS

Ye Olde Red Lion

Heol y Plas, Llannon, Carmarthenshire SA14 6AA
☎ *(01269) 841276* Steven Ireland

 A Felinfoel Brewery tied house with two pumps serving Felinfoel ales.

A rural sixteenth-century pub with oak beams and log fires. Non-smoking and smoking dining areas. Food available every evening plus Saturday and Sunday lunchtimes. Children welcome.

OPEN *5–11pm Mon–Fri; 11am–11pm Sat; 12–10.30pm Sun.*

KENFIG

The Prince of Wales Inn

Kenfig, Bridgend CF33 4PR
☎ *(01656) 740356* Richard Ellis

 A freehouse serving up to four real ales at any one time. Tomos Watkin OSB and Brains Bitter are regularly available, plus a range of others, changing constantly, from a huge list that might include Wye Valley Prince's Pride or Morland Old Speckled Hen.

An olde-worlde pub with three open fires, a lounge and a function room (which houses the Sunday School). Food is available at lunchtime and evenings. Children allowed.

OPEN *11.30am–4pm and 6–11pm Mon–Fri; 11.30am–11pm Sat–Sun (10.30pm Sun).*

LLANBEDR

The Red Lion Inn

Llanbedr, Crickhowell, Powys NP8 1SR
☎ *(01873) 810754* Mr Hart

 Brains Rev James Original permanently available plus one guest from a range which includes Greene King Abbot Ale, Shepherd Neame Spitfire, Timothy Taylor Landlord, Elgood's Double Swan and Hook Norton and Cottage Brewing Company Ales.

A quiet, 300-year-old pub with beams and real fires. Non-smoking room and garden. Nearby campsite situated in a very beautiful spot in the Black Mountains. Recently refurbished kitchen serving home-cooked food at lunchtimes and evenings in summer and evenings only in winter. Children and dogs welcome. Bootwash provided outside for walkers and up-to-date toilets are always open.

OPEN *7–11pm Mon–Fri; 12–2.30pm Wed–Fri; 11am–11pm Sat; 12–4pm and 7–10.30pm Sun.*

LLANDOGO

The Sloop Inn

Llandogo, Monmouthshire NP5 4TW
☎ *(01594) 530291* Eddie Grace

 A freehouse with two real ales always on at any one time and more in summer. One session and one stronger ale always available.

Describes itself as more of an inn than a pub, family-orientated with accommodation and garden. Set in a beautiful village location in the Wye Valley. Food available every lunchtime and evening. On the A466.

OPEN *Winter: 12–2.30pm and 5.30–11pm Mon–Fri, 11am–11pm Sat–Sun (10.30pm Sun). Summer: all day, every day.*

LLANDOVERY

The White Swan

47 High Street, Llandovery, Carmarthenshire SA20 0DE
☎ *(01550) 720816* Ray Miller

A freehouse specialising in beers up to 4.2% ABV. Two always available, changed every two weeks.

A town pub offering darts, pool and a mixed local clientele. No juke box or fruit machines. No food. Children and dogs are welcome. The last pub on the way out of Llandovery, near the supermarket.

OPEN *12–3pm and 7–11pm (10.30pm Sun).*

LLANGORSE

The Castle Inn

Llangorse, Brecon, Powys LD3 7UB
☎ *(01874) 658225* Mr Williams

 A freehouse with two pumps serving ales from a range including Bateman XB, Morland Old Speckled Hen and many more.

An olde-worlde village inn with a 27-seater restaurant. Food available at lunchtime and evenings. Children allowed under supervision.

OPEN *12–3pm and 6–11pm Mon–Fri; 11am–11pm Sat; 12–10.30pm Sun.*

LLANGYNWYD

The Old House

Llangynwyd, Maesteg, Bridgend CF34 9SB
☎ *(01656) 733310* Richard David

 Up to four real ales available, often including Brains Bitter.

A traditional pub dating back to the twelfth century, run by same family for 35 years and currently whisky pub of the year. Food available at lunchtimes and evenings with fresh fish a speciality. Beautiful conservatory with panoramic views overlooking wonderful countryside. Large children's play area.

OPEN *All day, every day.*

LLANTILIO CROSSENNY

The Hostry Inn

Llantilio Crossenny, Abergavenny, Monmouthshire NP7 8SU
☎ *(01600) 780278* Pauline and Michael Parker

 A freehouse offering up to three real ales. Bullmastiff and Cardiff brews regularly available plus one from Wye Valley or elsewhere.

A small, welcoming, country pub on Offa's Dyke ramblers' path. Skittle alley, function room, non-smoking restaurant and non-smoking area in the bar. Food available lunchtime and evenings. Well-behaved children allowed. Located on the B4233, halfway between Monmouth and Abergavenny.

OPEN *11am–11pm Mon, Tues, Fri, Sat, Sun (10.30pm); closed lunchtime Oct–Mar.*

LLANTWIT MAJOR

Old Swan Inn

Church Street, Llantwit Major, Vale of Glamorgan CF61 1SB
☎ *(01446) 792230* Geoff Harper (manager)

 A freehouse serving a very wide-ranging selection of guest ales which change on a daily basis. Minimum of two guest ales during the week and four on weekends. Breweries favoured include Cottage, Everards, Bateman and Tomos Watkin/Hearns.

The pub, situated opposite the Old Town Hall, dates back to the fourteenth century and is one of the oldest buildings in the historic town centre. A busy local with two bars, popular for food – extensive menu served until 9.30pm. Children welcome. Beer garden.

OPEN *12–11pm (10.30pm Sun).*

LLANVIHANGEL CRUCORNEY

Skirrid Mountain Inn

Llanvihangel Crucorney, Abergavenny, Monmouthshire NP7 8DH
☎ *(01873) 890258* Heather Grant

 Ushers Best, Founders and seasonal beers usually available.

Historic, twelfth-century country inn of unique character, believed to be the oldest pub in Wales and situated in the beautiful Black Mountains. Well-known for good food and a friendly welcome. Food served all day, every day, except Sun and Mon evenings. Car park. Well-behaved children welcome, but no special facilities.

OPEN *11am–3pm and 6–11pm Mon–Fri; 11am–11pm Sat; 12–10.30pm Sun.*

MACHEN

The White Hart Inn

Nant y Ceisiad, Machen, Newport NP1 8QQ
☎ *(01633) 441005* Alan Carter

 A freehouse offering four real ales at any one time, changing frequently. Beers are never repeated (unless requested by customers), and come from small and micro-breweries all around the UK.

A very olde-worlde pub, designed as the interior of ship (the captain's cabin came from the Empress of France). Food available at lunchtime and evenings in a separate dining area which seats 100 people. Play area and beer garden. Children allowed. Located just off the main road (A448).

OPEN *11am–11pm Mon–Sat; 12–10.30pm Sun; closed 3.30–6pm in winter.*

MAMHILAD

Star Inn

*Folly Lane, Mamhilad, near Pontypool, Torfaen
NP4 0JF*
☎ *(01495) 785319*
Darren Munt and Tony Azzopardi

 A freehouse offering two frequently changing guest ales such as Badger's Best and Exmoor Gold.

Seventeenth-century village pub situated opposite a church with reputedly the oldest yew tree in Wales. Two drinking areas around a single bar plus a dining room. Cosy in winter with an open fire and woodburning stove. Beer garden in summer. Popular with walkers and boaty-types from the nearby Monmoutshire and Brecon canal. Food available lunchtimes and evenings. First beer festival held in 2002 and they hope to make these a regular feature on bank holiday weekends.

OPEN *12–2.30pm and 6–11pm Tues–Fri
(closed Mon); 11am–11pm Sat;
12–10.30pm Sun. Open all day during
school summer holidays.*

MONKNASH

Plough and Harrow

*Monknash, nr Cowbridge, Vale of Glamorgan
CF71 7QQ*
☎ *(01656) 890209* Andrew Davies

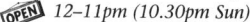 Five regular cask ale pumps often serving Wye Valley Hereford Pale Ale, Shepherd Neame Spitfire and Cottage Golden Arrow, plus guest ales served straight from the barrel. Beers from Bullmastiff are often on offer. Also a vast selection of bottled real ales, and cask cider (often Weston's Old Rosie).

This lively pub dates back to the twelfth century and is situated next to the ruins of an old priory in the village of Monknash. Two bars, the livelier of which has a huge hearth with roaring fire in the winter. Food served lunchtimes and evenings. Live music is a regular feature on Sunday nights. Large beer garden. Located only a short detour from the Glamorgan Heritage Coast footpath.

OPEN *12–11pm (10.30pm Sun).*

MUMBLES

The Park Inn

23 Park Street, Mumbles, Swansea SA3 4DA
☎ *(01792) 366738* Brian and Angela John

 There are six cask ale pumps at this traditional freehouse. Ales from Swansea Brewing Company feature – Three Cliffs is a favourite – and the beers change every week.

Built in a ninteenth-century terraced house in a seaside village. One bar where locals mix with tourists. Children welcome until 9pm, if eating. This pub takes part in the annual Mumbles Beer Festival over the August Bank Holiday weekend.

OPEN *12–2.30pm and 4–11pm Mon–Thur;
11am–11pm Fri–Sat; 12–10.30pm Sun.*

NEWPORT

St Julian Inn

Caerleon Road, Newport NP18 1QA
☎ *(01633) 243548* Mr SJ Williams

 A Unique Brewing Company pub serving four beers with two guests changed twice weekly. Wadworth 6X and Everards Tiger are regulars. Other brewers supported include Wye Valley, Cottage and B&T.

A pretty, family pub in a scenic location with balcony overlooking the River Usk. Food available Mon–Sat lunchtime and evenings. Children allowed.

OPEN *11am–11pm Mon–Sat; 12–10.30pm Sun.*

Wetherspoons

*Cambrian Retail Centre, Cambrian Road,
Newport NP9 4AD*
☎ *(01633) 251752* Paul McDonnell

 Five hand pumps serving a wide range of real ales that change on a weekly basis.

A busy pub with a wide-ranging clientele, old and young. Particularly lively in the evenings. Food available at lunchtime and evenings. No children. Next to the railway station.

OPEN *11am–11pm Mon–Sat; 12–10.30pm Sun.*

OGMORE

The Pelican In Her Piety

Ogmore, Bridgend CF32 0QP
☎ *(01656) 880049* Steve Fisher

Freehouse with six pumps serving Fuller's London Pride, Morland Old Speckled Hen, Greene King Abbot Ale and one regularly changing guest.

Unusually named (it's from a local family's coat of arms), eighteenth-century inn situated opposite Ogmore Castle on the river Ewenny. Recently refurbished to provide a restaurant serving food 12–2pm and 6–9pm. Child- and dog-friendly. Beer garden with spectacular views across the river. For further information, visit www.pelicanpub.co.uk.

OPEN *12–11pm (10.30pm Sun).*

PANT

Pant Cad Ifor Inn
Pant, Merthyr Tydfil CF48 2DD
☎ *(01685) 723688* Phillip Williams

 Up to six real ales available, with regulars including Wye Valley Butty Bach.

A small country pub on the outskirts of town. There is a steam railway 100 yards up the road. Coach parties are catered for. Food is available at lunchtimes (and evenings if pre-booked). Children allowed.

OPEN *11am–11pm Mon–Sat; 12–10.30pm Sun.*

PENALLT

The Boat Inn
Lone Lane, Penallt, Monmouth, Monmouthshire MP5 4AJ
☎ *(01600) 712615* Don and Pat Ellis

 Wadworth 6X and Greene King IPA are always available straight from the barrel, plus approximately six others, some from a rolling rota of about ten regulars, including Oakhill Bitter, and other occasionals.

A small riverside inn on the England–Wales border built into the hillside, with stone floors and simple decor. Live music on Tuesday and Thursday evenings. Very cosy with no juke box or games machines. Bar food available at lunchtimes and evenings. Car park on the side of the river, terrace gardens with ponds, streams and waterfalls. Children allowed. The car park is in Redbrook (Gloucestershire) on the A466, next to a football field. Follow the footpath over an old railway bridge across the Wye.

OPEN *11am–11pm Mon–Sat; 12–10.30pm Sun.*

PONTARDAWE

The Pontardawe Inn
Herbert Street, Pontardawe, Swansea SA8 4ED
☎ *(01792) 830791* Mr P Clayton

 A freehouse serving 170 guest beers per year. Shepherd Neame Early Bird and Everards Tiger are often available, plus a constantly changing range on seven pumps plus one straight from the barrel.

An olde-worlde pub with no juke box and no pool table. Four beer festivals are held every year and the pub is very lively during the town's annual folk music festival. Food served at lunchtime and in the evenings in a separate 28-seater restaurant. Children allowed until 9pm. Winner of CAMRA Regional Pub of the Year 2002. Three boules courts.

OPEN *11am–11pm Mon–Sat; 12–10.30pm Sun.*

RAGLAN

The Ship Inn
High Street, Raglan, Monmouthshire NP15 2DY
☎ *(01291) 690635* Jane Roper

A freehouse serving up to three guest beers at any one time.

A sixteenth-century olde-worlde coaching inn with beams and log fires. There is a well in the cobblestoned forecourt. Food available at lunchtime and evenings. Children allowed. Located just off the High Street, opposite the supermarket.

OPEN *12–11pm Mon; 11.30am–11pm Tues–Sat; 12–10.30pm Sun.*

RISCA

The Fox & Hounds
Park Road, Risca, Newport NP11 6PW
☎ *(01633) 612937* Mr J Madden

Three pumps serve an ever-changing range of beers, often including something from Wye Valley, such as Butty Bach, or brews from Cottage Spring or Cottage Brewery.

Village pub in an old stone building with beams and a fireplace. Food served every lunchtime 12–2.30pm, plus 5–7pm Mon–Thurs. Karaoke on Fridays, disco on Sundays. Children allowed. Two double letting rooms. Car park.

OPEN *11am–11pm Mon–Sat; 12–10.30pm Sun.*

ST BRIDES MAJOR

The Farmers Arms
Wick Road, St Brides Major, Vale of Glamorgan CF32 0SE
☎ *(01656) 880224/880329* Nigel Guy

Five cask pumps serving Ushers Best, Founders and Bishop's Tipple.

Nineteenth-century pub with patio garden overlooking the traditional village pond. Children welcome all day. Food served 12–2.30pm and 6.30–9.30pm Mon–Sat and 12–3.30pm and 6.30–9.30pm Sun.

OPEN *12–3.30pm and 6–11pm (10.30pm Sun).*

SEBASTOPOL

The Open Hearth

Wern Road, Sebastopol, Pontypool, Torfaen NP4 5DR

☎ *(01495) 763752* John and Emma Bennett

A freehouse with seven real ales always available. Regular favourites include Greene King Abbot Ale, Ruddles County and Fuller's London Pride.

A busy pub on the canal side, with excellent food and beer reputation. Winner of three regional CAMRA awards. Food available 12–2pm and 6.30–10pm every day in a separate non-smoking restaurant. No juke box or pool table. Mixed clientele of all ages. Children welcome, with children's room provided.

OPEN *11.30am–11pm Mon–Sat; 11am–11pm Sat; 12–10.30pm Sun.*

SHIRENEWTON

The Carpenters Arms

Shirenewton, Nr Chepstow, Monmouthshire
☎ *(01291) 64121* James Bennet

Fuller's London Pride, Wadworth 6X and Marston's Pedigree usually available with one or two guest beers such as Timothy Taylor Landlord, Greene King Abbot Ale, Gale's HSB, Fuller's ESB, Ringwood Old Thumper or Young's Special.

Atmospheric, traditional country inn crammed with antiques and memorabilia. Profusion of colour from the hanging baskets in summer months. Food served 12–2pm and 7–9.30pm Mon–Sat (until 10pm Fri–Sat). Car park. Family room. Located on the B4235 Chepstow/Usk road, just outside the village.

OPEN *11am–2.30pm and 6–11pm (10.30pm Sun).*

Tredegar Arms

Shirenewton, Nr Chepstow, Monmouthshire, NP16 6RQ
☎ *(01291) 641274* Sally Newham

Three real ale pumps, with Greene King IPA among the beers always on offer, plus a guest ale which changes regularly.

A pub since the mid nineteenth century although the building, which includes two bars and open fires, is considerably older. Situated in the centre of a picturesque Monouthshire village, a popular haunt for locals and occasional passing tourists. Food served lunchtimes and evenings. Children welcome. Outside patio area with seating and tables at the front of the pub.

OPEN *12–2.30pm and 6–11pm Mon–Fri; 12–11pm Sat; 12–4.30pm and 6–10.30pm Sun.*

SWANSEA

The Glamorgan Hotel

88 Argyle Street, Swansea SA1 3TA
☎ *(01792) 455120* Vince Carr

Two real ales on the guest pumps including Camerons Strongarm, Marston's Bitter and Banks's Bitter.

A broad-based local, no juke box. Food available lunchtime and evenings. Children allowed in the afternoons only.

OPEN *11am–11pm Mon–Sat; 12–10.30pm Sun.*

The New Inn

The Lone, Clydach, Near Swansea SA6 5SU
☎ *(01792) 842839* Peter Chatterton

A Whitbread-owned pub with one frequently changing guest ale.

A village inn with a restaurant and function room. Food available at lunchtime and evenings. Children allowed.

OPEN *11am–3pm and 6–11pm Mon–Thurs; 11am–11pm Fri–Sat; 12–10.30pm Sun.*

Plough and Harrow

Church Road, Llansamlet, Swansea SA7 9RL
☎ *(01792) 772263* Michael Bolter

Four real ale pumps serving Tomos Watkin beers such as OSB and Whoosh which come from the nearby brewery.

A village pub with a friendly atmosphere on the outskirts of Swansea, mainly frequented by locals. One large bar with an open fire and some outside seating. Children welcome. Food served lunchtimes and evenings.

OPEN *12–11pm (10.30pm Sun).*

The Potters Wheel

85–6 The Kingsway, Swansea SA1 5JE
☎ *(01792) 465113* Carl Jones

A JD Wetherspoon's pub with up to 10 real ales available.

A town-centre pub on the high street. No music, games or pool, non-smoking area. Food available all day. Children welcome.

OPEN *11am–11pm Mon–Sat; 12–10.30pm Sun.*

The Railway Inn
553 Gower Road, Upper Killay, Swansea SA2 7DS
☎ *(01792) 203946*
William Carter and Christine Hatton

A freehouse with three regular cask ales. Favourites include Original Wood, Deep Slade Dark and Bishop's Wood, all from the nearby Swansea Brewing Company, and Fuller's London Pride.

Dating back to 1864, this pub was a house until the 1930s. It stands next to the ticket office and station master's house on the old Clyne railway line which ran down the valley into Swansea. The line is now a cycle track and the pub is a popular stop-off point for cyclists, as well as locals and trippers to and from the nearby Gower peninsula. One main bar, separate lounge bar, open fires in the winter and a beer garden (two patios). Basic food is on offer lunchtimes and evenings. Children welcome until 7pm.

 11am–11pm Mon–Sat; 12–10.30pm Sun.

Woodman Inn
Mumbles Road, Blackpill, Swansea SA3 5AS
☎ *(01792) 402700* John Allan

Six pumps regularly serving three types of ale including Brains and at least one guest ale which will change regularly.

This old pub on the main tourist route to Swansea's beaches is under new owners who plan to make the most of its low beams and old-fashioned charm. Children welcome until 8pm.

 11am–11pm Mon–Sat; 12–10.30pm Sun.

TALYBONT-ON-USK

The Star Inn
Talybont-on-Usk, Brecon, Powys LD3 7YX
☎ *(01874) 676635* Mrs Coakham

A constantly changing range of beers, including brews from Felinfoel, Freeminers, Bullmastiff, Wadworth and Crown Buckley.

A riverside and canalside site, with lovely garden. Bar and restaurant food is available at lunchtime and evenings. Parking, garden, live music on Wednesdays. Children allowed. Accommodation. Less than a mile off the A40 between Brecon and Abergavenny (Brecon six miles, Abergavenny 14 miles).

 11am–11pm (10.30pm Sun) in summer; otherwise closed 3–6pm.

TINTERN

Cherry Tree Inn
Chapel Hill, Tintern, Monmouthshire, NP16 6TH
☎ *(01291) 689292* Stephen Pocock

Beers served straight from the barrel always include a choice of four real ales, and often up to six. Timothy Taylor Landlord and Morland Old Speckled Hen make frequent appearances. Guests include Fuller's London Pride and Spinning Dog Muttley's Revenge.

Low ceiling, beams, thick stone walls and single room bar, the Cherry Tree is a piece of living history – it has been a pub since the mid seventeenth century and the building is much older than that. Beer garden. Children welcome. Make the effort to find this gem of a pub and you'll not be disappointed.

 12–11pm (10.30pm Sun).

TONDU

Llynfi Arms
Maesteg Road, Tondu, Bridgend CF32 9DP
☎ *(01656) 720010* Pearl Fowler

One guest beer always available and changing every two weeks, from smaller independents such as Cottage, Fisherrow or Tomos Watkins.

The pub is close to Tondu railway station, and has two model trains running around the ceiling of the lounge bar. Food served 12–2pm and 7–9.30pm Wed–Sat and 12–2pm Sun. Booking advised Fri–Sun. Children welcome in the lounge bar at lunchtime.

 1–4pm and 7–11pm Mon–Tues; 12–4pm and 7–11pm Wed–Sat; 12–3pm and 7–10.30pm Sun.

TREDUNNOCK

The Newbridge Inn
Tredunnock, Usk, Monmouthshire NP5 1LY
☎ *(01633) 451000* Pascal Meril

A freehouse with Brains Rev James Original Ale always available, plus one guest, such as Fuller's London Pride or Brains St David's Ale.

A refurbished pub on the banks of the River Usk, featuring a unique interior design and original artwork and sculptures. Food available at lunchtimes and evenings. Children welcome. Village signposted off the Caerleon–Usk road, up the lane opposite the Cwrt Bleddyn Hotel.

 12–3pm and 6–11pm Tues–Sat; 12–3pm Sun.

TRELLECH

The Lion Inn

Trellech, Nr Monmouth, Monmouthshire
NP25 4PA
☎ *(01600) 860322* Tom and Debbie Zsigo

 A freehouse with four pumps. Bath SPA is always on offer, plus either Wadworth 6X, Fuller's London Pride or Wye Valley Butty Bach. A weekly guest is also served.

A traditional, stone-fronted, Grade II listed, sixteenth-century typical country pub with open fire, no fruit machines or juke box. Favours traditional pub games such as bar billiards and bar skittles plus many social evenings. Prize-winning food available every lunchtime and all evenings except Sunday. Well-behaved children and dogs allowed, but no dogs in the lounge.

OPEN *12–3pm and 7–11pm Mon; 12–3pm and 6–11pm Tues–Fri; 6.30–11pm Sat; closed Sunday evenings.*

The Trekkers

The Narth, Nr Trellech, Monmouthshire NP5 4QG
☎ *(01600) 860367* Mr and Mrs Flower

 A freehouse with two guest ales changed fortnightly. Greene King Abbot, Shepherd Neame Spitfire and Smiles Golden regularly available.

A local country pub, in the style of a log cabin, family-orientated with beer garden, swings and skittle alley. Traditional, homemade, British-bought food available in separate dining area lunchtimes and evenings. It is advisable to book for Sunday lunch.

OPEN *11am–2.30pm and 6–11pm Mon–Sat; 12–3pm and 7–10.30pm Sun.*

UPPER CWMTWRCH

The George IV Inn

Upper Cwmtwrch, Swansea Valley SA9 2XH
☎ *(01639) 830441*
Richard Thomas and Peter Tugwell

 A freehouse offering guest ales, particularly in the summer.

Friendly riverside rural pub and restaurant in a scenic valley in the foothills of the Black Mountains. Log fire, oak beams, antiques and plenty of olde-worlde atmosphere. Large beer garden and car park. Homemade food prepared in the open-plan kitchen and served during opening hours. Located just off the A4067 Brecon to Swansea road, not far from the famous Dan-yr-Ogof caves.

OPEN *12–3pm and 6pm–11pm Mon–Sat; 12–3pm and 7pm–10.30pm Sun.*

UPPER LLANOVER

The Goose & Cuckoo Inn

Upper Llanover, Abergavenny, Monmouthshire
NP7 9ER
☎ *(01873) 880277* Carol and Michael Langley

 A freehouse with three pumps, usually serving Brains Reverend James Original, Brakspear Bitter and beers from Bullmastiff.

A small, isolated, picturesque country pub with a log fire. The pub is family-orientated and has a collection of animals in the garden for the youngsters. No juke box or games machines, traditional games available including quoits, dominoes, cribbage and darts. Beer garden. Food available every lunchtime and evening, but Sunday lunch must be booked. Accomodation is available. Also an impressive 72 malt whiskies at the bar.

OPEN *11.30am–3pm and 7–11pm Tues–Thurs (closed Mon); all day Fri–Sun.*

UPPER TORFORA

The Queen Inn

Upper Cymbran Road, Upper Torfora, Cwmbran,
Torfaen NP44 1SN
☎ *(01633) 484252* Peter Crooks

 The guest beer is often from Cottage Spring, perhaps Four Seasons, Crow Valley Bitter, Drayman's Bitter, The Full Malty, or a celebration or seasonal ale.

Country inn on the edge of village in a 150-year-old stone building which is three cottages knocked into one. Food available. Restaurant, bar, lounge and garden. Children allowed. Car park. Off Henleys Way.

OPEN *12–3pm and 5–11pm (10.30pm Sun).*

USK

The Greyhound Inn

1 Chepstow Road, Usk, Monmouthshire NP5 1BL
☎ *(01291) 672074* Bob and Annette Burton

 A freehouse serving four beers including those from RCH, Brakspear, Greene King, Wye Valley, Shepherd Neame and Freeminer. The beers change fortnightly.

An early sixteenth-century pub on the edge of town. Bar, no juke box. Food available lunchtime and evenings. Children allowed.

OPEN *12–3pm and 6.30–11pm Mon–Sat; 12–3pm and 7–10.30pm Sun.*

The Kings Head Hotel
*18 Old Market Street, Usk, Monmouthshire
NP5 1AL*
☎ *(01291) 672963* S Musto

 A freehouse with four pumps serving Fuller's London Pride, Badger Tanglefoot and Timothy Taylor Landlord, plus one guest beer.

A fifteenth-century pub with accommodation. Open fireplace, function room and restaurant serving food at lunchtime and evenings. Children allowed.

OPEN *All day, every day.*

WICK

Lamb & Flag
*Church Street, Wick, Vale of Glamorgan
CF71 7QE*
☎ *(01656) 890278*
Tim Warrick and Gill Theophilus

 Two pumps dedicated to guest real ales such as Cottage Mallard Gold and local brew Bullmastiff Best Bitter.

Traditional sixteenth-century village pub (no juke box, no pool table) with mainly local clientele in the two bars and back lounge, but some tourists do drop in on their way to local beaches like Southerdown and Ogmore. Open fires in winter, outside seating in summer. Food available lunchtimes and evenings Mon–Fri, all day Sat–Sun.

OPEN *11.30am–3.30pm and 5–11pm Mon–Thur; 11.30am–11pm Fri–Sat; 12–10.30pm Sun.*

YSTALYFERA

Wern Fawr Inn
47 Wern Road, Ystalyfera, Swansea SA9 2LX
☎ *(01639) 843625* Mr Will Hopton

 The home of the Bryncelyn Brewery with the full range of own brews permanently available. All the home ales are named on a Buddy Holly theme. Also one guest, often from Wye Valley.

A village pub dating back to the 1850s. Background music is 1960s and 70s. No food. Beer garden. Children allowed.

BUDDY MARVELLOUS 4.0% ABV
Dark ruby mild beer.
CHH BITTER 4.5% ABV
A rich red-brown bitter with a good malt and hop balance.
OH BOY 4.5% ABV
A light-coloured ale with good aroma and taste.

OPEN *7–11pm only Mon–Sat; 12–3pm and 7–10.30pm Sun.*

Places Featured:

Abercych
Felinfoel
Haverfordwest
Horeb
Llanddarog
Llandeilo

Llansaint
Mynydd y Garreg
Narbeth
Pembroke
Upper Cwmtwrch

THE PUBS

ABERCYCH

The Nag's Head Inn

Abercych, Boncath, Pembrokeshire
☎ *(01239) 841200* Steven Jamieson

 A brewpub with Old Emrys brewed on the premises and always available plus three guests at any one time, which could be something like Morland Old Speckled Hen, Greene King Abbot, a Dorothy Goodbody's ale from Wye Valley or anything from a Welsh micro-brewery.

A friendly family-run riverside pub with flagstone floors and wooden beams. A large collection of beer bottles is on display. Bar and restaurant food available 12–2pm and 6–9pm daily. Separate non-smoking room. Children welcome with a dedicated menu and playground. Large car park. Situated on the B4332 between Cenarth Falls and Boncath.

 **OLD EMRYS 4.0% ABV**
Named after a late local man.

OPEN *11.30am–3pm and 6–11.30pm.*

FELINFOEL

The Royal Oak

Felinfoel Road, Felinfoel, Carmarthenshire SA14 8LA
☎ *(01554) 751140* Mrs M Cleland

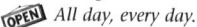 Tied to the nearby Felinfoel Brewery, with two hand pumps serving the Felinfoel ales.

An old-fashioned local opposite the brewery, with food available at lunchtime and evenings. Children allowed.

OPEN *All day, every day.*

HAVERFORDWEST

King's Arms Hotel

23 Dew Street, Haverfordwest, Dyfed
☎ *(01437) 763726* Chris Hudd

 Six beers always available from a list of approximately 150 brews per year.

An old, beamed and flagstoned pub in the town, just past the library. Street parking, function room. No children.

OPEN *11am–3pm and 6–11pm Mon–Sat; 12–3pm and 7–10.30pm Sun.*

HOREB

The Waunwyllt Inn

Horeb Road, Five Roads, Horeb, Llanelli, Carmarthenshire SA15 5AQ
☎ *(01269) 860209* Shaun Pawson

 A freehouse with four pumps serving a constantly changing selection of real ales. Examples include Shepherd Neame Bishop's Finger, Everards Tiger and others from Cottage, Brecknock and Tomos Watkin.

A popular country inn in a quiet hamlet outside Llanelli. Close to the Celtic Trail cycle route. Large beer garden, non-smoking dining area, five en-suite bedrooms. Food available at lunchtime and evenings. Children allowed. From Llanelli, take the B4309 towards Carmarthen.

OPEN *11am–11pm Mon–Sat and 12–10.30pm Sun in summer; 12–3pm and 6.30–11pm in winter.*

LLANDDAROG

The White Hart Thatched Inn

Llanddarog, Carmarthenshire SA32 8NT
☎ *(01267) 275395* Coles family

Cwrw Blasus ('tasty beer') is just one of the ales brewed and served here.

Beautiful rural village inn dating back to 1371, with open log fire, oak beams and old carved furniture. The antiques create an olde-worlde atmosphere. Delicious homemade meals are served in the dining room, with snacks and sandwiches available throughout the pub. The food is served during all opening times. Car park. Children welcome. On the B4310, just off the A48, not far from the National Botanic Garden of Wales.

BEETROOT 4.0% ABV
CWRW DU (BLACK BITTER) 4.0% ABV
NETTLE 4.0% ABV
PEAR 4.0% ABV
PLUM 4.0% ABV
TRADITIONAL LAGER 4.0–4.5% ABV
Occasional.
ROASTED BARLEY STOUT 4.1% ABV
CWRW BLASUS 4.3% ABV
CWRW NADOLIG 5.0% ABV
Spiced Christmas ale.

OPEN *11.30am–3pm and 6.30–11pm Mon–Sat; 12–3pm and 7–10.30pm Sun.*

LLANDEILO

The Castle Hotel
113 Rhosmaen Street, Llandeilo, Dyfed SA19 6EN
☎ *(01558) 823446* Simon Williams

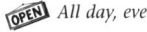 A Tomas Watkins tied house with award-winning ales such as Whoosh, Best, Old Style Bitter and Merlin's Stout permanently available. Other seasonal guests rotated on one hand pump.

A town-centre pub with two bars serving five adjoining rooms, 65-seater restaurant, beer garden. Bar and restaurant food served lunchtimes and evenings. Children allowed. Easy, free parking. Local CAMRA Pub of the Year 1999.

OPEN *All day, every day.*

LLANSAINT

The King's Arms
13 Maes yr Eglwys, Llansaint, Nr Kidwelly, Carmarthenshire SA17 5JE
☎ *(01267) 267487* John and Debbie Morris

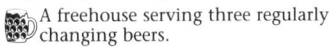 A freehouse serving three regularly changing beers.

Separate smoking and non-smoking dining areas – bar and restaurant food served lunchtimes and evenings. Log fire in season, beer garden, car park. Children allowed. Follow signs for Llansaint from Kidwelly – the pub nestles under the church tower. Accommodation available.

OPEN *12–2.30pm and 6.30–11pm (10.30pm Sun); closed Tues lunchtimes.*

MYNYDD Y GARREG

The Prince of Wales
Heol Meinciau, Mynydd y Garreg, Kidwelly, Carmarthenshire SA17 4RP
☎ *(01554) 890522* Gail and Richard Pickett

 A freehouse with six beers always available from a list that includes brews from Wye Valley, Bullmastiff and various Welsh micro-breweries. Please phone ahead for details of beers currently on tap. Real cider also available from Easter–Oct.

A 200-year-old cottage pub, in the same ownership since 1989, with a collection of cinema memorabilia and bric-à-brac. Bar and restaurant food available evenings – the restaurant is completely non-smoking. Car park and garden. No children. Take the Mynydd y Garreg turn from the Cydweli bypass, then just over a mile on the right.

OPEN *5–11pm (10.30pm Sun).*

NARBETH

The Kirkland Arms
East Gate, St James Street, Narbeth, Dyfed SA67 7DB
☎ *(01834) 860423* Mr Edger

 A Felinfoel Brewery tied pub with guest beers rotated on one pump. These might include York Yorkshire Terrier, Swansea Bishopswood Bitter, Wadworth 6X and many others changed on a weekly basis.

An old, traditional pub with pool table, games machines and beer garden. Fresh rolls and sandwiches served every day. Children allowed.

OPEN *11am–11pm Mon–Sat; 12–10.30pm Sun.*

PEMBROKE

The Castle Inn
17 Main Street, Pembroke, Pembrokeshire SA71 4JS
☎ *(01646) 682883* Nigel Temple

 A freehouse usually serving Charles Wells Bombardier and Wadworth 6X plus up to two guests.

A very old pub with long and narrow stone walls and beams. No food. Children allowed.

OPEN *11am–11pm Mon–Sat; 12–10.30pm Sun.*

The First & Last
London Road, Pembroke Dock, Pembrokeshire SA72 6TX
☎ *(01646) 682687* Richard Maynard

A freehouse with Charles Wells Bombardier or Brains SA usually available plus one other.

A local community pub with beer garden. Light lunches only served. Children allowed at lunchtime only.

OPEN *11am–11pm Mon–Sat; 12–10.30pm Sun.*

UPPER CWMTWRCH

The George IV Inn

Upper Cwmtwrch, Swansea Valley,
Carmarthenshire SA9 2XH
☎ *(01639) 830441* Coles family

 Cwmtwrch Ale (4.3% ABV), brewed especially for the pub by the Coles family brewery (White Hart Inn, Llanddarog), is always available, plus Cwrw Blasus, also from Coles.

Friendly, family-run, riverside rural pub and restaurant in a scenic valley in the foothills of the Black Mountains. Log fire, oak beams, antiques and plenty of olde-worlde atmosphere. Large beer garden, children's play area, car park. Delicious homemade food prepared in the open-plan kitchen and served during opening hours. Just off the A4067 Brecon to Swansea road, not far from the famous Dan-Yr-Ogof Caves.

OPEN *11.30am–3pm and 6.30–11pm Mon–Sat (closed all day Tues); 12–3pm and 7–10.30pm Sun.*

YOU TELL US

* *Bridge Inn,* Bridge Street, Chepstow
* *Garrd Fon,* Beach Road, Felinheli, Gwynedd
* *The Gatekeeper,* Westgate Street, Cardiff
* *Farmer's Arms,* Aberthin, near Cowbridge
* *The New Inn,* Bedwellty, Blackwood, Gwent

Places Featured:

JERSEY	GUERNSEY
Grouville	Castel
St Brelade	Forest
St Helier	St Martins
St Laurence	St Peter Port
St Ouen	St Peters
St Peter's Village	St Sampsons
	Vale

THE BREWERIES

THE GUERNSEY BREWERY CO. LTD

South Esplanade, St Peter Port, Guernsey GY1 1BJ
☎ *(01481) 720143*
www.bucktrouts.com/brewery.html

 BRAYE MILD 3.7% ABV
Malty, toffee flavour. Balancing hops.
SUNBEAM BITTER 4.2% ABV
Smooth, well-balanced. Dry bitter finish.

RW RANDALL LTD

*PO Box 154, Vauxlaurens Brewery, St Julian's
Avenue, St Peter Port, Guernsey GY1 3JG*
☎ *(01481) 720134*

 MILD 3.4% ABV
PATOIS ALE 5.0% ABV
Plus occasional brews.

THE PUBS

JERSEY

GROUVILLE

Seymour Inn

La Rocque, Grouville, Jersey JE3 9BU
☎ *(01534) 854558* Gary Boner

Guernsey Sunbeam and Tipsy Toad
Jimmy's usually available. The Tipsy
Toad special brews are also served.

Traditional country pub with two lounges,
bar and beer garden. Food served 12–2pm
and 6–8pm Mon–Sat. Car park. Children
welcome.

OPEN *10am–11pm Mon–Sat; 11am–11pm Sun.*

ST BRELADE

The Old Smugglers Inn

Ouaisne Bay, St Brelade, Jersey JE3 8AW
☎ *(01534) 741510* Nigel Godfrey

A genuine freehouse serving two guest
ales, changing daily, including beers
such as Greene King Abbot and brews from
Ringwood and Young's.

A pub dating from the eighteenth century,
with no music or fruit machines. Food is
served every day, and there is a non-smoking
dining area. Children welcome.

OPEN *All day, every day.*

ST HELIER

Lamplighter

Mulcaster Street, St Helier, Jersey JE2 3NJ
☎ *(01534) 723119* Dave Ellis

Marston's Pedigree usually available,
plus a guest beer which might be
Wadworth 6X.

Gas-lit pub with old wooden beams, rafters
and soft, pewter bar top. No music or
video games. Food served 12–2pm daily.
Children welcome but no special facilities.
Situated close to St Helier bus station.

OPEN *9.30am–11pm.*

The Prince of Wales Tavern

8 Hilgrove Street, St Helier, Jersey JE2 4SL
☎ *(01534) 737378* Graeme Channing

Although mainly serving beers from
national breweries, Wadworth 6X is
permanently available here.

Small, original old tavern with lovely beer
garden at the rear. No TV, no pool. Food
served 11am–2.30pm Mon–Fri. No children.

OPEN *10am–11pm Mon–Sat; 11am–2pm Sun.*

The Townhouse

57–9 New Street, St Helier, Jersey
☎ *(01534) 615000* Martin Kelly

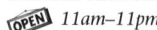 Mostly serves a selection of keg ales from The Jersey Brewery, but still worth a visit as Tipsy Toad Brewery's Jimmy's Bitter is also permanently available.

A pub in a converted warehouse with three function rooms for live music etc. Previous winner of CAMRA's Pub of the Year award. Bar and restaurant food available at lunchtime and evenings. Parking nearby. Children allowed.

OPEN *11am–11pm.*

ST LAWRENCE

The British Union

Main Road, St Lawrence, Jersey JE3 1NL
☎ *(01534) 861070* Alan Cheshire

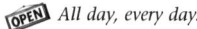 One guest, changed monthly, always features a beer from the Tipsy Toad Brewery.

An open-plan pub with two bars and games room. Small beer garden. Food available at lunchtime and evenings. Children allowed. Opposite St Lawrence Church

OPEN *All day, every day.*

ST OUEN

Le Moulin de Lecq

Greve de Lecq, St Ouen, Jersey JE3 2DT
☎ *(01534) 482818* Shaun Lynch (manager)

A freehouse offering guest ales such as Morland Old Speckled Hen, Greene King Abbot, and beers from Ringwood.

Built around a twelfth-century flour mill with working parts inside and outside the bar. One bar and small upstairs lounge, large outside seating area and adventure playground. Summer barbecues. Food served every lunchtime and evenings. Children welcome. In the north-west of the island.

OPEN *All day, every day.*

ST PETER'S VILLAGE

The Star

La Grande Route de St Pierre, St Peter's Village, Jersey JE3 7AA
☎ *(01534) 485556*

 Home of The Tipsy Toad Brewery. One cask ale is permanently brewed on the premises, plus seasonal specials.

Jersey's first brewpub is situated in renovated and restored Victorian premises. The result is a cosy pub with a family atmosphere. The brewing process can be observed through a wall of windows. Bar food is available at lunchtime and evenings. Family room and conservatory, outdoor children's play area. Baby-changing facilities and disabled toilets.

JIMMY'S BITTER 4.2% ABV
DIXIES WHEAT BEER 4.1% ABV
Summer.
NAOMH PADRAIG'S PORTER 4.4% ABV
Autumn.
FESTIVE TOAD 8.0% ABV
Christmas.

OPEN *10am–11.30pm.*

GUERNSEY

CASTEL

Hotel Fleur du Jardin

Kings Mills, Castel, Guernsey GY5 7JT
☎ *(01481) 257996* Keith Read

Guernsey Brewery Sunbeam plus one other local beer regularly served.

Fifteenth-century country inn with olde-worlde atmosphere, serving bar and restaurant meals at lunchtimes and evenings. A lovely beer garden with al fresco dining. Car park. Children welcome.

OPEN *11am–11.45pm Mon–Sat; 12–3pm Sun (Sun evenings with food only).*

FOREST

Venture Inn

New Road, (Rue de la Villiaze), Forest, Guernsey GY8 0HG
☎ *(01481) 263211* Tony and Kay Mollet

Randall's Patois usually available.

Country pub in the heart of the farming community. Log fire in the lounge during winter months. SIS Tele Betting, big-screen TV, pool and darts in locals' bar. Food served May–Sept, 12–2pm and 6–9pm Mon–Sat; Oct–Apr, 12–2pm Mon–Thurs, 12–2pm and 6–9pm Fri–Sat. Car park. Children's menu.

OPEN *10.30am–11.45pm Mon–Sat.*

ST MARTINS

The Captain's Hotel
La Fosse, St Martins, Guernsey GY4 6EF
☎ *(01481) 238990* Alison Delamare

 A Guernsey Brewery tied house with Sunbeam always available.

A traditional locals' pub, which is popular with tourists. Outside tables. Pentanque pitch. Food served in the bar and in separate bistro – parties catered for. Children and dogs allowed.

 10am–11.45pm.

ST PETER PORT

Albion House Tavern
Church Square, St Peter Port, Guernsey GY1 2LD
☎ *(01481) 723518* Amanda Roberts

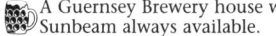 A Guernsey Brewery house with Sunbeam always available.

Spread over two floors with a large nautical-themed bar downstairs, sports bar and wine bar upstairs with pool tables. Food available every lunchtime and Mon–Thurs evenings. Children allowed. Situated right beside the Church, the pub actually features in *The Guinness Book of Records* as the pub closest to a Church in the UK!

 10.30am–11.45pm Mon–Sat; 12–3.30pm Sun (closed Sun evening).

The Banker's Draught
The Pollet, St Peter Port, Guernsey GY1 1WL
☎ *(01481) 723855* Glen Pontin

A Guernsey Brewery tied house with Sunbeam always available.

A big pub with varied clientele – business people, tourists and families. Video games machines and video juke box, live bands occasionally. Food served at lunchtime only. Children allowed.

10am–11.30pm Mon–Sat; 12–3.30pm Sun.

Cock & Bull
2 Lower Hauteville, St Peter Port, Guernsey
☎ *(01481) 722660* Stephen Taylor

 Ringwood Best Bitter, Fortyniner and Old Thumper always available, plus guests from breweries such as Stonehenge, Shepherd Neame, Hop Back, Rebellion, Greene King, Orkney, Crouch Vale, and many others.

Large, comfortable, friendly pub on three levels, with one bar and wooden flooring. The varied clientele includes university students. Irish music often featured on Thursday nights (with a little Irish dancing thrown in!), and there is acoustic music on Tuesday nights. Light snacks served 12–2pm Mon–Fri. Pool room, big-screen TV. Children welcome at lunchtimes only. Situated at the top of Cornet Street, on the way to Victor Hugo's house.

11.30am–2.30pm and 4–11.45pm Mon–Thurs; 11.30am–11.45pm Fri–Sat; closed Sun.

The Drunken Duck
La Charroterie, St Peter Port, Guernsey GY1 1EL
☎ *(01481) 725045* Charles Coyle

 One of only a few freehouses in Guernsey. Guests include Wadworth 6X, Shepherd Neame Spitfire and beers from Badger, to name but a few.

A small, friendly pub for young and old alike. Various promotional and fun nights. Bar snacks available all day. Ample parking from 5pm and at weekends.

11am–11.45pm Mon–Sat; 12–3.30pm Sun.

Prince of Wales Bars
Manor Place, St Peter Port, Guernsey GY1 2JN
☎ *(01481) 720166* Mrs Julie Lane

 Wadworth 6X regularly available, plus a guest beer, perhaps Morland Old Speckled Hen, Badger Tanglefoot or something from Tipsy Toad or Guernsey Brewery.

Town-centre freehouse, a rarity in Guernsey, with two bars known as The Coal Hole and The Prince Bar. Known locally for well-kept real ales. Food served at lunchtime only. Children welcome, but no special facilities. Situated opposite the Court House.

10am–11.45pm.

The Ship & Crown

Pier Steps, The Esplanade, St Peter Port, Guernsey
☎ *(01482) 721368* Mark Pontin

 Various Guernsey Brewery beers regularly available plus additional Tipsy Toad brews.

Large, lively, single-bar town pub with excellent views over the harbour. Walls covered in pictures of local shipwrecks and local history, including the German occupation during the Second World War. Food served 11am–3pm Mon–Sat, plus 12–3pm and 6–10pm Sun. Car park. Children welcome until 3pm.

OPEN *11am–11.45pm Mon–Sat; 12–3pm and 6–10pm Sun.*

ST PETERS

Longfrie Inn

Route du Longfrie, St Peters, Guernsey GY7 9RX
☎ *(01481) 263107* Phil and Pam Elliott

 A Guernsey Brewery tied house with Sunbeam always available.

A food-oriented pub with beams and log fires in winter. Beer garden. Live music and karaoke. Car Park. Accommodation. Children allowed.

OPEN *11am–11.45pm (summer); 12–3pm and 5.30–11.45pm (winter).*

ST SAMPSONS

Blind O'Reilly's

South Side, St Sampsons, Guernsey GY2 4QH
☎ *(01481) 244503* Mark O'Reilly

A Guernsey Brewery tied house with Sunbeam always available, plus house brews Cheap Pig and Pig's Ear on a guest basis.

A pub in two halves, with the front an Irish theme bar and the back a traditional family pub. Live music, festivals and entertainment. Food available at lunchtime. Children allowed.

OPEN *11am–11.45pm.*

Pony Inn

Les Capelles, St Sampsons, Guernsey GY2 4GX
☎ *(01481) 244374* Isoken Ogbeide

A Guernsey Brewery tied house with either Sunbeam or Pirates Ale always available.

A family-orientated two-bar pub with conservatory, patio, play area, Playstations and TV-screen games. Child-free zone for those who prefer a peaceful pint. Live music every Friday. Car park. Food available.

OPEN *10.30am–11.45pm.*

VALE

Houmet Tavern

Grande Havre, Vale, Guernsey GY6 8JR
☎ *(01481) 242214* Mr Franco Fasola

A Guernsey Brewery tied house with Bray Mild always available.

Comfortable lounge bar overlooking the sea. Non-smoking conservatory. Darts, pool, bar billiards. Beer garden. Car park. Food available Mon–Sat lunchtimes and Tues, Wed, Fri, Sat evenings. Children allowed, with special childrens' menu available.

OPEN *10am–11.45pm.*

YOU TELL US

* *The Coronation Inn,* 36 High Street, St Anne, Alderney
* *Le Friquet Hotel,* Castel, Guernsey

Places Featured:

Ballaugh
Castletown
Douglas
Laxey

Old Laxey
Peel
Ramsey

THE BREWERIES

BUSHY'S BREWERY

11 Church Street, Douglas, IM1 2AG
☎ *(01624) 611101*
www.bushys.com

RUBY 1874 MILD 3.5% ABV
BUSHY'S EXPORT BITTER 3.8% ABV
MANANNAN'S CLOAK 3.8% ABV
SUMMER ALE 3.8% ABV
Seasonal.
CELTIBRATION 4.0% ABV
Occasional.
OYSTER STOUT 4.2% ABV
Very occasional.
OLD BUSHY TAIL 4.5% ABV
OLD SHUNTER 4.5% ABV
Occasional.
PISTON BREW 4.5% ABV
Brewed for the TT races.
LOVELY JUBBELY 5.2% ABV
Winter brew.

THE PUBS

BALLAUGH

The Raven Inn

Main Road, Ballaugh
☎ *(01624) 897272* Steven Barrett

 Okells Bitter regularly served, plus a guest ale.

Small, friendly country pub next to Ballaugh Bridge. Good selection of home-cooked food served Thurs–Sat evenings. Traditional pub games and TV. Children welcome at lunchtime only and in the separate bistro during opening hours.

OPEN *12–11pm Mon–Thurs; 12–12 Fri–Sat; 12–11pm Sun. Times may vary during winter months.*

CASTLETOWN

The Sidings

Station Road, Castletown
☎ *(01624) 823282* Norman Turner

 Marston's Pedigree, Bushy's Castletown Bitter, Mild, Manannan's Cloak and seasonal brew usually available, plus two guest beers which might be from Bushy's, Everards, Greene King, Timothy Taylor, Wye Valley, Morland or Charles Wells.

Welcoming, traditional, beer-orientated pub which was once the railway station and is now situated alongside it. Chip-fat-free atmosphere! Bar snacks served 12–2.30pm. Car park. Beer garden. Children welcome at lunchtime only.

OPEN *11.30am–11pm Mon–Thurs; 11.30am–midnight Fri–Sat; 12–10.30pm Sun.*

DOUGLAS

Albert Hotel

3 Chapel Row, Douglas IM1 2BJ
☎ *(01624) 673632* Geoff Joughin

 Okells Mild, Bitter and Jough Manx Ale (house bitter) usually served. Occasional brews from Okells may also be available.

Town-centre, working man's local adjacent to the bus terminal. No food. No children.

OPEN *10am–11pm Mon–Thurs; 10am–midnight Fri–Sat; 12–11pm Sun.*

Old Market Inn

Chapel Row, Douglas IM1 2BJ
☎ *(01624) 675202* Breda Watters

 Okells Bitter and Bushy's Bitter regularly served.

A friendly atmosphere is to be found in this small, seventeenth-century tavern, popular with all ages. No food. No children.

OPEN *11am–11pm Mon–Wed; 10am–midnight Thurs–Fri; 12–3pm and 7–11pm Sun.*

Saddle Inn

Queen Street, Douglas
☎ *(01624) 673161* Christine Armstrong

 Okells Bitter and Mild regularly available, plus guest beers also from Okells.

Friendly quayside pub, popular with locals, visitors and motorcyclists throughout the year. Various memorabilia on display. No food.

 11.30am–11pm Mon–Thurs; 11.30am–midnight Fri–Sat; 12–11pm Sun.

LAXEY

Queens Hotel

New Road, Laxey
☎ *(01624) 861195* James Robert Hamer

 A Bushy's pub with Bushy's Ruby Mild, Castletown Bitter and Export plus Old Laxey Bosun Bitter regularly available, plus a guest beer which might, perhaps, be something from Cains Brewery.

Friendly village pub with single, open-plan bar and pool area. Large beer garden and adjacent to the electric railway. Live music on Saturday nights. The Laxey wheel is near by. Toasted sandwiches available. Car park. Children welcome, but no special facilities.

 12–11pm Mon–Thurs; 12–12 Fri–Sat; 12–11pm Sun.

OLD LAXEY

The Shore Hotel

Old Laxey IM4 7DA
☎ *(01624) 861509*

 A brewpub, home of the Old Laxey Brewing Company, with Bosun's Bitter always on offer, plus occasional appearances for Okells Bitter and Bushy's Bitter. Brewery tours can be arranged (phone for details).

Friendly village pub with river frontage close to the harbour and beach, featuring nautical charts, oil paintings of steam drifters and framed pictures of exotic fish from around the world! Food served in the bar or by the river 12–2pm. Background music only. Children's play area. Large car park. Website: www.welcome.to/shorehotel.

 BOSUN'S BITTER 3.8% ABV

 12–11pm Mon–Thurs; 12–12 Fri–Sat; 12–6pm and 7.30–11pm Sun.

PEEL

The White House

2 Tynwald Road, Peel IM5 1LA
☎ *(01624) 842252* Jamie Keig

 A freehouse serving Okells Mild and Bitter, Bushy's Bitter and Timothy Taylor Landlord plus regular guests.

A traditional pub with one main bar and four small adjoining rooms. CAMRA listed and Cask Marque approved. Live Manx music every Saturday. TV. Light bar snacks served in the bar area. Children allowed until 9pm.

 11am–11pm Mon–Thurs;11am–midnight Fri–Sat; 12–11pm Sun.

RAMSEY

The Stanley Hotel

West Quay, Ramsey
☎ *(01624) 812258* Colin Clarke

 Okells Mild and Bitter are permanent features, plus a guest beer from Coach House is also often available.

A small pub near the harbour. Food served 12–3pm daily. Children welcome at lunchtime only.

 11.30am–11pm (10.30pm Sun).

The Trafalgar Hotel

West Quay, Ramsey
☎ *(01624) 814601* James Kneen

 Okells Bitter, Cains Mild and Bitter usually available, plus a regularly changing guest beer which is often from Bushy's or Old Laxey.

Small, friendly and very traditional quayside pub, known for well-kept ales. Cask Marque accredited. Traditional, home-cooked food served at lunchtimes. Children welcome at lunchtime only.

 11am–11pm Mon–Thurs; 11am–midnight Fri–Sat; 12–3pm and 7–10.30pm Sun.

YOU TELL US

∗ *Samuel Webb,* Marina Road, Douglas
∗ *The Tramshunters Arms,* Sefton Hotel, Harris Promenade, Douglas

READER RECOMMENDATIONS

Research for the next edition of the guide is already underway and, to ensure that it will be as comprehensive and up-to-date as possible, we should be grateful for your help.

We hope that you will agree that every pub included this year is in the book on merit, but ownership and operation can change both for better and for worse. Equally, there are bound to be hidden gems that have so far escaped our attention and that really ought to be included next time around.

So, if what you discover does not live up to expectations, or if you know of another pub that we cannot afford to be without, please let us know. Either fill in the forms below or send your views on a separate piece of paper to:

The Editor, The Real Ale Pub Guide
Foulsham, Bennetts Close, Slough, Berkshire, SL1 5AP.

Alternatively, you can e-mail your comments to reception@foulsham.com

Please let us know if you would like additional forms. Every reply will be entered into a draw for one of five free copies of next year's guide. Thank you very much for your help.

Pub name: _____ Already in Yes ☐
Address: _____ the guide? No ☐

Comments: _____
_____
_____
_____

Your name: _____
Your address: _____
_____
_____ Tel: _____

Pub name: _____ Already in Yes ☐
Address: _____ the guide? No ☐

Comments: _____
_____
_____
_____

Your name: _____
Your address: _____
_____
_____ Tel: _____

QUESTIONNAIRE

Pub name: _____

Address: _____

Already in   Yes ☐
the guide?   No ☐

Comments: _____
_____
_____
_____

Your name: _____

Your address: _____
_____
_____ Tel: _____

Pub name: _____

Address: _____

Already in   Yes ☐
the guide?   No ☐

Comments: _____
_____
_____
_____

Your name: _____

Your address: _____
_____
_____ Tel: _____

Pub name: _____

Address: _____

Already in   Yes ☐
the guide?   No ☐

Comments: _____
_____
_____
_____

Your name: _____

Your address: _____
_____
_____ Tel: _____